THAT
GLIMPSE
OF
TRUTH

in memory of Deborah Rogers

THAT GLIMPSE OF TRUTH

100 OF THE FINEST SHORT STORIES EVER WRITTEN

Selected and Introduced by

DAVID MILLER

HEAD of ZEUS

First published in the UK in 2014 by Head of Zeus Ltd. Revised and updated edition published in the UK in 2015 by Head of Zeus Ltd.

In the compilation and introductory material © David Miller, 2014

9 7 5 6 8

A catalogue record for this book is available from the British Library.

ISBN (HB) 9781784080044
ISBN (E) 9781784080037

Typeset by PDQ, Bungay, Suffolk

Printed and bound in Leck,
Germany by CPI Books GmbH

Head of Zeus Ltd
Clerkenwell House
45-47 Clerkenwell Green
London EC1R 0HT
WWW.HEADOFZEUS.COM

CONTENTS

GLIMPSING WHO WE ARE

Tell me what you want, and I shall tell you who you are.

Anton Chekhov
A Dreary Story (1889)

Any anthology is a weird, wonky wonder: the one you hold in your hands is no different. Are all the short stories selected here *really* the "finest"? *Who* says – and *why*, let alone *how*?

There are several things to be stated at the outset: (1) choosing one hundred stories and stating they are the "finest" is an excellent way to start a discussion; (2) the form itself, the short story, exemplifies some of the finest writing that isn't poetry, that couldn't be a novel and (3) we are all aggravatingly, hopelessly, usefully, desperately subjective. Finally (4) the task is, frankly, impossible. How can anyone select a hundred short stories above the hundreds of thousands that sit beside them? Describing the process of judging a literary prize (for a novel), the British novelist Penelope Fitzgerald wrote in 1998:

> It's always the same, you make up your mind to remain calm, dispassionate and civilised. And then as the meetings go on, you become increasingly heated and quarrelsome. The book I wanted to win... didn't win, and I felt like weeping. And everyone complained, as they always do, that the judges must have lost their wits anyway.

Selecting the stories included here has had a similar feel. I've tried to remain dispassionate, searching for the finest, ending up being wholly and, I'd argue, usefully, passionate. I have spent weeks, then months, quarrelling with myself (and others) and, now there is a result, some will complain I've not included *a* or *y*, or *h* or *z* or given due attention to the burgeoning literary genre or scene in *delete as appropriate*. There are stories originally written in Hebrew, Spanish, French, Norwegian, Danish, Yiddish, Russian, German, Vietnamese, Japanese, and written in English from most continents, but it will be said there could be more Commonwealth writing here, that there is not enough science fiction, there's too much Russian, Irish and American and not enough Indian writing; that I have neglected gay, ghost (or gay ghost) stories, or crime fiction – and some of that is true, and not true, but I suspect each of those genres could hold a selection of over one hundred stories within their categories. We know that these days, whatever happens, someone will be there to complain, but this is a quality exercise, not a quota project. All I can say is that the experience of selecting the stories here has been blackly exhilarating, perhaps a little bit like it might be to appear on the literary equivalent of *Desert Island Discs* – my fate now has to be being told I've missed out authors whose names begin with X, Y, Z and the whole of the rest of the alphabet and, just, got it wrong, caused vast offence and – well, the list is as endless as this book could have been.

Philip Roth might – just – be a useful, if ignorant, ally here. He has written superb novels but is not a fine short story writer (according to me). In *American Pastoral* (1997) he wrote:

> The fact remains that getting people right is not what living is all about anyway. It's getting them wrong that is living, getting them wrong and wrong and wrong and then, on careful reconsideration, getting them wrong again. That's how we know we're alive: we're wrong.

What I have attempted to do is not get things right, but to reflect as many genres, as many moods, as many voices as I can curate, to show that a short story can do pretty much anything – tell the tale, untell the tale told, hide the teller; make you laugh, make you cry, show a world, be political, play and work and expand what fiction can do, and so on and so forth – as can any novel but, as a short story is already a distillation, it gives the writer a far harder task to achieve everything, not just any thing. Every thing in this book is as good as it can get.

It turns out, also, the choices made are personal, but they have to be: each of our reactions to any author is: most of our reading is reading what others have read before. The book is ordered by chronological date of birth of the author, as that seemed easiest. I have attempted to spread the notion of "finest" throughout the story of the "short story," as that should show how the world has changed since a man wrote how another could live in a fish (*very* magical realist) to how we simply look at one another when things go wrong (Cheever).

Given my own stipulations, I am still irritated by what I have not been able to include, for simple reasons of space, as much as I am surprised by who is not in the book – the novelists I admire who, for me, write better novels than stories (like Roth, or George Eliot, Shirley Hazzard, Graham Greene, John Updike, Evelyn Waugh) and who seem rarely to have written a short story (Anita Brookner, Robertson Davies, Alan Hollinghurst, Brian Moore), or the stories that were on their way to becoming novels (Raymond Chandler, Michael Cunningham, Evelyn Waugh) – the sort of short stories that read like five-finger exercises on a keyboard meant to be turned into a symphony.

Sometimes it is good to see a novelist as a novelist and realize short stories are for others, that they are – to use one of my most steady friend's best words – "beyond."

I hope the stories collected here reflect what writing is about: life, and its complications. The short story can be the most surprising form of fiction because it offers a magnitude of tellings. One or two pages can do it (Saki, Walser). So can many more (Carter, Pritchett). So can a series of questions, or answers, or footnotes (Ballard, Lydia Davis). Writers tell us how hard a short story is to get *right*: they are not wrong. One story included here was published originally on Twitter, which shows what you can do with as few words as you wish – FOR SALE: BABY'S SHOES. NEVER WORN.[1]

When Carver was twenty-seven, "back in 1966," he found he was

> having trouble concentrating my attention on long narrative fiction. For a time I experienced difficulty in trying to read it as well as in attempting to write it. My attention span had gone out on me; I no longer had the patience to try to write novels. It's an involved story, too tedious to talk about here. But I know it has much to do now with why I write poems and short stories. Get in, get out. Don't linger. Go on.

I had to look that last bit up, as I'd recalled the quote as a similarly snappy "Get in, get out, as quickly as you can."[2] Carver was a useful influence on my reading, as were those just before him, and his peers – but I had grown up with Saki being read to me at school, and then Roald Dahl's *Tales of the Unexpected* manipulating my adolescence, on television. At the same time, in my teens, each school-day morning when I opened my bedroom curtains, I could gaze on where Somerset Maugham's ashes had been interred.[3] One Christmas holiday, after he'd just won the 1982 Nobel Prize for Literature, and when I was nearly seventeen and stricken with some glandular thing, I asked my mother if she could buy anything by Gabriel García Márquez, and she came back from the WHSmith in Burgess Hill with the whole sodding lot reissued by Picador just to shut me up (which it did: I began reading his short stories, *Innocent Eréndira*).[4] I remember, very vividly, nipping out of school with £1.25 to buy Ian McEwan's *First Love, Last Rites* – short stories that seemed to me then, and still do now, to allow any writer to explore what can be done – and to which the answer is: almost anything.

At some stage I also realized writing can work at its most sublime when it does less. Carver admired one of the writers I hold most dear, V.S. Pritchett. Leo

---

[1] There is, sadly, no evidence that Ernest Hemingway actually wrote these words.

[2] In the last few years there has been the reassuring arrival of performing short plays without an interval – Richard Eyre's recent adaptation of Henrik Ibsen's *Ghosts* being the most splendid. Get in, get out, let the memory linger longer.

[3] There is a, probably apocryphal, story that Maugham was asked to come to the school to give a talk about how to write a story to the interested boys and, due to his stutter, Maugham kept the talk short, saying each needed the following ingredients – religion, aristocracy, sex, mystery and a sense of narrative drive. He asked the boys to write a story. No sooner had he sat down than a hand shot up and a boy said, "Sir! I've done it!" and then, when instructed, read out his effort, as follows: "My God!" said the Duchess. "I'm pregnant! Whose is it?"

[4] It seems strange that this now seems a period detail. In 1982, WHSmith stocked books by writers who won literary prizes. Indeed, V.S. Pritchett won one they sponsored in 1990. Perhaps they will stock this book – who knows?

Carey, writing recently in *The New Yorker* noted of Pritchett that:

> When he died, in 1997, the BBC ran an old documentary in which an actor read some of the stories (I can still remember how brilliantly he read "The Oedipus Complex") and Pritchett himself was interviewed. After a reading of a story that ends almost *in medias res*, the interviewer asked, "And we don't know what's going to happen next?" Pritchett said, "Yes. People don't know what's going to happen next in their lives, so we don't either."

In Carver's words, Pritchett's

> definition of a short story is "something glimpsed from the corner of the eye, in passing." Notice the "glimpse" part of this. First the glimpse. Then the glimpse gives life, turned into something that illuminates the moment and may, if we're lucky – that word again – have even further ranging consequences and meaning. The short story writer's task is to invest the glimpse with all that is in his power. He'll bring his intelligence and literary skill to bear (his talent), his sense of proportion and sense of the fitness of things: of how things out there really are and how he sees those things – like no one else sees them. And this is done through the use of clear and specific language, language used so as to bring to life the details that will light up the story for the reader. For the details to be concrete and convey meaning, the language must be accurate and precisely given. The words can be so precise they may even sound flat, but they can still carry; if used right they can hit all the notes.

For exactly half my life I have been lucky enough to hear writers hitting the right notes by working at a literary agency. The first story I placed was by Lorrie Moore ("Community Life"), the second was the last story by Angela Carter. I've come to work for Nicola Barker, John Burnside, Magnus Mills and Cynthia Ozick but also came to read for pleasure Muriel Spark, Denis Johnson, Shirley Hazzard, Alice Munro, Mavis Gallant, Richard Yates, Lydia Davis, and Jhumpa Lahiri. I remember standing to hear John McGahern read from his *Collected Stories* at Waterstones, Charing Cross Road, and peeing beside Joseph O'Connor in the urinals at the Purcell Rooms immediately after he had held an audience spell-bound with his story "True Believers" (not, sadly, included here for reasons of space) – not the moment to introduce yourself, or say anything, much.

Together with the reading I was doing by people who were alive, I tried to check myself, my taste: retain quality control – so, whilst I had Pritchett, I kept reading Chekhov, and in my mid-thirties, I discovered Joseph Conrad. Conrad is a great writer, but none of his novels is truly great: his short fiction is almost better than the baggy brilliance of *Nostromo*, or the clenched splendour of *Under Western Eyes* – "The Return", *Heart of Darkness*, "The Secret Sharer" or *The Shadow Line* count, but are all too long for inclusion here.[5] Conrad also wrote this, which is why the volume you have has the title it does:

[5] At the risk of embarrassing publishers, there is a howling need for a book comprising twenty best novellas, another stupidly overlooked form. There's also a real need for a prize for them.

My task which I am trying to achieve is, by the power of the written word, to make you hear, to make you feel – it is, before all, to make you see. That – and no more, and it is everything. If I succeed, you shall find there according to your deserts: encouragement, consolation, fear, charm – all you demand; and, perhaps, also that glimpse of truth for which you have forgotten to ask.

His is a superb challenge to any author, as good an explanation to any reader why anyone writes, or reads, fiction.

Twenty years ago, a friend of mine asked if I had ever read Ford Madox Ford's *The Good Soldier* and I replied, "No." His head rose from his burning cigarette, his eyes gleaming with what I took then for dismay, the grey in his hair sprinkled like the ash he was about to flick into the street. I had misread him because he then said, almost in italics, just after taking a drag, "Oh God, I envy you," and then he breathed out, the stub circling in the air to wherever it would land. When I asked him about the stories I was selecting here, he surprised me in knowing, bluntly, zilch. I now envy him, and – perhaps – you; if you haven't yet read any, or many, of these stories, I trust you'll find in most of them "that glimpse of truth for which you have forgotten to ask" as I shall continue to do so – to be endlessly surprised by, find some completion through, reading our finest form in fiction.

David Miller

Chiswick, London
10 May 2014

THE HARE AND THE TORTOISE

Aesop

Aesop (c. 620–564BC) was born in in Turkey and died in Greece, in the city of Delphi. He was probably a slave, was freed at some point and ended his days being thrown off a cliff on an exaggerated charge of theft from a temple whilst working as a diplomat for King Croesus of Lydia. All this may or may not be true and, indeed, he may or may not have written his fables, but they have endured and are often the first stories we come across.

The Hare was once boasting of his speed before the other animals. 'I have never yet been beaten,' said he, 'when I put forth my full speed. I challenge any one here to race with me.'

The Tortoise said quietly, 'I accept your challenge.'

'That is a good joke,' said the Hare, 'I could dance round you all the way.'

'Keep your boasting till you've beaten,' answered the Tortoise. 'Shall we race?'

So a course was fixed and a start was made.

The Hare darted almost out of sight at once, but soon stopped and, to show his contempt for the Tortoise, lay down to have a nap.

The Tortoise plodded on and plodded on, and when the Hare awoke from his nap, he saw the Tortoise just near the winning-post and could not run up in time to save the race.

Then said the Tortoise:

'Plodding wins the race.'

THE BOOK OF JONAH

Anon.

Isaac Bashevis Singer wrote in 1982, "Although the short story is not in vogue nowadays, I still believe that it constitutes the utmost challenge to the creative writer." He went on to praise Chekhov and Maupassant as well as "the sublime scribe of the Joseph story in the Book of Genesis," because they "knew exactly where they were going." **Anon.** (in this case) was probably writing in the late 5th or early 4th century BCE, and he – probably not, in this instance, she – also had a fine sense of irony.

Now the word of the LORD came unto Jonah the son of Amittai, saying, "Arise, go to Nineveh, that great city, and cry against it; for their wickedness is come up before me." But Jonah rose up to flee unto Tarshish from the presence of the LORD, and went down to Joppa; and he found a ship going to Tarshish: so he paid the fare thereof, and went down into it, to go with them unto Tarshish from the presence of the LORD. But the LORD sent out a great wind into the sea, and there was a mighty tempest in the sea, so that the ship was like to be broken. Then the mariners were afraid, and cried every man unto his god, and cast forth the wares that were in the ship into the sea, to lighten it of them. But Jonah was gone down into the sides of the ship; and he lay, and was fast asleep. So the shipmaster came to him, and said unto him,

"What meanest thou, O sleeper? arise, call upon thy God, if so be that God will think upon us, that we perish not." And they said every one to his fellow,

"Come, and let us cast lots, that we may know for whose cause this evil is upon us." So they cast lots, and the lot fell upon Jonah. Then said they unto him,

"Tell us, we pray thee, for whose cause this evil is upon us; What is thine occupation? and whence comest thou? what is thy country? and of what people art thou?" And he said unto them,

I am an Hebrew; and I fear the LORD, the God of heaven, which hath made the sea and the dry land. Then were the men exceedingly afraid, and said unto him,

"Why hast thou done this?" For the men knew that he fled from the presence of the LORD, because he had told them. Then said they unto him,

"What shall we do unto thee, that the sea may be calm unto us? for the sea wrought, and was tempestuous." And he said unto them,

"Take me up, and cast me forth into the sea; so shall the sea be calm unto you: for I know that for my sake this great tempest is upon you." Nevertheless the men rowed hard to bring it to the land; but they could not: for the sea wrought, and was tempestuous against them. Wherefore they cried unto the LORD, and said,

"We beseech thee, O LORD, we beseech thee, let us not perish for this man's life, and lay not upon us innocent blood: for thou, O LORD, hast done as it pleased thee." So they took up Jonah, and cast him forth into the sea: and the sea ceased from her raging.   Then the men feared the LORD exceedingly, and offered a sacrifice unto the LORD, and made vows.

Now the LORD had prepared a great fish to swallow up Jonah. And Jonah was in the belly of the fish three days and three nights.

Then Jonah prayed unto the LORD his God out of the fish's belly, and said,

"I cried by reason of mine affliction unto the LORD, and he heard me; out of the belly of hell cried I, and thou heardest my voice.   For thou hadst cast me into the deep, in the midst of the seas; and the floods compassed me about: all thy billows and thy waves passed over me.   Then I said, I am cast out of thy sight; yet I will look again toward thy holy temple. The waters compassed me about, even to the soul: the depth closed me round about, the weeds were wrapped about my head.   I went down to the bottoms of the mountains; the earth with her bars was about me for ever: yet hast thou brought up my life from corruption, O LORD my God.   When my soul fainted within me I remembered the LORD: and my prayer came in unto thee, into thine holy temple. They that observe lying vanities forsake their own mercy.   But I will sacrifice unto thee with the voice of thanksgiving; I will pay that that I have vowed. Salvation is of the LORD."   And the LORD spake unto the fish, and it vomited out Jonah upon the dry land.

And the word of the LORD came unto Jonah the second time, saying,

"Arise, go unto Nineveh, that great city, and preach unto it the preaching that I bid thee." So Jonah arose, and went unto Nineveh, according to the word of the LORD. Now Nineveh was an exceeding great city of three days' journey. And Jonah began to enter into the city a day's journey, and he cried, and said,

Yet forty days, and Nineveh shall be overthrown. So the people of Nineveh believed God, and proclaimed a fast, and put on sackcloth, from the greatest of them even to the least of them.   For word came unto the king of Nineveh, and he arose from his throne, and he laid his robe from him, and covered him with sackcloth, and sat in ashes.   And he caused it to be proclaimed and published through Nineveh by the decree of the king and his nobles, saying,

"Let neither man nor beast, herd nor flock, taste any thing: let them not feed, nor drink water: But let man and beast be covered with sackcloth, and cry mightily unto God: yea, let them turn every one from his evil way, and from the violence that is in their hands.   Who can tell if God will turn and repent, and turn away from his fierce anger, that we perish not?" And God saw their works, that they turned from their evil way; and God repented of the evil, that he had said that he would do unto them; and he did it not.

But it displeased Jonah exceedingly, and he was very angry.   And he prayed unto the LORD, and said,

"I pray thee, O LORD, was not this my saying, when I was yet in my country? Therefore I fled before unto Tarshish: for I knew that thou art a gracious God, and merciful, slow to anger, and of great kindness, and repentest thee of the evil. Therefore now, O LORD, take, I beseech thee, my life from me; for it is better for me to die than to live."   Then said the LORD,

"Doest thou well to be angry?" So Jonah went out of the city, and sat on the east side of the city, and there made him a booth, and sat under it in the shadow, till he might see what would become of the city. And the LORD God prepared a gourd, and made it to come up over Jonah, that it might be a shadow over his head, to deliver him from his grief. So Jonah was exceeding glad of the gourd. But God prepared a worm when the morning rose the next day, and it smote the gourd that it withered. And it came to pass, when the sun did arise, that God prepared a vehement east wind; and the sun beat upon the head of Jonah, that he fainted, and wished in himself to die, and said,

"It is better for me to die than to live." And God said to Jonah,

"Doest thou well to be angry for the gourd?" And he said,

"I do well to be angry, even unto death." Then said the LORD,

"Thou hast had pity on the gourd, for the which thou hast not laboured, neither madest it grow; which came up in a night, and perished in a night: And should not I spare Nineveh, that great city, wherein are more than sixscore thousand persons that cannot discern between their right hand and their left hand; and also much cattle?"

THE DECEITFUL MARRIAGE

Miguel de Cervantes

Miguel de Cervantes (1547–1616) was a playwright, poet and the author of *Don Quixote*, considered by many to be the first major European novel. He fought as a soldier in the Battle of Lepanto in 1571, spent five years as a slave in Algiers and then, after his release, worked buying supplies for the Spanish Armada and as a tax collector. He was born near, and died in, Madrid, and was buried on 23 April 1616, the day William Shakespeare died.

O ut of the hospital of the Resurrection, which is in Valladolid beyond the Puerta del Campo, came a soldier, using his sword as a staff, and with legs so weak and his face so yellow that you could see quite clearly that, although the weather was not very hot, he must have sweated out in three weeks all the fluid he had probably got in an hour. He was tottering slowly along as if he were just getting over an illness, and as he went in through the gate of the city he spotted a friend of his coming towards him, whom he had not seen for over six months. The friend, crossing himself as if he were seeing a ghost, said when he got up to him,

"What is this, Ensign Campuzano? Are you really in this part of the world? Upon my word I thought you were trailing a pike in Flanders, not dragging your sword along here. What is the meaning of this awful colour and this weakness of yours?"

Campuzano replied, "As for my being in this part of the world or not, Licenciate Peralta, the fact that you see me in it is sufficient answer; in reply to the other questions all I have to say is that I've just come out of that hospital, after sweating out fourteen buboes I got from a woman whom for my sins I took to myself."

"So you got married," observed Peralta.

"Yes sir," answered Campuzano.

"It must have been for love," said Peralta, "and marriages of that kind have the path to repentance already built in."

"I can't say whether it was for love," answered the ensign; "although I can assure you it was painful, because as a result of my marriage, or mismarriage, I was so afflicted with pain in both body and mind, that as far as my body is concerned, I've had to sweat it out forty times, and as for my mind, I can't find any cure for the pains. But I'm not in a fit condition for long conversation in the street, so I must ask you to excuse me. Some other day I'll tell you at leisure what has happened to me; for it is the most strange and unheard-of tale that you've ever come across in your whole life."

"That won't do," said the Licenciate; "for I want you to come with me to my lodgings, and we'll do penance together there. Stew is just right for invalids, and although there are only enough helpings for two, my servant can make do with a pie; and if you're feeling sufficiently recovered, a few rashers of ham will serve as hors d'oeuvre and the good will with which I offer it to you is worth more than anything, not only on this occasion but whenever you may desire."

Campuzano thanked him, and accepted the invitation and the offer. They went to San Lorenzo and heard Mass. Then Peralta took him off to his house, gave him what he had promised and offered him his services again, begging him as soon as he had finished to tell him the adventures he had said so much about. Campuzano was only too ready to oblige, and began as follows:

"You will remember, Licenciate Peralta, how I shared lodgings with Captain Pedro de Herrera, who is now in Flanders."

"I remember well," answered Peralta.

"Well one day," Campuzano went on, "as we had just finished a meal in that inn at La Solana, where we were staying, two good-looking women came in, with two maid-servants. One of them stood by the window and began to talk to the captain, and the other sat down on a chair beside me, keeping her veil lowered to her chin, and showing only what you could see through the thin material. Although I begged her out of courtesy to unveil herself, there was nothing doing, and this increased my desire to see her. It was still further increased by the fact that, whether by accident or design, she let me catch a glimpse of a snowy-white hand adorned with very fine jewels. At that time I was looking very smart, with that big chain which you must have seen me wearing, my hat with plumes and bands, my coloured army uniform so dashing, to my crazy way of thinking, that it seemed to me that I could conquer a woman just by looking at her. Anyway, I begged her to unveil herself, to which she replied, "Don't pester me; I have a house; get a page to follow me, for although I'm a more respectable person than this answer implies, if I find you are as discreet as you are handsome, I shall be glad for you to come and see me.""

"I kissed her hands out of gratitude for the great favour she was doing me, in return for which I promised her a heap of money. The captain finished his conversation, the ladies went off, and one of my servants followed them. The captain told me that what the lady wanted him to do was to take some letters to Flanders for her for another captain, who she said was her cousin, although he knew he was only her lover. I was inflamed with passion at the sight of those snowy hands, and dying to see her face; and so the next day my servant showed me the way, and I was allowed in quite freely. I found a very well-furnished house and a woman of about thirty, whom I recognized by her hands. She was not outstandingly beautiful, but she was sufficiently so for me to fall in love with her when I heard her speak, because her voice was so soft that when she spoke she touched my very soul. I had long amorous conversations with her; I boasted, wheedled, lied, offered, promised and went through all the motions I thought necessary to win her favours, but as she was used to hearing this sort of offer and argument, and even better ones, she appeared to be listening to me but without believing a word I said. The fact is that during the few days I spent visiting her our conversation was confined to trivialities, and I didn't manage to pick any of the fruit I desired.

"During the time I was visiting her I always found the house quite empty, with not a sign either of false relatives or real friends. She had as a servant a girl who was more crafty than stupid. In the end, treating my love-affair like a soldier who will soon be on the move, I put the pressure on my lady Doña Estefanía de Caicedo – for that's the name of the one who has reduced me to what I am – and she gave me this reply:

"'Ensign Campuzano, it would be sheer stupidity for me to pretend to you that I am a saint: I have been a sinner, and I still am; but not so much so that the neighbours gossip about me or that I attract the notice of the outside world. I inherited no property from my parents or from any other of my relatives, and yet my household effects are worth a good two and a half thousand crowns; and if they were auctioned would sell straight away. With this property I am looking for a husband whom I can cling to and obey; and apart from turning over a new leaf, I can promise him that I'll fall over myself to look after him and serve him. No prince has ever had a cook to make your mouth water more, or one more skilled in putting the finishing touches to the dishes I can give him when I'm in the mood for housekeeping and give my mind to it. I can act as butler, kitchen-maid and lady of the house. In fact, I know how to give orders and make people obey them. I waste nothing, and I manage to make a good deal of profit: I know how to make every *real* go a long way. My linen, of which I have a great deal and of the finest quality, is not from shops or drapers; it was spun by my own fingers and those of my maid-servants; and if it had been possible to weave it at home, it would have been woven there too. I am singing my own praises because it is only right that you should know these things. In short, what I mean to say is that I am looking for a husband to take care of me, give me orders and honour me, and not a lover to wait upon me and then hurl reproaches at me. If you are pleased to accept the prize you are being offered, here I am all ready to submit to any arrangement you choose, without offering myself for sale, which is the same as putting myself at the mercy of match-makers; for there's no one so well qualified to arrange things as the parties concerned.'

"At that time I had my brains in my heels rather than in my head, and as the pleasure seemed just then greater even than I had imagined it, and all that property in front of me as good as cash already, without stopping to look for any arguments beyond my own wishes, which had quite overcome my reason, I told her that I was the most fortunate of persons to have been presented with this heaven-sent miracle, a companion like this to be the mistress of my will and my possessions. These were not so small for, taking into account the chain I had round my neck and some other small jewels at home, with what I could get from the sale of some of my soldier's finery, they were worth over two thousand ducats. This, together with her twenty-five hundred, was enough to enable us to live in retirement in the village where I was born, and where I still had some property. This, added to the cash, and by selling our produce at the right season, could allow us to live happily and at ease. In short, our betrothal was settled there and then, we contrived to have ourselves registered as bachelor and spinster, and the banns were called on the three holy days which happened to come together at Easter time. On the fourth day we were married, two friends of mine being witnesses, with a youth she said was her cousin, to whom I swore kinship in the most civil way; just as I had behaved up to that moment with my new wife, though my intentions were so crooked and treacherous that I would rather not speak of them; for although I'm telling the truth, it's not the whole truth as I'd have to tell it at confession.

"My servant moved the trunk from my lodgings to my wife's house. In front of her I locked up my splendid chain in it; I showed her three or four more which, although not quite so big, were superior in workmanship, as well as three or four hatbands of various kinds; I let her see my finery and my plumes, and handed over to her four hundred odd *reales* that I had, for household expenses. The honeymoon lasted for six days, during which I took my ease like a humble son-in-law in the house of his rich father-in-law; I walked on rich carpets, slept on linen sheets, and basked in the light from silver candlesticks. I breakfasted in bed, got up at eleven, dined at twelve and at two took my siesta in the drawing-room, while Doña Estefanía and her maid danced attendance on me. My servant, who up to that time had always given me the impression of being lazy and slow, had become as swift as a deer. When Doña Estefanía was not at my side, she was to be found in the kitchen, preparing dishes to tempt my palate and stir up my appetite. My shirts, collars and handkerchiefs smelt just like the gardens of Aranjuez, with all the sweet-scented angel- and orange-water she sprinkled on them.

"The days flew by, like all the years which are subject to the law of time; and as they passed, seeing myself spoiled and waited on so well, the evil intentions with which I had embarked on that affair were changing. But it all came to an end one morning when, as I was with Doña Estefanía in bed, there was a loud knocking at the front door. The maid put her head out of the window, and withdrew it immediately.

"'Here's a fine sight!' she shrieked. 'She's come sooner than she said when she wrote the other day.'

"'Who's come, girl?' I asked her.

"'Who?' she answered. 'My lady Doña Clementa Bueso, and she's got with her Don Lope Meléndez de Almendárez, with two servants and Hortigosa, the duenna she took away with her.'

"'Hurry up, girl, for heaven's sake, open the door for them!', said Doña Estefanía. 'And you sir, if you love me, don't be upset or answer anything you may hear against me.'

"'And who will say anything to offend you, especially in my presence? Tell me: who are these people, whose arrival seems to have upset you so much?'

"'I've no time to explain to you now,' said Doña Estefanía; 'but you must know that everything that may happen here is a trick and is all part of a certain plan and purpose which you'll know about later.'

"And although I should have liked to reply to this, I was not given a chance, because the lady Doña Clementa Bueso came into the room then, dressed in green satin lustre with lots of gold lace edging, a cape of the same material and the same trimmings, a hat with green, white and red feathers and a rich gold band, and with a fine veil covering half her face. She came in accompanied by

Don Lope Meléndez de Almendárez, splendidly dressed in rich travelling clothes. The duenna Hortigosa was the first to speak.

"'Heavens! What is this? My mistress Doña Clementa's bed occupied, and occupied by a man? I can hardly believe my eyes. I must say Doña Estefanía has gone too far, taking advantage of my lady's good nature!'"

"'I should say she has, Hortigosa,' replied Doña Clementa; 'but it's all my fault! Will I never learn not to make the sort of friends who are only friends as long as it suits them?'

"To all this Doña Estefanía replied, 'Don't be upset, lady Clementa, and be sure that what you are seeing here in your home is not what you think. When the mystery is explained, I know I shall be blameless and you will have nothing to complain of.'

"By this time I had put on my breeches and doublet, and Doña Estefanía led me off by the hand to another room, and told me that this friend of hers wanted to play a trick on this Don Lope who was with her, and whom she wanted to marry; and that the trick was to give him to understand that the house and all its contents were hers, so that she could get him to give her a written promise of marriage, and once the marriage was over she didn't mind if the deceit was discovered, so confident was she of this Don Lope's great love for her. 'And then I'll get back my property, and no one will hold it against her or any other woman if she tries to get an honourable husband, even at the expense of a trick.'

"I answered that the gesture of friendship she was proposing was extremely generous, and that she should think seriously about it, because she might later have occasion to resort to the Law to get her property back. But she replied with so many arguments, setting forth so many obligations that she was under to be of even greater service to Doña Clementa that, much against my will and better judgement, I had to fall in with Doña Estefanía's wish. She assured me that the game would last only a week, during which we would go to stay with another friend of hers. She and I finished dressing and then she went in to say good-bye to Doña Clementa Bueso and to Don Lope Meléndez de Almendárez. She told my servant to pack the trunk and follow her, and I followed on too, without saying good-bye to anyone.

"Doña Estefanía stopped at the house of a friend of hers, and before we went in she spent some time talking to her, after which a girl came out and told me and my servant to go in. She took us to a little room, in which there were two beds so close together that they looked like one, because there was no space between them, and the sheets on them were touching each other. There we stopped for six days, and not an hour passed without our quarrelling, I telling her how stupid she had been to leave her house and property in someone else's hands, even if it had been her own mother's. I kept on at her so much that the lady of the house, one day when Doña Estefanía said she was going off to see how her affairs stood, wanted to know why I quarrelled so much with her, and what she had done to make me scold her, accusing her of crass stupidity rather than friendship. I told her the whole story, and when I got to the point of saying that I had married Doña Estefanía, and mentioned the dowry she had, and how silly she had been to leave her house and property to Doña Clementa, even with such a worthy purpose as that of winning an excellent husband like Don Lope, she began to cross herself rapidly, and repeated to herself so many times the words "Lord, what a wicked woman," that I was completely confused. At last she said to me,

"'Ensign, I don't know whether I am going against my conscience in telling you what I think would be just as much on my conscience if I kept silent about it, but at all events I must tell the truth. And the truth is that Doña Clementa Bueso is the real lady of the house and owns the property which was given to you as a dowry; everything that Doña Estefanía has told you is lies. She has neither house nor property, nor anything but the clothes she stands up in. And what gave her the occasion to practise this fraud was that Doña Clementa went off to do penance at Nuestra Señora de Guadalupe, leaving her house in the hands of Doña Estefanía to look after, for they are in fact great friends. And indeed, you can't blame the poor lady, since she's managed to pick up someone like you as a husband, Ensign.'

"Here she stopped speaking, and I was beginning to despair, and doubtless would have done so if my guardian angel hadn't come to the rescue at that moment by reminding me that I was a Christian and that the worst sin a human being could fall into was that of despair, for it was a devilish sin. This consideration or inspiration gave me some comfort, but not enough to prevent me putting on my cloak and sword and going off in search of Doña Estefanía, intending to inflict exemplary punishment on her. However luck, for better or worse, determined that I couldn't find Doña Estefanía, hard though I looked. I went to San Llorente, commended myself to Our Lady, sat down on a bench, and was so upset that I fell into a deep sleep, from which I shouldn't have stirred very quickly if I hadn't been awakened. Full of bitter thoughts I went to Doña Clementa's house, and found her completely at ease as the mistress of her house. I did not dare to say anything to her because Don Lope was there. I went back to my landlady's house, and she told me that she had told Doña Estefanía that I knew all about her plan and about the fraud, and that she had asked her how I had reacted to the news. She told her that I had taken it very badly, and that she thought I had gone to look for her, bent on doing her harm. Then she told me that Doña Estefanía had gone off with everything that was in the trunk, leaving me nothing but a single travelling suit.

"Here was a pretty kettle of fish! But I could feel the hand of God upon me again. I went to look at my trunk and found it open, like a tomb awaiting a corpse, and the corpse might well have been me, if my mind had been up to appreciating the full weight of my misfortune."

"It certainly was a grave misfortune," said Licenciate Peralta, "that Doña Estefanía went off with all those chains and hatbands, for, as they say, you can bear any trouble with a full stomach."

"I didn't mind the loss," answered the ensign; "for as they say: 'Don Simueque thought he was deceiving me with his squinting daughter, but by jove, I'm lop-sided myself, so he met his match.'"

"I don't know quite what the point of this is," said Peralta.

"The point is," answered the ensign, "that all that splendid pile of chains, hatbands and trinkets was worth no more than ten or twelve crowns."

"That is impossible," replied the licenciate. "The one that you were wearing round your neck looked as if it was worth more than two hundred ducats."

"Indeed it would have been," answered the ensign, "if truth matched appearance; but as all that glisters is not gold, the chains, hatbands, jewels and trinkets were in fact only artificial; but they were so well made that only a touchstone or fire could reveal it."

"In that case," said the licenciate, "as far as you and Doña Estefanía are concerned, you're quits."

"And so much so," answered the ensign, "that we can shuffle the cards and start again; but the trouble is, Licenciate, that she can get rid of my chains, but I can't get over the dirty trick she played on me. The fact is that whether I like it or not I've got the consequences for keeps."

"Give thanks to God, Mr Campuzano," said Peralta, "that she had feet and has gone off, and you're not obliged to look for her."

"That's true," replied the ensign. "All the same, even without looking for her, she's always in my mind, and wherever I am my disgrace goes with me."

"I don't know how to answer you," said Peralta, "except to remind you of a couple of verses of Petrarch, which go:

Che chi prende diletto di far frode,
Non si de' lamentar s'altri l'inganna.[1]

which being translated means: 'He who takes delight in deceiving others must not complain when he is deceived himself.'"

"I'm not complaining," answered the ensign, "but I am sorry for myself, for the guilty man does not fail to feel the pain of punishment because he recognizes his guilt. I can well see that I wanted to deceive and that I was deceived, because I was caught in my own trap; but I can't help feeling sorry for myself. And to crown it all, and this is the main point of my story – for this is what one can call this affair of mine – I found out that Doña Estefanía had been carried off by the cousin who I told you was at our wedding, and who had been her steady lover for a long time. I had no wish to look for her, for I'd have been looking for more trouble. I left my lodgings and I lost my hair within a few days, because my eyebrows and eyelashes began to moult, and gradually my hair went too, so I went bald before my time, suffering from a complaint they call 'alopecia', or in plain terms 'loss of hair'. I was really 'fleeced', because I had neither hair to comb nor money to spend. My sickness kept pace with my need, and as poverty tramples honour under foot and brings some to the gallows and others to the hospital, just as it makes others go begging and pleading at their enemies' doors, one of the greatest misfortunes which can come to an unhappy man; so in order not to have to pawn, for the sake of paying for a cure, the clothes which would have to cover me and protect my honour when I was well again, I waited until the time when they put on the sweat treatment in the hospital of the Resurrection, and then went in. I've been sweated forty times, and they say I'll stay well if I look after myself. I have a sword, and as for the rest, may God help me."

The licenciate, amazed at the things which he had told him, offered his sympathy again.

---

[1] *Trionfo d'amore*, Chapter 1.

"What you say surprises you, Señor Peralta, is nothing," said the ensign. "There are things I could tell you which surpass all imagination, for they go beyond the bounds of nature. But I'd like you to know that they are of such a kind that I think all my misfortunes well worth while if only because they brought me to the hospital, where I saw what I shall now relate, which neither you nor any one else in the world will ever credit."

All these preambles and commendations with which the ensign prefaced his account of what he had seen aroused the curiosity of Peralta. So much so that he pressed him to tell him straight away of the marvellous things he had to relate.

"You will have seen," said the ensign, "two dogs which go round with lanterns on them at night, accompanying the begging brothers, and lighting their way when they ask for alms."

"Yes, I have," replied Peralta.

"You will also have seen or heard," said the ensign, "the stories that are told about them: that if by chance people throw alms out of the windows and it falls on the ground, they rush up straight away with a light to look for what falls, and stop in front of the windows where they know people usually give them alms; and although they go along so meekly that they are more like lambs than dogs, in the hospital they're like lions, guarding the house with great care and vigilance."

"I've heard all this," said Peralta, "but there's no reason why that should surprise me."

"Well, what I'm going to tell you now will; and you must be prepared to believe it without crossing yourself or raising objections and difficulties. The fact is that I heard and as good as saw with my own eyes these two dogs, one of whom is called 'Scipio' and the other 'Berganza', who were lying one night (the one before I had the sweat treatment for the last time) on some old matting behind my bed; and in the middle of the night, when it was dark and I was lying awake, thinking of my past adventures and present misfortunes, I heard talking close by. I was listening attentively, to see if I could find out who was talking and what they were talking about, and soon after I realized by what they said that it was the two dogs 'Scipio' and 'Berganza' who were talking."

Campuzano had scarcely said this, when the licenciate got up and said, "This is where I must part company with you, Mr Campuzano; for up to now I've been hesitating whether or not to believe all that you had told me about your marriage; and what you are now telling me about hearing the dogs speak makes me declare that I don't believe any of it. For heaven's sake, Ensign, don't tell this rubbish to anyone except a close friend like me."

"Don't think I'm so ignorant," replied Campuzano, "that I don't realize that it's only by a miracle that animals can speak. I'm well aware that if thrushes, magpies and parrots talk, it's only the words that they learn and get by heart, and because these creatures have tongues which are made in such a way that they can pronounce them. This doesn't mean that they can speak and answer back with reasoned speech as these dogs were doing; and so, many times since I have heard them, I have been unwilling to believe myself, and have preferred to take as something I dreamed what in fact wide awake and with all my five senses as God was pleased to give them to me, I heard, listened to, noted and finally wrote down all in due order, without omitting a word. From this you may have sufficient proof to convince and persuade you to believe the truth of what I say. The things they discussed were many and varied, and more suitable for discussion by wise men than to be in the mouths of dogs; so that, since I could not have invented them off my own bat, in spite of myself and against my better judgement I have come to believe that I was not dreaming and that the dogs were talking."

"Good heavens," said the licenciate, "we're back to the time of Methuselah, when pumpkins talked; or Aesop's days when the cock conversed with the fox and animals talked to each other."

"I should be one of them, and the biggest beast of the lot," replied the ensign, "if I believed that those times had returned, and I should be an animal too if I didn't believe what I heard, and what I saw, and what I shall dare to swear with an oath which will bind and compel the most incredulous person to believe it. But although I may be wrong, and what I think is true is a dream and to persist in it were nonsense, won't it interest you, Mr Peralta, to see written down in the form of a colloquy the things that these dogs, or whatever they were, had to say?"

"Provided you don't weary yourself further in persuading me that you heard the dogs speaking," replied the licenciate, "I shall be very happy to listen to this colloquy, which as it was written down from the notes of your ingenious self, Ensign, I already adjudge to be good."

"Well, there's another point," said the ensign. "Since I was listening so attentively, my mind was in a delicate state, and my memory was also delicate, sharp and free of other concerns, thanks to the great quantity of raisins and almonds I had eaten, I learnt it off by heart and wrote it down the next day in almost the same words in which I had heard it, without looking for rhetorical colours to adorn it, nor adding or substracting anything to make it pleasing. The conversation did not take place all on one night, but on two consecutive nights, although I've recorded only one, when Berganza told his life story. I intend to write down his companion Scipio's, which was related on the second night, if I find that this one is credit-worthy or at least not deserving of scorn. I've got the colloquy tucked away in my shirt-front; I put it in the form of a colloquy to avoid the 'Scipio said', 'Berganza replied', which stretches out the narrative."

And saying this he took out a notebook and put it into the hands of the licenciate, who took it, laughing and apparently making a joke of all that he had heard and of what he was expecting to read.

"I shall recline in this chair," said the ensign, "while you so kindly read these dreams or absurdities, whose only virtue is that you can leave them alone when they annoy you."

"Take your ease," said Peralta, "for I shall soon get through my reading."

The ensign lay back, the licenciate opened the notebook, and saw that it began with this title:

"Tale and Colloquy that took place between 'Scipio' and 'Berganza', dogs belonging to the hospital of the Resurrection, which is in the city of Valladolid, outside the Puerta del Campo, and commonly known as the dogs of Mahudes."

THE CHILDREN OF HAMELN

Jacob and Wilhelm Grimm

Jacob (1785–1863) and Wilhelm (1786–1859), The Brothers Grimm, were born in Hanau and studied law and linguistics, working both together and separately. They collaborated on a German dictionary as well as a book of German legends and, with their fairy tales, had as much of an impact on the German imagination and language as Martin Luther's translation of the Bible.

In the year 1284 a mysterious man appeared in Hameln. He was wearing a coat of many colored, bright cloth, for which reason he was called the Pied Piper. He claimed to be a ratcatcher, and he promised that for a certain sum that he would rid the city of all mice and rats. The citizens struck a deal, promising him a certain price. The ratcatcher then took a small fife from his pocket and began to blow on it. Rats and mice immediately came from every house and gathered around him. When he thought that he had them all he led them to the River Weser where he pulled up his clothes and walked into the water. The animals all followed him, fell in, and drowned.

Now that the citizens had been freed of their plague, they regreted having promised so much money, and, using all kinds of excuses, they refused to pay him. Finally he went away, bitter and angry. He returned on June 26, Saint John's and Saint Paul's Day, early in the morning at seven o'clock (others say it was at noon), now dressed in a hunter's costume, with a dreadful look on his face and wearing a strange red hat. He sounded his fife in the streets, but this time it wasn't rats and mice that came to him, but rather children: a great number of boys and girls from their fourth year on. Among them was the mayor's grown daughter. The swarm followed him, and he led them into a mountain, where he disappeared with them.

All this was seen by a babysitter who, carrying a child in her arms, had followed them from a distance, but had then turned around and carried the news back to the town. The anxious parents ran in droves to the town gates seeking their children. The mothers cried out and sobbed pitifully. Within the hour messengers were sent everywhere by water and by land inquiring if the children – or any of them – had been seen, but it was all for naught.

In total, one hundred thirty were lost. Two, as some say, had lagged behind and came back. One of them was blind and the other mute. The blind one was not able to point out the place, but was able to tell how they had followed the piper. The mute one was able to point out the place, although he [or she] had heard nothing. One little boy in shirtsleeves had gone along with the others, but had turned back to fetch his jacket and thus escaped the tragedy, for when he returned, the others had already disappeared into a cave within a hill. This cave is still shown.

Until the middle of the eighteenth century, and probably still today, the street through which the children were led out to the town gate was called the *bunge-lose* (drumless, soundless, quiet) street, because no dancing or music was allowed there. Indeed, when a bridal procession on its way to church crossed this street, the musicians would have to stop playing. The mountain near Hameln where the the children disappeared is called Poppenberg. Two stone monuments in the form of crosses have been erected there, one on the left side and one on the right. Some say that the children were led into a cave, and that they came out again in Transylvania.

The citizens of Hameln recorded this event in their town register, and they came to date all their proclamations according to the years and days since the loss of their children.

According to Seyfried the 22nd rather than the 26th of June was entered into the town register.

The following lines were inscribed on the town hall:

> In the year 1284 after the birth of Christ
> From Hameln were led away
> One hundred thirty children, born at this place
> Led away by a piper into a mountain.

And on the new gate was inscribed: Centum ter denos cum magus ab urbe puellos duxerat ante annos CCLXXII condita porta fuit.

> [This gate was built 272 years after the magician led the 130 children from the city.]

In the year 1572 the mayor had the story portrayed in the church windows. The accompanying inscription has become largely illegible. In addition, a coin was minted in memory of the event.

THE RED SHOES

Hans Christian Andersen

Hans Christian Andersen (1805–1875) was a Danish story-teller best-known for his plays, travel writing, novels, poems and fairy tales. Born in Odense, he was educated there and in Copenhagen, where he trained to be an actor. Soon he focused on writing. He travelled to Sweden, Spain, Portugal and, in 1847, met and became friends with Dickens. He fell out of bed in 1872 and never properly recovered, dying in 1875. 'The Red Shoes' was written in 1845.

There was once a little girl, very nice and very pretty, but so poor that she had to go barefoot all summer. And in winter she had to wear thick wooden shoes that chafed her ankles until they were red, oh, as red as could be.

In the middle of the village lived Old Mother Shoemaker. She took some old scraps of red cloth and did her best to make them into a little pair of shoes. They were a bit clumsy, but well meant, for she intended to give them to the little girl. Karen was the little girl's name.

The first time Karen wore her new red shoes was on the very day when her mother was buried. Of course, they were not right for mourning, but they were all she had, so she put them on and walked barelegged after the plain wicker coffin.

Just then a large old carriage came by, with a large old lady inside it. She looked at the little girl and took pity upon her. And she went to the parson and said: "Give the little girl to me, and I shall take good care of her."

Karen was sure that this happened because she wore red shoes, but the old lady said the shoes were hideous, and ordered them burned. Karen was given proper new clothes. She was taught to read, and she was taught to sew. People said she was pretty, but her mirror told her, "You are more than pretty. You are beautiful."

It happened that the Queen came traveling through the country with her little daughter, who was a Princess. Karen went with all the people who flocked to see them at the castle. The little Princess, all dressed in white, came to the window to let them admire her. She didn't wear a train, and she didn't wear a gold crown, but she did wear a pair of splendid red morocco shoes. Of course, they were much nicer than the ones Old Mother Shoemaker had put together for little Karen, but there's nothing in the world like a pair of red shoes!

When Karen was old enough to be confirmed, new clothes were made for her, and she was to have new shoes. They went to the house of a thriving shoemaker, to have him take the measure of her little feet. In his shop were big glass cases, filled with the prettiest shoes and the shiniest boots. They looked most attractive but, as the old lady did not see very well, they did not attract her. Among the shoes there was a pair of red leather ones which were just like those the Princess had worn. How perfect they were! The shoemaker said he had made them for the daughter of a count, but that they did not quite fit her.

"They must be patent leather to shine so," said the old lady.

"Yes, indeed they shine," said Karen. As the shoes fitted Karen, the old lady bought them, but she had no idea they were red. If she had known that, she would never have let Karen wear them to confirmation, which is just what Karen did.

Every eye was turned toward her feet. When she walked up the aisle to the chancel of the church, it seemed to her as if even those portraits of bygone ministers and their wives, in starched ruffs and long black gowns – even they fixed their eyes upon her red shoes. She could think of nothing else, even when the pastor laid his hands upon her head and spoke of her holy baptism, and her covenant with God, and her duty as a Christian. The solemn organ rolled, the children sang sweetly, and the old choir leader sang too, but Karen thought of nothing except her red shoes.

Before the afternoon was over, the old lady had heard from everyone in the parish that the shoes were red. She told Karen it was naughty to wear red shoes to church. Highly improper! In the future she was always to wear black shoes to church, even though they were her old ones.

Next Sunday there was holy communion. Karen looked at her black shoes. She looked at her red ones. She kept looking at her red ones until she put them on.

It was a fair, sunny day. Karen and the old lady took the path through the cornfield, where it was rather dusty. At the church door they met an old soldier, who stood with a crutch and wore a long, curious beard. It was more reddish than white. In fact it was quite red. He bowed down to the ground, and asked the old lady if he might dust her shoes. Karen put out her little foot too.

"Oh, what beautiful shoes for dancing," the soldier said. "Never come off when you dance," he told the shoes, as he tapped the sole of each of them with his hand.

The old lady gave the soldier a penny, and went on into the church with Karen. All the people there stared at Karen's red shoes, and all the portraits stared too. When Karen knelt at the altar rail, and even when the chalice came to her lips, she could think only of her red shoes. It was as if they kept floating around in the chalice, and she forgot to sing the psalm. She forgot to say the Lord's Prayer.

Then church was over, and the old lady got into her carriage. Karen was lifting her foot to step in after her when the old soldier said, "Oh, what beautiful shoes for dancing!"

Karen couldn't resist taking a few dancing steps, and once she began her feet kept on dancing. It was as if the shoes controlled her. She danced round the corner of the church – she simply could not help it. The coachman had to run after her, catch her, and lift her into the carriage. But even there her feet went on dancing so that she gave the good old lady a terrible kicking. Only when she took her shoes off did her legs quiet down. When they got home the shoes were put away in a cupboard, but Karen would still go and look at them.

Shortly afterwards the old lady was taken ill, and it was said she could not recover. She required constant care and faithful nursing, and for this she depended on Karen. But a great ball was being given in the town, and Karen was invited. She looked at the old lady, who could not live in any case. She looked at the red shoes, for she thought there was no harm in looking. She put them on, for she thought there was no harm in that either. But then she went to the ball and began dancing. When she tried to turn to the right, the shoes turned to the left. When she wanted to dance up the ballroom, her shoes danced down. They danced down the stairs, into the street, and out through the gate of the town. Dance she did, and dance she must, straight into the dark woods.

Suddenly something shone through the trees, and she thought it was the moon, but it turned out to be the red-bearded soldier. He nodded and said, "Oh, what beautiful shoes for dancing."

She was terribly frightened, and tried to take off her shoes. She tore off her stockings, but the shoes had grown fast to her feet. And dance she did, for dance she must, over fields and valleys, in the rain and in the sun, by day and night. It was most dreadful by night. She danced over an unfenced graveyard, but the dead did not join her dance. They had better things to do. She tried to sit on a pauper's grave, where the bitter fennel grew, but there was no rest or peace for her there. And when she danced toward the open doors of the church, she saw it guarded by an angel with long white robes and wings that reached from his shoulders down to the ground. His face was grave and stern, and in his hand he held a broad, shining sword.

"Dance you shall!" he told her. "Dance in your red shoes until you are pale and cold, and your flesh shrivels down to the skeleton. Dance you shall from door to door, and wherever there are children proud and vain you must knock at the door till they hear you, and are afraid of you. Dance you shall. Dance always."

"Have mercy upon me!" screamed Karen. But she did not hear the angel answer. Her shoes swept her out through the gate, and across the fields, along highways and byways, forever and always dancing.

One morning she danced by a door she knew well. There was the sound of a hymn, and a coffin was carried out covered with flowers. Then she knew the old lady was dead. She was all alone in the world now, and cursed by the angel of God.

Dance she did and dance she must, through the dark night. Her shoes took her through thorn and briar that scratched her until she bled. She danced across the wastelands until she came to a lonely little house. She knew that this was where the executioner lived, and she tapped with her finger on his window pane.

"Come out!" she called. "Come out! I can't come in, for I am dancing."

The executioner said, "You don't seem to know who I am. I strike off the heads of bad people, and I feel my ax beginning to quiver."

"Don't strike off my head, for then I could not repent of my sins," said Karen. "But strike off my feet with the red shoes on them."

She confessed her sin, and the executioner struck off her feet with the red shoes on them. The shoes danced away with her little feet, over the fields into the deep forest. But he made wooden feet and a pair of crutches for her. He taught her a hymn that prisoners sing when they are sorry for what they have done. She kissed his hand that held the ax, and went back across the wasteland.

"Now I have suffered enough for those red shoes," she said. "I shall go and be seen again in the church." She hobbled to church as fast as she could, but when she got there the red shoes danced in front of her, and she was frightened and turned back.

All week long she was sorry, and cried many bitter tears. But when Sunday came again she said, "Now I have suffered and cried enough. I think I must be as good as many who sit in church and hold their heads high." She started out unafraid, but the moment she came to the church gate she saw her red shoes dancing before her. More frightened than ever, she turned away, and with all her heart she really repented.

She went to the pastor's house, and begged him to give her work as a servant. She promised to work hard, and do all that she could. Wages did not matter, if only she could have a roof over her head and be with good people. The pastor's wife took pity on her, and gave her work at the parsonage. Karen was faithful and serious. She sat quietly in the evening, and listened to every word when the pastor read the Bible aloud. The children were devoted to her, but when they spoke of frills and furbelows, and of being as beautiful as a queen, she would shake her head.

When they went to church next Sunday they asked her to go too, but with tears in her eyes she looked at her crutches, and shook her head. The others went to hear the word of God, but she went to her lonely little room, which was just big enough to hold her bed and one chair. She sat with her hymnal in her hands, and as she read it with a contrite heart she heard the organ roll. The wind carried the sound from the church to her window. Her face was wet with tears as she lifted it up, and said, "Help me, O Lord!"

Then the sun shone bright, and the white-robed angel stood before her. He was the same angel she had seen that night, at the door of the church. But he no longer held a sharp sword. In his hand was a green branch, covered with roses. He touched the ceiling with it. There was a golden star where it touched, and the ceiling rose high. He touched the walls and they opened wide. She saw the deep-toned organ. She saw the portraits of ministers and their wives. She saw the congregation sit in flower-decked pews, and sing from their hymnals. Either the church had come to the poor girl in her narrow little room, or it was she who had been brought to the church. She sat in the pew with the pastor's family. When they had finished the hymn, they looked up and nodded to her.

"It was right for you to come, little Karen," they said.

"It was God's own mercy," she told them.

The organ sounded and the children in the choir sang, softly and beautifully. Clear sunlight streamed warm through the window, right down to the pew where Karen sat. She was so filled with the light of it, and with joy and with peace, that her heart broke. Her soul traveled along the shaft of sunlight to heaven, where no one questioned her about the red shoes.

THE TELL-TALE HEART

Edgar Allan Poe

Edgar Allan Poe (1809–1849) wrote poetry, novels and criticism, and
is seen as one of the earliest practitioners of the short story, working
in all genres, including mystery and science fiction. He tried to make
a life from writing, which was not always entirely successful, although
he was determined that writing "Literature is the most noble of professions. In fact, it is about the only one fit for a man. For my own part,
there is no seducing me from the path." He died in Baltimore aged forty,
days after having been found delirious in the street.

TRUE! – nervous – very, very dreadfully nervous I had been and am; but
why will you say that I am mad? The disease had sharpened my senses
– not destroyed – not dulled them. Above all was the sense of hearing
acute. I heard all things in the heaven and in the earth. I heard many things in
hell. How, then, am I mad? Hearken! and observe how healthily – how calmly I
can tell you the whole story.

It is impossible to say how first the idea entered my brain; but once conceived,
it haunted me day and night. Object there was none. Passion there was none. I
loved the old man. He had never wronged me. He had never given me insult. For
his gold I had no desire. I think it was his eye! yes, it was this! He had the eye
of a vulture – a pale blue eye, with a film over it. Whenever it fell upon me, my
blood ran cold; and so by degrees – very gradually – I made up my mind to take
the life of the old man, and thus rid myself of the eye forever.

Now this is the point. You fancy me mad. Madmen know nothing. But you
should have seen me. You should have seen how wisely I proceeded – with what
caution – with what foresight – with what dissimulation I went to work! I was
never kinder to the old man than during the whole week before I killed him. And
every night, about midnight, I turned the latch of his door and opened it – oh so
gently! And then, when I had made an opening sufficient for my head, I put in a
dark lantern, all closed, closed, that no light shone out, and then I thrust in my
head. Oh, you would have laughed to see how cunningly I thrust it in! I moved
it slowly – very, very slowly, so that I might not disturb the old man's sleep. It
took me an hour to place my whole head within the opening so far that I could
see him as he lay upon his bed. Ha! would a madman have been so wise as this,
And then, when my head was well in the room, I undid the lantern cautiously-oh,
so cautiously – cautiously (for the hinges creaked) – I undid it just so much that
a single thin ray fell upon the vulture eye. And this I did for seven long nights –
every night just at midnight – but I found the eye always closed; and so it was

impossible to do the work; for it was not the old man who vexed me, but his Evil Eye. And every morning, when the day broke, I went boldly into the chamber, and spoke courageously to him, calling him by name in a hearty tone, and inquiring how he has passed the night. So you see he would have been a very profound old man, indeed, to suspect that every night, just at twelve, I looked in upon him while he slept.

Upon the eighth night I was more than usually cautious in opening the door. A watch's minute hand moves more quickly than did mine. Never before that night had I felt the extent of my own powers – of my sagacity. I could scarcely contain my feelings of triumph. To think that there I was, opening the door, little by little, and he not even to dream of my secret deeds or thoughts. I fairly chuckled at the idea; and perhaps he heard me; for he moved on the bed suddenly, as if startled. Now you may think that I drew back – but no. His room was as black as pitch with the thick darkness, (for the shutters were close fastened, through fear of robbers,) and so I knew that he could not see the opening of the door, and I kept pushing it on steadily, steadily.

I had my head in, and was about to open the lantern, when my thumb slipped upon the tin fastening, and the old man sprang up in bed, crying out – "Who's there?"

I kept quite still and said nothing. For a whole hour I did not move a muscle, and in the meantime I did not hear him lie down. He was still sitting up in the bed listening; – just as I have done, night after night, hearkening to the death watches in the wall.

Presently I heard a slight groan, and I knew it was the groan of mortal terror. It was not a groan of pain or of grief – oh, no! – it was the low stifled sound that arises from the bottom of the soul when overcharged with awe. I knew the sound well. Many a night, just at midnight, when all the world slept, it has welled up from my own bosom, deepening, with its dreadful echo, the terrors that distracted me. I say I knew it well. I knew what the old man felt, and pitied him, although I chuckled at heart. I knew that he had been lying awake ever since the first slight noise, when he had turned in the bed. His fears had been ever since growing upon him. He had been trying to fancy them causeless, but could not. He had been saying to himself – "It is nothing but the wind in the chimney – it is only a mouse crossing the floor," or "It is merely a cricket which has made a single chirp." Yes, he had been trying to comfort himself with these suppositions: but he had found all in vain. All in vain; because Death, in approaching him had stalked with his black shadow before him, and enveloped the victim. And it was the mournful influence of the unperceived shadow that caused him to feel – although he neither saw nor heard – to feel the presence of my head within the room.

When I had waited a long time, very patiently, without hearing him lie down, I resolved to open a little – a very, very little crevice in the lantern. So I opened it – you cannot imagine how stealthily, stealthily – until, at length a simple dim ray, like the thread of the spider, shot from out the crevice and fell full upon the vulture eye.

It was open – wide, wide open – and I grew furious as I gazed upon it. I saw it with perfect distinctness – all a dull blue, with a hideous veil over it that chilled the very marrow in my bones; but I could see nothing else of the old man's face or person: for I had directed the ray as if by instinct, precisely upon the damned spot.

And have I not told you that what you mistake for madness is but over-acuteness of the sense? – now, I say, there came to my ears a low, dull, quick sound, such as a watch makes when enveloped in cotton. I knew that sound well, too. It was the beating of the old man's heart. It increased my fury, as the beating of a drum stimulates the soldier into courage.

But even yet I refrained and kept still. I scarcely breathed. I held the lantern motionless. I tried how steadily I could maintain the ray upon the eve. Meantime the hellish tattoo of the heart increased. It grew quicker and quicker, and louder and louder every instant. The old man's terror must have been extreme! It grew louder, I say, louder every moment! – do you mark me well I have told you that I am nervous: so I am. And now at the dead hour of the night, amid the dreadful silence of that old house, so strange a noise as this excited me to uncontrollable terror. Yet, for some minutes longer I refrained and stood still. But the beating grew louder, louder! I thought the heart must burst. And now a new anxiety seized me – the sound would be heard by a neighbour! The old man's hour had come! With a loud yell, I threw open the lantern and leaped into the room. He shrieked once – once only. In an instant I dragged him to the floor, and pulled the heavy bed over him. I then smiled gaily, to find the deed so far done. But, for many minutes, the heart beat on with a muffled sound. This, however, did not vex me; it would not be heard through the wall. At length it ceased. The old man was dead. I removed the bed and examined the corpse. Yes, he was stone, stone dead. I placed my hand upon the heart and held it there many minutes. There was no pulsation. He was stone dead. His eve would trouble me no more.

If still you think me mad, you will think so no longer when I describe the wise precautions I took for the concealment of the body. The night waned, and I worked hastily, but in silence. First of all I dismembered the corpse. I cut off the head and the arms and the legs.

I then took up three planks from the flooring of the chamber, and deposited all between the scantlings. I then replaced the boards so cleverly, so cunningly, that no human eye – not even his – could have detected any thing wrong. There was nothing to wash out – no stain of any kind – no blood-spot whatever. I had been too wary for that. A tub had caught all – ha! ha!

When I had made an end of these labors, it was four o'clock – still dark as midnight. As the bell sounded the hour, there came a knocking at the street door. I went down to open it with a light heart, – for what had I now to fear? There entered three men, who introduced themselves, with perfect suavity, as officers of the police. A shriek had been heard by a neighbour during the night; suspicion of foul play had been aroused; information had been lodged at the police office, and they (the officers) had been deputed to search the premises.

I smiled, – for what had I to fear? I bade the gentlemen welcome. The shriek, I said, was my own in a dream. The old man, I mentioned, was absent in the country. I took my visitors all over the house. I bade them search – search well. I led them, at length, to his chamber. I showed them his treasures, secure, undisturbed. In the enthusiasm of my confidence, I brought chairs into the room, and desired them here to rest from their fatigues, while I myself, in the wild audacity of my perfect triumph, placed my own seat upon the very spot beneath which reposed the corpse of the victim.

The officers were satisfied. My manner had convinced them. I was singularly at ease. They sat, and while I answered cheerily, they chatted of familiar things. But, ere long, I felt myself getting pale and wished them gone. My head ached, and I fancied a ringing in my ears: but still they sat and still chatted. The ringing became more distinct: – It continued and became more distinct: I talked more freely to get rid of the feeling: but it continued and gained definiteness – until, at length, I found that the noise was not within my ears.

No doubt I now grew very pale; – but I talked more fluently, and with a heightened voice. Yet the sound increased – and what could I do? It was a low, dull, quick sound – much such a sound as a watch makes when enveloped in cotton. I gasped for breath – and yet the officers heard it not. I talked more quickly – more vehemently; but the noise steadily increased. I arose and argued about trifles, in a high key and with violent gesticulations; but the noise steadily increased. Why would they not be gone? I paced the floor to and fro with heavy strides, as if excited to fury by the observations of the men – but the noise steadily increased. Oh God! what could I do? I foamed – I raved – I swore! I swung the chair upon which I had been sitting, and grated it upon the boards, but the noise arose over all and continually increased. It grew louder – louder – louder! And still the men chatted pleasantly, and smiled. Was it possible they heard not? Almighty God! – no, no! They heard! – they suspected! – they knew! – they were making a mockery of my horror! – this I thought, and this I think. But anything was better than this agony! Anything was more tolerable than this derision! I could bear those hypocritical smiles no longer! I felt that I must scream or die! and now – again! – hark! louder! louder! louder! louder!

"Villains!" I shrieked, "dissemble no more! I admit the deed! – tear up the planks! here, here! – It is the beating of his hideous heart!"

THE NOSE

Nikolai Gogol

"You can't imagine how stupid the whole world has grown nowadays," **Nikolai Gogol** (1809–1852) once uttered, showing immediately how modern he is, "how old we are, how very little changes". Born in the Ukraine, Gogol wrote stories, plays, novels, journalism and died before he'd even reached forty-three. His work has inspired films, operas and made a huge impact on the lives of writers who followed him – Goncharov, Turgenev, Dostoyevsky, Bulgakov, and dozens of others not Russian. He is one of two writers included in this anthology to be found dead facedown. His corpse was buried, and the cross, bust and tombstone above him change regularly.

I

On the 25th March, 18—, a very strange occurrence took place in St Petersburg. On the Ascension Avenue there lived a barber of the name of Ivan Jakovlevitch. He had lost his family name, and on his signboard, on which was depicted the head of a gentleman with one cheek soaped, the only inscription to be read was, "Blood-letting done here."

On this particular morning he awoke pretty early. Becoming aware of the smell of fresh-baked bread, he sat up a little in bed, and saw his wife, who had a special partiality for coffee, in the act of taking some fresh-baked bread out of the oven.

"Today, Prasskovna Ossipovna," he said, "I do not want any coffee; I should like a fresh loaf with onions."

"The blockhead may eat bread only as far as I am concerned," said his wife to herself; "then I shall have a chance of getting some coffee." And she threw a loaf on the table.

For the sake of propriety, Ivan Jakovlevitch drew a coat over his shirt, sat down at the table, shook out some salt for himself, prepared two onions, assumed a serious expression, and began to cut the bread. After he had cut the loaf in two halves, he looked, and to his great astonishment saw something whitish sticking in it. He carefully poked round it with his knife, and felt it with his finger.

"Quite firmly fixed!" he murmured in his beard. "What can it be?"

He put in his finger, and drew out – a nose!

Ivan Jakovlevitch at first let his hands fall from sheer astonishment; then he rubbed his eyes and began to feel it. A nose, an actual nose; and, moreover, it seemed to be the nose of an acquaintance! Alarm and terror were depicted in

Ivan's face; but these feelings were slight in comparison with the disgust which took possession of his wife.

"Whose nose have you cut off, you monster?" she screamed, her face red with anger. "You scoundrel! You tippler! I myself will report you to the police! Such a rascal! Many customers have told me that while you were shaving them, you held them so tight by the nose that they could hardly sit still."

But Ivan Jakovlevitch was more dead than alive; he saw at once that this nose could belong to no other than to Kovaloff, a member of the Municipal Committee whom he shaved every Sunday and Wednesday.

"Stop, Prasskovna Ossipovna! I will wrap it in a piece of cloth and place it in the corner. There it may remain for the present; later on I will take it away."

"No, not there! Shall I endure an amputated nose in my room? You understand nothing except how to strop a razor. You know nothing of the duties and obligations of a respectable man. You vagabond! You good-for-nothing! Am I to undertake all responsibility for you at the police-office? Ah, you soap-smearer! You blockhead! Take it away where you like, but don't let it stay under my eyes!"

Ivan Jakovlevitch stood there flabbergasted. He thought and thought, and knew not what he thought.

"The devil knows how that happened!" he said at last, scratching his head behind his ear. "Whether I came home drunk last night or not, I really don't know; but in all probability this is a quite extraordinary occurrence, for a loaf is something baked and a nose is something different. I don't understand the matter at all." And Ivan Jakovlevitch was silent. The thought that the police might find him in unlawful possession of a nose and arrest him, robbed him of all presence of mind. Already he began to have visions of a red collar with silver braid and of a sword – and he trembled all over.

At last he finished dressing himself, and to the accompaniment of the emphatic exhortations of his spouse, he wrapped up the nose in a cloth and issued into the street.

He intended to lose it somewhere – either at somebody's door, or in a public square, or in a narrow alley; but just then, in order to complete his bad luck, he was met by an acquaintance, who showered inquiries upon him. "Hullo, Ivan Jakovlevitch! Whom are you going to shave so early in the morning?" etc., so that he could find no suitable opportunity to do what he wanted. Later on he did let the nose drop, but a sentry bore down upon him with his halberd, and said, "Look out! You have let something drop!" and Ivan Jakovlevitch was obliged to pick it up and put it in his pocket.

A feeling of despair began to take possession of him; all the more as the streets became more thronged and the merchants began to open their shops. At last he resolved to go to the Isaac Bridge, where perhaps he might succeed in throwing it into the Neva.

But my conscience is a little uneasy that I have not yet given any detailed information about Ivan Jakovlevitch, an estimable man in many ways.

Like every honest Russian tradesman, Ivan Jakovlevitch was a terrible drunkard, and although he shaved other people's faces every day, his own was always unshaved. His coat (he never wore an overcoat) was quite mottled, i.e. it had been black, but become brownish-yellow; the collar was quite shiny, and instead of the three buttons, only the threads by which they had been fastened were to be seen.

Ivan Jakovlevitch was a great cynic, and when Kovaloff, the member of the Municipal Committee, said to him, as was his custom while being shaved, "Your hands always smell, Ivan Jakovlevitch!" the latter answered, "What do they smell of?" "I don't know, my friend, but they smell very strong." Ivan Jakovlevitch after taking a pinch of snuff would then, by way of reprisals, set to work to soap him on the cheek, the upper lip, behind the ears, on the chin, and everywhere.

This worthy man now stood on the Isaac Bridge. At first he looked round him, then he leant on the railings of the bridge, as though he wished to look down and see how many fish were swimming past, and secretly threw the nose, wrapped in a little piece of cloth, into the water. He felt as though a ton weight had been lifted off him, and laughed cheerfully. Instead, however, of going to shave any officials, he turned his steps to a building, the sign-board of which bore the legend "Teas served here," in order to have a glass of punch, when suddenly he perceived at the other end of the bridge a police inspector of imposing exterior, with long whiskers, three-cornered hat, and sword hanging at his side. He nearly fainted; but the police inspector beckoned to him with his hand and said, "Come here, my dear sir."

Ivan Jakovlevitch, knowing how a gentleman should behave, took his hat off quickly, went towards the police inspector and said, "I hope you are in the best of health."

"Never mind my health. Tell me, my friend, why you were standing on the bridge."

"By heaven, gracious sir, I was on the way to my customers, and only looked down to see if the river was flowing quickly."

"That is a lie! You won't get out of it like that. Confess the truth."

"I am willing to shave Your Grace two or even three times a week gratis," answered Ivan Jakovlevitch.

"No, my friend, don't put yourself out! Three barbers are busy with me already, and reckon it a high honour that I let them show me their skill. Now then, out with it! What were you doing there?"

Ivan Jakovlevitch grew pale. But here the strange episode vanishes in mist, and what further happened is not known.

II

Kovaloff, the member of the Municipal Committee, awoke fairly early that morning, and made a droning noise – "Brr! Brr!" – through his lips, as he always did, though he could not say why. He stretched himself, and told his valet to give him a little mirror which was on the table. He wished to look at the heat-boil which had appeared on his nose the previous evening; but to his great astonishment, he saw that instead of his nose he had a perfectly smooth vacancy in his face. Thoroughly alarmed, he ordered some water to be brought, and rubbed his eyes with a towel. Sure enough, he had no longer a nose! Then he sprang out of bed, and shook himself violently! No, no nose any more! He dressed himself and went at once to the police superintendent.

But before proceeding further, we must certainly give the reader some information about Kovaloff, so that he may know what sort of a man this member of the Municipal Committee really was. These committee-men, who obtain that title by means of certificates of learning, must not be compared with the committee-men appointed for the Caucasus district, who are of quite a different kind. The learned committee-man – but Russia is such a wonderful country that when one committee-man is spoken of all the others from Riga to Kamschatka refer it to themselves. The same is also true of all other titled officials. Kovaloff had been a Caucasian committee-man two years previously, and could not forget that he had occupied that position; but in order to enhance his own importance, he never called himself "committee-man" but "Major."

"Listen, my dear," he used to say when he met an old woman in the street who sold shirt-fronts; "go to my house in Sadovaia Street and ask 'Does Major Kovaloff live here?' Any child can tell you where it is."

Accordingly we will call him for the future Major Kovaloff. It was his custom to take a daily walk on the Neffsky Avenue. The collar of his shirt was always remarkably clean and stiff. He wore the same style of whiskers as those that are worn by governors of districts, architects, and regimental doctors; in short, all those who have full red cheeks and play a good game of whist. These whiskers grow straight across the cheek towards the nose.

Major Kovaloff wore a number of seals, on some of which were engraved armorial bearings, and others the names of the days of the week. He had come to St Petersburg with the view of obtaining some position corresponding to his rank, if possible that of vice-governor of a province; but he was prepared to be content with that of a bailiff in some department or other. He was, moreover, not disinclined to marry, but only such a lady who could bring with her a dowry of two hundred thousand roubles. Accordingly, the reader can judge for himself what his sensations were when he found in his face, instead of a fairly symmetrical nose, a broad, flat vacancy.

To increase his misfortune, not a single droshky was to be seen in the street, and so he was obliged to proceed on foot. He wrapped himself up in his cloak, and held his handkerchief to his face as though his nose bled. "But perhaps it is all only my imagination; it is impossible that a nose should drop off in such a silly way," he thought, and stepped into a confectioner's shop in order to look into the mirror.

Fortunately no customer was in the shop; only small shop-boys were cleaning it out, and putting chairs and tables straight. Others with sleepy faces were carrying fresh cakes on trays, and yesterday's newspapers stained with coffee were still lying about. "Thank God no one is here!" he said to himself. "Now I can look at myself leisurely."

He stepped gingerly up to a mirror and looked.

"What an infernal face!" he exclaimed, and spat with disgust. "If there were only something there instead of the nose, but there is absolutely nothing."

He bit his lips with vexation, left the confectioner's, and resolved, quite contrary to his habit, neither to look nor smile at anyone on the street. Suddenly he halted as if rooted to the spot before a door, where something extraordinary happened. A carriage drew up at the entrance; the carriage door was opened, and a gentleman in uniform came out and hurried up the steps. How great was Kovaloff's terror and astonishment when he saw that it was his own nose!

At this extraordinary sight, everything seemed to turn round with him. He felt as though he could hardly keep upright on his legs; but, though trembling all over as though with fever, he resolved to wait till the nose should return to the carriage. After about two minutes the nose actually came out again. It wore a gold-embroidered uniform with a stiff, high collar, trousers of chamois leather, and a sword hung at its side. The hat, adorned with a plume, showed that it held the rank of a state-councillor. It was obvious that it was paying "duty-calls." It looked round on both sides, called to the coachman "Drive on," and got into the carriage, which drove away.

Poor Kovaloff nearly lost his reason. He did not know what to think of this extraordinary procedure. And indeed how was it possible that the nose, which only yesterday he had on his face, and which could neither walk nor drive, should wear a uniform. He ran after the carriage, which fortunately had stopped a short way off before the Grand Bazar of Moscow. He hurried towards it and pressed through a crowd of beggar-women with their faces bound up, leaving only two openings for the eyes, over whom he had formerly so often made merry.

There were only a few people in front of the Bazar. Kovaloff was so agitated that he could decide on nothing, and looked for the nose everywhere. At last he saw it standing before a shop. It seemed half buried in its stiff collar, and was attentively inspecting the wares displayed.

"How can I get at it?" thought Kovaloff. "Everything – the uniform, the hat, and so on – show that it is a state-councillor. How the deuce has that happened?"

He began to cough discreetly near it, but the nose paid him not the least attention.

"Honourable sir," said Kovaloff at last, plucking up courage, "honourable sir."

"What do you want?" asked the nose, and turned round.

"It seems to me strange, most respected sir – you should know where you belong – and I find you all of a sudden – where? Judge yourself."

"Pardon me, I do not understand what you are talking about. Explain yourself more distinctly."

"How shall I make my meaning plainer to him?" Then plucking up fresh courage, he continued, "Naturally – besides I am a Major. You must admit it is not befitting that I should go about without a nose. An old apple-woman on the Ascension Bridge may carry on her business without one, but since I am on the look out for a post; besides in many houses I am acquainted with ladies of high position – Madame Tchektyriev, wife of a state-councillor, and many others. So you see – I do not know, honourable sir, what you –" (here the Major shrugged his shoulders). "Pardon me; if one regards the matter from the point of view of duty and honour – you will yourself understand –"

"I understand nothing," answered the nose. "I repeat, please explain yourself more distinctly."

"Honourable sir," said Kovaloff with dignity, "I do not know how I am to understand your words. It seems to me the matter is as clear as possible. Or do you wish – but you are after all my own nose!"

The nose looked at the Major and wrinkled its forehead. "There you are wrong, respected sir; I am myself. Besides, there can be no close relations between us. To judge by the buttons of your uniform, you must be in quite a different department to mine." So saying, the nose turned away.

Kovaloff was completely puzzled; he did not know what to do, and still less what to think. At this moment he heard the pleasant rustling of a lady's dress, and there approached an elderly lady wearing a quantity of lace, and by her side her graceful daughter in a white dress which set off her slender figure to advantage, and wearing a light straw hat. Behind the ladies marched a tall lackey with long whiskers.

Kovaloff advanced a few steps, adjusted his cambric collar, arranged his seals which hung by a little gold chain, and with smiling face fixed his eyes on the graceful lady, who bowed lightly like a spring flower, and raised to her brow her little white hand with transparent fingers. He smiled still more when he spied under the brim of her hat her little round chin, and part of her cheek faintly tinted with rose-colour. But suddenly he sprang back as though he had been scorched. He remembered that he had nothing but an absolute blank in place of a nose, and tears started to his eyes. He turned round in order to tell the gentleman in uniform that he was only a state-councillor in appearance, but really a scoundrel and a rascal, and nothing else but his own nose; but the nose was no longer there. He had had time to go, doubtless in order to continue his visits.

His disappearance plunged Kovaloff into despair. He went back and stood for a moment under a colonnade, looking round him on all sides in hope of perceiving the nose somewhere. He remembered very well that it wore a hat with a plume in it and a gold-embroidered uniform; but he had not noticed the shape of the cloak, nor the colour of the carriages and the horses, nor even whether a lackey stood behind it, and, if so, what sort of livery he wore. Moreover, so many carriages were passing that it would have been difficult to recognise one, and even if he had done so, there would have been no means of stopping it.

The day was fine and sunny. An immense crowd was passing to and fro in the Neffsky Avenue; a variegated stream of ladies flowed along the pavement. There was his acquaintance, the Privy Councillor, whom he was accustomed to style "General," especially when strangers were present. There was Iarygin, his intimate friend who always lost in the evenings at whist; and there another Major, who had obtained the rank of committee-man in the Caucasus, beckoned to him.

"Go to the deuce!" said Kovaloff *sotto voce*. "Hi! coachman, drive me straight to the superintendent of police." So saying, he got into a droshky and continued to shout all the time to the coachman "Drive hard!"

"Is the police superintendent at home?" he asked on entering the front hall.

"No, sir," answered the porter, "he has just gone out."

"Ah, just as I thought!"

"Yes," continued the porter, "he has only just gone out; if you had been a moment earlier you would perhaps have caught him."

Kovaloff, still holding his handkerchief to his face, re-entered the droshky and cried in a despairing voice "Drive on!"

"Where?" asked the coachman.

"Straight on!"

"But how? There are cross-roads here. Shall I go to the right or the left?"

This question made Kovaloff reflect. In his situation it was necessary to have recourse to the police; not because the affair had anything to do with them directly but because they acted more promptly than other authorities. As for demanding any explanation from the department to which the nose claimed to belong, it would, he felt, be useless, for the answers of that gentleman showed that he regarded nothing as sacred, and he might just as likely have lied in this matter as in saying that he had never seen Kovaloff.

But just as he was about to order the coachman to drive to the police-station, the idea occurred to him that this rascally scoundrel who, at their first meeting, had behaved so disloyally towards him, might, profiting by the delay, quit the city secretly; and then all his searching would be in vain, or might last over a whole month. Finally, as though visited with a heavenly inspiration, he resolved to go directly to an advertisement office, and to advertise the loss of his nose, giving all its distinctive characteristics in detail, so that anyone who found it might bring it at once to him, or at any rate inform him where it lived. Having decided on this course, he ordered the coachman to drive to the advertisement office, and all the way he continued to punch him in the back – "Quick, scoundrel! quick!"

"Yes, sir!" answered the coachman, lashing his shaggy horse with the reins.

At last they arrived, and Kovaloff, out of breath, rushed into a little room where a grey-haired official, in an old coat and with spectacles on his nose, sat at a table holding his pen between his teeth, counting a heap of copper coins.

"Who takes in the advertisements here?" exclaimed Kovaloff.

"At your service, sir," answered the grey-haired functionary, looking up and then fastening his eyes again on the heap of coins before him.

"I wish to place an advertisement in your paper –"

"Have the kindness to wait a minute," answered the official, putting down figures on paper with one hand, and with the other moving two balls on his calculating-frame.

A lackey, whose silver-laced coat showed that he served in one of the houses of the nobility, was standing by the table with a note in his hand, and speaking in a lively tone, by way of showing himself sociable. "Would you believe it, sir, this little dog is really not worth twenty-four kopecks, and for my own part I would not give a farthing for it; but the countess is quite gone upon it, and offers a hundred roubles' reward to anyone who finds it. To tell you the truth, the tastes of these people are very different from ours; they don't mind giving five hundred or a thousand roubles for a poodle or a pointer, provided it be a good one."

The official listened with a serious air while counting the number of letters contained in the note. At either side of the table stood a number of housekeepers, clerks and porters, carrying notes. The writer of one wished to sell a barouche, which had been brought from Paris in 1814 and had been very little used; others wanted to dispose of a strong droshky which wanted one spring, a spirited horse seventeen years old, and so on. The room where these people were collected was very small, and the air was very close; but Kovaloff was not affected by it, for he had covered his face with a handkerchief, and because his nose itself was heaven knew where.

"Sir, allow me to ask you – I am in a great hurry," he said at last impatiently.

"In a moment! In a moment! Two roubles, twenty-four kopecks – one minute! One rouble, sixty-four kopecks!" said the grey-haired official, throwing their notes back to the housekeepers and porters. "What do you wish?" he said, turning to Kovaloff.

"I wish – " answered the latter, "I have just been swindled and cheated, and I cannot get hold of the perpetrator. I only want you to insert an advertisement to say that whoever brings this scoundrel to me will be well rewarded."

"What is your name, please?"

"Why do you want my name? I have many lady friends – Madame Tchekty-riev, wife of a state-councillor, Madame Podtotchina, wife of a Colonel. Heaven forbid that they should get to hear of it. You can simply write 'committee-man,' or, better, 'Major.'"

"And the man who has run away is your serf."

"Serf! If he was, it would not be such a great swindle! It is the nose which has absconded."

"H'm! What a strange name. And this Mr Nose has stolen from you a considerable sum?"

"Mr Nose! Ah, you don't understand me! It is my own nose which has gone, I don't know where. The devil has played a trick on me."

"How has it disappeared? I don't understand."

"I can't tell you how, but the important point is that now it walks about the city itself a state-councillor. That is why I want you to advertise that whoever gets hold of it should bring it as soon as possible to me. Consider; how can I live without such a prominent part of my body? It is not as if it were merely a little toe; I would only have to put my foot in my boot and no one would notice its absence. Every Thursday I call on the wife of M. Tchektyriev, the state-councillor; Madame Podtotchina, a Colonel's wife who has a very pretty daughter, is one of my acquaintances; and what am I to do now? I cannot appear before them like this."

The official compressed his lips and reflected. "No, I cannot insert an advertisement like that," he said after a long pause.

"What! Why not?"

"Because it might compromise the paper. Suppose everyone could advertise that his nose was lost. People already say that all sorts of nonsense and lies are inserted."

"But this is not nonsense! There is nothing of that sort in my case."

"You think so? Listen a minute. Last week there was a case very like it. An official came, just as you have done, bringing an advertisement for the insertion of which he paid two roubles, sixty-three kopecks; and this advertisement simply announced the loss of a black-haired poodle. There did not seem to be anything out of the way in it, but it was really a satire; by the poodle was meant the cashier of some establishment or other."

"But I am not talking of a poodle, but my own nose; i.e. almost myself."

"No, I cannot insert your advertisement."

"But my nose really has disappeared!"

"That is a matter for a doctor. There are said to be people who can provide you with any kind of nose you like. But I see that you are a witty man, and like to have your little joke."

"But I swear to you on my word of honour. Look at my face yourself."

"Why put yourself out?" continued the official, taking a pinch of snuff. "All the same, if you don't mind," he added with a touch of curiosity, "I should like to have a look at it."

The committee-man removed the handkerchief from before his face.

"It certainly does look odd," said the official. "It is perfectly flat like a freshly fried pancake. It is hardly credible."

"Very well. Are you going to hesitate any more? You see it is impossible to refuse to advertise my loss. I shall be particularly obliged to you, and I shall be glad that this incident has procured me the pleasure of making your acquaintance." The Major, we see, did not even shrink from a slight humiliation.

"It certainly is not difficult to advertise it," replied the official; "but I don't see what good it would do you. However, if you lay so much stress on it, you should apply to someone who has a skilful pen, so that he may describe it as a curious, natural freak, and publish the article in the *Northern Bee*" (here he took another pinch) "for the benefit of youthful readers" (he wiped his nose), "or simply as a matter worthy of arousing public curiosity."

The committee-man felt completely discouraged. He let his eyes fall absent-mindedly on a daily paper in which theatrical performances were advertised. Reading there the name of an actress whom he knew to be pretty, he involuntarily smiled, and his hand sought his pocket to see if he had a blue ticket – for in Kovaloff's opinion superior officers like himself should not take a lesser-priced seat; but the thought of his lost nose suddenly spoilt everything.

The official himself seemed touched at his difficult position. Desiring to console him, he tried to express his sympathy by a few polite words. "I much regret," he said, "your extraordinary mishap. Will you not try a pinch of snuff? It clears the head, banishes depression, and is a good preventive against hæmorrhoids."

So saying, he reached his snuff-box out to Kovaloff, skilfully concealing at the same time the cover, which was adorned with the portrait of some lady or other.

This act, quite innocent in itself, exasperated Kovaloff. "I don't understand what you find to joke about in the matter," he exclaimed angrily. "Don't you see that I lack precisely the essential feature for taking snuff? The devil take your snuff-box. I don't want to look at snuff now, not even the best, certainly not your vile stuff!"

So saying, he left the advertisement office in a state of profound irritation, and went to the commissary of police. He arrived just as this dignitary was reclining on his couch, and saying to himself with a sigh of satisfaction, "Yes, I shall make a nice little sum out of that."

It might be expected, therefore, that the committee-man's visit would be quite inopportune.

This police commissary was a great patron of all the arts and industries; but what he liked above everything else was a cheque. "It is a thing," he used to say, "to which it is not easy to find an equivalent; it requires no food, it does not take up much room, it stays in one's pocket, and if it falls, it is not broken."

The commissary accorded Kovaloff a fairly frigid reception, saying that the afternoon was not the best time to come with a case, that nature required one to rest a little after eating (this showed the committee-man that the commissary was acquainted with the aphorisms of the ancient sages), and that respectable people did not have their noses stolen.

The last allusion was too direct. We must remember that Kovaloff was a very sensitive man. He did not mind anything said against him as an individual, but he could not endure any reflection on his rank or social position. He even believed that in comedies one might allow attacks on junior officers, but never on their seniors.

The commissary's reception of him hurt his feelings so much that he raised his head proudly, and said with dignity, "After such insulting expressions on your part, I have nothing more to say." And he left the place.

He reached his house quite wearied out. It was already growing dark. After all his fruitless search, his room seemed to him melancholy and even ugly. In the vestibule he saw his valet Ivan stretched on the leather couch and amusing himself by spitting at the ceiling, which he did very cleverly, hitting every time the same spot. His servant's equanimity enraged him; he struck him on the forehead with his hat, and said, "You good-for-nothing, you are always playing the fool!"

Ivan rose quickly and hastened to take off his master's cloak.

Once in his room, the Major, tired and depressed, threw himself in an armchair and, after sighing a while, began to soliloquise:

"In heaven's name, why should such a misfortune befall me? If I had lost an arm or a leg, it would be less insupportable; but a man without a nose! Devil take it! – what is he good for? He is only fit to be thrown out of the window. If it had been taken from me in war or in a duel, or if I had lost it by my own fault! But it has disappeared inexplicably. But no! it is impossible," he continued after reflecting a few moments, "it is incredible that a nose can disappear like that – quite incredible. I must be dreaming, or suffering from some hallucination; perhaps I swallowed, by mistake instead of water, the brandy with which I rub my chin after being shaved. That fool of an Ivan must have forgotten to take it away, and I must have swallowed it."

In order to find out whether he were really drunk, the Major pinched himself so hard that he unvoluntarily uttered a cry. The pain convinced him that he was quite wide awake. He walked slowly to the looking-glass and at first closed his eyes, hoping to see his nose suddenly in its proper place; but on opening them, he started back. "What a hideous sight!" he exclaimed.

It was really incomprehensible. One might easily lose a button, a silver spoon, a watch, or something similar; but a loss like this, and in one's own dwelling!

After considering all the circumstances, Major Kovaloff felt inclined to suppose that the cause of all his trouble should be laid at the door of Madame Podtotchina, the Colonel's wife, who wished him to marry her daughter. He himself paid her court readily, but always avoided coming to the point. And when the lady one day told him point-blank that she wished him to marry her daughter, he gently drew back, declaring that he was still too young, and that he had to serve five years more before he would be forty-two. This must be the reason why the lady, in revenge, had resolved to bring him into disgrace, and had hired two sorceresses for that object. One thing was certain – his nose had not been cut off; no one had entered his room, and as for Ivan Jakovlevitch – he had been shaved by him on Wednesday, and during that day and the whole of Thursday his nose had been there, as he knew and well remembered. Moreover, if his nose had been cut off he would naturally have felt pain, and doubtless the wound would not have healed so quickly, nor would the surface have been as flat as a pancake.

All kinds of plans passed through his head: should he bring a legal action against the wife of a superior officer, or should he go to her and charge her openly with her treachery?

His reflections were interrupted by a sudden light, which shone through all the chinks of the door, showing that Ivan had lit the wax-candles in the vestibule. Soon Ivan himself came in with the lights. Kovaloff quickly seized a handkerchief and covered the place where his nose had been the evening before, so that his blockhead of a servant might not gape with his mouth wide open when he saw his master's extraordinary appearance.

Scarcely had Ivan returned to the vestibule than a stranger's voice was heard there.

"Does Major Kovaloff live here?" it asked.

"Come in!" said the Major, rising rapidly and opening the door.

He saw a police official of pleasant appearance, with grey whiskers and fairly full cheeks – the same who at the commencement of this story was standing at the end of the Isaac Bridge. "You have lost your nose?" he asked.

"Exactly so."

"It has just been found."

"What – do you say?" stammered Major Kovaloff.

Joy had suddenly paralysed his tongue. He stared at the police commissary on whose cheeks and full lips fell the flickering light of the candle.

"How was it?" he asked at last.

"By a very singular chance. It has been arrested just as it was getting into a carriage for Riga. Its passport had been made out some time ago in the name of an official; and what is still more strange, I myself took it at first for a gentleman. Fortunately I had my glasses with me, and then I saw at once that it was a nose. I am shortsighted, you know, and as you stand before me I cannot distinguish your nose, your beard, or anything else. My mother-in-law can hardly see at all."

Kovaloff was beside himself with excitement. "Where is it? Where? I will hasten there at once."

"Don't put yourself out. Knowing that you need it, I have brought it with me. Another singular thing is that the principal culprit in the matter is a scoundrel of a barber living in the Ascension Avenue, who is now safely locked up. I had long suspected him of drunkenness and theft; only the day before yesterday he stole some buttons in a shop. Your nose is quite uninjured." So saying, the police commissary put his hand in his pocket and brought out the nose wrapped up in paper.

"Yes, yes, that is it!" exclaimed Kovaloff. "Will you not stay and drink a cup of tea with me?"

"I should like to very much, but I cannot. I must go at once to the House of Correction. The cost of living is very high nowadays. My mother-in-law lives with me, and there are several children; the eldest is very hopeful and intelligent, but I have no means for their education."

After the commissary's departure, Kovaloff remained for some time plunged in a kind of vague reverie, and did not recover full consciousness for several moments, so great was the effect of this unexpected good news. He placed the recovered nose carefully in the palm of his hand, and examined it again with the greatest attention.

"Yes, this is it!" he said to himself. "Here is the heat-boil on the left side, which came out yesterday." And he nearly laughed aloud with delight.

But nothing is permanent in this world. Joy in the second moment of its arrival is already less keen than in the first, is still fainter in the third, and finishes by coalescing with our normal mental state, just as the circles which the fall of a pebble forms on the surface of water, gradually die away. Kovaloff began to meditate, and saw that his difficulties were not yet over; his nose had been recovered, but it had to be joined on again in its proper place.

And suppose it could not? As he put this question to himself, Kovaloff grew pale. With a feeling of indescribable dread, he rushed towards his dressing-table, and stood before the mirror in order that he might not place his nose crookedly. His hands trembled.

Very carefully he placed it where it had been before. Horror! It did not remain there. He held it to his mouth and warmed it a little with his breath, and then placed it there again; but it would not hold.

"Hold on, you stupid!" he said.

But the nose seemed to be made of wood, and fell back on the table with a strange noise, as though it had been a cork. The Major's face began to twitch feverishly. "Is it possible that it won't stick?" he asked himself, full of alarm. But however often he tried, all his efforts were in vain.

He called Ivan, and sent him to fetch the doctor who occupied the finest flat in the mansion. This doctor was a man of imposing appearance, who had magnificent black whiskers and a healthy wife. He ate fresh apples every morning, and cleaned his teeth with extreme care, using five different tooth-brushes for three-quarters of an hour daily.

The doctor came immediately. After having asked the Major when this misfortune had happened, he raised his chin and gave him a fillip with his finger just where the nose had been, in such a way that the Major suddenly threw back his head and struck the wall with it. The doctor said that did not matter; then, making him turn his face to the right, he felt the vacant place and said "H'm!" then he made him turn it to the left and did the same; finally he again gave him a fillip with his finger, so that the Major started like a horse whose teeth are being examined. After this experiment, the doctor shook his head and said, "No, it cannot be done. Rather remain as you are, lest something worse happen. Certainly one could replace it at once, but I assure you the remedy would be worse than the disease."

"All very fine, but how am I to go on without a nose?" answered Kovaloff. "There is nothing worse than that. How can I show myself with such a villainous appearance? I go into good society, and this evening I am invited to two parties. I know several ladies, Madame Tchektyriev, the wife of a state-councillor, Madame Podtotchina – although after what she has done, I don't want to have anything to do with her except through the agency of the police. I beg you," continued Kovaloff in a supplicating tone, "find some way or other of replacing it; even if it is not quite firm, as long as it holds at all; I can keep it in place sometimes with my hand, whenever there is any risk. Besides, I do not even dance, so that it is not likely to be injured by any sudden movement. As to your fee, be in no anxiety about that; I can well afford it."

"Believe me," answered the doctor in a voice which was neither too high nor too low, but soft and almost magnetic, "I do not treat patients from love of gain. That would be contrary to my principles and to my art. It is true that I accept fees, but that is only not to hurt my patients' feelings by refusing them. I could certainly replace your nose, but I assure you on my word of honour, it would only make matters worse. Rather let Nature do her own work. Wash the place often with cold water, and I assure you that even without a nose, you will be just as well as if you had one. As to the nose itself, I advise you to have it preserved in a bottle of spirits, or, still better, of warm vinegar mixed with two spoonfuls of brandy, and then you can sell it at a good price. I would be willing to take it myself, provided you do not ask too much."

"No, no, I shall not sell it at any price. I would rather it were lost again."

"Excuse me," said the doctor, taking his leave. "I hoped to be useful to you, but I can do nothing more; you are at any rate convinced of my good-will." So saying, the doctor left the room with a dignified air.

Kovaloff did not even notice his departure. Absorbed in a profound reverie, he only saw the edge of his snow-white cuffs emerging from the sleeves of his black coat.

The next day he resolved, before bringing a formal action, to write to the Colonel's wife and see whether she would not return to him, without further dispute, that of which she had deprived him.

The letter ran as follows:

"To Madame Alexandra Podtotchina,
"I hardly understand your method of action. Be sure that by adopting such a course you will gain nothing, and will certainly not succeed in making me marry your daughter. Believe me, the story of my nose has become well known; it is you and no one else who have taken the principal part in it. Its unexpected separation from the place which it occupied, its flight and its appearances sometimes in the disguise of an official, sometimes in proper person, are nothing but the consequence of unholy spells employed by you or by persons who, like you, are addicted to such honourable pursuits. On my part, I wish to inform you, that if the above-mentioned nose is not restored to-day to its proper place, I shall be obliged to have recourse to legal procedure.
"For the rest, with all respect, I have the honour to be your humble servant,
"Platon Kovaloff."

The reply was not long in coming, and was as follows:

"Major PLATON KOVALOFF, –
"Your letter has profoundly astonished me. I must confess that I had not expected such unjust reproaches on your part. I assure you that the official of whom you speak has not been at my house, either disguised or in his proper person. It is true that Philippe Ivanovitch Potantchikoff has paid visits at my house, and though he has actually asked for my daughter's hand, and was a man of good breeding, respectable and intelligent, I never gave him any hope.
"Again, you say something about a nose. If you intend to imply by that that I wished to snub you, i.e. to meet you with a refusal, I am very astonished because, as you well know, I was quite of the opposite mind. If after this you wish to ask for my daughter's hand, I should be glad to gratify you, for such has also been the object of my most fervent desire, in the hope of the accomplishment of which, I remain, yours most sincerely,
"ALEXANDRA PODTOTCHINA."

"No," said Kovaloff, after having reperused the letter, "she is certainly not guilty. It is impossible. Such a letter could not be written by a criminal." The committee-man was experienced in such matters, for he had been often officially deputed to conduct criminal investigations while in the Caucasus. "But then how and by what trick of fate has the thing happened?" he said to himself with a gesture of discouragement. "The devil must be at the bottom of it."

Meanwhile the rumour of this extraordinary event had spread all over the city, and, as is generally the case, not without numerous additions. At that period there was a general disposition to believe in the miraculous; the public had recently been impressed by experiments in magnetism. The story of the floating chairs in Koniouchennaia Street was still quite recent, and there was nothing astonishing in hearing soon afterwards that Major Kovaloff's nose was to be seen walking every day at three o'clock on the Neffsky Avenue. The crowd of curious spectators which gathered there daily was enormous. On one occasion someone spread a report that the nose was in Junker's stores and immediately the place was besieged by such a crowd that the police had to interfere and establish order. A certain speculator with a grave, whiskered face, who sold cakes at a theatre door, had some strong wooden benches made which he placed before the window of the stores, and obligingly invited the public to stand on them and look in, at the modest charge of twenty-four kopecks. A veteran colonel, leaving his house earlier than usual expressly for the purpose, had the greatest difficulty in elbowing his way through the crowd, but to his great indignation he saw nothing in the store window but an ordinary flannel waistcoat and a coloured lithograph representing a young girl darning a stocking, while an elegant youth in a waistcoat with large lappels watched her from behind a tree. The picture had hung in the same place for more than ten years. The colonel went off, growling savagely to himself, "How can the fools let themselves be excited by such idiotic stories?"

Then another rumour got abroad, to the effect that the nose of Major

Kovaloff was in the habit of walking not on the Neffsky Avenue but in the Tauris Gardens. Some students of the Academy of Surgery went there on purpose to see it. A high-born lady wrote to the keeper of the gardens asking him to show her children this rare phenomenon, and to give them some suitable instruction on the occasion.

All these incidents were eagerly collected by the town wits, who just then were very short of anecdotes adapted to amuse ladies. On the other hand, the minority of solid, sober people were very much displeased. One gentleman asserted with great indignation that he could not understand how in our enlightened age such absurdities could spread abroad, and he was astonished that the Government did not direct their attention to the matter. This gentleman evidently belonged to the category of those people who wish the Government to interfere in everything, even in their daily quarrels with their wives.

But here the course of events is again obscured by a veil.

III

Strange events happen in this world, events which are sometimes entirely improbable. The same nose which had masqueraded as a state-councillor, and caused so much sensation in the town, was found one morning in its proper place, i.e. between the cheeks of Major Kovaloff, as if nothing had happened.

This occurred on 7th April. On awaking, the Major looked by chance into a mirror and perceived a nose. He quickly put his hand to it; it was there beyond a doubt!

"Oh!" exclaimed Kovaloff. For sheer joy he was on the point of performing a dance barefooted across his room, but the entrance of Ivan prevented him. He told him to bring water, and after washing himself, he looked again in the glass. The nose was there! Then he dried his face with a towel and looked again. Yes, there was no mistake about it!

"Look here, Ivan, it seems to me that I have a heat-boil on my nose," he said to his valet.

And he thought to himself at the same time, "That will be a nice business if Ivan says to me 'No, sir, not only is there no boil, but your nose itself is not there!'"

But Ivan answered, "There is nothing, sir; I can see no boil on your nose."

"Good! Good!" exclaimed the Major, and snapped his fingers with delight.

At this moment the barber, Ivan Jakovlevitch, put his head in at the door, but as timidly as a cat which has just been beaten for stealing lard.

"Tell me first, are your hands clean?" asked Kovaloff when he saw him.

"Yes, sir."

"You lie."

"I swear they are perfectly clean, sir."

"Very well; then come here."

Kovaloff seated himself. Jakovlevitch tied a napkin under his chin, and in the twinkling of an eye covered his beard and part of his cheeks with a copious creamy lather.

"There it is!" said the barber to himself, as he glanced at the nose. Then he bent his head a little and examined it from one side. "Yes, it actually is the nose – really, when one thinks –" he continued, pursuing his mental soliloquy and still looking at it. Then quite gently, with infinite precaution, he raised two fingers in the air in order to take hold of it by the extremity, as he was accustomed to do.

"Now then, take care!" Kovaloff exclaimed.

Ivan Jakovlevitch let his arm fall and felt more embarrassed than he had ever done in his life. At last he began to pass the razor very lightly over the Major's chin, and although it was very difficult to shave him without using the olfactory organ as a point of support, he succeeded, however, by placing his wrinkled thumb against the Major's lower jaw and cheek, thus overcoming all obstacles and bringing his task to a safe conclusion.

When the barber had finished, Kovaloff hastened to dress himself, took a droshky, and drove straight to the confectioner's. As he entered it, he ordered a cup of chocolate. He then stepped straight to the mirror; the nose was there!

He returned joyfully, and regarded with a satirical expression two officers who were in the shop, one of whom possessed a nose not much larger than a waistcoat button.

After that he went to the office of the department where he had applied for the post of vice-governor of a province or Government bailiff. As he passed through the hall of reception, he cast a glance at the mirror; the nose was there! Then he went to pay a visit to another committee-man, a very sarcastic personage, to whom he was accustomed to say in answer to his raillery, "Yes, I know, you are the funniest fellow in St Petersburg."

On the way he said to himself, "If the Major does not burst into laughter at the sight of me, that is a most certain sign that everything is in its accustomed place."

But the Major said nothing. "Very good!" thought Kovaloff.

As he returned, he met Madame Podtotchina with her daughter. He accosted them, and they responded very graciously. The conversation lasted a long time, during which he took more than one pinch of snuff, saying to himself, "No, you haven't caught me yet, coquettes that you are! And as to the daughter, I shan't marry her at all."

After that, the Major resumed his walks on the Neffsky Avenue and his visits to the theatre as if nothing had happened. His nose also remained in its place as if it had never quitted it. From that time he was always to be seen smiling, in a good humour, and paying attentions to pretty girls.

IV

Such was the occurrence which took place in the northern capital of our vast empire. On considering the account carefully we see that there is a good deal which looks improbable about it. Not to speak of the strange disappearance of the nose, and its appearance in different places under the disguise of a councillor of state, how was it that Kovaloff did not understand that one cannot decently advertise for a lost nose? I do not mean to say that he would have had to pay too much for the advertisement – that is a mere trifle, and I am not one of those who attach too much importance to money; but to advertise in such a case is not proper nor befitting.

Another difficulty is – how was the nose found in the baked loaf, and how did Ivan Jakovlevitch himself – no, I don't understand it at all!

But the most incomprehensible thing of all is, how authors can choose such subjects for their stories. That really surpasses my understanding. In the first place, no advantage results from it for the country; and in the second place, no harm results either.

All the same, when one reflects well, there really is something in the matter.

Whatever may be said to the contrary, such cases do occur – rarely, it is true, but now and then actually.

THE SIGNAL-MAN

Charles Dickens

It still comes as a bit of a shock to me that **Charles Dickens** (1812–1870) produced five novellas, ten children, fifteen novels and hundreds of short stories and articles, dying at the age of fifty-eight. Influenced by Smollett and Fielding, he became *the* Victorian novelist, and his work has influenced countless authors who have written since his burial, against his wishes, in Westminster Abbey.

"Halloa! Below there!"

When he heard a voice thus calling to him, he was standing at the door of his box, with a flag in his hand, furled round its short pole. One would have thought, considering the nature of the ground, that he could not have doubted from what quarter the voice came; but, instead of looking up to where I stood on the top of the steep cutting nearly over his head, he turned himself about and looked down the Line. There was something remarkable in his manner of doing so, though I could not have said, for my life, what. But, I know it was remarkable enough to attract my notice, even though his figure was foreshortened and shadowed, down in the deep trench, and mine was high above him, so steeped in the glow of an angry sunset that I had shaded my eyes with my hand before I saw him at all.

"Halloa! Below!"

From looking down the Line, he turned himself about again, and, raising his eyes, saw my figure high above him.

"Is there any path by which I can come down and speak to you?"

He looked up at me without replying, and I looked down at him without pressing him too soon with a repetition of my idle question. Just then, there came a vague vibration in the earth and air, quickly changing into a violent pulsation, and an oncoming rush that caused me to start back, as though it had force to draw me down. When such vapour as rose to my height from this rapid train, had passed me and was skimming away over the landscape, I looked down again, and saw him re-furling the flag he had shown while the train went by.

I repeated my inquiry. After a pause, during which he seemed to regard me with fixed attention, he motioned with his rolled-up flag towards a point on my level, some two or three hundred yards distant. I called down to him, "All right!" and made for that point. There, by dint of looking closely about me, I found a rough zig-zag descending path notched out: which I followed.

The cutting was extremely deep, and unusually precipitate. It was made through a clammy stone that became oozier and wetter as I went down. For these reasons, I found the way long enough to give me time to recall a singular air of reluctance or compulsion with which he had pointed out the path.

When I came down low enough upon the zig-zag descent, to see him again, I saw that he was standing between the rails on the way by which the train had lately passed, in an attitude as if he were waiting for me to appear. He had his left hand at his chin, and that left elbow rested on his right hand crossed over his breast. His attitude was one of such expectation and watchfulness, that I stopped a moment, wondering at it.

I resumed my downward way, and, stepping out upon the level of the railroad and drawing nearer to him, saw that he was a dark sallow man, with a dark beard and rather heavy eyebrows. His post was in as solitary and dismal a place as ever I saw. On either side, a dripping-wet wall of jagged stone, excluding all view but a strip of sky; the perspective one way, only a crooked prolongation of this great dungeon; the shorter perspective in the other direction, terminating in a gloomy red light, and the gloomier entrance to a black tunnel, in whose massive architecture there was a barbarous, depressing, and forbidding air. So little sunlight ever found its way to this spot, that it had an earthy deadly smell; and so much cold wind rushed through it, that it struck chill to me, as if I had left the natural world.

Before he stirred, I was near enough to him to have touched him. Not even then removing his eyes from mine, he stepped back one step, and lifted his hand.

This was a lonesome post to occupy (I said), and it had riveted my attention when I looked down from up yonder. A visitor was a rarity, I should suppose; not an unwelcome rarity, I hoped? In me, he merely saw a man who had been shut up within narrow limits all his life, and who, being at last set free, had a newly-awakened interest in these great works. To such purpose I spoke to him; but I am far from sure of the terms I used, for, besides that I am not happy in opening any conversation, there was something in the man that daunted me.

He directed a most curious look towards the red light near the tunnel's mouth, and looked all about it, as if something were missing from it, and then looked at me.

That light was part of his charge? Was it not?

He answered in a low voice: "Don't you know it is?"

The monstrous thought came into my mind as I perused the fixed eyes and the saturnine face, that this was a spirit, not a man. I have speculated since, whether there may have been infection in his mind.

In my turn, I stepped back. But in making the action, I detected in his eyes some latent fear of me. This put the monstrous thought to flight.

"You look at me," I said, forcing a smile, "as if you had a dread of me."

"I was doubtful," he returned, "whether I had seen you before."

"Where?"

He pointed to the red light he had looked at.

"There?" I said.

Intently watchful of me, he replied (but without sound), Yes.

"My good fellow, what should I do there? However, be that as it may, I never was there, you may swear."

"I think I may," he rejoined. "Yes. I am sure I may."

His manner cleared, like my own. He replied to my remarks with readiness, and in well-chosen words. Had he much to do there? Yes; that was to say, he had enough responsibility to bear; but exactness and watchfulness were what was required of him, and of actual work – manual labour he had next to none. To change that signal, to trim those lights, and to turn this iron handle now and then, was all he had to do under that head. Regarding those many long and lonely hours of which I seemed to make so much, he could only say that the routine of his life had shaped itself into that form, and he had grown used to it. He had taught himself a language down here – if only to know it by sight, and to have formed his own crude ideas of its pronunciation, could be called learning it. He had also worked at fractions and decimals, and tried a little algebra; but he was, and had been as a boy, a poor hand at figures. Was it necessary for him when on duty, always to remain in that channel of damp air, and could he never rise into the sunshine from between those high stone walls? Why, that depended upon times and circumstances. Under some conditions there would be less upon the Line than under others, and the same held good as to certain hours of the day and night. In bright weather, he did choose occasions for getting a little above these lower shadows; but, being at all times liable to be called by his electric bell, and at such times listening for it with redoubled anxiety, the relief was less than I would suppose.

He took me into his box, where there was a fire, a desk for an official book in which he had to make certain entries, a telegraphic instrument with its dial face and needles, and the little bell of which he had spoken. On my trusting that he would excuse the remark that he had been well-educated, and (I hoped I might say without offence), perhaps educated above that station, he observed that instances of slight incongruity in such-wise would rarely be found wanting among large bodies of men; that he had heard it was so in workhouses, in the police force, even in that last desperate resource, the army; and that he knew it was so, more or less, in any great railway staff. He had been, when young (if I could believe it, sitting in that, hut; he scarcely could), a student of natural philosophy, and had attended lectures; but he had run wild, misused his opportunities, gone down, and never risen again. He had no complaint to offer about that. He had made his bed and he lay upon it. It was far too late to make another.

All that I have here condensed, he said in a quiet manner, with his grave dark regards divided between me and the fire. He threw in the word "Sir" from time to time, and especially when he referred to his youth: as though to request me to understand that he claimed to be nothing but what I found him. He was several times interrupted by the little bell, and had to read off messages, and send replies. Once, he had to stand without the door, and display a flag as a train passed, and make some verbal communication to the driver. In the discharge of his duties I observed him to be remarkably exact and vigilant, breaking off his discourse at a syllable, and remaining silent until what he had to do was done.

In a word, I should have set this man down as one of the safest of men to be employed in that capacity, but for the circumstance that while he was speaking to me he twice broke off with a fallen colour, turned his face towards the little bell when it did NOT ring, opened the door of the hut (which was kept shut to exclude the unhealthy damp), and looked out towards the red light near the mouth of the tunnel. On both of those occasions, he came back to the fire with the inexplicable air upon him which I had remarked, without being able to define, when we were so far asunder.

Said I when I rose to leave him: "You almost make me think that I have met with a contented man."

(I am afraid I must acknowledge that I said it to lead him on.)

"I believe I used to be so," he rejoined, in the low voice in which he had first spoken; "but I am troubled, sir, I am troubled."

He would have recalled the words if he could. He had said them, however, and I took them up quickly.

"With what? What is your trouble?"

"It is very difficult to impart, sir. It is very, very difficult to speak of. If ever you make me another visit, I will try to tell you."

"But I expressly intend to make you another visit. Say, when shall it be?"

"I go off early in the morning, and I shall be on again at ten to-morrow night, sir."

"I will come at eleven."

He thanked me, and went out at the door with me. "I'll show my white light, sir," he said, in his peculiar low voice, "till you have found the way up. When you have found it, don't call out! And when you are at the top, don't call out!"

His manner seemed to make the place strike colder to me, but I said no more than "Very well."

"And when you come down to-morrow night, don't call out! Let me ask you a parting question. What made you cry 'Halloa! Below there!' to-night?"

"Heaven knows," said I. "I cried something to that effect—"

"Not to that effect, sir. Those were the very words. I know them well."

"Admit those were the very words. I said them, no doubt, because I saw you below."

"For no other reason?"

"What other reason could I possibly have!"

"You had no feeling that they were conveyed to you in any supernatural way?"

"No."

He wished me good night, and held up his light. I walked by the side of the down Line of rails (with a very disagreeable sensation of a train coming behind me), until I found the path. It was easier to mount than to descend, and I got back to my inn without any adventure.

Punctual to my appointment, I placed my foot on the first notch of the zig-zag next night, as the distant clocks were striking eleven. He was waiting for me at the bottom, with his white light on. "I have not called out," I said, when we came close together; "may I speak now?" "By all means, sir." "Good night then, and here's my hand." "Good night, sir, and here's mine." With that, we walked side by side to his box, entered it, closed the door, and sat down by the fire.

"I have made up my mind, sir," he began, bending forward as soon as we were seated, and speaking in a tone but a little above a whisper, "that you shall not have to ask me twice what troubles me. I took you for someone else yesterday evening. That troubles me."

"That mistake?"

"No. That someone else."

"Who is it?"

"I don't know."

"Like me?"

"I don't know. I never saw the face. The left arm is across the face, and the right arm is waved. Violently waved. This way."

I followed his action with my eyes, and it was the action of an arm gesticulating with the utmost passion and vehemence: "For God's sake clear the way!"

"One moonlight night," said the man, "I was sitting here, when I heard a voice cry 'Halloa! Below there!' I started up, looked from that door, and saw this Some one else standing by the red light near the tunnel, waving as I just now showed you. The voice seemed hoarse with shouting, and it cried, 'Look out! Look out!' And then again 'Halloa! Below there! Look out!' I caught up my lamp, turned it on red, and ran towards the figure, calling, 'What's wrong? What has happened? Where?' It stood just outside the blackness of the tunnel. I advanced so close upon it that I wondered at its keeping the sleeve across its eyes. I ran right up at it, and had my hand stretched out to pull the sleeve away, when it was gone."

"Into the tunnel," said I.

"No. I ran on into the tunnel, five hundred yards. I stopped and held my lamp above my head, and saw the figures of the measured distance, and saw the wet stains stealing down the walls and trickling through the arch. I ran out again, faster than I had run in (for I had a mortal abhorrence of the place upon me), and I looked all round the red light with my own red light, and I went up the iron ladder to the gallery atop of it, and I came down again, and ran back here. I telegraphed both ways, 'An alarm has been given. Is anything wrong?' The answer came back, both ways: 'All well.'"

Resisting the slow touch of a frozen finger tracing out my spine, I showed him how that this figure must be a deception of his sense of sight, and how that figures, originating in disease of the delicate nerves that minister to the functions of the eye, were known to have often troubled patients, some of whom had become conscious of the nature of their affliction, and had even proved it by experiments upon themselves. "As to an imaginary cry," said I, "do but listen for a moment to the wind in this unnatural valley while we speak so low, and to the wild harp it makes of the telegraph wires!"

That was all very well, he returned, after we had sat listening for a while, and he ought to know something of the wind and the wires, he who so often passed long winter nights there, alone and watching. But he would beg to remark that he had not finished.

I asked his pardon, and he slowly added these words, touching my arm:

"Within six hours after the Appearance, the memorable accident on this Line happened, and within ten hours the dead and wounded were brought along through the tunnel over the spot where the figure had stood."

A disagreeable shudder crept over me, but I did my best against it. It was not to be denied, I rejoined, that this was a remarkable coincidence, calculated deeply to impress his mind. But it was unquestionable that remarkable coincidences did continually occur, and they must be taken into account in dealing with such a subject. Though to be sure I must admit, I added (for I thought I saw that he was going to bring the objection to bear upon me), men of common sense did not allow much for coincidences in making the ordinary calculations of life.

He again begged to remark that he had not finished.

I again begged his pardon for being betrayed into interruptions.

"This," he said, again laying his hand upon my arm, and glancing over his shoulder with hollow eyes, "was just a year ago. Six or seven months passed, and I had recovered from the surprise and shock, when one morning, as the day was breaking, I, standing at that door, looked towards the red light, and saw the spectre again." He stopped, with a fixed look at me.

"Did it cry out?"

"No. It was silent."

"Did it wave its arm?"

"No. It leaned against the shaft of the light, with both hands before the face. Like this."

Once more, I followed his action with my eyes. It was an action of mourning. I have seen such an attitude in stone figures on tombs.

"Did you go up to it?"

"I came in and sat down, partly to collect my thoughts, partly because it had turned me faint. When I went to the door again, daylight was above me, and the ghost was gone."

"But nothing followed? Nothing came of this?"

He touched me on the arm with his forefinger twice or thrice, giving a ghastly nod each time:

"That very day, as a train came out of the tunnel, I noticed, at a carriage window on my side, what looked like a confusion of hands and heads, and something waved. I saw it, just in time to signal the driver, Stop! He shut off, and put his brake on, but the train drifted past here a hundred and fifty yards or more. I ran after it, and, as I went along, heard terrible screams and cries. A beautiful young lady had died instantaneously in one of the compartments, and was brought in here, and laid down on this floor between us."

Involuntarily, I pushed my chair back, as I looked from the boards at which he pointed, to himself.

"True, sir. True. Precisely as it happened, so I tell it you."

I could think of nothing to say, to any purpose, and my mouth was very dry. The wind and the wires took up the story with a long lamenting wail.

He resumed. "Now, sir, mark this, and judge how my mind is troubled. The spectre came back, a week ago. Ever since, it has been there, now and again, by fits and starts."

"At the light?"

"At the Danger-light."

"What does it seem to do?"

He repeated, if possible with increased passion and vehemence, that former gesticulation of "For God's sake clear the way!"

Then, he went on. "I have no peace or rest for it. It calls to me, for many minutes together, in an agonised manner, 'Below there! Look out! Look out!' It stands waving to me. It rings my little bell—"

I caught at that. "Did it ring your bell yesterday evening when I was here, and you went to the door?"

"Twice."

"Why, see," said I, "how your imagination misleads you. My eyes were on the bell, and my ears were open to the bell, and if I am a living man, it did NOT ring at those times. No, nor at any other time, except when it was rung in the natural course of physical things by the station communicating with you."

He shook his head. "I have never made a mistake as to that, yet, sir. I have never confused the spectre's ring with the man's. The ghost's ring is a strange vibration in the bell that it derives from nothing else, and I have not asserted that the bell stirs to the eye. I don't wonder that you failed to hear it. But I heard it."

"And did the spectre seem to be there, when you looked out?"

"It WAS there."

"Both times?"

He repeated firmly: "Both times."

"Will you come to the door with me, and look for it now?"

He bit his under-lip as though he were somewhat unwilling, but arose. I opened the door, and stood on the step, while he stood in the doorway. There, was the Danger-light. There, was the dismal mouth of the tunnel. There, were the high wet stone walls of the cutting. There, were the stars above them.

"Do you see it?" I asked him, taking particular note of his face. His eyes were prominent and strained; but not very much more so, perhaps, than my own had been when I had directed them earnestly towards the same spot.

"No," he answered. "It is not there."

"Agreed," said I.

We went in again, shut the door, and resumed our seats. I was thinking how best to improve this advantage, if it might be called one, when he took up the conversation in such a matter of course way, so assuming that there could be no serious question of fact between us, that I felt myself placed in the weakest of positions.

"By this time you will fully understand, sir," he said, "that what troubles me so dreadfully, is the question, What does the spectre mean?"

I was not sure, I told him, that I did fully understand.

"What is its warning against?" he said, ruminating, with his eyes on the fire, and only by times turning them on me. "What is the danger? Where is the danger? There is danger overhanging, somewhere on the Line. Some dreadful calamity will happen. It is not to be doubted this third time, after what has gone before. But surely this is a cruel haunting of me. What can I do?"

He pulled out his handkerchief, and wiped the drops from his heated forehead.

"If I telegraph Danger, on either side of me, or on both, I can give no reason for it," he went on, wiping the palms of his hands. "I should get into trouble, and do no good. They would think I was mad. This is the way it would work:– Message: 'Danger! Take care!' Answer: 'What danger? Where?' Message: 'Don't know. But for God's sake take care!' They would displace me. What else could they do?"

His pain of mind was most pitiable to see. It was the mental torture of a conscientious man, oppressed beyond endurance by an unintelligible responsibility involving life.

"When it first stood under the Danger-light," he went on, putting his dark hair back from his head, and drawing his hands outward across and across his temples in an extremity of feverish distress, "why not tell me where that accident was to happen–if it must happen? Why not tell me how it could be averted–if it could have been averted? When on its second coming it hid its face, why not tell me instead: 'She is going to die. Let them keep her at home'? If it came, on those two occasions, only to show me that its warnings were true, and so to prepare me for the third, why not warn me plainly now? And I, Lord help me! A mere poor signalman on this solitary station! Why not go to somebody with credit to be believed, and power to act!"

When I saw him in this state, I saw that for the poor man's sake, as well as for the public safety, what I had to do for the time was, to compose his mind. Therefore, setting aside all question of reality or unreality between us, I represented to him that whoever thoroughly discharged his duty, must do well, and that at least it was his comfort that he understood his duty, though he did not understand these confounding Appearances. In this effort I succeeded far better than in the attempt to reason him out of his conviction. He became calm; the occupations incidental to his post as the night advanced, began to make larger demands on his attention; and I left him at two in the morning. I had offered to stay through the night, but he would not hear of it.

That I more than once looked back at the red light as I ascended the pathway, that I did not like the red light, and that I should have slept but poorly if my bed had been under it, I see no reason to conceal. Nor, did I like the two sequences of the accident and the dead girl. I see no reason to conceal that, either.

But, what ran most in my thoughts was the consideration how ought I to act, having become the recipient of this disclosure? I had proved the man to be intelligent, vigilant, painstaking, and exact; but how long might he remain so, in his state of mind? Though in a subordinate position, still he held a most important trust, and would I (for instance) like to stake my own life on the chances of his continuing to execute it with precision?

Unable to overcome a feeling that there would be something treacherous in my communicating what he had told me, to his superiors in the Company, without first being plain with himself and proposing a middle course to him, I ultimately resolved to offer to accompany him (otherwise keeping his secret for the present) to the wisest medical practitioner we could hear of in those parts, and to take his opinion. A change in his time of duty would come round next night, he had apprised me, and he would be off an hour or two after sunrise, and on again soon after sunset. I had appointed to return accordingly.

Next evening was a lovely evening, and I walked out early to enjoy it. The sun was not yet quite down when I traversed the field-path near the top of the deep cutting. I would extend my walk for an hour, I said to myself, half an hour on and half an hour back, and it would then be time to go to my signalman's box.

Before pursuing my stroll, I stepped to the brink, and mechanically looked down, from the point from which I had first seen him. I cannot describe the thrill that seized upon me, when, close at the mouth of the tunnel, I saw the appearance of a man, with his left sleeve across his eyes, passionately waving his right arm.

The nameless horror that oppressed me, passed in a moment, for in a moment I saw that this appearance of a man was a man indeed, and that there was a little group of other men standing at a short distance, to whom he seemed to be rehearsing the gesture he made. The Danger-light was not yet lighted. Against its shaft, a little low hut, entirely new to me, had been made of some wooden supports and tarpaulin. It looked no bigger than a bed.

With an irresistible sense that something was wrong–with a flashing self-re-proachful fear that fatal mischief had come of my leaving the man there, and causing no one to be sent to overlook or correct what he did–I descended the notched path with all the speed I could make.

"What is the matter?" I asked the men.

"Signalman killed this morning, sir."

"Not the man belonging to that box?"

"Yes, sir."

"Not the man I know?"

"You will recognise him, sir, if you knew him," said the man who spoke for the others, solemnly uncovering his own head and raising an end of the tarpaulin, "for his face is quite composed."

"O! how did this happen, how did this happen?" I asked, turning from one to another as the hut closed in again.

"He was cut down by an engine, sir. No man in England knew his work better. But somehow he was not clear of the outer rail. It was just at broad day. He had struck the light, and had the lamp in his hand. As the engine came out of the tunnel, his back was towards her, and she cut him down. That man drove her, and was showing how it happened. Show the gentleman, Tom."

The man, who wore a rough dark dress, stepped back to his former place at the mouth of the tunnel!

"Coming round the curve in the tunnel, sir," he said, "I saw him at the end, like as if I saw him down a perspective-glass. There was no time to check speed, and I knew him to be very careful. As he didn't seem to take heed of the whistle, I shut it off when we were running down upon him, and called to him as loud as I could call."

"What did you say?"

"I said, Below there! Look out! Look out! For God's sake clear the way!"

I started.

"Ah! it was a dreadful time, sir. I never left off calling to him. I put this arm before my eyes, not to see, and I waved this arm to the last; but it was no use."

Without prolonging the narrative to dwell on any one of its curious circumstances more than on any other, I may, in closing it, point out the coincidence that the warning of the Engine-Driver included, not only the words which the unfortunate Signalman had repeated to me as haunting him, but also the words which I myself- not he- had attached, and that only in my own mind, to the gesticulation he had imitated.

A SIMPLE HEART

Gustave Flaubert

Gustave Flaubert (1821–1880) wrote one of the great novels of the nineteenth century, *Madame Bovary*. Born in Rouen, he died there after suffering a haemorrhage. His other work includes *Sentimental Education*, *Dictionary of Received Ideas* as well as *Three Tales*, in which "A Simple Heart" was first published in 1877.

1

For half a century the housewives of Pont-l'Eveque had envied Madame Aubain her servant Felicite.

For a hundred francs a year, she cooked and did the housework, washed, ironed, mended, harnessed the horse, fattened the poultry, made the butter and remained faithful to her mistress – although the latter was by no means an agreeable person.

Madame Aubain had married a comely youth without any money, who died in the beginning of 1809, leaving her with two young children and a number of debts. She sold all her property excepting the farm of Toucques and the farm of Geffosses, the income of which barely amounted to 5,000 francs; then she left her house in Saint-Melaine, and moved into a less pretentious one which had belonged to her ancestors and stood back of the market-place. This house, with its slate-covered roof, was built between a passage-way and a narrow street that led to the river. The interior was so unevenly graded that it caused people to stumble. A narrow hall separated the kitchen from the parlour, where Madame Aubain sat all day in a straw armchair near the window. Eight mahogany chairs stood in a row against the white wainscoting. An old piano, standing beneath a barometer, was covered with a pyramid of old books and boxes. On either side of the yellow marble mantelpiece, in Louis XV. style, stood a tapestry armchair. The clock represented a temple of Vesta; and the whole room smelled musty, as it was on a lower level than the garden.

On the first floor was Madame's bed-chamber, a large room papered in a flowered design and containing the portrait of Monsieur dressed in the costume of a dandy. It communicated with a smaller room, in which there were two little cribs, without any mattresses. Next, came the parlour (always closed), filled with furniture covered with sheets. Then a hall, which led to the study, where books and papers were piled on the shelves of a book-case that enclosed three quarters of the big black desk. Two panels were entirely hidden under pen-and-ink sketches, Gouache landscapes and Audran engravings, relics of better times and vanished luxury. On the second floor, a garret-window lighted Felicite's room, which looked out upon the meadows.

She arose at daybreak, in order to attend mass, and she worked without interruption until night; then, when dinner was over, the dishes cleared away and the door securely locked, she would bury the log under the ashes and fall asleep in front of the hearth with a rosary in her hand. Nobody could bargain with greater obstinacy, and as for cleanliness, the lustre on her brass sauce-pans was the envy and despair of other servants. She was most economical, and when she ate she would gather up crumbs with the tip of her finger, so that nothing should be wasted of the loaf of bread weighing twelve pounds which was baked especially for her and lasted three weeks.

Summer and winter she wore a dimity kerchief fastened in the back with a pin, a cap which concealed her hair, a red skirt, grey stockings, and an apron with a bib like those worn by hospital nurses.

Her face was thin and her voice shrill. When she was twenty-five, she looked forty. After she had passed fifty, nobody could tell her age; erect and silent always, she resembled a wooden figure working automatically.

2

Like every other woman, she had had an affair of the heart. Her father, who was a mason, was killed by falling from a scaffolding. Then her mother died and her sisters went their different ways; a farmer took her in, and while she was quite small, let her keep cows in the fields. She was clad in miserable rags, beaten for the slightest offence and finally dismissed for a theft of thirty sous which she did not commit. She took service on another farm where she tended the poultry; and as she was well thought of by her master, her fellow-workers soon grew jealous.

One evening in August (she was then eighteen years old), they persuaded her to accompany them to the fair at Colleville. She was immediately dazzled by the noise, the lights in the trees, the brightness of the dresses, the laces and gold crosses, and the crowd of people all hopping at the same time. She was standing modestly at a distance, when presently a young man of well-to-do appearance, who had been leaning on the pole of a wagon and smoking his pipe, approached her, and asked her for a dance. He treated her to cider and cake, bought her a silk shawl, and then, thinking she had guessed his purpose, offered to see her home. When they came to the end of a field he threw her down brutally. But she grew frightened and screamed, and he walked off.

One evening, on the road leading to Beaumont, she came upon a wagon loaded with hay, and when she overtook it, she recognised Theodore. He greeted her calmly, and asked her to forget what had happened between them, as it "was all the fault of the drink."

She did not know what to reply and wished to run away.

Presently he began to speak of the harvest and of the notables of the village; his father had left Colleville and bought the farm of Les Ecots, so that now they would be neighbours. "Ah!" she exclaimed. He then added that his parents were looking around for a wife for him, but that he, himself, was not so anxious and preferred to wait for a girl who suited him. She hung her head. He then asked her whether she had ever thought of marrying. She replied, smilingly, that it was wrong of him to make fun of her. "Oh! no, I am in earnest," he said, and put his left arm around her waist while they sauntered along. The air was soft, the stars were bright, and the huge load of hay oscillated in front of them, drawn by four horses whose ponderous hoofs raised clouds of dust. Without a word from their driver they turned to the right. He kissed her again and she went home. The following week, Theodore obtained meetings.

They met in yards, behind walls or under isolated trees. She was not ignorant, as girls of well-to-do families are – for the animals had instructed her; – but her reason and her instinct of honour kept her from falling. Her resistance exasperated Theodore's love and so in order to satisfy it (or perchance ingenuously), he offered to marry her. She would not believe him at first, so he made solemn promises. But, in a short time he mentioned a difficulty; the previous year, his parents had purchased a substitute for him; but any day he might be drafted and the prospect of serving in the army alarmed him greatly. To Felicite his cowardice appeared a proof of his love for her, and her devotion to him grew stronger. When she met him, he would torture her with his fears and his entreaties. At last, he announced that he was going to the prefect himself for information, and would let her know everything on the following Sunday, between eleven o'clock and midnight.

When the time grew near, she ran to meet her lover.

But instead of Theodore, one of his friends was at the meeting-place.

He informed her that she would never see her sweetheart again; for, in order to escape the conscription, he had married a rich old woman, Madame Lehoussais, of Toucques.

The poor girl's sorrow was frightful. She threw herself on the ground, she cried and called on the Lord, and wandered around desolately until sunrise. Then she went back to the farm, declared her intention of leaving, and at the end of the month, after she had received her wages, she packed all her belongings in a handkerchief and started for Pont-l'Eveque.

In front of the inn, she met a woman wearing widow's weeds, and upon questioning her, learned that she was looking for a cook. The girl did not know very much, but appeared so willing and so modest in her requirements, that Madame Aubain finally said:

"Very well, I will give you a trial."

And half an hour later Felicite was installed in her house.

At first she lived in a constant anxiety that was caused by "the style of the household" and the memory of "Monsieur," that hovered over everything. Paul and Virginia, the one aged seven, and the other barely four, seemed made of some precious material; she carried them pig-a-back, and was greatly mortified when Madame Aubain forbade her to kiss them every other minute.

But in spite of all this, she was happy. The comfort of her new surroundings had obliterated her sadness.

Every Thursday, friends of Madame Aubain dropped in for a game of cards, and it was Felicite's duty to prepare the table and heat the foot-warmers. They arrived at exactly eight o'clock and departed before eleven.

Every Monday morning, the dealer in second-hand goods, who lived under the alley-way, spread out his wares on the sidewalk. Then the city would be filled with a buzzing of voices in which the neighing of horses, the bleating of lambs, the grunting of pigs, could be distinguished, mingled with the sharp sound of wheels on the cobble-stones. About twelve o'clock, when the market was in full swing, there appeared at the front door a tall, middle-aged peasant, with a hooked nose and a cap on the back of his head; it was Robelin, the farmer of Geffosses. Shortly afterwards came Liebard, the farmer of Toucques, short, rotund and ruddy, wearing a grey jacket and spurred boots.

Both men brought their landlady either chickens or cheese. Felicite would invariably thwart their ruses and they held her in great respect.

At various times, Madame Aubain received a visit from the Marquis de Gremanville, one of her uncles, who was ruined and lived at Falaise on the remainder of his estates. He always came at dinner-time and brought an ugly poodle with him, whose paws soiled their furniture. In spite of his efforts to appear a man of breeding (he even went so far as to raise his hat every time he said "My deceased father"), his habits got the better of him, and he would fill his glass a little too often and relate broad stories. Felicite would show him out very politely and say: "You have had enough for this time, Monsieur de Gremanville! Hoping to see you again!" and would close the door.

She opened it gladly for Monsieur Bourais, a retired lawyer. His bald head and white cravat, the ruffling of his shirt, his flowing brown coat, the manner in which he took snuff, his whole person, in fact, produced in her the kind of awe which we feel when we see extraordinary persons. As he managed Madame's estates, he spent hours with her in Monsieur's study; he was in constant fear of being compromised, had a great regard for the magistracy and some pretensions to learning.

In order to facilitate the children's studies, he presented them with an engraved geography which represented various scenes of the world; cannibals with feather head-dresses, a gorilla kidnapping a young girl, Arabs in the desert, a whale being harpooned, etc.

Paul explained the pictures to Felicite. And, in fact, this was her only literary education. The children's studies were under the direction of a poor devil employed at the town-hall, who sharpened his pocket-knife on his boots and was famous for his penmanship.

When the weather was fine, they went to Geffosses. The house was built in the centre of the sloping yard; and the sea looked like a grey spot in the distance. Felicite would take slices of cold meat from the lunch basket and they would sit down and eat in a room next to the dairy. This room was all that remained of a cottage that had been torn down. The dilapidated wall-paper trembled in the drafts. Madame Aubain, overwhelmed by recollections, would hang her head, while the children were afraid to open their mouths. Then, "Why don't you go and play?" their mother would say; and they would scamper off.

Paul would go to the old barn, catch birds, throw stones into the pond, or pound the trunks of the trees with a stick till they resounded like drums. Virginia would feed the rabbits and run to pick the wild flowers in the fields, and her flying legs would disclose her little embroidered pantalettes. One autumn evening, they struck out for home through the meadows. The new moon illumined part of the sky and a mist hovered like a veil over the sinuosities of the river. Oxen, lying in the pastures, gazed mildly at the passing persons. In the third field, however, several of them got up and surrounded them. "Don't be afraid," cried Felicite; and murmuring a sort of lament she passed her hand over the back of the nearest ox; he turned away and the others followed. But when they came to the next pasture, they heard frightful bellowing.

It was a bull which was hidden from them by the fog. He advanced towards the two women, and Madame Aubain prepared to flee for her life. "No, no! not so fast," warned Felicite. Still they hurried on, for they could hear the noisy breathing of the bull behind them. His hoofs pounded the grass like hammers, and presently he began to gallop! Felicite turned around and threw patches of grass in his eyes. He hung his head, shook his horns and bellowed with fury. Madame Aubain and the children, huddled at the end of the field, were trying to jump over the ditch. Felicite continued to back before the bull, blinding him with dirt, while she shouted to them to make haste.

Madame Aubain finally slid into the ditch, after shoving first Virginia and then Paul into it, and though she stumbled several times she managed, by dint of courage, to climb the other side of it.

The bull had driven Felicite up against a fence; the foam from his muzzle flew in her face and in another minute he would have disembowelled her. She had just time to slip between two bars and the huge animal, thwarted, paused.

For years, this occurrence was a topic of conversation in Pont-l'Eveque. But Felicite took no credit to herself, and probably never knew that she had been heroic.

Virginia occupied her thoughts solely, for the shock she had sustained gave her a nervous affection, and the physician, M. Poupart, prescribed the salt-water bathing at Trouville. In those days, Trouville was not greatly patronised. Madame Aubain gathered information, consulted Bourais, and made preparations as if they were going on an extended trip.

The baggage was sent the day before on Liebard's cart. On the following morning, he brought around two horses, one of which had a woman's saddle with a velveteen back to it, while on the crupper of the other was a rolled shawl that was to be used for a seat. Madame Aubain mounted the second horse, behind Liebard. Felicite took charge of the little girl, and Paul rode M. Lechaptois' donkey, which had been lent for the occasion on the condition that they should be careful of it.

The road was so bad that it took two hours to cover the eight miles. The two horses sank knee-deep into the mud and stumbled into ditches; sometimes they had to jump over them. In certain places, Liebard's mare stopped abruptly. He waited patiently till she started again, and talked of the people whose estates bordered the road, adding his own moral reflections to the outline of their histories. Thus, when they were passing through Toucques, and came to some windows draped with nasturtiums, he shrugged his shoulders and said: "There's a woman, Madame Lehoussais, who, instead of taking a young man –" Felicite could not catch what followed; the horses began to trot, the donkey to gallop, and they turned into a lane; then a gate swung open, two farm-hands appeared and they all dismounted at the very threshold of the farm-house.

Mother Liebard, when she caught sight of her mistress, was lavish with joyful demonstrations. She got up a lunch which comprised a leg of mutton, tripe, sausages, a chicken fricassee, sweet cider, a fruit tart and some preserved prunes; then to all this the good woman added polite remarks about Madame, who appeared to be in better health, Mademoiselle, who had grown to be "superb," and Paul, who had become singularly sturdy; she spoke also of their deceased grandparents, whom the Liebards had known, for they had been in the service of the family for several generations.

Like its owners, the farm had an ancient appearance. The beams of the ceiling were mouldy, the walls black with smoke and the windows grey with dust. The oak sideboard was filled with all sorts of utensils, plates, pitchers, tin bowls, wolf-traps. The children laughed when they saw a huge syringe. There was not a tree in the yard that did not have mushrooms growing around its foot, or a bunch of mistletoe hanging in its branches. Several of the trees had been blown down, but they had started to grow in the middle and all were laden with quantities of apples. The thatched roofs, which were of unequal thickness, looked like brown velvet and could resist the fiercest gales. But the wagon-shed was fast crumbling to ruins. Madame Aubain said that she would attend to it, and then gave orders to have the horses saddled.

It took another thirty minutes to reach Trouville. The little caravan dismounted in order to pass Les Ecores, a cliff that overhangs the bay, and a few minutes later, at the end of the dock, they entered the yard of the Golden Lamb, an inn kept by Mother David.

During the first few days, Virginia felt stronger, owing to the change of air and the action of the sea-baths. She took them in her little chemise, as she had no bathing suit, and afterwards her nurse dressed her in the cabin of a customs officer, which was used for that purpose by other bathers.

In the afternoon, they would take the donkey and go to the Roches-Noires, near Hennequeville. The path led at first through undulating grounds, and thence to a plateau, where pastures and tilled fields alternated. At the edge of the road, mingling with the brambles, grew holly bushes, and here and there stood large dead trees whose branches traced zigzags upon the blue sky.

Ordinarily, they rested in a field facing the ocean, with Deauville on their left, and Havre on their right. The sea glittered brightly in the sun and was as smooth as a mirror, and so calm that they could scarcely distinguish its murmur; sparrows chirped joyfully and the immense canopy of heaven spread over it all. Madame Aubain brought out her sewing, and Virginia amused herself by braiding reeds; Felicite wove lavender blossoms, while Paul was bored and wished to go home.

Sometimes they crossed the Toucques in a boat, and started to hunt for sea-shells. The outgoing tide exposed star-fish and sea-urchins, and the children tried to catch the flakes of foam which the wind blew away. The sleepy waves lapping the sand unfurled themselves along the shore that extended as far as the eye could see, but where land began, it was limited by the downs which separated it from the "Swamp," a large meadow shaped like a hippodrome. When they went home that way, Trouville, on the slope of a hill below, grew larger and larger as they advanced, and, with all its houses of unequal height, seemed to spread out before them in a sort of giddy confusion.

When the heat was too oppressive, they remained in their rooms. The dazzling sunlight cast bars of light between the shutters. Not a sound in the village, not a soul on the sidewalk. This silence intensified the tranquility of everything. In the distance, the hammers of some calkers pounded the hull of a ship, and the sultry breeze brought them an odour of tar.

The principal diversion consisted in watching the return of the fishing-smacks. As soon as they passed the beacons, they began to ply to windward. The sails were lowered to one third of the masts, and with their fore-sails swelled up like balloons they glided over the waves and anchored in the middle of the harbour. Then they crept up alongside of the dock and the sailors threw the quivering fish over the side of the boat; a line of carts was waiting for them, and women with white caps sprang forward to receive the baskets and embrace their men-folk.

One day, one of them spoke to Felicite, who, after a little while, returned to the house gleefully. She had found one of her sisters, and presently Nastasie Barette, wife of Leroux, made her appearance, holding an infant in her arms, another child by the hand, while on her left was a little cabin-boy with his hands in his pockets and his cap on his ear.

At the end of fifteen minutes, Madame Aubain bade her go.

They always hung around the kitchen, or approached Felicite when she and the children were out walking. The husband, however, did not show himself.

Felicite developed a great fondness for them; she bought them a stove, some shirts and a blanket; it was evident that they exploited her. Her foolishness annoyed Madame Aubain, who, moreover did not like the nephew's familiarity, for he called her son "thou"; – and, as Virginia began to cough and the season was over, she decided to return to Pont-l'Eveque.

Monsieur Bourais assisted her in the choice of a college. The one at Caen was considered the best. So Paul was sent away and bravely said good-bye to them all, for he was glad to go to live in a house where he would have boy companions.

Madame Aubain resigned herself to the separation from her son because it was unavoidable. Virginia brooded less and less over it. Felicite regretted the noise he made, but soon a new occupation diverted her mind; beginning from Christmas, she accompanied the little girl to her catechism lesson every day.

3

After she had made a curtsey at the threshold, she would walk up the aisle between the double lines of chairs, open Madame Aubain's pew, sit down and look around.

Girls and boys, the former on the right, the latter on the left-hand side of the church, filled the stalls of the choir; the priest stood beside the reading-desk; on one stained window of the side-aisle the Holy Ghost hovered over the Virgin; on another one, Mary knelt before the Child Jesus, and behind the altar, a wooden group represented Saint Michael felling the dragon.

The priest first read a condensed lesson of sacred history. Felicite evoked Paradise, the Flood, the Tower of Babel, the blazing cities, the dying nations, the shattered idols; and out of this she developed a great respect for the Almighty and a great fear of His wrath. Then, when she had listened to the Passion, she wept.

Why had they crucified Him who loved little children, nourished the people, made the blind see, and who, out of humility, had wished to be born among the poor, in a stable? The sowings, the harvests, the wine-presses, all those familiar things which the Scriptures mention, formed a part of her life; the word of God sanctified them; and she loved the lambs with increased tenderness for the sake of the Lamb, and the doves because of the Holy Ghost.

She found it hard, however, to think of the latter as a person, for was it not a bird, a flame, and sometimes only a breath? Perhaps it is its light that at night hovers over swamps, its breath that propels the clouds, its voice that renders church-bells harmonious. And Felicite worshipped devoutly, while enjoying the coolness and the stillness of the church.

As for the dogma, she could not understand it and did not even try. The priest discoursed, the children recited, and she went to sleep, only to awaken with a start when they were leaving the church and their wooden shoes clattered on the stone pavement.

In this way, she learned her catechism, her religious education having been neglected in her youth; and thenceforth she imitated all Virginia's religious practices, fasted when she did, and went to confession with her. At the Corpus-Christi Day they both decorated an altar.

She worried in advance over Virginia's first communion. She fussed about the shoes, the rosary, the book and the gloves. With what nervousness she helped the mother dress the child!

During the entire ceremony, she felt anguished. Monsieur Bourais hid part of the choir from view, but directly in front of her, the flock of maidens, wearing white wreaths over their lowered veils, formed a snow-white field, and she recognised her darling by the slenderness of her neck and her devout attitude. The bell tinkled. All the heads bent and there was a silence. Then, at the peals of the organ the singers and the worshippers struck up the Agnes Dei; the boys' procession began; behind them came the girls. With clasped hands, they advanced step by step to the lighted altar, knelt at the first step, received one by one the Host, and returned to their seats in the same order. When Virginia's turn came, Felicite leaned forward to watch her, and through that imagination which springs from true affection, she at once became the child, whose face and dress became hers, whose heart beat in her bosom, and when Virginia opened her mouth and closed her lids, she did likewise and came very near fainting.

The following day, she presented herself early at the church so as to receive communion from the cure. She took it with the proper feeling, but did not experience the same delight as on the previous day.

Madame Aubain wished to make an accomplished girl of her daughter; and as Guyot could not teach English or music, she decided to send her to the Ursulines at Honfleur.

The child made no objection, but Felicite sighed and thought Madame was heartless. Then, she thought that perhaps her mistress was right, as these things were beyond her sphere. Finally, one day, an old fiacre stopped in front of the door and a nun stepped out. Felicite put Virginia's luggage on top of the carriage, gave the coachman some instructions, and smuggled six jars of jam, a dozen pears and a bunch of violets under the seat.

At the last minute, Virginia had a fit of sobbing; she embraced her mother again and again, while the latter kissed her on the forehead, and said: "Now, be brave, be brave!" The step was pulled up and the fiacre rumbled off.

Then Madame Aubain had a fainting spell, and that evening all her friends, including the two Lormeaus, Madame Lechaptois, the ladies Rochefeuille, Messieurs de Houppeville and Bourais, called on her and tendered their sympathy.

At first the separation proved very painful to her. But her daughter wrote her three times a week and the other days she, herself, wrote to Virginia. Then she walked in the garden, read a little, and in this way managed to fill out the emptiness of the hours.

Each morning, out of habit, Felicite entered Virginia's room and gazed at the walls. She missed combing her hair, lacing her shoes, tucking her in her bed, and the bright face and little hand when they used to go out for a walk. In order to occupy herself she tried to make lace. But her clumsy fingers broke the threads; she had no heart for anything, lost her sleep and "wasted away," as she put it.

In order to have some distraction, she asked leave to receive the visits of her nephew Victor.

He would come on Sunday, after church, with ruddy cheeks and bared chest, bringing with him the scent of the country. She would set the table and they would sit down opposite each other, and eat their dinner; she ate as little as possible, herself, to avoid any extra expense, but would stuff him so with food that he would finally go to sleep. At the first stroke of vespers, she would wake him up, brush his trousers, tie his cravat and walk to church with him, leaning on his arm with maternal pride.

His parents always told him to get something out of her, either a package of brown sugar, or soap, or brandy, and sometimes even money. He brought her his clothes to mend, and she accepted the task gladly, because it meant another visit from him.

In August, his father took him on a coasting-vessel.

It was vacation time and the arrival of the children consoled Felicite. But Paul was capricious, and Virginia was growing too old to be thee-and-thou'd, a fact which seemed to produce a sort of embarrassment in their relations.

Victor went successively to Morlaix, to Dunkirk, and to Brighton; whenever he returned from a trip he would bring her a present. The first time it was a box of shells; the second, a coffee-cup; the third, a big doll of ginger-bread. He was growing handsome, had a good figure, a tiny moustache, kind eyes, and a little leather cap that sat jauntily on the back of his head. He amused his aunt by telling her stories mingled with nautical expressions.

One Monday, the 14th of July, 1819 (she never forgot the date), Victor announced that he had been engaged on a merchant-vessel and that in two days he would take the steamer at Honfleur and join his sailer, which was going to start from Havre very soon. Perhaps he might be away two years.

The prospect of his departure filled Felicite with despair, and in order to bid him farewell, on Wednesday night, after Madame's dinner, she put on her pattens and trudged the four miles that separated Pont-l'Eveque from Honfleur.

When she reached the Calvary, instead of turning to the right, she turned to the left and lost herself in coal-yards; she had to retrace her steps; some people she spoke to advised her to hasten. She walked helplessly around the harbour filled with vessels, and knocked against hawsers. Presently the ground sloped abruptly, lights flitted to and fro, and she thought all at once that she had gone mad when she saw some horses in the sky.

Others, on the edge of the dock, neighed at the sight of the ocean. A derrick pulled them up in the air, and dumped them into a boat, where passengers were bustling about among barrels of cider, baskets of cheese and bags of meal; chickens cackled, the captain swore and a cabin-boy rested on the railing, apparently indifferent to his surroundings. Felicite, who did not recognise him, kept shouting: "Victor!" He suddenly raised his eyes, but while she was preparing to rush up to him, they withdrew the gangplank.

The packet, towed by singing women, glided out of the harbour. Her hull squeaked and the heavy waves beat up against her sides. The sail had turned and nobody was visible; – and on the ocean, silvered by the light of the moon, the vessel formed a black spot that grew dimmer and dimmer, and finally disappeared.

When Felicite passed the Calvary again, she felt as if she must entrust that which was dearest to her to the Lord; and for a long while she prayed, with uplifted eyes and a face wet with tears. The city was sleeping; some customs officials were taking the air; and the water kept pouring through the holes of the dam with a deafening roar. The town clock struck two.

The parlour of the convent would not open until morning, and surely a delay would annoy Madame, so, in spite of her desire to see the other child, she went home. The maids of the inn were just arising when she reached Pont-l'Eveque.

So the poor boy would be on the ocean for months! His previous trips had not alarmed her. One can come back from England and Brittany; but America, the colonies, the islands, were all lost in an uncertain region at the very end of the world.

From that time on, Felicite thought solely of her nephew. On warm days she feared he would suffer from thirst, and when it stormed, she was afraid he would be struck by lightning. When she harkened to the wind that rattled in the chimney and dislodged the tiles on the roof, she imagined that he was being buffeted by the same storm, perched on top of a shattered mast, with his whole body bend backward and covered with sea-foam; or, – these were recollections of the engraved geography – he was being devoured by savages, or captured in a forest by apes, or dying on some lonely coast. She never mentioned her anxieties, however.

Madame Aubain worried about her daughter.

The sisters thought that Virginia was affectionate but delicate. The slightest emotion enervated her. She had to give up her piano lessons. Her mother insisted upon regular letters from the convent. One morning, when the postman failed to come, she grew impatient and began to pace to and fro, from her chair to the window. It was really extraordinary! No news since four days!

In order to console her mistress by her own example, Felicite said:

"Why, Madame, I haven't had any news since six months! –"

"From whom? –"

The servant replied gently:

"Why – from my nephew."

"Oh, yes, your nephew!" And shrugging her shoulders, Madame Aubain continued to pace the floor as if to say: "I did not think of it. – Besides, I do not care, a cabin-boy, a pauper! – but my daughter – what a difference! just think of it! –"

Felicite, although she had been reared roughly, was very indignant. Then she forgot about it.

It appeared quite natural to her that one should lose one's head about Virginia.

The two children were of equal importance; they were united in her heart and their fate was to be the same.

The chemist informed her that Victor's vessel had reached Havana. He had read the information in a newspaper.

Felicite imagined that Havana was a place where people did nothing but smoke, and that Victor walked around among negroes in a cloud of tobacco. Could a person, in case of need, return by land? How far was it from Pont-l'Eveque? In order to learn these things, she questioned Monsieur Bourais. He reached for his map and began some explanations concerning longitudes, and smiled with superiority at Felicite's bewilderment. At last, he took a pencil and pointed out an imperceptible black point in the scallops of an oval blotch, adding: "There it is." She bent over the map; the maze of coloured lines hurt her eyes without enlightening her; and when Bourais asked her what puzzled her, she requested him to show her the house Victor lived in. Bourais threw up his hands, sneezed, and then laughed uproariously; such ignorance delighted his soul; but Felicite failed to understand the cause of his mirth, she whose intelligence was so limited that she perhaps expected to see even the picture of her nephew!

It was two weeks later that Liebard came into the kitchen at market-time, and handed her a letter from her brother-in-law. As neither of them could read, she called upon her mistress.

Madame Aubain, who was counting the stitches of her knitting, laid her work down beside her, opened the letter, started, and in a low tone and with a searching look said: "They tell you of a – misfortune. Your nephew –"

He had died. The letter told nothing more.

Felicite dropped on a chair, leaned her head against the back, and closed her lids; presently they grew pink. Then, with drooping head, inert hands and staring eyes she repeated at intervals:

"Poor little chap! poor little chap!"

Liebard watched her and sighed. Madame Aubain was trembling.

She proposed to the girl to go to see her sister in Trouville.

With a single motion, Felicite replied that it was not necessary.

There was a silence. Old Liebard thought it about time for him to take leave. Then Felicite uttered:

"They have no sympathy, they do not care!"

Her head fell forward again, and from time to time, mechanically, she toyed with the long knitting-needles on the work-table.

Some women passed through the yard with a basket of wet clothes.

When she saw them through the window, she suddenly remembered her own wash; as she had soaked it the day before, she must go and rinse it now. So she arose and left the room.

Her tub and her board were on the bank of the Toucques. She threw a heap of clothes on the ground, rolled up her sleeves and grasped her bat; and her loud pounding could be heard in the neighbouring gardens. The meadows were empty, the breeze wrinkled the stream, at the bottom of which were long grasses that looked like the hair of corpses floating in the water. She restrained her sorrow and was very brave until night; but, when she had gone to her own room, she gave way to it, burying her face in the pillow and pressing her two fists against her temples.

A long while afterward, she learned through Victor's captain, the circumstances which surrounded his death. At the hospital they had bled him too much, treating him for yellow fever. Four doctors held him at one time. He died almost instantly, and the chief surgeon had said:

"Here goes another one!"

His parents had always treated him barbarously; she preferred not to see them again, and they made no advances, either from forgetfulness or out of innate hardness.

Virginia was growing weaker.

A cough, continual fever, oppressive breathing and spots on her cheeks indicated some serious trouble. Monsieur Popart had advised a sojourn in Provence. Madame Aubain decided that they would go, and she would have had her daughter come home at once, had it not been for the climate of Pont-l'Eveque.

She made an arrangement with a livery-stable man who drove her over to the convent every Tuesday. In the garden there was a terrace, from which the view extends to the Seine. Virginia walked in it, leaning on her mother's arm and treading the dead vine leaves. Sometimes the sun, shining through the clouds, made her blink her lids, when she gazed at the sails in the distance, and let her eyes roam over the horizon from the chateau of Tancarville to the lighthouses of Havre. Then they rested on the arbour. Her mother had bought a little cask of fine Malaga wine, and Virginia, laughing at the idea of becoming intoxicated, would drink a few drops of it, but never more.

Her strength returned. Autumn passed. Felicite began to reassure Madame Aubain. But, one evening, when she returned home after an errand, she met M. Boupart's coach in front of the door; M. Boupart himself was standing in the vestibule and Madame Aubain was tying the strings of her bonnet. "Give me my foot-warmer, my purse and my gloves; and be quick about it," she said.

Virginia had congestion of the lungs; perhaps it was desperate.

"Not yet," said the physician, and both got into the carriage, while the snow fell in thick flakes. It was almost night and very cold.

Felicite rushed to the church to light a candle. Then she ran after the coach which she overtook after an hour's chase, sprang up behind and held on to the straps. But suddenly a thought crossed her mind: "The yard had been left open; supposing that burglars got in!" And down she jumped.

The next morning, at daybreak, she called at the doctor's. He had been home, but had left again. Then she waited at the inn, thinking that strangers might bring her a letter. At last, at daylight she took the diligence for Lisieux.

The convent was at the end of a steep and narrow street. When she arrived about at the middle of it, she heard strange noises, a funeral knell. "It must be for some one else," thought she; and she pulled the knocker violently.

After several minutes had elapsed, she heard footsteps, the door was half opened and a nun appeared. The good sister, with an air of compunction, told her that "she had just passed away." And at the same time the tolling of Saint-Leonard's increased.

Felicite reached the second floor. Already at the threshold, she caught sight of Virginia lying on her back, with clasped hands, her mouth open and her head thrown back, beneath a black crucifix inclined toward her, and stiff curtains which were less white than her face. Madame Aubain lay at the foot of the couch, clasping it with her arms and uttering groans of agony. The Mother Superior was standing on the right side of the bed. The three candles on the bureau made red blurs, and the windows were dimmed by the fog outside. The nuns carried Madame Aubain from the room.

For two nights, Felicite never left the corpse. She would repeat the same prayers, sprinkle holy water over the sheets, get up, come back to the bed and contemplate the body. At the end of the first vigil, she noticed that the face had taken on a yellow tinge, the lips grew blue, the nose grew pinched, the eyes were sunken. She kissed them several times and would not have been greatly astonished had Virginia opened them; to souls like this the supernatural is always quite simple. She washed her, wrapped her in a shroud, put her into the casket, laid a wreath of flowers on her head and arranged her curls. They were blond and of an extraordinary length for her age. Felicite cut off a big lock and put half of it into her bosom, resolving never to part with it.

The body was taken to Pont-l'Eveque, according to Madame Aubain's wishes; she followed the hearse in a closed carriage.

After the ceremony it took three quarters of an hour to reach the cemetery. Paul, sobbing, headed the procession; Monsieur Bourais followed, and then came the principal inhabitants of the town, the women covered with black capes, and Felicite. The memory of her nephew, and the thought that she had not been able to render him these honours, made her doubly unhappy, and she felt as if he were being buried with Virginia.

Madame Aubain's grief was uncontrollable. At first she rebelled against God, thinking that he was unjust to have taken away her child – she who had never done anything wrong, and whose conscience was so pure! But no! she ought to have taken her South. Other doctors would have saved her. She accused herself, prayed to be able to join her child, and cried in the midst of her dreams. Of the latter, one more especially haunted her. Her husband, dressed like a sailor, had come back from a long voyage, and with tears in his eyes told her that he had received the order to take Virginia away. Then they both consulted about a hiding-place.

Once she came in from the garden, all upset. A moment before (and she showed the place), the father and daughter had appeared to her, one after the other; they did nothing but look at her.

During several months she remained inert in her room. Felicite scolded her gently; she must keep up for her son and also for the other one, for "her memory."

"Her memory!" replied Madame Aubain, as if she were just awakening, "Oh! yes, yes, you do not forget her!" This was an allusion to the cemetery where she had been expressly forbidden to go.

But Felicite went there every day. At four o'clock exactly, she would go through the town, climb the hill, open the gate and arrive at Virginia's tomb. It was a small column of pink marble with a flat stone at its base, and it was surrounded by a little plot enclosed by chains. The flower-beds were bright with blossoms. Felicite watered their leaves, renewed the gravel, and knelt on the ground in order to till the earth properly. When Madame Aubain was able to visit the cemetery she felt very much relieved and consoled.

Years passed, all alike and marked by no other events than the return of the great church holidays: Easter, Assumption, All Saints' Day. Household happenings constituted the only data to which in later years they often referred. Thus, in 1825, workmen painted the vestibule; in 1827, a portion of the roof almost killed a man by falling into the yard. In the summer of 1828, it was Madame's turn to offer the hallowed bread; at that time, Bourais disappeared mysteriously; and the old acquaintances, Guyot, Liebard, Madame Lechaptois, Robelin, old Gremanville, paralysed since a long time, passed away one by one. One night, the driver of the mail in Pont-l'Eveque announced the Revolution of July. A few days afterward a new sub-prefect was nominated, the Baron de Larsonniere, ex-consul in America, who, besides his wife, had his sister-in-law and her three grown daughters with him. They were often seen on their lawn, dressed in loose blouses, and they had a parrot and a negro servant. Madame Aubain received a call, which she returned promptly. As soon as she caught sight of them, Felicite would run and notify her mistress. But only one thing was capable of arousing her: a letter from her son.

He could not follow any profession as he was absorbed in drinking. His mother paid his debts and he made fresh ones; and the sighs that she heaved while she knitted at the window reached the ears of Felicite who was spinning in the kitchen.

They walked in the garden together, always speaking of Virginia, and asking each other if such and such a thing would have pleased her, and what she would probably have said on this or that occasion.

All her little belongings were put away in a closet of the room which held the two little beds. But Madame Aubain looked them over as little as possible. One summer day, however, she resigned herself to the task and when she opened the closet the moths flew out.

Virginia's frocks were hung under a shelf where there were three dolls, some hoops, a doll-house, and a basic which she had used. Felicite and Madame Aubain also took out the skirts, the handkerchiefs, and the stockings and spread them on the beds, before putting them away again. The sun fell on the piteous things, disclosing their spots and the creases formed by the motions of the body. The atmosphere was warm and blue, and a blackbird trilled in the garden; everything seemed to live in happiness. They found a little hat of soft brown plush, but it was entirely moth-eaten. Felicite asked for it. Their eyes met and filled with tears; at last the mistress opened her arms and the servant threw herself against her breast and they hugged each other and giving vent to their grief in a kiss which equalised them for a moment.

It was the first time that this had ever happened, for Madame Aubain was not of an expansive nature. Felicite was as grateful for it as if it had been some favour, and thenceforth loved her with animal-like devotion and a religious veneration.

Her kind-heartedness developed. When she heard the drums of a marching regiment passing through the street, she would stand in the doorway with a jug of cider and give the soldiers a drink. She nursed cholera victims. She protected Polish refugees, and one of them even declared that he wished to marry her. But they quarrelled, for one morning when she returned from the Angelus she found him in the kitchen coolly eating a dish which he had prepared for himself during her absence.

After the Polish refugees, came Colmiche, an old man who was credited with having committed frightful misdeeds in '93. He lived near the river in the ruins of a pig-sty. The urchins peeped at him through the cracks in the walls and threw stones that fell on his miserable bed, where he lay gasping with catarrh, with long hair, inflamed eyelids, and a tumour as big as his head on one arm.

She got him some linen, tried to clean his hovel and dreamed of installing him in the bake-house without his being in Madame's way. When the cancer broke, she dressed it every day; sometimes she brought him some cake and placed him in the sun on a bundle of hay; and the poor old creature, trembling and drooling, would thank her in his broken voice, and put out his hands whenever she left him. Finally he died; and she had a mass said for the repose of his soul.

That day a great joy came to her: at dinner-time, Madame de Larsonniere's servant called with the parrot, the cage, and the perch and chain and lock. A note from the baroness told Madame Aubain that as her husband had been promoted to a prefecture, they were leaving that night, and she begged her to accept the bird as a remembrance and a token of her esteem.

Since a long time the parrot had been on Felicite's mind, because he came from America, which reminded her of Victor, and she had approached the negro on the subject.

Once even, she had said:

"How glad Madame would be to have him!"

The man had repeated this remark to his mistress who, not being able to keep the bird, took this means of getting rid of it.

4

He was called Loulou. His body was green, his head blue, the tips of his wings were pink and his breast was golden.

But he had the tiresome tricks of biting his perch, pulling his feathers out, scattering refuse and spilling the water of his bath. Madame Aubain grew tired of him and gave him to Felicite for good.

She undertook his education, and soon he was able to repeat: "Pretty boy! Your servant, sir! I salute you, Marie!" His perch was placed near the door and several persons were astonished that he did not answer to the name of "Jacquot," for every parrot is called Jacquot. They called him a goose and a log, and these taunts were like so many dagger thrusts to Felicite. Strange stubbornness of the bird which would not talk when people watched him!

Nevertheless, he sought society; for on Sunday, when the ladies Rochefeuille, Monsieur de Houppeville and the new habitues, Onfroy, the chemist, Monsieur

Varin and Captain Mathieu, dropped in for their game of cards, he struck the window-panes with his wings and made such a racket that it was impossible to talk.

Bourais' face must have appeared very funny to Loulou. As soon as he saw him he would begin to roar. His voice re-echoed in the yard, and the neighbours would come to the windows and begin to laugh, too; and in order that the parrot might not see him, Monsieur Bourais edged along the wall, pushed his hat over his eyes to hide his profile, and entered by the garden door, and the looks he gave the bird lacked affection. Loulou, having thrust his head into the butcher-boy's basket, received a slap, and from that time he always tried to nip his enemy. Fabu threatened to ring his neck, although he was not cruelly inclined, notwithstanding his big whiskers and tattooings. On the contrary, he rather liked the bird, and, out of devilry, tried to teach him oaths. Felicite, whom his manner alarmed, put Loulou in the kitchen, took off his chain and let him walk all over the house.

When he went downstairs, he rested his beak on the steps, lifted his right foot and then his left one; but his mistress feared that such feats would give him vertigo. He became ill and was unable to eat. There was a small growth under his tongue like those chickens are sometimes afflicted with. Felicite pulled it off with her nails and cured him. One day, Paul was imprudent enough to blow the smoke of his cigar in his face; another time, Madame Lormeau was teasing him with the tip of her umbrella and he swallowed the tip. Finally he got lost.

She had put him on the grass to cool him and went away only for a second; when she returned, she found no parrot! She hunted among the bushes, on the bank of the river, and on the roofs, without paying any attention to Madame Aubain who screamed at her: "Take care! you must be insane!" Then she searched every garden in Pont-l'Eveque and stopped the passers-by to inquire of them: "Haven't you perhaps seen my parrot?" To those who had never seen the parrot, she described him minutely. Suddenly she thought she saw something green fluttering behind the mills at the foot of the hill. But when she was at the top of the hill she could not see it. A hod-carrier told her that he had just seen the bird in Saint-Melaine, in Mother Simon's store. She rushed to the place. The people did not know what she was talking about. At last she came home, exhausted, with her slippers worn to shreds, and despair in her heart. She sat down on the bench near Madame and was telling of her search when presently a light weight dropped on her shoulder – Loulou! What the deuce had he been doing? Perhaps he had just taken a little walk around the town!

She did not easily forget her scare; in fact, she never got over it. In consequence of a cold, she caught a sore throat; and some time later she had an earache. Three years later she was stone deaf, and spoke in a very loud voice even in church. Although her sins might have been proclaimed throughout the diocese without any shame to herself, or ill effects to the community, the cure thought it advisable to receive her confession in the vestry-room.

Imaginary buzzings also added to her bewilderment. Her mistress often said to her: "My goodness, how stupid you are!" and she would answer: "Yes, Madame," and look for something.

The narrow circle of her ideas grew more restricted than it already was; the bellowing of the oxen, the chime of the bells no longer reached her intelligence.

All things moved silently, like ghosts. Only one noise penetrated her ears; the parrot's voice.

As if to divert her mind, he reproduced for her the tick-tack of the spit in the kitchen, the shrill cry of the fish-vendors, the saw of the carpenter who had a shop opposite, and when the door-bell rang, he would imitate Madame Aubain: "Felicite! go to the front door."

They held conversations together, Loulou repeating the three phrases of his repertory over and over, Felicite replying by words that had no greater meaning, but in which she poured out her feelings. In her isolation, the parrot was almost a son, a love. He climbed upon her fingers, pecked at her lips, clung to her shawl, and when she rocked her head to and fro like a nurse, the big wings of her cap and the wings of the bird flapped in unison. When clouds gathered on the horizon and the thunder rumbled, Loulou would scream, perhaps because he remembered the storms in his native forests. The dripping of the rain would excite him to frenzy; he flapped around, struck the ceiling with his wings, upset everything, and would finally fly into the garden to play. Then he would come back into the room, light on one of the andirons, and hop around in order to get dry.

One morning during the terrible winter of 1837, when she had put him in front of the fire-place on account of the cold, she found him dead in his cage, hanging to the wire bars with his head down. He had probably died of congestion. But she believed that he had been poisoned, and although she had no proofs whatever, her suspicion rested on Fabu.

She wept so sorely that her mistress said: "Why don't you have him stuffed?"

She asked the advice of the chemist, who had always been kind to the bird.

He wrote to Havre for her. A certain man named Fellacher consented to do the work. But, as the diligence driver often lost parcels entrusted to him, Felicite resolved to take her pet to Honfleur herself.

Leafless apple-trees lined the edges of the road. The ditches were covered with ice. The dogs on the neighbouring farms barked; and Felicite, with her hands beneath her cape, her little black sabots and her basket, trotted along nimbly in the middle of the sidewalk. She crossed the forest, passed by the Haut-Chene, and reached Saint-Gatien.

Behind her, in a cloud of dust and impelled by the steep incline, a mail-coach drawn by galloping horses advanced like a whirlwind. When he saw a woman in the middle of the road, who did not get out of the way, the driver stood up in his seat and shouted to her and so did the postilion, while the four horses, which he could not hold back, accelerated their pace; the two leaders were almost upon her; with a jerk of the reins he threw them to one side, but, furious at the incident, he lifted his big whip and lashed her from her head to her feet with such violence that she fell to the ground unconscious.

Her first thought, when she recovered her senses, was to open the basket. Loulou was unharmed. She felt a sting on her right cheek; when she took her hand away it was red, for the blood was flowing.

She sat down on a pile of stones, and sopped her cheek with her handkerchief; then she ate a crust of bread she had put in her basket, and consoled herself by looking at the bird.

Arriving at the top of Ecquemanville, she saw the lights of Honfleur shining in the distance like so many stars; further on, the ocean spread out in a confused mass. Then a weakness came over her; the misery of her childhood, the disappointment of her first love, the departure of her nephew, the death of Virginia; all these things came back to her at once, and, rising like a swelling tide in her throat, almost choked her.

Then she wished to speak to the captain of the vessel, and without stating what she was sending, she gave him some instructions.

Fellacher kept the parrot a long time. He always promised that it would be ready for the following week; after six months he announced the shipment of a case, and that was the end of it. Really, it seemed as if Loulou would never come back to his home. "They have stolen him," thought Felicite.

Finally he arrived, sitting bold upright on a branch which could be screwed into a mahogany pedestal, with his foot in the air, his head on one side, and in his beak a nut which the naturalist, from love of the sumptuous, had gilded. She put him in her room.

This place, to which only a chosen few were admitted, looked like a chapel and a second-hand shop, so filled was it with devotional and heterogeneous things. The door could not be opened easily on account of the presence of a large wardrobe. Opposite the window that looked out into the garden, a bull's-eye opened on the yard; a table was placed by the cot and held a wash-basin, two combs, and a piece of blue soap in a broken saucer. On the walls were rosaries, medals, a number of Holy Virgins, and a holy-water basin made out of a cocoanut; on the bureau, which was covered with a napkin like an altar, stood the box of shells that Victor had given her; also a watering-can and a balloon, writing-books, the engraved geography and a pair of shoes; on the nail which held the mirror, hung Virginia's little plush hat! Felicite carried this sort of respect so far that she even kept one of Monsieur's old coats. All the things which Madame Aubain discarded, Felicite begged for her own room. Thus, she had artificial flowers on the edge of the bureau, and the picture of the Comte d'Artois in the recess of the window. By means of a board, Loulou was set on a portion of the chimney which advanced into the room. Every morning when she awoke, she saw him in the dim light of dawn and recalled bygone days and the smallest details of insignificant actions, without any sense of bitterness or grief.

As she was unable to communicate with people, she lived in a sort of somnambulistic torpor. The processions of Corpus-Christi Day seemed to wake her up. She visited the neighbours to beg for candlesticks and mats so as to adorn the temporary altars in the street.

In church, she always gazed at the Holy Ghost, and noticed that there was something about it that resembled a parrot. The likenesses appeared even more striking on a coloured picture by Espinal, representing the baptism of our Saviour. With his scarlet wings and emerald body, it was really the image of Loulou. Having bought the picture, she hung it near the one of the Comte d'Artois so that she could take them in at one glance.

They associated in her mind, the parrot becoming sanctified through the neighbourhood of the Holy Ghost, and the latter becoming more lifelike in her eyes, and more comprehensible. In all probability the Father had never chosen as messenger a dove, as the latter has no voice, but rather one of Loulou's ancestors.

And Felicite said her prayers in front of the coloured picture, though from time to time she turned slightly towards the bird.

She desired very much to enter in the ranks of the "Daughters of the Virgin." But Madame Aubain dissuaded her from it.

A most important event occurred: Paul's marriage.

After being first a notary's clerk, then in business, then in the customs, and a tax collector, and having even applied for a position in the administration of woods and forests, he had at last, when he was thirty-six years old, by a divine inspiration, found his vocation: registrature! and he displayed such a high ability that an inspector had offered him his daughter and his influence.

Paul, who had become quite settled, brought his bride to visit his mother.

But she looked down upon the customs of Pont-l'Eveque, put on airs, and hurt Felicite's feelings. Madame Aubain felt relieved when she left.

The following week they learned of Monsieur Bourais' death in an inn. There were rumours of suicide, which were confirmed; doubts concerning his integrity arose. Madame Aubain looked over her accounts and soon discovered his numerous embezzlements; sales of wood which had been concealed from her, false receipts, etc. Furthermore, he had an illegitimate child, and entertained a friendship for "a person in Dozule."

These base actions affected her very much. In March, 1853, she developed a pain in her chest; her tongue looked as if it were coated with smoke, and the leeches they applied did not relieve her oppression; and on the ninth evening she died, being just seventy-two years old.

People thought that she was younger, because her hair, which she wore in bands framing her pale face, was brown. Few friends regretted her loss, for her manner was so haughty that she did not attract them. Felicite mourned for her as servants seldom mourn for their masters. The fact that Madame should die before herself perplexed her mind and seemed contrary to the order of things, and absolutely monstrous and inadmissible. Ten days later (the time to journey from Besancon), the heirs arrived. Her daughter-in-law ransacked the drawers, kept some of the furniture, and sold the rest; then they went back to their own home.

Madame's armchair, foot-warmer, work-table, the eight chairs, everything was gone! The places occupied by the pictures formed yellow squares on the walls. They had taken the two little beds, and the wardrobe had been emptied of Virginia's belongings! Felicite went upstairs, overcome with grief.

The following day a sign was posted on the door; the chemist screamed in her ear that the house was for sale.

For a moment she tottered, and had to sit down.

What hurt her most was to give up her room, – so nice for poor Loulou! She looked at him in despair and implored the Holy Ghost, and it was this way that she contracted the idolatrous habit of saying her prayers kneeling in front of the bird. Sometimes the sun fell through the window on his glass eye, and lighted a spark in it which sent Felicite into ecstasy.

Her mistress had left her an income of three hundred and eighty francs. The garden supplied her with vegetables. As for clothes, she had enough to last her till the end of her days, and she economised on the light by going to bed at dusk.

She rarely went out, in order to avoid passing in front of the second-hand dealer's shop where there was some of the old furniture. Since her fainting spell, she dragged her leg, and as her strength was failing rapidly, old Mother Simon, who had lost her money in the grocery business, came very morning to chop the wood and pump the water.

Her eyesight grew dim. She did not open the shutters after that. Many years passed. But the house did not sell or rent. Fearing that she would be put out, Felicite did not ask for repairs. The laths of the roof were rotting away, and during one whole winter her bolster was wet. After Easter she spit blood.

Then Mother Simon went for a doctor. Felicite wished to know what her complaint was. But, being too deaf to hear, she caught only one word: "Pneumonia." She was familiar with it and gently answered: –"Ah! like Madame," thinking it quite natural that she should follow her mistress.

The time for the altars in the street drew near.

The first one was always erected at the foot of the hill, the second in front of the post-office, and the third in the middle of the street. This position occasioned some rivalry among the women and they finally decided upon Madame Aubain's yard.

Felicite's fever grew worse. She was sorry that she could not do anything for the altar. If she could, at least, have contributed something towards it! Then she thought of the parrot. Her neighbours objected that it would not be proper. But the cure gave his consent and she was so grateful for it that she begged him to accept after her death, her only treasure, Loulou. From Tuesday until Saturday, the day before the event, she coughed more frequently. In the evening her face was contracted, her lips stuck to her gums and she began to vomit; and on the following day, she felt so low that she called for a priest.

Three neighbours surrounded her when the dominie administered the Extreme Unction. Afterwards she said that she wished to speak to Fabu.

He arrived in his Sunday clothes, very ill at ease among the funereal surroundings.

"Forgive me," she said, making an effort to extend her arm, "I believed it was you who killed him!"

What did such accusations mean? Suspect a man like him of murder! And Fabu became excited and was about to make trouble.

"Don't you see she is not in her right mind?"

From time to time Felicite spoke to shadows. The women left her and Mother Simon sat down to breakfast.

A little later, she took Loulou and holding him up to Felicite:

"Say good-bye to him, now!" she commanded.

Although he was not a corpse, he was eaten up by worms; one of his wings was broken and the wadding was coming out of his body. But Felicite was blind now, and she took him and laid him against her cheek. Then Mother Simon removed him in order to set him on the altar.

5

The grass exhaled an odour of summer; flies buzzed in the air, the sun shone on the river and warmed the slated roof. Old Mother Simon had returned to Felicite and was peacefully falling asleep.

The ringing of bells woke her; the people were coming out of church. Felicite's delirium subsided. By thinking of the procession, she was able to see it as if she had taken part in it. All the school-children, the singers and the firemen walked on the sidewalks, while in the middle of the street came first the custodian of the church with his halberd, then the beadle with a large cross, the teacher in charge of the boys and a sister escorting the little girls; three of the smallest ones, with curly heads, threw rose leaves into the air; the deacon with outstretched arms conducted the music; and two incense-bearers turned with each step they took toward the Holy Sacrament, which was carried by M. le Cure, attired in his handsome chasuble and walking under a canopy of red velvet supported by four men. A crowd of people followed, jammed between the walls of the houses hung with white sheets; at last the procession arrived at the foot of the hill.

A cold sweat broke out on Felicite's forehead. Mother Simon wiped it away with a cloth, saying inwardly that some day she would have to go through the same thing herself.

The murmur of the crowd grew louder, was very distinct for a moment and then died away. A volley of musketry shook the window-panes. It was the postilions saluting the Sacrament. Felicite rolled her eyes, and said as loudly as she could:

"Is he all right?" meaning the parrot.

Her death agony began. A rattle that grew more and more rapid shook her body. Froth appeared at the corners of her mouth, and her whole frame trembled. In a little while could be heard the music of the bass horns, the clear voices of the children and the men's deeper notes. At intervals all was still, and their shoes sounded like a herd of cattle passing over the grass.

The clergy appeared in the yard. Mother Simon climbed on a chair to reach the bull's-eye, and in this manner could see the altar. It was covered with a lace cloth and draped with green wreaths. In the middle stood a little frame containing relics; at the corners were two little orange-trees, and all along the edge were silver candlesticks, porcelain vases containing sun-flowers, lilies, peonies, and tufts of hydrangeas. This mount of bright colours descended diagonally from the first floor to the carpet that covered the sidewalk. Rare objects arrested one's eye. A golden sugar-bowl was crowned with violets, earrings set with Alencon stones were displayed on green moss, and two Chinese screens with their bright landscapes were near by. Loulou, hidden beneath roses, showed nothing but his blue head which looked like a piece of lapis-lazuli.

The singers, the canopy-bearers and the children lined up against the sides of the yard. Slowly the priest ascended the steps and placed his shining sun on the lace cloth. Everybody knelt. There was deep silence; and the censers slipping on their chains were swung high in the air. A blue vapour rose in Felicite's room. She opened her nostrils and inhaled with a mystic sensuousness; then she closed her lids. Her lips smiled. The beats of her heart grew fainter and fainter, and vaguer, like a fountain giving out, like an echo dying away; – and when she exhaled her last breath, she thought she saw in the half-opened heavens a gigantic parrot hovering above her head.

DESIREE'S BABY

Kate Chopin

Born in St Louis Missouri, where she died, **Kate Chopin** (1850–1904) was mildly well-born, well-educated, and married by the time she was twenty. She gave birth to six children in eight years, whereupon Oscar Chopin died leaving a failed business and vast debts. She began to write – her second and best-known novel *The Awakening* was published in 1899. Her work never made a huge amount of money in her lifetime, but she touched on themes and topics well before others did. She is another of the writers who died two days after suffering a brain haemorrhage; in her case during a visit to the St Louis World's Fair on 20 August 1904. "To be an artist," she observed, "includes much; one must possess many gifts – absolute gifts – which have not been acquired by one's own efforts. And moreover, to succeed, the artist must possess the courageous soul."

As the day was pleasant, Madame Valmonde drove over to L'Abri to see Desiree and the baby.

It made her laugh to think of Desiree with a baby. Why, it seemed but yesterday that Desiree was little more than a baby herself; when Monsieur in riding through the gateway of Valmonde had found her lying asleep in the shadow of the big stone pillar.

The little one awoke in his arms and began to cry for "Dada." That was as much as she could do or say. Some people thought she might have strayed there of her own accord, for she was of the toddling age. The prevailing belief was that she had been purposely left by a party of Texans, whose canvas-covered wagon, late in the day, had crossed the ferry that Coton Mais kept, just below the plantation. In time Madame Valmonde abandoned every speculation but the one that Desiree had been sent to her by a beneficent Providence to be the child of her affection, seeing that she was without child of the flesh. For the girl grew to be beautiful and gentle, affectionate and sincere – the idol of Valmonde.

It was no wonder, when she stood one day against the stone pillar in whose shadow she had lain asleep, eighteen years before, that Armand Aubigny riding by and seeing her there, had fallen in love with her. That was the way all the Aubignys fell in love, as if struck by a pistol shot. The wonder was that he had not loved her before; for he had known her since his father brought him home from Paris, a boy of eight, after his mother died there. The passion that awoke in him that day, when he saw her at the gate, swept along like an avalanche, or like a prairie fire, or like anything that drives headlong over all obstacles.

Monsieur Valmonde grew practical and wanted things well considered: that is, the girl's obscure origin. Armand looked into her eyes and did not care. He was reminded that she was nameless. What did it matter about a name when he could give her one of the oldest and proudest in Louisiana? He ordered the corbeille from Paris, and contained himself with what patience he could until it arrived; then they were married.

Madame Valmonde had not seen Desiree and the baby for four weeks. When she reached L'Abri she shuddered at the first sight of it, as she always did. It was a sad looking place, which for many years had not known the gentle presence of a mistress, old Monsieur Aubigny having married and buried his wife in France, and she having loved her own land too well ever to leave it. The roof came down steep and black like a cowl, reaching out beyond the wide galleries that encircled the yellow stuccoed house. Big, solemn oaks grew close to it, and their thick-leaved, far-reaching branches shadowed it like a pall. Young Aubigny's rule was a strict one, too, and under it his negroes had forgotten how to be gay, as they had been during the old master's easy-going and indulgent lifetime.

The young mother was recovering slowly, and lay full length, in her soft white muslins and laces, upon a couch. The baby was beside her, upon her arm, where he had fallen asleep, at her breast. The yellow nurse woman sat beside a window fanning herself.

Madame Valmonde bent her portly figure over Desiree and kissed her, holding her an instant tenderly in her arms. Then she turned to the child.

"This is not the baby!" she exclaimed, in startled tones. French was the language spoken at Valmonde in those days.

"I knew you would be astonished," laughed Desiree, "at the way he has grown. The little cochon de lait! Look at his legs, mamma, and his hands and fingernails – real finger-nails. Zandrine had to cut them this morning. Isn't it true, Zandrine?"

The woman bowed her turbaned head majestically, "Mais si, Madame."

"And the way he cries," went on Desiree, "is deafening. Armand heard him the other day as far away as La Blanche's cabin."

Madame Valmonde had never removed her eyes from the child. She lifted it and walked with it over to the window that was lightest. She scanned the baby narrowly, then looked as searchingly at Zandrine, whose face was turned to gaze across the fields.

"Yes, the child has grown, has changed," said Madame Valmonde, slowly, as she replaced it beside its mother. "What does Armand say?"

Desiree's face became suffused with a glow that was happiness itself.

"Oh, Armand is the proudest father in the parish, I believe, chiefly because it is a boy, to bear his name; though he says not – that he would have loved a girl as well. But I know it isn't true. I know he says that to please me. And mamma," she added, drawing Madame Valmonde's head down to her, and speaking in a whisper, "he hasn't punished one of them – not one of them – since baby is born. Even Negrillon, who pretended to have burnt his leg that he might rest from work – he only laughed, and said Negrillon was a great scamp. Oh, mamma, I'm so happy; it frightens me."

What Desiree said was true. Marriage, and later the birth of his son had softened Armand Aubigny's imperious and exacting nature greatly. This was what made the gentle Desiree so happy, for she loved him desperately. When he frowned she trembled, but loved him. When he smiled, she asked no greater blessing of God. But Armand's dark, handsome face had not often been disfigured by frowns since the day he fell in love with her.

When the baby was about three months old, Desiree awoke one day to the conviction that there was something in the air menacing her peace. It was at first too subtle to grasp. It had only been a disquieting suggestion; an air of mystery among the blacks; unexpected visits from far-off neighbors who could hardly account for their coming. Then a strange, an awful change in her husband's manner, which she dared not ask him to explain. When he spoke to her, it was with averted eyes, from which the old love-light seemed to have gone out. He absented himself from home; and when there, avoided her presence and that of her child, without excuse. And the very spirit of Satan seemed suddenly to take hold of him in his dealings with the slaves. Desiree was miserable enough to die.

She sat in her room, one hot afternoon, in her peignoir, listlessly drawing through her fingers the strands of her long, silky brown hair that hung about her shoulders. The baby, half naked, lay asleep upon her own great mahogany bed, that was like a sumptuous throne, with its satin-lined half-canopy. One of La Blanche's little quadroon boys – half naked too – stood fanning the child slowly with a fan of peacock feathers. Desiree's eyes had been fixed absently and sadly upon the baby, while she was striving to penetrate the threatening mist that she felt closing about her. She looked from her child to the boy who stood beside him, and back again; over and over. "Ah!" It was a cry that she could not help; which she was not conscious of having uttered. The blood turned like ice in her veins, and a clammy moisture gathered upon her face.

She tried to speak to the little quadroon boy; but no sound would come, at first. When he heard his name uttered, he looked up, and his mistress was pointing to the door. He laid aside the great, soft fan, and obediently stole away, over the polished floor, on his bare tiptoes.

She stayed motionless, with gaze riveted upon her child, and her face the picture of fright.

Presently her husband entered the room, and without noticing her, went to a table and began to search among some papers which covered it.

"Armand," she called to him, in a voice which must have stabbed him, if he was human. But he did not notice. "Armand," she said again. Then she rose and tottered towards him. "Armand," she panted once more, clutching his arm, "look at our child. What does it mean? Tell me."

He coldly but gently loosened her fingers from about his arm and thrust the hand away from him. "Tell me what it means!" she cried despairingly.

"It means," he answered lightly, "that the child is not white; it means that you are not white."

A quick conception of all that this accusation meant for her nerved her with unwonted courage to deny it. "It is a lie; it is not true, I am white! Look at my hair, it is brown; and my eyes are gray, Armand, you know they are gray. And my skin is fair," seizing his wrist. "Look at my hand; whiter than yours, Armand," she laughed hysterically.

"As white as La Blanche's," he returned cruelly; and went away leaving her alone with their child.

When she could hold a pen in her hand, she sent a despairing letter to Madame Valmondé.

"My mother, they tell me I am not white. Armand has told me I am not white. For God's sake tell them it is not true. You must know it is not true. I shall die. I must die. I cannot be so unhappy, and live."

The answer that came was brief:

"My own Desiree: Come home to Valmondé; back to your mother who loves you. Come with your child."

When the letter reached Desiree she went with it to her husband's study, and laid it open upon the desk before which he sat. She was like a stone image: silent, white, motionless after she placed it there.

In silence he ran his cold eyes over the written words.

He said nothing. "Shall I go, Armand?" she asked in tones sharp with agonized suspense.

"Yes, go."

"Do you want me to go?"

"Yes, I want you to go."

He thought Almighty God had dealt cruelly and unjustly with him; and felt, somehow, that he was paying Him back in kind when he stabbed thus into his wife's soul. Moreover he no longer loved her, because of the unconscious injury she had brought upon his home and his name.

She turned away like one stunned by a blow, and walked slowly towards the door, hoping he would call her back.

"Good-by, Armand," she moaned.

He did not answer her. That was his last blow at fate.

Desiree went in search of her child. Zandrine was pacing the sombre gallery with it. She took the little one from the nurse's arms with no word of explanation, and descending the steps, walked away, under the live-oak branches.

It was an October afternoon; the sun was just sinking. Out in the still fields the negroes were picking cotton.

Desiree had not changed the thin white garment nor the slippers which she wore. Her hair was uncovered and the sun's rays brought a golden gleam from its brown meshes. She did not take the broad, beaten road which led to the far-off plantation of Valmondé. She walked across a deserted field, where the stubble bruised her tender feet, so delicately shod, and tore her thin gown to shreds.

She disappeared among the reeds and willows that grew thick along the banks of the deep, sluggish bayou; and she did not come back again.

Some weeks later there was a curious scene enacted at L'Abri. In the centre of the smoothly swept back yard was a great bonfire. Armand Aubigny sat in the wide hallway that commanded a view of the spectacle; and it was he who dealt out to a half dozen negroes the material which kept this fire ablaze.

A graceful cradle of willow, with all its dainty furbishings, was laid upon the pyre, which had already been fed with the richness of a priceless layette. Then there were silk gowns, and velvet and satin ones added to these; laces, too, and embroideries; bonnets and gloves; for the corbeille had been of rare quality.

The last thing to go was a tiny bundle of letters; innocent little scribblings that Desiree had sent to him during the days of their espousal. There was the remnant of one back in the drawer from which he took them. But it was not Desiree's; it was part of an old letter from his mother to his father. He read it. She was thanking God for the blessing of her husband's love:–

"But above all," she wrote, "night and day, I thank the good God for having so arranged our lives that our dear Armand will never know that his mother, who adores him, belongs to the race that is cursed with the brand of slavery."

THE HORLA

Guy de Maupassant

Sometimes known as the "father of the modern short story," **Guy de Maupassant** (1850–1893) was born near Dieppe. In a youth that would thrill any name-dropper, he became known to Flaubert, who introduced him to Zola and Turgenev, and he saved the English poet Swinburne from drowning aged just eighteen. He hated the Eiffel Tower, so had lunch at the restaurant at its base so he wouldn't have to look at it. He failed to slit his throat conclusively and died a year later in a private asylum in Paris. This strange story was published in 1887.

MAY 8. What a lovely day! I have spent all the morning lying on the grass in front of my house, under the enormous plantain tree which covers and shades and shelters the whole of it. I like this part of the country; I am fond of living here because I am attached to it by deep roots, the profound and delicate roots which attach a man to the soil on which his ancestors were born and died, to their traditions, their usages, their food, the local expressions, the peculiar language of the peasants, the smell of the soil, the hamlets, and to the atmosphere itself.

I love the house in which I grew up. From my windows I can see the Seine, which flows by the side of my garden, on the other side of the road, almost through my grounds, the great and wide Seine, which goes to Rouen and Havre, and which is covered with boats passing to and fro.

On the left, down yonder, lies Rouen, populous Rouen with its blue roofs massing under pointed, Gothic towers. Innumerable are they, delicate or broad, dominated by the spire of the cathedral, full of bells which sound through the blue air on fine mornings, sending their sweet and distant Iron clang to me, their metallic sounds, now stronger and now weaker, according as the wind is strong or light.

What a delicious morning it was! About eleven o'clock, a long line of boats drawn by a steam-tug, as big a fly, and which scarcely puffed while emitting its thick smoke, passed my gate.

After two English schooners, whose red flags fluttered toward the sky, there came a magnificent Brazilian three-master; it was perfectly white and wonderfully clean and shining. I saluted it, I hardly know why, except that the sight of the vessel gave me great pleasure.

May 12. I have had a slight feverish attack for the last few days, and I feel ill, or rather I feel low-spirited.

Whence come those mysterious influences which change our happiness into discouragement, and our self-confidence into diffidence? One might almost say that the air, the invisible air, is full of unknowable Forces, whose mysterious presence we have to endure. I wake up in the best of spirits, with an inclination to sing in my heart. Why? I go down by the side of the water, and suddenly, after walking a short distance, I return home wretched, as if some misfortune were awaiting me there. Why? Is it a cold shiver which, passing over my skin, has upset my nerves and given me a fit of low spirits? Is it the form of the clouds, or the tints of the sky, or the colors of the surrounding objects which are so changeable, which have troubled my thoughts as they passed before my eyes? Who can tell? Everything that surrounds us, everything that we see without looking at it, everything that we touch without knowing it, everything that we handle without feeling it, everything that we meet without clearly distinguishing it, has a rapid, surprising, and inexplicable effect upon us and upon our organs, and through them on our ideas and on our being itself.

How profound that mystery of the Invisible is! We cannot fathom it with our miserable senses: our eyes are unable to perceive what is either too small or too great, too near to or too far from us; we can see neither the inhabitants of a star nor of a drop of water; our ears deceive us, for they transmit to us the vibrations of the air in sonorous notes. Our senses are fairies who work the miracle of changing that movement into noise, and by that metamorphosis give birth to music, which makes the mute agitation of nature a harmony. So with our sense of smell, which is weaker than that of a dog, and so with our sense of taste, which can scarcely distinguish the age of a wine!

Oh! If we only had other organs which could work other miracles in our favor, what a number of fresh things we might discover around us!

May 16. I am ill, decidedly! I was so well last month! I am feverish, horribly feverish, or rather I am in a state of feverish enervation, which makes my mind suffer as much as my body. I have without ceasing the horrible sensation of some danger threatening me, the apprehension of some coming misfortune or of approaching death, a presentiment which is no doubt, an attack of some illness still unnamed, which germinates in the flesh and in the blood.

May 18. I have just come from consulting my medical man, for I can no longer get any sleep. He found that my pulse was high, my eyes dilated, my nerves highly strung, but no alarming symptoms. I must have a course of shower baths and of bromide of potassium.

May 25. No change! My state is really very peculiar. As the evening comes on, an incomprehensible feeling of disquietude seizes me, just as if night concealed some terrible menace toward me. I dine quickly, and then try to read, but I do not understand the words, and can scarcely distinguish the letters. Then I walk up and down my drawing-room, oppressed by a feeling of confused and irresistible fear, a fear of sleep and a fear of my bed.

About ten o'clock I go up to my room. As soon as I have entered I lock and bolt the door. I am frightened – of what? Up till the present time I have been frightened of nothing. I open my cupboards, and look under my bed; I listen – I listen – to what? How strange it is that a simple feeling of discomfort, of impeded or heightened circulation, perhaps the irritation of a nervous center, a slight congestion, a small disturbance in the imperfect and delicate functions of our living machinery, can turn the most light-hearted of men into a melancholy one, and make a coward of the bravest? Then, I go to bed, and I wait for sleep as a man might wait for the executioner. I wait for its coming with dread, and my heart beats and my legs tremble, while my whole body shivers beneath the warmth of the bedclothes, until the moment when I suddenly fall asleep, as a man throws himself into a pool of stagnant water in order to drown. I do not feel this perfidious sleep coming over me as I used to, but a sleep which is close to me and watching me, which is going to seize me by the head, to close my eyes and annihilate me.

I sleep – a long time – two or three hours perhaps – then a dream – no – a nightmare lays hold on me. I feel that I am in bed and asleep – I feel it and I know it – and I feel also that somebody is coming close to me, is looking at me, touching me, is getting on to my bed, is kneeling on my chest, is taking my neck between his hands and squeezing it – squeezing it with all his might in order to strangle me.

I struggle, bound by that terrible powerlessness which paralyzes us in our dreams; I try to cry out – but I cannot; I want to move – I cannot; I try, with the most violent efforts and out of breath, to turn over and throw off this being which is crushing and suffocating me – I cannot!

And then suddenly I wake up, shaken and bathed in perspiration; I light a candle and find that I am alone, and after that crisis, which occurs every night, I at length fall asleep and slumber tranquilly till morning.

June 2. My state has grown worse. What is the matter with me? The bromide does me no good, and the shower-baths have no effect whatever. Sometimes, in order to tire myself out, though I am fatigued enough already, I go for a walk in the forest of Roumare. I used to think at first that the fresh light and soft air, impregnated with the odor of herbs and leaves, would instill new life into my veins and impart fresh energy to my heart. One day I turned into a broad ride in the wood, and then I diverged toward La Bouille, through a narrow path, between two rows of exceedingly tall trees, which placed a thick, green, almost black roof between the sky and me.

A sudden shiver ran through me, not a cold shiver, but a shiver of agony, and so I hastened my steps, uneasy at being alone in the wood, frightened stupidly and without reason, at the profound solitude. Suddenly it seemed as if I were being followed, that somebody was walking at my heels, close, quite close to me, near enough to touch me.

I turned round suddenly, but I was alone. I saw nothing behind me except the straight, broad ride, empty and bordered by high trees, horribly empty; on the other side also it extended until it was lost in the distance, and looked just the same – terrible.

I closed my eyes. Why? And then I began to turn round on one heel very quickly, just like a top. I nearly fell down, and opened my eyes; the trees were dancing round me and the earth heaved; I was obliged to sit down. Then, ah! I no longer remembered how I had come! What a strange idea! What a strange, strange idea! I did not the least know. I started off to the right, and got back into the avenue which had led me into the middle of the forest.

June 3. I have had a terrible night. I shall go away for a few weeks, for no doubt a journey will set me up again.

July 2. I have come back, quite cured, and have had a most delightful trip into the bargain. I have been to Mont Saint-Michel, which I had not seen before.

What a sight, when one arrives as I did, at Avranches toward the end of the day! The town stands on a hill, and I was taken into the public garden at the extremity of the town. I uttered a cry of astonishment. An extraordinarily large bay lay extended before me, as far as my eyes could reach, between two hills which were lost to sight in the mist; and in the middle of this immense yellow bay, under a clear, golden sky, a peculiar hill rose up, somber and pointed in the midst of the sand. The sun had just disappeared, and under the still flaming sky stood out the outline of that fantastic rock which bears on its summit a pictur-esque monument.

At daybreak I went to it. The tide was low, as it had been the night before, and I saw that wonderful abbey rise up before me as I approached it. After several hours' walking, I reached the enormous mass of rock which supports the little town, dominated by the great church. Having climbed the steep and narrow street, I entered the most wonderful Gothic building that has ever been erected to God on earth, large as a town, and full of low rooms which seem buried beneath vaulted roofs, and of lofty galleries supported by delicate columns.

I entered this gigantic granite jewel, which is as light in its effect as a bit of lace and is covered with towers, with slender belfries to which spiral staircases ascend. The flying buttresses raise strange heads that bristle with chimeras. with devils, with fantastic animals, with monstrous flowers, are joined together by finely carved arches, to the blue sky by day, and to the black sky by night.

When I had reached the summit. I said to the monk who accompanied me: "Father, how happy you must be here!" And he replied: "It is very windy, Mon-sieur"; and so we began to talk while watching the rising tide, which ran over the sand and covered it with a steel cuirass.

And then the monk told me stories, all the old stories belonging to the place – legends, nothing but legends.

One of them struck me forcibly. The country people, those belonging to the Mornet, declare that at night one can hear talking going on in the sand, and also that two goats bleat, one with a strong, the other with a weak voice. Incredulous people declare that it is nothing but the screaming of the sea birds, which occa-sionally resembles bleatings, and occasionally human lamentations; but belated fishermen swear that they have met an old shepherd, whose cloak covered head they can never see, wandering on the sand, between two tides, round the little town placed so far out of the world. They declare he is guiding and walking before a he-goat with a man's face and a she-goat with a woman's face, both with white hair, who talk incessantly, quarreling in a strange language, and then suddenly cease talking in order to bleat with all their might.

"Do you believe it?" I asked the monk. "I scarcely know," he replied; and I continued: "If there are other beings besides ourselves on this earth, how comes it that we have not known it for so long a time, or why have you not seen them? How is it that I have not seen them?"

He replied: "Do we see the hundred-thousandth part of what exists? Look here; there is the wind, which is the strongest force in nature. It knocks down men, and blows down buildings, uproots trees, raises the sea into mountains of water, destroys cliffs and casts great ships on to the breakers; it kills, it whistles, it sighs, it roars. But have you ever seen it, and can you see it? Yet it exists for all that."

I was silent before this simple reasoning. That man was a philosopher, or perhaps a fool; I could not say which exactly, so I held my tongue. What he had said had often been in my own thoughts.

July 3. I have slept badly; certainly there is some feverish influence here, for my coachman is suffering in the same way as I am. When I went back home yesterday, I noticed his singular paleness, and I asked him: "What is the matter with you, Jean?"

"The matter is that I never get any rest, and my nights devour my days. Since your departure, Monsieur, there has been a spell over me."

However, the other servants are all well, but I am very frightened of having another attack, myself.

July 4. I am decidedly taken again; for my old nightmares have returned. Last night I felt somebody leaning on me who was sucking my life from between my lips with his mouth. Yes, he was sucking it out of my neck like a leech would have done. Then he got up, satiated, and I woke up, so beaten, crushed, and annihilated that I could not move. If this continues for a few days, I shall certainly go away again.

July 5. Have I lost my reason? What has happened? What I saw last night is so strange that my head wanders when I think of it!

As I do now every evening, I had locked my door; then, being thirsty, I drank half a glass of water, and I accidentally noticed that the water-bottle was full up to the cut-glass stopper.

Then I went to bed and fell into one of my terrible sleeps, from which I was aroused in about two hours by a still more terrible shock.

Picture to yourself a sleeping man who is being murdered, who wakes up with a knife in his chest, a gurgling in his throat, is covered with blood, can no longer breathe, is going to die and does not understand anything at all about it – there you have it.

Having recovered my senses, I was thirsty again, so I lighted a candle and went to the table on which my water-bottle was. I lifted it up and tilted it over my glass, but nothing came out. It was empty! It was completely empty! At first I could not understand it at all; then suddenly I was seized by such a terrible feeling that I had to sit down, or rather fall into a chair! Then I sprang up with a bound to look about me; then I sat down again, overcome by astonishment and fear, in front of the transparent crystal bottle! I looked at it with fixed eyes, trying to solve the puzzle, and my hands trembled! Some body had drunk the water, but who? I? I without any doubt. It could surely only be I? In that case I was a somnambulist – was living, without knowing it, that double, mysterious life which makes us doubt whether there are not two beings in us – whether a strange, unknowable, and invisible being does not, during our moments of mental and physical torpor, animate the inert body, forcing it to a more willing obedience than it yields to ourselves.

Oh! Who will understand my horrible agony? Who will understand the emotion of a man sound in mind, wide-awake, full of sense, who looks in horror at the disappearance of a little water while he was asleep, through the glass of a water-bottle! And I remained sitting until it was daylight, without venturing to go to bed again.

July 6. I am going mad. Again all the contents of my water-bottle have been drunk during the night; or rather I have drunk it!

But is it I? Is it I? Who could it be? Who? Oh! God! Am I going mad? Who will save me?

July 10. I have just been through some surprising ordeals. Undoubtedly I must be mad! And yet!

On July 6, before going to bed, I put some wine, milk, water, bread, and strawberries on my table. Somebody drank – I drank – all the water and a little of the milk, but neither the wine, nor the bread, nor the strawberries were touched.

On the seventh of July I renewed the same experiment, with the same results, and on July 8 I left out the water and the milk and nothing was touched.

Lastly, on July 9 I put only water and milk on my table, taking care to wrap up the bottles in white muslin and to tie down the stoppers. Then I rubbed my lips, my beard, and my hands with pencil lead, and went to bed.

Deep slumber seized me, soon followed by a terrible awakening. I had not moved, and my sheets were not marked. I rushed to the table. The muslin round the bottles remained intact; I undid the string, trembling with fear. All the water had been drunk, and so had the milk! Ah! Great God! I must start for Paris immediately.

July 12. Paris. I must have lost my head during the last few days! I must be the plaything of my enervated imagination, unless I am really a somnambulist, or I have been brought under the power of one of those influences – hypnotic suggestion, for example – which are known to exist, but have hitherto been inexplicable. In any case, my mental state bordered on madness, and twenty-four hours of Paris sufficed to restore me to my equilibrium.

Yesterday after doing some business and paying some visits, which instilled fresh and invigorating mental air into me, I wound up my evening at the Théâtre Français. A drama by Alexander Dumas the Younger was being acted, and his brilliant and powerful play completed my cure. Certainly solitude is dangerous for active minds. We need men who can think and can talk, around us. When we are alone for a long time, we people space with phantoms.

I returned along the boulevards to my hotel in excellent spirits. Amid the jostling of the crowd I thought, not without irony, of my terrors and surmises of the previous week, because I believed, yes, I believed, that an invisible being lived beneath my roof. How weak our mind is; how quickly it is terrified and unbalanced as soon as we are confronted with a small, incomprehensible fact. Instead of dismissing the problem with: "We do not understand because we cannot find the cause," we immediately imagine terrible mysteries and supernatural powers.

July 14. Fête of the Republic. I walked through the streets, and the crackers and flags amused me like a child. Still, it is very foolish to make merry on a set date, by Government decree. People are like a flock of sheep, now steadily patient, now in ferocious revolt. Say to it: "Amuse yourself," and it amuses itself. Say to it: "Go and fight with your neighbor," and it goes and fights. Say to it:

"Vote for the Emperor," and it votes for the Emperor; then say to it: "Vote for the Republic," and it votes for the Republic.

Those who direct it are stupid, too; but instead of obeying men they obey principles, a course which can only be foolish, ineffective, and false, for the very reason that principles are ideas which are considered as certain and unchangeable, whereas in this world one is certain of nothing, since light is an illusion and noise is deception.

July 16. I saw some things yesterday that troubled me very much.

I was dining at my cousin's, Madame Sablé, whose husband is colonel of the Seventy-sixth Chasseurs at Limoges. There were two young women there, one of whom had married a medical man, Dr. Parent, who devotes himself a great deal to nervous diseases and to the extraordinary manifestations which just now experiments in hypnotism and suggestion are producing.

He related to us at some length the enormous results obtained by English scientists and the doctors of the medical school at Nancy, and the facts which he adduced appeared to me so strange, that I declared that I was altogether incredulous.

"We are," he declared, "on the point of discovering one of the most important secrets of nature, I mean to say, one of its most important secrets on this earth, for assuredly there are some up in the stars, yonder, of a different kind of importance. Ever since man has thought, since he has been able to express and write down his thoughts, he has felt himself close to a mystery which is impenetrable to his coarse and imperfect senses, and he endeavors to supplement the feeble penetration of his organs by the efforts of his intellect. As long as that intellect remained in its elementary stage, this intercourse with invisible spirits assumed forms which were commonplace though terrifying. Thence sprang the popular belief in the supernatural, the legends of wandering spirits, of fairies, of gnomes, of ghosts, I might even say the conception of God, for our ideas of the Workman-Creator, from whatever religion they may have come down to us, are certainly the most mediocre, the stupidest, and the most unacceptable inventions that ever sprang from the frightened brain of any human creature. Nothing is truer than what Voltaire says: "If God made man in His own image, man has certainly paid Him back again."

"But for rather more than a century, men seem to have had a presentiment of something new. Mesmer and some others have put us on an unexpected track, and within the last two or three years especially, we have arrived at results really surprising."

My cousin, who is also very incredulous, smiled, and Dr. Parent said to her: "Would you like me to try and send you to sleep, Madame?"

"Yes, certainly."

She sat down in an easy-chair, and he began to look at her fixedly, as if to fascinate her. I suddenly felt myself somewhat discomposed; my heart beat rapidly and I had a choking feeling in my throat. I saw that Madame Sablé's eyes were growing heavy, her mouth twitched, and her bosom heaved, and at the end of ten minutes she was asleep.

"Go behind her," the doctor said to me; so I took a seat behind her. He put a visiting-card into her hands, and said to her: "This is a looking-glass; what do you see in it?"

She replied: "I see my cousin."

"What is he doing?"

"He is twisting his mustache."

"And now?"

"He is taking a photograph out of his pocket."

"Whose photograph is it?"

"His own."

That was true, for the photograph had been given me that same evening at the hotel.

"What is his attitude in this portrait?"

"He is standing up with his hat in his hand."

She saw these things in that card, in that piece of white pasteboard, as if she had seen them in a looking-glass.

The young women were frightened, and exclaimed: "That is quite enough! Quite, quite enough!"

But the doctor said to her authoritatively: "You will get up at eight o'clock to-morrow morning; then you will go and call on your cousin at his hotel and ask him to lend you the five thousand francs which your husband asks of you, and which he will ask for when he sets out on his coming journey."

Then he woke her up.

On returning to my hotel, I thought over this curious *séance* and I was assailed by doubts, not as to my cousin's absolute and undoubted good faith, for I had known her as well as if she had been my own sister ever since she was a child, but as to a possible trick on the doctor's part. Had not he, perhaps, kept a glass hidden in his hand, which he showed to the young woman in her sleep at the same time as he did the card? Professional conjurers do things which are just as singular.

However, I went to bed, and this morning, at about half past eight, I was awakened by my footman, who said to me: "Madame Sablé has asked to see you immediately, Monsieur." I dressed hastily and went to her.

She sat down in some agitation, with her eyes on the floor, and without raising her veil said to me: "My dear cousin, I am going to ask a great favor of you."

"What is it, cousin?"

"I do not like to tell you, and yet I must. I am in absolute want of five thousand francs."

"What, you?"

"Yes, I, or rather my husband, who has asked me to procure them for him."

I was so stupefied that I hesitated to answer. I asked myself whether she had not really been making fun of me with Dr. Parent, if it were not merely a very well-acted farce which had been got up beforehand. On looking at her attentively, however, my doubts disappeared. She was trembling with grief, so painful was this step to her, and I was sure that her throat was full of sobs.

I knew that she was very rich and so I continued: "What! Has not your husband five thousand francs at his disposal? Come, think. Are you sure that he commissioned you to ask me for them?"

She hesitated for a few seconds, as if she were making a great effort to search her memory, and then she replied: "Yes – yes, I am quite sure of it."

"He has written to you?"

She hesitated again and reflected, and I guessed the torture of her thoughts. She did not know. She only knew that she was to borrow five thousand francs of me for her husband. So she told a lie.

"Yes, he has written to me."

"When, pray? You did not mention it to me yesterday."

"I received his letter this morning."

"Can you show it to me?"

"No; no – no – it contained private matters, things too personal to ourselves. I burned it."

"So your husband runs into debt?"

She hesitated again, and then murmured: "I do not know."

Thereupon I said bluntly: "I have not five thousand francs at my disposal at this moment, my dear cousin."

She uttered a cry, as if she were in pair; and said: "Oh! oh! I beseech you, I beseech you to get them for me."

She got excited and clasped her hands as if she were praying to me! I heard her voice change its tone; she wept and sobbed, harassed and dominated by the irresistible order that she had received.

"Oh! oh! I beg you to – if you knew what I am suffering – I want them to-day."

I had pity on her: "You shall have them by and by, I swear to you."

"Oh! thank you! thank you! How kind you are."

I continued: "Do you remember what took place at your house last night?"

"Yes."

"Do you remember that Dr. Parent sent you to sleep?"

"Yes."

"Oh! Very well then; he ordered you to come to me this morning to borrow five thousand francs, and at this moment you are obeying that suggestion."

She considered for a few moments, and then replied: "But as it is my husband who wants them –"

For a whole hour I tried to convince her, but could not succeed, and when she had gone I went to the doctor. He was just going out, and he listened to me with a smile, and said: "Do you believe now?"

"Yes, I cannot help it."

"Let us go to your cousin's."

She was already resting on a couch, overcome with fatigue. The doctor felt her pulse, looked at her for some time with one hand raised toward her eyes, which she closed by degrees under the irresistible power of this magnetic influence. When she was asleep, he said:

"Your husband does not require the five thousand francs any longer! You must, therefore, forget that you asked your cousin to lend them to you, and, if he speaks to you about it, you will not understand him."

Then he woke her up, and I took out a pocket-book and said: "Here is what you asked me for this morning, my dear cousin." But she was so surprised, that I did not venture to persist; nevertheless, I tried to recall the circumstance to her, but she denied it vigorously, thought that I was making fun of her, and in the end, very nearly lost her temper.

There! I have just come back, and I have not been able to eat any lunch, for this experiment has altogether upset me.

July 19. Many people to whom I have told the adventure have laughed at me. I no longer know what to think. The wise man says: Perhaps?

July 21. I dined at Bougival, and then I spent the evening at a boatmen's ball. Decidedly everything depends on place and surroundings. It would be the height of folly to believe in the supernatural on the *Ile de la Grenouillière*.[1] But on the top of Mont Saint-Michel or in India, we are terribly under the influence of our surroundings. I shall return home next week.

1 Frog-island

July 30. I came back to my own house yesterday. Everything is going on well.

August 2. Nothing fresh; it is splendid weather, and I spend my days in watching the Seine flow past.

August 4. Quarrels among my servants. They declare that the glasses are broken in the cupboards at night. The footman accuses the cook, she accuses the needlewoman, and the latter accuses the other two. Who is the culprit? It would take a clever person to tell.

August 6. This time, I am not mad. I have seen – I have seen – I have seen! – I can doubt no longer – *I have seen it!*

I was walking at two o'clock among my rose-trees, in the full sunlight – in the walk bordered by autumn roses which are beginning to fall. As I stopped to look at a Géant de Bataille, which had three splendid blooms, I distinctly saw the stalk of one of the roses bend close to me, as if an invisible hand had bent it, and then break, as if that hand had picked it! Then the flower raised itself, following the curve which a hand would have described in carrying it toward a mouth, and remained suspended in the transparent air, alone and motionless, a terrible red spot, three yards from my eyes. In desperation I rushed at it to take it! I found nothing; it had disappeared. Then I was seized with furious rage against myself, for it is not wholesome for a reasonable and serious man to have such hallucinations.

But was it a hallucination? I turned to look for the stalk, and I found it immediately under the bush, freshly broken, between the two other roses which remained on the branch. I returned home, then, with a much disturbed mind; for I am certain now, certain as I am of the alternation of day and night, that there exists close to me an invisible being who lives on milk and on water, who can touch objects, take them and change their places; who is, consequently, endowed with a material nature, although imperceptible to sense, and who lives as I do, under my roof –

August 7. I slept tranquilly. He drank the water out of my decanter, but did not disturb my sleep.

I ask myself whether I am mad. As I was walking just now in the sun by the riverside, doubts as to my own sanity arose in me; not vague doubts such as I have had hitherto, but precise and absolute doubts. I have seen mad people, and I have known some who were quite intelligent, lucid, even clear-sighted in every concern of life, except on one point. They could speak clearly, readily, profoundly

---

[1] Frog-island.

on everything; till their thoughts were caught in the breakers of their delusions and went to pieces there, were dispersed and swamped in that furious and terrible sea of fogs and squalls which is called madness.

I certainly should think that I was mad, absolutely mad, if I were not conscious that I knew my state, if I could not fathom it and analyze it with the most complete lucidity. I should, in fact, be a reasonable man laboring under a hallucination. Some unknown disturbance must have been excited in my brain, one of those disturbances which physiologists of the present day try to note and to fix precisely, and that disturbance must have caused a profound gulf in my mind and in the order and logic of my ideas. Similar phenomena occur in dreams, and lead us through the most unlikely phantasmagoria, without causing us any surprise, because our verifying apparatus and our sense of control have gone to sleep, while our imaginative faculty wakes and works.

Was it not possible that one of the imperceptible keys of the cerebral finger-board had been paralyzed in me? Some men lose the recollection of proper names, or of verbs, or of numbers, or merely of dates, in consequence of an accident. The localization of all the avenues of thought has been accomplished nowadays; what, then, would there be surprising in the fact that my faculty of controlling the unreality of certain hallucinations should be destroyed for the time being?

I thought of all this as I walked by the side of the water. The sun was shining brightly on the river and made earth delightful, while it filled me with love for life, for the swallows, whose swift agility is always delightful in my eyes, for the plants by the riverside, whose rustling is a pleasure to my ears.

By degrees, however, an inexplicable feeling of discomfort seized me. It seemed to me as if some unknown force were numbing and stopping me, were preventing me from going further and were calling me back. I felt that painful wish to return which comes on you when you have left a beloved invalid at home, and are seized by a presentiment that he is worse.

I, therefore, returned despite of myself, feeling certain that I should find some bad news awaiting me, a letter or a telegram. There was nothing, however, and I was surprised and uneasy, more so than if I had had another fantastic vision.

August 8. I spent a terrible evening, yesterday. He does not show himself any more, but I feel that He is near me, watching me, looking at me, penetrating me, dominating me, and more terrible to me when He hides himself thus than if He were to manifest his constant and invisible presence by supernatural phenomena. However, I slept.

August 9. Nothing, but I am afraid.

August 10. Nothing; but what will happen to-morrow?

August 11. Still nothing. I cannot stop at home with this fear hanging over me and these thoughts in my mind; I shall go away.

August 12. Ten o'clock at night. All day long I have been trying to get away, and have not been able. I contemplated a simple and easy act of liberty, a carriage ride to Rouen – and I have not been able to do it. What is the reason?

August 13. When one is attacked by certain maladies, the springs of our physical being seem broken, our energies destroyed, our muscles relaxed, our bones to be as soft as our flesh, and our blood as liquid as water. I am experiencing the same in my moral being, in a strange and distressing manner. I have no longer any strength, any courage, any self-control, nor even any power to set my own will in motion. I have no power left to will anything, but some one does it for me and I obey.

August 14. I am lost! Somebody possesses my soul and governs it! Somebody orders all my acts, all my movements, all my thoughts. I am no longer master of myself, nothing except an enslaved and terrified spectator of the things which I do. I wish to go out; I cannot. He does not wish to; and so I remain, trembling and distracted in the armchair in which he keeps me sitting. I merely wish to get up and to rouse myself, so as to think that I am still master of myself: I cannot! I am riveted to my chair, and my chair adheres to the floor in such a manner that no force of mine can move us.

Then suddenly, I must, I must go to the foot of my garden to pick some strawberries and eat them – and I go there. I pick the strawberries and I eat them! Oh! my God! my God! Is there a God? If there be one, deliver me! save me! succor me! Pardon! Pity! Mercy! Save me! Oh! what sufferings! what torture! what horror!

August 15. Certainly this is the way in which my poor cousin was possessed and swayed, when she came to borrow five thousand francs of me. She was under the power of a strange will which had entered into her, like another soul, a parasitic and ruling soul. Is the world coming to an end?

But who is he, this invisible being that rules me, this unknowable being, this rover of a supernatural race?

Invisible beings exist, then! how is it, then, that since the beginning of the world they have never manifested themselves in such a manner as they do to me? I have never read anything that resembles what goes on in my house. Oh! If I could only leave it, if I could only go away and flee, and never return, I should be saved; but I cannot.

August 16. I managed to escape to-day for two hours, like a prisoner who finds the door of his dungeon accidentally open. I suddenly felt that I was free and that He was far away, and so I gave orders to put the horses in as quickly as possible, and I drove to Rouen. Oh! how delightful to be able to say to my coachman: "Go to Rouen!"

I made him pull up before the library, and I begged them to lend me Dr. Herrmann Herestauss's treatise on the unknown inhabitants of the ancient and modern world.

Then, as I was getting into my carriage, I intended to say: "To the railway station!" but instead of this I shouted – I did not speak; but I shouted – in such a loud voice that all the passers-by turned round: "Home!" and I fell back on to the cushion of my carriage, overcome by mental agony. He had found me out and regained possession of me.

August 17. Oh! What a night! what a night! And yet it seems to me that I ought to rejoice. I read until one o'clock in the morning! Herestauss, Doctor of Philosophy and Theogony, wrote the history and the manifestation of all those invisible beings which hover around man, or of whom he dreams. He describes their origin, their domains, their power; but none of them resembles the one which haunts me. One might say that man, ever since he has thought, has had a foreboding and a fear of a new being, stronger than himself, his successor in this world, and that, feeling him near, and not being able to foretell the nature of the unseen one, he has, in his terror, created the whole race of hidden beings, vague phantoms born of fear.

Having, therefore, read until one o'clock in the morning, I went and sat down at the open window, in order to cool my forehead and my thoughts in the calm night air. It was very pleasant and warm! How I should have enjoyed such a night formerly!

There was no moon, but the stars darted out their rays in the dark heavens. Who inhabits those worlds? What forms, what living beings, what animals are there yonder? Do those who are thinkers in those distant worlds know more than we do? What can they do more than we? What do they see which we do not? Will not one of them, some day or other, traversing space, appear on our earth to conquer it, just as formerly the Norsemen crossed the sea in order to subjugate nations feebler than themselves?

We are so weak, so powerless, so ignorant, so small – we who live on this particle of mud which revolves in liquid air.

I fell asleep, dreaming thus in the cool night air, and then, having slept for about three quarters of an hour, I opened my eyes without moving, awakened by an indescribably confused and strange sensation. At first I saw nothing, and then suddenly it appeared to me as if a page of the book, which had remained open on my table, turned over of its own accord. Not a breath of air had come in at my window, and I was surprised and waited. In about four minutes, I saw, I saw – yes I saw with my own eyes – another page lift itself up and fall down on the others, as if a finger had turned it over. My armchair was empty, appeared empty, but I knew that He was there, He, and sitting in my place, and that He was reading. With a furious bound, the bound of an enraged wild beast that wishes to disembowel its tamer, I crossed my room to seize him, to strangle him, to kill him! But before I could reach it, my chair fell over as if somebody had run away from me. My table rocked, my lamp fell and went out, and my window closed as if some thief had been surprised and had fled out into the night, shutting it behind him.

So He had run away; He had been afraid; He, afraid of me!

So to-morrow, or later – some day or other, I should be able to hold him in my clutches and crush him against the ground! Do not dogs occasionally bite and strangle their masters?

August 18. I have been thinking the whole day long. Oh! yes, I will obey Him, follow His impulses, fulfill all His wishes, show myself humble, submissive, a coward. He is the stronger; but an hour will come.

August 19. I know, I know, I know all! I have just read the following in the "Revue du Monde Scientifique": "A curious piece of news comes to us from Rio de Janeiro. Madness, an epidemic of madness, which may be compared to that contagious madness which attacked the people of Europe in the Middle Ages, is at this moment raging in the Province of San-Paulo. The frightened inhabitants are leaving their houses, deserting their villages, abandoning their land, saying that they are pursued, possessed, governed like human cattle by invisible, though tangible beings, by a species of vampire, which feeds on their life while they are asleep, and which, besides, drinks water and milk without appearing to touch any other nourishment.

"Professor Don Pedro Henriques, accompanied by several medical savants, has gone to the Province of San-Paulo, in order to study the origin and the manifestations of this surprising madness on the spot, and to propose such measures to the Emperor as may appear to him to be most fitted to restore the mad population to reason."

Ah! Ah! I remember now that fine Brazilian three-master which passed in front of my windows as it was going up the Seine, on the eighth of last May! I thought it looked so pretty, so white and bright! That Being was on board of her, coming from there, where its race sprang from. And it saw me! It saw my house, which was also white, and He sprang from the ship on to the land. Oh! Good heavens!

Now I know, I can divine. The reign of man is over, and he has come. He whom disquieted priests exorcised, whom sorcerers evoked on dark nights, without seeing him appear, He to whom the imaginations of the transient masters of the world lent all the monstrous or graceful forms of gnomes, spirits, genii, fairies, and familiar spirits. After the coarse conceptions of primitive fear, men more enlightened gave him a truer form. Mesmer divined him, and ten years ago physicians accurately discovered the nature of his power, even before He exercised it himself. They played with that weapon of their new Lord, the sway of a mysterious will over the human soul, which had become enslaved. They called it mesmerism, hypnotism, suggestion, I know not what? I have seen them diverting themselves like rash children with this horrible power! Woe to us! Woe to man! He has come, the – the – what does He call himself – the – I fancy that he is shouting out his name to me and I do not hear him – the – yes – He is shouting it out – I am listening – I cannot – repeat – it – Horla – I have heard – the Horla – it is He – the Horla – He has come! –

Ah! I the vulture has eaten the pigeon, the wolf has eaten the lamb; the lion has devoured the sharp-horned buffalo; man has killed the lion with an arrow, with a spear, with gunpowder; but the Horla will make of man what man has made of the horse and of the ox: his chattel, his slave, and his food, by the mere power of his will. Woe to us!

But, nevertheless, sometimes the animal rebels and kills the man who has subjugated it. I should also like – I shall be able to – but I must know Him, touch Him, see Him! Learned men say that eyes of animals, as they differ from ours, do not distinguish as ours do. And my eye cannot distinguish this newcomer who is oppressing me.

Why? Oh! Now I remember the words of the monk at Mont Saint-Michel: "Can we see the hundred-thousandth part of what exists? Listen; there is the wind which is the strongest force in nature; it knocks men down, blows down buildings, uproots trees, raises the sea into mountains of water, destroys cliffs, and casts great ships on to the breakers; it kills, it whistles, it sighs, it roars, – have you ever seen it, and can you see it? It exists for all that, however!"

And I went on thinking: my eyes are so weak, so imperfect, that they do not even distinguish hard bodies, if they are as transparent as glass! If a glass without quicksilver behind it were to bar my way, I should run into it, just like a bird which has flown into a room breaks its head against the windowpanes. A thousand things, moreover, deceive a man and lead him astray. How then is it surprising that he cannot perceive a new body which is penetrated and pervaded by the light?

A new being! Why not? It was assuredly bound to come! Why should we be the last? We do not distinguish it, like all the others created before us? The reason is, that its nature is more delicate, its body finer and more finished than ours. Our makeup is so weak, so awkwardly conceived; our body is encumbered with organs that are always tired, always being strained like locks that are too complicated; it lives like a plant and like an animal nourishing itself with difficulty on air, herbs, and flesh; it is a brute machine which is a prey to maladies, to malformations, to decay; it is broken-winded, badly regulated, simple and eccentric, ingeniously yet badly made, a coarse and yet a delicate mechanism, in brief, the outline of a being which might become intelligent and great.

There are only a few – so few – stages of development in this world, from the oyster up to man. Why should there not be one more, when once that period is accomplished which separates the successive products one from the other?

Why not one more? Why not, also, other trees with immense, splendid flowers, perfuming whole regions? Why not other elements beside fire, air, earth, and water? There are four, only four, nursing fathers of various beings! What a pity! Why should not there be forty, four hundred, four thousand! How poor everything is, how mean and wretched – grudgingly given, poorly invented, clumsily made! Ah! the elephant and the hippopotamus, what power! And the camel, what suppleness!

But the butterfly, you will say, a flying flower! I dream of one that should be as large as a hundred worlds, with wings whose shape, beauty, colors, and motion I cannot even express. But I see it – it flutters from star to star, refreshing them and perfuming them with the light and harmonious breath of its flight! And the people up there gaze at it as it passes in an ecstasy of delight!

What is the matter with me? It is He, the Horla who haunts me, and who makes me think of these foolish things! He is within me, He is becoming my soul; I shall kill him!

August 20. I shall kill Him. I have seen Him! Yesterday I sat down at my table and pretended to write very assiduously. I knew quite well that He would come prowling round me, quite close to me, so close that I might perhaps be able to touch him, to seize him. And then – then I should have the strength of desperation; I should have my hands, my knees, my chest, my forehead, my teeth to strangle him, to crush him, to bite him, to tear him to pieces. And I watched for him with all my overexcited nerves.

I had lighted my two lamps and the eight wax candles on my mantelpiece, as if, by this light I should discover Him.

My bed, my old oak bed with its columns, was opposite to me; on my right was the fireplace; on my left the door, which was carefully closed, after I had left it open for some time, in order to attract Him; behind me was a very high wardrobe with a looking-glass in it, which served me to dress by every day, and in which I was in the habit of inspecting myself from head to foot every time I passed it.

So I pretended to be writing in order to deceive Him, for He also was watching me, and suddenly I felt, I was certain, that He was reading over my shoulder, that He was there, almost touching my ear.

I got up so quickly, with my hands extended, that I almost fell. Horror! It was as bright as at midday, but I did not see myself in the glass! It was empty, clear, profound, full of light! But my figure was not reflected in it – and I, I was opposite to it! I saw the large, clear glass from top to bottom, and I looked at it with unsteady eyes. I did not dare advance; I did not venture to make a movement; feeling certain, nevertheless, that He was there, but that He would escape me again, He whose imperceptible body had absorbed my reflection.

How frightened I was! And then suddenly I began to see myself through a mist in the depths of the looking-glass, in a mist as it were, or through a veil of water; and it seemed to me as if this water were flowing slowly from left to right, and making my figure clearer every moment. It was like the end of an eclipse. Whatever hid me did not appear to possess any clearly defined outlines, but was a sort of opaque transparency, which gradually grew clearer.

At last I was able to distinguish myself completely, as I do every day when I look at myself.

I had seen Him! And the horror of it remained with me, and makes me shudder even now.

August 21. How could I kill Him, since I could not get hold of Him? Poison? But He would see me mix it with the water; and then, would our poisons have any effect on His impalpable body? No – no – no doubt about the matter. Then? – then?

August 22. I sent for a blacksmith from Rouen and ordered iron shutters of him for my room, such as some private hotels in Paris have on the ground floor, for fear of thieves, and he is going to make me a similar door as well. I have made myself out a coward, but I do not care about that!

September 10. Rouen, Hotel Continental. It is done; it is done – but is He dead? My mind is thoroughly upset by what I have seen.

Well then, yesterday, the locksmith having put on the iron shutters and door, I left everything open until midnight, although it was getting cold.

Suddenly I felt that He was there, and joy, mad joy took possession of me. I got up softly, and I walked to the right and left for some time, so that He might not guess anything; then I took off my boots and put on my slippers carelessly; then I fastened the iron shutters and going back to the door quickly I double-locked it with a padlock, putting the key into my pocket.

Suddenly I noticed that He was moving restlessly round me, that in his turn He was frightened and was ordering me to let Him out. I nearly yielded, though I did not quite, but putting my back to the door, I half opened it, just enough to allow me to go out backward, and as I am very tall, my head touched the lintel. I was sure that He had not been able to escape, and I shut Him up quite alone, quite alone. What happiness! I had Him fast. Then I ran downstairs into the drawing-room which was under my bedroom. I took the two lamps and poured all the oil on to the carpet, the furniture, everywhere; then I set fire to it and made my escape, after having carefully double locked the door.

I went and hid myself at the bottom of the garden, in a clump of laurel bushes. How long it was! how long it was! Everything was dark, silent, motionless, not a breath of air and not a star, but heavy banks of clouds which one could not see, but which weighed, oh! so heavily on my soul.

I looked at my house and waited. How long it was! I already began to think that the fire had gone out of its own accord, or that He had extinguished it, when one of the lower windows gave way under the violence of the flames, and a long, soft, caressing sheet of red flame mounted up the white wall, and kissed it as high as the roof. The light fell on to the trees, the branches, and the leaves, and a shiver of fear pervaded them also! The birds awoke; a dog began to howl, and it seemed to me as if the day were breaking! Almost immediately two other windows flew into fragments, and I saw that the whole of the lower part of my house was nothing but a terrible furnace. But a cry, a horrible, shrill, heart-rending cry, a woman's cry, sounded through the night, and two garret windows were opened! I had forgotten the servants! I saw the terror-struck faces, and the frantic waving of their arms!

Then, overwhelmed with horror, I ran off to the village, shouting: "Help! help! fire! fire!" Meeting some people who were already coming on to the scene, I went back with them to see!

By this time the house was nothing but a horrible and magnificent funeral pile, a monstrous pyre which lit up the whole country, a pyre where men were burning, and where He was burning also, He, He, my prisoner, that new Being, the new Master, the Horla!

Suddenly the whole roof fell in between the walls, and a volcano of flames darted up to the sky. Through all the windows which opened on to that furnace, I saw the flames darting, and I reflected that He was there, in that kiln, dead.

Dead? Perhaps? His body? Was not his body, which was transparent, indestructible by such means as would kill ours?

If He were not dead? Perhaps time alone has power over that Invisible and Redoubtable Being. Why this transparent, unrecognizable body, this body belonging to a spirit, if it also had to fear ills, infirmities, and premature destruction?

Premature destruction? All human terror springs from that! After man the Horla. After him who can die every day, at any hour, at any moment, by any accident, He came, He who was only to die at his own proper hour and minute, because He had touched the limits of his existence!

No – no – there is no doubt about it – He is not dead. Then – then – I suppose I must kill myself!

THE LAGOON

Joseph Conrad

Joseph Conrad (1857–1924) was born in Ukraine, in Berdychiv, the town where Balzac was married. He spoke three languages and wrote in his third. Having worked as a merchant seaman, he settled in England, mostly in Kent (where he died), and wrote works such as *Heart of Darkness, The Secret Agent, Under Western Eyes, Victory*. He is, arguably, a better writer than novelist, and his shorter fiction works impeccably. His influence ranges from authors including T.S. Eliot, Graham Greene, Shirley Hazzard, to Juan Gabriel Vásquez and John le Carré. He is buried in Canterbury.

The white man, leaning with both arms over the roof of the little house in the stern of the boat, said to the steersman –

"We will pass the night in Arsat's clearing. It is late."

The Malay only grunted, and went on looking fixedly at the river. The white man rested his chin on his crossed arms and gazed at the wake of the boat. At the end of the straight avenue of forests cut by the intense glitter of the river, the sun appeared unclouded and dazzling, poised low over the water that shone smoothly like a band of metal. The forests, somber and dull, stood motionless and silent on each side of the broad stream. At the foot of big, towering trees, trunkless nipa palms rose from the mud of the bank, in bunches of leaves enormous and heavy, that hung unstirring over the brown swirl of eddies. In the stillness of the air every tree, every leaf, every bough, every tendril of creeper and every petal of minute blossoms seemed to have been bewitched into an immobility perfect and final. Nothing moved on the river but the eight paddles that rose flashing regularly, dipped together with a single splash; while the steersman swept right and left with a periodic and sudden flourish of his blade describing a glinting semicircle above his head. The churned up water frothed alongside with a confused murmur. And the white man's canoe, advancing up stream in the short-lived disturbance of its own making, seemed to enter the portals of a land from which the very memory of motion had for ever departed.

The white man, turning his back upon the setting sun, looked along the empty and broad expanse of the sea-reach. For the last three miles of its course the wandering, hesitating river, as if enticed irresistibly by the freedom of an open horizon, flows straight into the sea, flows straight to the east – to the east that harbours both light and darkness. Astern of the boat the repeated call of some bird, a cry discordant and feeble, skipped along over the smooth water and lost itself, before it could reach the other shore, in the breathless silence of the world.

The steersman dug his paddle into the stream, and held hard with stiffened arms, his body thrown forward. The water gurgled aloud; and suddenly the long straight reach seemed to pivot on its centre, the forests swung in a semicircle, and the slanting beams of sunset touched the broadside of the canoe with a fiery glow, throwing the slender and distorted shadows of its crew upon the streaked glitter of the river. The white man turned to look ahead. The course of the boat had been altered at right-angles to the stream, and the carved dragon-head of its prow was pointing now at a gap in the fringing bushes of the bank. It glided through, brushing the overhanging twigs, and disappeared from the river like some slim and amphibious creature leaving the water for its lair in the forests.

The narrow creek was like a ditch: tortuous, fabulously deep; filled with gloom under the thin strip of pure and shining blue of the heaven. Immense trees soared up, invisible behind the festooned draperies of creepers. Here and there, near the glistening blackness of the water, a twisted root of some tall tree showed amongst the tracery of small ferns, black and dull, writhing and motionless, like an arrested snake. The short words of the paddlers reverberated loudly between the thick and somber walls of vegetation. Darkness oozed out from between the trees, through the tangled maze of the creepers, from behind the great fantastic and unstirring leaves; the darkness, mysterious and invincible; the darkness scented and poisonous of impenetrable forests.

The men poled in the shoaling water. The creek broadened, opening out into a wide sweep of a stagnant lagoon. The forests receded from the marshy bank, leaving a level strip of bright-green, reedy grass to frame the reflected blueness of the sky. A fleecy pink cloud drifted high above, trailing the delicate colouring of its image under the floating leaves and the silvery blossoms of the lotus. A little house, perched on high piles, appeared black in the distance. Near it, two tall nibong palms, that seemed to have come out of the forests in the background, leaned slightly over the ragged roof, with a suggestion of sad tenderness and care in the droop of their leafy and soaring heads.

The steersman, pointing with his paddle, said, "Arsat is there. I see his canoe fast between the piles."

The polers ran along the sides of the boat glancing over their shoulders at the end of the day's journey. They would have preferred to spend the night somewhere else than on this lagoon of weird aspect and ghostly reputation. Moreover, they disliked Arsat, first as a stranger, and also because he who repairs a ruined house, and dwells in it, proclaims that he is not afraid to live amongst the spirits that haunt the places abandoned by mankind. Such a man can disturb the course of fate by glances or words; while his familiar ghosts are not easy to propitiate by casual wayfarers upon whom they long to wreak the malice of their human master. White men care not for such things, being unbelievers and in league with the Father of Evil, who leads them unharmed through the invisible dangers of this world. To the warnings of the righteous they oppose an offensive pretence of disbelief. What is there to be done?

So they thought, throwing their weight on the end of their long poles. The big canoe glided on swiftly, noiselessly and smoothly, towards Arsat's clearing, till, in a great rattling of poles thrown down, and the loud murmurs of "Allah be praised!" it came with a gentle knock against the crooked piles below the house.

The boatmen with uplifted faces shouted discordantly, "Arsat! O Arsat!" Nobody came. The white man began to climb the rude ladder giving access to the bamboo platform before the house. The juragan of the boat said sulkily, "We will cook in the sampan, and sleep on the water."

"Pass my blankets and the basket," said the white man curtly.

He knelt on the edge of the platform to receive the bundle. Then the boat shoved off, and the white man, standing up, confronted Arsat, who had come out through the low door of his hut. He was a man young, powerful, with a broad chest and muscular arms. He had nothing on but his sarong. His head was bare. His big, soft eyes stared eagerly at the white man, but his voice and demeanor were composed as he asked, without any words of greeting –

"Have you medicine, Tuan?"

"No," said the visitor in a startled tone. "No. Why? Is there sickness in the house?"

"Enter and see," replied Arsat, in the same calm manner, and turning short round, passed again through the small doorway. The white man, dropping his bundles, followed.

In the dim light of the dwelling he made out on a couch of bamboos a woman stretched on her back under a broad sheet of red cotton cloth. She lay still, as if dead; but her big eyes, wide open, glittered in the gloom, staring upwards at the slender rafters, motionless and unseeing. She was in a high fever, and evidently unconscious. Her cheeks were sunk slightly, her lips were partly open, and on the young face there was the ominous and fixed expression – the absorbed, contemplating expression of the unconscious who are going to die. The two men stood looking down at her in silence.

"Has she been long ill?" asked the traveler.

"I have not slept for five nights," answered the Malay, in a deliberate tone. "At first she heard voices calling her from the water and struggled against me who held her. But since the sun of to-day rose she hears nothing – she hears not me. She sees nothing. She sees not me – me!"

He remained silent for a minute, then asked softly–

"Tuan, will she die?"

"I fear so," said the white man sorrowfully. He had known Arsat years ago, in a far country in times of trouble and danger, when no friendship is to be despised. And since his Malay friend had come unexpectedly to dwell in the hut on the lagoon with a strange woman, he had slept many times there, in his journeys up or down the river. He liked the man who knew how to keep faith in council and how to fight without fear by the side of his white friend. He liked him – not so much perhaps as a man likes his favorite dog – but still he liked him well enough to help and ask no questions, to think sometimes vaguely and hazily in the midst of his own pursuits, about the lonely man and the long-haired woman with audacious face and triumphant eyes, who lived together hidden by the forests – alone and feared.

The white man came out of the hut in time to see the enormous conflagration of sunset put out by the swift and stealthy shadows that, rising like a black and impalpable vapor above the tree-tops, spread over the heaven, extinguishing the crimson glow of floating clouds and the red brilliance of departing daylight. In a few moments all the stars came out above the intense blackness of the earth, and the great lagoon gleaming suddenly with reflected lights resembled an oval patch of night-sky flung down into the hopeless and abysmal night of the wilderness. The white man had some supper out of the basket, then collecting a few sticks that lay about the platform, made up a small fire, not for warmth, but for the sake of the smoke, which would keep off the mosquitos. He wrapped himself in his blankets and sat with his back against the reed wall of the house, smoking thoughtfully.

Arsat came through the doorway with noiseless steps and squatted down by the fire. The white man moved his outstretched legs a little.

"She breathes," said Arsat in a low voice, anticipating the expected question. "She breathes and burns as if with a great fire. She speaks not; she hears not – and burns!"

He paused for a moment, then asked in a quiet, incurious tone–

"Tuan . . . will she die?"

The white man moved his shoulders uneasily, and muttered in a hesitating manner–

"If such is her fate."

"No, Tuan," said Arsat calmly. "If such is my fate. I hear, I see, I wait. I remember . . . Tuan, do you remember the old days? Do you remember my brother?"

"Yes," said the white man. The Malay rose suddenly and went in. The other, sitting still outside, could hear the voice in the hut. Arsat said: "Hear me! Speak!" His words were succeeded by a complete silence. "O! Diamelen!" he cried suddenly. After that cry there was a deep sigh. Arsat came out and sank down again in his old place.

They sat in silence before the fire. There was no sound within the house, there was no sound near them; but far away on the lagoon they could hear the voices of the boatmen ringing fitful and distinct on the calm water. The fire in the bows of the sampan shone faintly in the distance with a hazy red glow. Then it died out. The voices ceased. The land and the water slept invisible, unstirring and mute. It was as though there had been nothing left in the world but the glitter of stars streaming, ceaseless and vain, through the black stillness of the night.

The white man gazed straight before him into the darkness with wide-open eyes. The fear and fascination, the inspiration and the wonder of death – of death near, unavoidable and unseen, soothed the unrest of his race and stirred the most indistinct, the most intimate of his thoughts. The ever-ready suspicion of evil, the gnawing suspicion that lurks in our hearts, flowed out into the stillness round him – into the stillness profound and dumb, and made it appear untrustworthy and infamous, like the placid and impenetrable mask of an unjustifiable violence. In that fleeting and powerful disturbance of his being the earth enfolded in the starlight peace became a shadowy country of inhuman strife, a battle-field of phantoms terrible and charming, august or ignoble, struggling ardently for the possession of our helpless hearts. An unquiet and mysterious country of inextinguishable desires and fears.

A plaintive murmur rose in the night; a murmur saddening and startling, as if the great solitudes of surrounding woods had tried to whisper into his ear the

wisdom of their immense and lofty indifference. Sounds hesitating and vague
floated in the air round him, shaped themselves slowly into words; and at last
flowed on gently in a murmuring stream of soft and monotonous sentences. He
stirred like a man waking up and changed his position slightly. Arsat, motionless
and shadowy, sitting with bowed head under the stars, was speaking in a low
and dreamy tone.

". . . for where can we lay down the heaviness of our trouble but in a friend's
heart? A man must speak of war and of love. You, Tuan, know what war is, and
you have seen me in time of danger seek death as other men seek life! A writing
may be lost; a lie may be written; but what the eye has seen is truth and remains
in the mind!"

"I remember," said the white man quietly. Arsat went on with mournful composure.

"Therefore I shall speak to you of love. Speak in the night. Speak before both
night and love are gone – and the eye of day looks upon my sorrow and my
shame; upon my blackened face; upon my burnt-up heart."

A sigh, short and faint, marked an almost imperceptible pause, and then his
words flowed on, without a stir, without a gesture.

"After the time of trouble and war was over and you went away from my
country in the pursuit of your desires, which we, men of the islands, cannot
understand, I and my brother became again, as we had been before, the sword-
bearers of the Ruler. You know we were men of family, belonging to a ruling
race, and more fit than any to carry on our right shoulder the emblem of power.
And in the time of prosperity Si Dendring showed us favor, as we, in time of
sorrow, had showed to him the faithfulness of our courage. It was a time of peace.
A time of deer-hunts and cock-fights; of idle talks and foolish squabbles between
men whose bellies are full and weapons are rusty. But the sower watched the young
rice-shoots grow up without fear, and the traders came and went, departed
lean and returned fat into the river of peace. They brought news too. Brought
lies and truth mixed together, so that no man knew when to rejoice and when
to be sorry. We heard from them about you also. They had seen you here and
had seen you there. And I was glad to hear, for I remembered the stirring times,
and I always remembered you, Tuan, till the time came when my eyes could see
nothing in the past, because they had looked upon the one who is dying there
– in the house."

He stopped to exclaim in an intense whisper, "O Mara bahia! O Calamity!"
then went on speaking a little louder.

"There's no worse enemy and no better friend than a brother, Tuan, for one
brother knows another, and in perfect knowledge is strength for good or evil. I
loved my brother. I went to him and told him that I could see nothing but one
face, hear nothing but one voice. He told me: 'Open your heart so that she can
see what is in it – and wait. Patience is wisdom. Inchi Midah may die or our
Ruler may throw off his fear of a woman!' . . . I waited! . . . You remember the
lady with the veiled face, Tuan, and the fear of our Ruler before her cunning
and temper. And if she wanted her servant, what could I do? But I fed the hunger of my heart on short glances and stealthy words. I loitered on the path to
the bath-houses in the daytime, and when the sun had fallen behind the forest I

crept along the jasmine hedges of the women's courtyard. Unseeing, we spoke to one another through the scent of flowers, through the veil of leaves, through the blades of long grass that stood still before our lips: so great was our prudence, so faint was the murmur of our great longing. The time passed swiftly . . . and there were whispers amongst women – and our enemies watched – my brother was gloomy, and I began to think of killing and of a fierce death. . . . We are of a people who take what they want – like you whites. There is a time when a man should forget loyalty and respect. Might and authority are given to rulers, but to all men is given love and strength and courage. My brother said, 'You shall take her from their midst. We are two who are like one.' And I answered, 'Let it be soon, for I find no warmth in sunlight that does not shine upon her.' Our time came when the Ruler and all the great people went to the mouth of the river to fish by torchlight. There were hundreds of boats, and on the white sand, between the water and the forests, dwellings of leaves were built for the households of the Rajahs. The smoke of cooking-fires was like a blue mist of the evening, and many voices rang in it joyfully. While they were making the boats ready to beat up the fish, my brother came to me and said, 'To-night!' I made ready my weapons, and when the time came our canoe took its place in the circle of boats carrying the torches. The lights blazed on the water, but behind the boats there was darkness. When the shouting began and the excitement made them like mad we dropped out. The water swallowed our fire, and we floated back to the shore that was dark with only here and there the glimmer of embers. We could hear the talk of slavegirls amongst the sheds. Then we found a place deserted and silent. We waited there. She came. She came running along the shore, rapid and leaving no trace, like a leaf driven by the wind into the sea. My brother said gloomily, 'Go and take her; carry her into our boat.' I lifted her in my arms. She panted. Her heart was beating against my breast. I said, 'I take you from those people. You came to the cry of my heart, but my arms take you into my boat against the will of the great!' 'It is right,' said my brother. 'We are men who take what we want and can hold it against many. We should have taken her in daylight.' I said, 'Let us be off;' for since she was in my boat I began to think of our Ruler's many men. 'Yes. Let us be off,' said my brother. 'We are cast out and this boat is our country now – and the sea is our refuge.' He lingered with his foot on the shore, and I entreated him to hasten, for I remembered the strokes of her heart against my breast and thought that two men cannot withstand a hundred. We left, paddling downstream close to the bank; and as we passed by the creek where they were fishing, the great shouting had ceased, but the murmur of voices was loud like the humming of insects flying at noonday. The boats floated, clustered together, in the red light of torches, under a black roof of smoke; and men talked of their sport. Men that boasted, and praised, and jeered – men that would have been our friends in the morning, but on that night were already our enemies. We paddled swiftly past. We had no more friends in the country of our birth. She sat in the middle of the canoe with covered face; silent as she is now; unseeing as she is now – and I had no regret at what I was leaving because I could hear her breathing close to me – as I can hear her now."

He paused, listened with his ear turned to the doorway, then shook his head and went on.

"My brother wanted to shout the cry of challenge – one cry only – to let the people know we were freeborn robbers that trusted our arms and the great sea. And again I begged him in the name of our love to be silent. Could I not hear her breathing close to me? I knew the pursuit would come quick enough. My brother loved me. He dipped his paddle without a splash. He only said, 'There is half a man in you now – the other half is in that woman. I can wait. When you are a whole man again, you will come back with me here to shout defiance. We are sons of the same mother.' I made no answer. All my strength and all my spirit were in my hands that held the paddle – for I longed to be with her in a safe place beyond the reach of men's anger and of women's spite. My love was so great, that I thought it could guide me to a country where death was unknown, if I could only escape from Inchi Midah's spite and from our Ruler's sword. We paddled with fury, breathing through our teeth. The blades bit deep into the smooth water. We passed out of the river; we flew in clear channels amongst the shallows. We skirted the black coast; we skirted the sand beaches where the sea speaks in whispers to the land; and the gleam of white sand flashed back past our boat, so swiftly she ran upon the water. We spoke not. Only once I said, 'Sleep, Diamelen, for soon you may want all your strength.' I heard the sweetness of her voice, but I never turned my head. The sun rose and still we went on. Water fell from my face like rain from a cloud. We flew in the light and heat. I never looked back, but I knew that my brother's eyes, behind me, were looking steadily ahead, for the boat went as straight as a bushman's dart, when it leaves the end of the sumpitan. There was no better paddler, no better steersman than my brother. Many times, together, we had won races in that canoe. But we never had put out our strength as we did then – then, when for the last time we paddled together! There was no braver or stronger man in our country than my brother. I could not spare the strength to turn my head and look at him, but every moment I heard the hiss of his breath getting louder behind me. Still he did not speak. The sun was high. The heat clung to my back like a flame of fire. My ribs were ready to burst, but I could no longer get enough air into my chest. And then I felt I must cry out with my last breath, 'Let us rest!' 'Good!' he answered; and his voice was firm. He was strong. He was brave. He knew not fear and no fatigue . . . My brother!'

A rumour powerful and gentle, a rumour vast and faint; the rumour of trembling leaves, of stirring boughs, ran through the tangled depths of the forests, ran over the starry smoothness of the lagoon, and the water between the piles lapped the slimy timber once with a sudden splash. A breath of warm air touched the two men's faces and passed on with a mournful sound – a breath loud and short like an uneasy sigh of the dreaming earth.

Arsat went on in an even, low voice.

"We ran our canoe on the white beach of a little bay close to a long tongue of land that seemed to bar our road; a long wooded cape going far into the sea. My brother knew that place. Beyond the cape a river has its entrance. Through the jungle of that land there is a narrow path. We made a fire and cooked rice. Then we slept on the soft sand in the shade of our canoe, while she watched. No sooner had I closed my eyes than I heard her cry of alarm. We leaped up. The sun was halfway down the sky already, and coming in sight in the opening of the bay we saw a prau manned by many paddlers. We knew it at once; it was one of our Rajah's praus. They were watching the shore, and saw us. They beat the gong, and turned the head of the prau into the bay. I felt my heart become weak within my breast. Diamelen sat on the sand and covered her face. There was no escape by sea. My brother laughed. He had the gun you had given him, Tuan, before you went away, but there was only a handful of powder. He spoke to me quickly: 'Run with her along the path. I shall keep them back, for they have no firearms, and landing in the face of a man with a gun is certain death for some. Run with her. On the other side of that wood there is a fisherman's house – and a canoe. When I have fired all the shots I will follow. I am a great runner, and before they can come up we shall be gone. I will hold out as long as I can, for she is but a woman – that can neither run nor fight, but she has your heart in her weak hands.' He dropped behind the canoe. The prau was coming. She and I ran, and as we rushed along the path I heard shots. My brother fired – once – twice – and the booming of the gong ceased. There was silence behind us. That neck of land is narrow. Before I heard my brother fire the third shot I saw the shelving shore, and I saw the water again: the mouth of a broad river. We crossed a grassy glade. We ran down to the water. I saw a low hut above the black mud, and a small canoe hauled up. I heard another shot behind me. I thought, 'That is his last charge.' We rushed down to the canoe; a man came running from the hut, but I leaped on him, and we rolled together in the mud. Then I got up, and he lay still at my feet. I don't know whether I had killed him or not. I and Diamelen pushed the canoe afloat. I heard yells behind me, and I saw my brother run across the glade. Many men were bounding after him. I took her in my arms and threw her into the boat, then leaped in myself. When I looked back I saw that my brother had fallen. He fell and was up again, but the men were closing round him. He shouted, 'I am coming!' The men were close to him. I looked. Many men. Then I looked at her. Tuan, I pushed the canoe! I pushed it into deep water. She was kneeling forward looking at me, and I said, 'Take your paddle,' while I struck the water with mine. Tuan, I heard him cry. I heard him cry my name twice; and I heard voices shouting, 'Kill! Strike!' I never turned back. I heard him calling my name again with a great shriek, as when life is going out together with the voice – and I never turned my head. My own name! . . . My brother! Three times he called – but I was not afraid of life. Was she not there in that canoe? And could I not with her find a country where death is forgotten – where death is unknown?"

The white man sat up. Arsat rose and stood, an indistinct and silent figure above the dying embers of the fire. Over the lagoon a mist drifting and low had crept, erasing slowly the glittering images of the stars. And now a great expanse of white vapour covered the land: flowed cold and grey in the darkness, eddied in noiseless whirls round the tree-trunks and about the platform of the house, which seemed to float upon a restless and impalpable illusion of a sea; seemed the only thing surviving the destruction of the world by that undulating and voiceless phantom of a flood. Only far away the tops of the trees stood outlined on the twinkle of heaven, like a somber and forbidding shore – a coast deceptive, pitiless and black.

Arsat's voice vibrated loudly in the profound peace.

"I had her there! I had her! To get her I would have faced all mankind. But I had her – and–"

His words went out ringing into the empty distances. He paused, and seemed to listen to them dying away very far – beyond help and beyond recall. Then he said quietly–

"Tuan, I loved my brother."

A breath of wind made him shiver. High above his head, high above the silent sea of mist the drooping leaves of the palms rattled together with a mournful and expiring sound. The white man stretched his legs. His chin rested on his chest, and he murmured sadly without lifting his head–

"We all love our brothers."

Arsat burst out with an intense whispering violence–

"What did I care who died? I wanted peace in my own heart."

He seemed to hear a stir in the house – listened – then stepped in noiselessly. The white man stood up. A breeze was coming in fitful puffs. The stars shone paler as if they had retreated into the frozen depths of immense space. After a chill gust of wind there were a few seconds of perfect calm and absolute silence. Then from behind the black and wavy line of the forests a column of golden light shot up into the heavens and spread over the semicircle of the eastern horizon. The sun had risen. The mist lifted, broke into drifting patches, vanished into thin flying wreaths; and the unveiled lagoon lay, polished and black, in the heavy shadows at the foot of the wall of trees. A white eagle rose over it with a slanting and ponderous flight, reached the clear sunshine and appeared dazzlingly brilliant for a moment, then soaring higher, became a dark and motionless speck before it vanished into the blue as if it had left the earth for ever. The white man, standing gazing upwards before the doorway, heard in the hut a confused and broken murmur of distracted words ending with a loud groan. Suddenly Arsat stumbled out with outstretched hands, shivered, and stood still for some time with fixed eyes. Then he said–

"She burns no more."

Before his face the sun showed its edge above the tree-tops, rising steadily. The breeze freshened; a great brilliance burst upon the lagoon, sparkled on the rippling water. The forests came out of the clear shadows of the morning, became distinct, as if they had rushed nearer – to stop short in a great stir of leaves, of nodding boughs, of swaying branches. In the merciless sunshine the whisper of unconscious life grew louder, speaking in an incomprehensible voice round the dumb darkness of that human sorrow. Arsat's eyes wandered slowly, then stared at the rising sun.

"I can see nothing," he said half aloud to himself.

"There is nothing," said the white man, moving to the edge of the platform and waving his hand to his boat. A shout came faintly over the lagoon and the sampan began to glide towards the abode of the friend of ghosts.

"If you want to come with me, I will wait all the morning," said the white man, looking away upon the water.

"No, Tuan," said Arsat softly. "I shall not eat or sleep in this house, but I must first see my road. Now I can see nothing – see nothing! There is no light and no peace in the world; but there is death – death for many. We were sons of the same mother – and I left him in the midst of enemies; but I am going back now."

He drew a long breath and went on in a dreamy tone.

"In a little while I shall see clear enough to strike – to strike. But she has died, and . . . now . . . darkness."

He flung his arms wide open, let them fall along his body, then stood still with unmoved face and stony eyes, staring at the sun. The white man got down into his canoe. The polers ran smartly along the sides of the boat, looking over their shoulders at the beginning of a weary journey. High in the stern, his head muffled up in white rags, the juragan sat moody, letting his paddle trail in the water. The white man, leaning with both arms over the grass roof of the little cabin, looked back at the shining ripple of the boat's wake. Before the sampan passed out of the lagoon into the creek he lifted his eyes. Arsat had not moved. In the searching clearness of crude sunshine he was still standing before the house, he was still looking through the great light of a cloudless day into the hopeless darkness of the world.

FLEET-FOOTED HESTER

George Gissing

George Gissing (1857–1903) was the subject of a fine *Private Eye* clerihew in the late 1980s, which read, if memory serves:

> If you haven't read Gissing
> You don't know what you're missing:
> Endless novels
> About whores in hovels.

He wrote over twenty novels, the best known being *New Grub Street*. He died from emphysema aged forty-six, three days after Christmas; rather uncharacteristically, H.G. Wells nursed him on his deathbed.

She was born and bred in Hackney – the third child of a burly, thick-witted soldier, who had married without leave. Her mother, a thin but wiry woman, took in washing, and supported the family. At sixteen, Hester had a splendid physique: strangers imagined her a fine girl of nineteen or twenty. It was then she ceased running races with the lads in London Fields, for she was engaged to John Rayner, a foreman at the gasworks.

In spite of her petticoats – she would not wear a frock that fell much below the ankle – Hester could beat all but the champion runner of that locality; the average youth had no chance against her. Running was her delight and glory. At the short distance she made capital records, and for "stay" she could have held her own in a public school paper-chase.

Of course John Rayner put an end to all that. It was her running, witnessed by chance when they were strangers to each other, that excited him to an uneasy interest. He made inquiries, sought out her parents, wooed, won a provisional assent; there was an understanding, however, that she should run no more, at all events, in places of public resort. Rayner's salary came to about two hundred a year; when he married he would take a house of his own; his wife must conform to the rules of civilisation. Hester willingly agreed, for, though she manifested no strong attachment, large prospects decidedly appealed to her, and she rejoiced in the envious admiration of girls who could not hope for a lover with more than thirty shillings a week.

Moreover, he was a man to be proud of. It would have been a calamity had Hester plighted her troth to some whippersnapper of a clerk or artisan, some mortal of poor blood and stinted stature. John Rayner was her male complement: a stalwart fellow, six feet or close upon it, of warm complexion, keen eye, independent bearing. Intellectually, altogether her superior, but a man of the open air, companionable, full of animal passions, little disposed to use his brains in the way of improving a very haphazard education. As a lad he had run away from home – somewhere in the North – and he throve well simply because he did not become a reprobate; for John there was no medium. For him, to fall in love meant something beyond the conception of common men. His fiery worship puzzled Hester, who as yet was by no means ripe for respondent passion.

She looked what she was, a noble savage. Her speech was the speech of Hackney, but on her lips it lost its excessive meanness, and became a fit expression of an elementary, not a degraded, mind. At school she had learnt little or nothing, yet idleness, in her case, seemed compatible with purity; an unconscious reserve kept her apart from the loose-tongued girls of the neighbourhood. She respected her body, was remarkable for cleanliness, aimed in attire at ease and decency, never at display. It was but rarely that she laughed; the sense of humour seemed quite lacking in her. But no one lived from day to day with more vigour of enjoyment. She had the appetite of a ploughboy. Notwithstanding her neglect of cheap triumphs, a vigorous ambition ruled her life. She boasted of John Rayner's four pounds a week because it seemed to her a very large income indeed; she liked the man because he seemed to her much stronger, and better-looking, and more authoritative than other men with whom she came in contact.

For half a year all went fairly well. Hester had worked at a pickle-factory, but Rayner, disapproving of this, secretly paid her mother an equivalent of the wages, that she might be kept at home. An elder sister, who had hitherto helped in the laundry, went out to work, and Hester took her place; not a very good arrangement, for the girl would not trouble herself to starch and iron skilfully; but it was only for a short time. At seventeen Hester was to be married.

Then befell a calamity. Challenged to run against a lad who boasted himself to be somewhat in the race-course, Hester could not resist the temptation. Late one evening she stole forth and ran the race – and was defeated. Soon hearing of this breach of their agreement, John Rayner came down in wrath. Had Hester been victorious in her contest, she might have bowed the head and asked pardon; mortification made her stubborn and resentful of chiding. There was a quarrel, of characteristic vigour on both sides, and for a week the two kept apart. The good offices of Hester's mother brought them together again, but John was not his old self; he had become suspicious, jealous. Presently he began to make inquiries concerning one Albert Batchelor, who seemed to be much at the house. He objected to this young man – a paper-hanger's assistant, smelling of hair-oil and of insolence. Hester wrathfully defended the acquaintance: she had known Albert Batchelor all her life: his object, if any at all, was to make love to her sister; Mr Rayner must be a little less of an autocrat, notwithstanding his place at the gasworks and his ample pay. Language of this kind brought the blood into John's face; there was a second conflict, more vigorous than the former. Hester tore the ring from her finger, and flung it to the ground – they were in Victoria Park.

"Tike it, and tike yerself off!" she exclaimed, with magnificent scorn, "I don't want nothin" to do with a man like you."

"I'm glad to hear it," was the furious answer. "It's very certain you won't do for me! Just send me back my letters, and – and anything else you've no use for."

"I'll very soon do that! And never show your bad-tempered face again near our 'ouse."

John turned his back and marched away. His letters and presents were returned – in a very ill-made parcel – and the rupture seemed final.

"You're a fool, that's what you are!" observed Hester's mother. "Now you may go to the pickles ag'in, and let your sister come back to the work as she didn't ought never to have left."

"I'll go precious quick, and glad of it!" Hester made retort.

But she ran no more races and perceptibly a change had come over her. Old friends gave place to new girls of more pretentious stamp than those Hester had formerly chosen. She dressed with corresponding increase of showiness, began to frequent the Standard Theatre whenever she had money to spare, and "carried on" with various young men. About this time her father died, which, on the whole, was a fortunate event, for he had grown of late too fond of rum, and might soon have been a serious burden upon the household which he had never exerted himself to assist. John Rayner heard the news, and one evening managed to encounter Hester in a street near her home. He spoke kindly, gently, but the girl answered only a few cold words and went her way.

A week later he saw her on Hackney Downs with Albert Batchelor. She was laughing noisily – a thing John had never known her do.

One night Hester stayed out so late that her mother threatened chastisement if the offence were repeated. That threat brought about another crisis in the girl's life. She left home, took lodgings for herself, and henceforth held little communication with her family.

For a space of two years John Rayner spoke not a word to the girl he loved, and in the meanwhile his circumstances underwent a notable change. First of all, owing to outrageous fits of temper, he was dismissed from his place as foreman; his employers offered him work in the carpenter's shop, a notable degradation. At first John scornfully refused, and left the works altogether; but in a few days – extraordinary thing in so proud a man – he returned as though humbled; he was willing to accept the inferior employment. Again he got into trouble, this time through drink; he was reduced to the smith's shop, and bore the disgrace without murmuring. Time went on; one day John fought with a fellow workman, and behaved like a wild beast. He had the choice given him of leaving the works altogether or "going to the heap." To go to the heap signified to labour as a loader of coke. John accepted his debasement, went to the heap, and toiled among the roughest men, making himself as one of them. He drank, and seemed to glory in the fate that had come upon him. To all appearances he was now a sturdy blackguard, coarse of language, violent in demeanour. He terrorised his companions; with him it was a word and a blow. His comely face had lost its tint of robust health; he wore grimy rags; his home was anywhere and nowhere.

Now of all these things Hester was well aware. An old friend of hers, a girl married at sixteen and widowed at twenty, knew John Rayner, and from time to time talked with him; this Mrs Heffron assiduously reported to Hester each calamitous step in John's history.

"It's because of you," she kept repeating. "If you was a girl with a 'art you'd go an' make it up with the poor man."

"Me! A likely thing!"

"He's awfully fond of you."

"How d'you know?" asked Hester, indifferently.

"'Cos he always says he don't care for you not a bit."

This, to be sure, was evidence. Hester mused, but would not discuss the matter. She talked a good deal just now of Albert Batchelor, whose employment kept him in South London, so that she saw him very seldom.

In the summer of this year Hester was just nineteen; she and Mrs Heffron went one Sunday morning into Victoria Park, taking it in turns to push a perambulator which contained the young widow's two-year-old child. At one point of their walk they passed a man who lay asleep on the grass; Hester went by without noticing him, but Mrs Heffron, suddenly casting back a glance, exclaimed in surpnse –

"Why, that's Mr Rayner!"

Her companion stopped and looked. John lay in profound slumber, head on arm. He had dressed himself decently this morning and was clean. For nearly a minute Hester gazed at him, then made a summoning motion and went on.

"A precious good job I didn't marry 'im!" she said.

"It's all your fault, Hetty," replied the other, looking back.

"No, it ain't. He'd have come low, anyway. He ain't half a man."

Albert Batchelor proposed marriage to Hester for the third time, but she would give him no definite reply. That she encouraged him was not to be doubted. This autumn he spent a good deal of time in her company: she allowed him to say what he liked, and constantly smiled, but a characteristic reserve appeared in her replies – when she made any. Frequently Hester spoke scarce twenty words in the course of an hour's walk. In fact, a strange silence had fallen upon her life, and she shunned ordinary companionship. Her temper was occasionally violent, but the old ardours never appeared in her; she had quite ceased to talk of her feats as a runner. In beauty, however, she had by no means fallen off; her lithe frame seemed to have reached the perfection of development, and her face had more expressiveness, consequently more charm, than when it was wont to be flushed with the fervour of physical contest. No one attacked Hester's reputation; her talk was still pure, and to all appearances she went fancy-free.

On an evening of September, Batchelor and she walked in a quiet road not far from her lodgings. Few people passed them, but presently they were both aware that an acquaintance approached, no other than John Rayner. He wore the coarse clothes in which he worked "at the heap." Hester fixed her eyes upon him; he saw her, but would not look, and carelessly he went by.

"Will you let him insult me like that?" said the girl, in a hard voice, the moment after John had passed.

"Insult you? What did he do?"

"Why, he looked at me as insultin' as he could – you must a'seen it. You're a nice man to walk with anyone!"

Her face was hot; she stood still, pointing after John's figure.

"It isn't the first time, neither," she added, with breathless rapidity. "If you let him go off like that I'll never speak to you again!"

Mr Batchelor was not exactly a combative man, though he had serviceable thews, and on occasion could face the enemy. The present affair annoyed him for he suspected that Hester had either imagined or invented the insult from Rayner; perhaps she wished to see John punished for the sake of old times. For an instant he hesitated.

"Coward!" cried the girl, with a face of bitter contempt.

That was more than Batchelor could endure.

"Hoigh!" he shouted, running after Rayner, who had reached a distance of twenty yards. "Hoigh, you! – jist stop, will you?"

The other turned in astonishment.

"Are you speaking to me?"

"Yis, I em. What d'ye mean by insultin' this young lydy? She says you looked at her insultin' and it ain't the first time neither. You jist come along 'ere an' apologise."

John gazed at the speaker in bewilderment, then at Hester, who had moved a few steps this way.

"She says I've insulted her?"

"Mind who you're calling she. Why, you're at it again, a turnin' up yer nose –"

"If you say another word to me," said John fiercely, "I'll leave you no nose to twist. Fool!"

He turned away, but at the same moment received a smart blow on the side of the face.

"That's your game, is it?" John remarked, again glancing towards Hester, who was leaning slightly forward, with eager gaze. "Look out for yourself, then!"

His coat was off, and in less than a minute Albert Batchelor measured his length on the pavement. There sounded from the spectator of the fight a short mocking laugh. Up again, not much the worse, her champion made excellent play with his fists: blood was on Rayner's cheek. Unable to plant another knock-down blow, John had still the best of it. Crash, and crash again, sounded his slogging hits. At length he damaged his opponent's front teeth and brought him to his knees.

"Had enough, you fool?" he asked.

Three or four people had assembled, and others were rushing up. A window in the nearest house flew open; women's voices were heard. The light of a lamp, shining full on Hester, showed her watching with fierce delight.

"I wouldn't give in, if I was you," she cried, tauntingly, to Batchelor.

Nor did he. The gathering crowd made it impossible. Another round was fought; it took perhaps, two minutes, and, in that space of time, Batchelor received so severe a thrashing that he tottered to the house steps, and sank there, helpless.

"Don't try it on again, young fellow," was John's parting advice, as he took up his coat and hustled through the throng.

At the same moment Hester went off in the opposite direction, an exulting smile in her eyes. Albert Batchelor never again sought her society.

On reaching home, Hester lit her lamp – it revealed a scrubby little bedroom with an attic window – took off her hat and jacket, and deliberately lay down on the bed. She lay there for an hour or more, gazing at nothing, smiling, her lips moving as though she talked to herself. At eleven o'clock she rose, put on her hat, and once more left the house. She walked as far as the spot where the fight had taken place. It was very quiet here, and very gloomy. A policeman approached and she spoke to him.

"P'liceman, can you tell me 'ow fur it is from 'ere to the corner of Beck Street?" she pointed.

"Cawn't say exactly. Five 'undred yards, dessay."

"Will you toime me while I run it there and back?"

The man laughed and made a joke, but in the end he consented to time her. Hester poised herself for a moment on her right foot, then sprang forward. She flew through the darkness and flew back again.

"Four minutes, two second," said the policeman. "Not bad, Miss!"

"Not bad? So that's all! Find me the girl as can do it better."

And she ran off in high spirits.

A few days after, as she came out of the pickle factory, Mrs Heffron met her with an item of news. John Rayner had left the gasworks, and, what was more, had resolved to leave England. He was going to the Cape; might be off in a week's time.

"What's that to me?" said Hester, snappishly.

"If I was you I wouldn't let a man like that go abroad. Mrs Crow's 'usband went to the Cape, and they've never heard of him again to this day."

"He may go to the devil for all I care," rejoined Hester, with unusual violence of phrase. And she walked away without heeding her friend.

They met again before long. Mrs Heffron's child was very ill; the mother had nursed it two days and two nights; she was worn out, and sent for Hester. The girl made herself useful, and promised to sit up half the night whilst Mrs Heffron slept in a room which her landlady put at her disposal.

"I've 'ed a letter from Mr Rayner to-day," said the widow, in an exhausted voice, as they sat by the child's bed.

"Oh!"

"He's goin' to-morrow. From Waterloo, first train in the morning."

"Best thing he can do, dessay."

Mrs Heffron took the crumpled letter out of her pocket and gazed at it.

"My God!" she exclaimed mournfully. "If it was me, Hetty, he wouldn't go."

Hester flashed a look at the thin face, pallid with fatigue. She said nothing; her eyes fell in abashment.

It was seven o'clock. Hester said she would go home for an hour, then return and watch over the child while the mother slept. But instead of going home, she walked to the nearest railway-station, which was Hackney Downs, and there, at the booking office, she put a question to the clerk.

"What's the first train from Waterloo in the mornin', please?"

"Main line?"

"To go to the Cape."

The clerk laughed.

"Southampton, I suppose you mean, then, or Plymouth. Five-fifty; ten minutes to six."

With this information, she presently returned to Mrs Heffron's lodging. It was arranged between them that Hester should sit up until two o'clock; the mother would then take her place. Mrs Heffron placed a watch on the mantelpiece, that her friend might call her, if necessary, when the time came. And at eight Hester seated herself, understanding perfectly what she had to do from time to time for the little sufferer.

Till midnight the child kept moaning and tossing on its bed. A dose of medicine given at that hour seemed to be of soothing effect. By half-past twelve all was quiet. Hester found the time go very slowly, for her mind was as feverish as the body of her little patient. One o'clock was striking; another hour –

How had it happened? From complete wakefulness she had sunk into profound sleep, without warning. It was the child's voice that wakened her, reproaching her conscience. She ran to the watch, and saw with great relief that it was only half-past two. Mrs Heffron must still be sleeping, poor thing. At any other time Hester would have let her sleep on, but now she was eager to get away. Half-past two – ten minutes to six; abundant time, but she must get away.

She called the mother, and told her what hour it was. They talked for a few minutes, then, with a promise to look in again that evening, Hester left the house.

Dark, and a cold morning; happily, no rain. Hester ran home, admitted herself with a latch-key, went silently up into her bedroom, and hurriedly made a change of dress. She put on her best things; a nice black straw hat, just purchased for the winter; a warm jacket, which showed the grace of her figure; a serge skirt; round her neck a boa of feathers, cheap imitation of a fashionable adornment. Then she stole forth again. It must be about three.

Deeply absorbed in her tumultuous thoughts, she walked at a quick pace as far as the crossing of City Road and Old Street. Here she spoke to a policeman, and asked him which direction she had better take for Waterloo Station. The reply was that she couldn't do better than go straight on to the Bank, then turn westward, and so to the Strand.

Very well; would he tell her what time it was? Just upon twenty-five minutes past five.

She staggered as though he had struck her. Twenty-five minutes past five? Then Mrs Heffron's watch had stopped. She saw in a flash of miserable enlightenment the misfortune that had befallen her.

"But," she panted, "I must be at Waterloo by ten minutes to six."

"You can't," replied the policeman stolidly – "unless you take a cab."

She felt in her pockets. Not a penny. In changing her dress she had left her purse behind; and she remembered that it contained only a few coppers.

"How far is it ?"

"A matter of three miles," was the leisurely answer. Five-and-twenty minutes: three miles. Without a word, without a look, Hester set off at her utmost speed.

Before reaching Finsbury Square, she pulled the boa from her neck, unbuttoned her jacket, loosely knotted the boa round her waist. As she came out into the open space between the Bank and the Mansion House, a clock pointed to one minute past the half-hour. She knew that it was now a straight run to the street which led out of the Strand towards Waterloo Bridge. But she must be prudent; agitation had made her heart beat violently; her breath came in painful pants; a "stitch" in the side, and it would be all over with her.

So along the Poultry, along Cheapside, she ran with self-restraint, yet quickly, her hands clutched at her sides. Clanging hoofs upon the asphalt suggested to her that she might get a lift, but it was only a parcels-post van, the driver perched high above his flaring lanterns; it soon outstripped her. On she sped between the tall, silent houses, the closed shops. Only one or two pedestrians saw her, and they turned in curiosity as she bounded by.

At the crossing from Cheapside into St. Paul's Churchyard a policeman, caped and with bull's-eye at his belt, put himself sharply in her way.

"What's up? Where are you going?"

Hester would have flown past, but a heavy hand arrested her. The constable insisted on explanations, and she sobbed them out all the time trying to tear herself away.

"Waterloo – the first train – ten minutes to six – someone goin' away –"

The bull's eye searched her face – bloodless, perspiring – and pried about her body.

"Let me go, Sir! Oh, let me go!"

She had lost two or three minutes, but was free again. Like a spirit of the wind, the wind itself blowing fiercely along with her from the north-east – she swept round the great Cathedral, and saw before her the descending lights of Ludgate Hill. How grateful she was for the downward slope! Her breath, much easier just when the policeman stopped her, had again become troubled with the heart-throbs of fear. At Ludgate Circus there came out from Blackfriars a market-cart, which turned westward, going to Covent Garden.

"Will you give me a lift?" she called out to the man who drove it.

Imprudent, perhaps; she might run quicker; but Fleet Street looked like a mountain before her. The man pulled up in a dawdling way, and began to gossip. Hester leapt to a seat beside him, and urged him on.

There was sudden revelation of busy life. She knew nothing of the newspaper trade; it astonished her to see buildings aflare with electric light; carts drawn up in a long row, side by side, along the pavement; trucks laden with huge bales; men labouring as if minutes meant life or death, as they did to her; for she felt that if she missed the train, if John Rayner were whirled away from her into the unknown, there would be nothing left to live for.

"Can't you go quicker?" she said feverishly.

The man asked questions; he was a chatterbox. Presently a big clock before her, that of the Law Courts, pointed, like the hand of fate, to twenty minutes before the hour. Oh! She could run quicker now that she had her breath again. Without a word she sprang down, fell violently on her hands and knees, was up and off. Moisture upon her hands – blood, the street-lamp showed. But the injury gave no pain.

The cart kept up with her; she would have burst the sinews of her heart rather than let it pass.

St. Clement Danes – the Strand. Here men were washing the road, drenching it with floods of water from a hose. Another great place of business, with bales flung about, men furiously at work, carts waiting or clattering away. She passed it like an arrow, and on, and on.

Somerset House – Wellington Street – the lights of Waterloo Bridge.

Again a policeman looked keenly at her, stepped forward. She shrieked at him, "The train! The train!" and he did not pursue. From the river a fierce wind smote upon her, caught her breath. Had she looked eastward she would have seen the dome of St. Paul's black against a red rift in the sky. To-day the sun rose at a few minutes past six; dawn was breaking.

Many workmen were crossing the bridge, and carts rattled in both directions. Her breast seemed bound with iron; her throat was parched; her temples throbbed and anguished. Quicker but she could not, she could not! Men were staring after her, and some shouted. She saw the station now; she was under the bridge. A railway servant, hurrying on before her, turned as she overtook him.

"The train – which way?" she gasped;

"Five-fifty? All right; you'll do it, my girl."

He showed the approach to the main line and Hester sped on. Up the sharp incline she raced with a mail-van. She saw the sparks struck out by the horses' hoofs. Behind came a newspaper cart, with deafening uproar.

The clock – the clock right before her! It was at a minute past the train time. Five minutes fast had she known it. On, in terror and agony! The outer platform was heaped with packages of newspapers, piles of them thrown back to await the slow train. A crowd of porters unloaded the vehicles, and rushed about with trucks. There was the sound of a jangling bell.

A long train, so long that she could not see the engine, waited with doors agape. No hurrying passengers; no confusion; trucks being briskly emptied into the vans, that was all. She was in time, but her eyes dazzled, and her limbs failed.

Then someone touched her. She turned. It was John Rayner. He had a rough new overcoat, a travelling cap, in his hand only a stout stick, and he looked at her with wide eyes of astonishment.

"What are you doing here?"

"I've come – I've run all the way –"

Her gasped words were barely intelligible.

"You came to see me off?"

Hester caught him by the hand in which he held his stick.

"Don't go! – I want you! – I'll marry you! –"

"Ho, ho! Then you must go with me. I've done with this country."

He drew his hand away, but kept his eyes fixed on hers.

"Go? To the Cape?"

"There's about one minute to get your ticket. I've got little enough money, but enough to pay your passage and leave us a pound or two when we get out there. Make your choice; a minute – less than a minute."

She tried to speak, but had no voice. John darted away from her to the booking-office, and returned with her ticket.

"Come along; my traps are in here."

He seized her by the arm and drew her along. She could not mount the step of the carriage. He lifted her in; placed her on the seat.

"But I haven't got no clothes – nothing!"

"I'll buy you some. We shall have two or three hours at Southampton before the ship sails. I say, how bad you look! Hetty!"

An official came to examine the tickets; he glanced with curiosity at the couple, then locked them in together. Again a bell rang.

"Hetty!"

She was all but fainting. John put his arms about her, kissed her forehead, her cheeks, her lips.

"I've run all the way –"

Insensibly, the train began to move. Hester did not know that she had started until they were rushing past Vauxhall.

And behind them the red rift of the eastern sky broadened into day.

A SCANDAL IN BOHEMIA

Sir Arthur Conan Doyle

Sir Arthur Conan Doyle (1859–1930) is best known as the creator of Sherlock Holmes. Born in Edinburgh, he died in East Sussex having written dozens of books, plays, romances, poetry and non-fiction. If that were not enough, he played in goal for Portsmouth Association Football Club, played cricket for the MCC, taking one wicket (that of W.G. Grace) and twice stood for Parliament, but was not elected. He also found time to father five children. He is probably the only writer included in this book to have been buried twice.

I

To Sherlock Holmes she is always *the* woman. I have seldom heard him mention her under any other name. In his eyes she eclipses and predominates the whole of her sex. It was not that he felt any emotion akin to love for Irene Adler. All emotions, and that one particularly, were abhorrent to his cold, precise but admirably balanced mind. He was, I take it, the most perfect reasoning and observing machine that the world has seen, but as a lover he would have placed himself in a false position. He never spoke of the softer passions, save with a gibe and a sneer. They were admirable things for the observer – excellent for drawing the veil from men's motives and actions. But for the trained reasoner to admit such intrusions into his own delicate and finely adjusted temperament was to introduce a distracting factor which might throw a doubt upon all his mental results. Grit in a sensitive instrument, or a crack in one of his own high-power lenses, would not be more disturbing than a strong emotion in a nature such as his. And yet there was but one woman to him, and that woman was the late Irene Adler, of dubious and questionable memory.

I had seen little of Holmes lately. My marriage had drifted us away from each other. My own complete happiness, and the home-centred interests which rise up around the man who first finds himself master of his own establishment, were sufficient to absorb all my attention, while Holmes, who loathed every form of society with his whole Bohemian soul, remained in our lodgings in Baker Street, buried among his old books, and alternating from week to week between cocaine and ambition, the drowsiness of the drug, and the fierce energy of his own keen nature. He was still, as ever, deeply attracted by the study of crime, and occupied his immense faculties and extraordinary powers of observation in following out those clews, and clearing up those mysteries which had been abandoned as hopeless by the official police. From time to time I heard some vague account of his doings: of his summons to Odessa in the case of the Trepoff murder, of his clearing up of the singular tragedy of the Atkinson brothers at Trincomalee, and finally of the mission which he had accomplished so delicately and successfully for the reigning family of Holland. Beyond these signs of his activity, however, which I merely shared with all the readers of the daily press, I knew little of my former friend and companion.

One night – it was on the twentieth of March, 1888 – I was returning from a journey to a patient (for I had now returned to civil practice), when my way led me through Baker Street. As I passed the well-remembered door, which must always be associated in my mind with my wooing, and with the dark incidents of the Study in Scarlet, I was seized with a keen desire to see Holmes again, and to know how he was employing his extraordinary powers. His rooms were brilliantly lit, and, even as I looked up, I saw his tall, spare figure pass twice in a dark silhouette against the blind. He was pacing the room swiftly, eagerly, with his head sunk upon his chest and his hands clasped behind him. To me, who knew his every mood and habit, his attitude and manner told their own story. He was at work again. He had risen out of his drug-created dreams and was hot upon the scent of some new problem. I rang the bell and was shown up to the chamber which had formerly been in part my own.

His manner was not effusive. It seldom was; but he was glad, I think, to see me. With hardly a word spoken, but with a kindly eye, he waved me to an armchair, threw across his case of cigars, and indicated a spirit case and a gasogene in the corner. Then he stood before the fire and looked me over in his singular introspective fashion.

"Wedlock suits you," he remarked. "I think, Watson, that you have put on seven and a half pounds since I saw you."

"Seven!" I answered.

"Indeed, I should have thought a little more. Just a trifle more, I fancy, Watson. And in practice again, I observe. You did not tell me that you intended to go into harness."

"Then, how do you know?"

"I see it, I deduce it. How do I know that you have been getting yourself very wet lately, and that you have a most clumsy and careless servant girl?"

"My dear Holmes," said I, "this is too much. You would certainly have been burned, had you lived a few centuries ago. It is true that I had a country walk on Thursday and came home in a dreadful mess, but as I have changed my clothes I can't imagine how you deduce it. As to Mary Jane, she is incorrigible, and my wife has given her notice, but there, again, I fail to see how you work it out."

He chuckled to himself and rubbed his long, nervous hands together.

"It is simplicity itself," said he; "my eyes tell me that on the inside of your left shoe, just where the firelight strikes it, the leather is scored by six almost parallel cuts. Obviously they have been caused by someone who has very carelessly scraped round the edges of the sole in order to remove crusted mud from it. Hence, you see, my double deduction that you had been out in vile weather, and that you had a particularly malignant boot-slitting specimen of the London slavey. As to your practice, if a gentleman walks into my rooms smelling of iodoform, with a black mark of nitrate of silver upon his right forefinger, and a bulge on the right side of his top-hat to show where he has secreted his stethoscope, I must be dull, indeed, if I do not pronounce him to be an active member of the medical profession."

I could not help laughing at the ease with which he explained his process of deduction. "When I hear you give your reasons," I remarked, "the thing always appears to me to be so ridiculously simple that I could easily do it myself, though at each successive instance of your reasoning I am baffled until you explain your process. And yet I believe that my eyes are as good as yours."

"Quite so," he answered, lighting a cigarette, and throwing himself down into an armchair. "You see, but you do not observe. The distinction is clear. For example, you have frequently seen the steps which lead up from the hall to this room."

"Frequently."

"How often?"

"Well, some hundreds of times."

"Then how many are there?"

"How many? I don't know."

"Quite so! You have not observed. And yet you have seen. That is just my point. Now, I know that there are seventeen steps, because I have both seen and observed. By-the-way, since you are interested in these little problems, and since you are good enough to chronicle one or two of my trifling experiences, you may be interested in this." He threw over a sheet of thick, pink-tinted note-paper which had been lying open upon the table. "It came by the last post," said he. "Read it aloud."

The note was undated, and without either signature or address.

"There will call upon you to-night, at a quarter to eight o'clock," it said, "a gentleman who desires to consult you upon a matter of the very deepest moment. Your recent services to one of the royal houses of Europe have shown that you are one who may safely be trusted with matters which are of an importance which can hardly be exaggerated. This account of you we have from all quarters received. Be in your chamber then at that hour, and do not take it amiss if your visitor wear a mask.

"This is indeed a mystery," I remarked. "What do you imagine that it means?"

"I have no data yet. It is a capital mistake to theorize before one has data. Insensibly one begins to twist facts to suit theories, instead of theories to suit facts. But the note itself. What do you deduce from it?"

I carefully examined the writing, and the paper upon which it was written.

"The man who wrote it was presumably well to do," I remarked, endeavoring to imitate my companion's processes. "Such paper could not be bought under half a crown a packet. It is peculiarly strong and stiff."

"Peculiar – that is the very word," said Holmes. "It is not an English paper at all. Hold it up to the light."

I did so, and saw a large "E" with a small "g," a "P," and a large "G" with a small "t" woven into the texture of the paper.

"What do you make of that?" asked Holmes.

"The name of the maker, no doubt; or his monogram, rather."

"Not at all. The 'G' with the small 't' stands for 'Gesellschaft,' which is the German for 'Company.' It is a customary contraction like our 'Co.' 'P,' of course, stands for 'Papier.' Now for the 'Eg.' Let us glance at our Continental Gazetteer." He took down a heavy brown volume from his shelves. "Eglow, Eglonitz – here we are, Egria. It is in a German-speaking country – in Bohemia, not far from Carlsbad. 'Remarkable as being the scene of the death of Wallenstein, and for its numerous glass-factories and paper-mills.' Ha, ha, my boy, what do you make of that?" His eyes sparkled, and he sent up a great blue triumphant cloud from his cigarette.

"The paper was made in Bohemia," I said.

"Precisely. And the man who wrote the note is a German. Do you note the peculiar construction of the sentence – 'This account of you we have from all quarters received.' A Frenchman or Russian could not have written that. It is the German who is so uncourteous to his verbs. It only remains, therefore, to discover what is wanted by this German who writes upon Bohemian paper and prefers wearing a mask to showing his face. And here he comes, if I am not mistaken, to resolve all our doubts."

As he spoke there was the sharp sound of horses' hoofs and grating wheels against the curb, followed by a sharp pull at the bell. Holmes whistled.

"A pair, by the sound," said he. "Yes," he continued, glancing out of the window. "A nice little brougham and a pair of beauties. A hundred and fifty guineas apiece. There's money in this case, Watson, if there is nothing else."

"I think that I had better go, Holmes."

"Not a bit, Doctor. Stay where you are. I am lost without my Boswell. And this promises to be interesting. It would be a pity to miss it."

"But your client –"

"Never mind him. I may want your help, and so may he. Here he comes. Sit down in that armchair, Doctor, and give us your best attention."

A slow and heavy step, which had been heard upon the stairs and in the passage, paused immediately outside the door. Then there was a loud and authoritative tap.

"Come in!" said Holmes.

A man entered who could hardly have been less than six feet six inches in height, with the chest and limbs of a Hercules. His dress was rich with a richness which would, in England, be looked upon as akin to bad taste. Heavy bands of astrakhan were slashed across the sleeves and fronts of his double-breasted coat, while the deep blue cloak which was thrown over his shoulders was lined with flame-colored silk and secured at the neck with a brooch which consisted of a single flaming beryl. Boots which extended halfway up his calves, and which were trimmed at the tops with rich brown fur, completed the impression of barbaric opulence which was suggested by his whole appearance. He carried a broad-brimmed hat in his hand, while he wore across the upper part of his face, extending down past the cheekbones, a black vizard mask, which he had apparently adjusted that very moment, for his hand was still raised to it as he entered. From the lower part of the face he appeared to be a man of strong character, with a thick, hanging lip, and a long, straight chin suggestive of resolution pushed to the length of obstinacy.

"You had my note?" he asked with a deep harsh voice and a strongly marked German accent. "I told you that I would call." He looked from one to the other of us, as if uncertain which to address.

"Pray take a seat," said Holmes. "This is my friend and colleague, Dr. Watson, who is occasionally good enough to help me in my cases. Whom have I the honor to address?"

"You may address me as the Count Von Kramm, a Bohemian nobleman. I understand that this gentleman, your friend, is a man of honor and discretion, whom I may trust with a matter of the most extreme importance. If not, I should much prefer to communicate with you alone."

I rose to go, but Holmes caught me by the wrist and pushed me back into my chair. "It is both, or none," said he. "You may say before this gentleman anything which you may say to me."

The Count shrugged his broad shoulders. "Then I must begin," said he, "by binding you both to absolute secrecy for two years; at the end of that time the matter will be of no importance. At present it is not too much to say that it is of such weight it may have an influence upon European history."

"I promise," said Holmes.

"And I."

"You will excuse this mask," continued our strange visitor. "The august person who employs me wishes his agent to be unknown to you, and I may confess at once that the title by which I have just called myself is not exactly my own."

"I was aware of it," said Holmes drily.

"The circumstances are of great delicacy, and every precaution has to be taken to quench what might grow to be an immense scandal and seriously compromise one of the reigning families of Europe. To speak plainly, the matter implicates the great House of Ormstein, hereditary kings of Bohemia."

"I was also aware of that," murmured Holmes, settling himself down in his armchair and closing his eyes.

Our visitor glanced with some apparent surprise at the languid, lounging figure of the man who had been no doubt depicted to him as the most incisive reasoner and most energetic agent in Europe. Holmes slowly reopened his eyes and looked impatiently at his gigantic client.

"If your Majesty would condescend to state your case," he remarked, "I should be better able to advise you."

The man sprang from his chair and paced up and down the room in uncontrollable agitation. Then, with a gesture of desperation, he tore the mask from his face and hurled it upon the ground. "You are right," he cried; "I am the King. Why should I attempt to conceal it?"

"Why, indeed?" murmured Holmes. "Your Majesty had not spoken before I was aware that I was addressing Wilhelm Gottsreich Sigismond von Ormstein, Grand Duke of Cassel-Felstein, and hereditary King of Bohemia."

"But you can understand," said our strange visitor, sitting down once more and passing his hand over his high white forehead, "you can understand that I am not accustomed to doing such business in my own person. Yet the matter was so delicate that I could not confide it to an agent without putting myself in his power. I have come incognito from Prague for the purpose of consulting you."

"Then, pray consult," said Holmes, shutting his eyes once more.

"The facts are briefly these: Some five years ago, during a lengthy visit to Warsaw, I made the acquaintance of the wellknown adventuress, Irene Adler. The name is no doubt farmiliar to you."

"Kindly look her up in my index, Doctor," murmured Holmes without opening his eyes. For many years he had adopted a system of docketing all paragraphs concerning men and things, so that it was difficult to name a subject or a person on which he could not at once furnish information. In this case I found her biography sandwiched in between that of a Hebrew rabbi and that of a staff-commander who had written a monograph upon the deep-sea fishes.

"Let me see!" said Holmes. "Hum! Born in New Jersey in the year 1858. Contralto – hum! La Scala, hum! Prima donna Imperial Opera of Warsaw – yes! Retired from operatic stage – ha! Living in London – quite so! Your Majesty, as I understand, became entangled with this young person, wrote her some compromising letters, and is now desirous of getting those letters back."

"Precisely so. But how –"

"Was there a secret marriage?"

"None."

"No legal papers or certificates?"

"None."

"Then I fail to follow your Majesty. If this young person should produce her letters for blackmailing or other purposes, how is she to prove their authenticity?"

"There is the writing."

"Pooh, pooh! Forgery."

"My private note-paper."

"Stolen."

"My own seal."

"Imitated."

"My photograph."

"Bought."

"We were both in the photograph."

"Oh, dear! That is very bad! Your Majesty has indeed committed an indiscretion."

"I was mad – insane."

"You have compromised yourself seriously."

"I was only Crown Prince then. I was young. I am but thirty now."

"It must be recovered."

"We have tried and failed."

"Your Majesty must pay. It must be bought."

"She will not sell."

"Stolen, then."

"Five attempts have been made. Twice burglars in my pay ransacked her house. Once we diverted her luggage when she travelled. Twice she has been waylaid. There has been no result."

"No sign of it?"

"Absolutely none."

Holmes laughed. "It is quite a pretty little problem," said he.

"But a very serious one to me," returned the King reproachfully.

"Very, indeed. And what does she propose to do with the photograph?"

"To ruin me."

"But how?"

"I am about to be married."

"So I have heard."

"To Clotilde Lothman von Saxe-Meningen, second daughter of the King of Scandinavia. You may know the strict principles of her family. She is herself the very soul of delicacy. A shadow of a doubt as to my conduct would bring the matter to an end."

"And Irene Adler?"

"Threatens to send them the photograph. And she will do it. I know that she will do it. You do not know her, but she has a soul of steel. She has the face of the most beautiful of women, and the mind of the most resolute of men. Rather than I should marry another woman, there are no lengths to which she would not go – none."

"You are sure that she has not sent it yet?"

"I am sure."

"And why?"

"Because she has said that she would send it on the day when the betrothal was publicly proclaimed. That will be next Monday."

"Oh, then we have three days yet," said Holmes with a yawn. "That is very fortunate, as I have one or two matters of importance to look into just at present. Your Majesty will, of course, stay in London for the present?"

"Certainly. You will find me at the Langham under the name of the Count Von Kramm."

"Then I shall drop you a line to let you know how we progress."

"Pray do so. I shall be all anxiety."

"Then, as to money?"

"You have carte blanche."

"Absolutely?"

"I tell you that I would give one of the provinces of my kingdom to have that photograph."

"And for present expenses?"

The King took a heavy chamois leather bag from under his cloak and laid it on the table.

"There are three hundred pounds in gold and seven hundred in notes," he said.

Holmes scribbled a receipt upon a sheet of his note-book and handed it to him.

"And Mademoiselle's address?" he asked.

"Is Briony Lodge, Serpentine Avenue, St. John's Wood."

Holmes took a note of it. "One other question," said he. "Was the photograph a cabinet?"

"It was."

"Then, good-night, your Majesty, and I trust that we shall soon have some good news for you. And good-night, Watson," he added, as the wheels of the royal brougham rolled down the street. "If you will be good enough to call to-morrow afternoon at three o'clock I should like to chat this little matter over with you."

II

At three o'clock precisely I was at Baker Street, but Holmes had not yet returned. The landlady informed me that he had left the house shortly after eight o'clock in the morning. I sat down beside the fire, however, with the intention of awaiting him, however long he might be. I was already deeply interested in his inquiry, for, though it was surrounded by none of the grim and strange features which were associated with the two crimes which I have already recorded, still, the nature of the case and the exalted station of his client gave it a character of its own. Indeed, apart from the nature of the investigation which my friend had on hand, there was something in his masterly grasp of a situation, and his keen, incisive reasoning, which made it a pleasure to me to study his system of work, and to follow the quick, subtle methods by which he disentangled the most inextricable mysteries. So accustomed was I to his invariable success that the very possibility of his failing had ceased to enter into my head.

It was close upon four before the door opened, and a drunken looking groom, ill-kempt and side-whiskered, with an inflamed face and disreputable clothes, walked into the room. Accustomed as I was to my friend's amazing powers in the use of disguises, I had to look three times before I was certain that it was indeed he. With a nod he vanished into the bedroom, whence he emerged in five minutes tweed-suited and respectable, as of old. Putting his hands into his pockets, he stretched out his legs in front of the fire and laughed heartily for some minutes.

"Well, really!" he cried, and then he choked and laughed again until he was obliged to lie back, limp and helpless, in the chair.

"What is it?"

"It's quite too funny. I am sure you could never guess how I employed my morning, or what I ended by doing."

"I can't imagine. I suppose that you have been watching the habits, and perhaps the house, of Miss Irene Adler."

"Quite so; but the sequel was rather unusual. I will tell you, however. I left the house a little after eight o'clock this morning in the character of a groom out of work. There is a wonderful sympathy and freemasonry among horsy men. Be one of them, and you will know all that there is to know. I soon found Briony Lodge. It is a bijou villa, with a garden at the back. but built out in front right up to the road, two stories. Chubb lock to the door. Large sitting-room on the right side, well furnished, with long windows almost to the floor, and those preposterous English window fasteners which a child could open. Behind there was nothing remarkable, save that the passage window could be reached from the top of the coach-house. I walked round it and examined it closely from every point of view, but without noting anything else of interest.

"I then lounged down the street and found, as I expected, that there was a mews in a lane which runs down by one wall of the garden. I lent the ostlers a hand in rubbing down their horses, and received in exchange twopence, a glass of half and half, two fills of shag tobacco, and as much information as I could desire about Miss Adler, to say nothing of half a dozen other people in the neighborhood in whom I was not in the least interested, but whose biographies I was compelled to listen to."

"And what of Irene Adler?" I asked.

"Oh, she has turned all the men's heads down in that part. She is the daintiest thing under a bonnet on this planet. So say the Serpentine-mews, to a man. She lives quietly, sings at concerts, drives out at five every day, and returns at seven sharp for dinner. Seldom goes out at other times, except when she sings. Has only one male visitor, but a good deal of him. He is dark, handsome, and dashing, never calls less than once a day, and often twice. He is a Mr. Godfrey Norton, of the Inner Temple. See the advantages of a cabman as a confidant. They had driven him home a dozen times from Serpentine-mews, and knew all about him. When I had listened to all they had to tell, I began to walk up and down near Briony Lodge once more, and to think over my plan of campaign.

"This Godfrey Norton was evidently an important factor in the matter. He was a lawyer. That sounded ominous. What was the relation between them, and what the object of his repeated visits? Was she his client, his friend, or his mistress? If the former, she had probably transferred the photograph to his keeping. If the latter, it was less likely. On the issue of this question depended whether I should continue my work at Briony Lodge, or turn my attention to the gentleman's chambers in the Temple. It was a delicate point and it widened the field of my inquiry. I fear that I bore you with these details, but I have to let you see my little difficulties, if you are to understand the situation."

"I am following you closely," I answered.

"I was still balancing the matter in my mind when a hansom cab drove up to Briony Lodge, and a gentleman sprang out. He was a remarkably handsome man, dark, aquiline, and moustached-evidently the man of whom I had heard. He appeared to be in a great hurry, shouted to the cabman to wait, and brushed past the maid who opened the door with the air of a man who was thoroughly at home.

"He was in the house about half an hour, and I could catch glimpses of him in the windows of the sitting-room, pacing up and down, talking excitedly, and waving his arms. Of her I could see nothing. Presently he emerged, looking even more flurried than before. As he stepped up to the cab, he pulled a gold watch from his pocket and looked at it earnestly, 'Drive like the devil,' he shouted, 'first to Gross & Hankey's in Regent Street, and then to the Church of St. Monica in the Edgeware Road. Half a guinea if you do it in twenty minutes!'

"Away they went, and I was just wondering whether I should not do well to follow them when up the lane came a neat little landau, the coachman with his coat only half-buttoned, and his tie under his ear, while all the tags of his harness were sticking out of the buckles. It hadn't pulled up before she shot out of the hall door and into it. I only caught a glimpse of her at the moment, but she was a lovely woman, with a face that a man might die for.

"'The Church of St. Monica, John,' she cried, 'and half a sovereign if you reach it in twenty minutes.'

"This was quite too good to lose, Watson. I was just balancing whether I should run for it, or whether I should perch behind her landau when a cab came through the street. The driver looked twice at such a shabby fare, but I jumped in before he could object. 'The Church of St. Monica,' said I, 'and half a sovereign if you reach it in twenty minutes.' It was twenty-five minutes to twelve, and of course it was clear enough what was in the wind.

"My cabby drove fast. I don't think I ever drove faster, but the others were there before us. The cab and the landau with their steaming horses were in front of the door when I arrived. I paid the man and hurried into the church. There was not a soul there save the two whom I had followed and a surpliced clergyman, who seemed to be expostulating with them. They were all three standing in a knot in front of the altar. I lounged up the side aisle like any other idler who has dropped into a church. Suddenly, to my surprise, the three at the altar faced round to me, and Godfrey Norton came running as hard as he could towards me.

"Thank God," he cried. "You'll do. Come! Come!"

"What then?" I asked.

"Come, man, come, only three minutes, or it won't be legal."

"I was half-dragged up to the altar, and before I knew where I was I found myself mumbling responses which were whispered in my ear and vouching for things of which I knew nothing, and generally assisting in the secure tying up of Irene Adler, spinster, to Godfrey Norton, bachelor. It was all done in an instant, and there was the gentleman thanking me on the one side and the lady on the other, while the clergyman beamed on me in front. It was the most preposterous position in which I ever found myself in my life, and it was the thought of it that started me laughing just now. It seems that there had been some informality about their license, that the clergyman absolutely refused to marry them without a witness of some sort, and that my lucky appearance saved the bridegroom from having to sally out into the streets in search of a best man. The bride gave me a sovereign, and I mean to wear it on my watch-chain in memory of the occasion."

"This is a very unexpected turn of affairs," said I; "and what then?"

"Well, I found my plans very seriously menaced. It looked as if the pair might take an immediate departure, and so necessitate very prompt and energetic measures on my part. At the church door, however, they separated, he driving back to the Temple, and she to her own house. 'I shall drive out in the park at five as usual,' she said as she left him. I heard no more. They drove away in different directions, and I went off to make my own arrangements."

"Which are?"

"Some cold beef and a glass of beer," he answered, ringing the bell. "I have been too busy to think of food, and I am likely to be busier still this evening. By the way, Doctor, I shall want your cooperation."

"I shall be delighted."

"You don't mind breaking the law?"

"Not in the least."

"Nor running a chance of arrest?"

"Not in a good cause."

"Oh, the cause is excellent!"

"Then I am your man."

"I was sure that I might rely on you."

"But what is it you wish?"

"When Mrs. Turner has brought in the tray I will make it clear to you. Now," he said as he turned hungrily on the simple fare that our landlady had provided, "I must discuss it while I eat, for I have not much time. It is nearly five now. In two hours we must be on the scene of action. Miss Irene, or Madame, rather, returns from her drive at seven. We must be at Briony Lodge to meet her."

"And what then?"

"You must leave that to me. I have already arranged what is to occur. There is only one point on which I must insist. You must not interfere, come what may. You understand?"

"I am to be neutral?"

"To do nothing whatever. There will probably be some small unpleasantness. Do not join in it. It will end in my being conveyed into the house. Four or five minutes afterwards the sitting-room window will open. You are to station yourself close to that open window."

"Yes."

"You are to watch me, for I will be visible to you."

"Yes."

"And when I raise my hand – so – you will throw into the room what I give you to throw, and will, at the same time, raise the cry of fire. You quite follow me?"

"Entirely."

"It is nothing very formidable," he said, taking a long cigarshaped roll from his pocket. "It is an ordinary plumber's smokerocket, fitted with a cap at either end to make it self-lighting. Your task is confined to that. When you raise your cry of fire, it will be taken up by quite a number of people. You may then walk to the end of the street, and I will rejoin you in ten minutes. I hope that I have made myself clear?"

"I am to remain neutral, to get near the window, to watch you, and at the signal to throw in this object, then to raise the cry of fire, and to wait you at the corner of the street."

"Precisely."

"Then you may entirely rely on me."

"That is excellent. I think, perhaps, it is almost time that I prepare for the new role I have to play."

He disappeared into his bedroom and returned in a few minutes in the character of an amiable and simple-minded Nonconformist clergyman. His broad black hat, his baggy trousers his white tie, his sympathetic smile, and general look of peering and benevolent curiosity were such as Mr. John Hare alone could have equalled. It was not merely that Holmes changed his costume. His expression, his manner, his very soul seemed to vary with every fresh part that he assumed. The stage lost a fine actor, even as science lost an acute reasoner, when he became a specialist in crime.

It was a quarter past six when we left Baker Street, and it still wanted ten minutes to the hour when we found ourselves in Serpentine Avenue. It was already dusk, and the lamps were just being lighted as we paced up and down in front of Briony Lodge, waiting for the coming of its occupant. The house was just such as I had pictured it from Sherlock Holmes's succinct description, but the locality appeared to be less private than I expected. On the contrary, for a small street in a quiet neighborhood, it was remarkably animated. There was a group of shabbily dressed men smoking and laughing in a corner, a scissors-grinder with his wheel, two guardsmen who were flirting with a nurse-girl, and several well-dressed young men who were lounging up and down with cigars in their mouths.

"You see," remarked Holmes, as we paced to and fro in front of the house, "this marriage rather simplifies matters. The photograph becomes a double-edged weapon now. The chances are that she would be as averse to its being seen by Mr. Godfrey Norton, as our client is to its coming to the eyes of his princess. Now the question is, Where are we to find the photograph?"

"Where, indeed?"

"It is most unlikely that she carries it about with her. It is cabinet size. Too large for easy concealment about a woman's dress. She knows that the King is capable of having her waylaid and searched. Two attempts of the sort have already been made. We may take it, then, that she does not carry it about with her."

"Where, then?"

"Her banker or her lawyer. There is that double possibility. But I am inclined to think neither. Women are naturally secretive, and they like to do their own secreting. Why should she hand it over to anyone else? She could trust her own guardianship, but she could not tell what indirect or political influence might be brought to bear upon a business man. Besides, remember that she had resolved to use it within a few days. It must be where she can lay her hands upon it. It must be in her own house."

"But it has twice been burgled."

"Pshaw! They did not know how to look."

"But how will you look?"

"I will not look."

"What then?"

"I will get her to show me."

"But she will refuse."

"She will not be able to. But I hear the rumble of wheels. It is her carriage. Now carry out my orders to the letter."

As he spoke the gleam of the side-lights of a carriage came round the curve of the avenue. It was a smart little landau which rattled up to the door of Briony Lodge. As it pulled up, one of the loafing men at the corner dashed forward to open the door in the hope of earning a copper, but was elbowed away by another loafer, who had rushed up with the same intention. A fierce quarrel broke out, which was increased by the two guardsmen, who took sides with one of the loungers, and by the scissorsgrinder, who was equally hot upon the other side. A blow was struck, and in an instant the lady, who had stepped from her carriage, was the centre of a little knot of flushed and struggling men, who struck savagely at each other with their fists and sticks. Holmes dashed into the crowd to protect the lady; but just as he reached her he gave a cry and dropped to the ground, with the blood running freely down his face. At his fall the guardsmen took to their heels in one direction and the loungers in the other, while a number of better-dressed people, who had watched the scuffle without taking part in it, crowded in to help the lady and to attend to the injured man. Irene Adler, as I will still call her, had hurried up the steps; but she stood at the top with her superb figure outlined against the lights of the hall, looking back into the street.

"Is the poor gentleman much hurt?" she asked.

"He is dead," cried several voices.

"No, no, there's life in him!" shouted another. "But he'll be gone before you can get him to hospital."

"He's a brave fellow," said a woman. "They would have had the lady's purse and watch if it hadn't been for him. They were a gang, and a rough one, too. Ah, he's breathing now."

"He can't lie in the street. May we bring him in, marm?"

"Surely. Bring him into the sitting-room. There is a comfortable sofa. This way, please!"

Slowly and solemnly he was borne into Briony Lodge and laid out in the principal room, while I still observed the proceedings from my post by the window. The lamps had been lit, but the blinds had not been drawn, so that I could see Holmes as he lay upon the couch. I do not know whether he was seized with compunction at that moment for the part he was playing, but I know that I never felt more heartily ashamed of myself in my life than when I saw the beautiful creature against whom I was conspiring, or the grace and kindliness with which she waited upon the injured man. And yet it would be the blackest treachery to Holmes to draw back now from the part which he had intrusted to me. I hardened my heart, and took the smoke-rocket from under my ulster. After all, I thought, we are not injuring her. We are but preventing her from injuring another.

Holmes had sat up upon the couch, and I saw him motion like a man who is in need of air. A maid rushed across and threw open the window. At the same instant I saw him raise his hand and at the signal I tossed my rocket into the room with a cry of "Fire!" The word was no sooner out of my mouth than the whole crowd of spectators, well dressed and ill – gentlemen, ostlers, and servant-maids – joined in a general shriek of "Fire!" Thick clouds of smoke curled through the room and out at the open window. I caught a glimpse of rushing figures, and a moment later the voice of Holmes from within assuring them that it was a false alarm. Slipping through the shouting crowd I made my way to the corner of the street, and in ten minutes was rejoiced to find my friend's arm in mine, and to get away from the scene of uproar. He walked swiftly and in silence for some few minutes until we had turned down one of the quiet streets which lead towards the Edgware Road.

"You did it very nicely, Doctor," he remarked. "Nothing could have been better. It is all right."

"You have the photograph?"

"I know where it is."

"And how did you find out?"

"She showed me, as I told you she would."

"I am still in the dark."

"I do not wish to make a mystery," said he, laughing. "The matter was perfectly simple. You, of course, saw that everyone in the street was an accomplice. They were all engaged for the evening."

"I guessed as much."

"Then, when the row broke out, I had a little moist red paint in the palm of my hand. I rushed forward, fell down. clapped my hand to my face, and became a piteous spectacle. It is an old trick."

"That also I could fathom."

"Then they carried me in. She was bound to have me in. What else could she do? And into her sitting-room. which was the very room which I suspected. It lay between that and her bedroom, and I was determined to see which. They laid me on a couch, I motioned for air, they were compelled to open the window and you had your chance."

"How did that help you?"

"It was all-important. When a woman thinks that her house is on fire, her instinct is at once to rush to the thing which she values most. It is a perfectly overpowering impulse, and I have more than once taken advantage of it. In the case of the Darlington substitution scandal it was of use to me, and also in the Arnsworth Castle business. A married woman grabs at her baby; an unmarried one reaches for her jewel-box. Now it was clear to me that our lady of to-day had nothing in the house more precious to her than what we are in quest of. She would rush to secure it. The alarm of fire was admirably done. The smoke and shouting were enough to shake nerves of steel. She responded beautifully. The photograph is in a recess behind a sliding panel just above the right bell-pull. She was there in an instant, and I caught a glimpse of it as she half-drew it out. When I cried out that it was a false alarm, she replaced it, glanced at the rocket, rushed from the room, and I have not seen her since. I rose, and, making my excuses, escaped from the house. I hesitated whether to attempt to secure the photograph at once; but the coachman had come in, and as he was watching me narrowly it seemed safer to wait. A little over-precipitance may ruin all."

"And now?" I asked.

"Our quest is practically finished. I shall call with the King to-morrow, and with you, if you care to come with us. We will be shown into the sitting-room to wait for the lady; but it is probable that when she comes she may find neither us nor the photograph. It might be a satisfaction to his Majesty to regain it with his own hands."

"And when will you call?"

"At eight in the morning. She will not be up, so that we shall have a clear field. Besides, we must be prompt, for this marriage may mean a complete change in her life and habits. I must wire to the King without delay."

We had reached Baker Street and had stopped at the door. He was searching his pockets for the key when someone passing said:

"Good-night, Mister Sherlock Holmes."

There were several people on the pavement at the time, but the greeting appeared to come from a slim youth in an ulster who had hurried by.

"I've heard that voice before," said Holmes, staring down the dimly lit street. "Now, I wonder who the deuce that could have been."

III

I slept at Baker Street that night, and we were engaged upon our toast and coffee in the morning when the King of Bohemia rushed into the room.

"You have really got it!" he cried, grasping Sherlock Holmes by either shoulder and looking eagerly into his face.

"Not yet."

"But you have hopes?"

"I have hopes."

"Then, come. I am all impatience to be gone."

"We must have a cab."

"No, my brougham is waiting."

"Then that will simplify matters." We descended and started off once more for Briony Lodge.

"Irene Adler is married," remarked Holmes.

"Married! When?"

"Yesterday."

"But to whom?"

"To an English lawyer named Norton."

"But she could not love him."

"I am in hopes that she does."

"And why in hopes?"

"Because it would spare your Majesty all fear of future annoyance. If the lady loves her husband, she does not love your Majesty. If she does not love your Majesty, there is no reason why she should interfere with your Majesty's plan."

"It is true. And yet – Well! I wish she had been of my own station! What a queen she would have made!" He relapsed into a moody silence, which was not broken until we drew up in Serpentine Avenue.

The door of Briony Lodge was open, and an elderly woman stood upon the steps. She watched us with a sardonic eye as we stepped from the brougham.

"Mr. Sherlock Holmes, I believe?" said she.

"I am Mr. Holmes," answered my companion, looking at her with a questioning and rather startled gaze.

"Indeed! My mistress told me that you were likely to call. She left this morning with her husband by the 5:15 train from Charing Cross for the Continent."

"What!" Sherlock Holmes staggered back, white with chagrin and surprise. "Do you mean that she has left England?"

"Never to return."

"And the papers?" asked the King hoarsely. "All is lost."

"We shall see." He pushed past the servant and rushed into the drawing-room, followed by the King and myself. The furniture was scattered about in every direction, with dismantled shelves and open drawers, as if the lady had hurriedly ransacked them before her flight. Holmes rushed at the bell-pull, tore back a small sliding shutter, and, plunging in his hand, pulled out a photograph and a letter. The photograph was of Irene Adler herself in evening dress, the letter was superscribed to "Sherlock Holmes, Esq. To be left till called for." My friend tore it open and we all three read it together. It was dated at midnight of the preceding night and ran in this way:

MY DEAR MR. SHERLOCK HOLMES,

You really did it very well. You took me in completely. Until after the alarm of fire, I had not a suspicion. But then, when I found how I had betrayed myself, I began to think. I had been warned against you months ago. I had been told that if the King employed an agent it would certainly be you. And your address had been given me. Yet, with all this, you made me reveal what you wanted to know. Even after I became suspicious, I found it hard to think evil of such a dear, kind old clergyman. But, you know, I have been trained as an actress myself. Male costume is nothing new to me. I often take advantage of the freedom which it gives. I sent John, the coachman, to watch you, ran up stairs, got into my walking-clothes, as I call them, and came down just as you departed.

Well, I followed you to your door, and so made sure that I was really an object of interest to the celebrated Mr. Sherlock Holmes. Then I, rather imprudently, wished you good-night, and started for the Temple to see my husband. We both thought the best resource was flight, when pursued by so formidable an antagonist; so you will find the nest empty when you call to-morrow. As to the photograph, your client may rest in peace. I love and am loved by a better man than he. The King may do what he will without hindrance from one whom he has cruelly wronged. I keep it only to safeguard myself, and to preserve a weapon which will always secure me from any steps which he might take in the future. I leave a photograph which he might care to possess; and I remain, dear Mr. Sherlock Holmes,

Very truly yours,

IRENE NORTON, nee ADLER.

"What a woman – oh, what a woman!" cried the King of Bohemia, when we had all three read this epistle. "Did I not tell you how quick and resolute she was? Would she not have made an admirable queen? Is it not a pity that she was not on my level?"

"From what I have seen of the lady she seems indeed to be on a very different level to your Majesty," said Holmes coldly. "I am sorry that I have not been able to bring your Majesty's business to a more successful conclusion."

"On the contrary, my dear sir," cried the King; "nothing could be more successful. I know that her word is inviolate. The photograph is now as safe as if it were in the fire."

"I am glad to hear your Majesty say so."

"I am immensely indebted to you. Pray tell me in what way I can reward you. This ring –" He slipped an emerald snake ring from his finger and held it out upon the palm of his hand.

"Your Majesty has something which I should value even more highly," said Holmes.

"You have but to name it."

"This photograph!"

The King stared at him in amazement.

"Irene's photograph!" he cried. "Certainly, if you wish it."

"I thank your Majesty. Then there is no more to be done in the matter. I have the honor to wish you a very good-morning." He bowed, and, turning away without observing the hand which the King had stretched out to him, he set off in my company for his chambers.

And that was how a great scandal threatened to affect the kingdom of Bohemia, and how the best plans of Mr. Sherlock Holmes were beaten by a woman's wit. He used to make merry over the cleverness of women, but I have not heard him do it of late. And when he speaks of Irene Adler, or when he refers to her photograph, it is always under the honorable title of the woman.

A LECTURE TOUR

Knut Hamsun

Knut Hamsun (1859–1952) is one of two Norwegians to have been awarded the Nobel Prize. Best known for his novel *Hunger* – perhaps the verbal equivalent of Edvard Munch's painting *The Scream* – he was the author of over a dozen novels, as well as poetry, plays, journalism and shorter fiction. It's probably best to gulp when reading that he sent Joseph Goebbels his Nobel Prize medal as a gift during the Second World War, but the Norwegian state fined him heftily for his political views.

I was going to give a lecture on modern literature in Drammen. I was short of money, and this seemed to me a good way to get hold of a little. I didn't think it would be all that difficult either. So one fine day in the late summer of 1886 I boarded a train bound for that splendid town.

I didn't know a soul in Drammen, nor did anyone there know me. Nor had I advertised my lecture in the papers, although earlier that summer, in an expansive moment, I had had 500 cards printed, and I intended to distribute these in the hotels and bars and large shops, to let people know what was in store for them. These cards were not wholly to my liking in that they contained a misprint in the spelling of my name; yet I was so comprehensively unknown in Drammen that a misprint was neither here nor there.

As I sat in the train I took stock of my situation. The prospects did not dishearten me. I had overcome many difficulties in my life with little or no money, and though I was not rich enough to live in a style befitting the dignity of my aesthetic mission in this town I was confident everything would be all right if I took care with my money. No fancy gestures now! As for food, I could always slip down to some basement-café after dark and get something to eat there, and I would lodge at a bed-and-breakfast that catered for travelling salesmen. Apart from that, what other outgoings would I have?

On the train I sat and studied my lecture. I was going to talk about the novelist Alexander Kielland. My fellow-passengers were a group of high-spirited farmers returning from a trip to Kristiania. They were passing a bottle round and offered me a drink, to which I said no thank you. Later, in the manner of all friendly drunks, they made other approaches to me; but I continued to ignore them until finally they realised, from my general demeanour and from all the notes I was making, that I was a learned man with a lot of important things on my mind. After that they left me in peace.

On arriving in Drammen I got off the train and carried my carpetbag over to a bench in order to compose myself before setting off into town. As it happens I had no use for this carpet-bag at all, I took it with me solely because I had heard that it was easier to book in and out of a bed-and-breakfast if one were carrying such a bag. It was anyway a wretched old worn-out yellow cloth bag, not really suitable for a travelling man of letters. My outfit, including a dark blue jacket, was considerably more respectable.

A hotel porter with writing on his hat came over and wanted to carry my bag.

I declined the offer, explaining that I had not yet made up my mind about a hotel, I had first to meet a couple of newspaper editors in town. It was I who was going to give this lecture on literature.

Well, I would need a hotel whatever, I had to stay somewhere, didn't I? His hotel was beyond all comparison the best in its class, with electric bells, a bath, a reading room. It's just round the corner here, up this street then left.

He picked up my bag by the strap.

I detained him.

Did I want to carry the bag to the hotel *myself?*

Well, I was going the same way as my bag so I might just as well hang it over the crook of my finger and that way we'd both get there.

At this the man looked at me, and realising that I was not a wealthy gentleman he headed off down towards the train again on the lookout for someone else. But there were no other travellers, so he returned and again began touting for my custom, persuading me finally that in fact he had come down to the station for the specific purpose of meeting me.

Well, that changed matters. The man had perhaps been sent by the committee of some society – the Workers' Educational Society, for example – who had got wind of my arrival. Drammen was obviously a town with an active cultural life and a healthy awareness of the need for good lectures. As a matter of fact, in this regard it seemed to me somewhat ahead of the capital itself, Kristiania.

"Of course you may carry my things," I said to the man. "Oh, by the way, I presume the hotel serves wine? Wine to drink with one's meal?"

"Wine? The best there is."

"Right. You can go now. I'll be along later. I must just pop into these newspaper offices."

The man looked as if he might know a thing or two so I took a chance on him:

"Which editor do you recommend? I can't be bothered to visit them all."

"Arentsen is the best man. Everyone goes to him."

Arentsen the editor was naturally not in his office, so I visited him at home. I told him my business, that I had come in the service of literature.

"Not much interest in such things here. We had a Swedish student come last year with a talk about everlasting peace. He lost money on it."

"I am going to talk about literature," I repeated.

"Yes," he said, "I realise that. I'm just warning you, you'll probably lose money on it."

Lose money on it? Priceless! Perhaps he thought I was a salesman travelling for a firm. I said merely:

"Is the large Workers" Hall available for hire?"

"No it isn't," he replied. "It's booked out for tomorrow evening by an anti-spiritualist. There are apes and wild beasts on the programme too. The only other venue I can suggest is the Park Pavilion."

"Do you recommend it?"

"It's very large. Spacious. The cost? Well, I don't know. It certainly won't cost you much. You'll have to speak to the committee."

I decided on the Park Pavilion. It sounded just right. Those Workers' Society halls were often such small, uncomfortable places. Who were the committee?

Carlsen the lawyer, so and so the furrier, and bookseller somebody else.

I set off for Carlsen the lawyer's house. He lived out in the country, and I walked and I walked until eventually the road came to an end. I told him my business, and that I wanted to hire the Park Pavilion. It sounded the perfect place for a unique event like a lecture on literature.

The lawyer thought for a moment, and then said he doubted that it was.

No? Was it really *so* big? Surely he could see for himself how unfortunate it would be if people had to be turned away at the door simply because there wasn't enough room for them inside.

But in fact the lawyer went on to advise me against the whole enterprise. There really wasn't much interest in such things here. Only last year we had a Swedish student . . .

"Yes yes, but his talk was about everlasting peace," I interrupted. "I'm going to talk about literature. Serious literature."

"In any case," he went on, "you've come at a bad time. An anti-spiritualist is doing a show at the Workers' Hall. He has apes and wild beasts with him."

I gave him a pitying smile. He seemed to believe what he said so I gave him up as hopeless.

"How much for the hire of the Park Pavilion?" I said curtly.

"Eight kroner," he replied. "I'll have to put it to the committee, but I can promise you an answer in two days' time. Informally I think I can safely say that the place is yours if you want it."

I did some quick mental arithmetic: two days' waiting would cost me three kroner, the hire of the pavilion eight, that was 11. A ticket-seller 12. An audience of 25 at 50 øre each would cover my entire outlay. The other couple of hundred who turned up would represent clear profit.

I agreed. The pavilion was hired.

At the hotel a maid asked:

"Do you want a room on the first or second floor?"

I replied quietly and modestly:

"I want a cheap room. The cheapest you have."

The maid looked me up and down, trying to work out if perhaps I was a gentleman who found his amusement in asking for cheap rooms. Wasn't I the one who had been asking the hotel porter about wine with the meals? Or was I being so modest in order to avoid embarrassing the hotel? Whatever, she opened a door. I caught my breath.

"Yes, it's empty all right," she said. "This is your room. Your bag's got put here already look."

There was no way out of it, so in I went. It was the finest room in the whole hotel.

"Where's the bed?"

"There. It's a sofa-bed. An ordinary bed in a room like this would spoil it. You just pull it out at night."

The maid left.

I was in a bad mood. My bag looked so scruffy in such surroundings, and after that long walk along the country roads my shoes were a mess. I swore out loud.

At once the maid popped her head round the door:

"Can I help you?"

Well how about that? All I have to do is open my mouth and a crowd of servants comes swarming in!

"No," I answered curtly. "I want some sandwiches."

She looks at me.

"Nothing hot?"

"No."

Then she understood. The stomach. It was spring. My bad time of the year.

When she came with the sandwiches she brought a wine-list too. The over-solicitous creature gave me no peace for the rest of the evening: "Would you like your blankets warmed?" "The bath's in there, if you want a bath . . ."

In the morning I hopped nervously out of bed and began dressing. I was freezing. Naturally, that damn sofa-bed had been much too short for me and I had slept badly. I rang. No one came. It must still be very early in the morning, I couldn't hear a sound from the streets, and when I was fully awake I realised that it was still not quite daylight.

I studied the room. It was the most elegant I had ever seen. With a sense of deepest foreboding I again rang, and then waited, up to my ankles in soft carpet. I was about to be stripped of every penny I had. Maybe I wouldn't even have enough to pay. In haste I began once again to count up how much I had. Then I hear footsteps outside and I stop.

But no one came. The footsteps were my imagination.

I started counting again, in a fearful state of uncertainty. Where was she now, that maid of yesterday, with her oppressive eagerness to be of service to me? Was the lazy creature still lying asleep somewhere, though it was now almost daylight?

At last she came, half-dressed, wearing just her shawl.

"Did you ring?"

"I would like the bill," I said with as much composure as possible.

"The bill?" Well that wasn't so easy. Madame was still asleep, it was only three o'clock. The maid stared at me, utterly confused. What sort of look was that to give a person? Was it any business of hers if I chose to leave the hotel at such an early hour?

"I can't help that," I said. "I want my bill now."

The maid left.

She was away an eternity. Compounding my unease was the thought that the room might be charged for by the hour, and that here I was wasting yet more of my money with all this useless waiting. I knew nothing about the way posh hotels are run and such a method of charging seemed highly likely to me. On top of that there was a notice above the hand-basin which said that any room not vacated by six o'clock in the evening would be charged for another day. Everything filled me with anxiety and spread confusion in my serious, literary head.

Finally the maid returned and knocked on the door:

Never, never will I forget fate's little joke that morning! Two kroner 70 øre – that was all! Nothing! A tip I might have given the maid to buy her hair-pins with! I tossed a few kroner onto the table – and then one more. "Keep the change, my friend!"

One had to show a certain amount of *savoir-faire*. Not to mention the fact that the maid deserved it, this rare and warm-hearted maid whom fate had de-posited in a Drammen hotel to be the butt of any traveller's whim. They don't make women like that any more, the race has died out. And how solicitous she was of me once she realised that she was dealing with a wealthy man:

"I'll get the porter to carry your bag."

"Certainly not! Certainly not!" I said, anxious to save her the bother. "It's just a carpet-bag, an old carpet-bag. I always have to have it with me when I'm away lecturing on literature. It's a little peculiarity of mine."

But my protests were in vain, the porter was ready and waiting for me out-side. As I came walking towards him he stared at my bag as though transfixed. Remarkable, the look such a man can give a bag, as if he's just burning up with the desire to be carrying it.

"I'll carry that," he said.

Surely I needed every penny I had left now? Was there any possibility of my coming into more money before giving my lecture? Thank you, I would carry the bag myself.

But the porter already had hold of it. That remarkably kind person didn't seem to find it any trouble at all. Payment seemed to be the last thing on his mind, and he carried it in such an innocent way, as though he was prepared to die for the owner of such a bag.

"Wait!" I called out and stopped. "Where do you think you're going with that bag?"

He smiled.

"That's for you to decide," he answered.

"Correct," said I. "That's for me to decide, not you."

We had already passed one bed-and-breakfast place in a basement-café and it was my idea to enquire for a room there. I had to get rid of the porter as quickly as possible, so that I could sneak back to the basement without him knowing.

I gave him a 50-øre piece.

Still he held his hand out.

"I carried the bag for you yesterday too," he said.

"That *is* for yesterday," I said.

"And I've just carried it now too," he said.

It was highway robbery.

"And this is for today," I said, tossing another 50-øre piece into his palm. "Now please get out of my sight."

The porter went. But he looked back several times and kept his eye on me.

I made my way to a bench and sat down. It was rather chilly, but once the sun had risen it warmed up. I dozed off and must have slept for quite a while, for when I awoke the street was full of people and smoke was curling up from the chimneys. I walked back to the basement-café and made an arrangement with the woman there. Bed-and-breakfast 50 øre per night.

After the two-day wait was over I again walked out to Carlsen the lawyer's house in the country. Again he advised me to cancel the lecture, but I would on no account be talked out of it. In the meantime I had paid for an insertion in Arentsen's newspaper giving the date, place and topic of my lecture.

When I then tried to pay for the pavilion, which would have left me temporarily without funds, Carlsen, a remarkable man, said:

"There's no need to pay until after the lecture."

I misunderstood him and took offence.

"Are you perhaps under the impression that I haven't got the eight kroner?"

"Goodness me no! But it's by no means certain you'll actually get the use of the pavilion, and if that happens then obviously there will be nothing to pay."

"I have already advertised the lecture," I told him.

He nodded.

"I saw that," he answered. Shortly afterwards he said:

"Will you still speak if less than fifty people turn up?"

I found this question actually rather offensive, but after thinking it over I said that fifty would be a poor showing, but that yes I would still do it.

"But not for just ten?"

At this I burst out laughing.

"You will forgive me. There are limits."

We spoke no more about it and I did not pay for the pavilion. Carlsen and I then began talking about literature. He rose in my estimation, and was clearly an interesting man, even though his views and opinions suffered by comparison with my own.

When we parted company he wished me a really good turn-out for the lecture that evening.

I returned to my basement in excellent spirits. The battleground was prepared – earlier in the day I had given a man 50 øre to walk round handing out my 500 cards, so now the whole town knew about the event.

My mood became strangely elevated, and as I contemplated the important task I was about to perform I became dissatisfied with my little basement home and its wretched occupants. Everyone wanted to know who I was and why I was living there. The landlady, the woman behind the counter, explained that I was a learned man who spent his whole day writing and studying and that people were not to bother me with questions. She was invaluable to me. The people who used the café were hungry working men and street porters in shirtsleeves who popped in to get themselves a cup of hot coffee or a lump of black pudding spread with butter and cheese. Sometimes they were unpleasant and abused the landlady because the waffles were stale or the eggs too small. When they found out I was going to lecture in the Park Pavilion itself they wanted to know how much tickets were. Some of them said they were interested in hearing me, but 50 øre was too much, and they began debating the ticket-price with me. I promised myself not to allow such people to upset me; they had absolutely no breeding at all.

There was a man in the room next to mine who spoke a horrible mixture of Swedish and Norwegian. The landlady referred to him as "the director". He always caused a stir when he breezed into the dining-room, not least because of his habit of dusting the seat of his chair with his handkerchief before sitting down. He was a real dandy, with an expensive way about him. I noticed that when he ordered a sandwich he was always most particular that it be served "on fresh bread and with best butter".

"Is it you who's giving the lecture?" he asked me.

"Yes he's the one," answered the landlady.

"You're taking a big chance," he said, continuing to address himself to me. "You don't even advertise. Haven't you seen the way I advertise?"

It dawned on me who he was: the anti-spiritualist, the man with the apes and the wild beasts.

"I advertise with posters *this* big," he went on. "I stick them up all over the place, wherever there's room. Big writing on them. You must have seen them. I've got drawings of the beasts on them too."

I pointed out that my lecture was on the subject of literature. Art, in a word. Intellectual matters.

"Doesn't make a damn bit of difference!" he scoffed. And then he compounded his insolence by saying that it would be a different matter if I worked for him. "I need a man to introduce the animals and I would prefer a stranger who isn't known to the people here. If someone they know gets up the audience starts shouting "Look, look, it's only Petterson, what does old Petterson know about wild beasts?"

I turned away in silent contempt, unwilling to dignify such shameless talk with a response.

"I'll pay you five kroner a night," he continued. "Think on it."

At this I rose from my seat and left the room. I had no choice. Clearly the director was afraid of the competition; worried that I would steal his audience away from him he was looking to make some sort of deal with me, to buy me off. Never! I said to myself. Never will I allow myself to be seduced into betraying the world of art. Mine is the way of the ideal.

At seven o'clock I carefully brushed my clothes and set off for the Park Pavilion. I knew my lecture well and my head was ringing with the lofty and elegant phrases I would be using. I felt a powerful certainty that it would go down well and in my mind I could hear already the telegraph wires jangling with the news of my success.

It rained. The weather was perhaps not so kind as it might have been. But a public hungry for literature would not allow themselves to be put off by a drop of rain. And the streets were full of people, couples walking arm in arm beneath umbrellas. It struck me that they were all going in the opposite direction to me, which is to say, not in the direction of the Park Pavilion. Where did they think they were going? Hm, must be the plebs on their way to see the apes at the Workers' Hall.

The ticket-seller was at his post.

"Anyone here yet?" I asked.

"Not yet," he answered. "But there's a good half-hour to go."

I went inside and took a walk round the massive auditorium, my footsteps echoing like hoof-beats. Ah God, if there were a full house sitting there now, row upon row of heads, men and women squashed together, all just waiting for the speaker! But not a soul!

I waited out the long half-hour. No one came. I wandered out and asked the ticket-seller what he made of the situation. He was cautious, but optimistic. In his opinion it wasn't lecturing weather, people didn't like going out when it was raining so heavily. Anyway, they would probably all turn up at the last minute.

And we waited.

At last a man came hurrying through the pouring rain, paid his 50 øre and went inside.

"Here they come," said the ticket-seller, nodding his head. "Drammen people have this terrible habit of turning up for things at the last minute."

We waited. No one else came. Eventually the only spectator joined us outside.

"Beastly weather," he said.

I recognised Carlsen the lawyer.

"I don't think you're going to get anyone this evening," he said, "It's pelting down!" Then, noticing my downcast expression, he added:

"I knew it when I saw the barometer. It sank much too quickly. That's the reason I advised you not to give your lecture."

But the ticket-seller was still on my side.

"We should wait another half-hour," he said. "Bound to be at least 20 or 30 turn up at the very last moment."

"I don't think so," said the lawyer, buttoning up his coat. "And while I remember," he added, "there is, naturally, nothing to pay for the hire of the pavilion."

He doffed his hat, said goodbye and left.

The ticket-seller and I waited another half-hour and continued to discuss the situation. It was an embarrassing business and I felt thoroughly humiliated. On top of that the lawyer had gone off without getting his money back. I was all for going after him, but the ticket-seller advised against it.

"I'll keep it," he said. "That way you only owe me another 50 øre."

But I gave him another krone. He'd stuck to his post and I wanted to show my appreciation. He thanked me warmly, we shook hands and off he went.

I wandered home, a beaten man. Numb with shame and disappointment I drifted through the streets scarcely knowing where my feet were taking me. To add to my distress I realised at a certain point that I no longer had the money for the train back to Kristiania.

The rain kept falling.

Presently I passed a large building. From the street I could see the lights of a box-office in the foyer. It was the Workers" Hall. Latecomers were still turning up, buying their tickets and disappearing through the great doors into the hall. I asked the ticket-seller how many were inside. The house was almost full.

That damned director. He'd beaten me in style.

I sneaked back to my lodgings and went quietly to bed, with nothing to eat and nothing to drink.

In the middle of the night there was a knock on the door and a man came in carrying a candle. It was the director.

"How did the lecture go?" he asked.

Under any other circumstances I would have thrown him out straightaway. Now, however, I was too crushed to put up any kind of front at all and I said merely that I had cancelled it.

He smiled.

"It wasn't the right weather for a lecture on serious literature," I explained. He should have been able to see that for himself.

He was still smiling.

"The barometer just collapsed," I said.

"I had standing-room only," he replied. Then he stopped smiling, apologised for disturbing me and explained his errand.

It was a most curious errand: he had come once again to offer me work as the presenter of his beasts.

I was mortally offended and asked him, very firmly, kindly to leave me in peace.

Instead he sat down on my bed with the candle in his hand.

"We can at least discuss it," he said. He explained that the local man he had hired to present the beasts had indeed been recognised by the audience. He himself – the director – had gone down extremely well with his exposure of the spiritualists' trickery; but his speaker, the man from Drammen, had ruined all his good work. "Look, it's Bjørn Pedersen," people shouted. "Where d'you get the badger from, Bjørn?" And Bjørn Pedersen, keeping to the script, explained that it wasn't a badger at all but a hyena from the African bush that had already eaten three missionaries. Then the people booed and jeered because they thought he was trying to make fools of them. "I don't understand it," said the director. "I blackened his face and put a wig on his head and still they recognised him."

I couldn't see what concern all this was of mine and I turned over to face the wall.

"Think on it!" said the director before he left. "I might stretch it to six kroner a night if you're good."

Never would I be a party to such vulgarity! A man had his honour to consider.

The following day the director approached me and asked me to look over the speech about the beasts, correct the grammar, brush up the language here and there. He offered me two kroner.

In spite of all, I accepted. I was doing the man a favour really, and it was, after all, a service in the cause of literature. Moreover, I needed the two kroner. Before commencing, however, I warned him in the strongest possible terms not to mention my involvement to anyone.

I spent all day on it, reworking the speech from beginning to end, injecting life and humour into the descriptions, adorning it with similes, warming more and more to my task. It was a work of art in itself to be able to make so much out of a few wretched animals. Late in the evening, when I read it out to the director, he said he had never heard a speech like it in his life, it had made a remarkable impression on him. In recognition of this he paid me not two but three kroner.

This both moved and encouraged me, and to some extent restored my faith in my literary mission.

"If only I had someone good enough to deliver such a lecture," he sighed. "But where is such a man to be found in Drammen?"

I began thinking. It really would be a disaster if a speech like that were to fall into the hands of some Bjørn Pedersen or other to mutilate with his atrocious delivery. The thought was almost unendurable.

"I might, perhaps, on certain conditions, consent to deliver the lecture," I said.

The director sat up.

"What conditions? I'll pay you seven kroner," he said.

"That's fine. My main condition is that it must remain a secret between you and me who the speaker is."

"I give you my word."

"Because as I'm sure you'll understand," I said, "a man with my mission in life can hardly let it get about that he gives talks on wild beasts."

No, he understood that.

"And of course, if it were not effectively my own composition from start to finish then I would not even contemplate doing it."

No, he understood that too.

"In that case I am quite prepared to help you out."

The director thanked me.

At seven o'clock we went together to the Workers' Hall for me to be shown the animals and given some basic instruction in how to deal with them.

There were two apes, a turtle, a bear, two wolf cubs and a badger.

There was nothing whatever in my "presentation" about wolves and badgers, though it abounded with references to a certain species of hyena from the African bush, a rare pine marten, and a sable, both "as mentioned in the Bible", and an enormous American grizzly. I had prepared an excellent joke about the turtle, that she was a real lady who would eat nothing but turtle soup.

"Where are the sable and the marten?" I asked.

"Here!" cried the director, pointing to the wolf cubs.

"And the hyena?"

He pointed decisively to the badger: "Here is the hyena."

I grew heated and angry. I said:

"This will not do at all. This is false pretences. I must believe in the truth of what I'm saying, with all my heart and soul."

"Let's not fall out over a trifle like this," said the director. He produced a bottle of brandy from somewhere and poured me a drink. To show that I had nothing personal against him, that it was just his dirty dealings I objected to, I accepted. We drank together.

"Please don't drop me in it," he said. "It's such a wonderful speech, and the beasts aren't that bad, not really that bad at all. Look at this great bear here. Give the speech, everything'll be all right."

The first spectators were filing into the hall and the director was becoming more and more anxious. His fate was in my hands, and it would become me to use my power with discretion. Moreover, I realised that it would be impossible to make the necessary alterations to my speech in the short time remaining before the show. And I did not see how anyone could put as much into the description of a badger as into an account of the ways of the ferocious hyena. Clearly, any alterations would only weaken my work to a degree I found indefensible. I informed the director of this.

He understood completely, and poured me another drink.

The performance began in front of a full house. The director himself – the anti-spiritualist – astounded everyone with his tricks. He pulled a string of hand-kerchiefs out of his nose, produced the Jack of Clubs from the pocket of an old woman sitting near the back of the house, and made a table walk across the floor without touching it. Finally he dematerialised himself, disappearing through a trapdoor in the floor of the stage. The audience went wild, the applause was thunderous. Now it was the turn of the beasts. The director brought them on one at a time, and it was my task to describe them.

I realised at once that I could not hope to emulate the director's success; however, I did hope that the more discerning members of the public might appreciate my presentation. In this I was not disappointed.

Once the turtle was out of the way I had only land-dwelling animals to deal with, and in my speech I had linked them all with the story of Noah, who kept two of every kind of animal that was unable to live in the water. But things dragged a bit and the audience's good mood seemed to have deserted it. The marten and the sable didn't get the recognition they deserved, not even when I mentioned how many expensive furs from the backs of these animals the Queen of Sheba was wearing when she visited King Solomon. And then gradually things began to improve. Inspired by my biblical subject-matter, and the two glasses of brandy, my speech grew colourful, rich, passionate. I threw my script aside, I improvised, extemporised, and when I was done the whole house applauded and there were even a few cries of "Bravo!"

"There's a brandy behind the curtain!" the director whispered to me.

I stepped back and located the glass. The bottle stood beside it. I sat down on a chair for a moment.

Meanwhile the director had brought out another animal and was waiting for me. I helped myself to another brandy and remained seated. The wait was obviously too much for the director, who presently began a presentation himself in his frightful mangle of a language. To my horror I realised that he was talking about the hyena; he even made a slip of the tongue and called it a badger. I rose indignantly and took the stage, gesturing for the director to step aside, and took over the presentation myself. The hyena was the climax of the whole show and I would have to surpass myself to rescue it now. I scoffed at the director, said he'd never seen a hyena in his life, and then swept into an account of the dissolute life of this savage beast. The brandies had their effect and my enthusiasm rose to dizzying heights. I could hear the passion and the fire in my own words as the hyena stood at the director's feet, blinking patiently with his little eyes. "Hold him tight!" I shouted to the director. "He's getting ready to pounce! He's after my guts! Keep your pistol cocked, he might break free!"

I must have alarmed the director himself. He pulled the hyena towards him with a jerk, the leash snapped, and the beast slipped between his legs. A great cry went up from the women and children out front and half the audience rose from their seats. For a moment the tension was unbearable. Then the hyena ran away from us with little tripping steps, across the stage and back into his little cage. The director slammed the door after him with a clang.

We all breathed out, and I concluded the presentation. This time we had been lucky, I said. After the show, this very evening, a heavy iron chain would be obtained for the monster. I bowed and stepped back.

The applause came like thunder. There were cries for the speaker, the speaker. I went on again and took another bow and if the truth be told I went down very well. The audience were still clapping as they went out of the door. Although there were some who were laughing.

The director was pleased and thanked me warmly for my support. He could certainly look forward to many more full houses.

A man was waiting for me outside as I left the hall. It was my ticket-seller from the Park Pavilion. He had heard the whole thing and was most enthusiastic and loud in his praise of my skills as a public speaker. On no account was I to give up the idea of lecturing in the pavilion, now was the time to advertise, now that people had heard me and knew what I could do. A repeat of the talk on the hyena, for example, would go down particularly well, especially if I brought the animal along with me.

But the following day that rascal of a director refused to pay me unless I gave an undertaking in writing to appear on his show the next evening. Otherwise I could sue him for it, he said. The cheat, the scoundrel! Eventually we reached a compromise under which he paid me five kroner. With the three he had already given me that made eight, which was enough to pay my fare back to Kristiania. He insisted on keeping my written speech, though I protested long about this, painfully aware of the abuse it would encounter. On the other hand it was undeniably his property and he had paid for it, so in the end I gave in. He was so inordinately appreciative of it.

"I've never heard a speech like it before," he said. "I remember yesterday, it gripped me the way no sermon ever has."

"You see?" I said. "That's the power literature has to move men's minds."

These were my last words to him. In the afternoon I caught the train back to Kristiania.

CREE QUEERY AND MYSY DROLLY

J.M. Barrie

Inside the tiny human frame of **J.M. Barrie** (1860–1937) was a literary
giant struggling to get out. Around five feet, three and a half inches tall,
he was born in Angus to a weaver, the ninth child of ten. Encouraged by
the family towards the ministry, he was educated at Glasgow Academy
and then the University of Edinburgh. He began writing journalism,
stories and novels, then plays; first parodying Ibsen, but soon work
like *The Admirable Crichton* and *Peter Pan* propelled him to become
one of the most successful writers of his generation. His emotional life
was more arid, but all is forgiven as he gave the copyright to his most
successful work to Great Ormond Street Hospital. He wrote, "We are
all of us failures, at least, the best of us are."

The children used to fling stones at Grinder Queery because he loved his
mother. I never heard the Grinder's real name. He and his mother were
Queery and Drolly, contemptuously so called, and they answered to
these names. I remember Cree best as a battered old weaver, who bent forward
as he walked, with his arms hanging limp as if ready to grasp the shafts of the
barrow behind which it was his life to totter up hill and down hill, a rope of
yarn suspended round his shaking neck and fastened to the shafts, assisting
him to bear the yoke and slowly strangling him. By and by there came a time
when the barrow and the weaver seemed both palsy-stricken, and Cree, gasping for breath, would stop in the middle of a brae, unable to push his load over
a stone. Then he laid himself down behind it to prevent the barrow's slipping
back. On those occasions only the barefooted boys who jeered at the panting
weaver could put new strength into his shrivelled arms. They did it by telling
him that he and Mysy would have to go to the "poorshouse" after all, at which
the gray old man would wince, as if "joukin" from a blow, and, shuddering,
rise and, with a desperate effort, gain the top of the incline. Small blame perhaps attached to Cree if, as he neared his grave, he grew a little dottle. His
loads of yarn frequently took him past the workhouse, and his eyelids quivered
as he drew near. Boys used to gather round the gate in anticipation of his coming, and make a feint of driving him inside. Cree, when he observed them, sat
down on his barrow-shafts terrified to approach, and I see them now pointing
to the workhouse till he left his barrow on the road and hobbled away, his legs
cracking as he ran.

It is strange to know that there was once a time when Cree was young and straight, a callant who wore a flower in his button-hole and tried to be a hero for a maiden's sake.

Before Cree settled down as a weaver, he was knife and scissor grinder for three counties, and Mysy, his mother, accompanied him wherever he went. Mysy trudged alongside him till her eyes grew dim and her limbs failed her, and then Cree was told that she must be sent to the pauper's home. After that a pitiable and beautiful sight was to be seen. Grinder Queery, already a feeble man, would wheel his grindstone along the long high-road, leaving Mysy behind. He took the stone on a few hundred yards, and then, hiding it by the roadside in a ditch or behind a paling, returned for his mother. Her he led – sometimes he almost carried her – to the place where the grindstone lay, and thus by double journeys kept her with him. Every one said that Mysy's death would be a merciful release – every one but Cree.

Cree had been a grinder from his youth, having learned the trade from his father, but he gave it up when Mysy became almost blind. For a time he had to leave her in Thrums with Dan'l Wilkie's wife, and find employment himself in Tilliedrum. Mysy got me to write several letters for her to Cree, and she cried while telling me what to say. I never heard either of them use a term of endearment to the other, but all Mysy could tell me to put in writing was: "Oh, my son Cree; oh, my beloved son; oh, I have no one but you; oh, thou God watch over my Cree!" On one of these occasions Mysy put into my hands a paper, which she said would perhaps help me to write the letter. It had been drawn up by Cree many years before, when he and his mother had been compelled to part for a time, and I saw from it that he had been trying to teach Mysy to write. The paper consisted of phrases such as "Dear son Cree," "Loving mother," "I am takin' my food weel," "Yesterday," "Blankets," "The peats is near done," "Mr. Dishart," "Come home, Cree." The grinder had left this paper with his mother, and she had written letters to him from it.

When Dan'l Wilkie objected to keeping a cranky old body like Mysy in his house, Cree came back to Thrums and took a single room with a hand-loom in it. The flooring was only lumpy earth, with sacks spread over it to protect Mysy's feet. The room contained two dilapidated old coffin-beds, a dresser, a high-backed arm-chair, several three-legged stools, and two tables, of which one could be packed away beneath the other. In one corner stood the wheel at which Cree had to fill his own pirns. There was a plate-rack on one wall, and near the chimney-piece hung the wag-at-the-wall clock, the time-piece that was common-est in Thrums at that time, and that got this name because its exposed pendulum swung along the wall. The two windows in the room faced each other on op-posite walls, and were so small that even a child might have stuck in trying to crawl through them. They opened on hinges, like a door. In the wall of the dark passage leading from the outer door into the room was a recess where a pan and pitcher of water always stood wedded, as it were, and a little hole, known as the "bole," in the wall opposite the fire-place contained Cree's library. It consisted of Baxter's "Saints' Rest," Harvey's "Meditations," the "Pilgrim's Progress," a work on folk-lore, and several Bibles. The saut-backet, or salt-bucket, stood at the end of the fender, which was half of an old cart-wheel. Here Cree worked, whistling "Ower the watter for Chairlie" to make Mysy think that he was as gay as a mavis. Mysy grew querulous in her old age, and up to the end she thought of poor, done Cree as a handsome gallant. Only by weaving far on into the night could Cree earn as much as six shillings a week. He began at six o'clock in the morning, and worked until midnight by the light of his cruizey. The cruizey was all the lamp Thrums had in those days, though it is only to be seen in use now in a few old-world houses in the glens. It is an ungainly thing in iron, the size of a man's palm, and shaped not unlike the palm when contracted and deepened to hold a liquid. Whale-oil, lying open in the mould, was used, and the wick was a rash with the green skin peeled off. These rashes were sold by herd-boys at a halfpenny the bundle, but Cree gathered his own wicks. The rashes skin readily when you know how to do it. The iron mould was placed inside another of the same shape, but slightly larger, for in time the oil dripped through the iron, and the whole was then hung by a cleek or hook close to the person using it. Even with three wicks it gave but a stime of light, and never allowed the weaver to see more than the half of his loom at a time. Sometimes Cree used threads for wicks. He was too dull a man to have many visitors, but Mr. Dishart called occasionally and reproved him for telling his mother lies. The lies Cree told Mysy were that he was sharing the meals he won for her, and that he wore the overcoat which he had exchanged years before for a blanket to keep her warm.

There was a terrible want of spirit about Grinder Queery. Boys used to climb on to his stone roof with clods of damp earth in their hands, which they dropped down the chimney. Mysy was bedridden by this time, and the smoke threatened to choke her; so Cree, instead of chasing his persecutors, bargained with them. He gave them fly-hooks which he had busked himself, and when he had nothing left to give he tried to flatter them into dealing gently with Mysy by talking to them as men. One night it went through the town that Mysy now lay in bed all day listening for her summons to depart. According to her ideas this would come in the form of a tapping at the window, and their intention was to forestall the spirit. Dite Gow's boy, who is now a grown man, was hoisted up to one of the little windows, and he has always thought of Mysy since as he saw her then for the last time. She lay sleeping, so far as he could see, and Cree sat by the fireside looking at her.

Every one knew that there was seldom a fire in that house unless Mysy was cold. Cree seemed to think that the fire was getting low. In the little closet, which, with the kitchen, made up his house, was a corner shut off from the rest of the room by a few boards, and behind this he kept his peats. There was a similar receptacle for potatoes in the kitchen. Cree wanted to get another peat for the fire without disturbing Mysy. First he took off his boots, and made for the peats on tip-toe. His shadow was cast on the bed, however, so he next got down on his knees and crawled softly into the closet. With the peat in his hands he returned in the same way, glancing every moment at the bed where Mysy lay. Though Tammy Gow's face was pressed against a broken window, he did not hear Cree putting that peat on the fire. Some say that Mysy heard, but pretended not to do so for her son's sake; that she realized the deception he played on her and had not the heart to undeceive him. But it would be too sad to believe that. The boys left Cree alone that night.

The old weaver lived on alone in that solitary house after Mysy left him, and by and by the story went abroad that he was saving money. At first no one believed this except the man who told it, but there seemed after all to be something in it. You had only to hit Cree's trouser pocket to hear the money chinking, for he was afraid to let it out of his clutch. Those who sat on dykes with him when his day's labor was over said that the wearer kept his hand all the time in his pocket, and that they saw his lips move as he counted his hoard by letting it slip through his fingers. So there were boys who called "Miser Queery" after him instead of Grinder, and asked him whether he was saving up to keep himself from the workhouse.

But we had all done Cree wrong. It came out on his death-bed what he had been storing up his money for. Grinder, according to the doctor, died of getting a good meal from a friend of his earlier days after being accustomed to starve on potatoes and a very little oatmeal indeed. The day before he died this friend sent him half a sovereign, and when Grinder saw it he sat up excitedly in his bed and pulled his corduroys from beneath his pillow. The woman who, out of kindness, attended him in his last illness, looked on curiously while Cree added the sixpences and coppers in his pocket to the half-sovereign. After all they only made some two pounds, but a look of peace came into Cree's eyes as he told the woman to take it all to a shop in the town. Nearly twelve years previously Jamie Lownie had lent him two pounds, and though the money was never asked for, it preyed on Cree's mind that he was in debt. He paid off all he owed, and so Cree's life was not, I think, a failure.

THE LADY WITH THE DOG

Anton Chekhov

Anton Chekhov (1860–1904) was a doctor who dabbled with literature to dazzling effect. He stated: "Medicine is my legal wife but literature my mistress." He wrote plays and short stories. He died too soon. Anyone interested in knowing more should read V.S. Pritchett's biography of him, or simply read the epigraph (from a letter to his wife, the actress, Olga Knipper) to Julian Barnes' *Flaubert's Parrot* and wonder at the wisdom of the man.

I

IT was said that a new person had appeared on the sea-front: a lady with a little dog. Dmitri Dmitritch Gurov, who had by then been a fortnight at Yalta, and so was fairly at home there, had begun to take an interest in new arrivals. Sitting in Verney's pavilion, he saw, walking on the sea-front, a fair-haired young lady of medium height, wearing a béret; a white Pomeranian dog was running behind her.

And afterwards he met her in the public gardens and in the square several times a day. She was walking alone, always wearing the same béret, and always with the same white dog; no one knew who she was, and every one called her simply "the lady with the dog."

"If she is here alone without a husband or friends, it wouldn't be amiss to make her acquaintance," Gurov reflected.

He was under forty, but he had a daughter already twelve years old, and two sons at school. He had been married young, when he was a student in his second year, and by now his wife seemed half as old again as he. She was a tall, erect woman with dark eyebrows, staid and dignified, and, as she said of herself, intellectual. She read a great deal, used phonetic spelling, called her husband, not Dmitri, but Dimitri, and he secretly considered her unintelligent, narrow, inelegant, was afraid of her, and did not like to be at home. He had begun being unfaithful to her long ago – had been unfaithful to her often, and, probably on that account, almost always spoke ill of women, and when they were talked about in his presence, used to call them "the lower race."

It seemed to him that he had been so schooled by bitter experience that he might call them what he liked, and yet he could not get on for two days together without "the lower race." In the society of men he was bored and not himself, with them he was cold and uncommunicative; but when he was in the company of women he felt free, and knew what to say to them and how to behave; and he was at ease with them even when he was silent. In his appearance, in his character, in his whole nature, there was something attractive and elusive which allured women and disposed them in his favour; he knew that, and some force seemed to draw him, too, to them.

Experience often repeated, truly bitter experience, had taught him long ago that with decent people, especially Moscow people – always slow to move and irresolute – every intimacy, which at first so agreeably diversifies life and appears a light and charming adventure, inevitably grows into a regular problem of extreme intricacy, and in the long run the situation becomes unbearable. But at every fresh meeting with an interesting woman this experience seemed to slip out of his memory, and he was eager for life, and everything seemed simple and amusing.

One evening he was dining in the gardens, and the lady in the béret came up slowly to take the next table. Her expression, her gait, her dress, and the way she did her hair told him that she was a lady, that she was married, that she was in Yalta for the first time and alone, and that she was dull there. . . . The stories told of the immorality in such places as Yalta are to a great extent untrue; he despised them, and knew that such stories were for the most part made up by persons who would themselves have been glad to sin if they had been able; but when the lady sat down at the next table three paces from him, he remembered these tales of easy conquests, of trips to the mountains, and the tempting thought of a swift, fleeting love affair, a romance with an unknown woman, whose name he did not know, suddenly took possession of him.

He beckoned coaxingly to the Pomeranian, and when the dog came up to him he shook his finger at it. The Pomeranian growled: Gurov shook his finger at it again.

The lady looked at him and at once dropped her eyes.

"He doesn't bite," she said, and blushed.

"May I give him a bone?" he asked; and when she nodded he asked courteously, "Have you been long in Yalta?"

"Five days."

"And I have already dragged out a fortnight here."

There was a brief silence.

"Time goes fast, and yet it is so dull here!" she said, not looking at him.

"That's only the fashion to say it is dull here. A provincial will live in Belyov or Zhidra and not be dull, and when he comes here it's 'Oh, the dulness! Oh, the dust!' One would think he came from Grenada."

She laughed. Then both continued eating in silence, like strangers, but after dinner they walked side by side; and there sprang up between them the light jesting conversation of people who are free and satisfied, to whom it does not matter where they go or what they talk about. They walked and talked of the strange light on the sea: the water was of a soft warm lilac hue, and there was a golden streak from the moon upon it. They talked of how sultry it was after a hot day. Gurov told her that he came from Moscow, that he had taken his degree in Arts, but had a post in a bank; that he had trained as an opera-singer, but had given it up, that he owned two houses in Moscow. . . . And from her he learnt that she had grown up in Petersburg, but had lived in S—— since her marriage two years before, that she was staying another month in Yalta, and that her husband, who needed a holiday too, might perhaps come and fetch her. She was not sure whether her husband had a post in a Crown Department or under the Provincial Council – and was amused by her own ignorance. And Gurov learnt, too, that she was called Anna Sergeyevna.

Afterwards he thought about her in his room at the hotel – thought she would certainly meet him next day; it would be sure to happen. As he got into bed he thought how lately she had been a girl at school, doing lessons like his own daughter; he recalled the diffidence, the angularity, that was still manifest in her laugh and her manner of talking with a stranger. This must have been the first time in her life she had been alone in surroundings in which she was followed, looked at, and spoken to merely from a secret motive which she could hardly fail to guess. He recalled her slender, delicate neck, her lovely grey eyes.

"There's something pathetic about her, anyway," he thought, and fell asleep.

II

A week had passed since they had made acquaintance. It was a holiday. It was sultry indoors, while in the street the wind whirled the dust round and round, and blew people's hats off. It was a thirsty day, and Gurov often went into the pavilion, and pressed Anna Sergeyevna to have syrup and water or an ice. One did not know what to do with oneself.

In the evening when the wind had dropped a little, they went out on the groyne to see the steamer come in. There were a great many people walking about the harbour; they had gathered to welcome some one, bringing bouquets. And two peculiarities of a well-dressed Yalta crowd were very conspicuous: the elderly ladies were dressed like young ones, and there were great numbers of generals.

Owing to the roughness of the sea, the steamer arrived late, after the sun had set, and it was a long time turning about before it reached the groyne. Anna Sergeyevna looked through her lorgnette at the steamer and the passengers as though looking for acquaintances, and when she turned to Gurov her eyes were shining. She talked a great deal and asked disconnected questions, forgetting next moment what she had asked; then she dropped her lorgnette in the crush.

The festive crowd began to disperse; it was too dark to see people's faces. The wind had completely dropped, but Gurov and Anna Sergeyevna still stood as though waiting to see some one else come from the steamer. Anna Sergeyevna was silent now, and sniffed the flowers without looking at Gurov.

"The weather is better this evening," he said. "Where shall we go now? Shall we drive somewhere?"

She made no answer.

Then he looked at her intently, and all at once put his arm round her and kissed her on the lips, and breathed in the moisture and the fragrance of the flowers; and he immediately looked round him, anxiously wondering whether any one had seen them.

"Let us go to your hotel," he said softly. And both walked quickly.

The room was close and smelt of the scent she had bought at the Japanese shop. Gurov looked at her and thought: "What different people one meets in the world!"

From the past he preserved memories of careless, good-natured women, who loved cheerfully and were grateful to him for the happiness he gave them, however brief it might be; and of women like his wife who loved without any genuine feeling, with superfluous phrases, affectedly, hysterically, with an expression that suggested that it was not love nor passion, but something more significant; and of two or three others, very beautiful, cold women, on whose faces he had caught a glimpse of a rapacious expression – an obstinate desire to snatch from life more than it could give, and these were capricious, unreflecting, domineering, unintelligent women not in their first youth, and when Gurov grew cold to them their beauty excited his hatred, and the lace on their linen seemed to him like scales.

But in this case there was still the diffidence, the angularity of inexperienced youth, an awkward feeling; and there was a sense of consternation as though some one had suddenly knocked at the door. The attitude of Anna Sergeyevna – "the lady with the dog" – to what had happened was somehow peculiar, very grave, as though it were her fall – so it seemed, and it was strange and inappropriate. Her face dropped and faded, and on both sides of it her long hair hung down mournfully; she mused in a dejected attitude like "the woman who was a sinner" in an old-fashioned picture.

"It's wrong," she said. "You will be the first to despise me now."

There was a water-melon on the table. Gurov cut himself a slice and began eating it without haste. There followed at least half an hour of silence.

Anna Sergeyevna was touching; there was about her the purity of a good, simple woman who had seen little of life. The solitary candle burning on the table threw a faint light on her face, yet it was clear that she was very unhappy.

"How could I despise you?" asked Gurov. "You don't know what you are saying."

"God forgive me," she said, and her eyes filled with tears. "It's awful."

"You seem to feel you need to be forgiven."

"Forgiven? No. I am a bad, low woman; I despise myself and don't attempt to justify myself. It's not my husband but myself I have deceived. And not only just now; I have been deceiving myself for a long time. My husband may be a good, honest man, but he is a flunkey! I don't know what he does there, what his work is, but I know he is a flunkey! I was twenty when I was married to him. I have been tormented by curiosity; I wanted something better. 'There must be a different sort of life,' I said to myself. I wanted to live! To live, to live! . . . I was fired by curiosity . . . you don't understand it, but, I swear to God, I could not control myself; something happened to me: I could not be restrained. I told my husband I was ill, and came here. . . . And here I have been walking about as though I were dazed, like a mad creature; . . . and now I have become a vulgar, contemptible woman whom any one may despise."

Gurov felt bored already, listening to her. He was irritated by the naïve tone, by this remorse, so unexpected and inopportune; but for the tears in her eyes, he might have thought she was jesting or playing a part.

"I don't understand," he said softly. "What is it you want?"

She hid her face on his breast and pressed close to him.

"Believe me, believe me, I beseech you . . . " she said. "I love a pure, honest life, and sin is loathsome to me. I don't know what I am doing. Simple people say: 'The Evil One has beguiled me.' And I may say of myself now that the Evil One has beguiled me."

"Hush, hush! . . . " he muttered.

He looked at her fixed, scared eyes, kissed her, talked softly and affectionately, and by degrees she was comforted, and her gaiety returned; they both began laughing.

Afterwards when they went out there was not a soul on the sea-front. The town with its cypresses had quite a deathlike air, but the sea still broke noisily on the shore; a single barge was rocking on the waves, and a lantern was blinking sleepily on it.

They found a cab and drove to Oreanda.

"I found out your surname in the hall just now: it was written on the board – Von Diderits," said Gurov. "Is your husband a German?"

"No; I believe his grandfather was a German, but he is an Orthodox Russian himself."

At Oreanda they sat on a seat not far from the church, looked down at the sea, and were silent. Yalta was hardly visible through the morning mist; white clouds stood motionless on the mountain-tops. The leaves did not stir on the trees, grasshoppers chirruped, and the monotonous hollow sound of the sea rising up from below, spoke of the peace, of the eternal sleep awaiting us. So it must have sounded when there was no Yalta, no Oreanda here; so it sounds now, and it will sound as indifferently and monotonously when we are all no more. And in this constancy, in this complete indifference to the life and death of each of us, there lies hid, perhaps, a pledge of our eternal salvation, of the unceasing movement of life upon earth, of unceasing progress towards perfection. Sitting beside a young woman who in the dawn seemed so lovely, soothed and spellbound in these magical surroundings – the sea, mountains, clouds, the open sky – Gurov thought how in reality everything is beautiful in this world when one reflects: everything except what we think or do ourselves when we forget our human dignity and the higher aims of our existence.

A man walked up to them – probably a keeper – looked at them and walked away. And this detail seemed mysterious and beautiful, too. They saw a steamer come from Theodosia, with its lights out in the glow of dawn.

"There is dew on the grass," said Anna Sergeyevna, after a silence.

"Yes. It's time to go home."

They went back to the town.

Then they met every day at twelve o'clock on the sea-front, lunched and dined together, went for walks, admired the sea. She complained that she slept badly, that her heart throbbed violently; asked the same questions, troubled now by jealousy and now by the fear that he did not respect her sufficiently. And often in the square or gardens, when there was no one near them, he suddenly drew her to him and kissed her passionately. Complete idleness, these kisses in broad daylight while he looked round in dread of some one's seeing them, the heat, the smell of the sea, and the continual passing to and fro before him of idle, well-dressed, well-fed people, made a new man of him; he told Anna Sergeyevna how beautiful she was, how fascinating. He was impatiently passionate, he would not move a step away from her, while she was often pensive and continually urged him to confess that he did not respect her, did not love her in the least, and thought of her as nothing but a common woman. Rather late almost every evening they drove somewhere out of town, to Oreanda or to the waterfall; and the expedition was always a success, the scenery invariably impressed them as grand and beautiful.

They were expecting her husband to come, but a letter came from him, saying that there was something wrong with his eyes, and he entreated his wife to come home as quickly as possible. Anna Sergeyevna made haste to go.

"It's a good thing I am going away," she said to Gurov. "It's the finger of destiny!"

· She went by coach and he went with her. They were driving the whole day. When she had got into a compartment of the express, and when the second bell had rung, she said:

"Let me look at you once more . . . look at you once again. That's right."

She did not shed tears, but was so sad that she seemed ill, and her face was quivering.

"I shall remember you . . . think of you," she said. "God be with you; be happy. Don't remember evil against me. We are parting forever – it must be so, for we ought never to have met. Well, God be with you."

The train moved off rapidly, its lights soon vanished from sight, and a minute later there was no sound of it, as though everything had conspired together to end as quickly as possible that sweet delirium, that madness. Left alone on the platform, and gazing into the dark distance, Gurov listened to the chirrup of the grasshoppers and the hum of the telegraph wires, feeling as though he had only just waked up. And he thought, musing, that there had been another episode or adventure in his life, and it, too, was at an end, and nothing was left of it but a memory. . . . He was moved, sad, and conscious of a slight remorse. This young woman whom he would never meet again had not been happy with him; he was genuinely warm and affectionate with her, but yet in his manner, his tone, and his caresses there had been a shade of light irony, the coarse condescension of a happy man who was, besides, almost twice her age. All the time she had called him kind, exceptional, lofty; obviously he had seemed to her different from what he really was, so he had unintentionally deceived her. . . .

Here at the station was already a scent of autumn; it was a cold evening.

"It's time for me to go north," thought Gurov as he left the platform. "High time!"

III

At home in Moscow everything was in its winter routine; the stoves were heated, and in the morning it was still dark when the children were having breakfast and getting ready for school, and the nurse would light the lamp for a short time. The frosts had begun already. When the first snow has fallen, on the first day of sledge-driving it is pleasant to see the white earth, the white roofs, to draw soft, delicious breath, and the season brings back the days of one's youth. The old limes and birches, white with hoar-frost, have a good-natured expression; they are nearer to one's heart than cypresses and palms, and near them one doesn't want to be thinking of the sea and the mountains.

Gurov was Moscow born; he arrived in Moscow on a fine frosty day, and when he put on his fur coat and warm gloves, and walked along Petrovka, and when on Saturday evening he heard the ringing of the bells, his recent trip and the places he had seen lost all charm for him. Little by little he became absorbed in Moscow life, greedily read three newspapers a day, and declared he did not read the Moscow papers on principle! He already felt a longing to go to restaurants, clubs, dinner-parties, anniversary celebrations, and he felt flattered at entertaining distinguished lawyers and artists, and at playing cards with a professor at the doctors' club. He could already eat a whole plateful of salt fish and cabbage.

In another month, he fancied, the image of Anna Sergeyevna would be shrouded in a mist in his memory, and only from time to time would visit him in his dreams with a touching smile as others did. But more than a month passed, real winter had come, and everything was still clear in his memory as though he had parted with Anna Sergeyevna only the day before. And his memories glowed more and more vividly. When in the evening stillness he heard from his study the voices of his children, preparing their lessons, or when he listened to a song or the organ at the restaurant, or the storm howled in the chimney, suddenly everything would rise up in his memory: what had happened on the groyne, and the early morning with the mist on the mountains, and the steamer coming from Theodosia, and the kisses. He would pace a long time about his room, remembering it all and smiling; then his memories passed into dreams, and in his fancy the past was mingled with what was to come. Anna Sergeyevna did not visit him in dreams, but followed him about everywhere like a shadow and haunted him. When he shut his eyes he saw her as though she were living before him, and she seemed to him lovelier, younger, tenderer than she was; and he imagined himself finer than he had been in Yalta. In the evenings she peeped out at him from the bookcase, from the fireplace, from the corner – he heard her breathing, the caressing rustle of her dress. In the street he watched the women, looking for some one like her.

He was tormented by an intense desire to confide his memories to some one. But in his home it was impossible to talk of his love, and he had no one outside; he could not talk to his tenants nor to any one at the bank. And what had he to talk of? Had he been in love, then? Had there been anything beautiful, poetical, or edifying or simply interesting in his relations with Anna Sergeyevna? And there was nothing for him but to talk vaguely of love, of woman, and no one guessed what it meant; only his wife twitched her black eyebrows, and said:

"The part of a lady-killer does not suit you at all, Dimitri."

One evening, coming out of the doctors' club with an official with whom he had been playing cards, he could not resist saying:

"If only you knew what a fascinating woman I made the acquaintance of in Yalta!"

The official got into his sledge and was driving away, but turned suddenly and shouted:

"Dmitri Dmitritch!"

"What?"

"You were right this evening: the sturgeon was a bit too strong!"

These words, so ordinary, for some reason moved Gurov to indignation, and struck him as degrading and unclean. What savage manners, what people! What senseless nights, what uninteresting, uneventful days! The rage for card-playing, the gluttony, the drunkenness, the continual talk always about the same thing. Useless pursuits and conversations always about the same things absorb the better part of one's time, the better part of one's strength, and in the end there is left a life grovelling and curtailed, worthless and trivial, and there is no escaping or getting away from it – just as though one were in a madhouse or a prison.

Gurov did not sleep all night, and was filled with indignation. And he had a headache all next day. And the next night he slept badly; he sat up in bed, thinking, or paced up and down his room. He was sick of his children, sick of the bank; he had no desire to go anywhere or to talk of anything.

In the holidays in December he prepared for a journey, and told his wife he was going to Petersburg to do something in the interests of a young friend – and he set off for S——. What for? He did not very well know himself. He wanted to see Anna Sergeyevna and to talk with her – to arrange a meeting, if possible.

He reached S—— in the morning, and took the best room at the hotel, in which the floor was covered with grey army cloth, and on the table was an inkstand, grey with dust and adorned with a figure on horseback, with its hat in its hand and its head broken off. The hotel porter gave him the necessary information; Von Diderits lived in a house of his own in Old Gontcharny Street – it was not far from the hotel: he was rich and lived in good style, and had his own horses; every one in the town knew him. The porter pronounced the name "Dridirits."

Gurov went without haste to Old Gontcharny Street and found the house. Just opposite the house stretched a long grey fence adorned with nails.

"One would run away from a fence like that," thought Gurov, looking from the fence to the windows of the house and back again.

He considered: to-day was a holiday, and the husband would probably be at home. And in any case it would be tactless to go into the house and upset her. If he were to send her a note it might fall into her husband's hands, and then it might ruin everything. The best thing was to trust to chance. And he kept walking up and down the street by the fence, waiting for the chance. He saw a beggar go in at the gate and dogs fly at him; then an hour later he heard a piano, and the sounds were faint and indistinct. Probably it was Anna Sergeyevna playing. The front door suddenly opened, and an old woman came out, followed by the familiar white Pomeranian. Gurov was on the point of calling to the dog, but his heart began beating violently, and in his excitement he could not remember the dog's name.

He walked up and down, and loathed the grey fence more and more, and by now he thought irritably that Anna Sergeyevna had forgotten him, and was perhaps already amusing herself with some one else, and that that was very natural in a young woman who had nothing to look at from morning till night but that confounded fence. He went back to his hotel room and sat for a long while on the sofa, not knowing what to do, then he had dinner and a long nap.

"How stupid and worrying it is!" he thought when he woke and looked at the dark windows: it was already evening. "Here I've had a good sleep for some reason. What shall I do in the night?"

He sat on the bed, which was covered by a cheap grey blanket, such as one sees in hospitals, and he taunted himself in his vexation:

"So much for the lady with the dog . . . so much for the adventure. . . . You're in a nice fix. . . . "

That morning at the station a poster in large letters had caught his eye. "The Geisha" was to be performed for the first time. He thought of this and went to the theatre.

"It's quite possible she may go to the first performance," he thought.

The theatre was full. As in all provincial theatres, there was a fog above the chandelier, the gallery was noisy and restless; in the front row the local dandies were standing up before the beginning of the performance, with their hands behind them; in the Governor's box the Governor's daughter, wearing a boa, was sitting in the front seat, while the Governor himself lurked modestly behind the curtain with only his hands visible; the orchestra was a long time tuning up; the stage curtain swayed. All the time the audience were coming in and taking their seats Gurov looked at them eagerly.

Anna Sergeyevna, too, came in. She sat down in the third row, and when Gurov looked at her his heart contracted, and he understood clearly that for him there was in the whole world no creature so near, so precious, and so important to him; she, this little woman, in no way remarkable, lost in a provincial crowd, with a vulgar lorgnette in her hand, filled his whole life now, was his sorrow and his joy, the one happiness that he now desired for himself, and to the sounds of the inferior orchestra, of the wretched provincial violins, he thought how lovely she was. He thought and dreamed.

A young man with small side-whiskers, tall and stooping, came in with Anna Sergeyevna and sat down beside her; he bent his head at every step and seemed to be continually bowing. Most likely this was the husband whom at Yalta, in a rush of bitter feeling, she had called a flunkey. And there really was in his long figure, his side-whiskers, and the small bald patch on his head, something of the flunkey's obsequiousness; his smile was sugary, and in his buttonhole there was some badge of distinction like the number on a waiter.

During the first interval the husband went away to smoke; she remained alone in her stall. Gurov, who was sitting in the stalls, too, went up to her and said in a trembling voice, with a forced smile:

"Good-evening."

She glanced at him and turned pale, then glanced again with horror, unable to believe her eyes, and tightly gripped the fan and the lorgnette in her hands, evidently struggling with herself not to faint. Both were silent. She was sitting, he was standing, frightened by her confusion and not venturing to sit down beside her. The violins and the flute began tuning up. He felt suddenly frightened; it seemed as though all the people in the boxes were looking at them. She got up and went quickly to the door; he followed her, and both walked senselessly along passages, and up and down stairs, and figures in legal, scholastic, and civil service uniforms, all wearing badges, flitted before their eyes. They caught glimpses of ladies, of fur coats hanging on pegs; the draughts blew on them, bringing a smell of stale tobacco. And Gurov, whose heart was beating violently, thought:

"Oh, heavens! Why are these people here and this orchestra! . . . "

And at that instant he recalled how when he had seen Anna Sergeyevna off at the station he had thought that everything was over and they would never meet again. But how far they were still from the end!

On the narrow, gloomy staircase over which was written "To the Amphitheatre," she stopped.

"How you have frightened me!" she said, breathing hard, still pale and overwhelmed. "Oh, how you have frightened me! I am half dead. Why have you come? Why?"

"But do understand, Anna, do understand . . . " he said hastily in a low voice. "I entreat you to understand. . . . "

She looked at him with dread, with entreaty, with love; she looked at him intently, to keep his features more distinctly in her memory.

"I am so unhappy," she went on, not heeding him. "I have thought of nothing but you all the time; I live only in the thought of you. And I wanted to forget, to forget you; but why, oh, why, have you come?"

On the landing above them two schoolboys were smoking and looking down, but that was nothing to Gurov; he drew Anna Sergeyevna to him, and began kissing her face, her cheeks, and her hands.

"What are you doing, what are you doing!" she cried in horror, pushing him away. "We are mad. Go away to-day; go away at once. . . . I beseech you by all that is sacred, I implore you. . . . There are people coming this way!"

Some one was coming up the stairs.

"You must go away," Anna Sergeyevna went on in a whisper. "Do you hear, Dmitri Dmitritch? I will come and see you in Moscow. I have never been happy; I am miserable now, and I never, never shall be happy, never! Don't make me suffer still more! I swear I'll come to Moscow. But now let us part. My precious, good, dear one, we must part!"

She pressed his hand and began rapidly going downstairs, looking round at him, and from her eyes he could see that she really was unhappy. Gurov stood for a little while, listened, then, when all sound had died away, he found his coat and left the theatre.

IV

And Anna Sergeyevna began coming to see him in Moscow. Once in two or three months she left S----, telling her husband that she was going to consult a doctor about an internal complaint – and her husband believed her, and did not believe her. In Moscow she stayed at the Slaviansky Bazaar hotel, and at once sent a man in a red cap to Gurov. Gurov went to see her, and no one in Moscow knew of it.

Once he was going to see her in this way on a winter morning (the messenger had come the evening before when he was out). With him walked his daughter, whom he wanted to take to school: it was on the way. Snow was falling in big wet flakes.

"It's three degrees above freezing-point, and yet it is snowing," said Gurov to his daughter. "The thaw is only on the surface of the earth; there is quite a different temperature at a greater height in the atmosphere."

"And why are there no thunderstorms in the winter, father?"

He explained that, too. He talked, thinking all the while that he was going to see her, and no living soul knew of it, and probably never would know. He had two lives: one, open, seen and known by all who cared to know, full of relative truth and of relative falsehood, exactly like the lives of his friends and acquaintances; and another life running its course in secret. And through some strange, perhaps accidental, conjunction of circumstances, everything that was essential, of interest and of value to him, everything in which he was sincere and did not deceive himself, everything that made the kernel of his life, was hidden from other people; and all that was false in him, the sheath in which he hid himself to conceal the truth – such, for instance, as his work in the bank, his discussions at the club, his "lower race," his presence with his wife at anniversary festivities – all that was open. And he judged of others by himself, not believing in what he saw, and always believing that every man had his real, most interesting life under the cover of secrecy and under the cover of night. All personal life rested on secrecy, and possibly it was partly on that account that civilised man was so nervously anxious that personal privacy should be respected.

After leaving his daughter at school, Gurov went on to the Slaviansky Bazaar. He took off his fur coat below, went upstairs, and softly knocked at the door. Anna Sergeyevna, wearing his favourite grey dress, exhausted by the journey and the suspense, had been expecting him since the evening before. She was pale; she looked at him, and did not smile, and he had hardly come in when she fell on his breast. Their kiss was slow and prolonged, as though they had not met for two years.

"Well, how are you getting on there?" he asked. "What news?"

"Wait; I'll tell you directly. . . . I can't talk."

She could not speak; she was crying. She turned away from him, and pressed her handkerchief to her eyes.

"Let her have her cry out. I'll sit down and wait," he thought, and he sat down in an arm-chair.

Then he rang and asked for tea to be brought him, and while he drank his tea she remained standing at the window with her back to him. She was crying from emotion, from the miserable consciousness that their life was so hard for them; they could only meet in secret, hiding themselves from people, like thieves! Was not their life shattered?

"Come, do stop!" he said.

It was evident to him that this love of theirs would not soon be over, that he could not see the end of it. Anna Sergeyevna grew more and more attached to him. She adored him, and it was unthinkable to say to her that it was bound to have an end some day; besides, she would not have believed it!

He went up to her and took her by the shoulders to say something affectionate and cheering, and at that moment he saw himself in the looking-glass.

His hair was already beginning to turn grey. And it seemed strange to him that he had grown so much older, so much plainer during the last few years. The shoulders on which his hands rested were warm and quivering. He felt compassion for this life, still so warm and lovely, but probably already not far from beginning to fade and wither like his own. Why did she love him so much? He always seemed to women different from what he was, and they loved in him not himself, but the man created by their imagination, whom they had been eagerly seeking all their lives; and afterwards, when they noticed their mistake, they loved him all the same. And not one of them had been happy with him. Time passed, he had made their acquaintance, got on with them, parted, but he had never once loved; it was anything you like, but not love.

And only now when his head was grey he had fallen properly, really in love – for the first time in his life.

Anna Sergeyevna and he loved each other like people very close and akin, like husband and wife, like tender friends; it seemed to them that fate itself had meant them for one another, and they could not understand why he had a wife and she a husband; and it was as though they were a pair of birds of passage, caught and forced to live in different cages. They forgave each other for what they were ashamed of in their past, they forgave everything in the present, and felt that this love of theirs had changed them both.

In moments of depression in the past he had comforted himself with any arguments that came into his mind, but now he no longer cared for arguments; he felt profound compassion, he wanted to be sincere and tender. . . .

"Don't cry, my darling," he said. "You've had your cry; that's enough. . . . Let us talk now, let us think of some plan."

Then they spent a long while taking counsel together, talked of how to avoid the necessity for secrecy, for deception, for living in different towns and not seeing each other for long at a time. How could they be free from this intolerable bondage?

"How? How?" he asked, clutching his head. "How?"

And it seemed as though in a little while the solution would be found, and then a new and splendid life would begin; and it was clear to both of them that they had still a long, long road before them, and that the most complicated and difficult part of it was only just beginning.

THE COP AND THE ANTHEM

O. Henry

O. Henry was the pen name of William Sydney Porter (1862–1910). Porter's mother died when he was three so, living with his father's mother,
he read to keep himself entertained. He became a chemist, moved from
North Carolina to Texas and got involved with a bohemian band, elop-
ing with a seventeen-year-old and marrying Athol Estes, with whom he
brought up a family. Accused of embezzlement, he fled to New Orleans
and then Honduras. Throughout, he wrote stories – for *Rolling Stone*
among others – and penned a story a week for a year for a magazine
in New York. Booze and diabetes helped him towards a grave in North
Carolina, and also to a legacy of American fiction remembered annually
in a prize named after him.

On his bench in Madison Square Soapy moved uneasily. When wild geese
honk high of nights, and when women without sealskin coats grow kind
to their husbands, and when Soapy moves uneasily on his bench in the
park, you may know that winter is near at hand.

A dead leaf fell in Soapy's lap. That was Jack Frost's card. Jack is kind to the
regular denizens of Madison Square, and gives fair warning of his annual call. At
the corners of four streets he hands his pasteboard to the North Wind, footman
of the mansion of All Outdoors, so that the inhabitants thereof may make ready.

Soapy's mind became cognisant of the fact that the time had come for him to
resolve himself into a singular Committee of Ways and Means to provide against
the coming rigour. And therefore he moved uneasily on his bench.

The hibernatorial ambitions of Soapy were not of the highest. In them there
were no considerations of Mediterranean cruises, of soporific Southern skies
drifting in the Vesuvian Bay. Three months on the Island was what his soul
craved. Three months of assured board and bed and congenial company, safe
from Boreas and bluecoats, seemed to Soapy the essence of things desirable.

For years the hospitable Blackwell's had been his winter quarters. Just as
his more fortunate fellow New Yorkers had bought their tickets to Palm Beach
and the Riviera each winter, so Soapy had made his humble arrangements for
his annual hegira to the Island. And now the time was come. On the previous
night three Sabbath newspapers, distributed beneath his coat, about his ankles and over his lap, had failed to repulse the cold as he slept on his bench
near the spurting fountain in the ancient square. So the Island loomed big and

timely in Soapy's mind. He scorned the provisions made in the name of charity for the city's dependents. In Soapy's opinion the Law was more benign than Philanthropy. There was an endless round of institutions, municipal and elee-mosynary, on which he might set out and receive lodging and food accordant with the simple life. But to one of Soapy's proud spirit the gifts of charity are encumbered. If not in coin you must pay in humiliation of spirit for every ben-efit received at the hands of philanthropy. As Caesar had his Brutus, every bed of charity must have its toll of a bath, every loaf of bread its compensation of a private and personal inquisition. Wherefore it is better to be a guest of the law, which though conducted by rules, does not meddle unduly with a gentleman's private affairs.

Soapy, having decided to go to the Island, at once set about accomplishing his desire. There were many easy ways of doing this. The pleasantest was to dine luxuriously at some expensive restaurant; and then, after declaring insolvency, be handed over quietly and without uproar to a policeman. An accommodating magistrate would do the rest.

Soapy left his bench and strolled out of the square and across the level sea of asphalt, where Broadway and Fifth Avenue flow together. Up Broadway he turned, and halted at a glittering cafe, where are gathered together nightly the choicest products of the grape, the silkworm and the protoplasm.

Soapy had confidence in himself from the lowest button of his vest upward. He was shaven, and his coat was decent and his neat black, ready-tied four-in-hand had been presented to him by a lady missionary on Thanksgiving Day. If he could reach a table in the restaurant unsuspected success would be his. The portion of him that would show above the table would raise no doubt in the waiter's mind. A roasted mallard duck, thought Soapy, would be about the thing – with a bottle of Chablis, and then Camembert, a demi-tasse and a cigar. One dollar for the cigar would be enough. The total would not be so high as to call forth any supreme manifestation of revenge from the cafe management; and yet the meat would leave him filled and happy for the journey to his winter refuge.

But as Soapy set foot inside the restaurant door the head waiter's eye fell upon his frayed trousers and decadent shoes. Strong and ready hands turned him about and conveyed him in silence and haste to the sidewalk and averted the ignoble fate of the menaced mallard.

Soapy turned off Broadway. It seemed that his route to the coveted island was not to be an epicurean one. Some other way of entering limbo must be thought of.

At a corner of Sixth Avenue electric lights and cunningly displayed wares behind plate-glass made a shop window conspicuous. Soapy took a cobble-stone and dashed it through the glass. People came running around the corner, a policeman in the lead. Soapy stood still, with his hands in his pockets, and smiled at the sight of brass buttons.

"Where's the man that done that?" inquired the officer excitedly.

"Don't you figure out that I might have had something to do with it?" said Soapy, not without sarcasm, but friendly, as one greets good fortune.

The policeman's mind refused to accept Soapy even as a clue. Men who smash windows do not remain to parley with the law's minions. They take to their heels. The policeman saw a man half way down the block running to catch a car. With drawn club he joined in the pursuit. Soapy, with disgust in his heart, loafed along, twice unsuccessful.

On the opposite side of the street was a restaurant of no great pretensions. It catered to large appetites and modest purses. Its crockery and atmosphere were thick; its soup and napery thin. Into this place Soapy took his accusive shoes and telltale trousers without challenge. At a table he sat and consumed beefsteak, flapjacks, doughnuts and pie. And then to the waiter be betrayed the fact that the minutest coin and himself were strangers.

"Now, get busy and call a cop," said Soapy. "And don't keep a gentleman waiting."

"No cop for youse," said the waiter, with a voice like butter cakes and an eye like the cherry in a Manhattan cocktail. "Hey, Con!"

Neatly upon his left ear on the callous pavement two waiters pitched Soapy. He arose, joint by joint, as a carpenter's rule opens, and beat the dust from his clothes. Arrest seemed but a rosy dream. The Island seemed very far away. A policeman who stood before a drug store two doors away laughed and walked down the street.

Five blocks Soapy travelled before his courage permitted him to woo capture again. This time the opportunity presented what he fatuously termed to himself a "cinch." A young woman of a modest and pleasing guise was standing before a show window gazing with sprightly interest at its display of shaving mugs and inkstands, and two yards from the window a large policeman of severe demeanour leaned against a water plug.

It was Soapy's design to assume the role of the despicable and execrated "masher." The refined and elegant appearance of his victim and the contiguity of the conscientious cop encouraged him to believe that he would soon feel the pleasant official clutch upon his arm that would insure his winter quarters on the right little, tight little isle.

Soapy straightened the lady missionary's readymade tie, dragged his shrinking cuffs into the open, set his hat at a killing cant and sidled toward the young woman. He made eyes at her, was taken with sudden coughs and "hems," smiled, smirked and went brazenly through the impudent and contemptible litany of the "masher." With half an eye Soapy saw that the policeman was watching him fixedly. The young woman moved away a few steps, and again bestowed her absorbed attention upon the shaving mugs. Soapy followed, boldly stepping to her side, raised his hat and said:

"Ah there, Bedelia! Don't you want to come and play in my yard?"

The policeman was still looking. The persecuted young woman had but to beckon a finger and Soapy would be practically en route for his insular haven. Already he imagined he could feel the cozy warmth of the station-house. The young woman faced him and, stretching out a hand, caught Soapy's coat sleeve.

"Sure, Mike," she said joyfully, "if you'll blow me to a pail of suds. I'd have spoke to you sooner, but the cop was watching."

With the young woman playing the clinging ivy to his oak Soapy walked past the policeman overcome with gloom. He seemed doomed to liberty.

At the next corner he shook off his companion and ran. He halted in the district where by night are found the lightest streets, hearts, vows and librettos.

Women in furs and men in greatcoats moved gaily in the wintry air. A sudden fear seized Soapy that some dreadful enchantment had rendered him immune to arrest. The thought brought a little of panic upon it, and when he came upon another policeman lounging grandly in front of a transplendent theatre he caught at the immediate straw of "disorderly conduct."

On the sidewalk Soapy began to yell drunken gibberish at the top of his harsh voice. He danced, howled, raved and otherwise disturbed the welkin.

The policeman twirled his club, turned his back to Soapy and remarked to a citizen.

"'Tis one of them Yale lads celebratin' the goose egg they give to the Hartford College. Noisy; but no harm. We've instructions to lave them be."

Disconsolate, Soapy ceased his unavailing racket. Would never a policeman lay hands on him? In his fancy the Island seemed an unattainable Arcadia. He buttoned his thin coat against the chilling wind.

In a cigar store he saw a well-dressed man lighting a cigar at a swinging light. His silk umbrella he had set by the door on entering. Soapy stepped inside, secured the umbrella and sauntered off with it slowly. The man at the cigar light followed hastily.

"My umbrella," he said, sternly.

"Oh, is it?" sneered Soapy, adding insult to petit larceny. "Well, why don't you call a policeman? I took it. Your umbrella! Why don't you call a cop? There stands one on the corner."

The umbrella owner slowed his steps. Soapy did likewise, with a presentiment that luck would again run against him. The policeman looked at the two curiously.

"Of course," said the umbrella man – "that is – well, you know how these mistakes occur – I – if it's your umbrella I hope you'll excuse me – I picked it up this morning in a restaurant – If you recognise it as yours, why – I hope you'll –"

"Of course it's mine," said Soapy, viciously.

The ex-umbrella man retreated. The policeman hurried to assist a tall blonde in an opera cloak across the street in front of a street car that was approaching two blocks away.

Soapy walked eastward through a street damaged by improvements. He hurled the umbrella wrathfully into an excavation. He muttered against the men who wear helmets and carry clubs. Because he wanted to fall into their clutches, they seemed to regard him as a king who could do no wrong.

At length Soapy reached one of the avenues to the east where the glitter and turmoil was but faint. He set his face down this toward Madison Square, for the homing instinct survives even when the home is a park bench.

But on an unusually quiet corner Soapy came to a standstill. Here was an old church, quaint and rambling and gabled. Through one violet-stained window a soft light glowed, where, no doubt, the organist loitered over the keys, making sure of his mastery of the coming Sabbath anthem. For there drifted out to Soapy's ears sweet music that caught and held him transfixed against the convolutions of the iron fence.

The moon was above, lustrous and serene; vehicles and pedestrians were few; sparrows twittered sleepily in the eaves – for a little while the scene might have been a country churchyard. And the anthem that the organist played cemented Soapy to the iron fence, for he had known it well in the days when his life contained such things as mothers and roses and ambitions and friends and immaculate thoughts and collars.

The conjunction of Soapy's receptive state of mind and the influences about the old church wrought a sudden and wonderful change in his soul. He viewed with swift horror the pit into which he had tumbled, the degraded days, unworthy desires, dead hopes, wrecked faculties and base motives that made up his existence.

And also in a moment his heart responded thrillingly to this novel mood. An instantaneous and strong impulse moved him to battle with his desperate fate. He would pull himself out of the mire; he would make a man of himself again; he would conquer the evil that had taken possession of him. There was time; he was comparatively young yet; he would resurrect his old eager ambitions and pursue them without faltering. Those solemn but sweet organ notes had set up a revolution in him. To-morrow he would go into the roaring downtown district and find work. A fur importer had once offered him a place as driver. He would find him to-morrow and ask for the position. He would be somebody in the world. He would –

Soapy felt a hand laid on his arm. He looked quickly around into the broad face of a policeman.

"What are you doin' here?" asked the officer.

"Nothin'," said Soapy.

"Then come along," said the policeman.

"Three months on the Island," said the Magistrate in the Police Court the next morning.

THE OTHER TWO

Edith Wharton

Edith Wharton (1862–1937) was fairly privileged: born into a monied American family, friends with Theodore Roosevelt, Henry James, Jean Cocteau, Andre Gide, Kenneth Clark and the like. She married and then divorced by 1913, and wrote over eighty-five stories, as well as novels including *The House of Mirth*, *Ethan Frome*, *The Buccaneers* and *The Age of Innocence*, the book that won a Pulitzer Prize for Fiction in 1921, making her the first woman novelist to be so awarded. She is a deliciously acute writer: "silence may be as variously shaded as speech," wise: "true originality consists not in a new manner but in a new vision," and wonderfully waspish: "the American landscape has no foreground and the American mind no background." She suffered a stroke in France in her mid-seventies, and is buried in Versailles.

I

Waythorn, on the drawing-room hearth, waited for his wife to come down to dinner.

It was their first night under his own roof, and he was surprised at his thrill of boyish agitation. He was not so old, to be sure – his glass gave him little more than the five-and-thirty years to which his wife confessed – but he had fancied himself already in the temperate zone; yet here he was listening for her step with a tender sense of all it symbolized, with some old trail of verse about the garlanded nuptial door-posts floating through his enjoyment of the pleasant room and the good dinner just beyond it.

They had been hastily recalled from their honeymoon by the illness of Lily Haskett, the child of Mrs. Waythorn's first marriage. The little girl, at Waythorn's desire, had been transferred to his house on the day of her mother's wedding, and the doctor, on their arrival, broke the news that she was ill with typhoid, but declared that all the symptoms were favorable. Lily could show twelve years of unblemished health, and the case promised to be a light one. The nurse spoke as reassuringly, and after a moment of alarm Mrs. Waythorn had adjusted herself to the situation. She was very fond of Lily – her affection for the child had perhaps been her decisive charm in Waythorn's eyes – but she had the perfectly balanced nerves which her little girl had inherited, and no woman ever wasted less tissue in unproductive worry. Waythorn was therefore quite prepared to see her come in presently, a little late because of a last look at Lily, but as serene and well-appointed as if her good-night kiss had been laid on the brow of health. Her composure was restful to him; it acted as ballast to his somewhat unstable sensibilities. As he pictured her bending over the child's bed he thought how soothing her presence must be in illness: her very step would prognosticate recovery.

His own life had been a gray one, from temperament rather than circumstance, and he had been drawn to her by the unperturbed gayety which kept her fresh and elastic at an age when most women's activities are growing either slack or febrile. He knew what was said about her; for, popular as she was, there had always been a faint undercurrent of detraction. When she had appeared in New York, nine or ten years earlier, as the pretty Mrs. Haskett whom Gus Varick had unearthed somewhere – was it in Pittsburgh or Utica? – society, while promptly accepting her, had reserved the right to cast a doubt on its own discrimination. Inquiry, however, established her undoubted connection with a socially reigning family, and explained her recent divorce as the natural result of a runaway match at seventeen; and as nothing was known of Mr. Haskett it was easy to believe the worst of him.

Alice Haskett's remarriage with Gus Varick was a passport to the set whose recognition she coveted, and for a few years the Varicks were the most popular couple in town. Unfortunately the alliance was brief and stormy, and this time the husband had his champions. Still, even Varick's stanchest supporters admitted that he was not meant for matrimony, and Mrs. Varick's grievances were of a nature to bear the inspection of the New York courts. A New York divorce is in itself a diploma of virtue, and in the semi-widowhood of this second separation Mrs. Varick took on an air of sanctity, and was allowed to confide her wrongs to some of the most scrupulous ears in town. But when it was known that she was to marry Waythorn there was a momentary reaction. Her best friends would have preferred to see her remain in the role of the injured wife, which was as becoming to her as crape to a rosy complexion. True, a decent time had elapsed, and it was not even suggested that Waythorn had supplanted his predecessor. Still, people shook their heads over him, and one grudging friend, to whom he affirmed that he took the step with his eyes open, replied oracularly: "Yes – and with your ears shut."

Waythorn could afford to smile at these innuendoes. In the Wall Street phrase, he had "discounted" them. He knew that society has not yet adapted itself to the consequences of divorce, and that till the adaptation takes place every woman who uses the freedom the law accords her must be her own social justification. Waythorn had an amused confidence in his wife's ability to justify herself. His expectations were fulfilled, and before the wedding took place Alice Varick's group had rallied openly to her support. She took it all imperturbably: she had a way of surmounting obstacles without seeming to be aware of them, and Waythorn looked back with wonder at the trivialities over which he had worn his nerves thin. He had the sense of having found refuge in a richer, warmer nature than his own, and his satisfaction, at the moment, was humorously summed up in the thought that his wife, when she had done all she could for Lily, would not be ashamed to come down and enjoy a good dinner.

The anticipation of such enjoyment was not, however, the sentiment expressed by Mrs. Waythorn's charming face when she presently joined him. Though she had put on her most engaging teagown she had neglected to assume the smile that went with it, and Waythorn thought he had never seen her look so nearly worried.

"What is it?" he asked. "Is anything wrong with Lily?"

"No; I've just been in and she's still sleeping." Mrs. Waythorn hesitated. "But something tiresome has happened."

He had taken her two hands, and now perceived that he was crushing a paper between them.

"This letter?"

"Yes – Mr. Haskett has written – I mean his lawyer has written."

Waythorn felt himself flush uncomfortably. He dropped his wife's hands.

"What about?"

"About seeing Lily. You know the courts –"

"Yes, yes," he interrupted nervously.

Nothing was known about Haskett in New York. He was vaguely supposed to have remained in the outer darkness from which his wife had been rescued, and Waythorn was one of the few who were aware that he had given up his business in Utica and followed her to New York in order to be near his little girl. In the days of his wooing, Waythorn had often met Lily on the doorstep, rosy and smiling, on her way "to see papa."

"I am so sorry," Mrs. Waythorn murmured.

He roused himself. "What does he want?"

"He wants to see her. You know she goes to him once a week."

"Well – he doesn't expect her to go to him now, does he?"

"No – he has heard of her illness; but he expects to come here."

"Here?"

Mrs. Waythorn reddened under his gaze. They looked away from each other.

"I'm afraid he has the right. . . . You'll see. . . ." She made a proffer of the letter.

Waythorn moved away with a gesture of refusal. He stood staring about the softly lighted room, which a moment before had seemed so full of bridal intimacy.

"I'm so sorry," she repeated. "If Lily could have been moved –"

"That's out of the question," he returned impatiently.

"I suppose so."

Her lip was beginning to tremble, and he felt himself a brute.

"He must come, of course," he said. "When is – his day?"

"I'm afraid – to-morrow."

"Very well. Send a note in the morning."

The butler entered to announce dinner.

Waythorn turned to his wife. "Come – you must be tired. It's beastly, but try to forget about it," he said, drawing her hand through his arm.

"You're so good, dear. I'll try," she whispered back.

Her face cleared at once, and as she looked at him across the flowers, between the rosy candle-shades, he saw her lips waver back into a smile.

"How pretty everything is!" she sighed luxuriously.

He turned to the butler. "The champagne at once, please. Mrs. Waythorn is tired."

In a moment or two their eyes met above the sparkling glasses. Her own were quite clear and untroubled: he saw that she had obeyed his injunction and forgotten.

II

Waythorn, the next morning, went down town earlier than usual. Haskett was not likely to come till the afternoon, but the instinct of flight drove him forth. He meant to stay away all day – he had thoughts of dining at his club. As his door closed behind him he reflected that before he opened it again it would have admitted another man who had as much right to enter it as himself, and the thought filled him with a physical repugnance.

He caught the "elevated" at the employees' hour, and found himself crushed between two layers of pendulous humanity. At Eighth Street the man facing him wriggled out and another took his place. Waythorn glanced up and saw that it was Gus Varick. The men were so close together that it was impossible to ignore the smile of recognition on Varick's handsome overblown face. And after all – why not? They had always been on good terms, and Varick had been divorced before Waythorn's attentions to his wife began. The two exchanged a word on the perennial grievance of the congested trains, and when a seat at their side was miraculously left empty the instinct of self-preservation made Waythorn slip into it after Varick.

The latter drew the stout man's breath of relief.

"Lord – I was beginning to feel like a pressed flower." He leaned back, looking unconcernedly at Waythorn. "Sorry to hear that Sellers is knocked out again."

"Sellers?" echoed Waythorn, starting at his partner's name.

Varick looked surprised. "You didn't know he was laid up with the gout?"

"No. I've been away – I only got back last night." Waythorn felt himself reddening in anticipation of the other's smile.

"Ah – yes; to be sure. And Sellers's attack came on two days ago. I'm afraid he's pretty bad. Very awkward for me, as it happens, because he was just putting through a rather important thing for me."

"Ah?" Waythorn wondered vaguely since when Varick had been dealing in "important things." Hitherto he had dabbled only in the shallow pools of speculation, with which Waythorn's office did not usually concern itself.

It occurred to him that Varick might be talking at random, to relieve the strain of their propinquity. That strain was becoming momentarily more apparent to Waythorn, and when, at Cortlandt Street, he caught sight of an acquaintance, and had a sudden vision of the picture he and Varick must present to an initiated eye, he jumped up with a muttered excuse.

"I hope you'll find Sellers better," said Varick civilly, and he stammered back: "If I can be of any use to you –" and let the departing crowd sweep him to the platform.

At his office he heard that Sellers was in fact ill with the gout, and would probably not be able to leave the house for some weeks.

"I'm sorry it should have happened so, Mr. Waythorn," the senior clerk said with affable significance. "Mr. Sellers was very much upset at the idea of giving you such a lot of extra work just now."

"Oh, that's no matter," said Waythorn hastily. He secretly welcomed the pressure of additional business, and was glad to think that, when the day's work was over, he would have to call at his partner's on the way home.

He was late for luncheon, and turned in at the nearest restaurant instead of going to his club. The place was full, and the waiter hurried him to the back of the room to capture the only vacant table. In the cloud of cigar-smoke Waythorn did not at once distinguish his neighbors; but presently, looking about him, he saw Varick seated a few feet off. This time, luckily, they were too far apart for conversation, and Varick, who faced another way, had probably not even seen him; but there was an irony in their renewed nearness.

Varick was said to be fond of good living, and as Waythorn sat despatching his hurried luncheon he looked across half enviously at the other's leisurely degustation of his meal. When Waythorn first saw him he had been helping himself with critical deliberation to a bit of Camembert at the ideal point of liquefaction, and now, the cheese removed, he was just pouring his cafe double from its little two-storied earthen pot. He poured slowly, his ruddy profile bent above the task, and one beringed white hand steadying the lid of the coffee-pot; then he stretched his other hand to the decanter of cognac at his elbow, filled a liqueur-glass, took a tentative sip, and poured the brandy into his coffee-cup.

Waythorn watched him in a kind of fascination. What was he thinking of – only of the flavor of the coffee and the liqueur? Had the morning's meeting left no more trace in his thoughts than on his face? Had his wife so completely passed out of his life that even this odd encounter with her present husband, within a week after her remarriage, was no more than an incident in his day? And as Waythorn mused, another idea struck him: had Haskett ever met Varick as Varick and he had just met? The recollection of Haskett perturbed him, and he rose and left the restaurant, taking a circuitous way out to escape the placid irony of Varick's nod.

It was after seven when Waythorn reached home. He thought the footman who opened the door looked at him oddly.

"How is Miss Lily?" he asked in haste.

"Doing very well, sir. A gentleman –"

"Tell Barlow to put off dinner for half an hour," Waythorn cut him off, hurrying upstairs.

He went straight to his room and dressed without seeing his wife. When he reached the drawing-room she was there, fresh and radiant. Lily's day had been good; the doctor was not coming back that evening.

At dinner Waythorn told her of Sellers's illness and of the resulting complications. She listened sympathetically, adjuring him not to let himself be overworked, and asking vague feminine questions about the routine of the office. Then she gave him the chronicle of Lily's day; quoted the nurse and doctor, and told him who had called to inquire. He had never seen her more serene and unruffled. It struck him, with a curious pang, that she was very happy in being with him, so happy that she found a childish pleasure in rehearsing the trivial incidents of her day.

After dinner they went to the library, and the servant put the coffee and liqueurs on a low table before her and left the room. She looked singularly soft and girlish in her rosy pale dress, against the dark leather of one of his bachelor armchairs. A day earlier the contrast would have charmed him.

He turned away now, choosing a cigar with affected deliberation.

"Did Haskett come?" he asked, with his back to her.

"Oh, yes – he came."

"You didn't see him, of course?"

She hesitated a moment. "I let the nurse see him."

That was all. There was nothing more to ask. He swung round toward her, applying a match to his cigar. Well, the thing was over for a week, at any rate. He would try not to think of it. She looked up at him, a trifle rosier than usual, with a smile in her eyes.

"Ready for your coffee, dear?"

He leaned against the mantelpiece, watching her as she lifted the coffee-pot. The lamplight struck a gleam from her bracelets and tipped her soft hair with brightness. How light and slender she was, and how each gesture flowed into the next! She seemed a creature all compact of harmonies. As the thought of Haskett receded, Waythorn felt himself yielding again to the joy of possessorship. They were his, those white hands with their flitting motions, his the light haze of hair, the lips and eyes. . . .

She set down the coffee-pot, and reaching for the decanter of cognac, measured off a liqueur-glass and poured it into his cup.

Waythorn uttered a sudden exclamation.

"What is the matter?" she said, startled.

"Nothing; only – I don't take cognac in my coffee."

"Oh, how stupid of me," she cried.

Their eyes met, and she blushed a sudden agonized red.

III

Ten days later, Mr. Sellers, still house-bound, asked Waythorn to call on his way downtown.

The senior partner, with his swaddled foot propped up by the fire, greeted his associate with an air of embarrassment.

"I'm sorry, my dear fellow; I've got to ask you to do an awkward thing for me."

Waythorn waited, and the other went on, after a pause apparently given to the arrangement of his phrases: "The fact is, when I was knocked out I had just gone into a rather complicated piece of business for – Gus Varick."

"Well?" said Waythorn, with an attempt to put him at his ease.

"Well – it's this way: Varick came to me the day before my attack. He had evidently had an inside tip from somebody, and had made about a hundred thousand. He came to me for advice, and I suggested his going in with Vanderlyn."

"Oh, the deuce!" Waythorn exclaimed. He saw in a flash what had happened. The investment was an alluring one, but required negotiation. He listened intently while Sellers put the case before him, and, the statement ended, he said: "You think I ought to see Varick?"

"I'm afraid I can't as yet. The doctor is obdurate. And this thing can't wait. I hate to ask you, but no one else in the office knows the ins and outs of it."

Waythorn stood silent. He did not care a farthing for the success of Varick's venture, but the honor of the office was to be considered, and he could hardly refuse to oblige his partner.

"Very well," he said, "I'll do it."

That afternoon, apprised by telephone, Varick called at the office. Waythorn, waiting in his private room, wondered what the others thought of it. The newspapers, at the time of Mrs. Waythorn's marriage, had acquainted their readers with every detail of her previous matrimonial ventures, and Waythorn could fancy the clerks smiling behind Varick's back as he was ushered in.

Varick bore himself admirably. He was easy without being undignified, and Waythorn was conscious of cutting a much less impressive figure. Varick had no head for business, and the talk prolonged itself for nearly an hour while Waythorn set forth with scrupulous precision the details of the proposed transaction.

"I'm awfully obliged to you," Varick said as he rose. "The fact is I'm not used to having much money to look after, and I don't want to make an ass of myself –" He smiled, and Waythorn could not help noticing that there was something pleasant about his smile. "It feels uncommonly queer to have enough cash to pay one's bills. I'd have sold my soul for it a few years ago!"

Waythorn winced at the allusion. He had heard it rumored that a lack of funds had been one of the determining causes of the Varick separation, but it did not occur to him that Varick's words were intentional. It seemed more likely that the desire to keep clear of embarrassing topics had fatally drawn him into one. Waythorn did not wish to be outdone in civility.

"We'll do the best we can for you," he said. "I think this is a good thing you're in."

"Oh, I'm sure it's immense. It's awfully good of you –" Varick broke off, embarrassed. "I suppose the thing's settled now – but if –"

"If anything happens before Sellers is about, I'll see you again," said Waythorn quietly. He was glad, in the end, to appear the more self-possessed of the two.

The course of Lily's illness ran smooth, and as the days passed Waythorn grew used to the idea of Haskett's weekly visit. The first time the day came round, he stayed out late, and questioned his wife as to the visit on his return. She replied at once that Haskett had merely seen the nurse downstairs, as the doctor did not wish any one in the child's sick-room till after the crisis.

The following week Waythorn was again conscious of the recurrence of the day, but had forgotten it by the time he came home to dinner. The crisis of the disease came a few days later, with a rapid decline of fever, and the little girl was pronounced out of danger. In the rejoicing which ensued the thought of Haskett passed out of Waythorn's mind and one afternoon, letting himself into the house with a latchkey, he went straight to his library without noticing a shabby hat and umbrella in the hall.

In the library he found a small effaced-looking man with a thinnish gray beard sitting on the edge of a chair. The stranger might have been a piano-tuner, or one of those mysteriously efficient persons who are summoned in emergencies to adjust some detail of the domestic machinery. He blinked at Waythorn through a pair of gold-rimmed spectacles and said mildly: "Mr. Waythorn, I presume? I am Lily's father."

Waythorn flushed. "Oh –" he stammered uncomfortably. He broke off, disliking to appear rude. Inwardly he was trying to adjust the actual Haskett to the image of him projected by his wife's reminiscences. Waythorn had been allowed to infer that Alice's first husband was a brute.

"I am sorry to intrude," said Haskett, with his over-the- counter politeness.

"Don't mention it," returned Waythorn, collecting himself. "I suppose the nurse has been told?"

"I presume so. I can wait," said Haskett. He had a resigned way of speaking, as though life had worn down his natural powers of resistance.

Waythorn stood on the threshold, nervously pulling off his gloves.

"I'm sorry you've been detained. I will send for the nurse," he said; and as he opened the door he added with an effort: "I'm glad we can give you a good report of Lily." He winced as the we slipped out, but Haskett seemed not to notice it.

"Thank you, Mr. Waythorn. It's been an anxious time for me."

"Ah, well, that's past. Soon she'll be able to go to you." Waythorn nodded and passed out.

In his own room, he flung himself down with a groan. He hated the womanish sensibility which made him suffer so acutely from the grotesque chances of life. He had known when he married that his wife's former husbands were both living, and that amid the multiplied contacts of modern existence there were a thousand chances to one that he would run against one or the other, yet he found himself as much disturbed by his brief encounter with Haskett as though the law had not obligingly removed all difficulties in the way of their meeting.

Waythorn sprang up and began to pace the room nervously. He had not suffered half so much from his two meetings with Varick. It was Haskett's presence in his own house that made the situation so intolerable. He stood still, hearing steps in the passage.

"This way, please," he heard the nurse say. Haskett was being taken upstairs, then: not a corner of the house but was open to him. Waythorn dropped into another chair, staring vaguely ahead of him. On his dressing-table stood a photograph of Alice, taken when he had first known her. She was Alice Varick then – how fine and exquisite he had thought her! Those were Varick's pearls about her neck. At Waythorn's instance they had been returned before her marriage. Had Haskett ever given her any trinkets – and what had become of them, Waythorn wondered? He realized suddenly that he knew very little of Haskett's past or present situation; but from the man's appearance and manner of speech he could reconstruct with curious precision the surroundings of Alice's first marriage. And it startled him to think that she had, in the background of her life, a phase of existence so different from anything with which he had connected her. Varick, whatever his faults, was a gentleman, in the conventional, traditional sense of the term: the sense which at that moment seemed, oddly enough, to have most meaning to Waythorn. He and Varick had the same social habits, spoke the same language, understood the same allusions. But this other man . . . it was grotesquely uppermost in Waythorn's mind that Haskett had worn a made-up tie attached with an elastic. Why should that ridiculous detail symbolize the whole man? Waythorn was exasperated by his own paltriness, but the fact of the tie expanded, forced itself on him, became as it were the key to Alice's past. He could see her, as Mrs. Haskett, sitting in a "front parlor" furnished in plush, with a pianola, and a copy of "Ben Hur" on the centre-table. He could see her going to the theatre with Haskett – or perhaps even to a "Church Sociable" – she in a "picture hat" and Haskett in a black frock-coat, a little creased, with the made-up tie on an elastic. On the way home they would stop and look at the illuminated shop-windows, lingering over the photographs of New York actresses. On Sunday afternoons Haskett would take her for a walk, pushing Lily ahead of them in a white enameled perambulator, and Waythorn had a vision of the people they would stop and talk to. He could fancy how pretty Alice must have looked, in a dress adroitly constructed from the hints of a New York fashion-paper; how she must have looked down on the other women, chafing at her life, and secretly feeling that she belonged in a bigger place.

For the moment his foremost thought was one of wonder at the way in which she had shed the phase of existence which her marriage with Haskett implied. It was as if her whole aspect, every gesture, every inflection, every allusion, were a studied negation of that period of her life. If she had denied being married to Haskett she could hardly have stood more convicted of duplicity than in this obliteration of the self which had been his wife.

Waythorn started up, checking himself in the analysis of her motives. What right had he to create a fantastic effigy of her and then pass judgment on it? She had spoken vaguely of her first marriage as unhappy, had hinted, with becoming reticence, that Haskett had wrought havoc among her young illusions. . . . It was a pity for Waythorn's peace of mind that Haskett's very inoffensiveness shed a new light on the nature of those illusions. A man would rather think that his wife has been brutalized by her first husband than that the process has been reversed.

IV

"Mr Waythorn, I don't like that French governess of Lily's."

Haskett, subdued and apologetic, stood before Waythorn in the library, revolving his shabby hat in his hand.

Waythorn, surprised in his armchair over the evening paper, stared back perplexedly at his visitor.

"You'll excuse my asking to see you," Haskett continued. "But this is my last visit, and I thought if I could have a word with you it would be a better way than writing to Mrs. Waythorn's lawyer."

Waythorn rose uneasily. He did not like the French governess either; but that was irrelevant.

"I am not so sure of that," he returned stiffly; "but since you wish it I will give your message to – my wife." He always hesitated over the possessive pronoun in addressing Haskett.

The latter sighed. "I don't know as that will help much. She didn't like it when I spoke to her."

Waythorn turned red. "When did you see her?" he asked.

"Not since the first day I came to see Lily – right after she was taken sick. I remarked to her then that I didn't like the governess."

Waythorn made no answer. He remembered distinctly that, after that first visit, he had asked his wife if she had seen Haskett. She had lied to him then, but she had respected his wishes since; and the incident cast a curious light on her character. He was sure she would not have seen Haskett that first day if she had divined that Waythorn would object, and the fact that she did not divine it was almost as disagreeable to the latter as the discovery that she had lied to him.

"I don't like the woman," Haskett was repeating with mild persistency. "She ain't straight, Mr. Waythorn – she'll teach the child to be underhand. I've noticed a change in Lily – she's too anxious to please – and she don't always tell the truth. She used to be the straightest child, Mr. Waythorn –" He broke off, his voice a little thick. "Not but what I want her to have a stylish education," he ended.

Waythorn was touched. "I'm sorry, Mr. Haskett; but frankly, I don't quite see what I can do."

Haskett hesitated. Then he laid his hat on the table, and advanced to the hearth-rug, on which Waythorn was standing. There was nothing aggressive in his manner; but he had the solemnity of a timid man resolved on a decisive measure.

"There's just one thing you can do, Mr. Waythorn," he said. "You can remind Mrs. Waythorn that, by the decree of the courts, I am entitled to have a voice in Lily's bringing up." He paused, and went on more deprecatingly: "I'm not the kind to talk about enforcing my rights, Mr. Waythorn. I don't know as I think a man is entitled to rights he hasn't known how to hold on to; but this business of the child is different. I've never let go there – and I never mean to."

The scene left Waythorn deeply shaken. Shamefacedly, in indirect ways, he had been finding out about Haskett; and all that he had learned was favorable. The little man, in order to be near his daughter, had sold out his share in a profitable business in Utica, and accepted a modest clerkship in a New York manufacturing house. He boarded in a shabby street and had few acquaintances. His passion for Lily filled his life. Waythorn felt that this exploration of Haskett was like groping about with a dark-lantern in his wife's past; but he saw now that there were recesses his lantern had not explored. He had never inquired into the exact circumstances of his wife's first matrimonial rupture. On the surface all had been fair. It was she who had obtained the divorce, and the court had given her the child. But Waythorn knew how many ambiguities such a verdict might cover. The mere fact that Haskett retained a right over his daughter implied an unsuspected compromise. Waythorn was an idealist. He always refused to recognize unpleasant contingencies till he found himself confronted with them, and then he saw them followed by a special train of consequences. His next days were thus haunted, and he determined to try to lay the ghosts by conjuring them up in his wife's presence.

When he repeated Haskett's request a flame of anger passed over her face; but she subdued it instantly and spoke with a slight quiver of outraged motherhood.

"It is very ungentlemanly of him," she said.

The word grated on Waythorn. "That is neither here nor there. It's a bare question of rights."

She murmured: "It's not as if he could ever be a help to Lily –"

Waythorn flushed. This was even less to his taste. "The question is," he repeated, "what authority has he over her?"

She looked downward, twisting herself a little in her seat. "I am willing to see him – I thought you objected," she faltered.

In a flash he understood that she knew the extent of Haskett's claims. Perhaps it was not the first time she had resisted them.

"My objecting has nothing to do with it," he said coldly; "if Haskett has a right to be consulted you must consult him."

She burst into tears, and he saw that she expected him to regard her as a victim.

Haskett did not abuse his rights. Waythorn had felt miserably sure that he would not. But the governess was dismissed, and from time to time the little man demanded an interview with Alice. After the first outburst she accepted the situation with her usual adaptability. Haskett had once reminded Waythorn of the piano-tuner, and Mrs. Waythorn, after a month or two, appeared to class him with that domestic familiar. Waythorn could not but respect the father's tenacity. At first he had tried to cultivate the suspicion that Haskett might be "up to" something, that he had an object in securing a foothold in the house. But in his heart Waythorn was sure of Haskett's single-mindedness; he even guessed in the latter a mild contempt for such advantages as his relation with the Waythorns might offer. Haskett's sincerity of purpose made him invulnerable, and his successor had to accept him as a lien on the property.

Mr. Sellers was sent to Europe to recover from his gout, and Varick's affairs hung on Waythorn's hands. The negotiations were prolonged and complicated; they necessitated frequent conferences between the two men, and the interests of the firm forbade Waythorn's suggesting that his client should transfer his business to another office.

Varick appeared well in the transaction. In moments of relaxation his coarse streak appeared, and Waythorn dreaded his geniality; but in the office he was concise and clear-headed, with a flattering deference to Waythorn's judgment. Their business relations being so affably established, it would have been absurd for the two men to ignore each other in society. The first time they met in a drawing-room, Varick took up their intercourse in the same easy key, and his hostess's grateful glance obliged Waythorn to respond to it. After that they ran across each other frequently, and one evening at a ball Waythorn, wandering through the remoter rooms, came upon Varick seated beside his wife. She colored a little, and faltered in what she was saying; but Varick nodded to Waythorn without rising, and the latter strolled on.

In the carriage, on the way home, he broke out nervously: "I didn't know you spoke to Varick."

Her voice trembled a little. "It's the first time – he happened to be standing near me; I didn't know what to do. It's so awkward, meeting everywhere – and he said you had been very kind about some business."

"That's different," said Waythorn.

She paused a moment. "I'll do just as you wish," she returned pliantly. "I thought it would be less awkward to speak to him when we meet."

Her pliancy was beginning to sicken him. Had she really no will of her own – no theory about her relation to these men? She had accepted Haskett – did she mean to accept Varick? It was "less awkward," as she had said, and her instinct was to evade difficulties or to circumvent them. With sudden vividness Waythorn saw how the instinct had developed. She was "as easy as an old shoe" – a shoe that too many feet had worn. Her elasticity was the result of tension in too many different directions. Alice Haskett – Alice Varick – Alice Waythorn – she had been each in turn, and had left hanging to each name a little of her privacy, a little of her personality, a little of the inmost self where the unknown god abides.

"Yes – it's better to speak to Varick," said Waythorn wearily.

V

The winter wore on, and society took advantage of the Waythorns' acceptance of Varick. Harassed hostesses were grateful to them for bridging over a social difficulty, and Mrs. Waythorn was held up as a miracle of good taste. Some experimental spirits could not resist the diversion of throwing Varick and his former wife together, and there were those who thought he found a zest in the propinquity. But Mrs. Waythorn's conduct remained irreproachable. She neither avoided Varick nor sought him out. Even Waythorn could not but admit that she had discovered the solution of the newest social problem.

He had married her without giving much thought to that problem. He had fancied that a woman can shed her past like a man. But now he saw that Alice was bound to hers both by the circumstances which forced her into continued relation with it, and by the traces it had left on her nature. With grim irony Waythorn compared himself to a member of a syndicate. He held so many shares in his wife's personality and his predecessors were his partners in the business. If there had been any element of passion in the transaction he would have felt less deteriorated by it. The fact that Alice took her change of husbands like a change of weather reduced the situation to mediocrity. He could have forgiven her for blunders, for excesses; for resisting Hackett, for yielding to Varick; for anything but her acquiescence and her tact. She reminded him of a juggler tossing knives; but the knives were blunt and she knew they would never cut her.

And then, gradually, habit formed a protecting surface for his sensibilities. If he paid for each day's comfort with the small change of his illusions, he grew daily to value the comfort more and set less store upon the coin. He had drifted into a dulling propinquity with Haskett and Varick and he took refuge in the cheap revenge of satirizing the situation. He even began to reckon up the advantages which accrued from it, to ask himself if it were not better to own a third of a wife who knew how to make a man happy than a whole one who had lacked opportunity to acquire the art. For it was an art, and made up, like all others, of concessions, eliminations and embellishments; of lights judiciously thrown and shadows skillfully softened. His wife knew exactly how to manage the lights, and he knew exactly to what training she owed her skill. He even tried to trace the source of his obligations, to discriminate between the influences which had combined to produce his domestic happiness: he perceived that Haskett's commonness had made Alice worship good breeding, while Varick's liberal construction of the marriage bond had taught her to value the conjugal virtues; so that he was directly indebted to his predecessors for the devotion which made his life easy if not inspiring.

From this phase he passed into that of complete acceptance. He ceased to satirize himself because time dulled the irony of the situation and the joke lost its humor with its sting. Even the sight of Haskett's hat on the hall table had ceased to touch the springs of epigram. The hat was often seen there now, for it had been decided that it was better for Lily's father to visit her than for the little girl to go to his boarding-house. Waythorn, having acquiesced in this arrangement, had been surprised to find how little difference it made. Haskett was never obtrusive, and the few visitors who met him on the stairs were unaware of his identity. Waythorn did not know how often he saw Alice, but with himself Haskett was seldom in contact.

One afternoon, however, he learned on entering that Lily's father was waiting to see him. In the library he found Haskett occupying a chair in his usual provisional way. Waythorn always felt grateful to him for not leaning back.

"I hope you'll excuse me, Mr. Waythorn," he said rising. "I wanted to see Mrs. Waythorn about Lily, and your man asked me to wait here till she came in."

"Of course," said Waythorn, remembering that a sudden leak had that morning given over the drawing-room to the plumbers.

He opened his cigar-case and held it out to his visitor, and Haskett's acceptance seemed to mark a fresh stage in their intercourse. The spring evening was chilly, and Waythorn invited his guest to draw up his chair to the fire. He meant to find an excuse to leave Haskett in a moment; but he was tired and cold, and after all the little man no longer jarred on him.

The two were inclosed in the intimacy of their blended cigar- smoke when the door opened and Varick walked into the room. Waythorn rose abruptly. It was the first time that Varick had come to the house, and the surprise of seeing him, combined with the singular inopportuneness of his arrival, gave a new edge to Waythorn's blunted sensibilities. He stared at his visitor without speaking.

Varick seemed too preoccupied to notice his host's embarrassment.

"My dear fellow," he exclaimed in his most expansive tone, "I must apologize for tumbling in on you in this way, but I was too late to catch you down town, and so I thought –" He stopped short, catching sight of Haskett, and his sanguine color deepened to a flush which spread vividly under his scant blond hair. But in a moment he recovered himself and nodded slightly. Haskett returned the bow in silence, and Waythorn was still groping for speech when the footman came in carrying a tea-table.

The intrusion offered a welcome vent to Waythorn's nerves. "What the deuce are you bringing this here for?" he said sharply.

"I beg your pardon, sir, but the plumbers are still in the drawing-room, and Mrs. Waythorn said she would have tea in the library." The footman's perfectly respectful tone implied a reflection on Waythorn's reasonableness.

"Oh, very well," said the latter resignedly, and the footman proceeded to open the folding tea-table and set out its complicated appointments. While this interminable process continued the three men stood motionless, watching it with a fascinated stare, till Waythorn, to break the silence, said to Varick: "Won't you have a cigar?"

He held out the case he had just tendered to Haskett, and Varick helped himself with a smile. Waythorn looked about for a match, and finding none, proffered a light from his own cigar. Haskett, in the background, held his ground mildly, examining his cigar-tip now and then, and stepping forward at the right moment to knock its ashes into the fire.

The footman at last withdrew, and Varick immediately began: "If I could just say half a word to you about this business –"

"Certainly," stammered Waythorn; "in the dining-room –"

But as he placed his hand on the door it opened from without, and his wife appeared on the threshold.

She came in fresh and smiling, in her street dress and hat, shedding a fragrance from the boa which she loosened in advancing.

"Shall we have tea in here, dear?" she began; and then she caught sight of Varick. Her smile deepened, veiling a slight tremor of surprise. "Why, how do you do?" she said with a distinct note of pleasure.

As she shook hands with Varick she saw Haskett standing behind him. Her smile faded for a moment, but she recalled it quickly, with a scarcely perceptible side-glance at Waythorn.

"How do you do, Mr. Haskett?" she said, and shook hands with him a shade less cordially.

The three men stood awkwardly before her, till Varick, always the most self-possessed, dashed into an explanatory phrase.

"We – I had to see Waythorn a moment on business," he stammered, brick-red from chin to nape.

Haskett stepped forward with his air of mild obstinacy. "I am sorry to intrude; but you appointed five o'clock –" he directed his resigned glance to the time-piece on the mantel.

She swept aside their embarrassment with a charming gesture of hospitality.

"I'm so sorry – I'm always late; but the afternoon was so lovely." She stood drawing her gloves off, propitiatory and graceful, diffusing about her a sense of ease and familiarity in which the situation lost its grotesqueness. "But before talking business," she added brightly, "I'm sure every one wants a cup of tea."

She dropped into her low chair by the tea-table, and the two visitors, as if drawn by her smile, advanced to receive the cups she held out.

She glanced about for Waythorn, and he took the third cup with a laugh.

"OH, WHISTLE, AND I'LL COME TO YOU, MY LAD"

M.R. James

M.R. James (1862–1936) was a Kentish curate's son. He went to Eton and King's College, Cambridge and became a distinguished medievalist. After his appointment as Dean, then Provost, of King's he became, in 1918, Provost of Eton. He visited Europe, frequently on a double tricycle. As they say, he never married, but left some of the most chilling, strange short stories written.

"I suppose you will be getting away pretty soon, now Full term is over, Professor," said a person not in the story to the Professor of Ontography, soon after they had sat down next to each other at a feast in the hospitable hall of St James's College.

The Professor was young, neat, and precise in speech.

"Yes," he said; "my friends have been making me take up golf this term, and I mean to go to the East Coast – in point of fact to Burnstow – (I dare say you know it) for a week or ten days, to improve my game. I hope to get off tomorrow."

"Oh, Parkins," said his neighbour on the other side, "if you are going to Burnstow, I wish you would look at the site of the Templars' preceptory, and let me know if you think it would be any good to have a dig there in the summer."

It was, as you might suppose, a person of antiquarian pursuits who said this, but, since he merely appears in this prologue, there is no need to give his entitlements.

"Certainly," said Parkins, the Professor: "if you will describe to me whereabouts the site is, I will do my best to give you an idea of the lie of the land when I get back; or I could write to you about it, if you would tell me where you are likely to be."

"Don't trouble to do that, thanks. It's only that I'm thinking of taking my family in that direction in the Long, and it occurred to me that, as very few of the English preceptories have ever been properly planned, I might have an opportunity of doing something useful on off-days."

The Professor rather sniffed at the idea that planning out a preceptory could be described as useful. His neighbour continued:

"The site – I doubt if there is anything showing above ground – must be down quite close to the beach now. The sea has encroached tremendously, as you know, all along that bit of coast. I should think, from the map, that it must be about three-quarters of a mile from the Globe Inn, at the north end of the town. Where are you going to stay?"

"Well, *at* the Globe Inn, as a matter of fact," said Parkins; "I have engaged a room there. I couldn't get in anywhere else; most of the lodging-houses are shut up in winter, it seems; and, as it is, they tell me that the only room of any size I can have is really a double-bedded one, and that they haven't a corner in which to store the other bed, and so on. But I must have a fairly large room, for I am taking some books down, and mean to do a bit of work; and though I don't quite fancy having an empty bed – not to speak of two – in what I may call for the time being my study, I suppose I can manage to rough it for the short time I shall be there."

"Do you call having an extra bed in your room roughing it, Parkins?" said a bluff person opposite. "Look here, I shall come down and occupy it for a bit; it'll be company for you."

The Professor quivered, but managed to laugh in a courteous manner.

"By all means, Rogers; there's nothing I should like better. But I'm afraid you would find it rather dull; you don't play golf, do you?"

"No, thank Heaven!" said rude Mr Rogers.

"Well, you see, when I'm not writing I shall most likely be out on the links, and that, as I say, would be rather dull for you, I'm afraid."

"Oh, I don't know! There's certain to be somebody I know in the place; but, of course, if you don't want me, speak the word, Parkins; I shan't be offended. Truth, as you always tell us, is never offensive."

Parkins was, indeed, scrupulously polite and strictly truthful. It is to be feared that Mr Rogers sometimes practised upon his knowledge of these characteristics. In Parkins's breast there was a conflict now raging, which for a moment or two did not allow him to answer. That interval being over, he said:

"Well, if you want the exact truth, Rogers, I was considering whether the room I speak of would really be large enough to accommodate us both comfortably; and also whether (mind, I shouldn't have said this if you hadn't pressed me) you would not constitute something in the nature of a hindrance to my work."

Rogers laughed loudly.

"Well done, Parkins!" he said. "It's all right. I promise not to interrupt your work; don't you disturb yourself about that. No, I won't come if you don't want me; but I thought I should do so nicely to keep the ghosts off." Here he might have been seen to wink and to nudge his next neighbour. Parkins might also have been seen to become pink. "I beg pardon, Parkins," Rogers continued; "I oughtn't to have said that. I forgot you didn't like levity on these topics."

"Well," Parkins said, "as you have mentioned the matter, I freely own that I do *not* like careless talk about what you call ghosts. A man in my position," he went on, raising his voice a little, "cannot, I find, be too careful about appearing to sanction the current beliefs on such subjects. As you know, Rogers, or as you ought to know; for I think I have never concealed my views –"

"No, you certainly have not, old man," put in Rogers *sotto voce*.

"– I hold that any semblance, any appearance of concession to the view that such things might exist is equivalent to a renunciation of all that I hold most sacred. But I'm afraid I have not succeeded in securing your attention."

"Your *undivided* attention, was what Dr Blimber actually *said*,"[1] Rogers interrupted, with every appearance of an earnest desire for accuracy. "But I beg your pardon, Parkins: I'm stopping you."

"No, not at all," said Parkins. "I don't remember Blimber; perhaps he was before my time. But I needn't go on. I'm sure you know what I mean."

"Yes, yes," said Rogers, rather hastily – "just so. We'll go into it fully at Burnstow, or somewhere."

In repeating the above dialogue I have tried to give the impression which it made on me, that Parkins was something of an old woman – rather henlike, perhaps, in his little ways; totally destitute, alas! of the sense of humour, but at the same time dauntless and sincere in his convictions, and a man deserving of the greatest respect. Whether or not the reader has gathered so much, that was the character which Parkins had.

On the following day Parkins did, as he had hoped, succeed in getting away from his college, and in arriving at Burnstow. He was made welcome at the Globe Inn, was safely installed in the large double-bedded room of which we have heard, and was able before retiring to rest to arrange his materials for work in apple-pie order upon a commodious table which occupied the outer end of the room, and was surrounded on three sides by windows looking out seaward; that is to say, the central window looked straight out to sea, and those on the left and right commanded prospects along the shore to the north and south respectively. On the south you saw the village of Burnstow. On the north no houses were to be seen, but only the beach and the low cliff backing it. Immediately in front was a strip – not considerable – of rough grass, dotted with old anchors, capstans, and so forth; then a broad path; then the beach. Whatever may have been the original distance between the Globe Inn and the sea, not more than sixty yards now separated them.

The rest of the population of the inn was, of course, a golfing one, and included few elements that call for a special description. The most conspicuous figure was, perhaps, that of an *ancien militaire*, secretary of a London club, and possessed of a voice of incredible strength, and of views of a pronouncedly Protestant type. These were apt to find utterance after his attendance upon the ministrations of the Vicar, an estimable man with inclinations towards a picturesque ritual, which he gallantly kept down as far as he could out of deference to East Anglian tradition.

Professor Parkins, one of whose principal characteristics was pluck, spent the greater part of the day following his arrival at Burnstow in what he had called improving his game, in company with this Colonel Wilson: and during the afternoon – whether the process of improvement were to blame or not, I am not sure – the Colonel's demeanour assumed a colouring so lurid that even Parkins jibbed at the thought of walking home with him from the links. He determined, after a short and furtive look at that bristling moustache and those incarnadined features, that it would be wiser to allow the influences of tea and tobacco to do what they could with the Colonel before the dinner-hour should render a meeting inevitable.

---

[1] Mr Rogers was wrong, *vide Dombey and Son*, Chapter xii.

"I might walk home tonight along the beach," he reflected – "yes, and take a look – there will be light enough for that – at the ruins of which Disney was talking. I don't exactly know where they are, by the way; but I expect I can hardly help stumbling on them."

This he accomplished, I may say, in the most literal sense, for in picking his way from the links to the shingle beach his foot caught, partly in a gorse-root and partly in a biggish stone, and over he went. When he got up and surveyed his surroundings, he found himself in a patch of somewhat broken ground covered with small depressions and mounds. These latter, when he came to examine them, proved to be simply masses of flints embedded in mortar and grown over with turf. He must, he quite rightly concluded, be on the site of the preceptory he had promised to look at. It seemed not unlikely to reward the spade of the explorer; enough of the foundations was probably left at no great depth to throw a good deal of light on the general plan. He remembered vaguely that the Templars, to whom this site had belonged, were in the habit of building round churches, and he thought a particular series of the humps or mounds near him did appear to be arranged in something of a circular form. Few people can resist the temptation to try a little amateur research in a department quite outside their own, if only for the satisfaction of showing how successful they would have been had they only taken it up seriously. Our Professor, however, if he felt something of this mean desire, was also truly anxious to oblige Mr Disney. So he paced with care the circular area he had noticed, and wrote down its rough dimensions in his pocket-book. Then he proceeded to examine an oblong eminence which lay east of the centre of the circle, and seemed to his thinking likely to be the base of a platform or altar. At one end of it, the northern, a patch of the turf was gone – removed by some boy or other creature *ferae naturae*. It might, he thought, be as well to probe the soil here for evidences of masonry, and he took out his knife and began scraping away the earth. And now followed another little discovery: a portion of soil fell inward as he scraped, and disclosed a small cavity. He lighted one match after another to help him to see of what nature the hole was, but the wind was too strong for them all. By tapping and scratching the sides with his knife, however, he was able to make out that it must be an artificial hole in masonry. It was rectangular, and the sides, top, and bottom, if not actually plastered, were smooth and regular. Of course it was empty. No! As he withdrew the knife he heard a metallic clink, and when he introduced his hand it met with a cylindrical object lying on the floor of the hole. Naturally enough, he picked it up, and when he brought it into the light, now fast fading, he could see that it, too, was of man's making – a metal tube about four inches long, and evidently of some considerable age.

By the time Parkins had made sure that there was nothing else in this odd receptacle, it was too late and too dark for him to think of undertaking any further search. What he had done had proved so unexpectedly interesting that he determined to sacrifice a little more of the daylight on the morrow to archaeology. The object which he now had safe in his pocket was bound to be of some slight value at least, he felt sure.

Bleak and solemn was the view on which he took a last look before starting homeward. A faint yellow light in the west showed the links, on which a few figures moving towards the club-house were still visible, the squat martello tower, the lights of Aldsey village, the pale ribbon of sands intersected at intervals by black wooden groynes, the dim and murmuring sea. The wind was bitter from the north, but was at his back when he set out for the Globe. He quickly rattled and clashed through the shingle and gained the sand, upon which, but for the groynes which had to be got over every few yards, the going was both good and quiet. One last look behind, to measure the distance he had made since leaving the ruined Templars' church, showed him a prospect of company on his walk, in the shape of a rather indistinct personage, who seemed to be making great efforts to catch up with him, but made little, if any, progress. I mean that there was an appearance of running about his movements, but that the distance between him and Parkins did not seem materially to lessen. So, at least, Parkins thought, and decided that he almost certainly did not know him, and that it would be absurd to wait until he came up. For all that, company, he began to think, would really be very welcome on that lonely shore, if only you could choose your companion. In his unenlightened days he had read of meetings in such places which even now would hardly bear thinking of. He went on thinking of them, however, until he reached home, and particularly of one which catches most people's fancy at some time of their childhood. "Now I saw in my dream that Christian had gone but a very little way when he saw a foul fiend coming over the field to meet him." "What should I do now," he thought, "if I looked back and caught sight of a black figure sharply defined against the yellow sky, and saw that it had horns and wings? I wonder whether I should stand or run for it. Luckily, the gentleman behind is not of that kind, and he seems to be about as far off now as when I saw him first. Well, at this rate he won't get his dinner as soon as I shall; and, dear me! it's within a quarter of an hour of the time now. I must run!"

Parkins had, in fact, very little time for dressing. When he met the Colonel at dinner, Peace – or as much of her as that gentleman could manage – reigned once more in the military bosom; nor was she put to flight in the hours of bridge that followed dinner, for Parkins was a more than respectable player. When, therefore, he retired towards twelve o'clock, he felt that he had spent his evening in quite a satisfactory way, and that, even for so long as a fortnight or three weeks, life at the Globe would be supportable under similar conditions – "especially," thought he, "if I go on improving my game."

As he went along the passages he met the boots of the Globe, who stopped and said:

"Beg your pardon, sir, but as I was a-brushing your coat just now there was somethink fell out of the pocket. I put it on your chest of drawers, sir, in your room, sir – a piece of a pipe or somethink of that, sir. Thank you, sir. You'll find it on your chest of drawers, sir – yes, sir. Good night, sir."

The speech served to remind Parkins of his little discovery of that afternoon. It was with some considerable curiosity that he turned it over by the light of his candles. It was of bronze, he now saw, and was shaped very much after the manner of the modern dog-whistle; in fact it was – yes, certainly it was – actually no more nor less than a whistle. He put it to his lips, but it was quite full of a fine, caked-up sand or earth, which would not yield to knocking, but must be loosened with a knife. Tidy as ever in his habits, Parkins cleared out the earth on to a piece of paper, and took the latter to the window to empty it out. The night was clear and bright, as he saw when he had opened the casement, and he stopped for an instant to look at the sea and note a belated wanderer stationed on the shore in front of the inn. Then he shut the window, a little surprised at the late hours people kept at Burnstow, and took his whistle to the light again. Why, surely there were marks on it, and not merely marks, but letters! A very little rubbing rendered the deeply-cut inscription quite legible, but the Professor had to confess, after some earnest thought, that the meaning of it was as obscure to him as the writing on the wall to Belshazzar. There were legends both on the front and on the back of the whistle. The one read thus:

FLA

FUR   BIS

FLE

The other:

QUIS EST ISTE QUI UENIT

"I ought to be able to make it out," he thought; "but I suppose I am a little rusty in my Latin. When I come to think of it, I don't believe I even know the word for a whistle. The long one does seem simple enough. It ought to mean, 'Who is this who is coming?' Well, the best way to find out is evidently to whistle for him."

He blew tentatively and stopped suddenly, startled and yet pleased at the note he had elicited. It had a quality of infinite distance in it, and, soft as it was, he somehow felt it must be audible for miles round. It was a sound, too, that seemed to have the power (which many scents possess) of forming pictures in the brain. He saw quite clearly for a moment a vision of a wide, dark expanse at night, with a fresh wind blowing, and in the midst a lonely figure – how employed, he could not tell. Perhaps he would have seen more had not the picture been broken by the sudden surge of a gust of wind against his casement, so sudden that it made him look up, just in time to see the white glint of a sea-bird's wing somewhere outside the dark panes.

The sound of the whistle had so fascinated him that he could not help trying it once more, this time more boldly. The note was little, if at all, louder than before, and repetition broke the illusion – no picture followed, as he had half hoped it might. "But what is this? Goodness! what force the wind can get up in a few minutes! What a tremendous gust! There! I knew that window-fastening was no use! Ah! I thought so – both candles out. It"s enough to tear the room to pieces."

The first thing was to get the window shut. While you might count twenty Parkins was struggling with the small casement, and felt almost as if he were pushing back a sturdy burglar, so strong was the pressure. It slackened all at once, and the window banged to and latched itself. Now to relight the candles and see what damage, if any, had been done. No, nothing seemed amiss; no glass even was broken in the casement. But the noise had evidently roused at least one member of the household: the Colonel was to be heard stumping in his stock-inged feet on the floor above, and growling.

Quickly as it had risen, the wind did not fall at once. On it went, moaning and rushing past the house, at times rising to a cry so desolate that, as Parkins disinterestedly said, it might have made fanciful people feel quite uncomfortable; even the unimaginative, he thought after a quarter of an hour, might be happier without it.

Whether it was the wind, or the excitement of golf, or of the researches in the preceptory that kept Parkins awake, he was not sure. Awake he remained, in any case, long enough to fancy (as I am afraid I often do myself under such conditions) that he was the victim of all manner of fatal disorders: he would lie counting the beats of his heart, convinced that it was going to stop work every moment, and would entertain grave suspicions of his lungs, brain, liver, etc. – suspicions which he was sure would be dispelled by the return of daylight, but which until then refused to be put aside. He found a little vicarious comfort in the idea that someone else was in the same boat. A near neighbour (in the darkness it was not easy to tell his direction) was tossing and rustling in his bed, too.

The next stage was that Parkins shut his eyes and determined to give sleep every chance. Here again over-excitement asserted itself in another form – that of making pictures. *Experto crede*, pictures do come to the closed eyes of one trying to sleep, and are often so little to his taste that he must open his eyes and disperse them.

Parkins's experience on this occasion was a very distressing one. He found that the picture which presented itself to him was continuous. When he opened his eyes, of course, it went; but when he shut them once more it framed itself afresh, and acted itself out again, neither quicker nor slower than before. What he saw was this: A long stretch of shore – shingle edged by sand, and intersected at short intervals with black groynes running down to the water – a scene, in fact, so like that of his afternoon's walk that, in the absence of any landmark, it could not be distinguished therefrom. The light was obscure, conveying an impression of gathering storm, late winter evening, and slight cold rain. On this bleak stage at first no actor was visible. Then, in the distance, a bobbing black object appeared; a moment more, and it was a man running, jumping, clambering over the groynes, and every few seconds looking eagerly back. The nearer he came the more obvious it was that he was not only anxious, but even terribly frightened, though his face was not to be distinguished. He was, moreover, almost at the end of his strength. On he came; each successive obstacle seemed to cause him more difficulty than the last. "Will he get over this next one?" thought Parkins; "it seems a little higher than the others." Yes; half climbing, half throwing himself, he did get over, and fell all in a heap on the other side (the side nearest to the spectator). There, as if really unable to get up again, he remained crouching under the groyne, looking up in an attitude of painful anxiety.

So far no cause whatever for the fear of the runner had been shown; but now there began to be seen, far up the shore, a little flicker of something light-coloured moving to and fro with great swiftness and irregularity. Rapidly growing larger, it, too, declared itself as a figure in pale, fluttering draperies, ill-defined. There was something about its motion which made Parkins very unwilling to see it at close quarters. It would stop, raise arms, bow itself toward the sand, then run stooping across the beach to the water-edge and back again; and then, rising upright, once more continue its course forward at a speed that was startling and terrifying. The moment came when the pursuer was hovering about from left to right only a few yards beyond the groyne where the runner lay in hiding. After two or three ineffectual castings hither and thither it came to a stop, stood upright, with arms raised high, and then darted straight forward towards the groyne.

It was at this point that Parkins always failed in his resolution to keep his eyes shut. With many misgivings as to incipient failure of eyesight, over-worked brain, excessive smoking, and so on, he finally resigned himself to light his candle, get out a book, and pass the night waking, rather than be tormented by this persistent panorama, which he saw clearly enough could only be a morbid reflection of his walk and his thoughts on that very day.

The scraping of match on box and the glare of light must have startled some creatures of the night – rats or what not – which he heard scurry across the floor from the side of his bed with much rustling. Dear, dear! the match is out! Fool that it is! But the second one burnt better, and a candle and book were duly procured, over which Parkins pored till sleep of a wholesome kind came upon him, and that in no long space. For about the first time in his orderly and prudent life he forgot to blow out the candle, and when he was called next morning at eight there was still a flicker in the socket and a sad mess of guttered grease on the top of the little table.

After breakfast he was in his room, putting the finishing touches to his golfing costume – fortune had again allotted the Colonel to him for a partner – when one of the maids came in.

"Oh, if you please," she said, "would you like any extra blankets on your bed, sir?"

"Ah! thank you," said Parkins. "Yes, I think I should like one. It seems likely to turn rather colder."

In a very short time the maid was back with the blanket.

"Which bed should I put it on, sir?" she asked.

"What? Why, that one – the one I slept in last night," he said, pointing to it.

"Oh yes! I beg your pardon, sir, but you seemed to have tried both of 'em; leastways, we had to make 'em both up this morning."

"Really? How very absurd!" said Parkins. "I certainly never touched the other, except to lay some things on it. Did it actually seem to have been slept in?"

"Oh yes, sir!" said the maid. "Why, all the things was crumpled and throwed about all ways, if you'll excuse me, sir – quite as if anyone 'adn't passed but a very poor night, sir."

"Dear me," said Parkins. "Well, I may have disordered it more than I thought when I unpacked my things. I'm very sorry to have given you the extra trouble, I'm sure. I expect a friend of mine soon, by the way – a gentleman from Cambridge – to come and occupy it for a night or two. That will be all right, I suppose, won't it?"

"Oh yes, to be sure, sir. Thank you, sir. It's no trouble, I'm sure," said the maid, and departed to giggle with her colleagues.

Parkins set forth, with a stern determination to improve his game.

I am glad to be able to report that he succeeded so far in this enterprise that the Colonel, who had been rather repining at the prospect of a second day's play in his company, became quite chatty as the morning advanced; and his voice boomed out over the flats, as certain also of our own minor poets have said, "like some great bourdon in a minster tower".

"Extraordinary wind, that, we had last night," he said. "In my old home we should have said someone had been whistling for it."

"Should you, indeed!" said Parkins. "Is there a superstition of that kind still current in your part of the country?"

"I don't know about superstition," said the Colonel. "They believe in it all over Denmark and Norway, as well as on the Yorkshire coast; and my experience is, mind you, that there's generally something at the bottom of what these country-folk hold to, and have held to for generations. But it's your drive" (or whatever it might have been: the golfing reader will have to imagine appropriate digressions at the proper intervals).

When conversation was resumed, Parkins said, with a slight hesitancy:

"Apropos of what you were saying just now, Colonel, I think I ought to tell you that my own views on such subjects are very strong. I am, in fact, a convinced disbeliever in what is called the 'supernatural'."

"What!" said the Colonel, "do you mean to tell me you don't believe in second-sight, or ghosts, or anything of that kind?"

"In nothing whatever of that kind," returned Parkins firmly.

"Well," said the Colonel, "but it appears to me at that rate, sir, that you must be little better than a Sadducee."

Parkins was on the point of answering that, in his opinion, the Sadducees were the most sensible persons he had ever read of in the Old Testament; but, feeling some doubt as to whether much mention of them was to be found in that work, he preferred to laugh the accusation off.

"Perhaps I am," he said; "but – Here, give me my cleek, boy! – Excuse me one moment, Colonel." A short interval. "Now, as to whistling for the wind, let me give you my theory about it. The laws which govern winds are really not at all perfectly known – to fisher-folk and such, of course, not known at all. A man or woman of eccentric habits, perhaps, or a stranger, is seen repeatedly on the beach at some unusual hour, and is heard whistling. Soon afterwards a violent wind rises; a man who could read the sky perfectly or who possessed a barometer could have foretold that it would. The simple people of a fishing-village have no barometers, and only a few rough rules for prophesying weather. What more natural than that the eccentric personage I postulated should be regarded as having raised the wind, or that he or she should clutch eagerly at the reputation of being able to do so? Now, take last night's wind: as it happens, I myself was whistling. I blew a whistle twice, and the wind seemed to come absolutely in answer to my call. If anyone had seen me –"

The audience had been a little restive under this harangue, and Parkins had, I fear, fallen somewhat into the tone of a lecturer; but at the last sentence the Colonel stopped.

"Whistling, were you?" he said. "And what sort of whistle did you use? Play this stroke first." Interval.

"About that whistle you were asking, Colonel. It's rather a curious one. I have it in my – No; I see I've left it in my room. As a matter of fact, I found it yesterday."

And then Parkins narrated the manner of his discovery of the whistle, upon hearing which the Colonel grunted, and opined that, in Parkins's place, he should himself be careful about using a thing that had belonged to a set of Papists, of whom, speaking generally, it might be affirmed that you never knew what they might not have been up to. From this topic he diverged to the enormities of the Vicar, who had given notice on the previous Sunday that Friday would be the Feast of St Thomas the Apostle, and that there would be service at eleven o'clock in the church. This and other similar proceedings constituted in the Colonel's view a strong presumption that the Vicar was a concealed Papist, if not a Jesuit; and Parkins, who could not very readily follow the Colonel in this region, did not disagree with him. In fact, they got on so well together in the morning that there was no talk on either side of their separating after lunch.

Both continued to play well during the afternoon, or, at least, well enough to make them forget everything else until the light began to fail them. Not until then did Parkins remember that he had meant to do some more investigating at the preceptory; but it was of no great importance, he reflected. One day was as good as another; he might as well go home with the Colonel.

As they turned the corner of the house, the Colonel was almost knocked down by a boy who rushed into him at the very top of his speed, and then, instead of running away, remained hanging on to him and panting. The first words of the warrior were naturally those of reproof and objurgation, but he very quickly discerned that the boy was almost speechless with fright. Inquiries were useless at first. When the boy got his breath he began to howl, and still clung to the Colonel's legs. He was at last detached, but continued to howl.

"What in the world *is* the matter with you? What have you been up to? What have you seen?" said the two men.

"Ow, I seen it wive at me out of the winder," wailed the boy, "and I don't like it."

"What window?" said the irritated Colonel. "Come, pull yourself together, my boy."

"The front winder it was, at the 'otel," said the boy.

At this point Parkins was in favour of sending the boy home, but the Colonel refused; he wanted to get to the bottom of it, he said; it was most dangerous to give a boy such a fright as this one had had, and if it turned out that people had been playing jokes, they should suffer for it in some way. And by a series of questions he made out this story: The boy had been playing about on the grass in front of the Globe with some others; then they had gone home to their teas, and he was just going, when he happened to look up at the front winder and see it a-wiving at him. *It* seemed to be a figure of some sort, in white as far as he knew – couldn't see its face; but it wived at him, and it warn't a right thing – not to say not a right person. Was there a light in the room? No, he didn"t think to look if there was a light. Which was the window? Was it the top one or the second one? The seckind one it was – the big winder what got two little uns at the sides.

"Very well, my boy," said the Colonel, after a few more questions. "You run away home now. I expect it was some person trying to give you a start. Another time, like a brave English boy, you just throw a stone – well, no, not that exactly, but you go and speak to the waiter, or to Mr Simpson, the landlord, and – yes – and say that I advised you to do so."

The boy's face expressed some of the doubt he felt as to the likelihood of Mr Simpson's lending a favourable ear to his complaint, but the Colonel did not appear to perceive this, and went on:

"And here's a sixpence – no, I see it's a shilling – and you be off home, and don't think any more about it."

The youth hurried off with agitated thanks, and the Colonel and Parkins went round to the front of the Globe and reconnoitred. There was only one window answering to the description they had been hearing.

"Well, that's curious," said Parkins; "it's evidently my window the lad was talking about. Will you come up for a moment, Colonel Wilson? We ought to be able to see if anyone has been taking liberties in my room."

They were soon in the passage, and Parkins made as if to open the door. Then he stopped and felt in his pockets.

"This is more serious than I thought," was his next remark. "I remember now that before I started this morning I locked the door. It is locked now, and, what is more, here is the key." And he held it up. "Now," he went on, "if the servants are in the habit of going into one's room during the day when one is away, I can only say that – well, that I don't approve of it at all." Conscious of a somewhat weak climax, he busied himself in opening the door (which was indeed locked) and in lighting candles. "No," he said, "nothing seems disturbed."

"Except your bed," put in the Colonel.

"Excuse me, that isn't my bed," said Parkins. "I don't use that one. But it does look as if someone has been playing tricks with it."

It certainly did: the clothes were bundled up and twisted together in a most tortuous confusion. Parkins pondered.

"That must be it," he said at last: "I disordered the clothes last night in un-packing, and they haven't made it since. Perhaps they came in to make it, and that boy saw them through the window; and then they were called away and locked the door after them. Yes, I think that must be it."

"Well, ring and ask," said the Colonel, and this appealed to Parkins as practical.

The maid appeared, and, to make a long story short, deposed that she had made the bed in the morning when the gentleman was in the room, and hadn't been there since. No, she hadn't no other key. Mr Simpson he kep' the keys; he'd be able to tell the gentleman if anyone had been up.

This was a puzzle. Investigation showed that nothing of value had been taken, and Parkins remembered the disposition of the small objects on tables and so forth well enough to be pretty sure that no pranks had been played with them. Mr and Mrs Simpson furthermore agreed that neither of them had given the duplicate key of the room to any person whatever during the day. Nor could Parkins, fair-minded man as he was, detect anything in the demeanour of master, mistress, or maid that indicated guilt. He was much more inclined to think that the boy had been imposing on the Colonel.

The latter was unwontedly silent and pensive at dinner and throughout the evening. When he bade good night to Parkins, he murmured in a gruff undertone:

"You know where I am if you want me during the night."

"Why, yes, thank you, Colonel Wilson, I think I do; but there isn't much prospect of my disturbing you, I hope. By the way," he added, "did I show you that old whistle I spoke of? I think not. Well, here it is."

The Colonel turned it over gingerly in the light of the candle.

"Can you make anything of the inscription?" asked Parkins, as he took it back.

"No, not in this light. What do you mean to do with it?"

"Oh, well, when I get back to Cambridge I shall submit it to some of the archaeologists there, and see what they think of it; and very likely, if they consider it worth having, I may present it to one of the museums."

"M!" said the Colonel. "Well, you may be right. All I know is that, if it were mine, I should chuck it straight into the sea. It's no use talking, I'm well aware, but I expect that with you it's a case of live and learn. I hope so, I'm sure, and I wish you a good night."

He turned away, leaving Parkins in act to speak at the bottom of the stair, and soon each was in his own bedroom.

By some unfortunate accident, there were neither blinds nor curtains to the windows of the Professor's room. The previous night he had thought little of this, but tonight there seemed every prospect of a bright moon rising to shine directly on his bed, and probably wake him later on. When he noticed this he was a good deal annoyed, but, with an ingenuity which I can only envy, he succeeded in rigging up, with the help of a railway-rug, some safety-pins, and a stick and umbrella, a screen which, if it only held together, would completely keep the moonlight off his bed. And shortly afterwards he was comfortably in that bed. When he had read a somewhat solid work long enough to produce a decided wish for sleep, he cast a drowsy glance round the room, blew out the candle, and fell back upon the pillow.

He must have slept soundly for an hour or more, when a sudden clatter shook him up in a most unwelcome manner. In a moment he realized what had happened: his carefully constructed screen had given way, and a very bright frosty moon was shining directly on his face. This was highly annoying. Could he possibly get up and reconstruct the screen? or could he manage to sleep if he did not?

For some minutes he lay and pondered over the possibilities; then he turned over sharply, and with all his eyes open lay breathlessly listening. There had been a movement, he was sure, in the empty bed on the opposite side of the room. Tomorrow he would have it moved, for there must be rats or something playing about in it. It was quiet now. No! the commotion began again. There was a rustling and shaking: surely more than any rat could cause.

I can figure to myself something of the Professor's bewilderment and horror, for I have in a dream thirty years back seen the same thing happen; but the reader will hardly, perhaps, imagine how dreadful it was to him to see a figure suddenly sit up in what he had known was an empty bed. He was out of his own bed in one bound, and made a dash towards the window, where lay his only weapon, the stick with which he had propped his screen. This was, as it turned out, the worst thing he could have done, because the personage in the empty bed, with a sudden smooth motion, slipped from the bed and took up a position, with out-spread arms, between the two beds, and in front of the door. Parkins watched it in a horrid perplexity. Somehow, the idea of getting past it and escaping through the door was intolerable to him; he could not have borne – he didn't know why – to touch it; and as for its touching him, he would sooner dash himself through the window than have that happen. It stood for the moment in a band of dark shadow, and he had not seen what its face was like. Now it began to move, in a stooping posture, and all at once the spectator realized, with some horror and some relief, that it must be blind, for it seemed to feel about it with its muffled arms in a groping and random fashion. Turning half away from him, it became suddenly conscious of the bed he had just left; and darted towards it, and bent over and felt the pillows in a way which made Parkins shudder as he had never in his life thought it possible. In a very few moments it seemed to know that the bed was empty, and then, moving forward into the area of light and facing the window, it showed for the first time what manner of thing it was.

Parkins, who very much dislikes being questioned about it, did once describe something of it in my hearing, and I gathered that what he chiefly remembers about it is a horrible, an intensely horrible, face *of crumpled linen*. What expression he read upon it he could not or would not tell, but that the fear of it went nigh to maddening him is certain.

But he was not at leisure to watch it for long. With formidable quickness it moved into the middle of the room, and, as it groped and waved, one corner of its draperies swept across Parkins's face. He could not – though he knew how perilous a sound was – he could not keep back a cry of disgust, and this gave the searcher an instant clue. It leapt towards him upon the instant, and the next moment he was half-way through the window backwards, uttering cry upon cry at the utmost pitch of his voice, and the linen face was thrust close into his own. At this, almost the last possible second, deliverance came, as you will have guessed: the Colonel burst the door open, and was just in time to see the dreadful group at the window. When he reached the figures only one was left. Parkins sank forward into the room in a faint, and before him on the floor lay a tumbled heap of bedclothes.

Colonel Wilson asked no questions, but busied himself in keeping everyone else out of the room and in getting Parkins back to his bed; and himself, wrapped in a rug, occupied the other bed for the rest of the night. Early on the next day Rogers arrived, more welcome than he would have been a day before, and the three of them held a very long consultation in the Professor's room. At the end of it the Colonel left the hotel door carrying a small object between his finger and thumb, which he cast as far into the sea as a very brawny arm could send it. Later on the smoke of a burning ascended from the back premises of the Globe.

Exactly what explanation was patched up for the staff and visitors at the hotel I must confess I do not recollect. The Professor was somehow cleared of the ready suspicion of delirium tremens, and the hotel of the reputation of a troubled house.

There is not much question as to what would have happened to Parkins if the Colonel had not intervened when he did. He would either have fallen out of the window or else lost his wits. But it is not so evident what more the creature that came in answer to the whistle could have done than frighten. There seemed to be absolutely nothing material about it save the bed-clothes of which it had made itself a body. The Colonel, who remembered a not very dissimilar occurrence in India, was of opinion that if Parkins had closed with it it could really have done very little, and that its one power was that of frightening. The whole thing, he said, served to confirm his opinion of the Church of Rome.

There is really nothing more to tell, but, as you may imagine, the Professor's views on certain points are less clear cut than they used to be. His nerves, too, have suffered: he cannot even now see a surplice hanging on a door quite unmoved, and the spectacle of a scarecrow in a field late on a winter afternoon has cost him more than one sleepless night.

MARY POSTGATE

Rudyard Kipling

Rudyard Kipling (1865–1936) was the first British writer to win the Nobel Prize for Literature, at the age of forty-two. Born in Bombay, he was brought back to England in 1870. His earliest works include *The Jungle Book, Just So Stories* and *Kim*. His son John died in the First World War, leading Kipling to take a role with the Imperial War Graves Commission. He was approached to be Poet Laureate, and to accept a knighthood, but delined both. He died two days before King George V, his ashes buried in Westminster Abbey, in Poets' Corner. The American poet and critic Randall Jarrell observed that "few men have written this many stories of this much merit . . . very few have written more and better stories."

Of Miss Mary Postgate, Lady McCausland wrote that she was "thoroughly conscientious, tidy, companionable, and ladylike. I am very sorry to part with her, and shall always be interested in her welfare." Miss Fowler engaged her on this recommendation, and to her surprise, for she had had experience of companions, found that it was true. Miss Fowler was nearer sixty than fifty at the time, but though she needed care she did not exhaust her attendant's vitality. On the contrary, she gave out, stimulatingly and with reminiscences. Her father had been a minor Court official in the days when the Great Exhibition of 1851 had just set its seal on Civilisation made perfect. Some of Miss Fowler's tales, none the less, were not always for the young. Mary was not young, and though her speech was as colourless as her eyes or her hair, she was never shocked. She listened unflinchingly to every one; said at the end, "How interesting!" or "How shocking!" as the case might be, and never again referred to it, for she prided herself on a trained mind, which "did not dwell on these things." She was, too, a treasure at domestic accounts, for which the village tradesmen, with their weekly books, loved her not. Otherwise she had no enemies; provoked no jealousy even among the plainest; neither gossip nor slander had ever been traced to her; she supplied the odd place at the Rector's or the Doctor's table at half an hour's notice; she was a sort of public aunt to very many small children of the village street, whose parents, while accepting everything would have been swift to resent what they called "patronage"; she served on the Village Nursing Committee as Miss Fowler's nominee when Miss Fowler was crippled by rheumatoid arthritis, and came out of six months" fort-nightly meetings equally respected by all the cliques.

And when Fate threw Miss Fowler's nephew, an unlovely orphan of eleven, on Miss Fowler's hands, Mary Postgate stood to her share of the business of education as practiced in private and public schools. She checked printed clothes-lists, and unitemised bills of extras; wrote to Head and House masters, matrons, nurses, and doctors, and grieved or rejoiced over half-term reports. Young Wyndham Fowler repaid her in his holidays by calling her "Gatepost," "Posty," or "Packthread," by thumping her between her narrow shoulders or by chasing her bleating, round the garden, her large mouth open, her large nose high in air at a stiff-necked shamble very like a camel's. Later on he filled the house with clamour, argument, and harangues as to his personal needs, likes and dislikes, and the limitations of "you women," reducing Mary to tears of physical fatigue, or, when he chose to be humorous, of helpless laughter. At crises, which multiplied as he grew older, she was his ambassadress and his interpretress to Miss Fowler, who had no large sympathy with the young; a vote in his interest at the councils on his future; his sewing-woman, strictly accountable for mislaid boots and garments; always his butt and his slave.

And when he decided to become a solicitor, and had entered an office in London; when his greeting had changed from "Hullo, Postey, you old beast," to "Mornin, Packthread" there came a war which, unlike all wars that Mary could remember, did not stay decently outside England and in the newspapers, but intruded on the lives of people whom she knew. As she said to Miss Fowler, it was "most vexatious." It took the Rector's son who was going into business with his elder brother; it took the Colonel's nephew on the eve of fruit-farming in Canada; it took Mrs. Grant's son who, his mother said, was devoted to the ministry; and, very early indeed, it took Wynn Fowler, who announced on a postcard that he had joined the Flying Corps and wanted a cardigan waistcoat.

"He must go, and he must have the waistcoat," said Miss Fowler. So Mary got the proper-sized needles and wool, while Miss Fowler told the men of her establishment – two gardeners and an old man, sixty – that those who could join the Army had better do so. The gardeners left. Cheape, the odd man, stayed on, and was promoted to the gardener's cottage. The cook, scorning to be limited in luxuries, also left, after a spirited scene with Miss Fowler, and took the house-maid with her. Miss Fowler gazetted Nellie, Cheape's seventeen-year-old daughter, to the vacant post; Mrs. Cheape to the rank of cook with occasional cleaning bouts; and the reduced establishment moved forward smoothly.

Wynn demanded an increase in his allowance. Miss Fowler, who always looked facts in the face, said, "He must have it. The chances are he won't live long to draw it, and if three hundred makes him happy –"

Wynn was grateful, and came over, in his tight-buttoned uniform, to say so. His training centre was not thirty miles away, and his talk was so technical that it had to be explained by charts of the various types of machines. He gave Mary such a chart.

"And you'd better study it, Postey," he said. "You'll be seeing a lot of 'em soon." So Mary studied the chart, but when Wynn next arrived to swell and exalt himself before his womenfolk, she failed badly in cross-examination, and he rated her as in the old days.

"You look more or less like a human being," he said in his new Service voice. "You must have had a brain at some time in your past. What have you done with it? Where'd you keep it? A sheep would know more than you do, Postey. You're lamentable. You are less use than an empty tin can, you dowey old cassowary."

"I suppose that's how your superior officer talks to you?" said Miss Fowler from her chair.

"But Postey doesn't mind," Wynn replied. "Do you, Packthread?"

"Why? Was Wynn saying anything? I shall get this right next time you come," she muttered, and knitted her pale brows again over the diagrams of Taubes, Farmans, and Zeppelins.

In a few weeks the mere land and sea battles which she read to Miss Fowler after breakfast passed her like idle breath. Her heart and her interest were high in the air with Wynn, who had finished "rolling" (whatever that might be) and gone on from a "taxi" to a machine more or less his own. One morning it circled over their very chimneys, alighted on Vegg's Heath, almost outside the garden gate, and Wynn came in, blue with cold, shouting for food. He and she drew Miss Fowler's bath-chair, as they had often done, along the Heath foot-path to look at the biplane. Mary observed that "it smelt very badly."

"Postey, I believe you think with your nose," said Wynn. "I know you don't with your mind. Now, what type's that?"

"I'll go and get the chart," said Mary.

"You're hopeless! You haven't the mental capacity of a white mouse," he cried, and explained the dials and the sockets for bomb-dropping till it was time to mount and ride the wet clouds once more.

"Ah!" said Mary, as the stinking thing flared upward. "Wait till our Flying Corps gets to work! Wynn says it's much safer than in the trenches."

"I wonder," said Miss Fowler. "Tell Cheape to come and tow me home again."

"It's all downhill. I can do it," said Mary, "if you put the brake on." She laid her lean self against the pushing-bar and home they trundled.

"Now, be careful you aren't heated and catch a chill," said overdressed Miss Fowler.

"Nothing makes me perspire," said Mary. As she bumped the chair under the porch she straightened her long back. The exertion had given her a colour, and the wind had loosened a wisp of hair across her forehead. Miss Fowler glanced at her.

"What do you ever think of, Mary?" she demanded suddenly.

"Oh, Wynn says he wants another three pairs of stockings – as thick as we can make them."

"Yes. But I mean the things that women think about Here you are, more than forty –"

"Forty-four," said truthful Mary.

"Well?"

"Well?" Mary offered Miss Fowler her shoulder as usual.

"And you've been with me ten years now."

"Let's see," said Mary. "Wynn was eleven when he came. He's twenty now, and I came two years before that. It must be eleven."

"Eleven! And you've never told me anything that matters in all that while. Looking back, it seems to me that I've done all the talking."

"I'm afraid I'm not much of a conversationalist. As Wynn says, I haven't the mind. Let me take your hat."

Miss Fowler, moving stiffly from the hip, stamped her rubber-tipped stick on the tiled hall floor. "Mary, aren't you anything except a companion? Would you ever have been anything except a companion?"

Mary hung up the garden hat on its proper peg. "No," she said after consideration. "I don't imagine I ever should. But I've no imagination, I'm afraid."

She fetched Miss Fowler her eleven-o'clock glass of Contrexeville.

That was the wet December when it rained six inches to the month, and the women went abroad as little as might be. Wynn's flying chariot visited them several times, and for two mornings (he had warned her by postcard) Mary heard the thresh of his propellers at dawn. The second time she ran to the window, and stared at the whitening sky. A little blur passed overhead. She lifted her lean arms towards it.

That evening at six o'clock there came an announcement in an official envelope that Second Lieutenant W. Fowler had been killed during a trial flight. Death was instantaneous. She read it and carried it to Miss Fowler.

"I never expected anything else," said Miss Fowler; "but I'm sorry it happened before he had done anything."

The room was whirling round Mary Postgate, but she found herself quite steady in the midst of it.

"Yes," she said. "It's a great pity he didn't die in action after he had killed somebody."

"He was killed instantly. That's one comfort," Miss Fowler went on.

"But Wynn says the shock of a fall kills a man at once – whatever happens to the tanks," quoted Mary.

The room was coming to rest now. She heard Miss Fowler say impatiently, "But why can't we cry, Mary?" and herself replying, "There's nothing to cry for. He has done his duty as much as Mrs. Grant's son did."

"And when he died, she came and cried all the morning," said Miss Fowler. "This only makes me feel tired – terribly tired. Will you help me to bed, please, Mary? – And I think I'd like the hot-water bottle."

So Mary helped her and sat beside, talking of Wynn in his riotous youth.

"I believe," said Miss Fowler suddenly, "that old people and young people slip from under a stroke like this. The middle-aged feel it most."

"I expect that's true," said Mary, rising. "I'm going to put away the things in his room now. Shall we wear mourning?"

"Certainly not," said Miss Fowler. "Except, of course, at the funeral. I can't go. You will. I want you to arrange about his being buried here. What a blessing it didn't happen at Salisbury!"

Every one, from the Authorities of the Flying Corps to the Rector, was most kind and sympathetic. Mary found herself for the moment in a world where bodies were in the habit of being despatched by all sorts of conveyances to all sorts of places. And at the funeral two young men in buttoned-up uniforms stood beside the grave and spoke to her afterwards.

"You're Miss Postgate, aren't you?" said one, "Fowler told me about you. He was a good chap – a first-class fellow – a great loss."

"Great loss!" growled his companion. "We're all awfully sorry."

"How high did he fall from?" Mary whispered.

"Pretty nearly four thousand feet, I should think, didn't he? You were up that day, Monkey?"

"All of that," the other child replied. "My bar made three thousand, and I wasn't as high as him by a lot."

"Then that's all right," said Mary. "Thank you very much."

They moved away as Mrs. Grant flung herself weeping on Mary's flat chest, under the lych-gate, and cried, "I know how it feels! I know how it feels!"

"But both his parents are dead," Mary returned, as she fended her off. "Perhaps they've all met by now," she added vaguely as she escaped towards the coach.

"I've thought of that too," wailed Mrs. Grant; "but then he'll be practically a stranger to them. Quite embarrassing!"

Mary faithfully reported every detail of the ceremony to Miss Fowler, who, when she described Mrs. Grant's outburst, laughed aloud.

"Oh, how Wynn would have enjoyed it! He was always utterly unreliable at funerals. D'you remember –" And they talked of him again, each piecing out the other's gaps. "And now," said Miss Fowler, "we'll pull up the blinds and we'll have a general tidy. That always does us good. Have you seen to Wynn's things?"

"Everything – since he first came," said Mary, "He was never destructive – even with his toys."

They faced that neat room.

"It can't be natural not to cry," Mary said at last. "I'm so afraid you'll have a reaction."

"As I told you, we old people slip from under the stroke. It's you I'm afraid for. Have you cried yet?"

"I can't. It only makes me angry with the Germans."

"That's sheer waste of vitality," said Miss Fowler. "We must live till the war's finished." She opened a full wardrobe. "Now, I've been thinking things over. This is my plan. All his civilian clothes can be given away – Belgian refugees, and so on."

Mary nodded. "Boots, collars, and gloves?"

"They came back yesterday with his Flying Corps clothes" – Mary pointed to a roll on the little iron bed.

"Ah, but keep his Service things. Some one may be glad of them later. Do you remember his sizes?"

"Five feet eight and a half; thirty-six inches round the chest. But he told me he's just put on an inch and a half. I'll mark it on a label and tie it on his sleeping-bag."

"So that disposes of that," said Miss Fowler, tapping the palm of one hand with the ringed third finger of the other. "What a waste it all is! We'll get his old school trunk to-morrow and pack his civilian clothes."

"And the rest?" said Mary. "His books and pictures and the games and the toys – and – and the rest?"

"My plan is to burn every single thing," said Miss Fowler. "Then we shall know where they are and no one can handle them afterwards. What do you think?"

"I think that would be much the best," said Mary. "But there's such a lot of them."

"We'll burn them in the destructor," said Miss Fowler.

This was an open-air furnace for the consumption of refuse; a little circular four-foot tower of pierced brick over an iron grating. Miss Fowler had noticed the design in a gardening journal years ago, and had had it built at the bottom of the garden. It suited her tidy soul, for it saved unsightly rubbish-heaps and the ashes lightened the stiff clay soil.

Mary considered for a moment, saw her way clear, and nodded again. They spent the evening putting away well-remembered civilian suits, underclothes that Mary had marked, and the regiments of very gaudy socks and ties. A second trunk was needed, and, after that, a little packing case, and it was late next day when Cheape and the local carrier lifted them to the cart. The Rector luckily knew of a friend's son, about five feet eight and a half inches high, to whom a complete Flying Corps outfit would be most acceptable, and sent his gardener's son down with a barrow to take delivery of it. The cap was hung up in Miss Fowler's bedroom, the belt in Miss Postgate's; for, as Miss Fowler said, they had no desire to make tea-party talk of them.

"That disposes of that," said Miss Fowler. "I'll leave the rest to you, Mary. I can't run up and down in the garden. You'd better take the big clothes-basket and get Nellie to help you."

"I shall take the wheel-barrow and do it myself," said Mary, and for once in her life closed her mouth.

Miss Fowler, in moments of irritation, had called Mary deadly methodical. She put on her oldest water-proof and gardening-hat and her ever-slipping go-loshes, for the weather was on the edge of more rain. She gathered firelighters from the kitchen, a half-scuttle of coals, and a faggot of brushwood. These she wheeled in the barrow down the mossed paths to the dank little laurel shrub-bery where the destructor stood under the drip of three oaks. She climbed the wire fence into the Rector's glebe just behind, and from his tenant's rick pulled two large armfuls of good hay, which she spread neatly on the fire-bars. Next, journey by journey, passing Miss Fowler's white face at the morning-room win-dow each time, she brought down in the towel-covered clothes-basket, on the wheel-barrow, thumbed and used Hentys, Marrayats, Levers, Stevensons, Bar-oness Orczys, Garvices, schoolbooks, and atlases, unrelated piles of the Motor Cyclist, the Light Car, and catalogues of Olympia Exhibitions; the remnants of a fleet of sailing-ships from nine-penney cutters to a three-guinea yacht; a prep-school dressing-gown; bats from three-and-sixpence to twenty-four shillings; cricket and tennis balls; disintegrated steam and clockwork locomotives with their twisted rails; a grey and red tin model of a submarine; a dumb gramophone and cracked records; golf-clubs that had to be broken across the knee, like his walking-sticks, and an assegai; photographs of private and public school cricket and football elevens, and his O.T.C. on the line of march; kodaks, and film-rolls; some pewters, and one real silver cup, for boxing competitions and Junior Hurdles; sheaves of school photographs; Miss Fowler's photograph; her own which he had borne off in fun and (good care she take not to ask!) had never re-turned; a playbox with a secret drawer; a load of flannels, belts, and jerseys, and a pair of spiked shoes unearthed in the attic; a packet of all the letters that Miss Fowler and she had ever written to him, kept for some absurd reason through all these years; a five-day attempt at a diary; framed pictures of racing motors in full Brooklands career, and load upon load of undistinguishable wreckage of tool-boxes, rabbit-hutches, electric batteries, tin soldiers, fret-saw outfits, and jig-saw puzzles.

Miss Fowler at the window watched her come and go, and said to herself, "Mary's an old woman. I never realised it before."

After lunch she recommended her to rest.

"I'm not in the least tired," said Mary. "I've got it all arranged. I'm going to the village at two o'clock for some paraffin. Nellie hasn't enough, and the walk will do me good."

She made one last quest round the house before she started, and found that she had overlooked nothing. It began to mist as soon as she had skirted Vegg's Heath, where Wynn used to descend – it seemed to her that she could almost hear the beat of his propellers overhead, but there was nothing to see. She hoisted her umbrella and lunged into the blind wet till she had reached the shelter of the empty village. As she came out of Mr. Kidd's shop with a bottle full of paraffin in her string shopping-bag, she met Nurse Eden, the village nurse, and fell into talk with her, as usual, about the village children. They were parting opposite the "Royal Oak" when a gun, they fancied, was fired immediately behind the house. It was followed by a child's shriek dying into a wail.

"Accident!" said Nurse Eden promptly, and dashed through the empty bar, followed by Mary. They found Mrs. Gerritt, the publican's wife, who could only gasp and point to the yard, where a little cart-lodge was sliding sideways amid a clatter of tiles. Nurse Eden snatched up a sheet drying before the fire, ran out, lifted something from the ground, and flung the sheet round it. The she turned scarlet and half her uniform too, as she bore the load into the kitchen. It was little Edna Gerritt, aged nine, whom Mary had known since her perambulator days.

"Am I hurted bad?" Edna asked, and died between Nurse Eden's dripping hands. The sheet fell aside and for an instant, before she could shut her eyes, Mary saw the ripped and shredded body.

"It's a wonder she spoke at all," said Nurse Eden. "What in God's name was it?"

"A bomb," said Mary.

"One o' the Zeppelins?"

"No. An aeroplane. I thought I heard it on the Heath but I fancied it was one of ours. It must have shut off its engines as it came down. That's why we didn't notice it."

"The filthy pigs!" said Nurse Eden, all white and shaken. "See the pickle I'm in! Go and tell Dr. Hennis, Miss Postgate." Nurse looked at the mother, who had dropped face down on the floor. "She's only in a fit. Turn her over."

Mary heaved Mrs. Gerritt right side up, and hurried off for the doctor. When she told her tale, he asked her to sit down in the surgery till he got her something.

"But I don't need it, I assure you," said she. "I don't think it would be wise to tell Miss Fowler about it, do you? Her heart is so irritable in this weather."

Dr. Hennis looked at her admiringly as he packed up his bag.

"No. Don't tell anybody till we're sure," he said, and hastened to the "Royal Oak," while Mary went on with the paraffin. The village behind her was as quiet as usual, for the news had not yet spread. She frowned a little to herself, the large nostrils expanded uglily from time to time as she muttered a phrase which Wynn who had never restrained himself before his women-folk, had applied to the enemy. "Bloody pagans! They are bloody pagans. But," she continued, falling back on the teaching that had made her what she was, "one mustn't let one's mind dwell on these things."

Before she reached the house Dr. Hennis, who was also a special constable, overtook her in his car.

"Oh, Miss Postgate," he said, "I wanted to tell you that that accident at the "Royal Oak" was due to Gerritt's stable tumbling down. It's been dangerous for a long time. It ought to have been condemned."

"I thought I heard an explosion too," said Mary.

"You might have been misled by the beams snapping. I've been looking at 'em. They were dry-rotted through and through. Of course, as they broke, they would make a noise just like a gun."

"Yes?" said Mary politely.

"Poor little Edna was playing underneath it," he went on, still holding her with his eyes, "and that and the tiles cut her to pieces, you see?"

"I saw it," said Mary, shaking her head. "I heard it too."

"Well, we cannot be sure." Dr. Hennis changed his tone completely. "I know both you and Nurse Eden (I've been speaking to her) are perfectly trustworthy, and I can rely on you not to say anything – yet at least. It is no good to stir up people unless –"

"Oh, I never do – anyhow," said Mary, and Dr. Hennis went on to the country town.

After all, she told herself, it might, just possibly, have been the collapse of the old stable that had done all those things to poor little Edna. She was sorry she had even hinted at other things, but Nurse Eden was discretion itself. By the time she reached home the affair seemed increasingly remote by its very monstrosity. As she came in, Miss Fowler told her that a couple of aeroplanes had passed half an hour ago.

"I though I heard them," she replied, "I'm going down to the garden now. I've got the paraffin."

"Yes, but – what have you got on your boots? They're soaking wet. Change them at once."

Not only did Mary obey, but she wrapped the boots in a newspaper, and put them into the string bag with the bottles. So, armed with the longest kitchen poker, she left.

"It's raining again," was Miss Fowler's last word, "but – I know you won't be happy till that's disposed of."

"It won't take long. I've got everything down there, and I've put the lid on the destructor to keep the wet out."

The shrubbery was filling with twilight by the same time she had completed her arrangements and sprinkled the sacrificial oil. As she lit the match that would burn her heart to ashes, she heard a groan or a grunt behind the dense Portugal laurels.

"Cheape?" she called impatiently, but Cheape, with his ancient lumbago, in his comfortable cottage would be the last man to profane the sanctuary. "Sheep," she concluded, and threw in the fuse. The pyre went up in a roar, and the immediate flame hastened the night around her."

"How Wynn would have loved this!" she thought, stepping back from the blaze.

By its light she saw, half hidden behind a laurel not five paces away, a bare-headed man sitting very stiffly at the foot of one of the oaks. A broken branch lay across his lap – one booted leg protruding from beneath it. His head moved ceaselessly from side to side, but his body was as still as the tree's trunk. He was dressed – she moved sideways to look more closely – in a uniform something like Lynn's with a flap buttoned across the chest. For an instant she had some idea that it might be one of the young flying men she had met at the funeral. But their heads were dark and glassy. This man's was as pale as a baby's, and so closely cropped that she could see the disgusting pink skin beneath. His lips moved.

"What do you say?" Mary moved towards him and stooped.

"Laty! Laty! Laty!" he muttered, while his hands picked at the dead wet leaves. There was no doubt as to his nationality. It made her so angry that she strode back to the destructor, though it was still too hot to use the poker there. Wynn's books seemed to be catching well. She looked up at the oak behind the man; several of the light upper and two or three rotten lower branches had broken and scattered their rubbish on the shrubbery path. On the lowest fork a helmet with dependent strings, showed like a bird's-nest in the light of a long-tongued flame. Evidently this person had fallen through the trees. Wynn had told her that it was quite possible for people to fall out of aeroplanes. Wynn told her, too, that trees were useful things to break an aviators fall, but in this case the aviator must have been broken or he would moved from his queer position. He seemed helpless except for his belt – and Mary loathed pistols. Months ago, after reading certain Belgian reports together, she and Miss Fowler had had dealings with one – a huge revolver with flat-nosed bullets, which latter, Wynn said, were forbidden by the rules of war to be used against civilised enemies. "They're good enough for us," Miss Fowler had replied. "Show Mary how it works." And Wynn, laughing at the mere possibility of any such need, had led the craven winking Mary into the Rector's disused quarry, and had shown her how to fire the terrible machine. It lay now in the top-left-hand drawer of her toilet-table – a memento not included in the burning. Wynn would be pleased to see how she was not afraid.

She slipped up to the house to get it. When she came through the rain, the eyes in the head were alive with expectation. The mouth even tried to smile. But at sight of the revolver its corners went down just like Edna Gerritt's. A tear trickled from one eye, and the head rolled from shoulder to shoulder as through trying to point out something.

"Cassee. Tout cassee [Broken. All broken]," it whimpered.

"What do you say?" said Mary disgustedly, keeping well to one side, though only the head moved.

"Cassee," it repeated. "Che me rends. Le medicin! Toctor! [I am hurt. The doctor (French) Doctor!]"

"Nein!" said she, bringing all her small German to bear with the big pistol. "Ich haben der todt Kinder gesehn [I have see the dead child]."

The head was still. Mary's hand dropped. She had been careful to keep her finger off the trigger for fear of accidents. After a few moments' waiting, she returned to the destructor, where the flames were falling, and churned up Wynn's charring books with the poker. Again the head groaned for the doctor.

"Stop that!" said Mary, and stamped her foot. "Stop that, you bloody pagan!"

The words came quite smoothly and naturally. They were Wynn's own words, and Wynn was a gentleman who for no consideration on earth would have torn little Edna into those vividly coloured strips and strings. But this thing hunched under the oak-tree had done that thing. It was no question of reading horrors out of newspapers to Miss Fowler. Mary had seen it with her own eyes on the "Royal Oak" kitchen table. She must not allow her mind to dwell upon it. Now Wynn was dead, and every thing connected with him was lumping and rustling and tinkling under her busy poker into red black dust and grey leaves of ash. The thing beneath the oak would die too. Mary had seen death more than once. She came of a family that had a knack of dying under, as she told Miss Fowler, "most distressing circumstances." She would stay where she was till she was entirely satisfied that It was dead – dead as dear papa in the late "eighties; aunt Mary in "eighty-nine; mamma in "ninety-one; cousin Dick in "ninety-five; Lady McCausland's housemaid in "ninety-nine; Lady McCausland's sister in nineteen hundred and one; Wynn burried five days ago; and Edna Gerritt still waiting for decent earth to hide her. As she thought – her underlip caught up by one faded canine, brows knit and nostrils wide – she wielded the poker with lunges that jarred the grating at the bottom, and careful scrapes round the brick-work above. She looked at her wrist-watch. It was getting on to half-past four, and the rain was coming down in earnest. Tea would be at five. If It did not die before that time, she would be soaked and would have to change. Meantime, and this occupied her, Wynn's things were burning well in spite of the hissing wet though now and again a book-back with a quite distinguishable title would be heaved up out of the mass. The exercise of stoking had given her a glow which seemed to reach to the marrow of her bones. She hummed – Mary never had a voice – to herself. She had never believed in all those advanced views – though Miss Fowler herself leaned a little that way – of woman's work in the world; but now she saw there was much to be said for them. This, for instance, was her work – work which no man, least of all Dr. Hennis, would ever have done. A man, at such a crisis, would be what Wynn called a "sportsman"; would leave everything to fetch help, and would certainly bring It into the house. Now a woman's business was to make a happy home for – for a husband and children. Failing these – it was not a thing one should allow one's mind to dwell upon – but –

"Stop it!" Mary cried once more across the shadows. "Nein, I tell you! Ich haben der todt Kinder gesehn."

But it was a fact. A woman who had missed these things could still be useful – more useful than a man in certain respects. She thumped like a paviour through the settling ashes at the secret thrill of it. The rain was damping the fire, but she could feel – it was too dark to see – that her work was done. There was a dull red glow at the bottom of the destructor, not enough to char the wooden lid if she slipped it half over against the driving wet. This arranged, she leaned on the poker and waited, while an increasing rapture laid hold on her. She ceased to think. She gave herself up to feel. Her long pleasure was broken by a sound that she had waited for in agony several times in her life. She leaned forward and listened, smiling. There could be no mistake. She closed her eyes and drank it in. Once it ceased abruptly.

"Go on," she murmured, half aloud. "That isn't the end."

Then the end came very distinctly in a lull between two rain-gusts. Mary Postgate drew her breath short between her teeth and shivered from head to foot. "That's all right," said she contentedly, and went up to the house, where she scandalised the whole routine by taking a luxurious hot bath before tea, and came down looking, as Miss Fowler said when she saw her lying all relaxed on the other sofa, "quite handsome!"

THE LOADED DOG

Henry Lawson

For **Henry Lawson** (1867–1922) "beer makes you feel the way you ought to feel without beer." Born to a Norwegian miner in New South Wales, Lawson was educated in NSW and read Dickens and Marryat. When an ear infection left him permanently deaf at fourteen, learning became difficult and he flunked most exams. He fell into writing for the *Brisbane Boomerang* and then the *Sydney Bulletin*, charting a path for what he called a sketch story: "the sketch story is the best of all." Drink ruined a disastrous marriage and he withdrew to a room he bought at Mrs Isabel Byers' Coffee Palace in North Sydney. Byers worked tirelessly as an advocate for his writing and he is now thought of as the first great Australian short story writer. When he died, he was the first person to be granted a state funeral on the grounds of having been a "distinguished citizen." His work should be much better known outside Australia.

D ave Regan, Jim Bently, and Andy Page were sinking a shaft at Stony Creek in search of a rich gold quartz reef which was supposed to exist in the vicinity. There is always a rich reef supposed to exist in the vicinity; the only questions are whether it is ten feet or hundreds beneath the surface, and in which direction. They had struck some pretty solid rock, also water which kept them baling. They used the old-fashioned blasting-powder and time-fuse. They'd make a sausage or cartridge of blasting-powder in a skin of strong calico or canvas, the mouth sewn and bound round the end of the fuse; they'd dip the cartridge in melted tallow to make it water-tight, get the drill-hole as dry as possible, drop in the cartridge with some dry dust, and wad and ram with stiff clay and broken brick. Then they'd light the fuse and get out of the hole and wait. The result was usually an ugly pot-hole in the bottom of the shaft and half a barrow-load of broken rock.

There was plenty of fish in the creek, fresh-water bream, cod, cat-fish, and tailers. The party were fond of fish, and Andy and Dave of fishing. Andy would fish for three hours at a stretch if encouraged by a "nibble" or a "bite" now and then – say once in twenty minutes. The butcher was always willing to give meat in exchange for fish when they caught more than they could eat; but now it was winter, and these fish wouldn't bite. However, the creek was low, just a chain of muddy water-holes, from the hole with a few bucketfuls in it to the sizable pool with an average depth of six or seven feet, and they could get fish by baling out the smaller holes or muddying up the water in the larger ones till the fish rose to the surface. There was the cat-fish, with spikes growing out of the sides of its head, and if you got pricked you'd know it, as Dave said. Andy took off his boots, tucked up his trousers, and went into a hole one day to stir up the mud with his feet, and he knew it. Dave scooped one out with his hand and got pricked, and he knew it too; his arm swelled, and the pain throbbed up into his shoulder, and down into his stomach too, he said, like a toothache he had once, and kept him awake for two nights – only the toothache pain had a "burred edge", Dave said.

Dave got an idea.

"Why not blow the fish up in the big water-hole with a cartridge?" he said. "I'll try it."

He thought the thing out and Andy Page worked it out. Andy usually put Dave's theories into practice if they were practicable, or bore the blame for the failure and the chaffing of his mates if they weren't.

He made a cartridge about three times the size of those they used in the rock. Jim Bently said it was big enough to blow the bottom out of the river. The inner skin was of stout calico; Andy stuck the end of a six-foot piece of fuse well down in the powder and bound the mouth of the bag firmly to it with whipcord. The idea was to sink the cartridge in the water with the open end of the fuse attached to a float on the surface, ready for lighting. Andy dipped the cartridge in melted bees'-wax to make it water-tight. "We'll have to leave it some time before we light it," said Dave, "to give the fish time to get over their scare when we put it in, and come nosing round again; so we'll want it well water-tight."

Round the cartridge Andy, at Dave's suggestion, bound a strip of sail canvas – that they used for making water-bags – to increase the force of the explosion, and round that he pasted layers of stiff brown paper – on the plan of the sort of fireworks we called "gun-crackers". He let the paper dry in the sun, then he sewed a covering of two thicknesses of canvas over it, and bound the thing from end to end with stout fishing-line. Dave's schemes were elaborate, and he often worked his inventions out to nothing. The cartridge was rigid and solid enough now – a formidable bomb; but Andy and Dave wanted to be sure. Andy sewed on another layer of canvas, dipped the cartridge in melted tallow, twisted a length of fencing-wire round it as an afterthought, dipped it in tallow again, and stood it carefully against a tent-peg, where he'd know where to find it, and wound the fuse loosely round it. Then he went to the camp-fire to try some potatoes which were boiling in their jackets in a billy, and to see about frying some chops for dinner. Dave and Jim were at work in the claim that morning.

They had a big black young retriever dog – or rather an overgrown pup, a big, foolish, four-footed mate, who was always slobbering round them and lashing their legs with his heavy tail that swung round like a stock-whip. Most of his head was usually a red, idiotic, slobbering grin of appreciation of his own silliness. He seemed to take life, the world, his two-legged mates, and his own instinct as a huge joke. He'd retrieve anything: he carted back most of the camp rubbish that Andy threw away. They had a cat that died in hot weather, and Andy threw it a good distance away in the scrub; and early one morning the dog found the cat, after it had been dead a week or so, and carried it back to camp, and laid it just inside the tent-flaps, where it could best make its presence known when the mates should rise and begin to sniff suspiciously in the sickly smothering atmosphere of the summer sunrise. He used to retrieve them when they went in swimming; he'd jump in after them, and take their hands in his mouth, and try to swim out with them, and scratch their naked bodies with his paws. They loved him for his good-heartedness and his foolishness, but when they wished to enjoy a swim they had to tie him up in camp.

He watched Andy with great interest all the morning making the cartridge, and hindered him considerably, trying to help; but about noon he went off to the claim to see how Dave and Jim were getting on, and to come home to dinner with them. Andy saw them coming, and put a panful of mutton-chops on the fire. Andy was cook to-day; Dave and Jim stood with their backs to the fire, as Bushmen do in all weathers, waiting till dinner should be ready. The retriever went nosing round after something he seemed to have missed.

Andy's brain still worked on the cartridge; his eye was caught by the glare of an empty kerosene-tin lying in the bushes, and it struck him that it wouldn't be a bad idea to sink the cartridge packed with clay, sand, or stones in the tin, to increase the force of the explosion. He may have been all out, from a scientific point of view, but the notion looked all right to him. Jim Bently, by the way, wasn't interested in their "damned silliness". Andy noticed an empty treacle-tin – the sort with the little tin neck or spout soldered on to the top for the convenience of pouring out the treacle – and it struck him that this would have made the best kind of cartridge-case: he would only have had to pour in the powder, stick the fuse in through the neck, and cork and seal it with bees'-wax. He was turning to suggest this to Dave, when Dave glanced over his shoulder to see how the chops were doing – and bolted. He explained afterwards that he thought he heard the pan spluttering extra, and looked to see if the chops were burning. Jim Bently looked behind and bolted after Dave. Andy stood stock-still, staring after them.

"Run, Andy! run!" they shouted back at him. "Run!!! Look behind you, you fool!" Andy turned slowly and looked, and there, close behind him, was the retriever with the cartridge in his mouth – wedged into his broadest and silliest grin. And that wasn't all. The dog had come round the fire to Andy, and the loose end of the fuse had trailed and waggled over the burning sticks into the blaze; Andy had slit and nicked the firing end of the fuse well, and now it was hissing and spitting properly.

Andy's legs started with a jolt; his legs started before his brain did, and he made after Dave and Jim. And the dog followed Andy.

Dave and Jim were good runners – Jim the best – for a short distance; Andy was slow and heavy, but he had the strength and the wind and could last. The dog leapt and capered round him, delighted as a dog could be to find his mates, as he thought, on for a frolic. Dave and Jim kept shouting back, "Don't foller us! don't foller us, you coloured fool!" but Andy kept on, no matter how they dodged. They could never explain, any more than the dog, why they followed each other, but so they ran, Dave keeping in Jim's track in all its turnings, Andy after Dave, and the dog circling round Andy – the live fuse swishing in all directions and hissing and spluttering and stinking. Jim yelling to Dave not to follow him, Dave shouting to Andy to go in another direction – to "spread out", and Andy roaring at the dog to go home. Then Andy's brain began to work, stimulated by the crisis: he tried to get a running kick at the dog, but the dog dodged; he snatched up sticks and stones and threw them at the dog and ran on again. The retriever saw that he'd made a mistake about Andy, and left him and bounded after Dave. Dave, who had the presence of mind to think that the fuse's time wasn't up yet, made a dive and a grab for the dog, caught him by the tail, and as he swung round snatched the cartridge out of his mouth and flung it as far as he could: the dog immediately bounded after it and retrieved it. Dave roared and cursed at the dog, who seeing that Dave was offended, left him and went after Jim, who was well ahead. Jim swung to a sapling and went up it like a native bear; it was a young sapling, and Jim couldn't safely get more than ten or twelve feet from the ground. The dog laid the cartridge, as carefully as if it was a kitten, at the foot of the sapling, and capered and leaped and whooped joyously round under Jim. The big pup reckoned that this was part of the lark – he was all right now – it was Jim who was out for a spree. The fuse sounded as if it were going a mile a minute. Jim tried to climb higher and the sapling bent and cracked. Jim fell on his feet and ran. The dog swooped on the cartridge and followed. It all took but a very few moments. Jim ran to a digger's hole, about ten feet deep, and dropped down into it – landing on soft mud – and was safe. The dog grinned sardonically down on him, over the edge, for a moment, as if he thought it would be a good lark to drop the cartridge down on Jim.

"Go away, Tommy," said Jim feebly, "go away."

The dog bounded off after Dave, who was the only one in sight now; Andy had dropped behind a log, where he lay flat on his face, having suddenly remembered a picture of the Russo-Turkish war with a circle of Turks lying flat on their faces (as if they were ashamed) round a newly-arrived shell.

There was a small hotel or shanty on the creek, on the main road, not far from the claim. Dave was desperate, the time flew much faster in his stimulated imagination than it did in reality, so he made for the shanty. There were several casual Bushmen on the verandah and in the bar; Dave rushed into the bar, banging the door to behind him. "My dog!" he gasped, in reply to the astonished stare of the publican, "the blanky retriever – he's got a live cartridge in his mouth –"

The retriever, finding the front door shut against him, had bounded round and in by the back way, and now stood smiling in the doorway leading from the passage, the cartridge still in his mouth and the fuse spluttering. They burst out of that bar. Tommy bounded first after one and then after another, for, being a young dog, he tried to make friends with everybody.

The Bushmen ran round corners, and some shut themselves in the stable. There was a new weather-board and corrugated-iron kitchen and wash-house on piles in the back-yard, with some women washing clothes inside. Dave and the publican bundled in there and shut the door – the publican cursing Dave and calling him a crimson fool, in hurried tones, and wanting to know what the hell he came here for.

The retriever went in under the kitchen, amongst the piles, but, luckily for those inside, there was a vicious yellow mongrel cattle-dog sulking and nursing his nastiness under there – a sneaking, fighting, thieving canine, whom neighbours had tried for years to shoot or poison. Tommy saw his danger – he'd had experience from this dog – and started out and across the yard, still sticking to the cartridge. Half-way across the yard the yellow dog caught him and nipped him. Tommy dropped the cartridge, gave one terrified yell, and took to the Bush. The yellow dog followed him to the fence and then ran back to see what he had dropped. Nearly a dozen other dogs came from round all the corners and under the buildings – spidery, thievish, cold-blooded kangaroo-dogs, mongrel sheep- and cattle-dogs, vicious black and yellow dogs – that slip after you in the dark, nip your heels, and vanish without explaining – and yapping, yelping small fry. They kept at a respectable distance round the nasty yellow dog, for it was dangerous to go near him when he thought he had found something which might be good for a dog to eat. He sniffed at the cartridge twice, and was just taking a third cautious sniff when –

It was very good blasting powder – a new brand that Dave had recently got up from Sydney; and the cartridge had been excellently well made. Andy was very patient and painstaking in all he did, and nearly as handy as the average sailor with needles, twine, canvas, and rope.

Bushmen say that that kitchen jumped off its piles and on again. When the smoke and dust cleared away, the remains of the nasty yellow dog were lying against the paling fence of the yard looking as if he had been kicked into a fire by a horse and afterwards rolled in the dust under a barrow, and finally thrown against the fence from a distance. Several saddle-horses, which had been "hanging-up" round the verandah, were galloping wildly down the road in clouds of dust, with broken bridle-reins flying; and from a circle round the outskirts, from every point of the compass in the scrub, came the yelping of dogs. Two of them went home, to the place where they were born, thirty miles away, and reached it the same night and stayed there; it was not till towards evening that the rest came back cautiously to make inquiries. One was trying to walk on two legs, and most of 'em looked more or less singed; and a little, singed, stumpy-tailed dog, who had been in the habit of hopping the back half of him along on one leg, had reason to be glad that he'd saved up the other leg all those years, for he needed it now. There was one old one-eyed cattle-dog round that shanty for years afterwards, who couldn't stand the smell of a gun being cleaned. He it was who had taken an interest, only second to that of the yellow dog, in the cartridge. Bushmen said that it was amusing to slip up on his blind side and stick a dirty ramrod under his nose: he wouldn't wait to bring his solitary eye to bear – he'd take to the Bush and stay out all night.

For half an hour or so after the explosion there were several Bushmen round behind the stable who crouched, doubled up, against the wall, or rolled gently on the dust, trying to laugh without shrieking. There were two white women in hysterics at the house, and a half-caste rushing aimlessly round with a dipper of cold water. The publican was holding his wife tight and begging her between her squawks, to "hold up for my sake, Mary, or I'll lam the life out of ye."

Dave decided to apologise later on, "when things had settled a bit," and went back to camp. And the dog that had done it all, "Tommy", the great, idiotic mongrel retriever, came slobbering round Dave and lashing his legs with his tail, and trotted home after him, smiling his broadest, longest, and reddest smile of amiability, and apparently satisfied for one afternoon with the fun he'd had.

Andy chained the dog up securely, and cooked some more chops, while Dave went to help Jim out of the hole.

And most of this is why, for years afterwards, lanky, easy-going Bushmen, riding lazily past Dave's camp, would cry, in a lazy drawl and with just a hint of the nasal twang –

"'Ello, Da-a-ve! How's the fishin' getting on, Da-a-ve?"

A COLD AUTUMN

Ivan Bunin

Ivan Bunin (1870–1953) won the Nobel Prize for Literature in 1933, the first Russian writer to do so. He was revered amongst anti-communist White Russian émigrés, and was seen as the heir to Chekhov and Tolstoy. His notable work includes *The Village*, and his 1917-1918 diary *Cursed Days*. He died in his flat in Paris, soon after his work became the first of exiled Russian writers to be published in the USSR.

In June of that year he was staying with us on the estate. He'd always been considered one of us, as his late father had been a friend and neighbour of my father's. On the fifteenth of June Franz Ferdinand was killed in Sarajevo. On the morning of the sixteenth the newspapers were delivered from the post office. Father emerged from his study carrying a Moscow evening paper and entered the dining-room, where he, Mama and I were still sitting at the table, and said:

"Well, my friends, it's war! The Austrian Crown Prince has been killed in Sarajevo. It's war!"

On St Peter's Day a crowd of visitors gathered at the house – it was father's name-day – and over dinner our engagement was announced. But on the nineteenth of July Germany declared war on Russia.

In September he came to us for just twenty-four hours, to say goodbye before going off to the front. (Everyone at that time thought that the war would soon be over, and our wedding had been postponed till the spring.) So this was our last evening together. After supper the servants brought in the samovar as usual and as he glanced at the windows which were steamed up from its heat, father said:

"What an astonishingly early and cold autumn!"

We sat quietly that evening, only occasionally exchanging the odd insignificant word, hiding our innermost thoughts and feelings with exaggerated calm. It was with the same affected simplicity that father had made his remark about the autumn. I went up to the door into the balcony and wiped the glass with a cloth: out in the garden the pure icy stars were sparkling with a sharp brilliance against the black sky. Father was smoking, leaning back in his armchair and absently gazing at the hot lamp suspended over the table; by its light Mama, in her spectacles, was carefully sewing a little silk bag – we knew what it was for – and the scene was both touching and chilling.

Father asked:

"So, you still want to set off in the morning rather than after lunch?"

"Yes, if I may, in the morning," he answered. "It's very sad, but I still haven't quite managed to see to everything at home."

Father let out a slight sigh:

"Well, as you wish, dear boy. Only in that case it's time Mama and I went to bed; we certainly don't want to miss seeing you off tomorrow . . ."

Mama stood up and made the sign of the cross over her son to be; he bent down and kissed her hand, and then father's. Left alone, we lingered in the dining-room; I decided to set out a game of patience, while he paced from one corner of the room to another. Then suddenly he asked:

"Shall we go for a little walk?"

My heart was growing heavier and heavier, and I answered indifferently:

"All right."

As he put on his coat in the entrance hall he was still deep in thought, and then with a sweet smile he suddenly recited some lines from Fet:

"What a cold autumn!
Put on your bonnet and shawl . . ."

"I don't have a bonnet," I said. "But how does it go on?"

"I don't remember. Something like:

"Look – through the darkening pine trees
A fire is arising . . ."

"What fire?"

"The rising moon, of course. There's a certain autumnal, rustic charm in those lines: 'Put on your bonnet and shawl.' That's our grandfathers' and grandmothers' time . . . Oh, my God, my God!"

"What is it?"

"Nothing, dearest love. But I do feel sad. Sad, but contented. I love you very, very much . . ."

We put our coats on, went through the dining-room out onto the balcony and then down into the garden. At first it was so dark I held onto his sleeve. Then the black boughs which were sprinkled with metallically brilliant stars began to stand out against the lightening sky. Stopping for a moment, he turned to face the house:

"Look how the windows are shining in a special autumn way. I shall remember this evening as long as I live."

I looked at the windows, and he embraced me in my Swiss cloak. I brushed my mohair scarf away from my face and tilted my head back slightly so he could kiss me. When he'd kissed me he looked into my face.

"How your eyes sparkle," he said. "Aren't you cold? The air's quite wintry. If I'm killed, you won't forget me straightaway?"

I found myself thinking: "Suppose he really is killed? Surely there won't come a time when I'll forget him – though in the end we do forget everything . . ."

And frightened by my own thought, I answered hurriedly:

"Don't talk like that. I wouldn't survive your death."

After a short pause he pronounced slowly:

"Anyway, if I am killed, I'll wait for you over there. You live, be happy for a while in the world, and then come to me."

I burst into tears . . .

In the morning he set off. Round his neck Mama hung that fateful little bag she'd been sewing the previous evening – it contained a small golden icon which had been carried to war by both her father and her grandfather – and we made the sign of the cross over him with nervously jerky despair. Watching him go, we stood on the porch in that state of stupefaction always experienced when saying farewell to someone before a long separation, and all we felt was the astonishing incongruity between ourselves and the joyful, sunny morning around us with its hoar-frost sparkling on the grass. We stood there for a while and then went back into the house. I walked through the rooms with my hands behind my back, not knowing what to do with myself, whether I should sob or sing at the top of my voice . . .

He was killed – what a strange word! – a month later, in Galicia. And since then a whole thirty years have passed. And I've experienced so much through those years which seem so long when you consider them carefully and go over in your memory all that magical, incomprehensible thing called the past which neither the mind nor the heart can grasp. In the spring of 1918, by which time my father and mother were both dead, I was living in Moscow, in the cellar of a house belonging to a woman trading in the Smolensk market who regularly mocked me with her "Well, your excellency, how are your circumstances?" I engaged in trade myself and, like many others at that time, I sold to soldiers in Caucasian fur caps and unbuttoned greatcoats some of the things I still had – a ring, a little cross, a moth-eaten fur collar – and then one day while trading on the corner of the Arbat and the Smolensk market I met a man with a rare beautiful soul, an elderly retired soldier; we soon got married and in April I went off with him to Yekaterinodar. It took almost two weeks to get there with him and his nephew, a boy of seventeen who was trying to make his way to the Volunteers – I disguised as a peasant-woman in bast shoes, he in a worn Cossack coat and with a newly-grown black and silver beard – and then we spent over two years on the Don and in the Kuban. In the winter, during a hurricane, we set sail from Novorossiysk for Turkey with a huge crowd of other refugees, and on the way, at sea, my husband died of typhus. After that, of all my nearest and dearest only three remained in the whole world – my husband's nephew, the latter's wife and their little girl, a child of seven months. But soon after this the nephew sailed off with his wife for the Crimea to join up with Wrangel, leaving the child on my hands. There they too disappeared without trace. And then I lived for a long time in Constantinople, earning a living for myself and the child by back-breaking manual labour. Then, like so many others, I wandered the world with her – Bulgaria, Serbia, Bohemia, Belgium, Paris, Nice . . . The little girl grew up long ago; she stayed in Paris and became a model Frenchwoman, very pretty and completely indifferent to me; she used to work in a confectioner's near the Madeleine, using her manicured hands with their silver fingernails to wrap up boxes in satin paper and gold string; and I lived, and am still living in Nice on what God provides . . . I saw Nice for the first time in 1912 – and could never have imagined in those happy days what the city would one day become for me!

So I did survive his death, even though I once impetuously said I wouldn't. But when I recall everything I've experienced since that time, I always ask myself: "What, when all is said and done, has there been in my life?" And I answer: "Only that cold autumn evening." Did it ever exist? Yes, it did. And that is all there's been in my life. All the rest has been a useless dream. But I believe, I do ardently believe that somewhere over there he is waiting for me – with the same love and the same youthfulness as on that evening. "You live, be happy for a while in the world, and then come to me . . ." I have lived, I have been happy for a while, and now, quite soon, I'll come.

SREDNI VASHTAR

Saki

Saki was the pen name of H.H. Munro (1870–1916). Born in Burma, he published mostly short stories before fighting with the Royal Fusiliers in the First World War. His last words, said towards the end of the Battle of Ancre before being shot by a sniper, were "Put that bloody cigarette out!"

Conradin was ten years old, and the doctor had pronounced his professional opinion that the boy would not live another five years. The doctor was silky and effete, and counted for little, but his opinion was endorsed by Mrs. De Ropp, who counted for nearly everything. Mrs. De Ropp was Conradin's cousin and guardian, and in his eyes she represented those three-fifths of the world that are necessary and disagreeable and real; the other two-fifths, in perpetual antagonism to the foregoing, were summed up in himself and his imagination. One of these days Conradin supposed he would succumb to the mastering pressure of wearisome necessary things – such as illnesses and coddling restrictions and drawn-out dullness. Without his imagination, which was rampant under the spur of loneliness, he would have succumbed long ago.

Mrs. De Ropp would never, in her honestest moments, have confessed to herself that she disliked Conradin, though she might have been dimly aware that thwarting him "for his good" was a duty which she did not find particularly irksome. Conradin hated her with a desperate sincerity which he was perfectly able to mask. Such few pleasures as he could contrive for himself gained an added relish from the likelihood that they would be displeasing to his guardian, and from the realm of his imagination she was locked out – an unclean thing, which should find no entrance.

In the dull, cheerless garden, overlooked by so many windows that were ready to open with a message not to do this or that, or a reminder that medicines were due, he found little attraction. The few fruit-trees that it contained were set jealously apart from his plucking, as though they were rare specimens of their kind blooming in an arid waste; it would probably have been difficult to find a market-gardener who would have offered ten shillings for their entire yearly produce. In a forgotten corner, however, almost hidden behind a dismal shrubbery, was a disused tool-shed of respectable proportions, and within its walls Conradin found a haven, something that took on the varying aspects of a playroom and a cathedral. He had peopled it with a legion of familiar phantoms, evoked partly from fragments of history and partly from his own brain, but it also boasted two inmates of flesh and blood. In one corner lived a raggedplumaged Houdan hen, on which the boy lavished an affection that had scarcely another outlet. Further back in the gloom stood a large hutch, divided into two compartments, one of which was fronted with close iron bars. This was the abode of a large polecat-ferret, which a friendly butcher-boy had once smuggled, cage and all, into its present quarters, in exchange for a long-secreted hoard of small silver. Conradin was dreadfully afraid of the lithe, sharp-fanged beast, but it was his most treasured possession. Its very presence in the tool-shed was a secret and fearful joy, to be kept scrupulously from the knowledge of the Woman, as he privately dubbed his cousin. And one day, out of Heaven knows what material, he spun the beast a wonderful name, and from that moment it grew into a god and a religion. The Woman indulged in religion once a week at a church near by, and took Conradin with her, but to him the church service was an alien rite in the House of Rimmon. Every Thursday, in the dim and musty silence of the tool-shed, he worshipped with mystic and elaborate ceremonial before the wooden hutch where dwelt Sredni Vashtar, the great ferret. Red flowers in their season and scarlet berries in the winter-time were offered at his shrine, for he was a god who laid some special stress on the fierce impatient side of things, as opposed to the Woman's religion, which, as far as Conradin could observe, went to great lengths in the contrary direction. And on great festivals powdered nutmeg was strewn in front of his hutch, an important feature of the offering being that the nutmeg had to be stolen. These festivals were of irregular occurrence, and were chiefly appointed to celebrate some passing event. On one occasion, when Mrs. De Ropp suffered from acute toothache for three days, Conradin kept up the festival during the entire three days, and almost succeeded in persuading himself that Sredni Vashtar was personally responsible for the toothache. If the malady had lasted for another day the supply of nutmeg would have given out.

The Houdan hen was never drawn into the cult of Sredni Vashtar. Conradin had long ago settled that she was an Anabaptist. He did not pretend to have the remotest knowledge as to what an Anabaptist was, but he privately hoped that it was dashing and not very respectable. Mrs. De Ropp was the ground plan on which he based and detested all respectability.

After a while Conradin's absorption in the tool-shed began to attract the notice of his guardian. "It is not good for him to be pottering down there in all weathers," she promptly decided, and at breakfast one morning she announced that the Houdan hen had been sold and taken away overnight. With her short-sighted eyes she peered at Conradin, waiting for an outbreak of rage and sorrow, which she was ready to rebuke with a flow of excellent precepts and reasoning. But Conradin said nothing: there was nothing to be said. Something perhaps in his white set face gave her a momentary qualm, for at tea that afternoon there was toast on the table, a delicacy which she usually banned on the ground that it was bad for him; also because the making of it "gave trouble," a deadly offence in the middle-class feminine eye.

"I thought you liked toast," she exclaimed, with an injured air, observing that he did not touch it.

"Sometimes," said Conradin.

In the shed that evening there was an innovation in the worship of the hutch-god. Conradin had been wont to chant his praises, tonight be asked a boon.

"Do one thing for me, Sredni Vashtar."

The thing was not specified. As Sredni Vashtar was a god he must be supposed to know. And choking back a sob as he looked at that other empty comer, Conradin went back to the world he so hated.

And every night, in the welcome darkness of his bedroom, and every evening in the dusk of the tool-shed, Conradin's bitter litany went up: "Do one thing for me, Sredni Vashtar."

Mrs. De Ropp noticed that the visits to the shed did not cease, and one day she made a further journey of inspection.

"What are you keeping in that locked hutch?" she asked. "I believe it's guinea-pigs. I'll have them all cleared away."

Conradin shut his lips tight, but the Woman ransacked his bedroom till she found the carefully hidden key, and forthwith marched down to the shed to complete her discovery. It was a cold afternoon, and Conradin had been bidden to keep to the house. From the furthest window of the dining-room the door of the shed could just be seen beyond the corner of the shrubbery, and there Conradin stationed himself. He saw the Woman enter, and then be imagined her opening the door of the sacred hutch and peering down with her short-sighted eyes into the thick straw bed where his god lay hidden. Perhaps she would prod at the straw in her clumsy impatience. And Conradin fervently breathed his prayer for the last time. But he knew as he prayed that he did not believe. He knew that the Woman would come out presently with that pursed smile he loathed so well on her face, and that in an hour or two the gardener would carry away his wonderful god, a god no longer, but a simple brown ferret in a hutch. And he knew that the Woman would triumph always as she triumphed now, and that he would grow ever more sickly under her pestering and domineering and superior wisdom, till one day nothing would matter much more with him, and the doctor would be proved right. And in the sting and misery of his defeat, he began to chant loudly and defiantly the hymn of his threatened idol:

> *Sredni Vashtar went forth,*
> *His thoughts were red thoughts and his teeth were white.*
> *His enemies called for peace, but he brought them death.*
> *Sredni Vashtar the Beautiful.*

And then of a sudden he stopped his chanting and drew closer to the window-pane. The door of the shed still stood ajar as it had been left, and the minutes were slipping by. They were long minutes, but they slipped by nevertheless. He watched the starlings running and flying in little parties across the lawn; he counted them over and over again, with one eye always on that swinging door. A sour-faced maid came in to lay the table for tea, and still Conradin stood and waited and watched. Hope had crept by inches into his heart, and now a look of triumph began to blaze in his eyes that had only known the wistful patience of defeat. Under his breath, with a furtive exultation, he began once again the pæan of victory and devastation. And presently his eyes were rewarded: out through that doorway came a long, low, yellow-and-brown beast, with eyes a-blink at the waning daylight, and dark wet stains around the fur of jaws and throat. Conradin dropped on his knees. The great polecat-ferret made its way down to a small brook at the foot of the garden, drank for a moment, then crossed a little plank bridge and was lost to sight in the bushes. Such was the passing of Sredni Vashtar.

"Tea is ready," said the sour-faced maid; "where is the mistress?" "She went down to the shed some time ago," said Conradin. And while the maid went to summon her mistress to tea, Conradin fished a toasting-fork out of the sideboard drawer and proceeded to toast himself a piece of bread. And during the toasting of it and the buttering of it with much butter and the slow enjoyment of eating it, Conradin listened to the noises and silences which fell in quick spasms beyond the dining-room door. The loud foolish screaming of the maid, the answering chorus of wondering ejaculations from the kitchen region, the scuttering foot-steps and hurried embassies for outside help, and then, after a lull, the scared sobbings and the shuffling tread of those who bore a heavy burden into the house.

"Whoever will break it to the poor child? I couldn't for the life of me!" exclaimed a shrill voice. And while they debated the matter among themselves, Conradin made himself another piece of toast.

THE BRIDE COMES TO YELLOW SKY

Stephen Crane

Stephen Crane (1871 – 1900) was a prolific American writer, who packed quite a bit into a short life. Born in Newark, New Jersey, he wrote his first story aged fourteen. He moved to New York in 1892, self-published his first novel *Maggie: A Girl of the Streets*. Over the next two years, Crane wrote *The Red Badge of Courage*, which is now deemed a classic. Crane left New York and met his common-law wife Cora, a brothel-keeper, on his way to cover the Greco-Turkish war of 1897. They then travelled to England where Crane befriended Conrad, Wells, Gosse, Garnett and Ford Madox Ford. In 1900, having suffered a lung hemorrhage, he and Cora left for Germany, where he died that summer, aged twenty-eight.

I

The great Pullman was whirling onward with such dignity of motion that a glance from the window seemed simply to prove that the plains of Texas were pouring eastward. Vast flats of green grass, dull-hued spaces of mesquite and cactus, little groups of frame houses, woods of light and tender trees, all were sweeping into the east, sweeping over the horizon, a precipice.

A newly married pair had boarded this coach at San Antonio. The man's face was reddened from many days in the wind and sun, and a direct result of his new black clothes was that his brick-colored hands were constantly performing in a most conscious fashion. From time to time he looked down respectfully at his attire. He sat with a hand on each knee, like a man waiting in a barber's shop. The glances he devoted to other passengers were furtive and shy.

The bride was not pretty, nor was she very young. She wore a dress of blue cashmere, with small reservations of velvet here and there and with steel buttons abounding. She continually twisted her head to regard her puff sleeves, very stiff, straight, and high. They embarrassed her. It was quite apparent that she had cooked, and that she expected to cook, dutifully. The blushes caused by the careless scrutiny of some passengers as she had entered the car were strange to see upon this plain, under-class countenance, which was drawn in placid, almost emotionless lines.

They were evidently very happy. "Ever been in a parlor-car before?" he asked, smiling with delight.

"No," she answered, "I never was. It's fine, ain't it?"

"Great! And then after a while we'll go forward to the diner and get a big layout. Finest meal in the world. Charge a dollar."

"Oh, do they?" cried the bride. "Charge a dollar? Why, that's too much – for us – ain't it, Jack?"

"Not this trip, anyhow," he answered bravely. "We're going to go the whole thing."

Later, he explained to her about the trains. "You see, it's a thousand miles from one end of Texas to the other, and this train runs right across it and never stops but four times." He had the pride of an owner. He pointed out to her the dazzling fittings of the coach, and in truth her eyes opened wider as she contemplated the sea-green figured velvet, the shining brass, silver, and glass, the wood that gleamed as darkly brilliant as the surface of a pool of oil. At one end a bronze figure sturdily held a support for a separated chamber, and at convenient places on the ceiling were frescoes in olive and silver.

To the minds of the pair, their surroundings reflected the glory of their marriage that morning in San Antonio. This was the environment of their new estate, and the man's face in particular beamed with an elation that made him appear ridiculous to the negro porter. This individual at times surveyed them from afar with an amused and superior grin. On other occasions he bullied them with skill in ways that did not make it exactly plain to them that they were being bullied. He subtly used all the manners of the most unconquerable kind of snobbery. He oppressed them, but of this oppression they had small knowledge, and they speedily forgot that infrequently a number of travelers covered them with stares of derisive enjoyment. Historically there was supposed to be something infinitely humorous in their situation.

"We are due in Yellow Sky at 3:42," he said, looking tenderly into her eyes.

"Oh, are we?" she said, as if she had not been aware of it. To evince surprise at her husband's statement was part of her wifely amiability. She took from a pocket a little silver watch, and as she held it before her and stared at it with a frown of attention, the new husband's face shone.

"I bought it in San Anton' from a friend of mine," he told her gleefully.

"It's seventeen minutes past twelve," she said, looking up at him with a kind of shy and clumsy coquetry. A passenger, noting this play, grew excessively sardonic, and winked at himself in one of the numerous mirrors.

At last they went to the dining-car. Two rows of negro waiters, in glowing white suits, surveyed their entrance with the interest and also the equanimity of men who had been forewarned. The pair fell to the lot of a waiter who happened to feel pleasure in steering them through their meal. He viewed them with the manner of a fatherly pilot, his countenance radiant with benevolence. The patronage, entwined with the ordinary deference, was not plain to them. And yet, as they returned to their coach, they showed in their faces a sense of escape.

To the left, miles down a long purple slope, was a little ribbon of mist where moved the keening Rio Grande. The train was approaching it at an angle, and the apex was Yellow Sky. Presently it was apparent that, as the distance from Yellow Sky grew shorter, the husband became commensurately restless. His brick-red hands were more insistent in their prominence. Occasionally he was even rather absent-minded and far-away when the bride leaned forward and addressed him.

As a matter of truth, Jack Potter was beginning to find the shadow of a deed weigh upon him like a leaden slab. He, the town marshal of Yellow Sky, a man known, liked, and feared in his corner, a prominent person, had gone to San Antonio to meet a girl he believed he loved, and there, after the usual prayers, had actually induced her to marry him, without consulting Yellow Sky for any part of the transaction. He was now bringing his bride before an innocent and unsuspecting community.

Of course, people in Yellow Sky married as it pleased them, in accordance with a general custom; but such was Potter's thought of his duty to his friends, or of their idea of his duty, or of an unspoken form which does not control men in these matters, that he felt he was heinous. He had committed an extraordinary crime. Face to face with this girl in San Antonio, and spurred by his sharp impulse, he had gone headlong over all the social hedges. At San Antonio he was like a man hidden in the dark. A knife to sever any friendly duty, any form, was easy to his hand in that remote city. But the hour of Yellow Sky, the hour of daylight, was approaching.

He knew full well that his marriage was an important thing to his town. It could only be exceeded by the burning of the new hotel. His friends could not forgive him. Frequently he had reflected on the advisability of telling them by telegraph, but a new cowardice had been upon him. He feared to do it. And now the train was hurrying him toward a scene of amazement, glee, and reproach. He glanced out of the window at the line of haze swinging slowly in towards the train.

Yellow Sky had a kind of brass band, which played painfully, to the delight of the populace. He laughed without heart as he thought of it. If the citizens could dream of his prospective arrival with his bride, they would parade the band at the station and escort them, amid cheers and laughing congratulations, to his adobe home.

He resolved that he would use all the devices of speed and plains-craft in making the journey from the station to his house. Once within that safe citadel he could issue some sort of a vocal bulletin, and then not go among the citizens until they had time to wear off a little of their enthusiasm.

The bride looked anxiously at him. "What's worrying you, Jack?"

He laughed again. "I'm not worrying, girl. I'm only thinking of Yellow Sky."

She flushed in comprehension.

A sense of mutual guilt invaded their minds and developed a finer tenderness. They looked at each other with eyes softly aglow. But Potter often laughed the same nervous laugh. The flush upon the bride's face seemed quite permanent.

The traitor to the feelings of Yellow Sky narrowly watched the speeding landscape. "We're nearly there," he said.

Presently the porter came and announced the proximity of Potter's home. He held a brush in his hand and, with all his airy superiority gone, he brushed Potter's new clothes as the latter slowly turned this way and that way. Potter fumbled out a coin and gave it to the porter, as he had seen others do. It was a heavy and muscle-bound business, as that of a man shoeing his first horse.

The porter took their bag, and as the train began to slow they moved forward to the hooded platform of the car. Presently the two engines and their long string of coaches rushed into the station of Yellow Sky.

"They have to take water here," said Potter, from a constricted throat and in mournful cadence, as one announcing death. Before the train stopped, his eye had swept the length of the platform, and he was glad and astonished to see there was none upon it but the station-agent, who, with a slightly hurried and anxious air, was walking toward the water-tanks. When the train had halted, the porter alighted first and placed in position a little temporary step.

"Come on, girl," said Potter hoarsely. As he helped her down they each laughed on a false note. He took the bag from the negro, and bade his wife cling to his arm. As they slunk rapidly away, his hang-dog glance perceived that they were unloading the two trunks, and also that the station-agent far ahead near the baggage-car had turned and was running toward him, making gestures. He laughed, and groaned as he laughed, when he noted the first effect of his marital bliss upon Yellow Sky. He gripped his wife's arm firmly to his side, and they fled. Behind them the porter stood chuckling fatuously.

II

The California Express on the Southern Railway was due at Yellow Sky in twenty-one minutes. There were six men at the bar of the "Weary Gentleman" saloon. One was a drummer who talked a great deal and rapidly; three were Texans who did not care to talk at that time; and two were Mexican sheep-herders who did not talk as a general practice in the "Weary Gentleman" saloon. The barkeeper's dog lay on the boardwalk that crossed in front of the door. His head was on his paws, and he glanced drowsily here and there with the constant vigilance of a dog that is kicked on occasion. Across the sandy street were some vivid green grass plots, so wonderful in appearance amid the sands that burned near them in a blazing sun that they caused a doubt in the mind. They exactly resembled the grass mats used to represent lawns on the stage. At the cooler end of the railway station a man without a coat sat in a tilted chair and smoked his pipe. The fresh-cut bank of the Rio Grande circled near the town, and there could be seen beyond it a great, plum-colored plain of mesquite.

Save for the busy drummer and his companions in the saloon, Yellow Sky was dozing. The new-comer leaned gracefully upon the bar, and recited many tales with the confidence of a bard who has come upon a new field.

" – and at the moment that the old man fell down stairs with the bureau in his arms, the old woman was coming up with two scuttles of coal, and, of course—"

The drummer's tale was interrupted by a young man who suddenly appeared in the open door. He cried: "Scratchy Wilson's drunk, and has turned loose with both hands." The two Mexicans at once set down their glasses and faded out of the rear entrance of the saloon.

The drummer, innocent and jocular, answered: "All right, old man. S'pose he has. Come in and have a drink, anyhow."

But the information had made such an obvious cleft in every skull in the room that the drummer was obliged to see its importance. All had become instantly solemn. "Say," said he, mystified, "what is this?" His three companions made the introductory gesture of eloquent speech, but the young man at the door forestalled them.

"It means, my friend," he answered, as he came into the saloon, "that for the next two hours this town won't be a health resort."

The barkeeper went to the door and locked and barred it. Reaching out of the window, he pulled in heavy wooden shutters and barred them. Immediately a solemn, chapel-like gloom was upon the place. The drummer was looking from one to another.

"But, say," he cried, "what is this, anyhow? You don't mean there is going to be a gun-fight?"

"Don't know whether there'll be a fight or not," answered one man grimly. "But there'll be some shootin' – some good shootin'."

The young man who had warned them waved his hand. "Oh, there'll be a fight fast enough if anyone wants it. Anybody can get a fight out there in the street. There's a fight just waiting."

The drummer seemed to be swayed between the interest of a foreigner and a perception of personal danger.

"What did you say his name was?" he asked.

"Scratchy Wilson," they answered in chorus.

"And will he kill anybody? What are you going to do? Does this happen often? Does he rampage around like this once a week or so? Can he break in that door?"

"No, he can't break down that door," replied the barkeeper. "He's tried it three times. But when he comes you'd better lay down on the floor, stranger. He's dead sure to shoot at it, and a bullet may come through."

Thereafter the drummer kept a strict eye upon the door. The time had not yet been called for him to hug the floor, but, as a minor precaution, he sidled near to the wall. "Will he kill anybody?" he said again.

The men laughed low and scornfully at the question.

"He's out to shoot, and he's out for trouble. Don't see any good in experimentin' with him."

"But what do you do in a case like this? What do you do?"

A man responded: "Why, he and Jack Potter—"

"But," in chorus, the other men interrupted, "Jack Potter's in San Anton'."

"Well, who is he? What's he got to do with it?"

"Oh, he's the town marshal. He goes out and fights Scratchy when he gets on one of these tears."

"Wow," said the drummer, mopping his brow. "Nice job he's got."

The voices had toned away to mere whisperings. The drummer wished to ask further questions which were born of an increasing anxiety and bewilderment; but when he attempted them, the men merely looked at him in irritation and motioned him to remain silent. A tense waiting hush was upon them. In the deep shadows of the room their eyes shone as they listened for sounds from the street. One man made three gestures at the barkeeper, and the latter, moving like a ghost, handed him a glass and a bottle. The man poured a full glass of whisky, and set down the bottle noiselessly. He gulped the whisky in a swallow, and turned again toward the door in immovable silence. The drummer saw that the barkeeper, without a sound, had taken a Winchester from beneath the bar. Later he saw this individual beckoning to him, so he tiptoed across the room.

"You better come with me back of the bar."

"No, thanks," said the drummer, perspiring. "I'd rather be where I can make a break for the back door."

Whereupon the man of bottles made a kindly but peremptory gesture. The drummer obeyed it, and finding himself seated on a box with his head below the level of the bar, balm was laid upon his soul at sight of various zinc and copper fittings that bore a resemblance to armor-plate. The barkeeper took a seat comfortably upon an adjacent box.

"You see," he whispered, "this here Scratchy Wilson is a wonder with a gun – a perfect wonder – and when he goes on the war trail, we hunt our holes – naturally. He's about the last one of the old gang that used to hang out along the river here. He's a terror when he's drunk. When he's sober he's all right – kind of simple – wouldn't hurt a fly – nicest fellow in town. But when he's drunk – whoo!"

There were periods of stillness. "I wish Jack Potter was back from San Anton'," said the barkeeper. "He shot Wilson up once – in the leg – and he would sail in and pull out the kinks in this thing."

Presently they heard from a distance the sound of a shot, followed by three wild yowls. It instantly removed a bond from the men in the darkened saloon. There was a shuffling of feet. They looked at each other. "Here he comes," they said.

III

A man in a maroon-colored flannel shirt, which had been purchased for purposes of decoration and made, principally, by some Jewish women on the east side of New York, rounded a corner and walked into the middle of the main street of Yellow Sky. In either hand the man held a long, heavy, blue-black revolver. Often he yelled, and these cries rang through a semblance of a deserted village, shrilly flying over the roofs in a volume that seemed to have no relation to the ordinary vocal strength of a man. It was as if the surrounding stillness formed the arch of a tomb over him. These cries of ferocious challenge rang against walls of silence. And his boots had red tops with gilded imprints, of the kind beloved in winter by little sledding boys on the hillsides of New England.

The man's face flamed in a rage begot of whisky. His eyes, rolling and yet keen for ambush, hunted the still doorways and windows. He walked with the creeping movement of the midnight cat. As it occurred to him, he roared menacing information. The long revolvers in his hands were as easy as straws; they were moved with an electric swiftness. The little fingers of each hand played sometimes in a musician's way. Plain from the low collar of the shirt, the cords of his neck straightened and sank, straightened and sank, as passion moved him. The only sounds were his terrible invitations. The calm adobes preserved their demeanor at the passing of this small thing in the middle of the street.

There was no offer of fight; no offer of fight. The man called to the sky. There were no attractions. He bellowed and fumed and swayed his revolvers here and everywhere.

The dog of the barkeeper of the "Weary Gentleman" saloon had not appreciated the advance of events. He yet lay dozing in front of his master's door. At sight of the dog, the man paused and raised his revolver humorously. At sight of the man, the dog sprang up and walked diagonally away, with a sullen head, and growling. The man yelled, and the dog broke into a gallop. As it was about to enter an alley, there was a loud noise, a whistling, and something spat the ground directly before it. The dog screamed, and, wheeling in terror, galloped headlong in a new direction. Again there was a noise, a whistling, and sand was kicked viciously before it. Fear-stricken, the dog turned and flurried like an animal in a pen. The man stood laughing, his weapons at his hips.

Ultimately the man was attracted by the closed door of the "Weary Gentleman" saloon. He went to it, and hammering with a revolver, demanded drink.

The door remaining imperturbable, he picked a bit of paper from the walk and nailed it to the framework with a knife. He then turned his back contemptuously upon this popular resort, and walking to the opposite side of the street, and spinning there on his heel quickly and lithely, fired at the bit of paper. He missed it by a half inch. He swore at himself, and went away. Later, he comfortably fusilladed the windows of his most intimate friend. The man was playing with this town. It was a toy for him.

But still there was no offer of fight. The name of Jack Potter, his ancient antagonist, entered his mind, and he concluded that it would be a glad thing if he should go to Potter's house and by bombardment induce him to come out and fight. He moved in the direction of his desire, chanting Apache scalp-music.

When he arrived at it, Potter's house presented the same still front as had the other adobes. Taking up a strategic position, the man howled a challenge. But this house regarded him as might a great stone god. It gave no sign. After a decent wait, the man howled further challenges, mingling with them wonderful epithets.

Presently there came the spectacle of a man churning himself into deepest rage over the immobility of a house. He fumed at it as the winter wind attacks a prairie cabin in the North. To the distance there should have gone the sound of a tumult like the fighting of 200 Mexicans. As necessity bade him, he paused for breath or to reload his revolvers.

IV

Potter and his bride walked sheepishly and with speed. Sometimes they laughed together shamefacedly and low.

"Next corner, dear," he said finally.

They put forth the efforts of a pair walking bowed against a strong wind. Potter was about to raise a finger to point the first appearance of the new home when, as they circled the corner, they came face to face with a man in a maroon-colored shirt who was feverishly pushing cartridges into a large revolver. Upon the instant the man dropped his revolver to the ground, and, like lightning, whipped another from its holster. The second weapon was aimed at the bridegroom's chest.

There was silence. Potter's mouth seemed to be merely a grave for his tongue. He exhibited an instinct to at once loosen his arm from the woman's grip, and he dropped the bag to the sand. As for the bride, her face had gone as yellow as old cloth. She was a slave to hideous rites gazing at the apparitional snake.

The two men faced each other at a distance of three paces. He of the revolver smiled with a new and quiet ferocity.

"Tried to sneak up on me," he said. "Tried to sneak up on me!" His eyes grew more baleful. As Potter made a slight movement, the man thrust his revolver venomously forward. "No, don't you do it, Jack Potter. Don't you move a finger toward a gun just yet. Don't you move an eyelash. The time has come for me to settle with you, and I'm goin' to do it my own way and loaf along with no interferin'. So if you don't want a gun bent on you, just mind what I tell you."

Potter looked at his enemy. "I ain't got a gun on me, Scratchy," he said. "Honest, I ain't." He was stiffening and steadying, but yet somewhere at the back of his mind a vision of the Pullman floated, the sea-green figured velvet, the shining brass, silver, and glass, the wood that gleamed as darkly brilliant as the surface of a pool of oil – all the glory of the marriage, the environment of the new estate. "You know I fight when it comes to fighting, Scratchy Wilson, but I ain't got a gun on me. You'll have to do all the shootin' yourself."

His enemy's face went livid. He stepped forward and lashed his weapon to and fro before Potter's chest. "Don't you tell me you ain't got no gun on you, you whelp. Don't tell me no lie like that. There ain't a man in Texas ever seen you without no gun. Don't take me for no kid." His eyes blazed with light, and his throat worked like a pump.

"I ain't takin' you for no kid," answered Potter. His heels had not moved an inch backward. "I'm takin' you for a damn fool. I tell you I ain't got a gun, and I ain't. If you're goin' to shoot me up, you better begin now. You'll never get a chance like this again."

So much enforced reasoning had told on Wilson's rage. He was calmer. "If you ain't got a gun, why ain't you got a gun?" he sneered. "Been to Sunday-school?"

"I ain't got a gun because I've just come from San Anton' with my wife. I'm married," said Potter. "And if I'd thought there was going to be any galoots like you prowling around when I brought my wife home, I'd had a gun, and don't you forget it."

"Married!" said Scratchy, not at all comprehending.

"Yes, married. I'm married," said Potter distinctly.

"Married?" said Scratchy. Seemingly for the first time he saw the drooping, drowning woman at the other man's side. "No!" he said. He was like a creature allowed a glimpse of another world. He moved a pace backward, and his arm with the revolver dropped to his side. "Is this the lady?" he asked.

"Yes, this is the lady," answered Potter.

There was another period of silence.

"Well," said Wilson at last, slowly, "I s'pose it's all off now."

"It's all off if you say so, Scratchy. You know I didn't make the trouble." Potter lifted his valise.

"Well, I 'low it's off, Jack," said Wilson. He was looking at the ground. "Married!" He was not a student of chivalry; it was merely that in the presence of this foreign condition he was a simple child of the earlier plains. He picked up his starboard revolver, and placing both weapons in their holsters, he went away. His feet made funnel-shaped tracks in the heavy sand.

CONSEQUENCES

Willa Cather

Willa Cather (1873–1947) was an American author who wrote highly praised novels depicting frontier life on the Great Plains. She was awarded the Pulitzer Prize in 1923 for her novel *One of Ours*. Cather received the Gold Medal for Fiction from the National Institute of Arts and Letters in 1944, an award given once a decade for an author's complete body of work. She once observed "Most of the basic material a writer works with is acquired before the age of fifteen", which is either inspiring, or depressing – and probably true.

Henry Eastman, a lawyer, aged forty, was standing beside the Flatiron Building in a driving November rainstorm, signaling frantically for a taxi. It was six-thirty, and everything on wheels was engaged. The streets were in confusion about him, the sky was in turmoil above him, and the Flatiron Building, which seemed about to blow down, threw water like a millshoot. Suddenly, out of the brutal struggle of men and cars and machines and people tilting at each other with umbrellas, a quiet, well-mannered limousine paused before him, at the curb, and an agreeable, ruddy countenance confronted him through the open window of the car.

"Don't you want me to pick you up, Mr. Eastman? I'm running directly home now."

Eastman recognized Kier Cavenaugh, a young man of pleasure, who lived in the house on Central Park South, where he himself had an apartment.

"Don't I?" he exclaimed, bolting into the car. "I'll risk getting your cushions wet without compunction. I came up in a taxi, but I didn't hold it. Bad economy. I thought I saw your car down on Fourteenth Street about half an hour ago."

The owner of the car smiled. He had a pleasant, round face and round eyes, and a fringe of smooth, yellow hair showed under the brim of his soft felt hat. "With a lot of little broilers fluttering into it? You did. I know some girls who work in the cheap shops down there. I happened to be downtown and I stopped and took a load of them home. I do sometimes. Saves their poor little clothes, you know. Their shoes are never any good."

Eastman looked at his rescuer. "Aren't they notoriously afraid of cars and smooth young men?" he inquired.

Cavenaugh shook his head. "They know which cars are safe and which are chancy. They put each other wise. You have to take a bunch at a time, of course. The Italian girls can never come along; their men shoot. The girls understand, all right; but their fathers don't. One gets to see queer places, sometimes, taking them home."

Eastman laughed drily. "Every time I touch the circle of your acquaintance, Cavenaugh, it's a little wider. You must know New York pretty well by this time."

"Yes, but I'm on my good behavior below Twenty-third Street," the young man replied with simplicity. "My little friends down there would give me a good character. They're wise little girls. They have grand ways with each other, a romantic code of loyalty. You can find a good many of the lost virtues among them."

The car was standing still in a traffic block at Fortieth Street, when Cavenaugh suddenly drew his face away from the window and touched Eastman's arm. "Look, please. You see that hansom with the bony gray horse – driver has a broken hat and red flannel around his throat. Can you see who is inside?"

Eastman peered out. The hansom was just cutting across the line, and the driver was making a great fuss about it, bobbing his head and waving his whip. He jerked his dripping old horse into Fortieth Street and clattered off past the Public Library grounds toward Sixth Avenue. "No, I couldn't see the passenger. Someone you know?"

"Could you see whether there was a passenger?" Cavenaugh asked.

"Why, yes. A man, I think. I saw his elbow on the apron. No driver ever behaves like that unless he has a passenger."

"Yes, I may have been mistaken," Cavenaugh murmured absent-mindedly.

Ten minutes or so later, after Cavenaugh's car had turned off Fifth Avenue into Fifty-eighth Street, Eastman exclaimed, "There's your same cabby, and his cart's empty. He's headed for a drink now, I suppose." The driver in the broken hat and the red flannel neck cloth was still brandishing the whip over his old gray. He was coming from the west now, and turned down Sixth Avenue, under the elevated.

Cavenaugh's car stopped at the bachelor apartment house between Sixth and Seventh Avenues where he and Eastman lived, and they went up in the elevator together. They were still talking when the lift stopped at Cavenaugh's floor, and Eastman stepped out with him and walked down the hall, finishing his sentence while Cavenaugh found his latch-key. When he opened the door, a wave of fresh cigarette smoke greeted them. Cavenaugh stopped short and stared into his hall-way. "Now how in the devil – !" he exclaimed angrily.

"Someone waiting for you? Oh, no, thanks. I wasn't coming in. I have to work tonight. Thank you, but I couldn't." Eastman nodded and went up the two flights to his own rooms.

Though Eastman did not customarily keep a servant he had this winter a man who had been lent to him by a friend who was abroad. Rollins met him at the door and took his coat and hat.

"Put out my dinner clothes, Rollins, and then get out of here until ten o'clock. I've promised to go to a supper tonight. I shan't be dining. I've had a late tea and I'm going to work until ten. You may put out some kumiss and biscuit for me."

Rollins took himself off, and Eastman settled down at the big table in his sitting-room. He had to read a lot of letters submitted as evidence in a breach of contract case, and before he got very far he found that long paragraphs in some of the letters were written in German. He had a German dictionary at his office, but none here. Rollins had gone, and anyhow, the bookstores would be closed. He remembered having seen a row of dictionaries on the lower shelf of one of Cavenaugh's bookcases. Cavenaugh had a lot of books, though he never read anything but new stuff. Eastman prudently turned down his student's lamp very low – the thing had an evil habit of smoking – and went down two flights to Cavenaugh's door.

The young man himself answered Eastman's ring. He was freshly dressed for the evening, except for a brown smoking jacket, and his yellow hair had been brushed until it shone. He hesitated as he confronted his caller, still holding the door knob, and his round eyes and smooth forehead made their best imitation of a frown. When Eastman began to apologize, Cavenaugh's manner suddenly changed. He caught his arm and jerked him into the narrow hall. "Come in, come in. Right along!" he said excitedly. "Right along," he repeated as he pushed Eastman before him into his sitting-room. "Well I'll—" He stopped short at the door and looked about his own room with an air of complete mystification. The back window was wide open and a strong wind was blowing in. Cavenaugh walked over to the window and stuck out his head, looking up and down the fire escape. When he pulled his head in, he drew down the sash.

"I had a visitor I wanted you to see," he explained with a nervous smile. "At least I thought I had. He must have gone out that way," nodding toward the window.

"Call him back. I only came to borrow a German dictionary, if you have one. Can't stay. Call him back."

Cavenaugh shook his head despondently. "No use. He's beat it. Nowhere in sight."

"He must be active. Has he left something?" Eastman pointed to a very dirty white glove that lay on the floor under the window.

"Yes, that's his."

Cavenaugh reached for his tongs, picked up the glove, and tossed it into the grate, where it quickly shriveled on the coals. Eastman felt that he had happened in upon something disagreeable, possibly something shady, and he wanted to get away at once. Cavenaugh stood staring at the fire and seemed stupid and dazed; so he repeated his request rather sternly, "I think I've seen a German dictionary down there among your books. May I have it?"

Cavenaugh blinked at him. "A German dictionary? Oh, possibly! Those were my father's. I scarcely know what there is." He put down the tongs and began to wipe his hands nervously with his handkerchief.

Eastman went over to the bookcase behind the Chesterfield, opened the door, swooped upon the book he wanted and stuck it under his arm. He felt perfectly certain now that something shady had been going on in Cavenaugh's rooms, and he saw no reason why he should come in for any hang-over. "Thanks. I'll send it back tomorrow," he said curtly as he made for the door.

Cavenaugh followed him. "Wait a moment. I wanted you to see him. You did see his glove," glancing at the grate.

Eastman laughed disagreeably. "I saw a glove. That's not evidence. Do your friends often use that means of exit? Somewhat inconvenient."

Cavenaugh gave him a startled glance. "Wouldn't you think so? For an old man, a very rickety old party? The ladders are steep, you know, and rusty." He approached the window again and put it up softly. In a moment he drew his head back with a jerk. He caught Eastman's arm and shoved him toward the window. "Hurry, please. Look! Down there." He pointed to the little patch of paved court four flights down.

The square of pavement was so small and the walls about it were so high, that it was a good deal like looking down a well. Four tall buildings backed upon the same court and made a kind of shaft, with flagstones at the bottom, and at the top a square of dark blue with some stars in it. At the bottom of the shaft Eastman saw a black figure, a man in a caped coat and a tall hat stealing cautiously around, not across the square of pavement, keeping close to the dark wall and avoiding the streak of light that fell on the flagstones from a window in the opposite house. Seen from that height he was of course fore-shortened and probably looked more shambling and decrepit than he was. He picked his way along with exaggerated care and looked like a silly old cat crossing a wet street. When he reached the gate that led into an alley way between two buildings, he felt about for the latch, opened the door a mere crack, and then shot out under the feeble lamp that burned in the brick arch over the gateway. The door closed after him.

"He'll get run in," Eastman remarked curtly, turning away from the window. "That door shouldn't be left unlocked. Any crook could come in. I'll speak to the janitor about it, if you don't mind," he added sarcastically.

"Wish you would." Cavenaugh stood brushing down the front of his jacket, first with his right hand and then with his left. "You saw him, didn't you?"

"Enough of him. Seems eccentric. I have to see a lot of buggy people. They don't take me in any more. But I'm keeping you and I'm in a hurry myself. Good night."

Cavenaugh put out his hand detainingly and started to say something; but Eastman rudely turned his back and went down the hall and out of the door. He had never felt anything shady about Cavenaugh before, and he was sorry he had gone down for the dictionary. In five minutes he was deep in his papers; but in the half hour when he was loafing before he dressed to go out, the young man's curious behavior came into his mind again.

Eastman had merely a neighborly acquaintance with Cavenaugh. He had been to a supper at the young man's rooms once, but he didn't particularly like Cavenaugh's friends; so the next time he was asked, he had another engagement. He liked Cavenaugh himself, if for nothing else than because he was so cheerful and trim and ruddy. A good complexion is always at a premium in New York, especially when it shines reassuringly on a man who does everything in the world to lose it. It encourages fellow mortals as to the inherent vigor of the human organism and the amount of bad treatment it will stand for. "Footprints that perhaps another," etc.

Cavenaugh, he knew, had plenty of money. He was the son of a Pennsylvania preacher, who died soon after he discovered that his ancestral acres were full of petroleum, and Kier had come to New York to burn some of the oil. He was thirty-two and was still at it; spent his life, literally, among the breakers. His motor hit the Park every morning as if it were the first time ever. He took people out to supper every night. He went from restaurant to restaurant, sometimes to half-a-dozen in an evening. The head waiters were his hosts and their cordiality made him happy. They made a life-line for him up Broadway and down Fifth Avenue. Cavenaugh was still fresh and smooth, round and plump, with a lustre to his hair and white teeth and a clear look in his round eyes. He seemed absolutely unwearied and unimpaired; never bored and never carried away.

Eastman always smiled when he met Cavenaugh in the entrance hall, serenely going forth to or returning from gladiatorial combats with joy, or when he saw him rolling smoothly up to the door in his car in the morning after a restful night in one of the remarkable new roadhouses he was always finding. Eastman had seen a good many young men disappear on Cavenaugh's route, and he admired this young man's endurance.

Tonight, for the first time, he had got a whiff of something unwholesome about the fellow – bad nerves, bad company, something on hand that he was ashamed of, a visitor old and vicious, who must have had a key to Cavenaugh's apartment, for he was evidently there when Cavenaugh returned at seven o'clock. Probably it was the same man Cavenaugh had seen in the hansom. He must have been able to let himself in, for Cavenaugh kept no man but his chauffeur; or perhaps the janitor had been instructed to let him in. In either case, and whoever he was, it was clear enough that Cavenaugh was ashamed of him and was mixing up in questionable business of some kind.

Eastman sent Cavenaugh's book back by Rollins, and for the next few weeks he had no word with him beyond a casual greeting when they happened to meet in the hall or the elevator. One Sunday morning Cavenaugh telephoned up to him to ask if he could motor out to a road-house in Connecticut that afternoon and have supper; but when Eastman found there were to be other guests he declined.

On New Year's eve Eastman dined at the University Club at six o'clock and hurried home before the usual manifestations of insanity had begun in the streets. When Rollins brought his smoking coat, he asked him whether he wouldn't like to get off early.

"Yes, sir. But won't you be dressing, Mr. Eastman?" he inquired.

"Not tonight." Eastman handed him a bill. "Bring some change in the morning. There'll be fees."

Rollins lost no time in putting everything to rights for the night, and Eastman couldn't help wishing that he were in such a hurry to be off somewhere himself. When he heard the hall door close softly, he wondered if there were any place, after all, that he wanted to go. From his window he looked down at the long lines of motors and taxis waiting for a signal to cross Broadway. He thought of some of their probable destinations and decided that none of those places pulled him very hard. The night was warm and wet, the air was drizzly. Vapor hung in clouds about the *Times* Building, half hid the top of it, and made a luminous haze along Broadway. While he was looking down at the army of wet, black carriage-tops and their reflected headlights and tail-lights, Eastman heard a ring at his door. He deliberated. If it were a caller, the hall porter would have telephoned up. It must be the janitor. When he opened the door, there stood a rosy young man in a tuxedo, without a coat or hat.

"Pardon. Should I have telephoned? I half thought you wouldn't be in."

Eastman laughed. "Come in, Cavenaugh. You weren't sure whether you wanted company or not, eh, and you were trying to let chance decide it? That was exactly my state of mind. Let's accept the verdict." When they emerged from the narrow hall into his sitting-room, he pointed out a seat by the fire to his guest. He brought a tray of decanters and soda bottles and placed it on his writing table.

Cavenaugh hesitated, standing by the fire. "Sure you weren't starting for somewhere?"

"Do I look it? No, I was just making up my mind to stick it out alone when you rang. Have one?" He picked up a tall tumbler.

"Yes, thank you. I always do."

Eastman chuckled. "Lucky boy! So will I. I had a very early dinner. New York is the most arid place on holidays," he continued as he rattled the ice in the glasses. "When one gets too old to hit the rapids down there, and tired of gobbling food to heathenish dance music, there is absolutely no place where you can get a chop and some milk toast in peace, unless you have strong ties of blood brotherhood on upper Fifth Avenue. But you, why aren't you starting for somewhere?"

The young man sipped his soda and shook his head as he replied:

"Oh, I couldn't get a chop, either. I know only flashy people, of course." He looked up at his host with such a grave and candid expression that Eastman decided there couldn't be anything very crooked about the fellow. His smooth cheeks were positively cherubic.

"Well, what's the matter with them? Aren't they flashing tonight?"

"Only the very new ones seem to flash on New Year's eve. The older ones fade away. Maybe they are hunting a chop, too."

"Well" – Eastman sat down – "holidays do dash one. I was just about to write a letter to a pair of maiden aunts in my old home town, up-state; old coasting hill, snow-covered pines, lights in the church windows. That's what you've saved me from."

Cavenaugh shook himself. "Oh, I'm sure that wouldn't have been good for you. Pardon me," he rose and took a photograph from the bookcase, a handsome man in shooting clothes. "Dudley, isn't it? Did you know him well?"

"Yes. An old friend. Terrible thing, wasn't it? I haven't got over the jolt yet."

"His suicide? Yes, terrible! Did you know his wife?"

"Slightly. Well enough to admire her very much. She must be terribly broken up. I wonder Dudley didn't think of that."

Cavenaugh replaced the photograph carefully, lit a cigarette, and standing before the fire began to smoke. "Would you mind telling me about him? I never met him, but of course I'd read a lot about him, and I can't help feeling interested. It was a queer thing."

Eastman took out his cigar case and leaned back in his deep chair. "In the days when I knew him best he hadn't any story, like the happy nations. Everything was properly arranged for him before he was born. He came into the world happy, healthy, clever, straight, with the right sort of connections and the right kind of fortune, neither too large nor too small. He helped to make the world an agreeable place to live in until he was twenty-six. Then he married as he should have married. His wife was a Californian, educated abroad. Beautiful. You have seen her picture?"

Cavenaugh nodded. "Oh, many of them."

"She was interesting, too. Though she was distinctly a person of the world, she had retained something, just enough of the large Western manner. She had the habit of authority, of calling out a special train if she needed it, of using all our ingenious mechanical contrivances lightly and easily, without over-rating them. She and Dudley knew how to live better than most people. Their house was the most charming one I have ever known in New York. You felt freedom there, and a zest of life, and safety – absolute sanctuary – from everything sordid or petty. A whole society like that would justify the creation of man and would make our planet shine with a soft, peculiar radiance among the constellations. You think I'm putting it on thick?"

The young man sighed gently. "Oh, no! One has always felt there must be people like that. I've never known any."

"They had two children, beautiful ones. After they had been married for eight years, Rosina met this Spaniard. He must have amounted to something. She wasn't a flighty woman. She came home and told Dudley how matters stood. He persuaded her to stay at home for six months and try to pull up. They were both fair-minded people, and I'm as sure as if I were the Almighty, that she did try. But at the end of the time, Rosina went quietly off to Spain, and Dudley went to hunt in the Canadian Rockies. I met his party out there. I didn't know his wife had left him and talked about her a good deal. I noticed that he never drank anything, and his light used to shine through the log chinks of his room until all hours, even after a hard day's hunting. When I got back to New York, rumors were creeping about. Dudley did not come back. He bought a ranch in Wyoming, built a big log house and kept splendid dogs and horses. One of his sisters went out to keep house for him, and the children were there when they were not in school. He had a great many visitors, and everyone who came back talked about how well Dudley kept things going.

"He put in two years out there. Then, last month, he had to come back on business. A trust fund had to be settled up, and he was administrator. I saw him at the club; same light, quick step, same gracious handshake. He was getting gray, and there was something softer in his manner; but he had a fine red tan on his face and said he found it delightful to be here in the season when everything is going hard. The Madison Avenue house had been closed since Rosina left it. He went there to get some things his sister wanted. That, of course, was the mistake. He went alone, in the afternoon, and didn't go out for dinner – found some sherry and tins of biscuit in the sideboard. He shot himself sometime that night. There were pistols in his smoking-room. They found burnt-out candles beside him in the morning. The gas and electricity were shut off. I suppose there, in his own house, among his own things, it was too much for him. He left no letters."

Cavenaugh blinked and brushed the lapel of his coat. "I suppose," he said slowly, "that every suicide is logical and reasonable, if one knew all the facts."

Eastman roused himself. "No, I don't think so. I've known too many fellows who went off like that – more than I deserve, I think – and some of them were absolutely inexplicable. I can understand Dudley; but I can't see why healthy bachelors, with money enough, like ourselves, need such a device. It reminds me of what Dr. Johnson said, that the most discouraging thing about life is the number of fads and hobbies and fake religions it takes to put people through a few years of it."

"Dr. Johnson? The specialist? Oh, the old fellow!" said Cavenaugh imperturbably. "Yes, that's interesting. Still I fancy if one knew the facts – Did you know about Wyatt?"

"I don't think so."

"You wouldn't, probably. He was just a fellow about town who spent money. He wasn't one of the *forestieri*, though. Had connections here and owned a fine old place over on Staten Island. He went in for botany, and had been all over, hunting things; rusts, I believe. He had a yacht and used to take a gay crowd down about the South Seas, botanizing. He really did botanize, I believe. I never knew such a spender – only not flashy. He helped a lot of fellows and he was awfully good to girls, the kind who come down here to get a little fun, who don't like to work and still aren't really tough, the kind you see talking hard for their dinner. Nobody knows what becomes of them, or what they get out of it, and there are hundreds of new ones every year. He helped dozens of 'em; it was he who got me curious about the little shop girls.

"Well, one afternoon when his tea was brought, he took prussic acid instead. He didn't leave any letters, either; people of any taste don't. They wouldn't leave any material reminder if they could help it. His lawyers found that he had just $314.72 above his debts when he died. He had planned to spend all his money, and then take his tea; he had worked it out carefully."

Eastman reached for his pipe and pushed his chair away from the fire. "That looks like a considered case, but I don't think philosophical suicides like that are common. I think they usually come from stress of feeling and are really, as the newspapers call them, desperate acts; done without a motive. You remember when Anna Karenina was under the wheels, she kept saying, 'Why am I here?'"

Cavenaugh rubbed his upper lip with his pink finger and made an effort to wrinkle his brows. "May I, please?" reaching for the whiskey. "But have you," he asked, blinking as the soda flew at him, "have you ever known, yourself, cases that were really inexplicable?"

"A few too many. I was in Washington just before Captain Jack Purden was married and I saw a good deal of him. Popular army man, fine record in the Philippines, married a charming girl with lots of money; mutual devotion. It was the gayest wedding of the winter, and they started for Japan. They stopped in San Francisco for a week and missed their boat because, as the bride wrote back to Washington, they were too happy to move. They took the next boat, were both good sailors, had exceptional weather. After they had been out for two weeks, Jack got up from his deck chair one afternoon, yawned, put down his book, and stood before his wife. 'Stop reading for a moment and look at me.' She laughed and asked him why. 'Because you happen to be good to look at.' He nodded to her, went back to the stern and was never seen again. Must have gone down to the lower deck and slipped overboard, behind the machinery. It was the luncheon hour, not many people about; steamer cutting through a soft green sea. That's one of the most baffling cases I know. His friends raked up his past, and it was as trim as a cottage garden. If he'd so much as dropped an ink spot on his fatigue uniform, they'd have found it. He wasn't emotional or moody; wasn't, indeed, very interesting; simply a good soldier, fond of all the pompous little formalities that make up a military man's life. What do you make of that, my boy?"

Cavenaugh stroked his chin. "It's very puzzling, I admit. Still, if one knew everything –"

"But we do know everything. His friends wanted to find something to help them out, to help the girl out, to help the case of the human creature."

"Oh, I don't mean things that people could unearth," said Cavenaugh uneasily. "But possibly there were things that couldn't be found out."

Eastman shrugged his shoulders. "It's my experience that when there are 'things' as you call them, they're very apt to be found. There is no such thing as a secret. To make any move at all one has to employ human agencies, employ at least one human agent. Even when the pirates killed the men who buried their gold for them, the bones told the story."

Cavenaugh rubbed his hands together and smiled his sunny smile.

"I like that idea. It's reassuring. If we can have no secrets, it means that we can't, after all, go so far afield as we might," he hesitated, "yes, as we might."

Eastman looked at him sourly. "Cavenaugh, when you've practised law in New York for twelve years, you find that people can't go far in any direction, except –" He thrust his forefinger sharply at the floor. "Even in that direction, few people can do anything out of the ordinary. Our range is limited. Skip a few baths, and we become personally objectionable. The slightest carelessness can rot a man's integrity or give him ptomaine poisoning. We keep up only by incessant cleansing operations, of mind and body. What we call character is held together by all sorts of tacks and strings and glue."

Cavenaugh looked startled. "Come now, it's not so bad as that, is it? I've always thought that a serious man, like you, must know a lot of Launcelots." When Eastman only laughed, the younger man squirmed about in his chair. He spoke again hastily, as if he were embarrassed. "Your military friend may have had personal experiences, however, that his friends couldn't possibly get a line on. He may accidentally have come to a place where he saw himself in too unpleasant a light. I believe people can be chilled by a draft from outside, somewhere."

"Outside?" Eastman echoed. "Ah, you mean the far outside! Ghosts, delusions, eh?"

Cavenaugh winced. "That's putting it strong. Why not say tips from the outside? Delusions belong to a diseased mind, don't they? There are some of us who have no minds to speak of, who yet have had experiences. I've had a little something in that line myself and I don't look it, do I?"

Eastman looked at the bland countenance turned toward him. "Not exactly. What's your delusion?"

"It's not a delusion. It's a haunt."

The lawyer chuckled. "Soul of a lost Casino girl?"

"No; an old gentleman. A most unattractive old gentleman, who follows me about."

"Does he want money?"

Cavenaugh sat up straight. "No. I wish to God he wanted anything – but the pleasure of my society! I'd let him clean me out to be rid of him. He's a real article. You saw him yourself that night when you came to my rooms to borrow a dictionary, and he went down the fire escape. You saw him down in the court."

"Well, I saw somebody down in the court, but I'm too cautious to take it for granted that I saw what you saw. Why, anyhow, should I see your haunt? If it was your friend I saw, he impressed me disagreeably. How did you pick him up?"

Cavenaugh looked gloomy. "That was queer, too. Charley Burke and I had motored out to Long Beach, about a year ago, sometime in October, I think. We had supper and stayed until late. When we were coming home, my car broke down. We had a lot of girls along who had to get back for morning rehearsals and things; so I sent them all into town in Charley's car, and he was to send a man back to tow me home. I was driving myself, and didn't want to leave my machine. We had not taken a direct road back; so I was stuck in a lonesome, woody place, no houses about. I got chilly and made a fire, and was putting in the time comfortably enough, when this old party steps up. He was in shabby evening clothes and a top hat, and had on his usual white gloves. How he got there, at three o'clock in the morning, miles from any town or railway, I'll leave it to you to figure out. *He* surely had no car. When I saw him coming up to the fire, I disliked him. He had a silly, apologetic walk. His teeth were chattering and I asked him to sit down. He got down like a clothes-horse folding up. I offered him a cigarette, and when he took off his gloves I couldn't help noticing how knotted and spotty his hands were. He was asthmatic, and took his breath with a wheeze. 'Haven't you got anything – refreshing in there?' he asked, nodding at the car. When I told him I hadn't, he sighed. 'Ah, you young fellows arc greedy. You drink it all up. You drink it all up, all up – up!' he kept chewing it over."

Cavenaugh paused and looked embarrassed again. "The thing that was most unpleasant is difficult to explain. The old man sat there by the fire and leered at me with a silly sort of admiration that was – well, more than humiliating. 'Gay boy, gay dog!' he would mutter, and when he grinned he showed his teeth, worn and yellow – shells. I remembered that it was better to talk casually to insane people; so I remarked carelessly that I had been out with a party and got stuck.

"'Oh yes, I remember,' he said, 'Flora and Lottie and Maybelle and Marcelline, and poor Kate.'

"He had named them correctly; so I began to think I had been hitting the bright waters too hard.

"Things I drank never had seemed to make me woody; but you can never tell when trouble is going to hit you. I pulled my hat down and tried to look as uncommunicative as possible; but he kept croaking on from time to time, like this: 'Poor Katie! Splendid arms, but dope got her. She took up with Eastern religions after she had her hair dyed. Got to going to a Swami's joint, and smoking opium. Temple of the Lotus, it was called, and the police raided it.'

"This was nonsense, of course; the young woman was in the pink of condition. I let him rave, but I decided that if something didn't come out for me pretty soon, I'd foot it across Long Island. There wasn't room enough for the two of us. I got up and took another try at my car. He hopped right after me.

"'Good car,' he wheezed, 'better than the little Ford.'

"I'd had a Ford before, but so has everybody; that was a safe guess.

"'Still,' he went on, 'that run in from Huntington Bay in the rain wasn't bad. Arrested for speeding, he-he.'

"It was true I had made such a run, under rather unusual circumstances, and had been arrested. When at last I heard my life-boat snorting up the road, my visitor got up, sighed, and stepped back into the shadow of the trees. I didn't wait to see what became of him, you may believe. That was visitation number one. What do you think of it?"

Cavenaugh looked at his host defiantly. Eastman smiled.

"I think you'd better change your mode of life, Cavenaugh. Had many returns?" he inquired.

"Too many, by far." The young man took a turn about the room and came back to the fire. Standing by the mantel he lit another cigarette before going on with his story.

"The second visitation happened in the street, early in the evening, about eight o'clock. I was held up in a traffic block before the Plaza. My chauffeur was driving. Old Nibbs steps up out of the crowd, opens the door of my car, gets in and sits down beside me. He had on wilted evening clothes, same as before, and there was some sort of heavy scent about him. Such an unpleasant old party! A thorough-going rotter; you knew it at once. This time he wasn't talkative, as he had been when I first saw him. He leaned back in the car as if he owned it, crossed his hands on his stick and looked out at the crowd – sort of hungrily.

"I own I really felt a loathing compassion for him.

"We got down the avenue slowly. I kept looking out at the mounted police. But what could I do? Have him pulled? I was afraid to. I was awfully afraid of getting him into the papers.

"'I'm going to the New Astor,' I said at last. 'Can I take you anywhere?'

"'No, thank you,' says he. 'I get out when you do. I'm due on West Forty-fourth. I'm dining tonight with Marcelline – all that is left of her!'

"He put his hand to his hat brim with a gruesome salute. Such a scandalous, foolish old face as he had! When we pulled up at the Astor, I stuck my hand in my pocket and asked him if he'd like a little loan.

"'No, thank you, but' – he leaned over and whispered, ugh! – 'but save a little, save a little. Forty years from now – a little – comes in handy. Save a little.'

"His eyes fairly glittered as he made his remark. I jumped out. I'd have jumped into the North River. When he tripped off, I asked my chauffeur if he'd noticed the man who got into the car with me. He said he knew someone was with me, but he hadn't noticed just when he got in. Want to hear any more?"

Cavenaugh dropped into his chair again. His plump cheeks were a trifle more flushed than usual, but he was perfectly calm. Eastman felt that the young man believed what he was telling him.

"Of course I do. It's very interesting. I don't see quite where you are coming out though."

Cavenaugh sniffed. "No more do I. I really feel that I've been put upon. I haven't deserved it any more than any other fellow of my kind. Doesn't it impress you disagreeably?"

"Well, rather so. Has anyone else seen your friend?"

"You saw him."

"We won't count that. As I said, there's no certainty that you and I saw the same person in the court that night. Has anyone else had a look in?"

"People sense him rather than see him. He usually crops up when I'm alone or in a crowd on the street. He never approaches me when I'm with people I know, though I've seen him hanging about the doors of theatres when I come out with a party; loafing around the stage exit, under a wall; or across on the street, in a doorway. To be frank, I'm not anxious to introduce him. The third time, it was I who came upon him. In November my driver, Harry, had a sudden attack of appendicitis. I took him to the Presbyterian Hospital in the car, early in the evening. When I came home, I found the old villain in my rooms. I offered him a drink, and he sat down. It was the first time I had seen him in a steady light, with his hat off.

"His face is lined like a railway map, and as to color – Lord, what a liver! His scalp grows tight to his skull, and his hair is dyed until it's perfectly dead, like a piece of black cloth."

Cavenaugh ran his fingers through his own neatly trimmed thatch, and seemed to forget where he was for a moment.

"I had a twin brother, Brian, who died when we were sixteen. I have a photograph of him on my wall, an enlargement from a kodak of him, doing a high jump, rather good thing, full of action. It seemed to annoy the old gentleman. He kept looking at it and lifting his eyebrows, and finally he got up, tip-toed across the room, and turned the picture to the wall.

"'Poor Brian! Fine fellow, but died young,' says he.

"Next morning, there was the picture, still reversed."

"Did he stay long?" Eastman asked interestedly.

"Half an hour, by the clock."

"Did he talk?"

"Well, he rambled."

"What about?"

Cavenaugh rubbed his pale eyebrows before answering.

"About things that an old man ought to want to forget. His conversation is highly objectionable. Of course he knows me like a book; everything I've ever done or thought. But when he recalls them, he throws a bad light on them, somehow. Things that weren't much off color, look rotten. He doesn't leave one a shred of self-respect, he really doesn't. That's the amount of it." The young man whipped out his handkerchief and wiped his face.

"You mean he really talks about things that none of your friends know?"

"Oh, dear, yes! Recalls things that happened in school. Anything disagreeable. Funny thing, he always turns Brian's picture to the wall."

"Does he come often?"

"Yes, oftener, now. Of course I don't know how he gets in downstairs. The hall boys never see him. But he has a key to my door. I don't know how he got it, but I can hear him turn it in the lock."

"Why don't you keep your driver with you, or telephone for me to come down?"

"He'd only grin and go down the fire escape as he did before. He's often done it when Harry's come in suddenly. Everybody has to be alone sometimes, you know. Besides, I don't want anybody to see him. He has me there."

"But why not? Why do you feel responsible for him?"

Cavenaugh smiled wearily. "That's rather the point, isn't it? Why do I? But I absolutely do. That identifies him, more than his knowing all about my life and my affairs."

Eastman looked at Cavenaugh thoughtfully. "Well, I should advise you to go in for something altogether different and new, and go in for it hard; business, engineering, metallurgy, something this old fellow wouldn't be interested in. See if you can make him remember logarithms."

Cavenaugh sighed. "No, he has me there, too. People never really change; they go on being themselves. But I would never make much trouble. Why can't they let me alone, damn it! I'd never hurt anybody, except, perhaps –"

"Except your old gentleman, eh?" Eastman laughed. "Seriously, Cavenaugh, if you want to shake him, I think a year on a ranch would do it. He would never be coaxed far from his favorite haunts. He would dread Montana."

Cavenaugh pursed up his lips. "So do I!"

"Oh, you think you do. Try it, and you'll find out. A gun and a horse beats all this sort of thing. Besides losing your haunt, you'd be putting ten years in the bank for yourself. I know a good ranch where they take people, if you want to try it."

"Thank you. I'll consider. Do you think I'm batty?"

"No, but I think you've been doing one sort of thing too long. You need big horizons. Get out of this."

Cavenaugh smiled meekly. He rose lazily and yawned behind his hand. "It's late, and I've taken your whole evening." He strolled over to the window and looked out. "Queer place, New York; rough on the little fellows. Don't you feel sorry for them, the girls especially? I do. What a fight they put up for a little fun! Why, even that old goat is sorry for them, the only decent thing he kept."

Eastman followed him to the door and stood in the hall, while Cavenaugh waited for the elevator. When the car came up Cavenaugh extended his pink, warm hand. "Good night."

The cage sank and his rosy countenance disappeared, his round-eyed smile being the last thing to go.

Weeks passed before Eastman saw Cavenaugh again. One morning, just as he was starting for Washington to argue a case before the Supreme Court, Cavenaugh telephoned him at his office to ask him about the Montana ranch he had recommended; said he meant to take his advice and go out there for the spring and summer.

When Eastman got back from Washington, he saw dusty trunks, just up from the trunk room, before Cavenaugh's door. Next morning, when he stopped to see what the young man was about, he found Cavenaugh in his shirt sleeves, packing.

"I'm really going; off tomorrow night. You didn't think it of me, did you?" he asked gaily.

"Oh, I've always had hopes of you!" Eastman declared. "But you are in a hurry, it seems to me."

"Yes, I am in a hurry." Cavenaugh shot a pair of leggings into one of the open trunks. "I telegraphed your ranch people, used your name, and they said it would be all right. By the way, some of my crowd are giving a little dinner for me at Rector's tonight. Couldn't you be persuaded, as it's a farewell occasion?" Cavenaugh looked at him. hopefully.

Eastman laughed and shook his head. "Sorry, Cavenaugh, but that's too gay a world for me. I've got too much work lined up before me. I wish I had time to stop and look at your guns, though. You seem to know something about guns. You've more than you'll need, but nobody can have too many good ones." He put down one of the revolvers regretfully. "I'll drop in to see you in the morning, if you're up."

"I shall be up, all right. I've warned my crowd that I'll cut away before midnight."

"You won't, though," Eastman called back over his shoulder as he hurried downstairs.

The next morning, while Eastman was dressing, Rollins came in greatly excited.

"I'm a little late, sir. I was stopped by Harry, Mr. Cavenaugh's driver. Mr. Cavenaugh shot himself last night, sir."

Eastman dropped his vest and sat down on his shoe-box. "You're drunk, Rollins," he shouted. "He's going away today!"

"Yes, sir. Harry found him this morning. Ah, he's quite dead, sir. Harry's telephoned for the coroner. Harry don't know what to do with the ticket."

Eastman pulled on his coat and ran down the stairway. Cavenaugh's trunks were stripped and piled before the door. Harry was walking up and down the hall with a long green railroad ticket in his hand and a look of complete stupidity on his face.

"What shall I do about this ticket, Mr. Eastman?" he whispered. "And what about his trunks? He had me tell the transfer people to come early. They may be here any minute. Yes, sir. I brought him home in the car last night, before twelve, as cheerful as could be."

"Be quiet, Harry. Where is he?"

"In his bed, sir."

Eastman went into Cavenaugh's sleeping-room. When he came back to the sitting-room, he looked over the writing table; railway folders, time-tables, receipted bills, nothing else. He looked up for the photograph of Cavenaugh's twin brother. There it was, turned to the wall. Eastman took it down and looked at it; a boy in track clothes, half lying in the air, going over the string shoulders first, above the heads of a crowd of lads who were running and cheering. The face was somewhat blurred by the motion and the bright sunlight. Eastman put the picture back, as he found it. Had Cavenaugh entertained his visitor last night, and had the old man been more convincing than usual?

"Well, at any rate, he's seen to it that the old man can't establish identity. What a soft lot they are, fellows like poor Cavenaugh!" Eastman thought of his office as a delightful place.

THE THREE HORSEMEN

G.K. Chesterton

G.K. Chesterton (1874–1936) was a novelist, Roman Catholic thinker, art critic, biographer and is best known for his novels – *The Napoleon of Notting Hill, The Man Who Was Tuesday* – as well as the Father Brown series of detective stories. A mesmerising speaker and polemicist, there are a few in the Roman Catholic community who are attempting to ensure he follows the path of John Henry Newman to beatification. A rather large man (weighing around 130 kg), he once suggested "Lying in bed would be an altogether perfect and supreme experience if only one had a coloured pencil long enough to draw on the ceiling." This story was first published in April 1935 and was described as "a memorable story by the world's most brilliant performer on the trapeze of surprise", which, given the size of his girth, is hilarious.

The curious and sometimes creepy effect which Mr. Pond produced upon me, despite his commonplace courtesy and dapper decorum, was possibly connected with some memories of childhood; and the vague verbal association of his name. He was a Government official who was an old friend of my father; and I fancy my infantile imagination had somehow mixed up the name of Mr. Pond with the pond in the garden. When one came to think of it, he was curiously like the pond in the garden. He was so quiet at all normal times, so neat in shape and so shiny, so to speak, in his ordinary reflections of earth and sky and the common daylight. And yet I knew there were some queer things in the pond in the garden. Once in a hundred times, on one or two days during the whole year, the pond would look oddly different; or there would come a flitting shadow or a flash in its flat serenity; and a fish or a frog or some more grotesque creature would show itself to the sky. And I knew there were monsters in Mr. Pond also: monsters in his mind which rose only for a moment to the surface and sank again. They took the form of monstrous remarks, in the middle of all his mild and rational remarks. Some people thought he had suddenly gone mad in the midst of his sanest conversation. But even they had to admit that he must have suddenly gone sane again.

Perhaps, again, this foolish fantasy was fixed in the youthful mind because, at certain moments, Mr. Pond looked rather like a fish himself. His manners were not only quite polite but quite conventional; his very gestures were conventional, with the exception of one occasional trick of plucking at his pointed beard which seemed to come on him chiefly when he was at last forced to be serious about one of his strange and random statements. At such moments he would stare owlishly in front of him and pull his beard, which had a comic effect of pulling his mouth open, as if it were the mouth of a puppet with hairs for wires. This odd, occasional opening and shutting of his mouth, without speech, had quite a startling similarity to the slow gaping and gulping of a fish. But it never lasted for more than a few seconds, during which, I suppose, he swallowed the unwelcome proposal of explaining what on earth he meant.

He was talking quite quietly one day to Sir Hubert Wotton, the well-known diplomatist; they were seated under gaily-striped tents or giant parasols in our own garden, and gazing towards the pond which I had perversely associated with him. They happened to be talking about a part of the world that both of them knew well, and very few people in Western Europe at all: the vast flats fading into fens and swamps that stretch across Pomerania and Poland and Russia and the rest; right away, for all I know, into the Siberian deserts. And Mr. Pond recalled that, across a region where the swamps are deepest and intersected by pools and sluggish rivers, there runs a single road raised on a high causeway with steep and sloping sides: a straight path safe enough for the ordinary pedestrian, but barely broad enough for two horsemen to ride abreast. That is the beginning of the story.

It concerned a time not very long ago, but a time in which horsemen were still used much more than they are at present, though already rather less as fighters than as couriers. Suffice it to say that it was in one of the many wars that have laid waste that part of the world – in so far as it is possible to lay waste such a wilderness. Inevitably it involved the pressure of the Prussian system on the nation of the Poles, but beyond that it is not necessary to expound the politics of the matter, or discuss its rights and wrongs here. Let us merely say, more lightly, that Mr. Pond amused the company with a riddle.

"I expect you remember hearing," said Pond, "of all the excitement there was about Paul Petrowski, the poet from Cracow, who did two things rather dangerous in those days: moving from Cracow and going to live in Poznan; and trying to combine being a poet with being a patriot. The town he was living in was held at the moment by the Prussians; it was situated exactly at the eastern end of the long causeway; the Prussian command having naturally taken care to hold the bridgehead of such a solitary bridge across such a sea of swamps. But their base for that particular operation was at the western end of the causeway; the celebrated Marshal Von Grock was in general command; and, as it happened, his own old regiment, which was still his favourite regiment, the White Hussars, was posted nearest to the beginning of the great embanked road. Of course, everything was spick and span, down to every detail of the wonderful white uniforms, with the flame-coloured baldrick slung across them; for this was just before the universal use of colours like mud and clay for all the uniforms in the world. I don't blame them for that; I sometimes feel the old epoch of heraldry was a finer thing than all that epoch of imitative colouring, that came in with natural history and the worship of chameleons and beetles. Anyhow, this crack regiment of cavalry in the Prussian service still wore its own uniform; and, as you will see, that was another element in the fiasco. But it wasn't only the uniforms; it was the uniformity. The whole thing went wrong because the discipline was too good. Grock's soldiers obeyed him too well; so he simply couldn't do a thing he wanted."

"I suppose that's a paradox," said Wotton, heaving a sigh. "Of course, it's very clever and all that; but really, it's all nonsense, isn't it? Oh, I know people say in a general way that there's too much discipline in the German army. But you can't have too much discipline in an army."

"But I don't say it in a general way," said Pond plaintively. "I say it in a particular way, about this particular case. Grock failed because his soldiers obeyed him. Of course, if one of his soldiers had obeyed him, it wouldn't have been so bad. But when two of his soldiers obeyed him – why, really, the poor old devil had no chance."

Wotton laughed in a guttural fashion. "I'm glad to hear your new military theory. You'd allow one soldier in a regiment to obey orders; but two soldiers obeying orders strikes you as carrying Prussian discipline a bit too far."

"I haven't got any military theory. I'm talking about a military fact," replied Mr. Pond placidly. "It is a military fact that Grock failed, because two of his soldiers obeyed him. It is a military fact that he might have succeeded, if one of them had disobeyed him. You can make up what theories you like about it afterwards."

"I don't go in much for theories myself," said Wotton rather stiffly, as if he had been touched by a trivial insult.

At this moment could be seen striding across the sun-chequered lawn, the large and swaggering figure of Captain Gahagan, the highly incongruous friend and admirer of little Mr. Pond. He had a flaming flower in his buttonhole and a grey top-hat slightly slanted upon his ginger-haired head; and he walked with a swagger that seemed to come out of an older period of dandies and duellists, though he himself was comparatively young. So long as his tall, broad-shouldered figure was merely framed against the sunlight, he looked like the embodiment of all arrogance. When he came and sat down, with the sun on his face, there was a sudden contradiction of all this in his very soft brown eyes, which looked sad and even a little anxious.

Mr. Pond, interrupting his monologue, was almost in a twitter of apologies: "I'm afraid I'm talking too much, as usual; the truth is I was talking about that poet, Petrowski, who was nearly executed in Poznan – quite a long time ago. The military authorities on the spot hesitated and were going to let him go, unless they had direct orders from Marshal Von Grock or higher; but Marshal Von Grock was quite determined on the poet's death; and sent orders for his execution that very evening. A reprieve was sent afterwards to save him; but as the man carrying the reprieve died on the way, the prisoner was released, after all."

"But as –" repeated Wotton mechanically.

"The man carrying the reprieve," added Gahagan somewhat sarcastically.

"Died on the way," muttered Wotton.

"Why then, of course, the prisoner was released," observed Gahagan in a loud and cheerful voice. "All as clear as clear can be. Tell us another of those stories, Grandpapa."

"It's a perfectly true story," protested Pond, "and it happened exactly as I say. It isn't any paradox or anything like that. Only, of course, you have to know the story to see how simple it is."

"Yes," agreed Gahagan. "I think I should have to know the story, before realizing how simple it is."

"Better tell us the story and have done with it," said Wotton shortly.

***

Paul Petrowski was one of those utterly unpractical men who are of prodigious importance in practical politics. His power lay in the fact that he was a national poet but an international singer. That is, he happened to have a very fine and powerful voice, with which he sang his own patriotic songs in half the concert halls of the world. At home, of course, he was a torch and trumpet of revolutionary hopes, especially then, in the sort of international crisis in which practical politicians disappear, and their place is taken by men either more or less practical than themselves. For the true idealist and the real realist have at least the love of action in common. And the practical politician thrives by offering practical objections to any action. What the idealist does may be unworkable, and what the man of action does may be unscrupulous; but in neither trade can a man win a reputation by doing nothing. It is odd that these two extreme types stood at the two extreme ends of that one ridge and road among the marshes – the Polish poet a prisoner in the town at one end, the Prussian soldier a commander in the camp at the other.

For Marshal Von Grock was a true Prussian, not only entirely practical but entirely prosaic. He had never read a line of poetry himself; but he was no fool. He had the sense of reality which belongs to soldiers; and it prevented him from falling into the asinine error of the practical politician. He did not scoff at visions; he only hated them. He knew that a poet or a prophet could be as dangerous as an army. And he was resolved that the poet should die. It was his one compliment to poetry; and it was sincere.

He was at the moment sitting at a table in his tent; the spiked helmet that he always wore in public was lying in front of him; and his massive head looked quite bald, though it was only closely shaven. His whole face was also shaven; and had no covering but a pair of very strong spectacles, which alone gave an enigmatic look to his heavy and sagging visage. He turned to a Lieutenant standing by, a German of the pale-haired and rather pudding-faced variety, whose blue saucer-eyes were staring vacantly.

"Lieutenant Von Hocheimer," he said, "did you say His Highness would reach the camp to-night?"

"Seven forty-five, Marshal," replied the Lieutenant, who seemed rather reluctant to speak at all, like a large animal learning a new trick of talking.

"Then there is just time," said Grock, "to send you with that order for execution, before he arrives. We must serve His Highness in every way, but especially in saving him needless trouble. He will be occupied enough reviewing the troops; see that everything is placed at His Highness's disposal. He will be leaving again for the next outpost in an hour."

The large Lieutenant seemed partially to come to life and made a shadowy salute. "Of course, Marshal, we must all obey His Highness."

"I said we must all serve His Highness," said the Marshal.

With a sharper movement than usual, he unhooked his heavy spectacles and rapped them down upon the table. If the pale blue eyes of the Lieutenant could have seen anything of the sort, or if they could have opened any wider even if they had, they might as well have opened wide enough at the transformation made by the gesture. It was like the removal of an iron mask. An instant before, Marshal Von Grock had looked uncommonly like a rhinoceros, with his heavy folds of leathery cheek and jaw. Now he was a new kind of monster: a rhinoceros with the eyes of an eagle. The bleak blaze of his old eyes would have told almost anybody that he had something within that was not merely heavy; at least, that there was a part of him made of steel and not only of iron. For all men live by a spirit, though it were an evil spirit, or one so strange to the commonalty of Christian men that they hardly know whether it be good or evil.

"I said we must all serve His Highness," repeated Grock. "I will speak more plainly, and say we must all save His Highness. Is it not enough for our kings that they should be our gods? Is it not enough for them to be served and saved? It is we who must do the serving and saving."

Marshal Von Grock seldom talked, or even thought, as more theoretical people would count thinking. And it will generally be found that men of his type, when they do happen to think aloud, very much prefer to talk to the dog. They have even a certain patronizing relish in using long words and elaborate arguments before the dog. It would be unjust to compare Lieutenant Von Hocheimer to a dog. It would be unjust to the dog, who is a much more sensitive and vigilant creature. It would be truer to say that Grock in one of his rare moments of reflection, had the comfort and safety of feeling that he was reflecting aloud in the presence of a cow or a cabbage.

"Again and again, in the history of our Royal House, the servant has saved the master," went on Grock, "and often got little but kicks for it, from the outer world at least, which always whines sentimentalism against the successful and the strong. But at least we were successful and we were strong. They cursed Bismarck for deceiving even his own master over the Ems telegram; but it made that master the master of the world. Paris was taken; Austria dethroned; and we were safe. To-night Paul Petrowski will be dead; and we shall again be safe. That is why I am sending you with his death-warrant at once. You understand that you are bearing the order for Petrowski's instant execution – and that you must remain to see it obeyed?"

The inarticulate Hocheimer saluted; he could understand that all right. And he had some qualities of a dog, after all: he was as brave as a bulldog; and he could be faithful to the death.

"You must mount and ride at once," went on Grock, "and see that nothing delays or thwarts you. I know for a fact that fool Arnheim is going to release Petrowski to-night, if no message comes. Make all speed."

And the Lieutenant again saluted and went out into the night; and mounting one of the superb white chargers that were part of the splendour of that splendid corps, began to ride along the high, narrow road along the ridge, almost like the top of a wall, which overlooked the dark horizon, the dim patterns and decaying colours of those mighty marshes.

Almost as the last echoes of his horse's hoofs died away along the causeway, Von Grock rose and put on his helmet and his spectacles and came to the door of his tent; but for another reason. The chief men of his staff, in full dress, were already approaching him; and all along the more distant lines there were the sounds of ritual salutation and the shouting of orders. His Highness the Prince had come.

His Highness the Prince was something of a contrast, at least in externals, to the men around him; and, even in other things, something of an exception in his world. He also wore a spiked helmet, but that of another regiment, black with glints of blue steel; and there was something half incongruous and half imaginatively appropriate, in some antiquated way, in the combination of that helmet with the long, dark, flowing beard, amid all those shaven Prussians. As if in keeping with the long, dark, flowing beard, he wore a long, dark, flowing cloak, blue with one blazing star on it of the highest Royal Order; and under the blue cloak he wore a black uniform. Though as German as any man, he was a very different kind of German; and something in his proud but abstracted face was consonant with the legend that the one true passion of his life was music.

In truth, the grumbling Grock was inclined to connect with that remote eccentricity the, to him, highly irritating and exasperating fact that the Prince did not immediately proceed to the proper review and reception by the troops, already drawn out in all the labyrinthine parade of the military etiquette of their nation; but plunged at once impatiently into the subject which Grock most desired to see left alone: the subject of this infernal Pole, his popularity and his peril; for the Prince had heard some of the man's songs sung in half the opera-houses of Europe.

"To talk of executing a man like that is madness," said the Prince, scowling under his black helmet. "He is not a common Pole. He is a European institution. He would be deplored and deified by our allies, by our friends, even by our fellow-Germans. Do you want to be the mad women who murdered Orpheus?"

"Highness," said the Marshal, "he would be deplored; but he would be dead. He would be deified; but he would be dead. Whatever he means to do, he would never do it. Whatever he is doing, he would do no more. Death is the fact of all facts; and I am rather fond of facts."

"Do you know nothing of the world?" demanded the Prince.

"I care nothing for the world," answered Grock, "beyond the last black and white post of the Fatherland."

"God in heaven," cried His Highness, "you would have hanged Goethe for a quarrel with Weimar!"

"For the safety of your Royal House," answered Grock, "without one instant's hesitation."

There was a short silence and the Prince said sharply and suddenly: "What does this mean?"

"It means that I had not an instant's hesitation," replied the Marshal steadily. "I have already myself sent orders for the execution of Petrowski."

The Prince rose like a great dark eagle, the swirl of his cloak like the sweep of mighty wings; and all men knew that a wrath beyond mere speech had made him a man of action. He did not even speak to Von Grock; but talking across him, at the top of his voice, called out to the second in command, General Von Voglen, a stocky man with a square head, who had stood in the background as motionless as a stone.

"Who has the best horse in your cavalry division, General? Who is the best rider?"

"Arnold Von Schacht has a horse that might beat a racehorse," replied the General promptly. "And rides it as well as a jockey. He is of the White Hussars."

"Very well," said the Prince, with the same new ring in his voice. "Let him ride at once after the man with this mad message and stop him. I will give him authority, which I think the distinguished Marshal will not dispute. Bring me pen and ink."

He sat down, shaking out the cloak, and they brought him writing materials; and he wrote firmly and with a flourish the order, overriding all other orders, for the reprieve and release of Petrowski the Pole.

Then amid a dead silence, in the midst of which old Grock stood with an unblinking stare like a stone idol of prehistoric times, he swept out of the room, trailing his mantle and sabre. He was so violently displeased that no man dared to remind him of the formal reviewing of the troops. But Arnold Von Schacht, a curly-haired active youth, looking more like a boy, but wearing more than one medal on the white uniform of the Hussars, clicked his heels, and received the folded paper from the Prince; then, striding out, he sprang on his horse and flew along the high, narrow road like a silver arrow or a shooting star.

The old Marshal went back slowly and calmly to his tent, slowly and calmly removed his spiked helmet and his spectacles, and laid them on the table as before. Then he called out to an orderly just outside the tent; and bade him fetch Sergeant Schwartz of the White Hussars immediately.

A minute later, there presented himself before the Marshal a gaunt and wiry man, with a great scar across his jaw, rather dark for a German, unless all his colours had been changed by years of smoke and storm and bad weather. He saluted and stood stiffly at attention, as the Marshal slowly raised his eyes to him. And vast as was the abyss between the Imperial Marshal, with Generals under him, and that one battered non-commissioned officer, it is true that of all the men who have talked in this tale, these two men alone looked and understood each other without words.

"Sergeant," said the Marshal, curtly, "I have seen you twice before. Once, I think, when you won the prize of the whole army for marksmanship with the carbine."

The sergeant saluted and said nothing.

"And once again," went on Von Grock, "when you were questioned for shooting that damned old woman who would not give us information about the ambush. The incident caused considerable comment at the time, even in some of our own circles. Influence, however, was exerted on your side. My influence."

The sergeant saluted again; and was still silent. The Marshal continued to speak in a colourless but curiously candid way.

"His Highness the Prince has been misinformed and deceived on a point essential to his own safety and that of the Fatherland. Under this error, he has rashly sent a reprieve to the Pole Petrowski, who is to be executed to-night. I repeat: who is to be executed to-night. You must immediately ride after Von Schacht, who carried the reprieve, and stop him."

"I can hardly hope to overtake him, Marshal," said Sergeant Schwartz. "He has the swiftest horse in the regiment, and is the finest rider."

"I did not tell you to overtake him. I told you to stop him," said Grock. Then he spoke more slowly: "A man may often be stopped or recalled by various signals: by shouting or shooting." His voice dragged still more ponderously, but without a pause. "The discharge of a carbine might attract his attention."

And then the dark sergeant saluted for the third time; and his grim mouth was again shut tight.

"The world is changed," said Grock, "not by what is said, or what is blamed or praised, but by what is done. The world never recovers from what is done. At this moment the killing of a man is a thing that must be done." He suddenly flashed his brilliant eyes of steel at the other, and added: "I mean, of course, Petrowski."

And Sergeant Schwartz smiled still more grimly; and he also, lifting the flap of the tent, went out into the darkness and mounted his horse and rode.

The last of the three riders was even less likely than the first to indulge in imaginative ideas for their own sake. But because he also was in some imperfect manner human, he could not but feel, on such a night and such an errand, the oppressiveness of that inhuman landscape. While he rode along that one abrupt ridge, there spread out to infinity all round him something a myriad times more inhuman than the sea. For a man could not swim in it, nor sail boats on it, nor do anything human with it; he could only sink in it, and practically without a struggle. The sergeant felt vaguely the presence of some primordial slime that was neither solid nor liquid nor capable of any form; and he felt its presence behind the forms of all things.

He was atheist, like so many thousands of dull, clever men in Northern Germany; but he was not that happier sort of pagan who can see in human progress a natural flowering of the earth. That world before him was not a field in which green or living things evolved and developed and bore fruit; it was only an abyss in which all living things would sink for ever as in a bottomless pit; and the thought hardened him for all the strange duties he had to do in so hateful a world. The grey-green blotches of flattened vegetation, seen from above like a sprawling map, seemed more like the chart of a disease than a development; and the land-locked pools might have been of poison rather than water. He remembered some humanitarian fuss or other about the poisoning of pools.

But the reflections of the sergeant, like most reflections of men not normally reflective, had a root in some subconscious strain on his nerves and his practical intelligence. The truth was that the straight road before him was not only dreary, but seemed interminably long. He would never have believed he could have ridden so far without catching some distant glimpse of the man he followed. Von Schacht must indeed have the fleetest of horses to have got so far ahead already; for, after all, he had only started, at whatever speed, within a comparatively short time. As Schwartz had said, he hardly expected to overtake him; but a very realistic sense of the distances involved had told him that he must very soon come in sight of him. And then, just as despair was beginning to descend and spread itself vaguely over the desolate landscape, he saw him at last.

A white spot, which slightly, slowly, enlarged into something like a white figure, appeared far ahead, riding furiously. It enlarged to that extent because Schwartz managed a spurt of riding furiously himself; but it was large enough to show the faint streak of orange across the white uniform that marked the regiment of the Hussars. The winner of the prize for shooting, in the whole army, had hit the white of smaller targets than that.

He unslung his carbine; and a shock of unnatural noise shook up all the wild fowl for miles upon the silent marshes. But Sergeant Schwartz did not trouble about them. What interested him was that, even at such a distance, he could see the straight, white figure turn crooked and alter in shape, as if the man had suddenly grown deformed. He was hanging like a humpback over the saddle; and Schwartz, with his exact eye and long experience, was certain that his victim was shot through the body; and almost certain that he was shot through the heart. Then he brought the horse down with a second shot; and the whole equestrian group heeled over and slipped and slid and vanished in one white flash into the dark fenland below.

The hard-headed sergeant was certain that his work was done. Hard-headed men of his sort are generally very precise about what they are doing; that is why they are so often quite wrong about what they do. He had outraged the comradeship that is the soul of armies; he had killed a gallant officer who was in the performance of his duty; he had deceived and defied his sovereign and committed a common murder without excuse of personal quarrel; but he had obeyed his superior officer and he had helped to kill a Pole. These two last facts for the moment filled his mind; and he rode thoughtfully back again to make his report to Marshal Von Grock. He had no doubts about the thoroughness of the work he had done. The man carrying the reprieve was certainly dead; and even if by some miracle he were only dying, he could not conceivably have ridden his dead or dying horse to the town in time to prevent the execution. No; on the whole it was much more practical and prudent to get back under the wing of his protector, the author of the desperate project. With his whole strength he leaned on the strength of the great Marshal.

And truly the great Marshal had this greatness about him; that after the monstrous thing he had done, or caused to be done, he disdained to show any fear of facing the facts on the spot or the compromising possibilities of keeping in touch with his tool. He and the sergeant, indeed, an hour or so later, actually rode along the ridge together, till they came to a particular place where the Marshal dismounted, but bade the other ride on. He wished the sergeant to go forward to the original goal of the riders, and see if all was quiet in the town after the execution, or whether there remained some danger from popular resentment.

"Is it here, then, Marshal?" asked the sergeant in a low voice. "I fancied it was further on; but it's a fact the infernal road seemed to lengthen out like a nightmare."

"It is here," answered Grock, and swung himself heavily from saddle and stirrup, and then went to the edge of the long parapet and looked down.

The moon had risen over the marshes and gone up strengthening in splendour and gleaming on dark waters and green scum; and in the nearest clump of reeds, at the foot of the slope, there lay, as in a sort of luminous and radiant ruin, all that was left of one of those superb white horses and white horsemen of his old brigade. Nor was the identity doubtful; the moon made a sort of aureole of the curled golden hair of young Arnold, the second rider and the bearer of the reprieve; and the same mystical moonshine glittered not only on baldrick and buttons, but on the special medals of the young soldier and the stripes and signs of his degree. Under such a glamorous veil of light, he might almost have been in the white armour of Sir Galahad; and there could scarcely have been a more horrible contrast than that between such fallen grace and youth below and the rocky and grotesque figure looking down from above. Grock had taken off his helmet again; and though it is possible that this was the vague shadow of some funereal form of respect, its visible effect was that the queer naked head and neck like that of a pachyderm glittered stonily in the moon, like the hairless head and neck of some monster of the Age of Stone. Rops, or some such etcher of the black, fantastic German schools, might have drawn such a picture: of a huge beast as inhuman as a beetle looking down on the broken wings and white and golden armour of some defeated champion of the Cherubim.

Grock said no prayer and uttered no pity; but in some dark way his mind was moved, as even the dark and mighty swamp will sometimes move like a living thing; and as such men will, when feeling for the first time faintly on their defence before they know not what, he tried to formulate his only faith and confront it with the stark universe and the staring moon.

"After and before the deed the German Will is the same. It cannot be broken by changes and by time, like that of those others who repent. It stands outside time like a thing of stone, looking forward and backward with the same face."

The silence that followed lasted long enough to please his cold vanity with a certain sense of portent; as if a stone figure had spoken in a valley of silence. But the silence began to thrill once more with a distant whisper which was the faint throb of horsehoofs; and a moment later the sergeant came galloping, or rather racing, back along the uplifted road, and his scarred and swarthy visage was no longer merely grim but ghastly in the moon.

"Marshal," he said, saluting with a strange stiffness, "I have seen Petrowski the Pole!"

"Haven't they buried him yet?" asked the Marshal, still staring down and in some abstraction.

"If they have," said Schwartz, "he has rolled the stone away and risen from the dead."

He stared in front of him at the moon and marshes; but, indeed, though he was far from being a visionary character, it was not these things that he saw, but rather the things he had just seen. He had, indeed, seen Paul Petrowski walking alive and alert down the brilliantly illuminated main avenue of that Polish town to the very beginning of the causeway; there was no mistaking the slim figure with plumes of hair and tuft of Frenchified beard which figured in so many private albums and illustrated magazines. And behind him he had seen that Polish town aflame with flags and firebrands and a population boiling with triumphant hero-worship, though perhaps less hostile to the government than it might have been, since it was rejoicing at the release of its popular hero.

"Do you mean," cried Grock with a sudden croaking stridency of voice, "that they have dared to release him in defiance of my message?"

Schwartz saluted again and said:

"They had already released him and they have received no message."

"Do you ask me, after all this," said Grock, "to believe that no messenger came from our camp at all?"

"No messenger at all," said the sergeant.

There was a much longer silence, and then Grock said, hoarsely: "What in the name of hell has happened? Can you think of anything to explain it all?"

"I have seen something," said the sergeant, "which I think does explain it all."

When Mr. Pond had told the story up to this point, he paused with an irritating blankness of expression.

"Well," said Gahagan impatiently, "and do you know anything that would explain it all?"

"Well, I think I do," said Mr. Pond meekly. "You see, I had to worry it out for myself, when the report came round to my department. It really did arise from an excess of Prussian obedience. It also arose from an excess of another Prussian weakness: contempt. And of all the passions that blind and madden and mislead men, the worst is the coldest: contempt.

"Grock had talked much too comfortably before the cow, and much too confidently before the cabbage. He despised stupid men even on his own staff; and treated Von Hocheimer, the first messenger, as a piece of furniture merely because he looked like a fool; but the Lieutenant was not such a fool as he looked. He also understood what the great Marshal meant, quite as well as the cynical sergeant, who had done such dirty work all his life. Hocheimer also understood the Marshal's peculiar moral philosophy: that an act is unanswerable even when it is indefensible. He knew that what his commander wanted was simply the corpse of Petrowski; that he wanted it anyhow, at the expense of any deception of princes or destruction of soldiers. And when he heard a swifter horseman behind him, riding to overtake him, he knew as well as Grock himself that the new messenger must be carrying with him the message of the mercy of the Prince. Von Schacht, that very young but gallant officer, looking like the very embodiment of all that more generous tradition of Germany that has been too much neglected in this tale, was worthy of the accident that made him the herald of a more generous policy. He came with the speed of that noble horsemanship that has left behind it in Europe the very name of chivalry, calling out to the other in a tone like a herald's trumpet to stop and stand and turn. And Von Hocheimer obeyed. He stopped, he reined in his horse, he turned in his saddle; but his hand held the carbine levelled like a pistol, and he shot the boy between the eyes.

"Then he turned again and rode on, carrying the death-warrant of the Pole. Behind him horse and man had crashed over the edge of the embankment, so that the whole road was clear. And along that clear and open road toiled in his turn the third messenger, marvelling at the interminable length of his journey; till he saw at last the unmistakable uniform of a Hussar like a white star disappearing in the distance, and he shot also. Only he did not kill the second messenger, but the first.

"That was why no messenger came alive to the Polish town that night. That was why the prisoner walked out of his prison alive. Do you think I was quite wrong in saying that Von Grock had two faithful servants, and one too many?"

MR KNOW-ALL

W. Somerset Maugham

William Somerset Maugham (1874–1965) was educated at The King's
School, Canterbury and went on to study medicinen at St Thomas's
hospital, but the success of his first novel, in 1897, began one of the
most successful literary careers of the last century. Maugham's books
include *Of Human Bondage*, *The Moon and Sixpence*, *The Painted Veil*
and *The Razor's Edge*, as well as a number of short story collections
and plays. In 1947 he instituted a prize in his name awarded to the best
British writer aged under 35, a prize won by both Kingsley and Martin
Amis, V.S. Naipaul, Doris Lessing, Seamus Heaney, Angela Carter, Alan
Hollinghurst, Lawrence Norfolk, Kate Summerscale, William Fiennes
and many others.

I was prepared to dislike Max Kelada even before I knew him. The war had
just finished and the passenger traffic in the ocean-going liners was heavy.
Accommodation was very hard to get and you had to put up with whatever
the agents chose to offer you. You could not hope for a cabin to yourself and
I was thankful to be given one in which there were only two berths. But when
I was told the name of my companion my heart sank. It suggested closed portholes and the night air rigidly excluded. It was bad enough to share a cabin for
fourteen days with anyone (I was going from San Francisco to Yokohama), but I
should have looked upon it with less dismay if my fellow-passenger's name had
been Smith or Brown.

When I went on board I found Mr. Kelada's luggage already below. I did not
like the look of it; there were too many labels on the suitcases, and the wardrobe
trunk was too big. He had unpacked his toilet things, and I observed that he
was a patron of the excellent Monsieur Coty; for I saw on the washing-stand
his scent, his hair-wash and his brilliantine. Mr. Kelada's brushes, ebony with his
monogram in gold, would have been all the better for a scrub. I did not at all like
Mr. Kelada. I made my way into the smoking-room. I called for a pack of cards
and began to play patience. I had scarcely started before a man came up to me
and asked me if he was right in thinking my name was so-and-so.

"I am Mr. Kelada," he added, with a smile that showed a row of flashing teeth,
and sat down.

"Oh, yes, we're sharing a cabin, I think."

"Bit of luck, I call it. You never know who you're going to be put in with.

I was jolly glad when I heard you were English. I'm all for us English sticking together when we're abroad, if you understand what I mean."

I blinked.

"Are you English?" I asked, perhaps tactlessly.

"Rather. You don't think I look like an American, do you? British to the backbone, that's what I am."

To prove it, Mr. Kelada took out of his pocket a passport and airily waved it under my nose.

King George has many strange subjects. Mr. Kelada was short and of a sturdy build, clean-shaven and dark-skinned, with a fleshy, hooked nose and very large, lustrous and liquid eyes. His long black hair was sleek and curly. He spoke with a fluency in which there was nothing English and his gestures were exuberant. I felt pretty sure that a closer inspection of that British passport would have betrayed the fact that Mr. Kelada was born under a bluer sky than is generally seen in England.

"What will you have?" he asked me.

I looked at him doubtfully. Prohibition was in force and to all appearances the ship was bone-dry. When I am not thirsty I do not know which I dislike more, ginger-ale or lemon-squash. But Mr. Kelada flashed an oriental smile at me.

"Whisky and soda or a dry Martini, you have only to say the word."

From each of his hip-pockets he fished a flask and laid them on the table before me. I chose the Martini, and calling the steward he ordered a tumbler of ice and a couple of glasses.

"A very good cocktail," I said.

"Well, there are plenty more where that came from, and if you've got any friends on board, you tell them you've got a pal who's got all the liquor in the world."

Mr. Kelada was chatty. He talked of New York and of San Francisco. He discussed plays, pictures, and politics. He was patriotic. The Union Jack is an impressive piece of drapery, but when it is flourished by a gentleman from Alexandria or Beirut, I cannot but feel that it loses somewhat in dignity. Mr. Kelada was familiar. I do not wish to put on airs, but I cannot help feeling that it is seemly in a total stranger to put mister before my name when he addresses me. Mr. Kelada, doubtless to set me at my ease, used no such formality. I did not like Mr. Kelada. I had put aside the cards when he sat down, but now thinking that for this first occasion our conversation had lasted long enough, I went on with my game.

"The three on the four," said Mr. Kelada.

There is nothing more exasperating when you are playing patience than to be told where to put the card you have turned up before you have had a chance to look for yourself.

"It's coming out, it's coming out," he cried. "The ten on the knave."

With rage and hatred in my heart I finished. Then he seized the pack.

"Do you like card tricks?"

"No, I hate card tricks," I answered.

"Well, I'll just show you this one."

He showed me three. Then I said I would go down to the dining-room and get my seat at table.

"Oh, that's all right," he said. "I've already taken a seat for you. I thought that as we were in the same state-room we might just as well sit at the same table."

I did not like Mr. Kelada.

I not only shared a cabin with him and ate three meals a day at the same table, but I could not walk round the deck without his joining me. It was impossible to snub him. It never occurred to him that he was not wanted. He was certain that you were as glad to see him as he was to see you. In your own house you might have kicked him downstairs and slammed the door in his face without the suspicion dawning on him that he was not a welcome visitor. He was a good mixer, and in three days knew everyone on board. He ran everything. He managed the sweeps, conducted the auctions, collected money for prizes at the sports, got up quoit and golf matches, organized the concert and arranged the fancy dress ball. He was everywhere and always. He was certainly the best-hated man in the ship. We called him Mr. Know-All, even to his face. He took it as a compliment. But it was at meal times that he was most intolerable. For the better part of an hour then he had us at his mercy. He was hearty, jovial, loquacious and argumentative. He knew everything better than anybody else, and it was an affront to his overweening vanity that you should disagree with him. He would not drop a subject, however unimportant, till he had brought you round to his way of thinking. The possibility that he could be mistaken never occurred to him. He was the chap who knew. We sat at the doctor's table. Mr. Kelada would certainly have had it all his own way, for the doctor was lazy and I was frigidly indifferent, except for a man called Ramsay who sat there also. He was as dogmatic as Mr. Kelada and resented bitterly the Levantine's cocksureness. The discussions they had were acrimonious and interminable.

Ramsay was in the American Consular Service, and was stationed at Kobe. He was a great heavy fellow from the Middle West, with loose fat under a tight skin, and he bulged out of his ready-made clothes. He was on his way back to resume his post, having been on a flying visit to New York to fetch his wife who had been spending a year at home. Mrs. Ramsay was a very pretty little thing, with pleasant manners and a sense of humour. The Consular Service is ill paid, and she was dressed always very simply; but she knew how to wear her clothes. She achieved an effect of quiet distinction. I should not have paid any particular attention to her but that she possessed a quality that may be common enough in women, but nowadays is not obvious in their demeanour. You could not look at her without being struck by her modesty. It shone in her like a flower on a coat.

One evening at dinner the conversation by chance drifted to the subject of pearls. There had been in the papers a good deal of talk about the culture pearls which the cunning Japanese were making, and the doctor remarked that they must inevitably diminish the value of real ones. They were very good already; they would soon be perfect. Mr. Kelada, as was his habit, rushed into the new topic. He told us all that was to be known about pearls. I do not believe Ramsay knew anything about them at all, but he could not resist the opportunity to have a fling at the Levantine, and in five minutes we were in the middle of a heated argument. I had seen Mr. Kelada vehement and voluble before, but never so voluble and vehement as now. At last something that Ramsay said stung him, for he thumped the table and shouted:

"Well, I ought to know what I am talking about. I'm going to Japan just to look into this Japanese pearl business. I'm in the trade and there's not a man in it who won't tell you that what I say about pearls goes. I know all the best pearls in the world, and what I don't know about pearls isn't worth knowing."

Here was news for us, for Mr. Kelada, with all his loquacity, had never told anyone what his business was. We only knew vaguely that he was going to Japan on some commercial errand. He looked round the table triumphantly.

"They'll never be able to get a culture pearl that an expert like me can't tell with half an eye." He pointed to a chain that Mrs. Ramsay wore. "You take my word for it, Mrs. Ramsay, that chain you're wearing will never be worth a cent less than it is now."

Mrs. Ramsay in her modest way flushed a little and slipped the chain inside her dress. Ramsay leaned forward. He gave us all a look and a smile flickered in his eyes.

"That's a pretty chain of Mrs. Ramsay's, isn't it?"

"I noticed it at once," answered Mr. Kelada. "Gee, I said to myself, those are pearls all right."

"I didn't buy it myself, of course. I'd be interested to know how much you think it cost."

"Oh, in the trade somewhere round fifteen thousand dollars. But if it was bought on Fifth Avenue I shouldn't be surprised to hear that anything up to thirty thousand was paid for it."

Ramsay smiled grimly.

"You'll be surprised to hear that Mrs. Ramsay bought that string at a department store the day before we left New York, for eighteen dollars."

Mr. Kelada flushed.

"Rot. It's not only real, but it's as fine a string for its size as I've ever seen."

"Will you bet on it? I'll bet you a hundred dollars it's imitation."

"Done."

"Oh, Elmer, you can't bet on a certainty," said Mrs. Ramsay.

She had a little smile on her lips and her tone was gently deprecating.

"Can't I? If I get a chance of easy money like that I should be all sorts of a fool not to take it."

"But how can it be proved?" she continued. "It's only my word against Mr. Kelada's."

"Let me look at the chain, and if it's imitation I'll tell you quickly enough. I can afford to lose a hundred dollars," said Mr. Kelada.

"Take it off, dear. Let the gentleman look at it as much as he wants."

Mrs. Ramsay hesitated a moment. She put her hands to the clasp.

"I can't undo it," she said. "Mr. Kelada will just have to take my word for it."

I had a sudden suspicion that something unfortunate was about to occur, but I could think of nothing to say.

Ramsay jumped up.

"I'll undo it."

He handed the chain to Mr. Kelada. The Levantine took a magnifying glass from his pocket and closely examined it. A smile of triumph spread over his smooth and swarthy face. He handed back the chain. He was about to speak.

Suddenly he caught sight of Mrs. Ramsay's face. It was so white that she looked as though she were about to faint. She was staring at him with wide and terrified eyes. They held a desperate appeal; it was so clear that I wondered why her husband did not see it.

Mr. Kelada stopped with his mouth open. He flushed deeply. You could almost *see* the effort he was making over himself.

"I was mistaken," he said. "It's a very good imitation, but of course as soon as I looked through my glass I saw that it wasn't real. I think eighteen dollars is just about as much as the damned thing's worth."

He took out his pocket-book and from it a hundred-dollar bill. He handed it to Ramsay without a word.

"Perhaps that'll teach you not to be so cocksure another time, my young friend," said Ramsay as he took the note.

I noticed that Mr. Kelada's hands were trembling.

The story spread over the ship as stories do, and he had to put up with a good deal of chaff that evening. It was a fine joke that Mr. Know-All had been caught out. But Mrs. Ramsay retired to her state-room with a headache.

Next morning I got up and began to shave. Mr. Kelada lay on his bed smoking a cigarette. Suddenly there was a small scraping sound and I saw a letter pushed under the door. I opened the door and looked out. There was nobody there. I picked up the letter and saw that it was addressed to Max Kelada. The name was written in block letters. I handed it to him.

"Who's this from?" He opened it. "Oh!"

He took out of the envelope, not a letter, but a hundred-dollar bill. He looked at me and again he reddened. He tore the envelope into little bits and gave them to me.

"Do you mind just throwing them out of the port-hole?"

I did as he asked, and then I looked at him with a smile.

"No one likes being made to look a perfect damned fool," he said.

"Were the pearls real?"

"If I had a pretty little wife I shouldn't let her spend a year in New York while I stayed at Kobe," said he.

At that moment I did not entirely dislike Mr. Kelada. He readied out for his pocket-book and carefully put in it the hundred-dollar note.

A LITTLE RAMBLE

Robert Walser

Robert Walser (1878–1956) was a Swiss writer who spent most of his life in mental institutions. He enjoyed long, solitary walks. He was found dead, in a field of snow, near the asylum where he had been living on Christmas Day 1956.

I walked through the mountains today. The weather was damp, and the entire region was gray. But the road was soft and in places very clean. At first I had my coat on; soon, however, I pulled it off, folded it together, and laid it upon my arm. The walk on the wonderful road gave me more and ever more pleasure; first it went up and then descended again. The mountains were huge, they seemed to go around. The whole mountainous world appeared to me like an enormous theatre. The road snuggled up splendidly to the mountain-sides. Then I came down into a deep ravine, a river roared at my feet, a train rushed past me with magnificent white smoke. The road went through the ravine like a smooth white stream, and as I walked on, to me it was as if the narrow valley were bending and winding around itself. Gray clouds lay on the mountains as though that were their resting place. I met a young traveller with a rucksack on his back, who asked if I had seen two other young fellows. No, I said. Had I come here from very far? Yes, I said, and went farther on my way. Not a long time, and I saw and heard the two young wanderers pass by with music. A village was especially beautiful with humble dwellings set thickly under the white cliffs. I encountered a few carts, otherwise nothing, and I had seen some children on the highway. We don't need to see anything out of the ordinary. We already see so much.

LORD EMSWORTH AND THE GIRL FRIEND

P.G. Wodehouse

One of the most-loved, successful and prolific authors, **P.G. Wodehouse** (1881–1975) is known for his novels, stories, plays, poems, song lyrics and journalism. The best known of his works are the Blandings novels and stories, the Psmith stories and the Jeeves and Wooster novels and stories. He became an American citizen in 1955, was knighted in 1975, and died a few weeks later on Valentine's Day. Only he could have admitted: "I know I was writing stories when I was five. I don't know what I did before that. Just loafed, I suppose."

THE day was so warm, so fair, so magically a thing of sunshine and blue skies and bird-song that anyone acquainted with Clarence, ninth Earl of Emsworth, and aware of his liking for fine weather, would have pictured him going about the place on this summer morning with a beaming smile and an uplifted heart. Instead of which, humped over the breakfast-table, he was directing at a blameless kippered herring a look of such intense bitterness that the fish seemed to sizzle beneath it. For it was August Bank Holiday, and Blandings Castle on August Bank Holiday became, in his lordship's opinion, a miniature Inferno.

This was the day when his park and grounds broke out into a noisome rash of swings, roundabouts, marquees, toy balloons and paper bags; when a tidal wave of the peasantry and its squealing young engulfed those haunts of immemorial peace. On August Bank Holiday he was not allowed to potter pleasantly about his gardens in an old coat: forces beyond his control shoved him into a stiff collar and a top hat and told him to go out and be genial. And in the cool of the quiet evenfall they put him on a platform and made him make a speech. To a man with a day like that in front of him fine weather was a mockery.

His sister, Lady Constance Keeble, looked brightly at him over the coffee-pot.

"What a lovely morning!" she said.

Lord Emsworth's gloom deepened. He chafed at being called upon – by this woman of all others – to behave as if everything was for the jolliest in the jolliest of all possible worlds. But for his sister Constance and her hawk-like vigilance, he might, he thought, have been able at least to dodge the top-hat.

"Have you got your speech ready?"

"Yes."

"Well, mind you learn it by heart this time and don't stammer and dodder as you did last year."

Lord Emsworth pushed plate and kipper away. He had lost his desire for food.

"And don't forget you have to go to the village this morning to judge the cottage gardens."

"All right, all right, all right," said his lordship testily. "I've not forgotten."

"I think I will come to the village with you. There are a number of those Fresh Air London children staying there now, and I must warn them to behave properly when they come to the Fête this afternoon. You know what London children are. McAllister says he found one of them in the gardens the other day, picking his flowers."

At any other time the news of this outrage would, no doubt, have affected Lord Emsworth profoundly. But now, so intense was his self-pity, he did not even shudder. He drank coffee with the air of a man who regretted that it was not hemlock.

"By the way, McAllister was speaking to me again last night about that gravel path through the yew alley. He seems very keen on it."

"Glug!" said Lord Emsworth – which, as any philologist will tell you, is the sound which peers of the realm make when stricken to the soul while drinking coffee.

Concerning Glasgow, that great commercial and manufacturing city in the county of Lanarkshire in Scotland, much has been written. So lyrically does the Encyclopædia Britannica deal with the place that it covers twenty-seven pages before it can tear itself away and go on to Glass, Glastonbury, Glatz and Glauber. The only aspect of it, however, which immediately concerns the present historian is the fact that the citizens it breeds are apt to be grim, dour, persevering, tenacious men; men with red whiskers who know what they want and mean to get it. Such a one was Angus McAllister, head-gardener at Blandings Castle.

For years Angus McAllister had set before himself as his earthly goal the construction of a gravel path through the Castle's famous yew alley. For years he had been bringing the project to the notice of his employer, though in anyone less whiskered the latter's unconcealed loathing would have caused embarrassment. And now, it seemed, he was at it again.

"Gravel path!" Lord Emsworth stiffened through the whole length of his stringy body. Nature, he had always maintained, intended a yew alley to be carpeted with a mossy growth. And, whatever Nature felt about it, he personally was dashed if he was going to have men with Clydeside accents and faces like dissipated potatoes coming along and mutilating that lovely expanse of green velvet. "Gravel path, indeed! Why not asphalt? Why not a few hoardings with advertisements of liver pills and a filling-station? That's what the man would really like."

Lord Emsworth felt bitter, and when he felt bitter he could be terribly sarcastic.

"Well, I think it is a very good idea," said his sister. "One could walk there in wet weather then. Damp moss is ruinous to shoes."

Lord Emsworth rose. He could bear no more of this. He left the table, the room and the house and, reaching the yew alley some minutes later, was revolted to find it infested by Angus McAllister in person. The head-gardener was standing gazing at the moss like a high priest of some ancient religion about to stick the gaff into the human sacrifice.

"Morning, McAllister," said Lord Emsworth coldly.

"Good morrrrning, your lorrudsheep."

There was a pause. Angus McAllister, extending a foot that looked like a violin-case, pressed it on the moss. The meaning of the gesture was plain. It expressed contempt, dislike, a generally anti-moss spirit: and Lord Emsworth, wincing, surveyed the man unpleasantly through his pince-nez. Though not often given to theological speculation, he was wondering why Providence, if obliged to make head-gardeners, had found it necessary to make them so Scotch. In the case of Angus McAllister, why, going a step farther, have made him a human being at all? All the ingredients of a first-class mule simply thrown away. He felt that he might have liked Angus McAllister if he had been a mule.

"I was speaking to her leddyship yesterday."

"Oh?"

"About the gravel path I was speaking to her leddyship."

"Oh?"

"Her leddyship likes the notion fine."

"Indeed! Well . . ."

Lord Emsworth's face had turned a lively pink, and he was about to release the blistering words which were forming themselves in his mind when suddenly he caught the head-gardener's eye and paused. Angus McAllister was looking at him in a peculiar manner, and he knew what that look meant. Just one crack, his eye was saying – in Scotch, of course – just one crack out of you and I tender my resignation. And with a sickening shock it came home to Lord Emsworth how completely he was in this man's clutches.

He shuffled miserably. Yes, he was helpless. Except for that kink about gravel paths, Angus McAllister was a head-gardener in a thousand, and he needed him. He could not do without him. That, unfortunately, had been proved by experiment. Once before, at the time when they were grooming for the Agricultural Show that pumpkin which had subsequently romped home so gallant a winner, he had dared to flout Angus McAllister. And Angus had resigned, and he had been forced to plead – yes, plead – with him to come back. An employer cannot hope to do this sort of thing and still rule with an iron hand. Filled with the coward rage that dares to burn but does not dare to blaze, Lord Emsworth coughed a cough that was undisguisedly a bronchial white flag.

"I'll – er – I'll think it over, McAllister."

"Mphm."

"I have to go to the village now. I will see you later."

"Mphm."

"Meanwhile, I will – er – think it over."

"Mphm."

The task of judging the floral displays in the cottage gardens of the little village of Blandings Parva was one to which Lord Emsworth had looked forward with pleasurable anticipation. It was the sort of job he liked. But now, even though he had managed to give his sister Constance the slip and was free from her threatened society, he approached the task with a downcast spirit. It is always unpleasant for a proud man to realize that he is no longer captain of his soul; that he is to all intents and purposes ground beneath the number twelve heel of a Glaswegian head-gardener; and, brooding on this, he judged the cottage gardens with a distrait eye. It was only when he came to the last on his list that anything like animation crept into his demeanour.

This, he perceived, peering over its rickety fence, was not at all a bad little garden. It demanded closer inspection. He unlatched the gate and pottered in. And a dog, dozing behind a water-butt, opened one eye and looked at him. It was one of those hairy, non-descript dogs, and its gaze was cold, wary and suspicious, like that of a stockbroker who thinks someone is going to play the confidence trick on him.

Lord Emsworth did not observe the animal. He had pottered to a bed of wall-flowers and now, stooping, he took a sniff at them.

As sniffs go, it was an innocent sniff, but the dog for some reason appeared to read into it criminality of a high order. All the indignant householder in him woke in a flash. The next moment the world had become full of hideous noises, and Lord Emsworth's preoccupation was swept away in a passionate desire to save his ankles from harm.

As these chronicles of Blandings Castle have already shown, he was not at his best with strange dogs. Beyond saying "Go away, sir!" and leaping to and fro with an agility surprising in one of his years, he had accomplished little in the direction of a reasoned plan of defence when the cottage door opened and a girl came out.

"Hoy!" cried the girl.

And on the instant, at the mere sound of her voice, the mongrel, suspending hostilities, bounded at the new-comer and writhed on his back at her feet with all four legs in the air. The spectacle reminded Lord Emsworth irresistibly of his own behaviour when in the presence of Angus McAllister.

He blinked at his preserver. She was a small girl, of uncertain age – possibly twelve or thirteen, though a combination of London fogs and early cares had given her face a sort of wizened motherliness which in some odd way caused his lordship from the first to look on her as belonging to his own generation. She was the type of girl you see in back streets carrying a baby nearly as large as herself and still retaining sufficient energy to lead one little brother by the hand and shout recrimination at another in the distance. Her cheeks shone from recent soaping, and she was dressed in a velveteen frock which was obviously the pick of her wardrobe. Her hair, in defiance of the prevailing mode, she wore drawn tightly back into a short pigtail.

"Er – thank you," said Lord Emsworth.

"Thank you, sir," said the girl.

For what she was thanking him, his lordship was not able to gather. Later, as their acquaintance ripened, he was to discover that this strange gratitude was a habit with his new friend. She thanked everybody for everything. At the moment, the mannerism surprised him. He continued to blink at her through his pince-nez.

Lack of practice had rendered Lord Emsworth a little rusty in the art of making conversation to members of the other sex. He sought in his mind for topics.

"Fine day."

"Yes, sir. Thank you, sir."

"Are you" – Lord Emsworth furtively consulted his list – "are you the daughter of – ah – Ebenezer Sprockett?" he asked, thinking, as he had often thought before, what ghastly names some of his tenantry possessed.

"No, sir. I'm from London, sir."

"Ah? London, eh? Pretty warm it must be there." He paused. Then, remembering a formula of his youth: "Er – been out much this Season?"

"No, sir."

"Everybody out of town now, I suppose? What part of London?"

"Drury Line, sir."

"What's your name? Eh, what?"

"Gladys, sir. Thank you, sir. This is Ern."

A small boy had wandered out of the cottage, a rather hard-boiled specimen with freckles, bearing surprisingly in his hand a large and beautiful bunch of flowers. Lord Emsworth bowed courteously and with the addition of this third party to the *tête-à-tête* felt more at his ease.

"How do you do," he said. "What pretty flowers."

With her brother's advent, Gladys, also, had lost diffidence and gained conversational aplomb.

"A treat, ain't they?" she agreed eagerly. "I got 'em for 'im up at the big 'ahse. Coo! The old josser the plice belongs to didn't arf chase me. 'E found me picking 'em and 'e sharted somefin at me and come runnin' after me, but I copped 'im on the shin wiv a stone and 'e stopped to rub it and I come away."

Lord Emsworth might have corrected her impression that Blandings Castle and its gardens belonged to Angus McAllister, but his mind was so filled with admiration and gratitude that he refrained from doing so. He looked at the girl almost reverently. Not content with controlling savage dogs with a mere word, this super-woman actually threw stones at Angus McAllister – a thing which he had never been able to nerve himself to do in an association which had lasted nine years – and, what was more, copped him on the shin with them. What nonsense, Lord Emsworth felt, the papers talked about the Modern Girl. If this was a specimen, the Modern Girl was the highest point the sex had yet reached.

"Ern," said Gladys, changing the subject, "is wearin' 'air-oil todiy."

Lord Emsworth had already observed this and had, indeed, been moving to windward as she spoke.

"For the Feet," explained Gladys.

"For the feet?" It seemed unusual.

"For the Feet in the pork this afternoon."

"Oh, you are going to the Fête?"

"Yes, sir, thank you, sir."

For the first time, Lord Emsworth found himself regarding that grisly social event with something approaching favour.

"We must look out for one another there," he said cordially. "You will remember me again? I shall be wearing" – he gulped – "a top hat."

"Ern's going to wear a stror penamaw that's been give 'im."

Lord Emsworth regarded the lucky young devil with frank envy. He rather fancied he knew that panama. It had been his constant companion for some six years and then had been torn from him by his sister Constance and handed over to the vicar's wife for her rummage-sale.

He sighed.

"Well, good-bye."

"Good-bye, sir. Thank you, sir."

Lord Emsworth walked pensively out of the garden and, turning into the little street, encountered Lady Constance.

"Oh, there you are, Clarence."

"Yes," said Lord Emsworth, for such was the case.

"Have you finished judging the gardens?"

"Yes."

"I am just going into this end cottage here. The vicar tells me there is a little girl from London staying there. I want to warn her to behave this afternoon. I have spoken to the others."

Lord Emsworth drew himself up. His pince-nez were slightly askew, but despite this his gaze was commanding and impressive.

"Well, mind what you say," he said authoritatively. "None of your district-visiting stuff, Constance."

"What do you mean?"

"You know what I mean. I have the greatest respect for the young lady to whom you refer. She behaved on a certain recent occasion – on two recent occasions – with notable gallantry and resource, and I won't have her ballyragged. Understand that!"

The technical title of the orgy which broke out annually on the first Monday in August in the park of Blandings Castle was the Blandings Parva School Treat, and it seemed to Lord Emsworth, wanly watching the proceedings from under the shadow of his top hat, that if this was the sort of thing schools looked on as pleasure he and they were mentally poles apart. A function like the Blandings Parva School Treat blurred his conception of Man as Nature's Final Word.

The decent sheep and cattle to whom this park normally belonged had been hustled away into regions unknown, leaving the smooth expanse of turf to children whose vivacity scared Lord Emsworth and adults who appeared to him to have cast aside all dignity and every other noble quality which goes to make a one hundred per cent British citizen. Look at Mrs Rossiter over there, for instance, the wife of Jno. Rossiter, Provisions, Groceries and Home-Made Jams. On any other day of the year, when you met her, Mrs Rossiter was a nice, quiet, docile woman who gave at the knees respectfully as you passed. To-day, flushed in the face and with her bonnet on one side, she seemed to have gone completely native. She was wandering to and fro drinking lemonade out of a bottle and employing her mouth, when not so occupied, to make a devastating noise with what he believed was termed a squeaker.

The injustice of the thing stung Lord Emsworth. This park was his own private park. What right had people to come and blow squeakers in it? How would Mrs Rossiter like it if one afternoon he suddenly invaded her neat little garden in the High Street and rushed about over her lawn, blowing a squeaker?

And it was always on these occasions so infernally hot. July might have ended in a flurry of snow, but directly the first Monday in August arrived and he had to put on a stiff collar out came the sun, blazing with tropic fury.

Of course, admitted Lord Emsworth, for he was a fair-minded man, this cut both ways. The hotter the day, the more quickly his collar lost its starch and ceased to spike him like a javelin. This afternoon, for instance, it had resolved itself almost immediately into something which felt like a wet compress. Severe as were his sufferings, he was compelled to recognize that he was that much ahead of the game.

A masterful figure loomed at his side.

"Clarence!"

Lord Emsworth's mental and spiritual state was now such that not even the advent of his sister Constance could add noticeably to his discomfort.

"Clarence, you look a perfect sight."

"I know I do. Who wouldn't in a rig-out like this? Why in the name of goodness you always insist . . ."

"Please don't be childish, Clarence. I cannot understand the fuss you make about dressing for once in your life like a reasonable English gentleman and not like a tramp."

"It's this top hat. It's exciting the children."

"What on earth do you mean, exciting the children?"

"Well, all I can tell you is that just now, as I was passing the place where they're playing football – Football! In weather like this! – a small boy called out something derogatory and threw a portion of a coco-nut at it."

"If you will identify the child," said Lady Constance warmly, "I will have him severely punished."

"How the dickens," replied his lordship with equal warmth, "can I identify the child? They all look alike to me. And if I did identify him, I would shake him by the hand. A boy who throws coco-nuts at top hats is fundamentally sound in his views. And stiff collars . . ."

"Stiff! That's what I came to speak to you about. Are you aware that your collar looks like a rag? Go in and change it at once."

"But, my dear Constance . . ."

"At once, Clarence. I simply cannot understand a man having so little pride in his appearance. But all your life you have been like that. I remember when we were children . . ."

Lord Emsworth's past was not of such a purity that he was prepared to stand and listen to it being lectured on by a sister with a good memory.

"Oh, all right, all right, all right," he said. "I'll change it, I'll change it."

"Well, hurry. They are just starting tea."

Lord Emsworth quivered.

"Have I got to go into that tea-tent?"

"Of course you have. Don't be so ridiculous. I do wish you would realize your position. As master of Blandings Castle . . ."

A bitter, mirthless laugh from the poor peon thus ludicrously described drowned the rest of the sentence.

It always seemed to Lord Emsworth, in analysing these entertainments, that the August Bank Holiday Saturnalia at Blandings Castle reached a peak of repulsiveness when tea was served in the big marquee. Tea over, the agony abated, to become acute once more at the moment when he stepped to the edge of the platform and cleared his throat and tried to recollect what the deuce he had planned to say to the goggling audience beneath him. After that, it subsided again and passed until the following August.

Conditions during the tea hour, the marquee having stood all day under a blazing sun, were generally such that Shadrach, Meshach and Abednego, had they been there, could have learned something new about burning fiery furnaces. Lord Emsworth, delayed by the revision of his toilet, made his entry when the meal was half over and was pleased to find that his second collar almost instantaneously began to relax its iron grip. That, however, was the only gleam of happiness which was to be vouchsafed him. Once in the tent, it took his experienced eye but a moment to discern that the present feast was eclipsing in frightfulness all its predecessors.

Young Blandings Parva, in its normal form, tended rather to the stolidly bovine than the riotous. In all villages, of course, there must of necessity be an occasional tough egg – in the case of Blandings Parva the names of Willie Drake and Thomas (Rat-Face) Blenkiron spring to the mind – but it was seldom that the local infants offered anything beyond the power of a curate to control. What was giving the present gathering its striking resemblance to a reunion of *sans-culottes* at the height of the French Revolution was the admixture of the Fresh Air London visitors.

About the London child, reared among the tin cans and cabbage stalks of Drury Lane and Clare Market, there is a breezy insouciance which his country cousin lacks. Years of back-chat with annoyed parents and relatives have cured him of any tendency he may have had towards shyness, with the result that when he requires anything he grabs for it, and when he is amused by any slight peculiarity in the personal appearance of members of the governing classes he finds no difficulty in translating his thoughts into speech. Already, up and down the long tables, the curate's unfortunate squint was coming in for hearty comment, and the front teeth of one of the school-teachers ran it a close second for popularity. Lord Emsworth was not, as a rule, a man of swift inspirations, but it occurred to him at this juncture that it would be a prudent move to take off his top hat before his little guests observed it and appreciated its humorous possibilities.

The action was not, however, necessary. Even as he raised his hand a rock cake, singing through the air like a shell, took it off for him.

Lord Emsworth had had sufficient. Even Constance, unreasonable woman though she was, could hardly expect him to stay and beam genially under conditions like this. All civilized laws had obviously gone by the board and Anarchy reigned in the marquee. The curate was doing his best to form a provisional government consisting of himself and the two school-teachers, but there was only one man who could have coped adequately with the situation and that was

King Herod, who – regrettably – was not among those present. Feeling like some aristocrat of the old régime sneaking away from the tumbril, Lord Emsworth edged to the exit and withdrew.

Outside the marquee the world was quieter, but only comparatively so. What Lord Emsworth craved was solitude, and in all the broad park there seemed to be but one spot where it was to be had. This was a red-tiled shed, standing beside a small pond, used at happier times as a lounge or retiring-room for cattle. Hurrying thither, his lordship had just begun to revel in the cool, cow-scented dimness of its interior when from one of the dark corners, causing him to start and bite his tongue, there came the sound of a subdued sniff.

He turned. This was persecution. With the whole park to mess about in, why should an infernal child invade this one sanctuary of his? He spoke with angry sharpness. He came of a line of warrior ancestors and his fighting blood was up.

"Who's that?"

"Me, sir. Thank you, sir."

Only one person of Lord Emsworth's acquaintance was capable of expressing gratitude for having been barked at in such a tone. His wrath died away and remorse took its place. He felt like a man who in error has kicked a favourite dog.

"God bless my soul!" he exclaimed. "What in the world are you doing in a cow-shed?"

"Please, sir, I was put."

"Put? How do you mean, put? Why?"

"For pinching things, sir."

"Eh? What? Pinching things? Most extraordinary. What did you – er – pinch?"

"Two buns, two jem-sengwiches, two apples and a slicer cake."

The girl had come out of her corner and was standing correctly at attention. Force of habit had caused her to intone the list of the purloined articles in the singsong voice in which she was wont to recite the multiplication-table at school, but Lord Emsworth could see that she was deeply moved. Tear-stains glistened on her face, and no Emsworth had ever been able to watch unstirred a woman's tears. The ninth Earl was visibly affected.

"Blow your nose," he said, hospitably extending his handkerchief.

"Yes, sir. Thank you, sir."

"What did you say you had pinched? Two buns . . ."

". . . Two jem-sengwiches, two apples and a slicer cake."

"Did you eat them?"

"No, sir. They wasn't for me. They was for Ern."

"Ern? Oh, ah, yes. Yes, to be sure. For Ern, eh?"

"Yes, sir."

"But why the dooce couldn't Ern have – er – pinched them for himself? Strong, able-bodied young feller, I mean."

Lord Emsworth, a member of the old school, did not like this disposition on the part of the modern young man to shirk the dirty work and let the woman pay.

"Ern wasn't allowed to come to the treat, sir."

"What! Not allowed? Who said he mustn't?"

"The lidy, sir."

"What lidy?"

"The one that come in just after you'd gorn this morning."

A fierce snort escaped Lord Emsworth. Constance! What the devil did Constance mean by taking it upon herself to revise his list of guests without so much as a . . . Constance, eh? He snorted again. One of these days Constance would go too far.

"Monstrous!" he cried.

"Yes, sir."

"High-handed tyranny, by Gad. Did she give any reason?"

"The lidy didn't like Ern biting 'er in the leg, sir."

"Ern bit her in the leg?"

"Yes, sir. Pliying 'e was a dorg. And the lidy was cross and Ern wasn't allowed to come to the treat, and I told 'im I'd bring 'im back somefing nice."

Lord Emsworth breathed heavily. He had not supposed that in these degenerate days a family like this existed. The sister copped Angus McAllister on the shin with stones, the brother bit Constance in the leg . . . It was like listening to some grand old saga of the exploits of heroes and demigods.

"I thought if I didn't 'ave nothing myself it would make it all right."

"Nothing?" Lord Emsworth started. "Do you mean to tell me you have not had tea?"

"No, sir. Thank you, sir. I thought if I didn't 'ave none, then it would be all right Ern 'aving what I would 'ave 'ad if I 'ad 'ave 'ad."

His lordship's head, never strong, swam a little. Then it resumed its equilibrium. He caught her drift.

"God bless my soul!" said Lord Emsworth. "I never heard anything so monstrous and appalling in my life. Come with me immediately."

"The lidy said I was to stop 'ere, sir."

Lord Emsworth gave vent to his loudest snort of the afternoon.

"Confound the lidy!"

"Yes, sir. Thank you, sir."

Five minutes later Beach, the butler, enjoying a siesta in the housekeeper's room, was roused from his slumbers by the unexpected ringing of a bell. Answering its summons, he found his employer in the library, and with him a surprising young person in a velveteen frock, at the sight of whom his eyebrows quivered and, but for his iron self-restraint, would have risen.

"Beach!"

"Your lordship?"

"This young lady would like some tea."

"Very good, your lordship."

"Buns, you know. And apples, and jem – I mean jam-sandwiches, and cake, and that sort of thing."

"Very good, your lordship."

"And she has a brother, Beach."

"Indeed, your lordship?"

"She will want to take some stuff away for him." Lord Emsworth turned to his guest. "Ernest would like a little chicken, perhaps?"

"Coo!"

"I beg your pardon?"

"Yes, sir. Thank you, sir."

"And a slice or two of ham?"

"Yes, sir. Thank you, sir."

"And – he has no gouty tendency?"

"No, sir. Thank you, sir."

"Capital! Then a bottle of that new lot of port, Beach. It's some stuff they've sent me down to try," explained his lordship. "Nothing special, you understand," he added apologetically, "but quite drinkable. I should like your brother's opinion of it. See that all that is put together in a parcel, Beach, and leave it on the table in the hall. We will pick it up as we go out."

A welcome coolness had crept into the evening air by the time Lord Emsworth and his guest came out of the great door of the castle. Gladys, holding her host's hand and clutching the parcel, sighed contentedly. She had done herself well at the tea-table. Life seemed to have nothing more to offer.

Lord Emsworth did not share this view. His spacious mood had not yet exhausted itself.

"Now, is there anything else you can think of that Ernest would like?" he asked. "If so, do not hesitate to mention it. Beach, can you think of anything?"

The butler, hovering respectfully, was unable to do so.

"No, your lordship. I ventured to add – on my own responsibility, your lordship – some hard-boiled eggs and a pot of jam to the parcel."

"Excellent! You are sure there is nothing else?"

A wistful look came into Glady's eyes.

"Could he 'ave some flarze?"

"Certainly," said Lord Emsworth. "Certainly, certainly, certainly. By all means. Just what I was about to suggest my – er – what *is* flarze?"

Beach, the linguist, interpreted.

"I think the young lady means flowers, your lordship."

"Yes, sir. Thank you, sir. Flarze."

"Oh?" said Lord Emsworth. "Oh? Flarze?" he said slowly. "Oh, ah, yes. Yes. I see. H'm!"

He removed his pince-nez, wiped them thoughtfully, replaced them, and gazed with wrinkling forehead at the gardens that stretched gaily out before him. Flarze! It would be idle to deny that those gardens contained flarze in full measure. They were bright with Achillea, Bignonia Radicans, Campanula, Digitalis, Euphorbia, Funkia, Gypsophila, Helianthus, Iris, Liatris, Monarda, Phlox Drummondi, Salvia, Thalictrum, Vinca and Yucca. But the devil of it was that Angus McAllister would have a fit if they were picked. Across the threshold of this Eden the ginger whiskers of Angus McAllister lay like a flaming sword.

As a general rule, the procedure for getting flowers out of Angus McAllister was as follows. You waited till he was in one of his rare moods of complaisance, then you led the conversation gently round to the subject of interior decoration, and then, choosing your moment, you asked if he could possibly spare a few to be put in vases. The last thing you thought of doing was to charge in and start helping yourself.

"I – er – . . ." said Lord Emsworth.

He stopped. In a sudden blinding flash of clear vision he had seen himself for what he was – the spineless, unspeakably unworthy descendant of ancestors who, though they may have had their faults, had certainly known how to handle employees. It was "How now, varlet!" and "Marry come up, thou malapert knave!" in the days of previous Earls of Emsworth. Of course, they had possessed certain advantages which he lacked. It undoubtedly helped a man in his dealings with the domestic staff to have, as they had had, the rights of the high, the middle and the low justice – which meant, broadly, that if you got annoyed with your head-gardener you could immediately divide him into four head-gardeners with a battle-axe and no questions asked – but even so, he realized that they were better men than he was and that, if he allowed craven fear of Angus McAllister to stand in the way of this delightful girl and her charming brother getting all the flowers they required, he was not worthy to be the last of their line.

Lord Emsworth wrestled with his tremors.

"Certainly, certainly, certainly," he said, though not without a qualm. "Take as many as you want."

And so it came about that Angus McAllister, crouched in his potting-shed like some dangerous beast in its den, beheld a sight which first froze his blood and then sent it boiling through his veins. Flitting to and fro through his sacred gardens, picking his sacred flowers, was a small girl in a velveteen frock. And – which brought apoplexy a step closer – it was the same small girl who two days before had copped him on the shin with a stone. The stillness of the summer evening was shattered by a roar that sounded like boilers exploding, and Angus McAllister came out of the potting-shed at forty-five miles per hour.

Gladys did not linger. She was a London child, trained from infancy to bear herself gallantly in the presence of alarms and excursions, but this excursion had been so sudden that it momentarily broke her nerve. With a horrified yelp she scuttled to where Lord Emsworth stood and, hiding behind him, clutched the tails of his morning-coat.

"Oo-er!" said Gladys.

Lord Emsworth was not feeling so frightfully good himself. We have pictured him a few moments back drawing inspiration from the nobility of his ancestors and saying, in effect, "That for McAllister!" but truth now compels us to admit that this hardy attitude was largely due to the fact that he believed the head-gardener to be a safe quarter of a mile away among the swings and roundabouts of the Fête. The spectacle of the man charging vengefully down on him with gleaming eyes and bristling whiskers made him feel like a nervous English infantryman at the Battle of Bannockburn. His knees shook and the soul within him quivered.

And then something happened, and the whole aspect of the situation changed.

It was, in itself, quite a trivial thing, but it had an astoundingly stimulating effect on Lord Emsworth's morale. What happened was that Gladys, seeking further protection, slipped at this moment a small, hot hand into his.

It was a mute vote of confidence, and Lord Emsworth intended to be worthy of it.

"He's coming," whispered his lordship's Inferiority Complex agitatedly.

"What of it?" replied Lord Emsworth stoutly.

"Tick him off," breathed his lordship's ancestors in his other ear.

"Leave it to me," replied Lord Emsworth.

He drew himself up and adjusted his pince-nez. He felt filled with a cool masterfulness. If the man tendered his resignation, let him tender his damned resignation.

"Well, McAllister?" said Lord Emsworth coldly.

He removed his top hat and brushed it against his sleeve.

"What is the matter, McAllister?"

He replaced his top hat.

"You appear agitated, McAllister."

He jerked his head militantly. The hat fell off. He let it lie. Freed from its loathsome weight he felt more masterful than ever. It had just needed that to bring him to the top of his form.

"This young lady," said Lord Emsworth, "has my full permission to pick all the flowers she wants, McAllister. If you do not see eye to eye with me in this matter, McAllister, say so and we will discuss what you are going to do about it, McAllister. These gardens, McAllister, belong to me, and if you do not – er – appreciate that fact you will, no doubt, be able to find another employer – ah – more in tune with your views. I value your services highly, McAllister, but I will not be dictated to in my own garden, McAllister. Er – dash it," added his lordship, spoiling the whole effect.

A long moment followed in which Nature stood still, breathless. The Achillea stood still. So did the Bignonia Radicans. So did the Campanula, the Digitalis, the Euphorbia, the Funkia, the Gypsophila, the Helianthus, the Iris, the Liatris, the Monarda, the Phlox Drummondi, the Salvia, the Thalictrum, the Vinca and the Yucca. From far off in the direction of the park there sounded the happy howls of children who were probably breaking things, but even these seemed hushed. The evening breeze had died away.

Angus McAllister stood glowering. His attitude was that of one sorely perplexed. So might the early bird have looked if the worm ear-marked for its breakfast had suddenly turned and snapped at it. It had never occurred to him that his employer would voluntarily suggest that he sought another position, and now that he had suggested it Angus McAllister disliked the idea very much. Blandings Castle was in his bones. Elsewhere, he would feel an exile. He fingered his whiskers, but they gave him no comfort.

He made his decision. Better to cease to be a Napoleon than be a Napoleon in exile.

"Mphm," said Angus McAllister.

"Oh, and by the way, McAllister," said Lord Emsworth, "that matter of the gravel path through the yew alley. I've been thinking it over, and I won't have it. Not on any account. Mutilate my beautiful moss with a beastly gravel path? Make an eyesore of the loveliest spot in one of the finest and oldest gardens in the United Kingdom? Certainly not. Most decidedly not. Try to remember, McAllister, as you work in the gardens of Blandings Castle, that you are not back in Glasgow, laying out recreation grounds. That is all, McAllister. Er – dash it – that is all."

"Mphm," said Angus McAllister.

He turned. He walked away. The potting-shed swallowed him up. Nature resumed its breathing. The breeze began to blow again. And all over the gardens birds who had stopped on their high note carried on according to plan.

Lord Emsworth took out his handkerchief and dabbed with it at his forehead. He was shaken, but a novel sense of being a man among men thrilled him. It might seem bravado, but he almost wished – yes, dash it, he almost wished – that his sister Constance would come along and start something while he felt like this.

He had his wish.

"Clarence!"

Yes, there she was, hurrying towards him up the garden path. She, like McAllister, seemed agitated. Something was on her mind.

"Clarence!"

"Don't keep saying "Clarence!" as if you were a dashed parrot," said Lord Emsworth haughtily. "What the dickens is the matter, Constance?"

"Matter? Do you know what the time is? Do you know that everybody is waiting down there for you to make your speech?"

Lord Emsworth met her eye sternly.

"I do not," he said. "And I don't care. I'm not going to make any dashed speech. If you want a speech, let the vicar make it. Or make it yourself. Speech! I never heard such dashed nonsense in my life." He turned to Gladys. "Now, my dear," he said, "if you will just give me time to get out of these infernal clothes and this ghastly collar and put on something human, we'll go down to the village and have a chat with Ern."

FORGOTTEN DREAMS

Stefan Zweig

Stefan Zweig (1881–1942) killed himself with barbiturates in 1942, in
Petrópolis, in Brazil, holding hands on a double bed with his second
wife. He was born in Vienna and, during the 1920s and 1930s, was one
of the most famous writers in the world.

The villa lay close to the sea.

The quiet avenues, lined with pine trees, breathed out the rich strength
of salty sea air, and a slight breeze constantly played around the orange
trees, now and then removing a colourful bloom from flowering shrubs as if
with careful fingers. The sunlit distance, where attractive houses built on hillsides
gleamed like white pearls, a lighthouse miles away rose steeply and straight as a
candle – the whole scene shone, its contours sharp and clearly outlined, and was
set in the deep azure of the sky like a bright mosaic. The waves of the sea, marked
by only the few white specks that were the distant sails of isolated ships, lapped
against the tiered terrace on which the villa stood; the ground then rose on and
on to the green of a broad, shady garden and merged with the rest of the park, a
scene drowsy and still, as if under some fairy-tale enchantment.

Outside the sleeping house on which the morning heat lay heavily, a narrow
gravel path ran like a white line to the cool viewing point. The waves tossed
wildly beneath it, and here and there shimmering spray rose, sparkling in rainbow colours as brightly as diamonds in the strong sunlight. There the shining
rays of the sun broke on the small groups of Vistulian pines standing close together, as if in intimate conversation, they also fell on a Japanese parasol with
amusing pictures on it in bright, glaring colours, now open wide.

A woman was leaning back in a soft basket chair in the shade of this parasol, her beautiful form comfortably lounging in the yielding weave of the
wicker. One slender hand, wearing no rings, dangled down as if forgotten, pet-
ting the gleaming, silky coat of a dog with gentle, pleasing movements, while
the other hand held a book on which her dark eyes, with their black lashes
and the suggestion of a smile in them, were concentrating. They were large
and restless eyes, their beauty enhanced by a dark, veiled glow. Altogether the
strong, attractive effect of the oval, sharply outlined face did not give the natural impression of simple beauty, but expressed the refinement of certain details
tended with careful, delicate coquetry. The apparently unruly confusion of her
fragrant, shining curls was the careful construction of an artist, and in the
same way the slight smile that hovered around her lips as she read, revealing
her white teeth, was the result of many years of practice in front of the mirror,

but had already become a firmly established part of the whole design and could not be laid aside now.

There was a slight crunch on the sand.

She looks without changing her position, like a cat lying basking in the dazzling torrent of warm sunlight and merely blinking apathetically at the newcomer with phosphorescent eyes.

The steps quickly come closer, and a servant in livery stands in front of her to hand her a small visiting card, then stands back a little way to wait.

She reads the name with that expression of surprise on her features that appears when you are greeted in the street with great familiarity by someone you do not know. For a moment, small lines appear above her sharply traced black eyebrows, showing how hard she is thinking, and then a happy light plays over her whole face all of a sudden, her eyes sparkle with high spirits as she thinks of the long-ago days of her youth, almost forgotten now. The name has aroused pleasant images in her again. Figures and dreams take on distinct shape once more, and become as clear as reality.

"Ah, yes," she said as she remembered, suddenly turning to the servant, "yes, of course show the gentleman up here."

The servant left, with a soft and obsequious tread. For a moment there was silence except for the never-tiring wind singing softly in the treetops, now full of the heavy golden midday light.

Then vigorous, energetic footsteps were heard on the gravel path, a long shadow fell at her feet, and a tall man stood before her. She had risen from her chair with a lively movement.

Their eyes met first. With a quick glance he took in the elegance of her figure, while a slight ironic smile came into her eyes. "It's really good of you to have thought of me," she began, offering him her slender and well-tended hand, which he touched respectfully with his lips.

"Dear lady, I will be honest with you, since this is our first meeting for years, and also, I fear, the last for many years to come. It is something of a coincidence that I am here; the name of the owner of the castle about which I was enquiring because of its magnificent position recalled you to my mind. So I am really here under false pretences."

"But nonetheless welcome for that, and in fact I myself could not remember your existence at first, although it was once of some significance to me."

Now they both smiled. The sweet, light fragrance of a first youthful, half-unspoken love, with all its intoxicating tenderness, had awoken in them like a dream on which you reflect ironically when you wake, although you really wish for nothing more than to dream it again, to live in the dream. The beautiful dream of young love that ventures only on half-measures, that desires and dares not ask, promises and does not give.

They went on talking. But there was already a warmth in their voices, an affectionate familiarity, that only a rosy if already half-faded secret like theirs can allow. In quiet words, broken by a peal of happy laughter now and then, they talked about the past, or forgotten poems, faded flowers, lost ribbons – little love tokens that they had exchanged in the little town where they spent their youth. The old stories that, like half-remembered legends, rang bells in their hearts that had long ago fallen silent, stifled by dust, were slowly, very slowly invested with a melancholy solemnity; the final notes of their youthful love, now dead, brought profound and almost sad gravity to their conversation.

His darkly melodious voice shook slightly as he said, "All that way across the ocean in America, I heard the news that you were engaged – I heard it at a time when the marriage itself had probably taken place."

She did not reply to that. Her thoughts were ten years back in the past. For several long minutes, a sultry silence hung in the air between them.

Then she asked, almost under her breath, "What did you think of me at the time?"

He looked up in surprise. "I can tell you frankly, since I am going back to my new country tomorrow. I didn't feel angry with you, I had no moments of confused, hostile indecision, since life had cooled the bright blaze of love to a dying glow of friendship by that time. I didn't understand you – I just felt sorry for you."

A faint tinge of red flew to her cheeks, and there was a bright glint in her eyes as she cried, in agitation, "Sorry for me! I can't imagine why."

"Because I was thinking of your future husband, that indolent financier with his mind always bent on making money – don't interrupt me, I really don't mean to insult your husband, whom I always respected in his way – and because I was thinking of you, the girl I had left behind. Because I couldn't see you, the independent idealist who had only ironic contempt for humdrum everyday life, as the conventional wife of an ordinary person."

"Then why would I have married him if it was as you say?"

"I didn't know exactly. Perhaps he had hidden qualities that escaped a superficial glance and came to light only in the intimacy of your life together. And I saw that as the easy solution to the riddle, because one thing I could not and would not believe."

"And that was?"

"That you had accepted him for his aristocratic title of Count and his millions. That was the one thing I considered impossible."

It was as if she had failed to hear those last words, for she was looking through her fingers, which glowed deep rose like a murex shell, staring far into the distance, all the way to the veils of mist on the horizon where the sky dipped its pale-blue garment into the dark magnificence of the waves.

He too was lost in thought, and had almost forgotten that last remark of his when, suddenly and almost inaudibly, she turned away from him and said, "And yet that is what happened."

He looked at her in surprise, almost alarm. She had settled back into her chair with slow and obviously artificial composure, and she went on in a soft melancholy undertone, barely moving her lips.

"None of you understood me when I was still a girl, shy and easily intimidated, not even you who were so close to me. Perhaps not even I myself. I think of it often now, and I don't understand myself at that time, because what do women still know about their girlish hearts that believed in miracles, whose dreams are like delicate little white flowers that will be blown away at the first breath of reality? And I was not like all the other girls who dreamt of virile, strong young heroes who would turn their yearnings into radiant happiness, their quiet guesses into delightful knowledge, and bring them release from the uncertain, ill-defined suffering that they cannot grasp, but that casts its shadow on their girlhood, becoming more menacing as it lies in wait for them. I never felt such things, my soul steered other dreams towards the hidden grove of the future that lay behind the enveloping mists of the coming days. My dreams were my own. I always dreamt of myself as a royal child out of one of the old books of fairy tales, playing with sparkling, radiant jewels, wearing sweeping dresses of great value – I dreamt of luxury and magnificence, because I loved them both. Ah, the pleasure of letting my hands pass over trembling, softly rustling silk, or laying my fingers down in the soft, darkly dreaming pile of a heavy velvet fabric, as if they were asleep! I was happy when I could wear jewels on my slender fingers as they trembled with happiness, when pale gemstones looked out of the thick torrent of my hair, like pearls of foam; my highest aim was to rest in the soft upholstery of an elegant vehicle. At the time I was caught up in a frenzied love of artistic beauty that made me despise my real, everyday life. I hated myself in my ordinary clothes, looking simple and modest as a nun, and I often stayed at home for days on end because I was ashamed of my humdrum appearance, I hid myself in my cramped, ugly room, and my dearest dream was to live alone beside the sea, on a property both magnificent and artistic, in shady, green garden walks that were never touched by the dirty hands of the common workaday world, where rich peace reigned – much like this place, in fact. My husband made my dreams come true, and because he could do that I married him."

She has fallen silent now, and her face is suffused with Bacchanalian beauty. The glow in her eyes has become deep and menacing, and the red in her cheeks burns more and more warmly.

There is a profound silence, broken only by the monotonous rhythmical song of the glittering waves breaking on the tiers of the terrace below, as if casting itself on a beloved breast.

Then he says softly, as if to himself, "But what about love?"

She heard that. A slight smile comes to her lips.

"Do you still have all the ideals, *all* the ideals that you took to that distant world with you? Are they all still intact, or have some of them died or withered away? Haven't they been torn out of you by force and flung in the dirt, where thousands of wheels carrying vehicles to their owners' destination in life crushed them? Or have you lost none of them?"

He nods sadly, and says no more.

Suddenly he carries her hand to his lips and kisses it in silence. Then he says, in a warm voice, "Goodbye, and I wish you well."

She returns his farewell firmly and honestly. She feels no shame at having unveiled her deepest secret and shown her soul to a man who has been a stranger to her for years. Smiling, she watches him go, thinks of the words he said about love, and the past comes up with quiet, inaudible steps to intervene between her and the present. And suddenly she thinks that *he* could have given her life its direction, and her ideas paint that strange notion in bright colours.

And slowly, slowly, imperceptibly, the smile on her dreaming lips dies away.

SOLID OBJECTS

Virginia Woolf

There are many things to say of **Virginia Woolf** (1882–1941). She was
a parody of the English, politically incorrect snob of the period, and
yet, once described Joseph Conrad's rather ample wife as a "mattress".
Born into a highly-strung, well-connected family, she married the writer
Leonard Woolf in 1912, and together they collaborated in managing
The Hogarth Press – publishing T.S. Eliot and Woolf's translation of
Dostoyesvsky's *The Devils* – as well as being the centre of a flourishing
intellectual group. Her work includes *Mrs Dalloway, Orlando, A Room
of One's Own* and, amongst others, this rather extraordinary story.

The only thing that moved upon the vast semicircle of the beach was one
small black spot. As it came nearer to the ribs and spine of the stranded
pilchard boat, it became apparent from a certain tenuity in its blackness
that this spot possessed four legs; and moment by moment it became more unmistakable that it was composed of the persons of two young men. Even thus in
outline against the sand there was an unmistakable vitality in them; an indescribable vigour in the approach and withdrawal of the bodies, slight though it was,
which proclaimed some violent argument issuing from the tiny mouths of the
little round heads. This was corroborated on closer view by the repeated lunging
of a walking-stick on the right-hand side. "You mean to tell me . . . You actually
believe . . ." thus the walking stick on the right-hand side next the waves seemed
to be asserting as it cut long straight stripes upon the sand.

"Politics be damned!" issued clearly from the body on the left-hand side, and,
as these words were uttered, the mouths, noses, chins, little moustaches, tweed
caps, rough boots, shooting coats, and check stockings of the two speakers
became clearer and clearer; the smoke of their pipes went up into the air; nothing was so solid, so living, so hard, red, hirsute and virile as these two bodies for
miles and miles of sea and sandhill.

They flung themselves down by the six ribs and spine of the black pilchard
boat. You know how the body seems to shake itself free from an argument, and
to apologize for a mood of exaltation; flinging itself down and expressing in the
looseness of its attitude a readiness to take up with something new – whatever it
may be that comes next to hand. So Charles, whose stick had been slashing the
beach for half a mile or so, began skimming flat pieces of slate over the water;
and John, who had exclaimed "Politics be damned!" began burrowing his fingers
down, down, into the sand. As his hand went further and further beyond the
wrist, so that he had to hitch his sleeve a little higher, his eyes lost their intensity,

or rather the background of thought and experience which gives an inscrutable depth to the eyes of grown people disappeared, leaving only the clear transparent surface, expressing nothing but wonder, which the eyes of young children display. No doubt the act of burrowing in the sand had something to do with it. He remembered that, after digging for a little, the water oozes round your fingertips; the hole then becomes a moat; a well; a spring; a secret channel to the sea. As he was choosing which of these things to make it, still working his fingers in the water, they curled round something hard – a full drop of solid matter – and gradually dislodged a large irregular lump, and brought it to the surface. When the sand coating was wiped off, a green tint appeared. It was a lump of glass, so thick as to be almost opaque; the smoothing of the sea had completely worn off any edge or shape, so that it was impossible to say whether it had been bottle, tumbler or window-pane; it was nothing but glass; it was almost a precious stone. You had only to enclose it in a rim of gold, or pierce it with a wire, and it became a jewel; part of a necklace, or a dull, green light upon a finger. Perhaps after all it was really a gem; something worn by a dark Princess trailing her finger in the water as she sat in the stern of the boat and listened to the slaves singing as they rowed her across the Bay. Or the oak sides of a sunk Elizabethan treasure-chest had split apart, and, rolled over and over, over and over, its emeralds had come at last to shore. John turned it in his hands; he held it to the light; he held it so that its irregular mass blotted out the body and extended right arm of his friend. The green thinned and thickened slightly as it was held against the sky or against the body. It pleased him; it puzzled him; it was so hard, so concentrated, so definite an object compared with the vague sea and the hazy shore.

Now a sigh disturbed him – profound, final, making him aware that his friend Charles had thrown all the flat stones within reach, or had come to the conclusion that it was not worth while to throw them. They ate their sandwiches side by side. When they had done, and were shaking themselves and rising to their feet, John took the lump of glass and looked at it in silence. Charles looked at it too. But he saw immediately that it was not flat, and filling his pipe he said with the energy that dismisses a foolish strain of thought:

"To return to what I was saying –"

He did not see, or if he had seen would hardly have noticed, that John, after looking at the lump for a moment, as if in hesitation, slipped it inside his pocket. That impulse, too, may have been the impulse which leads a child to pick up one pebble on a path strewn with them, promising it a life of warmth and security upon the nursery mantelpiece, delighting in the sense of power and benignity which such an action confers, and believing that the heart of the stone leaps with joy when it sees itself chosen from a million like it, to enjoy this bliss instead of a life of cold and wet upon the high road. "It might so easily have been any other of the millions of stones, but it was I, I, I!"

Whether this thought or not was in John's mind, the lump of glass had its place upon the mantelpiece, where it stood heavy upon a little pile of bills and letters and served not only as an excellent paper-weight, but also as a natural stopping place for the young man's eyes when they wandered from his book. Looked at again and again half consciously by a mind thinking of something else, any object mixes itself so profoundly with the stuff of thought that it loses its actual form and recomposes itself a little differently in an ideal shape which haunts the brain when we least expect it. So John found himself attracted to the windows of curiosity shops when he was out walking, merely because he saw something which reminded him of the lump of glass. Anything, so long as it was an object of some kind, more or less round, perhaps with a dying flame deep sunk in its mass, anything – china, glass, amber, rock, marble – even the smooth oval egg of a prehistoric bird would do. He took, also, to keeping his eyes upon the ground, especially in the neighbourhood of waste land where the household refuse is thrown away. Such objects often occurred there – thrown away, of no use to anybody, shapeless, discarded. In a few months he had collected four or five specimens that took their place upon the mantelpiece. They were useful, too, for a man who is standing for Parliament upon the brink of a brilliant career has any number of papers to keep in order – addresses to constituents, declarations of policy, appeals for subscriptions, invitations to dinner, and so on.

One day, starting from his rooms in the Temple to catch a train in order to address his constituents, his eyes rested upon a remarkable object lying half-hidden in one of those little borders of grass which edge the bases of vast legal buildings. He could only touch it with the point of his stick through the railings; but he could see that it was a piece of china of the most remarkable shape, as nearly resembling a starfish as anything – shaped, or broken accidentally, into five irregular but unmistakable points. The colouring was mainly blue, but green stripes or spots of some kind overlaid the blue, and lines of crimson gave it a richness and lustre of the most attractive kind. John was determined to possess it; but the more he pushed, the further it receded. At length he was forced to go back to his rooms and improvise a wire ring attached to the end of a stick, with which, by dint of great care and skill, he finally drew the piece of china within reach of his hands. As he seized hold of it he exclaimed in triumph. At that moment the clock struck. It was out of the question that he should keep his appointment. The meeting was held without him. But how had the piece of china been broken into this remarkable shape? A careful examination put it beyond doubt that the star shape was accidental, which made it all the more strange, and it seemed unlikely that there should be another such in existence. Set at the opposite end of the mantelpiece from the lump of glass that had been dug from the sand, it looked like a creature from another world – freakish and fantastic as a harlequin. It seemed to be pirouetting through space, winking light like a fitful star. The contrast between the china so vivid and alert, and the glass so mute and contemplative, fascinated him, and wondering and amazed he asked himself how the two came to exist in the same world, let alone to stand upon the same narrow strip of marble in the same room. The question remained unanswered.

He now began to haunt the places which are most prolific of broken china, such as pieces of waste land between railway lines, sites of demolished houses, and commons in the neighbourhood of London. But china is seldom thrown from a great height; it is one of the rarest of human actions. You have to find in conjunction a very high house, and a woman of such reckless impulse and passionate prejudice that she flings her jar or pot straight from the window without thought of who is below. Broken china was to be found in plenty, but broken in some trifling domestic accident, without purpose or character. Nevertheless, he was often astonished as he came to go into the question more deeply, by the immense variety of shapes to be found in London alone, and there was still more cause for wonder and speculation in the differences of qualities and designs. The finest specimens he would bring home and place upon his mantelpiece, where, however, their duty was more and more of an ornamental nature, since papers needing a weight to keep them down became scarcer and scarcer.

He neglected his duties, perhaps, or discharged them absent-mindedly, or his constituents when they visited him were unfavourably impressed by the appearance of his mantelpiece. At any rate he was not elected to represent them in Parliament, and his friend Charles, taking it much to heart and hurrying to condole with him, found him so little cast down by the disaster that he could only suppose that it was too serious a matter for him to realize all at once.

In truth, John had been that day to Barnes Common, and there under a furze bush had found a very remarkable piece of iron. It was almost identical with the glass in shape, massy and globular, but so cold and heavy, so black and metallic, that it was evidently alien to the earth and had its origin in one of the dead stars or was itself the cinder of a moon. It weighed his pocket down; it weighed the mantelpiece down; it radiated cold. And yet the meteorite stood upon the same ledge with the lump of glass and the star-shaped china.

As his eyes passed from one to another, the determination to possess objects that even surpassed these tormented the young man. He devoted himself more and more resolutely to the search. If he had not been consumed by ambition and convinced that one day some newly-discovered rubbish heap would reward him, the disappointments he had suffered, let alone the fatigue and derision, would have made him give up the pursuit. Provided with a bag and a long stick fitted with an adaptable hook, he ransacked all deposits of earth; raked beneath matted tangles of scrub; searched all alleys and spaces between walls where he had learned to expect to find objects of this kind thrown away. As his standard became higher and his taste more severe the disappointments were innumerable, but always some gleam of hope, some piece of china or glass curiously marked or broken lured him on. Day after day passed. He was no longer young. His career – that is his political career – was a thing of the past. People gave up visiting him. He was too silent to be worth asking to dinner. He never talked to anyone about his serious ambitions; their lack of understanding was apparent in their behaviour.

He leaned back in his chair now and watched Charles lift the stones on the mantelpiece a dozen times and put them down emphatically to mark what he was saying about the conduct of the Government, without once noticing their existence.

"What was the truth of it, John?" asked Charles suddenly, turning and facing him. "What made you give it up like that all in a second?"

"I've not given it up," John replied.

"But you've not the ghost of a chance now," said Charles roughly.

"I don't agree with you there," said John with conviction. Charles looked at him and was profoundly uneasy; the most extraordinary doubts possessed him; he had a queer sense that they were talking about different things. He looked round to find some relief for his horrible depression, but the disorderly appearance of the room depressed him still further. What was that stick, and the old carpet bag hanging against the wall? And then those stones? Looking at John, something fixed and distant in his expression alarmed him. He knew only too well that his mere appearance upon a platform was out of the question.

"Pretty stones," he said as cheerfully as he could; and saying that he had an appointment to keep, he left John – for ever.

EVELINE

James Joyce

James Joyce (1882–1941) is considered by some to be one of the most
influential writers of the last century. He wrote *Dubliners, A Portrait
of the Artist as a Young Man, Ulysses* and *Finnegans Wake*. Most of
his life was spent in exile, living in Paris, Zurich and Trieste. He died
after an operation on a perforated ulcer, and is buried in Zurich. After
reading *Ulysses*, and whilst analyzing Joyce's daughter Lucia, Carl Jung
concluded Joyce was suffering from schizophrenia.

She sat at the window watching the evening invade the avenue. Her head
was leaned against the window curtains and in her nostrils was the odour
of dusty cretonne. She was tired.

Few people passed. The man out of the last house passed on his way home;
she heard his footsteps clacking along the concrete pavement and afterwards
crunching on the cinder path before the new red houses. One time there used to
be a field there in which they used to play every evening with other people's children. Then a man from Belfast bought the field and built houses in it – not like
their little brown houses but bright brick houses with shining roofs. The children
of the avenue used to play together in that field – the Devines, the Waters, the
Dunns, little Keogh the cripple, she and her brothers and sisters. Ernest, however,
never played: he was too grown up. Her father used often to hunt them in out of
the field with his blackthorn stick; but usually little Keogh used to keep nix and
call out when he saw her father coming. Still they seemed to have been rather
happy then. Her father was not so bad then; and besides, her mother was alive.
That was a long time ago; she and her brothers and sisters were all grown up her
mother was dead. Tizzie Dunn was dead, too, and the Waters had gone back to
England. Everything changes. Now she was going to go away like the others, to
leave her home.

Home! She looked round the room, reviewing all its familiar objects which
she had dusted once a week for so many years, wondering where on earth all the
dust came from. Perhaps she would never see again those familiar objects from
which she had never dreamed of being divided. And yet during all those years she
had never found out the name of the priest whose yellowing photograph hung on
the wall above the broken harmonium beside the coloured print of the promises
made to Blessed Margaret Mary Alacoque. He had been a school friend of her
father. Whenever he showed the photograph to a visitor her father used to pass
it with a casual word:

"He is in Melbourne now."

She had consented to go away, to leave her home. Was that wise? She tried to weigh each side of the question. In her home anyway she had shelter and food; she had those whom she had known all her life about her. Of course she had to work hard, both in the house and at business. What would they say of her in the Stores when they found out that she had run away with a fellow? Say she was a fool, perhaps; and her place would be filled up by advertisement. Miss Gavan would be glad. She had always had an edge on her, especially whenever there were people listening.

"Miss Hill, don't you see these ladies are waiting?"

"Look lively, Miss Hill, please."

She would not cry many tears at leaving the Stores.

But in her new home, in a distant unknown country, it would not be like that. Then she would be married – she, Eveline. People would treat her with respect then. She would not be treated as her mother had been. Even now, though she was over nineteen, she sometimes felt herself in danger of her father's violence. She knew it was that that had given her the palpitations. When they were growing up he had never gone for her like he used to go for Harry and Ernest, because she was a girl but latterly he had begun to threaten her and say what he would do to her only for her dead mother's sake. And no she had nobody to protect her. Ernest was dead and Harry, who was in the church decorating business, was nearly always down somewhere in the country. Besides, the invariable squabble for money on Saturday nights had begun to weary her unspeakably. She always gave her entire wages – seven shillings – and Harry always sent up what he could but the trouble was to get any money from her father. He said she used to squander the money, that she had no head, that he wasn't going to give her his hard-earned money to throw about the streets, and much more, for he was usually fairly bad on Saturday night. In the end he would give her the money and ask her had she any intention of buying Sunday's dinner. Then she had to rush out as quickly as she could and do her marketing, holding her black leather purse tightly in her hand as she elbowed her way through the crowds and returning home late under her load of provisions. She had hard work to keep the house together and to see that the two young children who had been left to her charge went to school regularly and got their meals regularly. It was hard work – a hard life – but now that she was about to leave it she did not find it a wholly undesirable life.

She was about to explore another life with Frank. Frank was very kind, manly, open-hearted. She was to go away with him by the night-boat to be his wife and to live with him in Buenos Ayres where he had a home waiting for her. How well she remembered the first time she had seen him; he was lodging in a house on the main road where she used to visit. It seemed a few weeks ago. He was standing at the gate, his peaked cap pushed back on his head and his hair tumbled forward over a face of bronze. Then they had come to know each other. He used to meet her outside the Stores every evening and see her home. He took her to see The Bohemian Girl and she felt elated as she sat in an unaccustomed part of the theatre with him. He was awfully fond of music and sang a little. People knew that they were courting and, when he sang about the lass that loves a sailor, she always felt pleasantly confused. He used to call her Poppens out of fun. First of all it had been an excitement for her to have a fellow and then she had begun to like him. He had tales of distant countries. He had started as a deck boy at a pound a month on a ship of the Allan Line going out to Canada. He told her the names of the ships he had been on and the names of the different services. He had sailed through the Straits of Magellan and he told her stories of the terrible Patagonians. He had fallen on his feet in Buenos Ayres, he said, and had come over to the old country just for a holiday. Of course, her father had found out the affair and had forbidden her to have anything to say to him.

"I know these sailor chaps," he said.

One day he had quarrelled with Frank and after that she had to meet her lover secretly.

The evening deepened in the avenue. The white of two letters in her lap grew indistinct. One was to Harry; the other was to her father. Ernest had been her favourite but she liked Harry too. Her father was becoming old lately, she noticed; he would miss her. Sometimes he could be very nice. Not long before, when she had been laid up for a day, he had read her out a ghost story and made toast for her at the fire. Another day, when their mother was alive, they had all gone for a picnic to the Hill of Howth. She remembered her father putting on her mother's bonnet to make the children laugh.

Her time was running out but she continued to sit by the window, leaning her head against the window curtain, inhaling the odour of dusty cretonne. Down far in the avenue she could hear a street organ playing. She knew the air. Strange that it should come that very night to remind her of the promise to her mother, her promise to keep the home together as long as she could. She remembered the last night of her mother's illness; she was again in the close dark room at the other side of the hall and outside she heard a melancholy air of Italy. The organ-player had been ordered to go away and given sixpence. She remembered her father strutting back into the sickroom saying:

"Damned Italians! coming over here!"

As she mused the pitiful vision of her mother's life laid its spell on the very quick of her being – that life of commonplace sacrifices closing in final craziness. She trembled as she heard again her mother's voice saying constantly with foolish insistence:

"Derevaun Seraun! Derevaun Seraun!"

She stood up in a sudden impulse of terror. Escape! She must escape! Frank would save her. He would give her life, perhaps love, too. But she wanted to live. Why should she be unhappy? She had a right to happiness. Frank would take her in his arms, fold her in his arms. He would save her.

She stood among the swaying crowd in the station at the North Wall. He held her hand and she knew that he was speaking to her, saying something about the passage over and over again. The station was full of soldiers with brown baggages. Through the wide doors of the sheds she caught a glimpse of the black mass of the boat, lying in beside the quay wall, with illumined portholes. She answered nothing. She felt her cheek pale and cold and, out of a maze of distress, she prayed to God to direct her, to show her what was her duty. The boat blew a long mournful whistle into the mist. If she went, tomorrow she would be on the sea with Frank, steaming towards Buenos Ayres. Their passage had been booked.

Could she still draw back after all he had done for her? Her distress awoke a nausea in her body and she kept moving her lips in silent fervent prayer.

A bell clanged upon her heart. She felt him seize her hand:

"Come!"

All the seas of the world tumbled about her heart. He was drawing her into them: he would drown her. She gripped with both hands at the iron railing.

"Come!"

No! No! No! It was impossible. Her hands clutched the iron in frenzy. Amid the seas she sent a cry of anguish.

"Eveline! Evvy!"

He rushed beyond the barrier and called to her to follow. He was shouted at to go on but he still called to her. She set her white face to him, passive, like a helpless animal. Her eyes gave him no sign of love or farewell or recognition.

A HUNGER ARTIST

Franz Kafka

We should never have read the work of **Franz Kafka** (1883–1924) but his literary executor, Max Brod, ignored Kafka's wishes to burn everything unread. Kafka himself burned most of his work as his life neared an end from tuberculosis; he seems to have died from a condition in his throat which made eating too painful for him. He was editing "The Hunger Artist" on his deathbed. Today Kafka is seen as one of the most important figures in modernism. In *Metamorphosis*, he wrote "I cannot make you understand. I cannot make anyone understand what is happening inside me. I cannot even explain it to myself."

In the last decades interest in hunger artists has declined considerably. Whereas in earlier days there was good money to be earned putting on major productions of this sort under one's own management, nowadays that is totally impossible. Those were different times. Back then the hunger artist captured the attention of the entire city. From day to day while the fasting lasted, participation increased. Everyone wanted to see the hunger artist at least once a day. During the later days there were people with subscription tickets who sat all day in front of the small barred cage. And there were even viewing hours at night, their impact heightened by torchlight. On fine days the cage was dragged out into the open air, and then the hunger artist was put on display particularly for the children. While for grown-ups the hunger artist was often merely a joke, something they participated in because it was fashionable, the children looked on amazed, their mouths open, holding each other's hands for safety, as he sat there on scattered straw – spurning a chair – in black tights, looking pale, with his ribs sticking out prominently, sometimes nodding politely, answering questions with a forced smile, even sticking his arm out through the bars to let people feel how emaciated he was, but then completely sinking back into himself, so that he paid no attention to anything, not even to what was so important to him, the striking of the clock, which was the single furnishing in the cage, but merely looking out in front of him with his eyes almost shut and now and then sipping from a tiny glass of water to moisten his lips.

Apart from the changing groups of spectators there were also constant observers chosen by the public – strangely enough they were usually butchers – who, always three at a time, were given the task of observing the hunger artist day and night, so that he didn't get anything to eat in some secret manner. It was, however, merely a formality, introduced to reassure the masses, for those who understood knew well enough that during the period of fasting the hunger artist would never, under any circumstances, have eaten the slightest thing, not even if compelled by force. The honour of his art forbade it. Naturally, none of the watchers understood that. Sometimes there were nightly groups of watchers who carried out their vigil very laxly, deliberately sitting together in a distant corner and putting all their attention into playing cards there, clearly intending to allow the hunger artist a small refreshment, which, according to their way of thinking, he could get from some secret supplies. Nothing was more excruciating to the hunger artist than such watchers. They depressed him. They made his fasting terribly difficult. Sometimes he overcame his weakness and sang during the time they were observing, for as long as he could keep it up, to show people how unjust their suspicions about him were. But that was little help. For then they just wondered among themselves about his skill at being able to eat even while singing. He much preferred the observers who sat down right against the bars and, not satisfied with the dim backlighting of the room, illuminated him with electric flashlights, which the impresario made available to them. The glaring light didn't bother him in the slightest. Generally he couldn't sleep at all, and he could always doze off a little under any lighting and at any hour, even in an over-crowded, noisy auditorium. With such observers, he was very happily prepared to spend the entire night without sleeping. He was ready to joke with them, to recount stories from his nomadic life and then, in turn, to listen to their stories – doing everything just to keep them awake, so that he could keep showing them, once again, that he had nothing to eat in his cage and that he was fasting as none of them could. He was happiest, however, when morning came and a lavish breakfast was brought for them at his own expense, on which they hurled themselves with the appetite of healthy men after a hard night's work without sleep. True, there were still people who wanted to see in this breakfast an unfair means of influencing the observers, but that was going too far, and if they were asked whether they wanted to undertake the observers' night shift for its own sake, without the breakfast, they excused themselves. But nonetheless they stood by their suspicions.

However, it was, in general, part of fasting that these doubts were inextricably associated with it. For, in fact, no one was in a position to spend time watching the hunger artist every day and night without interruption, so no one could know, on the basis of his own observation, whether this was a case of truly continuous, flawless fasting. The hunger artist himself was the only one who could know that and, at the same time, the only spectator capable of being completely satisfied with his own fasting. But the reason he was never satisfied was something different. Perhaps it was not fasting at all which made him so very emaciated that many people, to their own regret, had to stay away from his performance, because they couldn't bear to look at him. For he was also so skeletal out of dissatisfaction with himself, because he alone knew something that even initiates didn't know – how easy it was to fast. It was the easiest thing in the world. About this he did not remain silent, but people did not believe him. At best they thought he was being modest. Most of them, however, believed he was a publicity seeker or a total swindler, for whom, at all events, fasting was easy, because he understood how to make it easy, and then still had the nerve to half admit it. He had to accept all that. Over the years he had become accustomed to it. But this dissatisfaction kept gnawing at his insides all the time and never yet – and this one had to say to his credit – had he left the cage of his own free will after any period of fasting. The impresario had set the maximum length of time for the fast at forty days – he would never allow the fasting go on beyond that point, not even in the cosmopolitan cities. And, in fact, he had a good reason. Experience had shown that for about forty days one could increasingly whip up a city's interest by gradually increasing advertising, but that then the public turned away – one could demonstrate a significant decline in popularity. In this respect, there were, of course, small differences among different towns and among different countries, but as a rule it was true that forty days was the maximum length of time. So then on the fortieth day the door of the cage – which was covered with flowers – was opened, an enthusiastic audience filled the amphitheatre, a military band played, two doctors entered the cage in order to take the necessary measurements of the hunger artist, the results were announced to the auditorium through a megaphone, and finally two young ladies arrived, happy about the fact that they were the ones who had just been selected by lot, and sought to lead the hunger artist down a couple of steps out of the cage, where on a small table a carefully chosen hospital meal was laid out. And at this moment the hunger artist always fought back. Of course, he still freely laid his bony arms in the helpful outstretched hands of the ladies bending over him, but he did not want to stand up. Why stop right now after forty days? He could have kept going for even longer, for an unlimited length of time. Why stop right now, when he was in his best form, indeed, not yet even in his best fasting form? Why did people want to rob him of the fame of fasting longer, not just so that he could become the greatest hunger artist of all time, which, in fact, he probably was already, but also so that he could surpass himself in some unimaginable way, for he felt there were no limits to his capacity for fasting. Why did this crowd, which pretended to admire him so much, have so little patience with him? If he kept going and kept fasting even longer, why would they not tolerate it? Then, too, he was tired and felt good sitting in the straw. Now he was supposed to stand up straight and tall and go to eat, something which, when he merely imagined it, made him feel nauseous right away. With great difficulty he repressed mentioning this only out of consideration for the women. And he looked up into the eyes of these women, apparently so friendly but in reality so cruel, and shook his excessively heavy head on his feeble neck. But then happened what always happened. The impresario came forward without a word – the music made talking impossible – raised his arms over the hunger artist, as if inviting heaven to look upon its work here on the straw, this unfortunate martyr, something the hunger artist certainly was, only in a completely different sense, grabbed the hunger artist around his thin waist, in the process wanting with his exaggerated caution to make people believe that here he had to deal with something fragile, and handed him over – not without secretly shaking him a little, so that the hunger artist's legs and upper body swung back and forth uncontrollably – to the women, who had in the meantime turned as pale as death. At this point, the hunger artist endured everything. His head lay on his chest – it was as if it had inexplicably rolled around and just stopped there – his body was arched back, his legs, in an impulse of self-preservation, pressed themselves together at the knees, but scraped the ground, as if they were not really on the floor but were looking for the real ground, and the entire weight of his body, admittedly very small, lay against one of the women, who appealed for help with flustered breath, for she had not imagined her post of honour would be like this, and then stretched her neck as far as possible, to keep her face from the least contact with the hunger artist, but then, when she couldn't manage this and her more fortunate companion didn't come to her assistance but trembled and remained content to hold in front of her the hunger artist's hand, that small bundle of knuckles, she broke into tears, to the delighted laughter of the auditorium, and had to be relieved by an attendant who had been standing ready for some time. Then came the meal. The impresario put a little food into the mouth of the hunger artist, now dozing as if he were fainting, and kept up a cheerful patter designed to divert attention away from the hunger artist's condition. Then a toast was proposed to the public, which was supposedly whispered to the impresario by the hunger artist, the orchestra confirmed everything with a great fanfare, people dispersed, and no one had the right to be dissatisfied with the event, no one except the hunger artist – he was always the only one.

He lived this way, taking small regular breaks, for many years, apparently in the spotlight, honoured by the world, but for all that, his mood was usually gloomy, and it kept growing gloomier all the time, because no one understood how to take it seriously. But how was he to find consolation? What was there left for him to wish for? And if a good-natured man who felt sorry for him ever wanted to explain to him that his sadness probably came from his fasting, then it could happen, especially at an advanced stage of the fasting, that the hunger artist responded with an outburst of rage and began to shake the cage like an animal, frightening everyone. But the impresario had a way of punishing moments like this, something he was happy to use. He would make an apology for the hunger artist to the assembled public, conceding that the irritability had been provoked only by his fasting, which well-fed people did not readily understand and which was capable of excusing the behaviour of the hunger artist. From there, he would move on to speak about the equally hard to understand claim of the hunger artist that he could go on fasting for much longer than he was doing. He would praise the lofty striving, the good will, and the great self-denial no doubt contained in this claim, but then would try to contradict it simply by producing photographs, which were also on sale, for in the pictures one could see the hunger artist on the fortieth day of his fast, in bed, almost dead from exhaustion. Although the hunger artist was very familiar with this perversion of the truth, it always strained his nerves again and was too much for him. What was a result of the premature ending of the fast people were now proposing as its cause! It was impossible to fight against this lack of understanding, against this world of misunderstanding. In good faith he always still listened eagerly to the impresario at the bars of his cage, but each time, once the photographs came out, he would let go of the bars and, with a sigh, sink back into the straw, and a reassured public could come up again and view him.

When those who had witnessed such scenes thought back on them a few years later, often they were unable to understand themselves. For, in the meantime, that change mentioned above had set it. It happened almost immediately. There may have been more profound reasons for it, but who bothered to discover what they were? At any rate, one day the pampered hunger artist saw himself abandoned by the crowd of pleasure seekers, who preferred to stream to other attractions. The impresario chased around half of Europe one more time with him, to see whether he could still re-discover the old interest here and there. It was all futile. It was as if a secret agreement against the fasting performances had really developed everywhere. Naturally, the truth is that it could not have happened so quickly, and people later remembered some things which in the days of intoxicating success they had not paid sufficient attention to, some inadequately suppressed indications, but now it was too late to do anything to counter them. Of course, it was certain that the popularity of fasting would return once more someday, but for those now alive that was no consolation. What was the hunger artist to do now? The man whom thousands of people had cheered on could not display himself in show booths at small fun fairs, and the hunger artist was not only too old to take up a different profession, but was fanatically devoted to fasting more than anything else. So he said farewell to the impresario, an incomparable companion on his life's road, and let himself be hired by a large circus. In order to spare his own feelings, he didn't even look at the terms of his contract at all.

A large circus with its huge number of men, animals, and gimmicks, which are constantly being let go and replenished, can use anyone at any time, even a hunger artist, provided, of course, his demands are modest. Moreover, in this particular case it was not only the hunger artist himself who was engaged, but also his old and famous name. In fact, given the characteristic nature of his art, which was not diminished by his advancing age, one could never claim that a worn-out artist, who no longer stood at the pinnacle of his ability, wanted to escape to a quiet position in the circus. On the contrary, the hunger artist declared that he could fast just as well as in earlier times – something that was entirely credible. Indeed, he even affirmed that if people would let him do what he wanted – and he was promised this without further ado – he would really now legitimately amaze the world for the first time, an assertion which, however, given the mood of the time, something the hunger artist in his enthusiasm easily overlooked, only brought smiles from the experts.

However, the hunger artist had also not forgotten his sense of the way things really were, and he took it as self-evident that people would not set him and his cage up as some star attraction in the middle of the arena, but would move him outside in some other readily accessible spot near the animal stalls. Huge brightly painted signs surrounded the cage and announced what there was to look at there. During the intervals in the main performance, when the general public pushed out towards the menagerie in order to see the animals, they could hardly avoid moving past the hunger artist and stopping there a moment. They would perhaps have remained with him longer, if those pushing up behind them in the narrow passageway, who did not understand this pause on the way to the animal stalls they wanted to see, had not made a longer peaceful observation impossible. This was also the reason why the hunger artist began to tremble before these visiting hours, which he naturally used to long for as the main purpose of his life. In the early days he could hardly wait for the pauses in the performances. He had looked forward with delight to the crowd pouring around him, until he became convinced only too quickly – and even the most stubborn, almost deliberate self-deception could not hold out against the experience – that, judging by their intentions, most of these people were, time and again without exception, only visiting the menagerie. And this view from a distance still remained his most beautiful moment. For when they had come right up to him, he immediately got an earful from the shouting and cursing of the two steadily increasing groups, the ones who wanted to take their time looking at the hunger artist, not with any understanding but on a whim or from mere defiance – for him these ones were soon the more painful – and a second group of people whose only demand was to go straight to the animal stalls. Once the large crowds had passed, the late-comers would arrive, and although there was nothing preventing these people any more from sticking around for as long as they wanted, they rushed past with long strides, almost without a sideways glance, to get to the animals in time. And it was an all-too-rare stroke of luck when the father of a family came by with his children, pointed his finger at the hunger artist, gave a detailed explanation about what was going on here, and talked of earlier years, when he had been present at similar but incomparably more magnificent performances, and then the children, because they had been inadequately prepared at school and in life, always stood around still uncomprehendingly. What was fasting to them? But nonetheless the brightness of the look in their searching eyes revealed something of new and more gracious times coming. Perhaps, the hunger artist said to himself sometimes, everything would be a little better if his location were not quite so near the animal stalls. That way it would be easy for people to make their choice, to say nothing of the fact that he was very upset and constantly depressed by the stink from the stalls, the animals' commotion at night, the pieces of raw meat dragged past him for the carnivorous beasts, and the roars at feeding time. But he did not dare to approach the administration about it. In any case, he had the animals to thank for the crowds of visitors among whom, now and then, there could also be one destined for him. And who knew where they would hide him if he wished to remind them of his existence and, along with that, of the fact that, strictly speaking, he was only an obstacle on the way to the menagerie.

A small obstacle, at any rate, a constantly diminishing obstacle. People became accustomed to thinking it strange that in these times they would want to pay attention to a hunger artist, and with this habitual awareness the judgment on him was pronounced. He might fast as well as he could – and he did – but nothing could save him any more. People went straight past him. Try to explain the art of fasting to anyone! If someone doesn't feel it, then he cannot be made to understand it. The beautiful signs became dirty and illegible. People tore them down, and no one thought of replacing them. The small table with the number of days the fasting had lasted, which early on had been carefully renewed every day, remained unchanged for a long time, for after the first weeks the staff grew tired of even this small task. And so the hunger artist kept fasting on and on, as he once had dreamed about in earlier times, and he had no difficulty at all managing to achieve what he had predicted back then, but no one was counting the days – no one, not even the hunger artist himself, knew how great his achievement was by this point, and his heart grew heavy. And when, once in a while, a person strolling past stood there making fun of the old number and talking of a swindle, that was in a sense the stupidest lie which indifference and innate maliciousness could invent, for the hunger artist was not being deceptive – he was working honestly – but the world was cheating him of his reward.

Many days went by once more, and this, too, came to an end. Finally the cage caught the attention of a supervisor, and he asked the attendant why they had left this perfectly useful cage standing here unused with rotting straw inside. Nobody knew, until one man, with the help of the table with the number on it, remembered the hunger artist. They pushed the straw around with poles and found the hunger artist in there. "Are you still fasting?" the supervisor asked. "When are you finally going to stop?" "Forgive me everything," whispered the hunger artist. Only the supervisor, who was pressing his ear up against the cage, understood him. "Certainly," said the supervisor, tapping his forehead with his finger in order to indicate to the staff the state the hunger artist was in, "we forgive you." "I always wanted you to admire my fasting," said the hunger artist. "But we do admire it," said the supervisor obligingly. "But you shouldn't admire it," said the hunger artist. "Well then, we don't admire it," said the supervisor, "but why shouldn't we admire it?" "Because I had to fast. I can't do anything else," said the hunger artist. "Just look at you," said the supervisor, "why can't you do anything else?" "Because," said the hunger artist, lifting his head a little and, with his lips pursed as if for a kiss, speaking right into the supervisor's ear so that he wouldn't miss anything, "because I couldn't find a food which tasted good to me. If I had found that, believe me, I would not have made a spectacle of myself and would have eaten to my heart's content, like you and everyone else." Those were his last words, but in his failing eyes there was still the firm, if no longer proud, conviction that he was continuing to fast.

"All right, tidy this up now," said the supervisor. And they buried the hunger artist along with the straw. But in his cage they put a young panther. Even for a person with the dullest mind it was clearly refreshing to see this wild animal prowling around in this cage, which had been dreary for such a long time. It lacked nothing. Without thinking about it for any length of time, the guards brought the animal food whose taste it enjoyed. It never seemed once to miss its freedom. This noble body, equipped with everything necessary, almost to the point of bursting, even appeared to carry freedom around with it. That seem to be located somewhere or other in its teeth, and its joy in living came with such strong passion from its throat that it was not easy for spectators to keep watching. But they controlled themselves, kept pressing around the cage, and had no desire at all to move on.

THE RING

Isak Dinesen

Karen Blixen (1885–1962), aka **Isak Dinesen**, is best known for having a farm in Africa: a coffee plantation she managed with her husband and cousin Baron Bror Blixen-Finecke. They divorced in 1925, a collapse in the price of coffee forced her return to her native Denmark and she began publishing her writing in earnest. Her style is Romantic, almost deliberately old-fashioned, a latter-day Grimm sister.

On a summer morning a hundred and fifty years ago a young Danish squire and his wife went out for a walk on their land. They had been married a week. It had not been easy for them to get married, for the wife's family was higher in rank and wealthier than the husband's. But the two young people, now twenty-four and nineteen years old, had been set on their purpose for ten years; in the end her haughty parents had had to give in to them.

They were wonderfully happy. The stolen meetings and secret, tearful love letters were now things of the past. To God and man they were one; they could walk arm in arm in broad daylight and drive in the same carriage, and they would walk and drive so till the end of their days. Their distant paradise had descended to earth and had proved, surprisingly, to be filled with the things of everyday life: with jesting and railleries, with breakfasts and suppers, with dogs, haymaking and sheep. Sigismund, the young husband, had promised himself that from now there should be no stone in his bride's path, nor should any shadow fall across it. Lovisa, the wife, felt that now, every day and for the first time in her young life, she moved and breathed in perfect freedom because she could never have any secret from her husband.

To Lovisa – whom her husband called Lise – the rustic atmosphere of her new life was a matter of wonder and delight. Her husband's fear that the existence he could offer her might not be good enough for her filled her heart with laughter. It was not a long time since she had played with dolls; as now she dressed her own hair, looked over her linen press and arranged her flowers she again lived through an enchanting and cherished experience: one was doing everything gravely and solicitously, and all the time one knew one was playing.

It was a lovely July morning. Little woolly clouds drifted high up in the sky, the air was full of sweet scents. Lise had on a white muslin frock and a large Italian straw hat. She and her husband took a path through the park; it wound on across the meadows, between small groves and groups of trees, to the sheep field. Sigismund was going to show his wife his sheep. For this reason she had not brought her small white dog, Bijou, with her, for he would yap at the lambs and frighten them, or he would annoy the sheep dogs. Sigismund prided himself on his sheep; he had studied sheep-breeding in Mecklenburg and England, and had brought back with him Cotswold rams by which to improve his Danish stock. While they walked he explained to Lise the great possibilities and difficulties of the plan.

She thought: "How clever he is, what a lot of things he knows!" and at the same time: "What an absurd person he is, with his sheep! What a baby he is! I am a hundred years older than he."

But when they arrived at the sheepfold the old sheepmaster Mathias met them with the sad news that one of the English lambs was dead and two were sick. Lise saw that her husband was grieved by the tidings; while he questioned Mathias on the matter she kept silent and only gently pressed his arm. A couple of boys were sent off to fetch the sick lambs, while the master and servant went into the details of the case. It took some time.

Lise began to gaze about her and to think of other things. Twice her own thoughts made her blush deeply and happily, like a red rose, then slowly her blush died away, and the two men were still talking about sheep. A little while after their conversation caught her attention. It had turned to a sheep thief.

This thief during the last months had broken into the sheepfolds of the neighborhood like a wolf, had killed and dragged away his prey like a wolf and like a wolf had left no trace after him. Three nights ago the shepherd and his son on an estate ten miles away had caught him in the act. The thief had killed the man and knocked the boy senseless, and had managed to escape. There were men sent out to all sides to catch him, but nobody had seen him.

Lise wanted to hear more about the horrible event, and for her benefit old Mathias went through it once more. There had been a long fight in the sheep house, in many places the earthen floor was soaked with blood. In the fight the thief's left arm was broken; all the same, he had climbed a tall fence with a lamb on his back. Mathias added that he would like to string up the murderer with these two hands of his, and Lise nodded her head at him gravely in approval. She remembered Red Ridinghood's wolf, and felt a pleasant little thrill running down her spine.

Sigismund had his own lambs in his mind, but he was too happy in himself to wish anything in the universe ill. After a minute he said: "Poor devil."

Lise said: "How can you pity such a terrible man? Indeed Grandmamma was right when she said that you were a revolutionary and a danger to society!" The thought of Grandmamma, and of the tears of past days, again turned her mind away from the gruesome tale she had just heard.

The boys brought the sick lambs and the men began to examine them carefully, lifting them up and trying to set them on their legs; they squeezed them here and there and made the little creatures whimper. Lise shrank from the show and her husband noticed her distress.

"You go home, my darling," he said, "this will take some time. But just walk ahead slowly, and I shall catch up with you."

So she was turned away by an impatient husband to whom his sheep meant more than his wife. If any experience could be sweeter than to be dragged out by him to look at those same sheep, it would be this. She dropped her large summer hat with its blue ribbons on the grass and told him to carry it back for her, for she wanted to feel the summer air on her forehead and in her hair. She walked on very slowly, as he had told her to do, for she wished to obey him in everything. As she walked she felt a great new happiness in being altogether alone, even without Bijou. She could not remember that she had ever before in all her life been altogether alone. The landscape around her was still, as if full of promise, and it was hers. Even the swallows cruising in the air were hers, for they belonged to him, and he was hers.

She followed the curving edge of the grove and after a minute or two found that she was out of sight to the men by the sheep house. What could now, she wondered, be sweeter than to walk along the path in the long flowering meadow grass, slowly, slowly, and to let her husband overtake her there? It would be sweeter still, she reflected, to steal into the grove and to be gone, to have vanished from the surface of the earth from him when, tired of the sheep and longing for her company, he should turn the bend of the path to catch up with her.

An idea struck her; she stood still to think it over.

A few days ago her husband had gone for a ride and she had not wanted to go with him, but had strolled about with Bijou in order to explore her domain. Bijou then, gamboling, had led her straight into the grove. As she had followed him, gently forcing her way into the shrubbery, she had suddenly come upon a glade in the midst of it, a narrow space like a small alcove with hangings of thick green and golden brocade, big enough to hold two or three people in it. She had felt at that moment that she had come into the very heart of her new home. If today she could find the spot again she would stand perfectly still there, hidden from all the world. Sigismund would look for her in all directions; he would be unable to understand what had become of her and for a minute, for a short minute – or, perhaps, if she was firm and cruel enough, for five – he would realize what a void, what an unendurably sad and horrible place the universe would be when she was no longer in it. She gravely scrutinized the grove to find the right entrance to her hiding-place, then went in.

She took great care to make no noise at all, therefore advanced exceedingly slowly. When a twig caught the flounces of her ample skirt she loosened it softly from the muslin, so as not to crack it. Once a branch took hold of one of her long golden curls; she stood still, with her arms lifted, to free it. A little way into the grove the soil became moist; her light steps no longer made any sound upon it. With one hand she held her small handkerchief to her lips, as if to emphasize the secretness of her course. She found the spot she sought and bent down to divide the foliage and make a door to her sylvan closet. At this the hem of her dress caught her foot and she stopped to loosen it. As she rose she looked into the face of a man who was already in the shelter.

He stood up erect, two steps off. He must have watched her as she made her way straight toward him.

She took him in in one single glance. His face was bruised and scratched, his hands and wrists stained with dark filth. He was dressed in rags, barefooted, with tatters wound round his naked ankles. His arms hung down to his sides, his right hand clasped the hilt of a knife. He was about her own age. The man and the woman looked at each other.

This meeting in the wood from beginning to end passed without a word; what happened could only be rendered by pantomime. To the two actors in the pantomime it was timeless; according to a clock it lasted four minutes.

She had never in her life been exposed to danger. It did not occur to her to sum up her position, or to work out the length of time it would take to call her husband or Mathias, whom at this moment she could hear shouting to his dogs. She beheld the man before her as she would have beheld a forest ghost: the apparition itself, not the sequels of it, changes the world to the human who faces it.

Although she did not take her eyes off the face before her she sensed that the alcove had been turned into a covert. On the ground a couple of sacks formed a couch; there were some gnawed bones by it. A fire must have been made here in the night, for there were cinders strewn on the forest floor.

After a while she realized that he was observing her just as she was observing him. He was no longer just run to earth and crouching for a spring, but he was wondering, trying to know. At that she seemed to see herself with the eyes of the wild animal at bay in his dark hiding-place: her silently approaching white figure, which might mean death.

He moved his right arm till it hung down straight before him between his legs. Without lifting the hand he bent the wrist and slowly raised the point of the knife till it pointed at her throat. The gesture was mad, unbelievable. He did not smile as he made it, but his nostrils distended, the corners of his mouth quivered a little. Then slowly he put the knife back in the sheath by his belt.

She had no object of value about her, only the wedding ring which her husband had set on her finger in church, a week ago. She drew it off, and in this movement dropped her handkerchief. She reached out her hand with the ring toward him. She did not bargain for her life. She was fearless by nature, and the horror with which he inspired her was not fear of what he might do to her. She commanded him, she besought him to vanish as he had come, to take a dreadful figure out of her life, so that it should never have been there. In the dumb movement her young form had the grave authoritativeness of a priestess conjuring down some monstrous being by a sacred sign.

He slowly reached out his hand to hers, his finger touched hers, and her hand was steady at the touch. But he did not take the ring. As she let it go it dropped to the ground as her handkerchief had done.

For a second the eyes of both followed it. It rolled a few inches toward him and stopped before his bare foot. In a hardly perceivable movement he kicked it away and again looked into her face. They remained like that, she knew not how long, but she felt that during that time something happened, things were changed.

He bent down and picked up her handkerchief. All the time gazing at her, he again drew his knife and wrapped the tiny bit of cambric round the blade. This was difficult for him to do because his left arm was broken. While he did it his face under the dirt and sun-tan slowly grew whiter till it was almost phosphorescent. Fumbling with both hands, he once more stuck the knife into the sheath. Either the sheath was too big and had never fitted the knife, or the blade was much worn – it went in. For two or three more seconds his gaze rested on her face; then he lifted his own face a little, the strange radiance still upon it, and closed his eyes.

The movement was definitive and unconditional. In this one motion he did what she had begged him to do: he vanished and was gone. She was free.

She took a step backward, the immovable, blind face before her, then bent as she had done to enter the hiding-place, and glided away as noiselessly as she had come. Once outside the grove she stood still and looked round for the meadow path, found it and began to walk home.

Her husband had not yet rounded the edge of the grove. Now he saw her and helloed to her gaily; he came up quickly and joined her.

The path here was so narrow that he kept half behind her and did not touch her. He began to explain to her what had been the matter with the lambs. She walked a step before him and thought: All is over.

After a while he noticed her silence, came up beside her to look at her face and asked, "What is the matter?"

She searched her mind for something to say, and at last said: "I have lost my ring."

"What ring?" he asked her.

She answered, "My wedding ring."

As she heard her own voice pronounce the words she conceived their meaning.

Her wedding ring. "With this ring" – dropped by one and kicked away by another – "with this ring I thee wed." With this lost ring she had wedded herself to something. To what? To poverty, persecution, total loneliness. To the sorrows and the sinfulness of this earth. "And what therefore God has joined together let man not put asunder."

"I will find you another ring," her husband said. "You and I are the same as we were on our wedding day; it will do as well. We are husband and wife today too, as much as yesterday, I suppose."

Her face was so still that he did not know if she had heard what he said. It touched him that she should take the loss of his ring so to heart. He took her hand and kissed it. It was cold, not quite the same hand as he had last kissed. He stopped to make her stop with him.

"Do you remember where you had the ring on last?" he asked.

"No," she answered.

"Have you any idea," he asked, "where you may have lost it?"

"No," she answered. "I have no idea at all."

THE ROCKING-HORSE WINNER

D.H. Lawrence

E.M. Forster described **D.H. Lawrence** (1885–1930) on his death as "the greatest imaginative novelist of our generation." Most people thought him a pornographer. His novels include *Sons and Lovers, The Rainbow* and *Lady Chatterley's Lover*. Born in Nottingham, he travelled widely to Australia, the USA, New Mexico and Italy. He died in Vence in France, from tuberculosis. His wife, Frieda, was a relative of Manfred von Richthofen, the "Red Baron".

There was a woman who was beautiful, who started with all the advantages, yet she had no luck. She married for love, and the love turned to dust. She had bonny children, yet she felt they had been thrust upon her, and she could not love them. They looked at her coldly, as if they were finding fault with her. And hurriedly she felt she must cover up some fault in herself. Yet what it was that she must cover up she never knew. Nevertheless, when her children were present, she always felt the centre of her heart go hard. This troubled her, and in her manner she was all the more gentle and anxious for her children, as if she loved them very much. Only she herself knew that at the centre of her heart was a hard little place that could not feel love, no, not for anybody. Everybody else said of her: "She is such a good mother. She adores her children." Only she herself, and her children themselves, knew it was not so. They read it in each other's eyes.

There were a boy and two little girls. They lived in a pleasant house, with a garden, and they had discreet servants, and felt themselves superior to anyone in the neighbourhood.

Although they lived in style, they felt always an anxiety in the house. There was never enough money. The mother had a small income, and the father had a small income, but not nearly enough for the social position which they had to keep up. The father went into town to some office. But though he had good prospects, these prospects never materialised. There was always the grinding sense of the shortage of money, though the style was always kept up.

At last the mother said: "I will see if I can't make something." But she did not know where to begin. She racked her brains, and tried this thing and the other, but could not find anything successful. The failure made deep lines come into her face. Her children were growing up, they would have to go to school. There must be more money, there must be more money. The father, who was always very handsome and expensive in his tastes, seemed as if he never would be able to do anything worth doing. And the mother, who had a great belief in herself, did not succeed any better, and her tastes were just as expensive.

And so the house came to be haunted by the unspoken phrase: There must be more money! There must be more money! The children could hear it all the time though nobody said it aloud. They heard it at Christmas, when the expensive and splendid toys filled the nursery. Behind the shining modern rocking-horse, behind the smart doll's house, a voice would start whispering: "There must be more money! There must be more money!" And the children would stop playing, to listen for a moment. They would look into each other's eyes, to see if they had all heard. And each one saw in the eyes of the other two that they too had heard. "There must be more money! There must be more money!"

It came whispering from the springs of the still-swaying rocking-horse, and even the horse, bending his wooden, champing head, heard it. The big doll, sitting so pink and smirking in her new pram, could hear it quite plainly, and seemed to be smirking all the more self-consciously because of it. The foolish puppy, too, that took the place of the teddy-bear, he was looking so extraordinarily foolish for no other reason but that he heard the secret whisper all over the house: "There must be more money!"

Yet nobody ever said it aloud. The whisper was everywhere, and therefore no one spoke it. Just as no one ever says: "We are breathing!" in spite of the fact that breath is coming and going all the time.

"Mother," said the boy Paul one day, "why don't we keep a car of our own? Why do we always use uncle's, or else a taxi?"

"Because we're the poor members of the family," said the mother.

"But why are we, mother?"

"Well – I suppose," she said slowly and bitterly, "it's because your father has no luck."

The boy was silent for some time.

"Is luck money, mother?" he asked, rather timidly.

"No, Paul. Not quite. It's what causes you to have money."

"Oh!" said Paul vaguely. "I thought when Uncle Oscar said filthy lucker, it meant money."

"Filthy lucre does mean money," said the mother. "But it's lucre, not luck."

"Oh!" said the boy. "Then what is luck, mother?"

"It's what causes you to have money. If you're lucky you have money. That's why it's better to be born lucky than rich. If you're rich, you may lose your money. But if you're lucky, you will always get more money."

"Oh! Will you? And is father not lucky?"

"Very unlucky, I should say," she said bitterly.

The boy watched her with unsure eyes.

"Why?" he asked.

"I don't know. Nobody ever knows why one person is lucky and another unlucky."

"Don't they? Nobody at all? Does nobody know?"

"Perhaps God. But He never tells."

"He ought to, then. And are'nt you lucky either, mother?"

"I can't be, it I married an unlucky husband."

"But by yourself, aren't you?"

"I used to think I was, before I married. Now I think I am very unlucky indeed."

"Why?"

"Well – never mind! Perhaps I'm not really," she said.

The child looked at her to see if she meant it. But he saw, by the lines of her mouth, that she was only trying to hide something from him.

"Well, anyhow," he said stoutly, "I'm a lucky person."

"Why?" said his mother, with a sudden laugh.

He stared at her. He didn't even know why he had said it.

"God told me," he asserted, brazening it out.

"I hope He did, dear!", she said, again with a laugh, but rather bitter.

"He did, mother!"

"Excellent!" said the mother, using one of her husband's exclamations.

The boy saw she did not believe him; or rather, that she paid no attention to his assertion. This angered him somewhere, and made him want to compel her attention.

He went off by himself, vaguely, in a childish way, seeking for the clue to 'luck'. Absorbed, taking no heed of other people, he went about with a sort of stealth, seeking inwardly for luck. He wanted luck, he wanted it, he wanted it. When the two girls were playing dolls in the nursery, he would sit on his big rocking-horse, charging madly into space, with a frenzy that made the little girls peer at him uneasily. Wildly the horse careered, the waving dark hair of the boy tossed, his eyes had a strange glare in them. The little girls dared not speak to him.

When he had ridden to the end of his mad little journey, he climbed down and stood in front of his rocking-horse, staring fixedly into its lowered face. Its red mouth was slightly open, its big eye was wide and glassy-bright.

"Now!" he would silently command the snorting steed. "Now take me to where there is luck! Now take me!"

And he would slash the horse on the neck with the little whip he had asked Uncle Oscar for. He knew the horse could take him to where there was luck, if only he forced it. So he would mount again and start on his furious ride, hoping at last to get there.

"You'll break your horse, Paul!" said the nurse.

"He's always riding like that! I wish he'd leave off!" said his elder sister Joan.

But he only glared down on them in silence. Nurse gave him up. She could make nothing of him. Anyhow, he was growing beyond her.

One day his mother and his Uncle Oscar came in when he was on one of his furious rides. He did not speak to them.

"Hallo, you young jockey! Riding a winner?" said his uncle.

"Aren't you growing too big for a rocking-horse? You're not a very little boy any longer, you know," said his mother.

But Paul only gave a blue glare from his big, rather close-set eyes. He would speak to nobody when he was in full tilt. His mother watched him with an anxious expression on her face.

At last he suddenly stopped forcing his horse into the mechanical gallop and slid down.

"Well, I got there!" he announced fiercely, his blue eyes still flaring, and his sturdy long legs straddling apart.

"Where did you get to?" asked his mother.

"Where I wanted to go," he flared back at her.

"That's right, son!" said Uncle Oscar. "Don't you stop till you get there. What's the horse's name?"

"He doesn't have a name," said the boy.

"Get's on without all right?" asked the uncle.

"Well, he has different names. He was called Sansovino last week."

"Sansovino, eh? Won the Ascot. How did you know this name?"

"He always talks about horse-races with Bassett," said Joan.

The uncle was delighted to find that his small nephew was posted with all the racing news. Bassett, the young gardener, who had been wounded in the left foot in the war and had got his present job through Oscar Cresswell, whose batman he had been, was a perfect blade of the 'turf'. He lived in the racing events, and the small boy lived with him.

Oscar Cresswell got it all from Bassett.

"Master Paul comes and asks me, so I can't do more than tell him, sir," said Bassett, his face terribly serious, as if he were speaking of religious matters.

"And does he ever put anything on a horse he fancies?"

"Well – I don't want to give him away – he's a young sport, a fine sport, sir. Would you mind asking him himself? He sort of takes a pleasure in it, and perhaps he'd feel I was giving him away, sir, if you don't mind.

Bassett was serious as a church.

The uncle went back to his nephew and took him off for a ride in the car.

"Say, Paul, old man, do you ever put anything on a horse?" the uncle asked.

The boy watched the handsome man closely.

"Why, do you think I oughtn't to?" he parried.

"Not a bit of it! I thought perhaps you might give me a tip for the Lincoln."

The car sped on into the country, going down to Uncle Oscar's place in Hampshire.

"Honour bright?" said the nephew.

"Honour bright, son!" said the uncle.

"Well, then, Daffodil."

"Daffodil! I doubt it, sonny. What about Mirza?"

"I only know the winner," said the boy. "That's Daffodil."

"Daffodil, eh?"

There was a pause. Daffodil was an obscure horse comparatively.

"Uncle!"

"Yes, son?"

"You won't let it go any further, will you? I promised Bassett."

"Bassett be damned, old man! What's he got to do with it?"

"We're partners. We've been partners from the first. Uncle, he lent me my first five shillings, which I lost. I promised him, honour bright, it was only between me and him; only you gave me that ten-shilling note I started winning with, so I thought you were lucky. You won't let it go any further, will you?"

The boy gazed at his uncle from those big, hot, blue eyes, set rather close together. The uncle stirred and laughed uneasily.

"Right you are, son! I'll keep your tip private. How much are you putting on him?"

"All except twenty pounds," said the boy. "I keep that in reserve."

The uncle thought it a good joke.

"You keep twenty pounds in reserve, do you, you young romancer? What are you betting, then?"

"I'm betting three hundred," said the boy gravely. "But it's between you and me, Uncle Oscar! Honour bright?"

"It's between you and me all right, you young Nat Gould," he said, laughing. "But where's your three hundred?"

"Bassett keeps it for me. We're partners."

"You are, are you! And what is Bassett putting on Daffodil?"

"He won't go quite as high as I do, I expect. Perhaps he'll go a hundred and fifty."

"What, pennies?" laughed the uncle.

"Pounds," said the child, with a surprised look at his uncle. "Bassett keeps a bigger reserve than I do."

Between wonder and amusement Uncle Oscar was silent. He pursued the matter no further, but he determined to take his nephew with him to the Lincoln races.

"Now, son," he said, "I'm putting twenty on Mirza, and I'll put five on for you on any horse you fancy. What's your pick?"

"Daffodil, uncle."

"No, not the fiver on Daffodil!"

"I should if it was my own fiver," said the child.

"Good! Good! Right you are! A fiver for me and a fiver for you on Daffodil."

The child had never been to a race-meeting before, and his eyes were blue fire. He pursed his mouth tight and watched. A Frenchman just in front had put his money on Lancelot. Wild with excitement, he flayed his arms up and down, yelling "Lancelot! Lancelot!" in his French accent.

Daffodil came in first, Lancelot second, Mirza third. The child, flushed and with eyes blazing, was curiously serene. His uncle brought him four five-pound notes, four to one.

"What am I to do with these?" he cried, waving them before the boys eyes.

"I suppose we'll talk to Bassett," said the boy. "I expect I have fifteen hundred now; and twenty in reserve; and this twenty."

His uncle studied him for some moments.

"Look here, son!" he said. "You're not serious about Bassett and that fifteen hundred, are you?"

"Yes, I am. But it's between you and me, uncle. Honour bright?"

"Honour bright all right, son! But I must talk to Bassett."

"If you'd like to be a partner, uncle, with Bassett and me, we could all be partners. Only, you'd have to promise, honour bright, uncle, not to let it go beyond us three. Bassett and I are lucky, and you must be lucky, because it was your ten shillings I started winning with . . ."

Uncle Oscar took both Bassett and Paul into Richmond Park for an afternoon, and there they talked.

"It's like this, you see, sir," Bassett said. "Master Paul would get me talking about racing events, spinning yarns, you know, sir. And he was always keen on knowing if I'd made or if I'd lost. It's about a year since, now, that I put five shillings on Blush of Dawn for him: and we lost. Then the luck turned, with that ten shillings he had from you: that we put on Singhalese. And since that time, it's been pretty steady, all things considering. What do you say, Master Paul?"

"We're all right when we're sure," said Paul. "It's when we're not quite sure that we go down."

"Oh, but we're careful then," said Bassett.

"But when are you sure?" smiled Uncle Oscar.

"It's Master Paul, sir," said Bassett in a secret, religious voice. "It's as if he had it from heaven. Like Daffodil, now, for the Lincoln. That was as sure as eggs."

"Did you put anything on Daffodil?" asked Oscar Cresswell.

"Yes, sir, I made my bit."

"And my nephew?"

Bassett was obstinately silent, looking at Paul.

"I made twelve hundred, didn't I, Bassett? I told uncle I was putting three hundred on Daffodil."

"That's right," said Bassett, nodding.

"But where's the money?" asked the uncle.

"I keep it safe locked up, sir. Master Paul he can have it any minute he likes to ask for it."

"What, fifteen hundred pounds?"

"And twenty! And forty, that is, with the twenty he made on the course."

"It's amazing!" said the uncle.

"If Master Paul offers you to be partners, sir, I would, if I were you: if you'll excuse me," said Bassett.

Oscar Cresswell thought about it.

"I'll see the money," he said.

They drove home again, and, sure enough, Bassett came round to the garden-house with fifteen hundred pounds in notes. The twenty pounds reserve was left with Joe Glee, in the Turf Commission deposit.

"You see, it's all right, uncle, when I'm sure! Then we go strong, for all we're worth, don't we, Bassett?"

"We do that, Master Paul."

"And when are you sure?" said the uncle, laughing.

"Oh, well, sometimes I'm absolutely sure, like about Daffodil," said the boy; "and sometimes I have an idea; and sometimes I haven't even an idea, have I, Bassett? Then we're careful, because we mostly go down."

"You do, do you! And when you're sure, like about Daffodil, what makes you sure, sonny?"

"Oh, well, I don't know," said the boy uneasily. "I'm sure, you know, uncle; that's all."

"It's as if he had it from heaven, sir," Bassett reiterated.

"I should say so!" said the uncle.

But he became a partner. And when the Leger was coming on Paul was 'sure' about Lively Spark, which was a quite inconsiderable horse. The boy insisted on putting a thousand on the horse, Bassett went for five hundred, and Oscar

Cresswell two hundred. Lively Spark came in first, and the betting had been ten to one against him. Paul had made ten thousand.

"You see," he said. "I was absolutely sure of him."

Even Oscar Cresswell had cleared two thousand.

"Look here, son," he said, "this sort of thing makes me nervous."

"It needn't, uncle! Perhaps I shan't be sure again for a long time."

"But what are you going to do with your money?" asked the uncle.

"Of course," said the boy, "I started it for mother. She said she had no luck, because father is unlucky, so I thought if I was lucky, it might stop whispering."

"What might stop whispering?"

"Our house. I hate our house for whispering."

"What does it whisper?"

"Why – why" – the boy fidgeted – "why, I don't know. But it's always short of money, you know, uncle."

"I know it, son, I know it."

"You know people send mother writs, don't you, uncle?"

"I'm afraid I do," said the uncle.

"And then the house whispers, like people laughing at you behind your back. It's awful, that is! I thought if I was lucky -"

"You might stop it," added the uncle.

The boy watched him with big blue eyes, that had an uncanny cold fire in them, and he said never a word.

"Well, then!" said the uncle. "What are we doing?"

"I shouldn't like mother to know I was lucky," said the boy.

"Why not, son?"

"She'd stop me."

"I don't think she would."

"Oh!" – and the boy writhed in an odd way – "I don't want her to know, uncle."

"All right, son! We'll manage it without her knowing."

They managed it very easily. Paul, at the other's suggestion, handed over five thousand pounds to his uncle, who deposited it with the family lawyer, who was then to inform Paul's mother that a relative had put five thousand pounds into his hands, which sum was to be paid out a thousand pounds at a time, on the mother's birthday, for the next five years.

"So she'll have a birthday present of a thousand pounds for five successive years," said Uncle Oscar. "I hope it won't make it all the harder for her later."

Paul's mother had her birthday in November. The house had been 'whispering' worse than ever lately, and, even in spite of his luck, Paul could not bear up against it. He was very anxious to see the effect of the birthday letter, telling his mother about the thousand pounds.

When there were no visitors, Paul now took his meals with his parents, as he was beyond the nursery control. His mother went into town nearly every day. She had discovered that she had an odd knack of sketching furs and dress materials, so she worked secretly in the studio of a friend who was the chief 'artist' for the leading drapers. She drew the figures of ladies in furs and ladies in silk and sequins for the newspaper advertisements. This young woman artist earned several thousand pounds a year, but Paul's mother only made several hundreds, and she was again dissatisfied. She so wanted to be first in something, and she did not succeed, even in making sketches for drapery advertisements.

She was down to breakfast on the morning of her birthday. Paul watched her face as she read her letters. He knew the lawyer's letter. As his mother read it, her face hardened and became more expressionless. Then a cold, determined look came on her mouth. She hid the letter under the pile of others, and said not a word about it.

"Didn't you have anything nice in the post for your birthday, mother?" said Paul.

"Quite moderately nice," she said, her voice cold and hard and absent.

She went away to town without saying more.

But in the afternoon Uncle Oscar appeared. He said Paul's mother had had a long interview with the lawyer, asking if the whole five thousand could not be advanced at once, as she was in debt.

"What do you think, uncle?" said the boy.

"I leave it to you, son."

"Oh, let her have it, then! We can get some more with the other," said the boy.

"A bird in the hand is worth two in the bush, laddie!" said Uncle Oscar.

"But I'm sure to know for the Grand National; or the Lincolnshire; or else the Derby. I'm sure to know for one of them," said Paul.

So Uncle Oscar signed the agreement, and Paul's mother touched the whole five thousand. Then something very curious happened. The voices in the house suddenly went mad, like a chorus of frogs on a spring evening. There were certain new furnishings, and Paul had a tutor. He was really going to Eton, his father's school, in the following autumn. There were flowers in the winter, and a blossoming of the luxury Paul's mother had been used to. And yet the voices in the house, behind the sprays of mimosa and almond-blossom, and from under the piles of iridescent cushions, simply trilled and screamed in a sort of ecstasy: "There must be more money! Oh-h-h; there must be more money. Oh, now, now-w! Now-w-w – there must be more money! – more than ever! More than ever!"

It frightened Paul terribly. He studied away at his Latin and Greek with his tutor. But his intense hours were spent with Bassett. The Grand National had gone by: he had not 'known', and had lost a hundred pounds. Summer was at hand. He was in agony for the Lincoln. But even for the Lincoln he didn't 'know', and he lost fifty pounds. He became wild-eyed and strange, as if something were going to explode in him.

"Let it alone, son! Don't you bother about it!" urged Uncle Oscar. But it was as if the boy couldn't really hear what his uncle was saying.

"I've got to know for the Derby! I've got to know for the Derby!" the child reiterated, his big blue eyes blazing with a sort of madness.

His mother noticed how overwrought he was.

"You'd better go to the seaside. Wouldn't you like to go now to the seaside, instead of waiting? I think you'd better," she said, looking down at him anxiously, her heart curiously heavy because of him.

But the child lifted his uncanny blue eyes.

"I couldn't possibly go before the Derby, mother!" he said. "I couldn't possibly!"

"Why not?" she said, her voice becoming heavy when she was opposed. "Why not? You can still go from the seaside to see the Derby with your Uncle Oscar, if that that's what you wish. No need for you to wait here. Besides, I think you care too much about these races. It's a bad sign. My family has been a gambling family, and you won't know till you grow up how much damage it has done. But it has done damage. I shall have to send Bassett away, and ask Uncle Oscar not to talk racing to you, unless you promise to be reasonable about it: go away to the seaside and forget it. You're all nerves!"

"I'll do what you like, mother, so long as you don't send me away till after the Derby," the boy said.

"Send you away from where? Just from this house?"

"Yes," he said, gazing at her.

"Why, you curious child, what makes you care about this house so much, suddenly? I never knew you loved it."

He gazed at her without speaking. He had a secret within a secret, something he had not divulged, even to Bassett or to his Uncle Oscar.

But his mother, after standing undecided and a little bit sullen for some moments, said: "Very well, then! Don't go to the seaside till after the Derby, if you don't wish it. But promise me you won't think so much about horse-racing and events as you call them!"

"Oh no," said the boy casually. "I won't think much about them, mother. You needn't worry. I wouldn't worry, mother, if I were you."

"If you were me and I were you," said his mother, "I wonder what we should do!"

"But you know you needn't worry, mother, don't you?" the boy repeated.

"I should be awfully glad to know it," she said wearily.

"Oh, well, you can, you know. I mean, you ought to know you needn't worry," he insisted.

"Ought I? Then I'll see about it," she said.

Paul's secret of secrets was his wooden horse, that which had no name. Since he was emancipated from a nurse and a nursery-governess, he had had his rocking-horse removed to his own bedroom at the top of the house.

"Surely you're too big for a rocking-horse!" his mother had remonstrated.

"Well, you see, mother, till I can have a real horse, I like to have some sort of animal about," had been his quaint answer.

"Do you feel he keeps you company?" she laughed.

"Oh yes! He's very good, he always keeps me company, when I'm there," said Paul.

So the horse, rather shabby, stood in an arrested prance in the boy's bedroom.

The Derby was drawing near, and the boy grew more and more tense. He hardly heard what was spoken to him, he was very frail, and his eyes were really uncanny. His mother had sudden strange seizures of uneasiness about him. Sometimes, for half an hour, she would feel a sudden anxiety about him that was almost anguish. She wanted to rush to him at once, and know he was safe.

Two nights before the Derby, she was at a big party in town, when one of her rushes of anxiety about her boy, her first-born, gripped her heart till she could hardly speak. She fought with the feeling, might and main, for she believed in common sense. But it was too strong. She had to leave the dance and go downstairs to telephone to the country. The children's nursery-governess was terribly surprised and startled at being rung up in the night.

"Are the children all right, Miss Wilmot?"

"Oh yes, they are quite all right."

"Master Paul? Is he all right?"

"He went to bed as right as a trivet. Shall I run up and look at him?"

"No," said Paul's mother reluctantly. "No! Don't trouble. It's all right. Don't sit up. We shall be home fairly soon." She did not want her son's privacy intruded upon.

"Very good," said the governess.

It was about one o'clock when Paul's mother and father drove up to their house. All was still. Paul's mother went to her room and slipped off her white fur cloak. She had told her maid not to wait up for her. She heard her husband downstairs, mixing a whisky and soda.

And then, because of the strange anxiety at her heart, she stole upstairs to her son's room. Noiselessly she went along the upper corridor. Was there a faint noise? What was it?

She stood, with arrested muscles, outside his door, listening. There was a strange, heavy, and yet not loud noise. Her heart stood still. It was a soundless noise, yet rushing and powerful. Something huge, in violent, hushed motion. What was it? What in God's name was it? She ought to know. She felt that she knew the noise. She knew what it was.

Yet she could not place it. She couldn't say what it was. And on and on it went, like a madness.

Softly, frozen with anxiety and fear, she turned the door-handle.

The room was dark. Yet in the space near the window, she heard and saw something plunging to and fro. She gazed in fear and amazement.

Then suddenly she switched on the light, and saw her son, in his green pyjamas, madly surging on the rocking-horse. The blaze of light suddenly lit him up, as he urged the wooden horse, and lit her up, as she stood, blonde, in her dress of pale green and crystal, in the doorway.

"Paul!" she cried. "Whatever are you doing?"

"It's Malabar!" he screamed in a powerful, strange voice. "It's Malabar!"

His eyes blazed at her for one strange and senseless second, as he ceased urging his wooden horse. Then he fell with a crash to the ground, and she, all her tormented motherhood flooding upon her, rushed to gather him up.

But he was unconscious, and unconscious he remained, with some brain-fever. He talked and tossed, and his mother sat stonily by his side.

"Malabar! It's Malabar! Bassett, Bassett, I know! It's Malabar!"

So the child cried, trying to get up and urge the rocking-horse that gave him his inspiration.

"What does he mean by Malabar?" asked the heart-frozen mother.

"I don't know," said the father stonily.

"What does he mean by Malabar?" she asked her brother Oscar.

"It's one of the horses running for the Derby," was the answer.

And, in spite of himself, Oscar Cresswell spoke to Bassett, and himself put a thousand on Malabar: at fourteen to one.

The third day of the illness was critical: they were waiting for a change. The boy, with his rather long, curly hair, was tossing ceaselessly on the pillow. He neither slept nor regained consciousness, and his eyes were like blue stones. His mother sat, feeling her heart had gone, turned actually into a stone.

In the evening Oscar Cresswell did not come, but Bassett sent a message, saying could he come up for one moment, just one moment? Paul's mother was very angry at the intrusion, but on second thoughts she agreed. The boy was the same. Perhaps Bassett might bring him to consciousness.

The gardener, a shortish fellow with a little brown moustache and sharp little brown eyes, tiptoed into the room, touched his imaginary cap to Paul's mother, and stole to the bedside, staring with glittering, smallish eyes at the tossing, dying child.

"Master Paul!" he whispered. "Master Paul! Malabar came in first all right, a clean win. I did as you told me. You've made over seventy thousand pounds, you have; you've got over eighty thousand. Malabar came in all right, Master Paul."

"Malabar! Malabar! Did I say Malabar, mother? Did I say Malabar? Do you think I'm lucky, mother? I knew Malabar, didn't I? Over eighty thousand pounds! I call that lucky, don't you, mother? Over eighty thousand pounds! I knew, didn't I know I knew? Malabar came in all right. If I ride my horse till I'm sure, then I tell you, Bassett, you can go as high as you like. Did you go for all you were worth, Bassett?"

"I went a thousand on it, Master Paul."

"I never told you, mother, that if I can ride my horse, and get there, then I'm absolutely sure – oh, absolutely! Mother, did I ever tell you? I am lucky!"

"No, you never did," said his mother.

But the boy died in the night.

And even as he lay dead, his mother heard her brother's voice saying to her, "My God, Hester, you're eighty-odd thousand to the good, and a poor devil of a son to the bad. But, poor devil, poor devil, he's best gone out of a life where he rides his rocking-horse to find a winner."

A MARRIED MAN'S STORY

Katherine Mansfield

One has to say, **Katherine Mansfield** (1888–1923) certainly packed quite
a bit in to what ended up as a short life. Born in New Zealand, she travelled
in Europe before settling in London in 1908, having clocked up lovers of
both sexes, before marrying a singing teacher over a decade older than her,
who she managed to leave on the day of their wedding. She befriended D.H.
Lawrence and Virginia Woolf and became the lover of John Middleton
Murry, who she married in 1918, only to leave him a fortnight later.
She suffered a fatal haemorrhage after running up a flight of stairs. In
between all this, she somehow left an astonishing array of poems, letters
and stories.

It is evening. Supper is over. We have left the small, cold dining room; we have
come back to the sitting room where there is a fire. All is as usual. I am sitting at my writing table which is placed across a corner so that I am behind
it, as it were, and facing the room. The lamp with the green shade is alight; I
have before me two large books of reference, both open, a pile of papers. . . .
All the paraphernalia, in fact, of an extremely occupied man. My wife, with our
little boy on her lap, is in a low chair before the fire. She is about to put him to
bed before she clears away the dishes and piles them up in the kitchen for the
servant girl to-morrow morning. But the warmth, the quiet, and the sleepy baby
have made her dreamy. One of his red woollen boots is off; one is on. She sits,
bent forward, clasping the little bare foot, staring into the glow, and as the fire
quickens, falls, flares again, her shadow – an immense *Mother and Child* – is
here and gone again upon the wall. . . .

Outside it is raining. I like to think of that cold drenched window behind the
blind, and beyond, the dark bushes in the garden, their broad leaves bright with
rain, and beyond the fence, the gleaming road with the two hoarse little gutters
singing against each other, and the wavering reflections of the lamps, like fishes'
tails. . . . While I am here, I am there, lifting my face to the dim sky, and it seems
to me it must be raining all over the world – that the whole earth is drenched,
is sounding with a soft quick patter or hard steady drumming, or gurgling and
something that is like sobbing and laughing mingled together, and that light
playful splashing that is of water falling into still lakes and flowing rivers. And
all at one and the same moment I am arriving in a strange city, slipping under
the hood of the cab while the driver whips the cover off the breathing horse,
running from shelter to shelter, dodging someone, swerving by someone else. I
am conscious of tall houses, their doors and shutters sealed against the night,

of dripping balconies and sodden flower pots, I am brushing through deserted gardens and peering into moist smelling summer-houses (you know how soft and almost crumbling the wood of a summer-house is in the rain), I am standing on the dark quayside, giving my ticket into the wet red hand of the old sailor in an oilskin – How strong the sea smells! How loudly those tied-up boats knock against one another! I am crossing the wet stackyard, hooded in an old sack, carrying a lantern, while the house-dog, like a soaking doormat, springs, shakes himself over me. And now I am walking along a deserted road – it is impossible to miss the puddles and the trees are stirring – stirring. . . .

But one could go on with such a catalogue for ever – on and on – until one lifted the single arum lily leaf and discovered the tiny snails clinging, until one counted . . . and what then? Aren't those just the signs, the traces of my feeling? The bright green streaks made by someone who walks over the dewy grass? Not the feeling itself. And as I think that, a mournful glorious voice begins to sing in my bosom. Yes, perhaps that is nearer what I mean. What a voice! What power! What velvety softness! Marvellous!

Suddenly my wife turns round quickly. She knows – how long has she known? – that I am not "working"! It is strange that with her full, open gaze, she should smile so timidly – and that she should say in such a hesitating voice: "What are you thinking?"

I smile and draw two fingers across my forehead in the way I have. "Nothing," I answer softly.

At that she stirs, and still trying not to make it sound important, she says: "Oh, but you must have been thinking of something!"

Then I really meet her gaze, meet it fully, and I fancy her face quivers. Will she never grow accustomed to these simple – one might say – everyday little lies? Will she never learn not to expose herself – or to build up defences?

"Truly, I was thinking of nothing!"

There! I seem to see it dart at her. She turns away, pulls the other red sock off the baby – sits him up, and begins to unbutton him behind. I wonder if that little soft rolling bundle sees anything, feels anything? Now she turns him over on her knee, and in this light, his soft arms and legs waving, he is extraordinarily like a young crab. A queer thing is I can't connect him with my wife and myself; I've never accepted him as ours. Each time when I come into the hall and see the perambulator, I catch myself thinking: "H'm, someone has brought a baby." Or, when his crying wakes me at night, I feel inclined to blame my wife for having brought the baby in from outside. The truth is, that though one might suspect her of strong maternal feelings, my wife doesn't seem to me the type of woman who bears children in her own body. There's an immense difference! Where is that . . . animal ease and playfulness, that quick kissing and cuddling one has been taught to expect of young mothers? She hasn't a sign of it. I believe that when she ties its bonnet she feels like an aunt and not a mother. But of course I may be wrong; she may be passionately devoted. . . . I don't think so. At any rate, isn't it a trifle indecent to feel like this about one's own wife? Indecent or not, one has these feelings. And one other thing. How can I reasonably expect my wife, *a broken-hearted woman*, to spend her time tossing the baby? But that is beside the mark. She never even began to toss when her heart was whole.

And now she has carried the baby to bed. I hear her soft deliberate steps moving between the dining room and the kitchen, there and back again, to the tune of the clattering dishes. And now all is quiet. What is happening now? Oh, I know just as surely as if I'd gone to see – she is standing in the middle of the kitchen, facing the rainy window. Her head is bent, with one finger she is tracing something – nothing – on the table. It is cold in the kitchen; the gas jumps; the tap drips; it's a forlorn picture. And nobody is going to come behind her, to take her in his arms, to kiss her soft hair, to lead her to the fire and to rub her hands warm again. Nobody is going to call her or to wonder what she is doing out there. And she knows it. And yet, being a woman, deep down, deep down, she really does expect the miracle to happen; she really could embrace that dark, dark deceit, rather than live – like this.

To live like this . . . I write those words, very carefully, very beautifully. For some reason I feel inclined to sign them, or to write underneath – Trying a New Pen. But seriously, isn't it staggering to think what may be contained in one innocent-looking little phrase? It tempts me – it tempts me terribly. Scene. The supper-table. My wife has just handed me my tea. I stir it, lift the spoon, idly chase and then carefully capture a speck of tea-leaf, and having brought it ashore, I murmur, quite gently, "How long shall we continue to live – like – this?" And immediately there is that famous "blinding flash and deafening roar. Huge pieces of débris (I must say I like débris) are flung into the air . . . and when the dark clouds of smoke have drifted away . . ." But this will never happen; I shall never know it. It will be found upon me "intact" as they say. "Open my heart and you will see . . ."

Why? Ah, there you have me! There is the most difficult question of all to answer. Why do people stay together? Putting aside "for the sake of the children", and "the habit of years" and "economic reasons" as lawyers' nonsense – it's not much more – if one really does try to find out why it is that people don't leave each other, one discovers a mystery. It is because they can't; they are bound. And nobody on earth knows what are the bands that bind them except those two. Am I being obscure? Well, the thing itself isn't so frightfully crystal clear, is it? Let me put it like this. Supposing you are taken, absolutely, first into his confidence and then into hers. Supposing you know all there is to know about the situation. And having given it not only your deepest sympathy but your most honest impartial criticism, you declare, very calmly (but not without the slightest suggestion of relish – for there is – I swear there is – in the very best of us – something that leaps up and cries "A-ahh!" for joy at the thought of destroying), "Well, my opinion is that you two people ought to part. You'll do no earthly good together. Indeed, it seems to me, it's the duty of either to set the other free." What happens then? He – and she – agree. It is their conviction too. You are only saying what they have been thinking all last night. And away they go to act on your advice, immediately . . . And the next time you hear of them they are still together. You see – you've reckoned without the unknown quantity – which is their secret relation to each other – and that they can't disclose even if they want to. Thus far you may tell and no further. Oh, don't misunderstand me! It need not necessarily have anything to do with their sleeping together . . . But this brings me to a thought I've often half entertained. Which is, that human beings, as we know them, don't choose each other at all. It is the owner, the second self inhabiting them, who makes the choice for his own particular purposes, and – this may sound absurdly far-fetched – it's the second self in the other which responds. Dimly – dimly – or so it has seemed to me – we realise this, at any rate to the extent that we realise the hopelessness of trying to escape. So that, what it all amounts to is – if the impermanent selves of my wife and me are happy – *tant mieux pour nous* – if miserable – *tant pis*. . . . But I don't know, I don't know. And it may be that it's something entirely individual in me – this sensation (yes, it is even a sensation) of how extraordinarily *shell-like* we are as we are – little creatures, peering out of the sentry-box at the gate, ogling through our glass case at the entry, wan little servants, who never can say for certain, even, if the master is out or in . . .

The door opens . . . My wife. She says: "I am going to bed."

And I look up vaguely, and vaguely say: "You are going to bed."

"Yes." A tiny pause. "Don't forget – will you? – to turn out the gas in the hall."

And again I repeat: "The gas in the hall."

There was a time – the time before – when this habit of mine (it really has become a habit now – it wasn't one then) was one of our sweetest jokes together. It began, of course, when, on several occasions, I really was deeply engaged and I didn't hear. I emerged only to see her shaking her head and laughing at me, "You haven't heard a word!"

"No. What did you say?"

Why should she think that so funny and charming? She did; it delighted her. "Oh, my darling, it's so like you! It's so – so – ." And I knew she loved me for it – knew she positively looked forward to coming in and disturbing me, and so – as one does – I played up. I was guaranteed to be wrapped away every evening at 10.30 p.m. But now? For some reason I feel it would be crude to stop my performance. It's simplest to play on. But what is she waiting for to-night? Why doesn't she go? Why prolong this? She is going. No, her hand on the door-knob, she turns round again, and she says in the most curious, small, breathless voice, "You're not cold?"

Oh, it's not fair to be as pathetic as that! That was simply damnable, I shudder all over before I manage to bring out a slow "No-o," while my left hand ruffles the reference pages.

She is gone; she will not come back again to-night. It is not only I who recognise that; the room changes, too. It relaxes, like an old actor. Slowly the mask is rubbed off; the look of strained attention changes to an air of heavy, sullen brooding. Every line, every fold breathes fatigue. The mirror is quenched; the ash whitens; only my shy lamp burns on . . . But what a cynical indifference to me it all shows! Or should I perhaps be flattered? No, we understand each other. You know those stories of little children who are suckled by wolves and accepted by the tribe, and how for ever after they move freely among their fleet grey brothers? Something like that has happened to me. But wait – that about the wolves won't do. Curious!

Before I wrote it down, while it was still in my head, I was delighted with it. It seemed to express, and more, to suggest, just what I wanted to say. But written, I can smell the falseness immediately and the ... source of the smell is in that word fleet. Don't you agree? Fleet, grey brothers! "Fleet." A word I never use. When I wrote "wolves" it skimmed across my mind like a shadow and I couldn't resist it. Tell me! Tell me! Why is it so difficult to write simply – and not only simply but *sotto voce*, if you know what I mean? That is how I long to write. No fine effects – no bravuras. But just the plain truth, as only a liar can tell it.

I light a cigarette, lean back, inhale deeply – and find myself wondering if my wife is asleep. Or is she lying in her cold bed, staring into the dark with those trustful, bewildered eyes? Her eyes are like the eyes of a cow being driven along a road. "Why am I being driven – what harm have I done? But I really am not responsible for that look; it's her natural expression. One day, when she was turning out a cupboard, she found a little old photograph of herself, taken when she was a girl at school. In her confirmation dress, she explained. And there were the eyes, even then. I remember saying to her: "Did you always look so sad?" Leaning over my shoulder, she laughed lightly. "Do I look sad? I think it's just ... me." And she waited for me to say something about it. But I was marvelling at her courage at having shown it to me at all. It was a hideous photograph! And I wondered again if she realised how plain she was, and comforted herself with the idea that people who loved each other didn't criticise but accepted everything, or if she really rather liked her appearance and expected me to say something complimentary. Oh, that was base of me! How could I have forgotten all the countless times when I have known her turn away, avoid the light, press her face into my shoulders. And above all, how could I have forgotten the afternoon of our wedding day, when we sat on the green bench in the Botanical Gardens and listened to the band, how, in an interval between two pieces, she suddenly turned to me and said in the voice in which one says: "Do you think the grass is damp?" or "Do you think it's time for tea?" . . . "Tell me – do you think physical beauty is so very important?" I don't like to think how often she rehearsed that question. And do you know what I answered? At that moment, as if at my command, there came a great gush of hard bright sound from the band. And I managed to shout above it – cheerfully – "I didn't hear what you said." Devilish! Wasn't it? Perhaps not wholly. She looked like the poor patient who hears the surgeon say, "It will certainly be necessary to perform the operation – but not now!"

But all this conveys the impression that my wife and I were never really happy together. Not true! Not true! We were marvellously, radiantly happy. We were a model couple. If you had seen us together, any time, any place, if you had followed us, tracked us down, spied, taken us off our guard, you still would have been forced to confess, "I have never seen a more ideally suited pair." Until last autumn.

But really to explain what happened then I should have to go back and back, I should have to dwindle until my tiny hands clutched the bannisters, the stair-rail was higher than my head, and I peered through to watch my father padding softly up and down. There were coloured windows on the landings. As he came up, first his bald head was scarlet; then it was yellow. How frightened I was! And when they put me to bed, it was to dream that we were living inside one of my father's big coloured bottles. For he was a chemist. I was born nine years after my parents were married; I was an only child, and the effort to produce even me – small, withered bud I must have been – sapped all my mother's strength. She never left her room again. Bed, sofa, window, she moved between the three. Well I can see her, on the window days, sitting, her cheek in her hand, staring out. Her room looked over the street. Opposite there was a wall plastered with advertisement for travelling shows and circuses and so on. I stand beside her, and we gaze at the slim lady in a red dress hitting a dark gentleman over the head with her parasol, or at the tiger peering through the jungle while the clown, close by, balances a bottle on his nose, or at a little golden-haired girl sitting on the knee of an old black man in a broad cotton hat ... She says nothing. On sofa days there is a flannel dressing-gown that I loathe, and a cushion that keeps on slipping off the hard sofa. I pick it up. It has flowers and writing sewn on. I ask what the writing says, and she whispers, "Sweet Repose!" In bed her fingers plait, in tight little plaits, the fringe of the quilt, and her lips are thin. And that is all there is of my mother, except the last queer "episode" that comes later ...

My father – curled up in the corner on the lid of a round box that held sponges, I stared at my father so long it's as though his image, cut off at the waist by the counter, has remained solid in my memory. Perfectly bald, polished head, shaped like a thin egg, creased creamy cheeks, little bags under the eyes, large pale ears like handles. His manner was discreet, sly, faintly amused and tinged with impudence. Long before I could appreciate it I knew the mixture . . . I even used to copy him in my corner, bending forward, with a small reproduction of his faint sneer. In the evening his customers were, chiefly, young women; some of them came in every day for his famous five-penny pick-me-up. Their gaudy looks, their voices, their free ways, fascinated me. I longed to be my father, handing them across the counter the little glass of bluish stuff they tossed off so greedily. God knows what it was made of. Years after I drank some, just to see what it tasted like, and I felt as though someone had given me a terrific blow on the head; I felt stunned. One of those evenings I remember vividly. It was cold; it must have been autumn, for the flaring gas was lighted after my tea. I sat in my corner and my father was mixing something; the shop was empty. Suddenly the bell jangled and a young woman rushed in, crying so loud, sobbing so hard, that it didn't sound real. She wore a green cape trimmed with fur and a hat with cherries dangling. My father came from behind the screen. But she couldn't stop herself at first. She stood in the middle of the shop and wrung her hands, and moaned. I've never heard such crying since. Presently she managed to gasp out, "Give me a pick-me-up." Then she drew a long breath, trembled away from him and quavered: "I've had *bad news*!" And in the flaring gaslight I saw the whole side of her face was puffed up and purple; her lip was cut, and her eyelid looked as though it was gummed fast over the wet eye. My father pushed the glass across the counter, and she took her purse out of her stocking and paid him. But she couldn't drink; clutching the glass, she stared in front of her as if she could not believe what she saw. Each time she put her head back the tears spurted out again. Finally she put the glass down. It was no use. Holding the cape with one hand, she ran in the same way out of the shop again. My father gave no sign. But long after she had gone I crouched in my corner, and when I think back it's as though I felt my whole body vibrating – "So that's what it is outside," I thought. "That's what it's like out there."

Do you remember your childhood? I am always coming across these marvellous accounts by writers who declare that they remember "everything, everything". I certainly don't. The dark stretches, the blanks, are much bigger than the bright glimpses. I seem to have spent most of my time like a plant in a cupboard. Now and again, when the sun shone, a careless hand thrust me out on to the window-sill, and a careless hand whipped me in again – and that was all. But what happened in the darkness – I wonder? Did one grow? Pale stem . . . timid leaves . . . white, reluctant bud. No wonder I was hated at school. Even the masters shrank from me. I somehow knew that my soft hesitating voice disgusted them. I knew, too, how they turned away from my shocked, staring eyes. I was small and thin, and I smelled of the shop; my nickname was Gregory Powder. School was a tin building stuck on the raw hillside. There were dark red streaks like blood in the oozing clay banks of the playground. I hide in the dark passage, where the coats hang, and am discovered there by one of the masters. "What are you doing there in the dark?" His terrible voice kills me; I die before his eyes. I am standing in a ring of thrust-out heads; some are grinning, some look greedy, some are spitting. And it is always cold. Big crushed up clouds press across the sky; the rusty water in the school tank is frozen; the bell sounds numb. One day they put a dead bird in my overcoat pocket. I found it just when I reached home. Oh, what a strange flutter there was at my heart, when I drew out that terribly soft, cold little body, with the legs thin as pins and the claws wrung. I sat on the back door step in the yard and put the bird in my cap. The feathers round the neck looked wet and there was a tiny tuft just above the closed eyes that stood up too. How tightly the beak was shut; I could not see the mark where it was divided. I stretched out one wing and touched the soft, secret down underneath; I tried to make the claws curl round my little finger. But I didn't feel sorry for it – no! I wondered. The smoke from our kitchen chimney poured downwards, and flakes of soot floated – soft, light in the air. Through a big crack in the cement yard a poor-looking plant with dull reddish flowers had pushed its way. I looked at the dead bird again . . . And that is the first time that I remember singing, rather . . . listening to a silent voice inside a little cage that was me.

But what has all this to do with my married happiness? How can all this affect my wife and me? Why – to tell what happened last autumn – do I run all this way back into the Past? The Past – what is the Past? I might say the star-shaped flake of soot on a leaf of the poor-looking plant, and the bird lying on the quilted lining of my cap, and my father's pestle and my mother's cushion, belong to it. But that is not to say they are any less mine than they were when I looked upon them with my very eyes, and touched them with these fingers. No, they are more; they are a living part of me. Who am I, in fact, as I sit here at this table, but my own past? If I deny that, I am nothing. And if I were to try and divide my life into childhood, youth, early manhood and so on, it would be a kind of affectation; I should know I was doing it just because of the pleasantly important sensation it gives one to rule lines, and to use green ink for childhood, red for the next stage, and purple for the period of adolescence. For, one thing I have learnt, one thing I do believe is, Nothing Happens Suddenly. Yes, that is my religion, I suppose . . .

My mother's death, for instance. Is it more distant from me to-day than it was then? It is just as close, as strange, as puzzling, and in spite of all the countless times I have recalled the circumstances, I know no more now than I did then whether I dreamed them or whether they really occurred. It happened when I was thirteen and I slept in a little strip of a room on what was called the Half Landing. One night I woke up with a start to see my mother, in her nightgown, without even the hated flannel dressing-gown, sitting on my bed. But the strange thing which frightened me was, she wasn't looking at me. Her head was bent; the short thin tail of hair lay between her shoulders; her hands were pressed between her knees, and my bed shook; she was shivering. It was the first time I had ever seen her out of her own room. I said, or I think I said, "Is that you, mother?" And as she turned round I saw in the moonlight how queer she looked. Her face looked small – quite different. She looked like one of the boys at the school baths, who sits on a step, shivering just like that, and wants to go in and yet is frightened.

"Are you awake?" she said. Her eyes opened; I think she smiled. She leaned towards me. "I've been poisoned," she whispered. "Your father's poisoned me." And she nodded. Then, before I could say a word, she was gone, and I thought I heard the door shut. I sat quite still; I couldn't move. I think I expected something else to happen. For a long time I listened for something; there wasn't a sound. The candle was by my bed, but I was too frightened to stretch out my hand for the matches. But even while I wondered what I ought to do, even while my heart thumped – everything became confused. I lay down and pulled the blankets round me. I fell asleep, and the next morning my mother was found dead of failure of the heart.

Did that visit happen? Was it a dream? Why did she come to tell me? Or why, if she came, did she go away so quickly? And her expression – so joyous under the frightened look – was that real? I believed it fully the afternoon of the funeral, when I saw my father dressed up for his part, hat and all. That tall hat so gleaming black and round was like a cork covered with black sealing-wax, and the rest of my father was awfully like a bottle, with his face for the label – *Deadly Poison*. It flashed into my mind as I stood opposite him in the hall. And Deadly Poison, or old D.P., was my private name for him from that day.

Late, it grows late. I love the night. I love to feel the tide of darkness rising slowly and slowly washing, turning over and over, lifting, floating, all that lies strewn upon the dark beach, all that lies hid in rocky hollows. I love, I love this strange feeling of drifting – whither? After my mother's death I hated to go to bed. I used to sit on the window-sill, folded up, and watch the sky. It seemed to me the moon moved much faster than the sun. And one big, bright green star I chose for my own. My star! But I never thought of it beckoning to me or twinkling merrily for my sake. Cruel, indifferent, splendid – it burned in the airy night. No matter – it was mine! But growing close up against the window there was a creeper with small, bunched up pink and purple flowers. These did know me. These, when I touched them at night, welcomed my fingers; the little tendrils, so weak, so delicate, knew I would not hurt them. When the wind moved the leaves I felt I understood their shaking. When I came to the window, it seemed to me the flowers said among themselves, "The boy is here."

As the months passed, there was often a light in my father's room below. And I heard voices and laughter. "He's got some woman with him," I thought. But it meant nothing to me. Then the gay voice, the sound of the laughter, gave me the idea it was one of the girls who used to come to the shop in the evenings – and gradually I began to imagine which girl it was. It was the dark one in the red coat and skirt, who once had given me a penny. A merry face stooped over me – warm breath tickled my neck – there were little beads of black on her long lashes, and when she opened her arms to kiss me, there came a marvellous wave of scent! Yes, that was the one. Time passed, and I forgot the moon and my green star and my shy creeper – I came to the window to wait for the light in my father's window, to listen for the laughing voice, until one night I dozed and I dreamed she came again – again she drew me to her, something soft, scented, warm and merry hung over me like a cloud. But when I tried to see, her eyes only mocked me, her red lips opened and she hissed, "Little sneak! little sneak!" But not as if she were angry, as if she understood, and her smile somehow was like a rat . . . hateful!

The night after, I lighted the candle and sat down at the table instead. By and by, as the flame steadied, there was a small lake of liquid wax, surrounded by a white, smooth wall. I took a pin and made little holes in this wall and then sealed them up faster than the wax could escape. After a time I fancied the candle flame joined in the game; it leapt up, quivered, wagged; it even seemed to laugh. But while I played with the candle and smiled and broke off the tiny white peaks of wax that rose above the wall and floated them on my lake, a feeling of awful dreariness fastened on me – yes, that is the word. It crept up from my knees to my thighs, into my arms; I ached all over with misery. And I felt so strangely that I couldn't move. Something bound me there by the table – I couldn't even let the pin drop that I held between my finger and thumb. For a moment I came to a stop, as it were.

Then the shrivelled case of the bud split and fell, the plant in the cupboard came into flower. "Who am I?" I thought. "What is all this?" And I looked at my room, at the broken bust of the man called Hahnemann on top of the cupboard, at my little bed with the pillow like an envelope. I saw it all, but not as I had seen before . . . Everything lived, but everything. But that was not all. I was equally alive and – it's the only way I can express it – the barriers were down between us – I had come into my own world!

The barriers were down. I had been all my life a little outcast; but until that moment no one had "accepted" me; I had lain in the cupboard – or the cave forlorn. But now – I was taken, I was accepted, claimed. I did not consciously turn away from the world of human beings; I had never known it; but I from that night did beyond words consciously turn towards my silent brothers . . .

THE FALL OF THE IDOL

Richmal Crompton

Richmal Crompton (1890–1969) is known worldwide for her Just William stories. Born in Lancashire, she moved to London, trained as a school mistress, but had to stop teaching when she lost the use of her right leg through polio. She died in Bromley in 1969 having written plays and nearly fifty novels. In most of them, William is aged eleven.

Willustration William was bored. He sat at his desk in the sunny schoolroom and gazed dispassionately at a row of figures on the blackboard.

"It isn't *sense*," he murmured scornfully.

Miss Drew was also bored, but, unlike William, she tried to hide the fact.

"If the interest on a hundred pounds for one year is five pounds," she said wearily, then, "William Brown, do sit up and don't look so stupid!"

William changed his position from that of lolling over one side of his desk to that of lolling over the other, and began to justify himself.

"Well, I can't unner*stand* any of it. It's enough to make anyone look stupid when he can't unner*stand* any of it. I can't think why people go on givin' people bits of money for givin' 'em lots of money and go on an' on doin' it. It dun't seem sense. Anyone's a mug for givin' anyone a hundred pounds just 'cause he says he'll go on givin' him five pounds and go on stickin' to his hundred pounds. How's he to *know* he will? Well," he warmed to his subject, "what's to stop him not givin' any five pounds once he's got hold of the hundred pounds an' goin' on stickin' to the hundred pounds –"

Miss Drew checked him by a slim, upraised hand.

"William," she said patiently, "just listen to me. Now suppose," her eyes roved round the room and settled on a small red-haired boy, "suppose that Eric wanted a hundred pounds for something and you lent it to him –"

"I wun't lend Eric a hundred pounds," he said firmly, "'cause I ha'n't got it. I've only got 3½d, an' I wun't lend that to Eric, 'cause I'm not such a mug, 'cause I lent him my mouth organ once an' he bit a bit off an' –"

Miss Drew interrupted sharply. Teaching on a hot afternoon is rather trying.

"You'd better stay in after school, William, and I'll explain."

William scowled, emitted his monosyllable of scornful disdain "Huh!" and relapsed into gloom.

He brightened, however, on remembering a lizard he had caught on the way to school, and drew it from its hiding place in his pocket. But the lizard had abandoned the unequal struggle for existence among the stones, top, penknife, bits of putty, and other small objects that inhabited William's pocket. The housing problem had been too much for it.

William in disgust shrouded the remains in blotting paper, and disposed of it in his neighbour's inkpot. The neighbour protested and an enlivening scrimmage ensued.

Finally the lizard was dropped down the neck of an inveterate enemy of William's in the next row, and was extracted only with the help of obliging friends. Threats of vengeance followed, couched in blood-curdling terms, and written on blotting paper.

Meanwhile Miss Drew explained Simple Practice to a small but earnest coterie of admirers in the front row. And William, in the back row, whiled away the hours for which his father paid the education authorities a substantial sum.

But his turn was to come.

At the end of afternoon school one by one the class departed, leaving William only nonchalantly chewing an India rubber and glaring at Miss Drew.

"Now, William."

Miss Drew was severely patient.

William went up to the platform and stood by her desk.

"You see, if someone borrows a hundred pounds from someone else –"

She wrote down the figures on a piece of paper, bending low over her desk. The sun poured in through the window, showing the little golden curls in the nape of her neck. She lifted to William eyes that were stern and frowning, but blue as blue above flushed cheeks.

"Don't you *see*, William?" she said.

There was a faint perfume about her, and William the devil-may-care pirate and robber-chief, the stern despiser of all things effeminate, felt the first dart of the malicious blind god. He blushed and simpered.

"Yes, I see all about it now," he assured her. "You've explained it all plain now. I cudn't unner*stand* it before. It's a bit soft – in't it – anyway, to go lending hundred pounds about just 'cause someone says they'll give you five pounds next year. Some folks is mugs. But I do unner*stand* now. I cudn't unner*stand* it before."

"You'd have found it simpler if you hadn't played with dead lizards all the time," she said wearily, closing her books.

William gasped.

He went home her devoted slave. Certain members of the class always deposited dainty bouquets on her desk in the morning. William was determined to outshine the rest. He went into the garden with a large basket and a pair of scissors the next morning before he set out for school.

It happened that no one was about. He went first to the hothouse. It was a riot of colour. He worked there with a thoroughness and concentration worthy of a nobler cause. He came out staggering beneath a piled-up basket of hothouse blooms. The hothouse itself was bare and desolate.

Hearing a sound in the back garden he hastily decided to delay no longer, but to set out to school at once. He set out as unostentatiously as possible.

Miss Drew, entering her classroom, was aghast to see instead of the usual small array of buttonholes on her desk, a mass of already withering hothouse flowers completely covering her desk and chair.

William was a boy who never did things by halves.

"Good Heavens!" she cried in consternation.

William blushed with pleasure.

He changed his seat to one in the front row. All that morning he sat, his eyes fixed on her earnestly, dreaming of moments in which he rescued her from robbers and pirates (here he was somewhat inconsistent with his own favourite role of robber-chief and pirate), and bore her fainting in his strong arms to safety. Then she clung to him in love and gratitude, and they were married at once by the Archbishops of Canterbury and York.

William would have no half measures. They were to be married by the Archbishops of Canterbury and York, or else the Pope. He wasn't sure that he wouldn't rather have the Pope. He would wear his black pirate suit with the skull and crossbones. No, that would not do –

"What have I just been saying, William?" said Miss Drew.

William coughed and gazed at her soulfully.

"'Bout lendin' money?" he said, hopefully.

"William!" she snapped. "This isn't an arithmetic lesson. I'm trying to teach you about the Armada."

"Oh, *that*!" said William brightly and ingratiatingly. "Oh, yes."

"Tell me something about it."

"I don't *know* anything – not jus' yet –"

"I've been *telling* you about it. I do wish you'd listen," she said despairingly.

William relapsed into silence, nonplussed, but by no means cowed.

When he reached home that evening he found that the garden was the scene of excitement and hubbub. One policeman was measuring the panes of glass in the conservatory door, and another was on his knees examining the beds near. His grown-up sister, Ethel, was standing at the front door.

"Every single flower has been stolen from the conservatory some time this morning," she said excitedly. "We've only just been able to get the police. William, did you see anyone about when you went to school this morning?"

William pondered deeply. His most guileless and innocent expression came to his face.

"No," he said at last. "No, Ethel, I didn't see nobody."

William coughed and discreetly withdrew.

That evening he settled down at the library table, spreading out his books around him, a determined frown upon his small face.

His father was sitting in an armchair by the window reading the evening paper.

"Father," said William suddenly, "s'pose I came to you an' said you was to give me a hundred pounds an' I'd give you five pounds next year an' so on, would you give it me?"

"I should not, my son," said his father firmly.

William sighed.

"I knew there was something wrong with it," he said.

Mr Brown returned to the leading article, but not for long.

"Father, what was the date of the Armada?"

"Good Heavens! How should I know? I wasn't there."

William sighed.

"Well, I'm tryin' to write about it and why it failed an' – why did it fail?"

Mr Brown groaned, gathered up his paper, and retired to the dining-room.

He had almost finished the leading article when William appeared, his arms full of books, and sat down quietly at the table.

"Father, what's the French for "my aunt is walking in the garden"?"

"What on earth are you doing?" said Mr Brown irritably.

"I'm doing my home lessons," said William virtuously.

"I never even knew you had the things to do."

"No," William admitted gently, "I don't generally take much bother over them, but I'm goin' to now – 'cause Miss Drew" – he blushed slightly and paused – "'cause Miss Drew" – he blushed more deeply and began to stammer, "'c – 'cause Miss Drew" – he was almost apoplectic.

Mr Brown quietly gathered up his paper and crept out to the verandah, where his wife sat with the week's mending.

"William's gone raving mad in the dining-room," he said pleasantly, as he sat down. "Takes the form of a wild thirst for knowledge, and a babbling of a Miss Drawing, or Drew, or something. He's best left alone."

Mrs Brown merely smiled placidly over the mending.

Mr Brown had finished one leading article and begun another before William appeared again. He stood in the doorway frowning and stern.

"Father, what's the capital of Holland?"

"Good Heavens!" said his father. "Buy him an encyclopedia. Anything, anything. What does he think I am? What –"

"I'd better set apart a special room for his homework," said Mrs Brown soothingly, "now that he's beginning to take such an interest."

"A room!" echoed his father bitterly. "He wants a whole house."

Miss Drew was surprised and touched by William's earnestness and attention the next day. At the end of the afternoon school he kindly offered to carry her books home for her. He waved aside all protests. He marched home by her side discoursing pleasantly, his small freckled face beaming devotion.

"I like pirates, don't you, Miss Drew? An' robbers an' things like that? Miss Drew, would you like to be married to a robber?"

He was trying to reconcile his old beloved dream of his future estate with the new one of becoming Miss Drew's husband.

"No," she said firmly.

His heart sank.

"Nor a pirate?" he said sadly.

"No."

"They're quite nice really – pirates," he assured her.

"I think not."

"Well," he said resignedly, "we'll jus' have to go huntin' wild animals and things. That'll be all right."

"Who?" she said, bewildered.

"Well – jus' you wait," he said darkly.

Then: "Would you rather be married by the Archbishop of York or the Pope?"

"The Archbishop, I think," she said gravely.

He nodded.

"All right."

She was distinctly amused. She was less amused the next evening. Miss Drew had a male cousin – a very nice-looking male cousin, with whom she often went for walks in the evening. This evening, by chance, they passed William's house, and William, who was in the garden, threw aside his temporary role of pirate and joined them. He trotted happily on the other side of Miss Drew. He entirely monopolised the conversation. The male cousin seemed to encourage him, and this annoyed Miss Drew. He refused to depart in spite of Miss Drew's strong hints. He had various items of interest to impart, and he imparted them with the air of one assured of an appreciative hearing. He had found a dead rat the day before and given it to his dog, but his dog didn't like 'em dead and neither did the ole cat, so he'd buried it. Did Miss Drew like all those flowers he'd got her the other day? He was afraid that he cudn't bring any more like that jus' yet. Were there pirates now? Well, what would folks do to one if there was one? He din't see why there shun't be pirates now. He thought he'd start it, anyway. He'd like to shoot a lion. He was goin' to one day. He'd shoot a lion an' a tiger. He'd bring the skin home to Miss Drew, if she liked. He grew recklessly generous. He'd bring home lots of skins of all sorts of animals for Miss Drew.

"Don't you think you ought to be going home, William?" said Miss Drew coldly.

William hastened to reassure her.

"Oh, no – not for ever so long yet," he said.

"Isn't it your bedtime?"

"Oh, no – not yet – not for ever so long."

The male cousin was giving William his whole attention.

"What does Miss Drew teach you at school, William?" he said.

"Oh, jus' ornery things. Armadas an' things. An' 'bout lending a hundred pounds. That's a norful *soft* thing. I unner*stand* it," he added hastily, fearing further explanation, "but it's *soft*. My father thinks it is, too, an' he oughter *know*. He's bin abroad lots of times. He's bin chased by a bull, my father has –"

The shades of night were falling fast when William reached Miss Drew's house still discoursing volubly. He was drunk with success. He interpreted his idol's silence as the silence of rapt admiration.

He was passing through the gate with his two companions with the air of one assured of welcome, when Miss Drew shut the gate upon him firmly.

"You'd better go home now, William," she said.

William hesitated.

"I don't mind comin' in a bit," he said. "I'm not tired."

But Miss Drew and the male cousin were already halfway up the walk.

William turned his steps homeward. He met Ethel near the gate.

"William, where *have* you been? I've been looking for you everywhere. It's *hours* past your bedtime."

"I was goin' for a walk with Miss Drew."

"But you should have come home at your bedtime."

"I don't think she wanted me to go," he said with dignity. "I think it wun't of bin p'lite."

William found that a new and serious element had entered his life. It was not without its disadvantages. Many had been the little diversions by which William had been wont to while away the hours of instruction. In spite of his devotion to Miss Drew, he missed the old days of carefree exuberance, but he kept his new seat in the front row, and clung to his role of earnest student. He was beginning to find also, that a conscientious performance of home lessons limited his activities after school hours, but at present he hugged his chains. Miss Drew, from her seat on the platform, found William's soulful concentrated gaze somewhat embarrassing, and his questions even more so.

As he went out of school he heard her talking to another mistress.

"I'm very fond of syringa," she was saying. "I'd love to have some."

William decided to bring her syringa, handfuls of syringa, armfuls of syringa.

He went straight home to the gardener.

"No, I ain't got no syringa. Please step off my rosebed, Mister William. No, there ain't any syringa in this 'ere garding. I dunno for why. Please leave my 'ose pipe alone, Mister William."

"Huh!" ejaculated William, scornfully turning away.

He went round the garden. The gardener had been quite right. There were guelder roses everywhere, but no syringa.

He climbed the fence and surveyed the next garden. There were guelder roses everywhere, but no syringa. It must have been some peculiarity in the soil.

William strolled down the road, scanning the gardens as he went. All had guelder roses. None had syringa.

Suddenly he stopped.

On a table in the window of a small house at the bottom of the road was a vase of syringa. He did not know who lived there. He entered the garden cautiously. No one was about.

He looked into the room. It was empty. The window was open at the bottom.

He scrambled in, removing several layers of white paint from the windowsill as he did so. He was determined to have that syringa. He took it dripping from the vase, and was preparing to depart, when the door opened and a fat woman appeared upon the threshold. The scream that she emitted at sight of William curdled the very blood in his veins. She dashed to the window, and William, in self-defence, dodged round the table and out of the door. The back door was open, and William blindly fled by it. The fat woman did not pursue. She was leaning out of the window, and her shrieks rent the air.

"Police! Help! Murder! Robbers!"

The quiet little street rang with the raucous sounds.

William felt cold shivers creeping up and down his spine. He was in a small back garden from which he could see no exit.

Meanwhile the shrieks were redoubled.

"Help! *Help! Help!*"

Then came sounds of the front door opening and men's voices.

"Hello! Who is it? What is it?"

William glared round wildly. There was a hen house in the corner of the garden, and into this he dashed, tearing open the door and plunging through a mass of flying feathers and angry, disturbed hens.

William crouched in a corner of the dark hen house determinedly clutching his bunch of syringa.

Distant voices were at first all he could hear. Then they came nearer, and he heard the fat lady's voice loudly declaiming.

"He was quite a small man, but with such an evil face. I just had one glimpse of him as he dashed past me. I'm sure he'd have murdered me if I hadn't cried for help. Oh, the coward! And a poor defenceless woman! He was standing by the silver table. I disturbed him at his work of crime. I feel so upset. I shan't sleep for nights. I shall see his evil, murderous face. And a poor unarmed woman!"

"Can you give us no details, madam?" said a man's voice. "Could you recognise him again?"

"*Anywhere!*" she said firmly. "Such a criminal face. You've no idea how upset I am. I might have been a lifeless corpse now, if I hadn't had the courage to cry for help."

"We're measuring the footprints, madam. You say he went out by the front door?"

"I'm convinced he did. I'm convinced he's hiding in the bushes by the gate. Such a low face. My nerves are absolutely jarred."

"We'll search the bushes again, madam," said the other voice wearily, "but I expect he has escaped by now."

"The brute!" said the fat lady. "Oh, the *brute*! And that *face*. If I hadn't had the courage to cry out –"

The voices died away and William was left alone in a corner of the hen house.

A white hen appeared in the little doorway, squawked at him angrily, and retired, cackling indignation. Visions of lifelong penal servitude or hanging passed before William's eyes. He'd rather be executed, really. He hoped they'd execute him.

Then he heard the fat lady bidding goodbye to the policeman. Then she came to the back garden evidently with a friend, and continued to pour forth her troubles.

"And he *dashed* past me, dear. Quite a small man, but with such an evil face."

A black hen appeared in the little doorway, and with an angry squawk at William, returned to the back garden.

"I think you're *splendid*, dear," said the invisible friend. "How you had the *courage*."

The white hen gave a sardonic scream.

"You'd better come in and rest, darling," said the friend.

"I'd better," said the fat lady in a plaintive, suffering voice. "I do feel very . . . shaken. . . . "

Their voices ceased, the door was closed, and all was still.

Cautiously, very cautiously, a much dishevelled William crept from the hen house and round the side of the house. Here he found a locked side-gate over which he climbed, and very quietly he glided down to the front gate and to the road.

"Where's William this evening?" said Mrs Brown. "I do hope he won't stay out after his bedtime."

"Oh, I've just met him," said Ethel. "He was going up to his bedroom. He was covered with hen feathers and holding a bunch of syringa."

"Mad!" sighed his father. "Mad! Mad! Mad!"

The next morning William laid a bunch of syringa upon Miss Drew's desk. He performed the offering with an air of quiet, manly pride. Miss Drew recoiled.

"*Not* syringa, William. I simply can't *bear* the smell!"

William gazed at her in silent astonishment for a few moments.

Then: "But you *said* . . . you *said* . . . you said you were fond of syringa an' that you'd like to have them."

"Did I say syringa?" said Miss Drew vaguely. "I meant guelder roses."

William's gaze was one of stony contempt.

He went slowly back to his old seat at the back of the room.

That evening he made a bonfire with several choice friends, and played Red Indians in the garden. There was a certain thrill in returning to the old life.

"Hello!" said his father, encountering William creeping on all fours among the bushes. "I thought you did home lessons now?"

William arose to an upright position.

"I'm not goin' to take much bother over 'em now," said William. "Miss Drew, she can't talk straight. She dunno what she *means*."

"That's always the trouble with women," agreed his father. "William says his idol has feet of clay," he said to his wife, who had approached.

"I dunno as she's got feet of clay," said William, the literal. "All I say is she can't talk straight. I took no end of trouble an' she dunno what she means. I think her feet's all right. She walks all right. 'Sides, when they make folks false feet, they make 'em of wood, not clay."

MY FIRST FEE

Isaac Babel

Isaac Babel (1894–1940) was a journalist, playwright and author of *Red Cavalry* and *Odessa Tales*, as well as stories of his youth. *The Collected Stories of Isaac Babel* were published in 2002. Born near Odessa, he moved to Petrograd, met Maxim Gorky and began making a living as a writer. He was shot, having been made to confess to being a Trotskyite spy, aged forty-five, a victim of Stalin's Great Purge on account of his love for the wife of an NKVD chief. Babel's last words were "I am innocent . . . I am asking for only one thing – let me finish my work." He was exonerated under Krushchev in 1954.

To be in Tiflis in spring, to be twenty years old, and not to be loved – that is a misfortune. Such a misfortune befell me. I was working as a proof-reader for the printing press of the Caucasus Military District. The Kura River bubbled beneath the windows of my attic. The sun in the morning, rising from behind the mountains, lit up the river's murky knots. I was renting a room in the attic from a newlywed Georgian couple. My landlord was a butcher at the Eastern Bazaar. In the room next door, the butcher and his wife, in the grip of love, thrashed about like two large fish trapped in a jar. The tails of these crazed fish thumped against the partition, rocking the whole attic, which was blackened by the piercing sun, ripping it from its rafters and whisking it off to eternity. They could not part their teeth, clenched in the obstinate fury of passion. In the mornings, Milyet, the young bride, went out to get bread. She was so weak that she had to hold on to the banister. Her delicate little foot searched for each step, and there was a vague blind smile on her lips, like that of a woman recovering from a long illness. Laying her palm on her small breasts, she bowed to everyone she met in the street – the Assyrian grown green with age, the kerosene seller, and the market shrews with faces gashed by fiery wrinkles, who were selling hanks of sheep's wool. At night the thumping and babbling of my neighbors was followed by a silence as piercing as the whistle of a cannonball.

To be twenty years old, to live in Tiflis, and to listen at night to the tempests of other people's silence – that is a misfortune. To escape it, I ran out of the house and down to the Kura River, where I was over-powered by the bathhouse steam of Tiflis springtime. It swept over me, sapping my strength. I roamed through the hunchbacked streets, my throat parched. A fog of springtime sultriness chased me back to my attic, to that forest of blackened stumps lit by the moon. I had no choice but to look for love. Needless to say, I found it. For better or worse, the woman I chose turned out to be a prostitute. Her name was Vera. Every evening

I went creeping after her along Golovinsky Boulevard, unable to work up the courage to talk to her. I had neither money for her nor words – those dull and ceaselessly burrowing words of love. Since childhood, I had invested every drop of my strength in creating tales, plays, and thousands of stories. They lay on my heart like a toad on a stone. Possessed by demonic pride, I did not want to write them down too soon. I felt that it was pointless to write worse than Tolstoy. My stories were destined to survive oblivion. Dauntless thought and grueling passion are only worth the effort spent on them when they are draped in beautiful raiment. But how does one sew such raiment?

A man who is caught in the noose of an idea and lulled by its serpentine gaze finds it difficult to bubble over with meaningless, burrowing words of love. Such a man is ashamed of shedding tears of sadness. He is not quick-witted enough to be able to laugh with happiness. I was a dreamer, and did not have the knack for the thoughtless art of happiness. Therefore I was going to have to give Vera ten rubles of my meager earnings.

I made up my mind and went to stand watch outside the doors of the Simpatia tavern. Georgian princes in blue Circassian jackets and soft leather boots sauntered past in casual parade. They picked their teeth with silver toothpicks and eyed the carmine-painted Georgian women with large feet and slim hips. There was a shimmer of turquoise in the twilight. The blossoming acacias howled along the streets in their petal-shedding bass voices. Waves of officials in white coats rolled along the boulevard. Balsamic streams of air came flowing toward them from the Karzbek Mountains.

Vera came later, as darkness was falling. Tall, her face a radiant white, she hovered before the apish crowd, as the Mother of God hovers before the prow of a fishing boat. She came up to the doors of the Simpatia. I hesitated, then followed her.

"Off to Palestine?"

Vera's wide, pink back was moving in front of me. She turned around.

"What?"

She frowned, but her eyes were laughing.

"Where does your path take you?"

The words crackled in my mouth like dry firewood. Vera came over and walked in step with me.

"A tenner – would that be fine with you?"

I agreed so quickly that she became suspicious.

"You sure you have ten rubles?"

We went through the gates and I handed her my wallet. She opened it and counted twenty-one rubles, narrowing her gray eyes and moving her lips. She rearranged the coins, sorting gold with gold and silver with silver.

"Give me ten," Vera said, handing me back my wallet. "We'll spend five, and the rest you can keep to get by. When's your next payday?"

I told her that I would get paid again in four days. We went back into the street. Vera took me by the arm and leaned her shoulder against mine. We walked up the cooling street. The sidewalk was covered with wilted vegetables.

"I'd love to be in Borzhom right now in this heat," she said.

Vera's hair was tied with a ribbon. The lightning of the street lamps flashed and bounced off it.

"So hightail it to Borzhom!"

That's what I said – "hightail it." For some reason, that's the expression I used.

"No dough," Vera answered with a yawn, forgetting all about me. She forgot all about me because her day was over and she had made easy money off me. She knew that I wouldn't call the police, and that I wasn't going to steal her money along with her earrings during the night.

We went to the foot of St. David's Mountain. There, in a tavern, I ordered some kebabs. Without waiting for our food to be brought, Vera went and sat with a group of old Persian men who were discussing business. They were leaning on propped-up sticks, wagging their olive-colored heads, telling the tavern keeper that it was time for him to expand his trade. Vera barged into their conversation, taking the side of the old men. She was for the idea of moving the tavern to Mikhailovsky Boulevard. The tavern keeper was sighing, paralyzed by uncertainty and caution. I ate my kebabs alone. Vera's bare arms poured out of the silk of her sleeves. She banged her fist on the table, her earrings dancing among long, lackluster backs, orange beards, and painted nails. By the time she came back to our table, her kebabs had become cold. Her face was flushed with excitement.

"There's no budging that man – he's such a mule! I swear, he could make a fortune with Eastern cooking on Mikhailovsky Boulevard!"

Friends of Vera's passed by our table one after another: princes in Circassian jackets, officers of a certain age, storekeepers in heavy silk coats, and potbellied old men with sunburned faces and little green pimples on their cheeks. It was pushing midnight when we got to the hotel, but there too Vera had countless things to do. An old woman was getting ready to go to her son in Armavir. Vera rushed over to help her, kneeling on her suitcase to force it shut, tying pillows together with cords, and wrapping pies in oilpaper. Clutching her rust-brown handbag, the squat little old woman hurried in her gauze hat from room to room to say good-bye. She shuffled down the hallway in her rubber boots, sobbing and smiling through all her wrinkles. The whole to-do took well over an hour. I waited for Vera in a musty room with three-legged armchairs and a clay oven. The corners of the room were covered with damp splotches.

I had been tormented and dragged around town for such a long time that even my feeling of love seemed to me an enemy, a dogged enemy.

Other people's life bustled in the hallway with peals of sudden laughter. Flies were dying in a jar filled with milky liquid. Each fly was dying in its own way – one in drawn-out agony, its death throes violent, another with a barely visible shudder. A book by Golovin about the life of the Boyars lay on the threadbare tablecloth next to the jar. I opened the book. Letters lined themselves up in a row and then fell into a jumble. In front of me, framed by the window, rose a stony hillside with a crooked Turkish road winding up it. Vera came into the room.

"We've just sent off Fedosya Mavrikevna," she said. "I swear, she was just like a mother to all of us. The poor old thing has to travel all alone with no one to help her!"

Vera sat down on the bed with her knees apart. Her eyes had wandered off to immaculate realms of tenderness and friendship. Then she saw me sitting there in my double-breasted jacket. She clasped her hands and stretched.

"I guess you're tired of waiting. Don't worry, we'll do it now."

But I simply couldn't figure out what exactly it was that Vera was intending to do. Her preparations resembled those of a surgeon preparing for an operation. She lit the kerosene burner and put a pot of water on it. She placed a clean towel over the bed frame and hung an enema bag over the headboard, a bag with a white tube dangling against the wall. When the water was hot, Vera poured it into the enema bag, threw in a red crystal, and pulled her dress off over her head. A large woman with sloping shoulders and rumpled stomach stood in front of me. Her flaccid nipples hung blindly to the sides.

"Come over here, you little rabbit, while the water's getting ready," my beloved said.

I didn't move. Despair froze within me. Why had I exchanged my loneliness for this den filled with poverty-stricken anguish, for these dying flies and furniture with legs missing?

O Gods of my youth! How different this dreary jumble was from my neighbors' love with its rolling, drawn-out moans.

Vera put her hands under her breasts and jiggled them.

"Why do you sit half dead, hanging your head?" she sang. "Come over here!"

I didn't move. Vera pressed her shirt to her stomach and sat down again on the bed.

"Or are you sorry you gave me the money?"

"I don't care about the money."

I said this in a cracking voice.

"What do you mean, you don't care? You a thief or something?"

"I'm not a thief."

"You work for thieves?"

"I'm a boy."

"Well, I can see you're not a cow," Vera mumbled. Her eyes were falling shut. She lay down and, pulling me over to her, started rubbing my body.

"A boy!" I shouted. "You understand what I'm saying? An Armenian's boy!"

O Gods of my youth! Five out of the twenty years I'd lived had gone into thinking up stories, thousands of stories, sucking my brain dry. These stories lay on my heart like a toad on a stone. One of these stories, pried loose by the power of loneliness, fell onto the ground. It was to be my fate, it seems, that a Tiflis prostitute was to be my first reader. I went cold at the suddenness of my invention, and told her the story about the boy and the Armenian. Had I been lazier and given less thought to my craft, I would have made up a drab story about a son thrown out by his rich official of a father – the father a despot, the mother a martyr. I didn't make such a mistake. A well-thought-out story doesn't need to resemble real life. Life itself tries with all its might to resemble a well-crafted story. And for this reason, and also because it was necessary for my listener, I had it that I was born in the town of Alyoshki in the district of Kherson. My father worked as a draftsman in the office of a river steamship company. He toiled night and day over his drawing board so that he could give us children an education, but we took after our mother, who was fond of fun and food. When I was ten I began stealing money from my father, and a few years later ran away to Baku to live with some relatives on my mother's side. They introduced me to Stepan Ivanovich, an Armenian. I became friends with him, and we lived together for four years.

"How old were you then?"

"Fifteen."

Vera was waiting to hear about the evil deeds of the Armenian who had corrupted me.

"We lived together for four years," I continued, "and Stepan Ivanovich turned out to be the most generous and trusting man I had ever met – the most conscientious and honorable man. He trusted every single friend of his to the fullest. I should have learned a trade in those four years, but I didn't lift a finger. The only thing on my mind was billiards. Stepan Ivanovich's friends ruined him. He gave them bronze promissory notes, and his friends went and cashed them right away."

Bronze promissory notes! I myself had no idea how I came up with that. But it was a very good idea. Vera believed everything once she heard "bronze promissory notes." She wrapped herself in her shawl and her shawl shuddered on her shoulders.

"They ruined Stepan Ivanovich. He was thrown out of his apartment and his furniture was auctioned off. He became a traveling salesman. When he lost all his money I left him and went to live with a rich old man, a church warden."

Church warden! I stole the idea from some novel, but it was the invention of a mind too lazy to create a real character.

I said church warden, and Vera's eyes blinked and slipped out from under my spell. To regain my ground, I squeezed asthma into the old man's yellow chest.

"Asthma attacks whistled hoarsely inside his yellow chest. The old man would jump up from his bed in the middle of the night and, moaning, breath in the kerosene-colored night of Baku. He died soon after. The asthma suffocated him." I told her that my relatives would have nothing to do with me and that here I was, in Tiflis, with twenty rubles to my name, the very rubles she had counted in that entrance on Golovinsky Boulevard. The waiter at the hotel where I was staying promised to send me rich clients, but up to now had only sent me taproom keepers with tumbling bellies, men who love their country, their songs, and their wine and who don't think twice about trampling on a foreign soul or a foreign woman, like a village thief will trample on his neighbor's garden.

And I started jabbering about low-down taproom keepers, bits of information I had picked up somewhere. Self-pity tore my heart to pieces; I had been completely ruined. I quaked with sorrow and inspiration. Streams of icy sweat trickled down my face like snakes winding through grass warmed by the sun. I fell silent, began to cry, and turned away. My story had come to an end. The kerosene burner had died out a long time ago. The water had boiled and cooled down again. The enema tube was dangling against the wall. Vera walked silently over to the window. Her back, dazzling and sad, moved in front of me. Outside the window the sun was beginning to light the mountain crevices.

"The things men do," Vera whispered, without turning around. "My God, the things men do!"

She stretched out her bare arms and opened the shutters all the way. The cooling flagstones on the street hissed. The smell of water and dust came rolling up the carriageway. Vera's head drooped.

"In other words, you're a whore. One of us – a bitch," she said.

I hung my head.

"Yes, I'm one of you – a bitch."

Vera turned around to face me. Her shirt hung in twisted tatters from her body.

"The things men do," she repeated more loudly. "My God, the things men do. So . . . have you ever been with a woman?"

I pressed my icy lips to her hand.

"No. . . . How could I have? Who would have wanted me?"

My head shook beneath her breasts, which rose freely above me. Her stretched nipples bounced against my cheeks, opening their moist eyelids and cavorting like calves. Vera looked at me from above.

"My little sister," she whispered, settling down on the floor next to me. "My little whorelet sister."

Now tell me, dear reader, I would like to ask you something: have you ever watched a village carpenter helping a fellow carpenter build a hut for himself and seen how vigorous, strong, and cheerful the shavings fly as they plane the wooden planks? That night a thirty-year-old woman taught me her trade. That night I learned secrets that you will never learn, experienced love that you will never experience, heard women's words that only other women hear. I have forgotten them. We are not supposed to remember them.

It was morning when we fell asleep. We were awakened by the heat of our bodies, a heat that weighed the bed down like a stone. When we awoke we laughed together. That day I didn't go to the printing press. We drank tea in the bazaar of the old quarters. A placid Turk carrying a samovar wrapped in a towel poured tea, crimson as a brick, steaming like blood freshly spilled on the earth. The smoking fire of the sun blazed on the walls of our glasses. The drawn-out braying of donkeys mingled with the hammering of blacksmiths. Copper pots were lined up under canopies, on faded carpets. Dogs were burrowing their muzzles into ox entrails. A caravan of dust flew toward Tiflis, the town of roses and mutton fat. The dust carried off the crimson fire of the sun. The Turk poured tea and kept count of the rolls we ate. The world was beautiful just for our sake. Covered in beads of sweat, I turned my glass upside down. I paid the Turk and pushed two golden five-ruble coins over to Vera. Her chunky leg was lying over mine. She pushed the money away and pulled in her leg.

"Do you want us to quarrel, my little sister?"

No, I didn't want to quarrel. We agreed to meet again in the evening, and I slipped back into my wallet the two golden fivers – my first fee.

Since that day many years have passed, and I have often been given money by editors, men of letters, and Jews selling books. For victories that were defeats, for defeats that turned into victories, for life and death, they paid me a trivial fee, much lower than the fee I was paid in my youth by my first reader. But I am not bitter. I am not bitter because I know that I will not die until I snatch one more gold ruble (and definitely not the last one!) from love's hands.

BABYLON REVISITED

F. Scott Fitzgerald

F. Scott Fitzgerald (1896–1940) wrote four novels, including *The Great Gatsby* and *Tender is the Night*, and a host of stories that reflected the age he lived in, between the wars. Born in Minnesota, he hung around Princeton for a while writing, and met Zelda Sayre, who he married in 1920. The Fitzgeralds lived in Paris for a while, but – in the words of Ira Gershwin's 'The Saga of Jenny' – "gin and rum and destiny, they play funny tricks", and Fitzgerald was dead, aged forty-four.

"And where's Mr. Campbell?" Charlie asked.

"Gone to Switzerland. Mr. Campbell's a pretty sick man, Mr. Wales."

"I'm sorry to hear that. And George Hardt?" Charlie inquired.

"Back in America, gone to work."

"And where is the Snow Bird?"

"He was in here last week. Anyway, his friend, Mr. Schaeffer, is in Paris."

Two familiar names from the long list of a year and a half ago. Charlie scribbled an address in his notebook and tore out the page.

"If you see Mr. Schaeffer, give him this," he said. "It's my brother-in-law's address. I haven't settled on a hotel yet."

He was not really disappointed to find Paris was so empty. But the stillness in the Ritz bar was strange and portentous. It was not an American bar any more – he felt polite in it, and not as if he owned it. It had gone back into France. He felt the stillness from the moment he got out of the taxi and saw the doorman, usually in a frenzy of activity at this hour, gossiping with a *chasseur* by the servants' entrance.

Passing through the corridor, he heard only a single, bored voice in the once-clamorous women's room. When he turned into the bar he travelled the twenty feet of green carpet with his eyes fixed straight ahead by old habit; and then, with his foot firmly on the rail, he turned and surveyed the room, encountering only a single pair of eyes that fluttered up from a newspaper in the corner. Charlie asked for the head barman, Paul, who in the latter days of the bull market had come to work in his own custom-built car – disembarking, however, with due nicety at the nearest corner. But Paul was at his country house today and Alix giving him information.

"No, no more," Charlie said, "I'm going slow these days."

Alix congratulated him: "You were going pretty strong a couple of years ago."

"I'll stick to it all right," Charlie assured him. "I've stuck to it for over a year and a half now."

"How do you find conditions in America?"

"I haven't been to America for months. I'm in business in Prague, representing a couple of concerns there. They don't know about me down there."

Alix smiled.

"Remember the night of George Hardt's bachelor dinner here?" said Charlie. "By the way, what's become of Claude Fessenden?"

Alix lowered his voice confidentially: "He's in Paris, but he doesn't come here any more. Paul doesn't allow it. He ran up a bill of thirty thousand francs, charging all his drinks and his lunches, and usually his dinner, for more than a year. And when Paul finally told him he had to pay, he gave him a bad check."

Alix shook his head sadly.

"I don't understand it, such a dandy fellow. Now he's all bloated up –" He made a plump apple of his hands.

Charlie watched a group of strident queens installing themselves in a corner.

"Nothing affects them," he thought. "Stocks rise and fall, people loaf or work, but they go on forever." The place oppressed him. He called for the dice and shook with Alix for the drink.

"Here for long, Mr. Wales?"

"I'm here for four or five days to see my little girl."

"Oh-h! You have a little girl?"

Outside, the fire-red, gas-blue, ghost-green signs shone smokily through the tranquil rain. It was late afternoon and the streets were in movement; the *bistros* gleamed. At the corner of the Boulevard des Capucines he took a taxi. The Place de la Concorde moved by in pink majesty; they crossed the logical Seine, and Charlie felt the sudden provincial quality of the Left Bank.

Charlie directed his taxi to the Avenue de l'Opera, which was out of his way. But he wanted to see the blue hour spread over the magnificent façade, and imagine that the cab horns, playing endlessly the first few bars of *La Plus que Lent,* were the trumpets of the Second Empire. They were closing the iron grill in front of Brentano's Book-store, and people were already at dinner behind the trim little bourgeois hedge of Duval's. He had never eaten at a really cheap restaurant in Paris. Five-course dinner, four francs fifty, eighteen cents, wine included. For some odd reason he wished that he had.

As they rolled on to the Left Bank and he felt its sudden provincialism, he thought, "I spoiled this city for myself. I didn't realize it, but the days came along one after another, and then two years were gone, and everything was gone, and I was gone."

He was thirty-five, and good to look at. The Irish mobility of his face was sobered by a deep wrinkle between his eyes. As he rang his brother-in-law's bell in the Rue Palatine, the wrinkle deepened till it pulled down his brows; he felt a cramping sensation in his belly. From behind the maid who opened the door darted a lovely little girl of nine who shrieked "Daddy!" and flew up, struggling like a fish, into his arms. She pulled his head around by one ear and set her cheek against his.

"My old pie," he said.

"Oh, daddy, daddy, daddy, daddy, dads, dads, dads!"

She drew him into the salon, where the family waited, a boy and girl his daughter's age, his sister-in-law and her husband. He greeted Marion with his voice pitched carefully to avoid either feigned enthusiasm or dislike, but her response was more frankly tepid, though she minimized her expression of unalterable distrust by directing her regard toward his child. The two men clasped hands in a friendly way and Lincoln Peters rested his for a moment on Charlie's shoulder.

The room was warm and comfortably American. The three children moved intimately about, playing through the yellow oblongs that led to other rooms; the cheer of six o'clock spoke in the eager smacks of the fire and the sounds of French activity in the kitchen. But Charlie did not relax; his heart sat up rigidly in his body and he drew confidence from his daughter, who from time to time came close to him, holding in her arms the doll he had brought.

"Really extremely well," he declared in answer to Lincoln's question. "There's a lot of business there that isn't moving at all, but we're doing even better than ever. In fact, damn well. I'm bringing my sister over from America next month to keep house for me. My income last year was bigger than it was when I had money. You see, the Czechs –"

His boasting was for a specific purpose; but after a moment, seeing a faint restiveness in Lincoln's eye, he changed the subject:

"Those are fine children of yours, well brought up, good manners."

"We think Honoria's a great little girl too."

Marion Peters came back from the kitchen. She was a tall woman with worried eyes, who had once possessed a fresh American loveliness. Charlie had never been sensitive to it and was always surprised when people spoke of how pretty she had been. From the first there had been an instinctive antipathy between them.

"Well, how do you find Honoria?" she asked.

"Wonderful. I was astonished how much she's grown in ten months. All the children are looking well."

"We haven't had a doctor for a year. How do you like being back in Paris?"

"It seems very funny to see so few Americans around."

"I'm delighted," Marion said vehemently. "Now at least you can go into a store without their assuming you're a millionaire. We've suffered like everybody, but on the whole it's a good deal pleasanter."

"But it was nice while it lasted," Charlie said. "We were a sort of royalty, almost infallible, with a sort of magic around us. In the bar this afternoon" – he stumbled, seeing his mistake – "there wasn't a man I knew."

She looked at him keenly. "I should think you'd have had enough of bars."

"I only stayed a minute. I take one drink every afternoon, and no more."

"Don't you want a cocktail before dinner?" Lincoln asked.

"I take only one drink every afternoon, and I've had that."

"I hope you keep to it," said Marion.

Her dislike was evident in the coldness with which she spoke, but Charlie only smiled; he had larger plans. Her very aggressiveness gave him an advantage, and he knew enough to wait. He wanted them to initiate the discussion of what they knew had brought him to Paris.

At dinner he couldn't decide whether Honoria was most like him or her mother. Fortunate if she didn't combine the traits of both that had brought them to disaster. A great wave of protectiveness went over him. He thought he knew what to do for her. He believed in character; he wanted to jump back a whole generation and trust in character again as the eternally valuable element. Everything wore out.

He left soon after dinner, but not to go home. He was curious to see Paris by night with clearer and more judicious eyes than those of other days. He bought *astrapontin* for the Casino and watched Josephine Baker go through her chocolate arabesques.

After an hour he left and strolled toward Montmartre, up the Rue Pigalle into the Place Blanche. The rain had stopped and there were a few people in evening clothes disembarking from taxis in front of cabarets, and *cocottes* prowling singly or in pairs, and many Negroes. He passed a lighted door from which issued music, and stopped with the sense of familiarity; it was Bricktop's, where he had parted with so many hours and so much money. A few doors farther on he found another ancient rendezvous and incautiously put his head inside. Immediately an eager orchestra burst into sound, a pair of professional dancers leaped to their feet and a maître d'hôtel swooped toward him, crying, "Crowd just arriving, sir!" But he withdrew quickly.

"You have to be damn drunk," he thought.

Zelli's was closed, the bleak and sinister cheap hotels surrounding it were dark; up in the Rue Blanche there was more light and a local, colloquial French crowd. The Poet's Cave had disappeared, but the two great mouths of the Café of Heaven and the Café of Hell still yawned – even devoured, as he watched, the meager contents of a tourist bus – a German, a Japanese, and an American couple who glanced at him with frightened eyes.

So much for the effort and ingenuity of Montmartre. All the catering to vice and waste was on an utterly childish scale, and he suddenly realized the meaning of the word "dissipate" – to dissipate into thin air; to make nothing out of something. In the little hours of the night every move from place to place was an enormous human jump, an increase of paying for the privilege of slower and slower motion.

He remembered thousand-franc notes given to an orchestra for playing a single number, hundred-franc notes tossed to a doorman for calling a cab.

But it hadn't been given for nothing.

It had been given, even the most wildly squandered sum, as an offering to destiny that he might not remember the things most worth remembering, the things that now he would always remember – his child taken from his control, his wife escaped to a grave in Vermont.

In the glare of a *brasserie* a woman spoke to him. He bought her some eggs and coffee, and then, eluding her encouraging stare, gave her a twenty-franc note and took a taxi to his hotel.

II

He woke upon a fine fall day – football weather. The depression of yesterday was gone and he liked the people on the streets. At noon he sat opposite Honoria at Le Grand Vatel, the only restaurant he could think of not reminiscent of champagne dinners and long luncheons that began at two and ended in a blurred and vague twilight.

"Now, how about vegetables? Oughtn't you to have some vegetables?"

"Well, yes."

"Here's *épinards* and *chou-fleur* and carrots and *haricots*."

"I'd like *chou-fleur*."

"Wouldn't you like to have two vegetables?"

"I usually only have one at lunch."

The waiter was pretending to be inordinately fond of children. *"Qu'elle est mignonne la petite? Elle parle exactement comme une Française."*

"How about dessert? Shall we wait and see?"

The waiter disappeared. Honoria looked at her father expectantly.

"What are we going to do?"

"First, we're going to that toy store in the Rue Saint-Honoré and buy you anything you like. And then we're going to the vaudeville at the Empire."

She hesitated. "I like it about the vaudeville, but not the toy store."

"Why not?"

"Well, you brought me this doll." She had it with her. "And I've got lots of things. And we're not rich any more, are we?"

"We never were. But today you are to have anything you want."

"All right," she agreed resignedly.

When there had been her mother and a French nurse he had been inclined to be strict; now he extended himself, reached out for a new tolerance; he must be both parents to her and not shut any of her out of communication.

"I want to get to know you," he said gravely. "First let me introduce myself. My name is Charles J. Wales, of Prague."

"Oh, daddy!" her voice cracked with laughter.

"And who are you, please?" he persisted, and she accepted a role immediately: "Honoria Wales, Rue Palatine, Paris."

"Married or single?"

"No, not married. Single."

He indicated the doll. "But I see you have a child, madame."

Unwilling to disinherit it, she took it to her heart and thought quickly: "Yes, I've been married, but I'm not married now. My husband is dead."

He went on quickly, "And the child's name?"

"Simone. That's after my best friend at school."

"I'm very pleased that you're doing so well at school."

"I'm third this month," she boasted. "Elsie" – that was her cousin – "is only about eighteenth, and Richard is about at the bottom."

"You like Richard and Elsie, don't you?"

"Oh, yes. I like Richard quite well and I like her all right."

Cautiously and casually he asked: "And Aunt Marion and Uncle Lincoln – which do you like best?"

"Oh, Uncle Lincoln, I guess."

He was increasingly aware of her presence. As they came in, a murmur of ". . . adorable" followed them, and now the people at the next table bent all their silences upon her, staring as if she were something no more conscious than a flower.

"Why don't I live with you?" she asked suddenly. "Because mamma's dead?"

"You must stay here and learn more French. It would have been hard for daddy to take care of you so well."

"I don't really need much taking care of any more. I do everything for myself."

Going out of the restaurant, a man and a woman unexpectedly hailed him.

"Well, the old Wales!"

"Hello there, Lorraine. . . . Dunc."

Sudden ghosts out of the past: Duncan Schaeffer, a friend from college. Lorraine Quarrles, a lovely, pale blonde of thirty; one of a crowd who had helped them make months into days in the lavish times of three years ago.

"My husband couldn't come this year," she said, in answer to his question. "We're poor as hell. So he gave me two hundred a month and told me I could do my worst on that. . . . This your little girl?"

"What about coming back and sitting down?" Duncan asked.

"Can't do it." He was glad for an excuse. As always, he felt Lorraine's passionate, provocative attraction, but his own rhythm was different now.

"Well, how about dinner?" she asked.

"I'm not free. Give me your address and let me call you."

"Charlie, I believe you're sober," she said judicially. "I honestly believe he's sober, Dunc. Pinch him and see if he's sober."

Charlie indicated Honoria with his head. They both laughed.

"What's your address?" said Duncan sceptically.

He hesitated, unwilling to give the name of his hotel.

"I'm not settled yet. I'd better call you. We're going to see the vaudeville at the Empire."

"There! That's what I want to do," Lorraine said. "I want to see some clowns and acrobats and jugglers. That's just what we'll do, Dunc."

"We've got to do an errand first," said Charlie. "Perhaps we'll see you there."

"All right, you snob. . . . Good-by, beautiful little girl."

"Good-by."

Honoria bobbed politely.

Somehow, an unwelcome encounter. They liked him because he was functioning, because he was serious; they wanted to see him, because he was stronger than they were now, because they wanted to draw a certain sustenance from his strength.

At the Empire, Honoria proudly refused to sit upon her father's folded coat. She was already an individual with a code of her own, and Charlie was more and more absorbed by the desire of putting a little of himself into her before she crystallized utterly. It was hopeless to try to know her in so short a time.

Between the acts they came upon Duncan and Lorraine in the lobby where the band was playing.

"Have a drink?"

"All right, but not up at the bar. We'll take a table."

"The perfect father."

Listening abstractedly to Lorraine, Charlie watched Honoria's eyes leave their table, and he followed them wistfully about the room, wondering what they saw. He met her glance and she smiled.

"I liked that lemonade," she said.

What had she said? What had he expected? Going home in a taxi afterward, he pulled her over until her head rested against his chest.

"Darling, do you ever think about your mother?"

"Yes, sometimes," she answered vaguely.

"I don't want you to forget her. Have you got a picture of her?"

"Yes, I think so. Anyhow, Aunt Marion has. Why don't you want me to forget her?"

"She loved you very much."

"I loved her too."

They were silent for a moment.

"Daddy, I want to come and live with you," she said suddenly.

His heart leaped; he had wanted it to come like this.

"Aren't you perfectly happy?"

"Yes, but I love you better than anybody. And you love me better than anybody, don't you, now that mummy's dead?"

"Of course I do. But you won't always like me best, honey. You'll grow up and meet somebody your own age and go marry him and forget you ever had a daddy."

"Yes, that's true," she agreed tranquilly.

He didn't go in. He was coming back at nine o'clock and he wanted to keep himself fresh and new for the thing he must say then.

"When you're safe inside, just show yourself in that window."

"All right. Good-by, dads, dads, dads, dads."

He waited in the dark street until she appeared, all warm and glowing, in the window above and kissed her fingers out into the night.

III

They were waiting. Marion sat behind the coffee service in a dignified black dinner dress that just faintly suggested mourning. Lincoln was walking up and down with the animation of one who had already been talking. They were as anxious as he was to get into the question. He opened it almost immediately:

"I suppose you know what I want to see you about – why I really came to Paris."

Marion played with the black stars on her necklace and frowned.

"I'm awfully anxious to have a home," he continued. "And I'm awfully anxious to have Honoria in it. I appreciate your taking in Honoria for her mother's sake, but things have changed now" – he hesitated and then continued more forcibly – "changed radically with me, and I want to ask you to reconsider the matter. It would be silly for me to deny that about three years ago I was acting badly –"

Marion looked up at him with hard eyes.

"– but all that's over. As I told you, I haven't had more than a drink a day for over a year, and I take that drink deliberately, so that the idea of alcohol won't get too big in my imagination. You see the idea?"

"No," said Marion succinctly.

"It's a sort of stunt I set myself. It keeps the matter in proportion."

"I get you," said Lincoln. "You don't want to admit it's got any attraction for you."

"Something like that. Sometimes I forget and don't take it. But I try to take it. Anyhow, I couldn't afford to drink in my position. The people I represent are more than satisfied with what I've done, and I'm bringing my sister over from Burlington to keep house for me, and I want awfully to have Honoria too. You know that even when her mother and I weren't getting along well we never let anything that happened touch Honoria. I know she's fond of me and I know I'm able to take care of her and – well, there you are. How do you feel about it?"

He knew that now he would have to take a beating. It would last an hour or two hours, and it would be difficult, but if he modulated his inevitable resentment to the chastened attitude of the reformed sinner, he might win his point in the end.

Keep your temper, he told himself. You don't want to be justified. You want Honoria.

Lincoln spoke first: "We've been talking it over ever since we got your letter last month. We're happy to have Honoria here. She's a dear little thing, and we're glad to be able to help her, but of course that isn't the question –"

Marion interrupted suddenly. "How long are you going to stay sober, Charlie?" she asked.

"Permanently, I hope."

"How can anybody count on that?"

"You know I never did drink heavily until I gave up business and came over here with nothing to do. Then Helen and I began to run around with –"

"Please leave Helen out of it. I can't bear to hear you talk about her like that."

He stared at her grimly; he had never been certain how fond of each other the sisters were in life.

"My drinking only lasted about a year and a half – from the time we came over until I – collapsed."

"It was time enough."

"It was time enough," he agreed.

"My duty is entirely to Helen," she said. "I try to think what she would have wanted me to do. Frankly, from the night you did that terrible thing you haven't really existed for me. I can't help that. She was my sister."

"Yes."

"When she was dying she asked me to look out for Honoria. If you hadn't been in a sanitarium then, it might have helped matters."

He had no answer.

"I'll never in my life be able to forget the morning when Helen knocked at my door, soaked to the skin and shivering, and said you'd locked her out."

Charlie gripped the sides of the chair. This was more difficult than he expected; he wanted to launch out into a long expostulation and explanation, but he only said: "The night I locked her out –" and she interrupted, "I don't feel up to going over that again."

After a moment's silence Lincoln said: "We're getting off the subject. You want Marion to set aside her legal guardianship and give you Honoria. I think the main point for her is whether she has confidence in you or not."

"I don't blame Marion," Charlie said slowly, "but I think she can have entire confidence in me. I had a good record up to three years ago. Of course, it's within human possibilities I might go wrong any time. But if we wait much longer I'll lose Honoria's childhood and my chance for a home." He shook his head, "I'll simply lose her, don't you see?"

"Yes, I see," said Lincoln.

"Why didn't you think of all this before?" Marion asked.

"I suppose I did, from time to time, but Helen and I were getting along badly. When I consented to the guardianship, I was flat on my back in a sanitarium and the market had cleaned me out. I knew I'd acted badly, and I thought if it would bring any peace to Helen, I'd agree to anything. But now it's different. I'm functioning, I'm behaving damn well, so far as –"

"Please don't swear at me," Marion said.

He looked at her, startled. With each remark the force of her dislike became more and more apparent. She had built up all her fear of life into one wall and faced it toward him. This trivial reproof was possibly the result of some trouble with the cook several hours before. Charlie became increasingly alarmed at leaving Honoria in this atmosphere of hostility against himself; sooner or later it would come out, in a word here, a shake of the head there, and some of that distrust would be irrevocably implanted in Honoria. But he pulled his temper down out of his face and shut it up inside him; he had won a point, for Lincoln realized the absurdity of Marion's remark and asked her lightly since when she had objected to the word "damn."

"Another thing," Charlie said: "I'm able to give her certain advantages now. I'm going to take a French governess to Prague with me. I've got a lease on a new apartment –"

He stopped, realizing that he was blundering. They couldn't be expected to accept with equanimity the fact that his income was again twice as large as their own.

"I suppose you can give her more luxuries than we can," said Marion. "When you were throwing away money we were living along watching every ten francs. . . . I suppose you'll start doing it again."

"Oh, no," he said. "I've learned. I worked hard for ten years, you know – until I got lucky in the market, like so many people. Terribly lucky. It didn't seem any use working any more, so I quit. It won't happen again."

There was a long silence. All of them felt their nerves straining, and for the first time in a year Charlie wanted a drink. He was sure now that Lincoln Peters wanted him to have his child.

Marion shuddered suddenly; part of her saw that Charlie's feet were planted on the earth now, and her own maternal feeling recognized the naturalness of his desire; but she had lived for a long time with a prejudice – a prejudice founded on a curious disbelief in her sister's happiness, and which, in the shock of one terrible night, had turned to hatred for him. It had all happened at a point in her life where the discouragement of ill health and adverse circumstances made it necessary for her to believe in tangible villainy and a tangible villain.

"I can't help what I think!" she cried out suddenly. "How much you were responsible for Helen's death, I don't know. It's something you'll have to square with your own conscience."

An electric current of agony surged through him; for a moment he was almost on his feet, an unuttered sound echoing in his throat. He hung on to himself for a moment, another moment.

"Hold on there," said Lincoln uncomfortably. "I never thought you were responsible for that."

"Helen died of heart trouble," Charlie said dully.

"Yes, heart trouble." Marion spoke as if the phrase had another meaning for her.

Then, in the flatness that followed her outburst, she saw him plainly and she knew he had somehow arrived at control over the situation. Glancing at her husband, she found no help from him, and as abruptly as if it were a matter of no importance, she threw up the sponge.

"Do what you like!" she cried, springing up from her chair. "She's your child. I'm not the person to stand in your way. I think if it were my child I'd rather see her –" She managed to check herself. "You two decide it. I can't stand this. I'm sick. I'm going to bed."

She hurried from the room; after a moment Lincoln said:

"This has been a hard day for her. You know how strongly she feels –" His voice was almost apologetic: "When a woman gets an idea in her head."

"Of course."

"It's going to be all right. I think she sees now that you – can provide for the child, and so we can't very well stand in your way or Honoria's way."

"Thank you, Lincoln."

"I'd better go along and see how she is."

"I'm going."

He was still trembling when he reached the street, but a walk down the Rue Bonaparte to the quais set him up, and as he crossed the Seine, fresh and new by the quai lamps, he felt exultant. But back in his room he couldn't sleep. The image of Helen haunted him. Helen whom he had loved so until they had senselessly begun to abuse each other's love, tear it into shreds. On that terrible February night that Marion remembered so vividly, a slow quarrel had gone on for hours. There was a scene at the Florida, and then he attempted to take her home, and then she kissed young Webb at a table; after that there was what she had hysterically said. When he arrived home alone he turned the key in the lock in wild anger. How could he know she would arrive an hour later alone, that there would be a snowstorm in which she wandered about in slippers, too confused to find a taxi? Then the aftermath, her escaping pneumonia by a miracle, and all the attendant horror. They were "reconciled," but that was the beginning of the end, and Marion, who had seen with her own eyes and who imagined it to be one of many scenes from her sister's martyrdom, never forgot.

Going over it again brought Helen nearer, and in the white, soft light that steals upon half sleep near morning he found himself talking to her again. She said that he was perfectly right about Honoria and that she wanted Honoria to be with him. She said she was glad he was being good and doing better. She said a lot of other things – very friendly things – but she was in a swing in a white dress, and swinging faster and faster all the time, so that at the end he could not hear clearly all that she said.

IV

He woke up feeling happy. The door of the world was open again. He made plans, vistas, futures for Honoria and himself, but suddenly he grew sad, remembering all the plans he and Helen had made. She had not planned to die. The present was the thing – work to do and someone to love. But not to love too much, for he knew the injury that a father can do to a daughter or a mother to a son by attaching them too closely: afterward, out in the world, the child would seek in the marriage partner the same blind tenderness and, failing probably to find it, turn against love and life.

It was another bright, crisp day. He called Lincoln Peters at the bank where he worked and asked if he could count on taking Honoria when he left for Prague. Lincoln agreed that there was no reason for delay. One thing – the legal guardianship. Marion wanted to retain that a while longer. She was upset by the whole matter, and it would oil things if she felt that the situation was still in her control for another year. Charlie agreed, wanting only the tangible, visible child.

Then the question of a governess. Charlie sat in a gloomy agency and talked to a cross Béarnaise and to a buxom Breton peasant, neither of whom he could have endured. There were others whom he would see tomorrow.

He lunched with Lincoln Peters at Griffons, trying to keep down his exultation.

"There's nothing quite like your own child," Lincoln said. "But you understand how Marion feels too."

"She's forgotten how hard I worked for seven years there," Charlie said. "She just remembers one night."

"There's another thing." Lincoln hesitated. "While you and Helen were tearing around Europe throwing money away, we were just getting along. I didn't touch any of the prosperity because I never got ahead enough to carry anything but my insurance. I think Marion felt there was some kind of injustice in it – you not even working toward the end, and getting richer and richer."

"It went just as quick as it came," said Charlie.

"Yes, a lot of it stayed in the hands of *chasseurs* and saxophone players and maîtres d'hôtel – well, the big party's over now. I just said that to explain Marion's feeling about those crazy years. If you drop in about six o'clock tonight before Marion's too tired, we'll settle the details on the spot."

Back at his hotel, Charlie found a *pneumatique* that had been redirected from the Ritz bar where Charlie had left his address for the purpose of finding a certain man.

DEAR CHARLIE: You were so strange when we saw you the other day that I wondered if I did something to offend you. If so, I'm not conscious of it. In fact, I have thought about you too much for the last year, and it's always been in the back of my mind that I might see you if I came over here. We *did* have such good times that crazy spring, like the night you and I stole the butcher's tricycle, and the time we tried to call on the president and you had the old derby rim and the wire cane. Everybody seems so old lately, but I don't feel old a bit. Couldn't we get together some time today for old time's sake? I've got a vile hang-over for the moment, but will be feeling better this afternoon and will look for you about five in the sweat-shop at the Ritz.

Always devotedly,
LORRAINE.

His first feeling was one of awe that he had actually, in his mature years, stolen a tricycle and pedalled Lorraine all over the Étoile between the small hours and dawn. In retrospect it was a nightmare. Locking out Helen didn't fit in with any other act of his life, but the tricycle incident did – it was one of many. How many weeks or months of dissipation to arrive at that condition of utter irresponsibility?

He tried to picture how Lorraine had appeared to him then – very attractive; Helen was unhappy about it, though she said nothing. Yesterday, in the restaurant, Lorraine had seemed trite, blurred, worn away. He emphatically did not want to see her, and he was glad Alix had not given away his hotel address. It was a relief to think, instead, of Honoria, to think of Sundays spent with her and of saying good morning to her and of knowing she was there in his house at night, drawing her breath in the darkness.

At five he took a taxi and bought presents for all the Peters – a piquant cloth doll, a box of Roman soldiers, flowers for Marion, big linen handkerchiefs for Lincoln.

He saw, when he arrived in the apartment, that Marion had accepted the inevitable. She greeted him now as though he were a recalcitrant member of the family, rather than a menacing outsider. Honoria had been told she was going; Charlie was glad to see that her tact made her conceal her excessive happiness. Only on his lap did she whisper her delight and the question "When?" before she slipped away with the other children.

He and Marion were alone for a minute in the room, and on an impulse he spoke out boldly:

"Family quarrels are bitter things. They don't go according to any rules. They're not like aches or wounds; they're more like splits in the skin that won't heal because there's not enough material. I wish you and I could be on better terms."

"Some things are hard to forget," she answered. "It's a question of confidence." There was no answer to this and presently she asked, "When do you propose to take her?"

"As soon as I can get a governess. I hoped the day after tomorrow."

"That's impossible. I've got to get her things in shape. Not before Saturday."

He yielded. Coming back into the room, Lincoln offered him a drink.

"I'll take my daily whisky," he said.

It was warm here, it was a home, people together by a fire. The children felt very safe and important; the mother and father were serious, watchful. They had things to do for the children more important than his visit here. A spoonful of medicine was, after all, more important than the strained relations between Marion and himself. They were not dull people, but they were very much in the grip of life and circumstances. He wondered if he couldn't do something to get Lincoln out of his rut at the bank.

A long peal at the door-bell; the *bonne à tout faire* passed through and went down the corridor. The door opened upon another long ring, and then voices, and the three in the salon looked up expectantly; Lincoln moved to bring the corridor within his range of vision, and Marion rose. Then the maid came back along the corridor, closely followed by the voices, which developed under the light into Duncan Schaeffer and Lorraine Quarrles.

They were gay, they were hilarious, they were roaring with laughter. For a moment Charlie was astounded; unable to understand how they ferreted out the Peters' address.

"Ah-h-h!" Duncan wagged his finger roguishly at Charlie. "Ah-h-h!"

They both slid down another cascade of laughter. Anxious and at a loss, Charlie shook hands with them quickly and presented them to Lincoln and Marion. Marion nodded, scarcely speaking. She had drawn back a step toward the fire; her little girl stood beside her, and Marion put an arm about her shoulder.

With growing annoyance at the intrusion, Charlie waited for them to explain themselves. After some concentration Duncan said:

"We came to invite you out to dinner. Lorraine and I insist that all this shishi, cagy business 'bout your address got to stop."

Charlie came closer to them, as if to force them backward down the corridor.

"Sorry, but I can't. Tell me where you'll be and I'll phone you in half an hour."

This made no impression. Lorraine sat down suddenly on the side of a chair, and focussing her eyes on Richard, cried, "Oh, what a nice little boy! Come here, little boy." Richard glanced at his mother, but did not move. With a perceptible shrug of her shoulders, Lorraine turned back to Charlie:

"Come and dine. Sure your cousins won' mine. See you so sel'om. Or solemn."

"I can't," said Charlie sharply. "You two have dinner and I'll phone you."

Her voice became suddenly unpleasant. "All right, we'll go. But I remember once when you hammered on my door at four A.M. I was enough of a good sport to give you a drink. Come on, Dunc."

Still in slow motion, with blurred, angry faces, with uncertain feet, they retired along the corridor.

"Good night," Charlie said.

"Good night!" responded Lorraine emphatically.

When he went back into the salon Marion had not moved, only now her son was standing in the circle of her other arm. Lincoln was still swinging Honoria back and forth like a pendulum from side to side.

"What an outrage!" Charlie broke out. "What an absolute outrage!" Neither of them answered. Charlie dropped into an armchair, picked up his drink, set it down again and said:

"People I haven't seen for two years having the colossal nerve –"

He broke off. Marion had made the sound "Oh!" in one swift, furious breath, turned her body from him with a jerk and left the room.

Lincoln set down Honoria carefully.

"You children go in and start your soup," he said, and when they obeyed, he said to Charlie:

"Marion's not well and she can't stand shocks. That kind of people make her really physically sick."

"I didn't tell them to come here. They wormed your name out of somebody. They deliberately –"

"Well, it's too bad. It doesn't help matters. Excuse me a minute."

Left alone, Charlie sat tense in his chair. In the next room he could hear the children eating, talking in monosyllables, already oblivious to the scene between their elders. He heard a murmur of conversation from a farther room and then the ticking bell of a telephone receiver picked up, and in a panic he moved to the other side of the room and out of earshot.

In a minute Lincoln came back. "Look here, Charlie. I think we'd better call off dinner for tonight. Marion's in bad shape."

"Is she angry with me?"

"Sort of," he said, almost roughly. "She's not strong and –"

"You mean she's changed her mind about Honoria?"

"She's pretty bitter right now. I don't know. You phone me at the bank tomorrow."

"I wish you'd explain to her I never dreamed these people would come here. I'm just as sore as you are."

"I couldn't explain anything to her now."

Charlie got up. He took his coat and hat and started down the corridor. Then he opened the door of the dining room and said in a strange voice, "Good night, children."

Honoria rose and ran around the table to hug him.

"Good night, sweetheart," he said vaguely, and then trying to make his voice more tender, trying to conciliate something, "Good night, dear children."

V

Charlie went directly to the Ritz bar with the furious idea of finding Lorraine and Duncan, but they were not there, and he realized that in any case there was nothing he could do. He had not touched his drink at the Peters', and now he ordered a whisky-and-soda. Paul came over to say hello.

"It's a great change," he said sadly. "We do about half the business we did. So many fellows I hear about back in the States lost everything, maybe not in the first crash, but then in the second. Your friend George Hardt lost every cent, I hear. Are you back in the States?"

"No, I'm in business in Prague."

"I heard that you lost a lot in the crash."

"I did," and he added grimly, "but I lost everything I wanted in the boom."

"Selling short."

"Something like that."

Again the memory of those days swept over him like a nightmare – the people they had met travelling; then people who couldn't add a row of figures or speak a coherent sentence. The little man Helen had consented to dance with at the ship's party, who had insulted her ten feet from the table; the women and girls carried screaming with drink or drugs out of public places –

– The men who locked their wives out in the snow, because the snow of twenty-nine wasn't real snow. If you didn't want it to be snow, you just paid some money.

He went to the phone and called the Peters' apartment; Lincoln answered.

"I called up because this thing is on my mind. Has Marion said anything definite?"

"Marion's sick," Lincoln answered shortly. "I know this thing isn't altogether your fault, but I can't have her go to pieces about it. I'm afraid we'll have to let it slide for six months; I can't take the chance of working her up to this state again."

"I see."

"I'm sorry, Charlie."

He went back to his table. His whisky glass was empty, but he shook his head when Alix looked at it questioningly. There wasn't much he could do now except send Honoria some things; he would send her a lot of things tomorrow. He thought rather angrily that this was just money – he had given so many people money. . . .

"No, no more," he said to another waiter. "What do I owe you?"

He would come back some day; they couldn't make him pay forever. But he wanted his child, and nothing was much good now, beside that fact. He wasn't young any more, with a lot of nice thoughts and dreams to have by himself. He was absolutely sure Helen wouldn't have wanted him to be so alone.

PIERRE MENARD, AUTHOR OF THE *QUIXOTE*

Jorge Luis Borges

Jorge Luis Borges (1899–1986) would have been remembered in dictionaries of quotations if only for his comment about the Falklands War (or *La Guerra de las Malvinas*) of 1982 being "a fight between two bald men over a comb", but he was also the author of *Fictions*, *The Book of Imaginary Beings* and a posthumously published collection of stories.

The visible *œuvre* left by this novelist can be easily and briefly enumerated; unpardonable, therefore, are the omissions and additions perpetrated by Mme. Henri Bachelier in a deceitful catalog that a certain newspaper, whose Protestant leanings are surely no secret, has been so inconsiderate as to inflict upon that newspaper's deplorable readers – few and Calvinist (if not Masonic arid circumcised) though they be. Menard's true friends have greeted that catalog with alarm, and even with a degree of sadness. One might note that only yesterday were we gathered before his marmoreal place of rest, among the dreary cypresses, and already Error is attempting to tarnish his bright Memory. . . . Most decidedly, a brief rectification is imperative.

I am aware that it is easy enough to call my own scant authority into question. I hope, nonetheless, that I shall not be prohibited from mentioning two high testimonials. The baroness de Bacourt (at whose unforgettable *vendredis* I had the honor to meet the mourned-for poet) has been so kind as to approve the lines that follow. Likewise, the countess de Bagnoregio, one of the rarest and most cultured spirits of the principality of Monaco (now of Pittsburgh, Pennsylvania, following her recent marriage to the international philanthropist Simon Kautzsch – a man, it grieves me to say, vilified and slandered by the victims of his disinterested operations), has sacrificed "to truth and to death" (as she herself has phrased it) the noble reserve that is the mark of her distinction, and in an open letter, published in the magazine *Luxe*, bestows upon me her blessing. Those commendations are sufficient, I should think.

I have said that the *visible* product of Menard's pen is easily enumerated. Having examined his personal files with the greatest care, I have established that this body of work consists of the following pieces:

a) a symbolist sonnet that appeared twice (with variants) in the review *La Conque* (in the numbers for March and October, 1899);

b) a monograph on the possibility of constructing a poetic vocabulary from concepts that are neither synonyms nor periphrastic locutions for the concepts that inform common speech, "but are, rather, ideal objects created by convention essentially for the needs of poetry" (Nîmes, 1901);

c) a monograph on "certain connections or affinities" between the philosophies of Descartes, Leibniz, and John Wilkins (Nîmes, 1903);

d) a monograph on Leibniz' *Characteristica universalis* (Nîmes, 1904);

e) a technical article on the possibility of enriching the game of chess by eliminating one of the rook's pawns (Menard proposes, recommends, debates, and finally rejects this innovation);

f) a monograph on Ramon Lull's *Ars magna generalis* (Nîmes, 1906);

g) a translation, with introduction and notes, of Ruy López de Segura's *Libro de la invención liberal y arte del juego del axedrez* (Paris, 1907);

h) drafts of a monograph on George Boole's symbolic logic;

i) a study of the essential metrical rules of French prose, illustrated with examples taken from Saint-Simon (*Revue des langues romanes*, Montpellier, October 1909);

j) a reply to Luc Durtain (who had countered that no such rules existed), illustrated with examples taken from Luc Durtain (*Revue des langues romanes*, Montpellier, December 1909);

k) a manuscript translation of Quevedo's *Aguja de navegar cultos*, titled *La boussole des précieux*;

l) a foreword to the catalog of an exhibit of lithographs by Carolus Hourcade (Nîmes, 1914);

m) a work entitled *Les problèmes d'un problème* (Paris, 1917), which discusses in chronological order the solutions to the famous problem of Achilles and the tortoise (two editions of this work have so far appeared; the second bears an epigraph consisting of Leibniz' advice "*Ne craignez point, monsieur, la tortue,*" and brings up to date the chapters devoted to Russell and Descartes);

n) a dogged analysis of the "syntactical habits" of Toulet (*N.R.F.*, March 1921) (Menard, I recall, affirmed that censure and praise were sentimental operations that bore not the slightest resemblance to criticism);

o) a transposition into alexandrines of Paul Valéry's *Cimetière marin* (*N.R.F.*, January 1928);

p) a diatribe against Paul Valéry, in Jacques Reboul's *Feuilles pour la suppression de la realité* (which diatribe, I might add parenthetically, states the exact reverse of Menard's true opinion of Valéry; Valéry understood this, and the two men's friendship was never imperiled);

q) a "definition" of the countess de Bagnoregio, in the "triumphant volume" (the phrase is that of another contributor, Gabriele d'Annunzio) published each year by that lady to rectify the inevitable biases of the popular press and to present "to the world and all of Italy" a true picture of her person, which was so exposed (by reason of her beauty and her bearing) to erroneous and/or hasty interpretations;

r) a cycle of admirable sonnets dedicated to the baroness de Bacourt (1934);

s) a handwritten list of lines of poetry that owe their excellence to punctuation.[1]

---

[1] Mme. Henri Bachelier also lists a literal translation of Quevedo's literal translation of St. Francis de Sales's *Introduction à la vie dévote*. In Pierre Menard's library there is no trace of such a work. This must be an instance of one of our friend's droll jokes, misheard or misunderstood.

This is the full extent (save for a few vague sonnets of occasion destined for Mme. Henri Bachelier's hospitable, or greedy, *album des souvenirs*) of the *visible* lifework of Pierre Menard, in proper chronological order. I shall turn now to the other, the subterranean, the interminably heroic production – the *œuvre nonpareil*, the *œuvre* that must remain – for such are our human limitations! – unfinished. This work, perhaps the most significant writing of our time, consists of the ninth and thirty-eighth chapters of Part I of *Don Quixote* and a fragment of Chapter XXII. I know that such a claim is on the face of it absurd; justifying that "absurdity" shall be the primary object of this note.[2]

Two texts, of distinctly unequal value, inspired the undertaking. One was that philological fragment by Novalis – number 2005 in the Dresden edition, to be precise – which outlines the notion of *total identification* with a given author. The other was one of those parasitic books that set Christ on a boulevard, Hamlet on La Cannabière, or don Quixote on Wall Street. Like every man of taste, Menard abominated those pointless travesties, which, Menard would say, were good for nothing but occasioning a plebeian delight in anachronism or (worse yet) captivating us with the elementary notion that all times and places are the same, or are different. It might be more interesting, he thought, though of contradictory and superficial execution, to attempt what Daudet had so famously suggested: conjoin in a single figure (Tartarin, say) both the Ingenious Gentleman don Quixote and his squire. . . .

Those who have insinuated that Menard devoted his life to writing a contemporary *Quixote* besmirch his illustrious memory. Pierre Menard did not want to compose *another* Quixote, which surely is easy enough – he wanted to compose *the* Quixote. Nor, surely, need one have to say that his goal was never a mechanical transcription of the original; he had no intention of *copying* it. His admirable ambition was to produce a number of pages which coincided – word for word and line for line – with those of Miguel de Cervantes.

"My purpose is merely astonishing," he wrote me on September 30, 1934, from Bayonne. "The final term of a theological or metaphysical proof – the world around us, or God, or chance, or universal Forms – is no more final, no more uncommon, than my revealed novel. The sole difference is that philosophers publish pleasant volumes containing the intermediate stages of their work, while I am resolved to suppress those stages of my own." And indeed there is not a single draft to bear witness to that years-long labor.

Initially, Menard's method was to be relatively simple: Learn Spanish, return to Catholicism, fight against the Moor or Turk, forget the history of Europe from 1602 to 1918 – *be* Miguel de Cervantes. Pierre Menard weighed that course (I know he pretty thoroughly mastered seventeenth-century Castilian) but he discarded it as too easy. Too impossible, rather!, the reader will say. Quite so, but the undertaking was impossible from the outset, and of all the impossible ways of bringing it about, this was the least interesting. To be a popular novelist of the seventeenth century in the twentieth seemed to Menard to be a diminution. Being, somehow, Cervantes, and arriving thereby at the

---

[2] I did, I might say, have the secondary purpose of drawing a small sketch of the figure of Pierre Menard – but how dare I complete with the gilded pages I am told the baroness de Bacourt is even now preparing, or with the delicate sharp *crayon* of Carolus Hourcade

Quixote – that looked to Menard less challenging (and therefore less interesting) than continuing to be Pierre Menard and coming to the Quixote *through the experiences of Pierre Menard*. (It was that conviction, by the way, that obliged him to leave out the autobiographical foreword to Part II of the novel. Including the prologue would have meant creating another character – "Cervantes" – and also presenting Quixote through that character's eyes, not Pierre Menard's. Menard, of course, spurned that easy solution.) "The task I have undertaken is not *in essence* difficult," I read at another place in that letter. "If I could just be immortal, I could do it." Shall I confess that I often imagine that he did complete it, and that I read the Quixote – the *entire* Quixote – as if Menard had conceived it? A few nights ago, as I was leafing through Chapter XXVI (never attempted by Menard), I recognized our friend's style, could almost hear his voice in this marvelous phrase: "the nymphs of the rivers, the moist and grieving Echo." That wonderfully effective linking of one adjective of emotion with another of physical description brought to my mind a line from Shakespeare, which I recall we discussed one afternoon:

Where a malignant and a turban'd Turk . . .

Why the Quixote? my reader may ask. That choice, made by a Spaniard, would not have been incomprehensible, but it no doubt is so when made by a *Symboliste* from Nîmes, a devotee essentially of Poe – who begat Baudelaire, who begat Mallarmé, who begat Valéry, who begat M. Edmond Teste. The letter mentioned above throws some light on this point. "The *Quixote*," explains Menard,

> deeply interests me, but does not seem to me – *comment dirai-je?* – inevitable. I cannot imagine the universe without Poe's ejaculation "Ah, bear in mind this garden was enchanted!" or the *Bateau ivre* or the *Ancient Mariner*, but I know myself able to imagine it without the *Quixote*. (I am speaking, of course, of my personal ability, not of the historical resonance of those works.) The *Quixote* is a contingent work; the *Quixote* is not necessary. I can premeditate committing it to writing, as it were – I can write it – without falling into a tautology. At the age of twelve or thirteen I read it – perhaps read it cover to cover, I cannot recall. Since then, I have carefully reread certain chapters, those which, at least for the moment, I shall not attempt. I have also glanced at the interludes, the comedies, the *Galatea*, the Exemplary Novels, the no doubt laborious *Travails of Persiles and Sigismunda*, and the poetic *Voyage to Parnassus*. . . . My general recollection of the *Quixote*, simplified by forgetfulness and indifference, might well be the equivalent of the vague foreshadowing of a yet unwritten book. Given that image (which no one can in good conscience deny me), my problem is, without the shadow of a doubt, much more difficult than Cervantes'. My obliging predecessor did not spurn the collaboration of chance; his method of composition for the immortal book was a bit *à la diable*, and he was often swept along by the inertiæ of the language and the imagination. I have assumed the mysterious obligation to reconstruct, word for word, the

novel that for him was spontaneous. This game of solitaire I play is governed by two polar rules: the first allows me to try out formal or psychological variants; the second forces me to sacrifice them to the "original" text and to come, by irrefutable arguments, to those eradications. . . . In addition to these first two artificial constraints there is another, inherent to the project. Composing the *Quixote* in the early seventeenth century was a reasonable, necessary, perhaps even inevitable undertaking; in the early twentieth, it is virtually impossible. Not for nothing have three hundred years elapsed, freighted with the most complex events. Among those events, to mention but one, is the *Quixote* itself.

In spite of those three obstacles, Menard's fragmentary Quixote is more subtle than Cervantes'. Cervantes crudely juxtaposes the humble provincial reality of his country against the fantasies of the romance, while Menard chooses as his "reality" the land of Carmen during the century that saw the Battle of Lepanto and the plays of Lope de Vega. What burlesque brushstrokes of local color that choice would have inspired in a Maurice Barrès or a Rodríguez Larreta*! Yet Menard, with perfect naturalness, avoids them. In his work, there are no gypsy goings-on or conquistadors or mystics or Philip IIs or *autos da fé*. He ignores, overlooks – or banishes – local color. That disdain posits a new meaning for the "historical novel." That disdain condemns *Salammbô*, with no possibility of appeal.

No less amazement visits one when the chapters are considered in isolation. As an example, let us look at Part I, Chapter XXXVIII, "which treats of the curious discourse that Don Quixote made on the subject of arms and letters." It is a matter of common knowledge that in that chapter, don Quixote (like Quevedo in the analogous, and later, passage in *La hora de todos*) comes down against letters and in favor of arms. Cervantes was an old soldier; from him, the verdict is understandable. But that *Pierre Menard*'s don Quixote – a contemporary of *La trahison des clercs* and Bertrand Russell – should repeat those cloudy sophistries! Mme. Bachelier sees in them an admirable (typical) subordination of the author to the psychology of the hero; others (lacking all perspicacity) see them as a *transcription* of the Quixote; the baroness de Bacourt, as influenced by Nietzsche. To that third interpretation (which I consider irrefutable), I am not certain I dare to add a fourth, though it agrees very well with the almost divine modesty of Pierre Menard: his resigned or ironic habit of putting forth ideas that were the exact opposite of those he actually held. (We should recall that diatribe against Paul Valéry in the ephemeral Surrealist journal edited by Jacques Reboul.) The Cervantes text and the Menard text are verbally identical, but the second is almost infinitely richer. (More *ambiguous*, his detractors will say – but ambiguity is richness.)

It is a revelation to compare the *Don Quixote* of Pierre Menard with that of Miguel de Cervantes. Cervantes, for example, wrote the following (Part I, Chapter IX):

. . . truth, whose mother is history, rival of time, depository of deeds, witness of the past, exemplar and adviser to the present, and the future's counselor.

This catalog of attributes, written in the seventeenth century, and written by the "ingenious layman" Miguel de Cervantes, is mere rhetorical praise of history. Menard, on the other hand, writes:

> . . . truth, whose mother is history, rival of time, depository of deeds, witness of the past, exemplar and adviser to the present, and the future's counselor.

History, the *mother* of truth! – the idea is staggering. Menard, a contemporary of William James, defines history not as a *delving into* reality but as the very *fount* of reality. Historical truth, for Menard, is not "what happened"; it is what we *believe* happened. The final phrases – *exemplar and adviser to the present, and the future's counselor* – are brazenly pragmatic.

The contrast in styles is equally striking. The archaic style of Menard – who is, in addition, not a native speaker of the language in which he writes – is somewhat affected. Not so the style of his precursor, who employs the Spanish of his time with complete naturalness.

There is no intellectual exercise that is not ultimately pointless. A philosophical doctrine is, at first, a plausible description of the universe; the years go by, and it is a mere chapter – if not a paragraph or proper noun – in the history of philosophy. In literature, that "falling by the wayside," that loss of "relevance," is even better known. The Quixote, Menard remarked, was first and foremost a pleasant book; it is now an occasion for patriotic toasts, grammatical arrogance, obscene *de luxe* editions. Fame is a form – perhaps the worst form – of incomprehension.

Those nihilistic observations were not new; what was remarkable was the decision that Pierre Menard derived from them. He resolved to anticipate the vanity that awaits all the labors of mankind; he undertook a task of infinite complexity, a task futile from the outset. He dedicated his scruples and his nights "lit by midnight oil" to repeating in a foreign tongue a book that already existed. His drafts were endless; he stubbornly corrected, and he ripped up thousands of handwritten pages. He would allow no one to see them, and took care that they not survive him.[3] In vain have I attempted to reconstruct them.

I have reflected that it is legitimate to see the "final" Quixote as a kind of palimpsest, in which the traces – faint but not undecipherable – of our friend's "previous" text must shine through. Unfortunately, only a second Pierre Menard, reversing the labors of the first, would be able to exhume and revive those Troys. . . .

"Thinking, meditating, imagining," he also wrote me, "are not anomalous acts – they are the normal respiration of the intelligence. To glorify the occasional exercise of that function, to treasure beyond price ancient and foreign thoughts, to recall with incredulous awe what some *doctor universalis* thought, is to confess our own languor, or our own *barbarie*. Every man should be capable of all ideas, and I believe that in the future he shall be."

---

3 I recall his square-ruled notebooks, his black crossings-out, his peculiar typographical symbols, and his insect-like handwriting. In the evening, he liked to go out for walks on the outskirts of Nîmes; he would often carry along a notebook and make ???

Menard has (perhaps unwittingly) enriched the slow and rudimentary art of reading by means of a new technique – the technique of deliberate anachronism and fallacious attribution. That technique, requiring infinite patience and concentration, encourages us to read the *Odyssey* as though it came after the *Æneid*, to read Mme. Henri Bachelier's *Le jardin du Centaure* as though it were written by Mme. Henri Bachelier. This technique fills the calmest books with adventure. Attributing the *Imitatio Christi* to Louis Ferdinand Céline or James Joyce – is that not sufficient renovation of those faint spiritual admonitions?

SUNDAY AFTERNOON

Elizabeth Bowen

Born in Dublin **Elizabeth Bowen** (1899–1973) moved to England when she was eight, deciding at art school she should become a writer. She had a dull, sexless marriage, pepped up by a variety of affairs with either sex. Her books include *The House in Paris, The Heat of the Day* and *Eva Trout*. She died from lung cancer and was buried next to her husband in County Cork. Her *Collected Stories* was published in 1980. She once said she was interested in "life with the lid on and what happens when the lid comes off."

"So here you are!" exclaimed Mrs Vesey to the newcomer who joined the group on the lawn. She reposed for an instant her light, dry fingers on his. "Henry has come from London," she added. Acquiescent smiles from the others round her showed that the fact was already known – she was no more than indicating to Henry the role that he was to play. "What are your experiences? – Please tell us. But nothing dreadful: we are already feeling a little sad."

"I am sorry to hear that," said Henry Russel, with the air of one not anxious to speak of his own affairs. Drawing a cane chair into the circle, he looked from face to face with concern. His look travelled on to the screen of lilac, whose dark purple, pink-silver, and white plumes sprayed out in the brilliance of the afternoon. The late May Sunday blazed, but was not warm: something less than a wind, a breath of coldness, fretted the edge of things. Where the lilac barrier ended, across the sun-polished meadows, the Dublin mountains continued to trace their hazy, today almost colourless line. The coldness had been admitted by none of the seven or eight people who, in degrees of elderly beauty, sat here full in the sun, at this sheltered edge of the lawn: they continued to master the coldness, or to deny it, as though with each it were some secret *malaise*. An air of fastidious, stylized melancholy, an air of being secluded behind glass, characterized for Henry these old friends in whose shadow he had grown up. To their pleasure at having him back among them was added, he felt, a taboo or warning – he was to tell a little, but not much. He could feel with a shock, as he sat down, how insensibly he had deserted, these last years, the aesthetic of living that he had got from them. As things were, he felt over him their suspended charm. The democratic smell of the Dublin thus, on which he had made the outward journey to join them, had evaporated from his person by the time he was half-way up Mrs Vesey's chestnut avenue. Her house, with its fanlights and tall windows, was a villa in the Italian sense, just near enough to the city to make the country's sweetness particularly acute. Now, the sensations of wartime, that locked his inside being, began as surely to be dispelled – in the influence of this eternalized Sunday afternoon.

"Sad?" he said, "that is quite wrong."

"These days, our lives seem unreal," said Mrs Vesey – with eyes that penetrated his point of view. "But, worse than that, this afternoon we discover that we all have friends who have died."

"Lately?" said Henry, tapping his fingers together.

"Yes, in all cases," said Ronald Cuffe – with just enough dryness to show how much the subject had been beginning to tire him. "Come, Henry, we look to you for distraction. To us, these days you are quite a figure. In fact, from all we have heard of London, it is something that you should be alive. Are things there as shocking as they say – or are they more shocking?" he went on, with distaste.

"Henry's not sure," said someone, "he looks pontifical."

Henry, in fact, was just beginning to twiddle this far-off word "shocking" round in his mind, when a diversion caused some turning of heads. A young girl stepped out of a window and began to come their way across the lawn. She was Maria, Mrs Vesey's niece. A rug hung over her bare arm: she spread out the rug and sat down at her aunt's feet. With folded arms, and her fingers on her thin pointed elbows, she immediately fixed her eyes on Henry Russel. "Good afternoon," she said to him, in a mocking but somehow intimate tone.

The girl, like some young difficult pet animal, seemed in a way to belong to everyone there. Miss Ria Store, the patroness of the arts who had restlessly been refolding her fur cape, said: "And where have *you* been, Maria?"

"Indoors."

Someone said, "On this beautiful afternoon?"

"Is it?" said Maria, frowning impatiently at the grass.

"Instinct," said the retired judge, "now tells Maria it's time for tea."

"No, this does," said Maria, nonchalantly showing her wrist with the watch on it. "It keeps good time, thank you, Sir Isaac." She returned her eyes to Henry. "What have you been saying?"

"You interrupted Henry. He was just going to speak."

"*Is* it so frightening?" Maria said.

"The bombing?" said Henry. "Yes. But as it does not connect with the rest of life, it is difficult, you know, to know what one feels. One's feelings seem to have no language for anything so preposterous. As for thoughts –"

"At that rate," said Maria, with a touch of contempt, "your thoughts would not be interesting."

"Maria," said somebody, "that is no way to persuade Henry to talk."

"About what is important," announced Maria, "it seems that no one can tell one anything. There is really nothing, till one knows it oneself."

"Henry is probably right," said Ronald Cuffe, "in considering that this – this outrage is *not* important. There is no place for it in human experience; it apparently cannot make a place of its own. It will have no literature."

"Literature!" said Maria. "One can see, Mr Cuffe, that *you* have always been safe!"

"Maria," said Mrs Vesey, "you're rather pert."

Sir Isaac said, "What does Maria expect to know?"

Maria pulled off a blade of grass and bit it. Something calculating and passionate appeared in her; she seemed to be crouched up inside herself. She said to Henry sharply: "But you'll go back, of course?"

"To London? Yes – this is only my holiday. Anyhow, one cannot stay long away."

Immediately he had spoken Henry realized how subtly this offended his old friends. Their position was, he saw, more difficult than his own, and he could not have said a more cruel thing. Mrs Vesey, with her adept smile that was never entirely heartless, said: "Then we must hope your time here will be pleasant. Is it so very short?"

"And be careful, Henry," said Ria Store, "or you will find Maria stowed away in your baggage. And there would be an embarrassment, at an English port! We can feel her planning to leave us at any time."

Henry said, rather flatly: "Why should not Maria travel in the ordinary way?"

"Why should Maria travel at all? There is only one journey now – into danger. We cannot feel that that is necessary for, her."

Sir Isaac added: "We fear, however, that this is the journey Maria wishes to make."

Maria, curled on the lawn with the nonchalance of a feline creature, through this kept her eyes cast down. Another cold puff came through the lilac, soundlessly knocking the blooms together. One woman, taken quite unawares, shivered – then changed this into a laugh. There was an aside about love from Miss Store, who spoke with a cold, abstracted knowledge – "Maria has no experience, none whatever; she hopes to meet heroes – she meets none. So now she hopes to find heroes across the sea. Why, Henry, she might make a hero of you."

"It is not that," said Maria, who had heard. Mrs Vesey bent down and touched her shoulder; she sent the girl into the house to see if tea were ready. Presently they all rose and followed – in twos and threes, heads either erect composedly or else deliberately bowed in thought. Henry knew the idea of summer had been relinquished: they would not return to the lawn again. In the dining-room – where the white walls and the glass of the pictures held the reflections of summers – burned the log fire they were so glad to see. With her shoulder against the mantelpiece stood Maria, watching them take their places at the round table. Everything Henry had heard said had fallen off her – in these few minutes all by herself she had started in again on a fresh phase of living that was intact and pure. So much so, that Henry felt the ruthlessness of her disregard for the past, even the past of a few minutes ago. She came forward and put her hands on two chairs – to show she had been keeping a place for him.

Lady Ottery, leaning across the table, said: "I must ask you – we heard you had lost everything. But that cannot be true?"

Henry said, unwillingly: "It's true that I lost my flat, and everything in my flat."

"*Henry*," said Mrs Vesey, "all your beautiful things?"

"Oh dear," said Lady Ottery, overpowered, "I thought that could not be possible. I ought not to have asked."

Ria Store looked at Henry critically. "You take this too calmly. What has happened to you?"

"It was some time ago. And it happens to many people."

"But not to everyone," said Miss Store. "I should see no reason, for instance, why it should happen to me."

"One cannot help looking at you," said Sir Isaac. "You must forgive our amazement. But there was a time, Henry, when I think we all used to feel that we knew you well. If this is not a painful question, at this juncture, why did you not send your valuables out of town? You could have even shipped them over to us."

"I was attached to them. I wanted to live with them."

"And now," said Miss Store, "you live with nothing, for ever. Can you really feel that that is life?"

"I do. I may be easily pleased. It was by chance I was out when the place was hit. You may feel – and I honour your point of view – that I should have preferred, at my age, to go into eternity with some pieces of glass and jade and a dozen pictures. But, in fact, I am very glad to remain. To exist."

"On what level?"

"On any level."

"Come, Henry," said Ronald Cuffe, "that is a cynicism one cannot like in you. You speak of your age: to us, of course, that is nothing. You are at your maturity."

"Forty-three."

Maria gave Henry an askance look, as though, after all, he were not a friend. But she then said. "Why should he wish he was dead?" Her gesture upset some tea on the lace cloth, and she idly rubbed it up with her handkerchief. The tug her rubbing gave to the cloth shook a petal from a Chinese peony in the centre bowl on to a plate of cucumber sandwiches. This little bit of destruction was watched by the older people with fascination, with a kind of appeasement, as though it were a guarantee against something worse.

"Henry is not young and savage, like you are. Henry's life is – or was – an affair of attachments," said Ria Store. She turned her eyes, under their lids, on Henry. "I wonder how much of you *has* been blown to blazes."

"I have no way of knowing," he said. "Perhaps you have?"

"Chocolate cake?" said Maria.

"Please."

For chocolate layer cake, the Vesey cook had been famous since Henry was a boy of seven or eight. The look, then the taste, of the brown segment linked him with Sunday afternoons when he had been brought here by his mother; then, with a phase of his adolescence when he had been unable to eat, only able to look round. Mrs Vesey's beauty, at that time approaching its last lunar quarter, had swum on him when he was about nineteen. In Maria, child of her brother's late marriage, he now saw that beauty, or sort of physical genius, at the start. In Maria, this was without hesitation, without the halting influence that had bound Mrs Vesey up – yes and bound Henry up, from his boyhood, with her – in a circle of quizzical half-smiles. In revenge, he accused the young girl who moved him – who seemed framed, by some sort of anticipation, for the new catastrophic *outward* order of life – of brutality, of being without spirit. At his age, between two generations, he felt cast out. He felt Mrs Vesey might not forgive him for having left her for a world at war.

Mrs Vesey blew out the blue flame under the kettle, and let the silver trapdoor down with a snap. She then gave exactly one of those smiles – at the same time, it was the smile of his mother's friend. Ronald Cuffe picked the petal from the sandwiches and rolled it between his fingers, waiting for her to speak.

"It is cold, *indoors*," said Mrs Vesey. "Maria, put another log on the fire – Ria, you say the most unfortunate things. We must remember Henry has had a shock. – Henry, let us talk about something better. You work in an office, then, since the war?"

"In a Ministry – in an office, yes."

"Very hard? – Maria, that is all you would do if you went to England: work in an office. This is not like a war history, you know."

Maria said: "It is not in history yet." She licked round her lips for the rest of the chocolate taste, then pushed her chair a little back from the table. She looked secretively at her wrist-watch. Henry wondered what the importance of time could be.

He learned what the importance of time was when, on his way down the avenue to the bus, he found Maria between two chestnut trees. She slanted up to him and put her hand on the inside of his elbow. Faded dark-pink stamen from the flowers above them had moulted down on to her hair. "You have ten minutes more, really she said. "They sent you off ten minutes before your time. They are frightened someone would miss the bus and come back; then every-thing would have to begin again. As it is always the same, you would not think it would be so difficult for my aunt."

"Don't talk like that; it's unfeeling; I don't like it," said Henry, stiffening his elbow inside Maria's grasp.

"Very well, then: walk to the gate, then back. I shall be able to hear your bus coming. It's true what they said – I'm intending to go away. They will have to make up something without me."

"Maria, I can't like you. Everything you say is destructive and horrible."

"Destructive? – I thought you didn't mind."

"I still want the past."

"Then how weak you are," said Maria. "At tea I admired you. The past – things done over and over again with more trouble than they were ever worth? – However, there's no time to talk about that. Listen, Henry: I must have your address. I suppose you *have* an address now?" She stopped him, just inside the white gate with the green drippings: here he blew stamen off a page of his note-book, wrote on the page and tore it out for her. "Thank you," said Maria, "I might turn up – if I wanted money, or anything. But there will be plenty to do: I can drive a car."

Henry said: "I want you to understand that I won't be party to this – *in any way.*"

She shrugged and said: "You want *them* to understand" – and sent a look back to the house. Whereupon, on his entire being, the suspended charm of the afternoon worked. He protested against the return to the zone of death, and perhaps never ever seeing all this again. The cruciform lilac flowers, in all their purples, and the colourless mountains behind Mrs Vesey's face besought him. The moment he had been dreading, returning desire, flooded him in this tunnel of avenue, with motors swishing along the road outside and Maria standing staring at him. He adored the stoicism of the group he had quitted – with their little fears and their great doubts – the grace of the thing done over again. He thought, with nothing left but our brute courage, we shall be nothing but brutes.

"What is the matter?" Maria said. Henry did not answer: they turned and walked to and fro inside the gates. Shadow played over her dress and hair: feeling the disenchantedness of his look at her she asked again, uneasily, "What's the matter?"

"You know," he said, "when you come away from here, no one will care any more that you are Maria. You will no longer be Maria, as a matter of fact. Those looks, those things that are said to you – they make you, you silly little girl. You are you only inside their spell. You may think action is better – but who will care for you when you only act? You will have an identity number, but no identity. Your whole existence has been in contradistinction. You may think you want an ordinary fate – but there is no ordinary fate. And that extraordinariness in the fate of each of us is only recognized by your aunt. I admit that her view of life is too much for me – that is why I was so stiff and touchy today. But where shall we be when nobody has a view of life?"

"You don't expect me to understand you, do you?"

"Even your being a savage, even being scornful – yes, even that you have got from them. – Is that my bus?"

"At the other side of the river: it has still got to cross the bridge – Henry –" she put her face up. He touched it with kisses thoughtful and cold. "Goodbye," he said, "Miranda."

"– Maria –"

"Miranda. This is the end of *you*. Perhaps it is just as well."

"I'll be seeing you –"

"You'll come round my door in London – with your little new number chained to your wrist."

"The trouble with you is, you're half old."

Maria ran out through the gates to stop the bus, and Henry got on to it and was quickly carried away.

HOW TO WRITE A SHORT STORY

Sean O'Faolain

Sean O'Faolain (1900–1991), the son of a police constable, was born over a pub in Cork. After studying at University College, Cork, he served as a courier and publicity officer for the IRA. It was Joseph Conrad who wrote, in *The Secret Agent*, "The terrorist and the policeman both come from the same basket." It is possible this has never been so nearly true. O'Faolain started to have his writing published in 1932. His work includes biographies, travel books, a study of the short story and a memoir. Married to the writer Eileen, he was the father of Julia O'Faolain.

One wet January night, some six months after they had met, young Morgan Myles, our country librarian, was seated in the doctor's pet armchair, on one side of the doctor's fire, digesting the pleasant memory of a lavish dinner, while leafing the pages of a heavy photographic album and savouring a warm brandy. From across the hearth the doctor was looking admiringly at his long, ballooning Gaelic head when, suddenly, Morgan let out a cry of delight.

"Good Lord, Frank! There's a beautiful boy! One of Raphael's little angels." He held up the open book for Frank to see. "Who was he?"

The doctor looked across at it and smiled.

"Me. Aged twelve. At school in Mount Saint Bernard."

"That's in England. I didn't know you went to school in England."

"Alas!"

Morgan glanced down at twelve, and up at sixty.

"It's not possible, Frank!"

The doctor raised one palm six inches from the arm of his chair and let it fall again.

"It so happened that I was a ridiculously beautiful child."

"Your mother must have been gone about you. And," with a smile, "the girls too."

"I had no interest in girls. Nor in boys either, though by your smile you seem to say so. But there was one boy who took a considerable interest in me."

Morgan at once lifted his nose like a pointer. At this period of his life he had rested from writing poetry and was trying to write short stories. For weeks he had read nothing but Maupassant. He was going to out-Maupassant Maupassant. He was going to write stories that would make poor old Maupassant turn as green as the grass on his grave.

"Tell me about it," he ordered. "Tell me every single detail."

"There is nothing to it. Or at any rate, as I now know, nothing abnormal. But, at that age!" – pointing with his pipestem. "I was as innocent as . . . Well, as innocent as a child of twelve! Funny that you should say that about Raphael's angels. At my preparatory school here – it was a French order – Sister Angélique used to call me her petit *ange*, because, she said, I had '*une tête d'ange et une voix d'ange*.' She used to make me sing solo for them at Benediction, dressed in a red soutane, a white lacy surplice and a purple bow tie.

"After that heavenly place Mount Saint Bernard was ghastly. Mobs of howling boys. Having to play games; rain, hail or snow. I was a funk at games. When I'd see a fellow charging me at rugger I'd at once pass the ball or kick for touch. I remember the coach cursing me. 'Breen, you're a bloody little coward, there are boys half your weight on this field who wouldn't do a thing like that.' And the constant discipline. The constant priestly distrust. Watching us like jail warders."

"Can you give me an example of that?" Morgan begged. "Mind you, you could have had that, too, in Ireland. Think of Clongowes. It turns up in Joyce. And he admired the Jesuits!"

"Yes, I can give you an example. It will show you how innocent I was. A month after I entered Mount Saint Bernard I was so miserable that I decided to write to my mother to take me away. I knew that every letter had to pass under the eyes of the Prefect of Discipline, so I wrote instead to Sister Angélique asking her to pass on the word to my mother. The next day old Father George Lee – he's long since dead – summoned me to his study. 'Breen!' he said darkly, holding up my unfortunate letter, 'you have tried to do a very underhand thing, something for which I could punish you severely. Why did you write this letter *in French*?'" The doctor sighed. "I was a very truthful little boy. My mother had brought me up to be truthful simply by never punishing me for anything I honestly owned up to. I said, "I wrote it in French, sir, because I hoped you wouldn't be able to understand it." He turned his face away from me but I could tell from his shoulders that he was laughing. He did not cane me, he just tore up the letter, told me never to try to deceive him again, and sent me packing with my tail between my legs."

"The old bastard!" Morgan said sympathetically, thinking of the lonely little boy.

"No, no! He was a nice old man. And a good classical scholar, I later discovered. But that day as I walked down the long corridor, with all its photographs of old boys who had made good, I felt the chill of the prison walls!"

"But this other boy?" Morgan insinuated, "Didn't his friendship help at all?"

The doctor rose and stood with his back to the fire staring fixedly in front of him.

(He rises, Morgan thought, his noble eyes shadowed. No! God damn it, no! Not noble. Shadowed? Literary word. Pensive? Blast it, that's worse. "Pensive eve!" Romantic fudge. His eyes are dark as a rabbit's droppings. That's got it! In his soul . . . Oh, Jase!)

"Since I was so lonely I suppose he *must* have helped. But he was away beyond me. Miles above me. He was a senior. He was the captain of the school."

"His name," Morgan suggested, "was, perhaps, Cyril?"

"We called him Bruiser. I would rather not tell you his real name."

"Because he is still alive," Morgan explained, "and remembers you vividly to this day."

"He was killed at the age of twenty."

"In the war! In the heat of battle."

"By a truck in Oxford. Two years after he went up there from Mount Saint Bernard. I wish I knew what happened to him in those two years. I can only hope that before he died he found a girl."

"A girl? I don't follow. Oh yes! Of course, yes, I take your point."

(He remembers with tenderness? No. With loving kindness! No! With benevolence? Dammit, no! With his wonted chivalry to women? But he remembered irritably that the old man sitting opposite to him was a bachelor. And a virgin?)

"What happened between the pair of ye? 'Brothers and companions in tribulation on the isle that is called Patmos'?"

The doctor snorted.

"Brothers? I have told you I was twelve. Bruiser was eighteen. The captain of the school. Captain of the rugby team. Captain of the tennis team. First in every exam. Tops. Almost a man. I looked up to him as a shining hero. I never understood what he saw in me. I have often thought since that he may have been amused by my innocence. Like the day he said to me, 'I suppose, Rosy,' that was my nickname, I had such rosy cheeks, 'suppose you think you are the best-looking fellow in the school?' I said, 'No, I don't, Bruiser. I think there's one fellow better-looking than me, Jimmy Simcox.'"

"Which he, of course, loyally refused to believe!"

The old doctor laughed heartily.

"He laughed heartily."

"A queer sense of humour!"

"I must confess I did not at the time see the joke. Another day he said, 'Would you like, Rosy, to sleep with me?'"

Morgan's eyes opened wide. Now they were getting down to it.

"I said, 'Oh, Bruiser, I don't think you would like that at all. I'm an awful chatterbox in bed. Whenever I sleep with my Uncle Tom he's always saying to me, "Will you for God's sake, stop your bloody gabble and let me sleep."' He laughed for five minutes at that."

"I don't see much to laugh at. He should have sighed. I will make him sigh. Your way makes him sound a queer hawk. And nothing else happened between ye but this sort of innocent gabble? Or are you keeping something back? Hang it, Frank, there's no story at all in this!"

"Oh, he used sometimes to take me on his lap. Stroke my bare knee. Ruffle my hair. Kiss me."

"How did you like that?"

"I made nothing of it. I was used to being kissed by my elders – my mother, my bachelor uncles, Sister Angélique, heaps of people." The doctor laughed. "I laugh at it now. But his first kiss! A few days before, a fellow named Calvert said to me, 'Hello, pretty boy, would you give me a smuck?' I didn't know what a smuck was. I said, 'I'm sorry, Calvert, but I haven't got one.' The story must have gone around the whole school. The next time I was alone with Bruiser he taunted me. I can hear his angry, toploftical English voice. 'You are an innocent mug, Rosy! A smuck is a kiss. Would you let *me* kiss you?' I said, 'Why not?' He put his arm around my neck in a vice and squashed his mouth to my mouth, hard, sticky. I thought I'd choke. 'O Lord,' I thought, 'this is what he gets from playing rugger. This is a rugger kiss.' And, I was thinking, 'His poor mother! Having to put up with this from him every morning and every night.' When he let me go, he said, 'Did you like that?' Not wanting to hurt his feelings I said, imitating his English voice, 'It was all right, Bruiser! A bit like ruggah, isn't it?' He laughed again and said, 'All right? Well, never mind. I shan't rush you.'"

Morgan waved impatiently.

"Look here, Frank! I want to get the background to all this. The telling detail, you know. 'The little actual facts' as Stendhal called them. You said the priests watched you all like hawks. The constant discipline, you said. The constant priestly distrust. How did ye ever manage to meet alone?"

"It was very simple. He was the captain of the school. The apple of their eye. He could fool them. He knew the ropes. After all, he had been there for five years. I remember old Father Lee saying to me once, 'You are a very lucky boy, Breen, it's not every junior that the captain of the school would take an interest in. You ought to feel very proud of his friendship.' We used to have a secret sign about our meetings. Every Wednesday morning when he would be walking out of chapel, leading the procession, if that day was all right for us he used to put his right hand in his pocket. If for any reason it was not all right he would put his left hand in his pocket. I was always on the aisle of the very last row. Less than the dust. Watching for the sign like a hawk. We had a double check. I'd then find a note in my overcoat in the cloakroom. All it ever said was, 'The same place.' He was very careful. He only took calculated risks. If he had lived he would have made a marvellous politician, soldier or diplomat."

"And where would ye meet? I know! By the river. Or in the woods? 'Enter these enchanted woods ye who dare!'"

"No river. No woods. There was a sort of dirty old trunk room upstairs, under the roof, never used. A rather dark place with only one dormer window. It had double doors. He used to lock the outside one. There was a big cupboard there – for cricket bats or something. 'If anyone comes,' he told me, 'you will have time to pop in there.' He had it all worked out. Cautious man! I had to be even more cautious, stealing up there alone. One thing that made it easier for us was that I was so much of a junior and he was so very much of a senior, because, you see, those innocent guardians of ours had the idea that the real danger lay between the seniors and the middles, or the middles and the juniors, but never between the seniors and the juniors. They kept the seniors and the middles separated by iron bars and stone walls. Any doctor could have told them that in cold climates like ours the really dangerous years are not from fifteen up but from eighteen to anything, up or down. It simply never occurred to them that any senior could possibly be interested in any way in a junior. I, of course, had no idea of what he was up to. I had not even reached the age of puberty. In fact I honestly don't believe he quite knew himself what he was up to."

"But, dammit, you must have had some idea! The secrecy, the kissing, alone, up there in that dim, dusty box room, not a sound but the wind in the slates."

"Straight from the nuns? *Un petit ange?* I thought it was all just pally fun."

Morgan clapped his hands.

"I've got it! An idyll! Looking out dreamily over the fields from that dusty dormer window? That's it, that's the ticket. Did you ever read that wonderful story by Maupassant – it's called *An Idyll* – about two young peasants meeting in a train, a poor, hungry young fellow who has just left home, and a girl with her first baby. He looked so famished that she took pity on him like a mother, opened her blouse and gave him her breast. When he finished he said, 'That was my first meal in three days.' Frank! You are telling me the most beautiful story I ever heard in my whole life."

"You think so?" the doctor said morosely. "I think he was going through hell all that year. At eighteen? On the threshold of manhood? In love with a child of twelve? That is, if you will allow that a youth of eighteen may suffer as much from love as a man twenty years older. To me the astonishing thing is that he did so well all that year at his studies and at sports. Killing the pain of it, I suppose? Or trying to? But the in between? What went on in the poor devil in between?"

Morgan sank back dejectedly.

"I'm afraid this view of the course doesn't appeal to me at all. All I can see is the idyll idea. After all, I mean, nothing happened!"

Chafing, he watched his friend return to his armchair, take another pipe from the rack, fill it slowly and ceremoniously from a black tobacco jar and light it with care. Peering through the nascent smoke, Morgan leaned slowly forward.

"Or did something happen?"

"Yes," the doctor resumed quietly. "Every year, at the end of the last term, the departing captain was given a farewell dinner. I felt sad that morning because we had not met for a whole week. And now, in a couple of days we would be scattered and I would never see him again."

"Ha, ha! You see, you too were in love!"

"Of course I was, I was hooked," the doctor said with more than a flicker of impatience. "However . . . That Wednesday as he passed me in the chapel aisle he put his right hand in his pocket. I belted off at once to my coat hanging in the cloakroom and found his note. It said, 'At five behind the senior tennis court.' I used always chew up his *billet doux* immediately I read it. He had ordered me to. When I read this one my mouth went so dry with fear that I could hardly swallow it. He had put me in an awful fix. To meet alone in the box room was risky enough, but for anybody to climb over the wall into the seniors' grounds was unheard of. If I was caught I would certainly be flogged. I might very well be expelled. And what would my mother and father think of me then? On top of all I was in duty bound to be with all the other juniors at prep at five o'clock, and to be absent from studies without permission was another crime of the first order. After lunch I went to the Prefect of Studies and asked him to excuse me from prep because I had an awful headache. He wasn't taken in one bit. He just ordered me to be at my place in prep as usual. The law! Orders! Tyranny! There was only one thing for it, to dodge prep, knowing well that whatever else happened later I would pay dearly for it."

"And what about him? He knew all this. And he knew that if *he* was caught they couldn't do anything to him. The captain of the school? Leaving in a few days? It was very unmanly of him to put you to such a risk. His character begins to emerge, and not very pleasantly. Go on!"

The doctor did not need the encouragement. He looked like a small boy sucking a man's pipe.

"I waited until the whole school was at study and then I crept out into the empty grounds. At that hour the school, the grounds, everywhere, was as silent as the grave. Games over. The priests at their afternoon tea. Their charges safely under control. I don't know how I managed to get over that high wall, but when I fell scrambling down on the other side, there he was. 'You're bloody late,' he said crossly. 'How did you get out of prep? What excuse did you give?' When I told him he flew into a rage. 'You little fool!' he growled. 'You've balloxed it all up. They'll know you dodged. They'll give you at least ten on the backside for this.' He was carrying a cane. Seniors at Saint Bernard's did carry walking sticks. I'd risked so much for him, and now he was so angry with me that I burst into tears. He put his arms around me – I thought, to comfort me – but after that all I remember from that side of the wall was him pulling down my short pants, holding me tight, I felt something hard, like his cane, and the next thing I knew I was wet. I thought I was bleeding. I thought he was gone mad. When I smelled whiskey I thought, 'He is trying to kill me.' 'Now run,' he ordered me, 'and get back to prep as fast as you can.'"

Morgan covered his eyes with his hand.

"He shoved me up to the top of the wall. As I peered around I heard his footsteps running away. I fell down into the shrubs on the other side and I immediately began to vomit and vomit. There was a path beside the shrubs. As I lay there puking I saw a black-soutaned priest approaching slowly along the path. He was an old, old priest named Constable. I did not stir. Now, I felt, I'm for it. This is the end. I am certain he saw me but he passed by as if he had not seen me. I got back to the study hall, walked up to the Prefect's desk and told him I was late because I had been sick. I must have looked it because he at once sent me to the matron in the infirmary. She took my temperature and put me to bed. It was summer. I was the only inmate of the ward. One of those evenings of prolonged daylight."

"You poor little bugger!" Morgan groaned in sympathy.

"A detail comes back to me. It was the privilege of seniors attending the captain's dinner to send down gifts to the juniors' table – sweets, fruit, a cake, for a younger brother or some special protégé. Bruiser ordered a whole white blancmange with a rosy cherry on top of it to be sent to me. He did not know I was not in the dining hall so the blacmange was brought up to me in the infirmary. I vomited again when I saw it. The matron, with my more than ready permission, took some of it for herself and sent the rest back to the juniors' table, 'with Master Breen's compliments.' I am sure it was gobbled greedily. In the morning the doctor saw me and had me sent home to Ireland immediately."

"Passing the buck," said Morgan sourly, and they both looked at a coal that tinkled from the fire into the fender.

The doctor peered quizzically at the hissing coal.

"Well?" he slurred around his pipestem. "There is your lovely idyll."

Morgan did not lift his eyes from the fire. Under a downdraft from the chimney a few specks of grey ashes moved clockwise on the worn hearth. He heard a car hissing past the house on the wet macadam. His eyebrows had gone up over his spectacles in two Gothic arches.

"I am afraid," he said at last, "it is no go. Not even a Maupassant could have made a story out of it. And Chekhov wouldn't have wanted to try. Unless the two boys lived on, and on, and met years afterwards in Moscow or Yalta or somewhere, each with a wife and a squad of kids, and talked of everything except their schooldays. You are sure you never did hear of him, or from him, again?"

"Never! Apart from the letter he sent with the blancmange and the cherry."

Morgan at once leaped alive.

"A letter? Now we are on to something! What did he say to you in it? Recite every word of it to me! Every syllable. I'm sure you have not forgotten one word of it. No!" he cried excitedly. "You have kept it. Hidden away somewhere all these years. Friendship surviving everything. Fond memories of . . ."

The doctor sniffed.

"I tore it into bits unread and flushed it down the W.C."

"Oh, God blast you, Frank!" Morgan roared. "That was the climax of the whole thing. The last testament. The final revelation. The summing up. The *document humain*. And you 'just tore it up!' Let's reconstruct it. 'Dearest Rosy, As long as I live I will never forget your innocence, your sweetness, your . . .'"

"My dear boy!" the doctor protested mildly. "I am sure he wrote nothing of the sort. He was much too cautious, and even the captain was not immune from censorship. Besides, sitting in public glory at the head of the table? It was probably a place-card with something on the lines of, 'All my sympathy, sorry, better luck next term.' A few words, discreet, that I could translate any way I liked."

Morgan raised two despairing arms.

"If that was all the damned fellow could say to you after that appalling experience, he was a character of no human significance whatever, a shallow creature, a mere agent, a catalyst, a cad. The story becomes your story."

"I must admit I have always looked on it in that way. After all it did happen to me... Especially in view of the sequel."

"Sequel? What sequel? I can't have sequels. In a story you always have to observe unity of time, place and action. Everything happening at the one time, in the same place, between the same people. *The Necklace. Boule de Suif. The Maison Tellier.* The examples are endless. What was this bloody sequel?"

The doctor puffed thoughtfully.

"In fact there were two sequels. Even three sequels. And all of them equally important."

"In what way were they important?"

"It was rather important to me that after I was sent home I was in the hospital for four months. I could not sleep. I had constant nightmares, always the same one – me running through a wood and him running after me with his cane. I could not keep down my food. Sweating hot. Shivering cold. The vomiting was recurrent. I lost weight. My mother was beside herself with worry. She brought doctor after doctor to me, and only one of them spotted it, an old, blind man from Dublin named Whiteside. He said, 'That boy has had some kind of shock,' and in private he asked me if some boy, or man, had interfered with me. Of course, I denied it hotly."

"I wish I was a doctor," Morgan grumbled. "So many writers were doctors. Chekhov. William Carlos Williams. Somerset Maugham. A.J. Cronin."

The doctor ignored the interruption.

"The second sequel was that when I at last went back to Mount Saint Bernard my whole nature changed. Before that I had been dreamy and idle. During my last four years at school I became their top student. I suppose psychologists would say nowadays that I compensated by becoming extroverted. I became a crack cricket player. In my final year I was the college champion at billiards. I never became much good at rugger but I no longer minded playing it and I wasn't all that bad. If I'd been really tops at it, or at boxing, or swimming I might very well have ended up as captain of the school. Like him."

He paused for so long that Morgan became alerted again.

"And the third sequel?" he prompted.

"I really don't know why I am telling you all this. I have never told a soul about it before. Even still I find it embarrassing to think about, let alone to talk about. When I left Mount Saint Bernard and had taken my final at the College of Surgeons I went on to Austria to continue my medical studies. In Vienna I fell in with a young woman. The typical blonde fräulein, handsome, full of life, outgoing, wonderful physique, what you might call an outdoor girl, free as the wind, frank as the daylight. She taught me skiing. We used to go mountain climbing together. I don't believe she knew the meaning of the word fear. She was great fun and the best of company. Her name was Brigitte. At twenty-six she was already a woman of the world. I was twenty-four, and as innocent of women as . . . as . . ."

To put him at his ease Morgan conceded his own embarrassing confession.

"As I am, at twenty-four."

"You might think that what I am going to mention could not happen to a doctor, however young, but on our first night in bed, immediately she touched my body I vomited. I pretended to her that I had eaten something that upset me. You can imagine how nervous I felt all through the next day wondering what was going to happen that night. Exactly the same thing happened that night. I was left with no option. I told her the whole miserable story of myself and Bruiser twelve years before. As I started to tell her I had no idea how she was going to take it. Would she leave me in disgust? Be coldly sympathetic? Make a mock of me? Instead, she became wild with what I can only call gleeful curiosity. 'Tell me more, *mein Schätzerl*,' she begged. 'Tell me everything! What exactly did he do to you? I want to know it all. This is *wunderbar*. Tell me! Oh do tell me!' I did tell her, and on the spot everything became perfect between us. We made love like Trojans. That girl saved my sanity."

In a silence Morgan gazed at him. Then coldly: –

"Well, of course, this is another story altogether. I mean I don't see how I can possibly blend these two themes together. I mean no writer worth his salt can say things like, 'Twelve long years passed over his head. Now read on.' I'd have to leave her out of it. She is obviously irrelevant to the main theme. Whatever the hell the main theme is." Checked by an ironical glance he poured the balm. "Poor Frank! I foresee it all. You adored her. You wanted madly to marry her.

Her parents objected. You were star-crossed lovers. You had to part."

"I never thought of marrying the bitch. She had the devil's temper. We had terrible rows. Once we threw plates at one another. We would have parted anyway. She was a lovely girl but quite impossible. Anyway, towards the end of that year my father fell seriously ill. Then my mother fell ill. Chamberlain was in Munich that year. Everybody knew the war was coming. I came back to Ireland that autumn. For keeps.

"But you tried again and again to find out what happened to her. And failed. She was swallowed up in the fire and smoke of war. I don't care what you say, Frank, you *must* have been heartbroken."

The doctor lifted a disinterested shoulder.

"A student's love affair? Of thirty and more years ago?"

No! He had never enquired. Anyway if she was alive now what would she be but a fat, blowsy old baggage of sixty-three? Morgan, though shocked, guffawed dutifully. There was the real Maupassant touch. In his next story a touch like that! The clock on the mantelpiece whirred and began to tinkle the hour. Morgan opened the album for a last look at the beautiful child. Dejectedly he slammed it shut, and rose.

"There is too much in it," he declared. "Too many strands. Your innocence. His ignorance. Her worldliness. Your forgetting her. Remembering him. Confusion and bewilderment. The ache of loss? Loss? *Lost Innocence?* Would that be a theme? But nothing rounds itself off. You are absolutely certain you never heard of him again after that day behind the tennis courts?"

They were both standing now. The rain brightly spotted the midnight window.

"In my first year in Surgeons, about three years after Bruiser was killed, I lunched one day with his mother and my mother at the Shelbourne Hotel in Dublin. By chance they had been educated at the same convent in England. They talked about him. My mother said, 'Frank here knew him in Mount Saint Bernard.' His mother smiled condescendingly at me. 'No, Frank. You were too young to have met him.' 'Well,' I said, 'I did actually speak to him a couple of times, and he was always very kind to me.' She said sadly, 'He was kind to everybody. Even to perfect strangers.'"

Morgan thrust out an arm and a wildly wagging finger.

"Now, *there* is a possible shape! Strangers to begin. Strangers to end! What a title! *Perfect Strangers.*" He blew out a long, impatient breath and shook his head. "But that is a fourth sequel! I'll think about it," as if he were bestowing a great favour. "But it isn't a story as it stands. I would have to fake it up a lot. Leave out things. Simplify. Mind you, I could still see it as an idyll. Or I could if only you hadn't torn up his last, farewell letter, which I still don't believe at all said what you said it said. If only we had that letter I bet you any money we could haul in the line and land our fish."

The doctor knocked out the dottle of his pipe against the fireguard, and throating a yawn looked at the fading fire.

"I am afraid I have been boring you with my reminiscences."

"Not at all, Frank! By no means! I was most interested in your story. And I do honestly mean what I said. I really will think about it. I promise. Who was it," he asked in the hall as he shuffled into his overcoat and his muffler and moved out to the wet porch, the tail of his raincoat rattling in the wind, "said that the two barbs of childhood are its innocence and its ignorance?" He failed to remember. He threw up his hand. "Ach, to hell with it for a story! It's all too bloody convoluted for me. And to hell with Maupassant, too! That vulgarian oversimplified everything. And he's full of melodrama. A besotted Romantic at heart! Like all the bloody French."

The doctor peeped out at him through three inches of door. Morgan, standing with his back to the arrowy night, suddenly lit up as if a spotlight had shone on his face.

"I know what I'll do with it!" he cried. "I'll turn it into a poem about a sea-shell!"

"About a seashell!"

"Don't you remember?" In his splendid voice Morgan chanted above the rain and wind: – "'*A curious child holding to his ear/ The convolutions of a smooth-lipped seashell/ To which, in silence hushed . . .*' How the hell does it go? '. . . *his very soul listened to the murmurings of his native sea.*' It's as clear as daylight, man! You! Me! Everyone! Always wanting to launch a boat in search of some far-off golden sands. And something or somebody always holding us back. 'The Curious Child'. *There's* a title!"

"Ah, well!" the doctor said, peering at him blankly. "There it is! As your friend Maupassant might have said, '*C'est la vie!*'"

"*La vie!*" Morgan roared, now on the gravel beyond the porch, indifferent to the rain pelting on his bare head. "That trollop? She's the one who always bitches up everything. No, Frank! For me there is only one fountain of truth, one beauty, one perfection. Art, Frank! Art! and bugger *la vie!*"

At the untimely verb the doctor's drooping eyelids shot wide open.

"It is a view," he said courteously and let his hand be shaken fervently a dozen times.

"I can never repay you, Frank. A splendid dinner. A wonderful story. Marvellous inspiration. I must fly. I'll be writing it all night!" – and vanished head down through the lamplit rain, one arm uplifted triumphantly behind him.

The doctor slowly closed his door, carefully locked it, bolted it, tested it, and prudently put its chain in place. He returned to his sitting room, picked up the cinder that had fallen into the hearth and tossed it back into the remains of his fire, then stood, hand on mantelpiece, looking down at it. What a marvellous young fellow! He would be tumbling and tossing all night over that story. Then he would be around in the morning apologizing, and sympathizing, saying, "Of course, Frank, I do realize that it was a terribly sad experience for both of you."

Gazing at the ashes his whole being filled with memory after memory like that empty vase in his garden being slowly filled by drops of rain.

A FAMILY MAN

V.S. Pritchett

V.S. Pritchett (1900–1997)was the best short story writer in English during the twentieth century. There should be no argument about this. He was born in 1900 and died ninety-seven years later having written two brilliant memoirs – *A Cab at the Door* and *Midnight Oil* – and several excellent biographies, including *Chekhov*. Chatto & Windus published his *Collected Short Stories* and *Collected Essays* in 1991, and it says something about our culture that neither are still in print.

Late in the afternoon, when she had given him up and had even changed out of her pink dress into her smock and jeans and was working once more at her bench, the doorbell rang. William had come, after all. It was in the nature of their love affair that his visits were fitful: he had a wife and children. To show that she understood the situation, even found the curious satisfaction of reverie in his absences that lately had lasted several weeks, Berenice dawdled yawning to the door. As she slipped off the chain, she called back into the empty flat, "It's all right, Father. I'll answer it.'

William had told her to do this because she was a woman living on her own: the call would show strangers that there was a man there to defend her. Berenice's voice was mocking, for she thought his idea possessive and ridiculous; not only that, she had been brought up by Quakers and thought it wrong to tell or act a lie. Sometimes, when she opened the door to him, she would say, "Well! Mr Cork', to remind him he was a married man. He had the kind of shadowed handsomeness that easily gleams with guilt, and for her this gave their affair its piquancy.

But now – when she opened the door – no William, and the yawn, its hopes and its irony, died on her mouth. A very large woman, taller than herself, filled the doorway from top to bottom, an enormous blob of pink jersey and green skirt, the jersey low and loose at the neck, a face and body inflated to the point of speechlessness. She even seemed to be asleep with her large blue eyes open.

"Yes?" said Berenice.

The woman woke up and looked unbelievingly at Berenice's feet, which were bare, for she liked to go about barefoot at home, and said, "Is this Miss Foster's place?"

Berenice was offended by the word "place". "This is Miss Foster's residence. I am she."

"Ah," said the woman, babyish no longer but sugary. "I was given your address at the College. You teach at the College, I believe? I've come about the repair."

"A repair? I make jewellery," said Berenice. "I do not do repairs."

"They told me at the College you were repairing my husband's flute. I am Mrs Cork."

Berenice's heart stopped. Her wrist went weak and her hand drooped on the door handle, and a spurt of icy air shot up her body to her face and then turned to boiling heat as it shot back again. Her head suddenly filled with chattering voices saying, Oh, God. How frightful! William, you didn't tell her? Now, what are you, you, you going to do. And the word "Do, do" clattered on in her head.

"Cork?" said Berenice. "Flute?"

"Florence Cork," said the woman firmly, all sleepy sweetness gone.

"Oh, yes. I am sorry. Mrs Cork. Of course, yes. Oh, do come in. I'm so sorry. We haven't met, how very nice to meet you. William's – Mr Cork's – flute! His flute. Yes, I remember. How d'you do? How is he? He hasn't been to the College for months. Have you seen him lately – how silly, of course you have. Did you have a lovely holiday? Did the children enjoy it? I would have posted it, only I didn't know your address. Come in, please, come in."

"In here?" said Mrs Cork and marched into the front room where Berenice worked. Here, in the direct glare of Berenice's working lamp, Florence Cork looked even larger and even pregnant. She seemed to occupy the whole of the room as she stood in it, memorizing everything – the bench, the pots of paint-brushes, the large designs pinned to the wall, the rolls of paper, the sofa covered with papers and letters and sewing, the pink dress which Berenice had thrown over a chair. She seemed to be consuming it all, drinking all the air.

But here, in the disorder of which she was very vain, which indeed fascinated her, and represented her talent, her independence, a girl's right to a life of her own, and above all, being barefooted, helped Berenice recover her breath.

"It is such a pleasure to meet you. Mr Cork has often spoken of you to us at the College. We're quite a family there. Please sit. I'll move the dress. I was mending it."

But Mrs Cork did not sit down. She gave a sudden lurch towards the bench, and seeing her husband's flute there propped against the wall, she grabbed it and swung it above her head as if it were a weapon.

"Yes," said Berenice, who was thinking, Oh, dear, the woman's drunk, "I was working on it only this morning. I had never seen a flute like that before. Such a beautiful silver scroll. I gather it's very old, a German one, a presentation piece given to Mr Cork's father. I believe he played in a famous orchestra – where was it? – Bayreuth or Berlin? You never see a scroll like that in England, not a delicate silver scroll like that. It seems to have been dropped somewhere or have had a blow. Mr Cork told me he had played it in an orchestra himself once, Covent Garden or somewhere . . ."

She watched Mrs Cork flourish the flute in the air.

"A blow," cried Mrs Cork, now in a rich voice. "I'll say it did. I threw it at him."

And then she lowered her arm and stood swaying on her legs as she confronted Berenice and said, "Where is he?"

"Who?" said Berenice in a fright.

"My husband!" Mrs Cork shouted. "Don't try and soft-soap me with all that twaddle. Playing in an orchestra! Is that what he has been stuffing you up with? I know what you and he are up to. He comes every Thursday. He's been here since half past two. I know. I have had this place watched."

She swung round to the closed door of Berenice's bedroom. "What's in there?" she shouted and advanced to it.

"Mrs Cork," said Berenice as calmly as she could. "Please stop shouting. I know nothing about your husband. I don't know what you are talking about." And she placed herself before the door of the room. "And please stop shouting. That is my father's room." And, excited by Mrs Cork's accusation, she said, "He is a very old man and he is not well. He is asleep in there."

"In there?" said Mrs Cork.

"Yes, in there."

"And what about the other rooms? Who lives upstairs?"

"There are no other rooms," said Berenice. "I live here with my father. Up-stairs? Some new people have moved in."

Berenice was astonished by these words of hers, for she was a truthful young woman and was astonished, even excited, by a lie so vast. It seemed to glitter in the air as she spoke it.

Mrs Cork was checked. She flopped down on the chair on which Berenice had put her dress.

"My dress, if you please," said Berenice and pulled it away.

"If you don't do it here," said Mrs Cork, quietening and with tears in her eyes, "you do it somewhere else."

"I don't know anything about your husband. I only see him at the College like the other teachers. I don't know anything about him. If you will give me the flute, I will pack it up for you and I must ask you to go."

"You can't deceive me. I know everything. You think because you are young you can do what you like," Mrs Cork muttered to herself and began rummaging in her handbag.

For Berenice one of the attractions of William was that their meetings were erratic. The affair was like a game: she liked surprise above all. In the intervals when he was not there, the game continued for her. She liked imagining what he and his family were doing. She saw them as all glued together as if in some enduring and absurd photograph, perhaps sitting in their suburban garden, or standing beside a motorcar, always in the sun, but William himself, dark-faced and busy in his gravity, a step or two back from them.

"Is your wife beautiful?" she asked him once when they were in bed.

William in his slow serious way took a long time to answer. He said at last, "Very beautiful."

This had made Berenice feel exceedingly beautiful herself. She saw his wife as a raven-haired, dark-eyed woman and longed to meet her. The more she imagined her, the more she felt for her, the more she saw eye to eye with her in the pleasant busy middle ground of womanish feelings and moods, for as a woman living alone she felt a firm loyalty to her sex. During this last summer when the family were on holiday she had seen them glued together again as they sat with dozens of other families in the aeroplane that was taking them abroad, so that it seemed to her that the London sky was rumbling day after day, night after night, with matrimony thirty thousand feet above the city, the countryside, the sea and its beaches where she imagined the legs of their children running across the sand, William flushed with his responsibilities, his wife turning to brown her back in the sun. Berenice was often out and about with her many friends, most of whom were married. She loved the look of harassed contentment, even the tired faces of the husbands, the alert looks of their spirited wives. Among the married she felt her singularity. She listened to their endearments and to their bickerings. She played with their children, who ran at once to her. She could not bear the young men who approached her, talking about themselves all the time, flashing with the slapdash egotism of young men trying to bring her peculiarity to an end. Among families she felt herself to be strange and necessary – a necessary secret. When William had said his wife was beautiful, she felt so beautiful herself that her bones seemed to turn to water.

But now the real Florence sat rummaging in her bag before her, this balloon-like giant, first babyish and then shouting accusations, the dreamt-of Florence vanished. This real Florence seemed unreal and incredible. And William himself changed. His good looks began to look commonplace and shady: his seriousness became furtive, his praise of her calculating. He was shorter than his wife, his face now looked hang-dog, and she saw him dragging his feet as obediently he followed her. She resented that this woman had made her tell a lie, strangely intoxicating though it was to do so, and had made her feel as ugly as his wife was. For she must be, if Florence was what he called "beautiful". And not only ugly, but pathetic and without dignity.

Berenice watched warily as the woman took a letter from her handbag.

"Then what is this necklace?" she said, blowing herself out again.

"What necklace is this?" said Berenice.

"Read it. You wrote it."

Berenice smiled with astonishment: she knew she needed no longer defend herself. She prided herself on fastidiousness: she had never in her life written a letter to a lover – it would be like giving something of herself away, it would be almost an indecency. She certainly felt it to be very wrong to read anyone else's letters, as Mrs Cork pushed the letter at her. Berenice took it in two fingers, glanced and turned it over to see the name of the writer.

"This is not my writing," she said. The hand was sprawling; her own was scratchy and small. "Who is Bunny? Who is Rosie?"

Mrs Cork snatched the letter and read in a booming voice that made the words ridiculous: "'I am longing for the necklace. Tell that girl to hurry up. Do bring it next time. And darling, don't forget the flute!!! Rosie.' What do you mean, who is Bunny?" Mrs Cork said. "You know very well. Bunny is my husband."

Berenice turned away and pointed to a small poster that was pinned to the wall. It contained a photograph of a necklace and three brooches she had shown at an exhibition in a very fashionable shop known for selling modern jewellery. At the bottom of the poster, elegantly printed, were the words

Created by Berenice

Berenice read the words aloud, reciting them as if they were a line from a poem: "My name is Berenice," she said.

It was strange to be speaking the truth. And it suddenly seemed to her, as she recited the words, that really William had never been to her flat, that he had never been her lover, and had never played his silly flute there, that indeed he was the most boring man at the College and that a chasm separated her from this woman, whom jealousy had made so ugly.

Mrs Cork was still swelling with unbelief, but as she studied the poster, despair settled on her face. "I found it in his pocket," she said helplessly.

"We all make mistakes, Mrs Cork," Berenice said coldly across the chasm. And then, to be generous in victory, she said, "Let me see the letter again."

Mrs Cork gave her the letter and Berenice read it and at the word "flute" a doubt came into her head. Her hand began to tremble and quickly she gave the letter back. "Who gave you my address – I mean, at the College?" Berenice accused. "There is a rule that no addresses are given. Or telephone numbers."

"The girl," said Mrs Cork, defending herself.

"Which girl? At Enquiries?"

"She fetched someone."

"Who was it?" said Berenice.

"I don't know. It began with a W, I think," said Mrs Cork.

"Wheeler?" said Berenice. "There is a Mr Wheeler."

"No, it wasn't a man. It was a young woman. With a W – Glowitz."

"That begins with a G," said Berenice.

"No," said Mrs Cork out of her muddle, now afraid of Berenice. "Glowitz was the name."

"Glowitz," said Berenice, unbelieving. "Rosie Glowitz. She's not young."

"I didn't notice," said Mrs Cork. "Is her name Rosie?"

Berenice felt giddy and cold. The chasm between herself and Mrs Cork closed up.

"Yes," said Berenice and sat on the sofa, pushing letters and papers away from herself. She felt sick. "Did you show her the letter?" she said.

"No," said Mrs Cork, looking masterful again for a moment. "She told me you were repairing the flute."

"Please go," Berenice wanted to say but she could not get her breath to say it. "You have been deceived. You are accusing the wrong person. I thought your husband's name was William. He never called himself Bunny. We all call him William at the College. Rosie Glowitz wrote this letter." But that sentence, "Bring the flute", was too much – she was suddenly on the side of this angry woman, she wished she could shout and break out into rage. She wanted to grab the flute that lay on Mrs Cork's lap and throw it at the wall and smash it.

"I apologize, Miss Foster," said Mrs Cork in a surly voice. The glister of tears in her eyes, the dampness on her face, dried. "I believe you. I have been worried out of my mind – you will understand."

Berenice's beauty had drained away. The behaviour of one or two of her lovers had always seemed self-satisfied to her, but William, the most unlikely one, was the oddest. He would not stay in bed and gossip but he was soon out staring at the garden, looking older, as if he were travelling back into his life: then, hardly saying anything, he dressed, turning to stare at the garden again as his head came out of his shirt or he put a leg into his trousers, in a manner that made her think he had completely forgotten. Then he would go into her front room, bring back the flute and go out to the garden seat and play it. She had done a cruel caricature of him once because he looked so comical, his long lip drawn down at the mouthpiece, his eyes lowered as the thin high notes, so sad and lascivious, seemed to curl away like wisps of smoke into the trees. Sometimes she laughed, sometimes she smiled, sometimes she was touched, sometimes angry and bewildered. One proud satisfaction was that the people upstairs had complained.

She was tempted, now that she and this clumsy woman were at one, to say to her, "Aren't men extraordinary! Is this what he does at home, does he rush out to your garden, bold as brass, to play that silly thing?" And then she was scornful. "To think of him going round to Rosie Glowitz's and half the gardens of London doing this!"

But she could not say this, of course. And so she looked at poor Mrs Cork with triumphant sympathy. She longed to break Rosie Glowitz's neck and to think of some transcendent appeasing lie which would make Mrs Cork happy again, but the clumsy woman went on making everything worse by asking to be forgiven. She said "I am truly sorry" and "When I saw your work in the shop I wanted to meet you. That is really why I came. My husband has often spoken of it."

Well, at least, Berenice thought, she can tell a lie too. Suppose I gave her everything I've got, she thought. Anything to get her to go. Berenice looked at the drawer of her bench, which was filled with beads and pieces of polished stone and crystal. She felt like getting handfuls of it and pouring it all on Mrs Cork's lap.

"Do you work only in silver?" said Mrs Cork, dabbing her eyes.

"I am," said Berenice, "working on something now."

And even as she said it, because of Mrs Cork's overwhelming presence, the great appeasing lie came out of her, before she could stop herself. "A present," she said. "Actually," she said, "we all got together at the College. A present for Rosie Glowitz. She's getting married again. I expect that is what the letter is about. Mr Cork arranged it. He is very kind and thoughtful."

She heard herself say this with wonder. Her other lies had glittered, but this one had the beauty of a newly discovered truth.

"You mean Bunny's collecting the money?" said Mrs Cork.

"Yes," said Berenice.

A great laugh came out of Florence Cork. "The big spender," she said, laughing. "Collecting other people's money. He hasn't spent a penny on us for thirty years. And you're all giving this to that woman I talked to who has been married twice? Two wedding presents!"

Mrs Cork sighed.

"You fools. Some women get away with it, I don't know why," said Mrs Cork, still laughing. "But not with my Bunny," she said proudly and as if with alarming meaning. "He doesn't say much. He's deep, is my Bunny!"

"Would you like a cup of tea?" said Berenice politely, hoping she would say no and go.

"I think I will," Mrs Cork said comfortably. "I'm so glad I came to see you. And," she added, glancing at the closed door, "what about your father? I expect he could do with a cup."

Mrs Cork now seemed wide awake and it was Berenice who felt dazed, drunk-ish, and sleepy.

"I'll go and see," she said.

In the kitchen she recovered and came back trying to laugh, saying, "He must have gone for his little walk in the afternoon, on the quiet."

"You have to keep an eye on them at that age," said Mrs Cork.

They sat talking and Mrs Cork said, "Fancy Mrs Glowitz getting married again." And then absently, "I cannot understand why she says 'Bring the flute.'"

"Well," said Berenice agreeably, "he played it at the College party."

"Yes," said Mrs Cork. "But at a wedding, it's a bit pushy. You wouldn't think it of my Bunny, but he *is* pushing."

They drank their tea and then Mrs Cork left. Berenice felt an enormous kiss on her face and Mrs Cork said, "Don't be jealous of Mrs Glowitz, dear. You'll get your turn," as she went.

Berenice put the chain on the door and went to her bedroom and lay on the bed.

How awful married people are, she thought. So public, sprawling over every-one and everything, always lying to themselves and forcing you to lie to them. She got up and looked bitterly at the empty chair under the tree at first and then she laughed at it and went off to have a bath so as to wash all those lies off her truthful body. Afterwards she rang up a couple called Brewster who told her to come round. She loved the Brewsters, so perfectly conceited as they were, in the burdens they bore. She talked her head off. The children stared at her.

"She's getting old. She ought to get married," Mrs Brewster said. "I wish she wouldn't swoosh her hair around like that. She'd look better if she put it up."

GIMPEL THE FOOL

Isaac Bashevis Singer

Isaac Bashevis Singer (1902–1991) was born in Poland and emigrated to the USA in 1935. Although his father and grandfather had been rabbis, he seemed to think he was more sceptic, private in his own faith. He wrote in Hebrew and adopted Yiddish, as he claimed "Yiddish contains vitamins that other languages don't have." He also thought the short story "constitutes the utmost challenge to a creative writer." He won the 1978 Nobel Prize for Literature. Once asked why he was a vegetarian he answered, "I did it for the health of the chickens."

I

I AM Gimpel the fool. I don't think myself a fool. On the contrary. But that's what folks call me. They gave me the name while I was still in school. I had seven names in all: imbecile, donkey, flax-head, dope, glump, ninny, and fool. The last name stuck. What did my foolishness consist of? I was easy to take in. They said, "Gimpel, you know the rabbi's wife has been brought to childbed?" So I skipped school. Well, it turned out to be a lie. How was I supposed to know? She hadn't had a big belly. But I never looked at her belly. Was that really so foolish? The gang laughed and hee-hawed, stomped and danced and chanted a good-night prayer. And instead of the raisins they give when a woman's lying in, they stuffed my hand full of goat turds. I was no weakling. If I slapped someone he'd see all the way to Cracow. But I'm really not a slugger by nature. I think to myself: Let it pass. So they take advantage of me.

I was coming home from school and heard a dog barking. I'm not afraid of dogs, but of course I never want to start up with them. One of them may be mad, and if he bites there's not a Tartar in the world who can help you. So I made tracks. Then I looked around and saw the whole market place wild with laughter. It was no dog at all but Wolf-Leib the thief. How was I supposed to know it was he? It sounded like a howling bitch.

When the pranksters and leg-pullers found that I was easy to fool, every one of them tried his luck with me. "Gimpel, the czar is coming to Frampol; Gimpel, the moon fell down in Turbeen; Gimpel, little Hodel Furpiece found a treasure behind the bathhouse." And I like a golem believed everyone. In the first place, everything is possible, as it is written in *The Wisdom of the Fathers*, I've forgotten just how. Second, I had to believe when the whole town came down on me! If I ever dared to say, "Ah, you're kidding!" there was trouble. People got angry. "What do you mean! You want to call everyone a liar?" What was I to do? I believed them, and I hope at least that did them some good.

I was an orphan. My grandfather who brought me up was already bent toward the grave. So they turned me over to a baker, and what a time they gave me there! Every woman or girl who came to bake a batch of noodles had to fool me at least once. "Gimpel, there's a fair in Heaven; Gimpel, the rabbi gave birth to a calf in the seventh month; Gimpel, a cow flew over the roof and laid brass eggs." A student from the yeshiva came once to buy a roll, and he said, "You, Gimpel, while you stand here scraping with your baker's shovel the Messiah has come. The dead have arisen." "What do you mean?" I said. "I heard no one blowing the ram's horn!" He said, "Are you deaf?" And all began to cry, "We heard it, we heard!" Then in came Rietze the candle-dipper and called out in her hoarse voice, "Gimpel, your father and mother have stood up from the grave. They're looking for you."

To tell the truth, I knew very well that nothing of the sort had happened, but all the same, as folks were talking, I threw on my wool vest and went out. Maybe something had happened. What did I stand to lose by looking? Well, what a cat music went up! And then I took a vow to believe nothing more. But that was no go either. They confused me so that I didn't know the big end from the small.

I went to the rabbi to get some advice. He said, "It is written, better to be a fool all your days than for one hour to be evil. You are not a fool. They are the fools. For he who causes his neighbor to feel shame loses Paradise himself." Nevertheless, the rabbi's daughter took me in. As I left the rabbinical court she said, "Have you kissed the wall yet?" I said, "No; what for?" She answered, "It's the law; you've got to do it after every visit." Well, there didn't seem to be any harm in it. And she burst out laughing. It was a fine trick. She put one over on me, all right.

I wanted to go off to another town, but then everyone got busy matchmaking, and they were after me so they nearly tore my coat tails off. They talked at me and talked until I got water on the car. She was no chaste maiden, but they told me she was virgin pure. She had a limp, and they said it was deliberate, from coyness. She had a bastard, and they told me the child was her little brother. I cried, "You're wasting your time. I'll never marry that whore." But they said indignantly, "What a way to talk! Aren't you ashamed of yourself? We can take you to the rabbi and have you fined for giving her a bad name." I saw then that I wouldn't escape them so easily and I thought: They're set on making me their butt. But when you're married the husband's the master, and if that's all right with her it's agreeable to me too. Besides, you can't pass through life unscathed, nor expect to.

I went to her clay house, which was built on the sand, and the whole gang, hollering and chorusing, came after me. They acted like bear-baiters. When we came to the well they stopped all the same. They were afraid to start anything with Elka. Her mouth would open as if it were on a hinge, and she had a fierce tongue. I entered the house. Lines were strung from wall to wall and clothes were drying. Barefoot she stood by the tub, doing the wash. She was dressed in a worn hand-me-down gown of plush. She had her hair put up in braids and pinned across her head. It took my breath away, almost, the reek of it all.

Evidently she knew who I was. She took a look at me and said, "Look who's here! He's come, the drip. Grab a seat."

I told her all; I denied nothing. "Tell me the truth," I said, "are you really a virgin, and is that mischievous Yechiel actually your little brother? Don't be deceitful with me, for I'm an orphan."

"I'm an orphan myself," she answered, "and whoever tries to twist you up, may the end of his nose take a twist. But don't let them think they can take advantage of me. I want a dowry of fifty guilders, and let them take up a collection besides. Otherwise they can kiss my you-know-what." She was very plainspoken. I said, "It's the bride and not the groom who gives a dowry." Then she said, "Don't bargain with me. Either a flat yes or a flat no. Go back where you came from."

I thought: No bread will ever be baked from *this* dough. But ours is not a poor town. They consented to everything and proceeded with the wedding. It so happened that there was a dysentery epidemic at the time. The ceremony was held at the cemetery gates, near the little corpse-washing hut. The fellows got drunk. While the marriage contract was being drawn up I heard the most pious high rabbi ask, "Is the bride a widow or a divorced woman?" And the sexton's wife answered for her, "Both a widow and divorced." It was a black moment for me. But what was I to do, run away from under the marriage canopy?

There was singing and dancing. An old granny danced opposite me, hugging a braided white hallah. The master of revels made a "God 'a mercy" in memory of the bride's parents. The schoolboys threw burrs, as on Tishe b'Av fast day. There were a lot of gifts after the sermon: a noodle board, a kneading trough, a bucket, brooms, ladles, household articles galore. Then I took a look and saw two strapping young men carrying a crib. "What do we need this for?" I asked. So they said, "Don't rack your brains about it. It's all right, it'll come in handy." I realized I was going to be rooked. Take it another way though, what did I stand to lose? I reflected: I'll see what comes of it. A whole town can't go altogether crazy.

II

At night I came where my wife lay, but she wouldn't let me in. "Say, look here, is this what they married us for?" I said. And she said, "My monthly has come." "But yesterday they took you to the ritual bath, and that's afterwards, isn't it supposed to be?" "Today isn't yesterday," said she, "and yesterday's not today. You can beat it if you don't like it." In short, I waited.

Not four months later, she was in childbed. The townsfolk hid their laughter with their knuckles. But what could I do? She suffered intolerable pains and clawed at the walls. "Gimpel," she cried, "I'm going. Forgive me!" The house filled with women. They were boiling pans of water. The screams rose to the welkin.

The thing to do was to go to the house of prayer to repeat psalms, and that was what I did.

The townsfolk liked that, all right. I stood in a corner saying psalms and prayers, and they shook their heads at me. "Pray, pray!" they told me. "Prayer never made any woman pregnant." One of the congregation put a straw to my mouth and said, "Hay for the cows." There was something to that too, by God!

She gave birth to a boy. Friday at the synagogue the sexton stood up before the Ark, pounded on the reading table, and announced, "The wealthy Reb Gimpel invites the congregation to a feast in honor of the birth of a son." The whole house of prayer rang with laughter. My face was flaming. But there was nothing I could do. After all, I *was* the one responsible for the circumcision honors and rituals.

Half the town came running. You couldn't wedge another soul in. Women brought peppered chick-peas, and there was a keg of beer from the tavern. I ate and drank as much as anyone, and they all congratulated me. Then there was a circumcision, and I named the boy after my father, may he rest in peace. When all were gone and I was left with my wife alone, she thrust her head through the bed-curtain and called me to her.

"Gimpel," said she, "why are you silent? Has your ship gone and sunk?"

"What shall I say?" I answered. "A fine thing you've done to me! If my mother had known of it she'd have died a second time."

She said, "Are you crazy, or what?"

"How can you make such a fool," I said, "of one who should be the lord and master?"

"What's the matter with you?" she said. "What have you taken it into your head to imagine?"

I saw that I must speak bluntly and openly. "Do you think this is the way to use an orphan?" I said. "You have borne a bastard."

She answered, "Drive this foolishness out of your head. The child is yours."

"How can he be mine?" I argued. "He was born seventeen weeks after the wedding."

She told me then that he was premature. I said, "Isn't he a little too premature?" She said, she had had a grandmother who carried just as short a time and she resembled this grandmother of hers as one drop of water does another. She swore to it with such oaths that you would have believed a peasant at the fair if he had used them. To tell the plain truth, I didn't believe her; but when I talked it over next day with the school-master, he told me that the very same thing had happened to Adam and Eve. Two they went up to bed, and four they descended.

"There isn't a woman in the world who is not the granddaughter of Eve," he said.

That was how it was; they argued me dumb. But then, who really knows how such things are?

I began to forget my sorrow. I loved the child madly, and he loved me too. As soon as he saw me he'd wave his little hands and want me to pick him up, and when he was colicky I was the only one who could pacify him. I bought him a little bone teething ring and a little gilded cap. He was forever catching the evil eye from someone, and then I had to run to get one of those abracadabras for him that would get him out of it. I worked like an ox. You know how expenses go up when there's an infant in the house. I don't want to lie about it; I didn't dislike Elka either, for that matter. She swore at me and cursed, and I couldn't get enough of her. What strength she had! One of her looks could rob you of the power of speech. And her orations! Pitch and sulphur, that's what they were full of, and yet somehow also full of charm. I adored her every word. She gave me bloody wounds though.

In the evening I brought her a white loaf as well as a dark one, and also poppyseed rolls I baked myself. I thieved because of her and swiped everything I could lay hands on: macaroons, raisins, almonds, cakes. I hope I may be forgiven for stealing from the Saturday pots the women left to warm in the baker's oven. I would take out scraps of meat, a chunk of pudding, a chicken leg or head, a piece of tripe, whatever I could nip quickly. She ate and became fat and handsome.

I had to sleep away from home all during the week, at the bakery. On Friday nights when I got home she always made an excuse of some sort. Either she had heartburn, or a stitch in the side, or hiccups, or headaches. You know what women's excuses are. I had a bitter time of it. It was rough. To add to it, this little brother of hers, the bastard, was growing bigger. He'd put lumps on me, and when I wanted to hit back she'd open her mouth and curse so powerfully I saw a green haze floating before my eyes. Ten times a day she threatened to divorce me. Another man in my place would have taken French leave and disappeared. But I'm the type that bears it and says nothing. What's one to do? Shoulders are from God, and burdens too.

One night there was a calamity in the bakery; the oven burst, and we almost had a fire. There was nothing to do but go home, so I went home. Let me, I thought, also taste the joy of sleeping in bed in midweek. I didn't want to wake the sleeping mite and tiptoed into the house. Coming in, it seemed to me that I heard not the snoring of one but, as it were, a double snore, one a thin enough snore and the other like the snoring of a slaughtered ox. Oh, I didn't like that! I didn't like it at all. I went up to the bed, and things suddenly turned black. Next to Elka lay a man's form. Another in my place would have made an uproar, and enough noise to rouse the whole town, but the thought occurred to me that I might wake the child. A little thing like that – why frighten a little swallow, I thought. All right then, I went back to the bakery and stretched out on a sack of flour and till morning I never shut an eye. I shivered as if I had had malaria. "Enough of being a donkey," I said to myself. "Gimpel isn't going to be a sucker all his life. There's a limit even to the foolishness of a fool like Gimpel."

In the morning I went to the rabbi to get advice, and it made a great commotion in the town. They sent the beadle for Elka right away. She came, carrying the child. And what do you think she did? She denied it, denied everything, bone and stone! "He's out of his head," she said. "I know nothing of dreams or divinations." They yelled at her, warned her, hammered on the table, but she stuck to her guns: it was a false accusation, she said.

The butchers and the horse-traders took her part. One of the lads from the slaughterhouse came by and said to me, "We've got our eye on you, you're a marked man." Meanwhile, the child started to bear down and soiled itself. In the rabbinical court there was an Ark of the Covenant, and they couldn't allow that, so they sent Elka away.

I said to the rabbi, "What shall I do?"

"You must divorce her at once," said he.

"And what if she refuses?" I asked.

He said, "You must serve the divorce. That's all you'll have to do."

I said, "Well, all right, Rabbi. Let me think about it."

"There's nothing to think about," said he. "You mustn't remain under the same roof with her."

"And if I want to see the child?" I asked.

"Let her go, the harlot," said he, "and her brood of bastards with her."

The verdict he gave was that I mustn't even cross her threshold – never again, as long as I should live.

During the day it didn't bother me so much. I thought: It was bound to happen, the abscess had to burst. But at night when I stretched out upon the sacks I felt it all very bitterly. A longing took me, for her and for the child. I wanted to be angry, but that's my misfortune exactly, I don't have it in me to be really angry. In the first place – this was how my thoughts went – there's bound to be a slip sometimes. You can't live without errors. Probably that lad who was with her led her on and gave her presents and what not, and women are often long on hair and short on sense, and so he got around her. And then since she denies it so, maybe I was only seeing things? Hallucinations do happen. You see a figure or a mannikin or something, but when you come up closer it's nothing, there's not a thing there. And if that's so, I'm doing her an injustice. And when I got so far in my thoughts I started to weep. I sobbed so that I wet the flour where I lay. In the morning I went to the rabbi and told him that I had made a mistake. The rabbi wrote on with his quill, and he said that if that were so he would have to reconsider the whole case. Until he had finished I wasn't to go near my wife, but I might send her bread and money by messenger.

III

Nine months passed before all the rabbis could come to an agreement. Letters went back and forth. I hadn't realized that there could be so much erudition about a matter like this.

Meanwhile, Elka gave birth to still another child, a girl this time. On the Sabbath I went to the synagogue and invoked a blessing on her. They called me up to the Torah, and I named the child for my mother-in-law – may she rest in peace. The louts and loudmouths of the town who came into the bakery gave me a going over. All Frampol refreshed its spirits because of my trouble and grief. However, I resolved that I would always believe what I was told. What's the good of *not* believing? Today it's your wife you don't believe; tomorrow it's God Himself you won't take stock in.

By an apprentice who was her neighbor I sent her daily a corn or a wheat loaf, or a piece of pastry, rolls or bagels, or, when I got the chance, a slab of pudding, a slice of honeycake, or wedding strudel – whatever came my way. The apprentice was a goodhearted lad, and more than once he added something on his own. He had formerly annoyed me a lot, plucking my nose and digging me in the ribs, but when he started to be a visitor to my house he became kind and friendly. "Hey, you, Gimpel," he said to me, "you have a very decent little wife and two fine kids. You don't deserve them."

"But the things people say about her," I said.

"Well, they have long tongues," he said, "and nothing to do with them but babble. Ignore it as you ignore the cold of last winter."

One day the rabbi sent for me and said, "Are you certain, Gimpel, that you were wrong about your wife?"

I said, "I'm certain."

"Why, but look here! You yourself saw it."

"It must have been a shadow," I said.

"The shadow of what?"

"Just of one of the beams, I think."

"You can go home then. You owe thanks to the Yanover rabbi. He found an obscure reference in Maimonides that favored you."

I seized the rabbi's hand and kissed it.

I wanted to run home immediately. It's no small thing to be separated for so long a time from wife and child. Then I reflected: I'd better go back to work now, and go home in the evening. I said nothing to anyone, although as far as my heart was concerned it was like one of the Holy Days. The women teased and twitted me as they did every day, but my thought was: Go on, with your loose talk. The truth is out, like the oil upon the water. Maimonides says it's right, and therefore it is right!

At night, when I had covered the dough to let it rise, I took my share of bread and a little sack of flour and started homeward. The moon was full and the stars were glistening, something to terrify the soul. I hurried onward, and before me darted a long shadow. It was winter, and a fresh snow had fallen. I had a mind to sing, but it was growing late and I didn't want to wake the householders. Then I felt like whistling, but I remembered that you don't whistle at night because it brings the demons out. So I was silent and walked as fast as I could.

Dogs in the Christian yards barked at me when I passed, but I thought: Bark your teeth out! What are you but mere dogs? Whereas I am a man, the husband of a fine wife, the father of promising children.

As I approached the house my heart started to pound as though it were the heart of a criminal. I felt no fear, but my heart went thump! thump! Well, no drawing back. I quietly lifted the latch and went in. Elka was asleep. I looked at the infant's cradle. The shutter was closed, but the moon forced its way through the cracks. I saw the newborn child's face and loved it as soon as I saw it – immediately – each tiny bone.

Then I came nearer to the bed. And what did I see but the apprentice lying there beside Elka. The moon went out all at once. It was utterly black, and I trembled. My teeth chattered. The bread fell from my hands, and my wife waked and said, "Who is that, ah?"

I muttered, "It's me."

"Gimpel?" she asked. "How come you're here? I thought it was forbidden."

"The rabbi said," I answered and shook as with a fever.

"Listen to me, Gimpel," she said, "go out to the shed and see if the goat's all right. It seems she's been sick." I have forgotten to say that we had a goat. When I heard she was unwell I went into the yard. The nannygoat was a good little creature. I had a nearly human feeling for her.

With hesitant steps I went up to the shed and opened the door. The goat stood there on her four feet. I felt her everywhere, drew her by the horns, examined her udders, and found nothing wrong. She had probably eaten too much bark. "Good night, little goat," I said. "Keep well." And the little beast answered with a "Maa" as though to thank me for the good will.

I went back. The apprentice had vanished.

"Where," I asked, "is the lad?"

"What lad?" my wife answered.

"What do you mean?" I said. "The apprentice. You were sleeping with him."

"The things I have dreamed this night and the night before," she said, "may they come true and lay you low, body and soul! An evil spirit has taken root in you and dazzles your sight." She screamed out, "You hateful creature! You moon calf! You spook! You uncouth man! Get out, or I'll scream all Frampol out of bed!"

Before I could move, her brother sprang out from behind the oven and struck me a blow on the back of the head. I thought he had broken my neck. I felt that something about me was deeply wrong, and I said, "Don't make a scandal. All that's needed now is that people should accuse me of raising spooks and dybbuks." For that was what she had meant. "No one will touch bread of my baking."

In short, I somehow calmed her.

"Well," she said, "that's enough. Lie down, and be shattered by wheels."

Next morning I called the apprentice aside. "Listen here, brother!" I said. And so on and so forth. "What do you say?" He stared at me as though I had dropped from the roof or something.

"I swear," he said, "you'd better go to an herb doctor or some healer. I'm afraid you have a screw loose, but I'll hush it up for you." And that's how the thing stood.

To make a long story short, I lived twenty years with my wife. She bore me six children, four daughters and two sons. All kinds of things happened, but I neither saw nor heard. I believed, and that's all. The rabbi recently said to me, "Belief in itself is beneficial. It is written that a good man lives by his faith."

Suddenly my wife took sick. It began with a trifle, a little growth upon the breast. But she evidently was not destined to live long; she had no years. I spent a fortune on her. I have forgotten to say that by this time I had a bakery of my own and in Frampol was considered to be something of a rich man. Daily the healer came, and every witch doctor in the neighborhood was brought. They decided to use leeches, and after that to try cupping. They even called a doctor from Lublin, but it was too late. Before she died she called me to her bed and said, "Forgive me, Gimpel."

I said, "What is there to forgive? You have been a good and faithful wife."

"Woe, Gimpel!" she said. "It was ugly how I deceived you all these years. I want to go clean to my Maker, and so I have to tell you that the children are not yours."

If I had been clouted on the head with a piece of wood it couldn't have bewildered me more.

"Whose are they?" I asked.

"I don't know," she said. "There were a lot . . . but they're not yours." And as she spoke she tossed her head to the side, her eyes turned glassy, and it was all up with Elka. On her whitened lips there remained a smile.

I imagined that, dead as she was, she was saying, "I deceived Gimpel. That was the meaning of my brief life."

IV

One night, when the period of mourning was done, as I lay dreaming on the flour sacks, there came the Spirit of Evil himself and said to me, "Gimpel, why do you sleep?"

I said, "What should I be doing? Eating kreplech?"

"The whole world deceives you," he said, "and you ought to deceive the world in your turn."

"How can I deceive all the world?" I asked him.

He answered, "You might accumulate a bucket of urine every day and at night pour it into the dough. Let the sages of Frampol eat filth."

"What about the judgment in the world to come?" I said.

"There is no world to come," he said. "They've sold you a bill of goods and talked you into believing you carried a cat in your belly. What nonsense!"

"Well then," I said, "and is there a God?"

He answered, "There is no God either."

"What," I said, "*is* there, then?"

"A thick mire."

He stood before my eyes with a goatish beard and horn, long-toothed, and with a tail. Hearing such words, I wanted to snatch him by the tail, but I tumbled from the flour sacks and nearly broke a rib. Then it happened that I had to answer the call of nature, and, passing, I saw the risen dough, which seemed to say to me, "Do it!" In brief, I let myself be persuaded.

At dawn the apprentice came. We kneaded the bread, scattered caraway seeds on it, and set it to bake. Then the apprentice went away, and I was left sitting in the little trench by the oven, on a pile of rags. Well, Gimpel, I thought, you've revenged yourself on them for all the shame they've put on you. Outside the frost glittered, but it was warm beside the oven. The flames heated my face. I bent my head and fell into a doze.

I saw in a dream, at once, Elka in her shroud. She called to me, "What have you done, Gimpel?"

I said to her, "It's all your fault," and started to cry.

"You fool!" she said. "You fool! Because I was false is everything false too? I never deceived anyone but myself. I'm paying for it all, Gimpel. They spare you nothing here."

I looked at her face. It was black; I was startled and waked, and remained sitting dumb. I sensed that everything hung in the balance. A false step now and I'd lose eternal life. But God gave me His help. I seized the long shovel and took out the loaves, carried them into the yard, and started to dig a hole in the frozen earth.

My apprentice came back as I was doing it. "What are you doing boss?" he said, and grew pale as a corpse.

"I know what I'm doing," I said, and I buried it all before his very eyes.

Then I went home, took my hoard from its hiding place, and divided it among the children. "I saw your mother tonight," I said. "She's turning black, poor thing."

They were so astounded they couldn't speak a word.

"Be well," I said, "and forget that such a one as Gimpel ever existed." I put on my short coat, a pair of boots, took the bag that held my prayer shawl in one hand, my stock in the other, and kissed the mezuzah. When people saw me in the street they were greatly surprised.

"Where are you going?" they said.

I answered, "Into the world." And so I departed from Frampol.

I wandered over the land, and good people did not neglect me. After many years I became old and white; I heard a great deal, many lies and falsehoods, but the longer I lived the more I understood that there were really no lies. Whatever doesn't really happen is dreamed at night. It happens to one if it doesn't happen to another, tomorrow if not today, or a century hence if not next year. What difference can it make? Often I heard tales of which I said, "Now this is a thing that cannot happen." But before a year had elapsed I heard that it actually had come to pass somewhere.

Going from place to place, eating at strange tables, it often happens that I spin yarns – improbable things that could never have happened – about devils, magicians, windmills, and the like. The children run after me, calling, "Grandfather, tell us a story." Sometimes they ask for particular stories, and I try to please them. A fat young boy once said to me, "Grandfather, it's the same story you told us before." The little rogue, he was right.

So it is with dreams too. It is many years since I left Frampol, but as soon as I shut my eyes I am there again. And whom do you think I see? Elka. She is standing by the washtub, as at our first encounter, but her face is shining and her eyes are as radiant as the eyes of a saint, and she speaks outlandish words to me, strange things. When I wake I have forgotten it all. But while the dream lasts I am comforted. She answers all my queries, and what comes out is that all is right. I weep and implore, "Let me be with you." And she consoles me and tells me to be patient. The time is nearer than it is far. Sometimes she strokes and kisses me and weeps upon my face. When I awaken I feel her lips and taste the salt of her tears.

No doubt the world is entirely an imaginary world, but it is only once removed from the true world. At the door of the hovel where I lie, there stands the plank on which the dead are taken away. The grave-digger Jew has his spade ready. The grave waits and the worms are hungry; the shrouds are prepared – I carry them in my beggar's sack. Another *shnorrer* is waiting to inherit my bed of straw. When the time comes I will go joyfully. Whatever may be there, it will be real, without complication, without ridicule, without deception. God be praised: there even Gimpel cannot be deceived.

GUESTS OF THE NATION

Frank O'Connor

Born in Cork, Ireland, **Frank O'Connor** (1903–1966) was brought
up by his adored mother. He joined the IRA when he was fifteen and
was imprisoned for his views between 1922 and 1923. He worked
as a teacher, librarian and in the theatre, most notably the Abbey
Theatre in Dublin. He began publishing his work in 1931 – this
story was his first – and wrote novels, criticism, history, travel writing,
autobiography and translated poetry. Asked by *The Paris Review* in 1957
why he preferred the short story, he said "because it's the nearest thing I
know to lyric poetry." Although he lived in the USA from the early 1950s,
he suffered a fatal heart attack in Dublin and was buried there.

At dusk the big Englishman, Belcher, would shift his long legs out of the
ashes and say "Well, chums, what about it ?" and Noble and myself
would say "All right, chum" (for we had picked up some of their curious
expressions), and the little Englishman, Hawkins, would light the lamp and bring
out the cards. Sometimes Jeremiah Donovan would come up and supervise the
game, and get excited over Hawkins' cards, which he always played badly, and
shout at him as if he was one of our own, "Ah, you divil, why didn't you play
the tray?"

But ordinarily Jeremiah was a sober and contented poor devil like the big
Englishman, Belcher, and was looked up to only because he was a fair hand
at documents, though he was slow even with them. He wore a small cloth hat
and big gaiters over his long pants, and you seldom saw him with his hands
out of his pockets. He reddened when you talked to him, tilting from toe to
heel and back, and looking down all the, time at his big farmer's feet. Noble
and myself used to make fun of his broad accent, because we were both from
the town.

I could not at the time see the point of myself and Noble guarding Belcher
and Hawkins at all, for it was my belief that you could have planted that pair
down anywhere from this to Claregalway and they'd have taken root there like
a native weed. I never in my short experience saw two men take to the country
as they did.

They were passed on to us by the Second Battalion when the search for them
became too hot, and Noble and myself, being young, took them over with a
natural feeling of responsibility, but Hawkins made us look like fools when he
showed that he knew the country better than we did.

"You're the bloke they call Bonaparte," he says to me. "Mary Brigid

O'Connell told me to ask what you'd done with the pair of her brother's socks you borrowed."

For it seemed, as they explained it, that the Second had little evenings, and some of the girls of the neighborhood turned up, and, seeing they were such decent chaps, our fellows could not leave the two Englishmen out. Hawkins learned to dance "The Walls of Limerick," "The Siege of Ennis" and "The Waves of Tory" as well as any of them, though he could not return the compliment, because our lads at that time did not dance foreign dances on principle.

So whatever privileges Belcher and Hawkins had with the Second they just took naturally with us, and after the first couple of days we gave up all pretence of keeping an eye on them. Not that they could have got far, because they had accents you could cut with a knife, and wore khaki tunics and overcoats with civilian pants and boots, but I believe myself they never had any idea of escaping and were quite content to be where they were.

It was a treat to see how Belcher got off with the old woman in the house where we were staying. She was a great warrant to scold, and cranky even with us, but before ever she had a chance of giving our guests, as I may call them, a lick of her tongue, Belcher had made her his friend for life. She was breaking sticks, and Belcher, who had not been more than ten minutes in the house, jumped up and went over to her.

"Allow me, madam," he said, smiling his queer little smile. "Please allow me," and he took the hatchet from her. She was too surprised to speak, and after that, Belcher would be at her heels, carrying a bucket, a basket or a load of turf. As Noble said, he got into looking before she leapt, and hot water, or any little thing she wanted, Belcher would have ready for her. For such a huge man (and though I am five foot ten myself I had to look up at him) he had an uncommon lack of speech. It took us a little while to get used to him, walking in and out like a ghost, without speaking. Especially because Hawkins talked enough for a platoon, it was strange to hear Belcher with his toes in the ashes come out with a solitary "Excuse me, chum," or "That's right, chum." His one and only passion was cards, and he was a remarkably good card player. He could have skinned myself and Noble, but whatever we lost to him, Hawkins lost to us, and Hawkins only played with the money Belcher gave him.

Hawkins lost to us because he had too much old gab, and we probably lost to Belcher for the same reason. Hawkins and Noble argued about religion into the early hours of the morning, and Hawkins worried the life out of Noble, who had a brother a priest, with a string of questions that would puzzle a cardinal. Even in treating of holy subjects, Hawkins had a deplorable tongue. I never met a man who could mix such a variety of cursing and bad language into any argument. He was a terrible man, and a fright to argue. He never did a stroke of work, and when he had no one else to argue with, he got stuck in the old woman.

He met his match in her, for when he tried to get her to complain profanely of the drought she gave him a great comedown by blaming it entirely on Jupiter Pluvius (a deity neither Hawkins nor I had ever heard of, though Noble said that among the pagans it was believed that he had something to do with the rain). Another day he was swearing at the capitalists for starting the German war when the old lady laid down her iron, puckered up her little crab's mouth and said:

"Mr. Hawkins, you can say what you like about the war, and think you'll deceive me because I'm only a simple poor countrywoman, but I know what started the war. It was the Italian Count that stole the heathen divinity out of the temple of Japan. Believe me, Mr. Hawkins, nothing but sorrow and want can follow people who disturb the hidden powers."

A queer old girl, all right.

II

One evening we had our tea and Hawkins lit the lamp and we all sat into cards. Jeremiah Donovan came in too, and sat and watched us for a while, and it suddenly struck me that he had no great love for the two Englishmen. It came as a surprise to me because I had noticed nothing of it before.

Late in the evening a really terrible argument blew up between Hawkins and Noble about capitalists and priests and love of country.

"The capitalists pay the priests to tell you about the next world so that you won't notice what the bastards are up to in this," said Hawkins

"Nonsense, man !" said Noble, losing his temper.

"Before ever a capitalist was thought of people believed in the next world."

Hawkins stood up as though he was preaching.

"Oh, they did, did they?" he said with a sneer. "They believed all the things you believe – isn't that what you mean? And you believe God created Adam, and Adam created Shem, and Shem created Jehoshophat. You believe all that silly old fairytale about Eve and Eden and the apple. Well listen to me, chum! If you're entitled to a silly belief like that, I'm entitled to my own silly belief - which is that the first thing your God created was a bleeding capitalist, with morality and Rolls-Royce complete. Am I right, chum?" he says to Belcher.

"You're right, chum," says Belcher with a smile, and he got up from the table to stretch his long legs into the fire and stroke his moustache. So, seeing that Jeremiah Donovan was going, and that there was no knowing when the argument about religion would be over, I went out with him. We strolled down to the village together, and then he stopped, blushing and mumbling, and said I should be behind, keeping guard. I didn't like the tone he took with me, and anyway I was bored with life in the cottage, so I replied by asking what the hell we wanted to guard them for at all.

He looked at me in surprise and said: "I thought you knew we were keeping them as hostages."

"Hostages?" I said.

"The enemy have prisoners belonging to us, and now they're talking of shooting them," he said. " If they shoot our prisoners, we'll shoot theirs."

"Shoot Belcher and Hawkins?" I said.

"What else did you think we were keeping them for?" he said. "Wasn't it very unforeseen of you not to warn Noble and myself of that in the beginning?" I said.

"How was it?" he said. "You might have known that much."

"We could not know it, Jeremiah Donovan," I said. "How could we when they were on our hands so long?"

"The enemy have our prisoners as long and longer," he said.

"That's not the same thing at all," said I.

"What difference is there?" said he.

I couldn't tell him, because I knew he wouldn't understand. If it was only an old dog that you had to take to the vet's, you'd try and not get too fond of him, but Jeremiah Donovan was not a man who would ever be in danger of that.

"And when is this to be decided?" I said.

"We might hear tonight," he said. "Or tomorrow or the next day at latest. So if it's only hanging round that's a trouble to you, you'll be free soon enough."

It was not the hanging round that was a trouble to me at all by this time. I had worse things to worry about. When I got back to the cottage the argument was still on. Hawkins was holding forth in his best style, maintaining that there was no next world, and Noble saying that there was; but I could see that Hawkins had had the best of it.

"Do you know what, chum?" he was saying with a saucy smile." I think you're just as big a bleeding unbeliever as I am. You say you believe in the next world, and you know just as much about the next world as I do, which is sweet damn-all. What's heaven? You don't know. Where's heaven? You don't know. You know sweet damn-all ! I ask you again, do they wear wings?"

"Very well, then," said Noble. "They do. Is that enough for you? They do wear wings."

"Where do they get them then? Who makes them? Have they a factory for wings? Have they a sort of store where you hand in, your chit and take your bleeding wings?"

"You're an impossible man to argue with," said Noble. "Now, listen to me –" And they were off again.

It was long after midnight when we locked up and went to bed. As I blew out the candle I told Noble. He took it very quietly. When we'd been in bed about an hour he asked if I thought we should tell the Englishmen. I didn't, because I doubted if the English would shoot our men. Even if they did, the Brigade officers, who were always up and down to the Second Battalion and knew the Englishmen well, would hardly want to see them plugged. "I think so too," said Noble. "It would be great cruelty to put the wind up them now."

"It was very unforeseen of Jeremiah Donovan, anyhow," said I. It was next morning that we found it so hard to face Belcher and Hawkins. We went about the house all day, scarcely saying a word. Belcher didn't seem to notice; he was stretched into the ashes as usual, with his usual look of waiting in quietness for something unforeseen to happen, but Hawkins noticed it and put it down to Noble's being beaten in the argument of the night before.

"Why can't you take the discussion in the proper spirit?" he said severely. "You and your Adam and Eve! I'm a Communist, that's what I am. Communist or Anarchist, it all comes to much the same thing." And he went round the house, muttering when the fit took him: "Adam and Eve! Adam and Eve! Nothing better to do with their time than pick bleeding apples !"

III

I don't know how we got through that day, but I was very glad when it was over, the tea things were cleared away, and Belcher said in his peaceable way: "Well, chums, what about it?" We sat round the table and Hawkins took out the cards, and just then I heard Jeremiah Donovan's footsteps on the path and a dark presentiment crossed my mind. I rose from the table and caught him before he reached the door.

"What do you want?" I asked.

"I want those two soldier friends of yours," he said, getting red. "Is that the way, Jeremiah Donovan?" I asked.

"That's the way. There were four of our lads shot this morning, one of them a boy of sixteen."

"That's bad," I said.

At that moment Noble followed me out, and the three of us walked down the path together, talking in whispers. Feeney, the local intelligence officer, was standing by the gate.

"What are you going to do about it?" I asked Jeremiah Donovan.

"I want you and Noble to get them out; tell them they're being shifted again; that'll be the quietest way."

"Leave me out of that," said Noble, under his breath. Jeremiah Donovan looked at him hard.

"All right," he says. "You and Feeney get a few tools from the shed and dig a hole by the far end of the bog. Bonaparte and myself will be after you. Don't let anyone see you with the tools. I wouldn't like it to go beyond ourselves."

We saw Feeney and Noble go round to the shed and went in ourselves. I left Jeremiah Donovan to do the explanations. He told them that he had orders to send them back to the Second Battalion. Hawkins let out a mouthful of curses, and you could see that though Belcher didn't say anything, he was a bit upset too. The old woman was for having them stay in spite of us, and she didn't stop advising them until Jeremiah Donovan lost his temper and turned on her. He had a nasty temper, I noticed. It was pitch-dark in the cottage by this time, but no one thought of lighting the lamp, and in the darkness the two Englishmen fetched their topcoats and said good-bye to the old woman.

"Just as a man makes a home of a bleeding place, some bastard at headquarters thinks you're too cushy and shunts you off," said Hawkins shaking her hand.

"A thousand thanks, madam," said Belcher, "A thousand thanks for everything" – as though he'd made it up.

We went round to the back of the house and down towards the bog. It was only then that Jeremiah Donovan told them. He was shaking with excitement.

"There were four of our fellows shot in Cork this morning and now you're to be shot as a reprisal."

"What are you talking about?" snaps Hawkins. "It's bad enough being mucked about as we are without having to put up with your funny jokes."

"It isn't a joke," says Donovan. "I'm sorry, Hawkins, but it's true," and begins on the usual rigmarole about duty and how unpleasant it is. I never noticed that people who talk a lot about duty find it much of a trouble to them.

"Oh, cut it out!" said Hawkins.

"Ask Bonaparte," said Donovan, seeing that Hawkins wasn't taking him seriously. "Isn't it true, Bonaparte?"

"It is," I said, and Hawkins stopped. "Ah, for Christ's sake, chum!"

"I mean it, chum," I said.

"You don't sound as if you meant it."

"If he doesn't mean it, I do," said Donovan, working himself up.

"What have you against me, Jeremiah Donovan?"

"I never said I had anything against you. But why did your people take out four of your prisoners and shoot them in cold blood?"

He took Hawkins by the arm and dragged him on, but it was impossible to make him understand that we were in earnest. I had the Smith and Wesson in my pocket and I kept fingering it and wondering what I'd do if they put up a fight for it or ran, and wishing to God they'd do one or the other. I knew if they did run for it, that I'd never fire on them. Hawkins wanted to know was Noble in it, and when we said yes, he asked us why Noble wanted to plug him. Why did any of us want to plug him? What had he done to us? Weren't we all chums? Didn't we understand him and didn't he understand us? Did we imagine for an instant that he'd shoot us for all the so-and-so officers in the so-and-so British Army?

By this time we'd reached the bog, and I was so sick I couldn't even answer him. We walked along the edge of it in the darkness, and every now and then Hawkins would call a halt and begin all over again, as if he was wound up, about our being chums, and I knew that nothing but the sight of the grave would convince him that we had to do it. And all the time I was hoping that something would happen; that they'd run for it or that Noble would take over the responsibility from me. I had the feeling that it was worse on Noble than on me.

IV

At last we saw the lantern in the distance and made towards it. Noble was carrying it, and Feeney was standing somewhere in the darkness behind him, and the picture of them so still and silent in the bogland brought it home to me that we were in earnest, and banished the last bit of hope I had.

Belcher, on recognising Noble, said: "Hallo, chum," in his quiet way, but Hawkins flew at him at once, and the argument began all over again, only this time Noble had nothing to say for himself and stood with his head down, holding the lantern between his legs.

It was Jeremiah Donovan who did the answering. For the twentieth time, as though it was haunting his mind, Hawkins asked if anybody thought he'd shoot Noble.

"Yes, you would," said Jeremiah Donovan. "No, I wouldn't, damn you!"

"You would, because you'd know you'd be shot for not doing it."

"I wouldn't, not if I was to be shot twenty times over. I wouldn't shoot a pal. And Belcher wouldn't – isn't that right, Belcher?"

"That's right, chum," Belcher said, but more by way of answering the question than of joining in the argument. Belcher sounded as though whatever unforeseen thing he'd always been waiting for had come at last.

"Anyway, who says Noble would be shot if I wasn't ? What do you think I'd do if I was in his place, out in the middle of a blasted bog?"

"What would you do?" asked Donovan.

"I'd go with him wherever he was going, of course. Share my last bob with him and stick by him through thick and thin. No one can ever say of me that I let down a pal."

"We had enough of this," said Jeremiah Donovan, cocking his revolver. "Is there any message you want to send?"

"No, there isn't."

"Do you want to say your prayers?"

Hawkins came out with a cold-blooded remark that even shocked me and turned on Noble again.

"Listen to me, Noble," he said. "You and me are chums. You can't come over to my side, so I'll come over to your side. That show you I mean what I say? Give me a rifle and I'll go along with you and the other lads."

Nobody answered him. We knew that was no way out.

"Hear what I'm saying?" he said. "I'm through with it. I'm a deserter or anything else you like. I don't believe in your stuff, but it's no worse than mine. That satisfy you?"

Noble raised his head, but Donovan began to speak and he lowered it again without replying.

"For the last time, have you any messages to send?" said Donovan in a cold, excited sort of voice.

"Shut up, Donovan! You don't understand me, but these lads do. They're not the sort to make a pal and kill a pal. They're not the tools of any capitalist."

I alone of the crowd saw Donovan raise his Webley to the back of Hawkins's neck, and as he did so I shut my eyes and tried to pray. Hawkins had begun to say something else when Donovan fired, and as I opened my eyes at the bang, I saw Hawkins stagger at the knees and lie out flat at Noble's feet, slowly and as quiet as a kid falling asleep, with the lantern-light on his lean legs and bright farmer's boots. We all stood very still, watching him settle out in the last agony.

Then Belcher took out a handkerchief and began to tie it about his own eyes (in our excitement we'd forgotten to do the same for Hawkins), and, seeing it wasn't big enough, turned and asked for the loan of mine. I gave it to him and he knotted the two together and pointed with his foot at Hawkins, "He's not quite dead." he said. "Better give him another," Sure enough, Hawkins's left knee was beginning to rise. I bent down and put my gun to his head; then, recollecting myself, I got up again. Belcher understood what was in my mind.

"Give him his first," he said, "I don't mind. Poor bastard, we don't know what's happening to him now."

I knelt and fired. By this time I didn't seem to know what I was doing. Belcher, who was fumbling a bit awkwardly with the handkerchiefs, came out with a laugh as he heard the shot. It was the first time I had heard him laugh and it sent a shudder down my back; it sounded so unnatural.

"Poor bugger!" he said quietly. "And last night he was so curious about it all. It's very queer, chums, I always think. Now he knows as much about it as they'll ever let him know, and last night he was all in the dark."

Donovan helped him to tie the handkerchiefs about his eyes.

"Thanks, chum," he said. Donovan asked if there were any messages he wanted sent.

"No, chum," he said. "Not for me. If any of you would like to write to Hawkins's mother, you'll find a letter from her in his pocket. He and his mother were great chums. But my missus left me eight years ago. Went away with another fellow and took the kid with her. I like the feeling of a home, as you may have noticed, but I couldn't start another again after that."

It was an extraordinary thing, but in those few minutes Belcher said more than in all the weeks before. It was just as if the sound of the shot had started a flood of talk in him and he could go on the whole night like that, quite happily, talking about himself. We stood around like fools now that he couldn't see us any longer. Donovan looked at Noble, and Noble shook his head. Then Donovan raised his Webley, and at that moment Belcher gave his queer laugh again, he may have thought we were talking about him, or perhaps he noticed the same thing I'd noticed and couldn't understand it.

"Excuse me, chums," he said. "I feel I'm talking the hell of a lot, and so silly, about my being so handy about a house and things like that. But this thing came on me suddenly. You'll forgive me, I'm sure."

"You don't want to say a prayer?" asked Donovan.

"No, churn," he said. "I don't think it would help. I'm ready, and you boys want to get it over."

"You understand that we're only doing our duty? said Donovan.

Belcher's head was raised like a blind man's, so that you could only see his chin and the top of his nose in the lantern-light.

"I never could make out what duty was myself," he said. "I think you're all good lads, if that's what you mean. I'm not complaining."

Noble, just as if he couldn't bear any more of it, raised his fist at Donovan, and in a flash Donovan raised his gun and fired. The big man went over like a sack of meal, and this time there was no need of a second shot.

I don't remember much about the burying, but that it was worse than all the rest because we had to carry them to the grave. It was all mad lonely with nothing but a patch of lantern-light between ourselves and the dark, and birds hooting and screeching all round, disturbed by the guns. Noble went through Hawkins's belongings to find the letter from his mother, and then joined his hands together. He did the same with Belcher. Then, when we'd filled in the grave, we separated from Jeremiah Donovan and Feeney and took our tools back to the shed. All the way we didn't speak a word. The kitchen was dark and as we'd left it, and the old woman was sitting over the hearth, saying her beads. We walked past her into the room, and Noble struck a match to light the lamp. She rose quietly and came to the doorway with all her cantankerousness gone.

"What did ye do with them?" she asked in a whisper, and Noble started so that the match went out in his hand.

"What's that?" he asked without turning round.

"I heard ye", she said.

"What did you hear?" asked Noble.

"I heard ye. Do ye think I didn't hear ye, putting the spade back in the houseen?"

Noble struck another match and this time the lamp lit for him.

"Was that what ye did to them?" she asked.

Then, by God, in the very doorway, she fell on her knees and began praying, and after looking at her for a minute or two Noble did the same by the fireplace. I pushed my way out past her and left them at it. I stood at the door, watching the stars and listening to the shrieking of the birds dying out over the bogs. It is so strange what you feel at times like that that you can't describe it. Noble says he saw everything ten times the size, as though there were nothing in the whole world but that little patch of bog with the two Englishmen stiffening into it, but with me it was as if the patch of bog where the Englishmen were was a million miles away, and even Noble and the old woman, mumbling behind me, and the birds and the bloody stars were all far away, and I was somehow very small and very lost and lonely like a child astray in the snow. And anything that happened to me afterwards, I never felt the same about again.

LOVE

William Maxwell

William Maxwell (1908–2000) was *The New Yorker's* fiction editor for
many years but, since his death, his own work has come to be highly
appreciated. He edited many of the best-known writers of the last
century including Nabokov, Updike, Salinger, Cheever, Gallant, Welty
and Bashevis Singer. He was married for fifty-five years, dying eight days
after his wife, Emily, a painter.

MISS *Vera Brown*, she wrote on the blackboard, letter by letter in flaw-
lessly oval Palmer method. Our teacher for the fifth grade. The name
might as well have been graven in stone.

As she called the roll, her voice was as gentle as the expression in her beautiful
dark-brown eyes. She reminded me of pansies. When she called on Alvin Ahrens
to recite and he said, "I know but I can't say," the class snickered but she said,
"Try," encouragingly, and waited, to be sure that he didn't know the answer,
and then said, to one of the hands waving in the air, "Tell Alvin what one-fifth
of three-eighths is." If we arrived late to school, red-faced and out of breath and
bursting with the excuse we had thought up on the way, before we could speak
she said, "I'm sure you couldn't help it. Close the door, please, and take your
seat." If she kept us after school it was not to scold us but to help us past the
hard part.

Somebody left a big red apple on her desk for her to find when she came into
the classroom, and she smiled and put it in her desk, out of sight. Somebody else
left some purple asters, which she put in her drinking glass. After that the presents kept coming. She was the only pretty teacher in the school. She never had
to ask us to be quiet or to stop throwing erasers. We would not have dreamed of
doing anything that would displease her.

Somebody wormed it out of her when her birthday was. While she was out of
the room the class voted to present her with flowers from the greenhouse. Then
they took another vote and sweet peas won. When she saw the florist's box waiting on her desk, she said, "Oh?"

"Look inside," we all said.

Her delicate fingers seemed to take forever to remove the ribbon. In the end,
she raised the lid of the box and exclaimed.

"Read the card!" we shouted.

Many Happy Returns to Miss Vera Brown, from the Fifth Grade, it said.

She put her nose in the flowers and said, "Thank you all very, very much," and
then turned our minds to the spelling lesson for the day.

After school we escorted her downtown in a body to a special matinee of D. W. Griffith's *Hearts of the World*. She was not allowed to buy her ticket. We paid for everything.

We meant to have her for our teacher forever. We intended to pass right up through sixth, seventh, and eighth grades and on into high school taking her with us. But that isn't what happened. One day there was a substitute teacher. We expected our real teacher to be back the next day but she wasn't. Week after week passed and the substitute continued to sit at Miss Brown's desk, calling on us to recite and giving out tests and handing them back with grades on them, and we went on acting the way we had when Miss Brown was there because we didn't want her to come back and find we hadn't been nice to the substitute. One Monday morning she cleared her throat and said that Miss Brown was sick and not coming back for the rest of the term.

In the fall we had passed on into the sixth grade and she was still not back. Benny Irish's mother found out that she was living with an aunt and uncle on a farm a mile or so beyond the edge of town. One afternoon after school Benny and I got on our bikes and rode out to see her. At the place where the road turned off to go to the cemetery and the Chautauqua grounds, there was a red barn with a huge circus poster on it, showing the entire inside of the Sells-Floto Circus tent and everything that was going on in all three rings. In the summertime, riding in the backseat of my father's open Chalmers, I used to crane my neck as we passed that turn, hoping to see every last tiger and flying-trapeze artist, but it was never possible. The poster was weather-beaten now, with loose strips of paper hanging down.

It was getting dark when we wheeled our bikes up the lane of the farmhouse where Miss Brown lived.

"You knock," Benny said as we started up on the porch.

"No, you do it," I said.

We hadn't thought ahead to what it would be like to see her. We wouldn't have been surprised if she had come to the door herself and thrown up her hands in astonishment when she saw who it was, but instead a much older woman opened the door and said, "What do you want?"

"We came to see Miss Brown," I said.

"We're in her class at school," Benny explained.

I could see that the woman was trying to decide whether she should tell us to go away, but she said, "I'll find out if she wants to see you," and left us standing on the porch for what seemed like a long time. Then she appeared again and said, "You can come in now."

As we followed her through the front parlor I could make out in the dim light that there was an old-fashioned organ like the kind you used to see in country churches, and linoleum on the floor, and stiff uncomfortable chairs, and family portraits behind curved glass in big oval frames.

The room beyond it was lighted by a coal-oil lamp but seemed ever so much darker than the unlighted room we had just passed through. Propped up on pillows in a big double bed was our teacher, but so changed. Her arms were like sticks, and all the life in her seemed concentrated in her eyes, which had dark circles around them and were enormous. She managed a flicker of recognition but I was struck dumb by the fact that she didn't seem glad to see us. She didn't belong to us anymore. She belonged to her illness.

Benny said, "I hope you get well soon."

The angel who watches over little boys who know but they can't say it saw to it that we didn't touch anything. And in a minute we were outside, on our bicycles, riding through the dusk toward the turn in the road and town.

A few weeks later I read in the Lincoln *Evening Courier* that Miss Vera Brown, who taught the fifth grade in Central School, had died of tuberculosis, aged twenty-three years and seven months.

Sometimes I went with my mother when she put flowers on the graves of my grandparents. The cinder roads wound through the cemetery in ways she understood and I didn't, and I would read the names on the monuments: Brower, Cadwallader, Andrews, Bates, Mitchell. In loving memory of. Infant daughter of. Beloved wife of. The cemetery was so large and so many people were buried there, it would have taken a long time to locate a particular grave, if you didn't know where it was already. But I know, the way I sometimes know what is in wrapped packages, that the elderly woman who let us in and who took care of Miss Brown during her last illness went to the cemetery regularly and poured the rancid water out of the tin receptacle that was sunk below the level of the grass at the foot of her grave, and filled it with fresh water from a nearby faucet and arranged the flowers she had brought in such a way as to please the eye of the living and the closed eyes of the dead.

PETRIFIED MAN

Eudora Welty

Eudora Welty (1909–2001) mostly wrote novels and stories set in the American South, where she was born and died, in Jackson, Mississippi. Her 1973 novel *The Optimist's Daughter* won the Pulitzer Prize. She published over forty stories in her lifetime, many of them winning awards, and she became the first living writer to have her work included in the Library of America.

Reach in my purse and git me a cigarette without no powder in it if you kin, Mrs. Fletcher, honey," said Leota to her ten o'clock shampoo-and-set customer. "I don't like no perfumed cigarettes."

Mrs. Fletcher gladly reached over to the lavender shelf under the lavender-framed mirror, shook a hair net loose from the clasp of the patent-leather bag, and slapped her hand down quickly on a powder puff which burst out when the purse was opened.

"Why, look at the peanuts, Leota!" said Mrs. Fletcher in her marvelling voice.

"Honey, them goobers has been in my purse a week if they's been in it a day. Mrs. Pike bought them peanuts."

"Who's Mrs. Pike?" asked Mrs. Fletcher, settling back. Hidden in this den of curling fluid and henna packs, separated by a lavender swing-door from the other customers, who were being gratified in other booths, she could give her curiosity its freedom. She looked expectantly at the black part in Leota's yellow curls as she bent to light the cigarette.

"Mrs. Pike is this lady from New Orleans," said Leota, puffing, and pressing into Mrs. Fletcher's scalp with strong red-nailed fingers. "A friend, not a customer. You see, like maybe I told you last time, me and Fred and Sal and Joe all had us a fuss, so Sal and Joe up and moved out, so we didn't do a thing but rent out their room. So we rented it to Mrs. Pike. And Mr. Pike." She flicked an ash into the basket of dirty towels. "Mrs. Pike is a very decided blonde. *She* bought me the peanuts."

"She must be cute," said Mrs. Fletcher.

"Honey, 'cute' ain't the word for what she is. I'm tellin' you, Mrs. Pike is attractive. She has her a good time. She's got a sharp eye out, Mrs. Pike has."

She dashed the comb through the air, and paused dramatically as a cloud of Mrs. Fletcher's hennaed hair floated out of the lavender teeth like a small storm-cloud.

"Hair fallin'."

"Aw, Leota."

"Uh-huh, commencin' to fall out," said Leota, combing again, and letting fall another cloud.

"Is it any dandruff in it?" Mrs. Fletcher was frowning, her hair-line eyebrows diving down toward her nose, and her wrinkled, beady-lashed eyelids batting with concentration.

"Nope." She combed again. "Just fallin' out."

"Bet it was that last perm'nent you gave me that did it," Mrs. Fletcher said cruelly. "Remember you cooked me fourteen minutes."

"You had fourteen minutes comin' to you," said Leota with finality.

"Bound to be somethin'," persisted Mrs. Fletcher. "Dandruff, dandruff. I couldn't of caught a thing like that from Mr. Fletcher, could I?"

"Well," Leota answered at last, "you know what I heard in here yestiddy, one of Thelma's ladies was settin' over yonder in Thelma's booth gittin' a machine-less, and I don't mean to insist or insinuate or anything, Mrs. Fletcher, but Thelma's lady just happ'med to throw out – I forgotten what she was talkin' about at the time that you was p-r-e-g., and lots of times that'll make your hair do awful funny, fall out and God knows what all. It just ain't our fault, is the way I look at it."

There was a pause. The women stared at each other in the mirror.

"Who was it?" demanded Mrs. Fletcher.

"Honey, I really couldn't say," said Leota. "Not that you look it."

"Where's Thelma? I'll get it out of her," said Mrs. Fletcher.

"Now, honey, I wouldn't go and git mad over a little thing like that," Leota said, combing hastily, as though to hold Mrs. Fletcher down by the hair. "I'm sure it was somebody didn't mean no harm in the world. How far gone are you?"

"Just wait," said Mrs. Fletcher, and shrieked for Thelma, who came in and took a drag from Leota's cigarette.

"Thelma, honey, throw your mind back to yes-tiddy if you kin," said Leota, drenching Mrs. Fletcher's hair with a thick fluid and catching the overflow in a cold wet towel at her neck.

"Well, I got my lady half wound for a spiral," said Thelma doubtfully.

"This won't take but a minute," said Leota. "Who is it you got in there, old Horse Face? Just cast your mind back and try to remember who your lady was yestiddy who happ'm to mention that my customer was pregnant, that's all. She's dead to know."

Thelma drooped her blood-red lips and looked over Mrs. Fletcher's head into the mirror. "Why, honey, I ain't got the faintest," she breathed. "I really don't recollect the faintest. But I'm sure she meant no harm. I declare, I forgot my hair finally got combed and thought it was a stranger behind me."

"Was it that Mrs. Hutchinson?" Mrs. Fletcher was tensely polite.

"Mrs. Hutchinson? Oh, Mrs. Hutchinson." Thelma batted her eyes. "Naw, precious, she come on Thursday and didn't ev'm mention your name. I doubt if she ev'm knows you're on the way."

"Thelma!" cried Leota staunchly.

"All I know is, whoever it is 'll be sorry some day. Why, I just barely knew it myself!" cried Mrs. Fletcher. "Just let her wait!"

"Why? What're you gonna do to her?"

It was a child's voice, and the women looked down. A little boy was making tents with aluminum wave pinchers on the floor under the sink.

"Billy Boy, hon, mustn't bother nice ladies," Leota smiled. She slapped him brightly and behind her back waved Thelma out of the booth. "Ain't Billy Boy a sight? Only three years old and already just nuts about the beauty-parlor business."

"I never saw him here before," said Mrs. Fletcher, still unmollified.

"He ain't been here before, that's how come," said Leota. "He belongs to Mrs. Pike. She got her a job but it was Fay's Millinery. He oughtn't to try on those ladies' hats, they come down over his eyes like I don't know what. They just git to look ridiculous, that's what, an' of course he's gonna put 'em on: hats. They tole Mrs. Pike they didn't appreciate him hangin' around there. Here, he couldn't hurt a thing."

"Well! I don't like children that much," said Mrs. Fletcher.

"Well!" said Leota moodily.

"Well! I'm almost tempted not to have this one," said Mrs. Fletcher. "That Mrs. Hutchinson! Just looks straight through you when she sees you on the street and then spits at you behind your back."

"Mr. Fletcher would beat you on the head if you didn't have it now," said Leota reasonably. "After going this far."

Mrs. Fletcher sat up straight. "Mr. Fletcher can't do a thing with me."

"He can't!" Leota winked at herself in the mirror.

"No, siree, he can't. If he so much as raises his voice against me, he knows good and well I'll have one of my sick headaches, and then I'm just not fit to live with. And if I really look that pregnant already –"

"Well, now, honey, I just want you to know – I habm't told any of my ladies and I ain't goin' to tell 'em – even that you're losin' your hair. You just get you one of those Stork-a-Lure dresses and stop worryin'. What people don't know don't hurt nobody, as Mrs. Pike says."

"Did you tell Mrs. Pike?" asked Mrs. Fletcher sulkily.

"Well, Mrs. Fletcher, look, you ain't ever goin' to lay eyes on Mrs. Pike or her lay eyes on you, so what difference does it make in the long run?"

"I knew it!" Mrs. Fletcher deliberately nodded her head so as to destroy a ringlet Leota was working on behind her ear. "Mrs. Pike!"

Leota sighed. "I reckon I might as well tell you. It wasn't any more Thelma's lady tole me you was pregnant than a bat."

"Not Mrs. Hutchinson?"

"Naw, Lord! It was Mrs. Pike."

"Mrs. Pike!" Mrs. Fletcher could only sputter and let curling fluid roll into her ear. "How could Mrs. Pike possibly know I was pregnant or otherwise, when she doesn't even know me? The nerve of some people!"

"Well, here's how it was. Remember Sunday?"

"Yes," said Mrs. Fletcher.

"Sunday, Mrs. Pike an' me was all by ourself. Mr. Pike and Fred had gone over to Eagle Lake, sayin' they was goin' to catch 'em some fish, but they didn't a course. So we was settin' in Mrs. Pike's car, it's a 1939 Dodge –"

"1939, eh," said Mrs. Fletcher.

"– An' we was gettin' us a Jax beer apiece – that's the beer that Mrs. Pike says is made right in N.O., so she won't drink no other kind. So I seen you drive up to the drugstore an' run in for just a secont, leavin' I reckon Mr. Fletcher in the car, an' come runnin' out with looked like a perscription. So I says to Mrs. Pike, just to be makin' talk, 'Right yonder's Mrs. Fletcher, and I reckon that's Mr. Fletcher – she's one of my regular customers,' I says."

"I had on a figured print," said Mrs. Fletcher tentatively.

"You sure did," agreed Leota. "So Mrs. Pike, she give you a good look – she's very observant, a good judge of character, cute as a minute, you know – and she says, 'I bet you another Jax that lady's three months on the way.' "

"What gall!" said Mrs. Fletcher. "Mrs. Pike!"

"Mrs. Pike ain't goin' to bite you," said Leota. "Mrs. Pike is a lovely girl, you'd be crazy about her, Mrs. Fletcher. But she can't sit still a minute. We went to the travellin' freak show yestiddy after work. I got through early – nine o'clock. In the vacant store next door. What, you ain't been?"

"No, I despise freaks," declared Mrs. Fletcher.

"Aw. Well, honey, talkin' about bein' pregnant an' all, you ought to see those twins in a bottle, you really owe it to yourself."

"What twins?" asked Mrs. Fletcher out of the side of her mouth.

"Well, honey, they got these two twins in a bottle, see? Born joined plumb together – dead a course." Leota dropped her voice into a soft lyrical hum. "They was about this long – pardon – must of been full time, all right, wouldn't you say? – an' they had these two heads an' two faces an' four arms an' four legs, all kind of joined *here*. See, this face looked this-a-way, and the other face looked that-a-way, over their shoulder, see. Kinda pathetic."

"Glah !" said Mrs. Fletcher disapprovingly.

"Well, ugly? Honey, I mean to tell you – their parents was first cousins and all like that. Billy Boy, git me a fresh towel from off Teeny's stack – this 'n's wringin' wet – an' quit ticklin' my ankles with that curler. I declare! He don't miss nothin'."

"Me and Mr. Fletcher aren't one speck of kin, or he could never of had me," said Mrs. Fletcher placidly.

"Of course not!" protested Leota. "Neither is me an' Fred, not that we know of. Well, honey, what Mrs. Pike liked was the pygmies. They've got these pygmies down there, too, an' Mrs. Pike was just wild about 'em. You know, the teeniniest men in the universe? Well, honey, they can just rest back on their little bohunkus an' roll around an' you can't hardly tell if they're sittin' or standin'. That'll give you some idea. They're about forty-two years old. Just suppose it was your husband!"

"Well, Mr. Fletcher is five foot nine and one half," said Mrs. Fletcher quickly.

"Fred's five foot ten," said Leota, "but I tell him he's still a shrimp, account of I'm so tall." She made a deep wave over Mrs. Fletcher's other temple with the comb. "Well, these pygmies are a kind of a dark brown, Mrs. Fletcher. Not bad-lookin' for what they are, you know."

"I wouldn't care for them," said Mrs. Fletcher. "What does that Mrs. Pike see in them?"

"Aw, I don't know," said Leota. "She's just cute, that's all. But they got this man, this petrified man, that ever'thing ever since he was nine years old, when it goes through his digestion, see, somehow Mrs. Pike says it goes to his joints and has been turning to stone."

"How awful!" said Mrs. Fletcher.

"He's forty-two too. That looks like a bad age."

"Who said so, that Mrs. Pike? I bet she's forty-two," said Mrs. Fletcher.

"Naw," said Leota, "Mrs. Pike's thirty-three, born in January, an Aquarian. He could move his head – like this. A course his head and mind ain't a joint, so to speak, and I guess his stomach ain't, either – not yet, anyways. But see – his food, he eats it, and it goes down, see, and then he digests it" – Leota rose on her toes for an instant – "and it goes out to his joints and before you can say 'Jack Robinson,' it's stone – pure stone. He's turning to stone. How'd you like to be married to a guy like that? All he can do, he can move his head just a quarter of an inch. A course he *looks* just *terrible*."

"I should think he would," said Mrs. Fletcher frostily. "Mr. Fletcher takes bending exercises every night of the world. I make him."

"All Fred does is lay around the house like a rug. I wouldn't be surprised if he woke up some day and couldn't move. The petrified man just sat there moving his quarter of an inch though," said Leota reminiscently.

"Did Mrs. Pike like the petrified man?" asked Mrs. Fletcher.

"Not as much as she did the others," said Leota deprecatingly. "And then she likes a man to be a good dresser, and all that."

"Is Mr. Pike a good dresser?" asked Mrs. Fletcher sceptically.

"Oh, well, yeah," said Leota, "but he's twelve or fourteen years older'n her. She ast Lady Evangeline about him."

"Who's Lady Evangeline?" asked Mrs. Fletcher.

"Well, it's this mind reader they got in the freak show," said Leota. "Was real good. Lady Evangeline is her name, and if I had another dollar I wouldn't do a thing but have my other palm read. She had what Mrs. Pike said was the 'sixth mind' but she had the worst manicure I ever saw on a living person."

"What did she tell Mrs. Pike?" asked Mrs. Fletcher.

"She told her Mr. Pike was as true to her as he could be and besides, would come into some money."

"Humph!" said Mrs. Fletcher. "What does he do?"

"I can't tell," said Leota, "because he don't work. Lady Evangeline didn't tell me enough about my nature or anything. And I would like to go back and find out some more about this boy. Used to go with this boy until he got married to this girl. Oh, shoot, that was about three and a half years ago, when you was still goin' to the Robert E. Lee Beauty Shop in Jackson. He married her for her money. Another fortune-teller tole me that at the time. So I'm not in love with him any more, anyway, besides being married to Fred, but Mrs. Pike thought, just for the hell of it, see, to ask Lady Evangeline was he happy."

"Does Mrs. Pike know everything about you already?" asked Mrs. Fletcher unbelievingly. "Mercy!"

"Oh, yeah, I tole her ever'thing about ever'thing, from now on back to I don't know when – to when I first started goin' out," said Leota. "So I ast Lady Evangeline for one of my questions, was he happily married, and she says, just like she was glad I ask her, 'Honey,' she says, 'naw, he idn't. You write down this day, March 8, 1941,' she says, 'and mock it down: three years from today him and her won't be occupyin' the same bed.' There it is, up on the wall with them other dates – see, Mrs. Fletcher? And she says, 'Child, you ought to be glad you didn't git him, because he's so mercenary.' So I'm glad I married Fred. He sure ain't mercenary, money don't mean a thing to him. But I sure would like to go back and have my other palm read."

"Did Mrs. Pike believe in what the fortuneteller said?" asked Mrs. Fletcher in a superior tone of voice.

"Lord, yes, she's from New Orleans. Ever'body in New Orleans believes ever'thing spooky. One of 'em in New Orleans before it was raided says to Mrs. Pike one summer she was goin' to go from State to State and meet some grey-headed men, and, sure enough, she says she went on a beautician convention up to Chicago. . . ."

"Oh!" said Mrs. Fletcher. "Oh, is Mrs. Pike a beautician too?"

"Sure she is," protested Leota. "She's a beautician. I'm goin' to git her in here if I can. Before she married. But it don't leave you. She says sure enough, there was three men who was a very large part of making her trip what it was, and they all three had grey in their hair and they went in six States. Got Christmas cards from 'em. Billy Boy, go see if Thelma's got any dry cotton. Look how Mrs. Fletcher's a-drippin'."

"Where did Mrs. Pike meet Mr. Pike?" asked Mrs. Fletcher primly.

"On another train," said Leota.

"I met Mr. Fletcher, or rather he met me, in a rental library," said Mrs. Fletcher with dignity, as she watched the net come down over her head.

"Honey, me an' Fred, we met in a rumble seat eight months ago and we was practically on what you might call the way to the altar inside of half an hour," said Leota in a guttural voice, and bit a bobby pin open. "Course it don't last. Mrs. Pike says nothin' like that ever lasts."

"Mr. Fletcher and myself are as much in love as the day we married," said Mrs. Fletcher belligerently as Leota stuffed cotton into her ears.

"Mrs. Pike says it don't last," repeated Leota in a louder voice. "Now go git under the dryer. You can turn yourself on, can't you? I'll be back to comb you out. Durin' lunch I promised to give Mrs. Pike a facial. You know – free. Her bein' in the business, so to speak."

"I bet she needs one," said Mrs. Fletcher, letting the swing-door fly back against Leota. "Oh, pardon me."

A week later, on time for her appointment, Mrs. Fletcher sank heavily into Leota's chair after first removing a drug-store rental book, called *Life Is Like That*, from the seat. She stared in a discouraged way into the mirror.

"You can tell it when I'm sitting down, all right," she said.

Leota seemed preoccupied and stood shaking out a lavender cloth. She began to pin it around Mrs. Fletcher's neck in silence.

"I said you sure can tell it when I'm sitting straight on and coming at you this way," Mrs. Fletcher said.

"Why, honey, naw you can't," said Leota gloomily. "Why, I'd never know. If somebody was to come up to me on the street and say, 'Mrs. Fletcher is pregnant!' I'd say, 'Heck, she don't look it to me.' "

"If a certain party hadn't found it out and spread it around, it wouldn't be too late even now," said Mrs. Fletcher frostily, but Leota was almost choking her with the cloth, pinning it so tight, and she couldn't speak clearly. She paddled her hands in the air until Leota wearily loosened her.

"Listen, honey, you're just a virgin compared to Mrs. Montjoy," Leota was going on, still absent-minded. She bent Mrs. Fletcher back in the chair and, sighing, tossed liquid from a teacup on to her head and dug both hands into her scalp. "You know Mrs. Montjoy – her husband's that premature-grey-headed fella?"

"She's in the Trojan Garden Club, is all I know," said Mrs. Fletcher.

"Well, honey," said Leota, but in a weary voice, "she come in here not the week before and not the day before she had her baby – she come in here the very selfsame day, I mean to tell you. Child, we was all plumb scared to death. There she was! Come for her shampoo an' set. Why, Mrs. Fletcher, in an hour an' twenty minutes she was layin' up there in the Babtist Hospital with a seb'm-pound son. It was that close a shave. I declare, if I hadn't been so tired I would of drank up a bottle of gin that night."

"What gall," said Mrs. Fletcher. "I never knew her at all well."

"See, her husband was waitin' outside in the car, and her bags was all packed an' in the back seat, an' she was all ready, 'cept she wanted her shampoo an' set. An' havin' one pain right after another. Her husband kep' comin' in here, scared-like, but couldn't do nothin' with her a course. She yelled bloody murder, too, but she always yelled her head off when I give her a perm'nent."

"She must of been crazy," said Mrs. Fletcher. "How did she look?"

"Shoot!" said Leota.

"Well, I can guess," said Mrs. Fletcher. "Awful."

"Just wanted to look pretty while she was havin' her baby, is all," said Leota airily. "Course, we was glad to give the lady what she was after – that's our motto – but I bet a hour later she wasn't payin' no mind to them little end curls. I bet she wasn't thinkin' about she ought to have on a net. It wouldn't of done her no good if she had."

"No, I don't suppose it would," said Mrs. Fletcher.

"Yeah man! She was a-yellin'. Just like when I give her perm'nent."

"Her husband ought to make her behave. Don't it seem that way to you?" asked Mrs. Fletcher. "He ought to put his foot down."

"Ha," said Leota. "A lot he could do. Maybe some women is soft."

"Oh, you mistake me, I don't mean for her to get soft – far from it! Women have to stand up for themselves, or there's just no telling. But now you take me – I ask Mr. Fletcher's advice now and then, and he appreciates it, especially on something important, like is it time for a permanent – not that I've told him about the baby. He says, 'Why, dear, go ahead!' Just ask their *advice*."

"Huh! If I ever ast Fred's advice we'd be floatin' down the Yazoo River on a houseboat or somethin' by this time," said Leota. "I'm sick of Fred. I told him to go over to Vicksburg."

"Is he going?" demanded Mrs. Fletcher.

"Sure. See, the fortune-teller – I went back and had my other palm read, since we've got to rent the room agin – said my lover was goin' to work in Vicksburg, so I don't know who she could mean, unless she meant Fred. And Fred ain't workin' here – that much is so."

"Is he going to work in Vicksburg?' asked Mrs. Fletcher. "And –"

"Sure. Lady Evangeline said so. Said the future is going to be brighter than the present. He don't want to go, but I ain't gonna put up with nothin' like that. Lays around the house an' bulls – did bull – with that good-for-nothin' Mr. Pike. He says if he goes who'll cook, but I says I never get to eat anyway – not meals. Billy Boy, take Mrs. Grover that *Screen Secrets* and leg it."

Mrs. Fletcher heard stamping feet go out the door.

"Is that that Mrs. Pike's little boy here again?" she asked, sitting up gingerly.

"Yeah, that's still him." Leota stuck out her tongue.

Mrs. Fletcher could hardly believe her eyes. "Well! How's Mrs. Pike, your attractive new friend with the sharp eyes who spreads it around town that perfect strangers are pregnant?" she asked in a sweetened tone.

"Oh, Mizziz Pike." Leota combed Mrs. Fletcher's hair with heavy strokes.

"You act like you're tired," said Mrs. Fletcher.

"Tired? Feel like it's four o'clock in the afternoon already," said Leota. "I ain't told you the awful luck we had, me and Fred? It's the worst thing you ever heard of. Maybe *you* think Mrs. Pike's got sharp eyes. Shoot, there's a limit! Well, you know, we rented out our room to this Mr. and Mrs. Pike from New Orleans when Sal an' Joe Fentress got mad at us 'cause they drank up some home-brew we had in the closet – Sal an' Joe did. So, a week ago Sat'day Mr. and Mrs. Pike moved in. Well, I kinda fixed up the room, you know – put a sofa pillow on the couch and picked some ragged robbins and put in a vase, but they never did say they appreciated it. Anyway, then I put some old magazines on the table."

"I think that was lovely," said Mrs. Fletcher.

"Wait. So, come night 'fore last, Fred and this Mr. Pike, who Fred just took up with, was back from they said they was fishin', bein' as neither one of 'em has got a job to his name, and we was all settin' around in their room. So Mrs. Pike was settin' there, readin' a old *Startling G-Man Tales* that was mine, mind you, I'd bought it myself, and all of a sudden she jumps! – into the air – you'd 'a' thought she'd set on a spider – an' says, 'Canfield' – ain't that silly, that's Mr. Pike – 'Canfield, my God A'mighty,' she says, 'honey,' she says, 'we're rich, and you won't have to work.' Not that he turned one hand anyway. Well, me and Fred rushes over to her, and Mr. Pike, too, and there she sets, pointin' her finger at a photo in my copy of *Startling G-Man*. 'See that man?' yells Mrs. Pike. 'Remember him, Canfield?' 'Never forget a face,' says Mr. Pike. 'It's Mr. Petrie, that we stayed with him in the apartment next to ours in Toulouse Street in N.O. for six weeks. Mr. Petrie.' 'Well,' says Mrs. Pike, like she can't hold out one secont longer, 'Mr. Petrie is wanted for five hundred dollars cash, for rapin' four women in California, and I know where he is.' "

"Mercy!" said Mrs. Fletcher. "Where was he?"

At some time Leota had washed her hair and now she yanked her up by the back locks and sat her up.

"Know where he was?"

"I certainly don't," Mrs. Fletcher said. Her scalp hurt all over.

Leota flung a towel around the top of her customer's head. "Nowhere else but in that freak show! I saw him just as plain as Mrs. Pike. *He* was the petrified man!"

"Who would ever have thought that!" cried Mrs. Fletcher sympathetically.

"So Mr. Pike says, 'Well whatta you know about that,' an' he looks real hard at the photo and whistles. And she starts dancin' and singin' about their good luck. She meant our bad luck! I made a point of tellin' that fortune-teller the next time I saw her. I said, 'Listen, that magazine was layin' around the house for a month, and there was the freak show runnin' night an' day, not two steps away from my own beauty parlor, with Mr. Petrie just settin' there waitin'. An' it had to be Mr. and Mrs. Pike, almost perfect strangers.' "

"What gall," said Mrs. Fletcher. She was only sitting there, wrapped in a turban, but she did not mind.

"Fortune-tellers don't care. And Mrs. Pike, she goes around actin' like she thinks she was Mrs. God," said Leota. "So they're goin' to leave tomorrow, Mr. and Mrs. Pike. And in the meantime I got to keep that mean, bad little ole kid here, gettin' under my feet ever' minute of the day an' talkin' back too."

"Have they gotten the five hundred dollars' reward already?" asked Mrs. Fletcher.

"Well," said Leota, "at first Mr. Pike didn't want to do anything about it. Can you feature that? Said he kinda liked that ole bird and said he was real nice to 'em, lent 'em money or somethin'. But Mrs. Pike simply tole him he could just go to hell, and I can see her point. She says, 'You ain't worked a lick in six months, and here I make five hundred dollars in two seconts, and what thanks do I get for it? You go to hell, Canfield,' she says. So," Leota went on in a despondent voice, "they called up the cops and they caught the ole bird, all right, right there in the freak show where I saw him with my own eyes, thinkin' he was petrified. He's the one. Did it under his real name – Mr. Petrie. Four women in California, all in the month of August. So Mrs. Pike gits five hundred dollars. And my magazine, and right next door to my beauty parlor. I cried all night, but Fred said it wasn't a bit of use and to go to sleep, because the whole thing was just a sort of coincidence – you know: can't do nothin' about it. He says it put him clean out of the notion of goin' to Vicksburg for a few days till we rent out the room agin – no tellin' who we'll git this time."

"But can you imagine anybody knowing this old man, that's raped four women?" persisted Mrs. Fletcher, and she shuddered audibly. "Did Mrs. Pike *speak* to him when she met him in the freak show?"

Leota had begun to comb Mrs. Fletcher's hair. "I says to her, I says, 'I didn't notice you fallin' on his neck when he was the petrified man – don't tell me you didn't recognize your fine friend?' And she says, 'I didn't recognize him with that white powder all over his face. He just looked familiar.' Mrs. Pike says, 'and lots of people look familiar.' But she says that ole petrified man did put her in mind of somebody. She wondered who it was! Kep' her awake, which man she'd ever knew it reminded her of. So when she seen the photo, it all come to her. Like a flash. Mr. Petrie. The way he'd turn his head and look at her when she took him in his breakfast."

"Took him in his breakfast!" shrieked Mrs. Fletcher. "Listen – don't tell me. I'd 'a' felt something."

"Four women. I guess those women didn't have the faintest notion at the time they'd be worth a hunderd an' twenty-five bucks a piece some day to Mrs. Pike.

We ast her how old the fella was then, an' she says he musta had one foot in the grave, at least. Can you beat it?"

"Not really petrified at all, of course," said Mrs. Fletcher meditatively. She drew herself up. "I'd 'a' felt something," she said proudly.

"Shoot! I did feel somethin'," said Leota. "I tole Fred when I got home I felt so funny. I said, 'Fred, that ole petrified man sure did leave me with a funny feelin'.' He says, 'Funny-haha or funny-peculiar?' and I says, 'Funny-peculiar.' " She pointed her comb into the air emphatically.

"I'll bet you did," said Mrs. Fletcher.

They both heard a crackling noise.

Leota screamed, "Billy Boy! What you doin' in my purse?"

"Aw, I'm just eatin' these ole stale peanuts up," said Billy Boy.

"You come here to me!" screamed Leota, recklessly flinging down the comb, which scattered a whole ashtray full of bobby pins and knocked down a row of Coca-Cola bottles. "This is the last straw!"

"I caught him! I caught him!" giggled Mrs. Fletcher. "I'll hold him on my lap. You bad, bad boy, you! I guess I better learn how to spank little old bad boys," she said.

Leota's eleven o'clock customer pushed open the swing-door upon Leota paddling him heartily with the brush, while he gave angry but belittling screams which penetrated beyond the booth and filled the whole curious beauty parlor. From everywhere ladies began to gather round to watch the paddling. Billy Boy kicked both Leota and Mrs. Fletcher as hard as he could, Mrs. Fletcher with her new fixed smile.

Billy Boy stomped through the group of wild-haired ladies and went out the door, but flung back the words, "If you're so smart, why ain't you rich?"

THE SWIMMER

John Cheever

John Cheever (1912–1982) was awarded the National Book Award for
his first novel in 1958, *The Wapshot Chronicle*, and the Howells Medal
for Fiction from the National Academy of Letters in 1965. His journals
show he was a complicated man, but his stories breathe an elegance and
simplicity that is rare to find. Hearing Richard Ford read, and talk, about
another Cheever masterpiece "Reunion" on *The New Yorker* fiction pod-
cast is almost essential.

It was one of those midsummer Sundays when everyone sits around saying, 'I
drank too much last night.' You might have heard it whispered by the parishioners leaving church, heard it from the lips of the priest himself, struggling
with his cassock in the *vestiarium*, heard it from the golf links and the tennis courts, heard it from the wildlife preserve where the leader of the Audubon
group was suffering from a terrible hangover. I *drank* too much,' said Donald
Westerhazy. 'We all *drank* too much,' said Lucinda Merrill. 'It must have been the
wine,' said Helen Westerhazy. 'I *drank* too much of that claret.'

This was at the edge of the Westerhazys' pool. The pool, fed by an artesian
well with a high iron content, was a pale shade of green. It was a fine day. In
the west there was a massive stand of cumulus cloud so like a city seen from a
distance – from the bow of an approaching ship – that it might have had a name.
Lisbon. Hackensack. The sun was hot. Neddy Merrill sat by the green water, one
hand in it, one around a glass of gin. He was a slender man – he seemed to have
the especial slenderness of youth – and while he was far from young he had slid
down his banister that morning and given the bronze backside of Aphrodite on
the hall table a smack, as he jogged toward the smell of coffee in his dining room.
He might have been compared to a summer's day, particularly the last hours of
one, and while he lacked a tennis racket or a sail bag the impression was definitely one of youth, sport, and clement weather. He had been swimming and now he
was breathing deeply, stertorously as if he could gulp into his lungs the components of that moment, the heat of the sun, the intenseness of his pleasure. It all
seemed to flow into his chest. His own house stood in Bullet Park, eight miles to
the south, where his four beautiful daughters would have had their lunch and
might be playing tennis. Then it occurred to him that by taking a dogleg to the
southwest he could reach his home by water.

His life was not confining and the delight he took in this observation could
not be explained by its suggestion of escape. He seemed to see, with a cartogra-
pher's eye, that string of swimming pools, that quasi-subterranean stream that

curved across the county. He had made a discovery, a contribution to modern geography; he would name the stream Lucinda after his wife. He was not a practical joker nor was he a fool but he was determinedly original and had a vague and modest idea of himself as a legendary figure. The day was beautiful and it seemed to him that a long swim might enlarge and celebrate its beauty.

He took off a sweater that was hung over his shoulders and dove in. He had an inexplicable contempt for men who did not hurl themselves into pools. He swam a choppy crawl, breathing either with every stroke or every fourth stroke and counting somewhere well in the back of his mind the one-two one-two of a flutter kick. It was not a serviceable stroke for long distances but the domestication of swimming had saddled the sport with some customs and in his part of the world a crawl was customary. To be embraced and sustained by the light green water was less a pleasure, it seemed, than the resumption of a natural condition, and he would have liked to swim without trunks, but this was not possible, considering his project. He hoisted himself up on the far curb – he never used the ladder – and started across the lawn. When Lucinda asked where he was going he said he was going to swim home.

The only maps and charts he had to go by were remembered or imaginary but these were clear enough. First there were the Grahams, the Hammers, the Lears, the Howlands, and the Crosscups. He would cross Ditmar Street to the Bunkers and come, after a short portage, to the Levys, the Welchers, and the public pool in Lancaster. Then there were the Hallorans, the Sachses, the Biswangers, Shirley Adams, the Gilmartins, and the Clydes. The day was lovely, and that he lived in a world so generously supplied with water seemed like a clemency, a beneficence. His heart was high and he ran across the grass. Making his way home by an uncommon route gave him the feeling that he was a pilgrim, an explorer, a man with a destiny, and he knew that he would find friends all along the way; friends would line the banks of the Lucinda River.

He went through a hedge that separated the Westerhazys' land from the Grahams', walked under some flowering apple trees, passed the shed that housed their pump and filter, and came out at the Grahams' pool. 'Why, Neddy,' Mrs Graham said, 'what a marvelous surprise. I've been trying to get you on the phone all morning. Here, let me get you a drink.' He saw then, like any explorer, that the hospitable customs and traditions of the natives would have to be handled with diplomacy if he was ever going to reach his destination. He did not want to mystify or seem rude to the Grahams nor did he have the time to linger there. He swam the length of their pool and joined them in the sun and was rescued, a few minutes later, by the arrival of two carloads of friends from Connecticut. During the uproarious reunions he was able to slip away. He went down by the front of the Grahams' house, stepped over a thorny hedge, and crossed a vacant lot to the Hammers'. Mrs Hammer, looking up from her roses, saw him swim by although she wasn't quite sure who it was. The Lears heard him splashing past the open windows of their living room. The Howlands and the Crosscups were away. After leaving the Howlands' he crossed Ditmar Street and started for the Bunkers', where he could hear, even at that distance, the noise of a party.

The water refracted the sound of voices and laughter and seemed to suspend it in midair. The Bunkers' pool was on a rise and he climbed some stairs to a terrace where twenty-five or thirty men and women were drinking. The only person in the water was Rusty Towers, who floated there on a rubber raft. Oh, how bonny and lush were the banks of the Lucinda River! Prosperous men and women gathered by the sapphire-colored waters while caterer's men in white coats passed them cold gin. Overhead a red de Haviland trainer was circling around and around and around in the sky with something like the glee of a child in a swing. Ned felt a passing affection for the scene, a tenderness for the gathering, as if it was something he might touch. In the distance he heard thunder. As soon as Enid Bunker saw him she began to scream: 'Oh, look who's here! What a marvelous surprise! When Lucinda said that you couldn't come I though I'd *die*.' She made her way to him through the crowd, and when they had finished kissing she led him to the bar, a progress that was slowed by the fact that he stopped to kiss eight or ten other women and shake the hands of as many men. A smiling bartender he had seen at a hundred parties gave him a gin and tonic and he stood by the bar for a moment, anxious not to get stuck in any conversation that would delay his voyage. When he seemed about to be surrounded he dove in and swam close to the side to avoid colliding with Rusty's raft. At the far end of the pool he bypassed the Tomlinsons with a broad smile and jogged up the garden path. The gravel cut his feet but this was the only unpleasantness. The party was confined to the pool, and as he went toward the house he heard the brilliant, watery sound of voices fade, heard the noise of a radio from the Bunkers' kitchen, where someone was listening to a ball game. Sunday afternoon. He made his way through the parked cars and down the grassy border of their driveway to Alewives Lane. He did not want to be seen on the road in his bathing trunks but there was no traffic and he made the short distance to the Levys' driveway, marked with a PRIVATE PROPERTY sign and a green tube for *The New York Times*. All the doors and windows of the big house were open but there were no signs of life; not even a dog barked. He went around the side of the house to the pool and saw that the Levys had only recently left. Glasses and bottles and dishes of nuts were on a table at the deep end, where there was a bathhouse or gazebo, hung with Japanese lanterns. After swimming the pool he got himself a glass and poured a drink. It was his fourth or fifth drink and he had swum nearly half the length of the Lucinda River. He felt tired, clean, and pleased at that moment to be alone; pleased with everything.

It would storm. The stand of cumulus cloud – that city – had risen and darkened, and while he sat there he heard the percussiveness of thunder again. The de Haviland trainer was still circling overhead and it seemed to Ned that he could almost hear the pilot laugh with pleasure in the afternoon; but when there was another peal of thunder he took off for home. A train whistle blew and he wondered what time it had gotten to be. Four? Five? He thought of the provincial station at that hour, where a waiter, his tuxedo concealed by a raincoat, a dwarf with some flowers wrapped in newspaper, and a woman who had been crying would be waiting for the local. It was suddenly growing dark; it was that moment when the pin-headed birds seem to organize their song into some acute and knowledgeable recognition of the storm's approach. Then there was a fine noise of rushing water from the crown of an oak at his back, as if a spigot there had been turned. Then the noise of fountains came from the crowns of all the tall trees. Why did he love storms, what was the meaning of his excitement when the door sprang open and the rain wind fled rudely up the stairs, why had the simple task of shutting the windows of an old house seemed fitting and urgent, why did the first watery notes of a storm wind have for him the unmistakable sound of good news, cheer, glad tidings? Then there was an explosion, a smell of cordite, and rain lashed the Japanese lanterns that Mrs Levy had bought in Kyoto the year before last, or was it the year before that?

He stayed in the Levys' gazebo until the storm had passed. The rain had cooled the air and he shivered. The force of the wind had stripped a maple of its red and yellow leaves and scattered them over the grass and the water. Since it was mid-summer the tree must be blighted, and yet he felt a peculiar sadness at this sign of autumn. He braced his shoulders, emptied his glass, and started for the Welchers' pool. This meant crossing the Lindleys' riding ring and he was surprised to find it overgrown with grass and all the jumps dismantled. He wondered if the Lindleys had sold their horses or gone away for the summer and put them out to board. He seemed to remember having heard something about the Lindleys and their horses but the memory was unclear. On he went, barefoot through the wet grass, to the Welchers', where he found their pool was dry.

This breach in his chain of water disappointed him absurdly, and he felt like some explorer who seeks a torrential headwater and finds a dead stream. He was disappointed and mystified. It was common enough to go away for the summer but no one ever drained his pool. The Welchers had definitely gone away. The pool furniture was folded, stacked, and covered with a tarpaulin. The bathhouse was locked. All the windows of the house were shut, and when he went around to the driveway in front he saw a **FOR SALE** sign nailed to a tree. When had he last heard from the Welchers – when, that is, had he and Lucinda last regretted an invitation to dine with them? It seemed only a week or so ago. Was his memory failing or had he so disciplined it in the repression of unpleasant facts that he had damaged his sense of the truth? Then in the distance he heard the sound of a tennis game. This cheered him, cleared away all his apprehensions and let him regard the overcast sky and the cold air with indifference. This was the day that Neddy Merrill swam across the county. That was the day! He started off then for his most difficult portage.

Had you gone for a Sunday afternoon ride that day you might have seen him, close to naked, standing on the shoulders of Route 424, waiting for a chance to cross. You might have wondered if he was the victim of foul play, had his car broken down, or was he merely a fool. Standing barefoot in the deposits of the highway – beer cans, rags, and blowout patches – exposed to all kinds of ridicule, he seemed pitiful. He had known when he started that this was a part of his jour-ney – it had been on his maps—but confronted with the lines of traffic, worming through the summery light, he found himself unprepared. He was laughed at, jeered at, a beer can was thrown at him, and he had no dignity or humor to bring to the situation. He could have gone back, back to the Westerhazys', where Lucinda would still be sitting in the sun. He had signed nothing, vowed nothing, pledged nothing, not even to himself. Why, believing as he did, that all human obduracy was susceptible to common sense, was he unable to turn back? Why was he determined to complete his journey even if it meant putting his life in danger? At what point had this prank, this joke, this piece of horseplay become serious? He could not go back, he could not even recall with any clearness the green water at the Westerhazys', the sense of inhaling the day's components, the friendly and relaxed voices saying that they had *drunk* too much. In the space of an hour, more or less, he had covered a distance that made his return impossible.

An old man, tooling down the highway at fifteen miles an hour, let him get to the middle of the road, where there was a grass divider. Here he was exposed to the ridicule of the northbound traffic, but after ten or fifteen minutes he was able to cross. From here he had only a short walk to the Recreation Center at the edge of the village of Lancaster, where there were some handball courts and a public pool.

The effect of the water on voices, the illusion of brilliance and suspense, was the same here as it had been at the Bunkers' but the sounds here were louder, harsher, and more shrill, and as soon as he entered the crowded enclosure he was confronted with regimentation. 'ALL SWIMMERS MUST TAKE A SHOWER BEFORE USING THE POOL. ALL SWIMMERS MUST USE THE FOOTBATH. ALL SWIMMERS MUST WEAR THEIR IDENTIFICATION DISKS.' He took a shower, washed his feet in a cloudy and bitter solution, and made his way to the edge of the water. It stank of chlorine and looked to him like a sink. A pair of lifeguards in a pair of towers blew police whistles at what seemed to be regular intervals and abused the swimmers through a public address system. Neddy remembered the sapphire water at the Bunkers' with longing and thought that he might contaminate himself – damage his own prosperousness and charm – by swimming in this murk, but he reminded himself that he was an explorer, a pilgrim, and that this was merely a stagnant bend in the Lucinda River. He dove, scowling with distaste, into the chlorine and had to swim with his head above water to avoid collisions, but even so he was bumped into, splashed, and jostled. When he got to the shallow end both lifeguards were shouting at him: 'Hey, you, you without the identification disk, get outa the water.' He did, but they had no way of pursuing him and he went through the reek of suntan oil and chlorine out through the hurricane fence and passed the handball courts. By crossing the road he entered the wooded part of the Halloran estate. The woods were not cleared and the footing was treacherous and difficult until he reached the lawn and the clipped beech hedge that encircled their pool.

The Hallorans were friends, an elderly couple of enormous wealth who seemed to bask in the suspicion that they might be Communists. They were zealous reformers but they were not Communists, and yet when they were accused, as they sometimes were, of subversion, it seemed to gratify and excite them. Their beech hedge was yellow and he guessed this had been blighted like the Levys' maple. He called hullo, hullo, to warn the Hallorans of his approach, to palliate his invasion of their privacy. The Hallorans, for reasons that had never been explained to him, did not wear bathing suits. No explanations were in order, really. Their nakedness was a detail in their uncompromising zeal for reform and he stepped politely out of his trunks before he went through the opening in the hedge.

Mrs Halloran, a stout woman with white hair and a serene face, was reading the *Times*. Mr Halloran was taking beech leaves out of the water with a scoop.

They seemed not surprised or displeased to see him. Their pool was perhaps the oldest in the country, a fieldstone rectangle, fed by a brook. It had no filter or pump and its waters were the opaque gold of the stream.

'I'm swimming across the county,' Ned said.

'Why, I didn't know one could,' exclaimed Mrs Halloran.

'Well, I've made it from the Westerhazys',' Ned said. 'That must be about four miles.'

He left his trunks at the deep end, walked to the shallow end, and swam this stretch. As he was pulling himself out of the water he heard Mrs Halloran say, 'We've been *terribly* sorry to hear about all your misfortunes, Neddy.'

'My misfortunes?' Ned asked. 'I don't know what you mean.'

'Why, we heard that you'd sold the house and that your poor children. . . .'

'I don't recall having sold the house,' Ned said, 'and the girls are at home.'

'Yes,' Mrs Halloran sighed. 'Yes . . .' Her voice filled the air with an unseasonable melancholy and Ned spoke briskly. 'Thank you for the swim.'

'Well, have a nice trip,' said Mrs Halloran.

Beyond the hedge he pulled on his trunks and fastened them. They were loose and he wondered if, during the space of an afternoon, he could have lost some weight. He was cold and he was tired and the naked Hallorans and their dark water had depressed him. The swim was too much for his strength but how could he have guessed this, sliding down the banister that morning and sitting in the Westerhazys' sun? His arms were lame. His legs felt rubbery and ached at the joints. The worst of it was the cold in his bones and the feeling that he might never be warm again. Leaves were falling down around him and he smelled wood smoke on the wind. Who would be burning wood at this time of year?

He needed a drink. Whiskey would warm him, pick him up, carry him through the last of his journey, refresh his feeling that it was original and valorous to swim across the county. Channel swimmers took brandy. He needed a stimulant. He crossed the lawn in front of the Hallorans' house and went down a little path to where they had built a house for their only daughter, Helen, and her husband, Eric Sachs. The Sachses' pool was small and he found Helen and her husband there.

'Oh, *Neddy*,' Helen said. 'Did you lunch at Mother's?'

'Not *really*,' Ned said. 'I *did* stop to see your parents.' This seemed to be explanation enough. 'I'm terribly sorry to break in on you like this but I've taken a chill and I wonder if you'd give me a drink.'

'Why, I'd *love* to,' Helen said, 'but there hasn't been anything in this house to drink since Eric's operation. That was three years ago.'

Was he losing his memory, had his gift for concealing painful facts let him forget that he had sold his house, that his children were in trouble, and that his friend had been ill? His eyes slipped from Eric's face to his abdomen, where he saw three pale, sutured scars, two of them at least a foot long. Gone was his navel, and what, Neddy thought, would the roving hand, bed-checking one's gifts at 3 A.M., make of a belly with no navel, no link to birth, this breach in the succession?

'I'm sure you can get a drink at the Biswangers',' Helen said. 'They're having an enormous do. You can hear it from here. Listen!'

She raised her head and from across the road, the lawns, the gardens, the woods, the fields, he heard again the brilliant noise of voices over water. 'Well, I'll get wet,' he said, still feeling that he had no freedom of choice about his means of travel. He dove into the Sachses' cold water and, gasping, close to drowning, made his way from one end of the pool to the other. 'Lucinda and I want *terribly* to see you,' he said over his shoulder, his face set toward the Biswangers'. 'We're sorry it's been so long and we'll call you *very* soon.'

He crossed some fields to the Biswangers' and the sounds of revelry there. They would be honored to give him a drink, they would be happy to give him a drink. The Biswangers invited him and Lucinda for dinner four times a year, six weeks in advance. They were always rebuffed and yet they continued to send out their invitations, unwilling to comprehend the rigid and undemocratic realities of their society. They were the sort of people who discussed the price of things at cocktails, exchanged market tips during dinner, and after dinner told dirty stories to mixed company. They did not belong to Neddy's set – they were not even on Lucinda's Christmas-card list. He went toward their pool with feelings of indifference, charity, and some unease, since it seemed to be getting dark and these were the longest days of the year. The party when he joined it was noisy and large. Grace Biswanger was the kind of hostess who asked the optometrist, the veterinarian, the real-estate dealer, and the dentist. No one was swimming and the twilight, reflected on the water of the pool, had a wintry gleam. There was a bar and he started for this. When Grace Biswanger saw him she came toward him, not affectionately as he had every right to expect, but bellicosely.

'Why, this party has everything,' she said loudly, 'including a gate crasher.'

She could not deal him a social blow – there was no question about this and he did not flinch. 'As a gate crasher,' he asked politely, 'do I rate a drink?'

'Suit yourself,' she said. 'You don't seem to pay much attention to invitations.'

She turned her back on him and joined some guests, and he went to the bar and ordered a whiskey. The bartender served him but he served him rudely. His was a world in which the caterer's men kept the social score, and to be rebuffed by a part-time barkeep meant that he had suffered some loss of social esteem. Or perhaps the man was new and uninformed. Then he heard Grace at his back say: 'They went for broke overnight – nothing but income – and he showed up drunk one Sunday and asked us to loan him five thousand dollars . . .' She was always talking about money. It was worse than eating your peas off a knife. He dove into the pool, swam its length and went away.

The next pool on his list, the last but two, belonged to his old mistress, Shirley Adams. If he had suffered any injuries at the Biswangers' they would be cured here. Love – sexual roughhouse in fact – was the supreme elixir, the pain killer, the brightly colored pill that would put the spring back into his step, the joy of life in his heart. They had had an affair last week, last month, last year. He couldn't remember. It was he who had broken it off, his was the upper hand, and he stepped through the gate of the wall that surrounded her pool with nothing so considered as self-confidence. It seemed in a way to be his pool, as the lover, particularly the illicit lover, enjoys the possessions of his mistress with an authority unknown to holy matrimony. She was there, her hair the color of brass, but her figure, at the edge of the lighted, cerulean water, excited in him no profound memories. It had been, he thought, a lighthearted affair, although she had wept when he broke it off. She seemed confused to see him and he wondered if she was still wounded. Would she, God forbid, weep again?

'What do you want?' she asked.

'I'm swimming across the county.'

'Good Christ. Will you ever grow up?'

'What's the matter?'

'If you've come here for money,' she said, 'I won't give you another cent.'

'You could give me a drink.'

'I could but I won't. I'm not alone.'

'Well, I'm on my way.'

He dove in and swam the pool, but when he tried to haul himself up onto the curb he found that the strength in his arms and shoulders had gone, and he paddled to the ladder and climbed out. Looking over his shoulder he saw, in the lighted bathhouse, a young man. Going out onto the dark lawn he smelled chrysanthemums or marigolds – some stubborn autumnal fragrance – on the night air, strong as gas. Looking overhead he saw that the stars had come out, but why should he seem to see Andromeda, Cepheus, and Cassiopeia? What had become of the constellations of midsummer? He began to cry.

It was probably the first time in his adult life that he had ever cried, certainly the first time in his life that he had ever felt so miserable, cold, tired, and bewildered. He could not understand the rudeness of the caterer's barkeep or the rudeness of a mistress who had come to him on her knees and showered his trousers with tears. He had swam too long, he had been immersed too long, and his nose and his throat were sore from the water. What he needed then was a drink, some company, and some clean, dry clothes, and while he could have cut directly across the road to his home he went on to the Gilmartins' pool. Here, for the first time in his life, he did not dive but went down the steps into the icy water and swam a hobbled sidestroke that he might have learned as a youth. He staggered with fatigue on his way to the Clydes' and paddled the length of their pool, stopping again and again with his hand on the curb to rest. He climbed up the ladder and wondered if he had the strength to get home. He had done what he wanted, he had swum the county, but he was so stupefied with exhaustion that his triumph seemed vague. Stooped, holding on to the gateposts for support, he turned up the driveway of his own house.

The place was dark. Was it so late that they had all gone to bed? Had Lucinda stayed at the Westerhazys' for supper? Had the girls joined her there or gone someplace else? Hadn't they agreed, as they usually did on Sunday, to regret all their invitations and stay at home? He tried the garage doors to see what cars were in but the doors were locked and rust came off the handles onto his hands. Going toward the house, he saw that the force of the thunderstorm had knocked one of the rain gutters loose. It hung down over the front door like an umbrella rib, but it could be fixed in the morning. The house was locked, and he thought that the stupid cook or the stupid maid must have locked the place up until he remembered that it had been some time since they had employed a maid or a cook. He shouted, pounded on the door, tried to force it with his shoulder, and then, looking in at the windows, saw that the place was empty.

THE BLUSH

Elizabeth Taylor

The writer Elizabeth Jane Howard was once asked to write a biography
of **Elizabeth Taylor** (1912–1975) but she declined as she thought Taylor's
life had a lack of event. Born near Reading, the daughter of an insurance
inspector, she worked as a librarian and teacher and married a man who
ran a confectionary company. She died, aged sixty-three, from cancer.
She wrote: "The whole point is that writing has a pattern and life hasn't.
Life is so untidy. Art is so short and life so long. It is not possible to have
perfection in life but it is possible to have perfection in a novel." Her
work is not so much under-rated as under-read.

They were the same age – Mrs Allen and the woman who came every day
to do the housework. 'I shall never have children now,' Mrs Allen had begun to tell herself. Something had not come true; the essential part of her
life. She had always imagined her children in fleeting scenes and intimations; that
was how they had come to her, like snatches of a film. She had seen them plainly,
their chins tilted up as she tied on their bibs at meal-times; their naked bodies
had darted in and out of the water sprinkler on the lawn; and she had listened to
their voices in the garden and in the mornings from their beds. She had even cried
a little dreaming of the day when the eldest boy would go off to boarding-school;
she pictured the train going out of the station; she raised her hand and her throat
contracted and her lips trembled as she smiled. The years passing by had slowly
filched from her the reality of these scenes – the gay sounds; the grave peace she
had longed for; even the pride of grief.

She listened – as they worked together in the kitchen – to Mrs Lacey's troubles
with her family, her grumblings about her grown-up son who would not get up
till dinner-time on Sundays and then expected his mother to have cleaned his
shoes for him; about the girl of eighteen who was a hairdresser and too full of
dainty ways which she picked up from the women's magazines, and the adolescent girl who moped and glowered and answered back.

'My children wouldn't have turned out like that,' Mrs Allen thought, as she
made her murmured replies. 'The more you do for some, the more you may,'
said Mrs Lacey. But from gossip in the village which Mrs Allen heard she had
done all too little. The children, one night after another, for years and years,
had had to run out for parcels of fish and chips while their mother sat in the
Horse and Jockey drinking brown ale. On summer evenings, when they were
younger, they had hung about outside the pub: when they were bored they
pressed their foreheads to the window and looked in at the dark little bar, hear-

ing the jolly laughter, their mother's the loudest of all. Seeing their faces, she would swing at once from the violence of hilarity to that of extreme annoyance and, although ginger-beer and packets of potato crisps would be handed out through the window, her anger went out with them and threatened the children as they ate and drank.

'And she doesn't always care who she goes there *with*,' Mrs Allen's gardener told her.

'She works hard and deserves a little pleasure – she has her anxieties,' said Mrs Allen, who, alas, had none.

She had never been inside the Horse and Jockey, although it was nearer to her house than the Chequers at the other end of the village where she and her husband went sometimes for a glass of sherry on Sunday mornings. The Horse and Jockey attracted a different set of customers – for instance, people who sat down and drank, at tables all round the wall. At the Chequers no one ever sat down, but stood and sipped and chatted as at a cocktail party, and luncheons and dinners were served, which made it so much more respectable: no children hung about outside, because they were all at home with their nannies.

Sometimes in the evenings – so many of them – when her husband was kept late in London, Mrs Allen wished that she could go down to the Chequers and drink a glass of sherry and exchange a little conversation with someone; but she was too shy to open the door and go in alone: she imagined heads turning, a surprised welcome from her friends, who would all be safely in married pairs; and then, when she left, eyes meeting with unspoken messages and conjecture in the air.

Mrs Lacey left her at midday and then there was gardening to do and the dog to be taken for a walk. After six o'clock, she began to pace restlessly about the house, glancing at the clocks in one room after another, listening for her husband's car – the sound she knew so well because she had awaited it for such a large part of her married life. She would hear, at last, the tyres turning on the soft gravel, the door being slammed, then his footsteps hurrying towards the porch. She knew that it was a wasteful way of spending her years – and, looking back, she was unable to tell one of them from another – but she could not think what else she might do. Humphrey went on earning more and more money and there was no stopping him now. Her acquaintances, in wretched quandaries about where the next term's school-fees were to come from, would turn to her and say cruelly: 'Oh, *you're* all right, Ruth. You've no idea what you are spared.'

And Mrs Lacey would be glad when Maureen could leave school and 'get out earning'. '"I've got my geometry to do," she says, when it's time to wash up the tea-things. "I'll geometry you, my girl," I said. "When I was your age, I was out earning." '

Mrs Allen was fascinated by the life going on in that house and the children seemed real to her, although she had never seen them. Only Mr Lacey remained blurred and unimaginable. No one knew him. He worked in the town in the valley, six miles away, and he kept himself to himself; had never been known to show his face in the Horse and Jockey. 'I've got my own set,' Mrs Lacey said airily. 'After all, he's nearly twenty years older than me. I'll make sure neither of my girls follow my mistake. "I'd rather see you dead at my feet," I said to

Vera.' Ron's young lady was lucky; having Ron, she added. Mrs Allen found this strange, for Ron had always been painted so black; was, she had been led to believe, oafish, ungrateful, greedy and slow to put his hands in his pockets if there was any paying out to do. There was also the matter of his shoe-cleaning, for no young woman would do what his mother did for him – or said she did. Always, Mrs Lacey would sigh and say: 'Goodness me, if only I was their age and knew what I know now.'

She was an envious woman: she envied Mrs Allen her pretty house and her clothes and she envied her own daughters their youth. 'If I had your figure,' she would say to Mrs Allen. Her own had gone: what else could be expected, she asked, when she had had three children? Mrs Allen thought, too, of all the brown ale she drank at the Horse and Jockey and of the reminiscences of meals past which came so much into her conversations. Whatever the cause was, her flesh, slackly corseted, shook as she trod heavily about the kitchen. In summer, with bare arms and legs she looked larger than ever. Although her skin was very white, the impression she gave was at once colourful – from her orange hair and bright lips and the floral patterns that she always wore. Her red-painted toe-nails poked through the straps of her fancy sandals; turquoise-blue beads were wound round her throat.

Humphrey Allen had never seen her; he had always left for the station before she arrived, and that was a good thing, his wife thought. When she spoke of Mrs Lacey, she wondered if he visualised a neat, homely woman in a clean white overall. She did not deliberately mislead him, but she took advantage of his indifference. Her relationship with Mrs Lacey and the intimacy of their conversations in the kitchen he would not have approved, and the sight of those calloused feet with their chipped nail-varnish and yellowing heels would have sickened him.

One Monday morning, Mrs Lacey was later than usual. She was never very punctual and had many excuses about flat bicycle-tyres or Maureen being poorly. Mrs Allen, waiting for her, sorted out all the washing. When she took another look at the clock, she decided that it was far too late for her to be expected at all. For some time lately Mrs Lacey had seemed ill and depressed; her eyelids, which were chronically rather inflamed, had been more angrily red than ever and, at the sink or ironing-board, she would fall into unusual silences, was absent-minded and full of sighs. She had always liked to talk about the 'change' and did so more than ever as if with a desperate hopefulness.

'I'm sorry, but I was ever so sick,' she told Mrs Allen, when she arrived the next morning. 'I still feel queerish. Such heartburn. I don't like the signs, I can tell you. All I crave is pickled walnuts, just the same as I did with Maureen. I don't like the signs one bit. I feel I'll throw myself into the river if I'm taken that way again.'

Mrs Allen felt stunned and antagonistic. 'Surely not at your age,' she said crossly.

'You can't be more astonished than me,' Mrs Lacey said, belching loudly. 'Oh, pardon. I'm afraid I can't help myself.'

Not being able to help herself, she continued to belch and hiccough as she turned on taps and shook soap-powder into the washing-up bowl. It was because of this that Mrs Allen decided to take the dog for a walk. Feeling consciously fastidious and aloof she made her way across the fields, trying to disengage her thoughts from Mrs Lacey and her troubles; but unable to. 'Poor woman,' she thought again and again with bitter animosity.

She turned back when she noticed how the sky had darkened with racing, sharp-edged clouds. Before she could reach home, the rain began. Her hair, soaking wet, shrank into tight curls against her head; her woollen suit smelt like a damp animal. 'Oh, I am drenched,' she called out, as she threw open the kitchen door.

She knew at once that Mrs Lacey had gone, that she must have put on her coat and left almost as soon as Mrs Allen had started out on her walk, for nothing was done; the washing-up was hardly started and the floor was unswept. Among the stacked-up crockery a note was propped; she had come over funny, felt dizzy and, leaving her apologies and respects, had gone.

Angrily, but methodically, Mrs Allen set about making good the wasted morning. By afternoon, the grim look was fixed upon her face. 'How dare she?' she found herself whispering, without allowing herself to wonder what it was the woman had dared.

She had her own little ways of cosseting herself through the lonely hours, comforts which were growing more important to her as she grew older, so that the time would come when not to have her cup of tea at four-thirty would seem a prelude to disaster. This afternoon, disorganised as it already was, she fell out of her usual habit and instead of carrying the tray to the low table by the fire, she poured out her tea in the kitchen and drank it there, leaning tiredly against the dresser. Then she went upstairs to make herself tidy. She was trying to brush her frizzed hair smooth again when she heard the door bell ringing.

When she opened the door, she saw quite plainly a look of astonishment take the place of anxiety on the man's face. Something about herself surprised him, was not what he had expected. 'Mrs Allen?' he asked uncertainly and the astonishment remained when she had answered him.

'Well, I'm calling about the wife,' he said. 'Mrs Lacey that works here.'

'I was worried about her,' said Mrs Allen.

She knew that she must face the embarrassment of hearing about Mrs Lacey's condition and invited the man into her husband's study, where she thought he might look less out-of-place than in her brocade-smothered drawing-room. He looked about him resentfully and glared down at the floor which his wife had polished. With this thought in his mind, he said abruptly: 'It's all taken its toll.'

He sat down on a leather couch with his cap and his bicycle-clips beside him.

'I came home to my tea and found her in bed, crying,' he said. This was true. Mrs Lacey had succumbed to despair and gone to lie down. Feeling better at four o'clock, she went downstairs to find some food to comfort herself with; but the slice of dough-cake was ill-chosen and brought on more heartburn and floods of bitter tears.

'If she carries on here for a while, it's all got to be very different,' Mr Lacey said threateningly. He was nervous at saying what he must and could only bring out the words with the impetus of anger. 'You may or may not know that she's expecting.'

'Yes,' said Mrs Allen humbly. 'This morning she told me that she thought . . .'

'There's no "thought" about it. It's as plain as a pikestaff.' Yet in his eyes she could see disbelief and bafflement and he frowned and looked down again at the polished floor.

Twenty years older than his wife – or so his wife had said – he really, to Mrs Allen, looked quite ageless, a crooked, bow-legged little man who might have been a jockey once. The expression about his blue eyes was like a child's: he was both stubborn and pathetic.

Mrs Allen's fat spaniel came into the room and went straight to the stranger's chair and began to sniff at his corduroy trousers.

'It's too much for her,' Mr Lacey said. 'It's too much to expect.'

To Mrs Allen's horror she saw the blue eyes filling with tears. Hoping to hide his emotion, he bent down and fondled the dog, making playful thrusts at it with his fist closed.

He was a man utterly, bewilderedly at sea. His married life had been too much for him, with so much in it that he could not understand.

'Now I know, I will do what I can,' Mrs Allen told him. 'I will try to get some-one else in to do the rough.'

'It's the late nights that are the trouble,' he said. 'She comes in dog-tired. Night after night. It's not good enough. "Let them stay at home and mind their own children once in a while," I told her. "We don't need the money." '

'I can't understand,' Mrs Allen began. She was at sea herself now, but felt peril-ously near a barbarous, unknown shore and was afraid to make any movement towards it.

'I earn good money. For her to come out at all was only for extras. She likes new clothes. In the daytimes I never had any objection. Then all these cocktail parties begin. It beats me how people can drink like it night after night and pay out for someone else to mind their kids. Perhaps you're thinking that it's not my business, but I'm the one who has to sit at home alone till all hours and get my own supper and see next to nothing of my wife. I'm boiling over some nights. Once I nearly rushed out when I heard the car stop down the road. I wanted to tell your husband what I thought of you both.'

'My husband?' murmured Mrs Allen.

'What am I supposed to have, I would have asked him? Is she my wife or your sitter-in? Bringing her back at this time of night. And it's no use saying she could have refused. She never would.'

Mrs Allen's quietness at last defeated him and dispelled the anger he had tried to rouse in himself. The look of her, too, filled him with doubts, her grave, un-certain demeanour and the shock her age had been to him. He had imagined someone so much younger and – because of the cocktail parties – flighty. Instead, he recognised something of himself in her, a yearning disappointment. He picked up his cap and his bicycle-clips and sat looking down at them, turning them round in his hands. 'I had to come,' he said.

'Yes,' said Mrs Allen.

'So you won't ask her again?' he pleaded. 'It isn't right for her. Not now.'

'No, I won't,' Mrs Allen promised and she stood up as he did and walked over to the door. He stooped and gave the spaniel a final pat. 'You'll excuse my coming, I hope.'

'Of course.'

'It was no use saying any more to her. Whatever she's asked, she won't refuse. It's her way.'

Mrs Allen shut the front door after him and stood in the hall, listening to him wheeling his bicycle across the gravel. Then she felt herself beginning to blush. She was glad that she was alone, for she could feel her face, her throat, even the tops of her arms burning, and she went over to a looking-glass and studied with great interest this strange phenomenon.

IN DREAMS BEGIN RESPONSIBILITIES

Delmore Schwartz

Delmore Schwartz (1913–1966) was born in Brooklyn to Romanian Jews, Henry and Rose; their separation when Schwartz was nine had a profound effect on him. The story included here, taking its title from W.B. Yeats and written when Schwartz was twenty-five, reflects that experience. A great white hope of American poetry and letters, when he died, in the summer of 1966, from a heart attack after years of drinking too much and mental illness, it took two days for his body to be identified, so remote was he from those around him. In better days, he taught Lou Reed.

I

I think it is the year 1909. I feel as if I were in a motion picture theatre, the long arm of light crossing the darkness and spinning, my eyes fixed on the screen. This is a silent picture as if an old Biograph one, in which the actors are dressed in ridiculously old-fashioned clothes, and one flash succeeds another with sudden jumps. The actors too seem to jump about and walk too fast. The shots themselves are full of dots and rays, as if it were raining when the picture was photographed. The light is bad.

It is Sunday afternoon, June 12th, 1909, and my father is walking down the quiet streets of Brooklyn on his way to visit my mother. His clothes are newly pressed and his tie is too tight in his high collar. He jingles the coins in his pockets, thinking of the witty things he will say. I feel as if I had by now relaxed entirely in the soft darkness of the theatre; the organist peals out the obvious and approximate emotions on which the audience rocks unknowingly. I am anonymous, and I have forgotten myself. It is always so when one goes to the movies, it is, as they say, a drug.

My father walks from street to street of trees, lawns and houses, once in a while coming to an avenue on which a street-car skates and gnaws, slowly progressing. The conductor, who has a handle-bar mustache helps a young lady wearing a hat like a bowl with feathers on to the car. She lifts her long skirts slightly as she mounts the steps. He leisurely makes change and rings his bell. It is obviously Sunday, for everyone is wearing Sunday clothes, and the street-car's noises emphasize the quiet of the holiday. Is not Brooklyn the City of Churches? The shops are closed and their shades drawn, but for an occasional stationery store or drug-store with great green balls in the window.

My father has chosen to take this long walk because he likes to walk and think. He thinks about himself in the future and so arrives at the place he is to visit in a state of mild exaltation. He pays no attention to the houses he is passing, in which the Sunday dinner is being eaten, nor to the many trees which patrol each street, now coming to their full leafage and the time when they will room the whole street in cool shadow. An occasional carriage passes, the horse's hooves falling like stones in the quiet afternoon, and once in a while an automobile, looking like an enormous upholstered sofa, puffs and passes.

My father thinks of my mother, of how nice it will be to introduce her to his family. But he is not yet sure that he wants to marry her, and once in a while he becomes panicky about the bond already established. He reassures himself by thinking of the big men he admires who are married: William Randolph Hearst, and William Howard Taft, who has just become President of the United States.

My father arrives at my mother's house. He has come too early and so is suddenly embarrassed. My aunt, my mother's sister, answers the loud bell with her napkin in her hand, for the family is still at dinner. As my father enters, my grandfather rises from the table and shakes hands with him. My mother has run upstairs to tidy herself. My grandmother asks my father if he has had dinner, and tells him that Rose will be downstairs soon. My grandfather opens the conversation by remarking on the mild June weather. My father sits uncomfortably near the table, holding his hat in his hand. My grandmother tells my aunt to take my father's hat. My uncle, twelve years old, runs into the house, his hair tousled. he shouts a greeting to my father, who has often given him a nickel, and he runs upstairs. It is evident that the respect in which my father is held in this household is tempered by a good deal of mirth. He is impressive, yet he is very awkward.

II

Finally my mother comes downstairs, all dressed up, and my father being engaged in conversation with my grandfather becomes uneasy, not knowing whether to greet my mother or continue the conversation. He get up from the chair clumsily and says "hello" gruffly. My grandfather watches, examining their congruence, such as it is, with a critical eye, and meanwhile rubbing his bearded cheek roughly, as he always does when he reflects. He is worried; he is afraid that my father will not make a good husband for his oldest daughter. At this point something happens to the film, just as my father is saying something funny to my mother; I am awakened to myself and my unhappiness just as my interest was rising. The audience begins to clap impatiently. Then the trouble is cared for but the film has been returned to a portion just shown, and once more I see my grandfather rubbing his bearded cheek and pondering my father's character. It is difficult to get back into the picture once more and forget myself, but as my mother giggles at my father's words, the darkness drowns me.

My father and mother depart from the house, my father shaking hands with my mother once more, out of some unknown uneasiness. I stir uneasily also, slouched in the hard chair of the theatre. Where is the older uncle, my mother's older brother? He is studying in his bedroom upstairs, studying for his final examination at the College of the City of New York, having been dead of rapid pneumonia for the last twenty-one years. My mother and father walk down the same quiet streets once more. My mother is holding my father's arm and telling him of the novel which she has been reading; and my father utters judgments of the charaters as the plot is made clear to him. This is a habit which he very much enjoys, for he feels the utmost superiority and confidence when he approves and condemns the behavior of other people. At times he feels moved to utter a brief "Ugh" – whenever the story becomes what he would call sugary. This tribute is paid to his manliness. My mother feels satisfied by the interest which she has awakened; she is showing my father how intelligent she is, and how interesting.

The reach the avenue, and the street-car leisurely arrives. They are going to Coney Island this afternoon, although my mother considers that such pleasures are inferior. She has made up her mind to indulge only in a walk on the boardwalk and a pleasant dinner, avoiding the riotous amusements as being beneath the dignity of so dignified a couple.

My father tells my mother how much money he has made in the past week, exaggerating an amount which need not have been exaggerated. But my father has always felt that actualities somehow fall short. Suddenly I begin to weep. The determined old lady who sits next to me in the theatre is annoyed and looks at me with an angry face, and being intimidated, I stop. I drag out my handkerchief and dry my face, licking the drop which has fallen near my lips. Meanwhile I have missed something, for here are my mother and father alighting at the last stop, Coney Island.

III

They walk toward the boardwalk, and my father commands my mother to inhale the pungent air from the sea. They both breathe in deeply, both of them laughing as they do so. They have in common a great interest in health, although my father is strong and husky, my mother frail. Their minds are full of theories of what is good to eat and not good to eat, and sometimes they engage in heated discussions of the subject, the whole matter ending in my father's announcement, made with a scornful bluster, that you have to die sooner or later anyway. On the boardwalk's flagpole, the American flag is pulsing in an intermittent wind from the sea.

My father and mother go to the rail of the boardwalk and look down on the beach where a good many bathers are casually walking about. A few are in the surf. A peanut whistle pierces the air with its pleasant and active whine, and my father goes to buy peanuts. My mother remains at the rail and stares at the ocean. The ocean seems merry to her; it pointedly sparkles and again and again the pony waves are released. She notices the children digging in the wet sand, and the bathing costumes of the girls who are her own age. My father returns with the peanuts. Overhead the sun's lightning strikes and strikes, but neither of them are at all aware of it. The boardwalk is full of people dressed in their Sunday clothes and idly strolling. The tide does not reach as far as the boardwalk, and the strollers would feel no danger if it did. My mother and father lean on the rail of the boardwalk and absently stare at the ocean. The ocean is becoming rough; the waves come in slowly, tugging strength from far back. The moment before they somersault, the moment when they arch their backs so beautifully, showing green and white veins amid the black, that moment is intolerable. They finally crack, dashing fiercely upon the sand, actually driving, full force downward, against the sand, bouncing upward and forward, and at last petering out into a small stream which races up the beach and then is recalled. My parents gaze absentmindedly at the ocean, scarcely interested in its harshness. The sun overhead does not disturb them. But I stare at the terrible sun which breaks up sight, and the fatal, merciless, passionate ocean, I forget my parents. I stare fascinated and finally, shocked by the indifference of my father and mother, I burst out weeping once more. The old lady next to me pats me on the shoulder and says "There, there, all of this is only a movie, young man, only a movie," but I look up once more at the terrifying sun and the terrifying ocean, and being unable to control my tears, I get up and go to the men's room, stumbling over the feet of the other people seated in my row.

IV

When I return, feeling as if I had awakened in the morning sick for lack of sleep, several hours have apparently passed and my parents are riding on the merry-go-round. My father is on a black horse, my mother on a white one, and they seem to be making an eternal circuit for the single purpose of snatching the nickel rings which are attached to the arm of one of the posts. A hand-organ is playing; it is one with the ceaseless circling of the merry-go-round.

For a moment it seems that they will never get off the merry-go-round because it will never stop. I feel like one who looks down on the avenue from the 50th story of a building. But at length they do get off; even the music of the hand-organ has ceased for a moment. My father has acquired ten rings, my mother only two, although it was my mother who really wanted them.

They walk on along the boardwalk as the afternoon descends by imperceptible degrees into the incredible violet of dusk. Everything fades into a relaxed blow, even the ceaseless murmuring from the beach, and the revolutions of the merry-go-round. They look for a place to have dinner. My father suggests the best one on the boardwalk and my mother demurs, in accordance with her principles.

However they do go to the best place, asking for a table near the window, so that they can look out on the boardwalk and the mobile ocean. My father feels omnipotent as he places a quarter in the waiter's hand as he asks for a table. The place is crowded and here too there is music, this time from a kind of string trio. My father orders dinner with a fine confidence.

As the dinner is eaten, my father tells of his plans for the future, and my mother shows with expressive face how interested she is, and how impressed. My father becomes exultant. He is lifted up by the waltz that is being played, and his own future begins to intoxicate him. My father tells my mother that he is going to expand his business, for there is a great deal of money to be made. He wants to settle down. After all, he is twenty-nine, he has lived by himself since he was thirteen, he is making more and more money, and he is envious of his married friends when he visits them in the cozy security of their homes, surrounded, it seems, by the calm domestic pleasures, and by delightful children, and then, as the waltz reaches the moment when all the dancers swing madly, then, then with awful daring, then he asks my mother to marry him, although awkwardly enough and puzzled, even in his excitement, at how he had arrived at the proposal, and she, to make the whole business worse, begins to cry, and my father looks nervously about, not knowing at all what to do now, and my mother says: "It's all I've wanted from the moment I saw you," sobbing, and he finds all of this very difficult, scarcely to his taste, scarcely as he had thought it would, on his long walks over Brooklyn Bridge in the revery of a fine cigar, and it was then that I stood up in the theatre and shouted: "Don't do it. It's not too late to change your minds, both of you. Nothing good will come of it, only remorse, hatred, scandal, and two children whose characters are monstrous." The whole audience turned to look at me, annoyed, the usher came hurrying down the aisle flashing his searchlight, and the old lady next to me tugged me down into my seat, saying: "Be quiet. You'll be put out, and you paid thirty-five cents to come in." And so I shut my eyes because I could not bear to see what was happening. I sat there quietly.

V

But after awhile I began to take brief glimpses, and at length I watch again with thirsty interest, like a child who wants to maintain his sulk although offered the bribe of candy. My parents are now having their picture taken in a photographer's booth along the boardwalk. The place is shadowed in the mauve light which is apparently necessary. The camera is set to the side on its tripod and looks like a Martian man. The photographer is instructing my parents in how to pose. My father has his arm over my mother's shoulder, and both of them smile emphatically. The photographer brings my mother a bouquet of flowers to hold in her hand but she holds it at the wrong angle. Then the photographer covers himself with the black cloth which drapes the camera and all that one sees of him is one protruding arm and his hand which clutches the rubber ball which he will squeeze when the picture is finally taken. But he is not satisfied with their appearance. He feels with certainty that somehow there is something wrong in their pose. Again and again he issues from his hidden place with new directions Each suggestion merely makes matters worse. My father is becoming impatient. They try a seated pose. The photographer explains that he has pride, he is not interested in all of this for the money, he wants to make beautiful pictures. My father says: "Hurry up, will you? We haven't got all night." But the photographer only scurries about apologetically, and issues new directions. The photographer charms me. I approve of him with all my heart, for I know just how he feels, and as he criticizes each revised pose according to some uknown idea of rightness, I become quite hopeful. But then my father says angrily: "Come on, you've had enough time, we're not going to wait any longer." And the photographer, sighing unhappily, goes back under his black covering, holds out his hand, says: "One, two, three, Now!", and the picture is taken, with my father's smile turned to a grimace and my mother's bright and false. It takes a few minutes for the picture to be developed and as my parents sit in the curious light they become quite depressed.

VI

They have passed a fortune-teller's booth, and my mother wishes to go in, but my father does not. They begin to argue about it. My mother becomes stubborn, my father once more impatient, and then they begin to quarrel, and what my father would like to do is walk off and leave my mother there, but he knows that that would never do. My mother refuses to budge. She is near to tears, but she feels an uncontrollable desire to hear what the palm-reader will say. My father consents angrily, and they both go into a booth which is in a way like the photographer's, since it is draped in black cloth and its light is shadowed. The place is too warm, and my father keeps saying this is all nonsense, pointing to the crystal ball on the table. The fortune-teller, a fat, short woman, garbed in what is supposed to be Oriental robes, comes into the room from the back and greets them, speaking with an accent. But suddenly my father feels that the whole thing is intolerable; he tugs at my mother's arm, but my mother refuses to budge. And then, in terrible anger, my father lets go of my mother's arm and strides out, leaving my mother stunned. She moves to go after my father, but the fortune-teller holds her arm tightly and begs her not to do so, and I in my seat am shocked more than can ever be said, for I feel as if I were walking a tight-rope a hundred feet over a circus-audience and suddenly the rope is showing signs of breaking, and I get up from my seat and begin to shout once more the first words I can think of to communicate my terrible fear and once more the usher comes hurrying down the aisle flashing his search-light, and the old lady pleads with me, and the shocked audience has turned to stare at me, and I keep shouting: "What are they doing? Don't they know what they are doing? Why doesn't my mother go after my father? If she does not do that, what will she do? Doesn't my father know what he is doing?"—But the usher has seized my arm and is dragging me away, and as he does so, he says: "What are *you* doing? Don't you know that you can't do whatever you want to do? Why should a young man like you, with your whole life before you, get hysterical like this? Why don't you *think* of what you're doing? You can't act like this even if other people aren't around! You will be sorry if you do not do what you should do, you can't carry on like this, it is not right, you will find that out soon enough, everything you do matters too much," and he said that dragging me through the lobby of the theatre into the cold light, and I woke up into the bleak winter morning of my 21st birthday, the windowsill shining with its lip of snow, and the morning already begun.

RASPBERRY JAM

Angus Wilson

Angus Wilson's (1913–1991) writing has never truly been recognized for what it is: utterly and brilliantly English. He was born in Bexhill -on-Sea in 1913. He spent too much of his life reviewing, helping administer institutions (the British Museum, travelling for the British Council, teaching at the University of East Anglia) and died in near penury in Suffolk. *The Middle Age of Mrs Eliot* is a quiet masterpiece, as is *Anglo-Saxon Attitudes*, which should be made into a film.

"How are your funny friends at Potter's Farm, Johnnie?" asked his aunt from London.

"Very well, thank you, Aunt Eva," said the little boy in the window in a high prim voice. He had been drawing faces on his bare knee and now put down the indelible pencil. The moment that he had been dreading all day had arrived. Now they would probe and probe with their silly questions and the whole story of that dreadful tea party with his old friends would come tumbling out. There would be scenes and abuse and the old ladies would be made to suffer further. This he could not bear, for although he never wanted to see them again and had come, in brooding over the afternoon's events, almost to hate them, to bring them further misery, to be the means of their disgrace would be worse than any of the horrible things that had already happened. Apart from his fear of what might follow he did not intend to pursue the conversation himself, for he disliked his aunt's bright patronizing tone. He knew that she felt ill at ease with children and would soon lapse into that embarrassing "leg pulling" manner which some grown-ups used. For himself, he did not mind this but if she made silly jokes about the old ladies at Potter's Farm he would get angry and then Mummy would say all that about his having to learn to take a joke and about his being highly strung and where could he have got it from, not from her.

But he need not have feared. For though the grown-ups continued to speak of the old ladies as "Johnnie's friends", the topic soon became a general one. Many of the things the others said made the little boy bite his lip, but he was able to go on drawing on his knee with the feigned abstraction of a child among adults.

"My dear," said Johnnie's mother to her sister, "you really must meet them. They're the *most* wonderful pair of freaks. They live in a great barn of a farmhouse. The inside's like a museum, full of old junk mixed up with some really lovely things all mouldering to pieces. The family's been there for hundreds of years and they're madly proud of it. They won't let anyone do a single thing for them, although they're both well over sixty, and of course the result is that the place is in the most *frightful* mess. It's really rather ghastly and one oughtn't to laugh, but if you could *see* them, my dear. The elder one, Marian, wears a long tweed skirt almost to the ankles, she had a terrible hunting accident or something, and a school blazer. The younger one's said to have been a beauty, but she's really rather sinister now, inches thick in enamel and rouge and dressed in all colours of the rainbow, with dyed red hair which is constantly falling down. Of course, Johnnie's made tremendous friends with them and I must say they've been immensely kind to him, but what Harry will say when he comes back from Germany, I can't think. As it *is*, he's always complaining that the child is too much with women and has no friends of his own age."

"I don't honestly think you need worry about that, Grace," said her brother Jim, assuming the attitude of the sole male in the company, for of the masculinity of old Mr Codrington their guest he instinctively made little. "Harry ought to be very pleased with the way old Miss Marian's encouraged Johnnie's cricket and riding; it's pretty uphill work, too. Johnnie's not exactly a Don Bradman or a Gordon Richards, are you, old man? I like the old girl, personally. She's got a bee in her bonnet about the Bolsheviks, but she's stood up to those damned council people about the drainage like a good 'un; she does no end for the village people as well and says very little about it."

"I don't like the sound of 'doing good to the village' very much," said Eva, "it usually means patronage and disappointed old maids meddling in other people's affairs. It's only in villages like this that people can go on serving out sermons with gifts of soup."

"Curiously enough, Eva old dear," Jim said, for he believed in being rude to his progressive sister, "in this particular case you happen to be wrong. Miss Swindale is extremely broadminded. You remember, Grace," he said, addressing his other sister, "what she said about giving money to old Cooper, when the rector protested it would only go on drink – 'You have a perfect right to consign us all to hell, rector, but you must allow us the choice of how we get there.' Serve him damn well right for interfering too."

"Well, Jim darling," said Grace, "I must say she could hardly have the nerve to object to drink – the poor old thing has the most dreadful bouts herself. Sometimes when I can't get gin from the grocer's it makes me absolutely livid to think of all that secret drinking and the strange silences and sudden tears, and, my dear, the awful nightmares he has! About a fortnight ago, after he'd been at tea with the Miss Swindales, I don't know whether it was something he'd eaten there, but he made the most awful sobbing noise in the night. Sometimes I think it's just temper, like Harry. The other day at tea I only offered him some jam, my best home-made raspberry too, and he just screamed at me."

"You should take him to a child psychologist," said her sister.

"Well, darling, I expect you're right. It's so difficult to know whether they're frauds, everyone recommends somebody different. I'm sure Harry would disapprove too, and then think of the expense . . . You know how desperately poor we are, although I think I manage as well as anyone could . . ." At this point Mr Codrington took a deep breath and sat back, for on the merits of her household management Grace Allingham was at her most boring and could by no possible stratagem be restrained.

Upstairs, in the room which had been known as the nursery until his eleventh birthday, but was now called his bedroom, Johnnie was playing with his farm animals. The ritual involved in the game was very complicated and had a long history. It was on his ninth birthday that he had been given the farm set by his father. "Something a bit less babyish than those woolly animals of yours," he had said, and Johnnie had accepted them, since they made in fact no difference whatever to the games he played; games at which could Major Allingham have guessed he would have been distinctly puzzled. The little ducks, pigs and cows of lead no more remained themselves in Johnnie's games than had the pink woollen sheep and green cloth horses of his early childhood. Johnnie's world was a strange compound of the adult world in which he had always lived and a book world composed from Grimm, the Arabian Nights, Alice's adventures, natural history books and more recently the novels of Dickens and Jane Austen. His imagination was taken by anything odd – strange faces, strange names, strange animals, strange voices and catchphrases – all these appeared in his games. The black pig and the white duck were keeping a hotel; the black pig was called that funny name of Granny's friend – Mrs Gudgeon-Rogers. She was always holding her skirt tight round the knees and warming her bottom over the fire – like Mrs Coates, and whenever anyone in the hotel asked for anything she would reply, "Darling, I can't stop now. I've simply got to fly," like Aunt Sophie, and then she would fly out of the window. The duck was an Echidna, or Spiny Anteater who wore a picture hat and a fish train like in the picture of Aunt Eleanor; she used to weep a lot, because, like Granny when she described her games of bridge, she was "vulnerable" and she would yawn at the hotel guests and say, "Lord I am tired," like Lydia Bennet. The two collie dogs had "been asked to leave," like in the story of Mummy's friend Gertie who "got tight" at the Hunt Ball, they were going to be divorced and were consequently wearing "corespondent shoes". The lady collie who was called Minnie Mongelheim kept on saying, "That chap's got a proud stomach. Let him eat chaff," like Mr F's Aunt in *Little Dorrit*. The sheep, who always played the part of a bore, kept on and on talking like Daddy about "leg cuts and fine shots to cover"; sometimes when the rest of the animal guests got too bored the sheep would change into Grandfather Graham and tell a funny story about a Scotsman so that they were bored in a different way. Finally the cat who was a grand vizier and worked by magic would say, "All the ways round here belong to me," like the Red Queen, and he would have all the guests torn in pieces and flayed alive until Johnnie felt so sorry for them that the game would come to an end. Mummy was already saying that he was getting too old for the farm animals: one always seemed to be getting too old for something. In fact the animals were no longer necessary to Johnnie's games for most of the time now he liked to read and when he wanted to play games he would do so in his head without the aid of any toys, but he hated the idea of throwing things away because they were no longer needed. Mummy and Daddy were always throwing things away and never thinking of their feelings. When he had been much younger Mummy had given him an old petticoat to put in the dustbin, but

Johnnie had taken it to his room and hugged it and cried over it, because it was no longer wanted. Daddy had been very upset. Daddy was always being upset at what Johnnie did. Only the last time that he was home there had been an awful row, because Johnnie had tried to make up like old Mrs Langdon and could not wash the blue paint off his eyes. Daddy had beaten him and looked very hurt all day and said to Mummy that he'd "rather see him dead than grow up a cissie". No, it was better not to do imitations oneself, but to leave it to the animals.

This afternoon, however, Johnnie was not attending seriously to his game, he was sitting and thinking of what the grown-ups had been saying and of how he would never see his friends, the old ladies, again, and of how he never, never wanted to. This irrevocable separation lay like a black cloud over his mind, a constant darkness which was lit up momentarily by forks of hysterical horror, as he remembered the nature of their last meeting.

The loss of this friendship was a very serious one to the little boy. It had met so completely the needs and loneliness which are always great in a child isolated from other children and surrounded by unimaginative adults. In a totally unselfconscious way, half-crazy as they were and half-crazy even though the child sensed them to be, the Misses Swindale possessed just those qualities of which Johnnie felt most in need. To begin with they were odd and fantastic and highly coloured, and more important still they believed that such peculiarities were nothing to be ashamed of, indeed were often a matter for pride. "How delightfully odd," Miss Dolly would say in her drawling voice, when Johnnie told her how the duckbilled platypus had chosen spangled tights when Queen Alexandra had ordered her to be shot from a cannon at Brighton Pavilion. "What a delightfully extravagant creature that duckbilled platypus is, Caro Gabriele," for Miss Dolly had brought back a touch of Italian here and there from her years in Florence, whilst in Johnnie she fancied a likeness to the angel Gabriel. In describing her own dresses, too, which she would do for hours on end, extravagance was her chief commendation; "as for that gold and silver brocade ball dress," she would say and her voice would sink to an awed whisper, "it was richly fantastic." To Miss Marian, with her more brusque, masculine nature, Johnnie's imaginative powers were a matter of far greater wonder than to her sister and she treated them with even greater respect. In her bluff, simple way like some old-fashioned religious army officer or overgrown but solemn schoolboy, she too admired the eccentric and unusual. "What a lark!" she would say, when Johnnie told her how the Crown Prince had slipped in some polar bears dressed in pink ballet skirts to sing "Ta Ra Ra boomdeay" in the middle of a boring school concert which his royal duties had forced him to attend, "What a nice chap he must be to know." In talking of her late father, the general, whose memory she worshipped and of whom she had a never-ending flow of anecdotes, she would give an instance of his warm-hearted but distinctly eccentric behaviour and say in her gruff voice, "Wasn't it rum? That's the bit I like best." But in neither of the sisters was there the least trace of that self-conscious whimsicality which Johnnie had met and hated in so many grown-ups. They were the first people he had met who liked what he liked and as he liked it.

Their love of lost causes and their defence of the broken, the worn out and the forgotten met a deep demand in his nature, which had grown almost sickly sentimental in the dead, practical world of his home. He loved the disorder of the old eighteenth-century farm house, the collection of miscellaneous objects of all kinds that littered the rooms, and thoroughly sympathized with the sisters' magpie propensity to collect dress ends, feathers, string, old whistles and broken cups. He grew excited with them in their fights, to prevent drunken old men being taken to workhouses and cancerous old women to hospitals, though he sensed something crazy in their constant fear of intruders, bolsheviks and prying doctors. He would often try to change the conversation when Miss Marian became excited about spies in the village, or told him of how torches had been flashing all night in the garden and of how the vicar was slandering her father's memory in a whispering campaign. He felt deeply embarrassed when Miss Dolly insisted on looking into all the cupboards and behind the curtains to see, as she said, "if there were any eyes or ears where they were not wanted. For, Caro Gabriele, those who hate beauty are many and strong, those who love it are few."

It was, above all, their kindness and their deep affection which held the love-starved child. His friendship with Miss Dolly had been almost instantaneous. She soon entered into his fantasies with complete intimacy, and he was spellbound by her stories of the gaiety and beauty of Mediterranean life. They would play dressing-up games together and enacted all his favourite historical scenes. She helped him with his French, too, and taught him Italian words with lovely sounds; she praised his painting and helped him to make costume designs for some of his "characters". With Miss Marian, at first, there had been much greater difficulty. She was an intensely shy woman and took refuge behind a rather forbidding bluntness of manner. Her old-fashioned military airs and general "manly" tone, copied from her father, with which she approached small boys, reminded Johnnie too closely of his own father. "Head up, me lad," she would say, "shoulders straight." Once he had come very near to hating her, when after an exhibition of his absentmindedness she had said, "take care, Johnnie head in the air. You'll be lost in the clouds, me' lad, if you're not careful." But the moment after she had won his heart for ever, when with a little chuckle she continued, "Jolly good thing if you are, you'll learn things up there that we shall never know." On her side, as soon as she saw that she had won his affection, she lost her shyness and proceeded impulsively to load him with kindnesses. She loved to cook his favourite dishes for him and give him his favourite fruit from their kitchen garden. Her admiration for his precocity and imagination was open-eyed and childlike. Finally they had found a common love of Dickens and Jane Austen, which she had read with her father, and now they would sit for hours talking over the characters in their favourite books.

Johnnie's affection for them was intensely protective, and increased daily as he heard and saw the contempt and dislike with which they were regarded by many persons in the village. The knowledge that "they had been away" was nothing new to him when Mr Codrington had revealed it that afternoon. Once Miss Dolly had told him how a foolish doctor had advised her to go into a home, "for you know, caro, ever since I returned to these grey skies my health has not been very good. People here think me strange, I cannot attune myself to the cold northern soul. But it was useless to keep me there, I need beauty and warmth of colour, and there it was so drab. The people, too, were unhappy crazy creatures and I missed my music so dreadfully." Miss Marian had spoken more violently of it on one of her "funny" days, when from the depredations caused by the village boys to the orchard she had passed on to the strange man she had found spying in her father's library and the need for a high wall round the house to prevent people peering through the telescopes from Mr Hatton's house opposite. "They're frightened of us, though, Johnnie," she had said, "I'm too honest for them and Dolly's too clever. They're always trying to separate us. Once they took me away against my will. They couldn't keep me, I wrote to all sorts of big pots, friends of father's, you know, and they had to release me." Johnnie realized, too, that when his mother had said that she never knew which was the keeper, she had spoken more truly than she understood. Each sister was constantly alarmed for the other and anxious to hide the other's defects from an un-understanding world. Once when Miss Dolly had been telling him a long story about a young waiter who had slipped a note into her hand the last time she had been in London, Miss Marian called Johnnie into the kitchen to look at some pies she had made. Later she had told him not to listen if Dolly said "soppy things" because being so beautiful she did not realize that she was no longer young. Another day when Miss Marian had brought in the silver-framed photo of her father in full dress uniform and had asked Johnnie to swear an oath to clear the general's memory in the village, Miss Dolly had begun to play a mazurka on the piano. Later, she too had warned Johnnie not to take too much notice when her sister got excited. "She lives a little too much in the past, Gabriele. She suffered very much when our father died. Poor Marian, it is a pity perhaps that she is so good, she has had too little of the pleasures of life. But we must love her very much, caro, very much."

Johnnie had sworn to himself to stand by them and to fight the wicked people who said they were old and useless and in the way. But now, since that dreadful teaparty, he could not fight for them any longer, for he knew why they had been shut up and felt that it was justified. In a sense, too, he understood that it was to protect others that they had to be restrained, for the most awful memory of all that terrifying afternoon was the thought that he had shared with pleasure for a moment in their wicked game.

It was certainly most unfortunate that Johnnie should have been invited to tea on that Thursday, for the Misses Swindale had been drinking heavily on and off for the preceding week, and were by that time in a state of mental and nervous excitement that rendered them far from normal. A number of events had combined to produce the greatest sense of isolation in these old women whose sanity in any event hung by a precarious thread. Miss Marian had been involved in an unpleasant scene with the vicar over the new hall for the Young People's Club. She was, as usual, providing the cash for the building and felt extremely happy and excited at being consulted about the decorations. Though she did not care for the vicar, she set out to see him, determined that she would accommodate herself to changing times. In any case, since she was the benefactress, it was, she felt, particularly necessary that she should take a back seat; to have imposed her wishes in any way would have been most ill-bred. It was an unhappy chance that caused the vicar to harp upon the need for new fabrics for the chairs and even to digress upon the ugliness of the old upholstery, for these chairs had come from the late General Swindale's library. Miss Marian was immediately reminded of her belief that the vicar was attempting secretly to blacken her father's memory, nor was the impression corrected when he tactlessly suggested that the question of her father's taste was unimportant and irrelevant. She was more deeply wounded still to find in the next few days that the village shared the vicar's view that she was attempting to dictate to the boys' club by means of her money. "After all," as Mrs Grove at the Post Office said, "it's not only the large sums that count, Miss Swindale, it's all the boys' sixpences that they've saved up." "You've too much of your father's ways in you, that's the trouble, Miss Swindale," said Mr Norton, who was famous for his bluntness, "and they won't do nowadays."

She had returned from this unfortunate morning's shopping to find Mrs Calkett on the doorstep. Now the visit of Mrs Calkett was not altogether unexpected, for Miss Marian had guessed from chance remarks of her sister's that something "unfortunate" had happened with young Tony. When, however, the sharp-faced unpleasant little woman began to complain about Miss Dolly with innuendos and veiledly coarse suggestions, Miss Marian could stand it no longer and drove her away harshly. "How dare you speak about my sister in that disgusting way, you evil-minded little woman," she said. "You'd better be careful or you'll find yourself charged with libel." When the scene was over, she felt very tired. It was dreadful of course that anyone so mean and cheap should speak thus of anyone so fine and beautiful as Dolly, but it was also dreadful that Dolly should have made such a scene possible.

Things were not improved, therefore, when Dolly returned from Brighton at once elevated by a new conquest and depressed by its subsequent results. It seemed that the new conductor on the South-down, "that charming dark Italian-looking boy I was telling you about, my dear," had returned her a most intimate smile and pressed her hand when giving her change. Her own smiles must have been embarrassingly intimate, for a woman in the next seat had remarked loudly to her friend, "These painted old things. Really, I wonder the men don't smack their faces." "I couldn't help smiling," remarked Miss Dolly, "she was so evidently *jalouse*, my dear. I'm glad to say the conductor did not hear, for no doubt he would have felt it necessary to come to my defence, he was so completely *épris*." But, for once, Miss Marian was too vexed to play ball, she turned on her sister and roundly condemned her conduct, ending up by accusing her of bringing misery to them both and shame to their father's memory. Poor Miss Dolly just stared in bewilderment, her baby-blue eyes round with fright, tears washing the mascara from her eyelashes in black streams down the wrinkled vermilion of her cheeks. Finally she ran crying up to her room.

That night both the sisters began to drink heavily. Miss Dolly lay like some monstrous broken doll, her red hair streaming over her shoulders, her corsets unloosed and her fat body poking out of an old pink velvet ball dress – pink with red hair was always so audacious – through the most unexpected places in bulges of thick blue-white flesh. She sipped at glass after glass of gin, sometimes staring into the distance with bewilderment that she should find herself in such a condition, sometimes leering pruriently at some pictures of Johnny Weismuller in swimsuits that she had cut out of *Film Weekly*. At last she began to weep to think that she had sunk to this. Miss Marian sat at her desk and drank more deliberately from a cut glass decanter of brandy. She read solemnly through her father's letters, their old-fashioned earnest Victorian sentiments swimming ever more wildly before her eyes. But, at last, she, too, began to weep as she thought of how his memory would be quite gone when she passed away, and of how she had broken the promise that she had made to him on his deathbed to stick to her sister through thick and thin.

So they continued for two or three days with wild spasms of drinking and horrible, sober periods of remorse. They cooked themselves odd scraps in the kitchen, littering the house with unwashed dishes and cups, but never speaking, always avoiding each other. They didn't change their clothes or wash, and indeed made little alteration in their appearance. Miss Dolly put fresh rouge on her cheeks periodically and some pink roses in her hair which hung there wilting; she was twice sick over the pink velvet dress. Miss Marian put on an old scarlet hunting waistcoat of her father's, partly out of maudlin sentiment and partly because she was cold. Once she fell on the stairs and cut her forehead against the banisters; the red and white handkerchief which she tied round her head gave her the appearance of a tipsy pirate. On the fourth day, the sisters were reconciled and sat in Miss Dolly's room. That night they slept, lying heavily against each other on Miss Dolly's bed, open-mouthed and snoring, Miss Marian's deep guttural rattle contrasting with Miss Dolly's highpitched whistle. They awoke on Thursday morning, much sobered, to the realization that Johnnie was coming to tea that afternoon.

It was characteristic that neither spoke a word of the late debauch. Together they went out into the hot July sunshine to gather raspberries for Johnnie's tea. But the nets in the kitchen garden had been disarranged and the birds had got the fruit. The awful malignity of this chance event took some time to pierce through the fuddled brains of the two ladies, as they stood there grotesque and obscene in their staring pink and clashing red, with their heavy pouchy faces and bloodshot eyes showing up in the hard, clear light of the sun. But when the realization did get home it seemed to come as a confirmation of all the beliefs of persecution which had been growing throughout the drunken orgy. There is little doubt that they were both a good deal mad when they returned to the house.

Johnnie arrived punctually at four o'clock, for he was a small boy of exceptional politeness. Miss Marian opened the door to him, and he was surprised at her appearance in her red bandana and her scarlet waistcoat, and especially by her voice which, though friendly and gruff as usual, sounded thick and flat. Miss Dolly, too, looked more than usually odd with one eye closed in a kind of perpetual wink, and with her pink dress falling off her shoulders. She kept on laughing in a silly, high giggle. The shock of discovering that the raspberries were gone had driven them back to the bottle and they were both fairly drunk. They pressed upon the little boy, who was thirsty after his walk, two small glasses in succession, one of brandy, the other of gin, though in their sober mood the ladies would have died rather than have seen their little friend take strong liquor. The drink soon combined with the heat of the day and the smell of vomit that hung around the room to make Johnnie feel most strange. The walls of the room seemed to be closing in and the floor to be moving up and down like sea waves. The ladies' faces came up at him suddenly and then receded, now Miss Dolly's with great blobs of blue and scarlet and her eyes winking and leering, now Miss Marian's a huge white mass with her moustache grown large and black. He was only conscious by fits and starts of what they were doing or saying. Sometimes he would hear Miss Marian speaking in a flat, slow monotone. She seemed to be reading out her father's letters, snatches of which came to him clearly and then faded away. "There is so much to be done in our short sojourn on this earth, so much that may be done for good, so much for evil. Let us earnestly endeavour to keep the good steadfastly before us," then suddenly, "Major Campbell has told me of his decision to leave the regiment. I pray God hourly that he may have acted in full consideration of the Higher Will to which . . .", and once grotesquely, "Your Aunt Maud was here yesterday, she is a maddening woman and I consider it a just judgment upon the Liberal party that she should espouse its cause." None of these phrases meant anything to the little boy, but he was dimly conscious that Miss Marian was growing excited, for he heard her say, "That was our father. As Shakespeare says, 'He was a man take him all in all' Johnnie. We loved him, but there were those who sought to destroy him, for he was too big for them. But their day is nearly ended. Always remember that, Johnnie." It was difficult to hear all that the elder sister said, for Miss Dolly kept on drawling and giggling in his ear about a black charmeuse evening gown she had worn, and a young donkeyboy she had danced with in the fiesta at Asti. "*E come era bello, caro Gabriele, come era bello*. And afterwards . . . but I must spare the ears of one so young the details of the *arte dell' amore*" she added with a giggle and then with drunken dignity, "it would not be immodest I think to mention that his skin was like velvet. Only a few lire, too, just imagine." All this, too, was largely meaningless to the boy, though he remembered it in later years.

For a while he must have slept, since he remembered that later he could see and hear more clearly though his head ached terribly. Miss Dolly was seated at the piano playing a little jig and bobbing up and down like a mountainous pink blancmange, whilst Miss Marian more than ever like a pirate was dancing some sort of a hornpipe. Suddenly Miss Dolly stopped playing. "Shall we show him the prisoner?" she said solemnly. "Head up, shoulders straight," said Miss Marian in a parody of her old manner, "you're going to be very honoured, my lad. Promise you'll never betray that honour. You shall see one of the enemy punished. Our father gave us close instructions, 'Do good at all,' he said, 'but if you catch one of the enemy, remember you are soldier's daughters.' We shall obey that command." Meanwhile Miss Dolly had returned from the kitchen, carrying a little bird which was pecking and clawing at the net in which it had been caught and shrilling incessantly – it was a little bullfinch. "You're a very beautiful little bird," Miss Dolly whispered, "with lovely soft pink feathers and pretty grey wings. But you're a very naughty little bird too, *tante cattivo*. You came and took the fruit from us which we'd kept for our darling Gabriele." She began feverishly to pull the rose breast feathers from the bird, which piped more loudly and squirmed. Soon little trickles of red blood ran down among the feathers. "Scarlet and pink very daring combination," Miss Dolly cried. Johnnie watched from his chair, his heart beating fast. Suddenly Miss Marian stepped forward and holding the bird's head she thrust a pin into its eyes. "We don't like spies round here looking at what we are doing," she said in her flat, gruff voice. "When we find them we teach them a lesson so that they don't spy on us again." Then she took out a little pocket knife and cut into the bird's breast; its wings were beating more feebly now and its claws only moved spasmodically, whilst its chirping was very faint. Little yellow and white strings of entrails began to peep out from where she had cut. "Oh!" cried Miss Dolly, "I like the lovely colours , I don't like these worms." But Johnnie could bear it no longer, white and shaking he jumped from his chair and seizing the bird he threw it on the floor and then he stamped on it violently until it was nothing but a sodden crimson mass. "Oh, Gabriele, what have you done? You've spoilt all the soft, pretty colours. Why it's nothing now, it just looks like a lump of raspberry jam. Why have you done it, Gabriele?" cried Miss Dolly. But little Johnnie gave no answer, he had run from the room.

THE LAST MOHICAN

Bernard Malamud

Bernard Malamud (1914–1986) was born in Brooklyn, New York, the
son of Russian immigrants. He wrote eight novels and sixty-five short
stories – his novel *The Fixer* winning the National Book Award and
the Pulitzer Prize for Fiction. He once stated, "Life is a tragedy full of
joy." His advice to writers: "Write your heart out . . . Watch out for self-
deceit in fiction. Write truthfully but with cunning. . . . Teach yourself to
work in uncertainty . . . Write, complete, revise. If it doesn't work, begin
something else."

Fidelman, a self-confessed failure as a painter, came to Italy to prepare a
critical study of Giotto, the opening chapter of which he had carried across
the ocean in a new pigskin leather brief case, now gripped in his perspiring
hand. Also new were his gum-soled oxblood shoes, a tweed suit he had on despite the late-September sun slanting hot in the Roman sky, although there was
a lighter one in his bag; and a dacron shirt and set of cotton-dacron underwear,
good for quick and easy washing for the traveler. His suitcase, a bulky, two-
strapped affair which embarrassed him slightly, he had borrowed from his sister
Bessie. He planned, if he had any money left at the end of the year, to buy a new
one in Florence. Although he had been in not much of a mood when he had left
the U.S.A., Fidelman picked up in Naples, and at the moment, as he stood in
front of the Rome railroad station, after twenty minutes still absorbed in his first
sight of the Eternal City, he was conscious of a certain exaltation that devolved
on him after he had discovered that directly across the many-vehicled piazza
stood the remains of the Baths of Diocletian. Fidelman remembered having read
that Michelangelo had had a hand in converting the baths into a church and
convent, the latter ultimately changed into the museum that presently was there.
"Imagine," he muttered. "Imagine all that history."

In the midst of his imagining, Fidelman experienced the sensation of suddenly
seeing himself as he was, to the pinpoint, outside and in, not without bittersweet
pleasure; and as the well-known image of his face rose before him he was taken
by the depth of pure feeling in his eyes, slightly magnified by glasses, and the sensitivity of his elongated nostrils and often tremulous lips, nose divided from lips
by a mustache of recent vintage that looked, Fidelman thought, as if it had been
sculptured there, adding to his dignified appearance although he was a little on
the short side. But almost at the same moment, this unexpectedly intense sense of
his being – it was more than appearance – faded, exaltation having gone where
exaltation goes, and Fidelman became aware that there was an exterior source

to the strange, almost tri-dimensional reflection of himself he had felt as well as seen. Behind him, a short distance to the right, he had noticed a stranger – give a skeleton a couple of pounds – loitering near a bronze statue on a stone pedestal of the heavy-dugged Etruscan wolf suckling the infant Romulus and Remus, the man contemplating Fidelman already acquisitively so as to suggest to the traveler that he had been mirrored (lock, stock, barrel) in the other's gaze for some time, perhaps since he had stepped off the train. Casually studying him, though pretending no, Fidelman beheld a person of about his own height, oddly dressed in brown knickers and black, knee-length woolen socks drawn up over slightly bowed, broomstick legs, these grounded in small, porous, pointed shoes. His yellowed shirt was open at the gaunt throat, both sleeves rolled up over skinny, hairy arms. The stranger's high forehead was bronzed, his black hair thick behind small ears, the dark, close-shaven beard tight on the face; his experienced nose was weighted at the tip, and the soft brown eyes, above all, *wanted*. Though his expression suggested humility, he all but licked his lips as he approached the ex-painter.

"Shalom," he greeted Fidelman.

"Shalom," the other hesitantly replied, uttering the word – so far as he recalled – for the first time in his life. My God, he thought, a handout for sure. My first hello in Rome and it has to be a schnorrer.

The stranger extended a smiling hand. "Susskind," he said, "Shimon Susskind."

"Arthur Fidelman." Transferring his brief case to under his left arm while standing astride the big suitcase, he shook hands with Susskind. A blue-smocked porter came by, glanced at Fidelman's bag, looked at him, then walked away.

Whether he knew it or not Susskind was rubbing his palms contemplatively together.

"Parla italiano?"

"Not with ease, although I read it fluently. You might say I need the practice."

"Yiddish?"

"I express myself best in English."

"Let it be English then." Susskind spoke with a slight British intonation. "I knew you were Jewish," he said, "the minute my eyes saw you."

Fidelman chose to ignore the remark. "Where did you pick up your knowledge of English?"

"In Israel."

Israel interested Fidelman. "You live there?"

"Once, not now," Susskind answered vaguely. He seemed suddenly bored.

"How so?"

Susskind twitched a shoulder. "Too much heavy labor for a man of my modest health. Also I couldn't stand the suspense."

Fidelman nodded.

"Furthermore, the desert air makes me constipated. In Rome I am light hearted."

"A Jewish refugee from Israel, no less," Fidelman said good humoredly.

"I'm always running," Susskind answered mirthlessly. If he was light hearted, he had yet to show it.

"Where else from, if I may ask?"

"Where else but Germany, Hungary, Poland? Where not?"

"Ah, that's so long ago." Fidelman then noticed the gray in the man's hair. "Well, I'd better be going," he said. He picked up his bag as two porters hovered uncertainly nearby.

But Susskind offered certain services. "You got a hotel?"

"All picked and reserved."

"How long are you staying?"

What business is it of his? However, Fidelman courteously replied, "Two weeks in Rome, the rest of the year in Florence, with a few side trips to Siena, Assisi, Padua and maybe also Venice."

"You wish a guide in Rome?"

"Are you a guide?"

"Why not?"

"No," said Fidelman. "I'll look as I go along to museums, libraries, et cetera." This caught Susskind's attention. "What are you, a professor?"

Fidelman couldn't help blushing. "Not exactly, really just a student."

"From which institution?"

He coughed a little. "By that I mean a professional student, you might say. Call me Trofimov, from Chekov. If there's something to learn I want to learn it."

"You have some kind of a project?" the other persisted. "A grant?"

"No grant. My money is hard earned. I worked and saved a long time to take a year in Italy. I made certain sacrifices. As for a project, I'm writing on the painter Giotto. He was one of the most important –"

"You don't have to tell me about Giotto," Susskind interrupted with a little smile.

"You've studied his work?"

"Who doesn't know Giotto?"

"That's interesting to me," said Fidelman, secretly irritated. "How do you happen to know him?"

"How do you?"

"I've given a good deal of time and study to his work."

"So I know him too."

I'd better get this over with before it begins to amount up to something, Fidelman thought. He set down his bag and fished with a finger in his leather coin purse. The two porters watched with interest, one taking a sandwich out of his pocket, unwrapping the newspaper and beginning to eat.

"This is for yourself," Fidelman said.

Susskind hardly glanced at the coin as he let it drop into his pants pocket. The porters then left.

The refugee had an odd way of standing motionless, like a cigar store Indian about to burst into flight. "In your luggage," he said vaguely, "would you maybe have a suit you can't use? I could use a suit."

At last he comes to the point. Fidelman, though annoyed, controlled himself. "All I have is a change from the one you now see me wearing. Don't get the wrong idea about me, Mr. Susskind. I'm not rich. In fact, I'm poor. Don't let a few new clothes deceive you. I owe my sister money for them."

Susskind glanced down at his shabby, baggy knickers. "I haven't had a suit for years. The one I was wearing when I ran away from Germany, fell apart. One day I was walking around naked."

"Isn't there a welfare organization that could help you out – some group in the Jewish community, interested in refugees?"

"The Jewish organizations wish to give me what they wish, not what I wish," Susskind replied bitterly. "The only thing they offer me is a ticket back to Israel."

"Why don't you take it?"

"I told you already, here I feel free."

"Freedom is a relative term."

"Don't tell me about freedom."

He knows all about that, too, Fidelman thought. "So you feel free," he said, "but how do you live?"

Susskind coughed, a brutal cough.

Fidelman was about to say something more on the subject of freedom but left it unsaid. Jesus, I'll be saddled with him all day if I don't watch out.

"I'd better be getting off to the hotel." He bent again for his bag.

Susskind touched him on the shoulder and when Fidelman exasperatedly straightened up, the half dollar he had given the man was staring him in the eye.

"On this we both lose money."

"How do you mean?"

"Today the lira sells six twenty-three on the dollar, but for specie they only give you five hundred."

"In that case, give it here and I'll let you have a dollar." From his billfold Fidelman quickly extracted a crisp bill and handed it to the refugee.

"Not more?" Susskind sighed.

"Not more," the student answered emphatically.

"Maybe you would like to see Diocletian's bath? There are some enjoyable Roman coffins inside. I will guide you for another dollar."

"No, thanks." Fidelman said goodbye, and lifting the suitcase, lugged it to the curb. A porter appeared and the student, after some hesitation, let him carry it toward the line of small dark-green taxis in the piazza. The porter offered to carry the brief case too, but Fidelman wouldn't part with it. He gave the cab driver the address of the hotel, and the taxi took off with a lurch. Fidelman at last relaxed. Susskind, he noticed, had disappeared. Gone with his breeze, he thought. But on the way to the hotel he had an uneasy feeling that the refugee, crouched low, might be clinging to the little tire on the back of the cab; however, he didn't look out to see.

Fidelman had reserved a room in an inexpensive hotel not far from the station, with its very convenient bus terminal. Then, as was his habit, he got himself quickly and tightly organized. He was always concerned with not wasting time, as if it were his only wealth – not true, of course, though Fidelman admitted he was an ambitious person – and he soon arranged a schedule that made the most of his working hours. Mornings he usually visited the Italian libraries, searching their catalogues and archives, read in poor light, and made profuse notes. He napped for an hour after lunch, then at four, when the churches and museums were re-opening, hurried off to them with lists of frescoes and paintings he must see. He was anxious to get to Florence, at the same time a little unhappy at all he would not have time to take in in Rome. Fidelman promised himself to return again if he could afford it, perhaps in the spring, and look at anything he pleased.

After dark he managed to unwind himself and relax. He ate as the Romans did, late, enjoyed a half litre of white wine and smoked a cigarette. Afterward he liked to wander – especially in the old sections near the Tiber. He had read that here, under his feet, were the ruins of Ancient Rome. It was an inspiring business, he, Arthur Fidelman, after all, born a Bronx boy, walking around in all this history. History was mysterious, the remembrance of things unknown, in a way burdensome, in a way a sensuous experience. It uplifted and depressed, why he did not know, except that it excited his thoughts more than he thought good for him. This kind of excitement was all right up to a point, perfect maybe for a creative artist, but less so for a critic. A critic, he thought, should live on beans. He walked for miles along the winding river, gazing at the star-strewn skies. Once, after a couple of days in the Vatican Museum, he saw flights of angels – gold, blue, white – intermingled in the sky. "My God, I got to stop using my eyes so much," Fidelman said to himself. But back in his room he sometimes wrote till morning.

Late one night, about a week after his arrival in Rome, as Fidelman was writing notes on the Byzantine style mosaics he had seen during the day, there was a knock on the door, and though the student, immersed in his work, was not conscious he had said "Avanti," he must have, for the door opened, and instead of an angel, in came Susskind in his shirt and baggy knickers.

Fidelman, who had all but forgotten the refugee, certainly never thought of him, half rose in astonishment. "Susskind," he exclaimed, "how did you get in here?"

Susskind for a moment stood motionless, then answered with a weary smile, "I'll tell you the truth, I know the desk clerk."

"But how did you know where I live?"

"I saw you walking in the street so I followed you."

"You mean you saw me accidentally?"

"How else? Did you leave me your address?"

Fidelman resumed his seat. "What can I do for you, Susskind?" He spoke grimly.

The refugee cleared his throat. "Professor, the days are warm but the nights are cold. You see how I go around naked." He held forth bluish arms, goose-fleshed. "I came to ask you to reconsider about giving away your old suit."

"And who says it's an old suit?" Despite himself, Fidelman's voice thickened.

"One suit is new, so the other is old."

"Not precisely. I am afraid I have no suit for you, Susskind. The one I presently have hanging in the closet is a little more than a year old and I can't afford to give it away. Besides, it's gabardine, more like a summer suit."

"On me it will be for all seasons."

After a moment's reflection, Fidelman drew out his billfold and counted four single dollars. These he handed to Susskind.

"Buy yourself a warm sweater."

Susskind also counted the money. "If four," he said, "then why not five?"

Fidelman flushed. The man's warped nerve. "Because I happen to have four available," he answered. "That's twenty-five hundred lire. You should be able to buy a warm sweater and have something left over besides."

"I need a suit," Susskind said. "The days are warm but the nights are cold." He rubbed his arms. "What else I need I won't say."

"At least roll down your sleeves if you're so cold."

"That won't help me."

"Listen, Susskind," Fidelman said gently, "I would gladly give you the suit if I could afford to, but I can't. I have barely enough money to squeeze out a year for myself here. I've already told you I am indebted to my sister. Why don't you try to get yourself a job somewhere, no matter how menial? I'm sure that in a short while you'll work yourself up into a decent position."

"A job, he says," Susskind muttered gloomily. "Do you know what it means to get a job in Italy? Who will give me a job?"

"Who gives anybody a job? They have to go out and look for it."

"You don't understand, professor. I am an Israeli citizen and this means I can only work for an Israeli company. How many Israeli companies are there here? – maybe two, El Al and Zim, and even if they had a job, they wouldn't give it to me because I have lost my passport. I would be better off now if I were stateless. A stateless person shows his laissez passer and sometimes he can find a small job."

"But if you lost your passport why didn't you put in for a duplicate?"

"I did, but did they give it to me?"

"Why not?"

"Why not? They say I sold it."

"Had they reason to think that?"

"I swear to you somebody stole it from me."

"Under such circumstances," Fidelman asked, "how do you live?"

"How do I live?" He chomped with his teeth. "I eat air."

"Seriously?"

"Seriously, on air. I also peddle," he confessed, "but to peddle you need a license, and that the Italians won't give me. When they caught me peddling I was interned for six months in a work camp."

"Didn't they attempt to deport you?"

"They did, but I sold my mother's old wedding ring that I kept in my pocket so many years. The Italians are a humane people. They took the money and let me go but they told me not to peddle anymore."

"So what do you do now?"

"I peddle. What should I do, beg? – I peddle. But last spring I got sick and gave my little money away to the doctors. I still have a bad cough." He coughed fruitily. "Now I have no capital to buy stock with. Listen, professor, maybe we can go in partnership together? Lend me twenty thousand lire and I will buy ladies' nylon stockings. After I sell them I will return you your money."

"I have no funds to invest, Susskind."

"You will get it back, with interest."

"I honestly am sorry for you," Fidelman said, "but why don't you at least do something practical? Why don't you go to the Joint Distribution Committee, for instance, and ask them to assist you? That's their business."

"I already told you why. They wish me to go back, but I wish to stay here."

"I still think going back would be the best thing for you."

"No," cried Susskind angrily.

"If that's your decision, freely made, then why pick on me? Am I responsible for you then, Susskind?"

"Who else?" Susskind loudly replied.

"Lower your voice, please, people are sleeping around here," said Fidelman, beginning to perspire. "Why should I be?"

"You know what responsibility means?"

"I think so."

"Then you are responsible. Because you are a man. Because you are a Jew, aren't you?"

"Yes, goddamn it, but I'm not the only one in the whole wide world. Without prejudice, I refuse the obligation. I am a single individual and can't take on everybody's personal burden. I have the weight of my own to contend with."

He reached for his billfold and plucked out another dollar.

"This makes five. It's more than I can afford, but take it and after this please leave me alone. I have made my contribution."

Susskind stood there, oddly motionless, an impassioned statue, and for a moment Fidelman wondered if he would stay all night, but at last the refugee thrust forth a stiff arm, took the fifth dollar and departed.

Early the next morning Fidelman moved out of the hotel into another, less convenient for him, but far away from Shimon Susskind and his endless demands.

This was Tuesday. On Wednesday, after a busy morning in the library, Fidelman entered a nearby trattoria and ordered a plate of spaghetti with tomato sauce. He was reading his *Messaggero*, anticipating the coming of the food, for he was unusually hungry, when he sensed a presence at the table. He looked up, expecting the waiter, but beheld instead Susskind standing there, alas, unchanged.

Is there no escape from him? thought Fidelman, severely vexed. Is this why I came to Rome?

"Shalom, professor," Susskind said, keeping his eyes off the table. "I was passing and saw you sitting here alone, so I came in to say shalom."

"Susskind," Fidelman said in anger, "have you been following me again?"

"How could I follow you?" asked the astonished Susskind. "Do I know where you live now?"

Though Fidelman blushed a little, he told himself he owed nobody an explanation. So he had found out he had moved – good.

"My feet are tired. Can I sit five minutes?"

"Sit."

Susskind drew out a chair. The spaghetti arrived, steaming hot. Fidelman sprinkled it with cheese and wound his fork into several tender strands. One of the strings of spaghetti seemed to stretch for miles, so he stopped at a certain point and swallowed the forkful. Having foolishly neglected to cut the long spaghetti string he was left sucking it, seemingly endlessly. This embarrassed him.

Susskind watched with rapt attention.

Fidelman at last reached the end of the long spaghetti, patted his mouth with a napkin, and paused in his eating.

"Would you care for a plateful?"

Susskind, eyes hungry, hesitated. "Thanks," he said.

"Thanks yes or thanks no?"

"Thanks no." The eyes looked away.

Fidelman resumed eating, carefully winding his fork; he had had not too much practice with this sort of thing and was soon involved in the same dilemma with the spaghetti. Seeing Susskind still watching him, he soon became tense.

"We are not Italians, professor," the refugee said. "Cut it in small pieces with your knife. Then you will swallow it easier."

"I'll handle it as I please," Fidelman responded testily. "This is my business. You attend to yours."

"My business," Susskind sighed, "don't exist. This morning I had to let a wonderful chance get away from me. I had a chance to buy ladies' stockings at three hundred lire if I had money to buy half a gross. I could easily sell them for five hundred a pair. We would have made a nice profit."

"The news doesn't interest me."

"So if not ladies' stockings, I can also get sweaters, scarves, men's socks, also cheap leather goods, ceramics – whatever would interest you."

"What interests me is what you did with the money I gave you for a sweater."

"It's getting cold, professor," Susskind said worriedly. "Soon comes the November rains, and in winter the tramontana. I thought I ought to save your money to buy a couple of kilos of chestnuts and a bag of charcoal for my burner. If you sit all day on a busy street corner you can sometimes make a thousand lire. Italians like hot chestnuts. But if I do this I will need some warm clothes, maybe a suit."

"A suit," Fidelman remarked sarcastically, "why not an overcoat?"

"I have a coat, poor that it is, but now I need a suit. How can anybody come in company without a suit?"

Fidelman's hand trembled as he laid down his fork. "To my mind you are utterly irresponsible and I won't be saddled with you. I have the right to choose my own problems and the right to my privacy."

"Don't get excited, professor, it's bad for your digestion. Eat in peace." Susskind got up and left the trattoria.

Fidelman hadn't the appetite to finish his spaghetti. He paid the bill, waited ten minutes, then departed, glancing around from time to time to see if he were being followed. He headed down the sloping street to a small piazza where he saw a couple of cabs. Not that he could afford one, but he wanted to make sure Susskind didn't tail him back to his new hotel. He would warn the clerk at the desk never to allow anybody of the refugee's name or description even to make inquiries about him.

Susskind, however, stepped out from behind a plashing fountain at the center of the little piazza. Modestly addressing the speechless Fidelman, he said, "I don't wish to take only, professor. If I had something to give you, I would gladly give it to you."

"Thanks," snapped Fidelman, "just give me some peace of mind."

"That you have to find yourself," Susskind answered.

In the taxi Fidelman decided to leave for Florence the next day, rather than at the end of the week, and once and for all be done with the pest.

That night, after returning to his room from an unpleasurable walk in the Trastevere – he had a headache from too much wine at supper – Fidelman found his door ajar and at once recalled that he had forgotten to lock it, although he had as usual left the key with the desk clerk. He was at first frightened, but when he tried the armadio in which he kept his clothes and suitcase, it was shut tight. Hastily unlocking it, he was relieved to see his blue gabardine suit – a one-button jacket affair, the trousers a little frayed on the cuffs, but all in good shape and usable for years to come – hanging amid some shirts the maid had pressed for him; and when he examined the contents of the suitcase he found nothing missing, including, thank God, his passport and travelers' checks. Gazing around the room, Fidelman saw all in place. Satisfied, he picked up a book and read ten pages before he thought of his brief case. He jumped to his feet and began to search everywhere, remembering distinctly that it had been on the night table as he had lain on the bed that afternoon, re-reading his chapter. He searched under the bed and behind the night table, then again throughout the room, even on top of and behind the armadio. Fidelman hopelessly opened every drawer, no matter how small, but found neither the brief case, nor, what was worse, the chapter in it.

With a groan he sank down on the bed, insulting himself for not having made a copy of the manuscript, for he had more than once warned himself that something like this might happen to it. But he hadn't because there were some revisions he had contemplated making, and he had planned to retype the entire chapter before beginning the next. He thought now of complaining to the owner of the hotel, who lived on the floor below, but it was already past midnight and he realized nothing could be done until morning. Who could have taken it? The maid or hall porter? It seemed unlikely they would risk their jobs to steal a piece of leather goods that would bring them only a few thousand lire in a pawn shop. Possibly a sneak thief? He would ask tomorrow if other persons on the floor were missing something. He somehow doubted it. If a thief, he would then and there have ditched the chapter and stuffed the brief case with Fidelman's oxblood shoes, left by the bed, and the fifteen-dollar R. H. Macy sweater that lay in full view of the desk. But if not the maid or porter or a sneak thief, then who? Though Fidelman had not the slightest shred of evidence to support his suspicions he could think of only one person – Susskind. This thought stung him. But if Susskind, why? Out of pique, perhaps, that he had not been given the suit he had coveted, nor was able to pry it out of the armadio? Try as he would, Fidelman could think of no one else and no other reason. Somehow the peddler had followed him home (he suspected their meeting at the fountain) and had got into his room while he was out to supper.

Fidelman's sleep that night was wretched. He dreamed of pursuing the refugee in the Jewish catacombs under the ancient Appian Way, threatening him a blow on the presumptuous head with a seven-flamed candalabrum he clutched in his hand; while Susskind, clever ghost, who knew the ins and outs of all the crypts and alleys, eluded him at every turn. Then Fidelman's candles all blew out, leaving him sightless and alone in the cemeterial dark; but when the student arose in the morning and wearily drew up the blinds, the yellow Italian sun winked him cheerfully in both bleary eyes.

Fidelman postponed going to Florence. He reported his loss to the Questura, and though the police were polite and eager to help, they could do nothing for him. On the form on which the inspector noted the complaint, he listed the brief case as worth ten thousand lire, and for "valore del manuscritto" he drew a line. Fidelman, after giving the matter a good deal of thought, did not report Susskind, first, because he had absolutely no proof, for the desk clerk swore he had seen no stranger around in knickers; second, because he was afraid of the consequences for the refugee if he were written down "suspected thief" as well as "unlicensed peddler" and inveterate refugee. He tried instead to rewrite the chapter, which he felt sure he knew by heart, but when he sat down at the desk, there were important thoughts, whole paragraphs, even pages, that went blank in the mind. He considered sending to America for his notes for the chapter but they were in a barrel in his sister's attic in Levittown, among many notes for other projects. The thought of Bessie, a mother of five, poking around in his things, and the work entailed in sorting the cards, then getting them packaged and mailed to him across the ocean, wearied Fidelman unspeakably; he was certain she would send the wrong ones. He laid down his pen and went into the street, seeking Susskind. He searched for him in neighborhoods where he had seen him before, and though Fidelman spent hours looking, literally days, Susskind never appeared; or if he perhaps did, the sight of Fidelman caused him to vanish. And when the student inquired about him at the Israeli consulate, the clerk, a new man on the job, said he had no record of such a person or his lost passport; on the other hand, he was known at the Joint Distribution Committee, but by name and address only, an impossibility, Fidelman thought. They gave him a number to go to but the place had long since been torn down to make way for an apartment house.

Time went without work, without accomplishment. To put an end to this appalling waste Fidelman tried to force himself back into his routine of research and picture viewing. He moved out of the hotel, which he now could not stand for the harm it had done him (leaving a telephone number and urging he be called if the slightest clue turned up), and he took a room in a small pensione near the Stazione and here had breakfast and supper rather than go out. He was much concerned with expenditures and carefully recorded them in a notebook he had acquired for the purpose. Nights, instead of wandering in the city, feasting himself upon its beauty and mystery, he kept his eyes glued to paper, sitting steadfastly at his desk in an attempt to recreate his initial chapter, because he was lost without a beginning. He had tried writing the second chapter from notes in his possession but it had come to nothing. Always Fidelman needed something solid behind him before he could advance, some worthwhile accomplishment upon which to build another. He worked late, but his mood, or inspiration, or whatever it was, had deserted him, leaving him with growing anxiety, almost disorientation; of not knowing – it seemed to him for the first time in months – what he must do next, a feeling that was torture. Therefore he again took up his search for the refugee. He thought now that once he had settled it, knew that the man had or hadn't stolen his chapter – whether he recovered it or not seemed at the moment immaterial – just the knowing of it would ease his mind and again he would *feel* like working, the crucial element.

Daily he combed the crowded streets, searching for Susskind wherever people peddled. On successive Sunday mornings he took the long ride to the Porta Portese market and hunted for hours among the piles of second-hand goods and junk lining the back streets, hoping his brief case would magically appear, though it never did. He visited the open market at Piazza Fontanella Borghese, and observed the ambulant vendors at Piazza Dante. He looked among fruit and vegetable stalls set up in the streets, whenever he chanced upon them, and dawdled on busy street corners after dark, among beggars and fly-by-night peddlers. After the first cold snap at the end of October, when the chestnut sellers appeared throughout the city, huddled over pails of glowing coals, he sought in their faces the missing Susskind. Where in all of modern and ancient Rome was he? The man lived in the open air – he had to appear somewhere. Sometimes when riding in a bus or tram, Fidelman thought he had glimpsed somebody in a crowd, dressed in the refugee's clothes, and he invariably got off to run after whoever it was – once a man standing in front of the Banco di Santo Spirito, gone when Fidelman breathlessly arrived; and another time he overtook a person in knickers, but this one wore a monocle. Sir Ian Susskind?

In November it rained. Fidelman wore a blue beret with his trench coat and a pair of black Italian shoes, smaller, despite their pointed toes, than his burly oxbloods which overheated his feet and whose color he detested. But instead of visiting museums he frequented movie houses sitting in the cheapest seats and regretting the cost. He was, at odd hours in certain streets, several times accosted by prostitutes, some heart-breakingly pretty, one a slender, unhappy-looking girl with bags under her eyes whom he desired mightily, but Fidelman feared for his health. He had got to know the face of Rome and spoke Italian fairly fluently, but his heart was burdened, and in his blood raged a murderous hatred of the bandy-legged refugee – although there were times when he bethought himself he might be wrong – so Fidelman more than once cursed him to perdition.

One Friday night, as the first star glowed over the Tiber, Fidelman, walking aimlessly along the left riverbank, came upon a synagogue and wandered in among a crowd of Sephardim with Italianate faces. One by one they paused before a sink in an antechamber to dip their hands under a flowing faucet, then in the house of worship touched with loose fingers their brows, mouths, and breasts as they bowed to the Arc, Fidelman doing likewise. Where in the world am I? Three rabbis rose from a bench and the service began, a long prayer, sometimes chanted, sometimes accompanied by invisible organ music, but no Susskind anywhere. Fidelman sat at a desk-like pew in the last row, where he could inspect the congregants yet keep an eye on the door. The synagogue was unheated and the cold rose like an exudation from the marble floor. The student's freezing nose burned like a lit candle. He got up to go, but the beadle, a stout man in a high hat and short caftan, wearing a long thick silver chain around his neck, fixed the student with his powerful left eye.

"From New York?" he inquired, slowly approaching.

Half the congregation turned to see who.

"State, not city," answered Fidelman, nursing an active guilt for the attention he was attracting. Then, taking advantage of a pause, he whispered, "Do you happen to know a man named Susskind? He wears knickers."

"A relative?" The beadle gazed at him sadly.

"Not exactly."

"My own son – killed in the Ardeatine Caves." Tears stood forth in his eyes.

"Ah, for that I'm sorry."

But the beadle had exhausted the subject. He wiped his wet lids with pudgy fingers and the curious Sephardim turned back to their prayer books.

"Which Susskind?" the beadle wanted to know.

"Shimon."

He scratched his ear. "Look in the ghetto."

"I looked."

"Look again."

The beadle walked slowly away and Fidelman sneaked out.

The ghetto lay behind the synagogue for several crooked, well-packed blocks, encompassing aristocratic palazzi ruined by age and unbearable numbers, their discolored façades strung with lines of withered wet wash, the fountains in the piazzas, dirt-laden, dry. And dark stone tenements, built partly on centuries-old ghetto walls, inclined towards one another across narrow, cobblestoned streets. In and among the impoverished houses were the wholesale establishments of wealthy Jews, dark holes ending in jeweled interiors, silks and silver of all colors. In the mazed streets wandered the present-day poor, Fidelman among them, oppressed by history, although, he joked to himself, it added years to his life.

A white moon shone upon the ghetto, lighting it like dark day. Once he thought he saw a ghost he knew by sight, and hastily followed him through a thick stone passage to a blank wall where shone in white letters under a tiny electric bulb: VIETATO URINARE. Here was a smell but no Susskind.

For thirty lire the student bought a dwarfed, blackened banana from a street vendor (not S) on a bicycle, and stopped to eat. A crowd of ragazzi gathered to watch.

"Anybody here know Susskind, a refugee wearing knickers?" Fidelman announced, stooping to point with the banana where the pants went beneath the knees. He also made his legs a trifle bowed but nobody noticed.

There was no response until he had finished his fruit, then a thin-faced boy with brown liquescent eyes out of Murillo, piped: "He sometimes works in the Cimitero Verano, the Jewish section."

There too? thought Fidelman. "Works in the cemetery?" he inquired. "With a shovel?"

"He prays for the dead," the boy answered, "for a small fee."

Fidelman bought him a quick banana and the others dispersed.

In the cemetery, deserted on the Sabbath – he should have come Sunday – Fidelman went among the graves, reading legends carved on tombstones, many topped with small brass candelabra, whilst withered yellow chrysanthemums lay on the stone tablets of other graves, dropped stealthily, Fidelman imagined, on All Souls Day – a festival in another part of the cemetery – by renegade sons and daughters unable to bear the sight of their dead bereft of flowers, while the crypts of the goyim were lit and in bloom. Many were burial places, he read on the stained stones, of those who, for one reason or another, had died in the late large war, including an empty place, it said under a six-pointed star engraved upon a marble slab that lay on the ground, for "My beloved father/ Betrayed by the damned Fascists/ Murdered at Auschwitz by the barbarous Nazis/ *O Crime Orribile*." But no Susskind.

Three months had gone by since Fidelman's arrival in Rome. Should he, he many times asked himself, leave the city and this foolish search? Why not off to Florence, and there, amid the art splendors of the world, be inspired to resume his work? But the loss of his first chapter was like a spell cast over him. There were times he scorned it as a man-made thing, like all such, replaceable; other times he feared it was not the chapter per se, but that his volatile curiosity had become somehow entangled with Susskind's strange personality – Had he repaid generosity by stealing a man's life work? Was he so distorted? To satisfy himself, to know man, Fidelman had to know, though at what a cost in precious time and effort. Sometimes he smiled wryly at all this; ridiculous, the chapter grieved him for itself only – the precious thing he had created then lost – especially when he got to thinking of the long diligent labor, how painstakingly he had built each idea, how cleverly mastered problems of order, form, how impressive the finished product, Giotto reborn! It broke the heart. What else, if after months he was here, still seeking?

And Fidelman was unchangingly convinced that Susskind had taken it, or why would he still be hiding? He sighed much and gained weight. Mulling over his frustrated career, on the backs of envelopes containing unanswered letters from his sister Bessie he aimlessly sketched little angels flying. Once, studying his minuscule drawings, it occurred to him that he might someday return to painting, but the thought was more painful than Fidelman could bear.

One bright morning in mid-December, after a good night's sleep, his first in weeks, he vowed he would have another look at the Navicella and then be off to Florence. Shortly before noon he visited the porch of St Peter's, trying, from his remembrance of Giotto's sketch, to see the mosaic as it had been before its many restorations. He hazarded a note or two in shaky handwriting, then left the church and was walking down the sweeping flight of stairs, when he beheld at the bottom – his heart misgave him, was he still seeing pictures, a sneaky apostle added to the overloaded boatful? – ecco, Susskind! The refugee, in beret and long green G.I. raincoat, from under whose skirts showed his black-stockinged, rooster's ankles – indicating knickers going on above though hidden – was selling black and white rosaries to all who would buy. He held several strands of beads in one hand, while in the palm of the other a few gilded medallions glinted in the winter sun. Despite his outer clothing, Susskind looked, it must be said, unchanged, not a pound more of meat or muscle, the face though aged, ageless. Gazing at him, the student ground his teeth in remembrance. He was tempted quickly to hide, and unobserved observe the thief; but his impatience, after the long unhappy search, was too much for him. With controlled trepidation he approached Susskind on his left as the refugee was busily engaged on the right, urging a sale of beads upon a woman drenched in black.

"Beads, rosaries, say your prayers with holy beads."

"Greetings, Susskind," Fidelman said, coming shakily down the stairs, dissembling the Unified Man, all peace and contentment. "One looks for you everywhere and finds you here. Wie gehts?"

Susskind, though his eyes flickered, showed no surprise to speak of. For a moment his expression seemed to say he had no idea who was this, had forgotten Fidelman's existence, but then at last remembered – somebody long ago from another country, whom you smiled on, then forgot.

"Still here?" he perhaps ironically joked.

"Still," Fidelman was embarrassed at his voice slipping.

"Rome holds you?"

"Rome," faltered Fidelman, "– the air." He breathed deep and exhaled with emotion.

Noticing the refugee was not truly attentive, his eyes roving upon potential customers, Fidelman, girding himself, remarked, "By the way, Susskind, you didn't happen to notice – did you? – the brief case I was carrying with me around the time we met in September?"

"Brief case – what kind?" This he said absently, his eyes on the church doors.

"Pigskin. I had in it –" Here Fidelman's voice could be heard cracking, "– a chapter of a critical work on Giotto I was writing. You know, I'm sure, the Trecento painter?"

"Who doesn't know Giotto?"

"Do you happen to recall whether you saw, if, that is –" He stopped, at a loss for words other than accusatory.

"Excuse me – business." Susskind broke away and bounced up the steps two at a time. A man he approached shied away. He had beads, didn't need others.

Fidelman had followed the refugee. "Reward," he muttered up close to his ear. "Fifteen thousand for the chapter, and who has it can keep the brand new brief case. That's his business, no questions asked. Fair enough?"

Susskind spied a lady tourist, including camera and guide book. "Beads – holy beads." He held up both hands, but she was just a Lutheran, passing through.

"Slow today," Susskind complained as they walked down the stairs, "but maybe it's the items. Everybody has the same. If I had some big ceramics of the Holy Mother, they go like hot cakes – a good investment for somebody with a little cash."

"Use the reward for that," Fidelman cagily whispered, "buy Holy Mothers."

If he heard, Susskind gave no sign. At the sight of a family of nine emerging from the main portal above, the refugee, calling addio over his shoulder, fairly flew up the steps. But Fidelman uttered no response. I'll get the rat yet. He went off to hide behind a high fountain in the square. But the flying spume raised by the wind wet him, so he retreated behind a massive column and peeked out at short intervals to keep the peddler in sight.

At two o'clock, when St Peter's closed to visitors, Susskind dumped his goods into his raincoat pockets and locked up shop. Fidelman followed him all the way home, indeed the ghetto, although along a street he had not consciously been on before, which led into an alley where the refugee pulled open a left-handed door, and without transition, was "home." Fidelman, sneaking up close, caught a dim glimpse of an overgrown closet containing bed and table. He found no address on wall or door, nor, to his surprise, any door lock. This for a moment depressed him. It meant Susskind had nothing worth stealing. Of his own, that is. The student promised himself to return tomorrow, when the occupant was elsewhere.

Return he did, in the morning, while the entrepreneur was out selling religious articles, glanced around once and was quickly inside. He shivered – a pitch black freezing cave. Fidelman scratched up a thick match and confirmed bed and table, also a rickety chair, but no heat or light except a drippy candle stub in a saucer on the table. He lit the yellow candle and searched all over the place. In the table drawer a few eating implements plus safety razor, though where he shaved was a mystery, probably a public toilet. On a shelf above the thin-blanketed bed stood half a flask of red wine, part of a package of spaghetti, and a hard panino. Also an unexpected little fish bowl with a bony gold fish swimming around in Arctic seas. The fish, reflecting the candle flame, gulped repeatedly, threshing its frigid tail as Fidelman watched. He loves pets, thought the student. Under the bed he found a chamber pot, but nowhere a brief case with a fine critical chapter in it. The place was not more than an ice-box someone probably had lent the refugee to come in out of the rain. Alas, Fidelman sighed. Back in the pensione, it took a hot water bottle two hours to thaw him out; but from the visit he never fully recovered.

In this latest dream of Fidelman's he was spending the day in a cemetery all crowded with tombstones, when up out of an empty grave rose this long-nosed brown shade, Virgilio Susskind, beckoning.

Fidelman hurried over.

"Have you read Tolstoy?"

"Sparingly."

"Why is art?" asked the shade, drifting off.

Fidelman, willy nilly, followed, and the ghost, as it vanished, led him up steps going through the ghetto and into a marble synagogue.

The student, left alone, for no reason he could think of lay down upon the stone floor, his shoulders keeping strangely warm as he stared at the sunlit vault above. The fresco therein revealed this saint in fading blue, the sky flowing from his head, handing an, old knight in a thin red robe his gold cloak. Nearby stood a humble horse and two stone hills.

Giotto. San Francesco dona le vesti al cavaliere povero.

Fidelman awoke running. He stuffed his blue gabardine into a paper bag, caught a bus, and knocked early on Susskind's heavy portal.

"Avanti." The refugee, already garbed in beret and raincoat (probably his pajamas), was standing at the table, lighting the candle with a flaming sheet of paper. To Fidelman the paper looked the underside of a typewritten page. Despite himself, the student recalled in letters of fire his entire chapter.

"Here, Susskind," he said in a trembling voice, offering the bundle, "I bring you my suit. Wear it in good health."

The refugee glanced at it without expression. "What do you wish for it?"

"Nothing at all." Fidelman laid the bag on the table, called goodbye and left.

He soon heard footsteps clattering after him across the cobblestones.

"Excuse me, I kept this under my mattress for you." Susskind thrust at him the pigskin brief case.

Fidelman savagely opened it, searching frenziedly in each compartment, but the bag was empty. The refugee was already in flight. With a bellow the student started after him. "You bastard, you burned my chapter!"

"Have mercy," cried Susskind, "I did you a favor."

"I'll do you one and cut your throat."

"The words were there but the spirit was missing."

In a towering rage, Fidelman forced a burst of speed, but the refugee, light as the wind in his marvelous knickers, his green coattails flying, rapidly gained ground.

The ghetto Jews, framed in amazement in their medieval windows, stared at the wild pursuit. But in the middle of it, Fidelman, stout and short of breath, moved by all he had lately learned, had a triumphant insight.

"Susskind, come back," he shouted, half sobbing. "The suit is yours. All is forgiven."

He came to a dead halt but the refugee ran on. When last seen he was still running.

PARSON'S PLEASURE

Roald Dahl

Best known to millions of children for works like *James and the Giant Peach, Charlie and the Chocolate Factory* and *Matilda*, **Roald Dahl** (1916–1990) was also a master of the manipulative short story, many published in *The Sunday Times, Esquire* and *The New Yorker,* and adapted for television as *Tales of the Unexpected.* His screenplays include *You Only Live Twice* and *Chitty Chitty Bang Bang.* On writing he said, "A person is a fool to become a writer. His only compensation is absolute freedom."

Mr Boggis was driving the car slowly, leaning back comfortably in the seat with one elbow resting on the sill of the open window. How beautiful the countryside, he thought; how pleasant to see a sign or two of summer once again. The primroses especially. And the hawthorn. The hawthorn was exploding white and pink and red along the hedges and the primroses were growing underneath in little clumps, and it was beautiful.

He took one hand off the wheel and lit himself a cigarette. The best thing now, he told himself, would be to make for the top of Brill Hill. He could see it about half a mile ahead. And that must be the village of Brill, that cluster of cottages among the trees right on the very summit. Excellent. Not many of his Sunday sections had a nice elevation like that to work from.

He drove up the hill and stopped the car just short of the summit on the outskirts of the village. Then he got out and looked around. Down below, the countryside was spread out before him like a huge green carpet. He could see for miles. It was perfect. He took a pad and pencil from his pocket, leaned against the back of the car, and allowed his practised eye to travel slowly over the landscape.

He could see one medium farmhouse over on the right, back in the fields, with a track leading to it from the road. There was another larger one beyond it. There was a house surrounded by tall elms that looked as though it might be a Queen Anne, and there were two likely farms away over on the left. Five places in all, That was about the lot in this direction.

Mr Boggis drew a rough sketch on his pad showing the position of each so that he'd be able to find them easily when he was down below, then he got back into the car and drove up through the village to the other side of the hill. From there he spotted six more possibles – five farms and one big white Georgian house. He studied the Georgian house through his binoculars. It had a clean prosperous look, and the garden was well ordered. That was a pity. He ruled it out immediately. There was no point in calling on the prosperous.

In this square then, in this section there were ten possibles in all. Ten was a nice number, Mr Boggis told himself. Just the right amount for a leisurely afternoon's work. What time was it now? Twelve o'clock. He would have liked a pint of beer in the pub before he started but on Sundays they didn't open until one. Very well, he would have it later. He glanced at the notes on his pad. He decided to take the Queen Anne first, the house with the elms. It had looked nicely dilapidated through the binoculars. The people there could probably do with some money. He was always lucky with Queen Annes, anyway. Mr Boggis climbed back into the car, released the handbrake, and began cruising slowly down the hill without the engine.

Apart from the fact that he was at this moment disguised in the uniform of a clergyman there was nothing very sinister about Mr Cyril Boggis. By trade he was a dealer in antique furniture, with his own shop and showroom in the King's Road, Chelsea. His premises were not large, and generally he didn't do a great deal of business, but because he always bought cheap, very very cheap, and sold very very dear, he managed to make quite a tidy little income every year. He was a talented salesman and when buying or selling a piece he could slide smoothly into whichever mood suited the client best. He could become grave and charming for the aged obsequious for the rich, sober for the godly, masterful for the weak, mischievous for the widow, arch and saucy for the spinster. He was well aware of his gift, using it shamelessly on every possible occasion; and often, at the end of an unusually good performance, it was as much as he could do to prevent himself from turning aside and taking a bow or two as the thundering applause of the audience went rolling through the theatre.

In spite of this rather clownish quality of his, Mr Boggis was not a fool. In fact it was said of him by some that he probably knew as much about French, English and Italian furniture as anyone else in London. He also had surprisingly good taste, and he was quick to recognise and reject an ungraceful design, however genuine the article might be. His real love, naturally, was for the work of the great eighteenth-century English designers, Ince, Mayhew, Chippendale, Robert Adams, Manwaring, Inigo Jones, Hepplewhite, Kent Johnson, George Smith, Lock Sheraton, and the rest of them but even with these he occasionally drew the line. He refused for example, to allow a single piece from Chippendale's Chinese or Gothic period to come into his showroom and the same was true of some of the heavier Italian designs of Robert Adam.

During the past few years, Mr Boggis had achieved considerable fame among his friends in the trade by his ability to produce unusual and often quite rare items with astonishing regularity. Apparently the man had a source of supply that was almost inexhaustible, a sort of private warehouse, and it seemed that all he had to do was to drive out to it once a week and help himself. Whenever they asked him where he got the stuff, he would smile knowingly and wink and murmur something about a little secret.

The idea behind Mr Boggis's little secret was a simple one, and it had come to him as a result of something that had happened on a certain Sunday afternoon nearly nine years before, while he was driving in the country.

He had gone out in the morning to visit his old mother, who lived in Sevenoaks, and on the way back the fan-belt on his car had broken, causing the engine to overheat and the water to boil away. He had got out of the car and walked to the nearest house, a smallish farm building about fifty yards off the road and had asked the woman who answered the door if he could please have a jug of water.

While he was waiting for her to fetch it, he happened to glance in through the door to the living-room and there, not five yards from where he was standing, he spotted something that made him so excited the sweat began to come out all over the top of his head. It was a large oak armchair of a type that he had only seen once before in his life. Each arm as well as the panel at the back, was supported by a row of eight beautifully turned spindles. The back panel itself was decorated by an inlay of the most delicate floral design, and the head of a duck was carved to lie along half the length of either arm. Good God he thought. This thing is late fifteenth century!

He poked his head in further through the door, and there, by heavens, was another of them on the other side of the fireplace!

He couldn't be sure, but two chairs like that must be worth at least a thousand pounds up in London. And oh, what beauties they were!

When the woman returned Mr Boggis introduced himself and straight away asked if she would like to sell her chairs.

Dear me, she said. But why on earth should she want to sell her chairs?

No reason at all, except that he might be willing to give her a pretty nice price.

And how much would he give? They were definitely not for sale, but just out of curiosity, just for fun, you know, how much would he give?

Thirty-five pounds.

How much?

Thirty-five pounds.

Dear me, thirty-five pounds. Well, well, that was very interesting. She'd always thought they were valuable. They were very old. They were very comfortable too. She couldn't possibly do without them, not possibly. No, they were not for sale but thank you very much all the same.

They weren't really so very old Mr Boggis told her, and they wouldn't be at all easy to sell, but it just happened that he had a client who rather liked that sort of thing. Maybe he could go up another two pounds – call it thirty-seven. How about that?

They bargained for half an hour, and of course in the end Mr Boggis got the chairs and agreed to pay her something less than a twentieth of their value.

That evening, driving back to London in his old station-wagon with the two fabulous chairs tucked away snugly in the back Mr Boggis had suddenly been struck by what seemed to him to be a most remarkable idea.

"Look here", he said. "If there is good stuff in one farmhouse, then why not in others?" Why shouldn't he search for it? Why shouldn't he comb the country-side? He could do it on Sundays. In that way, it wouldn't interfere with his work at all. He never knew what to do with his Sundays.

So Mr Boggis bought maps, large scale maps of all the counties around London, and with a fine pen he divided each of them up into a series of squares. Each of these squares covered an actual area of five miles by five, which was about as much territory, he estimated as he could cope with on a single Sunday, were he to comb it thoroughly. He didn't want the towns and the villages. It was the comparatively isolated places, the large farmhouses and the rather dilapidated country mansions, that he was looking for and in this way, if he did one square each Sunday, fifty-two squares a year, he would gradually cover every farm and every country house in the home counties.

But obviously there was a bit more to it than that. Country folk are a suspicious lot So are the impoverished rich. You can't go about ringing their bells and expecting them to show you around their houses just for the asking, because they won't do it. That way you would never get beyond the front door. How then was he to gain admittance? Perhaps it would be best if he didn't let them know he was a dealer at all. He could be the telephone man, the plumber, the gas inspector. He could even be a clergyman. . . ."

From this point on, the whole scheme began to take on a more practical aspect. Mr Boggis ordered a large quantity of superior cards on which the following legend was engraved:

THE REVEREND
CYRIL WINNINGTON BOGGIS

President of the Society for the Preservation of Rare Furniture. In association with The Victoria and Albert Museum.

From now on, every Sunday, he was going to be a nice old parson spending his holiday travelling around on a labour of love for the "Society", compiling an inventory of the treasures that lay hidden in the country homes of England. And who in the world was going to kick him out when they heard that one?

Nobody.

And then once he was inside, if he happened to spot something he really wanted well – he knew a hundred different ways of dealing with that.

Rather to Mr Boggis's surprise, the scheme worked. In fact, the friendliness with which he was received in one house after another through the countryside was, in the beginning, quite embarrassing, even to him. A slice of cold pie, a glass of port, a cup of tea, a basket of plums, even a full sit-down Sunday dinner with the family, such things were constantly being pressed upon him. Sooner or later, of course, there had been some bad moments and a number of unpleasant incidents, but then nine years is more than four hundred Sundays, and that adds up to a great quantity of houses visited all in all, it had been an interesting, exciting, and lucrative business.

And now it was another Sunday and Mr Boggis was operating in the county of Buckinghamshire, in one of the most northerly squares on his map, about ten miles from Oxford and as he drove down the hill and headed for his first house, the dilapidated Queen Anne, he began to get the feeling that this was going to be one of his lucky days. He parked the car about a hundred yards from the gates and got out to walk the rest of the way. He never liked people to see his car until after a deal was completed. A dear old clergyman and a large station-wagon somehow never seemed quite right together. Also the short walk gave him time to examine the property closely from the outside and to assume the mood most likely to be suitable for the occasion. Mr Boggis strode briskly up the drive. He was a small fatlegged man with a belly. The face was round and rosy, quite perfect for the part, and the two large brown eyes that bulged out at you from this rosy face gave an impression of gentle imbecility. He was dressed in a black suit with the usual parson's dog-collar round his neck and on his head a soft black hat. He carried an old oak walking-stick which lent him in his opinion a rather rustic easy-going air.

He approached the front door and rang the bell. He heard the sound of footsteps in the hall and the door opened and suddenly there stood before him or rather above him, a gigantic woman dressed in riding-breeches. Even through the smoke of her cigarette he could smell the powerful odour of stables and horse manure that clung about her.

"Yes?" she asked looking at him suspiciously. "What is it you want?"

Mr Boggis, who half expected her to whinny any moment, raised his hat made a little bow, and handed her his card." I do apologise for bothering you," he said and then he waited watching her face as she read the message.

"I don't understand" she said handing back the card. "What is it you want?"

Mr Boggis explained about the Society for the Preservation of Rare Furniture.

"This wouldn't by any chance be something to do with the Socialist Party?" she asked, staring at him fiercely from under a pair of pale bushy brows.

From then on, it was easy. A Tory in riding-breeches, male or female, was always a sitting duck for Mr Boggis. He spent two minutes delivering an impassioned eulogy on the extreme Right Wing of the Conservative Party, then two more denouncing the Socialists. As a clincher, he made particular reference to the Bill that the Socialists had once introduced for the abolition of bloodsports in the country, and went on to inform his listener that his idea of heaven – "though you better not tell the bishop, my dear" – was a place where one could hunt the fox, the stag, and the hare with large packs of tireless hounds from morn till night every day of the week, including Sundays.

Watching her as he spoke, he could see the magic beginning to do its work. The woman was grinning now, showing Mr Boggis a set of enormous, slightly yellow teeth. "Madam," he cried "I beg of you please don't get me started on Socialism." At that point, she let out a great guffaw of laughter, raised an enormous red hand, and slapped him so hard on the shoulder that he nearly went over.

"Come in!" she shouted "I don't know what the hell you want but come on in!"

Unfortunately, and rather surprisingly, there was nothing of any value in the whole house, and Mr Boggis, who never wasted time on barren territory, soon made his excuses and took his leave. The whole visit had taken less than fifteen minutes, and that, he told himself as he climbed back into his car and started off for the next place, was exactly as it should be. From now on it was all farmhouses, and the nearest was about half a mile up the road. It was a large half-timbered brick building of considerable age, and there was a magnificent pear tree still in blossom covering almost the whole of the south wall.

Mr Boggis knocked on the door. He waited, but no one came. He knocked again, but still there was no answer, so he wandered around the back to look for the farmer among the cowsheds. There was no one there either. He guessed that they must all still be in church, so he began peering in the windows to see if he could spot anything interesting. There was nothing in the dining-room. Nothing in the library either. He tried the next window, the living-room, and there, right under his nose, in the little alcove that the window made, he saw a beautiful thing, a semicircular card-table in mahogany, richly veneered, and in the style of Hepplewhite, built around 1780.

"Ah-ha," he said aloud, pressing his face hard against glass. "Well done, Boggis."

But that was not all. There was a chair there as well, a single chair, and if he were not mistaken it was of an even finer quality than the table. Another Hepplewhite, wasn't it? And oh, what a beauty! The lattices on the back were finely carved with the honeysuckle, the husk, and the paterae, the caning on the seat was original, the legs were very gracefully turned and the two back ones had that peculiar outward splay that meant so much.

It was an exquisite chair. "Before this day is done," Mr Boggis said softly, "I shall have the pleasure of sitting down upon that lovely seat." He never bought a chair without doing this. It was a favourite test of his, and it was always an intriguing sight to see him lowering himself delicately into the seat, waiting for the "give", expertly gauging the precise but infinitesimal degree of shrinkage that the years had caused in the mortise and dovetail joints.

But there was no hurry, he told himself. He would return here later. He had the whole afternoon before him.

The next farm was situated some way back in the fields, and in order to keep his car out of sight Mr Boggis had to leave it on the road and walk about six hundred yards along a straight track that led directly into the back yard of the farmhouse. This place, he noticed as he approached, was a good deal smaller than the last, and he didn't hold out much hope for it. It looked rambling and dirty, and some of the sheds were clearly in bad repair.

There were three men standing in a close group in a corner of the yard, and one of them had two large black greyhounds with him on leashes. When the men caught sight of Mr Boggis walking forward in his black suit and parson's collar, they stopped talking and seemed suddenly to stiffen and freeze, becoming absolutely still, motionless, three faces turned towards him, watching him suspiciously as he approached.

The oldest of the three was a stumpy man with a wide frog mouth and small shifty eyes, and although Mr Boggis didn't know it his name was Rummins and he was the owner of the farm.

The tall youth beside him who appeared to have something wrong with one eye, was Bert; the son of Rummins.

The shortish flat-faced man with a narrow corrugated brow and immensely broad shoulders was Claud. Claud had dropped in on Rummins in the hope of getting a piece of pork or ham out of him from the pig that had been killed the day before. Claud knew about the killing – the noise of it had carried far across the fields – and he also knew that a man should have a government permit to do that sort of thing, and that Rummins didn't have one.

"Good afternoon," Mr Boggis said. "Isn't it a lovely day? "None of the three men moved. At that moment they were all thinking precisely the same thing – that somehow or other this clergyman who was certainly not the local fellow, had been sent to poke his nose into their business and to report what he found to the government.

"What beautiful dogs," Mr Boggis said. "I must say I've never been grey-hound-racing myself, but they tell me it's a fascinating sport."

Again the silence, and Mr Boggis glanced quickly from Rummins to Bert, then to Claud then back again to Rummins, and he noticed that each of them had the same peculiar expression on his face, something between a jeer and a challenge, with a contemptuous curl to the mouth and a sneer around the nose.

"Might I inquire if you are the owner?" Mr Boggis asked undaunted, address-ing himself to Rummins.

"What is it you want?"

"I do apologise for troubling you, especially on a Sunday."

Mr Boggis offered his card and Rummins took it and held it up close to his face. The other two didn't move, but their eyes swivelled over to one side, trying to see.

"And what exactly might you be wanting?" Rummins asked.

For the second time that morning, Mr Boggis explained at some length the aims and ideals of the Society for the Preservation of Rare Furniture.

"We don't have any," Rummins told him when it was over. "You're wasting your time."

"Now, just a minute, sir," Mr Boggis said raising a finger. "The last man who said that to me was an old farmer down in Sussex, and when he finally let me into his house, d'you know what I found? A dirty-looking old chair in the corner of the kitchen, and it turned out to be worth FOUR HUNDRED POUNDS! I showed him how to sell it, and he bought himself a new tractor with the money."

"What on earth are you talking about?" Claud said. "There ain't no chair in the world worth four hundred pound."

"Excuse me," Mr Boggis answered primly, "but there are plenty of chairs in England worth more than twice that figure. And you know where they are? They're tucked away in the farms and cottages all over the country, with the owners using them as steps and ladders and standing on them with hobnailed boots to reach a pot of jam out of the top cupboard or to hang a picture. This is the truth I'm telling you, my friends."

Rummins shifted uneasily on his feet.

"You mean to say all you want to do is go inside and stand there in the middle of the room and look around?"

"Exactly," Mr Boggis said. He was at last beginning to sense what the trouble might be. "I don't want to pry into your cupboards or into your larder. I just want to look at the furniture to see if you happen to have any treasures here, and then I can write about them in our Society magazine."

"You know what I think?" Rummins said, fixing him with his small wicked eyes. "I think you're after buying the stuff yourself. Why else would you be going to all this trouble?"

"Oh, dear me. I only wish I had the money. Of course, if I saw something that I took a great fancy to, and it wasn't beyond my means, I might be tempted to make an offer. But alas, that rarely happens."

"Well," Rummins said "I don't suppose there's any harm in your taking a look around if that's all you want." He led the way across the yard to the back door of the farmhouse, and Mr Boggis followed him; so did the son Bert, and Claud with his two dogs. They went through the kitchen where the only furniture was a cheap deal table with a dead chicken lying on it, and they emerged into a fairly large, exceedingly filthy living-room.

And there it was! Mr Boggis saw it at once, and he stopped dead in his tracks and gave a little shrill gasp of shock. Then he stood there for five, ten fifteen seconds at least, staring like an idiot, unable to believe, not daring to believe what he saw before him. It couldn't be true, not possibly! But the longer he stared, the more true it began to seem. After all, there it was standing against the wall right in front of him, as real and as solid as the house itself. And who in the world could possibly make a mistake about a thing like that? Admittedly it was painted white, but that made not the slightest difference. Some idiot had done that The paint could easily be stripped off. But good God! Just look at it! And in a place like this!

At this point Mr Boggis became aware of the three men, Rummins, Bert and Claud standing together in a group over by the fireplace, watching him intently. They had seen him stop and gasp and stare, and they must have seen his face turning red or maybe it was white, but in any event they had seen enough to spoil the whole goddamn business if he didn't do something about it quick. In a flash, Mr Boggis clapped one hand over his heart, staggered to the nearest chair, and collapsed into it breathing heavily.

"What's the matter with you?" Claud asked

"It's nothing," he gasped. "I'll be all right in a minute. Please – a glass of water. It's my heart"

Bert fetched him the water, handed it to him and stayed close beside him staring down at him with a fatuous leer on his face.

"I thought maybe you were looking at something," Rummins said. The wide frog-mouth widened a fraction further into a crafty grin, showing the stubs of several broken teeth.

"No, no," Mr Boggis said. "Oh dear me, no. It's just my heart. I'm so sorry. It happens every now and then. But it goes away quite quickly. I'll be all right in a couple of minutes."

He must have time to think, he told himself. More important still, he must have time to compose himself thoroughly before he said another word. Take it gently, Boggis. And whatever you do, keep calm. These people may be ignorant, but they are not stupid. They are suspicious and wary and sly. And if it is really true – no it couldn't be, it can't be true. . . .

He was holding one hand up over his eyes in a gesture of pain, and now, very carefully, secretly, he made a little crack between two of the fingers and peeked through.

Sure enough, the thing was still there, and on this occasion he took a good long look at it. Yes – he had been right the first time! There wasn't the slightest doubt about it! It was really unbelievable! What he saw was a piece of furniture that any expert would have given almost anything to acquire. To a layman, it might not have appeared particularly impressive, especially when covered over as it was with dirty white paint but to Mr Boggis it was a dealer's dream. He knew, as does every other dealer in Europe and America, that among the most celebrated and coveted examples of eighteenth-century English furniture in existence are the three famous pieces known as "The Chippendale Commodes". He knew their history backwards – that the first was "discovered" in 1920, in a house at Moreton-in-Marsh, and was sold at Sotheby's the same year; that the other two turned up in the same auction rooms a year later, both coming out of Raynham Hall, Norfolk. They all fetched enormous prices. He couldn't quite remember the exact figure for the first one, or even the second, but he knew for certain that the last one to be sold had fetched thirty-nine hundred guineas. And that was in 1921! Today the same piece would surely be worth ten thousand pounds. Some man, Mr Boggis couldn't remember his name, had made a study of these commodes fairly recently and had proved that all three must have come from the same workshop, for the veneers were all from the same log, and the same set of templates had been used in the construction of each. No invoices had been found for any of them but all the experts were agreed that these three commodes could have been executed only by Thomas Chippendale himself, with his own hands, at the most exalted period in his career.

And here, Mr Boggis kept telling himself as he peered cautiously through the crack in his fingers, here was the fourth Chippendale Commode! And he had found it! He would be rich! He would also be famous! Each of the other three was known throughout the furniture world by a special name – The Chastleton Commode, The First Raynham Commode, The Second Raynham Commode. This one would go down in history as The Boggis Commode! Just imagine the faces of the boys up there in London when they got a look at it tomorrow morning! And the luscious offers coming in from the big fellows over in the West End – Frank Partridge, Mallett, Jetley, and the rest of them! There would be a picture of it in The Times, and it would say, "The very fine Chippendale Commode which was recently discovered by Mr Cyril Boggis, a London dealer. . . ." Dear God, what a stir he was going to make!

This one here Mr Boggis thought, was almost exactly similar to the Second Raynham Commode. (All three the Chastleton and the two Raynhams, differed from one another in a number of small ways.) It was a most impressive handsome affair, built in the French rococo style of Chippendale's Directoire period, a kind of large fat chest-of-drawers set upon four carved and fluted legs that raised it about a foot from the ground. There were six drawers in all, two long ones in the middle and two shorter ones on either side. The serpentine front was magnificently ornamented along the top and sides and bottom, and also vertically between each set of drawers, with intricate carvings of festoons and scrolls and clusters. The brass handles, although partly obscured by white paint, appeared to be superb. It was, of course, a rather "heavy" piece, but the design had been executed with such elegance and grace that the heaviness was in no way offensive.

"How're you feeling now?" Mr Boggis heard someone saying.

"Thank you, thank you, I'm much better already. It passes quickly. My doctor says it's nothing to worry about really so long as I rest for a few minutes whenever it happens. Ah yes," he said, raising himself slowly to his feet. "That's better. I'm all right now."

A trifle unsteadily, he began to move around the room examining the furniture, one piece at a time, commenting upon it briefly. He could see at once that apart from the commode it was a very poor lot.

"Nice oak table," he said. "But I'm afraid it's not old enough to be of any interest. Good comfortable chairs, but quite modern, yes, quite modern. Now this cupboard, well, it's rather attractive, but again, not valuable. This chest-of-drawers" – he walked casually past the Chippendale Commode and gave it a little contemptuous flip with his fingers – "worth a few pounds, I dare say, but no more. A rather crude reproduction, I'm afraid. Probably made in Victorian times. Did you paint it white?"

"Yes," Rummins said, "Bert did it."

"A very wise move. It's considerably less offensive in white."

"That's a strong piece of furniture," Rummins said. "Some nice carving on it too."

"Machine-carved" Mr Boggis answered superbly, bending down to examine the exquisite craftsmanship. "You can tell it a mile off. But still, I suppose it's quite pretty in its way. It has its points."

He began to saunter off, then he checked himself and turned slowly back again. He placed the tip of one finger against the point of his chin, laid his head over to one side, and frowned as though deep in thought.

"You know what?" he said, looking at the commode, speaking so casually that his voice kept trailing off. "I've just remembered", I've been wanting a set of legs something like that for a long time. I've got a rather curious table in my own little home, one of those low things that people put in front of the sofa, sort of a coffee-table, and last Michaelmas, when I moved house, the foolish movers damaged the legs in the most shocking way. I'm very fond of that table. I always keep my big Bible on it, and all my sermon notes."

He paused, stroking his chin with the finger. "Now I was just thinking. These legs on your chest-of-drawers might be very suitable. Yes, they might indeed. They could easily be cut off and fixed on to my table."

He looked around and saw the three men standing absolutely still, watching him suspiciously, three pairs of eyes, all different but equally mistrusting, small pig-eyes for Rummins, large slow eyes for Claud, and two odd eyes for Bert, one of them very queer and boiled and misty pale, with a little black dot In the centre, like a fish eye on a plate.

Mr Boggis smiled and shook his head. "Come, come, what on earth am I saying? I'm talking as though I owned the piece myself. I do apologize."

"What you mean to say is you'd like to buy it," Rummins said.

"Well . . ." Mr Boggis glanced back at the commode, frowning. "I'm not sure. I might . . . and then again . . . on second thoughts . . . no . . . I think it might be a bit too much trouble. It's not worth it. I'd better leave it."

"How much were you thinking of offering?" Rummins asked.

"Not much, I'm afraid. You see, this is not a genuine antique. It's merely a reproduction."

"I'm not so sure about that," Rummins told him. "It's been in here over twenty years, and before that it was up at the Manor House. I bought it there myself at auction when the old Squire died. You can't tell me that thing's new."

"It's not exactly new, but it's certainly not more than about sixty years old."

"It's more than that," Rummins said. "Bert, where's that bit of paper you once found at the back of one of them drawers? That old bill."

The boy looked vacantly at his father.

Mr Boggis opened his mouth, then quickly shut it again without uttering a sound. He was beginning literally to shake with excitement, and to calm himself he walked over to the window and stared out at a plump brown hen pecking around for stray grains of corn in the yard.

"It was in the back of that drawer underneath all them rabbitsnares," Rummins was saying. "Go on and fetch it out and show it to the parson."

When Bert went forward to the commode, Mr Boggis turned round again. He couldn't stand not watching him. He saw him pull out one of the big middle drawers, and he noticed the beautiful way in which the drawer slid open. He saw Bert's hand dipping inside and rummaging around among a lot of wires and strings.

"You mean this?" Bert lifted out a piece of folded yellowing paper and carried it over to the father, who unfolded it and held it up close to his face.

"You can't tell me this writing ain't bloody old," Rummins said, and he held the paper out to Mr Boggis, whose whole arm was shaking as he took it. It was brittle and it crackled slightly between his fingers. The writing was in a long sloping copperplate hand:

Edward Montagu, Esq. Dr
To Thos. Chippendale

A large mahogany Commode Table of exceeding fine Wood very rich carved set upon fluted legs, two very neat shapd long drawers in the middle part and two ditto on each side,
with rich chasd Brass Handle and Ornaments,
the whole completely finished in the most
exquisite taste......... .f87

Mr Boggis was holding on to himself tight and fighting to suppress the excitement that was spinning round inside him and making him dizzy. Oh God, it was wonderful! With the invoice, the value had climbed even higher. What in heaven's name would it fetch now? Twelve thousand pounds? Fourteen? Maybe fifteen or even twenty? Who knows?

Oh, boy!

He tossed the paper contemptuously on to the table and said quietly, "It's exactly what I told you, a Victorian reproduction. This is simply the invoice that the seller – the man who made it and passed it off as an antique – gave to his client. I've seen lots of them. You'll notice that he doesn't say he made it himself. That would give the game away."

"Say what you like," Rummins announced, "but that's an old piece of paper."

"Of course it is, my dear friend. It's Victorian, late Victorian. About eighteen ninety. Sixty or seventy years old. I've seen hundreds of them. That was a time when masses of cabinetmakers did nothing else but apply themselves to faking the fine furniture of the century before."

"Listen, Parson," Rummins said, pointing at him with a thick dirty finger," I'm not saying as how you may not know a fair bit about this furniture business, but what I am saying is this: How on earth can you be so mighty sure it's a fake when you haven't even seen what it looks like underneath all that paint?"

"Come here," Mr Boggis said. "Come over here and I'll show you." He stood beside the commode and waited for them to gather round. "Now, anyone got a knife?"

Claud produced a horn-handled pocket knife, and Mr Boggis took it and opened the smallest blade. Then, working with apparent casualness but actually with extreme care, he began chipping off the white paint from a small area on the top of the commode. The paint flaked away cleanly from the old hard varnish underneath, and when he had cleared away about three square inches, he stepped back and said, "Now, take a look at that!"

It was beautiful – a warm little patch of mahogany, glowing like a topaz, rich and dark with the true colour of its two hundred years.

"What's wrong with it?" Rummins asked

"It's processed! anyone can see that!"

"How can you see it, Mister? You tell us."

Well, I must say that's a trifle difficult to explain. It's chiefly a matter of experience. My experience tells me that without the slightest doubt this wood has been processed with lime. That's what they use for mahogany, to give it that dark aged colour. For oak, they use potash salts, and for walnut it's nitric acid but for mahogany it's always lime."

The three men moved a little closer to peer at the wood. There was a slight stirring of interest among them now. It was always intriguing to hear about some new form of crookery or deception.

"Look closely at the grain. You see that touch of orange in among the dark redbrown. That's the sign of lime."

They leaned forward, their noses close to the wood first Rummins, then Claud, then Bert.

"And then there's the patina," Mr Boggis continued

"The what?"

He explained to them the meaning of this words applied to furniture.

"My dear friends, you've no idea the trouble these rascals will go to to imitate the hard beautiful bronze-like appearance of genuine patina. It's terrible, really terrible, and it makes me quite sick to speak of it!" He was spitting each word sharply off the tip of the tongue and making a sour mouth to show his extreme distaste. The men waited, hoping for more secrets.

"The time and trouble that some mortals will go to in order to deceive the innocent!" Mr Boggis cried. "It's perfectly disgusting! D'you know what they did here, my friends? I can recognise it clearly. I can almost see them doing it, the long, complicated ritual of rubbing the wood with linseed oil, coating it over with french polish that has been cunningly coloured, brushing it down with pumice-stone and oil, bees-waxing it with a wax that contains dirt and dust and finally giving it the heat treatment to crack the polish so that it looks like two-hundred-year-old varnish! It really upsets me to contemplate such knavery!"

The three men continued to gaze at the little patch of dark wood.

"Feel it!" Mr Boggis ordered. "Put your fingers on it! There, how does it feel, warm or cold?"

"Feels cold," Rummins said.

"Exactly, my friend! It happens to be a fact that faked patina is always cold to the touch. Real patina has a curiously warm feel to it."

"This feels normal," Rummins said, ready to argue.

"No, sir, it's cold. But of course it takes an experienced and sensitive finger-tip to pass a positive judgement. You couldn't really be expected to judge this any more than I could be expected to judge the quality of your barley. Everything in life, my dear sir, is experience."

The men were staring at this queer moon-faced clergyman with the bulging eyes, not quite so suspiciously now because he did seem to know a bit about his subject. But they were still a long way from trusting him.

Mr Boggis bent down and pointed to one of the metal drawer-handles on the commode. "This is another place where the fakers go to work," he said. "Old brass normally has a colour and character all of its own. Did you know that?"

They stared at him, hoping for still more secrets.

"But the trouble is that they've become exceedingly skilled at matching it. In fact it's almost impossible to tell the difference between "genuine old" and "faked old". I don't mind admitting that it has me guessing. So there's not really, any point in our scraping the paint off these handles, We wouldn't be any the wiser."

"How can you possibly make new brass look like old?" Claud said. "Brass doesn't rust, you know."

"You are quite right, my friend. But these scoundrels have their own secret methods."

"Such as what?" Claud asked. Any information of this nature was valuable, in his opinion. One never knew when it might come in handy.

"All they have to do," Mr Boggis said "is to place these handles overnight in a box of mahogany shavings saturated in sal ammoniac. The sal ammoniac turns the metal green but if you rub off the green, you will find underneath it a fine soft silvery-warm lustre, a lustre identical to that which comes with very old brass. Oh, it is so bestial, the things they do! With iron they have another trick."

"What do they do with iron?" Claud asked, fascinated.

"Iron's easy," Mr Boggis said. "Iron locks and plates and hinges are simply buried in common salt and they come out all rusted and pitted in no time."

"All right," Rummins said. "So you admit you can't tell about the handles. For all you know, they may be hundreds and hundreds of years old. Correct?"

"Ah," Mr Boggis whispered, fixing Rummins with two big bulging brown eyes. "That's where you're wrong. Watch this."

From his jacket pocket, he took out a small screwdriver. At the same time, although none of them saw him do it, he also took out a little brass screw which he kept well hidden in the palm of his hand. Then he selected one of the screws in the commode – there were four to each handle – and began carefully scraping all traces of white paint from its head. When he had done this, he started slowly to unscrew it.

"If this is a genuine old brass screw from the eighteenth century," he was saying, "the spiral will be slightly uneven and you'll be able to see quite easily that it has been hand-cut with a file. But if this brasswork is faked from more recent times, Victorian or later, then obviously the screw will be of the same period. It will be a mass-produced, machine-made article. Anyone can recognise a machine-made screw. Well, we shall see."

It was not difficult, as he put his hands over the old screw and drew it out, for Mr Boggis to substitute the new one hidden in his palm. This was another little trick of his, and through the years it had proved a most rewarding one. The pockets of his clergyman's jacket were always stocked with a quantity of cheap brass screws of various sizes.

"There you are," he said handing the modern screw to Rummins. "Take a look at that. Notice the exact evenness of the spiral? See it? Of course you do. It's just a cheap common little screw you yourself could buy today in any ironmonger's in the country."

The screw was handed round from the one to the other, each examining it carefully. Even Rummins was impressed now. Mr Boggis put the screwdriver back in his pocket together with the fine hand-cut screw that he'd taken from the commode, and then he turned and walked slowly past the three men towards the door.

"My dear friends," he said, pausing at the entrance to the kitchen, "it was so good of you to let me peep inside your little home – so kind. I do hope I haven't been a terrible old bore."

Rummins glanced up from examining the screw. "You didn't tell us what you were going to offer," he said.

"Ah," Mr Boggis said. "That's quite right. I didn't, did I? Well, to tell you the honest truth, I think it's all a bit too much trouble. I think I'll leave it."

"How much would you give?"

"You mean that you really wish to part with it?"

"I didn't say I wished to part with it. I asked you how much."

Mr Boggis looked across at the commode, and he laid his head first to one side, then to the other, and he frowned, and pushed out his lips, and shrugged his shoulders, and gave a little scornful wave of the hand as though to say the thing was hardly worth thinking about really, was it?

"Shall we say . . . ten pounds. I think that would be fair."

"Ten pounds!" Rummins cried, "Don't be so ridiculous, Parson, please!"

"It's worth more 'n that for firewood!" Claud said, disgusted, "Look here at the bill!" Rummins went on, stabbing that precious document so fiercely with his dirty fore-finger that Mr Boggis became alarmed. "It tells you exactly what it cost! Eighty-seven pounds! And that's when it was new. Now it's antique it's worth double! "If you'll pardon me, no, sir, it's not. It's a second-hand reproduction. But I'll tell you what, my friend – I'm being rather reckless, I can't help it – I'll go up as high as fifteen pounds. How's that?"

"Make it fifty," Rummins said.

A delicious little quiver like needles ran all the way down the back of Mr Boggis's legs and then under the soles of his feet. He had it now. It was his. No question about that. But the habit of buying cheap, as cheap as it was humanly possible to buy, acquired by years of necessity and practice, was too strong in him now to permit him to give in so easily.

"My dear man" he whispered softly, "I only want the legs. Possibly I could find some use for the drawers later on, but the rest of it the carcass itself, as your friend so rightly said, it's firewood, that's all."

"Make it thirty-five," Rummins said.

"I couldn't sir, I couldn't! It's not worth it. And I simply mustn't allow myself to haggle like this about a price. It's all wrong. I'll make you one final offer, and then I must go. Twenty pounds."

"I'll take it," Rummins snapped. "It's yours."

"Oh dear," Mr Boggis said, clasping his hands. "There I go again. I should never have started this in the first place."

"You can't back out now, Parson. A deal's a deal."

"Yes, yes, I know."

"How're you going to take it?"

"Well, let me see. Perhaps if I were to drive my car up into the yard, you gentlemen would be kind enough to help me load it?"

"In a car? This thing'll never go in a car! You'll need a truck for this!"

"I don't think so. Anyway, we'll see. My car's on the road. I'll be back in a jiffy, We'll manage it somehow, I'm sure."

Mr Boggis walked out into the yard and through the gate and then down the long track that led across the field towards the road. He found himself giggling quite uncontrollably, and there was a feeling inside him as though hundreds and hundreds of tiny bubbles were rising up from his stomach and bursting merrily in the top of his head, like sparkling-water. All the buttercups in the field were suddenly turning into golden sovereigns, glistening in the sunlight. The ground was littered with them, and he swung off the track on to the grass so that he could walk among them and tread on them and hear the little metallic tinkle they made as he kicked them around with his toes. He was finding it difficult to stop himself from breaking into a run. But clergymen never run; they walk slowly. Walk slowly, Boggis. Keep calm, Boggis. There's no hurry now. The commode is yours! Yours for twenty pounds, and it's worth fifteen or twenty thousand! The Boggis Commode! In ten minutes it'll be loaded into your car – it'll go in easily – and you'll be driving back to London and singing all the way! Mr Boggis driving the Boggis Commode home in the Boggis car. Historic occasion. What wouldn't a newspaperman give to get a picture of that! Should he arrange it? Perhaps he should. Wait and see. Oh, glorious day! Oh, lovely sunny summer day! Oh, glory be!

Back in the farmhouse, Rummins was saying, "Fancy that old bastard giving twenty pound for a load of junk like this."

"You did very nicely, Mr Rummins," Claud told him. "You think he'll pay you?"

"We don't put it in the car till he do."

"And what if it won't go in the car?" Claud asked. "You know what I think, Mr Rummins? You want my honest opinion ? I think the bloody thing's too big to go in the car. And then what happens? Then he's going to say to hell with it and just drive off without it and you'll never see him again. Nor the money either. He didn't seem all that keen on having it, you know."

Rummins paused to consider this new and rather alarming prospect.

"How can a thing like that possibly go in a car?" Claud went on relentlessly. "A parson never has a big car anyway. You ever seen a parson with a big car, Mr Rummins?"

"Can't say I have."

"Exactly! And now listen to me. I've got an idea. He told us, didn't he, that it was only the legs he was wanting. Right? So all we've got to do is to cut 'em off quick right here on the spot before he comes back, then it'll be sure to go in the car. All we're doing is saving him the trouble of cutting them off himself when he gets home. How about it Mr Rummins?" Claud's flat bovine face glimmered with a mawkish pride.

"It's not such a bad idea at that" Rummins said looking at the commode. "In fact it's a bloody good idea. Come on then, we'll have to hurry. You and Bert carry it out into the yard I'll get the saw. Take the drawers out first."

Within a couple of minutes, Claud and Bert had carried the commode outside and had laid it upside down in the yard amidst the chicken droppings and cow dung and mud. In the distance, half-way across the field they could see a small black figure striding along the path towards the road They paused to watch. There was something rather comical about the way in which this figure was conducting itself. Every now and again it would break into a trot then it did a kind of hop, skip, and jump, and once it seemed as though the sound of a cheerful song came rippling faintly to them from across the meadow.

"I reckon he's balmy," Claud said and Bert grinned darkly, rolling his misty eye slowly round in its socket

Rummins came waddling over from the shed squat and frog-like, carrying a long saw. Claud took the saw away from him and went to work.

"Cut 'em close," Rummins said. "Don't forget he's going to use "em on another table."

The mahogany was hard and very dry, and as Claud worked, a fine red dust sprayed out from the edge of the saw and fell softly to the ground. One by one, the legs came off, and when they were all severed Bert stooped down and arranged them carefully in a row.

Claud stepped back to survey the results of his labour. There was a longish pause.

"Just let me ask you one question, Mr Rummins," he said slowly. "Even now, could you put that enormous thing into the back of a car?"

"Not unless it was a van."

"Correct!" Claud cried. "And parsons don't have vans, you know. All they've got usually is piddling little Morris Eights or Austin Sevens."

"The legs is all he wants," Rummins said "If the rest of it won't go in, then he can leave it. He can't complain. He's got the legs."

"Now you know better'n that Mr Rummins," Claud said patiently. "You know damn well he's going to start knocking the price if he don't get every single bit of this into the car. A parson's just as cunning as the rest of 'em when it comes to money, don't you make any mistake about that. Especially this old boy. So why don't we give him his firewood now and be done with it. Where d'you keep the axe?"

"I reckon that's fair enough" Rummins said "Bert, go fetch the axe."

Bert went into the shed and fetched a tall woodcutter's axe and gave it to Claud. Claud spat on the palms of his hands and rubbed them together. Then, with a long-armed high-swinging action, he began fiercely attacking the legless carcass of the commode.

It was hard work, and it took several minutes before he had the whole thing more or less smashed to pieces.

"I'll tell you one thing," he said, straightening up, wiping his brow. That was a bloody good carpenter put this job together and I don't care what the parson says."

"We're just in time!" Rummins called out. "Here he comes!"

THE RED-HAIRED GIRL

Penelope Fitzgerald

Penelope Fitzgerald (1916–2000) is generally recognized as one of the most singular English writers of the last century. Her novels include *Offshore* (winner of the 1979 Booker Prize), *The Beginnings of Spring*, *The Gate of Angels* and *The Blue Flower* (winner of the National Book Critics' Circle Award in 1995). She did not begin writing in earnest until she was sixty, having worked at the BBC, edited a literary journal, run a bookshop and taught at a variety of schools.

Hackett, Holland, Parsons, Charrington and Dubois all studied in Paris, in the atelier of Vincent Bonvin. Dubois, although his name sounded French, wasn't, and didn't speak any either. None of them did except Hackett.

In the summer of 1882 they made up a party to go to Brittany. That was because they admired Bastien-Lepage, which old Bonvin certainly didn't, and because they wanted somewhere cheap, somewhere with characteristic types, absolutely natural, busy with picturesque occupations, and above all, plein air. "Your work cannot be really good unless you have caught a cold doing it," said Hackett.

They were poor enough, but they took a certain quantity of luggage – only the necessities. Their canvases needed rigging like small craft putting out of harbour, and the artists themselves, for plein air work, had brought overcoats, knickerbockers, gaiters, boots, wide-awakes, broad straw hats for sunny days. They tried, to begin with, St Briac-sur-Mer, which had been recommended to them in Paris, but it didn't suit. On, then, to Palourde, on the coast near Cancale. All resented the time spent moving about. It wasn't in the spirit of the thing, they were artists, not sightseers.

At Palourde, although it looked, and was, larger than St Briac, there was, if anything, less room. The Palourdais had never come across artists before, considered them as rich rather than poor, and wondered why they did not go to St Malo. Holland, Parsons, Charrington and Dubois, however, each found a room of sorts. What about their possessions? There were sail-lofts and potato-cellars in Palourde, but, it seemed, not an inch of room to spare. Their clothes, books and painting material had to go in some boats pulled up above the foreshore, awaiting repairs. They were covered with a piece of tarred sailcloth and roped down. Half the morning would have to be spent getting out what was wanted. Hackett, as interpreter, was obliged to ask whether there was any risk of their being stolen. The reply was that no one in Palourde wanted such things.

It was agreed that Hackett should take what appeared to be the only room in the constricted Hôtel du Port. "Right under the rafters," he wrote to his Intended, "a bed, a chair, a basin, a *broc* of cold water brought up once a day, no view from the window, but I shan't of course paint in my room anyway. I have propped up the canvases I brought with me against the wall. That gives me the sensation of having done something. The food, so far, you wouldn't approve of. Black porridge, later on pieces of black porridge left over from the morning and fried, fish soup with onions, onion soup with fish. The thing is to understand these people well, try to share their devotion to onions, and above all to secure a good model –" He decided not to add "who must be a young girl, otherwise I haven't much chance of any of the London exhibitions."

The Hôtel du Port was inconveniently placed at the top of the village. It had no restaurant, but Hackett was told that he could be served, if he wanted it, at half past six o'clock. The ground floor was taken up with the bar, so this service would be in a very small room at the back, opening off the kitchen.

After Hackett had sat for some time at a narrow table covered with rose-patterned oilcloth, the door opened sufficiently for a second person to edge into the room. It was a red-haired girl, built for hard use and hard wear, who without speaking put down a bowl of fish soup. She and the soup between them filled the room with a sharp, cloudy odour, not quite disagreeable, but it wasn't possible for her to get in and out, concentrating always on not spilling anything, without knocking the back of the chair and the door itself, first with her elbows, then with her rump. The spoons and the saltbox on the table trembled as though in a railway carriage. Then the same manoeuvre again, this time bringing a loaf of dark bread and a carafe of cider. No more need to worry after that, there was no more to come.

"I think I've found rather a jolly-looking model already," Hackett told the others. They, too, had not done so badly. They had set up their easels on the quay, been asked, as far as they could make out, to move them further away from the moorings, done so "with a friendly smile," said Charrington – "we find that goes a long way." They hadn't risked asking anyone to model for them, just started some sea-pieces between the handfuls of wind and rain. "We might come up to the hotel tonight and dine with you. There's nothing but fish soup in our digs."

Hackett discouraged them.

The hotelier's wife, when he had made the right preliminary enquiries from her about the red-haired girl, had answered – as she did, however, on all subjects – largely with silences. He didn't learn who her parents were, or even her family name. Her given name was Annik. She worked an all-day job at the Hôtel du Port, but she had one and a half hours free after her lunch and if she wanted to spend that being drawn or painted, well, there were no objections. Not in the hotel, however, where, as he could see, there was no room.

"I paint en plein air," said Hackett.

"You'll find plenty of that."

"I shall pay her, of course."

"You must make your own arrangements."

He spoke to the girl at dinner, during the few moments when she was conveniently trapped. When she had quite skilfully allowed the door to shut behind her and, soup-dish in hand, was recovering her balance, he said:

"Anny, I want to ask you something."

"I'm called Annik," she said. It was the first time he had heard her speak.

"All the girls are called that. I shall call you Anny. I've spoken about you to the patronne."

"Yes, she told me."

Anny was a heavy breather, and the whole tiny room seemed to expand and deflate as she stood pondering.

"I shall want you to come to the back door of the hotel, I mean the back steps down to the rue de Dol. Let us say tomorrow, at twelve forty-five."

"I don't know about the forty-five," she said. "I can't be sure about that."

"How do you usually know the time?" She was silent. He thought it was probably a matter of pride and she did not want to agree to anything too easily. But possibly she couldn't tell the time. She might be stupid to the degree of idiocy.

The Hôtel du Port had no courtyard. Like every other house in the street, it had a flight of stone steps to adapt to the change of level. After lunch the shops shut for an hour and the women of Palourde sat or stood, according to their age, on the top step and knitted or did crochet. They didn't wear costume any more, they wore white linen caps and jackets, long skirts, and, if they weren't going far, carpet slippers.

Anny was punctual to the minute. "I shall want you to stand quite still on the top step, with your back to the door. I've asked them not to open it."

Anny, also, was wearing carpet slippers. "I can't just stand here doing nothing."

He allowed her to fetch her crochet. Give a little, take a little. He was relieved, possibly a bit disappointed, to find how little interest they caused in the rue de Dol. He was used to being watched, quite openly, over his shoulder, as if he was giving a comic performance. Here even the children didn't stop to look.

"They don't care about our picture," he said, trying to amuse her. He would have liked a somewhat gentler expression. Certainly she was not a beauty. She hadn't the white skin of the dreamed-of red-haired girl, in fact her face and neck were covered with a faint but noticeable hairy down, as though proof against all weathers.

"How long will it take?" she asked.

"I don't know. As God disposes! An hour will do for today."

"And then you'll pay me?"

"No," he said, "I shan't do that. I shall pay you when the whole thing's finished. I shall keep a record of the time you've worked, and if you like you can keep one as well."

As he was packing up his box of charcoals he added: "I shall want to make a few colour notes tomorrow, and I should like you to wear a red shawl." It seemed that she hadn't one. "But you could borrow one, my dear. You could borrow one, since I ask you particularly."

She looked at him as though he were an imbecile.

"You shouldn't have said 'Since I ask you particularly'," Parsons told him that evening. "That will have turned her head."

"It can't have done," said Hackett.

"Did you call her 'my dear'?"

"I don't know, I don't think so."

"I've noticed you say "particularly" with a peculiar intonation, which may well have become a matter of habit," said Parsons, nodding sagely.

This is driving me crazy, thought Hackett. He began to feel a division which he had never so much as dreamed of in Paris between himself and his fellow students. They had been working all day, having managed to rent a disused and indeed almost unusable shed on the quay. It had once been part of the market where the fishermen's wives did the triage, sorting out the catch by size. Hackett, as before, had done the interpreting. He had plenty of time, since Anny could only be spared for such short intervals. But at least he had been true to his principles. Holland, Parsons, Charrington and Dubois weren't working in the open air at all. Difficulties about models forgotten, they were sketching each other in the shed. The background of Palourde's not very picturesque jetty could be dashed in later.

Anny appeared promptly for the next three days to stand, with her crochet, on the back steps. Hackett didn't mind her blank expression, having accepted from the first that she was never likely to smile. The red shawl, though – that hadn't appeared. He could, perhaps, buy one in St Malo. He ached for the contrast between the copper-coloured hair and the scarlet shawl. But he felt it wrong to introduce something from outside Palourde.

"Anny, I have to tell you that you've disappointed me."

"I told you I had no red shawl."

"You could have borrowed one."

Charrington, who was supposed to understand women, and even to have had a great quarrel with Parsons about some woman or other, only said: "She can't borrow what isn't there. I've been trying ever since we came here to borrow a decent tin-opener. I've tried to. make it clear that I'd give it back."

Best to leave the subject alone. But the moment Anny turned up next day he found himself saying: "You could borrow one from a friend, that was what I meant."

"I haven't any friends," said Anny.

Hackett paused in the business of lighting his pipe. "An empty life for you, then, Anny."

"You don't know what I want," she said, very low.

"Oh, everybody wants the same things. The only difference is what they will do to get them."

"You don't know what I want, and you don't know what I feel," she said, still in the same mutter. There was, however, a faint note of something more than the contradiction that came so naturally to her, and Hackett was a good-natured man.

"I'm sorry I said you disappointed me, Anny. The truth is I find it rather a taxing business, standing here drawing in the street."

"I don't know why you came here in the first place. There's nothing here, nothing at all. If it's oysters you want, they're better at Cancale. There's nothing here to tell one morning from another, except to see if it's raining . . . Once they brought in three drowned bodies, two men and a boy, a whole boat's crew, and laid them out on the tables in the fish market, and you could see blood and water running out of their mouths . . . You can spend your whole life here, wash, pray, do your work, and all the time you might just as well not have been born."

She was still speaking so that she could scarcely be heard. The passers-by went un-noticing down Palourde's badly paved street. Hackett felt disturbed. It had never occurred to him that she would speak, without prompting, at such length.

"I've received a telegram from Paris," said Parsons, who was standing at the shed door. "It's taken its time about getting here. They gave it me at the post office."

"What does it say?" asked Hackett, feeling it was likely to be about money.

"Well, that he's coming – Bonvin, I mean. As is my custom every summer, I am touring the coasts – it's a kind of informal inspection, you see. – Expect me, then, on the 27th for dinner at the Hôtel du Port."

"It's impossible." Parsons suggested that, since Dubois had brought his banjo with him, they might get up some kind of impromptu entertainment. But he had to agree that one couldn't associate old Bonvin with entertainment.

He couldn't, surely, be expected from Paris before six. But when they arrived, all of them except Hackett carrying their portfolios, at the hotel's front door, they recognized, from the moment it opened, the voice of Bonvin. Hackett looked round, and felt his head swim. The bar, dark, faded, pickled in its own long-standing odours, crowded with stools and barrels, with the air of being older than Palourde, as though Palourde had been built round it without daring to disturb it, was swept and emptied now except for a central table and chairs such as Hackett had never seen in the hotel. At the head of the table sat old Bonvin. "Sit down, gentlemen! I am your host!" The everyday malicious dry voice, but a different Bonvin, in splendid seaside dress, a yellow waistcoat, a cravat. Palourde was indifferent to artists, but Bonvin had imposed himself as a professor.

"They are used to me here. They keep a room for me which I think is not available to other guests and they are always ready to take a little trouble for me when I come."

The artists sat meekly down, while the patronne herself served them with a small glass of greenish-white muscadet.

"I am your host," repeated Bonvin. "I can only say that I am delighted to see pupils, for the first time, in Palourde, but I assure you I have others as far away as Corsica. Once a teacher, always a teacher! I sometimes think it is a passion which outlasts even art itself."

They had all assured each other, in Paris, that old Bonvin was incapable of teaching anything. Time spent in his atelier was squandered. But here, in the strangely transformed bar of the Hôtel du Port, with a quite inadequate drink in front of them, they felt overtaken by destiny. The patronne shut and locked the front door to keep out the world who might disturb the professor. Bonvin, not, after all, looking so old, called upon them to show their portfolios.

Hackett had to excuse himself to go up to his room and fetch the four drawings which he had made so far. He felt it an injustice that he had to show his things last.

Bonvin asked him to hold them up one by one, then to lay them out on the table. To Hackett he spoke magniloquently, in French.

"Yes, they are bad," he said, "but, M. Hackett, they are bad for two distinct reasons. In the first place, you should not draw the view from the top of a street if you cannot manage the perspective, which even a child, following simple mechanical rules, can do. The relationship in scale of the main figure to those lower down is quite, quite wrong. But there is something else amiss.

"You are an admirer, I know, of Bastien-Lepage, who has said, "There is nothing really lasting, nothing that will endure, except the sincere expression of the actual conditions of life." Conditions in the potato patch, in the hayfield, at the washtub, in the open street! That is pernicious nonsense. Look at this girl of yours. Evidently she is not a professional model, for she doesn't know how to hold herself. I see you have made a note that the colour of the hair is red, but that is the only thing I know about her. She's standing against the door like a beast waiting to be put back in its stall. It's your intention, I am sure, to do the finished version in the same way, in the dust of the street. Well, your picture will say nothing and it will be nothing. It is only in the studio that you can bring out the heart of the subject, and that is what we are sent into this world to do, M. Hackett, to paint the experiences of the heart."

(– Gibbering dotard, you can talk till your teeth fall out. I shall go on precisely as I have been doing, even if I can only paint her for an hour and a quarter a day. –) An evening of nameless embarrassment, with Hackett's friends coughing, shuffling, eating noisily, asking questions to which they knew the answer, and telling anecdotes of which they forgot the endings. Anny had not appeared, evidently she was considered unworthy; the patronne came in again, bringing not soup but the very height of Brittany's grand-occasion cuisine, a fricassee of chicken. Who would have thought there were chickens in Palourde?

Hackett woke in what he supposed were the small hours. So far he had slept dreamlessly in Palourde, had never so much as lighted his bedside candle. – Probably, he thought, Bonvin made the same unpleasant speech wherever he went. The old impostor was drunk with power – not with anything else, only half a bottle of muscadet and, later, a bottle of *gros-plant* between the six of them. – The sky had begun to thin and pale. It came to him that what had been keeping him awake was not an injustice of Bonvin's, but of his own. What had been the experiences of Anny's heart?

Bonvin, with his dressing cases and book-boxes, left early. The horse omnibus stopped once a week in the little Place François-René de Chateaubriand, at the entrance to the village. Having made his formal farewells, Bonvin caught the omnibus. Hackett was left in good time for his appointment with Anny.

She did not come that day, nor the next day, nor the day after. On the first evening he was served by the boot-boy, pitifully worried about getting in and out of the door, on the second by the hotel laundrywoman, on the third by the patronne. "Where is Anny?" She did not answer. For that in itself Hackett was prepared, but he tried again. "Is she ill?" "No, not ill." "Has she taken another job?" "No." He was beginning, he realized, in the matter of this plain and sullen girl, to sound like an anxious lover. "Shall I see her again?" He got no answer.

Had she drowned herself? The question reared up in his mind, like a savage dog getting up from its sleep. She had hardly seemed to engage herself enough with life, hardly seemed to take enough interest in it to wish no more of it. Boredom, though, and the withering sense of insignificance can bring one as low as grief. He had felt the breath of it at his ear when Bonvin had told him – for that was what it came to – that there was no hope of his becoming an artist. Anny was stupid, but no one is too stupid to despair.

There was no police station in Palourde, and if Anny were truly drowned, they would say nothing about it at the Hôtel du Port. Hackett had been in enough small hotels to know that they did not discuss anything that was bad for business. The red-haired body might drift anywhere, might be washed ashore anywhere between Pointe du Grouin and Cap Prehel.

That night it was the laundrywoman's turn to dish up the fish soup. Hackett thought of confiding in her, but did not need to. She said to him: "You mustn't keep asking the patronne about Anny, it disturbs her." Anny, it turned out, had been dismissed for stealing from the hotel – some money, and a watch. "You had better have a look through your things," the laundrywoman said, "and see there's nothing missing. One often doesn't notice till a good while afterwards."

THE LOTTERY

Shirley Jackson

Shirley Jackson (1916–1965) was born in San Francisco, educated at Syracuse and settled with her husband, the critic Stanley Edgar Hyman, in North Bennington, Vermont. She wrote six novels, two memoirs, children's books and countless stories including her most famous "The Lottery", published in *The New Yorker* in June 1948. She once observed "I delight in what I fear", and wrote "So long as you write it away regularly nothing can really hurt you." A heavy smoker, overweight, she died of heart failure in her sleep.

The morning of June 27th was clear and sunny, with the fresh warmth of a fun-summer day; the flowers were blossoming profusely and the grass was richly green. The people of the village began to gather in the square, between the post office and the bank, around ten o'clock; in some towns there were so many people that the lottery took two days and had to be started on June 26th, but in this village, where there were only about three hundred people, the whole lottery took less than two hours, so it could begin at ten o'clock in the morning and still be through in time to allow the villagers to get home for noon dinner.

The children assembled first, of course. School was recently over for the summer, and the feeling of liberty sat uneasily on most of them; they tended to gather together quietly for a while before they broke into boisterous play, and their talk was still of the classroom and the teacher; of books and reprimands. Bobby Martin had already stuffed his pockets full of stones, and the other boys soon followed his example, selecting the smoothest and roundest stones; Bobby and Harry Jones and Dickie Delacroix – the villagers pronounced this name "Deflacroy" – eventually made a great pile of stones in one corner of the square and guarded it against the raids of the other boys. The girls stood aside, talking among themselves, looking over their shoulders at the boys, and the very small children rolled in the dust or clung to the hands of their older brothers or sisters.

Soon the men began to gather, surveying their own children, speaking of planting and rain, tractors and taxes. They stood together, away from the pile of stones in the corner, and their jokes were quiet and they smiled rather than laughed. The women, wearing faded house dresses and sweaters, came shortly after their menfolk. They greeted one another and exchanged bits of gossip as they went to join their husbands. Soon the women, standing by their husbands, began to call to their children, and the children came reluctantly, having to be called four or five times. Bobby Martin ducked under his mother's grasping hand and ran, laughing, back to the pile of stones. His father spoke up sharply, and Bobby came quickly and took his place between his father and his oldest brother.

The lottery was conducted – as were the square dances, the teenage club, the Halloween program – by Mr. Summers, who had time and energy to devote to civic activities. He was a round-faced, jovial man and he ran the coal business, and people were sorry for him, because he had no children and his wife was a scold. When he arrived in the square, carrying the black wooden box, there was a murmur of conversation among the villagers, and he waved and called, "Little late today, folks." The postmaster, Mr. Graves, followed him, carrying a three-legged stool, and the stool was put in the center of the square and Mr. Summers set the black box down on it. The villagers kept their distance, leaving a space between themselves and the stool, and when Mr. Summers said, "Some of you fellows want to give me a hand?" there was a hesitation before two men, Mr. Martin and his oldest son, Baxter, came forward to hold the box steady on the stool while Mr. Summers stirred up the papers inside it.

The original paraphernalia for the lottery had been lost long ago, and the black box now resting on the stool had been put into use even before Old Man Warner, the oldest man in town, was born. Mr. Summers spoke frequently to the villagers about making a new box, but no one liked to upset even as much tradition as was represented by the black box. There was a story that the present box had been made with some pieces of the box that had preceded it, the one that had been constructed when the first people settled down to make a village here. Every year, after the lottery, Mr. Summers began talking again about a new box, but every year the subject was allowed to fade off without anything's being done. The black box grew shabbier each year, by now it was no longer completely black but splintered badly along one side to show the original wood color, and in some places faded or stained.

Mr. Martin and his oldest son, Baxter, held the black box securely on the stool until Mr. Summers had stirred the papers thoroughly with his hand. Because so much of the ritual had been forgotten or discarded, Mr. Summers had been successful in having slips of paper substituted for the chips of wood that had been used for generations. Chips of wood, Mr. Summers had argued, had been all very well when the village was tiny, but now that the population was more than three hundred and likely to keep on growing, it was necessary to use something that would fit more easily into the black box. The night before the lottery, Mr. Summers and Mr. Graves made up the slips of paper and put them in the box, and it was then taken to the safe of Mr. Summers' coal company and locked up until Mr. Summers was ready to take it to the square next morning. The rest of the year, the box was put away, sometimes one place, sometimes another; it had spent one year in Mr. Graves's barn and another year underfoot in the post office, and sometimes it was set on a shelf in the Martin grocery and left there.

There was a great deal of fussing to be done before Mr. Summers declared the lottery open. There were the lists to make up – of heads of families, heads of households in each family, members of each household in each family. There was the proper swearing-in of Mr. Summers by the postmaster, as the official of the lottery; at one time, some people remembered, there had been a recital of some sort, performed by the official of the lottery, a perfunctory, tuneless chant that had been rattled off duly each year; some people believed that the official of the lottery used to stand just so when he said or sang it, others believed that he was supposed to walk among the people, but years and years ago this part of the ritual had been allowed to lapse. There had been, also, a ritual salute, which the official of the lottery had had to use in addressing each person who came up to draw from the box, but this also had changed with time, until now it was felt necessary only for the official to speak to each person approaching. Mr. Summers was very good at all this; in his clean white shirt and blue jeans, with one hand resting carelessly on the black box, he seemed very proper and important as he talked interminably to Mr. Graves and the Martins.

Just as Mr. Summers finally left off talking and turned to the assembled villagers, Mrs. Hutchinson came hurriedly along the path to the square, her sweater thrown over her shoulders, and slid into place in the back of the crowd. "Clean forgot what day it was," she said to Mrs. Delacroix, who stood next to her, and they both laughed softly. "Thought my old man was out back stacking wood," Mrs. Hutchinson went on, "and then I looked out the window and the kids was gone, and then I remembered it was the twenty-seventh and came a-running." She dried her hands on her apron, and Mrs. Delacroix said, "You're in time, though. They're still talking away up there."

Mrs. Hutchinson craned her neck to see through the crowd and found her husband and children standing near the front. She tapped Mrs. Delacroix on the arm as a farewell and began to make her way through the crowd. The people separated good-humoredly to let her through; two or three people said, in voices just loud enough to be heard across the crowd, "Here comes your Missus Hutchinson," and "Bill, she made it after all." Mrs. Hutchinson reached her husband, and Mr. Summers, who had been waiting, said cheerfully, "Thought we were going to have to get on without you, Tessie." Mrs. Hutchinson said, grinning, "Wouldn't have me leave m'dishes in the sink, now, would you, Joe?" and soft laughter ran through the crowd as the people stirred back into position after Mrs. Hutchinson's arrival.

"Well, now," Mr. Summers said soberly, "guess we better get started, get this over with, so's we can go back to work. Anybody ain't here?"

"Dunbar," several people said. "Dunbar, Dunbar."

Mr. Summers consulted his list. "Clyde Dunbar," he said. "That's right. He's broke his leg, hasn't he? Who's drawing for him?"

"Me, I guess," a woman said, and Mr. Summers turned to look at her. "Wife draws for her husband," Mr. Summers said. "Don't you have a grown boy to do it for you, Janey?" Although Mr. Summers and everyone else in the village knew the answer perfectly well, it was the business of the official of the lottery to ask such questions formally. Mr. Summers waited with an expression of polite interest while Mrs. Dunbar answered.

"Horace's not but sixteen yet," Mrs. Dunbar said regretfully. "Guess I gotta fill in for the old man this year."

"Right," Mr. Summers said. He made a note on the list he was holding. Then he asked, "Watson boy drawing this year?"

A tall boy in the crowd raised his hand. "Here," he said. "I'm drawing for m'mother and me." He blinked his eyes nervously and ducked his head as several voices in the crowd said things like "Good fellow, Jack," and "Glad to see your mother's got a man to do it."

"Well," Mr. Summers said, "guess that's everyone. Old Man Warner make it?"

"Here," a voice said, and Mr. Summers nodded.

A sudden hush fell on the crowd as Mr. Summers cleared his throat and looked at the list. "All ready?" he called. "Now, I'll read the names – heads of families first – and the men come up and take a paper out of the box. Keep the paper folded in your hand without looking at it until everyone has had a turn. Everything clear?"

The people had done it so many times that they only half listened to the directions; most of them were quiet, wetting their lips, not looking around. Then Mr. Summers raised one hand high and said, "Adams." A man disengaged himself from the crowd and came forward. "Hi, Steve," Mr. Summers said, and Mr. Adams said, "Hi, Joe." They grinned at one another humorlessly and nervously. Then Mr. Adams reached into the black box and took out a folded paper. He held it firmly by one corner as he turned and went hastily back to his place in the crowd, where he stood a little apart from his family, not looking down at his hand.

"Allen," Mr. Summers said. "Anderson . . . Bentham."

"Seems like there's no time at all between lotteries any more," Mrs. Delacroix said to Mrs. Graves in the back row. "Seems like we got through with the last one only last week."

"Time sure goes fast," Mrs. Graves said.

"Clark . . . Delacroix."

"There goes my old man," Mrs. Delacroix said. She held her breath while her husband went forward.

"Dunbar," Mr. Summers said, and Mrs. Dunbar went steadily to the box while one of the women said, "Go on, Janey," and another said, "There she goes."

"We're next," Mrs. Graves said. She watched while Mr. Graves came around from the side of the box, greeted Mr. Summers gravely, and selected a slip of paper from the box. By now, all through the crowd there were men holding the small folded papers in their large hands, turning them over and over nervously. Mrs. Dunbar and her two sons stood together, Mrs. Dunbar holding the slip of paper.

"Harburt . . . Hutchinson."

"Get up there, Bill," Mrs. Hutchinson said, and the people near her laughed.

"Jones."

"They do say," Mr. Adams said to Old Man Warner, who stood next to him, "that over in the north village they're talking of giving up the lottery."

Old Man Warner snorted. "Pack of crazy fools," he said. "Listening to the young folks, nothing's good enough for *them*. Next thing you know, they'll be wanting to go back to living in caves, nobody work any more, live *that* way for a while. Used to be a saying; about 'Lottery in June, corn be heavy soon.' First thing you know, we'd all be eating stewed chickweed and acorns. There's *always* been a lottery," he added petulantly. "Bad enough to see young Joe Summers up there joking with everybody."

"Some places have already quit lotteries," Mrs. Adams said.

"Nothing but trouble in *that*," Old Man Warner said stoutly. "Pack of young fools."

"Martin." And Bobby Martin watched his father go forward. "Overdyke . . . Percy."

"I wish they'd hurry," Mrs. Dunbar said to her older son. "I wish they'd hurry."

"They're almost through," her son said.

"You get ready to run tell Dad," Mrs. Dunbar said.

Mr. Summers called his own name and then stepped forward precisely and selected a slip from the box. Then he called, "Warner."

"Seventy-seventh year I been in the lottery," Old Man Warner said as he went through the crowd. "Seventy-seventh time."

"Watson." The tall boy came awkwardly through the crowd. Someone said, "Don't be nervous, Jack," and Mr. Summers said, "Take your time, son."

"Zanini."

After that, there was a long pause, a breathless pause, until Mr. Summers, holding his slip of paper in the air, said, "All right, fellows." For a minute, no one moved, and then all the slips of paper were opened. Suddenly, all the women began to speak at once, saying, "Who is it?" "Who's got it?" "Is it the Dunbars?" "Is it the Watsons?" Then the voices began to say, "It's Hutchinson. It's Bill," "Bill Hutchinson's got it."

"Go tell your father," Mrs. Dunbar said to her older son.

People began to look around to see the Hutchinsons. Bill Hutchinson was standing quiet, staring down at the paper in his hand. Suddenly, Tessie Hutchinson shouted to Mr. Summers, "You didn't give him time enough to take any paper he wanted. I saw you. It wasn't fair!"

"Be a good sport, Tessie," Mrs. Delacroix called, and Mrs. Graves said, "All of us took the same chance."

"Shut up, Tessie," Bill Hutchinson said.

"Well, everyone," Mr. Summers said, "that was done pretty fast, and now we've got to be hurrying a little more to get done in time." He consulted his next list. "Bill," he said, "you draw for the Hutchinson family. You got any other households in the Hutchinsons?"

"There's Don and Eva," Mrs. Hutchinson yelled. "Make *them* take their chance!"

"Daughters draw with their husbands' families, Tessie," Mr. Summers said gently. "You know that as well as anyone else."

"It wasn't *fair*," Tessie said.

"I guess not, Joe," Bill Hutchinson said regretfully. "My daughter draws with her husband's family, that's only fair. And I've got no other family except the kids."

"Then, as far as drawing for families is concerned, it's you," Mr. Summers said in explanation, "and as far as drawing for households is concerned, that's you, too. Right?"

"Right," Bill Hutchinson said.

"How many lads, Bill?" Mr. Summers asked formally.

"Three," Bill Hutchinson said. "There's Bill, Jr., and Nancy, and little Dave. And Tessie and me."

"All right, then," Mr. Summers said. "Harry, you got their tickets back?"

Mr. Graves nodded and held up the slips of paper. "Put them in the box, then," Mr. Summers directed. "Take Bill's and put it in."

"I think we ought to start over," Mrs. Hutchinson said, as quietly as she could. "I tell you it wasn't *fair*. You didn't give him time enough to choose, everybody saw that."

Mr. Graves had selected the five slips and put them in the box, and he dropped all the papers but those onto the ground, where the breeze caught them and lifted them off.

"Listen, everybody," Mrs. Hutchinson was saying to the people around her.

"Ready, Bill?" Mr. Summers asked, and Bill Hutchinson, with one quick glance around at his wife and children, nodded.

"Remember," Mr. Summers said, "take the slips and keep them folded until each person has taken one. Harry, you help little Dave." Mr. Graves took the hand of the little boy, who came willingly with him up to the box. "Take a paper out of the box, Davy," Mr. Summers said. Davy put his hand into the box and laughed. "Take just one paper," Mr. Summers said. "Harry, you hold it for him." Mr. Graves took the child's hand and removed the folded paper from the tight fist and held it while little Dave stood next to him and looked up at him wonderingly.

"Nancy next," Mr. Summers said. Nancy was twelve, and her school friends breathed heavily as she went forward, switching her skirt, and took a slip daintily from the box. "Bill, Jr.," Mr. Summers said, and Billy, his face red and his feet over-large, nearly knocked the box over as he got a paper out. "Tessie," Mr. Summers said. She hesitated for a minute, looking around defiantly, and then set her lips and went up to the box. She snatched a paper out and held it behind her.

"Bill," Mr. Summers said, and Bill Hutchinson reached into the box and felt around, bringing his hand out at last with the slip of paper in it.

The crowd was quiet. A girl whispered, "I hope it's not Nancy," and the sound of the whisper reached the edges of the crowd.

"It's not the way it used to be," Old Man Warner said clearly. "People ain't the way they used to be."

"All right," Mr. Summers said. "Open the papers. Harry, you open little Dave's."

Mr. Graves opened the slip of paper and there was a general sigh through the crowd as he held it up and everyone could see that it was blank. Nancy and Bill, Jr., opened theirs at the same time, and both beamed and laughed, turning around to the crowd and holding their slips of paper above their heads.

"Tessie," Mr. Summers said. There was a pause, and then Mr. Summers looked at Bill Hutchinson, and Bill unfolded his paper and showed it. It was blank.

"It's Tessie," Mr. Summers said, and his voice was hushed. "Show us her paper, Bill."

Bill Hutchinson went over to his wife and forced the slip of paper out of her hand. It had a black spot on it, the black spot Mr. Summers had made the night before with the heavy pencil in the coal-company office. Bill Hutchinson held it up, and there was a stir in the crowd.

"All right, folks," Mr. Summers said. "Let's finish quickly."

Although the villagers had forgotten the ritual and lost the original black box, they still remembered to use stones. The pile of stones the boys had made earlier was ready; there were stones on the ground with the blowing scraps of paper that had come out of the box. Mrs. Delacroix selected a stone so large she had to pick it up with both hands and turned to Mrs. Dunbar. "Come on," she said. "Hurry up."

Mrs. Dunbar had small stones in both hands, and she said, gasping for breath, "I can't run at all. You'll have to go ahead and I'll catch up with you."

The children had stones already, and someone gave little Davy Hutchinson a few pebbles.

Tessie Hutchinson was in the center of a cleared space by now, and she held her hands out desperately as the villagers moved in on her. "It isn't fair," she said. A stone hit her on the side of the head.

Old Man Warner was saying, "Come on, come on, everyone." Steve Adams was in the front of the crowd of villagers, with Mrs. Graves beside him.

"It isn't fair, it isn't right," Mrs. Hutchinson screamed, and then they were upon her.

THE EXECUTOR

Muriel Spark

Muriel Spark (1918–2006) was the author of several novels, including *The Prime of Miss Jean Brodie*. It should be noted that whole novel was published by *The New Yorker* before volume publication. Her finest fiction was short – *The Driver's Seat* is a model of sheer genius which I read, like Melville's *Bartleby*, each year.

When my uncle died all the literary manuscripts went to a university foundation, except one. The correspondence went too, and the whole of his library. They came (a white-haired man and a young girl) and surveyed his study. Everything, they said, would be desirable and it would make a good price if I let the whole room go – his chair, his desk, the carpet, even his ashtrays. I agreed to this. I left everything in the drawers of the desk just as it was when my uncle died, including the bottle of Librium and a rusty razor blade.

My uncle died this way: he was sitting on the bank of the river, playing a fish. As the afternoon faded a man passed by, and then a young couple who made pottery passed him. As they said later, he was sitting peacefully awaiting the catch and of course they didn't disturb him. As night fell the colonel and his wife passed by; they were on their way home from their daily walk. They knew it was too late for my uncle to be simply sitting there, so they went to look. He had been dead, the doctor pronounced, from two to two and a half hours. The fish was still struggling with the bait. It was a mild heart attack. Everything my uncle did was mild, so different from everything he wrote. Yet perhaps not so different. He was supposed to be "far out", so one didn't know what went on out there. Besides, he had not long returned from a trip to London. They say, still waters run deep.

But far out was how he saw himself. He once said that if you could imagine modern literature as a painting, perhaps by Brueghel the Elder, the people and the action were in the foreground, full of colour, eating, stealing, copulating, laughing, courting each other, excreting, and stabbing each other, selling things, climbing trees. Then in the distance, at the far end of a vast plain, there he would be, a speck on the horizon, always receding and always there, and always a necessary and mysterious component of the picture; always there and never to be taken away, essential to the picture – a speck in the distance, which if you were to blow up the detail would simply be a vague figure, plodding on the other way.

I am no fool, and he knew it. He didn't know it at first, but he had seven months in which to learn that fact. I gave up my job in Edinburgh in the government office, a job with a pension, to come here to the lonely house among the Pentland Hills to live with him and take care of things. I think he imagined I was going to be another Elaine when he suggested the arrangement. He had no idea how much better I was for him than Elaine. Elaine was his mistress, that is the stark truth. "My common-law wife," he called her, explaining that in Scotland, by tradition, the woman you are living with is your wife. As if I didn't know all that nineteenth-century folklore; and it's long died out. Nowadays you have to do more than say "I marry you, I marry you, I marry you," to make a woman your wife. Of course, my uncle was a genius and a character. I allowed for that. Anyway, Elaine died and I came here a month later. Within a month I had cleared up the best part of the disorder. He called me a Scottish puritan girl, and at forty-one it was nice to be a girl and I wasn't against the Scottish puritanical attribution either since I am proud to be a Scot; I feel nationalistic about it. He always had that smile of his when he said it, so I don't know how he meant it. They say he had that smile of his when he was found dead, fishing.

"I appoint my niece Susan Kyle to be my sole literary executor." I don't wonder he decided on this course after I had been with him for three months. Probably for the first time in his life all his papers were in order. I went into Edinburgh and bought box-files and cover-files and I filed away all that mountain of papers, each under its separate heading. And I knew what was what. You didn't catch me filing away a letter from Angus Wilson or Saul Bellow in the same place as an ordinary "W" or "B", a Miss Mary Whitelaw or a Mrs Jonathan Brown. I knew the value of these letters, they went into a famous-persons file, bulging and of value. So that in a short time my uncle said, "There's little for me to do now, Susan, but die." Which I thought was melodramatic, and said so. But I could see he was forced to admire my good sense. He said, "You remind me of my mother, who prepared her shroud all ready for her funeral." His mother was my grandmother Janet Kyle. Why shouldn't she have sat and sewn her shroud? People in those days had very little to do, and here I was running the house and looking after my uncle's papers with only the help of Mrs Donaldson three mornings a week, where my grandmother had four pairs of hands for indoor help and three out. The rest of the family never went near the house after my grandmother died, for Elaine was always there with my uncle.

The property was distributed among the family, but I was the sole literary executor. And it was up to me to do what I liked with his literary remains. It was a good thing I had everything inventoried and filed, ready for sale. They came and took the total archive as they called it away, all the correspondence and manuscripts except one. That one I kept for myself. It was the novel he was writing when he died, an unfinished manuscript. I thought, Why not? Maybe I will finish it myself and publish it. I am no fool, and my uncle must have known how the book was going to end. I never read any of his correspondence, mind you; I was too busy those months filing it all in order. I did think, however, that I would read this manuscript and perhaps put an ending to it. There were already ten chapters. My uncle had told me there was only another chapter to go. So I said nothing to the Foundation about that one unfinished manuscript; I was only too glad when they had come and gone, and the papers were out of the house. I got the painters in to clean the study. Mrs Donaldson said she had never seen the house looking so like a house should be.

Under my uncle's will I inherited the house, and I planned eventually to rent rooms to tourists in the summer, bed and breakfast. In the meantime I set about reading the unfinished manuscript for it was only April, and I'm not a one to let the grass grow under my feet. I had learnt to decipher that old-fashioned handwriting of his which looked good on the page but was not too clear. My uncle had a treasure in me those last months of his life, although he said I was like a book without an index – all information, and no way of getting at it. I asked him to tell me what information he ever got out of Elaine, who never passed an exam in her life.

This last work of my uncle's was an unusual story for him, set in the seventeenth century here among the Pentland Hills. He had told me only that he was writing something strong and cruel, and that this was easier to accomplish in a historical novel. It was about the slow identification and final trapping of a witch, and I could see as I read it that he hadn't been joking when he said it was strong and cruel; he had often said things to frighten and alarm me, I don't know why. By chapter ten the trial of the witch in Edinburgh was only halfway through. Her fate depended entirely on chapter eleven, and on the negotiations that were being conducted behind the scenes by the opposing factions of intrigue. My uncle had left a pile of notes he had accumulated towards this novel, and I retained these along with the manuscript. But there was no sign in the notes as to how my uncle had decided to resolve the fate of the witch – whose name was Edith but that is by the way. I put the notebooks and papers away, for there were many other things to be done following the death of my famous uncle. The novel itself was written by hand in twelve notebooks. In the twelfth only the first two pages had been filled, the rest of the pages were blank; I am sure of this. The two filled pages came to the end of chapter ten. At the top of the next page was written "Chapter Eleven". I looked through the rest of the notebook to make sure my uncle had not made some note there on how he intended to continue; all blank, I am sure of it. I put the twelve notebooks, together with the sheaf of loose notes, in a drawer of the solid-mahogany dining-room sideboard.

A few weeks later I brought the notebooks out again, intending to consider how I might proceed with the completion of the book and so enhance its value. I read again through chapter ten; then, when I turned to the page where "Chapter Eleven" was written, there in my uncle's handwriting was the following:

Well, Susan, how do you feel about finishing my novel? Aren't you a greedy little snoot, holding back my unfinished work, when you know the Foundation paid for the lot? What about your puritanical principles? Elaine and I are waiting to see how you manage to write Chapter Eleven. Elaine asks me to add it's lovely to see you scouring and cleaning those neglected corners of the house. But don't you know, Jaimie is having you on. Where does he go after lunch?

– Your affect Uncle

I could hardly believe my eyes. The first shock I got was the bit about Jaimie, and then came the second shock, that the words were there at all. It was twelve-thirty at night and Jaimie had gone home. Jaimie Donaldson is the son of Mrs Donaldson, and it isn't his fault he's out of work. We have had experiences together, but nobody is to know that, least of all Mrs Donaldson who introduced him into the household merely to clean the windows and stoke the boiler. But the words? Where did they come from?

It is a lonely house, here in a fold of the Pentlands, surrounded by woods, five miles to the nearest cottage, six to Mrs Donaldson's, and the buses stop at ten p.m. I felt a great fear there in the dining-room, with the twelve notebooks on the table, and the pile of papers, a great cold, and a panic. I ran to the hall and lifted the telephone but didn't know how to explain myself or whom to phone. My story would sound like that of a woman gone crazy. Mrs Donaldson? The police? I couldn't think what to say to them at that hour of night. "I have found some words that weren't there before in my uncle's manuscript, and in his own hand." It was unthinkable. Then I thought perhaps someone had played me a trick. Oh no, I knew that this couldn't be. Only Mrs Donaldson had been in the dining-room, and only to dust, with me to help her. Jaimie had no chance to go there, not at all. I never used the dining-room now and had meals in the kitchen. But in fact I knew it wasn't them, it was Uncle. I wished with all my heart that I was a strong woman, as I had always felt I was, strong and sensible. I stood in the hall by the telephone, shaking. "O God, everlasting and almighty," I prayed, "make me strong and guide and lead me as to how Mrs Thatcher would conduct herself in circumstances of this nature."

I didn't sleep all night. I sat in the big kitchen stoking up the fire. Only once I moved, to go back into the dining-room and make sure that those words were there. Beyond a doubt they were, and in my uncle's handwriting – that handwriting it would take an expert forger to copy. I put the manuscript back in the drawer; I locked the dining-room door and took the key. My uncle's study, now absolutely empty, was above the kitchen. If he was haunting the house, I heard no sound from there or from anywhere else. It was a fearful night, waiting there by the fire.

Mrs Donaldson arrived in the morning, complaining that Jaimie was getting lazy; he wouldn't rise. Too many late nights.

"Where does he go after lunch?" I said.

"Oh, he goes for a round of golf after his dinner," she said. "He's always ready for a round of golf no matter what else there is to do. Golf is the curse of Scotland."

I had a good idea who Jaimie was meeting on the golf course, and I could almost have been grateful to Uncle for pointing out to me in that sly way of his that Jaimie wandered in the hours after the midday meal which we called lunch and they called their dinner. By five o'clock in the afternoon Jaimie would come here to the house to fetch up the coal, bank the fire, and so forth. But all afternoon he would be on the links with that girl who works at the manse, Greta, younger sister of Elaine, the one who moved in here openly, ruining my uncle's morals, leaving the house to rot. I always suspected that family. After Elaine died it came out he had even introduced her to all his friends; I could tell from the letters of condolence, how they said things like "He never got over the loss of Elaine" and "He couldn't live without her". And sometimes he called me Elaine by mistake. I was furious. Once, for example, I said, "Uncle, stop pacing about down here. Go up to your study and do your scribbling; I'll bring you a cup of cocoa." He said, with that glaze-eyed look he always had when he was interrupted in his thoughts, "What's come over you, Elaine?" I said, "I'm not Elaine, thank you very much." "Oh, of course," he said, "you are not Elaine, you are most certainly not her." If the public that read his books by the tens of thousands could have seen behind the scenes, I often wondered what they would have thought. I told him so many a time, but he smiled in that sly way, that smile he still had on his face when they found him fishing and stone dead.

After Mrs Donaldson left the house, at noon, I went up to my bedroom, half dropping from lack of sleep. Mrs Donaldson hadn't noticed anything; you could be falling down dead – they never look at you. I slept till four. It was still light. I got up and locked the doors, front and back. I pulled the curtains shut, and when Jaimie rang the bell at five o'clock I didn't open, I just let him ring. Eventually he went away. I expect he had plenty to wonder about. But I wasn't going to make him welcome before the fire and get him his supper, and take off my clothes there in the back room on the divan with him, in front of the television, while Uncle and Elaine were looking on, even though it is only Nature. No, I turned on the television for myself. You would never believe, it was a programme on the Scottish BBC about Uncle. I switched to TV One, and got a quiz show. And I felt hungry, for I'd eaten nothing since the night before.

But I couldn't face any supper until I had assured myself about that manuscript. I was fairly certain by now that it was a dream. "Maybe I've been overworking," I thought to myself. I had the key of the dining-room in my pocket and I took it and opened the door; I closed the curtains, and I went to the drawer and took out the notebook.

Not only were the words that I had read last night there, new words were added, a whole paragraph:

Look up the Acts of the Apostles, Chapter 5, verses 1 to 10. See what happened to Ananias and Sapphira his wife. You're not getting on very fast with your scribbling, are you, Susan? Elaine and I were under the impression you were going to write Chapter Eleven. Why don't you take a cup of cocoa and get on with it? First read Acts, V, 1–10.

– Your affec Uncle

Well, I shoved the book in the drawer and looked round the dining-room. I looked under the table and behind the curtains. It didn't look as if anything had been touched. I got out of the room and locked the door, I don't know how. I went to fetch my Bible, praying, "O God omnipotent and all-seeing direct and instruct me as to the way out of this situation, astonishing as it must appear to Thee." I looked up the passage:

But a certain man named Ananias, with Sapphira his wife, sold a possession.
And kept back part of the price, his wife also being privy to it, and brought
a certain part and laid it at the apostles' feet.
But Peter said, Ananias, why hath Satan filled thine heart to lie to the Holy
Ghost, and to keep back part of the land?

I didn't read any more because I knew how it went on. Ananias and Sapphira,
his wife, were both struck dead for holding back the portion of the sale for themselves. This was Uncle getting at me for holding back his manuscript from the
Foundation. That's an impudence, I thought, to make such a comparison from
the Bible, when he was an open and avowed sinner himself.

I thought it all over for a while. Then I went into the dining-room and got out
that last notebook. Something else had been written since I had put it away, not
half an hour before:

Why don't you get on with Chapter Eleven? We're waiting for it.

I tore out the page, put the book away and locked the door. I took the page to
the fire and put it on to burn. Then I went to bed.

This went on for a month. My uncle always started the page afresh with
"Chapter Eleven", followed by a new message. He even went so far as to put in
that I had kept back bits of the housekeeping money, although, he wrote, I was
well paid enough. That's a matter of opinion, and who did the economising, anyway? Always, after reading Uncle's disrespectful comments, I burned the page,
and we were getting near the end of the notebook. He would say things to show
he followed me round the house, and even knew my dreams. When I went into
Edinburgh for some shopping he knew exactly where I had been and what I'd
bought. He and Elaine listened in to my conversations on the telephone if I rang
up an old friend. I didn't let anyone in the house except Mrs Donaldson. No
more Jaimie. He even knew if I took a dose of salts and how long I had sat in the
bathroom, the awful old man.

Mrs Donaldson one morning said she was leaving. She said to me, "Why don't
you see a doctor?" I said, "Why?" But she wouldn't speak.

One day soon afterwards a man rang me up from the Foundation. They didn't
want to bother me, they said, but they were rather puzzled. They had found in
Uncle's letters many references to a novel. *The Witch of the Pentlands*, which he
had been writing just before his death; and they had found among the papers
a final chapter to this novel, which he had evidently written on loose pages on
a train, for a letter of his, kindly provided by one of his many correspondents,
proved this. Only they had no idea where the rest of the manuscript could be.
In the end the witch Edith is condemned to be burned, but dies of her own will
power before the execution, he said, but there must be ten more chapters leading
up to it. This was Uncle's most metaphysical work, and based on a true history,
the man said, and he must stress that it was very important.

I said that I would have a look. I rang back that afternoon and said I had
found the whole book in a drawer in the dining-room.

So the man came to get it. On the phone he sounded very suspicious, in case there were more manuscripts. "Are you sure that's everything? You know, the Foundation's price included the whole archive. No, don't trust it to the mail, I'll be there tomorrow at two."

Just before he arrived I took a good drink, whisky and soda, as, indeed, I had been taking from sheer need all the past month. I had brought out the notebooks. On the blank page was written:

Goodbye, Susan. It's lovely being a speck in the distance.

Your affec Uncle

THE SMALLEST WOMAN IN THE WORLD

Clarice Lispector

Like Joseph Conrad, the great Brazilian author **Clarice Lispector** (1920–1977) was born in Ukraine. Her family fled to Romania and then Brazil. Her first novel, *Near to the Wildheart,* was published when she was twenty-three. She married a diplomat, unhappily, and lived in the UK, Italy, Switzerland and the USA before returning to Brazil. She burned herself badly after falling asleep smoking a cigarette. Colm Tóibín said of her "Lispector had an ability to write as though no one had ever written before."

In the depths of Equatorial Africa the French explorer, Marcel Pretre, hunter and man of the world, came across a tribe of surprisingly small pygmies. Therefore he was even more surprised when he was informed that a still smaller people existed, beyond forests and distances. So he plunged farther on.

In the Eastern Congo, near Lake Kivu, he really did discover the smallest pygmies in the world. And – like a box within a box within a box – obedient, perhaps, to the necessity nature sometimes feels of outdoing herself – among the smallest pygmies in the world there was the smallest of the smallest pygmies in the world.

Among mosquitoes and lukewarm trees, among leaves of the most rich and lazy green, Marcel Pretre found himself facing a woman seventeen and three-quarter inches high, full-grown, black, silent – "Black as a monkey," he informed the press – who lived in a treetop with her little spouse. In the tepid miasma of the jungle, that swells the fruits so early and gives them an almost intolerable sweetness, she was pregnant.

So there she stood, the smallest woman in the world. For an instant, in the buzzing heat, it seemed as if the Frenchman had unexpectedly reached his final destination. Probably only because he was not insane, his soul neither wavered nor broke its bounds. Feeling an immediate necessity for order and for giving names to what exists, he called her Little Flower. And in order to be able to classify her among the recognizable realities, he immediately began to collect facts about her.

Her race will soon be exterminated. Few examples are left of this species, which, if it were not for the sly dangers of Africa, might have multiplied. Besides disease, the deadly effluvium of the water, insufficient food, and ranging beasts, the great threat to the Likoualas are the savage Bahundes, a threat that surrounds them in the silent air, like the dawn of battle. The Bahundes hunt them with nets, like monkeys. And eat them. Like that: they catch them in nets and *eat* them. The tiny race, retreating, always re-treating, has finished hiding away in the heart of Africa, where the lucky explorer discovered it. For strategic defense, they live in the highest trees. The women descend to grind and cook corn and to gather greens; the men, to hunt. When a child is born, it is left free almost immediately. It is true that, what with the beasts, the child frequently cannot enjoy this freedom for very long. But then it is true that it cannot be lamented that for such a short life there had been any long, hard work. And even the language that the child learns is short and simple, merely the essentials. The Likoualas use few names; they name things by gestures and animal noises. As for things of the spirit, they have a drum. While they dance to the sound of the drum, a little male stands guard against the Bahundes, who come from no one knows where.

That was the way, then, that the explorer discovered, standing at his very feet, the smallest existing human thing. His heart beat, because no emerald in the world is so rare. The teachings of the wise men of India are not so rare. The richest man in the world has never set eyes on such strange grace. Right there was a woman that the greed of the most exquisite dream could never have imagined. It was then that the explorer said timidly, and with a delicacy of feeling of which his wife would never have thought him capable: "You are Little Flower."

At that moment, Little Flower scratched herself where no one scratches. The explorer – as if he were receiving the highest prize for chastity to which an idealistic man dares aspire – the explorer, experienced as he was, looked the other way.

A photograph of Little Flower was published in the colored supplement of the Sunday papers, life-size. She was wrapped in a cloth, her belly already very big. The flat nose, the black face, the splay feet. She looked like a dog.

On that Sunday, in an apartment, a woman seeing the picture of Little Flower in the paper didn't want to look a second time because "It gives me the creeps."

In another apartment, a lady felt such perverse tenderness for the smallest of the African women that – an ounce of prevention being worth a pound of cure – Little Flower could never be left alone to the tenderness of that lady. Who knows to what murkiness of love tenderness can lead? The woman was upset all day, almost as if she were missing something. Besides, it was spring and there was a dangerous leniency in the air.

In another house, a little girl of five, seeing the picture and hearing the comments, was extremely surprised. In a houseful of adults, this little girl had been the smallest human being up until now. And, if this was the source of all caresses, it was also the source of the first fear of the tyranny of love. The existence of Little Flower made the little girl feel – with a deep uneasiness that only years and years later, and for very different reasons, would turn into thought – made her feel, in her first wisdom, that "sorrow is endless."

In another house, in the consecration of spring, a girl about to be married felt an ecstasy of pity: "Mama, look at her little picture, poor little thing! Just look how sad she is!"

"But," said the mother, hard and defeated and proud, "it's the sadness of an animal. It isn't human sadness."

"Oh, Mama!" said the girl, discouraged.

In another house, a clever little boy had a clever idea: "Mummy, if I could put this little woman from Africa in little Paul's bed when he's asleep? When he woke up wouldn't he be frightened? Wouldn't he howl? When he saw her sitting on his bed? And then we'd play with her! She would be our toy!"

His mother was setting her hair in front of the bathroom mirror at the moment, and she remembered what a cook had told her about life in an orphanage. The orphans had no dolls, and, with terrible maternity already throbbing in their hearts, the little girls had hidden the death of one of the children from the nun. They kept the body in a cupboard and when the nun went out they played with the dead child, giving her baths and things to eat, punishing her only to be able to kiss and console her. In the bathroom, the mother remembered this, and let fall her thoughtful hands, full of curlers. She considered the cruel necessity of loving. And she considered the malignity of our desire for happiness. She considered how ferociously we need to play. How many times we will kill for love. Then she looked at her clever child as if she were looking at a dangerous stranger. And she had a horror of her own soul that, more than her body, had engendered that being, adept at life and happiness. She looked at him attentively and with uncomfortable pride, that child who had already lost two front teeth, evolution evolving itself, teeth falling out to give place to those that could bite better. "I'm going to buy him a new suit," she decided, looking at him, absorbed. Obstinately, she adorned her gap-toothed son with fine clothes; obstinately, she wanted him very clean, as if his cleanliness could emphasize a soothing superficiality, obstinately perfecting the polite side of beauty. Obstinately drawing away from, and drawing him away from, something that ought to be "black as a monkey." Then, looking in the bathroom mirror, the mother gave a deliberately refined and social smile, placing a distance of insuperable millenniums between the abstract lines of her features and the crude face of Little Flower. But, with years of practice, she knew that this was going to be a Sunday on which she would have to hide from herself anxiety, dreams, and lost millenniums.

In another house, they gave themselves up to the enthralling task of measuring the seventeen and three-quarter inches of Little Flower against the wall. And, really, it was a delightful surprise: she was even smaller than the sharpest imagination could have pictured. In the heart of each member of the family was born, nostalgic, the desire to have that tiny and indomitable thing for itself, that thing spared having been eaten, that permanent source of charity. The avid family soul wanted to devote itself. To tell the truth, who hasn't wanted to own a human being just for himself? Which, it is true, wouldn't always be convenient; there are times when one doesn't want to have feelings.

"I bet if she lived here it would end in a fight," said the father, sitting in the armchair and definitely turning the page of the newspaper. "In this house everything ends in a fight."

"Oh, you, José – always a pessimist," said the mother.

"But, Mama, have you thought of the size her baby's going to be?" said the oldest little girl, aged thirteen, eagerly.

The father stirred uneasily behind his paper.

"It should be the smallest black baby in the world," the mother answered, melting with pleasure. "Imagine her serving our table, with her big little belly!"

"That's enough!" growled father.

"But you have to admit," said the mother, unexpectedly offended, "that it is something very rare. You're the insensitive one."

And the rare thing itself?

In the meanwhile, in Africa, the rare thing herself, in her heart – and who knows if the heart wasn't black, too, since once nature has erred she can no longer be trusted – the rare thing herself had something even rarer in her heart, like the secret of her own secret: a minimal child. Methodically, the explorer studied the little belly of the smallest mature human being. It was at this moment that the explorer, for the first time since he had known her, instead of feeling curiosity, or exhaltation, or victory, or the scientific spirit, felt sick.

The smallest woman in the world was laughing.

She was laughing, warm, warm – Little Flower was enjoying life. The rare thing herself was experiencing the ineffable sensation of not having been eaten yet. Not having been eaten yet was something that at any other time would have given her the agile impulse to jump from branch to branch. But, in this moment of tranquility, amid the thick leaves of the Eastern Congo, she was not putting this impulse into action – it was entirely concentrated in the smallness of the rare thing itself. So she was laughing. It was a laugh such as only one who does not speak laughs. It was a laugh that the explorer, constrained, couldn't classify. And she kept on enjoying her own soft laugh, she who wasn't being devoured. Not to be devoured is the most perfect feeling. Not to be devoured is the secret goal of a whole life. While she was not being eaten, her bestial laughter was as delicate as joy is delicate. The explorer was baffled.

In the second place, if the rare thing herself was laughing, it was because, within her smallness, a great darkness had begun to move.

The rare thing herself felt in her breast a warmth that might be called love. She loved that sallow explorer. If she could have talked and had told him that she loved him, he would have been puffed up with vanity. Vanity that would have collapsed when she added that she also loved the explorer's ring very much, and the explorer's boots. And when that collapse had taken place, Little Flower would not have understood why. Because her love for the explorer – one might even say "profound love," since, having no other resources, she was reduced to profundity – her profound love for the explorer would not have been at all diminished by the fact that she also loved his boots. There is an old misunderstanding about the word love, and, if many children are born from this misunderstanding, many others have lost the unique chance of being born, only because of a susceptibility that demands that it be me! me! that is loved, and not my money. But in the humidity of the forest these cruel refinements do not exist, and love is not to be eaten, love is to find a boot pretty, love is to like the strange color of a man who isn't black, love is to laugh for love of a shiny ring. Little Flower blinked with love, and laughed warmly, small, gravid, warm.

The explorer tried to smile back, without knowing exactly to what abyss his smile responded, and then he was embarrassed as only a very big man can be embarrassed. He pretended to adjust his explorer's hat better; he colored, prudishly. He turned a lovely color, a greenish-pink, like a lime at sunrise. He was undoubtedly sour.

Perhaps adjusting the symbolic helmet helped the explorer to get control of himself, severely recapture the discipline of his work, and go on with his note-taking. He had learned how to understand some of the tribe's few articulate words, and to interpret their signs. By now, he could ask questions.

Little Flower answered "Yes." That it was very nice to have a tree of her own to live in. Because – she didn't say this but her eyes became so dark that they said it – because it is good to own, good to own, good to own. The explorer winked several times.

Marcel Pretre had some difficult moments with himself. But at least he kept busy taking notes. Those who didn't take notes had to manage as best they could:

"Well," suddenly declared one old lady, folding up the newspaper decisively, "well, as I always say: God knows what He's doing."

THE WEDDING RING

Mavis Gallant

Mavis Gallant (1922–2014) was born in Montreal but left Canada for Europe and lived most of her life in Paris, where she died. She wrote a number of novels, *Green Water, Green Sky* and *A Fairly Good Time*, and many stories, most of which appeared first in *The New Yorker*. Her advice to any author was simple, and brief: "Read Chekhov." She refused to analyze her own work saying, "I want a story to be perfectly clear and I don't want it to be boring. *C'est tout.*"

On my windowsill is a pack of cards, a bell, a dog's brush, a book about a girl named Jewel who is a Christian Scientist and won't let anyone take her temperature, and a white jug holding field flowers. The water in the jug has evaporated; the sand-and-amber flowers seem made of paper. The weather bulletin for the day can be one of several: No sun. A high arched yellow sky. Or, creamy clouds, stillness. Long motionless grass. The earth soaks up the sun. Or, the sky is higher than it ever will seem again, and the sun far away and small.

From the window, a field full of goldenrod, then woods; to the left as you stand at the front door of the cottage, the mountains of Vermont.

The screen door slams and shakes my bed. That was my cousin. The couch with the India print spread in the next room has been made up for him. He is the only boy cousin I have, and the only American relation my age. We expected him to be homesick for Boston. When he disappeared the first day, we thought we would find him crying with his head in the wild cucumber vine; but all he was doing was making the outhouse tidy, dragging out of it last year's magazines. He discovers a towel abandoned under his bed by another guest, and shows it to each of us. He has unpacked a trumpet, a hatchet, a pistol, and a water bottle. He is ready for anything except my mother, who scares him to death.

My mother is a vixen. Everyone who sees her that summer will remember, later, the gold of her eyes and the lovely movement of her head. Her hair is true russet. She has the bloom women have sometimes when they are pregnant or when they have fallen in love. She can be wild, bitter, complaining, and ugly as a witch, but that summer is her peak. She has fallen in love.

My father is – I suppose – in Montreal. The guest who seems to have replaced him except in authority over me (he is still careful, still courts my favor) drives us to a movie. It is a musical full of monstrously large people. My cousin sits intent, bites his nails, chews a slingshot during the love scenes. He suddenly dives down in the dark to look for lost, mysterious objects. He has seen so many movies that this one is nearly over before he can be certain he has seen it before. He always knows what is going to happen and what they are going to say next.

At night we hear the radio – disembodied voices in a competition, identifying tunes. My mother, in the living room, seen from my bed, plays solitaire and says from time to time, "That's an old song I like," and "When you play solitaire, do you turn out two cards or three?" My cousin is not asleep either; he stirs on his couch. He shares his room with the guest. Years later we will be astonished to realize how young the guest must have been – twenty-three, perhaps twenty-four. My cousin, in his memories, shared a room with a middle-aged man. My mother and I, for the first and last time, ever, sleep in the same bed. I see her turning out the cards, smoking, drinking cold coffee from a breakfast cup. The single light on the table throws the room against the black window. My cousin and I each have an extra blanket. We forget how the evening sun blinded us at suppertime – how we gasped for breath.

My mother remarks on my hair, my height, my teeth, my French, and what I like to eat, as if she had never seen me before. Together, we wash our hair in the stream. The stones at the bottom are the color of trout. There is a smell of fish and wildness as I kneel on a rock, as she does, and plunge my head in the water. Bubbles of soap dance in place, as if rooted, then the roots stretch and break. In a delirium of happiness I memorize ferns, moss, grass, seedpods. We sunbathe on camp cots dragged out in the long grass. The strands of wet hair on my neck are like melting icicles. Her "Never look straight at the sun" seems extravagantly concerned with my welfare. Through eyelashes I peep at the milky-blue sky. The sounds of this blissful moment are the radio from the house; my cousin opening a ginger-ale bottle; the stream, persistent as machinery. My mother, still taking extraordinary notice of me, says that while the sun bleaches her hair and makes it light and fine, dark hair (mine) turns ugly – "like a rusty old stove lid" – and should be covered up. I dart into the cottage and find a hat: a wide straw hat, belonging to an unknown summer. It is so large I have to hold it with a hand flat upon the crown. I may look funny with this hat on, but at least I shall never be like a rusty old stove lid. The cots are empty; my mother has gone. By mistake, she is walking away through the goldenrod with the guest, turned up from God knows where. They are walking as if they wish they were invisible, of course, but to me it is only a mistake, and I call and run and push my way between them. He would like to take my hand, or pretends he would like to, but I need my hand for the hat.

My mother is developing one of her favorite themes – her lack of roots. To give the story greater power, or because she really believes what she is saying at that moment, she gets rid of an extra parent: "I never felt I had any stake anywhere until my parents died and I had their graves. The graves were my only property. I felt I belonged somewhere."

Graves? What does she mean? My grandmother is still alive.

"That's so sad," he says.

"Don't you ever feel that way?"

He tries to match her tone. "Oh, I wouldn't care. I think everything was meant to be given away. Even a grave would be a tie. I'd pretend not to know where it was."

"My father and mother didn't get along, and that prevented me feeling close to any country," says my mother. This may be new to him, but, like my cousin at a musical comedy, I know it by heart, or something near it. "I was divorced from the landscape, as they were from each other. I was too taken up wondering what was going to happen next. The first country I loved was somewhere in the north of Germany. I went there with my mother. My father was dead and my mother was less tense and I was free of their troubles. That is the truth," she says, with some astonishment.

The sun drops, the surface of the leaves turns deep blue. My father lets a parcel fall on the kitchen table, for at the end of one of her long, shattering, analytical letters she has put "P.S. Please bring a four-pound roast and some sausages." Did the guest depart? He must have dissolved; he is no longer visible. To show that she is loyal, has no secrets, she will repeat every word that was said. But my father, now endlessly insomniac and vigilant, looks as if it were he who had secrets, who is keeping something back.

The children – hostages released – are no longer required. In any case, their beds are needed for Labor Day weekend. I am to spend six days with my cousin in Boston – a stay that will, in fact, be prolonged many months. My mother stands at the door of the cottage in nightgown and sweater, brown-faced, smiling. The tall field grass is gray with cold dew. The windows of the car are frosted with it. My father will put us on a train, in care of a conductor. Both my cousin and I are used to this.

"He and Jane are like sister and brother," she says – this of my cousin and me, who do not care for each other.

Uncut grass. I saw the ring fall into it, but I am told I did not – I was already in Boston. The weekend party, her chosen audience, watched her rise, without warning, from the wicker chair on the porch. An admirer of Russian novels, she would love to make an immediate, Russian gesture, but cannot. The porch is screened, so, to throw her wedding ring away, she must have walked a few steps to the door and *then* made her speech, and flung the ring into the twilight, in a great spinning arc. The others looked for it next day, discreetly, but it had disappeared. First it slipped under one of those sharp bluish stones, then a beetle moved it. It left its print on a cushion of moss after the first winter. No one else could have worn it. My mother's hands were small, like mine.

OLD FRIENDS

Shusaku Endo

Shusaku Endo (1923–1996) was born in Tokyo. He and his mother converted to Roman Catholicism after his parents' divorce. Endo won many awards – in the West, he is perhaps best known for his novels *Silence* and *Scandal*, as well as the collection of stories *Stained Glass Elegies*.

I had just returned from a wintry Poland and was still recovering from jet lag when I received an unexpected phone call from an old friend.

He was parish priest at a tiny church in Mikage, between Osaka and Kobe. Though he was three years younger than me, there was scarcely a hair left on his head. Come to think of it, when we were children, his father had shown up at church each Sunday with a shiny pate, too.

"Shū-chan!" He called me by the same familiar name he had used forty years before, when we had played catch together in the churchyard where red oleanders blossomed. I thought of his hairless head, and I found it amusing that this bald, fiftyish man was still squawking out "Shū-chan!"

"Shū-chan, I know you're awfully busy. But do you think you could come out here next Sunday? To tell the truth . . ."

To tell the truth, he was calling because it was going to be the twenty-fifth anniversary of his investiture as a priest. He wanted to have a little get-together with some of his old friends, and wondered if I could come.

"Who's going to be there?"

"Akira-san, and Koike Yat-chan, and Eitarō."

One after another he listed the names of friends I had not seen for many, many years. Ah, are they still alive? I mused. It was like standing on a hill at nightfall and looking down at a river twisting its way across a plain.

"Can you come?"

"Yes. I'll arrange it one way or another."

No matter how much trouble it took, I had to go for the sake of my old friend. If I missed this opportunity, I might never see him again. We had reached that age.

I booked reservations on a Saturday-afternoon flight. Into my tiny flight bag I stuffed the first book I came across on my shelf – a paperback collection of poems by Itō Shizuo.

Above the path the moorhen travels
There is no need for a fragrant morning breeze,
No need for lacy clouds

I opened the book on the packed airplane and read these opening lines. Slowly, placidly, I tasted the verses with my tongue. They were delicious.

The rays of the sun had grown faint when I arrived at Itami Airport. My old friend had come to meet me, bringing along a student in tow. He clutched his beret in his hand and said, "Thank you for coming."

His hairline had receded even further than when I had last seen him several years before, and drops of perspiration glistened on his scalp. I tried to remember what he had looked like as a child, but for the life of me I couldn't summon up an image of his face. I recalled that he had been a clumsy child and a poor catcher when we played ball, but life had utterly wiped away all other traces of his youth.

We were riding along the highway towards Kobe in a Corolla driven by the student when my old friend suddenly remembered something and said, "Say, listen. Father Bosch says he's going to come too."

"Father Bosch?"

"I'll bet you're eager to see him, Shū-chan. He was always giving you the devil, wasn't he?"

I was glad I had come. I hadn't seen Father Bosch for over thirty years. Just after the war ended, this French priest had been released from the concentration camp in Takatsuki, but I was already living in Tokyo by then.

What my old friend said was true. As a child, I had often been scolded by the French cleric, who was in his forties at the time and sported a beard. Once when we were playing baseball in the church courtyard, a ball I had hurled smashed a window in his rectory. He appeared with a red face like that of Chung K'uei the demon-killer and dragged me off by my ear. When my dog came bounding into the chapel in the middle of Mass and startled the congregation, he roared that I was not to come to church any more.

"It's been so long. How old is he now?"

"Seventy-two. His health has deteriorated a bit, so he's been recuperating at the monastery in Nigawa. But he's going to come."

"He's in bad health? What's the problem?"

"It's not any particular disease, but you know he was pretty badly treated by the MPs during the war. I suppose that's resurfaced now that he's getting along in years."

The highway we were racing along looked nothing like I remembered it. The tracks of the railway I had taken to school as a child had been torn out and replaced by a strip of scruffy bushes. The black-shingled houses that had lined both sides of the road were transformed into bowling alleys and service stations that basked in the afternoon sun.

I could still remember the day Father Bosch was taken away by the military police. I did not see it happen. I had just returned home from middle school, and two or three Catholic housewives were there, telling my mother all the horrifying details. Plainclothes police and MPs had stormed into the rectory without taking off their shoes, rifled through every drawer in the place, and then taken the Father away. The housewives chattered timorously among themselves, unable to believe the accusation that the priest was a spy.

In those days every foreigner was suspect. The police and the military authorities kept an even closer watch on Catholic priests. Later we learned that Father

Bosch had been arrested because of a camera and a photo album that he owned. They had come across a photograph of an airplane factory in his album.

From that day, Mass was no longer celebrated at the church. Even so, I heard that plainclothes detectives still came to survey the place from time to time. Rumours circulated that Father Bosch was being treated brutally by the military police. But we knew nothing of what was really going on.

The church in my old friend's parish at Mikage was hardly an imposing structure. On a plot of land barely sixteen hundred square metres stood the tiny church, the wooden rectory and a nursery school. While he made some phone calls, I watched absently as some children tossed a ball back and forth in the school playground.

One bespectacled boy was having trouble catching the balls flung at him by a chubby little fellow. His awkwardness made me think of my own youth. It had taken me until I was this old to realize that, at some time or other in their lives, people all taste the same sorrows and trials. Who could say that this boy was not experiencing the same grief I had felt forty years before?

My friend finished his work and came in to say, "Everyone should be arriving between 5.40 and six o'clock. Do you want to wait here, or would you rather go into the chapel?"

To mark his anniversary, he was planning to celebrate Mass at six o'clock for his childhood friends who had been good enough to attend.

I entered the chapel alone and sat down. Two kerosene stoves had been placed in the aisle separating the men's pews from the women's; their blue flames flickered, but the chapel was still icy cold.

While I waited for the others to arrive, I thought about Father Bosch. It was now some thirty years since the end of the war, but he had remained here in Japan, labouring in the churches at Akashi and Kakogawa. He never thought of abandoning the people who had inflicted such cruel tortures upon him. Undoubtedly one day his bones would be laid to rest in this land.

These thoughts were prompted by the experiences I had had in Poland just two weeks earlier. A powdery snow had swirled through the sky over Warsaw each day, and at dusk a grey mist had enveloped the round domes of the churches and the squares gloomily overlooking the gates at the triumphal arch. People wearing fur caps shivered as they walked like livestock past the denuded trees in the squares. That dark, desolate vista had reminded me of the war, and in truth the scars of war were in evidence everywhere in that country. While I was in Poland I met a number of men and women who had survived the living hells at Auschwitz and Dachau. They rarely touched on their memories of those days, but there was one woman who rolled back the sleeve of her dress and showed me the convict number tattooed on her arm. "This is what it was like," she muttered sadly. The four digits clung to her slender forearm like ink stains. "Now perhaps you will understand."

As a child, she told me, she had spent a year in the Auschwitz camp. With the innocent eyes of youth she had looked on day after day as scores of her fellow prisoners were beaten, kicked, lynched, and slaughtered in the gas chambers.

"I am a Catholic, and I know I am supposed to forgive others . . . But I have no desire to forgive them."

Her eyes were riveted on mine as she spoke. Her breath reeked of onions.

"Never?"

"I doubt if I will ever forgive them."

Her despairing sigh echoed in my ears throughout my stay in Poland.

As I rubbed my hands together and waited in the unyielding pew for my old friend to celebrate the six o'clock Mass, I heard those words ringing in my ears once again. I could even smell the onions that fouled her breath.

Who is to say that Father Bosch doesn't feel the same way? I thought. Perhaps within the very depths of his heart there is one ineffaceable spot that will never be able to forgive the Japanese who flogged and trampled and tortured him.

Behind me the door to the chapel squeaked open. The sound of hesitant foot-steps followed. I turned and saw three men standing with their overcoats over their arms. I had not seen them for many years, but I knew at a glance that they were Akira-san, Koike Yat-chan, and Eitarō. Layers of life and labour and age had piled up like dust on their youthful faces, too. Yat-chan saw me, raised a hand in greeting, and pointed me out to his companions. We merely exchanged glances; then they seated themselves in the cold chapel, where we maintained a respectful silence.

Our old friend appeared, dressed in his Mass vestments and reverently carry-ing the chalice swathed in a white cloth. At the altar decorated with two lighted candles, he began to intone the Mass. The chapel was silent, with just four of us in attendance, and the only other sound was an occasional cough from Akira-san.

Half-way through the Mass, where normally on the Sabbath he would deliver a sermon, our old friend blessed us with the sign of the cross and said:

"Thank you all very much. It is a great joy for me to be able to celebrate Mass for friends who once played in the same churchyard with me. Now twenty-five years have passed since I became a priest." His salutation was spoken in standard Tokyo speech laced with a bit of the Osaka dialect.

"I am the only one of our group who joined the priesthood, but I have contin-ued to pray for the welfare of each one of you."

There were footsteps at the rear of the chapel; slowly, quietly they made their way forward, determined not to interrupt the priest's remarks. From the sound I visualized a bent old man. Father Bosch slipped into a seat at the front of the chapel and brought his palms together. His short-cropped hair was virtually white, and the shadows of physical debilitation and the loneliness of life were etched on his slender back. As I looked at his back, it occurred to me that shortly this priest would die here in Japan.

Sushi was served in the rectory dining-room. We clustered around Father Bosch, drinking beer and watered-down whisky. Both Yat-chan, now the manager of an auto-parts factory, and Akira-san, a pharmacist, were flushed red with liquor, and they related one tale after another from their youthful days.

"Father. Shū-chan was really rotten, wasn't he?" Yat-chan called to Father Bosch. "Do you remember when he shinnied up the church steeple and pissed from up there?"

"Yes, I remember." He smiled in my direction and said, "I did have to repri-mand you a lot."

"I was scared to death of you, Father."

"I would have had a mess on my hands if I'd let you go unchastened. As it was, I received a lot of complaints from the Women's Society. I really would have been in trouble if I hadn't scolded you."

"Shū-chan was definitely on the black list with those old ladies of the Women's Society. We never thought he'd turn out to be a novelist."

"I'm sure you didn't," I grinned sardonically. "I never dreamed I'd end up this way, either."

Father Bosch took only a sip or two of beer and swallowed down a few pieces of sushi. He had lived in Japan for many years, but there was still a trace of awkwardness in the way he used his chopsticks.

The kerosene stove warmed the room with a soft, tranquil blue flame. From the depths of my memory, the faces of each of the parishioners who had once come to church on Sundays, at Easter, and at Christmas, floated up. These were faces I had forgotten for a long while.

As I drank down my umpteenth glass of diluted whisky, I remarked, "There was that university student named Komaki – do you remember? What's he doing these days? He used to play with us sometimes."

"Didn't you hear?" my old friend responded. "He was killed in the war."

I had heard nothing about it, since I had moved to Tokyo just after the defeat.

"Yamazaki and Kurita's father were killed too."

"I knew about them."

"The war was a terrible time," Yat-chan muttered, staring at the rim of his glass. "Just because we were Christians, they called us traitors and enemies at school and threw stones at us to torment us."

There was silence for a moment.

Then suddenly everyone's eyes turned towards Father Bosch. We had indeed been persecuted, but he alone had been subjected to torture.

For just an instant, a look of confusion and embarrassment flashed across his face. Then he forced a smile for our benefit. To me it looked like a smile filled with pain. I thought of the oniony breath of the Polish woman when she had said, "I doubt if I will ever forgive them."

Someone asked, "Are you tired, Father?"

"No, I'm fine," he mumbled, his eyes fixed on the floor. "I only feel pain in the winter when it is cold. When spring comes, I am fine again. That is the way it always is."

A GOOD MAN IS HARD TO FIND

Flannery O'Connor

There is no cure for lupus, a disease that mercilessly attacks the body's auto-connective tissue, which is why the great American short story writer **Flannery O'Connor** (1925–1964) died aged thirty-nine. The only child of a Roman Catholic estate agent, from whom she inherited the disease, she studied at the Iowa Writer's Workshop where she began writing the novel *Wise Blood,* shortly after being diagnosed. She wrote thirty-two stories and one other novel, *The Violent Bear It Away. The Complete Stories* won the National Book Award in the USA eight years after her death, a volume later named the "Best of the National Book Awards" in 2009. She wrote of the story "I find most people know what a story is until they sit down to write one."

The grandmother didn't want to go to Florida. She wanted to visit some of her connections in east Tennessee and she was seizing at every chance to change Bailey's mind. Bailey was the son she lived with, her only boy. He was sitting on the edge of his chair at the table, bent over the orange sports section of the Journal. "Now look here, Bailey," she said, "see here, read this," and she stood with one hand on her thin hip and the other rattling the newspaper at his bald head. "Here this fellow that calls himself The Misfit is aloose from the Federal Pen and headed toward Florida and you read here what it says he did to these people. Just you read it. I wouldn't take my children in any direction with a criminal like that aloose in it. I couldn't answer to my conscience if I did."

Bailey didn't look up from his reading so she wheeled around then and faced the children's mother, a young woman in slacks, whose face was as broad and innocent as a cabbage and was tied around with a green head-kerchief that had two points on the top like rabbit's ears. She was sitting on the sofa, feeding the baby his apricots out of a jar. "The children have been to Florida before," the old lady said. "You all ought to take them somewhere else for a change so they would see different parts of the world and be broad. They never have been to east Tennessee."

The children's mother didn't seem to hear her but the eight-year-old boy, John Wesley, a stocky child with glasses, said, "If you don't want to go to Florida, why dontcha stay at home?" He and the little girl, June Star, were reading the funny papers on the floor.

"She wouldn't stay at home to be queen for a day," June Star said without raising her yellow head.

"Yes and what would you do if this fellow, The Misfit, caught you?" the grandmother asked.

"I'd smack his face," John Wesley said.

"She wouldn't stay at home for a million bucks," June Star said. "Afraid she'd miss something. She has to go everywhere we go."

"All right, Miss," the grandmother said. "Just re- member that the next time you want me to curl your hair."

June Star said her hair was naturally curly.

The next morning the grandmother was the first one in the car, ready to go. She had her big black valise that looked like the head of a hippopotamus in one corner, and underneath it she was hiding a basket with Pitty Sing, the cat, in it. She didn't intend for the cat to be left alone in the house for three days because he would miss her too much and she was afraid he might brush against one of her gas burners and accidentally asphyxiate himself. Her son, Bailey, didn't like to arrive at a motel with a cat.

She sat in the middle of the back seat with John Wesley and June Star on either side of her. Bailey and the children's mother and the baby sat in front and they left Atlanta at eight forty-five with the mileage on the car at 55890. The grandmother wrote this down because she thought it would be interesting to say how many miles they had been when they got back. It took them twenty minutes to reach the outskirts of the city.

The old lady settled herself comfortably, removing her white cotton gloves and putting them up with her purse on the shelf in front of the back window. The children's mother still had on slacks and still had her head tied up in a green kerchief, but the grandmother had on a navy blue straw sailor hat with a bunch of white violets on the brim and a navy blue dress with a small white dot in the print. Her collars and cuffs were white organdy trimmed with lace and at her neckline she had pinned a purple spray of cloth violets containing a sachet. In case of an accident, anyone seeing her dead on the highway would know at once that she was a lady.

She said she thought it was going to be a good day for driving, neither too hot nor too cold, and she cautioned Bailey that the speed limit was fifty-five miles an hour and that the patrolmen hid themselves behind billboards and small clumps of trees and sped out after you before you had a chance to slow down. She pointed out interesting details of the scenery: Stone Mountain; the blue granite that in some places came up to both sides of the highway; the brilliant red clay banks slightly streaked with purple; and the various crops that made rows of green lace-work on the ground. The trees were full of silver-white sunlight and the meanest of them sparkled. The children were reading comic magazines and their mother and gone back to sleep.

"Let's go through Georgia fast so we won't have to look at it much," John Wesley said.

"If I were a little boy," said the grandmother, "I wouldn't talk about my native state that way. Tennessee has the mountains and Georgia has the hills."

"Tennessee is just a hillbilly dumping ground," John Wesley said, "and Georgia is a lousy state too."

"You said it," June Star said.

"In my time," said the grandmother, folding her thin veined fingers, "children were more respectful of their native states and their parents and everything else. People did right then. Oh look at the cute little pickaninny!" she said and pointed to a Negro child standing in the door of a shack. "Wouldn't that make a picture, now?" she asked and they all turned and looked at the little Negro out of the back window. He waved

"He didn't have any britches on," June Star said.

"He probably didn't have any," the grandmother explained. "Little riggers in the country don't have things like we do. If I could paint, I'd paint that picture," she said.

The children exchanged comic books.

The grandmother offered to hold the baby and the children's mother passed him over the front seat to her. She set him on her knee and bounced him and told him about the things they were passing. She rolled her eyes and screwed up her mouth and stuck her leathery thin face into his smooth bland one. Occasionally he gave her a faraway smile. They passed a large cotton field with five or fix graves fenced in the middle of it, like a small island. "Look at the graveyard!" the grandmother said, pointing it out. "That was the old family burying ground. That belonged to the plantation."

"Where's the plantation?" John Wesley asked.

"Gone With the Wind" said the grandmother. "Ha. Ha."

When the children finished all the comic books they had brought, they opened the lunch and ate it. The grandmother ate a peanut butter sandwich and an olive and would not let the children throw the box and the paper napkins out the window. When there was nothing else to do they played a game by choosing a cloud and making the other two guess what shape it suggested. John Wesley took one the shape of a cow and June Star guessed a cow and John Wesley said, no, an automobile, and June Star said he didn't play fair, and they began to slap each other over the grandmother.

The grandmother said she would tell them a story if they would keep quiet. When she told a story, she rolled her eyes and waved her head and was very dramatic. She said once when she was a maiden lady she had been courted by a Mr. Edgar Atkins Teagarden from Jasper, Georgia. She said he was a very good-looking man and a gentleman and that he brought her a watermelon every Saturday afternoon with his initials cut in it, E. A. T. Well, one Saturday, she said, Mr. Teagarden brought the watermelon and there was nobody at home and he left it on the front porch and returned in his buggy to Jasper, but she never got the watermelon, she said, because a nigger boy ate it when he saw the initials, E. A. T. ! This story tickled John Wesley's funny bone and he giggled and giggled but June Star didn't think it was any good. She said she wouldn't marry a man that just brought her a watermelon on Saturday. The grandmother said she would have done well to marry Mr. Teagarden because he was a gentle man and had bought Coca-Cola stock when it first came out and that he had died only a few years ago, a very wealthy man.

They stopped at The Tower for barbecued sandwiches. The Tower was a part stucco and part wood filling station and dance hall set in a clearing outside of

Timothy. A fat man named Red Sammy Butts ran it and there were signs stuck here and there on the building and for miles up and down the highway saying, TRY RED SAMMY'S FAMOUS BARBECUE. NONE LIKE FAMOUS RED SAMMY'S! RED SAM! THE FAT BOY WITH THE HAPPY LAUGH. A VETERAN! RED SAMMY'S YOUR MAN!

Red Sammy was lying on the bare ground outside The Tower with his head under a truck while a gray monkey about a foot high, chained to a small chinaberry tree, chattered nearby. The monkey sprang back into the tree and got on the highest limb as soon as he saw the children jump out of the car and run toward him.

Inside, The Tower was a long dark room with a counter at one end and tables at the other and dancing space in the middle. They all sat down at a board table next to the nickelodeon and Red Sam's wife, a tall burnt-brown woman with hair and eyes lighter than her skin, came and took their order. The children's mother put a dime in the machine and played "The Tennessee Waltz," and the grandmother said that tune always made her want to dance. She asked Bailey if he would like to dance but he only glared at her. He didn't have a naturally sunny disposition like she did and trips made him nervous. The grandmother's brown eyes were very bright. She swayed her head from side to side and pretended she was dancing in her chair. June Star said play something she could tap to so the children's mother put in another dime and played a fast number and June Star stepped out onto the dance floor and did her tap routine.

"Ain't she cute?" Red Sam's wife said, leaning over the counter. "Would you like to come be my little girl?"

"No I certainly wouldn't," June Star said. "I wouldn't live in a broken-down place like this for a million bucks!" and she ran back to the table.

"Ain't she cute?" the woman repeated, stretching her mouth politely.

"Arn't you ashamed?" hissed the grandmother.

Red Sam came in and told his wife to quit lounging on the counter and hurry up with these people's order. His khaki trousers reached just to his hip bones and his stomach hung over them like a sack of meal swaying under his shirt. He came over and sat down at a table nearby and let out a combination sigh and yodel. "You can't win," he said. "You can't win," and he wiped his sweating red face off with a gray handkerchief. "These days you don't know who to trust," he said. "Ain't that the truth?"

"People are certainly not nice like they used to be," said the grandmother.

"Two fellers come in here last week," Red Sammy said, "driving a Chrysler. It was a old beat-up car but it was a good one and these boys looked all right to me. Said they worked at the mill and you know I let them fellers charge the gas they bought? Now why did I do that?"

"Because you're a good man!" the grandmother said at once.

"Yes'm, I suppose so," Red Sam said as if he were struck with this answer.

His wife brought the orders, carrying the five plates all at once without a tray, two in each hand and one balanced on her arm. "It isn't a soul in this green world of God's that you can trust," she said. "And I don't count nobody out of that, not nobody," she repeated, looking at Red Sammy.

"Did you read about that criminal, The Misfit, that's escaped?" asked the grandmother.

"I wouldn't be a bit surprised if he didn't attack this place right here," said the woman. "If he hears about it being here, I wouldn't be none surprised to see him. If he hears it's two cent in the cash register, I wouldn't be a tall surprised if he . . ."

"That'll do," Red Sam said. "Go bring these people their Co'-Colas," and the woman went off to get the rest of the order.

"A good man is hard to find," Red Sammy said. "Everything is getting terrible. I remember the day you could go off and leave your screen door unlatched. Not no more."

He and the grandmother discussed better times. The old lady said that in her opinion Europe was entirely to blame for the way things were now. She said the way Europe acted you would think we were made of money and Red Sam said it was no use talking about it, she was exactly right. The children ran outside into the white sunlight and looked at the monkey in the lacy chinaberry tree. He was busy catching fleas on himself and biting each one carefully between his teeth as if it were a delicacy.

They drove off again into the hot afternoon. The grandmother took cat naps and woke up every few minutes with her own snoring. Outside of Toombsboro she woke up and recalled an old plantation that she had visited in this neighborhood once when she was a young lady. She said the house had six white columns across the front and that there was an avenue of oaks leading up to it and two little wooden trellis arbors on either side in front where you sat down with your suitor after a stroll in the garden. She recalled exactly which road to turn off to get to it. She knew that Bailey would not be willing to lose any time looking at an old house, but the more she talked about it, the more she wanted to see it once again and find out if the little twin arbors were still standing. "There was a secret:-panel in this house," she said craftily, not telling the truth but wishing that she were, "and the story went that all the family silver was hidden in it when Sherman came through but it was never found . . ."

"Hey!" John Wesley said. "Let's go see it! We'll find it! We'll poke all the woodwork and find it! Who lives there? Where do you turn off at? Hey Pop, can't we turn off there?"

"We never have seen a house with a secret panel!" June Star shrieked. "Let's go to the house with the secret panel! Hey Pop, can't we go see the house with the secret panel!"

"It's not far from here, I know," the grandmother said. "It wouldn't take over twenty minutes."

Bailey was looking straight ahead. His jaw was as rigid as a horseshoe. "No," he said.

The children began to yell and scream that they wanted to see the house with the secret panel. John Wesley kicked the back of the front seat and June Star hung over her mother's shoulder and whined desperately into her ear that they never had any fun even on their vacation, that they could never do what THEY wanted to do. The baby began to scream and John Wesley kicked the back of the seat so hard that his father could feel the blows in his kidney.

"All right!" he shouted and drew the car to a stop at the side of the road. "Will you all shut up? Will you all just shut up for one second? If you don't shut up, we won't go anywhere."

"It would be very educational for them," the grandmother murmured.

"All right," Bailey said, "but get this: this is the only time we're going to stop for anything like this. This is the one and only time."

"The dirt road that you have to turn down is about a mile back," the grandmother directed. "I marked it when we passed."

"A dirt road," Bailey groaned.

After they had turned around and were headed toward the dirt road, the grandmother recalled other points about the house, the beautiful glass over the front doorway and the candle-lamp in the hall. John Wesley said that the secret panel was probably in the fireplace.

"You can't go inside this house," Bailey said. "You don't know who lives there."

"While you all talk to the people in front, I'll run around behind and get in a window," John Wesley suggested.

"We'll all stay in the car," his mother said.

They turned onto the dirt road and the car raced roughly along in a swirl of pink dust. The grandmother recalled the times when there were no paved roads and thirty miles was a day's journey. The dirt road was hilly and there were sudden washes in it and sharp curves on dangerous embankments. All at once they would be on a hill, looking down over the blue tops of trees for miles around, then the next minute, they would be in a red depression with the dust-coated trees looking down on them.

"This place had better turn up in a minute," Bailey said, "or I'm going to turn around."

The road looked as if no one had traveled on it in months.

"It's not much farther," the grandmother said and just as she said it, a horrible thought came to her. The thought was so embarrassing that she turned red in the face and her eyes dilated and her feet jumped up, upsetting her valise in the corner. The instant the valise moved, the newspaper top she had over the basket under it rose with a snarl and Pitty Sing, the cat, sprang onto Bailey's shoulder.

The children were thrown to the floor and their mother, clutching the baby, was thrown out the door onto the ground; the old lady was thrown into the front seat. The car turned over once and landed right-side-up in a gulch off the side of the road. Bailey remained in the driver's seat with the cat gray-striped with a broad white face and an orange nose clinging to his neck like a caterpillar.

As soon as the children saw they could move their arms and legs, they scrambled out of the car, shouting, "We've had an ACCIDENT!" The grandmother was curled up under the dashboard, hoping she was injured so that Bailey's wrath would not come down on her all at once. The horrible thought she had had before the accident was that the house she had remembered so vividly was not in Georgia but in Tennessee.

Bailey removed the cat from his neck with both hands and flung it out the window against the side of a pine tree. Then he got out of the car and started looking for the children's mother. She was sitting against the side of the red gutted ditch, holding the screaming baby, but she only had a cut down her face and a broken shoulder. "We've had an ACCIDENT!" the children screamed in a frenzy of delight.

"But nobody's killed," June Star said with disappointment as the grandmother limped out of the car, her hat still pinned to her head but the broken front brim standing up at a jaunty angle and the violet spray hanging off the side. They all sat down in the ditch, except the children, to recover from the shock. They were all shaking.

"Maybe a car will come along," said the children's mother hoarsely.

"I believe I have injured an organ," said the grandmother, pressing her side, but no one answered her. Bailey's teeth were clattering. He had on a yellow sport shirt with bright blue parrots designed in it and his face was as yellow as the shirt. The grandmother decided that she would not mention that the house was in Tennessee.

The road was about ten feet above and they could see only the tops of the trees on the other side of it. Behind the ditch they were sitting in there were more woods, tall and dark and deep. In a few minutes they saw a car some distance away on top of a hill, coming slowly as if the occupants were watching them. The grandmother stood up and waved both arms dramatically to attract their attention. The car continued to come on slowly, disappeared around a bend and appeared again, moving even slower, on top of the hill they had gone over. It was a big black battered hearselike automobile. There were three men in it.

It came to a stop just over them and for some minutes, the driver looked down with a steady expressionless gaze to where they were sitting, and didn't speak. Then he turned his head and muttered something to the other two and they got out. One was a fat boy in black trousers and a red sweat shirt with a silver stallion embossed on the front of it. He moved around on the right side of them and stood staring, his mouth partly open in a kind of loose grin. The other had on khaki pants and a blue striped coat and a gray hat pulled down very low, hiding most of his face. He came around slowly on the left side. Neither spoke.

The driver got out of the car and stood by the side of it, looking down at them. He was an older man than the other two. His hair was just beginning to gray and he wore silver-rimmed spectacles that gave him a scholarly look. He had a long creased face and didn't have on any shirt or undershirt. He had on blue jeans that were too tight for him and was holding a black hat and a gun. The two boys also had guns.

"We've had an ACCIDENT!" the children screamed.

The grandmother had the peculiar feeling that the bespectacled man was someone she knew. His face was as familiar to her as if she had known him all her life but she could not recall who he was. He moved away from the car and began to come down the embankment, placing his feet carefully so that he wouldn't slip. He had on tan and white shoes and no socks, and his ankles were red and thin. "Good afternoon," he said. "I see you all had you a little spill."

"We turned over twice!" said the grandmother.

"Once", he corrected. "We seen it happen. Try their car and see will it run, Hiram," he said quietly to the boy with the gray hat.

"What you got that gun for?" John Wesley asked. "Whatcha gonna do with that gun?"

"Lady," the man said to the children's mother, "would you mind calling them children to sit down by you? Children make me nervous. I want all you all to sit down right together there where you're at."

"What are you telling US what to do for?" June Star asked.

Behind them the line of woods gaped like a dark open mouth. "Come here," said their mother.

"Look here now," Bailey began suddenly, "we're in a predicament! We're in . . ."

The grandmother shrieked. She scrambled to her feet and stood staring. "You're The Misfit!" she said. "I recognized you at once!"

"Yes'm," the man said, smiling slightly as if he were pleased in spite of himself to be known, "but it would have been better for all of you, lady, if you hadn't of reckernized me."

Bailey turned his head sharply and said something to his mother that shocked even the children. The old lady began to cry and The Misfit reddened.

"Lady," he said, "don't you get upset. Sometimes a man says things he don't mean. I don't reckon he meant to talk to you thataway."

"You wouldn't shoot a lady, would you?" the grandmother said and removed a clean handkerchief from her cuff and began to slap at her eyes with it.

The Misfit pointed the toe of his shoe into the ground and made a little hole and then covered it up again. "I would hate to have to," he said.

"Listen," the grandmother almost screamed, "I know you're a good man. You don't look a bit like you have common blood. I know you must come from nice people!"

"Yes mam," he said, "finest people in the world." When he smiled he showed a row of strong white teeth. "God never made a finer woman than my mother and my daddy's heart was pure gold," he said. The boy with the red sweat shirt had come around behind them and was standing with his gun at his hip. The Misfit squatted down on the ground. "Watch them children, Bobby Lee," he said. "You know they make me nervous." He looked at the six of them huddled together in front of him and he seemed to be embarrassed as if he couldn't think of anything to say. "Ain't a cloud in the sky," he remarked, looking up at it. "Don't see no sun but don't see no cloud neither."

"Yes, it's a beautiful day," said the grandmother. "Listen," she said, "you shouldn't call yourself The Misfit because I know you're a good man at heart. I can just look at you and tell."

"Hush!" Bailey yelled. "Hush! Everybody shut up and let me handle this!" He was squatting in the position of a runner about to sprint forward but he didn't move.

"I pre-chate that, lady," The Misfit said and drew a little circle in the ground with the butt of his gun.

"It'll take a half a hour to fix this here car," Hiram called, looking over the raised hood of it.

"Well, first you and Bobby Lee get him and that little boy to step over yonder with you," The Misfit said, pointing to Bailey and John Wesley. "The boys want to ast you something," he said to Bailey. "Would you mind stepping back in them woods there with them?"

"Listen," Bailey began, "we're in a terrible predicament! Nobody realizes what this is," and his voice cracked. His eyes were as blue and intense as the parrots in his shirt and he remained perfectly still.

The grandmother reached up to adjust her hat brim as if she were going to the woods with him but it came off in her hand. She stood staring at it and after a second she let it fall on the ground. Hiram pulled Bailey up by the arm as if he were assisting an old man. John Wesley caught hold of his father's hand and Bobby Lee followed. They went off toward the woods and just as they reached the dark edge, Bailey turned and supporting himself against a gray naked pine trunk, he shouted, "I'll be back in a minute, Mamma, wait on me!"

"Come back this instant!" his mother shrilled but they all disappeared into the woods.

"Bailey Boy!" the grandmother called in a tragic voice but she found she was looking at The Misfit squatting on the ground in front of her. "I just know you're a good man," she said desperately. "You're not a bit common!"

"Nome, I ain't a good man," The Misfit said after a second ah if he had considered her statement carefully, "but I ain't the worst in the world neither. My daddy said I was a different breed of dog from my brothers and sisters. 'You know,' Daddy said, 'it's some that can live their whole life out without asking about it and it's others has to know why it is, and this boy is one of the latters. He's going to be into everything!'" He put on his black hat and looked up suddenly and then away deep into the woods as if he were embarrassed again. "I'm sorry I don't have on a shirt before you ladies," he said, hunching his shoulders slightly. "We buried our clothes that we had on when we escaped and we're just making do until we can get better. We borrowed these from some folks we met," he explained.

"That's perfectly all right," the grandmother said. "Maybe Bailey has an extra shirt in his suitcase."

"I'll look and see terrectly," The Misfit said.

"Where are they taking him?" the children's mother screamed.

"Daddy was a card himself," The Misfit said. "You couldn't put anything over on him. He never got in trouble with the Authorities though. Just had the knack of handling them."

"You could be honest too if you'd only try," said the grandmother. "Think how wonderful it would be to settle down and live a comfortable life and not have to think about somebody chasing you all the time."

The Misfit kept scratching in the ground with the butt of his gun as if he were thinking about it. "Yestm, somebody is always after you," he murmured.

The grandmother noticed how thin his shoulder blades were just behind his hat because she was standing up looking down on him. "Do you every pray?" she asked.

He shook his head. All she saw was the black hat wiggle between his shoulder blades. "Nome," he said.

There was a pistol shot from the woods, followed closely by another. Then silence. The old lady's head jerked around. She could hear the wind move through the tree tops like a long satisfied insuck of breath. "Bailey Boy!" she called.

"I was a gospel singer for a while," The Misfit said. "I been most everything. Been in the arm service both land and sea, at home and abroad, been twict married, been an undertaker, been with the railroads, plowed Mother Earth, been in a tornado, seen a man burnt alive oncet," and he looked up at the children's mother and the little girl who were sitting close together, their faces white and their eyes glassy; "I even seen a woman flogged," he said.

"Pray, pray," the grandmother began, "pray, pray . . ."

I never was a bad boy that I remember of," The Misfit said in an almost dreamy voice, "but somewheres along the line I done something wrong and got sent to the penitentiary. I was buried alive," and he looked up and held her attention to him by a steady stare.

"That's when you should have started to pray," she said. "What did you do to get sent to the penitentiary that first time?"

"Turn to the right, it was a wall," The Misfit said, looking up again at the cloudless sky. "Turn to the left, it was a wall. Look up it was a ceiling, look down it was a floor. I forget what I done, lady. I set there and set there, trying to remember what it was I done and I ain't recalled it to this day. Oncet in a while, I would think it was coming to me, but it never come."

"Maybe they put you in by mistake," the old lady said vaguely.

"Nome," he said. "It wasn't no mistake. They had the papers on me."

"You must have stolen something," she said.

The Misfit sneered slightly. "Nobody had nothing I wanted," he said. "It was a head-doctor at the penitentiary said what I had done was kill my daddy but I known that for a lie. My daddy died in nineteen ought nineteen of the epidemic flu and I never had a thing to do with it. He was buried in the Mount Hopewell Baptist churchyard and you can go there and see for yourself."

"If you would pray," the old lady said, "Jesus would help you."

"That's right," The Misfit said.

"Well then, why don't you pray?" she asked trembling with delight suddenly.

"I don't want no hep," he said. "I'm doing all right by myself."

Bobby Lee and Hiram came ambling back from the woods. Bobby Lee was dragging a yellow shirt with bright blue parrots in it.

"Thow me that shirt, Bobby Lee," The Misfit said. The shirt came flying at him and landed on his shoulder and he put it on. The grandmother couldn't name what the shirt reminded her of. "No, lady," The Misfit said while he was buttoning it up, "I found out the crime don't matter. You can do one thing or you can do another, kill a man or take a tire off his car, because sooner or later you're going to forget what it was you done and just be punished for it."

The children's mother had begun to make heaving noises as if she couldn't get her breath. "Lady," he asked, "would you and that little girl like to step off yonder with Bobby Lee and Hiram and join your husband?"

"Yes, thank you," the mother said faintly. Her left arm dangled helplessly and she was holding the baby, who had gone to sleep, in the other. "Hep that lady up, Hiram," The Misfit said as she struggled to climb out of the ditch, "and Bobby Lee, you hold onto that little girl's hand."

"I don't want to hold hands with him," June Star said. "He reminds me of a pig."

The fat boy blushed and laughed and caught her by the arm and pulled her off into the woods after Hiram and her mother.

Alone with The Misfit, the grandmother found that she had lost her voice. There was not a cloud in the sky nor any sun. There was nothing around her but woods. She wanted to tell him that he must pray. She opened and closed her mouth several times before anything came out. Finally she found herself saying, "Jesus. Jesus," meaning, Jesus will help you, but the way she was saying it, it sounded as if she might be cursing.

"Yes'm, The Misfit said as if he agreed. "Jesus shown everything off balance. It was the same case with Him as with me except He hadn't committed any crime and they could prove I had committed one because they had the papers on me. Of course," he said, "they never shown me my papers. That's why I sign myself now. I said long ago, you get you a signature and sign everything you do and keep a copy of it. Then you'll know what you done and you can hold up the crime to the punishment and see do they match and in the end you'll have something to prove you ain't been treated right. I call myself The Misfit," he said, "because I can't make what all I done wrong fit what all I gone through in punishment."

There was a piercing scream from the woods, followed closely by a pistol report. "Does it seem right to you, lady, that one is punished a heap and another ain't punished at all?"

"Jesus!" the old lady cried. "You've got good blood! I know you wouldn't shoot a lady! I know you come from nice people! Pray! Jesus, you ought not to shoot a lady. I'll give you all the money I've got!"

"Lady," The Misfit said, looking beyond her far into the woods, "there never was a body that give the undertaker a tip."

There were two more pistol reports and the grandmother raised her head like a parched old turkey hen crying for water and called, "Bailey Boy, Bailey Boy!" as if her heart would break.

"Jesus was the only One that ever raised the dead," The Misfit continued, "and He shouldn't have done it. He shown everything off balance. If He did what He said, then it's nothing for you to do but thow away everything and follow Him, and if He didn't, then it's nothing for you to do but enjoy the few minutes you got left the best way you can by killing somebody or burning down his house or doing some other meanness to him. No pleasure but meanness," he said and his voice had become almost a snarl.

"Maybe He didn't raise the dead," the old lady mumbled, not knowing what she was saying and feeling so dizzy that she sank down in the ditch with her legs twisted under her.

"I wasn't there so I can't say He didn't," The Misfit said. "I wisht I had of been there," he said, hitting the ground with his fist. "It ain't right I wasn't there because if I had of been there I would of known. Listen lady," he said in a high voice, "if I had of been there I would of known and I wouldn't be like I am now." His voice seemed about to crack and the grandmother's head cleared for an instant. She saw the man's face twisted close to her own as if he were going to cry and she murmured, "Why you're one of my babies. You're one of my own children !" She reached out and touched him on the shoulder. The Misfit sprang back as if a snake had bitten him and shot her three times through the chest. Then he put his gun down on the ground and took off his glasses and began to clean them.

Hiram and Bobby Lee returned from the woods and stood over the ditch, looking down at the grandmother who half sat and half lay in a puddle of blood with her legs crossed under her like a child's and her face smiling up at the cloud-less sky.

Without his glasses, The Misfit's eyes were red-rimmed and pale and defense-less-looking. "Take her off and thow her where you thown the others," he said, picking up the cat that was rubbing itself against his leg.

"She was a talker, wasn't she?" Bobby Lee said, sliding down the ditch with a yodel.

"She would of been a good woman," The Misfit said, "if it had been some-body there to shoot her every minute of her life."

"Some fun!" Bobby Lee said.

"Shut up, Bobby Lee," The Misfit said. "It's no real pleasure in life."

LIVE BAIT

Frank Tuohy

Frank Tuohy (1925–1999) is an astonishingly under-rated writer who left a perfectly formed backlist, now utterly out of print. Born in East Sussex, he worked as an academic for most of his life, often working abroad for the British Council, perhaps a reason for his being overlooked. His work in Poland inspired his first novel *The Ice Saints*. He won a number of awards, including the James Tait Black Memorial Prize, the Geoffrey Faber Memorial Prize and the E.M. Forster Award. He suffered a heart attack in Cyprus and returned to die in Somerset, having begun work on a novel. On his death Francis King, in the *Independent*, wrote "Even at his second best he was better than most of his contemporaries at their best."

I

You travel southward toward the channel shore: there are petrol stations at intervals, council estates, a builder's yard, a used-tire depot, industrialized farmland. In patches of woodland, signposts at the ends of drives point to special schools, private nursing homes. Some show the headquarters of dubious-sounding companies or institutes: the large ugly mansions resound with the rattle of typewriters and the slow scythe-like rhythms of photocopying machines.

Long ago a house like this would shelter a different life, a life which was undergone in heavily furnished drawing rooms, bathrooms where taps poured out scalding niagaras, kitchens where food was fiercely boiled on enormous ranges. In the dining room, the mahogany sideboard smelled of pepper and Harvey's sauce, and contained a blue-glass bottle of indigestion mixture: "The Hon. Mrs. Peverill, to be taken as required."

Even then, families were getting smaller, visitors from outside were fewer. Daughters and sons-in-law were likely to be in India, in Bermuda, in Hong Kong. Grandchildren appeared for school holidays, but for them there were fewer suitable friendships available – the wrong sort of child might quite easily get invited to a children's party.

Of two boys bicycling one morning to Braxby Place, one belonged to this category. Andrew, small for his age, which was thirteen, was snub-nosed, crooked, and guilty. Jeremy, his companion, was altogether easier to commend, a handsome boy with blond hair and a milky complexion. The Peverills were distant connections of his mother; this was sufficient to allow him to approach the house without apprehension.

The drive was nearly half a mile long. For the first part the boys rode between cliffs of rhododendrons and conifers, where it was still damp and chill in the early morning. Then they came out into parkland. Oaks and horse chestnuts stood at intervals, and between them there was the flash of water.

The lake, which must long ago have been a stone quarry, was hidden among woods and outcrops of rock. They lost sight of it again as the drive went uphill. Neither of the boys liked to be the first to get off and walk. Andrew's bike was a woman's, which belonged to his mother. He was careful to mount and dismount in the masculine fashion, even though this sometimes hurt. Standing upright on the pedals, he zigzagged to and fro, dodging away from the trimmed edges, until he got to the top of the slope. There he waited for Jeremy who, in spite of his low-curved handlebars and three-speed gear, was usually first to start walking. They saw pergolas covered with climbing roses, clumps of pampas grass, a mon- key-puzzle tree, and then the house, of glazed brick, turreted, and with mullioned windows. There was a line of plate-glass windows to a winter garden, where blinds were already pulled down against the morning sunlight.

"Shouldn't we go around to the back?" Andrew asked.

"Of course not." Jeremy pulled the bell handle. They were still a bit winded by the ascent, and against the noise of their breathing they could hear the bell ringing far away and then the muffled opening and closing of doors, the slow approach of heavy feet.

"I've come about fishing in the lake."

"Mr. Jeremy Cathcart is it, sir? Yes, we're expecting you." The butler turned a large, purplish face toward the other.

"I'm his friend."

The butler switched back to Jeremy: "Mrs. Peverill asked you to come up for tea at half past four, sir."

"Please thank her and say I'll come. By the way, which is the best way to the lake?"

The butler pointed out the path. "You can leave your bicycle in the stables."

"Thank you." Jeremy's voice to people like that was taut and high-pitched.

While Andrew listened he realized that, against the excitement of fishing in the lake, there would be the dull anxiety about what he should do at teatime. Should he bicycle home by himself, or slope off into the shrubbery and wait for Jeremy to emerge? He knew he was saddled with some intangible burden that people like Jeremy did not possess.

In the stable yard, the boys leaned their bicycles against a wall and unstrapped the rods and fishing bags. A man who had been hammering something came to a doorway and pointed the way down to the lake.

"Good luck," he said. "There's a big jack down there."

"How big?" Andrew asked.

"Must be all of twenty pounds."

Jeremy thanked the man in the same high voice he had used to the butler. He led the way down a cart track.

Andrew followed him. He felt deaf. Twenty pounds: the man's words had caused a sort of minor explosion in his head. Suddenly the sky was lower and the air had grown darker. The smell of crushed vegetation was strong and heavy, and some gilded flies were buzzing upward from a dead bird. The track went downhill sharply and under some beech trees it opened out at the shore of the lake. The big pike was waiting like something in time rather than place: it was a sort of dread, like the anticipation of being swished at school, or the holidays approaching their end, only there was wild pleasure in it as well.

A wooden jetty projected a few yards out, surrounded by water lily leaves. A moorhen took off suddenly, skittering over the leaves, and settled fretfully among some undergrowth.

Andrew put down his rod and bag and walked out along the jetty. Halfway along some of the boards were missing; he knelt down and could make out some small fish circling slowly in the shafts of light going down into deep water. He went on to the end of the jetty. The lake stretched for about two hundred yards, the surface mostly packed with water lily leaves. On the opposite side birch trees grew on a rocky outcrop; from a cave underneath you could just distinguish the prow of a rowboat sticking out. Nearer, a shoal of small fish flipped through the surface, followed by a broad gulping swirl of water. A pike was feeding, probably a small one. To get out there you would need stronger tackle than any they had with them; live bait and hooks with wire traces; and, most of all perhaps, the boat which lay in the cave across the lake.

A rattling sound distracted him: Jeremy was peeing into some dock leaves beside the path. Andrew went and unbuttoned beside him. He watched his steam rising off the leaves.

Jeremy shuddered and stopped. "We'll both have to fish off the jetty," he said.

"It looks jolly good," Andrew said. Impatience made him button up too quickly, so that the last drops trickled warm and sore on the inside of his thigh.

The gardener's news of the big pike forced him to keep a check on his eagerness. He would not be allowed to come here without Jeremy, and Jeremy could very easily get bored with him and with fishing in the lake. Later in the holidays, Jeremy would go to relations who lived in Ireland, where there'd be trout and salmon, and perhaps some rough shooting. The number of claims Andrew could make was limited; he was not even Jeremy's best friend at school.

When the hook was baited with a worm and the float sitting upright beyond the lily leaves, Andrew felt at ease in the continual mild excitement that came from fishing and from being alive. Of course there would always be a gulf of apprehension ahead. If he avoided thinking about what he would do this afternoon, while Jeremy was having tea at the house, then there was next term to think about, when he would sit the entrance scholarship to his Public School. It had been implied that, if he failed, he would be cast into some sort of outer darkness, and his mother would be disappointed and weep. Nobody had ever explained why this had to happen; why it was that Jeremy, for instance, should proceed to Harrow without trouble, having been put down for the school at his birth.

By mid-afternoon, he knew Jeremy was growing restive. They had caught four perch, and had eaten the sandwiches and fruit they had brought with them. The sun was straight ahead of them. A wood pigeon dived and soared in the empty air over the lake.

There was a splash nearby. "That was a pike," Jeremy said. "A monster pike."

Andrew opened his eyes and saw the core of Jeremy's apple floating in circles of water.

He was appalled at this breach of the conventions, but knew better than to protest.

"Let's explore around the other side," he suggested.

They fought their way through a thicket of rhododendrons, and emerged on to a path which led down to the boathouse. At the bottom of some steps, slippery with moss, there was an iron gate. The boat, with the oars shipped in it, could be seen just beyond it. The boys shook the gate, but it was locked.

"We need the key."

"I suppose I could ask them at the house," Jeremy said.

"Could you? That would be super."

Jeremy seemed less confident suddenly. "I could try."

The path went around the lake through two tunnels in the rock and ended up near the jetty. Coming back there was comforting, an arrival at a place already known.

"I must go up to tea," Jeremy said. "They'll be waiting for me."

II

Andrew lurked under some elders near a potting shed, where lawn mowers had been emptied through the years. He was used to lurking: there was a lot of time to waste at school or in the holidays, and there were other times when it was better to keep out of people's sight. He had a great experience of damp corners by broken sheds, of hollows full of bedsprings and buckets without bottoms, and of streams littered with empty tins. In such places he pondered the possibility of hiding himself completely, of keeping absolutely still, blending with the background, taking on a protective coloration like a bird or an animal. He tried this now for a time, but got bored; the only person to find him would be the friendly gardener who had told them about the big pike.

He picked up a dry elder twig and began digging into the pile of rotten grass cuttings. It was full of worms, the active ones with brown and yellow rings which are best for fishing. However, he had left his bait tin with the bicycles. He was wondering whether to go for it, which would have meant coming into view of the windows of the house, when he received a blow on his left shoulder.

He yelped, and turned around. It was Jeremy Cathcart.

"I've been told to fetch you. You're expected too."

Andrew wiped his hands on his trousers. "Jesus."

"Yes, come on." Jeremy jerked his head and led the way. Andrew followed him at an undignified stumble.

Andrew had never seen anybody quite so old as the small old woman who was sitting in a basket chair in the winter garden. Her white hair was drawn tightly back, and her hands and forehead were deeply spotted like a seagull's egg. She wore a dark gray dress with a lace front, and a circular cairngorm brooch on a black ribbon around her neck.

"Let me see him," Mrs. Peverill said. "He'll have to come closer."

He was accustomed to soft, smiling old women who doted and said silly things. This one, however, looked at him without apparent friendliness.

"Yer Jeremy's friend?"

"Yes, that's right."

"What's yer father do?"

"He's in the Air Force. In Egypt."

"That used not to be well thought of, as a career."

The man standing beside her said: "That would hardly enter into it, Mother."

The man, who looked very nearly as old as Mrs. Peverill herself, smiled broadly at Andrew, who smiled back with an attempt at confidence.

"They had better sit down," Mrs. Peverill said. "Get me a cup of tea," she added to her son.

Major Peverill walked across to the table. He was a tall old man, wearing a gray tweed knickerbocker suit, with ribbed stockings and garter-tabs. The back of his neck was wispy, with a smile of flesh above the collar.

"Tea for them too."

"What's happened to Burgess?"

"I told him to go and find Rowena. Nurse Partridge thought she might come down."

"Is this a – a wise departure?"

"What?"

"Rowena's descent among us."

Mrs. Peverill drank some tea and dabbed at her mouth with a handkerchief. "She knows Jeremy. From children's parties." She replaced her cup and stared at Andrew.

"The Air Force," she said with sudden scorn. "Times change, I suppose."

The cups rattled continuously in the saucers, as Major Peverill handed the boys their tea. Andrew tried hard to return his smile.

"The little wretch keeps grinning at me," Major Peverill muttered angrily.

Jeremy kicked Andrew under the table. Andrew sat with his eyes lowered. He felt his face heating up and a terrifying desire to giggle. Major Peverill had not been smiling at him at all; he suffered from a tightening of the facial muscles which gave him protruding eyes and this fixed grimace. Viewed from the side, the old man's head was like a bird's: an ostrich, an emu, or a cassowary. In a magazine his mother took, Andrew had seen an advertisement with a sketch of a bird's grinning head, which asked "Can you change my expression?" If you could, using the smallest number of lines, you were offered free tuition by world-famous, but unnamed, artists.

Major Peverill was like this bird; he should have been smiling cheerfully but he looked tense and ruffled with his feathery wisps of hair. Could he, or anyone, change his expression?

Mrs. Peverill spoke to Andrew in a clear voice as though he were deaf. "My granddaughter is staying with us. She has not been well."

He nodded stupidly. At his age, he felt panicky at the thought of girls not being well.

While she spoke, the girl had come out of the hall into the winter garden. Jeremy jumped to his feet. At school he was well known for good manners and so Andrew copied him.

Mrs. Peverill said: "Rowena, you remember Jeremy."

Jeremy greeted her with his foppish skill.

"This is one of Jeremy's school friends."

The girl looked at Andrew without smiling. She was a large girl with a round face and dark hair plaited into two pigtails. Though she was two or three years older, she did not scare him. There was a sadness in her eyes that reminded you of the oppressed look you saw in boys at Chalgrove Park. Boys at school looked like this after the master in charge of the Navy set had twisted the short hairs in front of their ears. Even if this girl ended up despising him – a condition he was completely accustomed to – Andrew felt himself enlisted on her side.

The girl pulled down her tweed skirt and straightened together large feet in brown regulation school shoes.

"Did they send up Nurse Partridge's tea?" Mrs. Peverill asked.

"I think so."

"What does that mean?"

"Yes they did. They did. They did."

The old lady's face seemed to slam shut, like a box. A silence, long, resonant, and uncoiling, followed.

"Jeremy has come to fish in our lake," Major Peverill said.

"I hope they haven't caught anything," Rowena said quickly.

Andrew broke out. "Yes, we did. Four perch."

She gave him an angry intense look, which pleased him more than anything that had happened so far.

"Well, I think you're jolly cruel. Don't tell me anything about it."

Major Peverill put down a rock cake he was munching. "They're just mud fish. No one minds about mud fish. The gardener's boy used to catch them."

"I made the gardener's boy put them back," Rowena said. "Please promise you will, too."

"We usually put most of them back." He felt he had to be the spokesman for fishing. Jeremy was an uncertain ally: his politeness made him agree with people easily and talk lightly of things that were enormously important. The boys might be argued out of returning to the lake, because of danger or inconvenience, and the holidays would be spoiled, and the big pike would go on swimming there forever.

The girl, however, soon changed the subject. She told him about India, where she had been until two years ago and where her parents still lived. While he talked to her Andrew realized that, for him too, it would be easy to agree with everything she said, in part because he liked her, in part because she seemed hurt and ill at ease. The grandmother was watching them all the time, while eating a rock cake, bits of which fell down from her mouth. Jeremy and Major Peverill were having a conversation about cricket.

In the end the girl leaned over to Andrew and whispered: "Look, I've got to go now. Nothing about you. I hope to see you another time."

She stood up and the grandmother said: "Is anything the matter, Rowena?"

"No, nothing. I'm going, that's all." She pushed back her chair and it fell over.

"Try not to be clumsy, Rowena."

Major Peverill had also got to his feet. "I'll ring for Nurse Partridge," he said.

The girl stared at him, and then averted her gaze with contempt. She walked away between the palm trees, and then they could hear her footsteps breaking into a run across the tiled floor of the hall.

There was another ear-splitting silence. In the end, Jeremy stood up.

"I'm afraid we ought to go," he said. "It takes about three quarters of an hour to get home."

He went over and kissed the old lady's withered cheek. Andrew thanked her. She nodded to him but did not say anything.

"Give them one chocolate each," she said to her son. "Outside. I don't like the sound of chewing."

The boys went out into the hall. While they waited for Major Peverill they were watched by dozens of glittering eyes: the walls were lined with cases of stuffed seabirds, hovering on wires or squatting on papier-mâché rocks which the taxidermist had left unwhitened by droppings.

There turned out to be few chocolates remaining in the large ornate box. While Andrew's fingers searched among the crisp empty frills, the old man said to him: "I hope you were properly grateful to Mrs. Peverill. It's a great privilege for a boy like you, a great privilege."

"I did say thank you."

"You mustn't expect to come here frequently. There will be no question of that. Jeremy understands. It is different for him."

Andrew nodded. He was used to the absolute oddity of grown-ups. Major Peverill, however, didn't seem to be quite the same as a grown-up: he reminded you of an enormous boy from another school.

Major Peverill put his hand down hard on Andrew's shoulder, kneading it, and said in a scoffing voice: "You're very lucky to be at Chalgrove Park. It used to be one of the best private schools in the country."

"Yes, it is."

"Well, we had better just say it used to be. People of your parents' class must find it rather expensive."

Andrew quoted the words he had often heard spoken hushed and meaningly above his head. "I'm there on special terms."

The old man cackled mirthlessly. "Good God, he admits it. The little brat admits it."

When the boys had escaped into the open air, Andrew asked: "What did he mean by that?"

Jeremy kicked a stone across the drive. "Oh, he's bats. At least, everybody says he's bats. We'd better eat our chocolates."

Andrew examined his chocolate, which had a sort of greenish bloom on it. He bit a piece off it, and a taste of sour mold spread through his mouth. He spat it out and started retching. Jeremy was doing the same thing. They glanced at each other and suddenly burst into loud moans, and ended up butting each other, falling about on the grass and whooping with laughter.

When they were tired of doing this, they looked up. Major Peverill was standing behind the plate-glass front of the winter garden, so close to the glass that his nose made a pale circle against it.

"Ought we to go back and apologize?"

"No, let's go home. He doesn't matter."

While they were getting their bicycles, Andrew asked: "Is he Rowena's uncle?"

"Sort of. Not really. She's adopted. They were too old to have children when they were married."

"Who were?"

"Her parents. I mean, they weren't her parents. Mrs. Peverill's daughter. You know."

Andrew was uncertain that he did know, but guessed it was something that older people found embarrassing, like the prolonged absence of his own father and the continual presence at home of his mother's friend, Group-Captain Weare.

"How do you know about Rowena?"

"The nannies all talked about it at children's parties."

They were both embarrassed by this conversation. They found it rather awful to admit they had ever been younger than they now were. At school people blushed and lied when it was discovered that they had younger brothers or, much worse, sisters. No one knew what exacting god laid down such conditions. But his judgment could follow you, Andrew had discovered, even into dreams.

III

He free-wheeled down through the village and over the bridge that crossed the dull little river he had fished in since he was ten. Beyond the railway crossing there was a huge advertisement: BOVRIL – PREVENTS THAT SINKING FEELING.

His home was not far from the railway station, a red-brick villa which had "Braeside" painted on the fanlight above the front door. The adjoining houses were called "Ambleside" and "Glen Lomond." All three of the houses had upright pianos in the front rooms, but his mother was the only qualified pianist there and in the summer when the windows were open he could always recognize her playing as he drew near the three houses. He could also tell what was happening from what was being played: the thumping scales and chords when she was giving a lesson, or the stumbling of one of her pupils through a party piece; her own playing of Chopin or Schumann, and the casades of jazz which meant that Group-Captain Weare had come on one of his visits.

His mother was full of random enthusiasms and intensities, about a new friend or a letter from an old one, or about her new novel from the library, which lay with its suede bookmark on the brass-topped Indian table in the sitting room. To Andrew she was gentle-skinned and warm, and smelt of sweetish cake crumbs. Recently, though, he had begun to practice looking at her as though he had no idea who she was. Then he saw a small plump woman with reddish-blonde hair and a soft complexion, a cigarette in the corner of her mouth, her rings parked on the side of the piano, playing with marked expression, the backs of the small plump hands arched, poised and pouncing at the notes of a piece by her favorite Billy Mayerl, which fell in tinsely cascades, while Godfrey Weare sat on the settee trying to hook a dottle out of his pipe.

When she was playing the piano, she could not hear the ticking sound of the bicycle as he wheeled it along the cinder path to the back of the house. In the shed at the back where he kept his things, there were also two trunks; not the tin ones, which his father had taken to Egypt, but a traveling trunk of his mother's, and an old round-topped one, which was locked. This contained, among other objects, the sea-fishing tackle they had bought to fish for pollack in Devon about four years ago.

He would ask his mother to open the trunk after supper. It was full of his father's belongings and they had a sort of malign aura about them. Whenever he remembered them, he got the sinking feeling in the Bovril advertisement, and he remembered the time when his mother's sweet, woeful voice told him that his father had gone on leave to Cyprus with a Greek lady. After that, he had heard her crying once or twice, when he was in a different room.

He took his fishing bag into the kitchen. You could hear the piano thumping away, just beyond the thin wall. He opened the fishing bag and let out a sharp exciting gust of wet rubber and fish slime. He took out his two fish and then turned the bag inside out and left it under a running tap. The two perch looked less interesting in death, the prickly fins folded down and the dark stripes fading. He got out a rusty kitchen knife and ripped them open from the vent upwards and pulled out their insides. There was no sinking feeling anymore as he did this, which proved you could train yourself to do anything, like becoming a vet or a medical student. He washed out the cleaned fish, rubbed salt into them and put them on a white plate in the larder; he would have them for breakfast tomorrow.

When his mother had stopped playing, he went through to the sitting room.

"There he is! How long have you been in? Come and kiss Mummy."

Godfrey Weare was in uniform, but kept a somewhat odd appearance. His jacket stuck out over his large behind, and his hair stuck out where it had been sorely clipped.

"Hullo, Andrew old man."

"Hullo." He had no way of addressing Godfrey Weare at all. If he had been obliged to shout to him in the street, he would have had to shout "I say."

"Did you catch anything? He's been on the Peverills' estate, Braxby Park."

"It's a super lake. I caught three perch and I gave one to Jeremy, who caught one. We met a man who said there was a giant pike in the lake." He decided it would be embarrassing to admit having tea up at the house.

At supper he asked: "Can I open the big trunk in the shed?"

His mother looked agitated. "What do you want to do that for? They're not your things."

He spoke with his mouth full. "Sea tackle. It'd do for pike."

His mother said: "I think we had better discuss this another time. Some more ham, Godfrey?"

"I need it. I need it after supper."

"That's enough." She was trembling, obviously, enraged at him.

Godfrey Weare caught his eye and winked. It was an attempt at ingratiation; Andrew despised him for doing this when he could have no idea what the dispute was about.

IV

On the second day, they caught nothing at all. The weather had grown much warmer; dragonflies hovered and made sudden turns above the water lilies. Half-way through the afternoon, Jeremy announced that he was returning home early because he had relations coming to tea. Andrew felt let down; he wondered if this excuse were true, or whether it marked the beginning of a desertion. He decided to stay on alone.

He fished with the lighter of his two rods off the jetty. The lake water was dark, reflecting the massed green leaves of summer. He watched two dragonflies in a mating dance settle on his float.

Then, among all the other sounds, he heard a long way off something approaching through the undergrowth: there was a crash of heavy footsteps, followed by sharp breathing. He wondered whether to hide and watch, but decided to hold his ground as the footsteps drew nearer, crashing on dry foliage and twigs.

The girl came out on to the path by the jetty. She was dark in the face, and there were bits of greenery stuck to her long plaits.

"I took a shortcut. I thought I wasn't going to make it."

"Are you running away?" he asked.

This seemed to him a feasible form of activity. From some boarding schools people did it all the time, though rarely from Chalgrove Park, which had a high reputation.

"No, not really. I just had to get away from them for a bit. Gosh, I'm thirsty. Have you got anything to drink? I could drink the lake."

"I've got some Tizer."

He fished out the bottle and undid it. She drank straight from the bottle without wiping it, and this impressed him a good deal. He noticed she was wearing the same blouse and herringbone tweed skirt as the first time they had met. He thought it was odd to wear school clothes in the summer holidays, especially for a girl.

She handed back the bottle. "That was fine. Where's Jeremy got to?"

"He had to go back. His aunts were coming to tea." He blushed. "I suppose I shouldn't be here alone, actually."

"Don't worry. Nobody ever comes here." She inspected him in silence for a moment. He thought she was going to attack him for fishing, which she had seemed to disapprove of. Instead she asked him: "Were you shy up at the house the other day?"

"Not really."

"You looked shy. You looked as though you'd never been anywhere like that before, or met anybody like them." He turned away to pull in his line and examine the bait. Nothing had touched it yet.

"Uncle Maurice is a bit peculiar. Did you notice?"

"Well, I suppose so."

"Suppose so? You don't know much, do you?"

He was silent, not knowing whether to like her or to hate her. The pigtails certainly fascinated him; they were secured at the ends with twisted rubber bands, and had been so tightly plaited that bits of hair seemed to have broken under protest. She tossed them around her shoulders with confidence, but somehow this seemed the only thing she was confident about. Liking her completely would be like succumbing to a bully at school – one of those bullies who tried to frighten you because they themselves were frightened. Outram, for instance, a big bland boy with smooth, almost concave, knees. Rowena had a distinct look of Outram.

"My grandmother's terribly rich, did you know?"

"No, I didn't."

"Well, she is. That's why she thinks she's perfect. Lots of rich old women get like that, you know. Even if their husbands leave them or shoot themselves in the gunroom or die of drink, they go on thinking themselves perfect. She's like that."

He did not know what to make of this, except to think that she must have heard it from somebody grown-up.

Quite close by, a musical voice shouted: "Cooee! Cooee!"

"Don't worry. It's only Nurse Partridge. I ran away from her."

"Why do you have to have a nurse?"

"She's been here since I got ill at school. She's Australian. My parents employ her," she added with some grandeur. "They can afford it, you see."

Without turning his head, he began to watch the girl cautiously. He had hoped to be alone when Jeremy left, and here she was extremely close to him, with her large tweed behind planted on the bank beside him and her regulation shoes staring at him with the bright eyeholes of the laces. She was as close as Outram was when he sneaked up behind you and pinched the chilblains on your ears with stamp tweezers. Andrew imagined pulling her pigtails until she would weaken and cry out and honor him.

"Cooee!"

The nurse's voice, raised in forced cheerfulness, re-echoed among the sandstone rocks: if she came any nearer, there was risk of frightening the fish. A silence followed. The nurse must have been approaching along one of the paths that twisted downhill through the rhododendrons.

"I'd better go," Rowena said. "Will you come here again?"

"I'd like to come every day but it depends on Jeremy."

"Honestly, no one ever comes down here. You can get in without going near the house. There's a gap in the wall on the main road. See you tomorrow, then."

V

He was surprised that he missed her when she had gone. It was as though nothing would be quite as exciting and interesting as before. Then he saw that his float had moved a long way over towards the water lilies. He pulled in the line and found a small roach deeply hooked. He did not unhook it, but left it swimming in the clear water under the jetty. Back on the bank, he drew his father's sea rod out of its canvas case.

Dusk was approaching and small fish began to flip through the black surface of the lake. Andrew felt gloomy and guilty and treacherous at what he was doing. Yesterday he had stood by while his mother had unlocked the big trunk. There was a strong smell of mothballs and pipe tobacco. His father's remaining possessions included a winter overcoat, a porkpie hat with a salmon fly in it, a pair of brogues, some sports jackets and gray flannel bags. When she saw them, his mother made a little sharp sobbing noise, as though she had cut her finger. She pointed to three tin boxes at one end of the trunk.

"Those are the things you want, aren't they? Hurry up and get them out."

His mother held her face averted. When he had collected the boxes, she smoothed out the clothes again and slammed the lid of the trunk shut. He wanted to comfort her but she pulled herself away.

"No, don't touch me. You've no idea of what you're making me do."

He had an apprehensive feeling as he thought of the world of childhood closeness dying out, of there being nobody he could touch anymore. He already knew that he was physically unattractive, because people didn't much like him leaning on them at school. The naval master, who would often tickle Jeremy Cathcart to the verge of asphyxiation, usually pushed Andrew away. But his mother's coldness would be temporary; she was too changeable and excitable to stay in one mood for long. She would get up from the piano and dance him around the room, saying: "You haven't a spark of rhythm in your body. Watch me." He would trample on her feet and they'd collapse on the settee together, weak with laughter, until she'd suddenly stare closely at his face and say: "Why are you so ugly? I can't imagine where you came from."

He threaded the flax line through the four white porcelain rings on the sea rod, and knotted on the weighted wire trace with a single triangle hook. Then he pulled out the roach, unhooked it and laid it on the still-warm boards of the jetty. He slipped one barbed point of the triangle under the back fin and felt the slight crunch of the hook entering living flesh. The little fish wriggled and then lay still gasping, trying to recover. He let it swim around in the water and it seemed to accept its fate.

He pulled several yards of line off the reel and let them fall at his feet. Then he cast out, releasing the line as the live bait swung out in front of him, so that it hit the black water about fifteen yards out. The slack line whipped through into the fading rings of water until none of it was left and the reel began ticking, faster and faster. He was not sure what was happening, except that he could see the line cutting through the surface towards the water lilies and knew he had stop it. He put his hand on the reel and it was like having the whole lake moving. The reel jerked down and he held on in panic. The line snapped and sprang back in a tangle.

A great wave of loss rose up and hit him. He dropped the rod, and back on the bank he threw himself down with his hands on his crotch, moaning and jeering at himself and shouting all the bad words he knew.

It took him about five minutes to recover. He had no more live bait or tackle, it was growing dark and he knew he would have to go home. But he kept staring at the lake, the reed beds and the water lilies, as though by force of will he could bring the big pike out of the water. He packed up the rods and put the bag over his shoulder. Then, as he looked once more at the lake, a gray shape on the bank, which his eyes must have raced across again and again, turned into the figure of a man standing quite still, watching him.

His insides leaped upwards. Fear was confused with the sense that he had been watched making a fool of himself.

"Boy! Boy!" the figure called out to him. "Come here! Don't be frightened."

Andrew was already on the cart track that led up through the woods. He ran without stopping until he arrived at the bicycle in the stable yard. For the first time he looked back: nobody was following him.

He strapped the two rods to the bar of the bicycle. He was able to free-wheel most of the way down the long drive; between the big gate posts he stopped to look at his watch, which showed eight o'clock. He had promised to be home by half past six. He switched on the bicycle lamp, which threw an uneasy circle of light on the cow parsley at the road's edge, and seemed to make the surrounding darkness darker. When he set off, two cars approached him from behind: he thought he was being followed, but the cars roared off down the long straight road. Each time they passed his shadow leaped out and staggered down the long wall of the Braxby estate. By the lights from the second car, he saw the gap in the wall which Rowena had told him about. It had been roughly blocked off with a stack of dead thornbushes, but you could get through these fairly easily. Obviously the girl could be trusted about things like that.

A third car was slow in passing. It seemed to pause about thirty yards behind him. When he turned to look at it he got the full glare of the headlights in his eyes. Somehow he convinced himself that this time he was being pursued by the man, whoever he was, who had been watching by the lake. He pedaled as hard as he could but the road began to go uphill and he sensed the car drawing nearer until it was beside him.

Then suddenly, his mother's voice was shouting: "Stop at once, you little fool."

He recognized the car as Group-Captain Weare's Sunbeam. He swiveled the bicycle around so that the lamp shone in the car window at his mother's white furious face and Godfrey Weare's, concerned and keen. The moment he saw them he knew that no excuses would be worth making. For his own self-respect he had to sulk and say nothing.

His mother got out and stood beside him. "Get in," she said.

"What about the bike?"

There was a cottage not far off on the other side of the road. His mother wheeled the bicycle toward it. Andrew sat on the bench seat next to Group-Captain Weare, who fiddled around with his pipe and tobacco pouch. They were silent; his mother would be giving them the clue to how the scene was to be carried out.

"I told them one of us would fetch it tomorrow." She got in beside Andrew and when he brushed against her, she shrank away. "Don't touch me," she said. "You've upset me very much."

He moved closer to Godfrey Weare's massive gray-flannel thigh. Neither of them was likely to speak while his mother was in a bad temper.

However, she could not be silent for long. After about a mile she said: "I rang up Mrs. Carthcart and she told me Jeremy had been back since four o'clock. I felt such a fool."

They were approaching the village when she said: "She was most unfriendly, I thought." While they were getting out of the car, she took his arm: "I don't know why you want to chum up with that boy. They're a lot of snobs if you ask me."

He pulled himself away, although his heart sank with pity for her and her obtuseness. How could she know that he had to proceed with immense caution in order to have any friends at all? People at school were pretty good at estimating just how much you were worth in the popularity stakes. The fact that Jeremy lived nearby had been a piece of God-given good luck.

He refused anything to eat and went up to his bedroom.

After a time his mother started to play the piano, and later the wireless was switched on to dance music from Radio Luxembourg. He heard the Sunbeam drive off at about ten o'clock. He felt starved, but going downstairs would be a defeat, and his mother knew very well how to turn honorable defeat into abject surrender. He lay back determined to punish himself and her by keeping awake as long as he could.

He hoped his mother's telephone call hadn't spoiled things between him and Jeremy. Even though the girl had told him about the gap in the wall, he still needed Jeremy's help in getting the key to the boat. If you hooked the pike from the shore, it would always head straight for the water lilies and break the line; with the boat there was a chance of keeping it out in the open water. Jeremy had as good as promised to get hold of the key.

When the last train had gone through, the village was quiet. Beyond it, the sleeping fields stretched out towards Braxby Park, five miles away, a place cut off from the rest of the world. When he thought of it, he imagined a special darkness in the air overhead, like a sepia photograph. At the bottom of the lake the great pike lay with the hook stinging in its jaw; it had to keep fanning its pectoral fins, otherwise it would rise slowly upward through the water. Up at the house, the girl was fast asleep; perhaps the Australian nurse had administered some broken-up pill, so that Rowena slept with her mouth open, her plump arms outside the white sheets. When he thought about her, he knew he was frightened of her and that he enjoyed his fear. But now she was a captive, guarded by the nurse, the peculiar uncle, and the hard old lady. Who was the man at nightfall at the edge of the lake? He might have been a keeper, or the gardener, or the butler from the house. By the time Andrew had got around to this, the evidence of dreams indicated that the man was Godfrey Weare, and the girl and his mother kept changing identities, and he himself was running through the rhododendrons from the unseen Australian nurse, so that he wet himself and people stared at him and told him he was completely impossible.

VI

Each taking one oar, they rowed out toward the open water. The sun was already high up, shining blurred through the treetops, and it would soon enter the empty patch of sky above the lake. Andrew knew that they had arrived too late and the expedition would probably fail. He had planned for today with passion but had forgotten to cross his fingers.

After the previous day at the lake, he had fallen asleep in his clothes. He woke early and changed into pajamas before his mother called him. She was still angry with him, but three children were arriving for piano lessons and she could not give him much attention.

The first part of his plan involved getting some money. A small girl was thumping out scales in the front room, and he saw his mother's handbag on a table in the narrow hallway. Almost without touching it, he fished out a ten shilling note. It was the first time he had ever done this, and he found that the action disturbed him a good deal. Probably his mother would have given him extra pocket money if he had asked for it: he stole from her because he wanted to be able not to love her.

He spent the ten shilling note on wire traces and triangle hooks at the village tobacconist's shop. In the afternoon he went to collect the bicycle from the cottage near Braxby Park and later he fished for gudgeon in the stream near the village. He caught eight of them. Two were stiff and white next morning but the rest, for live bait, were now in a paint tin at the bottom of the boat.

They shipped the oars. There was no anchor but the boat stayed, held in the water lilies by the open water. It was Jeremy's fault that they had arrived so late. He had refused to come out until the middle of the morning; he had needed a good deal of persuasion before he would ask the butler for the key to the boathouse. Then he had pretended to be unable to unlock the iron gate at the top of the steps. Now the rods were out and nothing was happening. While they sat looking at the rays of sunlight fanning down into the deep water or watched the wood pigeons rocketing across the sky, Andrew could feel Jeremy getting bored again. It was like a weakening fever, he felt it infecting himself and breaking down his own will.

"Cooee! Cooee!"

This time it was the girl herself, who must have adopted from her nurse this Antipodean call sign. She was standing on the jetty on the other side of the lake, her pale face and blouse shining out against the shadow of the trees. They waved to her, hoping she would go away.

"Give me a ride."

"No, we can't. We're fishing."

"Come on, do. Please."

"You'll scare the fish," Andrew called.

"You'll sink the boat," Jeremy said. "You're too fat," he added more quietly.

"What was that?"

They both giggled, and whispered together: "Too fat, too fat."

"Please take me."

"No." Inside himself, Andrew was already twisted with shame and sorrow and ready to surrender. With Jeremy there, however, it was easy to fall back into shared silliness.

"I think you're both beastly," Rowena said. Then the tall navy-blue shape of the nurse appeared beside her. Some sort of heated discussion followed, which ended with both of them walking off together under the beech trees.

After the girl had gone, the boys avoided looking at each other for some time. Andrew felt saddened. Everything about her, even the ugly plaits and the fawn stockings which wrinkled over her round knees, struck him with a guilty and pleasurable melancholy, like singing "The Day Thou Gavest" at Sunday evening service.

A little later there was a splash near the boat, and a gingerpop bottle surfaced among the weeds.

"That was a bloody silly thing to do."

"Wa-wa. Why don't you cry about it?" Jeremy wriggled around to face him. "Who are you to go about giving the orders, that's what I'd like to know."

He picked up one of the oars and slapped it up and down on the surface of the water. The sounds echoed from the rocks and startled a flight of pigeons.

"Why did you do that?"

Jeremy mumbled something under his breath.

"I didn't hear. Why did you do that?"

"Because you stink, that's why."

Andrew began to reel in his line. Jeremy had got into a terrific rage: obviously the girl's presence and the way they had both reacted to it had made him feel guilty and angry too.

"Why don't you just admit you stink and be done with it?"

"I don't."

"Of course you stink, it's famous. You fart worse than anyone else in Lower Changing Room. Only last term I heard someone say "I'm not going in there because that oik's farted.""

"Let's go back."

"I'll say whether we go back or not, you little oik. This boat belongs to my friends, doesn't it? You haven't got any friends."

Andrew began to untwist the ferrules of his rod. His eyes were getting hot and blurred.

"You haven't got any friends because you are an oik. You live in a house in a row. Your mother's as common as muck. You remember when she rang us up the other day at home? Well, we all thought it must be one of the servants' friends."

By the conventions of Chalgrove Park, Jeremy's attack had gone through three stages. You could tell people they stank and be easily forgiven: it was a matter of style. Even being an oik could still be considered a temporary matter, arising out of one particular piece of behavior. But to attack somebody's "people" to his face was to break a tabu. Jeremy did it so that they would never be able to speak to each other again.

A few moments later they realized that this created difficulties. They were in the middle of the lake, aware to their fingertips of the black depth of water underneath them, and the hundred yards which lay between them and the boathouse.

Without speaking they rowed with quick, light strokes, shaking off the lily stems, and glided in under the rock. Together they slid the boat on to dry land. There were five live bait remaining. Andrew sank the tin in shallow water, which could enter the holes pierced in the lid. Jeremy had hurried ahead and did not see him do this. As he had done earlier, Jeremy found the lock too stiff to move; he handed Andrew the key again. Andrew stood in front of the iron gate and turned the key, but made sure that it did not click shut. He jammed a stone under the gate: it would appear to be locked but he could always get in when he wanted.

At the front of the house, Jeremy waited to return the key to the butler.

Andrew lingered for a little, and then called "Good-bye," when it seemed unlikely that the other could hear him. It was strange to be alone, bicycling home in the empty middle of the afternoon, as though he was entering on a newer harsher period of his life. Next term when he and Jeremy met at Chalgrove Park, they would not speak to each other anymore. This would not cause any problems, because they had always belonged to different gangs; in any case, the unwritten laws compelled a certain shame about knowing each other in the holidays.

Finding the front door of "Braeside" closed on the chain, he pushed it open as far as he could and shouted.

After some minutes, his mother came downstairs in her dressing-gown. "I wondered who on earth it was. I was resting. I thought you said you'd be out all day."

"It was no good. Too hot."

She opened the door in silence.

Trying to please her, he said: "I had a row with Jeremy Cathcart."

She did not respond to this but turned away, pulling the dressing-gown more tightly around her.

"Is there anything to eat?"

"Take some biscuits. You ought to be out in the open air."

"All right, I'm going. You won't catch me staying around this dump."

This remark, too, had no visible effect on her. He took a handful of ginger-snaps from the kitchen. Her unusual silence retained him for a moment. Then he shuffled off, kicking a stone along down the path in front of him. But the silence persisted until he heard her close the door again.

He crossed the main road by the Bovril advertisement, and walked uphill until he reached the Recreation Ground. Stuck in the middle of the country, it was an odd, townish place with its park seats, sandpit and swings, and a cricket pavilion of darkgreen corrugated iron. Everything here seemed much-handled and grimy, and Woodbine packets and sweet papers were trodden into the earth.

Some boys were playing cricket in the middle of the field. He sat on a bench and watched them while he ate the gingersnaps. On three sides of the Recreation Ground there were rows of young pine trees. The fourth side overlooked the village and the railway station. Four cars were parked in front of the station, one of them a Sunbeam, the same color as Godfrey Weare's. But it couldn't be Godfrey Weare's; why should he travel anywhere by train? With a telescope, he would be able to focus on the number plate and be sure.

A little later, though, he saw Godfrey Weare coming across the road near the Bovril advertisement, could not mistake the penguin walk, the large behind, and the bouncing cock's tail of hair. Godfrey Weare got into the Sunbeam. He reversed, went forward to pause by the main road, and then he drove across the level crossing toward London.

VII

The pike was firmly hooked and it fought strongly. He could glimpse it down below, a dull gold bar flashing in the deep water. Then, apparently surrendering, it rose slowly upward, but when its long head broke the surface it shook with new violence, knocking against the side of the boat. The broad tail fin twisted out, thrashing the water with a noise that echoed across the lake.

He dropped the tip of the rod, and the fish lay captive alongside the boat, with the back fin just out of the water. It was not really large, probably about four pounds, and he had already decided to let it go. If you fished alone, you caught more but there was nobody to witness the result. At home his mother seemed too distracted to pretend any interest.

Nevertheless, he watched the fish with triumph and pleasure. He looked at his watch: it was half past eight in the morning. The sun had not yet risen above the trees and the water was black and dead-looking. He willed himself to remember this moment, its surroundings, and what he was feeling. Whatever lay ahead, like school examinations, he hoped such feelings would continue, although, whenever you looked at adults, it seemed unlikely that they should. He leaned over the side of the boat and the pike turned over showing one flat furious eye. He hauled it into the boat and stuck a piece of wood into its mouth. Talking to it, he tried to get the hook free past the rows of tiny teeth. The hook finally yielded and came out dragging a large piece of living gristle. Appalled by what he had done he heaved the fish back into the water. It sank and then surfaced again, lying on its side. It flapped for a time, righted itself and disappeared. At least he had tried to save it; perhaps it would survive after all.

He was covered with fish slime and he longed to pee. He had observed his bearings from the trees on the shore, and so he rowed without looking back until he saw the rock walls on either side of him. The boat gritted on the floor of the cave.

He jumped out and collided with a buttoned, tweed-covered mass, smelling of tobacco, that felt like an old armchair. In the reflected light from the water, he could just make out the face with the startled permanent grin, like a pike's.

Andrew put down his head and tried to get past to the steps that led to the open air.

Major Peverill put out large wrinkled hands to stop him. "Where are you off to? There's no hurry."

"I must go out. I – I want to be excused."

"What does that mean? Oh, I understand." The old man laughed. "You can do it here. We are all men here."

There was a long pause while Andrew faced the wall. Outside the sun had begun to strike the lake water. He wondered what had happened to the pike he had caught, and whether it would die.

"Well, aren't you going to?"

"I can't," he admitted. He buttoned up and turned around again.

"Where's the other boy?"

"He didn't – want to come today."

"So you're alone?" The old man observed him with a livelier interest. "The brat's alone. Do you mind me calling you 'brat'?"

Andrew stood on one leg and then the other. The immediate urgency seemed to have gone, but he was contorted with something which was like shyness but much stronger.

"After all, why shouldn't I call you 'brat'? You are a brat, aren't you? Come here."

"No, I don't want to."

"You don't know what you want, at your age. You have to be shown. How old are you, brat?"

"Twelve and three quarters." Andrew went quiet and respectful; Chalgrove Park had trained him to behave like this unthinkingly in front of adults. "Excuse me, I'll just get my things."

He took his rod and fishing bag out of the boat. He went in front up the steps, while the old man's fingers pinched his backside and tried to get up his shorts. When he reached the last step, he ran as hard as he could.

"Come here, damn you. Here."

Out of breath at the top of the slope, Andrew looked down through a gap in the rhododendrons. He saw Major Peverill standing there, calling for him like a dog. He was so accustomed to obeying schoolmasters that he still felt he was in some way breaking the rules by not going down again. Now, too, he noticed a droop of sadness and frustration about the old man which made him obscurely sorry.

He returned home to hear his mother giving a piano lesson.

She had reached the point in the proceedings when she would firmly displace the pupil from the stool and take over, letting loose a stampede of chords, arpeggios, and glissandi, twisting around, showing her teeth and saying "Lovely thing, isn't it?" All of this he took for showing-off and it embarrassed him deeply. Even the noise of it made him cringe going past the window. In the kitchen he poured out a big glass of orange Kia-Ora, which he took upstairs to his bedroom, together with one of his mother's library books, which he had just started to read.

He heard the front door open and close. His mother came upstairs and stood in his bedroom doorway, with an airy and mysterious look about her.

"Isn't that book too old for you?"

"No, it isn't. I like it."

"You'll tire your eyes." She turned over his hairbrush and dug his comb deeply into it. "What are you going to do with yourself all afternoon? Godfrey wants me to go out with him."

"Read. Can I have a bath? I stink of fish."

His mother affected an expression of amused tolerance. She went back downstairs, where he heard her singing as she drifted from room to room.

The geyser flared up and subsided to a steady flame. In the bath, hot water pounded on to rusty stains where the taps had been weeping. When he came back from undressing, the bathroom window had steamed up. Wiping a patch clear, he looked out at the bright noon light over the neighboring gardens, yellow and green privet hedge and creosoted sheds. On one of the sheds a wooden airplane was spinning in a light breeze.

He waited till the bath was nearly full, before turning off the taps. While he looked at himself in the mirror his fingers explored the silky hair which had started growing in a line just above his cock. Now, with a pair of nail scissors, he trimmed the hairs off neatly, so that that part was quite bare again, as it had been a few weeks ago.

VIII

For some time he did not visit Braxby Park, except when he dreamed about it at night, and then it appeared as though he hardly ever left it. In dreams there were several ways of arriving there. Once or twice it was through his preparatory school: toward the end of the holidays his dream life usually attempted to make bridges between the opposing worlds, and his school dream was of drifting without will from the bare classrooms and dormitories, along the corridors, through the swing doors into the Headmaster's part of the house. There, in carpeted rooms lit by roaring log fires, the Headmaster's wife would discover him and expel him with ignominy. Sometimes now, however, the school corridors led directly into Braxby Park, and he met Rowena, who told him: "We thought you would keep away and not cause trouble. No wonder we are disappointed."

But on other occasions it was through unvisited rooms upstairs at "Braeside." Once he had found them (you knew these rooms existed but somehow they escaped your memory) the lake and the jetty were easily visible from the windows. Later, though, he was running down the paths between the rhododendrons and, although Braxby Park was behind him, there was some bias in his footsteps which pulled him back to the front door where Major Peverill was waiting. He awoke full of of apprehension from these encounters, blinking their persistent sad twilight out of his eyes, which seemed unaccustomed to the ordinary light of morning.

On the last evening of the holidays, he was back at the lake with his fishing tackle. As he had expected, the boathouse was securely locked again; he followed the path around until he reached the jetty. Now, in September, the shadows were already long, and some of the trees had golden reflections in the still water.

He took a long time assembling his rods, paying elaborate attention to each knot, in order to avoid tomorrow in his thoughts. His mother had told him that Godfrey Weare had very kindly offered to take him back to Chalgrove Park in the Sunbeam. It would mean leaving him at school a good deal earlier than usual, because Godfrey Weare and his mother would be driving on to Brighton, to dine together and see a show. She couldn't realize the sharp twinge she caused by announcing jolly plans for the time when he would be out of the way.

In some ways he was surprised to find himself here this evening, nearly a month after his last visit. In the village street he had run into Jeremy, returned from Ireland: with a single instinct they had cut each other dead. Then this morning he had discovered three frogs in some long grass at the end of the garden. He had read Izaak Walton's *Compleat Angler* and he remembered the instruction for using them as live bait: "Use him as though you love him, that he may live the longer." A frog would not only live longer but swim out into the clear water. Suddenly his passion was aroused all over again. Nevertheless, he was almost sure that this was the last time he would come here. The future was getting fuller and fuller of other things; part of his childhood was being crowded out, not because he wanted to let it go, but because there was nobody to share it with.

In spite of Izaak Walton, he had found the business of hooking on the frog rather appalling: you needed somebody else at hand to encourage you to do such things. He hoped to catch a small fish for live bait on the lighter of the two rods. By the time everything was ready, moths were starting to flutter clumsily and rooks were going home across the pale sky. His two floats lay far out on the pale water, the smaller one motionless, the larger one trembling, agitated by the desperately swimming frog.

Later, he heard footsteps approaching. He thought it better to disappear, in case it was Major Peverill. He climbed to the top of the rocks nearby and, hidden by a holly tree, looked down. It was the girl.

This time she was wearing a flowered dress, a shapeless effort with smocking and puffed sleeves. It was accompanied by the same crinkled stockings and sturdy shoes. The great difference was the hair, no longer in plaits but flowing loose on to her shoulders. It still framed her face but in a way that made it less round and doll-like. He scrambled down the slope toward her.

"I thought these must be your things. What's been happening to you?"

"Oh, I've been very busy," he said.

She laughed, as though he was too young to be eligible for this word. "When Uncle Maurice said he had found you down here, I came back several times."

"I'm sorry."

"In the end, I guessed that he had probably frightened you and you wouldn't come back. 'The poor boy's frightened,' I thought."

He blushed so hard his face was ready to explode. She was teasing him but, now that the pigtails had gone, you couldn't really tell what she mightn't know.

Now she went to the end of the jetty, pushing her hair back behind her ears and posing in profile against the water.

"It's nice that you've come back," she said.

"This is the last time."

"Why's that?"

"Because I've got to go back to school tomorrow."

"Have you caught the big fish yet?"

"Not yet." He felt embarrassed by something which two months ago had been the most important thing in the world.

"Not yet!"

She laughed. All at once, she pulled her long hair in a curtain over her eyes and, staring through it with a funny spooky face, she turned on him, waving her arms with the hands ready for clutching. He nearly fell off the jetty.

"Nervous, aren't you?"

To get a bit of his own back, he asked: "Where's that Australian person?"

Rowena stroked her hair into place behind her ears, and looked remote. "Oh, she left. Ages ago, actually. I'm going to school in Switzerland after Christmas."

While they were talking he had forgotten to keep watch on his two floats. The smaller one was still there, but the other had vanished. He picked up the sea rod and pulled hard. The float jerked back from where the water lilies had hidden it. He reeled the line in, and prepared to cast again.

"You've caught a little frog. Look, it's wriggling."

He tried not to let this display of female ignorance put him off his stroke. He cast out smoothly towards the middle of the lake.

"Didn't you see it?" she asked him in wonder.

"That was the bait. When you're fishing for pike, live frogs are good bait."

She stared as though she could not believe him. "But that's horrible. It must hurt it dreadfully. Do you know what you are? You're a sadist."

"What's that mean?"

"If you don't know, I'm certainly not going to tell you. Poor, poor little thing."

"They don't feel like we do."

"You little beast. You mean *you* don't feel."

He laughed. "No, they don't really."

He watched her doubtfully. No boy would ever make a fuss like this: at Chal-grove Park you could easily collect a crowd by burning a worm or an insect with a magnifying glass. He was quite shocked to see that she was crying in earnest.

"They all said you were horrible. They were quite right."

"Who said?"

Rowena did not answer, but turned around and fled, large and splay-footed, into the darkening woods.

"Who said? Tell me," he called after her.

He followed her to a point where the path forked, and the rhododendrons were too tall to allow him to see which way she had taken. Her tears had scattered his wits completely. Returning, still thinking about her last statement and not looking where he went, he tripped headlong over an elbow of tree-root sticking out of the path.

With the skin grazed off both his knees, he limped back to the jetty. There, a curious noise hung in the air. He could not identify it until he noticed that the big rod had fallen over and the noise came from the ratchet of the reel as the line was being dragged off it.

He grabbed the rod and held on. Whatever had seized the bait was now in the middle of the lake, fighting deep down. Though he was still sniveling with pain, the usual mixture of rage and glee took hold of him. Each time he started regaining some line, the fish headed off again, and he knew it must be deeply hooked because its strength was fighting directly against his own. This made him sure that it was the same pike he had hooked on the day Jeremy had gone home early.

After about ten minutes his arms began to ache. Hot water ran down his leg, though he hadn't felt himself peeing, and made the scraped knee sting. His eyes stung too, and he wiped the back of his hand against them. He couldn't see any better because it was getting dark, although a piece of the setting sun was still visible through the trees on the opposite shore.

By now he knew the battle was going his way: the fish had tired itself fighting out there in the open, and each failing effort gave him a little more slack line, so that he could steer it nearer the water lilies around the jetty. Suddenly he saw the rounded back fin, the one near the tail, break the surface: it was like a dark sail against the luminous water.

All his dreams came to a quiet conclusion as the pike slid gently towards him. To keep it from tangling among the lilies, he held the rod as high as he could. This brought the great head out of the water, the body looped and thrashed wildly, but the hook held. Gradually he eased the pike alongside the jetty, like a liner coming into dock, and into the shallow water. He dropped the rod and plunged in on top of the fish and manhandled it on to the bank. In the wild stink of mud and marsh gas it lay there, huge and terrible to him. While he watched it, a mounting sense of triumph began to break through all the webs of disbelief.

To stop the line from tangling, he cut the knot above the wire trace. The pike gave a number of violent heaves, and its scales became covered with dry leaves and earth. The two eyes that glared from the corners of the head belonged now to a monster of the woods more than the water. In the twilight, Andrew lay on the ground and worshipped it.

For a time, the only noise seemed to be of the blood pounding in his ears. This turned into the murmur of voices, not far off. He had just time to heave the big pike down the bank. By the faint shine that still came from the lake, he could see it indignantly right itself and then the furious swirl with which it regained the deep water.

When he had clambered once more on to the top of his rock, he was aware of several people approaching down the path between the rhododendrons. They carried electric torches, and soon you could see the long cylinders of light shifting to and fro, stopped by tree trunks and then reaching out again among the shadows.

He heard Major Peverill's voice, high-pitched like a well-bred sneeze. "The poor girl got back to the house in a terrible state."

Other voices answered, in the lower tones of country people accustomed to agreement.

"He should not have been allowed to come here in the first place." By now Major Peverill was standing about directly below. "It was a misunderstanding, which must be put right without more ado."

There was complete darkness under the holly tree on the rock. Andrew kept his head down, in case a beam of torchlight should sweep across to show his face as a pale patch among the bristling leaves. If you hated people enough, he thought, you could hold out as long as they could. In a short while they would find his gear lying where he had left it by the lake. It would hardly make much difference; they knew he was still here, but it was improbable that they would ever find him.

Soon after this, though, he saw other, different torches flash out on the far side of the lake. He heard his mother calling, and knew he would have to surrender.

THE PAGAN RABBI

Cynthia Ozick

Cynthia Ozick (b.1928) is the author of *Trust, The Messiah of Stock-holm, Heir to the Glimmering World* (or *The Bear Boy*) and *Foreign Bodies,* as well as a number of story collections, including *The Shawl, Dictation* as well as several collections of essays. She lives in New Rochelle with her husband. Her work has won the O. Henry Award three times, the PEN Malamud Award, the PEN Nabokov Award and the National Books Critic Circle Award. She was once described as "the Emily Dickinson of the Bronx", and said: "One *must* avoid ambition *in order to* write. Otherwise something else is the goal . . ."

> Rabbi Jacob said: "He who is walking along
> and studying, but then breaks off to remark,
> "How lovely is that tree!" or "How beautiful is that
> fallow field!" – Scripture regards such a one
> as having hurt his own being."
> – from The Ethics of the Fathers

When I heard that Isaac Kornfeld, a man of piety and brains, had hanged himself in the public park, I put a token in the subway stile and journeyed out to see the tree.

We had been classmates in the rabbinical seminary. Our fathers were both rabbis. They were also friends, but only in a loose way of speaking: in actuality our fathers were enemies. They vied with one another in demonstrations of charitableness, in the captious glitter of their scholia, in the number of their adherents. Of the two, Isaac's father was the milder. I was afraid of my father; he had a certain disease of the larynx, and if he even uttered something so trivial as "Bring the tea" to my mother, it came out splintered, clamorous, and vindictive.

Neither man was philosophical in the slightest. It was the one thing they agreed on. "Philosophy is an abomination," Isaac's father used to say. "The Greeks were philosophers, but they remained children playing with their dolls. Even Socrates, a monotheist, nevertheless sent money down to the temple to pay for incense to their doll."

"Idolatry is the abomination," Isaac argued, "not philosophy."

"The latter is the corridor to the former," his father said.

My own father claimed that if not for philosophy I would never have been brought to the atheism which finally led me to withdraw, in my second year, from the seminary. The trouble was not philosophy – I had none of Isaac's talent: his teachers later said of him that his imagination was so remarkable he could concoct holiness out of the fine line of a serif. On the day of his funeral the president of his college was criticized for having commented that, although a suicide could not be buried in consecrated earth, whatever earth enclosed Isaac Kornfeld was *ipso facto* consecrated. It should be noted that Isaac hanged himself several weeks short of his thirty-sixth birthday; he was then at the peak of his renown; and the president, of course, did not know the whole story. He judged by Isaac's reputation, which was at no time more impressive than just before his death.

I judged by the same, and marvelled that all that holy genius and intellectual surprise should in the end be raised no higher than the next-to-lowest limb of a delicate young oak, with burly roots like the toes of a gryphon exposed in the wet ground.

The tree was almost alone in a long rough meadow, which sloped down to a bay filled with sickly clams and a bad smell. The place was called Trilham's Inlet, and I knew what the smell meant: that cold brown water covered half the city's turds.

On the day I came to see the tree the air was bleary with fog. The weather was well into autumn and, though it was Sunday, the walks were empty. There was something historical about the park just then, with its rusting grasses and deserted monuments. In front of a soldiers' cenotaph a plastic wreath left behind months before by some civic parade stood propped against a stone frieze of identical marchers in the costume of an old war. A banner across the wreath's belly explained that the purpose of war is peace. At the margins of the park they were building a gigantic highway. I felt I was making my way across a battlefield silenced by the victory of the peace machines. The bulldozers had bitten far into the park, and the rolled carcasses of the sacrificed trees were already cut up into logs. There were dozens of felled maples, elms, and oaks. Their moist inner wheels breathed out a fragrance of barns, countryside, decay.

In the bottom-most meadow fringing the water I recognized the tree which had caused Isaac to sin against his own life. It looked curiously like a photograph – not only like that newspaper photograph I carried warmly in my pocket, which showed the field and its markers – the drinking-fountain a few yards off, the ruined brick wall of an old estate behind. The caption-writer had particularly remarked on the "rope". But the rope was no longer there; the widow had claimed it. It was his own prayer shawl that Isaac, a short man, had thrown over the comely neck of the next-to-lowest limb. A Jew is buried in his prayer shawl; the police had handed it over to Sheindel. I observed that the bark was rubbed at that spot. The tree lay back against the sky like a licked postage stamp. Rain began to beat it flatter yet. A stench of sewage came up like a veil in the nostril. It seemed to me I was a man in a photograph standing next to a grey blur of tree. I would stand through eternity beside Isaac's guilt if I did not run, so I ran that night to Sheindel herself.

I loved her at once. I am speaking now of the first time I saw her, though I don't exclude the last. The last – the last together with Isaac – was soon after my divorce; at one stroke I left my wife and my cousin's fur business to the small upstate city in which both had repined. Suddenly Isaac and Sheindel and two babies appeared in the lobby of my hotel – they were passing through: Isaac had a lecture engagement in Canada. We sat under scarlet neon and Isaac told how my father could now not speak at all.

"He keeps his vow," I said.

"No, no, he's a sick man," Isaac said. "An obstruction in the throat."

"I'm the obstruction. You know what he said when I left the seminary. He meant it, never mind how many years it is. He's never addressed a word to me since."

"We were reading together. He blamed the reading, who can blame *him*? Fathers like ours don't know how to love. They live too much indoors."

It was an odd remark, though I was too much preoccupied with my own resentments to notice. "It wasn't what we read," I objected, "Torah tells that an illustrious man doesn't have an illustrious son. Otherwise he wouldn't be humble like other people. This much scholarly stuffing I retain, Well, so my father always believed he was more illustrious than anybody, especially more than your father. *Therefore*," I delivered in Talmudic cadence, "what chance did I have? A nincompoop and no *Sitzfleish*. Now you, you could answer questions that weren't even invented yet. Then you invented them."

"Torah isn't a spade," Isaac said. "A man should have a livelihood. You had yours."

"The pelt of a dead animal isn't a living either, it's an indecency."

All the while Sheindel was sitting perfectly still; the babies, female infants in long stockings, were asleep in her arms. She wore a dark thick woollen hat – it was July – that covered every part of her hair. But I had once seen it in all its streaming black shine.

"And Jane?" Isaac asked finally.

"Speaking of dead animals, Tell my father – he won't answer a letter, he won't come to the telephone – that in the matter of the marriage he was right, but for the wrong reason. If you share a bed with a Puritan you'll come into it cold and you'll go out of it cold. Listen, Isaac, my father calls me an atheist, but between the conjugal sheets every Jew is a believer in miracles, even the lapsed."

He said nothing then. He knew I envied him his Sheindel and his luck. Unlike our fathers, Isaac had never condemned me for my marriage, which his father regarded as his private triumph over my father, and which my father, in his public defeat, took as an occasion for declaring me as one dead. He rent his clothing and sat on a stool for eight days, while Isaac's father came to watch him mourn, secretly satisfied, though aloud he grieved for all apostates. Isaac did not like my wife. He called her a tall yellow straw. After we were married he never said a word against her, but he kept away.

I went with my wife to his wedding. We took the early train down especially, but when we arrived the feast was well under way, and the guests far into the dancing.

"Look, look, they don't dance together," Jane said.

"Who?"

"The men and the women. The bride and the groom."

"Count the babies," I advised. "The Jews are also Puritans, but only in public."

The bride was enclosed all by herself on a straight chair in the centre of a spinning ring of young men. The floor heaved under their whirl. They stamped, the chandeliers shuddered, the guests cried out, the young men with linked arms spiralled and their skullcaps came flying off like centrifugal balloons. Isaac, a mist of black suit, a stamping foot, was lost in the planet's wake of black suits and emphatic feet. The dancing young men shouted bridal songs, the floor leaned like a plate, the whole room teetered.

Isaac had told me something of Sheindel. Before now I had never seen her. Her birth was in a concentration camp, and they were about to throw her against the electrified fence when an army mobbed the gate; the current vanished from the terrible wires, and she had nothing to show for it afterwards but a mark on her cheek like an asterisk, cut by a barb. The asterisk pointed to certain dry footnotes: she had no mother to show, she had no father to show, but she had, extraordinarily, God to show – she was known to be, for her age and sex, astonishingly learned. She was only seventeen.

"What pretty hair she has," Jane said.

Now Sheindel was dancing with Isaac's mother. All the ladies made a fence, and the bride, twirling with her mother-in-law, lost a shoe and fell against the long laughing row. The ladies lifted their glistering breasts in their lacy dresses and laughed; the young men, stamping two by two, went on shouting their wedding songs. Sheindel danced without her shoe, and the black river of her hair followed her.

"After today she'll have to hide it all," I explained.

Jane asked why.

"So as not to be a temptation to men," I told her, and covertly looked for my father. There he was, in a shadow, apart. My eyes discovered his eyes. He turned his back and gripped his throat.

"It's a very anthropological experience," Jane said.

"A wedding is a wedding," I answered her, "among us even more so."

"Is that your father over there, that little scowly man?"

To Jane all Jews were little. "My father the man of the cloth. Yes."

"A wedding is not a wedding," said Jane: we had had only a licence and a judge with bad breath.

"Everybody marries for the same reason."

"No," said my wife. "Some for love and some for spite."

"And everybody for bed."

"Some for spite," she insisted.

"I was never cut out for a man of the cloth," I said. "My poor father doesn't see that."

"He doesn't speak to you."

"A technicality. He's losing his voice."

"Well, he's not like you. He doesn't do it for spite," Jane said.

"You don't know him," I said.

He lost it altogether the very week Isaac published his first remarkable collection of responsa. Isaac's father crowed like a passionate rooster, and packed his wife and himself off to the Holy Land to boast on the holy soil. Isaac was a little relieved; he had just been made Professor of Mishnaic History, and his father's whims and pretences and foolish rivalries were an embarrassment. It is easy to honour a father from afar, but bitter to honour one who is dead. A surgeon cut out my father's voice, and he died without a word.

Isaac and I no longer met. Our ways were too disparate. Isaac was famous, if not in the world, certainly in the kingdom of jurists and scholars. By this time I had acquired a partnership in a small book store in a basement. My partner sold me his share, and I put up a new sign: "The Book Cellar"; for reasons more obscure than filial (all the same I wished my father could have seen it) I established a department devoted especially to not-quite-rare theological works, chiefly in Hebrew and Aramaic, though I carried some Latin and Greek. When Isaac's second volume reached my shelves (I had now expanded to street level), I wrote him to congratulate him, and after that we corresponded, not with any regularity. He took to ordering all his books from me, and we exchanged awkward little jokes. "I'm still in the jacket business," I told him, "but now I feel I'm where I belong. Last time I went too fur." "Sheindel is well, and Naomi and Esther have a sister," he wrote. And later: "Naomi, Esther, and Miriam have a sister." And still later: "Naomi, Esther, Miriam, and Ophra have a sister." It went on until there were seven girls. "There's nothing in Torah that prevents an illustrious man from having illustrious daughters," I wrote him when he said he had given up hope of another rabbi in the family. "But where do you find seven illustrious husbands?" he asked. Every order brought another quip, and we bantered back and forth in this way for some years.

I noticed that he read everything. Long ago he had inflamed my taste, but I could never keep up. No sooner did I catch his joy in Saadia Gaon than he had already sprung ahead to Yehudah Halevi. One day he was weeping with Dostoevsky and the next leaping in the air over Thomas Mann. He introduced me to Hegel and Nietzsche while our fathers wailed. His mature reading was no more peaceable than those frenzies of his youth, when I would come upon him in an abandoned classroom at dusk, his stocking feet on the windowsill, the light already washed from the lowest city clouds, wearing the look of a man half-sotted with print.

But when the widow asked me – covering a certain excess of alertness or irritation – whether to my knowledge Isaac had lately been ordering any books on horticulture, I was astonished.

"He bought so much," I demurred.

"Yes, yes, yes," she said. "How could you remember?"

She poured the tea and then, with a discreetness of gesture, lifted my dripping raincoat from the chair where I had thrown it and took it out of the room. It was a crowded apartment, not very neat, far from slovenly, cluttered with dolls and tiny dishes and an array of tricycles. The dining table was as large as a desert. An old-fashioned crocheted lace runner divided it into two nations, and on the end of this, in the neutral zone, so to speak, Sheindel had placed my cup. There was no physical relic of Isaac: not even a book.

She returned. "My girls are all asleep, we can talk. What an ordeal for you, weather like this and going out so far to that place."

It was impossible to tell whether she was angry or not. I had rushed in on her like the rainfall itself, scattering drops, my shoes stuck all over with leaves.

"I comprehend exactly why you went out there. The impulse of a detective," she said. Her voice contained an irony that surprised me. It was brilliantly and unmistakably accented, and because of this jaggedly precise. It was as if every word emitted a quick white thread of great purity, like hard silk, which she was then obliged to bite cleanly off. "You went to find something? An atmosphere? The sadness itself?"

"There was nothing to see," I said, and thought I was lunatic to have put myself in her way.

"Did you dig in the ground? He might have buried a note for goodbye."

"Was there a note?" I asked, startled.

"He left nothing behind for ordinary humanity like yourself."

I saw she was playing with me. "Rebbetzin Kornfeld," I said, standing up, "forgive me. My coat, please, and I'll go."

"Sit," she commanded. "Isaac read less lately, did you notice that?"

I gave her a civil smile. "All the same he was buying more and more."

"Think," she said. "I depend on you. You're just the one who might know. I had forgotten this. God sent you perhaps."

"Rebbetzin Kornfeld, I'm only a bookseller."

"God in his judgment sent me a bookseller. For such a long time Isaac never read at home. Think! Agronomy?"

"I don't remember anything like that. What would a Professor of Mishnaic History want with agronomy?"

"If he had a new book under his arm he would take it straight to the seminary and hide it in his office."

"I mailed to his office. If you like I can look up some of the titles –"

"You were in the park and you saw nothing?"

"Nothing." Then I was ashamed. "I saw the tree."

"And what is that? A tree is nothing."

"Rebbetzin Kornfeld," I pleaded, "it's a stupidity that I came here. I don't know myself why I came, I beg your pardon, I had no idea –"

"You came to learn why Isaac took his life. Botany? Or even, please listen, even mycology? He never asked you to send something on mushrooms? Or having to do with herbs? Manure? Flowers? A certain kind of agricultural poetry? A book about gardening? Forestry? Vegetables? Cereal growing?"

"Nothing, nothing like that," I said excitedly. "Rebbetzin Kornfeld, your husband was a rabbi!"

"I know what my husband was. Something to do with vines? Arbours? Rice? Think, think, think! Anything to do with land – meadows – goats – a farm, hay – anything at all, anything rustic or lunar –"

"Lunar! My God! Was he a teacher or a nurseryman? Goats! Was he a furrier? Sheindel, are you crazy? I was the furrier! What do you want from the dead?"

Without a word she replenished my cup, though it was more than half full, and sat down opposite me, on the other side of the lace boundary line. She leaned her face into her palms, but I saw her eyes. She kept them wide.

"Rebbetzin Kornfeld," I said, collecting myself, "with a tragedy like this –"

"You imagine I blame the books. I don't blame the books, whatever they were. If he had been faithful to his books he would have lived."

"He lived," I cried, "in books, what else?"

"No," said the widow.

"A scholar. A rabbi. A remarkable Jew!"

At this she spilled a furious laugh. "Tell me, I have always been very interested and shy to inquire. Tell me about your wife."

I intervened: "I haven't had a wife in years."

"What are they like, those people?"

"They're exactly like us, if you can think what we would be if we were like them."

"We are not like them. Their bodies are more to them than ours are to us. Our books are holy, to them their bodies are holy."

"Jane's was so holy she hardly ever let me get near it," I muttered to myself.

"Isaac used to run in the park, but he lost his breath too quickly. Instead he read in a book about runners with hats made of leaves."

"Sheindel, Sheindel, what did you expect of him? He was a student, he sat and he thought, he was a Jew."

She thrust her hands flat. "He was not."

I could not reply. I looked at her merely. She was thinner now than in her early young-womanhood, and her face had an in-between cast, poignant still at the mouth and jaw, beginning to grow coarse on either side of the nose.

"I think he was never a Jew," she said.

I wondered whether Isaac's suicide had unbalanced her.

"I'll tell you a story," she resumed. "A story about stories. These were the bed-time stories Isaac told Naomi and Esther: about mice that danced and children who laughed: When Miriam came he invented a speaking cloud. With Ophra it was a turtle that married a blade of withered grass. By Leah's time the stones had tears for their leglessness. Rebecca cried because of a tree that turned into a girl and could never grow colours again in autumn. Shiphrah, the littlest, believes that a pig has a soul."

"My own father used to drill me every night in sacred recitation. It was a terrible childhood."

"He insisted on picnics. Each time we went farther and farther into the country. It was a madness. Isaac never troubled to learn to drive a car, and there was always a clumsiness of baskets to carry and a clutter of buses and trains and seven exhausted wild girls. And he would look for special places – we couldn't settle just here or there, there had to be a brook or such-and-such a slope or else a little grove. And then, though he said it was all for the children's pleasure, he would leave them and go off alone and never come back until sunset, when everything was spilled and the air freezing and the babies crying."

"I was a grown man before I had the chance to go on a picnic," I admitted.

"I'm speaking of the beginning," said the widow. "Like you, wasn't I fooled? I was fooled, I was charmed. Going home with our baskets of berries and flowers we were a romantic huddle. Isaac's stories on those nights were full of dark invention. May God preserve me, I even begged him to write them down. Then suddenly he joined a club, and Sunday mornings he was up and away before dawn."

"A club? So early? What library opens at that hour?" I said, stunned that a man like Isaac should ally himself with anything so doubtful.

"Ah, you don't follow, you don't follow. It was a hiking club, they met under the moon. I thought it was a pity, the whole week Isaac was so inward, he needed air for the mind. He used to come home too fatigued to stand. He said he went for the landscape. I was like you, I took what I heard, I heard it all and never followed. He resigned from the hikers finally, and I believed all that strangeness was finished. He told me it was absurd to walk at such a pace, he was a teacher and not an athlete. Then he began to write."

"But he always wrote," I objected.

"Not this way. What he wrote was only fairy tales. He kept at it and for a while he neglected everything else. It was the strangeness in another form. The stories surprised me, they were so poor and dull. They were a little like the ideas he used to scare the girls with, but choked all over with notes, appendices, prefaces. It struck me then he didn't seem to understand he was only doing fairy tales. Yet they were really very ordinary – full of sprites, nymphs, gods, everything ordinary and old."

"Will you let me see them?"

"Burned, all burned."

"Isaac burned them?"

"You don't think I did! I see what you think."

It was true that I was marvelling at her hatred. I supposed she was one of those born to dread imagination. I was overtaken by a coldness for her, though the sight of her small hands with their tremulous staves of fingers turning and turning in front of her face like a gate on a hinge reminded me of where she was born and who she was. She was an orphan and had been saved by magic and had a terror of it. The coldness fled. "Why should you be bothered by little stories?" I inquired. "It wasn't the stories that killed him."

"No, no, not the stories," she said. "Stupid corrupt things. I was glad when he gave them up. He piled them in the bathtub and lit them with a match. Then he put a notebook in his coat pocket and said he would walk in the park. Week after week he tried all the parks in the city. I didn't dream what he could be after. One day he took the subway and rode to the end of the line, and this was the right park at last. He went every day after class, An hour going, an hour back. Two, three in the morning he came home. "Is it exercise?" I said. I thought he might be running again. He used to shiver with the chill of night and the dew. "No, I sit quite still," he said. "Is it more stories you do out there?" "No, I only jot down what I think." "A man should meditate in his own house, not by night near bad water," I said. Six, seven in the morning he came home. I asked him if he meant to find his grave in that place."

She broke off with a cough, half artifice and half resignation, so loud that it made her crane towards the bedrooms to see if she had awakened a child. "I don't sleep any more," she told me. "Look around you. Look, look everywhere, look on the windowsills. Do you see any plants, any common house plants? I went down one evening and gave them to the garbage collector. I couldn't sleep in the same space with plants. They are like little trees. Am I deranged? Take Isaac's notebook and bring it back when you can."

I obeyed. In my own room, a sparse place, with no ornaments but a few pretty stalks in pots, I did not delay and seized the notebook. It was a tiny affair, three inches by five, with ruled pages that opened on a coiled wire. I read searchingly, hoping for something not easily evident. Sheindel by her melancholy innuendo had made me believe that in these few sheets Isaac had revealed the reason for his suicide. But it was all a disappointment. There was not a word of any importance. After a while I concluded that, whatever her motives, Sheindel was playing with me again. She meant to punish me for asking the unaskable. My inquisitiveness offended her; she had given me Isaac's notebook not to enlighten but to rebuke. The handwriting was recognizable yet oddly formed, shaky and even senile, like that of a man outdoors and deskless who scribbles in his palm or on his lifted knee or leaning on a bit of bark; and there was no doubt that the wrinkled leaves, with their ragged corners, had been in and out of someone's pocket. So I did not mistrust Sheindel's mad anecdote; this much was true: a park, Isaac, a notebook, all at once, but signifying no more than that a professor with a literary turn of mind had gone for a walk. There was even a green stain straight across one of the quotations, as if the pad had slipped grasswards and been trodden on.

I have forgotten to mention that the notebook, though scantily filled, was in three languages. The Greek I could not read at all, but it had the shape of verse. The Hebrew was simply a miscellany, drawn mostly from Leviticus and Deuteronomy. Among these I found the following extracts, transcribed not quite verbatim:

Ye shall utterly destroy all the places of the gods, upon the high mountains, and upon the hills, and under every green tree.

And the soul that turneth after familiar spirits to go a-whoring after them, I will cut him off from among his people.

These, of course, were ordinary unadorned notes, such as any classroom lecturer might commonly make to remind himself of the text, with a phrase cut out here and there for the sake of speeding his hand. Or I thought it possible that Isaac might at that time have been preparing a paper on the Talmudic commentaries for these passages. Whatever the case, the remaining quotations, chiefly from English poetry, interested me only slightly more. They were the elegiac favourites of a closeted Romantic. I was repelled by Isaac's Nature: it wore a capital letter, and smelled like my own Book Cellar. It was plain to me that he had lately grown painfully academic: he could not see a weed's tassel without finding a classical reference for it. He had put down a snatch of Byron, a smudge of Keats (like his Scriptural copyings, these too were quick and fragmented), a pair of truncated lines from Tennyson, and this unmarked and clumsy quatrain:

And yet all is not taken. Still one Dryad
  Flits through the wood, one Oread skims the hill;
White in the whispering stream still gleams a Naiad;
  The beauty of the earth is haunted still.

All of this was so cloying and mooning and ridiculous, and so pedantic besides, that I felt ashamed for him. And yet there was almost nothing else, nothing to redeem him and nothing personal, only a sentence or two in his rigid self-controlled scholar's style, not unlike the starched little jokes of our correspondence. "I am writing at dusk sitting on a stone in Trilham's Inlet Park, within sight of Trilham's Inlet, a bay to the north of the city, and within two yards of a slender tree, *Quercus velutina*, the age of which, should one desire to measure it, can be ascertained by (God forbid) cutting the bole and counting the rings. The man writing is thirty-five years old and ageing too rapidly, which may be ascertained by counting the rings under his poor myopic eyes." Below this, deliberate and readily more legible than the rest, appeared three curious words:

Great Pan lives.

That was all. In a day or so I returned the notebook to Sheindel. I told myself that she had seven orphans to worry over, and repressed my anger at having been cheated.

She was waiting for me. "I am so sorry, there was a letter in the notebook, it had fallen out. I found it on the carpet after you left."

"Thank you, no," I said. "I've read enough out of Isaac's pockets."

"Then why did you come to see me to begin with?"

"I came," I said, just to see you."

"You came for Isaac." But she was more mocking than distraught. "I gave you everything you needed to see what happened and still you don't follow. Here." She held out a large law-sized paper. "Read the letter."

"I've read his notebook. If everything I need to fathom Isaac is in the notebook I don't need the letter."

"It's a letter he wrote to explain himself," she persisted.

"You told me Isaac left you no notes."

"It was not written to me."

I sat down on one of the dining-room chairs and Sheindel put the page before me on the table. It lay face up on the lace divider. I did not look at it.

"It's a love letter," Sheindel whispered. "When they cut him down they found the notebook in one pocket and the letter in the other."

I did not know what to say.

"The police gave me everything," Sheindel said. "Everything to keep."

"A love letter?" I repeated.

"That is what such letters are commonly called."

"And the police – they gave it to you, and that was the first you realized what" – I floundered after the inconceivable – "what could be occupying him?"

"What could be occupying him," she mimicked. "Yes. Not until they took the letter and the notebook out of his pocket."

"My God. His habit of life, his mind . . . I can't imagine it. You never guessed?"

"No."

"These trips to the park –"

"He had become aberrant in many ways. I have described them to you."

"But the park! Going off like that, alone – you didn't think he might be meeting a woman?"

"It was not a woman."

Disgust like a powder clotted my nose. "Sheindel, you're crazy."

"I'm crazy, is that it? Read his confession! Read it! How long can I be the only one to know this thing? Do you want my brain to melt? Be my confidant," she entreated so unexpectedly that I held my breath.

"You've said nothing to anyone?"

"Would they have recited such eulogies if I had? Read the letter!"

"I have no interest in the abnormal," I said coldly.

She raised her eyes and watched me for the smallest space. Without any change in the posture of her suppliant head her laughter began; I have never since heard sounds like those – almost mouselike in density for fear of waking her sleeping daughters, but so rational in intent that it was like listening to astonished sanity rendered into a cackling fugue. She kept it up for a minute and then calmed herself. "Please sit where you are. Please pay attention. I will read the letter to you myself."

She plucked the page from the table with an orderly gesture. I saw that this letter had been scrupulously prepared; it was closely written. Her tone was cleansed by scorn.

"'My ancestors were led out of Egypt by the hand of God,'" she read.

"Is this how a love letter starts out?"

She moved on resolutely. "'We were guilty of so-called abominations well-described elsewhere. Other peoples have been nourished on their mythologies. For aeons we have been weaned from all traces of the same.'"

I felt myself becoming impatient. The fact was I had returned with a single idea: I meant to marry Isaac's widow when enough time had passed to make it seemly. It was my intention to court her with great subtlety at first, so that I would not appear to be presuming on her sorrow. But she was possessed. "Sheindel, why do you want to inflict this treatise on me? Give it to the seminary, contribute it to a symposium of professors."

"I would sooner die."

At this I began to attend in earnest.

"'I will leave aside the wholly plausible position of so-called animism within the concept of the One God. I will omit a historical illumination of its continuous but covert expression even within the Fence of the Law. Creature, I leave these aside –'"

"What?" I yelped.

"'Creature,'" she repeated, spreading her nostrils. "'What is human history? What is our philosophy? What is our religion? None of these teaches us poor human ones that we are alone in the universe, and even without them we would know that we are not. At a very young age I understood that a foolish man would not believe in a fish had he not had one enter his experience. Innumerable forms exist and have come to our eyes, and to the still deeper eye of the lens of our instruments; from this minute perception of what already is, it is easy to conclude that further forms are possible, that all forms are probable. God created the world not for Himself alone, or I would not now possess this consciousness with which I am enabled to address thee, Loveliness.'"

"Thee," I echoed, and swallowed a sad bewilderment.

"You must let me go on," Sheindel said, and grimly went on. "'It is false history, false philosophy, and false religion which declare to us human ones that we live among Things. The arts of physics and chemistry begin to teach us differently, but their way of compassion is new, and finds few to carry fidelity to its logical and beautiful end. The molecules dance inside all forms, and within the molecules dance the atoms, and within the atoms dance still profounder sources of divine vitality. There is nothing that is Dead. There is no Non-life. Holy life subsists even in the stone, even in the bones of dead dogs and dead men. Hence in God's fecundating Creation there is no possibility of Idolatry, and therefore no possibility of committing this so-called abomination.'"

"My God, my God," I wailed. "Enough, Sheindel, it's more than enough, no more –"

"There is more," she said.

"I don't want to hear it."

"He stains his character for you? A spot, do you think? You will hear." She took up in a voice which all at once reminded me of my father's: it was unforgiving. "'Creature, I rehearse these matters though all our language is as breath to thee; as baubles for the juggler. Where we struggle to understand from day to day, and contemplate the grave for its riddle, the other breeds are born fulfilled in wisdom. Animal races conduct themselves without self-investigations; instinct is a higher and not a lower thing, Alas that we human ones – but for certain pitifully primitive approximations in those few reflexes and involuntary actions left to our bodies – are born bare of instinct! All that we unfortunates must resort to through science, art, philosophy, religion, all our imaginings and tormented strivings, all our meditations and vain questionings, all! – are expressed naturally and rightly in the beasts, the plants, the rivers, the stones. The reason is simple, it is our tragedy: our soul is included in us, it inhabits us, we contain it, when we seek our soul we must seek in ourselves. To *see* the soul, to confront it – that is divine wisdom. Yet how can we see into our dark selves? With the other races of being it is differently ordered. The soul of the plant does not reside in the chlorophyll, it may roam if it wishes, it may choose whatever form or shape it pleases. Hence the other breeds, being largely free of their soul and able to witness it, can live in peace. To see one's soul is to know all, to know all is to own the peace our philosophies futilely envisage. Earth displays two categories of soul: the free and the indwelling. We human ones are cursed with the indwelling –'"

"Stop!" I cried.

"I will not," said the widow.

"Please, you told me he burned his fairy tales."

"Did I lie to you? Will you say I lied?"

"Then for Isaac's sake why didn't you? If this isn't a fairy tale what do you want me to think it could be?"

"Think what you like."

"Sheindel," I said, "I beg you, don't destroy a dead man's honour. Don't look at this thing again, tear it to pieces, don't continue with it."

"I don't destroy his honour. He had none."

"Please! Listen to yourself! My God, who was the man? Rabbi Isaac Korn-feld! Talk of honour! Wasn't he a teacher? Wasn't he a scholar?"

"He was a pagan."

Her eyes returned without hesitation to their task. She commenced: "'All these truths I learned only gradually, against my will and desire. Our teacher Moses did not speak of them; much may be said under this head. It was not out of igno-rance that Moses failed to teach about those souls that are free. If I have learned what Moses knew, is this not because we are both men? He was a man, but God addressed him; it was God's will that our ancestors should no longer be slaves. Yet our ancestors, being stiff-necked, would not have abandoned their slavery in Egypt had they been taught of the free souls. They would have said: "Let us stay, our bodies will remain enslaved in Egypt, but our souls will wander at their pleasure in Zion, If the cactus-plant stays rooted while its soul roams, why not also a man?" And if Moses had replied that only the world of Nature has the gift of the free soul, while man is chained to his, and that a man, to free his soul, must also free the body that is its vessel, they would have scoffed. "How is it that men, and men alone, are different from the world of Nature? If this is so, then the condition of men is evil and unjust, and if this condition of ours is evil and unjust in general; what does it matter whether we are slaves in Egypt or citizens in Zion?" And they would not have done God's will and abandoned their slavery. Therefore Moses never spoke to them of the free souls, lest the people not do God's will and go out from Egypt.'"

In an instant a sensation broke in me – it was entirely obscure, there was nothing I could compare it with, and yet I was certain I recognized it. And then I did. It hurtled me into childhood – it was the crisis of insight one experiences when one has just read out, for the first time, that conglomeration of figurines which makes a word. In that moment I penetrated beyond Isaac's alphabet into his language. I saw that he was on the side of possibility: he was both sane and inspired. His intention was not to accumulate mystery but to dispel it.

"All that part is brilliant," I burst out.

Sheindel meanwhile had gone to the sideboard to take a sip of cold tea that was standing there. "In a minute," she said, and pursued her thirst. "I have heard of drawings surpassing Rembrandt daubed by madmen who when released from the fit couldn't hold the chalk. What follows is beautiful, I warn you."

"The man was a genius."

"Yes."

"Go on," I urged.

She produced for me her clownish jeering smile. She read: "'Sometimes in the desert journey on the way they would come to a watering place, and some quick spry boy would happen to glimpse the soul of the spring (which the wild Greeks afterwards called naiad), but not knowing of the existence of the free souls he would suppose only that the moon had cast a momentary beam across the water. Loveliness, with the same innocence of accident I discovered thee. Loveliness, Loveliness.'"

She stopped.

"Is that all?"

"There is more."

"Read it."

"The rest is the love letter."

"Is it hard for you?" But I asked with more eagerness than pity.

"I was that man's wife, he scaled the Fence of the Law. For this God preserved me from the electric fence. Read it for yourself."

Incontinently I snatched the crowded page.

"'Loveliness, in thee the joy, substantiation, and supernal succour of my theorem. How many hours through how many years I walked over the cilia-forests of our enormous aspiring vegetable-star, this light rootless seed that crawls in its single furrow, this shaggy mazy unimplanted cabbage-head of our earth! – never, all that time, all those days of unfulfilment, a white space like a desert thirst, never, never to grasp. I thought myself abandoned to the intrigue of my folly. At dawn, on a hillock, what seemed the very shape and seizing of the mound's nature – what was it? Only the haze of the sun-ball growing great through hoarfrost. The oread slipped from me, leaving her illusion; or was never there at all; or was there but for an instant, and ran away. What sly ones the free souls are! They have a comedy we human ones cannot dream: the laughing drunkard feels in himself the shadow of the shadow of the shadow of their wit, and only because he has made himself a vessel, as the two banks and the bed of a rivulet are the naiad's vessel. A naiad I may indeed have viewed whole: all seven of my daughters were once wading in a stream in a compact but beautiful park, of which I had much hope. The youngest being not yet two, and fretful, the older ones were told to keep her always by the hand, but they did not obey. I, having passed some way into the woods behind, all at once heard a scream and noise of splashes, and caught sight of a tiny body flying down into the water. Running back through the trees I could see the others bunched together, afraid, as the baby dived helplessly, all these little girls frozen in a garland – when suddenly one of them (it was too quick a movement for me to recognize which) darted to the struggler, who was now underwater, and pulled her up, and put an arm around her to soothe her. The arm was blue – blue. As blue as a lake. And fiercely, from my spot on the bank, panting, I began to count the little girls. I counted eight, thought myself not mad but delivered, again counted, counted seven, knew I had counted well before, knew I counted well even now. A blue-armed girl had come to wade among them. Which is to say the shape of a girl. I questioned my daughters: each in her fright believed one of the others had gone to pluck up the tiresome baby. None wore a dress with blue sleeves.'"

"Proofs," said the widow. "Isaac was meticulous, he used to account for all his proofs always."

"How?" My hand in tremor rustled Isaac's letter; the paper bleated as though whipped.

"By eventually finding a principle to cover them," she finished maliciously. Well, don't rest even for me, you don't oblige me. You have a long story to go, long enough to make a fever."

"Tea," I said hoarsely.

She brought me her own cup from the sideboard, and I believed as I drank that I swallowed some of her mockery and gall.

"Sheindel, for a woman so pious you're a great sceptic." And now the tremor had command of my throat.

"An atheist's statement," she rejoined. "The more piety, the more scepticism. A religious man comprehends this. Superfluity, excess of custom, and superstition would climb like a choking vine on the Fence of the Law if scepticism did not continually hack them away to make freedom for purity."

I then thought her fully worthy of Isaac. Whether I was worthy of her I evaded putting to myself; instead I gargled some tea and returned to the letter.

"'It pains me to confess,'" I read, "'how after that I moved from clarity to doubt and back again. I had no trust in my conclusions because all my experiences were evanescent. Everything certain I attributed to some other cause less certain. Every voice out of the moss I blamed on rabbits and squirrels. Every motion among leaves I called a bird, though there positively was no bird. My first sight of the Little People struck me as no more than a shudder of literary delusion, and I determined they could only be an instantaneous crop of mushrooms. But one night, a little after ten o'clock at the crux of summer – the sky still showed strings of light – I was wandering in this place, this place where they will find my corpse –'"

"Not for my sake," said Sheindel when I hesitated.

"It's terrible," I croaked, "terrible."

"Withered like a shell," she said, as though speaking of the cosmos; and I understood from her manner that she had a fanatic's acquaintance with this letter, and knew it nearly by heart. She appeared to be thinking the words faster than I could bring them out, and for some reason I was constrained to hurry the pace of my reading.

"'– where they will find my corpse withered like the shell of an insect,'" I rushed on. "'The smell of putrefaction lifted clearly from the bay. I began to speculate about my own body after I was dead – whether the soul would be set free immediately after the departure of life; or whether only gradually, as decomposition proceeded and more and more of the indwelling soul was released to freedom. But when I considered how a man's body is no better than a clay pot, a fact which none of our sages has ever contradicted, it seemed to me then that an indwelling soul by its own nature would be obliged to cling to its bit of pottery until the last crumb and grain had vanished into earth. I walked through the ditches of that black meadow grieving and swollen with self-pity. It came to me that while my poor bones went on decaying at their ease, my soul would have to linger inside them, waiting, despairing, longing to join the free ones. I cursed it for its gravity-despoiled, slow, interminably languishing purse of flesh; better to be encased in vapour, in wind, in a hair of a coconut! Who knows how long it takes the body of a man to shrink into gravel, and the gravel into sand, and the sand into vitamin? A hundred years? Two hundred, three hundred? A thousand perhaps! Is it not true that bones nearly intact are constantly being dug up by the paleontologists two million years after burial?' Sheindel," I interrupted, "this is death, not love. Where's the love letter to be afraid of here? I don't find it."

"Continue," she ordered. And then: "You see I'm not afraid.'

"Not of love?'

"No. But you recite much too slowly. Your mouth is shaking. Are you afraid of death?"

I did not reply.

"Continue," she said again. "Go rapidly. The next sentence begins with an extraordinary thought."

"'An extraordinary thought emerged in me. It was luminous, profound, and practical. More than that, it had innumerable precedents; the mythologies had documented it a dozen dozen times over. I recalled all those mortals reputed to have coupled with gods (a collective word, showing much common sense, signifying what our philosophies more abstrusely call Shekhina), and all that poignant miscegenation represented by centaurs, satyrs, mermaids, fauns, and so forth, not to speak of that even more famous mingling in Genesis, whereby the sons of God took the daughters of men for brides, producing giants and possibly also those abortions, leviathan and behemoth, of which we read in Job, along with unicorns and other chimeras and monsters abundant in Scripture, hence far from fanciful. There existed also the example of the succubus Lilith, who was often known to couple in the mediaeval ghetto even with pre-pubescent boys. By all these evidences I was emboldened in my confidence that I was surely not the first man to conceive such a desire in the history of our earth. Creature, the thought that took hold of me was this: if only I could couple with one of the free souls, the strength of the connection would likely wrest my own soul from my body – seize it, as if by a tongs, draw it out, so to say, to its own freedom. The intensity and force of my desire to capture one of these beings now became prodigious. I avoided my wife –'"

Here the widow heard me falter.

"Please," she commanded, and I saw creeping in her face the completed turn of a sneer.

"'– lest I be depleted of potency at that moment (which might occur in any interval, even, I assumed, in my own bedroom) when I should encounter one of the free souls. I was borne back again and again to the fetid viscosities of the Inlet, borne there as if on the rising stink of my own enduring and tedious putrefaction, the idea of which I could no longer shake off – I envisaged my soul as trapped in my last granule, and that last granule itself perhaps petrified, never to dissolve, and my soul condemned to minister to it throughout eternity! It seemed to me my soul must be released at once or be lost to sweet air forever. In a gleamless dark, struggling with this singular panic, I stumbled from ditch to ditch, strained like a blind dog for the support of solid verticality; and smacked my palm against bark. I looked up and in the black could not fathom the size of the tree – my head lolled forward, my brow met the trunk with all its gravings. I busied my fingers in the interstices of the bark's cuneiform. Then with forehead flat on the tree, I embraced it with both arms to measure it. My hands united on the other side. It was a young narrow weed, I did not know of what family. I reached to the lowest branch and plucked a leaf and made my tongue travel meditatively along its periphery to assess its shape: oak. The taste was sticky and exaltingly bitter. A jubilation lightly carpeted my groin. I then placed one hand (the other I kept around the tree's waist, as it were) in the bifurcation (disgustingly termed crotch) of that lowest limb and the elegant and devoutly firm torso, and caressed that miraculous juncture with a certain languor, which gradually changed to vigour. I was all at once savagely alert and deeply daring: I chose that single tree together with the ground near it for an enemy which in two senses would not yield: it would neither give nor give in. "Come, come," I called aloud to Nature. A wind blew out a braid of excremental malodour into the heated air. "Come," I called, "couple with me, as thou didst with Cadmus, Rhoecus, Tithonus, Endymion, and that king Numa Pompilius to whom thou didst give secrets. As Lilith comes without a sign, so come thou. As the sons of God came to copulate with women, so now let a daughter of Shekhina the Emanation reveal herself to me. Nymph, come now, come now."

"'Without warning I was flung to the ground. My face smashed into earth, and a flaky clump of dirt lodged in my open mouth. For the rest, I was on my knees, pressing down on my hands, with the fingernails clutching dirt. A superb ache lined my haunch. I began to weep because I was certain I had been ravished by some sinewy animal. I vomited the earth I had swallowed and believed I was defiled, as it is written: "Neither shalt thou lie with any beast." I lay sunk in the grass, afraid to lift my head to see if the animal still lurked. Through some curious means I had been fully positioned and aroused and exquisitely sated, all in half a second, in a fashion impossible to explain, in which, though I performed as with my own wife, I felt as if a preternatural rapine had been committed upon me. I continued prone, listening for the animal's breathing. Meanwhile, though every tissue of my flesh was gratified in its inmost awareness, a marvellous voluptuousness did not leave my body; sensual exultations of a wholly supreme and paradisal order, unlike anything our poets have ever defined, both flared and were intensely satisfied in the same moment. This salubrious and delightful perceptiveness excited my being for some time: a conjoining not dissimilar (in metaphor only; in actuality it cannot be described) from the magical contradiction of the tree and its issuance-of-branch at the point of bifurcation. In me were linked, *in the same instant*, appetite and fulfilment, delicacy and power, mastery and submissiveness, and other paradoxes of entirely remarkable emotional import.

"'Then I heard what I took to be the animal treading through the grass quite near my head, all cunningly; it withheld its breathing, then snored it out in a cautious and wisp-like whirr that resembled a light wind through rushes. With a huge energy (my muscular force seemed to have increased) I leaped up in fear of my life; I had nothing to use for a weapon but – oh, laughable! – the pen I had been writing with in a little notebook I always carried about with me in those days (and still keep on my person as a self-shaming souvenir of my insipidness, my bookishness, my pitiable conjecture and wishfulness in a time when, not yet knowing thee, I knew nothing). What I saw was not an animal but a girl no older than my oldest daughter, who was then fourteen. Her skin was as perfect as an eggplant's and nearly of that colour. In height she was half as tall as I was. The second and third fingers of her hands – this I noticed at once – were peculiarly fused, one slotted into the other, like the ligula of a leaf. She was entirely bald and had no ears but rather a type of gill or envelope, one only, on the left side. Her toes displayed the same oddity I had observed in her fingers. She was neither naked nor clothed – that is to say, even though a part of her body, from hip to just below the breasts (each of which appeared to be a kind of velvety colourless pear, suspended from a very short, almost invisible stem), was luxuriantly covered with a flossy or spore-like material, this was a natural efflorescence in the manner of, with us, hair. All her sexual portion was wholly visible, as in any field flower. Aside from these express deviations, she was commandingly human in aspect, if unmistakably flowerlike. She was, in fact, the reverse of our hackneyed euphuism, as when we say a young girl blooms like a flower – she, on the contrary, seemed a flower transfigured into the shape of the most stupendously lovely child I had ever seen. Under the smallest push of wind she bent at her superlative waist; this, I recognized, and not the exhalations of some lecherous beast, was the breathlike sound that had alarmed me at her approach: these motions of hers made the blades of grass collide. (She herself, having no lungs, did not "breathe".) She stood bobbing joyfully before me, with a face as tender as a morning-glory, strangely phosphorescent: she shed her own light, in effect, and I had no difficulty in confronting her beauty.

"'Moreover, by experiment I soon learned that she was not only capable of language, but that she delighted in playing with it. This she literally could do – if I had distinguished her hands before anything else, it was because she had held them out to catch my first cry of awe. She either caught my words like balls or let them roll, or caught them and then darted off to throw them into the Inlet. I discovered that whenever I spoke I more or less pelted her; but she liked this, and told me ordinary human speech only tickled and amused, whereas laughter, being highly plosive, was something of an assault. I then took care to pretend much solemnity, though I was lightheaded with rapture. Her own "voice" I apprehended rather than heard – which she, unable to imagine how we human ones are prisoned in sensory perception, found hard to conceive. Her sentences came to me not as a series of differentiated frequencies but (impossible to develop this idea in language) as a diffused cloud of field fragrances; yet to say that I assimilated her thought through the olfactory nerve would be a pedestrian distortion. All the same it was clear that whatever she said reached me in a shimmer of pellucid perfumes, and I understood her meaning with an immediacy of glee and with none of the ambiguities and suspiciousness of motive that surround our human communication.

"'Through this medium she explained that she was a dryad and that her name was Iripomoňoéià (as nearly as I can render it in our narrowly limited orthography, and in this dunce's alphabet of ours which is notoriously impervious to odoriferous categories). She told me what I had already seized: that she had given me her love in response to my call.

"'Wilt thou come to any man who calls?" I asked.

"'All men call, whether realizing it or not. I and my sisters sometimes come to those who do not realize. Almost never, unless for sport, do we come to that man who calls knowingly – he wishes only to inhabit us out of perversity or boastfulness or to indulge a dreamed-of disgust."

"'Scripture does not forbid sodomy with the plants," I exclaimed, but she did not comprehend any of this and lowered her hands so that my words would fly past her uncaught. "I too called thee knowingly, not for perversity but for love of Nature."

"""I have caught men's words before as they talked of Nature, you are not the first. It is not Nature they love so much as Death they fear. So Coryĺyĭyb my cousin received it in a season not long ago coupling in a harbour with one of your kind, one called Spinoza, one that had catarrh of the lung. I am of Nature and immortal and so I cannot pity your deaths. But return tomorrow and say Iripomoňoéià." Then she chased my last word to where she had kicked it, behind the tree. She did not come back. I ran to the tree and circled it diligently but she was lost for that night.

"'Loveliness, all the foregoing, telling of my life and meditations until now, I have never before recounted to thee or any other. The rest is beyond mean telling: those rejoicings from midnight to dawn, when the greater phosphorescence of the whole shouting sky frightened thee home! How in a trance of happiness we coupled in the ditches, in the long grasses, behind a fountain, under a broken wall, once recklessly on the very pavement, with a bench for roof and trellis! How I was taught by natural arts to influence certain chemistries engendering explicit marvels, blisses, and transports no man has slaked himself with since Father Adam pressed out the forbidden chlorophyll of Eden! Loveliness, Loveliness, none like thee. No brow so sleek, no elbow-crook so fine, no eye so green, no waist so pliant, no limbs so pleasant and acute. None like immortal Iripomoňoéià.

"'Creature, the moon filled and starved twice, and there was still no end to the glorious archaic newness of Iripomoňoéià.

"'Then last night. Last night! I will record all with simplicity.

"'We entered a shallow ditch. In a sweet-smelling voice of extraordinary red-olence – so intense in its sweetness that even the barbaric stinks and wind-lifted farts of the Inlet were overpowered by it – Iripomoňoéià inquired of me how I felt without my soul. I replied that I did not know this was my condition. "Oh yes, your body is now an empty packet, that is why it is so light. Spring." I sprang in air and rose effortlessly. "You have spoiled yourself, spoiled yourself with confusions," she complained, "now by morning your body will be crumpled and withered and ugly, like a leaf in its sere hour, and never again after tonight will this place see you." "Nymph!" I roared, amazed by levitation. "Oh, oh, that damaged," she cried, "you hit my eye with that noise," and she wafted a deeper aroma, a leek-like mist, one that stung the mucous membranes. A white bruise disfigured her petally lid. I was repentant and sighed terribly for her injury. "Beauty marred is for our kind what physical hurt is for yours," she reproved me. Where you have pain, we have ugliness. Where you profane yourselves by immorality, we are profaned by ugliness. Your soul has taken leave of you and spoils our pretty game." "Nymph!" I whispered, "heart, treasure, if my soul is separated how is it I am unaware?"

"""Poor man," she answered, "you have only to look and you will see the thing." Her speech had now turned as acrid as an herb, and all that place reeked bitterly. "You know I am a spirit. You know I must flash and dart. All my sisters flash and dart. Of all races we are the quickest. Our very religion is all-of-a-sudden. No one can hinder us, no one may delay us. But yesterday you undertook to detain me in your embrace, you stretched your kisses into years, you called me your treasure and your heart endlessly, your soul in its slow greed kept me close and captive, all the while knowing well how a spirit cannot stay and will not be fixed. I made to leap from you, but your obstinate soul held on until it was snatched straight from your frame and escaped with me. I saw it hurled out onto the pavement, the blue beginning of day was already seeping down, so I ran away and could say nothing until this moment."

"'My soul is free? Free entirely? And can be seen?'"

"'Free. If I could pity any living thing under the sky I would pity you for the sight of your soul. I do not like it, it conjures against me.'"

"'My soul loves thee,' I urged in all my triumph, 'it is freed from the thousand-year grave!' I jumped out of the ditch like a frog, my legs had no weight; but the dryad sulked in the ground, stroking her ugly violated eye. "Iripomoňoéià, my soul will follow thee with thankfulness into eternity."

"I would sooner be followed by the dirty fog. I do not like that soul of yours. It conjures against me. It denies me, it denies every spirit and all my sisters and every nereid of the harbour, it denies all our multiplicity, and all gods diversiform, it spites even Lord Pan, it is an enemy, and you, poor man, do not know your own soul. Go, look at it, there it is on the road."

"'I scudded back and forth under the moon.

"'Nothing, only a dusty old man trudging up there.'"

"'A quite ugly old man?'"

"'Yes, that is all. My soul is not there.'"

"'With a matted beard and great fierce eyebrows?'"

"'Yes, yes, one like that is walking on the road. He is half bent over under the burden of a dusty old bag. The bag is stuffed with books – I can see their ravelled bindings sticking out.'"

"'And he reads as he goes?'"

"'Yes, he reads as he goes.'"

"'What is it he reads?'"

"'Some huge and terrifying volume, heavy as a stone.' I peered forward in the moonlight. 'A Tractate. A Tractate of the Mishnah. Its leaves are so worn they break as he turns them, but he does not turn them often because there is much matter on a single page. He is so sad! Such antique weariness broods in his face! His throat is striped from the whip. His cheeks are folded like ancient flags, he reads the Law and breathes the dust.'"

"'And are there flowers on either side of the road?'"

"'Incredible flowers! Of every colour! And noble shrubs like mounds of green moss! And the cricket crackling in the field. He passes indifferent through the beauty of the field. His nostrils sniff his book as if flowers lay on the clotted page, but the flowers lick his feet. His feet are bandaged, his notched toenails gore the path. His prayer shawl droops on his studious back. He reads the Law and breathes the dust and doesn't see the flowers and won't heed the cricket spitting in the field.'"

"'That,' said the dryad, 'is your soul.' And was gone with all her odours.

"'My body sailed up to the road in a single hop. I alighted near the shape of the old man and demanded whether he were indeed the soul of Rabbi Isaac Kornfeld. He trembled but confessed. I asked if he intended to go with his books through the whole future without change, always with his Tractate in his hand, and he answered that he could do nothing else.

"'Nothing else! You, who I thought yearned for the earth! You, an immortal, free, and caring only to be bound to the Law!'"

"'He held a dry arm fearfully before his face, and with the other arm hitched up his merciless bag on his shoulder. "Sir," he said, still quavering, "didn't you wish to see me with your own eyes?"

"'I know your figure!' I shrieked. "Haven't I seen that figure a hundred times before? On a hundred roads? It is not mine! I will not have it be mine!'"

"'If you had not contrived to be rid of me, I would have stayed with you till the end. The dryad, who does not exist, lies. It was not I who clung to her but you, my body. Sir, all that has no real existence lies. In your grave beside you I would have sung you David's songs, I would have moaned Solomon's voice to your last grain of bone. But you expelled me, your ribs exile me from their fate, and I will walk here alone always, in my garden" – he scratched on his page – "with my precious birds" – he scratched at the letters – "and my darling trees" – he scratched at the tall side-column of commentary.

"'He was so impudent in his bravery – for I was all fleshliness and he all floppy wraith – that I seized him by the collar and shook him up and down, while the books on his back made a vast rubbing one on the other, and bits of shredding leather flew out like a rain.

"'The sound of the Law,' he said, "is more beautiful than the crickets. The smell of the Law is more radiant than the moss. The taste of the Law exceeds clear water."

"'At this nervy provocation – he more than any other knew my despair – I grabbed his prayer shawl by its tassels and whirled around him once or twice until I had unwrapped it from him altogether, and wound it on my own neck and in one bound came to the tree.

"'Nymph!' I called to it. "Spirit and saint! Iripomoňoéià, come! None like thee, no brow so sleek, no elbow-crook so fine, no eye so green, no waist so pliant, no limbs so pleasant and acute. For pity of me, come, come."

"'But she does not come.

"'Loveliness, come.'

"'She does not come.

"'Creature, see how I am coiled in the snail of this shawl as if in a leaf. I crouch to write my words. Let soul call thee lie, but body . . .

"'. . . body . . .

"'. . . fingers twist, knuckles dark as wood, tongue dries like grass, deeper now into silk . . .

"'. . . silk of pod of shawl, knees wilt, knuckles wither, neck . . .'"

Here the letter suddenly ended.

"You see? A pagan!" said Sheindel, and kept her spiteful smile. It was thick with audacity.

"You don't pity him," I said, watching the contempt that glittered in her teeth.

"Even now you don't see? You can't follow?"

"Pity him," I said.

"He who takes his own life does an abomination." For a long moment I considered her. You don't pity him? You don't pity him at all?"

"Let the world pity me."

"Goodbye," I said to the widow.

"You won't come back?"

I gave what amounted to a little bow of regret.

"I told you you came just for Isaac! But Isaac" – I was in terror of her cough, which was unmistakably laughter – "Isaac disappoints. "A scholar. A rabbi. A remarkable Jew!" Ha! He disappoints you?"

"He was always an astonishing man."

"But not what you thought," she insisted. "An illusion."

"Only the pitiless are illusory. Go back to that park, Rebbetzin," I advised her.

"And what would you like me to do there? Dance around a tree and call Greek names to the weeds?"

"Your husband's soul is in that park. Consult it." But her low derisive cough accompanied me home: whereupon I remembered her earlier words and dropped three green house plants down the toilet; after a journey of some miles through conduits they straightway entered Trilham's Inlet, where they decayed amid the civic excrement.

BROKEN HOMES

William Trevor

Born in Cork, **William Trevor** (b.1928) is recognized as being one of the undisputed masters of the short story of the last century. His work has won the Whitbread Prize three times, been shortlisted for the Booker Prize five times and he has won the 1999 David Cohen Prize as well as made an honorary knight in 2002. "There is an element of autobiography in all fiction in that pain or distress, or pleasure, is based on the author's own. But in my case that is as far as it goes," he once observed.

"I really think you're marvellous," the man said.

He was small and plump, with a plump face that had a greyness about it where he shaved; his hair was grey also, falling into a fringe on his forehead. He was untidily dressed, a turtle-necked red jersey beneath a jacket that had a ballpoint pen and a pencil sticking out of the breast pocket. When he stood up his black corduroy trousers developed concertina creases. Nowadays you saw a lot of men like this, Mrs Malby said to herself.

"We're trying to help them," he said, "and of course we're trying to help you. The policy is to foster a deeper understanding." He smiled, displaying small evenly-arranged teeth. "Between the generations," he added.

"Well, of course it's very kind," Mrs Malby said.

He shook his head. He sipped the instant coffee she'd made for him and nibbled the edge of a pink wafer biscuit. As if driven by a compulsion, he dipped the biscuit into the coffee. He said:

"What age actually are you, Mrs Malby?"

"I'm eighty-seven."

"You really are splendid for eighty-seven."

He went on talking. He said he hoped he'd be as good himself at eighty-seven. He hoped he'd even be in the land of the living. "Which I doubt," he said with a laugh. "Knowing me."

Mrs Malby didn't know what he meant by that. She was sure she'd heard him quite correctly, but she could recall nothing he'd previously stated which indicated ill-health. She thought carefully while he continued to sip at his coffee and attend to the mush of biscuit. What he had said suggested that a knowledge of him would cause you to doubt that he'd live to old age. Had he already supplied further knowledge of himself which, due to her slight deafness, she had not heard? If he hadn't, why had he left everything hanging in the air like that? It was difficult to know how best to react, whether to smile or to display concern.

"So what I thought," he said, "was that we could send the kids on Tuesday. Say start the job Tuesday morning, eh, Mrs Malby?"

"It's extremely kind of you."

"They're good kids."

He stood up. He remarked on her two budgerigars and the geraniums on her window-sill. Her sitting-room was as warm as toast, he said; it was freezing outside.

"It's just that I wondered," she said, having made up her mind to say it, "if you could possibly have come to the wrong house?"

"Wrong? *Wrong*? You're Mrs Malby, aren't you?" He raised his voice. "You're Mrs Malby, love?"

"Oh, yes, it's just that my kitchen isn't really in need of decoration."

He nodded. His head moved slowly and when it stopped his dark eyes stared at her from beneath his grey fringe. He said, quite softly, what she'd dreaded he might say: that she hadn't understood.

"I'm thinking of the community, Mrs Malby. I'm thinking of you here on your own above a greengrocer's shop with your two budgies. You can benefit my kids, Mrs Malby; they can benefit you. There's no charge of any kind whatsoever. Put it like this, Mrs Malby: it's an experiment in community relations." He paused. He reminded her of a picture there'd been in a history book, a long time ago, History with Miss Deacon, a picture of a Roundhead. "So you see, Mrs Malby," he said, having said something else while he was reminding her of a Roundhead.

"It's just that my kitchen is really quite nice."

"Let's have a little look, shall we?"

She led the way. He glanced at the kitchen's shell-pink walls, and at the white paintwork. It would cost her nearly a hundred pounds to have it done, he said; and then, to her horror, he began all over again, as if she hadn't heard a thing he'd been saying. He repeated that he was a teacher, from the school called the Tite Comprehensive. He appeared to assume that she wouldn't know the Tite Comprehensive, but she did: an ugly sprawl of glass and concrete buildings, children swinging along the pavements, shouting obscenities. The man repeated what he had said before about these children: that some of them came from broken homes. The ones he wished to send to her on Tuesday morning came from broken homes, which was no joke for them. He felt, he repeated, that we all had a special duty where such children were concerned.

Mrs Malby again agreed that broken homes were to be deplored. It was just, she explained, that she was thinking of the cost of decorating a kitchen which didn't need decorating. Paint and brushes were expensive, she pointed out.

"Freshen it over for you," the man said, raising his voice. "First thing Tuesday, Mrs Malby."

He went away, and she realized that he hadn't told her his name. Thinking she might be wrong about that, she went over their encounter in her mind, going back to the moment when her doorbell had sounded. "I'm from Tite Comprehensive," was what he'd said. No name had been mentioned, of that she was positive.

In her elderliness Mrs Malby liked to be sure of such details. You had to work quite hard sometimes at eighty-seven, straining to hear, concentrating carefully in order to be sure of things. You had to make it clear you understood because people often imagined you didn't. Communication was what it was called nowadays, rather than conversation.

Mrs Malby was wearing a blue dress with a pattern of darker blue flowers on it. She was a woman who had been tall but had shrunk a little with age and had become slightly bent. Scant white hair crowned a face that was touched with elderly freckling. Large brown eyes, once her most striking feature, were quieter than they had been, tired behind spectacles now. Her husband, George, the owner of the greengrocer's shop over which she lived, had died five years ago; her two sons, Eric and Roy, had been killed in the same month – June 1942 – in the same desert retreat.

The greengrocer's shop was unpretentious, in an unpretentious street in Fulham called Agnes Street. The people who owned it now, Jewish people called King, kept an eye on Mrs Malby. They watched for her coming and going and if they missed her one day they'd ring her doorbell to see that she was all right. She had a niece in Ealing who looked in twice a year, and another niece in Islington, who was crippled with arthritis. Once a week Mrs Grove and Mrs Halbert came round with Meals on Wheels. A social worker, Miss Tingle, called; and the Reverend Bush called. Men came to read the meters.

In her elderliness, living where she'd lived since her marriage in 1920, Mrs Malby was happy. The tragedy in her life – the death of her sons – was no longer a nightmare, and the time that had passed since her husband's death had allowed her to come to terms with being on her own. All she wished for was to continue in these same circumstances until she died, and she did not fear death. She did not believe she would be re-united with her sons and her husband, not at least in a specific sense, but she could not believe, either, that she would entirely cease to exist the moment she ceased to breathe. Having thought about death, it seemed likely to Mrs Malby that after it came she'd dream, as in sleep. Heaven and hell were surely no more than flickers of such pleasant dreaming, or flickers of a nightmare from which there was no waking release. No loving omnipotent God, in Mrs Malby's view, doled out punishments and reward: human conscience, the last survivor, did that. The idea of a God, which had puzzled Mrs Malby for most of her life, made sense when she thought of it in terms like these, when she forgot about the mystic qualities claimed for a Church and for Jesus Christ. Yet fearful of offending the Reverend Bush, she kept such conclusions to herself when he came to see her.

All Mrs Malby dreaded now was becoming senile and being forced to enter the Sunset Home in Richmond, of which the Reverend Bush and Miss Tingle warmly spoke. The thought of a communal existence, surrounded by other elderly people, with sing-songs and card-games, was anathema to her. All her life she had hated anything that smacked of communal jolliness, refusing even to go on coach trips. She loved the house above the greengrocer's shop. She loved walking down the stairs and out on to the street, nodding at the Kings as she went by the shop, buying birdseed and eggs and fire-lighters, and fresh bread from Len Skipps, a man of sixty-two whom she'd remembered being born.

The dread of having to leave Agnes Street ordered her life. With all her visitors she was careful, constantly on the look-out for signs in their eyes which might mean they were diagnosing her as senile. It was for this reason that she listened so intently to all that was said to her, that she concentrated, determined to let nothing slip by. It was for this reason that she smiled and endeavoured to appear agreeable and co-operative at all times. She was well aware that it wasn't going to be up to her to state that she was senile, or to argue that she wasn't, when the moment came.

After the teacher from Tite Comprehensive School had left, Mrs Malby continued to worry. The visit from this grey-haired man had bewildered her from the start. There was the oddity of his not giving his name, and then the way he'd placed a cigarette in his mouth and had taken it out again, putting it back in the packet. Had he imagined cigarette smoke would offend her? He could have asked, but in fact he hadn't even referred to the cigarette. Nor had he said where he'd heard about her: he hadn't mentioned the Reverend Bush, for instance, or Mrs Grove and Mrs Halbert, or Miss Tingle. He might have been a customer in the greengrocer's shop, but he hadn't given any indication that that was so. Added to which, and most of all, there was the consideration that her kitchen wasn't in the least in need of attention. She went to look at it again, beginning to wonder if there were things about it she couldn't see. She went over in her mind what the man had said about community relations. It was difficult to resist men like that, you had to go on repeating yourself and after a while you had to assess if you were sounding senile or not. There was also the consideration that the man was trying to do good, helping children from broken homes.

"Hi," a boy with long blond hair said to her on the Tuesday morning. There were two other boys with him, one with a fuzz of dark curls all round his head, the other red-haired, a greased shock that hung to his shoulders. There was a girl as well, thin and beaky-faced, chewing something. Between them they carried tins of paint, brushes, cloths, a blue plastic bucket, and a transistor radio. "We come to do your kitchen out," the blond boy said. "You Mrs Wheeler then?"

"No, no. I'm Mrs Malby."

"That's right, Billo," the girl said. "Malby."

"I thought he says Wheeler."

"Wheeler's the geyser in the paint shop," the fuzzy-haired boy said.

"Typical Billo," the girl said.

She let them in, saying it was very kind of them. She led them to the kitchen, remarking on the way that strictly speaking it wasn't in need of decoration, as they could see for themselves. She'd been thinking it over she added: she wondered if they'd just like to wash the walls down, which was a task she found difficult to do herself?

They'd do whatever she wanted, they said, no problem. They put their paint tins on the table. The red-haired boy turned on the radio. "Welcome back to Open House," a cheery voice said and then reminded its listeners that it was the voice of Pete Murray. It said that a record was about to be played for someone in Upminster.

"Would you like some coffee?" Mrs Malby suggested above the noise of the transistor.

"Great," the blond boy said.

They all wore blue jeans with patches on them. The girl had a T-shirt with the words *I Lay Down With Jesus* on it. The others wore T-shirts of different colours, the blond boy's orange, the fuzzy one's light blue, the red haired one's red. *Hot Jam-roll* a badge on the chest of the blond boy said; *Jaws* and *Bay City Rollers* other badges said.

Mrs Malby made them Nescafé while they listened to the music. They lit cigarettes, leaning about against the electric stove and against the edge of the table and against a wall. They didn't say anything because they were listening. "That's a load of crap," the red-haired boy pronounced eventually, and the others agreed. Even so they went on listening. "Pete Murray's crappy," the girl said.

Mrs Malby handed them the cups of coffee, drawing their attention to the sugar she'd put out for them on the table, and to the milk. She smiled at the girl. She said again that it was a job she couldn't manage any more, washing walls.

"Get that, Billo?" the fuzzy-haired boy said. "Washing walls."

"Who loves ya, baby?" Billo replied.

Mrs Malby closed the kitchen door on them, hoping they wouldn't take too long because the noise of the transistor was so loud. She listened to it for a quarter of an hour and then she decided to go out and do her shopping.

In Len Skipps' she said that four children from the Tite Comprehensive had arrived in her house and were at present washing her kitchen walls. She said it again to the man in the fish shop and the man was surprised. It suddenly occurred to her that of course they couldn't have done any painting because she hadn't discussed colours with the teacher. She thought it odd that the teacher hadn't mentioned colours and wondered what colour the paint tins contained. It worried her a little that all that hadn't occurred to her before.

"Hi, Mrs Wheeler," the boy called Billo said to her in her hall. He was standing there combing his hair, looking at himself in the mirror of the hall-stand. Music was coming from upstairs.

There were yellowish smears on the stair-carpet, which upset Mrs Malby very much. There were similar smears on the landing carpet. "Oh, but please," Mrs Malby cried, standing in the kitchen doorway. "Oh, please, go!" she cried.

Yellow emulsion paint partially covered the shell-pink of one wall. Some had spilt from the tin on to the black-and-white vinyl of the floor and had been walked through. The boy with fuzzy hair was standing on a draining-board applying the same paint to the ceiling. He was the only person in the kitchen.

He smiled at Mrs Malby, looking down at her. "Hi, Mrs Wheeler," he said.

"But I said only to wash them," she cried.

She felt tired, saying that. The upset of finding the smears on the carpets and of seeing the hideous yellow plastered over the quiet shell-pink had already taken a toll. Her emotional outburst had caused her face and neck to become warm. She felt she'd like to lie down.

"Eh, Mrs Wheeler?" The boy smiled at her again, continuing to slap paint on to the ceiling. A lot of it dripped back on top of him, on to the draining-board and on to cups and saucers and cutlery, and on to the floor. "D'you fancy the colour, Mrs Wheeler?" he asked her.

All the time the transistor continued to blare, a voice inexpertly singing, a tuneless twanging. The boy referred to this sound, pointing at the transistor with his paint-brush, saying it was great. Unsteadily she crossed the kitchen and turned the transistor off. "Hey, sod it, missus," the boy protested angrily.

"I said to wash the walls. I didn't even choose that colour."

The boy, still annoyed because she'd turned off the radio, was gesturing crossly with the brush. There was paint in the fuzz of his hair and on his T-shirt and his face. Every time he moved the brush about paint flew off it. It speckled the windows, and the small dresser, and the electric stove and the taps and the sink.

"Where's the sound gone?" the boy called Billo demanded, coming into the kitchen and going straight to the transistor.

"I didn't want the kitchen painted," Mrs Malby said again. "I told you."

The singing from the transistor recommenced, louder than before. On the draining-board the fuzzy-haired boy began to sway, throwing his body and his head about.

"Please stop him painting," Mrs Malby shouted as shrilly as she could.

"Here," the boy called Billo said, bundling her out on to the landing and closing the kitchen door. "Can't hear myself think in there."

"I don't want it painted."

"What's that, Mrs Wheeler?"

"My name isn't Wheeler. I don't want my kitchen painted. I told you."

"Are we in the wrong house? Only we was told –"

"Will you please wash that paint off?"

"If we come to the wrong house –"

"You haven't come to the wrong house. Please tell that boy to wash off the paint he's put on."

"Did a bloke from the Comp come in to see you, Mrs Wheeler? Fat bloke?"

"Yes, yes, he did."

"Only he give instructions –"

"Please would you tell that boy?"

"Whatever you say, Mrs Wheeler."

"And wipe up the paint where it's spilt on the floor. It's been trampled out, all over my carpets."

"No problem, Mrs Wheeler."

Not wishing to return to the kitchen herself, she ran the hot tap in the bathroom on to the sponge-cloth she kept for cleaning the bath. She found that if she rubbed hard enough at the paint on the stair-carpet and on the landing carpet it began to disappear. But the rubbing tired her. As she put away the sponge-cloth, Mrs Malby had a feeling of not quite knowing what was what. Everything that had happened in the last few hours felt like a dream; it also had the feeling of plays she had seen on television; the one thing it wasn't like was reality. As she paused in her bathroom, having placed the sponge-cloth on a ledge under the hand-basin, Mrs Malby saw herself standing there, as she often did in a dream: she saw her body hunched within the same blue dress she'd been wearing when the teacher called, and two touches of red in her pale face, and her white hair tidy on her head, and her fingers seeming fragile. In a dream anything could happen next: she might suddenly find herself forty years younger, Eric and Roy might be alive. She might be even younger; Dr Ramsey might be telling her she was pregnant. In a television play it would be different: the children who had come to her house might kill her. What she hoped for from reality was that order would be restored in her kitchen, that all the paint would be washed away from her walls as she had wiped it from her carpets, that the misunderstanding would be over. For an instant she saw herself in her kitchen, making tea for the children, saying it didn't matter. She even heard herself adding that in a life as long as hers you became used to everything.

She left the bathroom; the blare of the transistor still persisted. She didn't want to sit in her sitting-room, having to listen to it. She climbed the stairs to her bedroom, imagining the coolness there, and the quietness.

"Hey," the girl protested when Mrs Malby opened her bedroom door.

"Sod off, you guys," the boy with the red hair ordered.

They were in her bed. Their clothes were all over the floor. Her two budgerigars were flying about the room. Protruding from sheets and blankets she could see the boy's naked shoulders and the back of his head. The girl poked her face up from under him. She gazed at Mrs Malby. "It's not them," she whispered to the boy. "It's the woman."

"Hi there, missus." The boy twisted his head round. From the kitchen, still loudly, came the noise of the transistor.

"Sorry," the girl said.

"Why are they up here? Why have you let my birds out? You've no right to behave like this."

"We needed sex," the girl explained.

The budgerigars were perched on the looking-glass on the dressing-table, beadily surveying the scene.

"They're really great, them budgies," the boy said.

Mrs Malby stepped through their garments. The budgerigars remained where they were. They fluttered when she seized them but they didn't offer any resistance. She returned with them to the door.

"You had no right," she began to say to the two in her bed, but her voice had become weak. It quivered into a useless whisper, and once more she thought that what was happening couldn't be happening. She saw herself again, standing unhappily with the budgerigars.

In her sitting-room she wept. She returned the budgerigars to their cage and sat in an armchair by the window that looked out over Agnes Street. She sat in sunshine, feeling its warmth but not, as she might have done, delighting in it. She wept because she had intensely disliked finding the boy and girl in her bed. Images from the bedroom remained vivid in her mind. On the floor the boy's boots were heavy and black, composed of leather that did not shine. The girl's shoes were green, with huge heels and soles. The girl's underclothes were purple, the boy's dirty. There'd been an unpleasant smell of sweat in her bedroom.

Mrs Malby waited, her head beginning to ache. She dried away her tears, wiping at her eyes and cheeks with a handkerchief. In Agnes Street people passed by on bicycles, girls from the polish factory returning home to lunch, men from the brickworks. People came out of the greengrocer's with leeks and cabbages in baskets, some carrying paper bags. Watching these people in Agnes Street made her feel better, even though her headache was becoming worse. She felt more composed, and more in control of herself.

"We're sorry," the girl said again, suddenly appearing, teetering on her clumsy shoes. "We didn't think you'd come up to the bedroom."

She tried to smile at the girl, but found it hard to do so. She nodded instead.

"The others put the birds in," the girl said. "Meant to be a joke, that was."

She nodded again. She couldn't see how it could be a joke to take two budgerigars from their cage, but she didn't say that.

"We're getting on with the painting now," the girl said. "Sorry about that."

She went away and Mrs Malby continued to watch the people in Agnes Street. The girl had made a mistake when she'd said they were getting on with the painting: what she'd meant was that they were getting on with washing it off. The girl had come straight downstairs to say she was sorry; she hadn't been told by the boys in the kitchen that the paint had been applied in error. When they'd gone, Mrs Malby said to herself, she'd open her bedroom window wide in order to get rid of the odour of sweat. She'd put clean sheets on her bed.

From the kitchen, above the noise of the transistor, came the clatter of raised voices. There was laughter and a crash, and then louder laughter. Singing began, attaching itself to the singing from the transistor.

She sat for twenty minutes and then she went and knocked on the kitchen door, not wishing to push the door open in case it knocked someone off a chair. There was no reply. She opened the door gingerly.

More yellow paint had been applied. The whole wall around the window was covered with it, and most of the wall behind the sink. Half of the ceiling had it on it; the woodwork that had been white was now a glossy dark blue. All four of the children were working with brushes. A tin of paint had been upset on the floor.

She wept again, standing there watching them, unable to prevent her tears. She felt them running warmly on her cheeks and then becoming cold. It was in this kitchen that she had cried first of all when the two telegrams had come in 1942, believing when the second one arrived that she would never cease to cry. It would have seemed ridiculous at the time, to cry just because her kitchen was all yellow.

They didn't see her standing there. They went on singing, slapping the paint-brushes back and forth. There'd been neat straight lines where the shell-pink met the white of the woodwork, but now the lines were any old how. The boy with the red hair was applying the dark-blue gloss.

Again the feeling that it wasn't happening possessed Mrs Malby. She'd had a dream a week ago, a particularly vivid dream in which the Prime Minister had stated on television that the Germans had been invited to invade England since England couldn't manage to look after herself any more. That dream had been most troublesome because when she'd woken up in the morning she'd thought it was something she'd seen on television, that she'd actually been sitting in her sitting-room the night before listening to the Prime Minister saying that he and the Leader of the Opposition had decided the best for Britain was invasion. After thinking about it, she'd established that of course it hadn't been true; but even so she'd glanced at the headlines of newspapers when she went out shopping.

"How d'you fancy it?" the boy called Billo called out to her, smiling across the kitchen at her, not noticing that she was upset. "Neat, Mrs Wheeler?"

She didn't answer. She went downstairs and walked out of her hall-door, into Agnes Street and into the greengrocer's that had been her husband's. It never closed in the middle of the day; it never had. She waited and Mr King appeared, wiping his mouth. "Well then, Mrs Malby?" he said.

He was a big man with a well-kept black moustache and Jewish eyes. He didn't smile much because smiling wasn't his way, but he was in no way morose, rather the opposite.

"So what can I do for you?" he said.

She told him. He shook his head and repeatedly frowned as he listened. His expressive eyes widened. He called his wife.

While the three of them hurried along the pavement to Mrs Malby's open hall-door it seemed to her that the Kings doubted her. She could feel them thinking that she must have got it all wrong, that she'd somehow imagined all this stuff about yellow paint and pop music on a radio, and her birds flying around her bedroom while two children were lying in her bed. She didn't blame them; she knew exactly how they felt. But when they entered her house the noise from the transistor could at once be heard.

The carpet of the landing was smeared again with the paint. Yellow footprints led to her sitting-room and out again, back to the kitchen.

"You bloody young hooligans," Mr King shouted at them. He snapped the switch on the transistor. He told them to stop applying the paint immediately. "What the hell d'you think you're up to?" he demanded furiously.

"We come to paint out the old ma's kitchen," the boy called Billo explained, unruffled by Mr King's tone. "We was carrying out instructions, mister."

"So it was instructions to spill the blooming paint all over the floor? So it was instructions to cover the windows with it and every knife and fork in the place? So it was instructions to frighten the life out of a poor woman by messing about in her bedroom?"

"No one frightens her, mister."

"You know what I mean, son."

Mrs Malby returned with Mrs King and sat in the cubbyhole behind the shop, leaving Mr King to do his best. At three o'clock he arrived back, saying that the children had gone. He telephoned the school and after a delay was put in touch with the teacher who'd been to see Mrs Malby. He made this telephone call in the shop but Mrs Malby could hear him saying that what had happened was a disgrace. "A woman of eighty-seven," Mr King protested, "thrown into a state of misery. There'll be something to pay on this, you know."

There was some further discussion on the telephone, and then Mr King replaced the receiver. He put his head into the cubbyhole and announced that the teacher was coming round immediately to inspect the damage. "What can I entice you to?" Mrs Malby heard him asking a customer, and a woman's voice replied that she needed tomatoes, a cauliflower, potatoes and Bramleys. She heard Mr King telling the woman what had happened, saying that it had wasted two hours of his time.

She drank the sweet milky tea which Mrs King had poured her. She tried not to think of the yellow paint and the dark-blue gloss. She tried not to remember the scene in the bedroom and the smell there'd been, and the new marks that had appeared on her carpets after she'd wiped off the original ones. She wanted to ask Mr King if these marks had been washed out before the paint had had a chance to dry, but she didn't like to ask this because Mr King had been so kind and it might seem like pressing him.

"Kids nowadays," Mrs King said. "I just don't know."

"Birched they should be," Mr King said, coming into the cubbyhole and picking up a mug of the milky tea. "I'd birch the bottoms off them."

Someone arrived in the shop. Mr King hastened from the cubbyhole. "What can I entice you to, sir?" Mrs Malby heard him politely enquiring and the voice of the teacher who'd been to see her replied. He said who he was and Mr King wasn't polite any more. An experience like that, Mr King declared thunderously, could have killed an eighty-seven-year-old stone dead.

Mrs Malby stood up and Mrs King came promptly forward to place a hand under her elbow. They went into the shop like that. "Three and a half p," Mr King was saying to a woman who'd asked the price of oranges. "The larger ones at four."

Mr King gave the woman four of the smaller size and accepted her money. He called out to a youth who was passing by on a bicycle, about to start an afternoon paper round. He was a youth who occasionally assisted him on Saturday mornings: Mr King asked him now if he would mind the shop for ten minutes since an emergency had arisen. Just for once, Mr King argued, it wouldn't matter if the evening papers were a little late.

"Well, you can't say they haven't brightened the place up, Mrs Malby," the teacher said in her kitchen. He regarded her from beneath his grey fringe. He touched one of the walls with the tip of a finger. He nodded to himself, appearing to be satisfied.

The painting had been completed, the yellow and the dark-blue gloss. Where the colours met there were untidily jagged lines. All the paint that had been spilt on the floor had been wiped away, but the black-and-white vinyl had become dull and grubby in the process. The paint had also been wiped from the windows and from other surfaces, leaving them smeared. The dresser had been wiped down and was smeary also. The cutlery and the taps and the cups and saucers had all been washed or wiped.

"Well, you wouldn't believe it!" Mrs King exclaimed. She turned to her husband. However had he managed it all? she asked him. "You should have seen the place!" she said to the teacher.

"It's just the carpets," Mr King said. He led the way from the kitchen to the sitting-room, pointing at the yellow on the landing carpet and on the sitting-room one. "The blooming stuff dried," he explained, "before we could get to it. That's where compensation comes in." He spoke sternly, addressing the teacher. "I'd say she has a bob or two owing."

Mrs King nudged Mrs Malby, drawing attention to the fact that Mr King was doing his best for her. The nudge suggested that all would be well because a sum of money would be paid, possibly even a larger sum than was merited. It suggested also that Mrs Malby in the end might find herself doing rather well.

"Compensation?" the teacher said, bending down and scratching at the paint on the sitting-room carpet. "I'm afraid compensation's out of the question."

"She's had her carpets ruined," Mr King snapped quickly. "This woman's been put about, you know."

"She got her kitchen done free," the teacher snapped back at him.

"They released her pets. They got up to tricks in a bed. You'd no damn right –"

"These kids come from broken homes, sir. I'll do my best with your carpets, Mrs Malby."

"But what about my kitchen?" she whispered. She cleared her throat because her whispering could hardly be heard. "My kitchen?" she whispered again.

"What about it, Mrs Malby?"

"I didn't want it painted."

"Oh, don't be silly now."

The teacher took his jacket off and threw it impatiently on to a chair. He left the sitting-room. Mrs Malby heard him running a tap in the kitchen.

"It was best to finish the painting, Mrs Malby," Mr King said. "Otherwise the kitchen would have driven you mad, half done like that. I stood over them till they finished it."

"You can't take paint off, dear," Mrs King said, "once it's on. You've done wonders, Leo," she said to her husband. "Young devils."

"We'd best be getting back," Mr King said.

"It's quite nice, you know," his wife added. "Your kitchen's quite cheerful, dear."

The Kings went away and the teacher rubbed at the yellow on the carpets with her washing-up brush. The landing carpet was marked anyway, he pointed out, poking a finger at the stains left behind by the paint she'd removed herself with the sponge-cloth from the bathroom. She must be delighted with the kitchen, he said.

She knew she mustn't speak. She'd known she mustn't when the Kings had been there; she knew she mustn't now. She might have reminded the Kings that she'd chosen the original colours in the kitchen herself. She might have complained to the man as he rubbed at her carpets that the carpets would never be the same again. She watched him, not saying anything, not wishing to be regarded as a nuisance. The Kings would have considered her a nuisance too, agreeing to let children into her kitchen to paint it and then making a fuss. If she became a nuisance the teacher and the Kings would drift on to the same side, and the Reverend Bush would somehow be on that side also, and Miss Tingle, and even Mrs Grove and Mrs Halbert. They would agree among themselves that what had happened had to do with her elderliness, with her not understanding that children who brought paint into a kitchen were naturally going to use it.

"I defy anyone to notice that," the teacher said, standing up, gesturing at the yellow blurs that remained on her carpets. He put his jacket on. He left the washing-up brush and the bowl of water he'd been using on the floor of her sitting-room. "All's well that ends well," he said. "Thanks for your co-operation, Mrs Malby."

She thought of her two sons, Eric and Roy, not knowing quite why she thought of them now. She descended the stairs with the teacher, who was cheerfully talking about community relations. You had to make allowances, he said, for kids like that; you had to try and understand; you couldn't just walk away.

Quite suddenly she wanted to tell him about Eric and Roy. In the desire to talk about them she imagined their bodies, as she used to in the past, soon after they'd been killed. They lay on desert sand, desert birds swooped down on them. Their four eyes were gone. She wanted to explain to the teacher that they'd been happy, a contented family in Agnes Street, until the war came and smashed everything to pieces. Nothing had been the same afterwards. It hadn't been easy to continue with nothing to continue for. Each room in the house had contained different memories of the two boys growing up. Cooking and cleaning had seemed pointless. The shop which would have been theirs would have to pass to someone else.

And yet time had soothed the awful double wound. The horror of the emptiness had been lived with, and if having the Kings in the shop now wasn't the same as having your sons there at least the Kings were kind. Thirty-four years after the destruction of your family you were happy in your elderliness because time had been merciful. She wanted to tell the teacher that also, she didn't know why, except that in some way it seemed relevant. But she didn't tell him because it would have been difficult to begin, because in the effort there'd be the danger of seeming senile. Instead she said goodbye, concentrating on that. She said she was sorry, saying it just to show she was aware that she hadn't made herself clear to the children. Conversation had broken down between the children and herself, she wanted him to know she knew it had.

He nodded vaguely, not listening to her. He was trying to make the world a better place, he said. "For kids like that, Mrs Malby. Victims of broken homes."

DREAM CARGOES

J.G. Ballard

J.G. Ballard (1930–2009) is best known for his semi-autobiographical novel *Empire of the Sun*, filmed to great acclaim. Before his death he was rightly applauded for a late sequence of novels that thrilled in examining the possibility of violence in modern society – *Cocaine Nights, Super-Cannes, Millenium People* and *Kingdom Come*. His stories are sublime, inventive, questing, genre-bending, and he is one of the five writers in this volume when it became hardest to chose the finest as his range is so wide.

Across the lagoon an eager new life was forming, drawing its spectrum of colours from a palette more vivid than the sun's. Soon after dawn, when Johnson woke in Captain Galloway's cabin behind the bridge of the *Prospero*, he watched the lurid hues, cyanic blues and crimsons, playing against the ceiling above his bunk. Reflected in the metallic surface of the lagoon, the tropical foliage seemed to concentrate the Caribbean sunlight, painting on the warm air a screen of electric tones that Johnson had only seen on the nightclub façades of Miami and Vera Cruz.

He stepped onto the tilting bridge of the stranded freighter, aware that the island's vegetation had again surged forward during the night, as if it had miraculously found a means of converting darkness into these brilliant leaves and blossoms. Shielding his eyes from the glare, he searched the 600 yards of empty beach that encircled the *Prospero*, disappointed that there was no sign of Dr Chambers' rubber inflatable. For the past three mornings, when he woke after an uneasy night, he had seen the craft beached by the inlet of the lagoon. Shaking off the overlit dreams that rose from the contaminated waters, he would gulp down a cup of cold coffee, jump from the stern rail and set off between the pools of leaking chemicals in search of the American biologist.

It pleased Johnson that she was so openly impressed by this once barren island, a left-over of nature seven miles from the north-east coast of Puerto Rico. In his modest way he knew that he was responsible for the transformation of the nondescript atoll, scarcely more than a forgotten garbage dump left behind by the American army after World War II. No one, in Johnson's short life, had ever been impressed by him, and the biologist's silent wonder gave him the first sense of achievement he had ever known.

Johnson had learned her name from the labels on the scientific stores in the inflatable. However, he had not yet approached or even spoken to her, embarrassed by his rough manners and shabby seaman's clothes, and the engrained chemical stench that banned him from sailors' bars all over the Caribbean. Now, when she failed to appear on the fourth morning, he regretted all the more that he had never worked up the courage to introduce himself.

Through the acid-streaked windows of the bridge-house he stared at the terraces of flowers that hung from the forest wall. A month earlier, when he first arrived at the island, struggling with the locked helm of the listing freighter, there had been no more than a few stunted palms growing among the collapsed army huts and water-tanks buried in the dunes.

But already, for reasons that Johnson preferred not to consider, a wholly new vegetation had sprung to life. The palms rose like flagpoles into the vivid Caribbean air, pennants painted with a fresh green sap. Around them the sandy floor was thick with flowering vines and ground ivy, blue leaves like dappled metal foil, as if some midnight gardener had watered them with a secret plant elixir while Johnson lay asleep in his bunk.

He put on Galloway's peaked cap and examined himself in the greasy mirror. Stepping into the open deck behind the wheel-house, he inhaled the acrid chemical air of the lagoon. At least it masked the odours of the captain's cabin, a rancid bouquet of ancient sweat, cheap rum and diesel oil. He had thought seriously of abandoning Galloway's cabin and returning to his hammock in the forecastle, but despite the stench he felt that he owed it to himself to remain in the cabin. The moment that Galloway, with a last disgusted curse, had stepped into the freighter's single lifeboat he, Johnson, had become the captain of this doomed vessel.

He had watched Galloway, the four Mexican crewmen and the weary Portuguese engineer row off into the dusk, promising himself that he would sleep in the captain's cabin and take his meals at the captain's table. After five years at sea, working as cabin boy and deck hand on the lowest grade of chemical waste carrier, he had a command of his own, this antique freighter, even if the *Prospero*'s course was the vertical one to the sea-bed of the Caribbean.

Behind the funnel the Liberian flag of convenience hung in tatters, its fabric rotted by the acid air. Johnson stepped onto the stern ladder, steadying himself against the sweating hull-plates, and jumped into the shallow water. Careful to find his feet, he waded through the bilious green foam that leaked from the steel drums he had jettisoned from the freighter's deck.

When he reached the clear sand above the tide-line he wiped the emerald dye from his jeans and sneakers. Leaning to starboard in the lagoon, the *Prospero* resembled an exploded paint-box. The drums of chemical waste on the foredeck still dripped their effluent through the scuppers. The more sinister below-decks cargo – nameless organic by-products that Captain Galloway had been bribed to carry and never entered into his manifest – had dissolved the rusty plates and spilled an eerie spectrum of phosphorescent blues and indigos into the lagoon below.

Frightened of these chemicals, which every port in the Caribbean had rejected, Johnson had begun to jettison the cargo after running the freighter aground. But the elderly diesels had seized and the winch had jarred to a halt, leaving only a few of the drums on the nearby sand with their death's head warnings and eroded seams.

Johnson set off along the shore, searching the sea beyond the inlet of the lagoon for any sign of Dr Chambers. Everywhere a deranged horticulture was running riot. Vivid new shoots pushed past the metal debris of old ammunition boxes, filing cabinets and truck tyres. Strange grasping vines clambered over the scarlet caps of giant fungi, their white stems as thick as sailors' bones. Avoiding them, Johnson walked towards an old staff car that sat in an open glade between the palms. Wheel-less, its military markings obliterated by the rain of decades, it had settled into the sand, vines encircling its roof and windshield.

Deciding to rest in the car, which once perhaps had driven an American general around the training camps of Puerto Rico, he tore away the vines that had wreathed themselves around the driver's door pillar. As he sat behind the steering wheel it occurred to Johnson that he might leave the freighter and set up camp on the island. Nearby lay the galvanised iron roof of a barrack hut, enough material to build a beach house on the safer, seaward side of the island.

But Johnson was aware of an unstated bond between himself and the derelict freighter. He remembered the last desperate voyage of the *Prospero*, which he had joined in Vera Cruz, after being duped by Captain Galloway. The short voyage to Galveston, the debarkation port, would pay him enough to ship as a deck passenger on an inter-island boat heading for the Bahamas. It had been three years since he had seen his widowed mother in Nassau, living in a plywood bungalow by the airport with her invalid boyfriend.

Needless to say, they had never berthed at Galveston, Miami or any other of the ports where they had tried to unload their cargo. The crudely sealed cylinders of chemical waste-products, supposedly en route to a reprocessing plant in southern Texas, had begun to leak before they left Vera Cruz. Captain Galloway's temper, like his erratic seamanship and consumption of rum and tequila, increased steadily as he realised that the Mexican shipping agent had abandoned them to the seas. Almost certainly the agent had pocketed the monies allocated for reprocessing and found it more profitable to let the ancient freighter, now refused entry to Vera Cruz, sail up and down the Gulf of Mexico until her corroded keel sent her conveniently to the bottom.

For two months they had cruised forlornly from one port to another, boarded by hostile maritime police and customs officers, public health officials and journalists alerted to the possibility of a major ecological disaster. At Kingston, Jamaica, a television launch trailed them to the ten-mile limit, at Santo Domingo a spotter plane of the Dominican navy was waiting for them when they tried to slip into harbour under the cover of darkness. Greenpeace power-boats intercepted them outside Tampa, Florida, when Captain Galloway tried to dump part of his cargo. Firing flares across the bridge of the freighter, the US Coast Guard dispatched them into the Gulf of Mexico in time to meet the tail of Hurricane Clara.

When at last they recovered from the storm the cargo had shifted, and the *Prospero* listed ten degrees to starboard. Fuming chemicals leaked across the decks from the fractured seams of the waste drums, boiled on the surface of the sea and sent up a cloud of acrid vapour that left Johnson and the Mexican crewmen coughing through makeshift face-masks, and Captain Galloway barricading himself into his cabin with his tequila bottle.

First Officer Pereira had saved the day, rigging up a hose-pipe that sprayed the leaking drums with a torrent of water, but by then the *Prospero* was taking in the sea through its strained plates. When they sighted Puerto Rico the captain had not even bothered to set a course for port. Propping himself against the helm, a bottle in each hand, he signalled Pereira to cut the engines. In a self-pitying monologue, he cursed the Mexican shipping agent, the US Coast Guard, the world's agro-chemists and their despicable science that had deprived him of his command. Lastly he cursed Johnson for being so foolish ever to step aboard this ill-fated ship. As the *Prospero* lay doomed in the water, Pereira appeared with his already packed suitcase, and the captain ordered the Mexicans to lower the life-boat.

It was then that Johnson made his decision to remain on board. All his life he had failed to impose himself on anything – running errands as a six-year-old for the Nassau airport shoe-blacks, cadging pennies for his mother from the irritated tourists, enduring the years of school where he had scarcely learned to read and write, working as a dishwasher at the beach restaurants, forever conned out of his wages by the thieving managers. He had always reacted to events, never initiated anything on his own. Now, for the first time, he could become the captain of the *Prospero* and master of his own fate. Long before Galloway's curses faded into the dusk Johnson had leapt down the companionway ladder into the engine room.

As the elderly diesels rallied themselves for the last time Johnson returned to the bridge. He listened to the propeller's tired but steady beat against the dark ocean, and slowly turned the *Prospero* towards the north-west. Five hundred miles away were the Bahamas, and an endless archipelago of secret harbours. Somehow he would get rid of the leaking drums and even, perhaps, ply for hire between the islands, renaming the old tub after his mother, Velvet Mae. Meanwhile Captain Johnson stood proudly on the bridge, oversize cap on his head, 300 tons of steel deck obedient beneath his feet.

By dawn the next day he was completely lost on an open sea. During the night the freighter's list had increased. Below decks the leaking chemicals had etched their way through the hull plates, and a phosphorescent steam enveloped the bridge. The engine room was a knee-deep vat of acid brine, a poisonous vapour rising through the ventilators and coating every rail and deck-plate with a lurid slime.

Then, as Johnson searched desperately for enough timber to build a raft, he saw the old World War II garbage island seven miles from the Puerto Rican coast. The lagoon inlet was unguarded by the US Navy or Greenpeace speedboats. He steered the *Prospero* across the calm surface and let the freighter settle into the shallows. The inrush of water smothered the cargo in the hold. Able to breathe again, Johnson rolled into Captain Galloway's bunk, made a space for himself among the empty bottles and slept his first dreamless sleep.

"Hey, you! Are you all right?" A woman's hand pounded on the roof of the staff car. "What *are* you doing in there?"

Johnson woke with a start, lifting his head from the steering wheel. While he slept the lianas had enveloped the car, climbing up the roof and windshield pillars. Vivid green tendrils looped themselves around his left hand, tying his wrist to the rim of the wheel.

Wiping his face, he saw the American biologist peering at him through the leaves, as if he were the inmate of some bizarre zoo whose cages were the bodies of abandoned motor-cars. He tried to free himself, and pushed against the driver's door.

"Sit back! I'll cut you loose."

She slashed at the vines with her clasp knife, revealing her fierce and determined wrist. When Johnson stepped onto the ground she held his shoulders, looking him up and down with a thorough eye. She was no more than thirty, three years older than himself, but to Johnson she seemed as self-possessed and remote as the Nassau school-teachers. Yet her mouth was more relaxed than those pursed lips of his childhood, as if she were genuinely concerned for Johnson.

"You're all right," she informed him. "But I wouldn't go for too many rides in that car."

She strolled away from Johnson, her hands pressing the burnished copper trunks of the palms, feeling the urgent pulse of awakening life. Around her shoulders was slung a canvas bag holding a clipboard, sample jars, a camera and reels of film.

"My name's Christine Chambers," she called out to Johnson. "I'm carrying out a botanical project on this island. Have you come from the stranded ship?"

"I'm the captain," Johnson told her without deceit. He reached into the car and retrieved his peaked cap from the eager embrace of the vines, dusted it off and placed it on his head at what he hoped was a rakish angle. "She's not a wreck – I beached her here for repairs."

"Really? For repairs?" Christine Chambers watched him archly, finding him at least as intriguing as the giant scarlet-capped fungi. "So you're the captain. But where's the crew?"

"They abandoned ship." Johnson was glad that he could speak so honestly. He liked this attractive biologist and the way she took a close interest in the island. "There were certain problems with the cargo."

"I bet there were. You were lucky to get here in one piece." She took out a notebook and jotted down some observation on Johnson, glancing at his pupils and lips. "Captain, would you like a sandwich? I've brought a picnic lunch – you look as if you could use a square meal."

"Well . . ." Pleased by her use of his title, Johnson followed her to the beach, where the inflatable sat on the sand. Clearly she had been delayed by the weight of stores: a bell tent, plastic coolers, cartons of canned food, and a small office cabinet. Johnson had survived on a diet of salt beef, cola and oatmeal biscuits he cooked on the galley stove.

For all the equipment, she was in no hurry to unload the stores, as if unsure of sharing the island with Johnson, or perhaps pondering a different approach to her project, one that involved the participation of the human population of the island.

Trying to reassure her, as they divided the sandwiches, he described the last voyage of the *Prospero*, and the disaster of the leaking chemicals. She nodded while he spoke, as if she already knew something of the story.

"It sounds to me like a great feat of seamanship," she complimented him. "The crew who abandoned ship – as it happens, they reported that she went down near Barbados. One of them, Galloway I think he was called, claimed they'd spent a month in an open boat."

"Galloway?" Johnson assumed the pursed lips of the Nassau schoolmarms. "One of my less reliable men. So no one is looking for the ship?"

"No. Absolutely no one."

"And they think she's gone down?"

"Right to the bottom. Everyone in Barbados is relieved there's no pollution. Those tourist beaches, you know."

"They're important. And no one in Puerto Rico thinks she's here?"

"No one except me. This island is my research project," she explained. "I teach biology at San Juan University, but I really want to work at Harvard. I can tell you, lectureships are hard to come by. Something very interesting is happening here, with a little luck . . ."

"It is interesting," Johnson agreed. There was a conspiratorial note to Dr Christine's voice that made him uneasy. "A lot of old army equipment is buried here – I'm thinking of building a house on the beach."

"A good idea . . . even if it takes you four or five months. I'll help you out with any food you need. But be careful." Dr Christine pointed to the weal on his arm, a temporary reaction against some invading toxin in the vine sap. "There's something else that's interesting about this island, isn't there?"

"Well . . ." Johnson stared at the acid stains etching through the *Prospero*'s hull and spreading across the lagoon. He had tried not to think of his responsibility for these dangerous and unstable chemicals. "There are a few other things going on here."

"A few other things?" Dr Christine lowered her voice. "Look, Johnson, you're sitting in the middle of an amazing biological experiment. No one would allow it to happen anywhere in the world – if they knew, the US Navy would move in this afternoon."

"Would they take away the ship?"

"They'd take it away and sink it in the nearest ocean trench, then scorch the island with flame-throwers."

"And what about me?"

"I wouldn't like to say. It might depend on how advanced . . ." She held his shoulder reassuringly, aware that her vehemence had shocked him. "But there's no reason why they should find out. Not for a while, and by then it won't matter. I'm not exaggerating when I say that you've probably created a new kind of life."

As they unloaded the stores Johnson reflected on her words. He had guessed that the chemicals leaking from the *Prospero* had set off the accelerated growth, and that the toxic reagents might equally be affecting himself. In Galloway's cabin mirror he inspected the hairs on his chin and any suspicious moles. The weeks at sea, inhaling the acrid fumes, had left him with raw lungs and throat, and an erratic appetite, but he had felt better since coming ashore.

He watched Christine step into a pair of thigh-length rubber boots and move into the shallow water, ladle in hand, looking at the plant and animal life of the lagoon. She filled several specimen jars with the phosphorescent water, and locked them into the cabinet inside the tent.

"Johnson – you couldn't let me see the cargo manifest?"

"Captain . . . Galloway took it with him. He didn't list the real cargo."

"I bet he didn't." Christine pointed to the vermilion-shelled crabs that scuttled through the vivid filaments of kelp, floating like threads of blue electric cable. "Have you noticed? There are no dead fish or crabs – and you'd expect to see hundreds. That was the first thing I spotted. And it isn't just the crabs – you look pretty healthy . . ."

"Maybe I'll be stronger?" Johnson flexed his sturdy shoulders.

". . . in a complete daze, mentally, but I imagine that will change. Meanwhile, can you take me on board? I'd like to visit the *Prospero*."

"Dr Christine . . ." Johnson held her arm, trying to restrain this determined woman. He looked at her clear skin and strong legs. "It's too dangerous, you might fall through the deck."

"Fair enough. Are the containers identified?"

"Yes, there's no secret." Johnson did his best to remember. "Organo . . ."

"Organo-phosphates? Right – what I need to know is which containers are leaking and roughly how much. We might be able to work out the exact chemical reactions – you may not realise it, Johnson, but you've mixed a remarkably potent cocktail. A lot of people will want to learn the recipe, for all kinds of reasons . . ."

Sitting in the colonel's chair on the porch of the beach-house, Johnson gazed contentedly at the luminous world around him, a fever-realm of light and life that seemed to have sprung from his own mind. The jungle wall of cycads, giant tamarinds and tropical creepers crowded the beach to the waterline, and the reflected colours drowned in swatches of phosphoresence that made the lagoon resemble a cauldron of electric dyes.

So dense was the vegetation that almost the only free sand lay below Johnson's feet. Every morning he would spend an hour cutting back the flowering vines and wild magnolia that inundated the metal shack. Already the foliage was crushing the galvanised iron roof. However hard he worked – and he found himself too easily distracted – he had been unable to keep clear the inspection pathways which Christine patrolled on her weekend visits, camera and specimen jars at the ready.

Hearing the sound of her inflatable as she neared the inlet of the lagoon, Johnson surveyed his domain with pride. He had found a metal card-table buried in the sand, and laid it with a selection of fruits he had picked for Christine that morning. To Johnson's untrained eye they seemed to be strange hybrids of pomegranate and pawpaw, cantaloupe and pineapple. There were giant tomato-like berries and clusters of purple grapes each the size of a baseball. Together they glowed through the overheated light like jewels set in the face of the sun.

By now, four months after his arrival on the *Prospero*, the one-time garbage island had become a unique botanical garden, generating new species of trees, vines and flowering plants every day. A powerful life-engine was driving the island. As she crossed the lagoon in her inflatable Christine stared at the aerial terraces of vines and blossoms that had sprung up since the previous weekend.

The dead hulk of the *Prospero*, daylight visible through its acid-etched plates, sat in the shallow water, the last of its chemical wastes leaking into the lagoon. But Johnson had forgotten the ship and the voyage that had brought him here, just as he had forgotten his past life and unhappy childhood under the screaming engines of Nassau airport. Lolling back in his canvas chair, on which was stencilled "Colonel Pottle, US Army Engineer Corps", he felt like a plantation owner who had successfully subcontracted a corner of the original Eden. As he stood up to greet Christine he thought only of the future, of his pregnant bride and the son who would soon share the island with him.

"Johnson! My God, what have you been doing?" Christine ran the inflatable onto the beach and sat back, exhausted by the buffetting waves. "It's a botanical mad-house!"

Johnson was so pleased to see her that he forgot his regret over their weekly separations. As she explained, she had her student classes to teach, her project notes and research samples to record and catalogue.

"Dr Christine . . . ! I waited all day!" He stepped into the shallow water, a carmine surf filled with glowing animalcula, and pulled the inflatable onto the sand. He helped her from the craft, his eyes avoiding her curving abdomen under the smock.

"Go on, you can stare . . ." Christine pressed his hand to her stomach. "How do I look, Johnson?"

"Too beautiful for me, and the island. We've all gone quiet."

"That is gallant – you've become a poet, Johnson."

Johnson never thought of other women, and knew that none could be so beautiful as this lady biologist bearing his child. He spotted a plastic cooler among the scientific equipment.

"Christine – you've brought me ice-cream . . ."

"Of course I have. But don't eat it yet. We've a lot to do, Johnson."

He unloaded the stores, leaving to the last the nylon nets and spring-mounted steel frames in the bottom of the boat. These bird-traps were the one cargo he hated to unload. Nesting in the highest branches above the island was a flock of extravagant aerial creatures, sometime swallows and finches whose jewelled plumage and tail-fans transformed them into gaudy peacocks. He had set the traps reluctantly at Christine's insistence. He never objected to catching the phosphorescent fish with their enlarged fins and ruffs of external gills, which seemed to prepare them for life on the land, or the crabs and snails in their baroque armour. But the thought of Christine taking these rare and beautiful birds back to her laboratory made him uneasy – he guessed that they would soon end their days under the dissection knife.

"Did you set the traps for me, Johnson?"

"I set all of them and put in the bait."

"Good." Christine heaped the nets onto the sand. More and more she seemed to hurry these days, as if she feared that the experiment might end. "I can't understand why we haven't caught one of them."

Johnson gave an eloquent shrug. In fact he had eaten the canned sardines, and released the one bird that had strayed into the trap below the parasol of a giant cycad. The nervous creature with its silken scarlet wings and kite-like tail feathers had been a dream of flight. "Nothing yet – they're clever, those birds."

"Of course they are – they're a new species." She sat in Colonel Pottle's chair, photographing the table of fruit with her small camera. "Those grapes are huge – I wonder what sort of wine they'd make. Champagne of the gods, grand cru . . ."

Warily, Johnson eyed the purple and yellow globes. He had eaten the fish and crabs from the lagoon, when asked by Christine, with no ill effects, but he was certain that these fruits were intended for the birds. He knew that Christine was using him, like everything else on the island, as part of her experiment. Even the child she had conceived after their one brief act of love, over so quickly that he was scarcely sure it had ever occurred, was part of the experiment. Perhaps the child would be the first of a new breed of man and he, Johnson, errand runner for airport shoe-shine boys, would be the father of an advanced race that would one day repopulate the planet.

As if aware of his impressive physique, she said: "You look wonderfully well, Johnson. If this experiment ever needs to be justified . . ."

"I'm very strong now – I'll be able to look after you and the boy."

"It might be a girl – or something in between." She spoke in a matter-of-fact way that always surprised him. "Tell me, Johnson, what do you do while I'm away?"

"I think about you, Dr Christine."

"And I certainly think about you. But do you sleep a lot?"

"No. I'm busy with my thoughts. The time goes very quickly."

Christine casually opened her note-pad. "You mean the hours go by without you noticing?"

"Yes. After breakfast I fill the oil-lamp and suddenly it's time for lunch. But it can go more slowly, too. If I look at a falling leaf in a certain way it seems to stand still."

"Good. You're learning to control time. Your mind is enlarging, Johnson."

"Maybe I'll be as clever as you, Dr Christine."

"Ah, I think you're moving in a much more interesting direction. In fact, Johnson, I'd like you to eat some of the fruit. Don't worry, I've already analysed it, and I'll have some myself." She was cutting slices of the melon-sized apple. "I want the baby to try some."

Johnson hesitated, but as Christine always reminded him, none of the new species had revealed a single deformity.

The fruit was pale and sweet, with a pulpy texture and a tang like alcoholic mango. It slightly numbed Johnson's mouth and left a pleasant coolness in the stomach.

A diet for those with wings.

"Johnson! Are you sick?"

He woke with a start, not from sleep but from an almost too-clear examination of the colour patterns of a giant butterfly that had settled on his hand. He looked up from his chair at Christine's concerned eyes, and at the dense vines and flowering creepers that crowded the porch, pressing against his shoulders. The amber of her eyes was touched by the same overlit spectrum that shone through the trees and blossoms. Everything on the island was becoming a prism of itself.

"Johnson, wake up!"

"I am awake. Christine . . . I didn't hear you come."

"I've been here for an hour." She touched his cheeks, searching for any sign of fever and puzzled by Johnson's distracted manner. Behind her, the inflatable was beached on the few feet of sand not smothered by the vegetation. The dense wall of palms, lianas and flowering plants had collapsed onto the shore. Engorged on the sun, the giant fruits had begun to split under their own weight, and streams of vivid juice ran across the sand, as if the forest was bleeding.

"Christine? You came back so soon . . . ?" It seemed to Johnson that she had left only a few minutes earlier. He remembered waving goodbye to her and sitting down to finish his fruit and admire the giant butterfly, its wings like the painted hands of a circus clown.

"Johnson – I've been away for a week." She held his shoulder, frowning at the unstable wall of rotting vegetation that towered a hundred feet into the air. Cathedrals of flower-decked foliage were falling into the waters of the lagoon.

"Johnson, help me to unload the stores. You don't look as if you've eaten for days. Did you trap the birds?"

"Birds? No, nothing yet." Vaguely Johnson remembered setting the traps, but he had been too distracted by the wonder of everything to pursue the birds. Graceful, feather-tipped wraiths like gaudy angels, their crimson plumage leaked its ravishing hues onto the air. When he fixed his eyes onto them they seemed suspended against the sky, wings fanning slowly as if shaking the time from themselves.

He stared at Christine, aware that the colours were separating themselves from her skin and hair. Superimposed images of herself, each divided from the others by a fraction of a second, blurred the air around her, an exotic plumage that sprang from her arms and shoulders. The staid reality that had trapped them all was beginning to dissolve. Time had stopped and Christine was ready to rise into the air . . .

He would teach Christine and the child to fly.

"Christine, we can all learn."

"What, Johnson?"

"We can learn to fly. There's no time any more – everything's too beautiful for time."

"Johnson, look at my watch."

"We'll go and live in the trees, Christine. We'll live with the high flowers . . ."

He took her arm, eager to show her the mystery and beauty of the sky people they would become. She tried to protest, but gave in, humouring Johnson as he led her gently from the beach-house to the wall of inflamed flowers. Her hand on the radio-transmitter in the inflatable, she sat beside the crimson lagoon as Johnson tried to climb the flowers towards the sun. Steadying the child within her, she wept for Johnson, only calming herself two hours later when the siren of a naval cutter crossed the inlet.

"I'm glad you radioed in," the US Navy lieutenant told Christine. "One of the birds reached the base at San Juan. We tried to keep it alive but it was crushed by the weight of its own wings. Like everything else on this island."

He pointed from the bridge to the jungle wall. Almost all the over-crowded canopy had collapsed into the lagoon, leaving behind only a few of the original palms with their bird traps. The blossoms glowed through the water like thousands of drowned lanterns.

"How long has the freighter been here?" An older civilian, a government scientist holding a pair of binoculars, peered at the riddled hull of the *Prospero*. Below the beach-house two sailors were loading the last of Christine's stores into the inflatable. "It looks as if it's been stranded there for years."

"Six months," Christine told him. She sat beside Johnson, smiling at him encouragingly. "When Captain Johnson realised what was going on he asked me to call you."

"Only six? That must be roughly the life-cycle of these new species. Their cellular clocks seem to have stopped – instead of reproducing, they force-feed their own tissues, like those giant fruit that contain no seeds. The life of the individual becomes the entire life of the species." He gestured towards the impassive Johnson. "That probably explains our friend's altered time sense – great blocks of memory were coalescing in his mind, so that a ball thrown into the air would never appear to land . . ."

A tide of dead fish floated past the cutter's bow, the gleaming bodies like discarded costume jewellery.

"You weren't contaminated in any way?" the lieutenant asked Christine. "I'm thinking of the baby."

"No, I didn't eat any of the fruit," Christine said firmly. "I've been here only twice, for a few hours."

"Good. Of course, the medical people will do all the tests."

"And the island?"

"We've been ordered to torch the whole place. The demolition charges are timed to go off in just under two hours, but we'll be well out of range. It's a pity, in a way."

"The birds are still here," Christine said, aware of Johnson staring at the trees.

"Luckily, you've trapped them all." The scientist offered her the binoculars. "Those organic wastes are hazardous things – God knows what might happen if human beings were exposed to long-term contact. All sorts of sinister alterations to the nervous system – people might be happy to stare at a stone all day."

Johnson listened to them talking, glad to feel Christine's hand in his own. She was watching him with a quiet smile, aware that they shared the conspiracy. She would try to save the child, the last fragment of the experiment, and he knew that if it survived it would face a fierce challenge from those who feared it might replace them.

But the birds endured. His head had cleared, and he remembered the visions that had given him a brief glimpse of another, more advanced world. High above the collapsed canopy of the forest he could see the traps he had set, and the great crimson birds sitting on their wings. At least they could carry the dream forward.

Ten minutes later, when the inflatable had been winched onto the deck, the cutter set off through the inlet. As it passed the western headland the lieutenant helped Christine towards the cabin. Johnson followed them, then pushed aside the government scientist and leapt from the rail, diving cleanly into the water. He struck out for the shore a hundred feet away, knowing that he was strong enough to climb the trees and release the birds, with luck a mating pair who would take him with them in their escape from time.

THE CHILDREN STAY

Alice Munro

How does one chose *one* story by **Alice Munro** (b.1931)? This is a problem I've had with Ballard, Chekhov, Cheever, McGahern, Maugham, Pritchett, Spark: this book could have included at least three from each, and been no less 'fine'. Munro won the 2009 Man Booker International Prize and the 2013 Nobel Prize for Literature for her work, most of which has been short stories. Cynthia Ozick once described her as "our Chekhov." There is little else to say.

Thirty years ago, a family was spending a holiday together on the east coast of Vancouver Island. A young father and mother, their two small daughters, and an older couple, the husband's parents.

What perfect weather. Every morning, every morning it's like this, the first pure sunlight falling through the high branches, burning away the mist over the still water of Georgia Strait. The tide out, a great empty stretch of sand still damp but easy to walk on, like cement in its very last stage of drying. The tide is actually less far out; every morning, the pavilion of sand is shrinking, but it still seems ample enough. The changes in the tide are a matter of great interest to the grandfather, not so much to anyone else.

Pauline, the young mother, doesn't really like the beach as well as she likes the road that runs behind the cottages for a mile or so north till it stops at the bank of the little river that runs into the sea.

If it wasn't for the tide, it would be hard to remember that this is the sea. You look across the water to the mountains on the mainland, the ranges that are the western wall of the continent of North America. These humps and peaks coming clear now through the mist and glimpsed here and there through the trees, by Pauline as she pushes her daughter's stroller along the road, are also of interest to the grandfather. And to his son Brian, who is Pauline's husband. The two men are continually trying to decide which is what. Which of these shapes are actual continental mountains and which are improbable heights of the islands that ride in front of the shore? It's hard to sort things out when the array is so complicated and parts of it shift their distance in the day's changing light.

But there is a map, set up under glass, between the cottages and the beach. You can stand there looking at the map, then looking at what's in front of you, looking back at the map again, until you get things sorted out. The grandfather and Brian do this every day, usually getting into an argument – though you'd think there would not be much room for disagreement with the map right there. Brian chooses to see the map as inexact. But his father will not hear a word of criticism about any aspect of this place, which was his choice for the holiday. The map, like the accommodation and the weather, is perfect.

Brian's mother won't look at the map. She says it boggles her mind. The men laugh at her, they accept that her mind is boggled. Her husband believes that this is because she is a female. Brian believes that it's because she's his mother. Her concern is always about whether anybody is hungry yet, or thirsty, whether the children have their sun hats on and have been rubbed with protective lotion. And what is the strange bite on Caitlin's arm that doesn't look like the bite of a mosquito? She makes her husband wear a floppy cotton hat and thinks that Brian should wear one too – she reminds him of how sick he got from the sun, that summer they went to the Okanagan, when he was a child. Sometimes Brian says to her, "Oh, dry up, Mother." His tone is mostly affectionate, but his father may ask him if that's the way he thinks he can talk to his mother nowadays.

"She doesn't mind," says Brian.

"How do you know?" says his father.

"Oh for Pete's sake," says his mother.

Pauline slides out of bed as soon as she's awake every morning, slides out of reach of Brian's long, sleepily searching arms and legs. What wakes her are the first squeaks and mutters of the baby, Mara, in the children's room, then the creak of the crib as Mara – sixteen months old now, getting to the end of babyhood – pulls herself up to stand hanging on to the railing. She continues her soft amiable talk as Pauline lifts her out – Caitlin, nearly five, shifting about but not waking, in her nearby bed – and as she is carried into the kitchen to be changed, on the floor. Then she is settled into her stroller, with a biscuit and a bottle of apple juice, while Pauline gets into her sundress and sandals, goes to the bathroom, combs out her hair – all as quickly and quietly as possible. They leave the cottage; they head past some other cottages for the bumpy unpaved road that is still mostly in deep morning shadow, the floor of a tunnel under fir and cedar trees.

The grandfather, also an early riser, sees them from the porch of his cottage, and Pauline sees him. But all that is necessary is a wave. He and Pauline never have much to say to each other (though sometimes there's an affinity they feel, in the midst of some long-drawn-out antics of Brian's or some apologetic but insistent fuss made by the grandmother; there's an awareness of not looking at each other, lest their look should reveal a bleakness that would discredit others).

On this holiday Pauline steals time to be by herself – being with Mara is still almost the same thing as being by herself. Early morning walks, the late-morning hour when she washes and hangs out the diapers. She could have had another hour or so in the afternoons, while Mara is napping. But Brian has fixed up a shelter on the beach, and he carries the playpen down every day, so that Mara can nap there and Pauline won't have to absent herself. He says his parents may be offended if she's always sneaking off. He agrees though that she does need some time to go over her lines for the play she's going to be in, back in Victoria, this September.

Pauline is not an actress. This is an amateur production, but she is not even an amateur actress. She didn't try out for the role, though it happened that she had already read the play. *Eurydice* by Jean Anouilh. But then, Pauline has read all sorts of things.

She was asked if she would like to be in this play by a man she met at a barbecue, in June. The people at the barbecue were mostly teachers and their wives or husbands – it was held at the house of the principal of the high school where Brian teaches. The woman who taught French was a widow – she had brought her grown son who was staying for the summer with her and working as a night clerk in a downtown hotel. She told everybody that he had got a job teaching at a college in western Washington State and would be going there in the fall.

Jeffrey Toom was his name. "Without the *B*," he said, as if the staleness of the joke wounded him. It was a different name from his mother's, because she had been widowed twice, and he was the son of her first husband. About the job he said, "No guarantee it'll last, it's a one-year appointment."

What was he going to teach?

"Dram-ah," he said, drawing the word out in a mocking way.

He spoke of his present job disparagingly, as well.

"It's a pretty sordid place," he said. "Maybe you heard – a hooker was killed there last winter. And then we get the usual losers checking in to OD or bump themselves off."

People did not quite know what to make of this way of talking and drifted away from him. Except for Pauline.

"I'm thinking about putting on a play," he said. "Would you like to be in it?" He asked her if she had ever heard of a play called *Eurydice*.

Pauline said, "You mean Anouilh's?" and he was unflatteringly surprised. He immediately said he didn't know if it would ever work out. "I just thought it might be interesting to see if you could do something different here in the land of Noël Coward."

Pauline did not remember when there had been a play by Noël Coward put on in Victoria, though she supposed there had been several. She said, "We saw *The Duchess of Malfi* last winter at the college. And the little theater did *A Resounding Tinkle*, but we didn't see it."

"Yeah. Well," he said, flushing. She had thought he was older than she was, at least as old as Brian (who was thirty, though people were apt to say he didn't act it), but as soon as he started talking to her, in this offhand, dismissive way, never quite meeting her eyes, she suspected that he was younger than he'd like to appear. Now with that flush she was sure of it.

As it turned out, he was a year younger than she was. Twenty-five.

She said that she couldn't be Eurydice; she couldn't act. But Brian came over to see what the conversation was about and said at once that she must try it.

"She just needs a kick in the behind," Brian said to Jeffrey. "She's like a little mule, it's hard to get her started. No, seriously, she's too self-effacing, I tell her that all the time. She's very smart. She's actually a lot smarter than I am."

At that Jeffrey did look directly into Pauline's eyes – impertinently and searchingly – and she was the one who was flushing.

He had chosen her immediately as his Eurydice because of the way she looked. But it was not because she was beautiful. "I'd never put a beautiful girl in that part," he said. "I don't know if I'd ever put a beautiful girl on stage in anything. It's too much. It's distracting."

So what did he mean about the way she looked? He said it was her hair, which was long and dark and rather bushy (not in style at that time), and her pale skin ("Stay out of the sun this summer") and most of all her eyebrows.

"I never liked them," said Pauline, not quite sincerely. Her eyebrows were level, dark, luxuriant. They dominated her face. Like her hair, they were not in style. But if she had really disliked them, wouldn't she have plucked them?

Jeffrey seemed not to have heard her. "They give you a sulky look and that's disturbing," he said. "Also your jaw's a little heavy and that's sort of Greek. It would be better in a movie where I could get you close up. The routine thing for Eurydice would be a girl who looked ethereal. I don't want ethereal."

As she walked Mara along the road, Pauline did work at the lines. There was a speech at the end that was giving her trouble. She bumped the stroller along and repeated to herself, "'You are terrible, you know, you are terrible like the angels. You think everybody's going forward, as brave and bright as you are – oh, don't look at me, please, darling, don't look at me – perhaps I'm not what you wish I was, but I'm here, and I'm warm, I'm kind, and I love you. I'll give you all the happiness I can. Don't look at me. Don't look. Let me live.'"

She had left something out. "'Perhaps I'm not what you wish I was, but you feel me here, don't you? I'm warm and I'm kind – '"

She had told Jeffrey that she thought the play was beautiful.

He said, "Really?" What she'd said didn't please or surprise him – he seemed to feel it was predictable, superfluous. He would never describe a play in that way. He spoke of it more as a hurdle to be got over. Also a challenge to be flung at various enemies. At the academic snots – as he called them – who had done *The Duchess of Malfi*. And at the social twits – as he called them – in the little theater. He saw himself as an outsider heaving his weight against these people, putting on his play – he called it his – in the teeth of their contempt and opposition. In the beginning Pauline thought that this must be all in his imagination and that it was more likely these people knew nothing about him. Then something would happen that could be, but might not be, a coincidence. Repairs had to be done on the church hall where the play was to be performed, making it unobtainable. There was an unexpected increase in the cost of printing advertising posters. She found herself seeing it his way. If you were going to be around him much, you almost had to see it his way – arguing was dangerous and exhausting.

"Sons of bitches," said Jeffrey between his teeth, but with some satisfaction. "I'm not surprised."

The rehearsals were held upstairs in an old building on Fisgard Street. Sunday afternoon was the only time that everybody could get there, though there were fragmentary rehearsals during the week. The retired harbor pilot who played Monsieur Henri was able to attend every rehearsal, and got to have an irritating familiarity with everybody else's lines. But the hairdresser – who had experience only with Gilbert and Sullivan but now found herself playing Eurydice's mother – could not leave her shop for long at any other time. The bus driver who played her lover had his daily employment as well, and so had the waiter who played Orphée (he was the only one of them who hoped to be a real actor). Pauline had to depend on sometimes undependable high-school baby-sitters – for the first six weeks of the summer Brian was busy teaching summer school – and Jeffrey himself had to be at his hotel job by eight o'clock in the evenings. But on Sunday afternoons they were all there. While other people swam at Thetis Lake, or thronged Beacon Hill Park to walk under the trees and feed the ducks, or drove far out of town to the Pacific beaches, Jeffrey and his crew labored in the dusty high-ceilinged room on Fisgard Street. The windows were rounded at the top as in some plain and dignified church, and propped open in the heat with whatever objects could be found – ledger books from the 1920s belonging to the hat shop that had once operated downstairs, or pieces of wood left over from the picture frames made by the artist whose canvases were now stacked against one wall and apparently abandoned. The glass was grimy, but outside the sunlight bounced off the sidewalks, the empty gravelled parking lots, the low stuccoed buildings, with what seemed a special Sunday brightness. Hardly anybody moved through these downtown streets. Nothing was open except the occasional hole-in-the-wall coffee shop or fly-specked convenience store.

Pauline was the one who went out at the break to get soft drinks and coffee. She was the one who had the least to say about the play and the way it was going – even though she was the only one who had read it before – because she alone had never done any acting. So it seemed proper for her to volunteer. She enjoyed her short walk in the empty streets – she felt as if she had become an urban person, someone detached and solitary, who lived in the glare of an important dream. Sometimes she thought of Brian at home, working in the garden and keeping an eye on the children. Or perhaps he had taken them to Dallas Road – she recalled a promise – to sail boats on the pond. That life seemed ragged and tedious compared to what went on in the rehearsal room – the hours of effort, the concentration, the sharp exchanges, the sweating and tension. Even the taste of the coffee, its scalding bitterness, and the fact that it was chosen by nearly everybody in preference to a fresher-tasting and maybe more healthful drink out of the cooler seemed satisfying to her. And she liked the look of the shop-windows. This was not one of the dolled-up streets near the harbor – it was a street of shoe- and bicycle-repair shops, discount linen and fabric stores, of clothes and furniture that had been so long in the windows that they looked secondhand even if they weren't. On some windows sheets of golden plastic as frail and crinkled as old cellophane were stretched inside the glass to protect the merchandise from the sun. All these enterprises had been left behind just for this one day, but they had a look of being fixed in time as much as cave paintings or relics under sand.

When she said that she had to go away for the two-week holiday Jeffrey looked thunderstruck, as if he had never imagined that things like holidays could come into her life. Then he turned grim and slightly satirical, as if this was just another blow that he might have expected. Pauline explained that she would miss only the one Sunday – the one in the middle of the two weeks – because she and Brian were driving up the island on a Monday and coming back on a Sunday morning. She promised to get back in time for rehearsal. Privately she wondered how she would do this – it always took so much longer than you expected to pack up and get away. She wondered if she could possibly come back by herself, on the morning bus. That would probably be too much to ask for. She didn't mention it.

She couldn't ask him if it was only the play he was thinking about, only her absence from a rehearsal that caused the thundercloud. At the moment, it very likely was. When he spoke to her at rehearsals there was never any suggestion that he ever spoke to her in any other way. The only difference in his treatment of her was that perhaps he expected less of her, of her acting, than he did of the others. And that would be understandable to anybody. She was the only one chosen out of the blue, for the way she looked – the others had all shown up at the audition he had advertised on the signs put up in cafés and bookstores around town. From her he appeared to want an immobility or awkwardness that he didn't want from the rest of them. Perhaps it was because, in the latter part of the play, she was supposed to be a person who had already died.

Yet she thought they all knew, the rest of the cast all knew, what was going on, in spite of Jeffrey's offhand and abrupt and none too civil ways. They knew that after every one of them had straggled off home, he would walk across the room and bolt the staircase door. (At first Pauline had pretended to leave with the rest and had even got into her car and circled the block, but later such a trick had come to seem insulting, not just to herself and Jeffrey, but to the others whom she was sure would never betray her, bound as they all were under the temporary but potent spell of the play.)

Jeffrey crossed the room and bolted the door. Every time, this was like a new decision, which he had to make. Until it was done, she wouldn't look at him. The sound of the bolt being pushed into place, the ominous or fatalistic sound of the metal hitting metal, gave her a localized shock of capitulation. But she didn't make a move, she waited for him to come back to her with the whole story of the afternoon's labor draining out of his face, the expression of matter-of-fact and customary disappointment cleared away, replaced by the live energy she always found surprising.

"So. Tell us what this play of yours is about," Brian's father said. "Is it one of those ones where they take their clothes off on the stage?"

"Now don't tease her," said Brian's mother.

Brian and Pauline had put the children to bed and walked over to his parents' cottage for an evening drink. The sunset was behind them, behind the forests of Vancouver Island, but the mountains in front of them, all clear now and hard-cut against the sky, shone in its pink light. Some high inland mountains were capped with pink summer snow.

"Nobody takes their clothes off, Dad," said Brian in his booming schoolroom voice. "You know why? Because they haven't got any clothes on in the first place. It's the latest style. They're going to put on a bare-naked *Hamlet* next. Bare-naked *Romeo and Juliet*. Boy, that balcony scene where Romeo is climbing up the trellis and he gets stuck in the rosebushes –"

"Oh, Brian," said his mother.

"The story of Orpheus and Eurydice is that Eurydice died," Pauline said. "And Orpheus goes down to the underworld to try to get her back. And his wish is granted, but only if he promises not to look at her. Not to look back at her. She's walking behind him –"

"Twelve paces," said Brian. "As is only right."

"It's a Greek story, but it's set in modern times," said Pauline. "At least this version is. More or less modern. Orpheus is a musician travelling around with his father – they're both musicians – and Eurydice is an actress. This is in France."

"Translated?" Brian's father said.

"No," said Brian. "But don't worry, it's not in French. It was written in Transylvanian."

"It's so hard to make sense of anything," Brian's mother said with a worried laugh. "It's so hard, with Brian around."

"It's in English," Pauline said.

"And you're what's-her-name?"

She said, "I'm Eurydice."

"He get you back okay?"

"No," she said. "He looks back at me, and then I have to stay dead."

"Oh, an unhappy ending," Brian's mother said.

"You're so gorgeous?" said Brian's father skeptically. "He can't stop himself from looking back?"

"It's not that," said Pauline. But at this point she felt that something had been achieved by her father-in-law, he had done what he meant to do, which was the same thing that he nearly always meant to do, in any conversation she had with him. And that was to break through the structure of some explanation he had asked her for, and she had unwillingly but patiently given, and, with a seemingly negligent kick, knock it into rubble. He had been dangerous to her for a long time in this way, but he wasn't particularly so tonight.

But Brian did not know that. Brian was still figuring out how to come to her rescue.

"Pauline is gorgeous," Brian said.

"Yes indeed," said his mother.

"Maybe if she'd go to the hairdresser," his father said. But Pauline's long hair was such an old objection of his that it had become a family joke. Even Pauline laughed. She said, "I can't afford to till we get the veranda roof fixed." And Brian laughed boisterously, full of relief that she was able to take all this as a joke. It was what he had always told her to do.

"Just kid him back," he said. "It's the only way to handle him."

"Yeah, well, if you'd got yourselves a decent house," said his father. But this like Pauline's hair was such a familiar sore point that it couldn't rouse anybody. Brian and Pauline had bought a handsome house in bad repair on a street in Victoria where old mansions were being turned into ill-used apartment buildings. The house, the street, the messy old Garry oaks, the fact that no basement had been blasted out under the house, were all a horror to Brian's father. Brian usually agreed with him and tried to go him one further. If his father pointed at the house next door all criss-crossed with black fire escapes, and asked what kind of neighbors they had, Brian said, "Really poor people, Dad. Drug addicts." And when his father wanted to know how it was heated, he'd said, "Coal furnace.

Hardly any of them left these days, you can get coal really cheap. Of course it's dirty and it kind of stinks."

So what his father said now about a decent house might be some kind of peace signal. Or could be taken so.

Brian was an only son. He was a math teacher. His father was a civil engineer and part owner of a contracting company. If he had hoped that he would have a son who was an engineer and might come into the company, there was never any mention of it. Pauline had asked Brian whether he thought the carping about their house and her hair and the books she read might be a cover for this larger disappointment, but Brian had said, "Nope. In our family we complain about just whatever we want to complain about. We ain't subtle, ma'am."

Pauline still wondered, when she heard his mother talking about how teachers ought to be the most honored people in the world and they did not get half the credit they deserved and that she didn't know how Brian managed it, day after day. Then his father might say, "That's right," or, "I sure wouldn't want to do it, I can tell you that. They couldn't pay me to do it."

"Don't worry Dad," Brian would say. "They wouldn't pay you much."

Brian in his everyday life was a much more dramatic person than Jeffrey. He dominated his classes by keeping up a parade of jokes and antics, extending the role that he had always played, Pauline believed, with his mother and father. He acted dumb, he bounced back from pretended humiliations, he traded insults. He was a bully in a good cause – a chivvying cheerful indestructible bully.

"Your boy has certainly made his mark with us," the principal said to Pauline. "He has not just survived, which is something in itself. He has made his mark."

Your boy.

Brian called his students boneheads. His tone was affectionate, fatalistic. He said that his father was the King of the Philistines, a pure and natural barbarian. And that his mother was a dishrag, good-natured and worn out. But however he dismissed such people, he could not be long without them. He took his students on camping trips. And he could not imagine a summer without this shared holiday. He was mortally afraid, every year, that Pauline would refuse to go along. Or that, having agreed to go, she was going to be miserable, take offense at something his father said, complain about how much time she had to spend with his mother, sulk because there was no way they could do anything by themselves. She might decide to spend all day in their own cottage, reading and pretending to have a sunburn.

All those things had happened, on previous holidays. But this year she was easing up. He told her he could see that, and he was grateful to her.

"I know it's an effort," he said. "It's different for me. They're my parents and I'm used to not taking them seriously."

Pauline came from a family that took things so seriously that her parents had got a divorce. Her mother was now dead. She had a distant, though cordial, relationship with her father and her two much older sisters. She said that they had nothing in common. She knew Brian could not understand how that could be a reason. She saw what comfort it gave him, this year, to see things going so well. She had thought it was laziness or cowardice that kept him from breaking the arrangement, but now she saw that it was something far more positive. He needed to have his wife and his parents and his children bound together like this, he needed to involve Pauline in his life with his parents and to bring his parents to some recognition of her – though the recognition, from his father, would always be muffled and contrary, and from his mother too profuse, too easily come by, to mean much. Also he wanted Pauline to be connected, he wanted the children to be connected, to his own childhood – he wanted these holidays to be linked to holidays of his childhood with their lucky or unlucky weather, car troubles or driving records, boating scares, bee stings, marathon Monopoly games, to all the things that he told his mother he was bored to death hearing about. He wanted pictures from this summer to be taken, and fitted into his mother's album, a continuation of all the other pictures that he groaned at the mention of.

The only time they could talk to each other was in bed, late at night. But they did talk then, more than was usual with them at home, where Brian was so tired that often he fell immediately asleep. And in ordinary daylight it was often hard to talk to him because of his jokes. She could see the joke brightening his eyes (his coloring was very like hers – dark hair and pale skin and gray eyes, but her eyes were cloudy and his were light, like clear water over stones). She could see it pulling at the corners of his mouth, as he foraged among your words to catch a pun or the start of a rhyme – anything that could take the conversation away, into absurdity. His whole body, tall and loosely joined together and still almost as skinny as a teenager's, twitched with comic propensity. Before she married him, Pauline had a friend named Gracie, a rather grumpy-looking girl, subversive about men. Brian had thought her a girl whose spirits needed a boost, and so he made even more than the usual effort. And Gracie said to Pauline, "How can you stand the nonstop show?"

"That's not the real Brian," Pauline had said. "He's different when we're alone." But looking back, she wondered how true that had ever been. Had she said it simply to defend her choice, as you did when you had made up your mind to get married?

So talking in the dark had something to do with the fact that she could not see his face. And that he knew she couldn't see his face.

But even with the window open on the unfamiliar darkness and stillness of the night, he teased a little. He had to speak of Jeffrey as Monsieur le Directeur, which made the play or the fact that it was a French play slightly ridiculous. Or perhaps it was Jeffrey himself, Jeffrey's seriousness about the play, that had to be called in question.

Pauline didn't care. It was such a pleasure and a relief to her to mention Jeffrey's name.

Most of the time she didn't mention him; she circled around that pleasure. She described all the others, instead. The hairdresser and the harbor pilot and the waiter and the old man who claimed to have once acted on the radio. He played Orphée's father and gave Jeffrey the most trouble, because he had the stubbornest notions of his own, about acting.

The middle-aged impresario Monsieur Dulac was played by a twenty-four-year-old travel agent. And Mathias, who was Eurydice's former boyfriend, presumably around her own age, was played by the manager of a shoe store, who was married and a father of children.

Brian wanted to know why Monsieur le Directeur hadn't cast these two the other way round.

"That's the way he does things," Pauline said. "What he sees in us is something only he can see."

For instance, she said, the waiter was a clumsy Orphée.

"He's only nineteen, he's so shy Jeffrey has to keep at him. He tells him not to act like he's making love to his grandmother. He has to tell him what to do. *Keep your arms around her a little longer, stroke her here a little*. I don't know how it's going to work – I just have to trust Jeffrey, that he knows what he's doing."

" 'Stroke her here a little'?" said Brian. "Maybe I should come around and keep an eye on these rehearsals."

When she had started to quote Jeffrey Pauline had felt a giving-way in her womb or the bottom of her stomach, a shock that had travelled oddly upwards and hit her vocal cords. She had to cover up this quaking by growling in a way that was supposed to be an imitation (though Jeffrey never growled or ranted or carried on in any theatrical way at all).

"But there's a point about him being so innocent," she said hurriedly. "Being not so physical. Being awkward." And she began to talk about Orphée in the play, not the waiter. Orphée has a problem with love or reality. Orphée will not put up with anything less than perfection. He wants a love that is outside of ordinary life. He wants a perfect Eurydice.

"Eurydice is more realistic. She's carried on with Mathias and with Monsieur Dulac. She's been around her mother and her mother's lover. She knows what people are like. But she loves Orphée. She loves him better in a way than he loves her. She loves him better because she's not such a fool. She loves him like a human person."

"But she's slept with those other guys," Brian said.

"Well with Mr. Dulac she had to, she couldn't get out of it. She didn't want to, but probably after a while she enjoyed it, because after a certain point she couldn't help enjoying it."

So Orphée is at fault, Pauline said decidedly. He looks at Eurydice on purpose, to kill her and get rid of her because she is not perfect. Because of him she has to die a second time.

Brian, on his back and with his eyes wide open (she knew that because of the tone of his voice) said, "But doesn't he die too?"

"Yes. He chooses to."

"So then they're together?"

"Yes. Like Romeo and Juliet. *Orphée is with Eurydice at last*. That's what Monsieur Henri says. That's the last line of the play. That's the end." Pauline rolled over onto her side and touched her cheek to Brian's shoulder – not to start anything but to emphasize what she said next. "It's a beautiful play in one way, but in another it's so silly. And it isn't really like *Romeo and Juliet* because it isn't bad luck or circumstances. It's on purpose. So they don't have to go on with life and get married and have kids and buy an old house and fix it up and –"

"And have affairs," said Brian. "After all, they're French."

Then he said, "Be like my parents."

Pauline laughed. "Do they have affairs? I can imagine."

"Oh sure," said Brian. "I meant their life."

"Logically I can see killing yourself so you won't turn into your parents," Brian said. "I just don't believe anybody would do it."

"Everybody has choices," Pauline said dreamily. "Her mother and his father are both despicable in a way, but Orphée and Eurydice don't have to be like them. They're not corrupt. Just because she's slept with those men doesn't mean she's corrupt. She wasn't in love then. She hadn't met Orphée. There's one speech where he tells her that everything she's done is sticking to her, and it's disgusting. Lies she's told him. The other men. It's all sticking to her forever. And then of course Monsieur Henri plays up to that. He tells Orphée that he'll be just as bad and that one day he'll walk down the street with Eurydice and he'll look like a man with a dog he's trying to lose."

To her surprise, Brian laughed.

"No," she said. "That's what's stupid. It's not inevitable. It's not inevitable at all."

They went on speculating, and comfortably arguing, in a way that was not usual, but not altogether unfamiliar to them. They had done this before, at long intervals in their married life – talked half the night about God or fear of death or how children should be educated or whether money was important. At last they admitted to being too tired to make sense any longer, and arranged themselves in a comradely position and went to sleep.

Finally a rainy day. Brian and his parents were driving into Campbell River to get groceries, and gin, and to take Brian's father's car to a garage, to see about a problem that had developed on the drive up from Nanaimo. This was a very slight problem, but there was the matter of the new-car warranty's being in effect at present, so Brian's father wanted to get it seen to as soon as possible. Brian had to go along, with his car, just in case his father's car had to be left in the garage. Pauline said that she had to stay home because of Mara's nap.

She persuaded Caitlin to lie down too – allowing her to take her music box to bed with her if she played it very softly. Then Pauline spread the script on the kitchen table and drank coffee and went over the scene in which Orphée says that it's intolerable, at last, to stay in two skins, two envelopes with their own blood and oxygen sealed up in their solitude, and Eurydice tells him to be quiet.

"*Don't talk. Don't think. Just let your hand wander, let it be happy on its own.*"

Your hand is my happiness, says Eurydice. Accept that. Accept your happiness. Of course he says he cannot.

Caitlin called out frequently to ask what time it was. She turned up the sound of the music box. Pauline hurried to the bedroom door and hissed at her to turn it down, not to wake Mara.

"If you play it like that again I'll take it away from you. Okay?"

But Mara was already rustling around in her crib, and in the next few minutes there were sounds of soft, encouraging conversation from Caitlin, designed to get her sister wide awake. Also of the music being quickly turned up and then down. Then of Mara rattling the crib railing, pulling herself up, throwing her bottle out onto the floor, and starting the bird cries that would grow more and more desolate until they brought her mother.

"I didn't wake her," Caitlin said. "She was awake all by herself. It's not raining anymore. Can we go down to the beach?"

She was right. It wasn't raining. Pauline changed Mara, told Caitlin to get her bathing suit on and find her sand pail. She got into her own bathing suit and put her shorts over it, in case the rest of the family arrived home while she was down there. ("Dad doesn't like the way some women just go right out of their cottages in their bathing suits," Brian's mother had said to her. "I guess he and I just grew up in other times.") She picked up the script to take it along, then laid it down. She was afraid that she would get too absorbed in it and take her eyes off the children for a moment too long.

The thoughts that came to her, of Jeffrey, were not really thoughts at all – they were more like alterations in her body. This could happen when she was sitting on the beach (trying to stay in the half shade of a bush and so preserve her pallor, as Jeffrey had ordered) or when she was wringing out diapers or when she and Brian were visiting his parents. In the middle of Monopoly games, Scrabble games, card games. She went right on talking, listening, working, keeping track of the children, while some memory of her secret life disturbed her like a radiant explosion. Then a warm weight settled, reassurance filling up all her hollows. But it didn't last, this comfort leaked away, and she was like a miser whose windfall has vanished and who is convinced such luck can never strike again. Longing buckled her up and drove her to the discipline of counting days. Sometimes she even cut the days into fractions to figure out more exactly how much time had gone.

She thought of going into Campbell River, making some excuse, so that she could get to a phone booth and call him. The cottages had no phones – the only public phone was in the hall of the lodge. But she did not have the number of the hotel where Jeffrey worked. And besides that, she could never get away to Campbell River in the evening. She was afraid that if she called him at home in the daytime his mother the French teacher might answer. He said his mother hardly ever left the house in the summer. Just once, she had taken the ferry to Vancouver for the day. Jeffrey had phoned Pauline to ask her to come over. Brian was teaching, and Caitlin was at her play group.

Pauline said, "I can't. I have Mara."

Jeffrey said, "Who? Oh. Sorry." Then "Couldn't you bring her along?"

She said no.

"Why not? Couldn't you bring some things for her to play with?"

No, said Pauline. "I couldn't," she said. "I just couldn't." It seemed too dangerous to her, to trundle her baby along on such a guilty expedition. To a house where cleaning fluids would not be bestowed on high shelves, and all pills and cough syrups and cigarettes and buttons put safely out of reach. And even if she escaped poisoning or choking, Mara might be storing up time bombs – memories of a strange house where she was strangely disregarded, of a closed door, noises on the other side of it.

"I just wanted you," Jeffrey said. "I just wanted you in my bed."

She said again, weakly, "No."

Those words of his kept coming back to her. *I wanted you in my bed.* A half-joking urgency in his voice but also a determination, a practicality, as if "in my bed" meant something more, the bed he spoke of taking on larger, less material dimensions.

Had she made a great mistake with that refusal? With that reminder of how fenced in she was, in what anybody would call her real life?

The beach was nearly empty – people had got used to its being a rainy day. The sand was too heavy for Caitlin to make a castle or dig an irrigation system – projects she would only undertake with her father, anyway, because she sensed that his interest in them was wholehearted, and Pauline's was not. She wandered a bit forlornly at the edge of the water. She probably missed the presence of other children, the nameless instant friends and occasional stone-throwing water-kicking enemies, the shrieking and splashing and falling about. A boy a little bigger than she was and apparently all by himself stood knee-deep in the water farther down the beach. If these two could get together it might be all right; the whole beach experience might be retrieved. Pauline couldn't tell whether Caitlin was now making little splashy runs into the water for his benefit or whether he was watching her with interest or scorn.

Mara didn't need company, at least for now. She stumbled towards the water, felt it touch her feet and changed her mind, stopped, looked around, and spotted Pauline. "Paw. Paw," she said, in happy recognition. "Paw" was what she said for "Pauline," instead of "Mother" or "Mommy." Looking around overbalanced her – she sat down half on the sand and half in the water, made a squawk of surprise that turned to an announcement, then by some determined ungraceful maneuvers that involved putting her weight on her hands, she rose to her feet, wavering and triumphant. She had been walking for half a year, but getting around on the sand was still a challenge. Now she came back towards Pauline, making some reasonable, casual remarks in her own language.

"Sand," said Pauline, holding up a clot of it. "Look. Mara. Sand."

Mara corrected her, calling it something else – it sounded like "whap." Her thick diaper under her plastic pants and her terry-cloth playsuit gave her a fat bottom, and that, along with her plump cheeks and shoulders and her sidelong important expression, made her look like a roguish matron.

Pauline became aware of someone calling her name. It had been called two or three times, but because the voice was unfamiliar she had not recognized it. She stood up and waved. It was the woman who worked in the store at the lodge. She was leaning over the balcony and calling, "Mrs. Keating. Mrs. Keating? Telephone, Mrs. Keating."

Pauline hoisted Mara onto her hip and summoned Caitlin. She and the little boy were aware of each other now – they were both picking up stones from the bottom and flinging them out into the water. At first she didn't hear Pauline, or pretended not to.

"Store," called Pauline. "Caitlin. Store." When she was sure Caitlin would follow – it was the word "store" that had done it, the reminder of the tiny store in the lodge where you could buy ice cream and candy and cigarettes and mixer – she began the trek across the sand and up the flight of wooden steps above the sand and the salal bushes. Halfway up she stopped, said, "Mara, you weigh a ton," and shifted the baby to her other hip. Caitlin banged a stick against the railing.

"Can I have a Fudgsicle? Mother? Can I?"

"We'll see."

"Can I please have a Fudgsicle?"

"Wait."

The public phone was beside a bulletin board on the other side of the main hall and across from the door to the dining room. A bingo game had been set up in there, because of the rain.

"Hope he's still hanging on," the woman who worked in the store called out. She was unseen now behind her counter.

Pauline, still holding Mara, picked up the dangling receiver and said breathlessly, "Hello?" She was expecting to hear Brian telling her about some delay in Campbell River or asking her what it was she had wanted him to get at the drugstore. It was just the one thing – calamine lotion – so he had not written it down.

"Pauline," said Jeffrey. "It's me."

Mara was bumping and scrambling against Pauline's side, anxious to get down. Caitlin came along the hall and went into the store, leaving wet sandy footprints. Pauline said, "Just a minute, just a minute." She let Mara slide down and hurried to close the door that led to the steps. She did not remember telling Jeffrey the name of this place, though she had told him roughly where it was. She heard the woman in the store speaking to Caitlin in a sharper voice than she would use to children whose parents were beside them.

"Did you forget to put your feet under the tap?"

"I'm here," said Jeffrey. "I didn't get along well without you. I didn't get along at all."

Mara made for the dining room, as if the male voice calling out "Under the N –" was a direct invitation to her.

"Here. Where?" said Pauline.

She read the signs that were tacked up on the bulletin board beside the phone.

No Person under Fourteen Years of Age Not Accompanied by Adult Allowed in Boats or Canoes.

Fishing Derby.

Bake and Craft Sale, St. Bartholomew's Church.

Your Life Is in Your Hands. Palms and Cards Read. Reasonable and Accurate. Call Claire. "In a motel. In Campbell River."

Pauline knew where she was before she opened her eyes. Nothing surprised her. She had slept but not deeply enough to let go of anything.

She had waited for Brian in the parking area of the lodge, with the children, and had asked him for the keys. She had told him in front of his parents that there was something else she needed, from Campbell River. He asked, What was it? And did she have any money?

"Just something," she said, so he would think that it was tampons or birth control supplies, that she didn't want to mention. "Sure."

"Okay but you'll have to put some gas in," he said.

Later she had to speak to him on the phone. Jeffrey said she had to do it.

"Because he won't take it from me. He'll think I kidnapped you or something. He won't believe it."

But the strangest thing of all the things that day was that Brian did seem, immediately, to believe it. Standing where she had stood not so long before, in the public hallway of the lodge – the bingo game over now but people going past, she could hear them, people on their way out of the dining room after dinner – he said, "Oh. Oh. Oh. Okay" in a voice that would have to be quickly controlled, but that seemed to draw on a supply of fatalism or foreknowledge that went far beyond that necessity.

As if he had known all along, all along, what could happen with her.

"Okay," he said. "What about the car?"

He said something else, something impossible, and hung up, and she came out of the phone booth beside some gas pumps in Campbell River.

"That was quick," Jeffrey said. "Easier than you expected."

Pauline said, "I don't know."

"He may have known it subconsciously. People do know."

She shook her head, to tell him not to say any more, and he said, "Sorry." They walked along the street not touching or talking.

They'd had to go out to find a phone booth because there was no phone in the motel room. Now in the early morning looking around at leisure – the first real leisure or freedom she'd had since she came into that room – Pauline saw that there wasn't much of anything in it. Just a junk dresser, the bed without a headboard, an armless upholstered chair, on the window a Venetian blind with a broken slat and curtain of orange plastic that was supposed to look like net and that didn't have to be hemmed, just sliced off at the bottom. There was a noisy air conditioner – Jeffrey had turned it off in the night and left the door open on the chain, since the window was sealed. The door was shut now. He must have got up in the night and shut it.

This was all she had. Her connection with the cottage where Brian lay asleep or not asleep was broken, also her connection with the house that had been an expression of her life with Brian, of the way they wanted to live. She had no furniture anymore. She had cut herself off from all the large solid acquisitions like the washer and dryer and the oak table and the refinished wardrobe and the chandelier that was a copy of the one in a painting by Vermeer. And just as much from those things that were particularly hers – the pressed-glass tumblers that she had been collecting and the prayer rug which was of course not authentic, but beautiful. Especially from those things. Even her books, she might have lost. Even her clothes. The skirt and blouse and sandals she had put on for the trip to Campbell River might well be all she had now to her name. She would never go back to lay claim to anything. If Brian got in touch with her to ask what was to be done with things, she would tell him to do what he liked – throw everything into garbage bags and take it to the dump, if that was what he liked. (In fact she knew that he would probably pack up a trunk, which he did, sending on, scrupulously, not only her winter coat and boots but things like the waist cincher she had worn at her wedding and never since, with the prayer rug draped over the top of everything like a final statement of his generosity, either natural or calculated.)

She believed that she would never again care about what sort of rooms she lived in or what sort of clothes she put on. She would not be looking for that sort of help to give anybody an idea of who she was, what she was like. Not even to give herself an idea. What she had done would be enough, it would be the whole thing.

What she was doing would be what she had heard about and read about. It was what Anna Karenina had done and what Madame Bovary had wanted to do. It was what a teacher at Brian's school had done, with the school secretary. He had run off with her. That was what it was called. Running off with. Taking off with. It was spoken of disparagingly, humorously, enviously. It was adultery taken one step further. The people who did it had almost certainly been having an affair already, committing adultery for quite some time before they became desperate or courageous enough to take this step. Once in a long while a couple might claim their love was unconsummated and technically pure, but these people would be thought of – if anybody believed them – as being not only very serious and high-minded but almost devastatingly foolhardy, almost in a class with those who took a chance and gave up everything to go and work in some poor and dangerous country.

The others, the adulterers, were seen as irresponsible, immature, selfish, or even cruel. Also lucky. They were lucky because the sex they had been having in parked cars or the long grass or in each other's sullied marriage beds or most likely in motels like this one must surely have been splendid. Otherwise they would never have got such a yearning for each other's company at all costs or such a faith that their shared future would be altogether better and different in kind from what they had in the past.

Different in kind. That was what Pauline must believe now – that there was this major difference in lives or in marriages or unions between people. That some of them had a necessity, a fatefulness, about them that others did not have. Of course she would have said the same thing a year ago. People did say that, they seemed to believe that, and to believe that their own cases were all of the first, the special kind, even when anybody could see that they were not and that these people did not know what they were talking about. Pauline would not have known what she was talking about.

It was too warm in the room. Jeffrey's body was too warm. Conviction and contentiousness seemed to radiate from it, even in sleep. His torso was thicker than Brian's; he was pudgier around the waist. More flesh on the bones, yet not so slack to the touch. Not so good-looking in general – she was sure most people would say that. And not so fastidious. Brian in bed smelled of nothing. Jeffrey's skin, every time she'd been with him, had had a baked-in, slightly oily or nutty smell. He didn't wash last night – but then, neither did she. There wasn't time. Did he even have a toothbrush with him? She didn't. But she had not known she was staying.

When she met Jeffrey here it was still in the back of her mind that she had to concoct some colossal lie to serve her when she got home. And she – they

– had to hurry. When Jeffrey said to her that he had decided that they must stay together, that she would come with him to Washington State, that they would have to drop the play because things would be too difficult for them in Victoria, she had looked at him just in the blank way you'd look at somebody the moment that an earthquake started. She was ready to tell him all the reasons why this was not possible, she still thought she was going to tell him that, but her life was coming adrift in that moment. To go back would be like tying a sack over her head.

All she said was "Are you sure?"

He said, "Sure." He said sincerely, "I'll never leave you."

That did not seem the sort of thing that he would say. Then she realized he was quoting – maybe ironically – from the play. It was what Orphée says to Eurydice within a few moments of their first meeting in the station buffet.

So her life was falling forwards; she was becoming one of those people who ran away. A woman who shockingly and incomprehensibly gave everything up. For love, observers would say wryly. Meaning, for sex. None of this would happen if it wasn't for sex.

And yet what's the great difference there? It's not such a variable procedure, in spite of what you're told. Skins, motions, contact, results. Pauline isn't a woman from whom it's difficult to get results. Brian got them. Probably anybody would, who wasn't wildly inept or morally disgusting.

But nothing's the same, really. With Brian – especially with Brian, to whom she has dedicated a selfish sort of goodwill, with whom she's lived in married complicity – there can never be this stripping away, the inevitable flight, the feelings she doesn't have to strive for but only to give in to like breathing or dying. That she believes can only come when the skin is on Jeffrey, and the weight that bears down on her has Jeffrey's heart in it, also his habits, thoughts, peculiarities, his ambition and loneliness (that for all she knows may have mostly to do with his youth).

For all she knows. There's a lot she doesn't know. She hardly knows anything about what he likes to eat or what music he likes to listen to or what role his mother plays in his life (no doubt a mysterious but important one, like the role of Brian's parents). One thing she's pretty sure of – whatever preferences or prohibitions he has will be definite.

She slides out from under Jeffrey's hand and from under the top sheet which has a harsh smell of bleach, she slips down to the floor where the bedspread is lying and wraps herself quickly in that rag of greenish-yellow chenille. She doesn't want him to open his eyes and see her from behind and note the droop of her buttocks. He's seen her naked efore, but generally in a more forgiving moment.

She rinses her mouth and washes herself,using the bar of soap that is about the size of two thin squares of chocolate and firm as stone. She's hard-used between the legs, swollen and stinking. Urinating takes an effort, and it seems she's constipated. Last night when they went out and got hamburgers she found she could not eat. Presumably she'll learn to do all these things again, they'll resume their natural importance in her life. At the moment it's as if she can't quite spare the attention.

She has some money in her purse. She has to go out and buy a toothbrush, toothpaste, deodorant, shampoo. Also vaginal jelly. Last night they used condoms the first two times but nothing the third time.

She didn't bring her watch and Jeffrey doesn't wear one. There's no clock in the room, of course. She thinks it's early – there's still an early look to the light in spite of the heat. The stores probably won't be open, but there'll be someplace where she can get coffee.

Jeffrey has turned onto his other side. She must have wakened him, just for a moment.

They'll have a bedroom. A kitchen, an address. He'll go to work. She'll go to the Laundromat Maybe she'll go to work too. Selling things, waiting on tables, tutoring students. She knows French and Latin – do they teach French and Latin in American high schools? Can you get a job if you're not an American? Jeffrey isn't.

She leaves him the key. She'll have to wake him to get back in. There's nothing to write a note with, or on.

It is early. The motel is on the highway at the north end of town, beside the bridge. There's no traffic yet. She scuffs along under the cottonwood trees for quite a while before a vehicle of any kind rumbles over the bridge – though the traffic on it shook their bed regularly late into the night.

Something is coming now. A truck. But not just a truck – there's a large bleak fact coming at her. And it has not arrived out of nowhere – it's been waiting cruelly nudging at her ever since she woke up, or even all night.

Caitlin and Mara.

Last night on the phone, after speaking in such a flat and controlled and almost agreeable voice – as if he prided himself on not being shocked, not objecting or pleading – Brian cracked open. He said with contempt and fury and no concern for whoever might hear him, "Well then – what about the kids?"

The receiver began to shake against Pauline's ear.

She said, "We'll talk –" but he did not seem to hear her.

"The children," he said, in this same shivering and vindictive voice. Changing the word "kids" to "children" was like slamming a board down on her – a heavy formal, righteous threat.

"The children stay," Brian said. "Pauline. Did you hear me?"

"No," said Pauline. "Yes I heard you but –"

"All right. You heard me. Remember. The children stay."

It was all he could do. To make her see what she was doing what she was ending, and to punish her if she did so. Nobody would blame him. There might be finagling, there might be bargaining, there would certainly be humbling of herself, but there it was like a round cold stone in her gullet, like a cannonball. And it would remain here unless she changed her mind entirely. The children stay.

Their car – hers and Brian's – was still sitting in the motel parking lot. Brian would have to ask his father or his mother to drive him up here today to get it. She had the keys in her purse. There were spare keys – he would surely bring them. She unlocked the car door and threw her keys on the seat and locked the door on the inside and shut it.

Now she couldn't go back. She couldn't get into the car and drive back and say that she'd been insane. If she did that he would forgive her, but he'd never get over it and neither would she. They'd go on, though, as people did.

She walked out of the parking lot, she walked along the sidewalk, into town.

The weight of Mara on her hip, yesterday. The sight of Caitlin's footprints on the floor.

Paw. Paw.

She doesn't need the keys to get back to them, she doesn't need the car. She could beg a ride on the highway. Give in, give in, get back to them any way at all, how can she not do that?

A sack over her head.

A fluid choice, the choice of fantasy, is poured out on the ground and instantly hardens; it has taken its undeniable shape.

This is acute pain. It will become chronic. Chronic means that it will be permanent but perhaps not constant. It may also mean that you won't die of it. You won't get free of it, but you won't die of it. You won't feel it every minute, but you won't spend many days without it. And you'll learn some tricks to dull it or banish it, trying not to end up destroying what you incurred this pain to get. It isn't his fault. He's still an innocent or a savage, who doesn't know there's a pain so durable in the world. Say to yourself, You lose them anyway. They grow up. For a mother there's always waiting this private slightly ridiculous desolation. They'll forget this time, in one way or another they'll disown you. Or hang around till you don't know what to do about them, the way Brian has.

And still, what pain. To carry along and get used to until it's only the past she's grieving for and not any possible present.

Her children have grown up. They don't hate her. For going away or staying away. They don't forgive her, either. Perhaps they wouldn't have forgiven her anyway, but it would have been for something different.

Caitlin remembers a little about the summer at the lodge, Mara nothing. One day Caitlin mentions it to Pauline, calling it "that place Grandma and Grandpa stayed at."

"The place we were at when you went away," she says. "Only we didn't know till later you went away with Orphée."

Pauline says, "It wasn't Orphée."

"It wasn't Orphée? Dad used to say it was. He'd say, And then your mother ran away with Orphée."

"Then he was joking," says Pauline.

"I always thought it was Orphée. It was somebody else then."

"It was somebody else connected with the play. That I lived with for a while."

"Not Orphée."

"No. Never him."

UNDER THE ROSE

Julia O'Faolain

Julia O'Faolain (b.1932) is the daughter of Sean O'Faolain. Married to
the historian Lauro Martines, she is the author of several collections of
stories and novels, including *The Irish Signorina*, *No Country for Young
Men* and a memoir, *Trespassers*. She lives in London.

D an said – to be sure, there was only his word for this; but who would
invent such a thing? – that, in their teens, his brother and he had ravaged
their sister on the parsonage kitchen table. Their father was a parson,
and when the rape took place the household was at Evensong. Dan described a
fume of dust motes sliced by thin, surgical light, a gleam of pinkish copper pans
and, under his nose, the pith of the deal table. Outside the door, his sister's dog
had howled. The truth was, said Dan, that she herself did not resist much. She'd
been fifteen, and the unapologetic Dan was now twenty. It had, he claimed, been
a liberation for all three.

"The Bible's full of it," he'd wind up. "Incest!"

The story was for married women only. Dan specialized in unhappy wives.
Mal mariées. He sang a song about them in French, easing open the tight, alien
vowels and letting the slur of his voice widen their scope: *ma-uhl mah-urrr-
ee-yeh*. It was a Limerick voice, and those who resisted its charm said that the
further Dan Lydon got from Limerick the broader his accent grew. The resistant
tended to be men; women always liked Dan. To hear him lilt, "My lo-hove is
lo-ike a r-red, r-red r-ro-rose" was, as respected matrons would tell you, like listening to grand opera. His vibrancy fired them. It kindled and dazzled like those
beams you saw in paintings of the Holy Ghost, and his breath had a pulse to it,
even when all he was ordering was the same again, please, and a packet of fags.
Words, moving in his mouth like oysters, put town dwellers in mind of rural
forebears and of the damp, reticent lure of the countryside.

The parsonage of Dan's youth lay in the grasslands watered by the River
Shannon, flat country shadowed by those cloud formations known as mackerel
backs and mare's tails – arrangements as chameleon as himself. He was a bright-
haired, smiling boy, who first reached Dublin in 1943, a time when the Japanese
minister rode with a local hunt and the German one did not always get the cold
shoulder. Dan's allegiance was to the noble Soviets, but he was alive, too, to sexual raciness blown in like pollen from the war zones. Change fizzed; neutrality
opened fields of choice, and values had rarely been shiftier.

"So where is your sister now?"

Mrs. Connors did and did not believe his story.

"Tea?" she offered. Tea was his hour. Husbands tended to be at work. Mr. Connors was a civil servant.

Dan took his tea. "She had to be married off," he admitted. "She has a sweet little boy."

Mrs. Connors dared: "Yours?"

"Or my brother's? I'd like there to be one I *knew* was mine." His eyes held hers. Putting down the cup, he turned her wrist over, slid back the sleeve, and traced the artery with a finger.

"The blue-veined child!" he murmured. "Don't you think children conceived in passion are special? Fruits of willfulness! Surely they become poets? Or Napoleons?"

Phyllis Connors was sure Napoleon's family had been legitimate. On her honeymoon, before the war, she had visited Corsica. "Their mother was addressed as Madame Mère."

"Was that the model Connors held up to you? 'Madame Mère'!" Dan teased. "On your honeymoon! What a clever cuss!"

The teasing could seem brotherly; but Dan's brotherliness was alarming. Indeed, Phyllis's offer to be a sister to him had touched off the nonsense – what else could it be? – about incest.

Nonsense or not, it unsettled her.

He was predatory. A known idler. Wolfed her sandwiches as though he had had no lunch – and maybe he hadn't? The parson had washed his hands of him. But Dan had a new spiritual father in a poet who had stopped the university from kicking him out. Dan's enthusiasm for poetry – he was, he said, writing it full-time – so captivated the poet that he had persuaded the provost to waive mundane requirements and insure that the boy's scholarship (paid by a fund for sons of needy parsons) be renewed. Surely, urged Dan's advocate, the alma mater of Burke and Sam Beckett could be flexible with men of stellar promise? Talents did not mature at the rate of seed potatoes, and Ireland's best-known export was fractious writers. Let's try to keep this one at home.

The poet, who ran a magazine, needed someone to do the legwork and when need be plug gaps with pieces entitled "Where the Red Flag Flies," "A Future for Cottage Industries?," or "Folk Memories of West Clare." Dan could knock these off at speed, and the connection gave him prestige with the fellow-undergraduates, at whose verse readings he starred.

It was at one of these that Phyllis Connors had first heard him recite. The verse had not been his. That, he explained, must stay sub rosa. Did she know that Jack Yeats, the painter, kept a rose on his easel when painting his mad, marvellous pictures of horse dealers, fiddlers, and fairs? Art in progress was safest under the rose.

After tea, Dan talked of procreation and of how men in tropical lands like Ecuador thought sex incomplete without it. That was the earth's wisdom speaking through them. R.C.s – look at their Madonnas – had the same instincts. Dan, the parson's son, defended the Pope, whose church had inherited the carnal wit of the ancients. "The sower went out to sow his seed. . . ."

Talk like this unnerved Phyllis, who was childless and unsure what was being offered. What farmer, asked Dan, would scatter with an empty hand? "Your women are your fields," he quoted, from the Koran. "Go freely into your fields!" Then he extolled the beauty of pregnant women – bloomy as June meadows – and recited a poem about changelings: "Come away, O human child. . . ."

Phyllis, thinking him a child himself, might have surrendered to the giddiest request. But Dan made none. Instead, he went home to his lodgings, leaving her to gorge her needs on the last of the sandwiches.

He came back, though, for her house was near the poet's, and after drudging with his galleys would drop by to cup hands, sculpt air, praise her hips, and eat healthy amounts of whatever was for tea. Refreshed, he liked to intone poems about forest gods and fairy folk. "And if any gaze on our rushing band," he chanted, "We come between him and the deed of his hand, We come between him and the hope of his heart."

Why did he not come after what he implied was the hope of his own heart? Wondering made her think of him more than she might otherwise have done, and so did seeing him in the Singing Kettle, eating doughnuts with the poet's wife. Peering through trickles in a steamy window, she thought she saw the word "love" on his lips. Or was it "dove"? His motto, "Let the doves settle!" meant "Take things as they come."

Phyllis decided that some doves needed to be snared.

Soon she was pregnant, and when she went into the Hatch Street Nursing Home to give birth Dan brought her a reproduction of Piero della Francesca's Madonna del Parto, with the pale slash where the Virgin, easing her gown off her round belly, shows underlinen more intimate than skin. His finger on Phyllis's stomach sketched an identical white curve. He teased the nurses, relished the fertility all about, and was happy as a mouse in cheese.

It turned out that the poet's wife was here, too, and for the same reason. Her room was on another floor, so Dan yoyoed up and down. Sometimes he brought gifts that had to be divided: fruit, for instance, from the poet, who still used Dan to run errands. Or books, review copies from the magazine. When a nurse let drop that the poet's wife had the same Piero Madonna on her side table, Phyllis wrapped hers in a nappy and put it in the trash. If there had been a fireplace, she would have burned it, as she had been trained to do with unwanted religious objects.

Her baby received her husband's first name, and the poet's baby the poet's. Dan – though neither couple asked him to be godfather – presented both infants with christening mugs. One had been his and the other his brother's, and both were made of antique Dublin silver. Early Georgian. The official godfathers, fearing odious comparisons, returned their purchases to Weirs Jewellers and bought cutlery. Phyllis wondered if Dan's brother knew what had happened to his mug. Though the war was now over, he was still overseas with the British Army.

"He'll not be back," Dan assured her, and revealed that the parsonage had been a dour and penurious place. Its congregation had dwindled since the R.C. natives took over the country in '21, and attendance some Sundays amounted to less than six. Pride had throttled Dan's widowed father, who did menial work behind the scenes and made his children collect firewood, polish silver, and dine on boiled offal.

"He wouldn't want the mug," said Dan. "Too many bad memories!" The brothers had left as soon as they could, and getting their sister pregnant had been a parting gift. "If we hadn't, she'd still be Daddy's slave."

Some years went by, and Dan was a student still, of a type known to Dubliners as "chronic," one of a ragged brigade who, recoiling from a jobless job market, harked back to the tribally condoned wandering scholars of long ago. This connection was often all that raised the chronics above tramps or paupers, and the lifeline was frail.

But out of the blue, opportunity came Dan's way. The poet, who had to go into the hospital, asked him to bring out an issue of the magazine bearing on its masthead the words "Guest Editor: Daniel Lydon." Here was challenge! Dan toyed excitedly with the notion of publishing his secret poetry, which he yearned, yet feared, to display. These urges warred in him until, having read and reread it, he saw that it had gone dead, leaking virtue like batteries kept too long in a drawer. Stewing, he fell behind with the magazine and had to ghostwrite several pieces to pad the thing out. As part of this process, he decided to publish photographs of A Changing Ireland. Hydrofoils, reapers-and-binders, ballpoint pens, and other such innovations were shown next to Neolithic barrows. The Knights of Columbanus in full fig appeared cheek by jowl with an electric band. Portraits of "the last Gaelic storyteller" and some "future Irishmen" rounded out the theme. The future Irishmen, three small boys with their heads arranged like the leaves of a shamrock, were recognizably Dan's nephew and the recipients of his christening mugs – and what leaped to the eye was their resemblance to himself. The caption "Changelings" drove the scandal home.

The poet, convalescing in his hospital bed after an operation for a gentleman's complaint, told his wife, in an insufficiently discreet hiss, that he had paid Dan to do his legwork, not to get his leg over. Reference was made to "cuckoo's eggs," and it was not long before echoes of this reached the ear of Mr. Connors, the proverbial quiet man whom it is dangerous to arouse. Connors, who had done a bit of hacking in his bachelor days, had a riding crop. Taking this to the student lodgings where Dan lived, he used it to tap smartly on the door.

When Dan opened this, Connors raised the crop. Dan yelled, and his neighbor, a fellow-Communist, who was on the varsity boxing team, came hurtling to the rescue. Assuming the row to be political and Connors a member of the Blue Shirts only reinforced his zeal. Shoving ensued; Connors fell downstairs; gawkers gathered, and the upshot was that an ambulance was called and the opinion bandied that the victim had broken his back. Some genuine Blue Shirts were meanwhile rustled up, men whose finest hours had been fighting for Franco, singing hymns to Cristo Re, and beating the sin out of Reds; they were spoiling for a scrap, and if it had not been for Dan's friend spiriting him out the back they might have sent him to join Mr. Connors – who, as it would turn out, had not been injured, after all, and was fit as a fiddle in a couple of weeks.

Dan, however, had by then prudently boarded the ferry to Holyhead, taking with him, like a subsidiary passport, the issue of the magazine bearing his name as "guest editor." It got him work with the BBC, which, in those days of live programming, needed men with a gift of the gab and was friendly to Celts. Louis MacNeice and Dylan Thomas were role models, liquid stimulants in high favor, and Dan was recruited straight off the boat.

So ran reports reaching Dublin. Pithy myths, these acquired an envious tinge as Dan's success was magnified, along with the sums he was earning for doing what he had formerly done for free: talking, singing, and gargling verse. Others were soon dreaming of jobs in a London whose airwaves vapored with gold. Hadn't Dubliners a known talent for transubstantiating eloquence into currency? And couldn't every one of us talk at least as well as Dan Lydon?

Declan Connors doubted it. Despite himself, he'd caught snatches of what nobody had the indecency to quote quite to his face: a saga featuring Dan as dispenser of sweet anointings to women. These, Connors understood, had needed preparation. Persuasion had been required, and Dan's boldness at it had grown legendary, as an athlete's prowess does with fans. The gossips relished Dan's gall, the airy way he could woo without promise or commitment – arguing, say, that in a war's wake more kids were needed and that his companion's quickened pulse was nature urging her to increase the supply. Nature! What a let out! Any man who could sell a line like that in Holy Ireland could sell heaters in hell.

"He's a one-man social service!" A wag raised his pint. "Offers himself up. 'Partake ye of my body.' He'd rather be consumed than consume!"

The wag drained his glass. His preferences ran the other way. So did those of the man next to him, whose tongue wrestled pinkly with ham frilling from a sandwich. All around, males guzzled: women, in this prosperous pub, were outnumbered ten to one. Connors, sipping his whiskey, thought, No wonder Lydon made out – we left him an open field!

He could no longer regret this, for after ten barren years of marriage, Phyllis had had three children in quick succession. It was as if something in her had been unlocked. He supposed there were jokes about this, too, but he didn't care. His master passion had turned out to be paternal, and Declan Junior was the apple of his eye. The younger two were girls and, as Phyllis spoiled them, he had to make things up to the boy.

For a while after the scandal, the couple had felt shy with each other, but they had no thoughts of divorce. You couldn't in Ireland, and it wasn't what they wanted. They were fond of each other – and, besides, there was Declan, of whom it was said behind Mr. Connors' shrugging back that he used his blood father's charm to wind his nominal father around his little finger. A seducer ab ovo.

Small-mindedness! Envy! Anyway, time heals, and when the boy was picked, surprisingly early, for his elementary-school soccer team, and later won ribbons for show jumping, Connors – a sportsman – knew him for his spiritual son. Even if the kid was a Lydon, he was a better one than Dan – whose brother, Connors recalled, had been decorated for gallantry in the war. Skimming the entry on Mendel in the encyclopedia, he learned that hereditary character was transmitted chancily and, remembering the poltroonish Dan draped over armchairs and cowering during their fight, decided that Declan Junior had nothing of his natural father's but his looks.

Connors still took an interest, though, in the news trickling back from London, where Dan's free lance was said to be cutting a swath: he had apparently acquired a new patron, a literary pundit who, though married, was partial to a handsome young man. And now Connors noted an odd thing: admiration was ousting envy and Dan's stature in the saga growing. Needless to say, his news was slow to reach Connors, since nobody who remembered their connection would wish to reopen old wounds. It came in scraps and, by the time he got them, these were as spare and smooth as broken glass licked by recurring tides.

As Connors heard it, then: Dan's new benefactor's marriage, though possibly unconsummated, was harmonious, for his wife had money. The couple made fashionable hosts, and Dan was soon glowing in their orbit – singing ballads, referring to his secret œuvre, and enlivening their soirees with tales of Irish mores. The pundit's wife, the story went, was a handsome, angry woman who had hated her father, but having agreed to inherit his money, would make no further concession to men, and slept only with those she could pity or control. As her husband didn't fit the bill, she had lovers. Dan was soon servicing both her and the husband who, being jealous and smitten, was in the dark about this.

Here the story fractures. In one version, she "gets preggers," which so shatters the husband that his violence leads to a miscarriage and Dan's subsequent flight to Paris. But there was an implausible symmetry to this, as though running dye from the Dublin episode had colored it; a likelier account has no pregnancy and the jealousy provoked by someone's indiscretion. Deliberate? Careless? Either way, Connors learned, Dan left England, the marriage collapsed, and the husband, previously a rather nerveless knight of the pen – who had, in his own words, "failed to grapple with his subjectivity" – finally did so in a book that raised him several rungs on the literary ladder. This was before the Wolfenden Report; homosexuality was a still painful subject, and his grappling was judged brave. Dan, as midwife to his lover's best writing, could be said to have done him a good turn.

Meanwhile, Declan Junior was in his teens, and his mother – noting that if you cut the heart from his name you'd be left with "Dan" – feared leaving him alone with his sisters. An idle fear: girls bored him, and so did poetry, to her relief. Not that Dan himself had yet published a line, but the appellation *Poète irlandais* clung to him, who had now – wonder of wonders! – married and settled in Paris. The word was that an old Spanish Civil War hero, whose memoirs Dan had been ghost-writing while sleeping with his daughter, had, on catching the pair in flagrante, sat on Dan's chest and said, "Marry her!" A bad day's work for the girl, tittered those Dubliners who still remembered him.

One or two had looked him up on trips abroad and reported that he was doing something nowadays for films. Script-doctoring, was it? And his wife had published poems before their marriage, but none since. Maybe she didn't want to shame him? Closer friends said the marriage was a good one, and that no forcing had been needed.

Why should it have been? Marisol was bright, young, had a river of dark hair, and gave Dan the tribal connection he had always coveted. His ravenous charm sprang from his childhood in that bleak parsonage. Marginal. Clanless. Left behind by the tide. Catholics – whose clan had dispersed his – did not appeal, but the Left did. The Spanish Civil War had been Dan's boyhood war, and the more romantic for having been lost. Dan loved a negative. What, he would argue, was there to say about success? The surprise was that the Anglo-Saxon ruling classes could still talk and didn't just beat their smug chests like chimps. If it weren't for their homosexuals, he claimed, they'd have no art. Art was for those whose reality needed suborning. It burrowed and queried; it . . . et cetera! Dan could still chatter like a covey of starlings, and the Limerick accent went down a treat in French, being, as people would soon start to say, *médiatique*.

Along came the sixties. The Youth Cult blossomed just as Dan – in his forties – began losing his hair. Juvenescence glowed in him, though, as in a golden autumn tree. His freshness was a triumph of essence over accident, and he became an acknowledged Youth Expert when he made a film about the graffiti of May '68. Graffiti, being, like pub talk, insolent, jubilant, and an end in itself, was right up his street, and he was soon in Hollywood working on a second film. It came to nothing, which confirmed the purity of his response to the ephemeral, and he continued to fly between Paris and California, dressed in light, summery suits and engaged in optimistic projects, some of which did throw his name onto a screen for a fleeting shimmer.

One evening in Paris, he came face to face with Connors and Phyllis in a *brasserie*. They were at different tables, and could have ignored each other. As their last encounter had led to Connors' departure from the scene in an ambulance and Dan's from Ireland, this might have seemed wise. Sportingly, however, Dan came over. Shiny and aglow, his forehead – higher than it used to be – damp with sweat. It was a hot night. Hand outstretched. A little self-deprecating. He had heard their news, as they had his, and congratulated Connors on a recent promotion. Family all well? Grand! Great! He was with *his*. Nodding at a tableful of Spaniards. Laughing at their noise. Then, ruefully, as two of his wrestling children knocked over a sauceboat, he said he'd better go and cope.

Soon the waiter brought two glasses of very old cognac with Dan's compliments. They accepted, toasted him, and, watching his gypsy table, remembered hearing that "the poor bastard" had saddled himself with a family of idlers whom he had to work overtime to support. Dan's father-in-law, it seemed, had emphysema. Marisol's brother yearned to be a pop star, and she herself kept producing children. How many had they? Phyllis counted three, who were dark like their mother and did not look at all like Declan Junior. As she and Connors left, they thanked Dan for the cognac.

Afterward, they discussed the encounter half sharply, half shyly. Looking out for each other's dignity. Not mentioning Declan Junior, whom Phyllis, her husband guessed, thought of as having two fathers. Blame could thus be moved about or dissolved in the whirligig of her brain. And she could play peekaboo, too, with romance. He suspected this because – the evening had brought it home to him – he, too, had an imaginative connection with Dan and had not liked what he saw in the *brasserie*. It had depressed him. Spilled gravy and domesticity cut Dan down to size, and a life-size Dan was a reproach, while the saga figure hadn't been at all. The connection to *that* Dan had, somehow, aureoled Connors' life and added a dimension to his fantasies. For a while, it had even made Phyllis more attractive to him. An adulterous wife was exciting – and he had often wondered whether it could have been that extra zest that had led to his begetting the two girls.

Water under the bridge, to be sure! The Dan Saga had not stimulated his sex life for years. What it did do was make him feel more benign than might have been expected of the sober civil servant he was. Broader, and even passionate. It was as if he himself had had a part in Dan's adventurings. That, of course, made no sense, or rather, the sense it made was private and – why not? – poetic. Dan, the unproductive poet, had, like Oscar Wilde, put his genius into his life: a fevering contagion. Or so Connors must have been feeling, unknown to himself. How else to explain the gloom provoked by the sighting in the *brasserie*? Phyllis didn't seem to feel it. But then, women saw what they wanted to see. Connors guessed that for her Dan Lydon was still a figure of romance.

It was around this time that Declan Junior began to disappoint his parents. A gifted athlete who handled his academic work with ease, he had come through university with flying colors and Connors, convinced that the boy could star in any firmament, had looked forward to seeing him join the diplomatic corps or go in for politics or journalism. Something with scope. Instead, what should their affable, graceful Declan do on graduating but take a humdrum job in a bank and announce that he was getting married! Yes. Now. There was no talking him out of it, and it was not a shotgun wedding, either. Indeed, Declan Junior was rather stuffy when asked about this. And when you met the girl you saw that it was unlikely. She was limp-haired, steady, and – well, dull. Here was their cuckoo, thought Connors, turning out too tame rather than too wild. If there was a Lydon gene at work, the resemblance was more to the family man he and Phyllis had glimpsed in Paris than to the satyr whose heredity they had feared. Had they worked too hard at stamping out the demon spark?

That, they learned, was still riskily smoldering in the vicinity of Lydon himself. Connors heard the latest bulletin by a fluke, for he had grown reclusive since Declan's wedding and more so after the christening, which came an impeccable ten months later. He was, to tell the truth, a touch down in the mouth. Brooding. Had Phyllis, he wondered, been cold with the boy when he was small? Could guilt have made her be? And might there be something, after all, to Freudian guff? Till now Connors had dismissed it, but there was Declan, married to a surrogate Mum. *Born* to be a Mum: she was pregnant again, and had tied her limp hair in a bun. Cartoonish, in orthopedic shoes, she wore a frilly apron and loved to make pastry. Declan was putting on weight! Ah, well.

The latest about Lydon was that, hungry for money, he had agreed to be a beard.

A what?

"You may well ask," said Connors' source, a man called Breen, who swore him to secrecy. Breen was on leave from the Irish Embassy in Rome, which, said he, was in a turmoil over the thing.

"But what *is* a . . . ?"

Breen looked over his shoulder; they'd met in the St. Stephen's Green Club. "I can't tell you here."

So Connors brought him home and settled him down with a whiskey, to tell his story before Phyllis came in. She was babysitting Declan III, known as Dicky-bird, who was at the crawling stage and tiring. His mother needed a rest.

Breen's hot spurts of shock revived Connors' spirits. The Dan Saga thrilled him in an odd, outraged way, much as the whiskey was warming and biting at his mouth. Recklessness, he thought welcomingly, a touch of folly to temper the norms and rules.

Lydon, said Breen, had been acting as cover for one of the candidates in the upcoming United States election, a married man who was having it off with an actress. Needing to seem above reproach – "You know American voters!" – the candidate had engaged Dan to pretend to be the woman's lover.

"He was what's called a beard – travelled with her, took her to parties, et cetera, then left the scene when the candidate had a free moment." The beard's function was to draw suspicion. For the real lover to seem innocent, the beard must suggest the rut. And Dan did. Though he was now fifty, an aura of youth and potency clung to him.

"It's all in the mind!" said Breen, shrugging.

Outside the window, someone had turned on a revolving lawn sprinkler and the family Labrador, a puppy called Muff, was leaping at its spray. That meant that Phyllis and the child were back from their walk.

Breen said that what Lydon's wife thought of his job nobody knew. The money must have been good. Or maybe she hadn't known – until she was kidnapped. Kidnapped? Yes. Hadn't he said? By mistake. At the Venice Film Festival. By Sardinian kidnappers who got wind of the story but took the wrong woman. "The candidate's rich, and they'd hoped for a big ransom." This had happened just three weeks ago.

Connors was stunned. A changeling, he thought, and felt a breath of shame. Play had turned dangerous, and he had been relishing Lydon's tomfoolery.

"The Yanks came to us," Breen told him, "asking us to handle the thing with discretion – after they'd got the actress back to the U.S. You could say we're *their* beard!" He grew grave, for there was a danger that the kidnappers could panic. "Sardinians are primeval and inbred, you know! Islanders! What? No, no, not like us. More basic! Crude! Their life way was easy to commercialize because it *was* so crude. With them, vengeance required blood as real as you'd put in blood sausage. Quantifiable! Material! We, by contrast, are casuists and symbol jugglers. Closers of eyes..."

A flick of embarrassment in Breen's own eye signalled a sudden recognition that this could seem to refer to the story – had he only now remembered it? – of Connors and Dan: a case of eyes closed to lost honor. With professional bland-ness, he tried to cover his gaffe with an account of the Embassy's dilemma: on the one hand, the papers must not learn of the thing. On the other, the kidnappers must be made to see that there was no money to be had. Breen castigated Lydon, whose sins were catching up with him. His poor wife, though...

Connors tried to remember her face in the Paris *brasserie*, but could not.

"That louser Lydon!" Breen, intending perhaps to express solidarity with Connors, threw out words like "parasite" and "sociopath." When you thought about it, a man like that was worse than the kidnappers. "He breaks down the barriers between us and them. He lets in anarchy. He sells the pass."

Connors tried to demur, but Breen, warming to his theme, blamed society's tolerance, for which it – "we" – must now pay. "Bastards like that trade on it." Someone, he implied, should have dealt with Lydon long ago.

Connors ignored the reproach. Off on a different tack, his mind was cutting through a tangle of shy, willed confusions. He recognized that what he felt for Dan was love or something closer. Far from being his enemy, Dan was a part of himself. Luminous alter ego? Partner in father-and grandfatherhood? Closing his ears to his companion's sermon, he looked out to where Phyllis and Dicky-bird had caught up with the golden Lab, on whose back the child kept trying to climb. Shaken off, he tried again: a rubbery *putto*, bouncing back like foam. The wild Lydon heritage had skipped a generation and here it was again.

Excited by the whirling spray, the puppy scampered through its prism while the infant held on to its tail. The child's hair was as blond as the dog's, and in the rainbow embrace the two gleamed like fountain statuary. They were Arcadian, anarchic, playful – and propelled by pooled energy.

"It's a terrible thing to happen," Connors conceded. "But I wouldn't blame Lydon. Blame the American candidate or the Italian state. Hypocrisy. Puritanism. Pretense. Lydon's innocent of all that. Blaming him is like, I don't know, blaming that dog out there." And he waved his glass of whiskey at the golden scene outside.

THE WINE BREATH

John McGahern

John McGahern (1934–2006) was born in Dublin and brought up in the west of Ireland. A graduate of University College, Dublin, he worked as a Primary School teacher before writing six highly acclaimed novels and four collections of short stories. He was the recipient of numerous awards and honours, including the Irish Times Award for *Amongst Women*, which was also shortlisted for the Man Booker Prize and made into a four-part television series. He once said, "When you're in danger of losing a thing it becomes precious and when it's around us, it's in tedious abundance and we take it for granted as if we're going to live forever, which we're not." He died in Dublin, in 2006. His *Collected Stories* was reissued earlier this year.

I f I were to die, I'd miss most the mornings and the evenings, he thought as he walked the narrow dirt-track by the lake in the late evening, and then wondered if his mind was failing, for how could anybody think anything so stupid: being a man he had no choice, he was doomed to die; and being dead he'd miss nothing, being nothing. It went against everything in his life as a priest.

The solid world, though, was everywhere around him. There was the lake, the road, the evening, and he was going to call on Gillespie. Gillespie was sawing. Gillespie was always sawing. The roaring rise-and-fall of the two-stroke stayed like a rent in the evening. When he got to the black gate there was Gillespie, his overalled bulk framed in the short avenue of alders, and he was sawing not alders but beech, four or five tractor-loads dumped in the front of the house. The priest put a hand to the black gate, bolted to the first of the alders, and was at once arrested by showery sunlight falling down the avenue. It lit up one boot holding the length of beech in place, it lit the arms moving the blade slowly up and down as it tore through the beech, white chips milling out on the chain.

Suddenly, as he was about to rattle the gate loudly to see if this would penetrate the sawing, he felt himself (bathed as in a dream) in an incredible sweetness of light. It was the evening light on snow. The gate on which he had his hand vanished, the alders, Gillespie's formidable bulk, the roaring of the saw. He was in another day, the lost day of Michael Bruen's funeral nearly thirty years before. All was silent and still there. Slow feet crunched on the snow. Ahead, at the foot of the hill, the coffin rode slowly forward on shoulders, its brown varnish and metal trappings dull in the glittering snow, riding just below the long waste of snow eight or ten feet deep over the whole countryside. The long dark line of mourners following the coffin stretched away towards Oakport Wood in the pathway cut through the snow. High on Killeelan Hill the graveyard evergreens rose out of the snow. The graveyard wall was covered, the narrow path cut up the side of the hill stopping at the little gate deep in the snow. The coffin climbed with painful slowness, as if it might never reach the gate, often pausing for the bearers to be changed; and someone started to pray, the prayer travelling down the whole mile-long line of the mourners as they shuffled behind the coffin in the narrow tunnel cut in the snow.

It was the day in February 1947 that they buried Michael Bruen. Never before or since had he experienced the Mystery in such awesomeness. Now, as he stood at the gate, there was no awe or terror, only the coffin moving slowly towards the dark trees on the hill, the long line of the mourners, and everywhere the blinding white light, among the half-buried thorn bushes and beyond Killeelan, on the covered waste of Gloria Bog, on the sides of Slieve an Iarainn.

He did not know how long he had stood in that lost day, in that white light, probably for no more than a moment. He could not have stood the intensity for any longer. When he woke out of it the grey light of the alders had reasserted itself. His hand was still on the bar of the gate. Gillespie was still sawing, bent over the saw-horse, his boot on the length of beechwood, completely enclosed in the roaring rise-and-fall of the saw. The priest felt as vulnerable as if he had suddenly woken out of sleep, shaken and somewhat ashamed to have been caught asleep in the actual day and life, without any protection of walls.

He was about to rattle the gate again, feeling a washed-out parody of a child or old man on what was after all nothing more than a poor errand: to tell the Gillespies that a bed had at long last been made available in the Regional Hospital for the operation on Mrs Gillespie's piles, when his eyes were caught again by the quality of the light. It was one of those late October days, small white clouds drifting about the sun, and the watery light was shining down the alder rows to fall on the white chips of the beechwood strewn all about Gillespie, some inches deep. It was the same white light as the light on snow. As he watched, the light went out on the beech chips, and it was the grey day again around Gillespie's sawing. It had been as simple as that. The suggestion of snow had been enough to plunge him into the lost day of Michael Bruen's funeral. Everything in that remembered day was so pure and perfect that he felt purged of all tiredness, was, for a moment, eager to begin life again.

Making sure that Gillespie hadn't noticed him at the gate, he turned back. The bed wouldn't be ready for another week. The news could wait a day or more. Before leaving he stole a last look at the dull white ground about the saw-horse. The most difficult things always seem to lie closest to us, to lie around our feet.

Ever since his mother's death he found himself stumbling into these dead days. Once, crushed mint in the garden had given him back a day he'd spent with her at the sea in such reality that he had been frightened, as if he'd suddenly fallen through time; it was as if the world of the dead was as available to him as the world of the living. It was also humiliating for him to realize that she must have been the mainspring of his days. Now that the mainspring was broken, the hands were weakly falling here and falling there. Today there had been the sudden light on the bits of white beech. He'd not have noticed it if he hadn't been alone, if Gillespie had not been so absorbed in his sawing. Before, there must have been some such simple trigger that he'd been too ashamed or bewildered to notice.

Stealthily and quickly he went down the dirt-track by the lake till he got to the main road. To the left was the church in a rookery of old trees, and behind it the house where he lived. Safe on the wide main road he let his mind go back to the beech chips. They rested there around Gillespie's large bulk, and paler still was the line of mourners following the coffin through the snow, a picture you could believe or disbelieve but not be in. In idle exasperation he began to count the trees in the hedge along the road as he walked: ash, green oak, whitehorn, ash; the last leaves a vivid yellow on the wild cherry, empty October fields in dull wet light behind the hedges. This, then, was the actual day, the only day that mattered, the day from which our salvation had to be won or lost: it stood solidly and impenetrably there, denying the weak life of the person, with nothing of the eternal other than it would dully endure, while the day set alight in his mind by the light of the white beech, though it had been nothing more than a funeral he had attended during a dramatic snowfall when a boy, seemed bathed in the eternal, seemed everything we had been taught and told of the world of God.

Dissatisfied, and feeling as tired again as he'd been on his way to Gillespie's, he did not go through the church gate with its circle and cross, nor did he call to the sexton locking up under the bellrope. In order to be certain of being left alone he went by the circular path at the side. A high laurel hedge hid the path from the graveyard and church. There he made coffee without turning on the light. Always when about to give birth or die cattle sought out a clean place in some corner of the field.

Michael Bruen had been a big kindly agreeable man, what was called a lovely man. His hair was a coarse grey. He wore loose-fitting tweeds with red cattleman's boots. When young he had been a policeman in Dublin. It was said he had either won or inherited money, and had come home to where he'd come from to buy the big Crossna farm, to marry and grow rich.

He had a large family. Men were employed on the farm. The yard and its big outhouses with the red roofs rang with work: cans, machinery, raillery, the sliding of hooves, someone whistling. Within the house, away from the yard, was the enormous cave of a kitchen, the long table down its centre, the fireplace at its end, the plates and pots and presses along the walls, sides of bacon wrapped in gauze hanging from hooks in the ceiling, the whole room full of the excitement and bustle of women.

Often as a boy the priest had gone to Michael Bruen's on some errand for his father. Once the beast was housed or the load emptied Michael would take him into the kitchen. The huge fire of wood blazed all the brighter because of the frost.

"Give this man something." Michael had led him. "Something solid that'll warm the life back into him."

"A cup of tea will do fine," he had protested in the custom.

"Nonsense. Don't pay him the slightest attention. Empty bags can't stand."

Eileen, the prettiest of Michael's daughters, laughed as she took down the pan. Her arms were white to the elbows with a fine dusting of flour.

"He'll remember this was a good place to come to when he has to start thinking about a wife." Michael's words gave licence to general hilarity.

It was hard to concentrate on Michael's questions about his father, so delicious was the smell of frying. The mug of steaming tea was put by his side. The butter melted on the fresh bread on the plate. There were sausages, liver, bacon, a slice of black-pudding and sweetest grisceens.

"Now set to," Michael laughed. "We don't want any empty bags leaving Bruen's."

Michael came with him to the gate when he left. "Tell your father it's ages since we had a drink in the Royal. And that if he doesn't search me out in the Royal the next Fair Day I'll have to go over and bate the lugs off him." As he shook his hand in the half-light of the yard lamp it was the last time he was to see him alive. Before the last flakes had stopped falling, when old people were searching back to "the great snows when Count Plunkett was elected" to find another such fall, Michael Bruen had died, and his life was already another such watermark of memory.

The snow lay eight feet deep on the roads, and dead cattle and sheep were found in drifts of fifteen feet in the fields. All of the people who hadn't lost sheep or cattle were in extraordinary good humour, their own ills buried for a time as deep as their envy of any other's good fortune in the general difficulty of the snow. It took days to cut a way out to the main road, the snow having to be cut in blocks breast-high out of a face of frozen snow. A wild cheer went up as the men at last cut through to the gang digging in from the main road. Another cheer greeted the first van to come in, Doherty's bread van, and it had hardly died when the hearse came with the coffin for Michael Bruen. That night they cut the path up the side of Killeelan Hill and found the family headstone beside the big yew just inside the gate and opened the grave. They hadn't finished digging when the first funeral bell came clearly over the snow the next day to tell them that the coffin had started on its way.

The priest hadn't thought of the day for years or of Michael Bruen till he had stumbled into it without warning by way of the sudden light on the beech chips. It did not augur well. There were days, especially of late, when he seemed to be lost in dead days, to see time present as a flimsy accumulating tissue over all the time that was lost. Sometimes he saw himself as an old man children were helping down to the shore, restraining the tension of their need to laugh as they pointed out a rock in the path he seemed about to stumble over, and then they had to lift their eyes and smile apologetically to the passersby while he stood staring out to sea, having forgotten all about the rock in his path. "It's this way we're going." He felt the imaginary tug on his sleeve, and he was drawn again into the tortuous existence of the everyday, away from the eternal of the sea or the lost light on frozen snow across Killeelan Hill.

Never before though had he noticed anything like the beech chips. There was the joy of holding what had eluded him for so long, in its amazing simplicity: but mastered knowledge was no longer knowledge unless it opened, became part of a greater knowledge, and what did the beech chips do but turn back to his own death?

Like the sudden snowfall and Michael Bruen's burial his life had been like any other, except to himself, and then only in odd visions of it, as a lost life. When it had been agreeable and equitable he had no vision of it at all.

The country childhood. His mother and father. The arrival at the shocking knowledge of birth and death. His attraction to the priesthood as a way of vanquishing death and avoiding birth. O hurry it, he thought. There is not much to a life. Many have it. There is not enough room. His father and mother were old when they married; he was "the fruit of old things", he heard derisively. His mother had been a seamstress. He could still see the needle flashing in her strong hands, that single needle-flash composed of thousands of hours.

"His mother had the vocation for him." Perhaps she had, perhaps all the mothers of the country had, it had so passed into the speech of the country, in all the forms of both beatification and derision; but it was out of fear of death he became a priest, which became in time the fear of life. Wasn't it natural to turn back to the mother in this fear? She was older than fear, having given him his life, and who would give a life if they knew its end? There was, then, his father's death, his acceptance of it, as he had accepted all poor fortune all his life long as his due, refusing to credit the good.

And afterwards his mother sold the land to "Horse" McLaughlin and came to live with him and was happy. She attended all the Masses and Devotions, took messages, and she sewed, though she had no longer any need, linen for the altar, soutanes and surplices, his shirts and all her own clothes. Sometimes her concern for him irritated him to exasperation but he hardly ever let it show. He was busy with the many duties of a priest. The fences on the past and future were secure. He must have been what is called happy, and there was a whole part of his life that, without his knowing, had come to turn to her for its own expression.

He discovered it when she began her death. He came home one summer evening to find all the lights on in the house. She was in the living-room, in the usual chair. The table was piled high with dresses. Round the chair was a pile of rags. She did not look up when he entered, her still strong hands tearing apart a herringbone skirt she had made only the year before.

"What on earth are you doing, Mother?" He caught her by the hands when she didn't answer.

"It's time you were up for Mass," she said.

"What are you doing with your dresses?"

"What dresses?"

"All the dresses you've just been tearing up."

"I don't know anything about dresses," and then he saw there was something wrong. She made no resistance when he led her up the stairs.

For some days she seemed absent and confused but, though he watched her carefully, she was otherwise very little different from her old self, and she did not appear ill. Then he came home one evening to find her standing like a child in the middle of the room, surrounded by an enormous pile of rags. She had taken up from where she'd been interrupted at the herring-bone skirt and torn up every dress or article of clothing she had ever made. After his initial shock he sent for the doctor.

"I'm afraid it's just the onset of senility," the doctor said.

"It's irreversible?"

The doctor nodded, "It very seldom takes such a violent form, but that's what it is. She'll have to be looked after." With a sadness that part of his life was over, he took her to the Home and saw her settled there.

She recognized him when he visited her there the first year, but without excitement, as if he was already far away; and then the day came when he had to admit that she no longer knew who he was, had become like a dog kennelled out too long. He was with her when she died. She'd turned her face towards him. There came a light of recognition in the eyes like a last glow of a match before it goes out, and then she died.

There was nothing left but his own life. There had been nothing but that all along, but it had been obscured, comfortably obscured.

He turned on the radio.

A man had lost both legs in an explosion. There was violence on the night-shift at Ford's. The pound had steadied towards the close but was still down on the day.

Letting his fingers linger on the knob he turned it off. The disembodied voice on the air was not unlike the lost day he'd stumbled into through the light on the beech chips, except it had nothing of its radiance – the funeral during the years he carried it around with him lost the sheltered burden of the everyday, had become light as the air in all the clarity of light. It was all timeless, and seemed at least a promise of the eternal.

He went to draw the curtain. She had made the red curtain too with its pale lining but hadn't torn it. How often must she have watched the moonlight on the still headstones beyond the laurel as it lay evenly on them this night. She had been afraid of ghosts: old priests who had lived in this house, who through whiskey or some other ill had neglected to say some Mass for the dead and because of the neglect the soul for whom the Mass should have been offered was forced to linger beyond its time in Purgatory, and the priest guilty of the omission could himself not be released until the living priest had said the Mass, and was forced to come at midnight to the house in all his bondage until the Mass was said.

"They must have been all good priests, Mother. Good steady old fellows like myself. They never come back," he used to assure her. He remembered his own idle words as he drew the curtain, lingering as much over the drawing of the curtain as he had lingered over the turning off of the radio. He would be glad of a ghost tonight, be glad of any visitation from beyond the walls of sense.

He took up the battered and friendly missal, which had been with him all his adult life, to read the office of the day. On bad days he kept it till late, the familiar words that changed with the changing year, that he had grown to love, and were as well his daily duty. It must be surely the greatest grace of life, the greatest freedom, to have to do what we love because it is also our duty. He wasn't able to read on this evening among the old familiar words for long. An annoyance came between him and the page, the Mass he had to repeat every day, the Mass in English. He wasn't sure whether he hated it or the guitar-playing priests more. It was humiliating to think that these had never been such a scourge when his mother had been alive. Was his life the calm vessel it had seemed, dully setting out and returning from the fishing grounds? Or had he been always what he seemed now? "Oh yes. There you go again," he heard the familiar voice in the empty room. "Complaining about the Mass in the vernacular. When you prefer the common names of flowers to their proper names," and the sharp, energetic, almost brutal laugh. It was Peter Joyce, he was not dead. Peter Joyce had risen to become a bishop at the other end of the country, an old friend he no longer saw.

"But they are more beautiful. Dog rose, wild woodbine, buttercup, daisy . . ."

He heard his own protest. It was in a hotel that they used to go to every summer on the Atlantic, a small hotel where you could read after dinner without fear of a rising roar from the bar beginning to outrival the Atlantic by ten o'clock.

"And, no doubt, the little rose of Scotland, sharp and sweet and breaks the heart," he heard his friend quote maliciously. "And it's not the point. The reason that names of flowers must be in Latin is that when flower lovers meet they know what they are talking about, no matter whether they're French or Greeks or Arabs. They have a universal language."

"I prefer the humble names, no matter what you say."

"Of course you do. And it's parochial sentimentalists like yourself who prefer the *smooth sowthistle* to *Sonchus oleraceus* that's the whole cause of your late lamented Mass in Latin disappearing. I have no sympathy with you. You people tire me."

The memory of that truculent argument dispelled his annoyance, as its simple logic had once taken his breath away, but he was curiously tired after the vividness of the recall. It was only by a sheer act of will, sometimes having to count the words, that he was able to finish his office. "I know one thing, Peter Joyce. I know that I know nothing," he murmured when he finished. But when he looked at the room about him he could hardly believe it was so empty and dead and dry, the empty chair where she should be sewing, the oaken table with the scattered books, the clock on the mantel. Wildly and aridly he wanted to curse, but his desire to curse was as unfair as life. He had not wanted it.

Then, quietly, he saw that he had a ghost all right, one that he had been walking around with for a long time, a ghost he had not wanted to recognize – his own death. He might as well get to know him well. It would never leave now and had no mortal shape. Absence does not cast a shadow.

All that was there was the white light of the lamp on the open book, on the white marble; the brief sun of God on beechwood, and the sudden light of that glistening snow, and the timeless mourners moving towards the yews on Killee-lan Hill almost thirty years ago. It was as good a day as any, if there ever was a good day to go.

Somewhere, outside this room that was an end, he knew that a young man, not unlike he had once been, stood on a granite step and listened to the door-bell ring, smiled as he heard a woman's footsteps come down the hallway, ran his fingers through his hair, and turned the bottle of white wine he held in his hands completely around as he prepared to enter a pleasant and uncomplicated evening, feeling himself immersed in time without end.

TOYFOLK

Edith Pearlman

Only recently discovered by readers outside America, **Edith Pearlman** (b.1936) won the 2011 PEN/Malamud Award and the National Book Critics Circle Award for Fiction for the stories collected in *Binocular Vision*. Ann Patchett wrote of them being "an exercise in imagination and compassion, a trip around the world, an example of what happens when talent meets discipline and a stunning intelligence."

In the town square Fergus was trying out his rudimentary Czech. "Stores are on the ground floors," he remarked. "People above."

"I speak only English," snapped the news vendor, in German. His left hand rested on the awning of his wheelbarrow. Index and middle fingers were missing – their ghosts pointed at Fergus's throat.

"The cobblestones were light gray once. Dark gray now," Fergus persisted.

"I have other magazines in the bottom of the barrow," the news vendor said, in French.

Fergus shook his head, though without censure. An old church stood aslant in the middle of the square. The minute hand of its clock twitched every sixty seconds. Would you go mad, hearing that forever? Would you come to need it, like kisses? A line of customers stuttered into the bakery, and the greengrocer moved sideways and sideways, sprinkling water on his cabbages. Under the October sun the whole little enterprise – church, stores, peaked facades – glistened as if shellacked.

"Good-bye," Fergus said to the news vendor.

"Au revoir, Toyman."

Fergus walked away, smiling.

He was a division head of ToyFolk. He came to a new place after a site had been selected, and he supervised the building of the factory and the hiring of the workers, and managed the facility for a while – ten years, usually; well, it never seemed that long.

The knitting shop – what a careful pyramid of yarns. A cat with a passion for some middle ball could set the whole thing tumbling. The druggist's window displayed old-fashioned brass scales. Then came the premises of an estate agent. A middle-aged woman sat composedly at a typewriter; a young woman peered into a computer screen with an expression of dismay.

And this next place? Perhaps the window meant to be revealing, but it had too many small panes. There was merchandise inside – women's accessories? He thought of Barbara, and of his daughters and daughter-in-law; and he went in.

Bells fixed to the door announced his presence. Something flipped onto his head and then bounced onto his shoes. A knitted clown.

"Oh!" said a woman's voice.

"Ah," said a man's.

Fergus picked up the clown and remained squatting, examining the miniature buttons of wood that ran down the torso. Each button had been carved by hand. He cradled the toy in his own hand, two fingers supporting the head. Finally he stood up, creaking just a little, and looked around.

Dolls. Dolls crowding each other on shelves like slaves on shipboard. Dolls democratically sharing a pram. Dolls of all sizes sitting one atop the other, the largest on a rocker, exhaustedly supporting the rest.

Noah's ark, the animals assembled on deck to wait for the dove.

Jack-in-the-boxes. Punch and Judy, on their sides, locked in each other's arms. A pint-size printing press.

Teddies . . . His eyes didn't sting, really; they remembered stinging. They remembered his children asleep, favorites crooked in their elbows. They remembered the plush of his own bear.

The man who had said "Ah" and the woman who had said "Oh" stood in front of a case of toys. They were in their middle forties. Barbara had been at her lanky best then – the rigors of child rearing past, the predations of age still ahead. For this woman, now staring at him with such assurance, beauty must be an old habit. Her pale face was surrounded by hair once blond and now transparent. Her chin was delicately cleft as if by a master chiseler. The irises of her gunmetal eyes were rimmed with a darker shade. She wore a flowered skirt, a blouse of a different flowered pattern, a shawl embroidered with yet another species.

The man's eyes were a gentle blue. He had a courtier's small beard, but he was dressed in black garments that suggested the peasant – baggy trousers, a loose vest over a T-shirt.

Fergus walked toward a shelf of windup toys. He stepped side-ways. In a case, tiny ballerinas posed before a mirror, and through the mirror he saw that a curtained archway led to a stockroom.

He glided again, and now the mirror gave him the handsome man and woman in their awful clothes.

"Is this a store?" he asked, turning toward them. "A museum?"

"We are a secondhand toy shop," the man answered. His accent was French. "That makes us a kind of museum. Most travelers come in only to look. But we get the occasional collector."

"We started out as a collection ourselves," the woman said. Her accent was Gallic, too. "We are also a workshop."

The man shrugged. "I turn out some wooden things."

"Bernard repairs appliances for the entire population."

"Anna exaggerates."

"My name is Fergus."

Bernard nodded. "The American. The president of ToyFolk."

"This town has no secrets," Anna explained.

Fergus laughed. "Not president. A division head."

"ToyFolk will bring prosperity," Anna said. "Everybody says so. Will you have some tea?"

Each new posting had brought its special friends. In Burgundy he and Barbara had hit it off with a cartoonist who raised sheep. In Lancashire they spent every Sunday with the dentist and his wife, disorganized, comical, their three children just the ages of Fergus and Barbara's own. In the Canaries the mayor, a bachelor, cleaved to them with nervous ardor. And now came this pair, served up like a final course. Toy people. What a blast.

"We always *have* brought prosperity," Fergus said, smiling at his hosts from the chair they had unfolded. Anna sat on a footstool; Bernard said he preferred to stand. "When we move on things are better than they were – they seem so, anyway. Delicious tea – blackberry?"

"Yes. And your family?" Anna asked.

"Kids all married, living in different states. Barbara joins me next week; she's in Minneapolis visiting our grandchild."

"I like your action figures," Bernard said abruptly. "They remind me of my lead soldiers. Only instead of pouring lead your factory molds plastic – yes?"

"Yes. Limbs and torsos and heads." Fergus cleared his throat. "Research indicates that as the market for action figures grows, the market for old-fashioned playthings grows also. So you and I are . . . collaborators."

"To be sure! But toys are not our living. We support ourselves with repairs."

"You support me," Anna murmured. Then she raised her chin as if staring down an enemy. She picked up a music box and put it on her knees and wound it up. Two figures in formal clothing twirled to "Cheek to Cheek," off tune here and there.

"I've tried to fix that cylinder," Bernard said, shrugging again. "It resists me. Will you come back for dinner?"

"I have appointments this evening," Fergus said. "And the innkeeper has invited me for a schnapps."

"Tomorrow, then," Anna said, as the song wound sourly down.

He came, flowers in one hand, wine in the other. In the rooms above the shop the couple lived snugly, kept company by overflow toys. Dolls fitted their rumps into the corners of chairs, peered over the top of a highboy. Cherry-colored rattles flourished in a pewter mug.

"They were dangerous, those rattles," Bernard said gravely. "Imagine putting paint on a plaything for a mouthing child. Some toys were foolish then."

"Some are foolish now," Fergus said. "There's a list, every Christmas, you hear it on the radio in France, in England . . ."

"Here, too," Bernard said. "And was anything ever deadlier than a slingshot?"

"Sanctioned by the Bible," Anna said. "Marbles, though . . . down the throat . . ." She shuddered, then produced that soldierly smile, and busied herself ladling the stew.

Photographs lined the passageway from kitchen to bathroom. Snapshots, really, but blown up and matted in ivory and framed in silver as if they were meant to hang in a gallery. All were of the same child – blond, light-eyed. At two she was solemn, in a draperied room, sharing a chair with a rag doll. At four she was solemn against the sea; this time the doll was a naked rubber baby. At six she smiled, clutching Raggedy Ann. At eight the girl with her Barbie stood straight as a stick in front of a constructed pond – could it have been the one at the Luxembourg Garden? Slatted chairs, smoking pensioners, and a toy boat sailing off to the right.

No further pictures.

He found himself unable to swallow.

After coffee he walked back to the inn across the floodlit square – the mayor had recently planted a light next to the church. At tables outside the café a few tourists bent toward each other in puppet conversations. In doorways pairs of men stood motionless. Smoke floated from their pipes. The news vendor stood beside his barrow. The church clock ticked.

Fergus looked up at tiled roofs, then at the mountains beyond. Visiting grandchildren would recognize this scene as the source of tales, he thought with a brief joy. The clock ticked. That girl.

It was still afternoon for Barbara. She was babysitting while their daughter did errands. "Hello!" she heard Fergus say, fizzing with anxious love. "How are you?"

She was fine, and the kids were, too. She had made telephone rounds yesterday. As usual he refused to take the whole for the parts, and asked after each in turn, and the spouses, too. "And the little fellow?"

"A genius, I do believe," she said. Their grandchild was six months old.

"Of course. And the rash?"

"Prickly heat, entirely gone." She would not fret him about the little patch of eczema. Then they talked about friends in France and England and the Canaries – Barbara kept up with everyone – and then Fergus asked whether she thought their son was really enjoying law school, and Barbara, who knew he hated it, said law school wasn't supposed to be enjoyable, was it? Perhaps he'd like practice. "Not everyone can be as fortunate in work as you've been." Immediately she regretted the remark; he did not want to be luckier than his children.

"The kids were my work," he said.

"Well, don't tell that to ToyFolk; they might renege on that nice retirement package." She thought of all those years on all those living room floors, the five of them, and wooden blocks and doll houses and action toys. The school conferences. The older daughter's flirtation with anorexia and the younger's brief attachment to a thug on a motorcycle. The army-brat hardness of all three of them . . . "Darling. They're on their own at last."

She heard two sounds, the first a resigned sigh, the second a catch of breath, as if he were constructing one of his catastrophes.

"I can't wait to see you," she said.

"Oh, and there's this couple . . ."

A cry upstairs. "The baby's awake."

"Till soon," said his soft voice.

Two nights later Fergus visited Anna and Bernard after dinner. In the living room Anna was repairing the headdress of a Japanese doll in a kimono. The kimono had an elaborate design of reeds and a river. The doll's face was dead white: faithful to life, the color of a powdered geisha. "Is that hair real?" Fergus asked.

"Some of it," Anna said.

"A museum would give – "

"She is not for sale."

At the dining table Bernard was playing chess with one of the druggist's sons. Bernard introduced Fergus to the boy, and motioned him to a chair; but he did not interrupt the play or his affectionate commentary. He revealed his plans to the child, offered suggestions for an opposing strategy, tolerated the distortion of his advice, allowed young Mirik to progress toward gentle defeat. The boy, cheeks aflame, said: "Tomorrow?"

"Tomorrow." Bernard's hand rested briefly on the plaid shoulder. Then Mirik ran through the living room, pausing to bow toward Anna.

"No knack for the game," Bernard summed up. "Such a sweet youngster."

On the night before Barbara's arrival Fergus came for another of Anna's stews. He brought brandy along with flowers and wine. After the meal Anna said her palate was as discriminating as flannel and she would excuse herself from wasting fine cognac.

Fergus said to Bernard, "I'd like to see your workshop."

"Let's take the bottle there."

From the stockroom downstairs they descended farther, spinning around a staircase to a stone basement. "This was once the wine cellar," Bernard said. An overbright fluorescent bar in the ceiling made Fergus's eyes water. Bernard pulled a string, and now the only light came from the church's flood lamp spilling weakly through a small high window. The two men sat at the worktable, surrounded by shelves of toasters and vacuum cleaners and radios, or their shadowy ghosts; by dolls without heads and marionettes without strings.

"Where did you learn toy making?" Fergus asked.

"Ah, I taught myself. I like to carve, and I am mechanical by nature, and I trained as an engineer. I was employed by a company in Paris."

"I studied engineering, too, at Georgia Tech. But it wasn't my bent. Management was more to my liking."

"A talent for organization, affability, languages. You could have been a diplomat . . ."

"I'm not canny. And I worry too much."

Bernard lit a pipe. "That must make you valuable to ToyFolk."

"Well, it does. I've never seen you smoke," Fergus said.

"Anna coughs."

What had felled the child in the photographs? A missile to the eye, a marble in the esophagus? A train wreck, the middle cars humping upward, the engine falling onto its side? Drowning? There were microorganisms resistant to medicine that could lodge in the chest and emit poisons; sooner or later the patient lay dead. He had spent his children's childhoods making mental lists of dire events, to forestall them.

He looked across the worktable at the smoking man, then looked away. His eye fell on a rectangular wooden box at the end of the table. One of its faces was glass. He reached for the thing. A crank protruded from the side. "Is this an old automaton?"

"A new one."

Fergus turned the crank. A bulb went on inside the box. A castle had been painted on the back wall. Three carved soldiers in breeches and jackets with epaulets pointed their rifles at a blind-folded figure in a peasant's smock. One soldier had a blond beard, another a jutting brow, the third a frivolous nose. Fergus continued to turn the crank. The soldiers lurched in unison. There was a tiny blasting sound. The blindfolded figure fell forward. The light went out. Fergus kept at the crank. The light went on: the scene as before – executioners poised, villain erect and waiting.

Fergus worked the toy for a while. Then he said: "What will you do with this?"

"Oh . . . we're fond of the estate agent's children, and at Christmas . . ."

"You have a rare talent."

"Oh, rare, no . . . It passes the time."

Fergus turned the crank again. "Yes," he said. "What doesn't pass the time? Managing factories, mastering languages, raising families . . ." He had said too much. "More brandy?" he asked, and poured without waiting for an answer, as if the bottle were still his.

Bernard drank. "Your action figures . . . they all have the same face, yes?"

"The same face," Fergus admitted. "Headgear distinguishes them, and costume . . . Children, young children, identify clothes, equipment, color."

"Features are too . . . subtle?"

"Well, research indicates . . ."

Bernard said: "After all, this is not for the estate agent's children." He paused. "I would like to give it to you."

"Oh, I – "

"Because you value it."

"– couldn't take such a gift." But he took it.

Barbara rode on a little train that chugged through the mountains. From her window she looked up at pines, down at a miniature town. She recognized it as charming: the ideal final posting for her sentimental man.

When the train halted she stepped briskly off, carrying one small suitcase and a sack of paperback novels. She wore new harlequin glasses bought in the hope that they would soften her bony face.

She leaped toward Fergus and he leaped toward her.

Then Fergus shouldered Barbara's books and picked up her suitcase. "Only a few blocks to the inn," he said. "Wherever we live we'll be able to walk everywhere. In two months we'll know everybody here. Have you eaten?"

"There was a nice little buffet car. I'll bet you know half of the citizens already. Let me take the books."

"I've met the officials," he said, not relinquishing the sack. "The lawyer, the estate agent," he enumerated as they walked downhill past soft old buildings. "A doctor, too; I met him at a party the contractor gave. All rather wooden, except for a crazy news vendor who speaks in tongues, sort of."

At the inn she met the innkeeper. Then: "What a model room!" she said when Fergus brought her upstairs. "That fat quilt. Stencils on the highboy. And what's this?" she said, spotting the automaton.

She listened to a description of a husband and wife who were devoted to toys. Then she picked up the box and turned the crank and watched an execution several times. "The chin below the blindfold," she said at last. "Such defiance. I'd like to meet the man who made this."

"You will. Are you tired, darling?" her husband asked.

"Not too tired. Darling."

Five days went by before Fergus and Barbara could get together with Bernard and Anna – five days of meetings, of house hunting, of the hiring of a tutor. "Though I'm not sure I have the stomach for another language," Barbara said. "I'll mime my way around."

At last the four met on a Saturday night in the dining room of the inn. Under his vest Bernard wore a button-down instead of a T-shirt. He looked like a woodman. Anna wore a cocktail dress – Fergus remembered that his mother had once owned one like it: blue taffeta, with a wide skirt.

The innkeeper sent over a bottle of wine. They bought a second bottle. Guests of the inn and citizens of the town came into the big room in pairs and groups.

"Saturday night," Anna remarked. "It's always like this."

At ten o'clock the innkeeper brought out his collection of big band records, and there was dancing in a glassed-in terrace that overlooked the square. Fergus danced with Barbara, then with Anna.

"I like your wife," she said.

"I like your village. I think we'll be happy here."

"I suspect you're happy everywhere."

"Happy enough," he said, cautiously. "We have a taste for small things."

"Here you can make a lot out of a little. Old tragedies like the news vendor's. His father had a fit and chopped off his fingers when he was twelve . . ."

"Good Lord." The music stopped.

"He speaks half a dozen languages, more when he's sober. Life's a game to him."

Music again: the big band records repeated. Couples again took the floor. Fergus smiled at the people he'd already met and wondered which would become intimates, which only friends.

"What other scandals can you tell me?" he asked.

"Bernard and I are a bit of a scandal . . . not being married, you know."

"I didn't know. That's not much of a scandal these days," he said lightly.

She gave him an offended stare. Though the floor had become crowded, he maneuvered her sideways, backward, forward, without colliding with anyone. He had always been a skillful dancer.

"*I* am married," she said at last. "Bernard isn't. I've seen you watching the photographs. Isn't she pretty?"

"She is your image."

"We lived in Paris. My husband owned jewelry shops. I designed brooches, necklaces. Ten years ago Bernard persuaded me to move in with him. I thought to divorce."

Divorce was not on his list of unbearables; it was simply unthinkable. "Custody?" he asked.

"We'd divide her."

"She liked dolls."

"She was careless with the antiques."

"Yes, well . . ."

"The bastard sent the whole collection in a taxi across town," she said, heatedly now. "As if they were groceries. He sold his business, and decamped with our daughter. I traced them to New York but never any further."

"That's kidnapping," Fergus said. "It can't be done."

"No? It was done."

"She would be . . . eighteen?"

"She *is* eighteen," Anna chided softly.

The song had not ended but they had stopped dancing. He stood with his heels together, stiff as a palace guard. Her fingers caressed the silk of her skirt. He took her right hand in his left and placed his own right on the small of her back and moved forward lightly, mechanically. "You and Bernard were young enough to have children together."

"Oh, young enough," she said, and nodded; this time she was not offended. "But I would have no further children until my first child was returned. Loyalty. It's how I'm made."

She smiled that brave little smile. Her spite uncoiled like a paper snake; Fergus felt its twitch. He imagined Bernard beset by his own longings: raising a rifle to his shoulder and training its sight on the hollow of her neck . . . Because the music was ending at last, and because Anna's outdated dress demanded some appreciative flourish, Fergus whirled her once and then urged her backward over his left arm. He did not bend over her as custom demanded, but instead looked fiercely at Barbara and the toyman standing profile to profile against the floodlit square.

Barbara felt the beam cast by his eyes, and turned to face it. He was holding Anna so oddly, like a garment. Anna, one hand clawing his upper arm, righted herself, looking aggrieved. Barbara tactfully shifted her own gaze to the square, where smoke rose from the pipes of standing men; and a café waiter stacked chairs, one on top of another on top of another; and the news vendor, the hour of repose come round, lifted the handles of the barrow and trundled it across the cobblestones, his footfalls managing to keep time with the church clock; ten unsteady steps . . . click; ten steps . . . click; ten steps . . .

"Tomorrow is Sunday," she heard Fergus loudly saying. His shoulder brushed hers. "We have to call the States early, because of the time difference," he said, somehow getting it wrong even after all these years, or pretending to; anyway, he rushed her away from their new friends with only the skimpiest of good-byes.

Fergus, in pajamas, sat on the billowing quilt, clipping his toe-nails into the wastebasket. Barbara, in her nightgown, brushed her short hair.

"I thought they'd lost her," he said.

"They lost sight of her."

"Bernard, a bereaved father, I thought. Well, bereaved in a way. His children were never allowed to be born." He got up and moved the wastebasket back to the corner of the room and put the clippers on the highboy.

"He's made other people's children his," Barbara said. Fergus, considering, put his elbow on the highboy. "A reasonable alternative to the terrors of parenthood, some would say," she added.

He gave her a look of distaste.

She countered with one of boldness. "Maybe even preferable."

"Some would say," he hurried to supply, sparing her the necessity of repeating the phrase, she who had experienced motherhood's joys in such reassuring milieus – just listen to that faithful clock. "Well, we know better," he said.

And waited for her assent.

And waited.

PRIVATE TUITION BY MR BOSE

Anita Desai

One of the quietest writers I've read, **Anita Desai** (b.1937) was shortlisted for the Booker Prize for *In Custody*, later filmed by Ismail Merchant. She has also been awarded the RSL's Benson Medal and the Sahitya Akademi Fellowship as well as, in 2014, the Padma Bhushan. Her work includes *The Zigzag Way*, *Baumgartner's Bombay*, *Clear Light of Day* and *Fasting, Feasting*.

Mr Bose gave his private tuition out on the balcony, in the evenings, in the belief that, since it faced south, the river Hooghly would send it a wavering breeze or two to drift over the rooftops, through the washing and the few pots of *tulsi* and marigold that his wife had placed precariously on the balcony rail, to cool him, fan him, soothe him. But there was no breeze: it was hot, the air hung upon them like a damp towel, gagging him and, speaking through this gag, he tiredly intoned the Sanskrit verses that should, he felt, have been roared out on a hill-top at sunrise.

"*Aum. Usa va asvasya medhyasya sirah . . .*"

It came out, of course, a mumble. Asked to translate, his pupil, too, scowled as he had done, thrust his fist through his hair and mumbled:

"Aum is the dawn and the head of a horse . . ."

Mr Bose protested in a low wail. "What horse, my boy? What horse?"

The boy rolled his eyes sullenly. "I don't know, sir, it doesn't say."

Mr Bose looked at him in disbelief. He was the son of a Brahmin priest who himself instructed him in the Mahabharata all morning, turning him over to Mr Bose only in the evening when he set out to officiate at weddings, *puja* and other functions for which he was so much in demand on account of his stately bearing, his calm and inscrutable face and his sensuous voice that so suited the Sanskrit language in which he, almost always, discoursed. And this was his son – this Pritam with his red-veined eyes and oiled locks, his stumbling fingers and shuffling feet that betrayed his secret life, its scruffiness, its gutters and drains full of resentment and destruction. Mr Bose suddenly remembered how he had seen him, from the window of a bus that had come to a standstill on the street due to a fist fight between the conductor and a passenger, Pritam slipping up the stairs, through the door, into a neon-lit bar off Park Street.

"The sacrificial horse," Mr Bose explained with forced patience. "Have you heard of Asvamedha, Pritam, the royal horse that was let loose to run through the kingdom before it returned to the capital and was sacrificed by the king?"

The boy gave him a look of such malice that Mr Bose bit the end of his moustache and fell silent, shuffling through the pages. "Read on, then," he mumbled and listened, for a while, as Pritam blundered heavily through the Sanskrit verses that rolled off his father's experienced tongue, and even Mr Bose's shy one, with such rich felicity. When he could not bear it any longer, he turned his head, slightly, just enough to be able to look out of the corner of his eye through the open door, down the unlit passage at the end of which, in the small, dimly lit kitchen, his wife sat kneading dough for bread, their child at her side. Her head was bowed so that some of her hair had freed itself of the long steel pins he hated so much and hung about her pale, narrow face. The red border of her sari was the only stripe of colour in that smoky scene. The child beside her had his back turned to the door so that Mr Bose could see his little brown buttocks under the short white shirt, squashed firmly down upon the woven mat. Mr Bose wondered what it was that kept him so quiet – perhaps his mother had given him a lump of dough to mould into some thick and satisfying shape. Both of them seemed bound together and held down in some deeply absorbing act from which he was excluded. He would have liked to break in and join them.

Pritam stopped reading, maliciously staring at Mr Bose whose lips were wavering into a smile beneath the ragged moustache. The woman, disturbed by the break in the recitation on the balcony, looked up, past the child, down the passage and into Mr Bose's face. Mr Bose's moustache lifted up like a pair of wings and, beneath them, his smile lifted up and out with almost a laugh of tenderness and delight. Beginning to laugh herself, she quickly turned, pulled down the corners of her mouth with mock sternness, trying to recall him to the path of duty, and picking up a lump of sticky dough, handed it back to the child, softly urging him to be quiet and let his father finish the lesson.

Pritam, the scabby, oil-slick son of a Brahmin priest, coughed theatrically – a cough imitating that of a favourite screen actor, surely, it was so false and overdone and suggestive. Mr Bose swung around in dismay, crying "Why have you stopped? Go on, go on."

"You weren't listening, sir."

Many words, many questions leapt to Mr Bose's lips, ready to pounce on this miserable boy whom he could hardly bear to see sitting beneath his wife's holy *tulsi* plant that she tended with prayers, water-can and oil-lamp every evening. Then, growing conscious of the way his moustache was agitating upon his upper lip, he said only, "Read.

"*Ahar va asvam purustan mahima nvajagata . . .*"

Across the road someone turned on a radio and a song filled with a pleasant, lilting *weltschmerz* twirled and sank, twirled and rose from that balcony to this. Pritam raised his voice, grinding through the Sanskrit consonants like some dying, diseased tram-car. From the kitchen only a murmur and the soft thumping of the dough in the pan could be heard – sounds as soft and comfortable as sleepy pigeons. Mr Bose longed passionately to listen to them, catch every faintest nuance of them, but to do this he would have to smash the radio, hurl the

Brahmin's son down the iron stairs . . . He curled up his hands on his knees and drew his feet together under him, horrified at this welling up of violence inside him, under his pale pink bush-shirt, inside his thin, ridiculously heaving chest. As often as Mr Bose longed to alter the entire direction of the world's revolution, as often as he longed to break the world apart into two halves and shake out of them – what? Festival fireworks, a woman's soft hair, blood-stained feathers? – he would shudder and pale at the thought of his indiscretion, his violence, this secret force that now and then threatened, clamoured, so that he had quickly to still it, squash it. After all, he must continue with his private tuitions: that was what was important. The baby had to have his first pair of shoes and soon he would be needing oranges, biscuits, plastic toys. "Read," said Mr Bose, a little less sternly, a little more sadly.

But, "It is seven, I can go home now," said Pritam triumphantly, throwing his father's thick yellow Mahabharata into his bag, knocking the bag shut with one fist and preparing to fly. Where did he fly to? Mr Bose wondered if it would be the neon-lit bar off Park Street. Then, seeing the boy disappear down the black stairs – the bulb had fused again – he felt it didn't matter, didn't matter one bit since it left him alone to turn, plunge down the passage and fling himself at the doorposts of the kitchen, there to stand and gaze down at his wife, now rolling out *purees* with an exquisite, back-and-forth rolling motion of her hands, and his son, trying now to make a spoon stand on one end.

She only glanced at him, pretended not to care, pursed her lips to keep from giggling, flipped the *puree* over and rolled it finer and flatter still. He wanted so much to touch her hair, the strand that lay over her shoulder in a black loop, and did not know how to – she was so busy. "Your hair is coming loose," he said.

"Go, go," she warned, "I hear the next one coming."

So did he, he heard the soft patting of sandals on the worn steps outside, so all he did was bend and touch the small curls of hair on his son's neck. They were so soft, they seemed hardly human and quite frightened him. When he took his hand away he felt the wisps might have come off onto his fingers and he rubbed the tips together wonderingly. The child let fall the spoon, with a magnificent ring, onto a brass dish and started at this discovery of percussion.

The light on the balcony was dimmed as his next pupil came to stand in the doorway. Quickly he pulled himself away from the doorpost and walked back to his station, tense with unspoken words and unexpressed emotion. He had quite forgotten that his next pupil, this Wednesday, was to be Upneet. Rather Pritam again than this once-a-week typhoon, Upneet of the flowered sari, ruby ear-rings and shaming laughter. Under this Upneet's gaze such ordinary functions of a tutor's life as sitting down at a table, sharpening a pencil and opening a book to the correct page became matters of farce, disaster and hilarity. His very bones sprang out of joint. He did not know where to look – everywhere were Upneet's flowers, Upneet's giggles. Immediately, at the very sight of the tip of her sandal peeping out beneath the flowered hem of her sari, he was a man broken to pieces, flung this way and that, rattling. Rattling.

Throwing away the Sanskrit books, bringing out volumes of Bengali poetry, opening to a poem by Jibanandan Das, he wondered ferociously: Why did she come? What use had she for Bengali poetry? Why did she come from that house across the road where the loud radio rollicked, to sit on his balcony, in view of his shy wife, making him read poetry to her? It was intolerable. Intolerable, all of it – except, only for the seventy-five rupees paid at the end of the month. Oranges, he thought grimly, and milk, medicines, clothes. And he read to her:

> "Her hair was the dark night of Vidisha,
> Her face the sculpture of Svarasti . . ."

Quite steadily he read, his tongue tamed and enthralled by the rhythm of the verse he had loved (copied on a sheet of blue paper, he had sent it to his wife one day when speech proved inadequate).

> "'Where have you been so long?' she asked,
> Lifting her bird's-nest eyes,
> Banalata Sen of Natore."

Pat-pat-pat. No, it was not the rhythm of the verse, he realized, but the tapping of her foot, green-sandalled, red-nailed, swinging and swinging to lift the hem of her sari up and up. His eyes slid off the book, watched the flowered hem swing out and up, out and up as the green-sandalled foot peeped out, then in, peeped out, then in. For a while his tongue ran on of its own volition:

> "All birds come home, and all rivers,
> Life's ledger is closed . . ."

But he could not continue – it was the foot, the sandal that carried on the rhythm exactly as if he were still reciting. Even the radio stopped its rollicking and, as a peremptory voice began to enumerate the day's disasters and achievements all over the world, Mr Bose heard more vigorous sounds from his kitchen as well. There too the lulling pigeon sounds had been crisply turned off and what he heard were bangs and rattles among the kitchen pots, a kettle-drum of commands, he thought. The baby, letting out a wail of surprise, paused, heard the nervous commotion continue and intensify and launched himself on a series of wails.

Mr Bose looked up, aghast. He could not understand how these two halves of the difficult world that he had been holding so carefully together, sealing them with reams of poetry, reams of Sanskrit, had split apart into dissonance. He stared at his pupil's face, creamy, feline, satirical, and was forced to complete the poem in a stutter:

> "Only darkness remains, to sit facing
>   Banalata Sen of Natore."

But the darkness was filled with hideous sounds of business and anger and command. The radio news commentator barked, the baby wailed, the kitchen pots clashed. He even heard his wife's voice raised, angrily, at the child, like a threatening stick. Glancing again at his pupil whom he feared so much, he saw precisely that lift of the eyebrows and that twist of a smile that disjointed him, rattled him.

"Er – please read," he tried to correct, to straighten that twist of eyebrows and lips. "Please read."

"But you have read it to me already," she laughed, mocking him with her eyes and laugh.

"The next poem," he cried, "read the next poem," and turned the page with fingers as clumsy as toes.

"It is much better when you read to me," she complained impertinently, but read, keeping time to the rhythm with that restless foot which he watched as though it were a snake-charmer's pipe, swaying. He could hear her voice no more than the snake could the pipe's – it was drowned out by the baby's wails, swelling into roars of self-pity and indignation in this suddenly hard-edged world.

Mr Bose threw a piteous, begging look over his shoulder at the kitchen. Catching his eye, his wife glowered at him, tossed the hair out of her face and cried, "Be quiet, be quiet, can't you see how busy your father is?" Red-eared, he turned to find Upneet looking curiously down the passage at this scene of domestic anarchy, and said, "I'm sorry, sorry – please read."

"I have read!" she exclaimed. "Didn't you hear me?"

"So much noise – I'm sorry," he gasped and rose to hurry down the passage and hiss, pressing his hands to his head as he did so, "Keep him quiet, can't you? Just for half an hour!"

"He is hungry," his wife said, as if she could do nothing about that.

"Feed him then," he begged.

"It isn't time," she said angrily.

"Never mind. Feed him, feed him."

"Why? So that you can read poetry to that girl in peace?"

"Shh!" he hissed, shocked, alarmed that Upneet would hear. His chest filled with the injustice of it. But this was no time for pleas or reason. He gave another desperate look at the child who lay crouched on the kitchen floor, rolling with misery. When he turned to go back to his pupil who was watching them interestedly, he heard his wife snatch up the child and tell him, "Have your food then, have it and eat it – don't you see how angry your father is?"

He spent the remaining half-hour with Upneet trying to distract her from observation of his domestic life. Why should it interest her? he thought angrily. She came here to study, not to mock, not to make trouble. He was her tutor, not her clown! Sternly, he gave her dictation but she was so hopeless – she learnt no Bengali at her convent school, found it hard even to form the letters of the Bengali alphabet – that he was left speechless. He crossed out her errors with his red pencil – grateful to be able to cancel out, so effectively, some of the ugliness of his life – till there was hardly a word left uncrossed and, looking up to see her reaction, found her far less perturbed than he. In fact, she looked quite mischievously pleased. Three months of Bengali lessons to end in this! She was as truimphant as he was horrified. He let fall the red pencil with a discouraged gesture. So, in complete discord, the lesson broke apart, they all broke apart and for a while Mr Bose was alone on the balcony, clutching at the rails, thinking that these bars of cooled iron were all that were left for him to hold. Inside all was a conflict of shame and despair, in garbled grammar.

But, gradually, the grammar rearranged itself according to rule, corrected itself. The composition into quiet made quite clear the exhaustion of the child, asleep or nearly so. The sounds of dinner being prepared were calm, decorative even. Once more the radio was tuned to music, sympathetically sad. When his wife called him in to eat, he turned to go with his shoulders beaten, sagging, an attitude repeated by his moustache.

"He is asleep," she said, glancing at him with a rather ashamed face, conciliatory.

He nodded and sat down before his brass tray. She straightened it nervously, waved a hand over it as if to drive away a fly he could not see, and turned to the fire to fry hot *purees* for him, one by one, turning quickly to heap them on his tray so fast that he begged her to stop.

"Eat more," she coaxed. "One more" – as though the extra *puree* were a peace offering following her rebellion of half an hour ago.

He took it with reluctant fingers but his moustache began to quiver on his lip as if beginning to wake up. "And you?" he asked. "Won't you eat now?"

About her mouth, too, some quivers began to rise and move. She pursed her lips, nodded and began to fill her tray, piling up the *purees* in a low stack.

"One more," he told her, "just one more," he teased, and they laughed.

ENTROPY

Thomas Pynchon

Thomas Pynchon (b.1937) is the author of *V, The Crying of Lot 49, Gravity's Rainbow, Vineland, Mason & Dixon, Against the Day, Inherent Vice, Bleeding Edge,* and a collection of stories, *Slow Learner* and no more need be known.

> Boris has just given me a summary of his views. He is a weather prophet. The weather will continue bad, he says. There will be more calamities, more death, more despair. Not the slightest indication of a change anywhere. . . . We must get into step, a lockstep toward the prison of death. There is no escape. The weather will not change.
>
> *– Tropic of Cancer*

Downstairs, Meatball Mulligan's lease-breaking party was moving into its 40th hour. On the kitchen floor, amid a litter of empty champagne fifths, were Sandor Rojas and three friends, playing spit in the ocean and staying awake on Heidseck and benzedrine pills. In the living room Duke, Vincent, Krinkles and Paco sat crouched over a 15-inch speaker which had been bolted into the top of a wastepaper basket, listening to 27 watts' worth of *The Heroes' Gate at Kiev*. They all wore hornrimmed sunglasses and rapt expressions, and smoked funny-looking cigarettes which contained not, as you might expect, tobacco, but an adulterated form of *cannabis sativa*. This group was the Duke di Angelis quartet. They recorded for a local label called Tambú and had to their credit one 10" LP entitled *Songs of Outer Space*. From time to time one of them would flick the ashes from his cigarette into the speaker cone to watch them dance around. Meatball himself was sleeping over by the window, holding an empty magnum to his chest as if it were a teddy bear. Several government girls, who worked for people like the State Department and NSA, had passed out on couches, chairs and in one case the bathroom sink.

This was in early February of '57 and back then there were a lot of American expatriates around Washington, D.C., who would talk, every time they met you, about how someday they were going to go over to Europe for real but right now it seemed they were working for the government. Everyone saw a fine irony in this. They would stage, for instance, polyglot parties where the newcomer was sort of ignored if he couldn't carry on simultaneous conversations in three or four languages. They would haunt Armenian delicatessens for weeks at a stretch and invite you over for bulghour and lamb in tiny kitchens whose walls were covered with bullfight posters. They would have affairs with sultry girls from Andalucía or the Midi who studied economics at George-town. Their Dôme was a collegiate Rathskeller out on Wisconsin Avenue called the Old Heidelberg and they had to settle for cherry blossoms instead of lime trees when spring came, but in its lethargic way their life provided, as they said, kicks.

At the moment, Meatball's party seemed to be gathering its second wind. Outside there was rain. Rain splatted against the tar paper on the roof and was fractured into a fine spray off the noses, eyebrows and lips of wooden gargoyles under the eaves, and ran like drool down the windowpanes. The day before, it had snowed and the day before that there had been winds of gale force and before that the sun had made the city glitter bright as April, though the calendar read early February. It is a curious season in Washington, this false spring. Somewhere in it are Lincoln's Birthday and the Chinese New Year, and a forlornness in the streets because cherry blossoms are weeks away still and, as Sarah Vaughan has put it, spring will be a little late this year. Generally crowds like the one which would gather in the Old Heidelberg on weekday afternoons to drink Würtzburger and to sing Lili Marlene (not to mention The Sweetheart of Sigma Chi) are inevitably and incorrigibly Romantic. And as every good Romantic knows, the soul (*spiritus, ruach, pneuma*) is nothing, substantially, but air; it is only natural that warpings in the atmosphere should be recapitulated in those who breathe it. So that over and above the public components – holidays, tourist attractions – there are private meanderings, linked to the climate as if this spell were a *stretto* passage in the year's fugue: haphazard weather, aimless loves, unpredicted commitments: months one can easily spend *in* fugue, because oddly enough, later on, winds, rains, passions of February and March are never remembered in that city, it is as if they had never been.

The last bass notes of *The Heroes' Gate* boomed up through the floor and woke Callisto from an uneasy sleep. The first thing he became aware of was a small bird he had been holding gently between his hands, against his body. He turned his head sidewise on the pillow to smile down at it, at its blue hunched-down head and sick, lidded eyes, wondering how many more nights he would have to give it warmth before it was well again. He had been holding the bird like that for three days: it was the only way he knew to restore its health. Next to him the girl stirred and whimpered, her arm thrown across her face. Mingled with the sounds of the rain came the first tentative, querulous morning voices of the other birds, hidden in philodendrons and small fan palms: patches of scarlet, yellow and blue laced through this Rousseau-like fantasy, this hothouse jungle it had taken him seven years to weave together. Hermetically sealed, it was a tiny enclave of regularity in the city's chaos, alien to the vagaries of the weather, of national politics, of any civil disorder. Through trial-and-error Callisto had perfected its ecological balance, with the help of the girl its artistic harmony, so that the swayings of its plant life, the stirrings of its birds and human inhabitants were all as integral as the rhythms of a perfectly-executed mobile. He and the girl could no longer, of course, be omitted from that sanctuary; they had become necessary to its unity. What they needed from outside was delivered. They did not go out.

"Is he all right," she whispered. She lay like a tawny question mark facing him, her eyes suddenly huge and dark and blinking slowly. Callisto ran a finger beneath the feathers at the base of the bird's neck; caressed it gently. "He's going to be well, I think. See: he hears his friends beginning to wake up." The girl had heard the rain and the birds even before she was fully awake. Her name was Aubade: she was part French and part Annamese, and she lived on her own curious and lonely planet, where the clouds and the odor of poincianas, the bitterness of wine and the accidental fingers at the small of her back or feathery against her breasts came to her reduced inevitably to the terms of sound: of music which emerged at intervals from a howling darkness of discordancy. "Aubade," he said, "go see." Obedient, she arose; padded to the window, pulled aside the drapes and after a moment said: "It is 37. Still 37." Callisto frowned. "Since Tuesday, then," he said. "No change." Henry Adams, three generations before his own, had stared aghast at Power; Callisto found himself now in much the same state over Thermodynamics, the inner life of that power, realizing like his predecessor that the Virgin and the dynamo stand as much for love as for power; that the two are indeed identical; and that love therefore not only makes the world go round but also makes the boccie ball spin, the nebula precess. It was this latter or sidereal element which disturbed him. The cosmologists had predicted an eventual heat-death for the universe (something like Limbo: form and motion abolished, heat-energy identical at every point in it); the meteorologists, day-to-day, staved it off by contradicting with a reassuring array of varied temperatures.

But for three days now, despite the changeful weather, the mercury had stayed at 37 degrees Fahrenheit. Leery at omens of apocalypse, Callisto shifted beneath the covers. His fingers pressed the bird more firmly, as if needing some pulsing or suffering assurance of an early break in the temperature.

It was that last cymbal crash that did it. Meatball was hurled wincing into consciousness as the synchronized wagging of heads over the wastebasket stopped. The final hiss remained for an instant in the room, then melted into the whisper of rain outside. "Aarrgghh," announced Meatball in the silence, looking at the empty magnum. Krinkles, in slow motion, turned, smiled and held out a cigarette. "Tea time, man," he said. "No, no," said Meatball. "How many times I got to tell you guys. Not at my place. You ought to know, Washington is lousy with Feds." Krinkles looked wistful. "Jeez, Meatball," he said, "you don't want to do nothing no more." "Hair of dog," said Meatball. "Only hope. Any juice left?" He began to crawl toward the kitchen. "No champagne, I don't think," Duke said. "Case of tequila behind the icebox." They put on an Earl Bostic side. Meatball paused at the kitchen door, glowering at Sandor Rojas. "Lemons," he said after some thought. He crawled to the refrigerator and got out three lemons and some cubes, found the tequila and set about restoring order to his nervous system. He drew blood once cutting the lemons and had to use two hands squeezing them and his foot to crack the ice tray but after about ten minutes he found himself, through some miracle, beaming down into a monster tequila sour. "That looks yummy," Sandor Rojas said. "How about you make me one." Meatball blinked at him. "*Kitchi lofass a shegitbe*," he replied automatically, and wandered away into the bathroom. "I say," he called out a moment later to no one in particular. "I say, there seems to be a girl or something sleeping in the sink." He took her by the shoulders and shook. "Wha," she said. "You don't look too comfortable," Meatball said. "Well," she agreed. She stumbled to the shower, turned on the cold water and sat down crosslegged in the spray. "That's better," she smiled.

"Meatball," Sandor Rojas yelled from the kitchen. "Somebody is trying to come in the window. A burglar, I think. A second-story man." "What are you worrying about," Meatball said. "We're on the third floor." He loped back into the kitchen. A shaggy woebegone figure stood out on the fire escape, raking his fingernails down the windowpane. Meatball opened the window. "Saul," he said.

"Sort of wet out," Saul said. He climbed in, dripping. "You heard, I guess."

"Miriam left you," Meatball said, "or something, is all I heard."

There was a sudden flurry of knocking at the front door. "Do come in," Sandor Rojas called. The door opened and there were three coeds from George Washington, all of whom were majoring in philosophy. They were each holding a gallon of Chianti. Sandor leaped up and dashed into the living room. "We heard there was a party," one blonde said. "Young blood," Sandor shouted. He was an ex-Hungarian freedom fighter who had easily the worst chronic case of what certain critics of the middle class have called Don Giovannism in the District of Columbia. *Purche porti la gonnella, voi sapete quel che fa.* Like Pavlov's dog: a contralto voice or a whiff of Arpège and Sandor would begin to salivate. Meatball regarded the trio blearily as they filed into the kitchen; he shrugged. "Put the wine in the icebox," he said "and good morning."

Aubade's neck made a golden bow as she bent over the sheets of foolscap, scribbling away in the green murk of the room. "As a young man at Princeton," Callisto was dictating, nestling the bird against the gray hairs of his chest, "Callisto had learned a mnemonic device for remembering the Laws of Thermodynamics: you can't win, things are going to get worse before they get better, who says they're going to get better. At the age of 54, confronted with Gibbs' notion of the universe, he suddenly realized that undergraduate cant had been oracle, after all. That spindly maze of equations became, for him, a vision of ultimate, cosmic heat-death. He had known all along, of course, that nothing but a theoretical engine or system ever runs at 100% efficiency; and about the theorem of Clausius, which states that the entropy of an isolated system always continually increases. It was not, however, until Gibbs and Boltzmann brought to this principle the methods of statistical mechanics that the horrible significance of it all dawned on him: only then did he realize that the isolated system – galaxy, engine, human being, culture, whatever – must evolve spontaneously toward the Condition of the More Probable. He was forced, therefore, in the sad dying fall of middle age, to a radical reëvaluation of everything he had learned up to then; all the cities and seasons and casual passions of his days had now to be looked at in a new and elusive light. He did not know if he was equal to the task. He was aware of the dangers of the reductive fallacy and, he hoped, strong enough not to drift into the graceful decadence of an enervated fatalism. His had always been a vigorous, Italian sort of pessimism: like Machiavelli, he allowed the forces of *virtù* and *fortuna* to be about 50/50; but the equations now introduced a random factor which pushed the odds to some unutterable and indeterminate ratio which he found himself afraid to calculate." Around him loomed vague hothouse shapes; the pitifully small heart fluttered against his own. Counterpointed against his words the girl heard the chatter of birds and fitful car honkings scattered along the wet morning and Earl Bostic's alto rising in occasional wild peaks through the floor. The architectonic purity of her world was constantly threatened by such hints of anarchy: gaps and excrescences and skew lines, and a shifting or tilting of planes to which she had continually to readjust lest the whole structure shiver into a disarray of discrete and meaningless signals. Callisto had described the process once as a kind of "feedback": she crawled into dreams each night with a sense of exhaustion, and a desperate resolve never to relax that vigilance. Even in the brief periods when Callisto made love to her, soaring above the bowing of taut nerves in haphazard double-stops would be the one singing string of her determination.

"Nevertheless," continued Callisto, "he found in entropy or the measure of disorganization for a closed system an adequate metaphor to apply to certain phenomena in his own world. He saw, for example, the younger generation responding to Madison Avenue with the same spleen his own had once reserved for Wall Street: and in American 'consumerism' discovered a similar tendency from the least to the most probable, from differentiation to sameness, from ordered individuality to a kind of chaos. He found himself, in short, restating Gibbs' prediction in social terms, and envisioned a heat-death for his culture in which ideas, like heat-energy, would no longer be transferred, since each point in it would ultimately have the same quantity of energy; and intellectual motion would, accordingly, cease." He glanced up suddenly. "Check it now," he said. Again she rose and peered out at the thermometer. "37," she said. "The rain has stopped." He bent his head quickly and held his lips against a quivering wing. "Then it will change soon," he said, trying to keep his voice firm.

Sitting on the stove Saul was like any big rag doll that a kid has been taking out some incomprehensible rage on. "What happened," Meatball said. "If you feel like talking, I mean."

"Of course I feel like talking," Saul said. "One thing I did, I slugged her."

"Discipline must be maintained."

"Ha, ha. I wish you'd been there. Oh Meatball, it was a lovely fight. She ended up throwing a *Handbook of Chemistry and Physics* at me, only it missed and went through the window, and when the glass broke I reckon something in her broke too. She stormed out of the house crying, out in the rain. No raincoat or anything."

"She'll be back."

"No."

"Well." Soon Meatball said: "It was something earth-shattering, no doubt. Like who is better, Sal Mineo or Ricky Nelson."

"What it was about," Saul said, "was communication theory. Which of course makes it very hilarious."

"I don't know anything about communication theory."

"Neither does my wife. Come right down to it, who does? That's the joke."

When Meatball saw the kind of smile Saul had on his face he said: "Maybe you would like tequila or something."

"No. I mean, I'm sorry. It's a field you can go off the deep end in, is all. You get where you're watching all the time for security cops: behind bushes, around corners. MUFFET is top secret."

"Wha."

"Multi-unit factorial field electronic tabulator."

"You were fighting about that."

"Miriam has been reading science fiction again. That and *Scientific American*. It seems she is, as we say, bugged at this idea of computers acting like people. I made the mistake of saying you can just as well turn that around, and talk about human behavior like a program fed into an IBM machine."

"Why not," Meatball said.

"Indeed, why not. In fact it is sort of crucial to communication, not to mention information theory. Only when I said that she hit the roof. Up went the balloon. And I can't figure out *why*. If anybody should know why, I should. I refuse to believe the government is wasting taxpayers' money on me, when it has so many bigger and better things to waste it on."

Meatball made a moue. "Maybe she thought you were acting like a cold, dehumanized amoral scientist type."

"My god," Saul flung up an arm. "Dehumanized. How much more human can I get? I worry, Meatball, I do. There are Europeans wandering around North Africa these days with their tongues torn out of their heads because those tongues have spoken the wrong words. Only the Europeans thought they were the right words."

"Language barrier," Meatball suggested.

Saul jumped down off the stove. "That," he said, angry, "is a good candidate for sick joke of the year. No, ace, it is *not* a barrier. If it is anything it's a kind of leakage. Tell a girl: 'I love you.' No trouble with two-thirds of that, it's a closed circuit. Just you and she. But that nasty four-letter word in the middle, *that's* the one you have to look out for. Ambiguity. Redundancy. Irrelevance, even. Leakage. All this is noise. Noise screws up your signal, makes for disorganization in the circuit."

Meatball shuffled around. "Well, now, Saul," he muttered, "you're sort of, I don't know, expecting a lot from people. I mean, you know. What it is is, most of the things we say, I guess, are mostly noise."

"Ha! Half of what you just said, for example."

"Well, you do it too."

"I know." Saul smiled grimly. "It's a bitch, ain't it."

"I bet that's what keeps divorce lawyers in business. Whoops."

"Oh I'm not sensitive. Besides," frowning, "you're right. You find I think that most 'successful' marriages – Miriam and me, up to last night – are sort of founded on compromises. You never run at top efficiency, usually all you have is a minimum basis for a workable thing. I believe the phrase is Togetherness."

"Aarrgghh."

"Exactly. You find that one a bit noisy, don't you. But the noise content is different for each of us because you're a bachelor and I'm not. Or wasn't. The hell with it."

"Well sure," Meatball said, trying to be helpful, "you were using different words. By 'human being' you meant something that you can look at like it was a computer. It helps you think better on the job or something. But Miriam meant something entirely –"

"The hell with it."

Meatball fell silent. "I'll take that drink," Saul said after a while.

The card game had been abandoned and Sandor's friends were slowly getting wasted on tequila. On the living room couch, one of the coeds and Krinkles were engaged in amorous conversation. "No," Krinkles was saying, "no, I can't put Dave *down*. In fact I give Dave a lot of credit, man. Especially considering his accident and all." The girl's smile faded. "How terrible," she said. "What accident?" "Hadn't you heard?" Krinkles said. "When Dave was in the army, just a private E-2, they sent him down to Oak Ridge on special duty. Something to do with the Manhattan Project. He was handling hot stuff one day and got an overdose of radiation. So now he's got to wear lead gloves all the time." She shook her head sympathetically. "What an awful break for a piano-player."

Meatball had abandoned Saul to a bottle of tequila and was about to go to sleep in a closet when the front door flew open and the place was invaded by five enlisted personnel of the U.S. Navy, all in varying stages of abomination. "This is the place," shouted a fat, pimply seaman apprentice who had lost his white hat. "This here is the hoorhouse that chief was telling us about." A stringy-looking 3rd class boatswain's mate pushed him aside and cased the living room. "You're right, Slab," he said. "But it don't look like much, even for Stateside. I seen better tail in Naples, Italy." "How much, hey," boomed a large seaman with adenoids, who was holding a Mason jar full of white lightning. "Oh, my god," said Meatball.

Outside the temperature remained constant at 37 degrees Fahrenheit. In the hothouse Aubade stood absently caressing the branches of a young mimosa, hearing a motif of sap-rising, the rough and unresolved anticipatory theme of those fragile pink blossoms which, it is said, insure fertility. That music rose in a tangled tracery: arabesques of order competing fugally with the improvised discords of the party downstairs, which peaked sometimes in cusps and ogees of noise. That precious signal-to-noise ratio, whose delicate balance required every calorie of her strength, seesawed inside the small tenuous skull as she watched Callisto, sheltering the bird. Callisto was trying to confront any idea of the heat-death now, as he nuzzled the feathery lump in his hands. He sought correspondences. Sade, of course. And Temple Drake, gaunt and hopeless in her little park in Paris, at the end of *Sanctuary*. Final equilibrium. *Nightwood*. And the tango. Any tango, but more than any perhaps the sad sick dance in Stravinsky's *L'Histoire du Soldat*. He thought back: what had tango music been for them after the war, what meanings had he missed in all the stately coupled automatons in the *cafés-dansants*, or in the metronomes which had ticked behind the eyes of his own partners? Not even the clean constant winds of Switzerland could cure the *grippe espagnole*: Stravinsky had had it, they all had had it. And how many musicians were left after Passchendaele, after the Marne? It came down in this case to seven: violin, double-bass. Clarinet, bassoon. Cornet, trombone. Tympani. Almost as if any tiny troupe of saltimbanques had set about conveying the same information as a full pit-orchestra. There was hardly a full complement left in Europe. Yet with violin and tympani Stravinsky had managed to communicate in that tango the same exhaustion, the same airlessness one saw in the slicked-down youths who were trying to imitate Vernon Castle, and in their mistresses, who simply did not care. *Ma maîtresse*. Celeste. Returning to Nice after the second war he had found that café replaced by a perfume shop which catered to American tourists. And no secret vestige of her in the cobblestones or in the old pension next door; no perfume to match her breath heavy with the sweet Spanish wine she always drank. And so instead he had purchased a Henry Miller novel and left for Paris, and read the book on the train so that when he arrived he had been given at least a little forewarning. And saw that Celeste and the others and even Temple Drake were not all that had changed. "Aubade," he said, "my head aches." The sound of his voice generated in the girl an answering scrap of melody. Her movement toward the kitchen, the towel, the cold water, and his eyes following her formed a weird and intricate canon; as she placed the compress on his forehead his sigh of gratitude seemed to signal a new subject, another series of modulations.

"No," Meatball was still saying, "no, I'm afraid not. This is not a house of ill repute. I'm sorry, really I am." Slab was adamant. "But the chief said," he kept repeating. The seaman offered to swap the moonshine for a good piece. Meatball looked around frantically, as if seeking assistance. In the middle of the room, the Duke di Angelis quartet were engaged in a historic moment. Vincent was seated and the others standing: they were going through the motions of a group having a session, only without instruments. "I say," Meatball said. Duke moved his head a few times, smiled faintly, lit a cigarette, and eventually caught sight of Meatball. "Quiet, man," he whispered. Vincent began to fling his arms around, his fists clenched; then, abruptly, was still, then repeated the performance. This went on for a few minutes while Meatball sipped his drink moodily. The navy had withdrawn to the kitchen. Finally at some invisible signal the group stopped tapping their feet and Duke grinned and said, "At least we ended together."

Meatball glared at him. "I say," he said. "I have this new conception, man," Duke said. "You remember your namesake. You remember Gerry."

"No," said Meatball. "I'll remember April, if that's any help."

"As a matter of fact," Duke said, "it was Love for Sale. Which shows how much you know. The point is, it was Mulligan, Chet Baker and that crew, way back then, out yonder. You dig?"

"Baritone sax," Meatball said. "Something about a baritone sax."

"But no piano, man. No guitar. Or accordion. You know what that means."

"Not exactly," Meatball said.

"Well first let me just say, that I am no Mingus, no John Lewis. Theory was never my strong point. I mean things like reading were always difficult for me and all –"

"I know," Meatball said drily. "You got your card taken away because you changed key on Happy Birthday at a Kiwanis Club picnic."

"Rotarian. But it occurred to me, in one of these flashes of insight, that if that first quartet of Mulligan's had no piano, it could only mean one thing."

"No chords," said Paco, the baby-faced bass.

"What he is trying to say," Duke said, "is no root chords. Nothing to listen to while you blow a horizontal line. What one does in such a case is, one *thinks* the roots."

A horrified awareness was dawning on Meatball. "And the next logical extension," he said.

"Is to think everything," Duke announced with simple dignity. "Roots, line, everything."

Meatball looked at Duke, awed. "But," he said.

"Well," Duke said modestly, "there are a few bugs to work out."

"But," Meatball said.

"Just listen," Duke said. "You'll catch on." And off they went again into orbit, presumably somewhere around the asteroid belt. After a while Krinkles made an embouchure and started moving his fingers and Duke clapped his hand to his forehead. "Oaf!" he roared. "The new head we're using, you remember, I wrote last night?" "Sure," Krinkles said, "the new head. I come in on the bridge. All your heads I come in then." "Right," Duke said. "So why –" "Wha," said Krinkles, "16 bars, I wait, I come in –" "16?" Duke said. "No. No, Krinkles. Eight you waited. You want me to sing it? A cigarette that bears a lipstick's traces, an airline ticket to romantic places." Krinkles scratched his head. "These Foolish Things, you mean." "Yes," Duke said, "yes, Krinkles. Bravo." "Not I'll Remember April," Krinkles said. "*Minghe morte*," said Duke. "I *figured* we were playing it a little slow," Krinkles said. Meatball chuckled. "Back to the old drawing board," he said. "No, man," Duke said, "back to the airless void." And they took off again, only it seemed Paco was playing in G sharp while the rest were in E flat, so they had to start all over.

In the kitchen two of the girls from George Washington and the sailors were singing Let's All Go Down and Piss on the Forrestal. There was a two-handed, bilingual *morra* game on over by the icebox. Saul had filled several paper bags with water and was sitting on the fire escape, dropping them on passersby in the street. A fat government girl in a Bennington sweatshirt, recently engaged to an ensign attached to the Forrestal, came charging into the kitchen, head lowered, and butted Slab in the stomach. Figuring this was as good an excuse for a fight as any, Slab's buddies piled in. The *morra* players were nose-to-nose, screaming *trois, sette* at the tops of their lungs. From the shower the girl Meatball had taken out of the sink announced that she was drowning. She had apparently sat on the drain and the water was now up to her neck. The noise in Meatball's apartment had reached a sustained, ungodly crescendo.

Meatball stood and watched, scratching his stomach lazily. The way he figured, there were only about two ways he could cope: (a) lock himself in the closet and maybe eventually they would all go away, or (b) try to calm everybody down, one by one. (a) was certainly the more attractive alternative. But then he started thinking about that closet. It was dark and stuffy and he would be alone. He did not feature being alone. And then this crew off the good ship Lollipop or whatever it was might take it upon themselves to kick down the closet door, for a lark. And if that happened he would be, at the very least, embarrassed. The other way was more a pain in the neck, but probably better in the long run.

So he decided to try and keep his lease-breaking party from deteriorating into total chaos: he gave wine to the sailors and separated the *morra* players; he introduced the fat government girl to Sandor Rojas, who would keep her out of trouble; he helped the girl in the shower to dry off and get into bed; he had another talk with Saul; he called a repairman for the refrigerator, which someone had discovered was on the blink. This is what he did until nightfall, when most of the revellers had passed out and the party trembled on the threshold of its third day.

Upstairs Callisto, helpless in the past, did not feel the faint rhythm inside the bird begin to slacken and fail. Aubade was by the window, wandering the ashes of her own lovely world; the temperature held steady, the sky had become a uniform darkening gray. Then something from downstairs – a girl's scream, an overturned chair, a glass dropped on the floor, he would never know what exactly – pierced that private time-warp and he became aware of the faltering, the constriction of muscles, the tiny tossings of the bird's head; and his own pulse began to pound more fiercely, as if trying to compensate. "Aubade," he called weakly, "he's dying." The girl, flowing and rapt, crossed the hothouse to gaze down at Callisto's hands. The two remained like that, poised, for one minute, and two, while the heartbeat ticked a graceful diminuendo down at last into stillness. Callisto raised his head slowly. "I held him," he protested, impotent with the wonder of it, "to give him the warmth of my body. Almost as if I were communicating life to him, or a sense of life. What has happened? Has the transfer of heat ceased to work? Is there no more . . ." He did not finish.

"I was just at the window," she said. He sank back, terrified. She stood a moment more, irresolute; she had sensed his obsession long ago, realized somehow that that constant 37 was now decisive. Suddenly then, as if seeing the single and unavoidable conclusion to all this she moved swiftly to the window before Callisto could speak; tore away the drapes and smashed out the glass with two exquisite hands which came away bleeding and glistening with splinters; and turned to face the man on the bed and wait with him until the moment of equilibrium was reached, when 37 degrees Fahrenheit should prevail both outside and inside, and forever, and the hovering, curious dominant of their separate lives should resolve into a tonic of darkness and the final absence of all motion.

ERRAND

Raymond Carver

The life of **Raymond Carver** (1938–1988) was cut short by lung cancer, rather than booze. Whilst his life may have been short, his legacy is large – together with Richard Ford and Tobias Wolff he came to incarnate the soul of North American writing in the 1970s and 1980s, what Bill Buford once termed "dirty realism". Carver's collections include *Will You Please Be Quiet, Please?*, *What We Talk About When We Talk About Love*, *Cathedral* and *Elephant*.

Chekhov. On the evening of 22 March 1897, he went to dinner in Moscow with his friend and confidant Alexei Suvorin. This Suvorin was a very rich newspaper and book publisher, a reactionary, a self-made man whose father was a private at the battle of Borodino. Like Chekhov, he was the grandson of a serf. They had that in common: each had peasant's blood in his veins. Otherwise, politically and temperamentally, they were miles apart. Nevertheless, Suvorin was one of Chekhov's few intimates, and Chekhov enjoyed his company.

Naturally, they went to the best restaurant in the city, a former town house called the Hermitage – a place where it could take hours, half the night even, to get through a ten-course meal that would, of course, include several wines, liqueurs, and coffee. Chekhov was impeccably dressed, as always – a dark suit and waistcoat, his usual pince-nez. He looked that night very much as he looks in the photographs taken of him during this period. He was relaxed, jovial. He shook hands with the maître d', and with a glance took in the large dining room. It was brilliantly illuminated by ornate chandeliers, the tables occupied by elegantly dressed men and women. Waiters came and went ceaselessly. He had just been seated across the table from Suvorin when suddenly, without warning, blood began gushing from his mouth. Suvorin and two waiters helped him to the gentlemen's room and tried to stanch the flow of blood with ice packs. Suvorin saw him back to his own hotel and had a bed prepared for Chekhov in one of the rooms of the suite. Later, after another hemorrhage, Chekhov allowed himself to be moved to a clinic that specialized in the treatment of tuberculosis and related respiratory infections. When Suvorin visited him there, Chekhov apologized for the "scandal" at the restaurant three nights earlier but continued to insist there was nothing seriously wrong. "He laughed and jested as usual," Suvorin noted in his diary, "while spitting blood into a large vessel."

Maria Chekhov, his younger sister, visited Chekhov in the clinic during the last days of March. The weather was miserable; a sleet storm was in progress, and frozen heaps of snow lay everywhere. It was hard for her to wave down a carriage to take her to the hospital. By the time she arrived she was filled with dread and anxiety.

"Anton Pavlovich lay on his back," Maria wrote in her *Memoirs*. "He was not allowed to speak. After greeting him, I went over to the table to hide my emotions." There, among bottles of champagne, jars of caviar, bouquets of flowers from well-wishers, she saw something that terrified her: a freehand drawing, obviously done by a specialist in these matters, of Chekhov's lungs. It was the kind of sketch a doctor often makes in order to show his patient what he thinks is taking place. The lungs were outlined in blue, but the upper parts were filled in with red. "I realized they were diseased," Maria wrote.

Leo Tolstoy was another visitor. The hospital staff were awed to find themselves in the presence of the country's greatest writer. The most famous man in Russia? Of course they had to let him in to see Chekhov, even though "nonessential" visitors were forbidden. With much obsequiousness on the part of the nurses and resident doctors, the bearded, fierce-looking old man was shown into Chekhov's room. Despite his low opinion of Chekhov's abilities as a playwright (Tolstoy felt the plays were static and lacking in any moral vision. "Where do your characters take you?" he once demanded of Chekhov. "From the sofa to the junk room and back"), Tolstoy liked Chekhov's short stories. Furthermore, and quite simply, he loved the man. He told Gorky, "What a beautiful, magnificent man: modest and quiet, like a girl. He even walks like a girl. He's simply wonderful." And Tolstoy wrote in his journal (everyone kept a journal or a diary in those days), "I am glad I love . . . Chekhov."

Tolstoy removed his woollen scarf and bearskin coat, then lowered himself into a chair next to Chekhov's bed. Never mind that Chekhov was taking medication and not permitted to talk, much less carry on a conversation. He had to listen, amazedly, as the Count began to discourse on his theories of the immortality of the soul. Concerning that visit, Chekhov later wrote, "Tolstoy assumes that all of us (humans and animals alike) will live on in a principle (such as reason or love) the essence and goals of which are a mystery to us. . . . I have no use for that kind of immortality. I don't understand it, and Lev Nikolayevich was astonished I didn't."

Nevertheless, Chekhov was impressed with the solicitude shown by Tolstoy's visit. But, unlike Tolstoy, Chekhov didn't believe in an afterlife and never had. He didn't believe in anything that couldn't be apprehended by one or more of his five senses. And as far as his outlook on life and writing went, he once told someone that he lacked "a political, religious, and philosophical world view. I change it every month, so I'll have to limit myself to the description of how my heroes love, marry, give birth, die, and how they speak."

Earlier, before his TB was diagnosed, Chekhov had remarked, "When a peasant has consumption, he says, 'There's nothing I can do. I'll go off in the spring with the melting of the snows.'" (Chekhov himself died in the summer, during a heat wave.) But once Chekhov's own tuberculosis was discovered he continually tried to minimize the seriousness of his condition. To all appearances, it was as if he felt, right up to the end, that he might be able to throw off the disease as he would a lingering catarrh. Well into his final days, he spoke with seeming conviction of the possibility of an improvement. In fact, in a letter written shortly before his end, he went so far as to tell his sister that he was "getting fat" and felt much better now that he was in Badenweiler.

Badenweiler is a spa and resort city in the western area of the Black Forest, not far from Basel. The Vosges are visible from nearly anywhere in the city, and in those days the air was pure and invigorating. Russians had been going there for years to soak in the hot mineral baths and promenade on the boulevards. In June, 1904, Chekhov went there to die.

Earlier that month, he'd made a difficult journey by train from Moscow to Berlin. He traveled with his wife, the actress Olga Knipper, a woman he'd met in 1898 during rehearsals for *The seagull*. Her contemporaries describe her as an excellent actress. She was talented, pretty, and almost ten years younger than the playwright. Chekhov had been immediately attracted to her, but was slow to act on his feelings. As always, he preferred a flirtation to marriage. Finally, after a three-year courtship involving many separations, letters, and the inevitable misunderstandings, they were at last married, in a private ceremony in Moscow, on 25 May 1901. Chekhov was enormously happy. He called Olga his "pony", and sometimes "dog" or "puppy". He was also fond of addressing her as "little turkey" or simply as "my joy".

In Berlin, Chekhov consulted with a renowned specialist in pulmonary disorders, a Dr Karl Ewald. But, according to an eyewitness, after the doctor examined Chekhov he threw up his hands and left the room without a word. Chekhov was too far gone for help: this Dr Ewald was furious with himself for not being able to work miracles, and with Chekhov for being so ill.

A Russian journalist happened to visit the Chekhovs at their hotel and sent back this dispatch to his editor: "Chekhov's days are numbered. He seems mortally ill, is terribly thin, coughs all the time, gasps for breath at the slightest movement, and is running a high temperature." This same journalist saw the Chekhovs off at Potsdam Station when they boarded their train for Badenweiler. According to his account, "Chekhov had trouble making his way up the small staircase at the station. He had to sit down for several minutes to catch his breath." In fact, it was painful for Chekhov to move: his legs ached continually and his insides hurt. The disease had attacked his intestines and spinal cord. At this point he had less than a month to live. When Chekhov spoke of his condition now, it was, according to Olga, "with an almost reckless indifference".

Dr Schwöhrer was one of the many Badenweiler physicians who earned a good living by treating the well-to-do who came to the spa seeking relief from various maladies. Some of his patients were ill and infirm, others simply old and hypochondriacal. But Chekhov's was a special case: he was clearly beyond help and in his last days. He was also very famous. Even Dr Schwöhrer knew his name: he'd read some of Chekhov's stories in a German magazine. When he examined the writer early in June, he voiced his appreciation of Chekhov's art but kept his medical opinions to himself. Instead, he prescribed a diet of cocoa, oatmeal drenched in butter, and strawberry tea. This last was supposed to help Chekhov sleep at night.

On 13 June, less than three weeks before he died, Chekhov wrote a letter to his mother in which he told her his health was on the mend. In it he said, "It's likely that I'll be completely cured in a week." Who knows why he said this? What could he have been thinking? He was a doctor himself, and he knew better. He was dying, it was as simple and as unavoidable as that. Nevertheless, he sat out on the balcony of his hotel room and read railway timetables. He asked for information on sailings of boats bound for Odessa from Marseilles. But he *knew*. At this stage he had to have known. Yet in one of the last letters he ever wrote he told his sister he was growing stronger by the day.

He no longer had any appetite for literary work, and hadn't for a long time. In fact, he had very nearly failed to complete *The Cherry Orchard* the year before. Writing that play was the hardest thing he'd ever done in his life. Toward the end, he was able to manage only six or seven lines a day. "I've started losing heart," he wrote Olga. "I feel I'm finished as a writer, and every sentence strikes me as worthless and of no use whatever." But he didn't stop. He finished his play in October 1903. It was the last thing he ever wrote, except for letters and a few entries in his notebook.

A little after midnight on 2 July 1904, Olga sent someone to fetch Dr Schwöhrer. It was an emergency: Chekhov was delirious. Two young Russians on holiday happened to have the adjacent room, and Olga hurried next door to explain what was happening. One of the youths was in his bed asleep, but the other was still awake, smoking and reading. He left the hotel at a run to find Dr Schwöhrer. "I can still hear the sound of the gravel under his shoes in the silence of that stifling July night," Olga wrote later on in her memoirs. Chekhov was hallucinating, talking about sailors, and there were snatches of something about the Japanese. "You don't put ice on an empty stomach," he said when she tried to place an ice pack on his chest.

Dr Schwöhrer arrived and unpacked his bag, all the while keeping his gaze fastened on Chekhov, who lay gasping in the bed. The sick man's pupils were dilated and his temples glistened with sweat. Dr Schwöhrer's face didn't register anything. He was not an emotional man, but he knew Chekhov's end was near. Still, he was a doctor, sworn to do his utmost, and Chekhov held on to life, however tenuously. Dr Schwöhrer prepared a hypodermic and administered an injection of camphor, something that was supposed to speed up the heart. But the injection didn't help – nothing, of course, could have helped. Nevertheless, the doctor made known to Olga his intention of sending for oxygen. Suddenly, Chekhov roused himself, became lucid, and said quietly, "What's the use? Before it arrives I'll be a corpse."

Dr Schwöhrer pulled on his big moustache and stared at Chekhov. The writer's cheeks were sunken and gray, his complexion waxen; his breath was raspy. Dr Schwöhrer knew the time could be reckoned in minutes. Without a word, without conferring with Olga, he went over to an alcove where there was a telephone on the wall. He read the instructions for using the device. If he activated it by holding his finger on a button and turning a handle on the side of the phone, he could reach the lower regions of the hotel – the kitchen. He picked up the receiver, held it to his ear, and did as the instructions told him. When someone finally answered, Dr Schwöhrer ordered a bottle of the hotel's best champagne.

"How many glasses?" he was asked. "Three glasses!" the doctor shouted into the mouthpiece. "And hurry, do you hear?" It was one of those rare moments of inspiration that can easily enough be overlooked later on, because the action is so entirely appropriate it seems inevitable.

The champagne was brought to the door by a tired-looking young man whose blond hair was standing up. The trousers of his uniform were wrinkled, the creases gone, and in his haste he'd missed a loop while buttoning his jacket. His appearance was that of someone who'd been resting (slumped in a chair, say, dozing a little), when off in the distance the phone had clamored in the early-morning hours – great God in Heaven! – and the next thing he knew he was being shaken awake by a superior and told to deliver a bottle of Moët to Room 211. "And hurry, do you hear?"

The young man entered the room carrying a silver ice bucket with the champagne in it and a silver tray with three cut-crystal glasses. He found a place on the table for the bucket and glasses, all the while craning his neck, trying to see into the other room, where someone panted ferociously for breath. It was a dreadful, harrowing sound, and the young man lowered his chin into his collar and turned away as the ratchety breathing worsened. Forgetting himself, he stared out the open window toward the darkened city. Then this big imposing man with a thick moustache pressed some coins into his hand – a large tip, by the feel of it – and suddenly the young man saw the door open. He took some steps and found himself on the landing, where he opened his hand and looked at the coins in amazement.

Methodically, the way he did everything, the doctor went about the business of working the cork out of the bottle. He did it in such a way as to minimize, as much as possible, the festive explosion. He poured three glasses and, out of habit, pushed the cork back into the neck of the bottle. He then took the glasses of champagne over to the bed. Olga momentarily released her grip on Chekhov's hand – a hand, she said later, that burned her fingers. She arranged another pillow behind his head. Then she put the cool glass of champagne against Chekhov's palm and made sure his fingers closed around the stem. They exchanged looks – Chekhov, Olga, Dr Schwöhrer. They didn't touch glasses. There was no toast. What on earth was there to drink to? To death? Chekhov summoned his remaining strength and said, "It's been so long since I've had champagne." He brought the glass to his lips and drank. In a minute or two Olga took the empty glass from his hand and set it on the nightstand. Then Chekhov turned onto his side. He closed his eyes and sighed. A minute later, his breathing stopped.

Dr Schwöhrer picked up Chekhov's hand from the bedsheet. He held his fingers to Chekhov's wrist and drew a gold watch from his vest pocket, opening the lid of the watch as he did so. The second hand on the watch moved slowly, very slowly. He let it move around the face of the watch three times while he waited for signs of a pulse. It was three o'clock in the morning and still sultry in the room. Badenweiler was in the grip of its worst heat wave in years. All the windows in both rooms stood open, but there was no sign of a breeze. A large, black-winged moth flew through a window and banged wildly against the electric lamp. Dr Schwöhrer let go of Chekhov's wrist. "It's over," he said. He closed the lid of his watch and returned it to his vest pocket.

At once Olga dried her eyes and set about composing herself. She thanked the doctor for coming. He asked if she wanted some medication – laudanum, perhaps, or a few drops of valerian. She shook her head. She did have one request, though: before the authorities were notified and the newspapers found out, before the time came when Chekhov was no longer in her keeping, she wanted to be alone with him for a while. Could the doctor help with this? Could he withhold, for a while anyway, news of what had just occurred?

Dr Schwöhrer stroked his moustache with the back of a finger. Why not? After all, what difference would it make to anyone whether this matter became known now or a few hours from now? The only detail that remained was to fill out a death certificate, and this could be done at his office later on in the morning, after he'd slept a few hours. Dr Schwöhrer nodded his agreement and prepared to leave. He murmured a few words of condolence. Olga inclined her head. "An honor," Dr Schwöhrer said. He picked up his bag and left the room and, for that matter, history.

It was at this moment that the cork popped out of the champagne bottle; foam spilled down onto the table. Olga went back to Chekhov's bedside. She sat on a footstool, holding his hand, from time to time stroking his face. "There were no human voices, no everyday sounds," she wrote. "There was only beauty, peace, and the grandeur of death."

She stayed with Chekhov until daybreak, when thrushes began to call from the garden below. Then came the sound of tables and chairs being moved about down there. Before long, voices carried up to her. It was then a knock sounded at the door. Of course she thought it must be an official of some sort – the medical examiner, say, or someone from the police who had questions to ask and forms for her to fill out, or maybe, just maybe, it could be Dr Schwöhrer returning with a mortician to render assistance in embalming and transporting Chekhov's remains back to Russia.

But, instead, it was the same blond young man who'd brought the champagne a few hours earlier. This time, however, his uniform trousers were neatly pressed, with stiff creases in front, and every button on his snug green jacket was fastened. He seemed quite another person. Not only was he wide awake but his plump cheeks were smooth-shaven, his hair was in place, and he appeared anxious to please. He was holding a porcelain vase with three long-stemmed yellow roses. He presented these to Olga with a smart click of his heels. She stepped back and let him into the room. He was there, he said, to collect the glasses, ice bucket, and tray, yes. But he also wanted to say that, because of the extreme heat, breakfast would be served in the garden this morning. He hoped this weather wasn't too bothersome; he apologized for it.

The woman seemed distracted. While he talked, she turned her eyes away and looked down at something in the carpet. She crossed her arms and held her elbows. Meanwhile, still holding his vase, waiting for a sign, the young man took in the details of the room. Bright sunlight flooded through the open windows. The room was tidy and seemed undisturbed, almost untouched. No garments were flung over chairs, no shoes, stockings, braces, or stays were in evidence, no open suitcases. In short, there was no clutter, nothing but the usual heavy pieces of hotel-room furniture. Then, because the woman was still looking down, he looked down, too, and at once spied a cork near the toe of his shoe. The woman did not see it – she was looking somewhere else. The young man wanted to bend over and pick up the cork, but he was still holding the roses and was afraid of seeming to intrude even more by drawing any further attention to himself. Reluctantly, he left the cork where it was and raised his eyes. Everything was in order except for the uncorked, half-empty bottle of champagne that stood alongside two crystal glasses over on the little table. He cast his gaze about once more. Through an open door he saw that the third glass was in the bedroom, on the nightstand. But someone still occupied the bed! He couldn't see a face, but the figure under the covers lay perfectly motionless and quiet. He noted the figure and looked elsewhere. Then, for a reason he couldn't understand, a feeling of uneasiness took hold of him. He cleared his throat and moved his weight to the other leg. The woman still didn't look up or break her silence. The young man felt his cheeks grow warm. It occurred to him, quite without his having thought it through, that he should perhaps suggest an alternative to breakfast in the garden. He coughed, hoping to focus the woman's attention, but she didn't look at him. The distinguished foreign guests could, he said, take breakfast in their rooms this morning if they wished. The young man (his name hasn't survived, and it's likely he perished in the Great War) said he would be happy to bring up a tray. Two trays, he added, glancing uncertainly once again in the direction of the bedroom.

He fell silent and ran a finger around the inside of his collar. He didn't understand. He wasn't even sure the woman had been listening. He didn't know what else to do now; he was still holding the vase. The sweet odor of the roses filled his nostrils and inexplicably caused a pang of regret. The entire time he'd been waiting, the woman had apparently been lost in thought. It was as if all the while he'd been standing there, talking, shifting his weight, holding his flowers, she had been someplace else, somewhere far from Badenweiler. But now she came back to herself, and her face assumed another expression. She raised her eyes, looked at him, and then shook her head. She seemed to be struggling to understand what on earth this young man could be doing there in the room holding a vase with three yellow roses. Flowers? She hadn't ordered flowers.

The moment passed. She went over to her handbag and scooped up some coins. She drew out a number of banknotes as well. The young man touched his lips with his tongue; another large tip was forthcoming, but for what? What did she want him to do? He'd never before waited on such guests. He cleared his throat once more.

No breakfast, the woman said. Not yet, at any rate. Breakfast wasn't the important thing this morning. She required something else. She needed him to go out and bring back a mortician. Did he understand her? Herr Chekhov was dead, you see. *Comprenezvous?* Young man? Anton Chekhov was dead. Now listen carefully to me, she said. She wanted him to go downstairs and ask someone at the front desk where he could go to find the most respected mortician in the city. Someone reliable, who took great pains in his work and whose manner was appropriately reserved. A mortician, in short, worthy of a great artist. Here, she said, and pressed the money on him. Tell them downstairs that I have specifically requested you to perform this duty for me. Are you listening? Do you understand what I'm saying to you?

The young man grappled to take in what she was saying. He chose not to look again in the direction of the other room. He had sensed that something was not right. He became aware of his heart beating rapidly under his jacket, and he felt perspiration break out on his forehead. He didn't know where he should turn his eyes. He wanted to put the vase down.

Please do this for me, the woman said. I'll remember you with gratitude. Tell them downstairs that I insist. Say that. But don't call any unnecessary attention to yourself or to the situation. Just say that this is necessary, that I request it – and that's all. Do you hear me? Nod if you understand. Above all, don't raise an alarm. Everything else, all the rest, the commotion – that'll come soon enough. The worst is over. Do we understand each other?

The young man's face had grown pale. He stood rigid, clasping the vase. He managed to nod his head.

After securing permission to leave the hotel he was to proceed quietly and resolutely, though without any unbecoming haste, to the mortician's. He was to behave exactly as if he were engaged on a very important errand, nothing more. He *was* engaged on an important errand, she said. And if it would help keep his movements purposeful he should imagine himself as someone moving down the busy sidewalk carrying in his arms a porcelain vase of roses that he had to deliver to an important man. (She spoke quietly, almost confidentially, as if to a relative or a friend.) He could even tell himself that the man he was going to see was expecting him, was perhaps impatient for him to arrive with his flowers. Nevertheless, the young man was not to become excited and run, or otherwise break his stride. Remember the vase he was carrying! He was to walk briskly, comporting himself at all times in as dignified a manner as possible. He should keep walking until he came to the mortician's house and stood before the door. He would then raise the brass knocker and let it fall, once, twice, three times. In a minute the mortician himself would answer.

This mortician would be in his forties, no doubt, or maybe early fifties – bald, solidly built, wearing steel-frame spectacles set very low on his nose. He would be modest, unassuming, a man who would ask only the most direct and necessary questions. An apron. Probably he would be wearing an apron. He might even be wiping his hands on a dark towel while he listened to what was being said. There'd be a faint whiff of formaldehyde on his clothes. But it was all right, and the young man shouldn't worry. He was nearly a grown-up now and shouldn't be frightened or repelled by any of this. The mortician would hear him out. He was a man of restraint and bearing, this mortician, someone who could help allay people's fears in this situation, not increase them. Long ago he'd acquainted himself with death in all its various guises and forms; death held no surprises for him any longer, no hidden secrets. It was this man whose services were required this morning.

The mortician takes the vase of roses. Only once while the young man is speaking does the mortician betray the least flicker of interest, or indicate that he's heard anything out of the ordinary. But the one time the young man mentions the name of the deceased, the mortician's eyebrows rise just a little. Chekhov, you say? Just a minute, and I'll be with you.

Do you understand what I'm saying, Olga said to the young man. Leave the glasses. Don't worry about them. Forget about crystal wineglasses and such. Leave the room as it is. Everything is ready now. We're ready. Will you go?

But at that moment the young man was thinking of the cork still resting near the toe of his shoe. To retrieve it he would have to bend over, still gripping the vase. He would do this. He leaned over. Without looking down, he reached out and closed it into his hand.

THE DYING ROOM

Georgina Hammick

Georgina Hammick (b.1939) was born in Hampshire, educated in Kenya
and England and later attended the Academie Julian in Paris as well as
the Salisbury School of Art. She is the author of *People for Lunch*, *Spoilt*
and *Green Man Running*.

I think I left my wireless in the drawing room, his mother said. Could you get
it? I'd be grateful.

His mother and he were in the kitchen. He took a big breath. He said, You
can't use that word any more, I'm sorry, we've decided.

What word are you talking about? his mother said. She took a tray of cheese
tartlets from the oven and put them on the table. His mother is a cook. She cooks
for her family when they're at home and she cooks professionally: for other
women's freezers and other women's lunch and dinner parties. She also supplies,
on a regular basis, her local delicatessen with pâtés and terrines and tarts and
quiches. Blast, these look a bit burnt to me, his mother said. Do they look burnt
to you? What word can't I use?

"Drawing room", he said. It's an anachronism, it's irrelevant. It's snobbish. It
has associations with mindless West End theatre. It's embarrassing.

His mother said nothing for a minute. She looked thoughtful; she looked
thoughtfully at her feet. Then she said, Who are "we"? "We" who have decided?

My sisters and I, he told her. Your children. All of them.

I see, his mother said. First I've heard of this, I have to say.

The point is, he said, our friends, the ones we bring here, find it offensive – or
a joke. And so do we. It is offensive, and ridiculous, to continue to use a word
that means nothing to ninety-nine per cent of the population, that ninety-nine
per cent of the population does not use.

Hang on a minute, his mother said, I just want to get this straight. You're
at university, and most of the people you bring here, from whatever background, are students too. Are you saying that this doesn't make you an elite
of some kind? Are you telling me that the words you use in your essays are
the words ninety-nine per cent of the population uses? Don't look at me like
that, his mother said. If you want to know, I don't feel that strongly about
"drawing room"; it's what your father called it, it's the habit of a lifetime,
but you can break habits. I have wondered about it. The room in question
is rather small for a drawing room. What word would you like me to use
instead? "Lounge"?

There were other words, he told his mother.

Are there? his mother said. What's wrong with "lounge"? I bet "lounge" is what ninety-nine per cent of the population uses. But if you don't like it, if its airport and hotel connotations bother you, how about "front room"? Will that do?

The room his mother calls the "drawing room" is at the back of the house and looks on to the back garden. It looks on to a square of lawn with three apple trees on it, two mixed borders either side and, beyond the lawn and divided from it by a box hedge, the vegetable garden: peasticks and bean poles and a rusty fruit cage and a potting shed. A cottage garden, his mother has always described it as.

I can't call it the "morning room", his mother murmured, more to herself than to him, because we tend to use it mostly in the evenings. I can't call it the "music room" because none of us plays an instrument, and because all those gramophones – those CD and tape-deck affairs – are in your bedrooms. To call it the "smoking room", though when you're at home accurate, would be tantamount to encouraging a health-wrecking practice I deplore.

His mother was mocking him. She was, as usual, refusing to address the issue, a serious and important one. She was declining to engage with the argument. He said so.

Address the issue? Engage with the argument? His mother turned the phrases over and weighed them in invisible scales. Engage with the argument. Is that an expression ninety-nine per cent of the pop . . .? Well, no matter. Where was I? I know, in the "parlour". I like "parlour", I rather go for "parlour". It's an old word. It conjures up monks in monasteries having a chinwag, it conjures up people in ruffs having a tête-à-tête. Then there's the ice-cream side of it, of course – oh, and massage, and nail buffing and leg waxing . . . Which reminds me . . .

Oh for God's sake, he said.

I like "parlour", his mother said. I think I like "parlour" best. But on the other hand – *parlare, parlatorium* – a bit too elitist, don't you think? On the whole?

Look, he said, there are other names for rooms, ordinary ones, not jokey or archaic or patronising, that you haven't mentioned yet, that you seem to be deliberately avoiding.

If you mean "sitting room", his mother said, I did think of it, it did occur to me, and then I thought, No, too safe, a compromise choice, with a whiff of amontillado about it.

It's less offensive than "drawing room". And it's more exact – people do tend to sit in rooms.

Probably it is for you, his mother said. You and your siblings and friends are great sitters. Great loungers and withdrawers too, I might say. But I don't have that much time for sitting. In the room that for the moment shall be nameless I tend to stand.

His mother was standing as she said this. She was standing by the stove, lifting the lid from the saucepan, giving the soup a stir. He was sitting on a chair at the table, lounging perhaps. He sat up. He stood up.

You haven't got an ashtray, his mother said, here, use this. By the way, his mother said, did I ever tell you about the misprint your father found in the local paper once? In an estate agent's advertisement? "Five bed, two bath, kitchen, dining room, shitting room"? Or perhaps it wasn't a misprint, who can say? This soup doesn't taste of anything much, his mother said, come and try it. Come and tell me what you think it needs.

He took the spoon from his mother's hand and tasted her soup. It's okay, he said, it's fine, could do with more salt. The name you're avoiding, he said, the name we use, as you must have noticed, that we want you to use, is "living room". A room for living in. The room where people live. Graham Greene wrote a play about it. No, he said (for he could see his mother was about to interrupt him), there are no jokes to be made. I defy you to be satirical about this one. "Living room" is accurate. And it's classless, it embraces all. The pathetic thing is (and he banged his fist on the table) it'd be impossible to have this argument anywhere else but here! It'd be meaningless anywhere but in Little England. Christ, what a shower!

Nineteen fifty-three, was it? his mother said, or nineteen fifty-four? The year I saw *The Living Room*. Dorothy Tutin was made a star overnight – don't think that sort of thing happens any more, does it? I'd seen her in *Much Ado* at the Phoenix, but . . . Look, it's accuracy I want to quiz you about, his mother said. Pass me that colander, would you. No not that one, the red one. Think for a moment – where are we having this conversation? If we can be said to live anywhere, it's the kitchen – except for your grandfather, poor man, who lives in the lavatory. No, we live in the kitchen and we make occasional forays – withdraw, if you like – into –

You're so clever, he said, you think everything can be reduced to a clever, silly, word game.

No, his mother said, no I don't, I just want to understand your motives, which I suspect are suspect.

Our motives, our motive, is clear, he said. There's nothing eccentric about it. We're egalitarians and we want to live in an egalitarian world. Drawing rooms – withdrawing rooms, as no doubt you'd prefer – have no place in that world. They have nothing to do with the real world as it is now. They have to do with privilege and power. They have to do with tribalism in the worst sense.

His mother took a bunch of parsley from a jam jar on the windowsill. Do come and see what these sparrows are up to! she said. Damn, you're too late, she said. She put the parsley on a chopping board. Then she took five soup bowls off the dresser and put them in the bottom oven. She straightened up.

He said, Look, doesn't it embarrass you when you say "drawing room" to Mrs Todd, for example? Doesn't it make you feel uncomfortable? Doesn't it? It does us, I can tell you.

His mother looked astonished. She said, You astonish me. Why ever should it? It doesn't embarrass her. I'll tell you how it works. I say to her, Oh Mrs Todd, the children were down at the weekend, and you know what that means, so I think the drawing room could do with some special attention . . . or she'll say to me, Thought I might do the lounge through today, Mrs Symonds – kids home Sunday, were they? Point is, we have our own language, a language we feel comfortable in, and we stick to it. Both of us. Not just me. Don't think it's just me. But we understand each other. We do. And – though you may not believe this – we're fond of each other. We've got a lot in common. We're both working women, we're both widows. We've been seeing each other twice a week now for what? – fifteen years. I know a lot about her life, I know all about our Malcolm and our Cheryl and our Diane and our Diane's baby Gary – who's teething at the moment incidentally – and she knows even more about my life. I remember her birthday, and she – unlike some I could mention – always remembers mine. I went to see her when she was in hospital, and she came to see me when I was. She came on the bus the day after my op, and then later in the week she got Malcolm to drive her over after work. Malcolm's pick-up is very unreliable, you know. He spends all his Sundays working on it, but even so it invariably fails its MOT. If it isn't the gear box it's the brakes, and if it isn't the brakes it's the exhaust . . . I'm very much afraid Malcolm was sold a pup.

If you're such good friends, he said, if you know everything there is to know about Mrs Todd's life, how come you don't call her by her first name? How come she doesn't call you by your first name?

Ah, you can't catch me there, his mother said. The answer is because she doesn't want it. I asked her once. She'd been here about a year, and I said, Mrs Todd, don't you think we've known each other long enough to call each other by our Christian names? Mine's Elizabeth, as I expect you know. And she said, Think I'd rather leave things the way they are, if it's all the same to you, Mrs Symonds. So we did. I did feel crushed at the time, I did feel a bit snubbed, but I don't think she meant to snub me. I really don't think she did.

About "living room", he said.

Oh that, his mother said. If that's what you're set on, I'll give it a try. But if you want to bring Mrs Todd into line, I fear you've got problems – she's a "lounge" person, definitely. "Definitely" is another of her words. She says "definitely" very often when I'd say "yes". Do you find your microwave has made life easier, Mrs Todd? I'll ask her, and she'll say, Oh definitely, definitely. It definitely do, definitely. Mrs Todd is a very definite person. If you think you can get her to turn her lounge into a living room, well, good luck.

I never said I wanted her to alter anything, he said. You're putting words into my mouth. I never said that. Of course she can keep her lounge. We want you to get rid of your drawing room, which is quite different. He hesitated. He said, We won't bring our friends here unless you do.

Can I have that in writing? his mother said. Joke, she said, when she saw his frown. Could you pass me that baking tray please. Actually, Kit, I don't like your tone. Dictatorship and blackmail seem to be the names of your game. Why? Couldn't you wait for evolution to do the job? You won't have to wait long. "Nurseries" – in houses large enough to have a nursery – are mostly "play-rooms" now. "Studies" have turned themselves into "telly rooms". "Drawing rooms" are dying even as we speak. By the time my generation is under the sod, the only "drawing rooms" left will be in palaces and stately homes. Truly, you won't have to wait long.

If you want to make yourself useful, you could lay the table, his mother said.

What I don't understand, his mother said, is why you have to be so heavy about all this. If your friends don't like the vocabulary I use, couldn't you make a joke of it? Couldn't you just tell them your mother is an eccentric old bat? That sort of confession would improve your street cred no end, I should've thought.

There isn't any point in going on with this, he said. There isn't any point in trying to have a serious discussion with you. You're the personification of the English disease, the English upper class disease, of superciliousness. Everything you've said this morning, and the way you've said it, is offensive, but you can't even see it, you can't even hear it. If you knew the way you sound to ordinary people! "Our Malcolm" and "our Joanne" – mocking and superior, that's how you sound.

Diane, his mother said, Diane, not Joanne. I wasn't mocking, I assure you, I was borrowing. I was repeating. And who's calling who ordinary? No one's that ordinary. In my experience most people, when you get to know them, are extraordinary. Look, if you're not going to lay the table, d'you think you could stop hovering and sit down?

I didn't mean "ordinary", he said, I meant "other". Other people. You mentioned palaces and stately homes a minute ago, he said. What you don't seem to understand is that this place is a palace to some of the friends I bring here. In fact that's exactly what Julie said the first time she came down. She walked in the door and said, God, it's a palace! You never told me your mother lived in a fucking palace, Kit.

I don't get this, his mother said. First it's "drawing room", then it's the way I talk, now it's this house. You keep moving the goal posts. Are you saying people shouldn't be allowed to live in five-bedroomed houses, in five-and-a-half- – if you count the box room – bedroomed houses in case other people, who live in two-bedroomed houses or flats, might think of them as palaces? Is that what you're saying? I happen to know that Julie liked this house. She came down early one morning that first visit – you were still in bed – and had breakfast with me. She said, I really love this place, Elizabeth – it's magic. I'm going to live in a place like this one day. We went round the garden and she knew the names of everything. Monkshood! she said, my dad won't have monkshood in the garden . . . I was fond of Julie. She was a very nice girl. I was sorry when you gave her the push.

Martin found you frightening, he said. D'you remember Martin?

That's okay, I found Martin frightening, his mother said.

When I say "frightening" I mean "posh", he said. I met Martin in the pub the other night and he seemed a bit down and fed up with life – well, with his job really – and I asked him if he'd like to get away to the country this weekend. He wanted to know if you were going to be there. I said probably you would, it was your house. And he said, Well, think I'll give it a miss then. No offence, but your mother and her "drawing rooms" and "wirelesses" and "gramophones" are a bit posh for me. He pronounced it "poshe".

Well that hurts certainly. Yes it does, his mother said. Could you come here a minute, I can't read this without my specs, does it say two ounces or four?

Martin spent a lot of his childhood in care, you know, he said. Four ounces, he said. He was shunted from council home to council home. From the age of seven, that is. Before that he lived in a one-room flat with his parents. They ate in it and slept in it and his parents screwed in it. A lot of pain went on in that living room. His father beat his mother up in it – night after night after night. Dreadful, bloody beatings. If Martin tried to stop him he got beaten up too.

That is very dreadful, his mother said. Poor child. Poor Martin. I didn't know that. I am very sorry indeed about that.

So you can probably see why "drawing rooms" and such would put him off, he said. Piss him off. I mean, what the fuck have they got to do with his life, or with anything he knows about? Like fucking nothing.

Yes I do see, his mother said. I understand now why he's on the defensive. What I don't understand is, why, if you're so fond of him, you didn't warn me about all this before he came down here. It would have saved me asking him all sorts of tactless questions about his life and family, and him having to skate round them – which is what he did do.

How patronising can you be! he said. Martin doesn't need explaining, or explaining away, by me or anyone. He is himself, he is a valuable human being.

His mother took her mixing bowl and egg whisk to the sink and ran the tap over them. She turned the tap off, twisting it hard. Remind me to get something done about this washer, she said. She said, Why do I get the feeling that, for you, only one sort of person, from one sort of background, is a valuable human being? Why do I get the impression that, in your view, a person has to have been brought up in an obviously deprived environment to know anything about pain?

I haven't said that, he said.

So much so that I feel I've failed you, that you'd have preferred to have had Martin's childhood, that kind of misery being the only passport – as you would see it – to full membership of the human race.

You're silent, his mother said. She tapped him on the shoulder. Hey, look at me.

He looked out of the window.

Let me remind you of your father's childhood, his mother said. It was a very comfortable, green-belt childhood. There was a cook, Inez I think, and a maid. Two maids. There was a nanny until your father went away to school. There was a big garden with a shrubbery one end to play in – though he had to play by himself most of the time, of course, being an only child. There was all that. There were also your grandparents who hated each other. They slept at different ends of the house, but in the evenings when your grandfather came home from his office they sat together in the drawing room in their own special chairs and tormented each other. Your grandmother had the edge, she was the cleverer. She was frustrated. Nowadays, I suppose, she'd have been a career woman, and perhaps not married. From all the evidence she despised men. While this ritual was going on, while they goaded and persecuted each other, your father was made to sit in a corner and play with his Meccano or read a book. He was not allowed to interrupt and he was not allowed to leave the room. At six-forty-five on the dot your grandmother would take a key from the bunch on the thin leather belt she always wore and unlock the drinks cupboard, and the serious whisky drinking – and the serious torturing – would begin.

I know about that, he said, you've told me about that.

There was no blood, his mother said, there were no visible bruises, just –

I've got the point, he said, you've made your point.

When your father was dying I thought about the nightmare he'd had to endure while he was growing up. I wondered if it might have been responsible in some way for his illness, if the stress of it had made him vulnerable, damaged his immune system. D'you think that's possible?

Could be, he said. Could be. I don't know.

I wish you'd known him, his mother said. That's the worst of it, your never knowing him, or rather being too young to remember him. That photograph on my dressing table, the one of you aged eighteen months or so with Daddy. You're looking up at him and you're hugging his knees. Now I remember that occasion – I took the photograph. I remember the way you ran, well, staggered up the garden – you were a very late walker, you know, very slow to get yourself off your bottom – and threw yourself at him. You nearly toppled him. And then I pressed the button. I remember that afternoon very well. I remember your father telling me there was no point in taking any photographs, the light was too poor . . . well, I remember it all. I remember how tired your father was. He was already ill but we didn't know. I remember that you had a tantrum about ten minutes before I took the photograph. You lay on the grass and kicked and screamed. But you don't remember. You don't remember him, and you don't remember you – or any of it. It's just a photograph to you.

Cass and Anna remember him, he said, they say they do. They've told me things.

He did his dying in the drawing room – as it was then called – his mother said. He wanted to be downstairs so he could see into the garden – walk into it to begin with. When he was given his death sentence, at Christmas, he set himself some targets. The start of the cricket season – on telly – was one. The peonies and irises out was another. We had wonderful irises in those days, the proper rhizomatous sort, the tall bearded ones, a huge bed of them your father made. He was passionate about his irises, quite boring about them. Irises are tricky things, they like being by themselves, they don't like being moved, they have to have full sun, you're supposed to divide them every three years immediately after flowering – it's quite a performance. It takes patience to grow good irises, and your father was not a patient man. He was a quick-tempered man. I was quite jealous of his irises and all the patient attention they got. Every weekend spent in the garden – or the bloody potting shed. Graham Greene has got a lot to answer for, if you ask me.

He had not known about the irises. He said, Did he see them? Were they out in time?

Some of them were out, the ordinary white flags, and the blue ones. The red peonies were out, the *officinalis*, but the pale ones weren't – you know, the Chinese ones. The ones he liked best weren't.

I don't think I knew he died in the living room, he said. I don't think you ever told me that.

He didn't die in it, his mother said. About three weeks before he died we moved him upstairs. It had become impossible to look after him properly downstairs, and it was too noisy. Small children – you were only two and obstreperous – kept bursting in. When they carried him upstairs, which was difficult because he was in agony, I waited at the top, on the landing; and when he saw me he said, Next time I go down these stairs, folks, it'll be feet first. He said it to make me laugh, to make the doctor and the nurse – who'd made a sort of chair for him out of their hands – laugh. It was brave to make that joke, but it was cruel too, because three weeks later when he did go down the stairs, in his coffin, I kept remembering him coming up, I kept hearing him say, Feet first.

If I don't talk about it much, his mother said, it's because I don't like thinking about it. I prefer to remember your father before he got that bloody disease. He was a different person before he got it. I don't mean just because he looked different – obviously if someone loses six stone in a short time he's going to seem different, he's going to feel unfamiliar – I suppose because we tend to think of a person's shape as being part of their personality, of being them – but that wasn't the real problem. The real problem I discovered was the gap there is between the living and the dying. An enormous, unbridgeable gap.

We're all dying though, aren't we, he said. From the moment we're born you could say we're dying.

Don't give me that, his mother said, don't give me that claptrap. Could you move your elbow please, I'm trying to lay the table. I want to give you a knife and fork.

Sit down, he said, stop working and sit down and talk to me. Just for five minutes. You never sit down and talk. You never tell me anything. You never tell me anything about you.

It's lunch time, his mother said, we can't talk now. Grandpa will be starving. Could you go and tell him it's ready and give him a hand down the stairs. I fear we're going to have to have a lift put in, you know, or –

What is lunch? he said. What are we having? Fish fingers and peas? he said hopefully, beefburgers and beans, sausage and chips?

I wish you hadn't mentioned sausages, his mother said, why did you have to mention sausages? Okay, I'll tell you, his mother said (as though he'd asked her to, which he hadn't, he hadn't said a word), why not? I'll tell you. When your father was dying, before he got to the point of not wanting anything to eat at all, the only thing he wanted was sausages. I'd put my head round the door and ask him, What d'you fancy for lunch today, darling? and he'd say, Bangers and mash. Then I'd go away and cook him something quite other – something I thought would be nourishing and easy to digest, that would slip down. I'd bring in the tray – he'd be sitting with his back to me, shoulders stooped, head supported by a hand, looking out at the garden – and he'd say, without turning his head because turning and twisting were very painful for him, Doesn't smell like bangers. And I'd say, You just wait and see. I'd put the tray down on a chair, and tuck a napkin under his chin and adjust the invalid table and wheel it up over his knees, and put the plate on it and whip the cover off and say, There! Doesn't that look delicious? And he'd stare down at the plate. I asked for bangers, he'd say eventually. I was expecting bangers.

I don't think I let him have bangers more than twice in the whole of that five months, the whole time he was dying, his mother said. I don't know why I didn't give him what he asked for. I've tried to work out why I didn't.

He said nothing for a minute. Then he said, You thought they'd be hard for him to digest, you thought they'd make him uncomfortable.

Did I? his mother said. What would a bit of discomfort have mattered? He was dying, for God's sake! He wanted bangers.

Say something! his mother said. I've shocked you, haven't I? I can tell.

No. No, you haven't, he said. Look, I'd better go and get Grandpa, I'd better go and find the girls.

Could you bring me my wireless at the same time? his mother said, I want to hear the news. I'm not sure where I left it, downstairs I think, in the – in some room or other.

LIZZIE'S TIGER

Angela Carter

Angela Carter (1940–1992) is best known for her novels *Nights at the Circus* and *Wise Children*, but might be better known for her journalism, criticism and her short stories. Perhaps her finest work in fiction were retellings of tales told before, especially *The Bloody Chamber* and her two Virago *Book of Fairy Tales*. Fearsomely intelligent – "a day without an argument is like an egg without salt," – and wickedly funny, her death, aged fifty-two from cancer, only makes me wonder at what she might have gone on to do. She said, "Reading a book is like re-writing it for yourself. You bring to a novel, anything you read, all your experience of the world. You bring your history and you read it in your own terms." The story here was one of the last she wrote.

When the circus came to town and Lizzie saw the tiger, they were living on Ferry Street, in a very poor way. It was the time of the greatest parsimony in their father's house; everyone knows the first hundred thousand is the most difficult and the dollar bills were breeding slowly, slowly, even if he practised a little touch of usury on the side to prick his cash in the direction of greater productivity. In another ten years' time, the War between the States would provide rich pickings for the coffin-makers, but, back then, back in the Fifties, well – if he had been a praying man, he would have gone down on his knees for a little outbreak of summer cholera or a touch, just a touch, of typhoid. To his chagrin, there had been nobody to bill when he had buried his wife.

For, at that time, the girls were just freshly orphaned. Emma was thirteen, Lizzie four – stern and square, a squat rectangle of a child. Emma parted Lizzie's hair in the middle, stretched it back over each side of her bulging forehead and braided it tight. Emma dressed her, undressed her, scrubbed her night and morning with a damp flannel, and humped the great lump of little girl around in her arms whenever Lizzie would let her, although Lizzie was not a demonstrative child and did not show affection easily, except to the head of the house, and then only when she wanted something. She knew where the power was and, intuitively feminine in spite of her gruff appearance, she knew how to court it.

That cottage on Ferry – very well, it was a slum; but the undertaker lived on unconcerned among the stiff furnishings of his defunct marriage. His bits and pieces would be admired today if they turned up freshly beeswaxed in an antique store, but in those days they were plain old-fashioned, and time would only make them more so in that dreary interior, the tiny house he never mended, eroding clapboard and diseased paint, mildew on the dark wallpaper with a brown pattern like brains, the ominous crimson border round the top of the walls, the sisters sleeping in one room in one thrifty bed.

On Ferry, in the worst part of town, among the dark-skinned Portuguese fresh off the boat with their earrings, flashing teeth and incomprehensible speech, come over the ocean to work the mills whose newly erected chimneys closed in every perspective; every year more chimneys, more smoke, more newcomers, and the peremptory shriek of the whistle that summoned to labour as bells had once summoned to prayer.

The hovel on Ferry stood, or, rather, leaned at a bibulous angle on a narrow street cut across at an oblique angle by another narrow street, all the old wooden homes like an upset cookie jar of broken gingerbread houses lurching this way and that way, and the shutters hanging off their hinges and windows stuffed with old newspapers, and the snagged picket fence and raised voices in unknown tongues and howling of dogs who, since puppyhood, had known of the world only the circumference of their chain. Outside the parlour window were nothing but rows of counterfeit houses that sometimes used to scream.

Such was the anxious architecture of the two girls' early childhood.

A hand came in the night and stuck a poster, showing the head of a tiger, on to a picket fence. As soon as Lizzie saw the poster, she wanted to go to the circus, but Emma had no money, not a cent. The thirteen-year-old was keeping house at that time, the last skivvy just quit with bad words on both sides. Every morning, Father would compute the day's expenses, hand Emma just so much, no more. He was angry when he saw the poster on the fence; he thought the circus should have paid him rental for the use. He came home in the evening, sweet with embalming fluid, saw the poster, purpled with fury, ripped it off, tore it up.

Then it was supper-time. Emma was no great shakes at cookery and Father, dismissing the possibility of another costly skivvy until such time as plague struck, already pondered the cost-efficiency of remarriage; when Emma served up her hunks of cod, translucently uncooked within, her warmed-over coffee and a dank loaf of baker's bread, it almost put him in a courting mood, but that is not to say his meal improved his temper. So that, when his youngest climbed kitten-like upon his knee and, lisping, twining her tiny fingers in his gunmetal watch-chain, begged small change for the circus, he answered her with words of unusual harshness, for he truly loved this last daughter, whose obduracy recalled his own.

Emma unhandily darned a sock.

"Get that child to bed before I lose my temper!"

Emma dropped the sock and scooped up Lizzie, whose mouth set in dour lines of affront as she was borne off. The square-jawed scrap, deposited on the rustling straw mattress – oat straw, softest and cheapest – sat where she had been dropped and stared at the dust in a sunbeam. She seethed with resentment. It was moist midsummer, only six o'clock and still bright day outside.

She had a whim of iron, this one. She swung her feet on to the stool upon which the girls climbed down out of bed, thence to the floor. The kitchen door stood open for air behind the screen door. From the parlour came the low murmur of Emma's voice as she read *The Providence Journal* aloud to Father.

Next-door's lean and famished hound launched itself at the fence in a frenzy of yapping that concealed the creak of Lizzie's boots on the back porch. Unobserved, she was off – off and away! – trotting down Ferry Street, her cheeks pink with self-reliance and intent. She would not be denied. The circus! The word tinkled in her head with a red sound, as if it might signify a profane church.

"That's a tiger," Emma had told her as, hand in hand, they inspected the poster on their fence.

"A tiger is a big cat," Emma added instructively.

How big a cat?

A *very* big cat.

A dumpy, red-striped, regular cat of the small, domestic variety greeted Lizzie with a raucous mew from atop a gatepost as she stumped determinedly along Ferry Street; our cat, Ginger, whom Emma, in a small ecstasy of sentimental whimsy presaging that of her latter protracted spinsterhood, would sometimes call Miss Ginger, or even Miss Ginger Cuddles. Lizzie, however, sternly ignored Miss Ginger Cuddles. Miss Ginger Cuddles sneaked. The cat put out a paw as Lizzie brushed past, as if seeking to detain her, as if to suggest she took second thoughts as to her escapade, but, for all the apparent decision with which Lizzie put one firm foot before the other, she had not the least idea where the circus might be and would not have got there at all without the help of a gaggle of ragged Irish children from Corkey Row, who happened by in the company of a lean, black and tan, barking dog of unforeseen breed that had *this* much in common with Miss Ginger Cuddles, it could go wither it pleased.

This free-ranging dog with its easy-going grin took a fancy to Lizzie and, yapping with glee, danced around the little figure in the white pinafore as it marched along. Lizzie reached out to pat its head. She was a fearless girl.

The child-gang saw her pet their dog and took a fancy to her for the same reason as crows settle on one particular tree. Their wild smiles circled round her. "Going to the circus, are ye? See the clown and the ladies dancing?" Lizzie knew nothing about clowns and dancers, but she nodded, and one boy took hold of one hand, another of the other, so they raced her off between them. They soon saw her little legs could not keep up their pace, so the ten-year-old put her up on his shoulders where she rode like a lord. Soon they came to a field on the edge of town.

"See the big top?" There was a red and white striped tent of scarcely imaginable proportions, into which you could have popped the entire house on Ferry, and the yard too, with enough room to spare inside for another house, and another – a vast red and white striped tent, with ripping naphtha flares outside and, besides this, all manner of other tents, booths and stalls, dotted about the field, but most of all she was impressed by the great number of people, for it seemed to her that the whole town must be out tonight, yet, when they looked closely at the throng, nowhere at all was anyone who looked like she did, or her father did, or Emma; nowhere that old New England lantern jaw, those ice-blue eyes.

She was a stranger among these strangers, for all here were those the mills had brought to town, the ones with different faces. The plump, pink-cheeked Lancashire mill-hands, with brave red neckerchiefs; the sombre features of the Canucks imbibing fun with characteristic gloom; and the white smiles of the

Portuguese, who knew how to enjoy themselves, laughter tripping off their tipsy-sounding tongues.

"Here y'are!" announced her random companions as they dumped her down and, feeling they had amply done their duty by their self-imposed charge, they capered off among the throng, planning, perhaps, to slither under the canvas and so enjoy the shows for free, or even to pick a pocket or two to complete the treat, who knows?

Above the field, the sky now acquired the melting tones of the end of the day, the plush, smoky sunsets unique to these unprecedented industrial cities, sunsets never seen in this world before the Age of Steam that set the mills in motion that made us all modern.

At sunset, the incomparably grave and massive light of New England acquires a monumental, a Roman sensuality; under this sternly voluptuous sky, Lizzie abandoned herself to the unpremeditated smells and never-before-heard noises – hot fat in a vat of frying doughnuts; horse-dung; boiling sugar; frying onions; popping corn; freshly churned earth; vomit; sweat; cries of vendors; crack of rifles from the range; singsong of the white-faced clown, who clattered a banjo, while a woman in pink fleshings danced upon a little stage. Too much for Lizzie to take in at once, too much for Lizzie to take in at all – too rich a feast for her senses, so that she was taken a little beyond herself and felt her head spinning, a vertigo, a sense of profound strangeness overcoming her.

All unnoticeably small as she was, she was taken up by the crowd and tossed about among insensitive shoes and petticoats, too close to the ground to see much else for long; she imbibed the frenetic bustle of the midway through her nose, her ears, her skin that twitched, prickled, heated up with excitement so that she began to colour up in the way she had, her cheeks marked with red, like the marbling on the insides of the family Bible. She found herself swept by the tide of the crowd to a long table where hard cider was sold from a barrel.

The white tablecloth was wet and sticky with spillage and gave forth a dizzy, sweet, metallic odour. An old woman filled tin mugs at the barrel spigot, mug after mug, and threw coins on to other coins into a tin box – splash, chink, clang. Lizzie clung on to the edge of the table to prevent herself being carried away again. Splash, chink, clang. Trade was brisk, so the old woman never turned the spigot off and cider cascaded on to the ground on the other side of the table.

The devil got into Lizzie, then. She ducked down and sneaked in under the edge of the tablecloth, to hide in the resonant darkness and crouch on the crushed grass in fresh mud, as she held out her unobserved hands under the discontinuous stream from the spigot until she collected two hollowed palmfuls, which she licked up, and smacked her lips. Filled, licked, smacked again. She was so preoccupied with her delicious thievery that she jumped half out of her skin when she felt a living, quivering thing thrust into her neck in that very sensitive spot where her braids divided. Something moist and intimate shoved inquisitively at the nape of her neck.

She craned round and came face to face with a melancholy piglet, decently dressed in a slightly soiled ruff. She courteously filled her palms with cider and offered it to her new acquaintance, who sucked it up eagerly. She squirmed to feel the wet quiver of the pig's curious lips against her hands. It drank, tossed its pink snout, and trotted off out the back way from the table.

Lizzie did not hesitate. She followed the piglet past the dried-cod smell of the cider-seller's skirts. The piglet's tail disappeared beneath a cart piled with fresh barrels that was pulled up behind the stall. Lizzie pursued the engaging piglet to find herself suddenly out in the open again, but this time in an abrupt margin of pitch black and silence. She had slipped out of the circus grounds through a hole in their periphery, and the dark had formed into a huge clot, the night, whilst Lizzie was underneath the table; behind her were the lights, but here only shadowy undergrowth, stirring, and then the call of a night bird.

The pig paused to rootle the earth, but when Lizzie reached out to stroke it, it shook its ears out of its eyes and took off at a great pace into the countryside. However, her attention was immediately diverted from this disappointment by the sight of a man who stood with his back to the lights, leaning slightly forward. The cider-barrel-spigot sound repeated itself. Fumbling with the front of his trousers, he turned round and tripped over Lizzie, because he was a little unsteady on his feet and she was scarcely to be seen among the shadows. He bent down and took hold of her shoulders.

"Small child," he said, and belched a puff of acridity into her face. Lurching a little, he squatted right down in front of her, so they were on the same level. It was so dark that she could see of his face only the hint of moustache above the pale half-moon of his smile.

"Small girl," he corrected himself, after a closer look. He did not speak like ordinary folks. He was not from around these parts. He belched again, and again tugged at his trousers. He took firm hold of her right hand and brought it tenderly up between his squatting thighs.

"Small girl, do you know what *this* is for?"

She felt buttons; serge; something hairy; something moist and moving. She didn't mind it. He kept his hand on hers and made her rub him for a minute or two. He hissed between his teeth: "Kissy, kissy from Missy?"

She *did* mind that and shook an obdurate head; she did not like her father's hard, dry, imperative kisses, and endured them only for the sake of power. Sometimes Emma touched her cheek lightly with unparted lips. Lizzie would allow no more. The man sighed when she shook her head, took her hand away from the crotch, softly folded it up on its fingers and gave her hand ceremoniously back to her.

"Gratuity," he said, felt in his pocket and flipped her a nickel. Then he straightened up and walked away. Lizzie put the coin in her pinafore pocket and, after a moment's thought, stumped off after the funny man along the still, secret edges of the field, curious as to what he might do next.

But now surprises were going on all round her in the bushes, mewings, squeaks, rustlings, although the funny man paid no attention to them, not even when a stately fat woman rose up under his feet, huge as a moon and stark but for her stays, but for black cotton stockings held up by garters with silk rosettes on them, but for a majestic hat of black leghorn with feathers. The woman addressed the drunken man angrily, in a language with a good many ks in it, but he ploughed on indifferently and Lizzie scuttled unseen after, casting an inquisitive backward glance. She had never seen a woman's naked breasts since she could remember, and this pair of melons jiggled entrancingly as the fat woman shook her fist in the wake of the funny man before she parted her thighs with a wet smack and sank down on her knees again in the grass in which something unseen moaned.

Then a person scarcely as tall as Lizzie herself, dressed up like a little drummer-boy, somersaulted – head over heels – directly across their paths, muttering to himself as he did so. Lizzie had just the time to see that, although he was small, he was not shaped quite right, for his head seemed to have been pressed into his shoulders with some violence, but then he was gone.

Don't think any of this frightened her. She was not the kind of child that frightens easily.

Then they were at the back of a tent, not the big, striped tent, but another, smaller tent, where the funny man fumbled with the flap much as he had fumbled with his trousers. A bright mauve, ammoniac reek pulsed out from this tent; it was lit up inside like a Chinese lantern and glowed. At last he managed to un-fasten and went inside. He did not so much as attempt to close up after him; he seemed to be in as great a hurry as the tumbling dwarf, so she slipped through too, but as soon as she was inside, she lost him, because there were so many other people there.

Feet of customers had worn all the grass from the ground and it had been replaced by sawdust, which soon stuck all over the mudpie Lizzie had become. The tent was lined with cages on wheels, but she could not see high enough to see what was inside them, yet, mixed with the everyday chatter around her, she heard strange cries that did not come from human throats, so she knew she was on the right track.

She saw what could be seen: a young couple, arm in arm, he whispering in her ear, she giggling; a group of three grinning, gaping youths, poking sticks within the bars; a family that went down in steps of size, a man, a woman, a boy, a girl, a boy, a girl, a boy, a girl, down to a baby of indeterminate sex in the woman's arms. There were many more present, but these were the people she took account of.

The gagging stench was worse than a summer privy and a savage hullabaloo went on all the time, a roaring as if the sea had teeth.

She eeled her way past skirts and trousers and scratched, bare legs of summer boys until she was standing beside the biggest brother of the staircase family at the front of the crowd, but still she could not see the tiger, even if she stood on tiptoe, she saw only wheels and the red and gold base of the cage, whereon was depicted a woman without any clothes, much like the one in the grass out-side only without the hat and stockings, and some foliage, with a gilded moon and stars. The brother of the staircase family was much older than she, per-haps twelve, and clearly of the lower class, but clean and respectable-looking, although the entire family possessed that pale, peculiar look characteristic of the mill operatives. The brother looked down and saw a small child in a filthy pinafore peering and straining upwards.

"Veux-tu voir le grand chat, ma petite?"

Lizzie did not understand what he said, but she knew what he was saying and nodded assent. Mother looked over the head of the good baby in the lace bonnet as her son heaved Lizzie up in his arms for a good look.

"*Les poux* . . ." she warned, but her son paid her no heed.

"*Voilà, ma petite!*"

The tiger walked up and down, up and down; it walked up and down like Satan walking about the world and it burned. It burned so brightly, she was scorched. Its tail, thick as her father's forearm, twitched back and forth at the tip. The quick, loping stride of the caged tiger; its eyes like yellow coins of a foreign currency; its round, innocent, toy-like ears; the stiff whiskers sticking out with an artificial look; the red mouth from which the bright noise came. It walked up and down on straw strewn with bloody bones.

The tiger kept its head down; questing hither and thither though in quest of what might not be told. All its motion was slung from the marvelous haunches it held so high you could have rolled a marble down its back, if it would have let you, and the marble would have run down an oblique angle until it rolled over the domed forehead on to the floor. In its hind legs the tense muscles keened and sang. It was a miracle of dynamic suspension. It reached one end of the cage in a few paces and whirled around upon itself in one liquid motion; nothing could be quicker or more beautiful than its walk. It was all raw, vivid, exasperated nerves. Upon its pelt it bore the imprint of the bars behind which it lived.

The young lad who kept hold of her clung tight as she lunged forward towards the beast, but he could not stop her clutching the bars of the cage with her little fingers and he tried but he could not dislodge them. The tiger stopped in its track halfway through its mysterious patrol and looked at her. Her pale-blue Calvinist eyes of New England encountered with a shock the flat, mineral eyes of the tiger.

It seemed to Lizzie that they exchanged this cool regard for an endless time, the tiger and herself.

Then something strange happened. The svelte beast fell to its knees. It was as if it had been subdued by the presence of this child, as if this little child of all the children in the world, might lead it towards a peaceable kingdom where it need not eat meat. But only "as if". All we could see was, it knelt. A crackle of shock ran through the tent; the tiger was acting out of character.

Its mind remained, however, a law unto itself. We did not know what it was thinking. How could we?

It stopped roaring. Instead it started to emit a rattling purr. Time somersaulted. Space diminished to the field of attractive force between the child and the tiger. All that existed in the whole world now were Lizzie and the tiger.

Then, oh! then. . . it came towards her, as if she were winding it to her on an invisible string by the exercise of pure will. I cannot tell you how much she loved the tiger, nor how wonderful she thought it was. It was the power of her love that forced it to come to her, on its knees, like a penitent. It dragged its pale belly across the dirty straw towards the bars where the little soft creature hung by its hooked fingers. Behind it followed the serpentine length of its ceaselessly twitching tail.

There was a wrinkle in its nose and it buzzed and rumbled and they never took their eyes off one another, though neither had the least idea what the other meant.

The boy holding Lizzie got scared and pummelled her little fists, but she would not let go a grip as tight and senseless as that of the newborn.

Crack! The spell broke.

The world bounded into the ring.

A lash cracked round the tiger's carnivorous head, and a glorious hero sprang into the cage brandishing in the hand that did not hold the whip a three-legged stool. He wore fawn breeches, black boots, a bright red jacket frogged with gold, a tall hat. A dervish, he; he beckoned, crouched, pointed with the whip, menaced with the stool, leaped and twirled in a brilliant ballet of mimic ferocity, the dance of the Taming of the Tiger, to whom the tamer gave no chance to fight at all.

The great cat unpeeled its eyes off Lizzie's in a trice, rose up on its hind legs and feinted at the whip like our puss Ginger feints at a piece of paper dangled from a string. It batted at the tamer with its enormous paws, but the whip continued to confuse, irritate and torment it and, what with the shouting, the sudden, excited baying of the crowd, the dreadful confusion of the signs surrounding it, habitual custom, a lifetime's training, the tiger whimpered, laid back its ears and scampered away from the whirling man to an obscure corner of the stage, there to cower, while its flanks heaved, the picture of humiliation.

Lizzie let go of the bars and clung, mudstains and all, to her young protector for comfort. She was shaken to the roots by the attack of the trainer upon the tiger and her four-year-old roots were very near the surface.

The tamer gave his whip a final, contemptuous ripple around his adversary's whispers that made it sink its huge head on the floor. Then he placed one booted foot on the tiger's skull and cleared his throat for speech. He was a hero. He was a tiger himself, but even more so, because he was a man.

"Ladies and gentlemen, boys and girls, this incomparable tiger known as the Scourge of Bengal, and brought alive-oh to Boston from its native jungle but three short months before this present time, now, at my imperious command, offers you a perfect imitation of docility and obedience. But do not let the brute deceive you. Brute it was, and brute it remains. Not for nothing did it receive the soubriquet of Scourge for, in its native habitat, it thought nothing of consuming a dozen brown-skinned heathen for its breakfast and following up with a couple of dozen more for dinner!"

A pleasing shudder tingled through the crowd.

"This tiger," and the beast whickered ingratiatingly when he named it, "is the veritable incarnation of blood lust and fury; in a single instant, it can turn from furry quiescence into three hundred pounds, yes, three hundred POUNDS of death-dealing fury.

"The tiger is the cat's revenge."

Oh, Miss Ginger, Miss Ginger Cuddles, who sat mewing censoriously on the gatepost as Lizzie passed by; who would have thought you seethed with such resentment!

The man's voice dropped to a confidential whisper and Lizzie, although she was in such a state, such nerves, recognized this was the same man as the one she had met behind the cider stall, although now he exhibited such erect mastery, not a single person in the tent would have thought he had been drinking.

"What is the nature of the bond between us, between the Beast and Man? Let me tell you. It is fear. Fear! Nothing but fear. Do you know how insomnia is the plague of the tamer of cats? How all night long, every night, we pace our quarters, impossible to close our eyes for brooding on what day, what hour, what moment the fatal beast will choose to strike?

"Don't think I cannot bleed, or that they have not wounded me. Under my clothes, my body is a palimpsest of scars, scar upon scar. I heal only to be once more broken open. No skin of mine that is not scar tissue. And I am always afraid, always; all the time in the ring, in the cage, now, this moment – this very moment, boys and girls, ladies and gentlemen, you see before you a man in the grip of mortal fear.

"Here and now I am in terror of my life.

"At this moment I am in this cage within a perfect death trap."

Theatrical pause.

"But," and here he knocked the tiger's nose with his whipstock, so that it howled with pain and affront, "but . . ." and Lizzie saw the secret frog he kept within his trousers shift a little, ". . . but I'm not half so scared of the big brute as it is of me!"

He showed his red maw in a laugh.

"For I bring to bear upon its killer instinct a rational man's knowledge of the power of fear. The whip, the stool, are instruments of bluff with which I create his fear in my arena. In my cage, among my cats, I have established a hierarchy of FEAR and among my cats you might well say I am top dog, because I know that all the time they want to kill me, that is their project, that it their intention... but as for them, they just don't know what I might do next. No, sir!"

As if enchanted by the notion, he laughed out loud again, but by now the tiger, perhaps incensed by the unexpected blow on the nose, rumbled out a clear and incontrovertible message of disaffection and, with a quick jerk of its sculptured head, flung the man's foot away so that, caught off-balance, he half toppled over. And then the tiger was no longer a thing of stillness, of hard edges and clear outlines, but a whizz of black and red, maw and canines, in the air. On him.

The crowd immediately bayed.

But the tamer, with enormous presence of mind, seeing as how he was drunk, and, in the circumstances, with almost uncanny physical agility, bounced backwards on his boot-heels and thrust the tool he carried in his left hand into the fierce tiger's jaws, leaving the tiger worrying, gnawing, destroying the harmless thing, as a ragged black boy quickly unlatched the cage door and out the tamer leaped, unscathed, amidst hurrahs.

Lizzie's stunned little face was now mottled all over with a curious reddish-purple, with the heat of the tent, with passion, with the sudden access of enlightenment.

To see the rest of the stupendous cat act, the audience would have had to buy another ticket for the Big Top, besides the ticket for the menagerie, for which it had already paid, so, reluctant on the whole to do that, in spite of the promise of clowns and dancing ladies, it soon got bored with watching the tiger splintering the wooden stool, and drifted off.

"*Eh bien, ma petite*," said her boy-nurse to her in a sweet, singsong, crooning voice. "*Tu as vu la bête! La bête du cauchemar!*"

The baby in the lace bonnet had slept peacefully through all this, but now began to stir and mumble. Its mother nudged her husband with her elbow.

"*On va, Papa?*"

The crooning, smiling boy brought his bright pink lips down on Lizzie's forehead for a farewell kiss. She could not bear that; she struggled furiously and shouted to be put down. With that, her cover broke and she burst out of her disguise of dirt and silence; half the remaining gawpers in the tent had kin been bleakly buried by her father, the rest owed him money. She was the most famous daughter in all Fall River.

"Well, if it ain't Andrew Borden's little girl! What are they Canucks doing with little Lizzie Borden?"

AT THE BEACH

Bernard MacLaverty

Bernard MacLaverty (b.1942) was born in Belfast but has lived in Scotland for most of his life. His work includes the novels *Lamb*, and *Cal* and the Booker shortlisted *Grace Notes*. His *Collected Stories* were published in 2013 when MacLaverty said, in an interview with the *Guardian:* "Frank O'Connor said that short stories are a place for loneliness while the novel is a public event. So for me that means it's a dram not a pint . . . when you have a pint at the bar there are people around you. It is about society. The short story is more often about an individual; it's having a dram, of an evening to yourself."

They sat opposite each other across the table in the small apartment. He was just out of bed. The first thing he had done was to peer through the slats of the shutters at the view – white apartments, two cranes and, beyond, the blue of the Mediterranean. He wore underpants and a shirt to cover his stomach. She had risen earlier to go to the Supermercado for some essentials. The *Welcome-pack* was only meant to get them through the night – tea-bags, some sachets of coffee, a packet of plain biscuits.

"The price of cereal would frighten you," she said. He nodded, trying to open the cardboard milk carton. "I'm not exactly sure what it is in pounds or pesetas but that packet of All-Bran costs the same as a bottle of brandy."

"It's worth it for the bowels. The bowels will thank me before the week's out." He tried to press back the winged flaps of the waxed carton but they bent and he couldn't get it open. "Fuck this." He stood up and raked noisily through the drawer of provided cutlery for a pair of scissors. She was looking in the cupboards under the sink.

"Hey – a toaster." She held it up. He smiled at its strange design – it was as if someone had removed the internal workings of an ordinary toaster. She plugged it in to see if it would work and the wires glowed red almost immediately. The socket was beneath the sink so the toaster could only sit on the floor. "Stamped with the skull and cross-bones of the Spanish Safety Mark." She put on two slices of bread.

"Is this goats' milk?" He made a face but persevered spooning the All-Bran into his mouth.

"I didn't get you a paper – they only had yesterday's. And we read yesterday's on the plane."

"We want a holiday from all that." He reached down and brushed an ant off his bare foot. "Did you sleep?"

"It was getting light through the shutters," she said. "The crickets went on all night. They're so bloody loud."

"What's it like outside?"

"Hot – and it'll get worse as the day goes on. The Supermarket has . . ." She laughed. "I was going to say central heating but I mean . . ." She wobbled her hand above her head.

"Air conditioning."

"Yeah – you come out onto the street and feel that hot wind – like somebody left a hair-dryer on. The Supermarket's a Spar, would you believe. I thought they only existed in Ireland. And I got Irish butter – here in Spain."

He killed an ant on the table with his thumb.

"These wee bastards are everywhere." He bent forward and stared down at the maroon tiled floor. "Look – Maureen."

"The toast." She hunkered down and turned the bread just as it was beginning to smoke.

When they had eaten breakfast they made love and after a while he said, "I love you," and when her breath had come back she said,

"Snap." She reached out and touched the side of his face. "I mean it, Jimmy," she said and smiled, hugging him to herself. Their faces were close enough to know they were both smiling.

In the plane Maureen had bought a long-distance Fly-Travel kit which contained light slippers and a neck pillow. It also included some stickers which said *Wake for Meals*. Jimmy stuck one on his forehead and pretended to be asleep. Maureen laughed when she saw it.

"It's what life's all about," he said. He put on his salesman's voice. "Have you seen our other bestselling sticker, sir? *We give birth astride the grave.*"

"Wake for meals." Maureen said it aloud again and laughed. "Let me have a shower – then we'll find out where this pleasure beach is."

He laughed and said, "We *know* where it is."

They followed the signs which said *Playa*. His hands were joined behind his back, she carried a bag with the camera and the towels and stuff. They stopped on the hill overlooking the beach to study which part of it would suit them best. The place was crowded and colourful.

Sun-beds were stacked at intervals. When they got down they took one each and camped near the beach bar. Jimmy sat on his like a sofa while Maureen stepped out of her dress. She had her bathing suit on. She stood putting sun cream on her shoulders and legs.

"Do my back," she said, handing him the bottle. She lay on her front on the sun-bed. He squeezed some cream into the palm of his hand and began to rub it into her skin. He looked around him. Most of the women were bare-breasted. Everyone seemed to be tanned. Mediterranean people with jet-black hair and dark olive eyes.

"We're pale as lard," Jimmy said.

"Only for a day or two. Who cares anyway – nobody knows us here."

"I care," he said – then after a pause, "Nipples the colour of mahogany."

"What?"

"Never mind."

"Act your age, Jimmy. They're young enough to be your daughters."

"I can look, can't I? Anyway, who's talking about girls – the boys have nipples, too."

When he finished doing her back he did his own arms and legs. He opened his shirt and saw the pallidness of his own skin. If anything, it was whiter than Maureen's.

"Don't forget the top of your feet and . . . your bald spot."

"I meant to buy a fucking hat." When he had his body covered with cream he joined his hands and rubbed the top of his head with his moist palms as if he was stretching. Then he lay down on his back. That way his gut was less noticeable.

"Do you miss the girls?" Maureen said.

"Like hell. It's about bloody time we got away by ourselves." He laughed and said, "It's like it used to be. Just you and me, baby."

"It's different now." Even though her eyes were closed she made an eye-shade cupping her hand over her brow. "Maybe better."

"God it's hot."

"That's what we paid all the money for."

"Did you remember to put the butter back in the fridge?" Maureen nodded.

"I hate butter when it's slime."

"I hate *anything* when it's slime."

"This place makes me so . . ." Jimmy looked around at the people sprawled near him. If they were reading books he could tell by the authors whether or not they were English-speaking. Jilly Cooper, Catherine Cookson, Elizabeth Jane Howard. Others who just lay there sunbathing gave no clue. So he lowered his voice. "It makes me so fucking randy."

A couple in their early twenties came up and kicked off their sandals. They dropped all their paraphernalia on the sand and began to undress. Jimmy watched the girl, who was wearing a flimsy beach dress of bright material like a sarong. Beneath she wore a one-piece black swimsuit. The lad pulled off his T-shirt. He was brown with a stomach as lean as a washboard. He said something to his girl-friend and she replied, laughing. They sounded German or Austrian. The girl el-bowed her way out of the shoulder straps of her bathing suit and rolled it down, baring her breasts. She continued rolling until the one-piece was like the bottom half of a bikini. They both sat down and the girl took a tube from her basket. She squirted a teaspoonful of white cream onto her midriff and began rubbing it up and over her breasts. They lifted and fell as her hand moved over them. She looked up in Jimmy's direction and he quickly turned his head towards Maureen.

"What?" said Maureen, sensing his movement.

"Nothing." He shook his head.

About mid-day Jimmy put his shirt on and they went up to the patio of the beach bar for a drink and something to eat. They sat in the shelter of a sun umbrella looking over the beach. The luminous shadow cast by the red material of the umbrella made them look a slightly better colour. Maureen leaned towards him and said,

"Don't look now but I hear Irish voices."

"Jesus – where?" Jimmy, with his elbows on the table, arched both hands over his brows and pretended to hide.

"Behind me and to the left."

Jimmy looked over her shoulder. There were three men around a table smoking. They all were wearing shirts and shorts. One of them had a heavy black moustache. Maureen was about to say something when Jimmy shushed her. He listened hard through the foreign talk and rattle of dishes. He heard some flat vowels – but they could have been Dutch or Scottish. American even.

"I'm not sure," said Jimmy.

"Well, I am."

"Let's steer well clear."

A waiter approached their table.

"Try your Spanish," said Maureen.

"Naw – it's embarrassing." But when the waiter opened his pad Jimmy said, "Dos cervezas, por favor."

"Grande o pequeño?"

Jimmy cleared his throat.

"Uno grande y uno pequeño," he said.

"That's one large and one small, sir."

Jimmy nodded. "Gracias."

"De nada." The waiter disappeared indoors to the restaurant. Jimmy raised his eyebrows in a show-off manner.

"Not bad at all," said Maureen. "I hate all the th's – like everybody's got a lisp."

When the beers came they toasted each other. Every time he raised his glass an ice-cold drip would fall down the open front of his shirt onto his belly and startle him. He cursed – thought there was a crack in the glass or the beer mat was wet.

"They put the stupid fuckin beer mat round the stem instead of underneath." Maureen pointed out to him it was condensation. The beer was cold – the air was hot – condensation formed on the outside of the glass – each time he picked it up it would drip on him. The beer mat round the stem was a none too successful attempt to prevent this.

"You're too smart for your own good," he said.

Maureen looked up at the menu displayed on the wall.

"We'll have to eat a paella some night."

"Yeah – seafood."

"It's a kind of enforced intimacy. They only do it for two people."

"No paella for spinsters."

"Or priests."

"If it was in Ireland they'd make it for *his Riverence* and throw the half of it out."

They both smiled at the thought. There was a long silence between them. Jimmy shifted his white plastic chair closer to hers. His voice dropped to a whisper.

"Who – I don't know whether I should ask this or not . . ."

"What?"

"Naw . . ."

"Go on."

"Who was the first man you ever did it with?" She stared at him. "You don't have to tell me – if you don't want to."

"I don't want to and it's none of your business." She spoke quietly and without anger.

"Can you remember the first time you had an orgasm? I mean – not even with somebody. By yourself, even."

"Not really. All that early stuff is smudged together."

"Come on," he whispered. "That's one of those questions like where were you when they shot Kennedy. Everybody knows. The first time that happens to you it's like being in an earthquake or something. You *remember*. It's like your first kiss . . ."

She hesitated and screwed her face up. "It might have been the back of a car . . ." He leaned forward to hear her better. "This is nonsense. Why do you want to know?"

"We've been married twenty-five years. We should have no privacy – no secrets from one another."

"This is just stirring up poison." She looked away from him at the sea. There were pedalos and wind surfers criss-crossing the bay.

"I just want to know."

"It's like picking scabs on your knee. No good'll come of it." She finished her beer and stood up. "I'm going for a swim."

When she had gone Jimmy sat staring at the white table top. He raised one finger at the waiter and said,

"La cuenta, por favor."

They swam and dried off, then reapplied the sun cream. They did each other's back.

"It was a bit nippy getting in at first," said Maureen. "I didn't expect that. But it was lovely when you got down."

The German or Austrian couple had gone off. Jimmy picked them out from the other bathers. They were playing knee-deep in the waves with a velcro ball and bats which fitted onto the hand. If the ball touched the glove even lightly it stuck fast.

Maureen settled down on her front, crossing her arms as a pillow for her cheek. She sighed.

"This is *so* nice. I deserve it."

"I'm sorry about that – that before the swim – up at the bar. But sometimes – there's a thing in me that . . . wants to *know* about you before I met you. There's a part of me that's jealous of the time when I didn't know you."

"Jimmy . . ."

"What?"

"You're starting again."

"Sorry."

"Where do you think the girls are? Right now," said Maureen.

"God knows. Half way across the Nevada desert. New Orleans? L.A.? I just hope they don't hitch. Them hitching makes me nervous. Bloody lorry-drivers."

"They'll be fine."

The German couple came up the beach, laughing, their hair sleeked and wet. The boy dropped the bat and ball game beside Maureen. The girl rolled down her bathing suit again and lay down on her back just a few feet from Jimmy. She was breathless. Her wet stomach rose and fell as she gasped for breath. Jimmy stared at her. Gradually over a minute or so her breathing became normal. She turned to get the sun on her back and her breasts appeared columnar before she eased herself down.

"How does that work?" Maureen asked.

"What?"

"That bat and ball game."

"Velcro."

"Oh . . ."

"Two materials – one has hooks, the other loops. When they hit they stick."

"I've only seen it used as a zip."

"It was one of those ideas that came from nature. The burr sticking to the animal hair."

"Clever balls."

"I've just expanded your world for you, Maureen. You should be grateful."

To avoid the risk of sunburn they went back to the apartment at three o'clock. They walked slowly through the heat.

"I feel utterly drained," said Maureen. There was a flight of steps to where their apartment was and they both paused half way up.

"It's the heat," said Jimmy and they both smiled at each other. He leaned against the wall which was in shadow. The stones forming the wall were round and porous.

"They build everything here out of Rice Crispies."

A lizard suddenly appeared on the sunlit side of the wall. "Behind you Maureen." She looked and stood still. It had come to a halt in an S-shape. It was bright green. With a flicker of movement it was gone as suddenly as it had appeared.

"Wasn't it lovely to see that?" said Maureen. "I've never seen one before. They move so fast."

"They're cold-blooded, that's why they seem so energetic in this heat. It's like us going for a run on a frosty morning."

"I feel my world expanding all the time."

The shutters were closed and the place was dark. They had a shower together and Maureen got to choose the luke-warm temperature of the water. Then they made love again.

"We'll not be able to stick the pace", said Jimmy, "– without the kids."

"Today is lovely but I don't want you – y'know – every time we close that door. We need our own space." She was boiling the kettle for a coffee and it seemed to take ages. The room was still dark but slivers of the harsh hot light and white buildings could be seen through the top slats of the shutters. Jimmy sat in his white towelling dressing-gown looking down at the table. The ant population had increased since the morning.

"They're after our toast crumbs," he said. They seemed to be forming a line to and from the table, clustering round a crumb or an almond flake from a biscuit. There were too many now to start killing them.

"Just let them be," said Maureen. "It's not as if they bite."

Jimmy was following the line to its source. Down the table leg and across the kitchen floor to the jamb of the bathroom door. There was a millimetre gap between the wood and the tiles and ants were disappearing into it. Others were coming out.

"There must be a nest somewhere."

"Or a hill," said Maureen.

"Maybe they've been on this route for ten million years," he said. "Somebody just built this place in their way fifty years ago. This is their track – why should they change just because some bastard of a developer puts a house in their way."

She poured two coffees and set one on the table for him. She side-stepped the shifting black line of ants and said,

"They do no harm to anybody."

He decided to watch one – it seemed sure of itself heading away from the table with news of food. It came face to face with others and seemed to kiss, swerve, carry on. Away from the main line there were outriders exploring – wandering aimlessly while in the main line the ants moved like blood cells in a vein.

"There's no point in killing one or two. The whole thing is the organism. It would be like trying to murder somebody cell by cell."

"Just let them be."

"The almond crumbs are yours," he said but still he flicked ants from his bare feet whenever he felt them there.

The next day they went to the beach and sat in the same place. Jimmy looked around and saw that Jilly Cooper, Catherine Cookson and Elizabeth Jane Howard were just behind him.

"We're all creatures of habit," he said. "It's as bad as the fucking staff room." The mid-day sun made the sand hot to the touch. Maureen had moved from Factor Fifteen and was putting on Factor Six. He did her back for her and she lay down.

"We agreed not to talk about things like that."

"Okay – okay."

"Until we get back."

They lay there roasting for about thirty minutes, Maureen flat out, Jimmy resting on his elbows taking in the view. He had bought a white floppy hat with little or no brim and a pair of sun-glasses in the Supermercado. The glasses gave him greater freedom to look around without noticeably moving his head.

"The Germans are absent," he said, "and no note."

"Which Germans?"

"The Velcro Germans."

"I didn't realise they were Germans. What is the Assistant Head's particular interest there?"

"Nothing. They just haven't turned up."

"Liar."

"The girl is a class act – a bit magnificent."

Maureen laughed and rubbed a little cream onto her nose with her little finger.

"Do you fancy a walk?" she said.

"Yeah sure." He put on his shirt and let it hang out over his shorts and they walked to the rocky cliff at the far end of the beach. People here were brown and mostly Spanish-speaking. There was a lot of laughing and shouting.

"It seems to be compulsory not to listen. People all speak at the same time."

"That's because you don't have the faintest idea what they're saying. Two people from Derry would sound just the same – if you didn't know – if your English . . ."

"They just seem to interrupt each other all the time."

They swam off the rocks and the water seemed warmer than the previous day. As they walked back across the beach Jimmy took Maureen's hand. They nudged up against each other and fleetingly she put her head against his shoulder.

"This is *so* good," she said. "I like Public Displays of Affection – no matter what you say."

"Why does it matter when nobody knows us?"

"I know us," she said. "Sometimes you can be so bloody parochial."

In the middle of the afternoon the German couple arrived and sat down about three feet to the left of the spot where they had been the day before. From behind his sunglasses Jimmy watched the girl undress. Today she wore the bottom half of a white bikini. He heard the boy use her name. *Heidrun*, he called her. Jimmy tried to nod hello to her but she didn't notice. She shook out, then spread a large towel, adjusting and flattening the corners. All her attention was taken up with her friend.

"They might as well be on a deserted beach in Donegal," said Jimmy, nodding at the couple. Heidrun knelt down on the spread towel and her boyfriend leaned over and nuzzled into her neck. They both lay down face to face, their feet pointing in Jimmy's direction.

"They'd be covered in goose-pimples," said Maureen. Jimmy stared at the gusset of the white bikini facing him. It was as if the closeness of the German couple had some influence on them and Jimmy and Maureen moved closer together. He whispered in her ear.

"Why is it that the only woman on the beach who seems to have any pubic hair is you?"

"You mean you go around looking?"

"A man cannot help but notice these things."

"You mean a Catholic repressed man. A lecher. A man with a problem."

"You lie there like some kind of a farmer's wife from the backabeyond or . . . or somebody from Moscow."

"I meant to do it before I came away – but with the rush and all . . . It's not that obvious – is it?" She looked down at herself.

"Not really but . . ."

"Anyway, who's looking at me in that tone of voice – at my age. Catch yourself on, Jimmy. Go and buy me an ice cream."

He got to his feet and put on his shirt. "What flavour?"

"The green one with the bits of chocolate in it."

"What's it called?"

"Jesus, you can point, can't you?"

He fiddled in her purse for pesetas, then went off towards the bar.

At the bar he noticed again the three suspected Irishmen from the first day. They sat beside the counter. Jimmy listened as he pointed out and bought the ice-cream. Maureen was right again. They were definitely from the North of Ireland. They were talking about football. Something about Manchester United and the English league. Two of them wore tartan shirts, the third a T-shirt with Guinness advertising on it.

When he got back to Maureen he gave her the ice-cream.

"I saw your friends up there. I think they're RUC men."

She licked the peppermint green and crunched a bit of the chocolate.

"What makes you think that?"

"I dunno. They look like Chief Constables or Inspectors. I feel sorry for them. If you were a policeman in the North where would *you* go for your holidays?"

She didn't answer. She nodded towards the German couple.

"There's been plenty of PDA since you left." She smiled and winked at Jimmy. The couple were lying with their faces an inch apart staring into each other's eyes. Occasionally the boy would trail the back of his knuckles down her naked side. Maureen beckoned Jimmy's ear to her mouth.

"Meine Liebe," she whispered.

That evening on the patio of *Nino's* they decided to have the seafood paella for two. They had been given complimentary glasses of a local sherry and Jimmy asked to have the order repeated. He would pay for them. As he suspected, when the waitress brought the drinks she said, "On the house."

Jimmy drank Maureen's second drink as well as his own two.

When the waiter brought the double paella he showed it to them. They both nodded in appreciation at its presentation. It was served from a much-used, blackened pan and the waiter made sure to divide everything equally. Three open navy blue mussel shells to one plate, three to the other. One red langoustine to you and one to you.

Maureen hated it – wet sloppy rice with too much salt and the most inaccessible parts of shellfish. Things that had to be broken open and scraped, recognisable creatures which had to have them backs snapped and their contents sucked. At one point Maureen raised her eyes and gave a warning to Jimmy. The three Northern Ireland men were sitting down at the next but one table from them. She scrutinised them.

"I'm sure they're not policemen." They were directly behind Jimmy and he had to twist in his chair to see them. One of them caught his eye and recognised him from the beach. They nodded politely to each other.

"They're like people out of a uniform of some kind," said Jimmy. "Maybe they're screws – from Long Kesh."

"Or security men."

Maureen gave up on the paella.

"How do you tell a lie in Spanish – it was lovely but there was too much of it?" There was a lull in the noise of conversation and dish-rattling and Maureen heard a name float across from the next but one table. Jimmy said,

"If you are not willing to talk about your early sexual experiences – I am."

"Not again."

"In those days I was a vicious bastard – every time I went out with a woman I went straight for the conjugular."

She laughed and said, "You think I didn't notice." She paused and looked at him. "You made that up."

"Of course I did. I just said it, didn't I?"

"No I mean you thought it up one day and then waited for a time when you could use it. Tonight's the night."

He nodded vigorously, pouring himself another glass of wine. Maureen put her hand over the top of her own glass.

Another, different name came floating across from the Northern Ireland table. Maureen made a face as if something was just dawning on her.

"I know," she said when she had swallowed the food in her mouth. "They're priests. The first name I heard was Conor and now there's Malachy."

"Catholic names don't make them priests."

"But black socks do."

"Keep your voice down. If we can hear them they can hear us."

"Two of them's wearing black socks," whispered Maureen. "It all fits now. Why would three aging men go away on holiday together?"

"A homosexual ring?"

"They never go *on* the beach. They never take their clothes off. They are keeping an eye on each other. Since the Bishop of Galway nobody trusts anybody else."

"One of them has a moustache."

Maureen looked over his shoulder and checked.

"So?"

"I've never seen a priest with a moustache."

"Maybe there's two of them priests and the one with the moustache is the priest's brother. You're right – the one with the moustache is wearing white towelling socks." Jimmy checked under the table. Maureen smiled and said, "There's nothing worse than a priest's brother. All the hang-ups and none of the courage."

"Are they drinking?"

"Yes."

"They probably *are* priests then." They laughed at each other. Jimmy reached out and covered her hand with his. "Would you like coffee or will we get another bottle?"

"Coffee is fine for me."

"I'm sorry to go on about this – but there must have been no shortage of men *trying it on* before me."

Maureen stared at him. "What is this – where did all this shite suddenly come from, Jimmy?"

"I've just been thinking. Seeing things that remind me. You were a very attractive woman when we first met . . ."

"Gee thanks . . ."

"No I don't mean that. You still are. I'm saying – in comparison to others in the field."

"In the field – you're making it sound like a cattle fair – have a good look at her teeth."

"That's a horse fair you're thinking of."

"Jimmy." She stared hard at him. "Teach me how to be right all the time?"

"It wouldn't work – two in the one family."

"Then one of us would have to leave," said Maureen. "It's that time of life. Everybody is leaving everybody else. They stayed together for the kids. Now that's over."

"You don't feel like that, do you?"

Maureen looked at him and smiled. She shook her head.

"Not yet."

They walked back to the apartment across the dark beach. They both took off their shoes and walked ankle deep at the water's edge. It was warmer than during the day. There was a white moon reflected on the water. They held hands again until Jimmy stopped for a piss in the sea. Maureen walked on.

In the apartment Jimmy fell down onto the sofa.

"I'm going to have a drink of that duty-free whiskey before it's all drunk."

"And who's liable to drink it?"

"Me." He grinned and rose to pour himself one. She laughed at him.

"Have you drunk all *that* since we came here?"

"Lay off. I'm on my holidays too."

"But we drink a bottle of wine – minus one glass for me – every night as well."

"Over dinner."

"That makes no difference."

"Plus a few beers. Maureen, will you stop counting. And some of that Spanish fucking gin."

"With no ice."

"Ice is where the bugs get in." He diluted his whiskey with bottled water *sin gas* he had bought for the purpose. "Speaking of which . . ." He moved to the bathroom and looked down at the tiled floor.

"Holy shit! Maureen will you take a look at this." He hunkered down and sipped his whiskey.

"Oh my God," said Maureen. What had been a trickle of ants was now a torrent – a stream that was moving both ways. From the chink in the bathroom tile they moved across the floor in a bristling stream to the table leg, up the table leg onto the table – into the cereal packets. The stream divided and part of it went to the rubbish bin where they had thrown their leftovers – melon rinds, tea-bags, stale bread.

"It's fizzin with them," said Maureen, lifting a bread wrapper from the bin between her finger and thumb. "Are they just a fact of life. Will we have to put up with them all the time we're here?"

"As long as they're not in the bed," said Jimmy. As he stood up some of his whiskey slopped over. The ants panicked, began moving faster. The stream parted and moved around the droplets of whiskey, ignoring it. "Why don't they get pissed?"

"Maybe they will do – after work," said Maureen.

"They're really prehistoric, aren't they. And so *silent*. In the movies there would be a soundtrack."

Maureen made tea with a tea-bag in a mug and they went out onto the small balcony. There was a candle in a bottle left by a previous tenant and Maureen lit it and set it on the white plastic table. Jimmy sipped his whiskey and put his feet up on the balcony rail.

"I just love being in my shirt-sleeves at this time of night. Can you imagine what it's like at home?" Maureen sighed a kind of agreement. The moon was low in the sky and criss-crossed by the struts of two cranes. Had the moon not been there the cranes would have been invisible. Jimmy nodded towards the candle.

"Somebody from the north. Remember that holiday in Norway?" Maureen nodded. "Candles everywhere. The kids loved it. Flames burning *outside* restaurants. Never pulling their curtains – you could follow people moving from room to room."

"You certainly did."

"The bills – light shining out of everywhere. Here it's the opposite. Shutters – keep the light out. It's impossible to get the slightest glimpse inside a Spanish or an Italian house." Jimmy sipped his whiskey and held it in his mouth for a while, savouring it. It was a thing he knew annoyed her. They didn't speak again for some time.

"You *really* don't like to talk about this stuff, do you?"

"No," she said.

"I just want to know what happened to you before I met you."

"I've told you everything there is to know – chapter and verse. Everything about my home and school . . ."

"But not sexually. You never mention anything about that." She sipped her mug of tea holding it with both hands – the way she would sip tea in the winter. "I'm jealous of not knowing you then. Your school uniform. Your First Communion. I am jealous of all the time I was not with you."

"That's a kind of adolescent – James Dean – kind of thing to say."

"I am jealous of every single sexual act *in which I was not involved.*"

She looked at his face in the candle light and realised he was serious.

"Jimmy, why are you torturing yourself about this? Leave it alone. Why should all this come up now – after twenty-five years? Maybe you feel threatened. Now that you're out of shape and balding you feel threatened."

"Fuck off."

"I'm going to bed." She got up and went the long way round the table so he wouldn't have to take his feet down off the balcony rail.

He heard her shut the latch on the bedroom door and the creak of the bed as she got into it. He poured himself another whiskey larger than the last because she was not there to see the size of it. He drank several more glasses equally large and listened to the crickets and the English voices that were continually passing in the street below.

When Maureen woke at 4 am he still had not come to bed. She found him in the chair, his head tilted back, his mouth open and slanting in his face.

"Are you okay, Jimmy?" She put her arm beneath his and got him to his feet.

He was mumbling something about "those fucking priests" as she eased him down onto the bed and started to take his shoes off.

He was sick the next day and, although he tried to hide the fact by going out of the room, Maureen could hear the crinkling of him in the bathroom pressing indigestion tablets out of their tinfoil pack. When she accused him of drinking foolishly he blamed the paella.

"You've never done that in your life before, Jimmy. Not to my knowledge."

"Got a bit pissed?"

"No – passed out – sitting in your seat."

"I fell asleep, for fucksake."

"I'm going to get you one of those wee stickers printed which says *Wake for Drinks*." Maureen went to the fridge to put away the butter.

"Oh my God," she said, "would you look at this?"

"What?"

"There's ants crawling up the rubber seal of the fridge door."

"We'll have to do something."

In the coolness of the Supermercado Maureen, with the help of a small Spanish dictionary, made herself understood to the man she liked at the checkout. She wanted to kill ants. The man nodded, went off down between the aisles and came back with an orange-coloured tube.

"You have children?" he asked.

"Yes – two girls."

He made a face which said – oh well, I don't think this is a good idea. He pointed at the black skull and crossbones on the side of the tube. Maureen realised what he meant and laughed at herself.

"My children are not here. They are big. Away." He smiled and raised an eyebrow which Maureen interpreted as – you don't look old enough to have grown-up children. It was soft soap but she still liked him.

"Where ants come in." He directed the nozzle downwards. Maureen nodded that she understood.

When she got back Jimmy was lying on the sofa still looking hung-over. She handed the tube to him and he insisted on looking up the instructions and ingredients in the dictionary.

"Jesus – it seems to be honey and arsenic."

"The guy says you have to put it down where they're coming in."

Jimmy heaved himself off the sofa and squatted down by the bathroom door. The stream of ants was now so dense that they blackened the floor in an inch-wide band. Millions coming, millions going. He unscrewed the lid and aimed the oily liquid into the crack they were pouring in and out of.

"Try this for size, my little ones." Several drops fell on the tiles of the bathroom floor. Jimmy stood up and washed his hands thoroughly. Maureen came to see the effect the stuff was having.

"They are going daft, Jimmy. They're all lining up to drink it. Look at them." The ants were now streaming in all directions but the main movement was to line up along the edge of the liquid. "They can't leave it alone. Look they're dying." The ones on the margin of the poison had ceased to move. Others nudged them aside to get at it. Maureen looked at the tile where the single drops had fallen. Ants had gathered round the edge of the drop and ceased to move.

"They're like eyelashes round an eye," said Maureen.

"Christ – it's very dramatic stuff." Jimmy looked down at the floor still drying his hands. "Goodnight Vienna."

Maureen went out to go to the beach. If Jimmy felt better he would join her later. She had to pass the Supermercado so she stepped inside and gave the thumbs up to the guy at the checkout about the efficiency of the ant stuff. He nodded his head and smiled.

It was on the way down the hill that it occurred to her that maybe he didn't know what she'd been referring to. She became embarrassed at the thought. Maybe he didn't even know who she was – a man like him would smile at all his customers.

It was nice to be on her own. She felt good about herself. Her tan was beginning to be evident without being red. The pale stripe beneath her watch-strap acted as a kind of indicator. She was in no hurry to get to the beach and walked towards the old town looking in shop windows. She did not want to buy anything – just to look. Most of the shops were closed and she realised that it was *siesta*. The streets were empty. It was eerie – like in a movie after the bomb had been dropped. The flat stones of the pavement were hot and shining and she got the notion that she would slip on them if she was not careful. Pasted to a wall were posters for a fiesta which coincided with their last night. There were to be fireworks starting at 11 pm in the square at the harbour front.

She was now moving through an area of the town where she hadn't been before. The façade of a church appeared as she came round a corner. It seemed to grow out of a terrace of houses and looked very old and very Spanish. She walked along the street towards it. She was not knowledgeable about these things but she guessed it was mediaeval. In the curved arch above the door white doves blew out their chests and made cooing, bubbling noises. The main door was huge and ancient – studded with iron nails, each shaped like a pyramid. There was a smaller door cut into it. She tried the handle but found it locked. Now that she was excluded she wanted to see the inside more than ever. Several yards to the left of the main door was another side door. She was unsure whether it belonged to the next house or the church. She tried the handle and it swung open.

"Ah . . ." She stepped in. It wasn't really inside the church but in a colonnade alongside. At this end it was dark and cool but the far end was brilliant with sunshine. In between the colonnade of columns, arches of shadow sliced onto the walkway. She had a memory of looking out from a dark wood into sunlight. The door closed behind her with a rattle as the catch clicked. There appeared to be no way into the church from here. She walked down the colonnade towards the sunshine, listening to the slight itching sound the soles of her shoes made with the sandstone floor. The arches were curved, held up by pillars of blond stone which got lighter and lighter as they neared the source of the sunlight. Was she sufficiently dressed to go into the church? Her white T-shirt left her arms bare, but nobody could object to her Bermuda-length shorts. She felt slightly nervous – like a child expecting to be scolded for trespassing or intruding where she had no right to be. What if some *Monsignor* were to turn the corner and begin shouting at her in Spanish, yelling at her that this was the Holy of Holies. She paused and thought of going back. But she was so curious to see what lay beyond the source of the light. She walked hesitantly down the arcade and came upon a small square. It took her breath. There was something about it which made her love it with an intensity she had rarely experienced. There was no fear now of being caught. In some way she felt she had the right to be here. It was a square or atrium made of the same blond stone as the columns which formed the cloisters around its perimeter. In the centre was what looked like a font set up on a dais of steps. It had a spindly canopy of wrought iron. Maureen moved near the font and turned slowly to look around her with her head tilted back, looking up. Windows, three sets in each wall, overlooked the small courtyard but there appeared to be no one living behind them. There were no shutters, no curtains. Empty rooms. The sun was almost directly overhead. When she sat down on the steps the stone was warm. She was aware of the absolute silence – aware that outside this cloister was the quietness of a town in *siesta*. Inside, everything was intensified. Suddenly the silence was broken by the clattering of wings as several white doves flew onto the tiled roof. Maureen stood up and climbed the steps to the font. She leaned her elbows on the rim and looked at the round hole or shaft in the middle of it. She gave a little jump and leaned on her forearms, her feet off the ground, and looked down into the shaft. There was a white disc at the bottom.

"It's a well." She unslung her bag from her shoulder and found a 25 peseta coin – the one with a hole in it – and dropped it down. Nothing happened and she was amazed at the silence. How could there be nothing? Where was the sound of the coin dropping into the water below –

spluck!

She couldn't believe the depth. She took another coin and dropped it and counted as if making an exposure. A thousand and one – silence – a thousand and two – silence – a thousand and three – still silence – a thou –

spluck!

She heaved herself up again and looked into the well. The disc of light at the bottom rippled. There was something so *right* about this place. It was affecting her body. Her knees began to tremble. She held tight to the well head. She had to sit down on the steps and lean her back against the font.

She sat for the best part of an hour, sunbathing and absorbing the place. Occasionally she changed her position on the steps or walked in and out of the shadow of the cloisters. The place emphasised her aloneness. It felt as if it had been made for her and she should share it with no one. The cloister was a well for light – the cloister was a well for water. The word *Omphalos* came into her head. She connected the word to a poem of Heaney's she'd read somewhere. The stone that marked the centre of the world. The navel.

The sunlight and the clarity of the air squeezed into such a small space by the surrounding roofs became a lens which made her see herself with more precision. She did not think of herself as a middle-aged woman – she was still the same person she had been all her life – a child being bathed by her own mother – a teenager kissing. She was the same bride, the same mother-to-be in white socks and stirrups on the delivery table. Her soul was the same as that younger girl. She *felt* the same.

Soul was a word. What did it mean? People talked of stripping away layers to reveal the soul. It was not buried deep within her. It wasn't like that at all. Her soul was herself – it was the way she treated other people, it was the love for her children, for the people around her and for people she had never seen but felt responsible for. Her soul was the way she treated the world – ants and all.

She smiled at herself. In this place she knew who she was. In the hour she'd been here it had become sacred. She would remember this haven – this cloister – for the rest of her life.

By the time she got to the beach Jimmy was already there. He was lying flat out on a sun-bed with his back to the sun. Maureen went up and nudged his elbow with her shin.

"Hi."

"Buenos días," he said. He looked up sideways at her. "Where have you been?"

"Around. I went up into the old town."

"See anything?"

"The shops were closed. So was the church. Siesta."

"What kept you?"

"Exploring. I had a coffee. Sat in an old courtyard for a while." It was too late in the day to get the value out of lying on a sun-bed so she began spreading a towel, having flapped it free of sand. "Oh there's a fiesta tomorrow night – fire-works, specially for us leaving."

"That's nice of them."

"How are you feeling now?"

"Hunky dory." But he groaned all the same when he was turning over to get the sun on his chest. He cradled the back of his head in his hands and from be-tween his feet watched the German girl and her boyfriend. "You missed it earlier on," he said. "I'm sure she was lying on his hand."

"Jimmy – leave them alone. Don't be such a . . . "

"Remember that?"

"Sometimes I don't know what goes on in men's minds." She took off her shorts and T-shirt and lay down on the carefully spread towel. The beach was noisy – an English crowd were shouting their heads off at the water's edge – there was a baby crying having its nappy changed – euro-pop played and dishes rattled constantly in the beach café. "Or whether they've got minds at all."

The next evening before they went out to eat they decided to try and get the whiskey "used up" before going home. Because it was their last night they decided to dress up a bit. They sat on the balcony while it was still light. Maureen had a small whiskey and he a much bigger one.

"I better leave enough for a nightcap," said Jimmy.

"But you'll be drinking all evening."

"A nightcap's a nightcap. We judged the bottle well."

"We?"

"Almost as well as the All-Bran. If we were to stay here a day longer the bowels would grind to a halt."

They sat staring at the view – the sea straight at the horizon – the white buildings, the palm trees, the cranes.

"I'm going to miss this," said Maureen. All that week they had seen no-one working on the unfinished apartments. The cranes were unmanned but they moved imperceptibly – at no time did they respond like a weather vane to the wind but whenever Maureen or Jimmy had occasion to look up the cranes would be in different positions and at different angles to each other.

"The recession must be hitting here too," said Jimmy.

"It's back to normal next week."

"Don't mention it – don't ruin our last night."

"I think – I've been thinking . . . now that the kids are practically gone I might try and get a job."

"Doing what?"

She shrugged.

"I might train for something."

"At your age?" said Jimmy. "No chance."

"Why do you always put me down?"

"I'm just being *realistic*, Maureen."

"I got three distinctions in A levels. I held a good job in the photo works up until you came along."

"They were the days of black and white." He laughed.

"They were the days when they sacked you for being pregnant."

He finished his whiskey and stood.

"We'd better go if we want to eat *and* firework. Do I look okay?"

"Yeah, fine." She picked a few grey hairs off the collar of his navy blazer and dusted away some dandruff.

"You look good," he said and kissed her.

During the meal in the restaurant Jimmy drank three-quarters of the bottle of wine. He dismissed white wine as not drinking at all – "imbibing for young girls", he called it. By the time they'd had their coffee Jimmy had finished the bottle. Maureen noticed that he was looking over her shoulder more than usual during the meal. She glanced round and saw an attractive, tanned girl in a white dress sitting by herself.

"She's lovely, isn't she?" said Jimmy.

Maureen nodded. "Why's she by herself?"

"Because her lover has just gone to the crapper."

"And there was me building a romantic story . . ."

"Do you want the rest of your wine?"

Maureen shook her head. He poured what was left of her glass into his.

"Get the bill, Jimmy." He put his arm in the air and attracted the attention of the waiter. Left alone again he said,

"A woman by herself is the most erotic thought a man can have."

"What d'you mean?"

"By herself she is the complete item. The brain, the body, the emotions. In the shower, in bed. Uninterfered with. Herself."

"I still don't understand."

"Sexy. Absorbed. Unreachable. Aloof. Detached."

"I thought sexy was the opposite of detached."

"A woman in a shop", said Jimmy, "by herself is absorbed – choosing something to wear – looking through a rack of dresses."

"Or even studying a book – or even *writing* a book."

"You're really fucking bolshie this evening."

The partner of the woman in white returned to the table.

"He's back," said Jimmy. Maureen twisted in her seat to see.

"They can't be married," she said. "She smiled at him. That's very early days. Second or third date."

"Remember that?"

She smiled and put her hand on his.

"I do," said Maureen. "Vividly."

"That was a time of finding out . . . of knowing everything there is to know . . . There must be no privacy between people in love."

"Crap Jimmy. You're talking the impossible. Anyway, there can never be a situation where you know *everything* about another person. It's harder to know one thing *for sure*."

"Maybe."

"When there's nothing left to know there's no mystery. We would all be so utterly predictable."

The waiter brought the bill and they paid and left. Maureen checked her watch and saw there were only a couple of minutes before the fireworks were due to start. They walked quickly towards the main square.

It was a large open area overlooking the harbour. At the back of the square were the dark shapes of civic buildings. Gardens and pavements and steps descended to the sea. There were trees of different varieties symmetrically spaced. Looped between the trees were what looked like fairy lights but they were not working. Jimmy pointed them out to Maureen and laughed.

"They're about as organised as the Irish," he said. "If they had a microphone it'd whine."

The square was filled with local people waiting for the fireworks. Amongst them, holidaymakers like Jimmy and Maureen were obvious.

Suddenly there was a whoosh of a rocket followed by an ear-shattering bang. Both Maureen and Jimmy jumped visibly. There was a sound of drums and the raucous piping noise of a shawm and ten or so figures pranced into the middle of the square.

"It's the fucking Ku-Klax-Klan," said Jimmy.

They were dressed in white overalls, some like sheets, some like rough suits. Their heads were hidden in triangular hoods with eye-slits. Two or three of them were whacking drums, all of them were dancing – leaping and cart-wheeling.

"I don't like the look of these guys."

"They're really spooky."

"Like drunk ghosts."

"They're more like your man – Miro," said Maureen. The figures danced and dervished around, whirling hand-held fireworks and scattering fire crackers amongst the crowd who screamed and jostled out of their way.

"Jumpin jinnies, we used to call those," shouted Maureen. The troupe of dancers pushed sculptures on wheels with fireworks attached – shapes of crescent moons, of angular trees, of whirling globes – from which rockets and Roman candles burst red and green and yellow over the heads of the public. Between the feet of the bystanders crackers exploded. The air was filled with screams of both adults and children as they leapt away from them.

"Jesus – this is so dangerous," said Jimmy. "They're breaking every regulation in the book." The drums pounded and the pipe screeched on. As the sculptures were swung round they gushed sparks – sometimes it looked as if the sculptures moved *because* of the sparks – jet-propelled.

"Those robes must be fire-proofed. This wouldn't be allowed at home. It scares the shit outa me – All-Bran or no All-Bran."

"It's so utterly primitive – prehistoric," said Maureen.

"How could it be prehistoric. Gunpowder was invented in the middle ages."

"There would have been an equivalent – fire, torches, sparks."

"Come on let's get outa here before somebody gets hurt."

The troupe had split up and before Jimmy and Maureen could move three dancers had run up the steps and appeared behind them. Close up their robes were embroidered with Miro-like symbols. One of them held aloft a thing that looked like the spokes of an umbrella. Suddenly it burst into roaring fire – five Catherine wheels with whistles on them spraying sparks in every direction. They rained down on the crowd – white magnesium sparks – drenching them in light and danger and everyone screamed and covered their heads with their hands.

"Fucking hell," shouted Jimmy. Maureen saw the white hot sparks bouncing off the cobblestones like dashing rain – white, intense, like welder's sparks. She tried to cover her head – she knew the skin of her shoulders was bare. But she felt nothing. Neither did Jimmy. They ran, Jimmy elbowing his way through the crowd away from the dancers, pulling Maureen after him by the hand. On the edge of the crowd they looked at each other and laughed.

"They're like kids' hand-held fireworks," said Jimmy. "They're harmless. Fuckin sparklers."

"Are you sure?"

"I'm not going back to check, I'll tell you that."

Again there was a series of enormous explosions just above their heads so that Maureen screamed out. What Jimmy had thought were broken fairy lights were fire crackers going off a few feet above their heads. They both ran holding hands.

They stopped at a small pavement area outside a bistro still in sight of the fireworks and they were both given a free sherry. The three supposed priests sat at a table near the door. They nodded recognition to each other. Jimmy ordered Menorcan gin and because he was going home the next evening allowed the barman to fill the glass with ice. They sat at the same side of the table, shoulder to shoulder, at a safe distance from the fireworks.

"It's pure street theatre," said Maureen. "The audience are involved because of their fear. The adrenalin flows. The costumes, the music, the fire –"

"It could never happen at home."

"Yeah, we kill people outright."

"The danger brings pleasure. It involves the audience totally."

"Look," said Jimmy. The young German couple were walking away from the fireworks. They had an arm around each other. They stopped to kiss and the boy slid both his hands down onto Heidrun's backside to hold her closer.

"They make a fine couple – even though we don't know their language." When the kiss was finished the lovers walked passed the bistro. The boy's hand was worming its way down the back of her shorts and Heidrun was leaning her blonde head against his shoulder.

Jimmy mimicked the gesture and laid his head on Maureen's bare shoulder.

"I'd still be interested to know how far you went with previous – the men before me? You knew some pretty good tricks."

She looked at him tight-lipped then moved away from his head.

"I wouldn't like to see you with another man *now* – but I'd like to have seen you with one *then*."

"This got us nowhere before," she said quietly. "Jimmy, give it a rest."

"No, why should I? Tell me about the first time you came, then."

"I would if I could – if it's SO important to you. But I can't so I won't. Would you like to ask your daughters this question the next time you see them?"

"Don't be stupid. That's a totally different thing."

"I don't see why."

"Why can't you tell me?" said Jimmy. "You're repressed. Why can't we talk openly about this?"

"It's *you* that's repressed," she almost shouted, "wanting to know stuff like that. It's becoming a fixation."

"It was a question I'd always wanted to ask. I thought – what better time. Holiday. Alone. No kids."

"No time is a good time for questions like that."

When she lifted her sherry her hand was shaking.

"Don't make such a big thing of it."

"When you do those kind of things with people there's a pact – a kind of unspoken thing – that it's private – that it's just between the two of you. Secrecy is a matter of honour."

"So you *have* done it."

"No – *don't be so stupid* – it could be just kissing or affection or kidding on or flirting. Whatever it was it's none of your fucking business."

She did not finish her sherry but got to her feet.

"I'm going home. You can stay here with your priests, if you like."

At about three o'clock Jimmy crawled into bed beside her and wakened her from a deep sleep. He was drunk and crying and apologising and patting her shoulder and telling her how good she was and how much she meant to him and that he would never ever ever ever leave her. He was a pest but that's the way he was and she could like it or lump it. But she was a wonderful woman.

"Jimmy, shut up – will you?" Now that he had disturbed her she got up and went to the bathroom. When she came back he was snoring loudly. She closed the latch of the bedroom door so that he wouldn't waken and tried to get some sleep on the sofa. She felt alone on the narrow rectangle of foam – lonely even – a very different feeling to the wonderful solitariness she had experienced in the cloisters. She couldn't sleep. The thought of leaving Jimmy came into her head but it seemed so impossibly difficult, not part of any reality. Nothing bad enough had happened – or good enough – to force her to examine the possibility seriously. Where would she live? How could she tell the girls? What would she tell her parents? Jimmy was right about getting a job. It seemed so much simpler to stay as they were. The status quo. People stayed together because it was the best arrangement. She slept eventually and in the morning she could not distinguish when her deliberations had tailed off and turned to dreaming.

"Jimmy, I think we should try and salvage something from the last day.' She spoke to wake him. Startled, he turned in the bed to face the room. Maureen had the large suitcase open on the floor. She was holding one of his jackets beneath her chin then folding the arms across the chest. She packed it into the case, then reached for another. Jimmy tried not to groan. He sat on the side of the bed and slowly realised he was still in his clothes. She must have taken his shoes off him. He put his bald head in his hands.

"Is the kettle boiled?"

"It was – a couple of hours ago."

He got up and finished the packet of All-Bran – bran dust at this stage. He made tea and a piece of toast in the skeletal toaster. Maureen continued to pack.

"What time's the flight?" he asked.

"Eighteen hundred hours."

"I hate those fucking times. What time is that?"

"Minus twelve. Six o'clock."

Jimmy had a shower and changed his clothes. After he cleaned his teeth he packed everything in sight into his wash-bag. He came out of the bathroom with a towel round his middle. He was grinning. Maureen was kneeling on the floor packing dirty washing into a Spar plastic bag.

"I've got the hang-over horn."

"Well, that's just too bad. There's things to be done."

"Indeed there are."

Maureen got a brush and a plastic dust-pan. The living room floor was scritchy with sand spilled from their shoes. Earlier in the week Jimmy had knocked over a tumbler and it had exploded on the tiled floor into a million tiny fragments. She thought she had swept them all up at the time but still she was finding dangerous shards in the dust.

Between the bathroom and the living room the dead ants still blackened the margins of the honey-poison. There was no mop and she had not wanted to sweep them up and make the floor sticky underfoot. Now it didn't seem to matter and she swept the whole mess onto the dust pan. Individual ants had lost their form and were now just black specks. She turned on the tap and washed them down the plug hole.

Jimmy was sent down the street to the waste-bins while she put any usable food in the fridge as a gift for whoever cleaned up. When he came back everything was done and the cases were sitting in the middle of the floor. Maureen was drinking a last coffee and there was one on the table for him.

He stood behind her chair and put his arms round her.

"I'm sorry," he said. "About last night. Going on and on about those . . ." He kissed the top of her hair.

"Jimmy – promise me. You mustn't annoy me about that again."

"Okay – scout's honour." He began massaging the muscles which joined her neck and shoulders.

"Oh – easy – that hurts."

"What time do we have to vacate this place?"

"Mid-day."

He bent over and whispered, "That gives us twenty minutes."

They left their luggage at the Tour company headquarters for the remaining hours and went down to the beach. They walked along to the rocky promontory at the far side.

"I've really enjoyed this," said Jimmy. "The whole thing."

"Who did you meet up with last night?"

"They said they were social workers. Which means they admitted to being priests in mufti. They were okay."

"What did you talk about?"

"I'm afraid eh . . . Large chunks of it are missing. We seemed to laugh a lot. I think they were every bit as pissed as I was."

"I don't like the look of them. They're the kind of people who'd go out of their way to take a short cut."

They sat on the rocks watching the sea swell in and out at their feet.

"It's very clear," said Jimmy. The water was blue-green, transparent.

"You can be a real pest when you come in like that. You look so *stupid*."

"Sorry."

They became aware of an old couple in bathing suits paddling into the sea close by the rocks, They looked like they were in their eighties. The woman wore a pink bathing cap which was shaped like a conical shell. Her wrinkled back was covered in moles or age spots as if someone had thrown a handful of wet sand at her back. The old man had the stub of an unlit cigar clamped in the corner of his mouth. Their skin was sallow. Mediterranean but paler than those around them for not having been exposed to the sun – although their faces and arms were the nut-brown colour of people who had worked in the open. The old man was taking the woman by the elbow and speaking loudly to her in Spanish, scolding her almost. But maybe she was deaf or could not hear, her ears being covered by the puce conical cap. She was shaking her head, her features cross. They were thigh-deep and wading. When the water rose to her waist she began to make small stirring motions with her hands as if she were performing the breast stroke. She made the sign of the cross. The old man shouted at her again. She dismissed him with a wave of her hand, then submerged herself by crouching down. She kept her face out of the water. The old man reached out from where he stood and cupped his hand under her chin. She began to make the breast-stroke motions with her arms, this time *in* the water. The old man shouted encouragement to her. She swam about ten or twelve strokes unaided until she swallowed sea water, coughed and threshed to her feet. The old man yelled and flung his damp cigar stub out to sea.

"Jesus – he's teaching her to swim." Jimmy turned and looked up at his wife. Maureen was somewhere between laughing and crying.

"That's magic," she said. "What a bloody magic thing to do."

REPORT ON THE SHADOW INDUSTRY

Peter Carey

Peter Carey (b.1943) is one of Australia's finest novelists. Born in Bacchus Marsh, his novels include the Man Booker Prize winning *Oscar and Lucinda* and *True History of the Kelly Gang*. He has also won the Commonwealth Writers' Prize twice and the Miles Franklin Literary Award three times. His most recent work includes *The Chemistry of Tears* and *Amnesia*. He lives in New York. He once said of his work, "If you ever read one of my books I hope you'll think it looks so easy. In fact, I wrote those chapters twenty times over, and over, and over, and if you want to write at a good level, you'll have to do that too."

1.

My friend S. went to live in America ten years ago and I still have the letter he wrote me when he first arrived, wherein he describes the shadow factories that were springing up on the west coast and the effects they were having on that society. "You see people in dark glasses wandering around the supermarkets at 2 a.m. There are great boxes all along the aisles, some as expensive as fifty dollars but most of them only five. There's always Muzak. It gives me the shits more than the shadows. The people don't look at one another. They come to browse through the boxes of shadows although the packets give no indication of what's inside. It really depresses me to think of people going out at two in the morning because they need to try their luck with a shadow. Last week I was in a super-market near Topanga and I saw an old negro tear the end off a shadow box. He was arrested almost immediately."

A strange letter ten years ago but it accurately describes scenes that have since become common in this country. Yesterday I drove in from the airport past shadow factory after shadow factory, large faceless buildings gleaming in the sun, their secrets guarded by ex-policemen with Alsatian dogs.

The shadow factories have huge chimneys that reach far into the sky, chimneys which billow forth smoke of different, brilliant colours. It is said by some of my more cynical friends that the smoke has nothing to do with any manufac-turing process and is merely a trick, fake evidence that technological miracles are being performed within the factories. The popular belief is that the smoke sometimes contains the most powerful shadows of all, those that are too large and powerful to be packaged. It is a common sight to see old women standing for hours outside the factories, staring into the smoke.

There are a few who say the smoke is dangerous because of carcinogenic chemicals used in the manufacture of shadows. Others argue that the shadow is a natural product and by its very nature chemically pure. They point to the advantages of the smoke: the beautifully coloured patterns in the clouds which serve as a reminder of the happiness to be obtained from a fully realized shadow. There may be some merit in this last argument, for on cloudy days the skies above our city are a wondrous sight, full of blues and vermilions and brilliant greens which pick out strange patterns and shapes in the clouds.

Others say that the clouds now contain the dreadful beauty of the apocalypse.

2.

The shadows are packaged in large, lavish boxes which are printed with abstract designs in many colours. The Bureau of Statistics reveals that the average house-holder spends 25 per cent of his income on these expensive goods and that this percentage increases as the income decreases.

There are those who say that the shadows are bad for people, promising an impossible happiness that can never be realized and thus detracting from the very real beauties of nature and life. But there are others who argue that the shadows have always been with us in one form or another and that the pack-aged shadow is necessary for mental health in an advanced technological society. There is, however, research to indicate that the high suicide rate in advanced countries is connected with the popularity of shadows and that there is a direct statistical correlation between shadow sales and suicide rates. This has been ex-plained by those who hold that the shadows are merely mirrors to the soul and that the man who stares into a shadow box sees only himself, and what beauty he finds there is his own beauty and what despair he experiences is born of the poverty of his spirit.

3.

I visited my mother at Christmas. She lives alone with her dogs in a poor part of town. Knowing her weakness for shadows I brought her several of the more expensive varieties which she retired to examine in the privacy of the shadow room.

She stayed in the room for such a long time that I became worried and knocked on the door. She came out almost immediately. When I saw her face I knew the shadows had not been good ones.

"I'm sorry," I said, but she kissed me quickly and began to tell me about a neighbour who had won the lottery.

I myself know, only too well, the disappointments of shadow boxes for I also have a weakness in that direction. For me it is something of a guilty secret, some-thing that would not be approved of by my clever friends.

I saw J. in the street. She teaches at the university.

"Ah-hah," she said knowingly, tapping the bulky parcel I had hidden under my coat. I know she will make capital of this discovery, a little piece of gossip to use at the dinner parties she is so fond of. Yet I suspect that she too has a weakness for shadows. She confessed as much to me some years ago during that strange misunderstanding she still likes to call "Our Affair". It was she who hinted at the feeling of emptiness, that awful despair that comes when one has failed to grasp the shadow.

4.

My own father left home because of something he had seen in a box of shadows. It wasn't an expensive box, either, quite the opposite — a little surprise my mother had bought with the money left over from her housekeeping. He opened it after dinner one Friday night and he was gone before I came down to breakfast on the Saturday. He left a note which my mother only showed me very recently. My father was not good with words and had trouble communicating what he had seen: "Words Cannot Express It What I feel Because of The Things I Saw In The Box Of Shadows You Bought Me."

5.

My own feelings about the shadows are ambivalent, to say the least. For here I have manufactured one more: elusive, unsatisfactory, hinting at greater beauties and more profound mysteries that exist somewhere before the beginning and somewhere after the end.

THE TEACHER'S STORY

Gita Mehta

Gita Mehta (b.1943) is the author of *Karma Cola*, *Raj* and *Snakes and Ladders*, as well as a beguiling book of interlinked tales, *A River Sutra*. Married with one son, she divides her time between the USA, India and England.

M aster Mohan was not a bitter man. Although he led an unhappy life his gentle nature disposed him to small acts of kindness; helping a stranger to dismount from a rickshaw, reaching into his pockets to find a boiled sweet for a child, and when he walked down the narrow streets leading to the avenue where he boarded the tram which took him to his music students, he was greeted warmly by the neighbours sitting on their tiny verandas to catch the breeze.

"Good evening, Master Mohan."

"A late class, tonight?"

"Walk under the streetlights coming home, Master Mohan. These days one must be careful."

Near the tram stop, the paanwallah smearing lime paste onto his paan leaves always shouted from inside his wooden stall,

"Master! Master! Let me give you a paan. A little betel leaf will help you through the pain of hearing your students sing."

Even though it meant losing his place in the queue Master Mohan stopped to talk to the paanwallah and listen to his gossip of the comings and goings in the quarter. And so he was the first to learn the great Quawwali singers from Nizam-uddin were coming to Calcutta.

"You should ask Mohammed-sahib to go with you. You are a teacher of music, he is a lover of poetry. And they are singing so nearby, in that mosque on the other side of the bazaar."

"But my wife will not go even that far to hear –"

"Wives! Don't talk to me of wives. I never take mine anywhere. Nothing destroys a man's pleasure like a wife."

Master Mohan knew the paanwallah was being kind. His wife's contempt for him was no secret on their street. The small houses were built on top of each other and his wife never bothered to lower her voice. Everyone knew she had come from a wealthier family than his and could barely survive on the money he brought back from his music lessons.

"What sins did I commit in my last life that I should be yoked to this apology for a man. See how you are still called Master Mohan as if you were only ten years old. Gupta-sahib you should be called. But who respects you enough to make even that small effort!"

Her taunts re-opened a wound which might have healed if only Master Mohan's wife had left him alone. The music teacher had acquired the name as a child singer when he had filled concert halls with admirers applauding the purity of his voice. His father, himself a music teacher, had saved every paisa from his earnings to spend on Master Mohan's training, praying his son's future would be secured with a recording contract.

But it takes a very long time for a poor music teacher to cultivate connections with the owners of recording studios. For four years Master Mohan's father had pleaded for assistance from the wealthy families at whose houses his son sang on the occasion of a wedding or a birthday. For four years he had stood outside recording studios, muffling his coughs as tuberculosis ate away at his lungs, willing himself to stay alive until his son's talent was recognised, urging the boy to practise for that first record which would surely astonish the world.

When the recording contract was finally offered, only weeks before the record was to be made, Master Mohan's voice had broken.

Every day his wife reminded him how his voice had not mellowed in the years that followed. "Your family has the evil eye. Whatever you touch is cursed, whatever you are given you lose."

Sometimes Master Mohan tried to escape his wife's taunts by reminding himself of those four years of happiness that had preceded the moment when the golden bowl of his voice had shattered and with it his life. As her shrill insults went on and and on, drilling into his brain, he found himself only able to remember his father's anguish that his son would have to abandon a great career as a singer, becoming just another music teacher like himself.

Master Mohan's father had made one last effort to help his son by engaging him in marriage to the daughter of a rich village landowner who loved music. He had lived long enough to see the marriage performed but not long enough to celebrate the birth of his two grandchildren, or to witness the avarice of his daughter-in-law when her own father died and her brothers took the family wealth, leaving her dependent on Master Mohan's earnings.

Prevented by pride from criticising her own family, Master Mohan's wife had held her husband responsible for the treachery of her brothers, raising their children to believe it was only Master Mohan's weakness and stupidity which had robbed them of the servants, the cars, the fancy clothes from foreign countries, which should have been their right.

"How can I ever forgive myself for burdening you with this sorry creature for a father? Come Babloo, come Dolly. Have some fruit. Let him make his own tea."

With such exactitude had she perfected her cruelty that Master Mohan's children despised their father's music as they despised him, allying themselves with their mother's neglect.

After giving music lessons all day Master Mohan was left to cook a meagre meal for himself, which he took up to the small roof terrace of the house to escape his household's contempt. But he could not escape the blaring film music from the radio, or the loud noise of the gramophone echoing up the narrow stone stairwell leading to the terrace. It set him coughing, sometimes so loudly that his wife, or his daughter and son, would run up the stairs yelling at him to be quiet. Though he tried Master Mohan could not stop coughing. It was a nervous reaction to his family's ability to silence the music he heard in his own head.

So when the paanwallah told him about the Quawwali singers Master Mohan found himself daydreaming on the tram. He had never heard the singers from Nizamuddin where Quawwali music had been born seven hundred years ago. But he knew Nizamuddin had been the fountain from which the poems and songs of the great Sufi mystics had flowed throughout India, and that even today its teachers still trained the finest Quawwali musicians in the country. He could not believe his good fortune – seven nights spent away from his wife and children listening to their music. And what is more, the music could be heard free.

On his way home that evening he stopped outside Mohammed-sahib's house. Finding him on his veranda, Master Mohan asked shyly if he would be listening to the Quawwali singers.

"Only if you accompany me. I am a poor fool who never knows what he is hearing unless it is explained to him."

So it was settled and the next week Master Mohan hardly heard his wife and children shouting at him as he cooked himself a simple meal, relishing the taste of it while they listened to their noisy film music.

"Make sure you do not wake up the whole house when you return!" his wife shouted behind him as he slipped into the street.

By the time Master Mohan and Mohammed-sahib reached the tent tethered to one side of the mosque the singing had begun and curious bazaar children crowded at the entrances.

Mohammed-sahib peered over their heads in disappointment. "We are too late. There is nowhere for us to sit."

Master Mohan refused to give up so easily. He squeezed past the children to look for a vacant place in the tent filled with people listening in rapt attention to the passionate devotional music breaking in waves over their heads.

He felt a familiar excitement as he led his friend to a small gap between the rows of people crushed against each other on the floor. The fluorescent lights winking from the struts supporting the tent, the musty odour of the cotton carpets covering the ground brought back the concerts of his childhood, and a constriction inside himself began to loosen.

On the podium nine performers sat cross-legged in a semi-circle around a harmonium and a pair of tablas. An old sheikh from Nizamuddin sat to one side, his white beard disappearing into the loose robes flowing around him. Every now and then a spectator, moved by the music, handed the sheikh money which he received as an offering to God before placing it near the tabla drums sending their throbbing beat into the night.

The more the singers were carried away by their music the more Master Mohan felt the weight that burdened him lighten, as if the ecstasy of the song being relayed from one throat to another was lifting him into a long-forgotten ecstasy himself.

Twice Mohammed-sahib got up to place money at the sheikh's feet. Master Mohan watched him stepping over crossed legs as he made his way to the stage, ashamed his own poverty prevented him from expressing gratitude to the singers for reviving emotions which he had thought dead.

After two hours Mohammed-sahib's funds and patience were exhausted, and he went home. Gradually the tent began to empty until only a few beggar children remained, asleep on the cotton carpets. Master Mohan looked at his watch. It was three o'clock in the morning.

In front of Master Mohan a young woman holding the hand of a child suddenly approached the podium to whisper to the sheikh. The sheikh leaned across to the singers wiping perspiration from their foreheads.

The lead singer nodded wearily and the young woman pulled the child behind her up the stairs. The boy stumbled twice, struggling to recover his balance. Then he was on the podium, both hands stretched in front of him. Master Mohan realised the boy was blind as the woman pushed him down next to the singers.

The lead singer sang a verse. The other singers took up the chorus. The lead singer sang another verse, his arm extended to the boy who could not see him. The singers prodded him and the startled child entered the song two octaves above the others.

"I prostrate my head to the blade of Your sword.
    O, the wonder of my submission.
    O, the wonder of Your protection."

It was a sound Master Mohan had only heard in his dreams.

"In the very spasm of death I see Your face.
    O, the wonder of Your protection.
    O, the wonder of my submission."

Until this moment he had believed such purity of tone was something which could only be imagined but never realised by the human voice.

He crept forward until he was sitting by the young woman.

"Who is that child?" he asked.

The young woman turned a pleasant face pinched by worry to him. "My brother, Imrat. This is the first song my father taught Imrat – the song of the children of the Nizamuddin Quawwali."

Tears glistened in the large eyes. Under the fluorescent lights Master Mohan thought they magnified her eyes into immense pearls. "Last year I brought Imrat with me to Calcutta to sell my embroidery. While we were here, terrible floods swept our village away. Our father, my husband, everybody was killed."

Master Mohan glanced at the stage. The singers were already intoxicated by the power of their combined voices, unable to distinguish the singular voice of the child from all the other voices praising God.

"Do not reveal the Truth in a world where blasphemy prevails.
    O wondrous Source of Mystery.
    O Knower of Secrets."

* * *

The woman covered her face with her hands. "I have been promised a job as a maidservant with a family who are leaving for the north of India but I cannot take my brother because he is blind. I hope the sheikh will take Imrat to Nizam-uddin until I can earn enough to send for him."

Master Mohan felt tears welling in his own eyes as he heard the high voice sing,

> "I prostrate my head to the blade of Your sword
>   O, the wonder of Your guidance.
>   O, the wonder of my submission."

The next evening Mohammed-sahib confessed, "I am not as musical as you, Master. God will forgive me for not accompanying you tonight."

So Master Mohan went alone to hear the Quawwali singers. The young woman and the blind child were sitting under the podium, still there when the other spectators had gone.

He waited all evening, hoping to hear the child's pure voice again but that night the boy did not join the singers on the stage. The following night and the next, Master Mohan was disappointed to see the young woman and her brother were not present at the Quawwali.

On the fourth night Master Mohan found himself the last listener to leave the tent. As he hurried through the deserted alleys of the dark bazaar he heard someone calling behind him, "Sahib, wait. For the love of Allah, listen to us."

He turned under the solitary street lamp at the end of the bazaar. The woman was pulling the child past the shuttered shops towards him.

"Please, sahib. The Quawwali singers are travelling around India. They cannot take my brother with them, and in two days I must start work or lose my job. You have a kind face, sahib. Can you keep Imrat? He is a willing worker. He will do the sweeping or chop your vegetables. Just feed him and give him a place to sleep until I can send for him."

A drunk stumbled towards the street lamp. "What's the woman's price, pimp? Offer me a bargain. She won't find another customer tonight."

The woman shrank into the darkness clutching the child in her arms. "For the love of Allah, sahib. Help us. We have nowhere to turn."

To his astonishment Master Mohan heard himself saying, "I am a music teacher. I will take your brother as my pupil. Now you must return to the safety of the mosque."

The woman turned obediently into the dark alley. Master Mohan was grateful she could not see the expression on his face or she must surely have recognised his fear at the offer he had made.

At the entrance to the tent he said, "I will come tomorrow evening to fetch the child."

The woman turned her face away to hide her gratitude, whispering, "Please, sahib, I have a last request. See my brother follows the practices of Islam."

The next morning Master Mohan went to the corner of the avenue to consult the paanwallah.

"You did what, Master? Do you know what your wife and children will do to that poor boy?"

"They would not harm a defenceless child!"

"Your wife will never permit you to keep the boy. Make some excuse to the sister. Get out of it somehow."

As they argued Mohammed-sahib joined them.

"I couldn't help myself." Master Mohan pleaded. "The girl was crying. If she loses her job how will she feed herself and a blind brother? This is no city for a young woman alone."

Mohammed-sahib pulled at his moustache. "You have done a very fine thing, my friend. Prohibit your wife from interfering in your affairs. It is you who feed and clothe your family and put a roof over their heads. Your decision as to who shall share that roof is final and irreversible." He slapped Master Mohan on the back and turned towards the tram stop.

The paanwallah shook his head. "That fellow is as puffed up as a peacock. It is easy for him to give advice when it costs him nothing. Don't go back for the child, Master."

But Master Mohan could not betray the young woman's trust, even when he returned to the tent that night and saw the sobbing boy clinging to his sister's legs. Master Mohan lifted the weeping child in his arms as the sister consoled her brother. "I'll write often. Study hard with your kind teacher until I send for you. You'll hardly notice the time until we are together again."

The child was asleep by the time Master Mohan reached his silent household. He crept up the stone stairs to the terrace and laid Imrat on the cloth mattress, pleased when the child rolled over onto his torn shawl and continued sleeping.

Well, you can imagine how his wife shrieked the next morning when she discovered what Master Mohan had done. As the days passed her rage did not diminish. In fact, it got worse. Each day Master Mohan returned from giving his music lessons in the city to find his wife waiting on the doorstep with fresh accusations about the blind boy's insolence, his clumsiness, his greed. She carried her attack into the kitchen when Master Mohan was trying to cook food for himself and Imrat, chasing behind him up the narrow stairwell so that everyone could hear her abuse raging over the rooftops.

When Master Mohan continued to refuse her demand that Imrat be thrown out into the street, Dolly and Babloo triumphantly joined in their mother's battle, complaining they no longer got enough to eat with another mouth sharing their food. In the evenings they placed their gramophone on the very top step of the stone staircase just outside the terrace, so the child could not hear the fragile drone of Master Mohan's tanpura strings giving the key for Imrat's music lesson. They teased Imrat by withholding his sister's letters, sometimes even tearing them up before Master Mohan had returned to the house and was able to read them to the waiting child.

Somehow Master Mohan discovered a strength in himself equal to his family's cruelty to Imrat. He arranged for the child's letters to be left with the paanwallah and on the rare occasions when he entered the house and found his family gone to visit friends he gently encouraged Imrat to stop cowering against the walls and become a child again. He would cook some special dish, letting the boy join in the preparations, encouraging him to eat his fill. Then he would take the child onto the roof terrace. Allowing his fingers to play over the strings of his tanpura until he found the note best suited to the boy's range Master Mohan would ask Imrat to sing.

Hearing the clear notes pierce the night, Master Mohan knew he had been made guardian of something rare, as if his own life until now had only been a purification to ready him for the task of tending this voice for the world.

Then one day the music teacher returned late from giving a music lesson and found his daughter holding Imrat down while his son tried to force pork into the child's mouth. The child's sightless eyes were wide open, tears streaming down his cheeks. For the first time in his life Master Mohan struck his children. "He's only nine years old. How can you torture a child so much younger than yourselves! Get out of this house until you learn civilised behaviour!"

With those words war was declared in Master Mohan's household. His wife accused Master Mohan of striking his own children out of preference for a blind beggar, unleashing such furious threats at the child that Master Mohan was worried Imrat would run away.

Mohammed-sahib would not agree to let Imrat live in his house, despite the music teacher's eloquent pleading. As he listened to Mohammed-sahib's elaborate excuses Master Mohan realised his friend wished to avoid the unpleasantness of dealing with his wife.

"I warned you, Master," the paanwallah said with satisfaction when he heard of Mohammed-sahib's response. "That man is just good for free advice. Now there is only one thing to do. Go to the park in the early mornings. Only goats and shepherds will disturb you there. Don't give up, Master. After all, there is a whole world in which to practise, away from the distractions of your house."

So the music teacher woke his young charge before dawn and they boarded the first tram of the morning to reach the great park that is the centre of Calcutta City.

When they arrived at the park Master Mohan led Imrat by the hand between the homeless men and women wrapped in tattered cloths asleep under the great English oaks turning red each time the neon signs flashed, past the goatherds gossiping by their aluminium canisters until it was time to milk the goats grazing on the grass, towards the white balustrades that enclosed the marble mausoleum of the Victoria Memorial.

The music teacher lowered his cane mat and his tanpura over the side of the balustrade before gently lifting Imrat onto the wall. Climbing over himself, he lifted the child down, both so silent in the dark the guard asleep in his sentry box was left undisturbed.

With a swishing sound Master Mohan unrolled his cane mat, still smelling of green fields, and seated Imrat sat next to him.

Then he played the first notes of the morning raga on his tanpura. To his delight Imrat repeated the scale faultlessly.

Master Mohan explained the significance of the raga, initiating Imrat into the mystery of the world's rebirth, when light disperses darkness and Vishnu rises from his slumbers to re-dream the universe.

Again Imrat sang the scale, but there was a new resonance in his voice. He could not see the faint blur of the picket fences ringing the race course in the distance, or the summit of Ochterlony's Needle breaking through the smoke from the illegal fires built by the street hawkers around the base of the obelisk. He could not even see the guard looking through his sentry box, his hand half-raised to expel them from the gardens, frozen in that gesture by the boy's voice. He only saw the power of the morning raga and dreaming visions of light he pushed his voice towards them, believing sight was only a half-tone away.

Afraid the raga would strain the child's voice Master Mohan asked Imrat to sing a devotional song. The boy obediently turned his head towards the warmth of the sun's first rays and sang,

> "The heat of Your presence
> Blinds my eyes.
> Blisters my skin.
> Shrivels my flesh.
>
> "Do not turn in loathing from me.
> O Beloved, can You not see
> Only Love disfigures me?"

Master Mohan patted Imrat's head. "That is a beautiful prayer. Where did you learn such a song?"

Tears clouded the clouded eyes. "It is a poem by Amir Rumi. My father said that one day he and I would sing it at Amir Rumi's tomb together."

The music teacher took the child in his arms. "You will still sing at Amir Rumi's tomb, I promise you. And your father will hear your voice from heaven. Come, sing it once more so I can listen properly."

The child blew his nose and again shocked the music teacher with the power of his voice.

> "Do not turn in loathing from me.
> O Beloved, can You not see
> Only Love disfigures me?"

At that moment a sudden belief took root in Master Mohan's mind. He was convinced God was giving him a second voice, greater than he had ever heard, greater than his own could ever have been. He was certain such a voice must only be used to praise God, lest fate exact a second revenge by robbing him of it.

Sure of his purpose as a teacher at last Master Mohan asked the boy, "Did your father ever teach you the prayers of Kabir? Do you know this hymn?"

He played some notes on his tanpura and Imrat responded with excitement, opening his throat full to contain the mystic's joy.

> "O servant, where do you seek Me?
> You will not find Me in temple or mosque,
> In Kaaba or in Kailash,
> In yoga or renunciation.

"Sings Kabir, 'O seeker, find God
In the breath of all breathing.'"

And now a most extraordinary thing happened. Someone threw a coin over the wall and it fell on the grass in front of Master Mohan. The music teacher stood up. On the other side of the balustrades, just visible in the first light of dawn, he saw a group of goatherds leaning on the wall.

By the next morning people were already waiting for them and the guard waved Master Mohan and Imrat benevolently through the gate. Word had spread in the park that a blind boy with the voice of an angel was singing in the gardens of the Victoria Memorial. In the darkness goat-herds, street hawkers, refugees with children huddled to their bodies, waited patiently for Imrat to practise the scales of the morning raga before Master Mohan permitted him to sing the devotional songs which would give them the endurance to confront the indignities of their lives for another day.

Morning after morning they listened to the music teacher instruct Imrat in the songs of Kabir and Mirabai, of Khusrau and Tulsidas, of Chisti and Chandidas, the wandering poets and mystics who had made India's soul visible to herself. Sometimes they even asked the boy to repeat a song and Master Mohan could see them responding to the purity of the lyrics translated with such innocence by Imrat's voice.

To show their gratitude they began to leave small offerings on the wall above the balustrade; fruit, coins, a few crumpled rupees. And when the morning lesson ended, the street vendors crowded around Master Mohan and Imrat to offer a glass of steaming sweet tea or a hot samosa straight off a scalding iron pan.

Within a week Imrat's audience had expanded. Wealthy people on their morning walks stopped at the balustrades, drawn by the beauty of Imrat singing,

"Some seek God in Mecca,
Some seek God in Benares.
Each finds his own path and the focus of his worship.

"Some worship Him in Mecca.
Some in Benares.
But I centre my worship on the eyebrow of my Beloved."

Over the weeks more and more people made the balustrade part of their morning routines, until Master Mohan was able to recognise many faces at the wall, and every day he smiled at a young woman who folded a ten rupee note, placing it in a crevice in the parapet.

When they dismounted from the tram, the paanwallah shouted his congratulations to fortify them against the raging wife waiting at the music teacher's house.

"Well, little Master Imrat. Your fame is spreading throughout Calcutta. Soon you will be rich. How much money did you make today?"

"Thirteen rupees." Imrat pulled the music teacher towards the sound of the paanwallah's voice. "How much have we got now?"

"Still a long way to go, Master Imrat. But here is another letter from your sister."

The paanwallah kept Imrat's money so Master Mohan's wife would not take it. It was Imrat's dream to earn enough money by his singing to live with his sister again and each time she wrote he sang with renewed force.

Perhaps it was the fervour in Imrat's voice the morning after he had received another letter from his sister that made the miracle happen.

As Imrat was ending his song a man in a blazer shouted, "Come on, come on, my good fellow. I haven't got all morning. Do you read English?"

The music teacher put down his tanpura and walked to the balustrade. The man handed him a paper without even looking at him, turning to the woman at his side. "Does the boy have a name or not? Can't sign a recording contract without a name."

Master Mohan pulled himself to his full height in defence of the child's dignity although the man in the blazer had his back to him. "He is blind and cannot read or write. But I am his guardian. I can sign for him."

"Jolly good. Turn up at the studio this afternoon so the engineers can do a preliminary test. That's what you want isn't it, Neena?"

His companion lifted her face and Master Mohan saw she was the woman who left ten rupees on the wall every day.

She smiled at Master Mohan's recognition. "Is this gifted child your son?"

Master Mohan shyly told her the story of Imrat, suppressing anything that might reflect well on himself, only praising the boy's talent. He could see the interest in her eyes but the man was pulling at her elbow. "Fascinating, fascinating. Well, be sure to be at the studio at four o'clock. The address in on the contract."

Master Mohan studied the paper. "It says nothing here about payment."

"Payment?" For the first time the man in the blazer looked at him. "Singing for coppers in the park and you dare ask for payment?"

"We are not beggars." Master Mohan could not believe his own temerity. "I am a music teacher. I give the boy his lessons here so as not to disturb our household."

The woman laid her hand on the man's arm. "Don't be such a bully, Ranjit. Offer him a thousand rupees. You'll see it is a good investment."

The man laughed indulgently. "You are the most demanding sister a man ever had. Here, give me that paper." He pulled a pen from his blazer and scribbled down the sum, signing his name after it.

Master Mohan folded the paper and put it carefully in his pocket. When he looked up he saw two men watching him from the other side of the wall. Their oiled hair and stained teeth frightened him, bringing back memories of the musicians who had waited outside the great houses where he had sung as a child, until the menfolk sent for the dancing girls who often did not even dance before musicians such as these led them to the bedrooms.

On their way home Imrat lifted his blind eyes to his teacher and whispered, "But how much money is a thousand rupees? Enough to find somewhere to live with you and my sister?"

The music teacher hugged the child. "If the record is a success you can be together with your sister. Now try and rest. This afternoon you must not be tired."

As they dismounted from the tram the paanwallah shouted, "Last night two musicians were asking about about you, Master. Did they come to hear Imrat today?"

Imrat interrupted the paanwallah. "We are going to make a record and get lots of money."

"A record, Master Imrat! Be sure you sing well. Then I will buy a gramophone to listen to you."

It was no surprise to Master Mohan that Imrat sang as he did that afternoon. The child could not see the microphone dangling from the wire covered with flies or the bored faces watching him behind the glass panel. He only saw himself in his sister's embrace and when the recording engineer ordered him to sing the studio reverberated with his joy.

"The boy has recording genius," an engineer admitted reluctantly as Imrat ended his song. "His timing is so exact we can print these as they are."

"Ranjit-sahib will be very pleased. I'll call him."

A few minutes later the man in the blazer strode into the office followed by his engineers. "Well done, young man. Now my sister will give me some peace at last. She has done nothing but talk about you since she first heard you sing."

He patted Imrat's head. "Come back in ten days. If the engineers are right and we do not have to make another recording I will give you a thousand rupees. What will a little chap like you do with so much money?"

But he was gone before Imrat could reply.

Master Mohan dared not hope for anything until the record was made. To prevent the child from believing too fervently that he would soon be reunited with his sister, the music teacher continued Imrat's lessons in the park, trying not to feel alarm when he saw the same two men always at the balustrade, smiling at him, nodding their heads in appreciation of Imrat's phrasing.

One day the men followed Master Mohan and Imrat to the tram, waiting until they were alone before approaching the music teacher with their offer.

"A great sahib wants to hear the boy sing."

"No, no. We are too busy." Master Mohan pushed Imrat before him. "The boy is making his first record. He must practise."

"Don't be a fool, brother. The sahib will pay handsomely to listen to his voice."

"Five thousand rupees, brother. Think of it."

"But your sahib can hear the child free every morning in the park."

They laughed and Master Mohan felt the old fear when he saw their be-tel-stained teeth. "Great men do not stand in a crowd, snatching their pleasure from the breeze, brother. They indulge their pleasures in the privacy of palaces."

"He must finish his recording first."

"Naturally. But after that . . ."

"We will be here every morning, Master."

"You will not escape us."

To Master Mohan's dismay the men waited each day at the park, leaning against the parapet until Imrat's small crowd of admirers had dispersed before edging up to the blind boy.

"Please, little Master Imrat, take pity on a man who worships music."

"The sahib's responsibilities prevented him from following his own calling as a singer."

"He could have been a great singer like you, Master Imrat, if he had not been forced to take care of his family business."

Master Mohan could see the smirking expressions on the faces of the two men as they tried to ingratiate themselves with Imrat.

"To hear you sing will relieve the pain of his own heart, denied what he has most loved in this life."

"If you sing well he will give you leaves from Tansen's tamarind tree to make your voice as immortal as Tansen's."

Master Mohan knew these men had once learned music as Imrat was doing now, until poverty had reduced them to pandering to the vices and whims of wealthy men. Even as he despised them he was relieved that Imrat's record would save him from such a life.

Now they turned their attention on Master Mohan.

"We have told the great sahib this boy has a voice which is heard only once in five hundred years."

"The sahib is a man of influence, brother. Perhaps he can arrange to have the boy invited to the Calcutta Music Festival."

The music teacher felt dizzy even imagining that his blind charge, who had been no better than a beggar only eight months ago, might be invited to sing in the company of India's maestros. The great singing teachers always attended the festival. One might even offer to train Imrat's pure voice, taking it to a perfection that had not been heard since Tansen himself sang before the Great Mogul. He nearly agreed but controlled himself enough to say again, "You must wait until the boy completes his recording."

Fortunately he did not have to think long about the temptation offerred by the two men.

On the day he took Imrat back to the recording studio, the young woman was also present in the office, seated on an armchair opposite her brother's desk.

"I played this record for the director of the radio station. He thinks Master Imrat has great promise, and must be taught by the best teachers available. A talent like his should not be exposed to the dust and germs in the park. There are empty rooms above one of our garages. He must live there."

The woman put her arm around the boy. "Wouldn't you like to stay with me? Your sister could work in my house and your teacher would come to see you every day."

The boy nodded happily and she handed two copies of the record and an envelope of money to Master Mohan. "So it is settled. As soon as his sister reaches Calcutta they will both move into my house."

Master Mohan took the records but left the envelope of money in the woman's hand for Imrat's sister.

"Are we to be given nothing for feeding and clothing this changeling you brought into our home?" Master Mohan's wife screamed when she learned her husband had left the boy's money with the studio owner. "What about the whole year we have kept him, restricting our own lives so he could become rich? Are your own children to receive nothing out of this, only blows and abuses?"

Her fury increased when Imrat's record was released and proved immediately popular.

In the weeks that followed the record was played over and over again on the radio by enthusiastic programmers. While Imrat waited for his sister to send news of her arrival in Calcutta, Master Mohan was informed by the recording studio that Imrat's record was disappearing from the record shops as fast as new copies could be printed.

Now his wife's rage was inflamed by jealousy. She could hear Imrat's record being played everywhere in the bazaars. Even the paanwallah had brought a gramophone to his stall, storing it behind the piles of wet leaves at his side. Each time a customer bought a paan the paanwallah cranked the machine and placed the record on the turntable, boasting, "I advised the music teacher to adopt the child. Even though he was only a blind beggar I was able to recognise the purity of his voice immediately."

A week before Imrat's sister was due to arrive in Calcutta, the music teacher's wife learned from Mohammed-sahib that her husband had refused to let Imrat perform at the home of a great sahib.

"And he was offering the sum of five thousand rupees to listen to the blind boy." Mohammed-sahib said in awe.

"Five thousand rupees!" Master Mohan's wife shrieked. "He turned down five thousand rupees when his own children do not have enough to eat and nothing to wear! Where can I find those men?"

That night the music teacher helped Imrat into the house. To his distress he found his wife entertaining the two men who had come so often to the park.

She waved a sheaf of notes in Master Mohan's face. "I have agreed the brat will sing before the sahib tonight. See, they have already paid me. Five thousand rupees will cover a little of what I have spent on this blind beggar over the last year."

The music teacher tried to object but Imrat intruded on his arguments. "I am not tired, Master-sahib."

"Waited on hand and foot by our entire household! Why should you be tired?" She grabbed the boy's arm. "I'm coming myself to make sure you sing properly to pay for all the meals you have eaten at our table."

The two men smiled victoriously at the music teacher. "Our rickshaws are waiting at the corner of the street."

As they rode to the great sahib's house Master Mohan felt tears on his cheeks. In a week Imrat would be gone, leaving him imprisoned again in his hateful household. He hugged Imrat to his chest, his sighs lost in the rasping breathing of the man straining between the wooden shafts of the rickshaw.

At the high iron gates of a mansion the rickshaws halted. A guard opened the gates and Master Mohan's wife seized Imrat's arm, pulling him roughly behind her as servants ushered them through a series of dimly lit chambers into a dark room empty of furniture.

Wooden shutters sealed the french doors on either side of the room, and large patches of paint peeled from the walls. The floor was covered by a Persian carpet which extended from the door to a raised platform. Above the platform two unused chandeliers hung from the ceiling, shrouded in muslin like corpses.

A man sat on the platform, his size exaggerated by the candles burning on either side of him. The musicians bowed to him obsequiously. The sahib ignored them. Still smiling the musicians climbed onto the platform where a harmonium and drums were placed in readiness for the concert.

"Come here, little Master," the great sahib said. "I am told you have a voice such as India has not heard for hundreds of years."

Master Mohan's wife released her hold on the boy and the music teacher led him to the platform grateful that Imrat could not see this empty room with its sealed wooden shutters, and the shadows flickering on the peeling walls.

As he helped him up the stairs the music teacher whispered in Imrat's ear, "Only sing the two songs from your record. Then we can go home."

"Soon I will be with my sister again," Imrat answered in a whisper as Master Mohan gently pushed him down in front of the two musicians. "Tonight I must thank Allah for his kindness."

For a few minutes only the music of the harmonium echoed through the heavy shadows of the room and Master Mohan could feel his wife shifting restlessly from foot to foot at his side. Then Imrat's clear voice pierced the darkness.

> "I prostrate my head to Your drawn sword.
>   O, the wonder of Your kindness
>   O, the wonder of my submission.

> "Do not reveal the Truth in a world where blasphemy prevails.
>   O wondrous Source of Mystery.
>   O Knower of Secrets."

The boy's sightless eyes seemed fixed on infinity and it seemed to Master Mohan that the candles in the shrouded chandeliers were leaping into flame, ignited by Imrat's innocent devotion as he sang,

> "In the very spasm of death I see Your face.
>   O, the wonder of my submission.
>   O, the wonder of Your protection."

Listening to the purity of each note Master Mohan felt himself being lifted into another dimension, into the mystic raptures of the Sufis who were sometimes moved to dance by such music. For the first time he understood why the Sufis believed that once a man began to dance in the transport of his ecstasy the singers must continue until the man stopped dancing lest the sudden breaking of the dancer's trance should kill him.

> "The heat of Your presence
>   Blinds my eyes.
>   Blisters my skin.
>   Shrivels my flesh."

The great sahib rose to his feet. Master Mohan wondered if the great sahib was about to dance as music poured out of that young throat which carried in it too great a knowledge of the world.

> "The heat of Your presence
> Blinds my eyes.
> Blisters my skin.

> "Do not turn in loathing from me.
> O Beloved, can You not see
> Only Love disfigures me."

In the flickering light of the candles Master Mohan thought he saw something glint in the sahib's hand. The musicians were smiling ingratiatingly, waiting for the great sahib to circle the boy's head with money before flinging it to them. Now Master Mohan could not see Imrat, dwarfed by the shadow of the man standing in front of him as he sang again,

> "I prostrate my head to Your drawn sword.
> O, the wonder of Your kindness
> O, the wonder of my submission.

> "Do not reveal the Truth in a world where blasphemy prevails.
> O wondrous Source of Mystery.
> O Knower of Secrets."

The great sahib turned around and Master Mohan thought he saw tears on his cheeks. "Such a voice is not human. What will happen to music if this is the standard by which God judges us?"

Imrat was not listening, intoxicated by the power issuing from his own throat.

> "In the very spasm of death I see Your face.
> O, the wonder of my submission.
> O, the wonder of Your protection . . ."

Master Mohan could hear his wife cursing. He did not know his own screams echoed the blind boy's as he screamed and screamed and screamed.

RADIO GANNET

Shena Mackay

Born in Edinburgh on D-Day, **Shena Mackay** (b.1944) grew up in Hampstead, Kent and lived much of her life in Surrey and south London before moving, in 2008, to Southampton. She first published a book aged seventeen, when her novellas *Dust Falls on Eugene Schlumburger* and *Toddler on the Run* were published in one volume. Her novels have won countless awards and, recently, *Heligoland* was shortlisted for both the Whitbread Novel Award and the Orange Prize. *The Orchard on Fire* was shortlisted for the Booker Prize in 1995. A selection of her stories was published as *The Atmospheric Railway*. She was once described as "the best writer in the world today."

There were two sisters, Norma and Dolly, christened Dorothy, who lived in a seaside town. Norma and her husband, Eric, resided in a large detached house in Cliftonville Crescent, while Dolly's caravan was berthed at the Ocean View Mobile Home Park, on the wrong side of the tracks of the miniature steam railway. Norma and Dolly's elder brother, Walter, was the curator of the small Sponge Museum founded by their grandfather.

Eastcliff-on-Sea was a town divided. The prizewinning municipal gardens overlooked Sandy Bay where all the beach huts had been bought up by Londoners wanting traditional bucket-and-spade holidays, and as their offspring watched the Punch and Judy show while eating their organic ice cream, or played a sedate game of crazy golf, they could see the lights of the funfair winking across the tracks, and hear the shouts of less privileged children on the rides and smell their burgers, doughnuts and candyfloss drifting on the breeze from the ramshackle plaza that was Ocean View.

Norma had five children and fourteen grandchildren, thus ensuring that she had somebody to worry about at any given moment. One particularly hot summer night, she lay awake fretting at the news that a giant asteroid was on course to hit the earth sometime in the future. She groped for her bedside radio and switched it on low so as not to disturb Eric. Her finger slipped on the dial and out of the radio came the squawk of a gull, followed by a voice singing "All you hear is Radio Gannet, Radio gaga, Radio Gannet. Greetings, all you night owls, this is Radio Gannet taking you through the wee small hours with Joanne and The Streamliners and their ever-lovin' 'Frankfurter Sandwiches'."

At the female DJ's voice, Norma sat bolt upright, hyperventilating. Over the music came the spluttering of fat in a pan, and a muffled expletive. It was the indisputable sound of her sister Dolly having a fry-up. "Whatever happened to the good old British banger?" grumbled Dolly. "Answers on a postcard, please."

Norma sat transfixed, picturing Dolly at the Baby Belling with her tail of grey-blonde hair hanging over her dressing gown, slipshod in downtrodden espadrilles, in that terrible caravan with its tangle of dead plants in rotting macramé potholders, Peruvian dream-catchers, etiolated things growing out of old margarine tubs, the encrusted saucers left out for hedgehogs by the door, the plastic gnomes bleached white by time. The budgie. The cat. The slugs.

She hadn't seen her sister since their father's funeral, when Dolly had grabbed the microphone from the vicar and launched into "Wind Beneath My Wings". Dolly was dressed in frayed denim, cowgirl boots and a kiss-me-quick cowgirl hat.

In the morning Norma dismissed the radio programme as a bad dream. She was taking a brace of grandchildren to buy their new school shoes for the autumn term. It was one of those days when people tell each other that "it's not the heat, it's the *humidity*". In the shoeshop they were served by an apathetic girl with a film of sweat on her upper lip who showed little enthusiasm for measuring the children's feet, gazing ahead as if watching a procession of Odor-Eaters marching into eternity. Music played in the background; a common family was creating havoc with the Barbie and Star Wars trainers. Norma looked fondly at her grandchildren. Their legs were the colour of downy, sun-kissed apricots in the sensible shoes she was insisting on. Suddenly, there it was again, the squawking gull, that idiotic jingle.

"This is Radio Gannet coming to you on – some kilohertz or other, I can never remember. Kilohertz – what's that in old money, anyway? I blame the boffins in Brussels, myself. This one's specially for you, all you metric martyrs out there: "Pennies from Heaven" – hang on, a road traffic report's just coming in. It's Mr Wilf Arnold ringing from the call box on the corner of Martello Street where a wheelie bin has overturned, shedding its load . . ."

As soon as she had paid for the shoes Norma hurried the children round to the Sponge Museum to consult her brother. Walter's nose had grown porous with the passing years; it was an occupational hazard.

"Great Uncle Walter, have you ever thought of making the museum a bit more interactive? You need a hands-on approach if you're going to compete in the modern world," said Matilda.

"Yeah, like Sea World. With octopuses and killer whales and sharks. Everything in here's dead," agreed Sam.

"There's far too much of this touchy-feely nonsense nowadays in my opinion," said Walter. Norma nodded agreement, imagining herself in the wet embrace of an octopus.

"Go and improve your minds," Walter told them. "And if you behave yourselves, you can choose a souvenir from the shop. How about a nice packet of Grow-Your-Own Loofah seeds?"

When they had slouched away, sniggering, Norma told Walter what she'd heard, recounting how Dolly had signed off, saying, "Keep those calls and e-mails coming, and as always, my thanks to Mr Tibbs, my producer."

"Mr Tibbs? Isn't that her cat?" said Walter.

"Exactly. She's totally bonkers – remember the spectacle she made of herself at the funeral? *I* wouldn't have said that Daddy was the wind beneath Dolly's wings, would you, Walter?"

He considered. "Well, he did sponsor her for that bungee jump off the pier, *and* he made her that fairy dress with glittery wings for her birthday."

"It was *my* birthday," said Norma.

"Yes, I'm afraid our father always indulged Dolly," admitted Walter.

"Well, look where it's got him. I hardly think even Daddy would approve of her latest venture. We can only trust that nobody we know will tune into Radio Gannet."

Walter's Rotarian connections and Norma's aspiration to serve as Eastcliff's Lady Mayoress hung unspoken between them.

"Radio Gannet, eh? How appropriate."

Walter remembered a plump little fairy flitting about the table at a children's party, touching cakes and jellies with the silver star at the tip of her magic wand. Norma thought about her sister's three helpings of tiramisu at her youngest son's wedding. She'd turned that into a karaoke too. Then the sound that she and Walter had been half-listening out for, that of a display cabinet toppling, recalled them to the present.

"Where is this so-called radio station to be found?" asked Walter.

"Oh, at the wrong end of the dial. Where you get all those foreign and religious programmes."

"But is she legal? I mean, do you think she's got a licence to broadcast? It could well be that our dear sister is a pirate, in which case something can be done to put a stop to her little game. Leave Dolly Daydream to me, Norma."

It was time for a weather check at Radio Gannet. "Let's see what Joey the weather girl has in store for us this afternoon. Over to you at the Weather Centre, Joey."

The Weather Centre was the budgerigar's cage which hung in the open doorway with strips of seaweed trailing from its bars. Dry seaweed denoted a fine spell, while when it turned plump and moist, rain was in the offing.

"Pretty boy, pretty boy," said Joey.

"Pretty dry – good news for all you holidaymakers, then. Uh oh," Dolly stretched out to touch a ribbon of kelp and found it dripping. The caravan park was shrouded in grey drizzle. "Joey says better pop the brolly in the old beach bag, just in case."

Joey was popular with the listeners. A recent beak problem had brought sackloads of cuttle-fish and millet from well-wishers, many of them students. "I'm only sending this ironically," one of them had written. Dolly was flattered; she knew that students do everything ironically nowadays; watch kids' TV, eat Pot Noodles; they even iron their jeans ironically. She placed her 78 of "Any Umbrellas" on the turntable, put her feet up and reached for the biscuit barrel.

Dolly was truly happy, having found her niche at last in public service broadcasting. Her *Send a Pet to Lourdes* campaign was coming along nicely and the coffers were swelling with milk-bottle tops and unused Green Shield stamps; the jigsaw swapshop was up and running, and the day care centre had asked her to put out an announcement that they had exceeded their quota of multi-coloured blankets. That *Unravel Your Unwanted Woolies and Make Something Useful* wheeze had been a triumph; the charity shops were full of its results. But fame, Dolly knew, came with a price. Like every celebrity, she had attracted a stalker. Hers had staring yellow eyes and a maniacal laugh. He tracked her through the plaza on pink webbed feet, he snatched ice lollies from her hand in the street, and chips from her polystyrene tray, tossing them aside if she hadn't put on enough vinegar. He brought a whole new meaning to "take-away" food.

Radio Gannet went off the airwaves altogether when Dolly had to go down the shops; at other times listeners heard only the gentle snoring of the presenter and her producer Mr Tibbs.

"Coming up – six things to do on a rainy day in Eastcliff, but now it's paper and pencils at the ready, for *Dolly's Dish of the Day*. And it's a scrummy Jammie Dodger coffee cheesecake recipe sent in by Mrs Elsie Majors of Spindrift, Ocean View Plaza. For this, you'll need four tablespoons of Camp Coffee, a large tin of condensed milk, a handful of peanuts for the garnish, and a packet of Jammie Dodgers, crushed. And here's a Dolly Tip for crushing the biscuits: place them in a plastic bag, tie securely, and bash them with a rolling pin. If you haven't got a plastic bag handy, the foot cut off an old pair of tights will do just as well . . .

"Thanking you kindly, Elsie," she concluded. "Your pipkin of Radio Gannet hedgerow jam is winging its way to you even as we speak."

Or will be, as soon as Dolly has soaked the label off that jar of Spar Mixed Berry and replaced the lid with one of her crochet covers.

In Cliftonville Crescent Norma and Eric were listening in horror as the programme continued.

"This one's for all you asylum seekers out there – 'They're Coming to Take Me Away Ha Ha'. That ought to get the politically correct brigade's knickers in a twist. Which reminds me, don't forget to text your entries for the Radio Gannet Political Correctness Gone Mad competition. 'Fly's in the sugar bowl, shoo fly shoo,'" she sang. "'Hey hey, skip to my loo . . .'" and Radio Gannet went temporarily off the air.

"Dolly inhabits a parallel universe," said Norma, scarlet with shame.

How it rained. Pennies from heaven. Stair rods. Cats and dogs. In the museum the sponges trembled and swelled in their glass cases, great sensitive blooms and castles and honeycombs saturated with the moisture in the air. Walter listened glumly to "Seasons in the Sun" on Radio Gannet. He'd been in touch with the authorities. Yet, like the man in the song, the stars that he'd reached were just starfish on the beach. His only visitors had been a couple of Canadian tourists on the Heritage Trail. Apparently they'd been misled by something they'd picked up on their hotel radio and were expecting an exhibition of sponge cakes through the ages. From King Alfred to Mr Kipling.

Dolly's voice broke into his thoughts.

"Joey at the Weather Centre has handed me a severe weather warning. 'How high's the water, Mamma? Six feet high and risin' . . .'"

Walter rushed out to check his sandbags.

That night a tremendous crash brought Norma and Eric leaping from their bed to the window. Norma had lain awake worrying about an asteroid hitting the earth. Now she was about to experience the collision of two worlds. Cresting a tsunami was her sister's caravan and then the whole parallel universe was deposited in Cliftonville Crescent. It was like a scene from a Stanley Spencer Resurrection; the entire population of Ocean View Mobile Home Park were struggling out of their caravans in their night clothes, clutching plastic bags doubtless filled with old Green Shield stamps and unwashed milk-bottle tops, and there was Dolly splashing through the debris with her producer Mr Tibbs, Joey the Weather Girl, and a herring gull perched on her head.

MARRIAGE LINES

Julian Barnes

Julian Barnes (b.1946) is the author of several novels, including *Flaubert's Parrot*, *Arthur & George*, *The Sense of an Ending*, three collections of stories, among them *Pulse*, volumes of essays, and, most recently, *Levels of Life*. He notes: "Reading is a majority skill but a minority art. Yet nothing can replace the exact, complicated, subtle communion between absent author and entranced, present reader." Asked what he used a computer for, he replied: "I use it for e-mail and shopping." He is an officer of L'ordre des Arts et des Lettres.

The twin otter was only half full as they took off from Glasgow: a few islanders returning from the mainland, plus some early-season weekenders with hiking boots and rucksacks. For almost an hour they flew just above the shifting brainscape of the clouds. Then they descended, and the jigsaw edges of the island appeared below them.

He had always loved this moment. The neck of headland, the long Atlantic beach of Traigh Eais, the large white bungalow they ritually buzzed, then a slow turn over the little humpy island of Orosay, and a final approach to the flat, sheeny expanse of Traigh Mhòr. In summer months, you could usually count on some boisterous mainland voice, keen perhaps to impress a girlfriend, shouting over the propellor noise, "Only commercial beach landing in the world!" But with the years he had grown indulgent even about that. It was part of the folklore of coming here.

They landed hard on the cockle beach and spray flew up between the wing struts as they raced through shallow puddles. Then the plane slewed side on to the little terminal building, and a minute later they were climbing down the rickety metal steps to the beach. A tractor with a flatbed trailer was standing by to trundle their luggage the dozen yards to a damp concrete slab which served as the carousel. They, their: he knew he must start getting used to the singular pronoun instead. This was going to be the grammar of his life from now on.

Calum was waiting for him, looking past his shoulder, scanning the other passengers. The same slight, grey-haired figure in a green windcheater who met them every year. Being Calum, he didn't ask; he waited. They had known one another, with a kind of intimate formality, for twenty years or so. Now that regularity, that repetition, and all it contained, was broken.

As the van dawdled along the single-track road, and waited politely in the passing bays, he told Calum the story he was already weary with repeating. The sudden tiredness, the dizzy spells, the blood tests, the scans, hospital, more hospital, the hospice. The speed of it all, the process, the merciless tramp of events. He told it without tears, in a neutral voice, as if it might have happened to someone else. It was the only way, so far, that he knew how.

Outside the dark stone cottage, Calum yanked on the handbrake. "Rest her soul," he said quietly, and took charge of the holdall.

The first time they had come to the island, they weren't yet married. She had worn a wedding ring as a concession to . . . what? – their imagined version of island morality? It made them feel both superior and hypocritical at the same time. Their room at Calum and Flora's B & B had whitewashed walls, rain drying on the window, and a view across the machair to the sharp rise of Beinn Mhartainn. On their first night, they had discovered a bed whose joints wailed against any activity grosser than the minimum required for the sober conception of children. They found themselves comically restricted. Island sex, they had called it, giggling quietly into each other's bodies.

He had bought new binoculars especially for that trip. Inland, there were larks and twites, wheatears and wagtails. On the shoreline, ringed plovers and pipits. But it was the seabirds he loved best, the cormorants and gannets, the shags and fulmars. He spent many a docile, wet-bottomed hour on the clifftops, thumb and middle finger bringing into focus their whirling dives, and their soaring independence. The fulmars were his favourites. Birds which spent their whole lives at sea, coming to land only to nest. Then they laid a single egg, raised the chick, and took to the sea again, skimming the waves, rising on the air currents, being themselves.

She had preferred flowers to birds. Sea pinks, yellow rattle, purple vetch, flag iris. There was something, he remembered, called self-heal. That was as far as his knowledge, and memory, went. She had never picked a single flower here, or anywhere else. To cut a flower was to speed its death, she used to say. She hated the sight of a vase. In the hospital, other patients, seeing the empty metal trolley at the foot of her bed, had thought her friends neglectful, and tried to pass on their excess bouquets. This went on until she was moved to her own room, and then the problem ceased.

That first year, Calum had shown them the island. One afternoon, on a beach where he liked to dig for razor clams, he had looked away from them and said, almost as if he was addressing the sea, "My grandparents were married by declaration, you know. That was all you needed in the old days. Approval and declaration. You were married when the moon was waxing and the tide running – to bring you luck. And after the wedding there'd be a rough mattress on the floor of an outbuilding. For the first night. The idea was that you begin marriage in a state of humility."

"Oh, that's wonderful, Calum," she had said. But he felt it was a rebuke – to their English manners, their presumption, their silent lie.

The second year, they had returned a few weeks after getting married. They wanted to tell everyone they met; but here was one place they couldn't. Perhaps this had been good for them – to be silly with happiness and obliged into silence. Perhaps it had been their own way of beginning marriage in a state of humility.

He sensed, nevertheless, that Calum and Flora had guessed. No doubt it wasn't difficult, given their new clothes and their daft smiles. On the first night Calum gave them whisky from a bottle without a label. He had many such bottles. There was a lot more whisky drunk than sold on this island, that was for sure.

Flora had taken out of a drawer an old sweater which had belonged to her grandfather. She laid it on the kitchen table, ironing it with her palms. In the old days, she explained, the women of these islands used to tell stories with their knitting. The pattern of this jersey showed that her grandfather had come from Eriskay, while its details, its decorations, told of fishing and faith, of the sea and the sand. And this series of zigzags across the shoulder – *these here, look* – represented the ups and downs of marriage. They were, quite literally, marriage lines.

Zigzags. Like any newly married couple, they had exchanged a glance of sly confidence, sure that for them there would be no downs – or at least, not like those of their parents, or of friends already making the usual stupid, predictable mistakes. They would be different; they would be different from anyone who had ever got married before.

"Tell them about the buttons, Flora," said Calum.

The pattern of the jersey told you which island its owner came from; the buttons at the neck told you precisely which family they belonged to. It must have been like walking around dressed in your own postcode, he thought.

A day or two later, he had said to Calum, "I wish everyone was still wearing those sweaters." Having no sense of tradition himself, he liked other people to display one.

"They had great use," replied Calum. "There was many a drowning you could only recognise by the jersey. And then by the buttons. Who the man was."

"I hadn't thought of that."

"Well, no reason for it. For you to know. For you to think."

There were moments when he felt this was the most distant place he had ever come to. The islanders happened to speak the same language as him, but that was just some strange, geographical coincidence.

This time, Calum and Flora treated him as he knew they would: with a tact and modesty he had once, stupidly, Englishly, mistaken for deference. They didn't press themselves upon him, or make a show of their sympathy. There was a touch on the shoulder, a plate laid before him, a remark about the weather.

Each morning, Flora would give him a sandwich wrapped in greaseproof paper, a piece of cheese and an apple. He would set off across the machair and up Beinn Mhartainn. He made himself climb to the top, from where he could see the island and its jigsaw edges, where he could feel himself alone. Then, binoculars in hand, he would head for the cliffs and the seabirds. Calum had once told him that on some of the islands, generations back, they used to make oil for their lamps from the fulmars. Odd how he had always kept this detail from her, for twenty years and more. The rest of the year round, he never thought of it. Then they would come to the island, and he would say to himself, I mustn't tell her what they did with the fulmars.

That summer she had nearly left him (or had he nearly left her? – at this distance, it was hard to tell) he had gone clam-digging with Calum. She had left them to pursue their sport, preferring to walk the damp, wavy line of the beach from which the sea had just retreated. Here, where the pebbles were barely bigger than sand grains, she liked to search for pieces of coloured glass – tiny shards of broken bottle, worn soft and smooth by water and time. For years he had watched the stooped walk, the inquisitive crouch, the picking, the discarding, the hoarding in the cupped left palm.

Calum explained how you looked for a small declivity in the sand, poured a little salt into it, then waited for the razor clam to shoot up a few inches from its lair. He wore an oven glove on his left hand, against the sharpness of the rising shell. You had to pull quickly, he said, seizing the clam before it disappeared again.

Mostly, despite Calum's expertise, nothing stirred, and they moved on to the next hollow in the sand. Out of the corner of his eye, he saw her wandering further along the beach, her back turned to him, self-sufficient, content with what she was doing, not giving him a thought.

As he handed Calum more salt, and saw the oven glove poised in anticipation, he found himself saying, man to man, "Bit like marriage, isn't it?"

Calum frowned slightly. "What's your meaning?"

"Oh, waiting for something to pop out of the sand. Then it turns out either there's nothing there, or something that cuts your hand open if you aren't bloody careful."

It had been a stupid thing to say. Stupid because he hadn't really meant it, more stupid because it was presumptuous. Silence told him that Calum found such talk offensive, to himself, to Flora, to the islanders generally.

Each day he walked, and each day soft rain soaked into him. He ate a sodden sandwich, and watched the fulmars skimming the sea. He walked to Greian Head and looked down over the flat rocks where the seals liked to congregate. One year, they had watched a dog swim all the way out from the beach, chase the seals off, and then parade up and down its rock like a new landowner. This year there was no dog.

On the vertiginous flank of Greian was part of an unlikely golf course where, year after year, they had never seen a single golfer. There was a small circular green surrounded by a picket fence to keep the cows off. Once, nearby, a sudden herd of bullocks had rushed at them, frightening her silly. He had stood his ground, waved his arms wildly, instinctively shouted the names of the political leaders he most despised, and somehow not been surprised that it had calmed them down. This year, there were no bullocks to be seen, and he missed them. He supposed they must have long gone to slaughter.

He remembered a crofter on Vatersay telling them about lazy beds. You cut a slice of turf, placed your potatoes on the open soil, relaid the turf upside down on top of them – and that was it. Time and rain and the warmth of the sun did the rest. Lazy beds – he saw her laughing at him, reading his mind, saying afterwards that this would be his idea of gardening, wouldn't it? He remembered her eyes shining like the damp glass jewellery she used to fill her palm with.

On the last morning, Calum drove him back to Traigh Mhòr in the van. Politicians had been promising a new airstrip so that modern planes could land. There was talk of tourist development and island regeneration, mixed with warnings about the current cost of subsidy. Calum wanted none of it, and nor did he. He knew that he would need the island to stay as still and unchanging as possible. He wouldn't come back if jets started landing on tarmac.

He checked in his holdall at the counter, and they went outside. Hanging over a low wall, Calum lit a cigarette. They looked out across the damp and bumpy sand of the cockle beach. The cloud was low, the windsock inert.

"These are for you," said Calum, handing him half a dozen postcards. He must have bought them at the café just now. Views of the island, the beach, the machair; one of the very plane waiting to take him away.

"But . . ."

"You will be needing the memory."

A few minutes later, the Twin Otter took off straight out across Orosay and the open sea. There was no farewell view of the island before that world below was shut out. In the enveloping cloud, he thought about marriage lines and buttons; about razor clams and island sex; about missing bullocks and fulmars being turned into oil; and then, finally, the tears came. Calum had known he would not be coming back. But the tears were not for that, or for himself, or even for her, for their memories. They were tears for his own stupidity. His presumption too.

He had thought he could recapture, and begin to say farewell. He had thought that grief might be assuaged, or if not assuaged, at least speeded up, hurried on its way a little, by going back to a place where they had been happy. But he was not in charge of grief. Grief was in charge of him. And in the months and years ahead, he expected grief to teach him many other things as well. This was just the first of them.

SOLID GEOMETRY

Ian McEwan

Ian McEwan (b.1948) is the highly acclaimed author of *Black Dogs, Enduring Love,* the Booker Prize-winning *Amsterdam, Atonement, On Chesil Beach, Solar, Sweet Tooth* and *The Children Act.* McEwan has not written a short story since his second collection in 1978, saying once, "They were a kind of laboratory for me, they allowed me to try out different things, to discover myself as a writer." Even as experiments, they showed McEwan's precision and craft as a writer from a very early stage.

In Melton Mowbray in 1875 at an auction of articles of 'curiosity and worth', my great-grandfather, in the company of M his friend, bid for the penis of Captain Nicholls who died in Horsemonger jail in 1873. It was bottled in a glass twelve inches long, and, noted my great-grandfather in his diary that night, 'in a beautiful state of preservation'. Also for auction was 'the unnamed portion of the late Lady Barrymore. It went to Sam Israels for fifty guineas.' My great-grandfather was keen on the idea of having the two items as a pair, and M dissuaded him. This illustrates perfectly their friendship. My great-grandfather the excitable theorist, M the man of action who knew when to bid at auctions. My great-grandfather lived for sixty-nine years. For forty-five of them, at the end of every day, he sat down before going to bed and wrote his thoughts in a diary. These diaries are on my table now, forty-five volumes bound in calf leather, and to the left sits Capt. Nicholls in the glass jar. My great-grandfather lived on the income derived from the patent of an invention of his father, a handy fastener used by corset-makers right up till the outbreak of the First World War. My great-grandfather liked gossip, numbers and theories. He also liked tobacco, good port, jugged hare and, very occasionally, opium. He liked to think of himself as a mathematician, though he never had a job, and never published a book. Nor did he ever travel or get his name in *The Times,* even when he died. In 1869 he married Alice, only daughter of the Rev. Toby Shadwell, co-author of a not highly regarded book on English wild flowers. I believe my great-grandfather to have been a very fine diarist, and when I have finished editing the diaries and they are published I am certain he will receive the recognition due to him. When my work is over I will take a long holiday, travel somewhere cold and clean and treeless, Iceland or the Russian Steppes. I used to think that at the end of it all I would try, if it was possible, to divorce my wife Maisie, but now there is no need at all.

Often Maisie would shout in her sleep and I would have to wake her.

'Put your arm around me,' she would say. 'It was a horrible dream. I had it once before. I was in a plane flying over a desert. But it wasn't really a desert. I took the plane lower and I could see there were thousands of babies heaped up, stretching away over the horizon, all of them naked and climbing over each another. I was running out of fuel and I had to land the plane. I tried to find a space, I flew on and kept looking for a space... '

'Go to sleep now,' I said through a yawn. 'It was only a dream.'

'No,' she cried. 'I mustn't go to sleep, not just yet.'

'Well, *I* have to sleep now,' I told her. 'I have to be up early in the morning.'

She shook my shoulder. 'Please don't go to sleep yet, don't leave me here.'

'I'm in the same bed,' I said. 'I won't leave you.'

'It makes no difference, don't leave me awake... ' But my eyes were already closing.

Lately I have taken up my great-grandfather's habit. Before going to bed I sit down for half an hour and think over the day. I have no mathematical whimsies or sexual theories to note down. Mostly I write out what Maisie has said to me and what I have said to Maisie. Sometimes, for complete privacy, I lock myself in the bathroom, sit on the toilet seat and balance the writing-pad on my knees. Apart from me there is occasionally a spider or two in the bathroom. They climb up the waste pipe and crouch perfectly still on the glaring white enamel. They must wonder where they have come to. After hours of crouching they turn back, puzzled, or perhaps disappointed they could not learn more. As far as I can tell, my great-grandfather made only one reference to spiders. On May 8th, 1906, he wrote, 'Bismarck is a spider.'

In the afternoons Maisie used to bring me tea and tell me her nightmares. Usually I was going through old newspapers, compiling indexes, cataloguing items, putting down this volume, picking up another. Maisie said she was in a bad way. Recently she had been sitting around the house all day glancing at books on psychology and the occult, and almost every night she had bad dreams. Since the time we exchanged physical blows, lying in wait to hit each other with the same shoe outside the bathroom, I had had little sympathy for her. Part of her problem was jealousy. She was very jealous... of my great-grandfather's forty-five volume diary, and of my purpose and energy in editing it. She was doing nothing. I was putting down one volume and picking up another when Maisie came in with the tea.

'Can I tell you my dream?' she asked. 'I was flying this plane over a kind of desert... '

'Tell me later, Maisie,' I said. 'I'm in the middle of something here.' After she had gone I stared at the wall in front of my desk and thought about M, who came to talk and dine with my great-grandfather regularly over a period of fifteen years up until his sudden and unexplained departure one evening in 1898. M, whoever he might have been, was something of an academic, as well as a man of action. For example, on the evening of August 9th, 1870, the two of them are talking about positions for lovemaking and M tells my great-grandfather that copulation *a posteriori* is the most natural way owing to the position of the clitoris and because other anthropoids favour this method. My great-grandfather, who copulated about half-a-dozen times in his entire life, and that with Alice during the first year of their marriage, wondered out loud what the Church's view was and straight away M is able to tell him that the seventh-century theologian Theodore considered copulation *a posteriori* a sin ranking with masturbation and therefore worthy of forty penances. Later in the same evening my great-grandfather produced mathematical evidence that the number of positions cannot exceed the prime number seventeen. M scoffed at this and told him he had seen a collection of drawings by Romano, a pupil of Raphael's, in which twenty-four positions were shown. And, he said, he had heard of Mr F. K. Forberg who had accounted for ninety. By the time I remembered the tea Maisie had left by my elbow it was cold.

An important stage in the deterioration of our marriage was reached as follows. I was sitting in the bathroom one evening writing out a conversation Maisie and I had had about the Tarot pack when suddenly she was outside, rapping on the door and rattling the door-handle.

'Open the door,' she called out. 'I want to come in.'

I said to her, 'You'll have to wait a few minutes more. I've almost finished.'

'Let me in now,' she shouted. 'You're not using the toilet.'

'Wait,' I replied, and wrote another line or two. Now Maisie was kicking the door.

'My period has started and I need to get something.' I ignored her yells and finished my piece, which I considered to be particularly important. If I left it till later certain details would be lost. There was no sound from Maisie now and I assumed she was in the bedroom. But when I opened the door she was standing right in my way with a shoe in her hand. She brought the heel of it sharply down on my head, and I only had time to move slightly to one side. The heel caught the top of my ear and cut it badly.

'There,' said Maisie, stepping round me to get to the bathroom, 'now we are both bleeding,' and she banged the door shut. I picked up the shoe and stood quietly and patiently outside the bathroom holding a handkerchief to my bleeding ear. Maisie was in the bathroom about ten minutes and as she came out I caught her neatly and squarely on the top of her head. I did not give her time to move. She stood perfectly still for a moment looking straight into my eyes.

'You worm,' she breathed, and went down to the kitchen to nurse her head out of my sight.

During supper yesterday Maisie claimed that a man locked in a cell with only the Tarot cards would have access to all knowledge. She had been doing a reading that afternoon and the cards were still spread about the floor.

'Could he work out the street plan of Valparaiso from the cards?' I asked.

'You're being stupid,' she replied.

'Could it tell him the best way to start a laundry business, the best way to make an omelette or a kidney machine?'

'You mind is so narrow,' she complained. 'You're so narrow, so predictable.'

'Could he,' I insisted, 'tell me who M is, or why... '

'Those things don't matter,' she cried. 'They're not necessary.'

'They are still knowledge. Could he find them out?'

She hesitated. 'Yes, he could.'

I smiled, and said nothing.

'What's so funny?' she said. I shrugged, and she began to get angry. She wanted to be disproved. 'Why did you ask all those pointless questions?'

I shrugged again. 'I just wanted to know if you really meant *everything*.'

Maisie banged the table and screamed, 'Damn you! Why are you always trying me out? Why don't you say something real?' And with that we both recognized we had reached the point where all our discussions led and we became bitterly silent.

Work on the diaries cannot proceed until I have cleared up the mystery surrounding M. After coming to dinner on and off for fifteen years and supplying my great-grandfather with a mass of material for his theories, M simply disappears from the pages of the diary. On Tuesday, December 6th, my great-grandfather invited M to dine on the following Saturday, and although M came, my great-grandfather in the entry for that day simply writes, 'M to dinner.' On any other day the conversation at these meals is recorded at great length. M had been to dinner on Monday, December 5th, and the conversation had been about geometry, and the entries for the rest of that week are entirely given over to the same subject. There is absolutely no hint of antagonism. Besides, my great-grandfather *needed* M. M provided his material, M knew what was going on, he was familiar with London and he had been on the Continent a number of times. He knew all about socialism and Darwin, he had an acquaintance in the free love movement, a friend of James Hinton. M was in the world in a way which my great-grandfather, who left Melton Mowbray only once in his lifetime, to visit Nottingham, was not. Even as a young man my great-grandfather preferred to theorize by the fireside; all he needed were the materials M supplied. For example, one evening in June 1884 M, who was just back from London, gave my great-grandfather an account of how the streets of the town were fouled and clogged by horse-dung. Now in that same week my great-grandfather had been reading the essay by Malthus called 'On the Principle of Population'. That night he made an excited entry in the diary about a pamphlet that he wanted to write and have published. It was to be called 'De Stercore Equorum'. The pamphlet was never published and probably never written, but there are detailed notes in the diary entries for the two weeks following that evening. In 'De Stercore Equorum' ('Concerning Horseshit') he assumes geometric growth in the horse population, and working from detailed street plans he predicted that the metropolis would be impassable by 1935. By impassable he took to mean an average thickness of one foot (compressed) in every major street. He described involved experiments outside his own stables to determine the compressibility of horse dung, which he managed to express mathematically. It was all pure theory, of course. His results rested on the assumption that no dung would be shovelled aside in the fifty years to come. Very likely it was M who talked my great-grandfather out of the project.

One morning, after a long dark night of Maisie's nightmares, we were lying side by side in bed and I said, 'What is it you really want? Why don't you go back to your job? These long walks, all this analysis, sitting around the house, lying in bed all morning, the Tarot pack, the nightmares... what is it you want?'

And she said, 'I want to get my head straight,' which she had said many times before.

I said, 'Your head, your mind, it's not like a hotel kitchen, you know, you can't throw stuff out like old tin cans. It's more like a river than a place, moving and changing all the time. You can't make rivers flow straight.'

'Don't go through all that again,' she said. 'I'm not trying to make rivers flow straight, I'm trying to get my head straight.'

'You've got to *do* something,' I told her. 'You can't do nothing. Why not go back to your job? You didn't have nightmares when you were working. You were never so unhappy when you were working.'

'I've got to stand back from all that,' she said, 'I'm not sure what any of it means.'

'Fashion,' I said, 'It's all fashion. Fashionable metaphors, fashionable reading, fashionable malaise. What do you care about Jung for example? You've read twelve pages in a month.'

'Don't go on,' she pleaded, 'you know it leads nowhere.'

But I went on.

'You've never been anywhere,' I told her, 'you've never done anything. You're a nice girl without even the blessing of an unhappy childhood. Your sentimental Buddhism, this junk-shop mysticism, joss-stick therapy, magazine astrology… none of it is yours, you've worked none of it out for yourself. You fell into it, you fell into a swamp of respectable intuitions. You haven't the originality or passion to intuit anything yourself beyond your own unhappiness. Why are you filling your mind with other people's mystic banalities and giving yourself nightmares?' I got out of bed, opened the curtains and began to get dressed.

'You talk like this was a fiction seminar,' Maisie said. 'Why are you trying to make things worse for me?' Self-pity began to well up from inside her, but she fought it down. 'When you are talking,' she went on, 'I can feel myself, you know, being screwed up like a piece of paper.'

'Perhaps we *are* in a fiction seminar,' I said grimly. Maisie sat up in bed staring at her lap. Suddenly her tone changed. She patted the pillow beside her and said softly,

'Come over here. Come and sit here. I want to touch you, I want you to touch me… ' But I was sighing, and already on my way to the kitchen.

In the kitchen I made myself some coffee and took it through to my study. It had occurred to me in my night of broken sleep that a possible clue to the disappearance of M might be found in the pages of geometry. I had always skipped through them before because mathematics does not interest me. On the Monday, December 5th, 1898, M and my great-grandfather discussed the *vescia piscis*, which apparently is the subject of Euclid's first proposition and a profound influence on the ground plans of many ancient religious buildings. I read through the account of the conversation carefully, trying to understand as best I could the geometry of it. Then, turning the page, I found a lengthy anecdote which M told my great-grandfather that same evening when the coffee had been brought in and the cigars were lit. Just as I was beginning to read Maisie came in.

'And what about you,' she said, as if there had not been an hour break in our exchange, 'all you have is books. Crawling over the past like a fly on a turd.'

I was angry, of course, but I smiled and said cheerfully, 'Crawling? Well at least I'm moving.'

'You don't speak to me any more,' she said, 'you play me like a pinball machine, for points.'

'Good morning, Hamlet,' I replied and sat in my chair waiting patiently for what she had to say next. But she did not speak, she left, closing the study door softly behind her.

'In September 1870,' M began to tell my great-grandfather,

I came into the possession of certain documents which not only invalidate everything fundamental to our science of solid geometry but also undermine the whole canon of our physical laws and force one to redefine one's place in Nature's scheme. These papers outweigh in importance the combined work of Marx and Darwin. They were entrusted to me by a young American mathematician, and they are the work of David Hunter, a mathematician too and a Scotsman. The American's name was Goodman. I had corresponded with his father over a number of years in connection with his work on the cyclical theory of menstruation which, incredibly enough, is still widely discredited in this country. I met the young Goodman in Vienna where, along with Hunter and mathematicians from a dozen countries, he had been attending an international conference on mathematics. Goodman was pale and greatly disturbed when I met him, and planned to return to America the following day even though the conference was not yet half complete. He gave the papers into my care with the instructions that I was to deliver them to David Hunter if I was ever to learn of his whereabouts. And then, only after much persuasion and insistence on my part, he told me what he had witnessed on the third day of the conference. The conference met every morning at nine thirty when a paper was read and a general discussion ensued. At eleven o'clock refreshments were brought in and many of the mathematicians would get up from the long, highly polished table round which they were all gathered and stroll about the large, elegant room and engage in informal discussions with their colleagues. Now, the conference lasted two weeks, and by a long-standing arrangement the most eminent of the mathematicians read their papers first, followed by the slightly less eminent, and so on, in a descending hierarchy throughout the two weeks, which caused, as it is wont to do among highly intelligent men, occasional but intense jealousies. Hunter, though a brilliant mathematician, was young and virtually unknown outside his university, which was Edinburgh. He had applied to deliver what he described as a very important paper on solid geometry, and since he was of little account in this pantheon he was assigned to read to the conference on the last day but one, by which time many of the most important figures would have returned to their respective countries. And so on the third morning, as the servants were bringing in the refreshments, Hunter stood up and suddenly addressed his colleagues just as they were rising from their seats. He was a large, shaggy man and, though young, he had about him a certain presence which reduced the hum of conversation to a complete silence.

'Gentlemen,' said Hunter, 'I must ask you to forgive this improper form of address, but I have something to tell you of the utmost importance. I have discovered the plane without a surface.' Amid derisive smiles and gentle bemused laughter, Hunter picked up from the table a large white sheet of paper. With a pocket-knife he made an incision along its surface about three inches long and slightly to one side of its centre. Then he made some rapid, complicated folds and, holding the paper aloft so all could see, he appeared to draw one corner of it through the incision, and as he did so it disappeared.

'Behold, gentlemen,' said Hunter, holding out his empty hands towards the company, 'the plane without a surface.'

Maisie came into my room, washed now and smelling faintly of perfumed soap. She came and stood behind my chair and placed her hands on my shoulders.

'What are you reading?' she said.

'Just bits of the diary which I haven't looked at before.'

She began to massage me gently at the base of my neck. I would have found it soothing if it had still been the first year of our marriage. But it was the sixth year and it generated a kind of tension which communicated itself the length of my spine. Maisie wanted something. To restrain her I placed my right hand on her left, and, mistaking this for affection, she leaned forward and kissed under my ear. Her breath smelled of toothpaste and toast. She tugged at my shoulder.

'Let's go in the bedroom,' she whispered. 'We haven't made love for nearly two weeks now.'

'I know,' I replied. 'You know how it is... with my work.' I felt no desire for Maisie or any other woman. All I wanted to do was turn the next page of my great-grandfather's diary. Maisie took her hands off my shoulders and stood by my side. There was such a sudden ferocity in her silence that I found myself tensing like a sprinter on the starting line. She stretched forward and picked up the sealed jar containing Capt. Nicholls. As she lifted it his penis drifted dreamily from one end of the glass to the other.

'You're so COMPLACENT,' Maisie shrieked, just before she hurled the glass bottle at the wall in front of my table. Instinctively I covered my face with my hand to shield off the shattering glass. As I opened my eyes I heard myself saying,

'Why did you do that? That belonged to my great-grandfather.' Amid the broken glass and the rising stench of formaldehyde lay Capt. Nicholls, slouched across the leather cover of a volume of the diary, grey, limp and menacing, transformed from a treasured curiosity into a horrible obscenity.

'That was terrible thing to do. Why did you do that?' I said again.

'I'm going for a walk,' Maisie replied, and slammed the door this time as she left the room.

I did not move from my chair for a long time. Maisie had destroyed an object of great value to me. It had stood in his study while he lived, and then it had stood in mine, linking my life with his. I picked a few splinters of glass from my lap and stared at the 160-year-old piece of another human on my table. I looked at it and thought of all the homunculi which had swarmed down its length. I thought of all the places it had been, Cape Town, Boston, Jerusalem, travelling in the dark, fetid inside of Capt. Nicholls's leather breeches, emerging occasionally into the dazzling sunlight to discharge urine in some jostling public place. I thought also of all the things it had touched, all the molecules, of Capt. Nicholls's exploring hands on lonely unrequited nights at sea, the sweating walls of cunts of young girls and old whores, their molecules must still exist today, a fine dust blowing from Cheapside to Leicestershire. Who knows how long it might have lasted in its glass jar. I began to clear up the mess. I brought the rubbish bucket in from the kitchen. I swept and picked up all the glass I could find and swabbed up the formaldehyde. Then, holding him by just one end, I tried to ease Capt. Nicholls on to a sheet of newspaper. My stomach heaved as the foreskin began to come away in my fingers. Finally, with my eyes closed, I succeeded, and wrapping him carefully in the newspaper, I carried him into the garden and buried him under the geraniums. All this time I tried to prevent my resentment towards Maisie filling my mind. I wanted to continue with M's story. Back in my chair I dabbed at a few spots of formaldehyde which had blotted the ink, and read on.

For as long a minute the room was frozen, and with each successive second it appeared to freeze harder. The first to speak was Dr Stanley Rose of Cambridge University, who had much to lose by Hunter's plane without a surface. His reputation, which was very considerable indeed, rested upon his 'Principles of Solid Geometry'.

'How dare you, sir. How dare you insult the dignity of this assembly with a worthless conjuror's trick.' And bolstered by the rising murmur of concurrence behind him, he added, 'You should be ashamed, young man, thoroughly ashamed.' With that, the room erupted like a volcano. With the exception of young Goodman, and of the servants who still stood by with the refreshments, the whole room turned on Hunter and directed at him a senseless babble of denunciation, invective and threat. Some thumped on the table in their fury, others waved their clenched fists. One very frail German gentleman fell to the floor in an apoplexy and had to be helped to a chair. And there stood Hunter, firm and outwardly unmoved, his head inclined slightly to one side, his fingers resting lightly on the surface of the long polished table. That such an uproar should follow a worthless conjuror's trick clearly demonstrated the extent of the underlying unease, and Hunter surely appreciated this. Raising his hand, and the company falling suddenly silent once more, he said,

'Gentlemen, your concern is understandable and I will effect another proof, the ultimate proof.' This said, he sat down and removed his shoes, stood up and removed his jacket, and then called for a volunteer to assist him, at which Goodman came forward. Hunter strode through the crowd to a couch which stood along one of the walls, and while he settled himself upon it he told the mystified Goodman that when he returned to England he should take with him Hunter's papers and keep them there until he came to collect them. When the mathematicians had gathered round the couch Hunter rolled on to his stomach and clasped his hands behind his back in a strange posture to fashion a hoop with his arms. He asked Goodman to hold his arms in that position for him, and rolled on his side where he began a number of strenuous jerking movements which enabled him to pass one of his feet through the hoop. He asked his assistant to turn him on his other side, where he performed the same movements again and succeeded in passing his other foot between his arms, and at the same time bent his trunk in such a way that his head was able to pass through the hoop in the opposite direction to his feet. With the help of his assistant he began to pass his legs and head past each other through the hoop made by his arms. It was then that the distinguished assembly vented, as one man, a single yelp of utter incredulity. Hunter was beginning to disappear, and now, as his legs and head passed through his arms with greater facility, seemed even to be drawn through by some invisible power, he was almost gone. And now... he was gone, quite gone, and nothing remained...

M's story put my great-grandfather in a frenzy of excitement. In his diary that night he recorded how he tried 'to prevail upon my guest to send for the papers upon the instant' even though it was by now two o'clock in the morning. M, however, was more skeptical about the whole thing. 'Americans,' he told my great-grandfather, 'often indulge in fantastic tales.' But he agreed to bring along the papers the following day. As it turned out M did not dine with my great-grandfather that night because of another engagement, but he called round in the late afternoon with the papers. Before he left he told my great-grandfather he had been through them a number of times and 'there was no sense to be had out of them'. He did not realize then how much he was underestimating my great-grandfather as an amateur mathematician. Over a glass of sherry in front of the drawing-room fire the two men arranged to dine again at the end of the week, on Saturday. For the next three days my great-grandfather hardly paused from his reading of Hunter's theorems to eat or sleep. The diary is full of nothing else. The pages are covered with scribbles, diagrams and symbols. It seems that Hunter had to devise a new set of symbols, virtually a whole new language, to express his ideas. By the end of the second day my great-grandfather had made his first breakthrough. At the bottom of a page of mathematical scribble he wrote, 'Dimensionality is a function of consciousness'. Turning to the entry for the next day I read the words, 'It disappeared in my hands'. He had re-established the plane without a surface. And there, spread out in front of me, were step by step instructions on how to fold the piece of paper. Turning the next page I suddenly understood the mystery of M's disappearance. Undoubtedly encouraged by my great-grandfather, he had taken part in a scientific experiment, probably in a spirit of great skepticism. For here my great-grandfather had drawn a series of small sketches illustrating what at first glance looked like yoga poses. Clearly they were the secret of Hunter's disappearing act.

My hands were trembling as I cleared a space on my desk. I selected a clean sheet of typing paper and laid it in front of me. I fetched a razor blade from the bathroom. I rummaged in a drawer and found an old pair of compasses, sharpened a pencil and fitted it in. I searched through the house till I found an accurate steel ruler I had once used for fitting window panes, and then I was ready. First I had to cut the paper to size. The piece that Hunter had so casually picked up from the table had obviously been carefully prepared beforehand. The length of the sides had to express a specific ratio. Using the compasses I found the centre of the paper and through this point I drew a line parallel to one of the sides and continued it right to the edge. Then I had to construct a rectangle whose measurements bore a particular relation to those of the sides of the paper. The centre of this rectangle occurred on the line in such a way as to dissect it by the Golden Mean. From the top of this rectangle I drew intersecting arcs, again of specified proportionate radii. This operation was repeated at the lower end of the rectangle, and when the two points of intersection were joined I had the line of incision. Then I started work on the folding lines. Each line seemed to express, in its length, angle of incline and point of intersection with other lines, some mysterious inner harmony of numbers. As I intersected arcs, drew lines and made folds, I felt I was blindly operating a system of the highest, most terrifying form of knowledge, the mathematics of the Absolute. By the time I had made the final fold the piece of paper was the shape of a geometric flower with three concentric rings arranged around the incision at the centre. There was something so tranquil and perfect about this design, something so remote and compelling, that as I stared into it I found myself going into a light trance and my mind becoming clear and inactive. I shook my head and glanced away. It was now time to turn the flower in on itself and pull it through the incision. This was a delicate operation and now my hands were trembling again. Only by staring into the centre of the design could I calm myself. With my thumbs I began to push the sides of the paper flower towards the centre, and as I did so I felt a numbness settle over the back of my skull. I pushed a little further, the paper glowed whiter for an instant and then it seemed to disappear. I say 'seemed' because at first I could not be sure whether I could feel it still in my hands and not see it, or see it but not feel it, or whether I could sense it had disappeared while its external properties remained. The numbness had spread right across my head and shoulders. My senses seemed inadequate to grasp what was happening. 'Dimensionality is a function of consciousness,' I thought. I brought my hands together and there was nothing between them, but even when I opened them again and saw nothing I could not be sure the paper flower had completely gone. An impression remained, an after-image not on the retina but on the mind itself. Just then the door opened behind me, and Maisie said,

'What are you doing?'

I returned as if from a dream to the room and to the faint smell of formaldehyde. It was a long, long time ago now, the destruction of Capt. Nicholls, but the smell revived my resentment, which spread through me like the numbness. Maisie slouched in the doorway, muffled in a thick coat and woolen scarf. She seemed a long way off, and as I looked at her my resentment merged into a familiar weariness of our marriage. I thought, why did she break the glass? Because she wanted to make love? Because she wanted a penis? Because she was jealous of my work, and wanted to smash the connection it had with my great-grandfather's life?

'Why did you do it?' I said out loud, involuntarily. Maisie snorted. She had opened the door and found me hunched over the table staring at my hands.

'Have you been sitting there all afternoon,' she asked, 'thinking about *that*?' She giggled. 'What happened to it anyway? Did you suck it off?'

'I buried it, ' I said, 'under the geraniums.'

She came into the room a little way and said in a serious tone, 'I'm sorry about that, I really am. I just did it before I knew what was happening. Do you forgive me?' I hesitated, and then, because my weariness had blossomed into a sudden resolution, I said,

'Yes, of course I forgive you. It was only a prick in pickle,' and we both laughed. Maisie came over to me and kissed me, and I returned the kiss, prising open her lips with my tongue.

'Are you hungry?' she said, when we were done with kissing. 'Shall I make you some supper?'

'Yes,' I said. 'I would love that.' Maisie kissed me on the top of my head and left the room, while I turned back to my studies, resolving to be as kind as I could possibly could to Maisie that evening.

Later we sat in the kitchen eating the meal Maisie had cooked and getting mildly drunk on a bottle of wine. We smoked a joint, the first one we had had together in a very long time. Maisie told me how she was going to get a job with the Forestry Commission planting trees in Scotland next summer. And I told Maisie about a conversation M and my great-grandfather had had about *a posteriori*, and about my great-grandfather's theory that there could not be more than the prime number seventeen positions for making love. We both laughed, and Maisie squeezed my hand, and lovemaking hung in the air between us, in the warm fug of the kitchen. Then we put our coats on and went for a walk. It was almost a full moon. We walked along the main road which runs outside our house and then turned down a narrow street of tightly packed houses with immaculate and minute front gardens. We did not talk much, but our arms were linked and Maisie told me how very stoned and happy she was. We came to a small park which was locked and we stood outside the gates looking up at the moon through the almost leafless braches. When we came home Maisie took a leisurely hot bath while I browsed in my study, checking on a few details. Our bedroom is a warm, comfortable room, luxurious in its way. The bed is seven foot by eight, and I made it myself in the first year of our marriage. Maisie made the sheets, dyed them a deep, rich blue and embroidered the pillow cases. The only light in the room shone through a rough old goatskin lampshade Maisie bought from a man who came to the door. It was a long time since I had taken an interest in the bedroom. We lay side by side in the tangle of sheets and rugs, Maisie voluptuous and drowsy after her bath and stretched full out, and I propped up on my elbow. Maisie said sleepily,

'I was walking along the river this afternoon. The trees are beautiful now, the oaks, the elms... there are two copper beeches about a mile past the footbridge, you should see them now... ahh, that feels good.' I had eased her onto her belly and was caressing her back as she spoke. 'There are blackberries, the biggest ones I've ever seen, growing all along the path, and elderberries, too. I'm going to make some wine this autumn... ' I leaned over her and kissed the nape of her neck and brought her arms behind her back. She liked to be manipulated in this way and she submitted warmly. 'And the river is really still,' she was saying. 'You know, reflecting the trees, and the leaves are dropping into the river. Before the winter comes we should go there together, by the river, in the leaves. I found this little place. No one goes there... ' Holding Maisie's arms in position with one hand, I worked her legs towards the 'hoop' with the other. '... I sat in this place for half an hour without moving, like a tree. I saw a water-rat running along the opposite bank, and different kinds of ducks landing on the river and taking off. I heard these plopping noises in the river but I didn't know what they were and I saw two orange butterflies, they almost came on my hand.' When I had her legs in place Maisie said, 'Position number eighteen,' and we both laughed softly. 'Let's go there tomorrow, to the river,' said Maisie as I carefully eased her head towards her arms. 'Careful, careful, that hurts,' she suddenly shouted, and tried to struggle. But it was too late now, her head and legs were in place in the hoop of her arms, and I was beginning to push them through, past each other. 'What's happening?' cried Maisie. Now the positioning of her limbs expressed the breathtaking beauty, the nobility of the human form, and, as in the paper flower, there was the fascinating power in its symmetry. I felt the trance coming on again and the numbness settling over the back of my head. As I drew her arms and legs through, Maisie appeared to turn in on herself like a sock. 'Oh God,' she sighed, 'what's happening?' and her voice sounded very far away. Then she was gone… and not gone. Her voice was quite tiny, 'What's happening?' and all that remained was the echo of her question above the deep-blue sheets.

EMERGENCY

Denis Johnson

Denis Johnson (b.1949) was born in Munich, in West Germany, and later lived in the Philippines and Japan. A student at Iowa, he was taught by Raymond Carver and is the author of *Angels*, a collection of stories, *Jesus' Son, Tree of Smoke, Train Dreams* – the latter two books were shortlisted for a Pulitzer Prize for fiction, the former won the National Book Award – and several volumes of poetry. Of his collection he once said, "What's funny about *Jesus' Son* is that I never wrote that book, I just wrote it down. I would tell these stories and people would say, You should write these things down."

I'd been working in the emergency room for about three weeks, I guess. This was in 1973, before the summer ended. With nothing to do on the overnight shift but batch the insurance reports from the daytime shifts, I just started wandering around, over to the coronary-care unit, down to the cafeteria, et cetera, looking for Georgie, the orderly, a pretty good friend of mine. He often stole pills from the cabinets.

He was running over the tiled floor of the operating room with a mop. "Are you still doing that?" I said.

"Jesus, there's a lot of blood here," he complained.

"Where?" The floor looked clean enough to me.

"What the hell were they doing in here?" he asked me.

"They were performing surgery, Georgie," I told him.

"There's so much goop inside of us, man," he said, "and it all wants to get out." He leaned his mop against a cabinet.

"What are you crying for?" I didn't understand.

He stood still, raised both arms slowly behind his head, and tightened his ponytail. Then he grabbed the mop and started making broad random arcs with it, trembling and weeping and moving all around the place really fast. "What am I *crying* for?" he said. "Jesus. Wow, oh boy, perfect."

I was hanging out in the E.R. with fat, quivering Nurse. One of the Family Service doctors that nobody liked came in looking for Georgie to wipe up after him. "Where's Georgie?" this guy asked.

"Georgie's in O.R.," Nurse said.

"Again?"

"No," Nurse said. "Still."

"Still? Doing what?"

"Cleaning the floor."

"Again?"

"No," Nurse said again. "Still."

Back in O.R., Georgie dropped his mop and bent over in the posture of a child soiling its diapers. He stared down with his mouth open in terror.

He said, "What am I going to do about these fucking *shoes*, man?"

"Whatever you stole," I said, "I guess you already ate it all, right?"

"Listen to how they squish," he said, walking around carefully on his heels.

"Let me check your pockets, man."

He stood still a minute, and I found his stash. I left him two of each, whatever they were. "Shift is about half over," I told him.

"Good. Because I really, really, really need a drink," he said. "Will you please help me get this blood mopped up?"

Around 3:30 a.m. a guy with a knife in his eye came in, led by Georgie.

"I hope *you* didn't do that to him," Nurse said.

"Me?" Georgie said. "No. He was like this."

"My wife did it," the man said. The blade was buried to the hilt in the outside corner of his left eye. It was a hunting knife kind of thing.

"Who brought you in?" Nurse said.

"Nobody. I just walked down. It's only three blocks," the man said.

Nurse peered at him. "We'd better get you lying down."

"Okay, I'm certainly ready for something like that," the man said.

She peered a bit longer into his face.

"Is your other eye," she said, "a glass eye?"

"It's plastic, or something artificial like that," he said.

"And you can see out of *this* eye?" she asked, meaning the wounded one.

"I can see. But I can't make a fist out of my left hand because this knife is doing something to my brain."

"My God," Nurse said.

"I guess I'd better get the doctor," I said.

"There you go," Nurse agreed.

They got him lying down, and Georgie says to the patient, "Name?"

"Terrence Weber."

"Your face is dark. I can't see what you're saying."

"Georgie," I said.

"What are you saying, man? I can't see."

Nurse came over, and Georgie said to her, "His face is dark."

She leaned over the patient. "How long ago did this happen, Terry?" she shouted down into his face.

"Just a while ago. My wife did it. I was asleep," the patient said.

"Do you want the police?"

He thought about it and finally said, "Not unless I die."

Nurse went to the wall intercom and buzzed the doctor on duty, the Family Service person. "Got a surprise for you," she said over the intercom. He took his time getting down the hall to her, because he knew she hated Family Service and her happy tone of voice could only mean something beyond his competence and potentially humiliating.

He peeked into the trauma room and saw the situation: the clerk – that is, me – standing next to the orderly, Georgie, both of us on drugs, looking down at a patient with a knife sticking up out of his face.

"What seems to be the trouble?" he said.

The doctor gathered the three of us around him in the office and said, "Here's the situation. We've got to get a team here, an entire team. I want a good eye man. A great eye man. The best eye man. I want a brain surgeon. And I want a really good gas man, get me a genius. I'm not touching that head. I'm just going to watch this one. I know my limits. We'll just get him prepped and sit tight. Orderly!"

"Do you mean me?" Georgie said. "Should I get him prepped?"

"Is this a hospital?" the doctor asked. "Is this the emergency room? Is that a patient? Are you the orderly?"

I dialled the hospital operator and told her to get me the eye man and the brain man and the gas man.

Georgie could be heard across the hall, washing his hands and singing a Neil Young song that went "Hello, cowgirl in the sand. Is this place at your command?"

"That person is not right, not at all, not one bit," the doctor said.

"As long as my instructions are audible to him it doesn't concern me," Nurse insisted, spooning stuff up out of a little Dixie cup. "I've got my own life and the protection of my family to think of."

"Well, okay, okay. Don't chew my head off," the doctor said.

The eye man was on vacation or something. While the hospital's operator called around to find someone else just as good, the other specialists were hurrying through the night to join us. I stood around looking at charts and chewing up more of Georgie's pills. Some of them tasted the way urine smells, some of them burned, some of them tasted like chalk. Various nurses, and two physicians who'd been tending somebody in I.C.U., were hanging out down here with us now.

Everybody had a different idea about exactly how to approach the problem of removing the knife from Terrence Weber's brain. But when Georgie came in from prepping the patient – from shaving the patient's eyebrow and disinfecting the area around the wound, and so on – he seemed to be holding the hunting knife in his left hand.

The talk just dropped off a cliff.

"Where," the doctor asked finally, "did you get that?"

Nobody said one thing more, not for quite a long time.

After a while, one of the I.C.U. nurses said, "Your shoelace is untied." Georgie laid the knife on a chart and bent down to fix his shoe.

There were twenty more minutes left to get through.

"How's the guy doing?" I asked.

"Who?" Georgie said.

It turned out that Terrence Weber still had excellent vision in the one good eye, and acceptable motor and reflex, despite his earlier motor complaint. "His vitals are normal," Nurse said. "There's nothing wrong with the guy. It's one of those things."

After a while you forget it's summer. You don't remember what the morning is. I'd worked two doubles with eight hours off in between, which I'd spent sleeping on a gurney in the nurse's station. Georgie's pills were making me feel like a giant helium-filled balloon, but I was wide awake. Georgie and I went out to the lot, to his orange pickup.

We lay down on a stretch of dusty plywood in the back of the truck with the daylight knocking against our eyelids and the fragrance of alfalfa thickening on our tongues.

"I want to go to church," Georgie said.

"Let's go to the county fair."

"I'd like to worship. I would."

"They have these injured hawks and eagles there. From the Humane Society," I said.

"I need a quiet chapel about now."

Georgie and I had a terrific time driving around. For a while the day was clear and peaceful. It was one of the moments you stay in, to hell with all the troubles of before and after. The sky is blue and the dead are coming back. Later in the afternoon, with sad resignation, the county fair bares it breasts. A champion of the drug LSD, a very famous guru of the love generation, is being interviewed amid a TV crew off to the left of the poultry cages. His eyeballs look like he bought them in a joke shop. It doesn't occur to me, as I pity this extraterrestrial, that in my life I've taken as much as he has.

After that, we got lost. We drove for hours, literally hours, but we couldn't find the road back to town.

Georgie started to complain. "That was the worst fair I've been to. Where were the rides?"

"They had rides," I said.

"I didn't see one ride."

A jackrabbit scurried out in front of us, and we hit it.

"There was a merry-go-round, a Ferris wheel, and a thing called the Hammer that people were bent over vomiting from after they got off," I said. "Are you completely blind?"

"What was that?"

"A rabbit."

"Something thumped."

"You hit him. *He* thumped."

Georgie stood on the brake pedal. "Rabbit stew."

He threw the truck in reverse and zigzagged back toward the rabbit. "Where's my hunting knife?" He almost ran over the poor animal a second time.

"We'll camp in the wilderness," he said. "In the morning we'll breakfast on its haunches." He was waving Terrence Weber's hunting knife around in what I was sure was a dangerous way.

In a minute he was standing at the edge of the fields, cutting the scrawny little thing up, tossing away its organs. "I should have been a doctor," he cried.

A family in a big Dodge, the only car we'd seen for a long time, slowed down and gawked out the windows as they passed by. The father said, "What is it, a snake?"

"No, it's not a snake," Georgie said. "It's a rabbit with babies inside it."

"Babies!" the mother said, and the father sped the car forward, over the protests of several little kids in the back.

Georgie came back to my side of the truck with his shirtfront stretched out in front of him as if he were carrying apples in it, or some such, but they were, in fact, slimy miniature bunnies. "No way I'm eating those things," I told him.

"Take them, take them. I gotta drive, take them," he said, dumping them in my lap and getting in on his side of the truck. He started driving along faster and faster, with a look of glory on his face. "We killed the mother and saved the children," he said.

"It's getting late," I said. "Let's get back to town."

"You bet." Sixty, seventy, eighty-five, just topping ninety.

"These rabbits better be kept warm." One at a time I slid the little things in between my shirt buttons and nestled them against my belly. "They're hardly moving," I told Georgie.

"We'll get some milk and sugar and all that, and we'll raise them up ourselves. They'll get as big as gorillas."

The road we were lost on cut straight through the middle of the world. It was still daytime, but the sun had no more power than an ornament or a sponge. In this light the truck's hood, which had been bright orange, had turned a deep blue.

Georgie let us drift to the shoulder of the road, slowly, slowly, as if he'd fallen asleep or given up trying to find his way.

"What is it?"

"We can't go on. I don't have any headlights," Georgie said.

We parked under a strange sky with a faint image of a quarter-moon superimposed on it.

There was a little woods beside us. This day had been dry and hot, the buck pines and what-all simmering patiently, but as we sat there smoking cigarettes it started to get very cold.

"The summer's over," I said.

That was the year when arctic clouds moved down over the Midwest and we had two weeks of winter in September.

"Do you realize it's going to snow?" Georgie asked me.

He was right, a gun-blue storm was shaping up. We got out and walked around idiotically. The beautiful chill! That sudden crispness, and the tang of evergreen stabbing us!

The gusts of snow twisted themselves around our heads while the night fell. I couldn't find the truck. We just kept getting more and more lost. I kept calling, "Georgie, can you see?" and he kept saying, "See what? See what?"

The only light visible was a streak of sunset flickering below the hem of the clouds. We headed that way.

We bumped softly down a hill toward an open field that seemed to be a military graveyard, filled with rows and rows of austere, identical markers over soldiers' graves. I'd never before come across this cemetery. On the farther side of the field, just beyond the curtains of snow, the sky was torn away and the angels were descending out of a brilliant blue summer, their huge faces streaked with light and full of pity. The sight of them cut through my heart and down the knuckles of my spine, and if there'd been anything in my bowels I would have messed my pants from fear.

Georgie opened his arms and cried out, "It's the drive-in, man!"

"The drive-in . . ." I wasn't sure what these words meant.

"They're showing movies in a fucking blizzard!" Georgie screamed.

"I see. I thought it was something else," I said.

We walked carefully down there and climbed through the busted fence and stood in the very back. The speakers, which I'd mistaken for grave markers, muttered in unison. Then there was tinkly music, of which I could very nearly make out the tune. Famous movie stars rode bicycles beside a river, laughing out of their gigantic, lovely mouths. If anybody had come to see this show, they'd left when the weather started. Not one car remained, not even a broken-down one from last week, or one left here because it was out of gas. In a couple of minutes, in the middle of a whirling square dance, the screen turned black, the cinematic summer ended, the snow went dark, there was nothing but my breath.

"I'm starting to get my eyes back," Georgie said in another minute.

A general greyness was giving birth to various shapes, it was true. "But which ones are close and which ones are far off?" I begged him to tell me.

By trial and error, with a lot of walking back and forth in wet shoes, we found the truck and sat inside it shivering.

"Let's get out of here," I said.

"We can't go anywhere without headlights."

"We've gotta get back. We're a long way from home."

"No, we're not."

"We must have come three hundred miles."

"We're right outside town, Fuckhead. We've just been driving around and around."

"This is no place to camp. I hear the Interstate over there."

"We'll just stay here till it gets late. We can drive home late. We'll be invisible."

We listened to the big rigs going from San Francisco to Pennsylvania along the Interstate, like shudders down a long hacksaw blade, while the snow buried us.

Eventually Georgie said, "We better get some milk for those bunnies."

"We don't have *milk*," I said.

"We'll mix sugar up with it."

"Will you forget about this milk all of a sudden?"

"They're mammals, man."

"Forget about those rabbits."

"Where are they, anyway?"

"You're not listening to me. I said, 'Forget the rabbits.'"

"Where are they?"

The truth was I'd forgotten all about them, and they were dead.

"They slid around behind me and got squashed," I said tearfully.

"They slid around *behind*?"

He watched while I pried them out from behind my back.

I picked them out one at a time and held them in my hands and we looked at them. There were eight. They weren't any bigger than my fingers, but everything was there.

Little feet! Eyelids! Even whiskers! "Deceased," I said.

Georgie asked, "Does everything you touch turn to shit? Does this happen to you every time?"

"No wonder they call me Fuckhead."

"It's a name that's going to stick."

"I realize that."

"'Fuckhead'is gonna ride you to your grave."

"I just said so. I agreed with you in advance," I said.

Or maybe that wasn't the time it snowed. Maybe it was the time we slept in the truck and I rolled over on the bunnies and flattened them. It doesn't matter. What's important for me to remember now is that early the next morning the snow was melted off the windshield and the daylight woke me up. A mist covered everything and, with the sunshine, was beginning to grow sharp and strange. The bunnies weren't a problem yet, or they'd already been a problem and were already forgotten, and there was nothing on my mind. I felt the beauty of the morning. I could understand how a drowning man might suddenly feel a deep thirst being quenched. Or how the slave might become a friend to his master. Georgie slept with his face right on the steering wheel.

I saw bits of snow resembling an abundance of blossoms on the stems of the drive-in speakers – no, revealing the blossoms that were always there. A bull elk stood still in the pasture beyond the fence, giving off an air of authority and stupidity. And a coyote jogged across the pasture and faded away among the saplings.

That afternoon we got back to work in time to resume everything as if it had never stopped happening and we'd never been anywhere else.

"The Lord," the intercom said, "is my shepherd." It did that each evening because this was a Catholic hospital. "Our Father, who art in Heaven," and so on.

"Yeah, yeah," Nurse said.

The man with the knife in his head, Terrence Weber, was released around suppertime. They'd kept him overnight and given him an eyepatch – all for no reason, really.

He stopped off at E.R. to say goodbye. "Well, those pills they gave me make everything taste terrible," he said.

"It could have been worse," Nurse said.

"Even my tongue."

"It's just a miracle you didn't end up sightless or at least dead," she reminded him.

The patient recognized me. He acknowledged me with a smile. "I was peeping on the lady next door while she was out there sunbathing," he said. "My wife decided to blind me."

He shook Georgie's hand. Georgie didn't know him. "Who are you supposed to be?" he asked Terrence Weber.

Some hours before that, Georgie had said something that had suddenly and completely explained the difference between us. We'd been driving back toward town, along the Old Highway, through the flatness. We picked up a hitch-hiker, a boy I knew. We stopped the truck and the boy climbed slowly up out of the fields as out of the mouth of a volcano. His name was Hardee. He looked even worse than we probably did.

"We got messed up and slept in the truck all night," I told Hardee.

"I had a feeling," Hardee said. "Either that or, you know, driving a thousand miles."

"That too," I said.

"Or you're sick or diseased or something."

"Who's this guy?" Georgie asked.

"This is Hardee. He lived with me last summer. I found him on the doorstep. What happened to your dog?" I asked Hardee.

"He's still down there."

"Yeah, I heard you went to Texas."

"I was working on a bee farm," Hardee said.

"Wow. Do those things sting you?"

"Not like you'd think," Hardee said. "You're part of their daily drill. It's all part of a harmony."

Outside, the same identical stretch of ground repeatedly rolled past our faces. The day was cloudless, blinding. But Georgie said, "Look at that," pointing straight ahead of us.

One star was so hot it showed, bright and blue, in the empty sky.

"I recognized you right away," I told Hardee. "But what happened to your hair? Who chopped it off?"

"I hate to say."

"Don't tell me."

"They drafted me."

"Oh no."

"Oh yeah. I'm AWOL. I'm bad AWOL. I got to get to Canada."

"Oh, that's terrible," I said to Hardee.

"Don't worry," Georgie said. "We'll get you there."

"How?"

"Somehow. I think I know some people. Don't worry. You're on your way to Canada."

That world! These days it's all been erased and they've rolled it up like a scroll and put it away somewhere. Yes, I can touch it with my fingers. But where is it?

After a while Hardee asked Georgie, "What do you do for a job," and Georgie said, "I save lives."

LET ME COUNT
THE TIMES

Martin Amis

Martin Amis (b.1949) is the author of over twenty books, including *The Rachel Papers, Dead Babies, Money* and *London Fields,* as well as a memoir, *Experience.* His most recent novel is *The Zone of Interest.* He lives in Brooklyn, New York.

Vernon made love to his wife three and a half times a week, and this was all right.

For some reason, making love always averaged out that way. Normally – though by no means invariably – they made love every second night. On the other hand Vernon had been known to make love to his wife seven nights running; for the next seven nights they would not make love – or perhaps they would once, in which case they would make love the following week only twice but four times the week after that – or perhaps only three times, in which case they would make love four times the next week but only twice the week after that – or perhaps only once. And so on. Vernon didn't know why, but making love always averaged out that way; it seemed invariable. Occasionally – and was it any wonder? – Vernon found himself wishing that the week contained only six days, or as many as eight, to render these calculations (which were always blandly corroborative in spirit) easier to deal with.

It was, without exception, Vernon himself who initiated their conjugal acts. His wife responded every time with the same bashful alacrity. Oral foreplay was by no means unknown between them. On average – and again it always averaged out like this, and again Vernon was always the unsmiling ring master – fellatio was performed by Vernon's wife every third coupling, or 60.8333 times a year, or 1.1698717 times a week. Vernon performed cunnilingus rather less often: every fourth coupling, on average, or 45.625 times a year, or .8774038 times a week. It would also be a mistake to think that this was the extent of their variations. Vernon sodomized his wife twice a year, for instance – on his birthday, which seemed fair enough, but also, ironically (or so *he* thought), on hers. He put it down to the expensive nights out they always had on these occasions, and more particularly to the effects of champagne. Vernon always felt desperately ashamed afterwards, and would be a limp spectre of embarrassment and remorse at breakfast the next day. Vernon's wife never said anything about it, which was something. If she ever did, Vernon would probably have stopped doing it. But she never did. The same sort of thing happened when Vernon ejaculated in his wife's mouth, which on average he did 1.2 times a year. At this point they had been married for ten years. That was convenient. What would it be like when they had been married for eleven years – or thirteen. Once, and only once, Vernon had been about to ejaculate in his wife's mouth when suddenly he had got a better idea: he ejaculated all over her face instead. She didn't say anything about that either, thank God. Why he had thought it a better idea he would never know. He didn't think it was a better idea now. It distressed him greatly to reflect that his rare acts of abandonment should expose a desire to humble and degrade the loved one. And she was the loved one. Still, he had only done it once. Vernon ejaculated all over his wife's face .001923 times a week. That wasn't very often to ejaculate all over your wife's face, now was it?

Vernon was a businessman. His office contained several electronic calculators. Vernon would often run his marital frequencies through these swift, efficient, and impeccably discreet machines. They always responded brightly with the same answer, as if to say, "Yes, Vernon, that's how often you do it," or "No, Vernon, you don't do it any more often than that." Vernon would spend whole lunch-hours crooked over the calculator. And yet he knew that all these figures were in a sense approximate. Oh, Vernon knew, Vernon knew. Then one day a powerful white computer was delivered to the accounts department. Vernon saw at once that a long-nursed dream might now take flesh: leap years. "Ah, Alice. I don't want to be disturbed, do you hear?" he told the cleaning lady sternly when he let himself into the office that night. "I've got some very important calculations to do in the accounts department." Just after midnight Vernon's hot red eyes stared up wildly from the display screen, where his entire sex life lay tabulated in recurring prisms of threes and sixes, in endless series, like mirrors placed face to face.

Vernon's wife was the only woman Vernon had ever known. He loved her and he liked making love to her quite a lot; certainly he had never craved any other outlet. When Vernon made love to his wife he thought only of her pleasure and her beauty: the infrequent but highly flattering noises she made through her evenly parted teeth, the divine plasticity of her limbs, the fever, the magic, and the safety of the moment. The sense of peace that followed had only a little to do with the probability that tomorrow would be a night off. Even Vernon's dreams were monogamous: the women who strode those slipped but essentially quotidian landscapes were mere icons of the self-sufficient female kingdom, nurses, nuns, bus-conductresses, parking wardens, policewomen. Only every now and then, once a week, say, or less, or not calculably, he saw things that made him suspect that life might have room for more inside – a luminous ribbon dappling the under-curve of a bridge, certain cloudscapes, intent figures hurrying through changing light.

All this, of course, was before Vernon's business trip.

It was not a particularly important business trip: Vernon's firm was not a particularly important firm. His wife packed his smallest suitcase and drove him to the station. On the way she observed that they had not spent a night apart for over four years – when she had gone to stay with her mother after that operation of hers. Vernon nodded in surprised agreement, making a few brisk calculations in his head. He kissed her goodbye with some passion. In the restaurant car he had a gin and tonic. He had another gin and tonic. As the train approached the thickening city Vernon felt a curious lightness play through his body. He thought of himself as a young man, alone. The city would be full of cabs, stray people, shadows, women, things happening.

Vernon got to his hotel at eight o'clock. The receptionist confirmed his reservation and gave him his key. Vernon rode the elevator to his room. He washed and changed, selecting, after some deliberation, the more sombre of the two ties his wife had packed. He went to the bar and ordered a gin and tonic. The cocktail waitress brought it to him at a table. The bar was scattered with city people: men, women who probably did things with men fairly often, young couples secretively chuckling. Directly opposite Vernon sat a formidable lady with a fur, a hat, and a cigarette holder. She glanced at Vernon twice or perhaps three times. Vernon couldn't be sure.

He dined in the hotel restaurant. With his meal he enjoyed half a bottle of good red wine. Over coffee Vernon toyed with the idea of going back to the bar for a crème de menthe – or a champagne cocktail. He felt hot; his scalp hummed; two hysterical flies looped round his head. He rode back to his room, with a view to freshening up. Slowly, before the mirror, he removed all his clothes. His pale body was inflamed with the tranquil glow of fever. He felt deliciously raw, tingling to his touch. What's happening to me? he wondered. Then, with relief, with shame, with rapture, he keeled backwards on to the bed and did something he hadn't done for over ten years.

Vernon did it three more times that night and twice again in the morning.

Four appointments spaced out the following day. Vernon's mission was to pick the right pocket calculator for daily use by all members of his firm. Between each demonstration – the Moebius strip of figures, the repeated wink of the decimal point – Vernon took cabs back to the hotel and did it again each time. "As fast as you can, driver," he found himself saying. That night he had a light supper sent up to his room. He did it five more times – or was it six? He could no longer be absolutely sure. But he was sure he did it three more times the next morning, once before breakfast and twice after. He took the train back at noon, having done it an incredible 18 times in 36 hours: that was – what? – 84 times a week, or 4,368 times a year. Or perhaps he had done it 19 times! Vernon was exhausted, yet in a sense he had never felt stronger. And here was the train giving him an erection all the same, whether he liked it or not.

"How was it?" asked his wife at the station.

"Tiring. But successful," admitted Vernon.

"Yes, you do look a bit whacked. We'd better get you home and tuck you up in bed for a while."

Vernon's red eyes blinked. He could hardly believe his luck.

Shortly afterwards Vernon was to look back with amused disbelief at his own faint-heartedness during those trail-blazing few days. Only in bed, for instance! Now, in his total recklessness and elation, Vernon did it everywhere. He hauled himself roughly on to the bedroom floor and did it there. He did it under the impassive gaze of the bathroom's porcelain and steel. With scandalized laughter he dragged himself out protesting to the garden tool shed and did it there. He did it lying on the kitchen table. For a while he took to doing it in the open air, in windy parks, behind hoardings in the town, on churned fields; it made his knees tremble. He did it in corridorless trains. He would rent rooms in cheap hotels for an hour, for half an hour, for ten minutes (how the receptionists stared). He thought of renting a little love-nest somewhere. Confusedly and very briefly he considered running off with himself. He started doing it at work, cautiously at first, then with nihilistic abandon, as if discovery was the very thing he secretly craved. Once, giggling coquettishly before and afterwards (the danger, the danger), he did it while dictating a long and tremulous letter to the secretary he shared with two other senior managers. After this he came to his senses somewhat and resolved to try only to do it at home.

"How long will you be, dear?" he would call over his shoulder as his wife opened the front door with her shopping-bags in her hands. An hour? Fine. Just a couple of minutes? Even better! He took to lingering sinuously in bed while his wife made their morning tea, deliciously sandwiched by the moist uxoriousness of the sheets. On his nights off from love-making (and these were invariable now: every other night, every other night) Vernon nearly always managed one while his wife, in the bathroom next door, calmly readied herself for sleep. She nearly caught him at it on several occasions. He found that especially exciting. At this point Vernon was still trying hectically to keep count; it was all there somewhere, gurgling away in the memory banks of the computer in the accounts department. He was averaging 3.4 times a day, or 23.8 times a week, or an insane 1,241 times a year. And his wife never suspected a thing.

Until now, Vernon's "sessions" (as he thought of them) had always been mentally structured round his wife, the only woman he had ever known – her beauty, the flattering noises she made, the fever, the safety. There were variations, naturally. A typical "session" would start with her undressing at night. She would lean out of her heavy brassière and submissively debark the tender checks of her panties. She would give a little gasp, half pleasure, half fear (how do you figure a woman?), as naked Vernon, obviously in sparkling form, emerged impressively from the shadows. He would mount her swiftly, perhaps even rather brutally. Her hands mimed their defencelessness as the great muscles rippled and plunged along Vernon's powerful back. "You're too big for me," he would have her say to him sometimes, or "That hurts, but I like it." Climax would usually be synchronized with his wife's howled request for the sort of thing Vernon seldom did to her in real life. But Vernon never did the things for which she yearned, oh no. He usually just ejaculated all over her face. She loved that as well of course (the bitch), to Vernon's transient disgust.

And then the strangers came.

One summer evening Vernon returned early from the office. The car was gone: as Vernon had shrewdly anticipated, his wife was out somewhere. Hurrying into the house, he made straight for the bedroom. He lay down and lowered his trousers – and then with a sensuous moan tugged them off altogether. Things started well, with a compelling preamble that had become increasingly popular in recent weeks. Naked, primed, Vernon stood behind the half-closed bedroom door. Already he could hear his wife's preparatory truffles of shy arousal. Vernon stepped forward to swing open the door, intending to stand there menacingly for a few seconds, his restless legs planted well apart. He swung open the door and stared. At what? At his wife sweatily grappling with a huge bronzed gypsy, who turned incuriously towards Vernon and then back again to the hysteria of volition splayed out on the bed before him. Vernon ejaculated immediately. His wife returned home within a few minutes. She kissed him on the forehead. He felt very strange.

The next time he tried, he swung open the door to find his wife upside down over the headboard, doing scarcely credible things to a hairy-shouldered Turk. The time after that, she had her elbows hooked round the back of her knee-caps as a 15 stone Chinaman feasted at his leisure on her imploring sobs. The time after that, two silent, glistening negroes were doing what the hell they liked with her. The two negroes, in particular, wouldn't go away; they were quite frequently joined by the Turk, moreover. Sometimes they would even let Vernon and his wife get started before they all came thundering in on them. And did Vernon's wife mind any of this? Mind? She liked it. Like it? She *loved* it! And so did Vernon, apparently. At the office Vernon soberly searched his brain for a single neutrino of genuine desire that his wife should do these things with these people. The very idea made him shout with revulsion. Yet, one way or another, he didn't mind it really, did he? One way or another, he liked it. He loved it. But he was determined to put an end to it.

His whole approach changed. "Right, my girl," he muttered to himself, "two can play at that game." To begin with, Vernon had affairs with all his wife's friends. The longest and perhaps the most detailed was with Vera, his wife's old school chum. He sported with her bridge-partners, her co-workers in the Charity. He fooled around with all her eligible relatives – her younger sister, that nice little niece of hers. One mad morning Vernon even mounted her hated mother. "But Vernon, what about . . .?" they would all whisper fearfully. But Vernon just shoved them on to the bed, twisting off his belt with an imperious snap. All the women out there on the edges of his wife's world – one by one, Vernon had the lot.

Meanwhile, Vernon's erotic dealings with his wife herself had continued much as before. Perhaps they had even profited in poignancy and gentleness from the pounding rumours of Vernon's nether life. With this latest development, however, Vernon was not slow to mark a new dimension, a disfavoured presence, in their bed. Oh, they still made love all right; but now there were two vital differences. Their acts of sex were no longer hermetic; the safety and the peace had gone: no longer did Vernon attempt to apply any brake to the chariot of his thoughts. Secondly – and perhaps even more crucially – their love-making was, without a doubt, *less frequent*. Six and a half times a fortnight, three times a week, five times a fortnight . . . : they were definitely losing ground. At first Vernon's mind was a chaos of back-logs, short-falls, restructured schedules, recuperation schemes. Later he grew far more detached about the whole business. Who said he had to do it three and a half times a week? Who said that this was all right? After ten nights of chaste sleep (his record up till now) Vernon watched his wife turn sadly on her side after her diffident goodnight. He waited several minutes, propped up on an elbow, glazedly eternalized in the potent moment. Then he leaned forward and coldly kissed her neck, and smiled as he felt her body's axis turn. He went on smiling. He knew where the real action was.

For Vernon was now perfectly well aware that any woman was his for the taking, any woman at all, at a nod, at a shrug, at a single convulsive snap of his peremptory fingers. He systematically serviced every woman who caught his eye in the street, had his way with them, and tossed them aside without a second thought. All the models in his wife's fashion magazines – they all trooped through his bedroom, too, in their turn. Over the course of several months he worked his way through all the established television actresses. An equivalent period took care of the major stars of the Hollywood screen. (Vernon bought a big glossy book to help him with this project. For his money, the girls of the Golden Age were the most daring and athletic lovers: Monroe, Russell, West, Dietrich, Dors, Ekberg. Frankly, you could keep your Welches, your Dunaways, your Fondas, your Keatons.) By now the roll-call of names was astounding. Vernon's prowess with them epic, unsurpassable. All the girls were saying that he was easily the best lover they had ever had.

One afternoon he gingerly peered into the pornographic magazines that blazed from the shelves of a remote newsagent. He made a mental note of the faces and figures, and the girls were duly accorded brief membership of Vernon's thronging harem. But he was shocked; he didn't mind admitting it: why should pretty young girls take their clothes off for money like that, like *that*? Why should men want to buy pictures of them doing it? Distressed and not a little confused, Vernon conducted the first great purge of his clamorous rumpus rooms. That night he paced through the shimmering corridors and becalmed ante-rooms dusting his palms and looking sternly this way and that. Some girls wept openly at the loss of their friends; others smiled up at him with furtive triumph. But he stalked on, slamming the heavy doors behind him.

Vernon now looked for solace in the pages of our literature. Quality, he told himself, was what he was after – quality, quality. Here was where the high-class girls hung out. Using the literature shelves in the depleted local library, Vernon got down to work. After quick flings with Emily, Griselda, and Criseyde, and a strapping weekend with the Good Wife of Bath, Vernon cruised straight on to Shakespeare and the delightfully wide-eyed starlets of the romantic comedies. He romped giggling with Viola over the Illyrian hills, slept in a glade in Arden with the willowy Rosalind, bathed nude with Miranda in a turquoise lagoon. In a single disdainful morning he splashed his way through all four of the tragic heroines: cold Cordelia (this was a bit of a frost, actually), bitter-sweet Ophelia (again rather constricted, though he quite liked her dirty talk), the snake-eyed Lady M. (Vernon had had to watch himself there) and, best of all, that sizzling sorceress Desdemona (Othello had *her* number all right. She *stank* of sex!). Following some arduous, unhygienic yet relatively brief dalliance with Restoration drama, Vernon soldiered on through the prudent matrons of the Great Tradition. As a rule, the more sedate and respectable the girls, the nastier and more complicated were the things Vernon found himself wanting to do to them (with lapsed hussies like Maria Bertram, Becky Sharp, or Lady Dedlock,

Vernon was in, out, and away, darting half-dressed over the rooftops). Pamela had her points, but Clarissa was the one who turned out to be the true co-artist of the oeuvres; Sophie Western was good fun all right, but the pious Amelia yodelled for the humbling high points in Vernon's sweltering repertoire. Again he had no very serious complaints about his one-night romances with the likes of Elizabeth Bennett and Dorothea Brooke; it was adult, sanitary stuff, based on a clear understanding of his desires and his needs; they knew that such men will take what they want; they knew that they would wake the next morning and Vernon would be gone. Give him a Fanny Price, though, or better, much better, a Little Nell, and Vernon would march into the bedroom rolling up his sleeves; and Nell and Fan would soon be ruing the day they'd ever been born. Did they mind the horrible things he did to them? Mind? When he prepared to leave the next morning, solemnly buckling his belt before the tall window – how they howled!

The possibilities seemed endless. Other literatures dozed expectantly in their dormitories. The sleeping lion of Tolstoy – Anna, Natasha, Masha, and the rest. American fiction – those girls would show even Vernon a trick or two. The sneaky Gauls – Vernon had a hunch that he and Madame Bovary, for instance, were going to get along just fine . . . One puzzled weekend, however, Vernon encountered the writings of D. H. Lawrence. Snapping *The Rainbow* shut on Sunday night, Vernon realized at once that this particular avenue of possibility – sprawling as it was, with its intricate trees and their beautiful diseases, and that distant prospect where sandy mountains loomed – had come to an abrupt and unanswerable end. He never knew women behaved like *that* . . . Vernon felt obscure relief and even a pang of theoretical desire when his wife bustled in last thing, bearing the tea-tray before her.

Vernon was now, on average, sleeping with his wife 1.15 times a week. Less than single figure love-making was obviously going to be some sort of crunch, and Vernon was making himself vigilant for whatever form the crisis might take. She hadn't, thank God, said anything about it, yet. Brooding one afternoon soon after the Lawrence débâcle, Vernon suddenly thought of something that made his heart jump. He blinked. He couldn't believe it. It was true. Not once since he had started his "sessions" had Vernon exacted from his wife any of the sly variations with which he had used to space out the weeks, the months, the years. Not once. It had simply never occurred to him. He flipped his pocket calculator on to his lap. Stunned, he tapped out the figures. She now owed him . . . Why, if he wanted, he could have an entire week of . . . They were behind with *that* to the tune of . . . Soon it would be time again for him to . . . Vernon's wife passed through the room. She blew him a kiss. Vernon resolved to shelve these figures but also to keep them up to date. They seemed to balance things out. He knew he was denying his wife something she ought to have; yet at the same time he was withholding something he ought not to give. He began to feel better about the whole business.

For it now became clear that no mere woman could satisfy him – not Vernon. His activities moved into an entirely new sphere of intensity and abstraction. Now, when the velvet curtain shot skywards, Vernon might be astride a black stallion on a marmoreal dune, his narrow eyes fixed on the caravan of defenceless Arab women straggling along beneath him; then he dug in his spurs and thundered down on them, swords twirling in either hand. Or else Vernon climbed from a wriggling human swamp of tangled naked bodies, playfully batting away the hands that clutched at him, until he was tugged down once again into the thudding mass of membrane and heat. He visited strange planets where women were metal, were flowers, were gas. Soon he became a cumulus cloud, a tidal wave, the East Wind, the boiling Earth's core, the air itself, wheeling round a terrified globe as whole tribes, races, ecologies fled and scattered under the continent-wide shadow of his approach.

It was after about a month of this new brand of skylarking that things began to go rather seriously awry.

The first hint of disaster came with sporadic attacks of *ejaculatio praecox*. Vernon would settle down for a leisurely session, would just be casting and scripting the cosmic drama about to be unfolded before him – and would look down to find his thoughts had been messily and pleasurelessly anticipated by the roguish weapon in his hands. It began to happen more frequently, sometimes quite out of the blue: Vernon wouldn't even notice until he saw the boyish, telltale stains on his pants last thing at night. (Amazingly, and rather hurtfully too, his wife didn't seem to detect any real difference. But he was making love to her only every ten or eleven days by that time.) Vernon made a creditable attempt to laugh the whole thing off, and, sure enough, after a while the trouble cleared itself up. What followed, however, was far worse.

To begin with, at any rate, Vernon blamed himself. He was so relieved, and so childishly delighted, by his newly recovered prowess that he teased out his "sessions" to unendurable, unprecedented lengths. Perhaps that wasn't wise . . . What was certain was that he overdid it. Within a week, and quite against his will, Vernon's "sessions" were taking between thirty and forty-five minutes; within two weeks, up to an hour and a half. It wrecked his schedules: all the lightning strikes, all the silky raids, that used to punctuate his life were reduced to dour campaigns which Vernon could perforce never truly win. "Vernon, are you ill?" his wife would say outside the bathroom door. "It's nearly *tea*-time." Vernon – slumped on the lavatory seat, panting with exhaustion – looked up wildly, his eyes startled, shrunken. He coughed until he found his voice. "I'll be straight out," he managed to say, climbing heavily to his feet.

Nothing Vernon could summon would deliver him. Massed, maddened, cartwheeling women – some of molten pewter and fifty feet tall, others indigo and no bigger than fountain-pens – hollered at him from the four corners of the universe. No help. He gathered all the innocents and subjected them to atrocities of unimaginable proportions, committing a million murders enriched with infamous tortures. He still drew a blank. Vernon, all neutronium, a supernova, a black sun, consumed the Earth and her sisters in his dead fire, bullocking through the solar system, ejaculating the Milky Way. That didn't work either. He was obliged to fake orgasms with his wife (rather skilfully, it seemed: she didn't say anything about it). His testicles developed a mighty migraine, whose slow throbs all day timed his heartbeat with mounting frequency and power, until at night Vernon's face was a sweating parcel of lard and his hands shimmered deliriously as he juggled the aspirins to his lips.

Then the ultimate catastrophe occurred. Paradoxically, it was heralded by a single, joyous, uncovenanted climax – again out of the blue, on a bus, one lunchtime. Throughout the afternoon at the office Vernon chuckled and gloated, convinced that finally all his troubles were at an end. It wasn't so. After a week of ceaseless experiment and scrutiny Vernon had to face the truth. The thing was dead. He was impotent.

"Oh my God," he thought, "I always knew something like this would happen to me some time." In one sense Vernon accepted the latest reverse with grim stoicism (by now the thought of his old ways filled him with the greatest disgust); in another sense, and with terror, he felt like a man suspended between two states: one is reality, perhaps, the other an unspeakable dream. And then when day comes he awakes with a moan of relief; but reality has gone and the nightmare has replaced it: the nightmare was really there all the time. Vernon looked at the house where they had lived for so long now, the five rooms through which his calm wife moved along her calm tracks, and he saw it all slipping away from him forever, all his peace, all the fever and the safety. And for what, for what?

"Perhaps it would be better if I just told her about the whole thing and made a clean breast of it," he thought wretchedly. "It wouldn't be easy, God knows, but in time she might learn to trust me again. And I really *am* finished with all that other nonsense. God, when I . . ." But then he saw his wife's face – capable, straightforward, confident – and the scar of dawning realization as he stammered out his shame. No, he could never tell her, he could never do that to her, no, not to her. She was sure to find out soon enough anyway. How could a man conceal that he had lost what made him a man? He considered suicide, but – "But I just haven't got the guts," he told himself. He would have to wait, to wait and melt in his dread.

A month passed without his wife saying anything. This had always been a make-or-break, last-ditch deadline for Vernon, and he now approached the coming confrontation as a matter of nightly crisis. All day long he rehearsed his excuses. To kick off with Vernon complained of a headache, on the next night of a stomach upset. For the following two nights he stayed up virtually until dawn – "preparing the annual figures," he said. On the fifth night he simulated a long coughing fit, on the sixth a powerful fever. But on the seventh night he just helplessly lay there, sadly waiting. Thirty minutes passed, side by side. Vernon prayed for her sleep and for his death.

"Vernon?" she asked.

"Mm-hm?" he managed to say – God, what a croak it was.

"Do you want to talk about this?"

Vernon didn't say anything. He lay there, melting, dying. More minutes passed. Then he felt her hand on his thigh.

Quite a long time later, and in the posture of a cowboy on the back of a bucking steer, Vernon ejaculated all over his wife's face. During the course of the preceding two and a half hours he had done to his wife everything he could possibly think of, to such an extent that he was candidly astonished that she was still alive. They subsided, mumbling soundlessly, and slept in each other's arms.

Vernon woke up before his wife did. It took him thirty-five minutes to get out of bed, so keen was he to accomplish this feat without waking her. He made breakfast in his dressing-gown, training every cell of his concentration on the small, sacramental tasks. Every time his mind veered back to the night before, he made a low growling sound, or slid his knuckles down the cheese-grater, or caught his tongue between his teeth and pressed hard. He closed his eyes and he could see his wife crammed against the headboard with that one leg sticking up in the air; he could hear the sound her breasts made as he two-handedly slapped them practically out of alignment. Vernon steadied himself against the refrigerator. He had an image of his wife coming into the kitchen – on crutches, her face black and blue. She couldn't very well not say anything about *that*, could she? He laid the table. He heard her stir. He sat down, his knees cracking, and ducked his head behind the cereal packet.

When Vernon looked up his wife was sitting opposite him. She looked utterly normal. Her blue eyes searched for his with all their light.

"Toast?" he bluffed.

"Yes please. Oh Vernon, wasn't it lovely?"

For an instant Vernon knew beyond doubt that he would now have to murder his wife and then commit suicide – or kill her and leave the country under an assumed name, start all over again somewhere, Romania, Iceland, the Far East, the New World.

"What, you mean the –?"

"Oh yes. I'm so happy. For a while I thought that we . . . I thought you were –"

"I –"

"– Don't, darling. You needn't say anything. I understand. And now everything's all right again. Ooh," she added. "You were naughty, you know."

Vernon nearly panicked all over again. But he gulped it down and said, quite nonchalantly, "Yes, I was a bit, wasn't I?"

"Very naughty. So *rude*. Oh Vernon . . ."

She reached for his hand and stood up. Vernon got to his feet too – or became upright by some new hydraulic system especially devised for the occasion. She glanced over her shoulder as she moved up the stairs.

"You mustn't do that too often, you know."

"Oh really?" drawled Vernon. "Who says?"

"*I* say. It would take the fun out of it. Well, not *too* often, anyway."

Vernon knew one thing: he was going to stop keeping count. Pretty soon, he reckoned, things would be more or less back to normal. He'd had his kicks: it was only right that the loved one should now have hers. Vernon followed his wife into the bedroom and softly closed the door behind them.

CUN

Nguyen Huy Thiep

Nguyen Huy Thiep (b.1950) has been described as Vietnam's most influential writer. He moved with his family to Hanoi aged ten and trained to be a teacher. When his collection *The General Retires* was published in 1987, it caused a sensation. To secure his livelihood he has worked as a potter, painter, and runs two restaurants in Hanoi. He has published plays and criticism. He published his first novel in 2007.

1. The Cause of the Story

Among the people I know, I have particular respect for the literary scholar K. He understands our literary debates well (which I must confess I don't). There are even times when people compare his articles with "whips" that lash "the horse of creation" unerringly along its path.

K is handsome, intelligent, and especially sensitive to other people's pain and suffering. On many occasions that I've been out with him, I've seen him slip away from places where there are beggars and cripples. In situations where he can't escape, he becomes very agitated. I've seen him turn pale and empty his pockets for a beggar or a cripple.

With me and other young writers of my generation K is very strict. He demands high standards in what he calls the *character* of a person. Hard work, sacrifice, dedication, sincerity, and, of course, good grammar are the qualities he requires. Such strictness means our friendship is stormy. However, this does not lessen my admiration for him. It had often occurred to me that there must be a very deep reason for K's unusual strictness and sensitivity. Then, once, after I'd been inquiring around the point, he suddenly let something unexpected slip.

"My father was Cun," he said. "Throughout his short life his only desire was to become a human being, but he never did."

On the basis of that utterance, I wrote this story.

2. The Story

Cun knew that death was about to claim him. His legs were already cold, and a deep chill was rising through his body. When it reached the top of his head, he knew it would be the end, his final parting with life.

Cun opened his mouth. His thirst was so great he could feel his throat shrivel. He had an enveloping bodily sense that his life was being cornered and crushed. He knew he could not escape this time. Death was upon him. It stuck out an invisible tongue and, black as night, slowly licked Cun's eyes closed.

More than ten years before, Cun was found in a drainpipe that had been sunk near a stream on the outskirts of the city. The stream was a pitch-black run-off of waste water. It was full of rubbish and supported patches of dust-covered water hyacinths. The broken cement drainpipe was laid across a small dirt road, so that the wind blew into it from both the stream on one side and the fields on the other. Cun lay in a pile of stinking rags and was purple with the cold. And if you are wondering why he did not die there and then, it was certainly because of old Ha.

Old Ha was a beggar at the market. It is not clear why he was groping around the drain on that day, but as he stood on the road he heard the sound of crying. It seemed to come from under the ground, as though it was welling up from hell. The old man shuddered. The afternoon was fading into evening as the last rays of the setting sun illuminated the creamy clouds on the horizon and swept forbidding streaks of wintry light across the face of the earth. The northern wind was howling around the low stalls in the deserted market-place. This was the right time of day for demons, and it was the kind of landscape in which ghosts could easily appear. Old Ha had lived almost all his life without fearing people, who only inspired love or hate in him. What he feared was inhuman.

The old man was limp with fear. The wailing was certainly real. He pricked up his ears and listened. It was the sound of a young child crying. Without knowing what he was doing, he ran stumbling down to the edge of the river. Still gripped by the sound of the crying, he looked towards the road, and there he saw a child lying in the drainpipe.

Old Ha came gradually to his senses when he realized it was not a ghost at all. With his soul back in his possession, he realized how fortunate he was that the demons had lost an opportunity to snatch it. He crawled back up to the drainpipe, stuck his hand inside it, and pulled out a small child. Its arms and legs were freezing cold.

The old man picked up the child in his arms and carried it back to his shelter in the market-place. He called the child Cun, which was a name people often gave to puppy dogs. This was because the child had really not developed into a human being. It was strangely deformed with an enormous hydrocephalic head and soft, seemingly boneless limbs. This meant that it couldn't stand upright, but fell over and lay flat on the ground. However, the extraordinary thing was that Cun had an unusually beautiful face.

Cun lived with the old man and did not perish because he possessed two odd powers. One of these was in his eyes, for they aroused fear in everyone around him. If people passed Cun without throwing a coin into the torn hat on the ground beside him, they did not feel at ease. The second of Cun's powers was his ability to bear extreme suffering: he could bear hunger and cold with such indifference that it seemed his body was made of some indestructible material.

Old Ha took a liking to the deformed child. With Cun he could more easily make money from begging, and he carried the child everywhere. At the Phu Giay Festival alone, he made as much as he had made in several years of begging by himself. His way of working was very simple. He would leave Cun lying on his back with his battered hat beside him in the middle of a crowd of people. That was all there was to it. Cun would squirm around, and his eyes would do the work: "Hey, Sir! Madam! You are human beings; think of someone like me who is not-yet-a-human." Old Ha, who would be hiding somewhere near by, would appear when the hat was full of money, gather it up, and leave. Sometimes, the old man slipped Cun a few crumbs of corn cake, the way people feed chickens they are taking to market.

Old Ha regarded Cun as a son. Naturally, he didn't pay much attention to the boy: he was busy. Just as people with other professions are always occupied, beggars have plenty to do too. In old Ha's world, the fate of a cripple didn't count for much. He never felt uneasy about leaving Cun weak with hunger or shaking with a fever when he went off drinking or gambling. The old man himself had been as hungry, as ill, and as cold as that many times. In the world of beggars, people use a child for two or three months to attract sympathy. Then, when the child dies, they throw it on to the rubbish heap, as though they are discarding a broken basket. There is no difficulty in finding another one. When you are cold and hungry, you don't care about anything, least of all ethics and human feelings.

As Cun grew up, he gradually became conscious of his fate, and this forced him into an awareness of the circumstances in which he lived. At the time of this growing awareness, there was war and many people died of starvation. The weather was very cold. Cun and old Ha lay rolled up in two gunny sacks on the veranda of a house, about a hundred metres from New Market on the outskirts of the city. Old Ha coughed repeatedly. He was very weak and had not been able to get up for a number of days. Occasionally, he coughed up blood.

"Cun, you've grown up. I'm about to die. You are about to lose me, your main support in life," old Ha whispered weakly. "Actually, I'm not your main support. You and I live together . . . like earthworms, crickets, bees, ants." The old man had a fit of coughing, then cried: "Human beings don't live like us. Good heavens, why do they persecute us like this? We only want to live like everyone else, but are not able to."

Cun listened attentively, then turned away and left old Ha to sob and wail to himself. He did not say anything. He was already familiar with the situation. He lifted his hand across the torn gunny sack to cover his belly. Cun sighed. He was exhausted. For more than ten years he had been a beggar, and there was nothing he did not know about the life of the downtrodden people. ". . . Who are beggars, we are beggars . . . with torn clothes and no rice we become beggars. . . ." He knew how the meaningless lives of people were filled with misfortune. They lived like him, like old Ha, like earthworms, crickets, bees, ants. Cun only suffered more because he was deformed. Cun was not a full human being; he found it too difficult to do what everyone else could do. As he got older, Cun saw increasingly that there was nothing easy about standing firmly on the face of the earth. He continued to tremble, continued to take three steps, overbalance, and fall on the ground. His arms and legs would not do what he wanted them to do.

Around the time of his awareness, Cun had also become anxious for no apparent reason. He didn't understand why he thought or dreamt so much of Dieu, the mistress of the house on whose veranda he and old Ha lay. Miss Dieu, who sold goods at the market, always gave off the strong scent of cheap perfume mixed, as country girls often mix it, with a touch of naphthalene. She had a pair of small eyes and a very delicate nose with quivering nostrils. She was full of mischievous jokes and laughter. She called Cun the "Blob-with-the-Beautiful-Face".

"Hey, Blob-with-the-Beautiful-Face! I'll give you a cent. Come to the door tomorrow morning. You are like the star of change bringing good fortune to this house. When people go to the market and see you, they rush in to do their shopping, as though they are ransacking the place."

Cun laughed timidly. He bent down to pick up the cent, but fell over on the ground. The coin was three bricks away from his hand. He stood up, held one knee to maintain his centre of gravity, and reached out with his free hand. Again, however, he fell obliquely to the right. The coin was now a further brick away from Cun. Miss Dieu laughed like a butterfly on the veranda of the house: "Hey, Blob-with-the-Beautiful-Face! You missed by a long way. Try and get up! Try once more and see how you fare!"

Cun was so pleased he laughed. Good heavens, he'd made her happy. Cun stood up. He tried to hold both knees. That seemed to work. That's it, that's it. . . . All he had to do was to try a little harder and lean over to the left so that he could reach the coin. He gasped and broke out into a sweat. Cun estimated the distance and smiled. Then, at the same moment as he leant out to pick up the coin, Dieu jumped down and moved the coin one brick to the side. She shrieked with laughter. Cun lost his poise and fell down. He smashed his head on the bricks and, although he was bleeding from the mouth, he ignored his injury. The woman's attractive nose made him suck in his breath as quickly as he could. She had never been as close to Cun as that.

Cun laughed heartily. If he had known how, he would have sung.

Old Ha sat quietly at the corner of the broken wall feeling pity as he looked at Cun. The old man stood up sluggishly, went over to the coin, picked it up, and put it into his pocket. Dieu stopped laughing. "You miserable old man," she snapped as her lips tightened impertinently. "The coin wasn't for you at all! I'm sure you'll spend it on drink."

Old Ha stood crestfallen like someone who had done something wrong and expected a thrashing. Dieu disappeared into the house, while old Ha squatted down and wiped the blood off Cun's mouth. He picked Cun up by the armpit and guided him towards the market.

Miss Dieu had gradually worked her way into Cun's life. He thought about her endlessly. He visualized her every move, heard her voice, imagined her laughter. He paid no attention to old Ha's tear-choked utterances as he lay beside him. Some time later, old Ha vomited and, as he did so, he pinched Cun's face so hard with his gnarled fingers that the burning pain suddenly brought Cun back to his senses. Cun opened his eyes. He was startled to see that old Ha's face had completely changed. It was waxen and distorted, so that the vertical flute above the upper-lip was tilted to one side. From out of the old man's mouth there lapped a flow of black blood. He tried incoherently to say something. He tried to press a small purse into Cun's hand. Cun crawled to his feet. He understood what had happened: death was appearing before him. It was there. It lurked very deep in the pupils of the old man's eyes and killed the colour in them. Cun sobbed. Although he was only very dimly aware of it, he had lost his mainstay, the mainstay of his earthly existence.

After old Ha's death, Cun's fate did not change radically. He was still hungry and cold. But, in the terrible winter of that year, Dieu married an unfeeling young man who carried merchandise. Cun followed every detail of her life, and his observations made him feel that she was not very happy.

Cun was not deceived. Three months after the wedding, the husband made off with his new wife's property and fled to the south with a lover. Dieu had lost everything. She fell ill and was so unhappy there were times when she contemplated suicide.

Nevertheless, her spirits eventually started to lift. The day that her illness seemed to pass and she began to recover her appetite was a gentle summer day. She sat in her room, looking out into the street. The sunlight shimmered on the canopies of the shady fig trees, the mango trees, and the ornamental shrubs. Nobody else was at home, and all that could be heard was the disconcerting sound of wood-borers grinding away in the corner of an empty closet.

Miss Dieu thought of the market and her small-goods shop. She wondered when she would be able to have another shop like that. She looked sadly out into the street. Then, suddenly, she saw Cun sitting up on the veranda, outside the door of her house. He was feeling for something with his hand in a purse. Miss Dieu kneeled down and looked out of the window as Cun opened a cloth envelope that old Ha had given him. The envelope was made of dark brown cloth with black stitching and was as small as a chicken's gizzard. Miss Dieu gave a sudden start when she saw some gold rings glittering in the palm of Cun's hand. She felt a chill run down her spine. Her arms and legs shuddered violently, and a thought flashed through her mind.

"Hey, Blob-with-the-Beautiful-Face!" She hurriedly pushed the door ajar and squatted down beside Cun. "What have you got in your hand there?"

Cun raised his head, stretched out his hand, and said in a tone of spontaneous pride: "Rings. These are the gold rings old Ha gave me."

"Real gold or fool's gold?" Miss Dieu inquired as she grabbed Cun's hand. "Let me have a look," she said, now holding three rather heavy rings in her hand. "Let me have a look."

Miss Dieu took each ring and let it fall gently on to a slab of stone. She listened carefully. She held the rings up so that they flashed in the sunlight. She put them into her mouth and bit them. "Good heavens, it's real gold," she gasped. "There's a whole family inheritance here. This Blob-with-the-Beautiful-Face is truly rich." She blanched, laughed, cried, and thumped Cun's body repeatedly with her small fist. "'Real gold is not brass. Don't test it in the flame that burns a golden heart.' You little puppy! How is it that I haven't known you till now?"

Cun, whose face had broken into a euphoric smile, swooned with bliss. "Come in here, come in here, you rich little puppy," Miss Dieu panted, as she closed the door and pressed Cun's body down into a chair. She put on the rings, then clasped her hands behind her. She stood right up close in front of Cun's face, and arched her body like a bow in front of him.

"Now? I'll bargain, OK!" Miss Dieu laughed. She spoke with her thoughts sparking like lightning flashes in her brain. "You must first give me these three rings. It doesn't matter if you don't have them. You are still a beggar. How about it? Do you agree? I'll give you whatever you want."

Cun nodded with the corners of his eyes full of tears. He felt only pleasure, for he had made her happy. She had recovered. She was strong. Cun was enraptured.

"How about it?" she cajoled, as she bent down and rubbed her forehead against Cun's. "What are you looking like that for?" She pealed with laughter. "Tell me, tell me. What do you want now?" Cun raised his hand, but only made a vague gesture in space, because he was unable to activate the sinews in his arm. People who light incense sticks in front of an altar also make gestures like that.

"All right, I understand now," Miss Dieu said. She sat down beside Cun and fondled him. "You are also a bastard! You men are all the same. . . . But it's OK. . . . It's all right. That's the price we women must pay. It's OK. I'm only afraid that you can't perform, that an ill-bred husband of mine still can't make me pregnant."

Miss Dieu pulled Cun out of the chair and slammed him on to the bed. Cun was terrified. He screwed his eyes closed and pushed his face down on to Dieu's quivering, vaguely blue, translucent nose. He was like someone flying in the clouds. He suddenly felt all the bitterness of his life flow away in a flood of unknown relief.

In the end, Cun had forgotten about all the time he had spent sitting in the street. "That means we're square!" He could hear the sound of Miss Dieu's voice somewhere; he understood that he had just experienced something really wonderful; he felt empty, but had a sense of surpassing exaltation that dizzied and dazzled him.

Cun did not comprehend that this was the only opportunity he would have in his miserable life to experience this feeling. But this opportunity, in all its strangeness, would give Cun a son in nine months' time.

Nine months later, Miss Dieu gave birth to a son. Some months before, she had said to Cun: "Hey, Blob-with-the-Beautiful-Face, you are about to have a child! I couldn't have believed that anything as strange as this would have happened either."

Cun was so happy he was beside himself. He didn't eat or drink, and all that was left of him was skin and bones. He could not believe he was going to have a child. Someone who was not-yet-a-human-being could still have a child. Cun visualized it very clearly: it would move strongly across the face of the earth, it would never lose its balance, it would smile as it went through life, it would wear a halo shining with many colours.

Cun lived in an agitated state during the last months of Miss Dieu's pregnancy. He became seriously ill; his greatest fear was that death would strike him before he knew what the child was like. He prayed daily for death's forbearance, and his prayers were answered. Death would wait until the minute his son was born, so that he could take his place on earth.

On exactly the day that Miss Dieu gave birth, Cun crawled from his stall in the market to the window of her house. It was drizzling, and the penetrating cold numbed Cun's body. His head was burning – from time to time, he passed out. Only a little over 100 metres was a great distance for Cun. Every metre he dragged himself along the road he struggled with death. It was there, as black as the night falling around him. Cun continued to edge himself along, metre by metre, as it pulled him back down into the mud.

While he dragged himself along with blood oozing out of his ear, he groaned. He reached the veranda outside the lamplight in the window and fainted. When he regained consciousness, Cun felt as though some immense object was pressing on his body.

Cun opened his mouth. Thirst. His throat felt dry. In all his weary life as a beggar, he had never been as thirsty as this. He tried to hold his breath to regain his strength. Alternatively, he passed out and regained consciousness, while he waited for a sign that his child was born. Then, in the middle of the night, Cun was suddenly startled by the sound of a trembling cry inside the house. It was the wailing of a newborn baby boy. Cun knew that his child was born.

Cun smiled blissfully and sank into unconsciousness. A very light wisp of wind glided over Cun's still face.

Cun was dead. It had really been short, this life of someone who was not-yet-a-human-being. It was the winter of the great famine of 1944.

3. Conclusion

After I'd finished writing Cun's story, I took it and read it to the literary critic K. He turned pale as the story unfolded.

"That's not correct!" he said, pulling the manuscript out of my hand. "You've fabricated the story! You need to get it straight. The reality was very different. How could you know what my father was like?"

K searched somewhere in the bookcase and found a pile of photographs. He flicked through the portraits for a moment, then pulled out a colour photo. He gave a gentle laugh that built up and faded away, while his soft hand touched the pressure point behind my elbow: "My father was Cun, but he wasn't like that! Do you see? This is my father's photo here!"

The photo was of a big fat man wearing a black silk shirt with a starched collar. He also wore a neatly trimmed moustache and was smiling at me.

UNSEEN TRANSLATION

Kate Atkinson

Kate Atkinson (b.1951) was born in York, studied in Dundee and currently lives in Edinburgh. Her first novel, *Behind the Scenes at the Museum,* won the 1995 Whitbread Book of the Year and began her career as one of the most popular and critically praised authors of her generation. Her other work includes *Case Histories, One Good Turn, When Will There Be Good News?, Started Early, Took My Dog* – a series of novels featuring Jackson Brodie, some of which have been adapted for television – as well as the 2002 collection *Not the End of the World* and, most recently *Life After Life*. She was appointed an MBE in 2011. "If you don't have a unique voice, then you're not a writer," she once observed, saying about creative writing courses: "I think you have to learn for yourself how to write."

UNSEEN TRANSLATION

Αρτεμιν αειδω χρυσηλαϖκατον, κελαδεινην,
παρθενον αιφδοιϖην, εϕλαϕηβοϖλον, ιοχεαιραν . . .

I sing of Artemis, whose shafts are of gold,
who cheers on the hounds, the pure maiden
shooter of stags, who delights in archery.

HOMERIC HYMN TO ARTEMIS

They had managed an entire afternoon in the Bird Gallery. From egg to skeleton, from common to extinct, from flightless to free, Missy and Arthur were on familiar terms with the avian world.

"Can we come back and do mammals tomorrow?" Arthur asked.

"If you like. There are a lot of them though, remember. You might want to subdivide them into categories."

"There were a lot of birds. We didn't subdivide them."

"True."

Missy believed that knowledge was best taken in small, digestible portions. Museums and galleries, in her opinion, were full of people wandering listlessly from exhibit to exhibit, their eyes glazed over with too much information and not enough knowledge.

"It's an established neurological fact," Missy told Arthur (Missy believed in using long words with children wherever possible), "that window shopping and museums are the two most tiring activities for the brain. A chronic insomniac could probably come into the Natural History Museum and fall asleep before he'd got past the diplodocus in the Central Hall." Arthur yawned.

"I've noticed you're very suggestible, Arthur."

"Is that bad?"

"No, it's a good thing, it makes my job much easier. Just make sure it's me that you take suggestions from, not someone else." The words "like your mother" remained unspoken, but understood, between them.

The Natural History Museum was closing, already echoing with emptiness and a promise of the secret life it led when no one was there. Missy imagined the birds shaking out their feathers and shuffling from one stiff leg to the other, cracking neck bones and easing off flight muscles. Diplodocus himself gave a little tidal tremor along the vertebrae of his huge backbone as if warming up for a leisurely evening stroll. They took no notice of him. Missy never bothered her charges too much with dinosaurs. She thought children (not to mention parents) were far too obsessed with them already.

Outside, the threat of summer rain had darkened the South Kensington sky to an otherworldly purple.

"Are we going home?" Arthur asked, rather indifferently.

"No, we're going to Patisserie Valerie for hot chocolate and cake. Unless you don't like that idea."

"Ha, ha."

Missy and Arthur had spent Arthur's school holidays picking and choosing from the capital's smorgasbord of culture. This week, for example, had begun with a short visit to the British Museum (where they spent most of their time admiring Jennings Dog), followed on Tuesday by a Mozart String Quartet at the Wigmore Hall, Wednesday was Shakespeare in the Park (*As You Like It* – "Very good" in Arthur's opinion) and yesterday it had been the eighteenth-century rooms of the National Gallery. Missy was pleased to find that Arthur was able to spend almost twenty minutes in near-silent contemplation of *Whistlejacket*. It was at that moment, as they sat companionably together considering Stubbs's huge ideal of a horse ("Essence of horse," Missy whispered in Arthur's ear), that Missy knew for certain that Arthur was a superior version of an eight-year-old boy.

Unfortunately, children were usually spoilt for life by the time Missy got her hands on them. At two years old they had acquired all the faults that would mar them for ever and Missy had to spend most of her time rectifying their old bad habits rather than instilling new good ones. Of course, that was why Missy was called in. She had a reputation, like a Jesuitical troubleshooter, a Marine Corps Mary Poppins – when all else failed, call in Missy Clark. They expected her to drop in from the skies on the end of an umbrella, like a parachutist floating into a country in the middle of a civil war, and rescue their children from bad behaviour.

Missy was tiring of this phase of her life. She was even thinking of returning to nursing, although not to the hellish half-world of the NHS. She was considering applying to a private clinic somewhere, plastic surgery perhaps – somewhere where people weren't actually ill. If she was to remain in this job beyond the age of forty (she was thirty-eight – a difficult age) then she needed a completely blank canvas on which to practise her art. A tabula rasa, untouched by another's hand. A new baby. That was what Romney Wright had offered. A baby so untouched that it wasn't even born yet.

Missy was never interviewed by an employer, she interviewed them. Not that she was looking for the perfect family – years of experience had taught her there was no such thing. All she wanted was a family capable of reformation, and failing that, then just one child in the family who could be rescued from the fate which awaited it (ordinariness). Missy made it a rule never to stay anywhere longer than two years.

"Think of me as the SAS," she said brightly, when the hugely pregnant Romney had engaged her two weeks before the birth of her second child. Romney – sometime wife of a rock star, glamour model and ironic game-show guest, "now concentrating on her acting career", but mostly famous for being famous – forgot to mention the first child until Missy was dictating her non-negotiable terms and conditions (own bedroom, kitchen, bathroom and sitting room; own car; one and a half days off a week; no nights; full-time maternity nurses for the first three months; pension allowance). In fact, it was only by chance that Arthur wandered into the room at that moment and asked Romney if anyone was going to make his tea or should he heat up some baked beans? Missy was pleased at this – she liked to see a self-sufficient child and had nothing against baked beans.

"Oh, and, of course, this is Arthur," Romney said carelessly in a grating kind of East London accent that was already beginning to annoy Missy. Hadn't elocution lessons been on the curriculum at Romney's stage school?

Missy did actually know about Arthur's existence as she had checked out Romney's (entirely tabloid) cuttings file ("My love for my little boy", "My single-parent hell", and so on) before arriving at Romney's Primrose Hill house.

"This is the new nanny, Arthur," Romney said.

"Oh," Arthur said, raising surprised eyebrows. Missy liked a child who didn't speak when he had nothing to say.

"Missy," Missy said to Arthur.

"Missy?" Romney repeated thoughtfully. "What kind of a name is that?"

"A nickname my father gave me. It stuck."

"Right. Well, Arthur's called Arthur because his dad was into like Camelot and all that stuff."

"I think it's a very good name," Missy said, smiling encouragingly at Arthur.

"It's a bit old-fashioned though, isn't it?" Romney frowned. "I mean "Arthur Wright" sounds like your grandad or something. But that was his dad all over, thought it was funny. His dad's Campbell Wright? Lead singer with Boak? Useless piece of Scottish string. Completely debauched, the lot of them." Romney pronounced "debauched" with relish as if it was only recently learned. Arthur, a solemn, bespectacled boy, said nothing. Missy had already looked up Boak on the internet. Romney was surprisingly accurate in her choice of vocabulary. Boak were debauched. In photographs they all wore Second World War gas masks, so it was impossible to see if Arthur looked like his father. He certainly didn't resemble his mother, at least not in any major particular, perhaps in the whorl of an ear, the oval of a nostril, nothing too relevant.

"What would you have called him?" Missy asked, intrigued by the idea that you could be the mother of a child and not name it.

"Zeus," Romney said, without hesitation.

"Zeus?"

"King of the gods," Romney explained helpfully. Arthur looked at Missy with absolutely no expression on his face. Missy liked a child who kept his own counsel.

"He wears glasses, of course." Romney sighed. "Arthur, not Zeus, obviously. When I was a kid," she carried on, when neither Arthur nor Missy had anything to add to this observation, "if you wore glasses you were like "speccy four-eyes" or "double-glazing" but now it's cool, like because of Harry Potter. And that kid in that Tom Cruise film. Or no, maybe not him, I don't think that kid was cool, was he? Of course, Campbell was very romantic then, now he's a wanker, but you should have seen our wedding – he planned it all himself – in a ruined castle, I rode over the drawbridge on a white horse and when we were pronounced man and wife – although it wasn't really a vicar, it was more of a shaman kind of bloke – they released butterflies, hundreds of butterflies, over our heads. It was really something, I never thought—"

Missy stood up abruptly; she could see that Romney was a talker. "I have to go now," she said. "When would you like me to start?"

"Tomorrow," Arthur said promptly. Missy was pleased to hear that he spoke a more civilized form of the English language than his mother.

"He's a funny one, isn't he?" Romney said, for no particular reason.

Missy allowed Arthur two cakes with his hot chocolate. She understood that sometimes one simply wasn't enough.

"What do you think she'll call the baby?" Arthur asked.

"Who are we talking about – the cat's mother? Wipe your fingers."

"You know who I mean. I bet it's something stupid."

Romney had been delivered of a baby girl the previous day and Missy and Arthur had visited her that morning in the hospital, in the private maternity wing that was like a five-star hotel. Romney had opted to be knocked unconscious and split open rather than give birth naturally. Missy favoured natural childbirth wherever possible. She thought it was character-forming for a child to have to fight its way into existence. Missy herself was a twin and had made sure she'd elbowed her way out first, ahead of her brother.

The father of Romney's baby was a multi-millionaire, Swiss-born financier who had led an impeccably boring life until a lifelong interest in West End musicals had led him to bankroll a doomed stage version of Charlotte Brontë's *Villette* in which Romney had a small and surprisingly naked part. In a moment of champagne-and-cocaine-fuelled incontinence at the opening night party, the Swiss financier had found himself in a backstage dressing-room toilet having frantic sex with Romney – a fact which he subsequently vehemently denied when it became tabloid knowledge. (" 'I am a love god!' Otto shouted in our steamy sex session.") Romney was now looking forward to the DNA tests to see just how wealthy Otto's seed would prove.

"I'm glad it's a girl," Arthur said, finishing off his second cake (both his chosen cakes had been chocolate). "I like girls. Do you know I used to have a male nanny once?"

"And? Was he all right?"

"So-so. He was Australian."

"How many nannies have you had, Arthur?"

"Five. I think."

"Why do they leave? Not because of you, you're not a difficult child."

"Thank you."

"What about the last one, my predecessor?"

Arthur shrugged.

"What does that mean? The shrugging?"

Arthur stood up and piled their dirty plates neatly. "We should go. The tube's going to be packed."

The rain held off as they walked to the underground. Missy thought it was important for a child to use public transport, to suffer dreary queues and biting winds. Even when working for the richest families she had made a point of hauling their children around the streets of London on buses and tubes and trains. She believed stoicism was a virtue that was badly in need of reviving.

They went into a newsagent's so that Missy could replenish essentials – she was never without Elastoplasts, safety pins, first-class stamps, tissues, extra-strong mints, Nurofen, cough sweets, Calpol, bottled water. The search for tissues led them past the newspaper and magazine racks which took up one wall. All of the top shelf was occupied by glossy girls presenting their buttocks or breasts to the camera.

"Difficult though it may be for you to believe, one day, sadly, you will probably find these images attractive," Missy told Arthur. "But for now you can buy a *Beano*."

Arthur wasn't listening. "Look," he said, pointing to the rack of tabloids beneath the naked women. Nearly every newspaper had a photograph of Romney Wright on the front, posing in her hospital bed – "Romney's bundle of joy", "Love-rat leaves Romney holding the baby", "Romney keeping mum about dad" (which was hardly true). Romney had managed to adopt a pose similar to the models in the pornographic magazines – her huge, milk-swollen breasts offered to the camera like gifts. The baby itself seemed incidental, almost invisible inside its shawl cocoon. Arthur skim-read the text. "They don't mention me," he said.

"That's a good thing."

"I know." Arthur gazed at the photographs of his mother as if she was an interesting stranger. "Do you think we'll like the baby?"

"What's not to like?"

Arthur gazed at his overexposed mother. Missy liked a wise child better than anyone but she considered the expression on Arthur's face to be knowledgeable well beyond his years.

"I realize you've already had far too much chocolate today and are probably as high as a kite, which is a technical term used by nannies, but, and against my better judgement, and you will rarely hear those words from my lips, Arthur, you can have a packet of chocolate buttons. Now come on, don't dawdle."

The baby was finally named. Romney toyed with a galaxy of goddesses ("Athene? Aphrodite? Artemis?") and gave up before reaching the end of the alphas.

"What did they do?" Arthur asked as they meandered ("from the river god Maeander, by the way") through the textile rooms of the V and A.

"Well," Missy said, "Athene was smug and thought she knew everything, Aphrodite was a troublemaker, and very irritating, I might add, and only Artemis had any sense."

"What did she do?"

"Virgin, close relationship with the moon, childbirth, wolves. Oh, and the chase."

"The chase?"

"Shot stags with silver arrows, that kind of thing."

Arthur looked horrified. "Shot stags?" he echoed ("from Echo – an unfortunate nymph. Show me one that isn't").

"It's a mythic thing, no stags were actually harmed during the . . . that kind of thing."

Romney had offered the choice of name to Arthur but reneged when he opted for "Jane", a name far too plain for Romney's tastes. In the end, she went for world geography. Romney's sister Johdi had a child called Africa and her friend Lily had a baby called India so Romney decided on China for Arthur's sister. "Like collecting countries," she said to Missy. "They'll be like NATO or something when they grow up."

"It could have been much worse," Missy said to Arthur. "Belgium, Luxemburg, New Zealand, Gibraltar, Uzbekistan. The list of worse is endless. That's not grammatical, by the way."

China, although in no way Chinese, was as delicate as porcelain with creamy skin and a rosy blush on her cheeks. She was more robust than her name implied but nevertheless received round-the-clock attention from a series of maternity nurses who themselves received round-the-clock attention from the nanny-cam in the nursery. Romney had a monitor in her bedroom so that she could watch the nurse watching her baby. Otto's DNA had finally been forced to own up as the culprit ("Kraut comes clean – 'China's mine' ") much to Romney's relief, although, "He wasn't a kraut," she said indignantly.

Autumn came. The Primrose Hill household was running smoothly – Romney was sated with money and sex, the sex in the stocky form of a soap star, Arthur was as happy as an eight-year-old boy can be at school ("OK, I suppose") and China was a dream of a child. Even the tabloid photographers had stopped camping on the doorstep and Missy was looking forward to the school break and some leaf-kicking time in London's parks with Arthur and the baby, when Romney suddenly announced that Arthur was going to visit his father for half-term.

"They have joint custody," Arthur explained over a boiled-egg tea down in the huge basement kitchen.

"And when did you last see him?"

Arthur thought for a long time. "Two years ago, I think. You have to come with me," he added matter-of-factly.

"Why?"

"Because he's on tour."

"On tour?"

"Oh yeah, didn't I say?" Romney said when Missy questioned her. "Boak are in the middle of like this huge world tour, actually I think they're always on it. Arthur's going to visit him when they're in Germany. Flying into Munich, flying out of Hamburg at the end of the week. All the arrangements have been made by his publicist, you're going too. And I tell you what, I'm going to give you your own credit card. How's that? One more thing for the kraut to pay for."

"He's Swiss," Missy reminded her.

"Same difference," Romney said.

"What about my hamster?" Arthur asked Missy.

"We'll ask Africa to look after him."

"What about the baby?"

"It's only a week," Missy said, "and babies are almost indestructible, you know." Romney, however, decided not to look after China herself but to go on a "detox meditation" in the Cotswolds with her friend Lily while China went to stay with her maternal grandmother, who had, in Romney's words, "been dying to get a shot at her".

"So China will be fine," Missy reassured Arthur. "After all, your grandmother managed to bring your mother up." Arthur gave Missy the most beautifully blank look.

"You can be very enigmatic sometimes, Arthur," Missy said ("from the Greek *ainigma*, derived from *ainos* – fable").

If they were on their way to partake of Boak's debauchery, there was no indication of it in Lufthansa business class, which was so clean and grey and lacking in decadence that Arthur, a nonchalant traveller, managed to study the Collins German phrase book that Missy had bought him in an Oxfam shop prior to the trip ("Why buy new?" she said to Arthur, "when you can buy cheap?") while Missy herself read a book about astronomy that she had taken out from the library. Missy thought it was important to use libraries. ("Why buy at all when you can borrow?") She wasn't particularly interested in astronomy but she believed an important part of her job was to impart as much general knowledge as possible to her charges, because if not her, then who?

"Did you know," Missy asked Arthur, "that they can weigh galaxies?"

"Sie führen mich an," Arthur said, consulting his phrase book.

"I'm sorry?"

"You're pulling my leg," he laughed, pleased that he knew something that Missy didn't.

Missy and Arthur were in possession of an extra-ordinarily detailed itinerary for the German leg of Boak's tour, prepared by the band's publicist, a girl called Lulu, who, as well as providing flight times, driver details and hotel reservations, had also given two different mobile numbers on which she could be contacted. The itinerary also informed them that they were going to travel around Germany on Boak's tour bus.

"What will that be like?" Missy asked Arthur, as the plane bumped lightly onto the runway at Munich airport. Arthur frowned, carefully searching for the right word.

"Extreme," he said finally.

There was no car to collect them at the airport, as promised by Lulu, but Missy had changed sterling into Deutschmarks at Heathrow and they caught a taxi to the hotel with the careless abandon of people on someone else's expenses.

The Bayerischer Hof had no record of any reservation. "Two rooms? In the name of Wright?" Missy persisted, showing the receptionist Lulu's careful itinerary. The receptionist regarded it politely as if it was a document from another civilization, far away in time and space, and beyond translation.

"Are Boak actually staying here?" Missy asked, wishing they weren't called such a stupid name. At first, the receptionist thought she was trying to say "book" and then "Björk". The smile on the receptionist's face grew stiff and tired. She called the manager.

"What does boak mean, anyway?" Missy asked Arthur as they waited.

"It's Scottish for sick."

"Ill sick or vomit sick?"

"Vomit sick."

The manager appeared, smiling sadly, and said that he very much regretted but the hotel never revealed details about its guests. It was growing late by now and Missy felt an uncharacteristic reluctance for battle. Arthur was sitting on their luggage, looking like a weary refugee, and Missy decided they would take a room anyway. She offered the brand-new gold credit card Romney had given her before they left. A few minutes later the hotel manager returned it to her and said in a low murmur that he was very sorry but the card was "not acceptable". He smiled even more sadly. Missy paid for the room on her own card.

"How much money do you have?" Arthur asked.

"Quite a lot actually," Missy said truthfully. "I've been saving for years."

"But you're not supposed to be paying."

"True. But it's only for one night. I expect your father'll turn up tomorrow."

"Das ist Pech," Arthur consoled.

The room was nice, although not the "luxury suite" promised by Lulu. The floors were clean and the sheets snappy with starch. Missy ordered cheese omelettes and apfelstrudel on room service. After they had eaten she phoned both the mobile numbers that Lulu had provided. One was completely dead, the other announced something impenetrable in a German that was well beyond the capacity of the phrase book. Missy phoned Romney's Primrose Hill number but there was no answer. On Romney's mobile a voice announced that it might not be switched on.

They filled in their breakfast cards – Arthur found this very exciting – and then watched an incomprehensible game show on television that even if they had been fluent in German they probably wouldn't have understood. They went to their beds at nine o'clock German time, eight o'clock Primrose Hill time, and they both slept as soundly as babies until the maid hammered on the door with their breakfast, long after the dawn had scattered her yellow robes across the skies.

After breakfast, which Arthur liked almost as much as the ordering of it, Missy tried all the phone numbers she had tried the previous evening, with the same result. "Es sind schlechte Zeiten," Arthur said, leafing industriously through his phrase book. "Wie schade."

Missy went down to reception and looked the sadly smiling manager in the eye in the same way that she looked at little boys when she particularly wanted them to tell her the truth.

"If you were me", she said to him, "and think about this carefully, would you stay another night in this unbelievably expensive hotel and wait for the band known, unfortunately, as Boak to turn up?"

"No," he said, "I wouldn't."

"Thank you."

"Look at it this way", Missy said to Arthur. "Our flight from Hamburg isn't for another week, we have enough money – even if it's mine – and we are in one of the great cultural cities of Western Europe in the half-term holidays, so we may as well enjoy ourselves."

They moved into a guest house on Karlstrasse, although they returned several times to the Bayerischer Hof to check that Boak hadn't suddenly materialized. "Hat jemand nach uns gefragt?" Arthur asked the sad manager. No, he replied, in English, they hadn't.

They trekked to the Olympiahalle and discovered a tour poster slashed with a banner in large red capitals, declaring that Boak's concert was "Entfällt".

"I think that means cancelled", Arthur said without bothering to consult the German dictionary they'd bought ("Sometimes you have no choice but to buy"). After that, they didn't bother returning to the Bayerischer Hof. Lulu and Romney remained unreachable by all means.

"Perhaps we're dead," Arthur suggested, "and we just don't know it."

"I think that's a rather fanciful explanation," Missy said.

In accord with Missy's beliefs, they visited museums and galleries in moderation – the Forum der Technik (but only the Planetarium), the Deutsches Museum (but only the coal mine), the Alte Pinakothek (but only pre-sixteenth-century paintings). Arthur stayed awake for the whole of the BMW museum – he wasn't an eight-year-old boy for nothing – but was asleep on his feet within minutes of going into the Residenz-Museum. The Frauenkirche and the Peterskirche had much the same effect on both of them. An expedition to the Schloss Nymphenburg might have been more of a success if it hadn't rained so much. Their favourite museum exhibit was a chance discovery, a stuffed creature, in the oddly named Jagd- und Fischereimuseum ("Hunting and fishing," Arthur supplied helpfully). The "Wolpertinger" was a curious Mitteleuropean chimera, a mix of rabbit, stag and duck, plus something less definable and more frightening. ("Distantly related to the rare wolfkin," Missy said.)

"Bavarian primeval creature", Arthur read from the guidebook the sad hotel manager had given them on their last visit to the Bayerischer Hof.

In truth, neither of them was much in the mood for history and culture and they spent a lot of time wandering in the Englischer Garten or drinking hot chocolate. Every day at midday they went and stood ritualistically in front of the glockenspiel on the Neues Rathaus and watched for all the brightly coloured figures to make their rounds.

"What did happen to your last nanny?" Missy asked as they waited for the glockenspiel to start. Arthur made a pinched sort of face.

"What," Missy encouraged, "she was murdered? She killed herself, she came back as a ghost and wandered round a lake? Fell in love with the master who had a mad wife in the attic and who became hideously disfigured in a fire?"

"You're not supposed to talk like that to eight-year-olds."

"Sorry."

"She left."

"Left?"

"Left. She said she wouldn't leave and she did. And I liked her." Arthur stuck his hands in his pockets and angrily kicked an imaginary stone on the ground. "I liked her and she promised she wouldn't leave and she did. And you'll leave." His face began to quiver and he kicked the ground harder. His shoe was getting scuffed. Missy tried to touch the small shoulders, heaving with suppressed tears, but Arthur grew suddenly hysterical and shook her off.

"You'll leave just like she did," he screamed. "You'll leave me and I hate you! I hate you, I hate you, I hate you!"

"Arthur—"

"Shut up, shut up, shut up!" he yelled, so wound up now that he could hardly breathe, and several passers-by regarded with curiosity the small English boy struggling furiously to escape his mother's grip.

"It feels as though we've been away years," Arthur said when the cab dropped them off at Munich airport.

"I know."

"Do you think anyone's missed us?"

"Can you see the Lufthansa sales desk?"

"Over there."

Arthur, Missy was relieved to see, was quite calm today, although his eyes were still red from crying – he had sobbed for hours, long after Missy had got him back to the Karlstrasse guest house, long after she had put him to bed with milk and honey cake offered by the sympathetic proprietress. "Die Kinder", she sighed, as if to be a child was the worst thing in the world. Arthur had finally fallen asleep, flushed and tear-stained, clutching onto Missy's hand. "I don't hate you, you know," he said, with a grief-stricken hiccup. "I love you really."

"I love you too," she said, kissing the top of his head, "and I promise I won't leave you and I never break promises. Ever. You'll leave me one day, though," she added softly when Arthur was asleep.

They waited in the queue at the ticket sales desk. The airport was hot and incredibly busy. So many airlines, so many destinations. Arthur read them off the departure board: "Paris, Rome, Lisbon, New York, London Heathrow."

"I think we should have bought these tickets earlier," Missy said, looking uncharacteristically distracted. Arthur yawned extravagantly. "Ich langweile mich", he said. "At least I learnt some German."

"Yes, you've done very well, Arthur," Missy said vaguely.

"Are you all right?"

"Mm."

The Lufthansa sales clerk regarded Missy's request for two single tickets to Hamburg with solemnity. She would gladly sell her them, she said, but all the Hamburg flights were full until that evening, did she still want to go?

"How about London?" Missy asked.

"I can get you on the next flight to Heathrow," the sales clerk said, "but not sitting together."

"It will be quicker for us just to go straight home," Missy said to Arthur.

"Mm," Arthur said.

Missy thought about buying a ticket for London. She thought for rather a long time so that the sales clerk grew agitated because of the long queue snaking and coiling and knotting behind Arthur and Missy.

"Arthur," Missy said finally, "have you ever been to Rome?"

"I don't think so."

"I can get you on a connecting flight to Rome leaving in half an hour," the sales clerk said hopefully.

"A lot of museums in Rome," Arthur said.

"A lot," Missy agreed.

"And there are other places too," Arthur said.

"Oh, yes," Missy agreed, "there are many places. So many places that you need never come back to where you started from."

"Which was Primrose Hill," Arthur said. He tugged at Missy's hand. "What about China?"

"China?" the sales clerk asked, looking agitated.

"Don't panic," Missy said to her ("from the Great God Pan, now dead, thank goodness"). "I don't know about China," Missy said solemnly to Arthur. "I'm afraid her fate may be to stay with Romney."

"You're going to have to hurry", the sales clerk said, "the gate will be closing soon."

They ran. They ran so fast Arthur was sure they were going to take off before they even got on the plane. Missy pulled him along by the hand and when he looked at her feet her sensible leather boots had turned into silver sandals and he wondered if that was why they were able to run so fast. The airport tannoy stopped announcing that passengers for Düsseldorf should go to the gate and instead broadcast the rousing sound of a hunting horn. For a few dizzy seconds Arthur saw the quiver of silver arrows on Missy's back, gleaming with moonshine. He saw her green, wolfish eyes light up with amusement as she shouted, "Come on, Arthur, hurry up", while a pack of hounds bayed and boiled around her silver-sandalled feet, eager for the chase.

D'ACCORD, BABY

Hanif Kureishi

Hanif Kureishi (b.1954), CBE, is a playwright, screenwriter and novelist whose work includes the films *My Beautiful Launderette, Venus, The Mother* and *Le Week-End*; the novels *The Buddha of Suburbia, Intimacy, Something To Tell You* and, most recently, *The Last Word*. His *Collected Essays* and *Collected Stories* are published by Faber & Faber.

All week Bill had been looking forward to this moment. He was about to fuck the daughter of the man who had fucked his wife. Lying in her bed, he could hear Celestine humming in the bathroom as she prepared for him.

It had been a long time since he'd been in a room so cold, with no heating. After a while he ventured to put his arms out over the covers, tore open a condom and laid the rubber on the cardboard box which served as a bedside table. He was about to prepare another, but didn't want to appear over-optimistic. One would achieve his objective. He would clear out then. Already there had been too many delays. The waltz, for instance, though it made him giggle. Nevertheless he had told Nicola, his pregnant wife, that he would be back by midnight. What could Celestine be doing in there? There wasn't even a shower; and the wind cut viciously through the broken window.

His wife had met Celestine's father, Vincent Ertel, the French ex-Maoist intellectual, in Paris. He had certainly impressed her. She had talked about him continually, which was bad enough, and then rarely mentioned him, which, as he understood now, was worse.

Nicola worked on a late-night TV discussion programme. For two years she had been eager to profile Vincent's progress from revolutionary to Catholic reactionary. It was, she liked to inform Bill – using a phrase that stayed in his mind – indicative of the age. Several times she went to see Vincent in Paris; then she was invited to his country place near Auxerre. Finally she brought him to London to record the interview. When it was done, to celebrate, she took him to Le Caprice for champagne, fishcakes and chips.

That night Bill had put aside the script he was directing and gone to bed early with a ruler, pencil and *The Brothers Karamazov*. Around the time that Nicola was becoming particularly enthusiastic about Vincent, Bill had made up his mind not only to study the great books – the most dense and intransigent, the ones from which he'd always flinched – but to underline parts of and even to memorise certain passages. The effort to concentrate was a torment, as his mind flew about. Yet most nights – even during the period when Nicola was preparing for her encounter with Vincent – he kept his light on long after she had put hers out. Determined to swallow the thickest pills of understanding, he would lie there muttering phrases he wanted to retain. One of his favourites was Emerson's: "We but half express ourselves, and are ashamed of that divine idea which each of us represents."

One night Nicola opened her eyes and with a quizzical look said, "Can't you be easier on yourself?"

Why? He wouldn't give up. He had read biology at university. Surely he couldn't be such a fool as to find these books beyond him? His need for knowledge, wisdom, nourishment was more than his need for sleep. How could a man have come to the middle of his life with barely a clue about who he was or where he might go? The heavy volumes surely represented the highest point to which man's thought had flown; they had to include guidance.

The close, leisurely contemplation afforded him some satisfaction – usually because the books started him thinking about other things. It was the part of the day he preferred. He slept well, usually. But at four, on the long night of the fish-cakes, he awoke and felt for Nicola across the bed. She wasn't there. Shivering, he walked through the house until dawn, imagining she'd crashed the car. After an hour he remembered she hadn't taken it. Maybe she and Vincent had gone on to a late-night place. She had never done anything like this before.

He could neither sleep nor go to work. He decided to sit at the kitchen table until she returned, whenever it was. He was drinking brandy, and normally he never drank before eight in the evening. If anyone offered him a drink before this time, he claimed it was like saying goodbye to the whole day. In the mid-eighties he'd gone to the gym in the early evening. For some days, though, goodbye was surely the most suitable word.

It was late afternoon before his wife returned, wearing the clothes she'd gone out in, looking dishevelled and uncertain. She couldn't meet his eye. He asked her what she'd been doing. She said "What d'you think?" and went into the shower.

He had considered several options, including punching her. But instead he fled the house and made it to a pub. For the first time since he'd been a student he sat alone with nothing to do. He was expected nowhere. He had no newspaper with him, and he liked papers; he could swallow the most banal and incredible thing provided it was on newsprint. He watched the passing faces and thought how pitiless the world was if you didn't have a safe place in it.

He made himself consider how unrewarding it was to constrain people. In-fidelities would occur in most relationships. These days every man and woman was a cuckold. And why not, when marriage was insufficient to satisfy most human need? Nicola had needed something and she had taken it. How bold and stylish. How petty to blame someone for pursuing any kind of love!

He was humiliated. The feeling increased over the weeks in a strange way. At work or waiting for the tube, or having dinner with Nicola – who had gained, he could see, a bustling, dismissive intensity of will or concentration – he found himself becoming angry with Vincent. For days on end he couldn't really think of anything else. It was as if the man were inhabiting him.

As he walked around Soho where he worked, Bill entertained himself by thinking of how someone might get even with a type like Vincent, were he so inclined. The possibility was quite remote but this didn't prevent him imagining stories from which he emerged with some satisfaction, if not credit. What incentive, distraction, energy and interest Vincent provided him with! This was almost the only creative work he got to do now.

A few days later he was presented with Celestine. She was sitting with a man in a newly opened café, drinking cappuccino. Life was giving him a chance. It was awful. He stood in the doorway pretending to look for someone and wondered whether he should take it.

Vincent's eldest daughter lived in London. She wanted to be an actress and Bill had auditioned her for a commercial a couple of years ago. He knew she'd obtained a small part in a film directed by an acquaintance of his. On this basis he went over to her, introduced himself, made the pleasantest conversation he could, and was invited to sit down. The man turned out to be a gay friend of hers. They all chatted. After some timorous vacillation Bill asked Celestine in a cool tone whether she'd have a drink with him later, in a couple of hours.

He didn't go home but walked about the streets. When he was tired he sat in a pub with the first volume of *Remembrance of Things Past*. He had decided that if he could read to the end of the whole book he would deserve a great deal of praise. He did a little underlining, which since school he had considered a sign of seriousness, but his mind wandered even more than usual, until it was time to meet her.

To his pleasure Bill saw that men glanced at Celestine when they could; others openly stared. When she fetched a drink they turned to examine her legs. This would not have happened with Nicola; only Vincent Ertel had taken an interest in her. Later, as he and Celestine strolled up the street looking for cabs, she agreed that he could come to her place at the end of the week.

It was a triumphant few days of gratification anticipated. He would do more of this. He had obviously been missing out on life's meaner pleasures. As Nicola walked about the flat, dressing, cooking, reading, searching for her glasses, he could enjoy despising her. He informed his two closest friends that the pleasures of revenge were considerable. Now his pals were waiting to hear of his coup.

Celestine flung the keys, wrapped in a tea-towel, out of the window. It was a hard climb: her flat was at the top of a run-down five-storey building in West London, an area of bedsits, students and itinerants. Coming into the living room he saw it had a view across a square. Wind and rain were sweeping into the cracked windows stuffed with newspaper. The walls were yellow, the carpet brown and stained. Several pairs of jeans were suspended on a clothes horse in front of a gas fire which gave off an odour and heated parts of the room while leaving others cold.

She persuaded him to remove his overcoat but not his scarf. Then she took him into the tiny kitchen with bare floorboards where, between an old sink and the boiler, there was hardly room for the two of them.

"I will be having us some dinner." She pointed to two shopping bags. "Do you like troot?"

"Sorry?"

It was trout. There were potatoes and green beans. After, they would have apple strudel with cream. She had been to the shops and gone to some trouble. It would take ages to prepare. He hadn't anticipated this, He left her there, saying he would fetch drink.

In the rain he went to the off-licence and was paying for the wine when he noticed through the window that a taxi had stopped at traffic lights. He ran out of the shop to hail the cab, but as he opened the door couldn't go through with it. He collected the wine and carried it back.

He waited in her living room while she cooked, pacing and drinking. She didn't have a TV. Wintry gales battered the window. Her place reminded him of rooms he'd shared as a student. He was about to say to himself, thank God I'll never have to live like this again, when it occurred to him that if he left Nicola, he might, for a time, end up in some unfamiliar place like this, with its stained carpet and old, broken fittings. How fastidious he'd become! How had it happened? What other changes had there been while he was looking in the other direction?

He noticed a curled photograph of a man tacked to the wall. It looked as though it had been taken at the end of the sixties. Bill concluded it was the hopeful radical who'd fucked his wife. He had been a handsome man, and with his pipe in his hand, long hair and open-necked shirt, he had an engaging look of self-belief and raffish pleasure. Bill recalled the slogans that had decorated Paris in those days. "Everything Is Possible", "Take Your Desires for Realities", "It Is Forbidden to Forbid". He'd once used them in a TV commercial. What optimism that generation had had! With his life given over to literature, ideas, conversation, writing and political commitment, ol' Vincent must have had quite a time. He wouldn't have been working constantly, like Bill and his friends.

The food was good. Bill leaned across the table to kiss Celestine. His lips brushed her cheek. She turned her head and looked out across the dark square to the lights beyond, as if trying to locate something.

He talked about the film industry and what the actors, directors and producers of the movies were really like. Not that he knew them personally, but they were gossiped about by other actors and technicians. She asked questions and laughed easily.

Things should have been moving along. He had to get up at 5.30 the next day to direct a commercial for a bank. He was becoming known for such well-paid but journeyman work. Now that Nicola was pregnant he would have to do more of it. It would be a struggle to find time for the screenwriting he wanted to do. It was beginning to dawn on him that if he was going to do anything worthwhile at his age, he had to be serious in a new way. And yet when he considered his ambitions, which he no longer mentioned to anyone – to travel overland to Burma while reading Proust, and other, more "internal" things – he felt a surge of shame, as if it was immature and obscene to harbour such hopes; as if, in some ways, it was already too late.

He shuffled his chair around the table until he and Celestine were sitting side by side. He attempted another kiss.

She stood up and offered him her hands. "Shall we dance?"

He looked at her in surprise. "Dance?"

"It will 'ot you up. Don't you . . . dance?"

"Not really."

"Why?"

"Why? We always danced like this." He shut his eyes and nodded his head as if attempting to bang in a nail with his forehead.

She kicked off her shoes.

"We dance like this. I'll illustrate you." She looked at him. "Take it off."

"What?"

"This stupid thing."

She pulled off his scarf. She shoved the chairs against the wall and put on a Chopin waltz, took his hand and placed her other hand on his back. He looked down at her dancing feet even as he trod on them, but she didn't object. Gently but firmly she turned and turned him across the room, until he was dizzy, her hair tickling his face. Whenever he glanced up she was looking into his eyes. Each time they crossed the room she trotted back, pulling him, amused. She seemed determined that he should learn, certain that this would benefit him.

"You require some practice," she said at last. He fell back into his chair, blowing and laughing. "But after a week, who knows, we could be having you work as a gigolo!"

It was midnight. Celestine came naked out of the bathroom smoking a cigarette. She got into bed and lay beside him. He thought of a time in New York when the company sent a white limousine to the airport. Once inside it, drinking whisky and watching TV as the limo passed over the East River towards Manhattan, he wanted nothing more than for his friends to see him.

She was on him vigorously and the earth was moving: either that, or the two single beds, on the juncture of which he was lying, were separating. He stuck out his arms to secure them, but with each lurch his head was being forced down into the fissure. He felt as if his ears were going to be torn off. The two of them were about to crash through onto the floor.

He rolled her over onto one bed. Then he sat up and showed her what would have happened. She started to laugh, she couldn't stop.

The gas meter ticked; she was dozing. He had never lain beside a lovelier face. He thought of what Nicola might have sought that night with Celestine's father. Affection, attention, serious talk, honesty, distraction. Did he give her that now? Could they give it to one another, and with a kid on the way?

Celestine was nudging him and trying to say something in his ear.

"You want what?" he said. Then, "Surely . . . no . . . no."

"Bill, yes."

He liked to think he was willing to try anything. A black eye would certainly send a convincing message to her father. She smiled when he raised his hand.

"I deserve to be hurt."

"No one deserves that."

"But you see . . . I do."

That night, in that freezing room, he did everything she asked, for as long as she wanted. He praised her beauty and her intelligence. He had never kissed anyone for so long, until he forgot where he was, or who they both were, until there was nothing they wanted, and there was only the most satisfactory peace.

He got up and dressed. He was shivering. He wanted to wash, he smelled of her, but he wasn't prepared for a cold bath.

"Why are you leaving?" She leaped up and held him. "Stay, stay, I haven't finished with you yet."

He put on his coat and went into the living room. Without looking back he hurried out and down the stairs. He pulled the front door, anticipating the fresh damp night air. But the door held. He had forgotten: the door was locked. He stood there.

Upstairs she was wrapped in a fur coat, looking out of the window.

"The key," he said.

"Old man," she said, laughing. "You are."

She accompanied him barefoot down the stairs. While she unlocked the door he mumbled, "Will you tell your father I saw you?"

"But why?"

He touched her face. She drew back. "You should put something on that," he said. "I met him once. He knows my wife."

"I rarely see him now," she said.

She was holding out her arms. They danced a few steps across the hall. He was better at it now. He went out into the street. Several cabs passed him but he didn't hail them. He kept walking. There was comfort in the rain. He put his head back and looked up into the sky. He had some impression that happiness was beyond him and everything was coming down, and that life could not be grasped but only lived.

THE TANGLING POINT

Tim Parks

Born in Manchester, **Tim Parks** (b.1954) has lived in Italy for most of his life, working as a translator – of works by Calasso, Calvino, Moravia, Tabucchi as well as Machiavelli's *The Prince* – and academic. His award-winning novels include *Goodness, Europa, Destiny, Judge Savage, Cleaver* and *Painting Death*; a memoir, *Teach Us To Sit Still,* and several travelogues and collections of essays. His blog at the *New York Review of Books* is shortly to be collected in one volume. He now lives and teaches in Milan.

Before the dinner my wife told me that her boss's daughter was obsessed by dogs. Her parents were worried about it, more than worried. In fact they had asked whether I might be able to help. I remarked that I had never heard that a love for animals constituted a pathology. My wife sighed and explained that the young woman, Emanuela, had a job teaching biology in a local school, but couldn't be persuaded to leave home, claiming she needed all her extra money for her dogs.

"How many does she have?"

"Only two of her own. It seems she's a dog saviour. She drives all over Europe saving dogs."

My wife had finally returned to work after many years as a housewife and mother. I was anxious that the job go well and that she be happy there. Our marriage had run out of steam many years ago, the last child was leaving home and there was the prospect that we would be able to separate without too much trauma. A good job – she was p.a. to the Director of a busy pharmaceutical concern – could only facilitate this, giving my wife something to rebuild her life around. Hence, when she said her boss had invited us to dinner, I agreed at once, hoping this indicated an investment on both sides in their new work relationship.

"I think he partly invited us so as to talk to you about her. He seemed very interested when I said you were a therapist."

We had arrived at the house, an attractive villa on the hills to the north of town. The automatic gate swung open, a yellow light flashing above one of the posts.

"What do you mean, 'saving dogs'?" I asked.

"It seems people alert her when they hear of a dog being mistreated and she goes and rescues the creature and finds it a good home."

"Sounds rather noble," I said.

"Think if one of our kids were doing that," my wife snapped back. "Be serious." It was a while since we had spent an evening together.

Signor Fanna was a tall, bulky man, rather sloppy by Italian standards, but he greeted us energetically and with evident pleasure, rather as if he might be a big playful dog himself. Behind him his wife leaned forward from a wheelchair; in her early sixties she was dryly polite and wore an elegant green silk blouse. "*Buona sera*, Dr Marks," she greeted me. I was struck by her lean wrists, braceleted in gold, but evidently powerful as she spun her wheelchair around and led the way to the dining room.

We went through the usual social rigmaroles, drinking something white and sharp. I was pleased to see that Signor Fanna was on easy and respectful terms with my wife, and she too seemed to have the measure of him, coming across as both sociable and sensible. For a few moments they talked about work and the arrangements for a conference in Germany that he was to be attending the following week.

"At which point I shall be left alone with the mad dog woman," his wife remarked coolly to me.

It seemed a curious thing to say for someone who must rely heavily on domestic help. Shouldn't Signora Fanna be glad to have her daughter around? I noticed that they did have an elderly Asian maid doing the cooking. Wearing a simple black dress that may or may not have been a uniform, this elderly woman brought in a plate of mixed hors d'oeuvres and laid it on the glass table top.

"I hear your daughter is something of an activist," I smiled.

"A terrorist, Dr Marks."

I laughed. "I see no bomb damage."

"Because we clean-up afterwards."

Swallowing a vol-au-vent, Signor Fanna turned towards us and sighed. "You've studied psychology, Dr Marks. Perhaps you could tell us what would induce a young woman to sacrifice everything to dogs. Is there anything we can do?"

It is one of the comedies of being a mental health therapist that people imagine you have magical powers of divination.

"Evidently she likes her dogs more than the things she is supposedly giving up," I said. "Why is it such a worry for you?"

"Honestly, she's driving us crazy," Signor Fanna began, but stopped. "You tell him, Elvira."

The woman on the wheelchair, who had evidently been a beauty in her day, pursed her lips and frowned. "Five or six years ago, we were expecting Emanuela to marry and leave home. She had a nice boyfriend she'd been seeing for some time. They'd lived together on and off. A young lawyer. Then it fell through because he couldn't put up with having dogs constantly lodged in his flat and even sleeping on his bed. It was sad, we'd actually become good friends with his parents, excellent people from Bologna. After the break-up she started bringing the dogs here. Every weekend she's off in the car driving hundreds, even thousands of kilometres, either to fetch dogs who've been abandoned or to take the strays she's gathered to some new home. Every afternoon after school all she does is feed and walk the dogs then get on the internet to plan her next 'raid'. That's what she calls them."

"She was so smart at school," Signor Fanna said. "Got an excellent degree in molecular biology from Milan. We had expected her to go into research. Instead she settled for work as a replacement teacher on the local school circuit. Now she's thirty-four and seems to have no plans beyond saving dogs."

"Last week she brought back a three-legged, leprous creature from Bari, or thereabouts. It cost a fortune just in petrol. Then there are veterinary expenses."

"Not to mention problems with the law. If she sees a dog kept on a short chain she simply steals it. Goes at night with a chain cutter. There've been two summonses. We had to put down bail."

My wife said to me, "Think if one of ours started doing that kind of thing, Ted!"

I looked around. "There are no dogs in here," I observed.

"Because we've insisted that this side of the house be kept dog free."

"Ah."

"But if we took you round the back, you'd need a gas mask. I've set up a fire-wall of air-fresheners," Signora Elvira explained with a pained smile.

I thought about it. "I must say I rather like dogs. They're always friendly. And hard-wired for obedience."

"We all like dogs," both of them wailed rather louder than was necessary. "Everybody does, but not scores of them, and not dogs with sores and wounded paws and pus in their eyes."

As I wondered what to say next my wife shot me a glance to remind me that these were not any old friends, and certainly not my clients. People want a therapist's advice for their nearest and dearest, but are not eager to find their own assumptions under scrutiny. Fortunately a tureen of smooth asparagus soup was served and we sat at table to eat. A fifth place had been set, I noticed, at the head of the table too, but no attempt had been made to call Emanuela. Perhaps the couple wanted the benefit of my advice before she arrived. Rather deliberately, I changed the subject to pharmaceuticals and Signor Fanna, a jowly expansive man, spoke happily of his work and the rather special situation, as he put it, in Italy where the industry faced the combined problems of a certain level of anarchy, a lot of petty corruption, and of course the Church doing everything possible to hinder the distribution of all products connected with contraception.

Signora Elvira seemed bored and left half her soup in her bowl.

"I've been given special instructions for how to speak to right-to-life lobby-ists," my wife confirmed cheerfully.

Then Emanuela walked in and the evening got interesting.

I had expected a loser, the dog craze covering up a young woman's fear of starting her own life away from home. Or a polemical young woman playing committed radical to her parents' bourgeois complacency; a do-gooder, a bore. Instead Emanuela banged open the door and strode in smiling, apologizing for being late. "I never make it anywhere on time," she laughed. She was wearing a grey wool dress on a shapely, freshly-showered body of medium height, feminine but healthily solid, and if her face was on the plain side, it nevertheless had plenty of character and presence. "No don't get up," she protested. "You must be Anita, and you're the husband."

"Ted."

"Right, the shrink."

Why had the girl been told that?

We talked for twenty minutes or so without any mention of dogs. The main dishes were brought by the discreet maid who seemed to be from the Philippines or thereabouts and I noticed that Emanuela's plate did not have meat on it, though she made no attempt to draw attention to her vegetarianism. She was a confident, outgoing young woman happy to discuss the school she worked in and her attitude to her teacher's role: "I try to give papà a hand," she laughed, telling the girls to get on the pill and the boys to use condoms."

Yet her parents were evidently unhappy with her. The mother in particular frowned constantly. Perhaps Signora Elvira was a devout catholic, I reflected, and didn't approve of these allusions to sex and contraception. Her husband had become cautious after his daughter's arrival, as if picking his way through a minefield. I suspected he could have got on with her if the mother were not present. As it was, all his attentions seemed aimed at getting my wife and his to talk together, about recipes and clothes and shopping centres. Perhaps her p.a.'s responsibilities were to include keeping the boss's invalid wife company while he was away.

"I hear you are a dog lover," I said as the tiramisu was placed before us.

"That's right," Emanuela agreed amiably. She concentrated on spooning up the mascarpone.

There was an expectant silence. I couldn't decide whether the Fannas wanted me to make some kind of effort to explore the dog thing or not. I was trying to be helpful.

With a dour smile, Signora Elvira said: "Emanuela's going up to Holland this weekend, aren't you, love?"

The 'love' was unexpected, and unexpectedly respectful. Emanuela nodded. "I thought we'd agreed not to talk about dogs anymore, Mamma."

"It's not every weekend one drives to Holland," Signor Fanna said.

My wife threw in a few enthusiastic remarks about Amsterdam in the spring and what wonderful people the Dutch were. "So liberal. No problems selling pharmaceuticals there!"

Emanuela put her spoon down. "Too liberal sometimes."

"How so?" I asked.

She hesitated, shot a glance at her parents. "There are no laws against deviant sexual behaviour in Holland. They let men rape dogs. This usually leads to the animals' death through internal bleeding."

"God!" My wife raised her napkin to her lips.

Signora Elvira's face was a mask of severity.

"Special brothels exist to provide dogs to an international clientele. Like the cafés where you can smoke dope. This weekend there will be a big animal rights demonstration. We're planning to free as many dogs as we can." She turned to her father who was looking a little queasy: "Do you mind if I take the SUV, Papà?"

Some time later, as we were preparing to leave, I said: "I'd love to see your dogs, Emanuela."

We were standing in the hallway. Signor Fanna had gone to get some papers he wanted my wife to deal with first thing the following morning. Signora Elvira had cheered up as the evening drew to a close and was evidently enjoying my wife's company. Perhaps Signor Fanna always introduced his p.a.s and their husbands to his wife to prevent any suspicion that there might be any illicit intimacy developing.

Emanuela assented readily enough and led the way down the hallway, through a door that crossed a spacious kitchen, then another door that led to a generous extension on the back of the house. At once there was a strong doggy smell, but nothing excessive, or not for those of us who've been brought up with dogs. The girl crouched down to greet a fine border collie that came scampering up to her, then stretched an arm to welcome a pretty beagle waggling behind. As she crouched, her wool dress tightened. The collie licked her face which she turned smilingly from side to side under his long wet tongue. Her thighs were strong and her back pleasantly full. The beagle yelped and pawed. Both dogs were beautifully glossy, in the pink of canine health, and the more Emanuela played with them, the more attractive her youth and evident good nature became.

"What my parents wanted you to pronounce on, though," she broke off, "was this."

Suddenly businesslike, she stood up and led me out through the extension and out of a back door into the garden. Immediately, from a low building at the far side of the lawn, an excited barking began. It was no more than a large garden shed, half hidden behind low bushes. Emanuela took a torch hanging under the eaves and pointed it through the window. Here there were ten or a dozen dogs all falling over each other to thrust their snouts against the window, yapping and snuffling and scratching. I could see at once that these were not such healthy specimens. One had an eye missing. One limped and whimpered.

"I always find a home for them in the end. It just takes a little time."

"That's very impressive," I said. "It must be hard work."

"There's a group of us, called Puppy Love."

She turned towards me. Because we had been peering in at small the window we were close to each other. It was impossible not to be aware of her body in the fresh dark, her lips faintly illuminated in the torchlight.

"Maybe you'd like to make a donation. We're not a registered charity yet, but I can guarantee that every cent would be spent on the dogs' welfare."

We began to walk back to the house.

"I've worked out that each dog I save and re-house costs on average around 400 Euros, just over a quarter of my monthly salary."

"Let me think about it."

"Of course. Take your time. I ask everybody I meet. Otherwise we wouldn't be able to do what we do."

I felt excited.

"How would I contact you, if I did decide to give?"

She mentioned a website. The name was easy to remember. There was a contact box. But before we crossed the threshold back into the house she stopped me. "Tell me something, though. I mean, you being a shrink. Why does it bother my parents so much? Especially Mamma. Why is she so hostile?"

I took a deep breath. This was tempting; an alliance against her parents would be an easy way to intimacy. I resisted.

"I suppose they wanted something different for you. As parents tend to do. They no doubt have some more conventional narrative of their daughter, happy in her middle-class marriage with a professional career that they can talk to their friends about." I hesitated, "Probably what makes it harder is that what you're doing is obviously generous and good. I mean, if one has to choose between dog rapists and dog rescuers, one plumps for the rescuers. On the other hand we'd all be happier not to think about such disturbing things at all. I suspect you confuse them. They're not sure how to behave. And of course," I smiled, "they could probably do without the barking in the garden. And the dogshit no doubt."

As I spoke and she watched me, standing a fraction closer than people ordinarily stand to each other, I sensed that very soon we would become lovers and I would be dedicating substantial sums of money to the salvation of Europe's abused dogs.

So it was. Emanuela was arrested in Holland. My wife told me that Signor Fanna had cancelled his trip to Germany to go to the Italian Consulate in Rotterdam. Signora Elvira, on the other hand, had kept her, my wife, on the phone for hours, expressing her indignation that her husband had allowed his daughter to get in the way of his work; she was all for leaving the girl to languish in a police cell. That way she'd be forced to wake up and take life seriously.

I wondered who fed and walked the dogs while Emanuela was away. My wife said she had no idea.

"Ask."

She looked puzzled. "Why?"

"Just curious. I found the whole set up rather intriguing."

"I thought you'd come to the conclusion that she was a nice girl with a good cause and the parents were making too much fuss."

"Just curious," I repeated. "By the way, do you know how Signora Elvira ended up in the wheelchair?"

My wife had no idea. Signor Fanna had never talked about it.

"He's extremely devoted to her," she said with a hint of bitterness.

The following week, Emanuela appeared on the regional TV news. She had been released with a caution. Quizzed by an interviewer on her return to Verona, she said. "I just don't like to think of animals being mistreated. Especially not to satisfy perverts. It's ugly and I want the world to be beautiful."

Watching, I was struck by how at ease she was with the questions and the camera; there was no shrillness, no preaching or proselytizing. As someone who daily spends hours every day in conversation with conflicted and unhappy people, I rarely see this: a young woman entirely at home with herself and her choices. It made her extremely desirable. The closing shots showed Emanuela crouching down to greet her collie and beagle on arriving home. It was a replay of the scene I had witnessed after our dinner, except that now she was wearing jeans and tee shirt. The collie pushed its wet nose into her breasts.

I would send her 400 euros a month, I wrote in the website contact box, on condition that I be allowed to see the dogs my money was helping. A few days later we met outside her school and she took me to a veterinary surgery where an obese black Labrador was sedated on a drip. He had been found half dead in a ditch.

The vet, in his late forties, greeted Emanuela with a warm embrace; she ruffled his hair, he tweaked her nose, and I understood at once that they had been lovers and that this was why he was willing to offer her his services for no more than the cost of the drugs. He greeted me and smiled, explaining that it was a daily occurrence in Verona for dogs to be found poisoned, either by dog haters who left spiked meatballs around, or by their owners who were fed up with them. In Italy it is illegal to put a healthy animal down. "So they fake a poisoning and take care to remove the dog's collar and identification, in case it survives."

Emanuela stroked the creature which was stretched out on a surgical table. "Come and say hello, Ted," she said in a low voice. I went to stand beside her and put a hand on the dog's matted fur. It twitched and a muscle shifted under the skin. She put her hand next to mine. It was actually quite strange to feel this threatened animal life beneath my fingers; the Labrador's bulk and odorous canine presence took on an unexpected solemnity - here were fifty kilos of sensitive suffering flesh that could not easily be ignored - and I knew it was the woman beside me who had made me feel this. Her hand invited mine to linger and to get to know the creature. Sitting in the car again we looked at each other and kissed.

Signora Elvira had fallen off a horse, my wife told me. "Twenty years ago."

"Ah."

I wondered aloud what her husband did about sex.

"Trust you," she grumbled. "It is possible for people to love each other without constant sex, you know."

It went unspoken that my wife hadn't made love for months if not years.

Emanuela had a more interesting version of events. Her mother, a successful doctor at the time, had been eager to get her daughter into horse-riding; she went around with a rather snobbish Rotary Club crowd. "One holiday, in Umbria, she hired these two horses and at a certain point mine took off. I couldn't control it. She was quite expert and galloped after me. Then I fell and she had to hit the brakes not to trample me. The horse crashed her into a wall."

"So it was your fault."

"She never actually said that."

Her mother was the one serious worry in Emanuela's life. "What can I do to make her happy" she moaned "or at least to get her off my back? Why is she constantly asking me when I plan to get real and move out of the house? She's obsessed."

We met once a week and made love in my studio. Often Emanuela brought a dog to show me, ostensibly the one my money was helping. The animals did not always take kindly to our embraces. Sometimes she invited me on a reconnaissance mission: I had to wander into a farmyard in some outlying village to see if it was true that a German Shepherd was being kept up to its knees in slime. On another occasion I was asked to drive a bull terrier to its new owner in Genova while she went to deal with an emergency in Trieste. As I drove, sacrificing a whole Sunday in the process and wondering how I would explain to my wife about the doggy smell in the car, I realized that this must be how all her relationships went. Men fell in love with her enthusiasm around dogs, her warmth, affection and contagious sense of purpose. It was impossible not to want to be touched and loved by this generous animal woman. Then they grew offended that the dogs always came first and the relationship cooled and died; after which ex-lovers might become occasional helpers, taking the dogs out for walks when she was away on a mission, perhaps getting a kiss or two as a reward, or maybe more. Emanuela was not a stingy girl. She had a finely developed sense of give and take.

As far as I was concerned, though, it was rather convenient that the dogs came first. After three children I had no interest in serious commitments with a young woman. And watching Emanuela I was beginning to understand her motivation and her gift: again and again she made you feel the individuality and irrefutable physical presence of each animal. However sick or crippled or aggressive or stinking they might be, these creatures couldn't be wished away; they really were there, living and suffering and snuffling at your crotch. Emanuela's response to their vitality brought out the animal in her too; she radiated life. I never minded when a promised session on my studio sofa was cancelled for a trip to some dog refuge with a carload of cheap feed. She liked my big Audi because it carried more than her old Vectra. And she was appreciative of my patience. "I'll make it up to you, darling," she whispered. This could go on forever, I thought.

But there was one animal Emanuela couldn't get rid of. She'd had a Doberman for a year and more and despaired of finding a home for it. Paralysed in one hind leg, abandoned by its owner when no longer able to run along a fence barking madly at every passerby, this ex guard dog was frustrated and irritable, snapping at the other dogs in the shed and making sure that there was a constant din in the garden, which of course gave Signora Elvira every excuse for insisting that the situation was unsustainable. On two occasions this grumpy creature had made the journey to generous adoptive families in distant country estates, but each time, after a week or so, these good people had asked to be relieved of the animal. So the Doberman - Kenny he was called - was brought back, not without expense and effort, and the strife began again. He nipped the other dogs' heels and necks, they yelped and barked. The paralysis also seemed to have affected his bladder. He peed in the shed. The stink was getting worse.

"You take him," Emanuela eventually said.

Yes, this is how she gets rid of her men, I thought, with an impossible test of love.

"Let me mull it over," I told her and I noticed that when we made love that afternoon she was particularly generous with her caresses. Sex was never easier or more affectionately physical than with Emanuela. She made you feel how fortunate you were to be alive and in possession of all your senses. In my mid fifties, I had clearly lucked out.

On the other hand, Kenny was one hell of an ugly dog.

"Signora Elvira phoned me today," my wife said. My wife had been in a better mood since she had started working again, so much so that I had begun to think that what with the affair I was enjoying and this new pleasantness at home, perhaps after all there would be no need to make major changes.

"She asked if you would be willing to see her."

"She didn't say why?"

"I thought it might be unwise to ask."

I drove over the following morning and found Signora Elvira smartly if sternly dressed with a black jacket and cream blouse.

"I never thought it would come to this," she said without any preamble, "but I was wondering if you would accept me for therapy, or analysis, or whatever it is exactly you do."

This was tricky. Ethically, it must be wrong for me to become the therapist of my lover's mother. On the other hand I could hardly state the impediment.

"I wonder if that's a good idea," I said "with my wife being your husband's p.a."

"Nonsense," she declared.

There was a prickliness about the woman that was intimidating and endearing. I hesitated.

"Dr Marks," she said determinedly "I need to learn how to stop being so unpleasant to my daughter, who after all helps me in all kinds of ways, something which is actually quite important for a woman on a wheelchair. The truth is I don't really understand why she irritates me so much. I was hoping you could guide me."

Intrigued, I stayed to listen. The truth is that inhibitions, and even professional vetoes, have less force as one grows older. I thought, why not?

Needless to say my wife was horrified when she found Kenny in the garden. The creature barked and bared its teeth. He had shat on our small lawn, a steamy liquid shit.

"Take it right back! At once. Whatever were you thinking of?"

I explained that as I had had come out of one of my sessions with Signora Elvira - for with her being wheelchair bound, I very unusually went to the client's house - Emanuela had buttonholed me and begged me, simply begged me to take the Doberman.

"Just temporarily, until she finds a permanent home. A good deed," I said. "Apparently it's the dog that most gets under her parents skin."

"You're going soft," my wife told me. But that evening she looked at me in a way she hadn't for some time.

I sat outside on a garden chair, something I never do, reading and talking to Kenny and trying to pat him whenever he came close. Already the neighbours had complained about the loud barking every time they opened and closed their front door. All day Kenny dragged his bad leg back and forth from the hedge on one side of the garden to the fence on the other, occasionally stopping to growl at me in between.

"How goes it, old pal?" I asked. "How does it feel to have a territory to defend again?"

Now, after making love, Emanuela gave me tips for winning the dog's confidence and imposing a minimum of discipline. She enjoyed getting me to pretend I was the Doberman and she was me. We laughed and tussled. I pretended to bite her fingers and she yelled, "Heel! Bad boy!" But there was also a new caution about Emanuela these days. She hadn't expected that I would take on Kenny. Even less that I would keep him. Perhaps she feared what I might ask in return. She certainly hadn't expected that I would become her mother's therapist.

"God knows what secrets you're learning," she fished.

"If you only knew!" I teased.

Nearly a year on it was still enormously exciting making love to Emanuela. It had cheered me up no end. Walking Kenny on the lead every evening, waiting while he dragged his bad leg, picking up his stinking shit in a plastic bag, pulling him away from the other dogs he was always determined to attack, I kept repeating: "I'm not doing this for you, you know, old mate. I'm doing it to keep a certain lady in my bed."

But Kenny didn't seem upset by this deviousness. He had started to lick my fingers and to sit when I told him to. My wife was impressed.

"I'd have never imagined you had it in you," she said and she too crouched down to stroke him. Kenny growled, but softly. My wife looked up and our eyes met: this was a very unusual occurrence.

"By the way," she said then "Signor Fanna seems rather nervous about your talks with his wife. He hadn't realised she was planning to go into analysis."

"I hope you reassured him that I never talk to you about my patients."

"Of course."

On another occasion I asked her, "Do you ever get the impression that Signor Fanna is a big shaggy dog? It's what I always think when I see him."

More and more often Signora Elvira's husband was contriving to be around when our therapy sessions ended. He would appear in the hallway smiling nervously like an expectant father and never failed to ask me how things were going.

My wife reflected. "Not a menacing dog," she said. "Not a Kenny." She hesitated. "Maybe one of those bouncy, friendly things that don't know what to do with their energy and always try to put their snouts in your crotch.

"So he has made a pass at you!"

"No!" she shook her head. "You know I didn't mean that." Very unusually, she smiled.

Having now guessed the Fanna family's unhappy secret, my problem, but it was also an interesting challenge as a therapist, was how to play it to everyone's advantage, my own included.

"Why do you think Emanuela's so fixated with these situations where people abuse dogs sexually?" Signora Elvira demanded. "You're a bit slow for an analyst aren't you?"

As it turned out my lover was now involved in a campaign to ban websites that showed men having sex with animals.

I sighed and smiled. If she wanted to bring it out in the open she would have to say it herself.

"We had such a great love life," Signora Elvira sighed "Gianni and I, and then of course it all ended very suddenly. I was bedridden for more than a year. And Emanuela had just turned twelve."

I listened. It was up to her.

"The fact is he still dotes on me. It's as if he's afraid that if he had sex with anyone else he'd lose me."

I nodded.

"I'm always telling him to find a pretty young p.a. who knows the ropes. Then what does he do? He employs someone like your wife and invites her here *with her husband*!"

So often the best policy for a therapist is simply to nod sympathetically.

"I wish I could help him, but I can't," she wailed. She cast around. It was as if she were furious that I wouldn't tell her what she needed to tell me. "If only Emanuela would find a man who would take her away. But she deliberately chooses people who can't or won't marry, or if they will she chases them off by giving them some impossible dog to look after."

Did she know about us? How similar to her father was I?

"What's the solution?" she asked. "Gianni is dying of guilt, without really being guilty," she added.

"Nobody dies of guilt," I told her. Actually, of the three of them I had the distinct impression that only Signora Elvira was suffering. The others were troubled only in so far as she was unhappy. That week Emanuela was interviewed on the radio about her campaign: "It's incredible," she said, "the lengths the Church goes to to stop people using contraceptives and day-after pills, while doing nothing nothing to prevent this monstrous abuse of dogs."

To me, out of the blue, she said, "The problem with Dad is he lives in the past. He always treats me like I was twelve years old. You know he doesn't even close the loo door when he pees?"

Her mother had already told me this.

At home my wife had become friendly with Kenny who now greeted her more enthusiastically than he did me. He even wagged his tail. She was buying him treats from the supermarket, a kindness she had once shown to me.

"It seems someone's given Emanuela the money to set up a dog refuge of her own," I told my wife a few months later. "She'll even have a place to live, over the shop, as it were. In Quinzano."

The small house was just out of town. I had had my eye on it for a while.

"But that's fantastic," she said. "Really fantastic. Signor Fanna will be so pleased. They've been dying for her to get out."

"I'm surprised he didn't tell you."

Having a heart to heart with Kenny after she had left for work, I told him:

"Kenny, mate, you and I are now approaching what, with my clients or lovers, I always call the tangling point."

The dog growled, tugging on a rubber bone I was holding; I yanked one way and he yanked the other. As any dog-lovers knows, it's a game that can go on for quite a while.

"What I mean, Kenny, is the point where it will be impossible to tell the story of your life without telling the story of mine. And vice versa of course. Impossible to talk about Dr Marks without mentioning Kenny."

Since I refused to let him win, the dog suddenly let go of the bone and barked fiercely. At which I actually fell off my chair. I couldn't believe it. I came crashing off my chair and cracked my head on the bottom shelf of the bookcase. It hurt like hell, a really sharp crack on the temple. Yet as I came to my senses I found I was laughing. Crumpled on the floor, my legs caught in the chair, I was laughing and sobbing together. It was strange. I was overcome with an emotion I still can't begin to explain. Meantime, slobbery red mouth and stinking breath only inches from my face, the dog was barking and barking and barking, and in his excitement piss had begun to dribble out from his hindquarters onto our best rug. I lunged up, grabbed his head and pulled it down squealing and growling next to mine.

"Thanks, Kenny," I told him as the creature fought like mad to get loose. "Thank you so much."

THE COLD OUTSIDE

John Burnside

John Burnside (b.1955) was born in Dunfermline and studied in Cambridge. He is a prize-winning poet – *Black Cat Bone* won both the T.S. Eliot and Forward Prize – and novelist – *A Summer of Drowning* won the Costa Novel of the Year in 2011 – as well as memoirist – *A Lie About My Father* won the 2006 Saltire Scottish Book of the Year. His collection of stories *Something Like Happy* won the 2013 Saltire Scottish Book of the Year. He lives, with his family, in Fife.

When the cancer came back, I wasn't surprised. I was upset for Caroline, knowing she'd have to be told eventually, and I was bothered about how Sall would take it, after last time. I was even sorry for Malky, because finding reliable drivers was difficult, and he'd always been a good boss. Still, I wasn't surprised, not when they told me. I'd been expecting something to go wrong since the summer, when Sall and I had talked about flying over to Montreal to see Caroline and meet her new boyfriend, then given up on the idea. Sall knew I was keen, of course: Caroline had always been Daddy's little girl, and, ever since she'd left, it had been an effort to hide how empty the house felt without her – an effort I'd sometimes failed to make. Sall probably knew as well as I did that I was on borrowed time, so to begin with she had gone through all the motions of planning the trip, but then she'd started talking about how expensive it was and how tiring it would be for me, having to drive over to Glasgow, then sit on the plane for seven hours, and then, after all that, there was immigration and customs, which took forever. The way she spoke, it was as if she'd made the journey herself, but she hadn't. She'd never even left Scotland, and all that talk about the Montreal customs was just stuff she'd picked up from Caroline, who'd been back three times in the six years since she got the job in Montreal. Not long before her last visit, though, she had met this new boyfriend and had started making a big thing about how it was our turn to go over there.

"I understand it's a long way," she'd said. "But you'll love it when you get there. You'll see. It'll be a nice holiday. Besides, Jim keeps asking me if you really exist. He thinks I made you up." She'd laughed, but the invitation was real, even if she didn't look at Sall when she said it but kept her eyes fixed on me. She was content to work around her mother for my sake, now that the two of them didn't have to live in the same house. For her, it was all about careful management, about avoiding those occasions when something might be said that couldn't be taken back. Even before she left, she had come and gone like a ghost, just so she didn't have to be with Sall. I'd never really understood why.

I once overheard Caroline say that her mother could start a fight in an empty room, but that wasn't altogether fair. The two of them just weren't able to sit together without arriving at some kind of disagreement or misunderstanding. It was a mismatch of personalities, something that happened all the time, in all kinds of situations. It was shocking only when it happened between a mother and her child.

Whenever Caroline extended one of those vague invitations, I wanted to tell her that we'd come over as soon as we could, but Sall always got in first. "We'll see" was all she'd say, and then she would go to work, undermining the idea. That was what she had done during the summer, making up excuses and problems and eventually talking the trip out of existence, till we ended up driving down to Hertfordshire instead, for a sad fortnight of rain and tea shops with Sall's brother Tom and his second wife. I'd understood what was going on, and I told myself that it was probably for the best, what with the history between them; still, that so-called holiday was more of an upset than I'd expected. At first, I just put it down to the usual disappointment with Sall's games and the way I never seemed to be able to stand up to her, but somewhere in the midst of it all, wandering around a grimy little bric-a-brac shop in Stevenage, I realized that I'd given up the last chance I would ever have to visit Montreal.

So the knowledge was there, sitting at the back of my mind, waiting to come true, when the doctor told me. I was almost ready for it: almost accepting, the way you're supposed to be in all the stories they tell about dying. Not completely but close, just waiting to hear how it was going to be, so I could walk out of the surgery and get on with what was left of my life. I had a matter of months, the specialist thought, and the idea crossed my mind that I could do anything I liked. I was free. Except that there wasn't anything I wanted to do that much, apart from seeing Caroline, and I knew what Sall would say to that now. I'd heard it all before: how I had never had any time for anybody but my little girl, how I'd spoiled her rotten. To hear Sall talk, you'd have thought that what happened between them was all my fault, but I looked back in my mind's eye and I tried to find a picture, one reliable image of the two of them happy together, and I couldn't. Not even when Caroline was a baby. I could see me standing at the window in the back bedroom, rocking her to sleep and singing her Christmas carols, because they were the only songs I could remember, and I could see the two of us, when Caroline was six, going around and around on the horses at Flamingo Park, while Sall sat off by herself, watching, a curious, slightly bewildered look on her face, as if she were ashamed or embarrassed about something. I could see Caroline laughing at my bad jokes as we drove to school in the mornings, and I saw us making a row of snowmen in the garden – four of them, all identical. That was why I liked driving, and that was why I didn't mind going back on the road so soon, because when I was out there, on my own, I would look at those pictures in my head and I would be happy.

Anyway, the day after I got the diagnosis, I was back at work, hauling treacle. When Malky called, that first evening, Sall told him I was fine, and that I'd be back in the morning. I didn't blame her for that; we needed the money. I suppose I should have been disappointed that she didn't want me at home, at least for a little while, but I wasn't. I knew it wasn't really her fault. She just didn't know how to deal with that kind of thing. Even before we left the surgery, I could feel her edging away, the way she always did whenever there was a problem. She slipped away into her own separate place, as she had done when we were first married and things weren't what either of us had expected, or during the long weeks after Caroline moved away and we were left stranded, speechless and unable to touch or even look at each other, alone together with the quiet of an empty house and a shelf's worth of pale photographs in the matching set of Shaker-style frames that Sall had bought at the Sue Ryder.

So I'm not blaming her. I was just as glad to go back on the road and not have to sit moping about the house. Besides, I've always liked pulling treacle – molasses, to give it its proper name. Every now and then, I run around the countryside, delivering the warm, dark slop that farmers use to supplement the fodder for their cattle, blending the treacle with barley to make a sweet malty mix that the beasts can't get enough of. I like going out on the farms, all quiet and lonely in the middle of the day; I like talking to the farmers and listening to their stories – men who have never been anywhere in all their born years save these hundred acres of ground, grown men haunted by their own holdings. To be honest, I like hauling treacle more than anything else. There are times when it's so thick and dark and solid you could walk on it, and we have to work hard to get it pumped out and into the big tanks, which are usually so old and creaky that you think they won't hold. Sometimes they don't. On a really warm day, one of the pipes, or maybe the wall of the tank, will give way, and there will be treacle everywhere: treacle and the smell of treacle that makes you dizzy, it's so sweet and strong.

It was hard work, but it was good being busy. It gave me less time to dwell. And I knew, when I started out that winter's morning, that I'd feel better coming home with a full day's work under my belt, knowing that I wasn't quite used up. I thought about that all day, driving round the farms in the frosty light – about how I would keep going till I couldn't go on anymore. All a man has is his work and his sense of himself, all the secret life he holds inside that nobody else can know. That was how it had always been, even at home: my real life was separate from the day-to-day business that Sall knew or cared enough about to make decisions. It wasn't that I didn't love her, at least to begin with; we got on well enough in the first few years. It was just that we'd always been private people, in our different ways. That was probably what made it possible for us to stay together after Caroline left. We knew how to keep ourselves to ourselves, a skill we had perfected through the years without even knowing how completely we had mastered it.

It was late in the afternoon, the sun just going down over the fields, the last of the light filtering through the trees and shrubs along the road by the old hospital. The first green of evening, my mother had always called it, sitting on the back step at home, watching the Peruvian lilies and the montbretia fade into the gloaming. I was never sure if that was a phrase of her own, or a quote from something, some radio drama, say, or a children's book she'd read to me in the days before memory. Usually, if I got home early, this was my time. While Sall made herself busy in the kitchen, I would sit in the dining room with the paper spread out on the table, or I would listen to the radio, staring out at the garden and fiddling with the dials to get a better signal. That day, though, I had pulled a long run, only just finishing up at Jacob's Well Farm when the dark set in. It had been a good day, but I knew I wasn't supposed to overdo it, so I was happy enough saying my goodbyes to Ben Walsh, who used to run Jacob's Well with his dad, and keeps it going himself now, his wife gone, no kids, both his parents dead. He had been living alone like that for some years by then, which was maybe why he paid so much attention to the few people he encountered. That day, it was attention I could have done without, but then he wasn't to know what my troubles were. He offered me a cup of tea, but he didn't seem to mind when I told him I'd better get on back. He gave me a solemn little smile and shook his head. "How's the missus?" he said. "Keeping all right?" He always talked about Sall as if she were an invalid.

"Can't complain," I said.

"That's good." He gave me an odd, shy look. "Still, if you don't mind me saying, you're looking a bit under the weather yourself."

"Oh, no," I said. "I'm fine."

"Yes?"

"I'm a bit tired, I suppose," I said. "It'll pass."

He nodded. He was curious and, I think, genuinely concerned, but he knew not to pursue it. "Well, I hope so," he said. "You take care of yourself. You don't want to be coming down with something, right before Christmas."

I managed a smile. "You can say that again," I said. "Anyway, this is the last of it, before the holidays. I'll get a good rest then. You take care, too." I shook his hand and got back into the rig. For a moment, I wished I'd said yes to the tea and stopped, not to talk about anything in particular but to keep company with the man for a while. I couldn't imagine that his Christmas would be that festive, with just him and the animals.

Then again, I couldn't imagine much of a Christmas for myself, now that everything was decided. I wasn't looking forward to the quiet of the holidays, or having to go through the motions with Sall, which she would want to do, because – well, it was Christmas. Maybe Caroline would ring, sometime in the middle of the afternoon, making the call first thing, so she could get on with the rest of the day knowing she'd done her duty. I hadn't said anything to her about the cancer, of course. I'd considered telling her the first time, but it would only have worried her, and then she might have felt duty-bound to come over. This time, I didn't even give it a second thought, because I knew for sure that I was going to die, and I wanted to do it in my own way. I wanted to let go of life with some kind of grace, or at least with some attention to what was happening, instead of just sitting quietly in the middle of some great drama between Sall and Caroline about what they thought I should do. That was how it had been through so much of my life: I hadn't missed any of the big events, but, at the same time, I hadn't felt entirely present while they were happening. Those last few weeks, though, I noticed everything. Like the way time would catch up with me all of a sudden, and I'd see myself opening a letter, or making a cup of tea: see myself from above, doing these ordinary little things and taking an odd pleasure in them, though I can't say why.

I'd notice things out on the road, too, things I'd seen a thousand times before and had liked without knowing why. Little details and imaginings I'd dismissed all my life as plain silliness suddenly became important. Like that stretch of road on the way back from the Glasgow run, when I would pass the turnoff for Larbert. I used to see it all the time: a blue road sign and a row of cherry-cola street lamps running off into the distance – Larbert, A9. It was odd how much I liked that sign. I'd never had reason to go to Larbert. We didn't do any runs in that direction, but maybe that was why I'd always liked the name. Larbert. It sounded like a place where the teen-age years went on forever, all gray days by the water and strange-tasting sweets that fizzed in your mouth, making you think of the possibility of sex. Not that I had ever known much about sex as a teen-ager, other than what I saw in films and the oddly pleasurable discomfort I felt when Rita Compton visited my sister.

That was the kind of stuff that was running through my head when I came across the boy, a few hundred yards into the woods, in the first of the heavy rain. I was thirty miles from home when it started, a thick sleet that might turn to snow later, or might come to nothing; it was already dark enough for headlights, but as I came into the woods, passing under the beech trees, it was like entering a little theatre, the lights flickering across the darkness, the woods black and still, like a backdrop. I'd always liked that about the woods, the way they suddenly closed in on me as if a story were about to be told. Like when I was a boy, and the announcer on "Listen with Mother" would say, "Are you sitting comfortably? Then I'll begin." Usually the road was empty, with maybe the odd set of head-lamps – not a person, not even a car, just an effect of the light – streaming past in the opposite direction. But that night the story contained another character, though he wasn't a character from any of the children's books I knew.

To begin with, I thought he was a woman. Maybe I wouldn't have stopped if I'd known otherwise. He certainly looked like a woman: a black dress, no coat, fish-net stockings, ankle boots, shoulder-length wavy hair. She was walking slow-ly, toward the far end of that little avenue of beech trees, and I couldn't make out much, but when my lights picked her out she turned, and I saw that there was something odd about her, something heavy. Not that I guessed right away that she was a boy. It was dark and rainy, and then, when I saw her properly, I was distracted by the bruises on her face: the bruises, the mess her hair was in, the dark stain that might have been blood on her right leg, just below the hem of the dress.

I didn't pick up hitchhikers much. I did in the early days, and I'd enjoyed the chat most of the time. Not always, but enough to make it worthwhile. More recently, though, I'd preferred being alone in the cab. Some nights, coming home in the dark, reeling off the narrow roads that ran to Perth or St. Andrews, re-membering the way by my own landmarks – the hedges and drystone dykes and the spaces between them that other people didn't even notice, tight angles of holly or lamplight as I came through a town – I would realize, with a pleasant rush of surprise, that I was fond of myself as I was, fond of my life, and yet, at the same time, not that worried about having to let it go. I had got past the stage when company seemed like a good thing on the road, and I have to admit that I thought about driving on that night, even after I'd noticed the gash on her leg. I didn't need complications, and by then everything that wasn't part of the usual schedule had come to seem unnecessarily complicated. Nevertheless, I made myself stop, and I pulled up alongside her – still thinking of this person on the road as a woman, possibly a woman in real difficulty – just to check, at least, that she was all right. I rolled down the window and leaned across to the passenger side. "You look like you ran into some trouble," I called out, trying to make myself heard above the engine and, at the same time, not to be so loud that I might frighten her.

The moment I put on the brake, she stopped walking – and that was when I realized that she wasn't a woman. She looked up, and I could see it in everything about her: the way she stood, the darkness in her face, the heaviness. It was a boy, not a woman. Not a man, either, just a boy of eighteen or twenty, fairly thickset and not at all feminine. When he looked up at me, I saw the fear in his face, behind the mass of wet makeup and mascara, a fear that he wanted, but couldn't quite manage, to hide. "I'm O.K.," he said, but he stayed where he was, stock still, waiting.

"Where are you headed?" I said, switching off the ignition and trying to keep the surprise out of my voice.

"Home," he said. Then he mumbled something else that I couldn't make out.

"What was that?" I said.

He shook his head. He seemed desperate, though I wasn't sure if he was desperate to be helped or to be left alone – at least, not until he spoke. "I'll be fine," he said.

I knew then that he wanted to trust me enough to get him home safe and dry. I also knew that he didn't trust anybody, not right at that moment, anyway. "Well," I said, "I'm Bill Harley. I'm on my way home from a long run delivering molasses, and it's nearly Christmas, so I'm not going to leave you out here in the dark."

Something changed in him then. Maybe it struck him as funny that I was talking about molasses, but he seemed to soften. He moved closer to the cab and tried to see inside. "I'm going home," he said. "It's just down this road." He looked up into my face. "I'll be fine," he added, though he sounded less convinced than before.

"Oh, come on," I said. "Do yourself a favor. We'll get you home, and you can get cleaned up." I swung the passenger-side door open.

The boy nodded. I suppose he'd sized me up and decided it was worth the risk. Or maybe he was just past caring and the promise of shelter was more than he could resist. "All right," he said. "It's very kind of you."

I nodded, then waited while he climbed in. He had a bit of trouble with that, what with the dress and the sling-back shoes, which I assumed he wasn't used to, but finally he got himself settled and pulled the door shut. I looked at him for a moment in the golden light from the overhead, then I started the engine as casually as I could. "Well," I said, raising my voice so he could hear me above the noise. "Where are you headed?"

"Coaltown?"

I nodded and turned back toward the road. It was a good twenty miles to Coaltown, not just down the road, but I had to pass it on my way home anyway. "O.K.," I said.

"You know it?"

"I used to work there," I said. "Long time ago."

"Well, he said. "You'll not find it much changed. I guarantee you that."

"I don't suppose I will," I said, releasing the hand brake. As I did, I caught sight of the gash on his leg. It looked nasty, but the bleeding seemed to have stopped. There was dirt all over his legs and hands, dirt and blood dried into the mesh of his fish-net stockings. His face was badly bruised, as if someone had punched him several times. I turned back toward the road, but I knew that he'd noticed me looking at him.

"I'm all right," he said. "Just a few cuts and grazes."

I shook my head. "It's a bit more than that," I said.

He let out a short, hard laugh, as if I'd made some joke at his expense. "I suppose it is," he said – and I detected something in his voice, more of a drift than a slur, that suggested he might be on something.

"Well," I said. "It's none of my business. But I've got a first-aid kit in the box behind you." I tilted my head toward the back. "If you want to get yourself sorted out."

"I'm fine," he said. "But thanks, anyway." He shot me a quick glance, then looked away. "I've had worse."

"Really?"

"Rules of the game," he said. "It's not as bad as it looks. I just went to the wrong party." He glanced out at the side mirror. "I suppose it was a mistake, going for the Aileen Wuornos look." I had to think about that for a moment, before I remembered who he was talking about, and he must have seen the realization dawn in my face, because he laughed again, louder and more confident this time. "Don't worry, Bill," he said. "I didn't bring the gun."

I had to smile at that. "Well," I said. "There's a relief."

He laughed again, but this time his laughter was good-humored and warm, and I was suddenly glad that I'd stopped. "So," he said. "Where are you headed, Bill Harley?"

"Home," I said, and I realized that I didn't want to think about home, at least for the moment. I wanted to be out on the road still, out on the road on a winter's night, with no set destination, passing the time with someone I'd never see again.

"Ah, yes," he said. "Home." He dwelled on the word for the moment before moving on. "Soon be Christmas," he said.

"Not long." I looked over at him; he was watching me, attentive, taking me in, maybe searching for something that he thought I wanted to keep hidden – and I had an image of Caroline, of how she had watched me like that sometimes when she was younger, hoping for a clue to what lay behind the façade that she thought I was working so hard to maintain. Maybe that was what made me say what I said next, surprising myself, and the boy. I didn't say it very loudly, and I wasn't really speaking to him, but it was loud enough to be audible above the noise of the engine. "One last Christmas," I said. "Better make the most of it, eh?"

It wasn't what I'd intended to say, though I wasn't sorry I'd said it. Still, I had no wish to pursue the notion any further, now that it was out – and I think he understood that, because, after allowing just enough space for what I might say next, he let it go without another word, and we drove on in silence, staring out from our separate places into the sleety darkness, our faces filling with light from time to time as a car passed from the opposite direction. It was slow going, then, but the silence didn't bother me; if anything, it felt strangely comfortable, like having a passenger in the cab and being alone at the same time. After a while, though, the boy picked up the conversation, slipping casually into the kind of slow-moving, pointless talk that goes on between people of good will who don't know each other well: stuff about football – I was surprised by that, though I suppose I shouldn't have been – and some documentary he'd seen on television. It could have been anybody in the cab with me, to begin with at least, but then he started talking about other things, minor stuff about his school days mostly, only it was funny and good-humored, and all the time I knew he was really talking about something else altogether, some other story about himself that he wanted to tell, not out of need but because it was interesting. Like his memory of the school atlas that he'd been given in geography class – how he had loved the way the world was all mapped out, all the colors and lines and borders perfect and just, so that it looked like the kind of world it would be a pleasure to inhabit, an utterly fictional world where you could never be lost, because everybody and everything belonged somewhere. I enjoyed that, for as long as it lasted, partly because it felt new, to be driving along like this, talking to a boy in a dress and runny makeup, but also because he was such good company. When we finally reached the turn for Coaltown, he leaned forward in his seat slightly. "If you drop me here, that'll be fine," he said.

I shook my head. I didn't want to leave him in the dark, on another stretch of featureless road. "I'll take you to your door," I said. "It's no trouble."

"Thanks, Bill," he said. "But I'd rather walk from here. No offense." He looked over at me, and, even out of the corner of my eye, I could see that he was hoping he hadn't somehow insulted me.

"None taken," I said, but I turned off the main road and carried on a few hundred yards toward the coast before I stopped.

"Thanks," he said.

"Don't mention it," I said.

He put his hand on the door, as if to go, then he turned and smiled, not so much at me as at something that had just crossed his mind. "It's not how you think it is," he said. I felt uneasy, as if he were breaking some prearranged code and had started telling me a secret that I wasn't supposed to know. "I'm happy with how things are, most of the time," he said, and it was as if he were talking to someone else, trying to persuade them that what he was saying was true. Someone else, or himself, or a little of both. "So that question in your mind," he said. "You might as well forget it."

I nodded, but I didn't say anything. I really didn't want to make something of it, even if there was a question in my mind, because it probably wasn't the question he thought I wanted to ask. I didn't need to know about his life, or what he did sexually, or what he wanted to do, or any of those things. I certainly didn't want to know what the wrong party had been, or how he had come by his cuts and bruises. Some part of me was curious about him, but it was his happiness that I was curious about – because I thought he wanted me to imagine him as happy, and I wondered why it mattered to him. Or maybe I was just surprised that he seemed to believe that happiness was possible – and probably that was why I asked him the question I thought he wanted to hear, because, even on such short acquaintance, I liked him and I wished him well, at least. It was a piece of shorthand, I suppose, for all the other questions, the ones about happiness and being alone and getting home safe. It was also nothing at all. "Do you know what you're doing?" I said.

The boy laughed. "Never," he said, with a little too much emphasis. "But you have to pretend, Bill." He regarded me for a moment. "If you don't pretend," he said, "you're lost."

I had no idea what he was talking about, but I understood anyway. He couldn't do anything else, was what he meant. He couldn't do anything different, and neither could anybody else. "Well," I said. "You be careful now."

He slid down off the seat and turned back toward me. "You, too, Bill," he said. He'd said my name again, and I suddenly realized that I didn't know his. "Have a good Christmas," he said.

"You, too," I said. Then I slipped into gear, released the hand brake, and pulled away, leaving him there in the slow, dark sleet. I didn't look back through the side mirror so I didn't see what he did next, and it wasn't until I was some miles farther down the road that I realized that he hadn't wanted to talk about himself at all, but was just giving me something back, and I felt sorry not to have understood it at the time, but glad, too, because, out on the road, in the cold, any gift is better than nothing.

After I dropped the boy off, the weather cleared a little, and the last ten miles took next to no time. I liked that final stretch, the road going straight along the coast for a while, the water big and empty to the south, the fields and low hills above spotted with light here and there from farmsteads and faraway cottages. By the time I turned off and began climbing the rise toward home, the sleet had stopped altogether; a few miles farther, I came within sight of my own village, not much more than a row of houses straggling along a back road, a brief distraction on the way to somewhere else. The lights here always seemed dull and brownish in comparison with the fairy-tale silver of the lights I'd seen from the high road, and it struck me, sometimes, coming home late, that I knew the place too well. I knew all the stories. I knew what the people were doing behind those windows. I could see the abandoned dinner tables and the stone sculleries, the muddy boots on the doormat, the piles of newly opened letters on the sideboard, the silent men sitting in worn armchairs in the kitchen, watching television.

When I reached my own cottage, I parked the rig in the lay-by opposite and let myself in through the side gate, coming across the garden to the back door, which was always left unlocked. The house was silent, almost dark; the one lamp burning was in the dining room, a room we hardly ever used, preferring to eat in the creaturely warmth of the kitchen. I wasn't surprised that Sall was in there, though: that was where we kept the things that her real life was made from – the best china and the family albums and the framed pictures from what she probably thought were better days. I opened the back door and went through the kitchen as quietly as I could – quieter, those last months, than I'd ever been before, as if the promise of death had revealed a carefulness in me that I'd never suspected – and I found Sall sleeping in the big armchair by the fireplace, a magazine on the floor by her feet, an empty mug cradled in her lap. Asleep like that, unguarded, her head leaning heavily to one side, she looked old and tired, but at least the worry that usually haunted her face was gone, and, as I stood watching her, it struck me that she was dreaming. I knew she would be upset if she woke up and found that I'd come home while she was sleeping, but I stood a moment longer, watching her dream and wondering how she had spent the day, what she had thought about, what she had done. After a moment, though, I felt uncomfortable spying on her like that, and I walked back through to the kitchen, to let her rest.

It was colder than ever now, but the sky had cleared, and a bright moon had emerged from the clouds, cold and white in a pool of indigo sky right above the garden. I put the kettle on, then I stepped outside and stood on the patio, looking over the fields to the stand of trees and the long stone wall that I knew were just beyond, black and irrefutably solid in the darkness. It was almost completely silent: from time to time, a dog barked at the end of the road, or the odd gust of wind caught in the beech hedge by Sall's flower border; then, after a minute or so, the kettle began to sing quietly, and, as I felt the silence slipping away, I tried to capture it all, to drink it all in, before Sall woke up and I wasn't alone anymore. This was my life, these were the times when I was true: in these half hours here and there when I felt alone in the house, or those fleeting moments out on the road, when I opened a gate and crossed an empty farmyard, a stranger, even to myself, in the quiet of the afternoon. The best part of the day was getting up at dawn and going down to the cool gray kitchen, the dark garden waiting at the door like some curious beast strayed in from the fields, a casual attentiveness in the coming light that seemed ready to include me, as it did everything else, in a soft, foreign stillness. That was the best, because I knew Sall would stay in bed until after I left, whether she was awake or not – though times like tonight were almost as good. It had become more frequent of late, this coming home and knowing that Sall was asleep somewhere, the magazine she had been reading slipped to the floor, a mug of tea cooling on a side table. It felt like coming home to another house, a place full of secrets, a childhood still there, intact among the green shadows under the stairs. First love, too – though not for Sall, as it happened, even though I'd never known anyone else, or not in that way. No: if thirty years of marriage and bringing up a child had taught me anything, it was that through everything, through all the Christmases and birthdays, through all the mishaps and misunderstandings, almost nothing had been shared. Everything that happened had happened to us separately, and, afterward, in my own mind, it all had a strangely abstract feel: a marriage inferred from picture books and Saturday matinées, a love that didn't quite materialize, a series of other lives that had involved me for a while then shied away, the way an animal does when you make the wrong move and remind it of what you really are.

The kettle was whistling now, and I thought to leave it, so that Sall would have to get up and turn off the gas. That way, I could pretend I hadn't seen her sleeping. It felt too close, seeing her like that. It was as if I were breaking the rules we had worked for years to set up, a system of small courtesies and avoidances and slow, fluid conversations that ran for days, pieces of hearsay and local news passed back and forth over meals and cups of tea to cover the bewildered quiet that had fallen upon us. It was awkward sometimes, but it did work, and it was better than any of the possible alternatives. For a moment, I thought of the boy on the road and wondered if it would ever come to this for him, if he would ever come home and find someone he cared for, but no longer loved, asleep in an armchair. It was a tender thought, I suppose, but it wasn't sad, or sentimental, and it had nothing to do with death. It was just a notion, passing through my mind, while I waited for the kettle to stop whistling.

Only it didn't stop, and after a while I walked back inside and turned off the gas myself. At exactly the same moment, Sall came through, her eyes bleary, an odd, faraway look on her face. She seemed surprised to see me, as if she hadn't heard the kettle at all but had just woken up in what she thought was an empty house – and it struck me, for the first time, how difficult it would be for her, having me die first.

"You're back," she said. It sounded like an accusation. She glanced at the clock, but she didn't say anything else.

"It was a long run," I said. "I just got in."

She nodded. "I haven't made you anything," she said. "I didn't know when you'd be finished."

"It's all right," I said. "I'm not that hungry."

She gave me a quick, scared look. "You've got to eat," she said.

"I'll have an omelette or something later," I said. "I was just making coffee, if you want some."

"I'll make it," she said. "You sit down. You've had a long day."

I nodded, but I didn't move. The door was still open, just enough that I could smell the cold outside, and I heard the dog barking – farther away now, it seemed, at the darker end of the road that ran past our house and into the hills, past the golden lights of farms and dairies and narrow sheep runs through the gorse, where snow was probably beginning to form – real snow this time, not the cold sleet I'd driven through in the woods where I met the boy. For a split second – no more – I wanted to get back in the rig and drive on, up into the darkness, into the origin of the approaching blizzard, just to be alone out there, the way that boy had been alone in the woods. Then, with Sall watching me curiously, and perhaps fearfully, I let go of that thought and went through to the living room, where the curtains were already drawn and the night was nothing more than a story to be told by a warm fire, with the radio humming quietly in the background, so that the world felt familiar and more or less happy, like the future that seemed possible when you didn't think about dying, or the pastel-colored maps in a childhood atlas that you couldn't help but go on trusting, even when you knew that they no longer meant what they said.

SUMMER OF '38

Colm Tóibín

Colm Tóibín (b.1955) was born in Wexford, Ireland. His work includes
The Heather Blazing, The Master, Brooklyn, The Testament of Mary and,
most recently, *Nora Webster*. He has been awarded the Encore Award,
the International IMPAC Dublin Literary Award, the Costa Novel Award
and been shortlisted for the Booker Prize several times. He lives in
Dublin.

Montse held the door of the lift open for her daughter and put her hand
in her coat pocket to make sure that she had her keys. She would walk
Ana to her car, which was parked nearby, then, once Ana had driven
away, continue on the short distance to the town center to get some groceries. It
was easier like this, easier than having Ana say goodbye to her in the apartment,
easier than hearing the lift door close, knowing that there was nothing except
the night ahead, no other sound but the traffic outside and the birdsong, which
would die out when darkness fell.

"Oh, I meant to say that the man – you know, the man from the electric company –" Ana looked at her as though the man were someone she should know.
"The one I told you about – he knew I was your daughter and he's writing a
book about the war in his spare time and he asked me where you lived."

"I don't know that man at all," Montse said as she closed the front door of
the building. "I've never had anyone from fecsa in the apartment. He is mixing
me up with someone else."

She liked to sound firm and in control. It saved her daughters from having to
worry about her living on her own.

"Well, anyway, he said he knows you, and I gave him the address. So if he calls
on you, that will be why."

"The war?"

"He's collecting information on the war."

"Does he think I was in the war?"

"I don't know what he's doing exactly. He's writing a book."

"Well, I am sure he can write it without my help."

"He's nice. I mean, if there's ever a problem with the electricity, he comes."

"Don't be giving my address out to people."

They had reached Ana's car. Montse saw that Ana was not even listening to
her. Her youngest daughter, the one who lived closest by, took things lightly. She
was, Montse thought, probably relieved that her weekly visit to her mother was
over and she was on her way home.

Montse went out three times a day, even in winter. There was always something to buy, if only a loaf of bread or a newspaper. It meant that she took some exercise and saw people.

The week after Ana had mentioned the man from the electric company, Montse saw him waiting at the front door of her building when she came home with a bag of fruit. She did know him, she realized; he was someone she often saw on the street. She must have been aware, too, that he worked for fecsa, although she couldn't think how she knew this. She didn't think she knew his name or anything else about him.

Once he had introduced himself, she realized that he wanted to come up to the apartment with her. She was unsure about this. Since Paco died, she had become protective of her own space and she disliked surprises. She even asked her daughters to phone at appointed times. But there was something both eager and easygoing in this man's manner and she knew that it would sound rude if she asked him to say whatever he had to say in the hallway of the building. Also, she thought, if something ever went wrong with her electricity, it would be useful to know a man who could fix it.

"Ana may have told you what I am doing," he said, once he was sitting in the armchair opposite hers with a glass of water in his hand.

She nodded but said nothing.

"I am trying to chart every event of the war, just in this valley and the mountains," he said.

"I wasn't involved in the war," she replied. "My father wasn't even involved. And I had no brothers."

"Oh, no, it wasn't to ask you anything, but to say that a retired general in Madrid – actually, he's from Badajoz – who was here during the war is coming back to show me where the dugouts were and exactly where the guns were positioned. He hasn't been here since then."

"One of Franco's generals?"

"Yes, though he wasn't a general during the war. I found his name and address and wrote to him. I didn't expect a reply, but he is coming. I spoke to him on the phone and the only person he remembered here, besides the other soldiers, was you. He remembered your name and said that he would like to see you. I asked around, because I didn't recognize your maiden name. I asked around without telling anyone why."

"And what is his name?"

"Ramirez. Rudolfo Ramirez. He was high up in the Army when he retired. I didn't ask him how old he was, but he sounded in good shape. Still drives a car."

Montse nodded calmly and then looked toward the window, as though distracted by something.

"There were a few of them," she said. "I'm not sure I would remember him. We didn't have much to do with them, as you can imagine."

"Anyway, he's coming here on Saturday of next week. There will be no big fuss – I've assured him of that. I've told no one that he is coming, except you. He'll show me what he needs to show me and then I'll take him to Lleida to catch the train back to Madrid. But he said that he would come for lunch at Mirella's, and when I told him that you were still living here he asked if you might join us."

"I'm here all right," she said, "but I don't go out much."

"I understand. But no one will know who he is. I could collect you and drop you back if that would suit you."

"The war was a long time ago." She was going to say something else and then hesitated. "It was fifty years ago. More."

"I know. It was hard for all of you who lived through it. The more I find out about it, the clearer it is how much it divided people. I'm trying to get the facts right while there is still time. It's history now – at least, for the younger generation it is."

She smiled.

"Anyway, yours was the name he gave me, and he seemed delighted to hear that you were well."

"I'm not sure I would know him. In fact, I'm sure I wouldn't."

"Shall I drop by next week and see what you think?"

"If you want, but I don't go out much. I've never been to Mirella's."

"Well, it's Saturday week at two o'clock, and, as I said, it would be just the three of us and no one any the wiser. He won't be in uniform, or anything like that."

"I'm sure he hasn't been in uniform for a long time if he was one of Franco's generals," she said, and then instantly regretted having sounded so sure, so up to date, since she wished to give the impression that she was old and living in her own world.

"It is good of him to come," the man said. "I was surprised."

Montse looked back toward the window and did not reply. She hoped that it was clear to her visitor that he should go.

Rudolfo would be over eighty now, she calculated. But he would still have something of what he had then, even if it lurked beneath sagging flesh and stiff hesitant movements. She pictured an old man getting slowly out of an old-fashioned car, his hair white, his frame frail. Maybe he would still have something of the effortless charm that had come to him that summer as naturally as light did to the morning.

It was the summer of '38, when the prisoners had all been taken to Lleida or Tremp. Those who had avoided capture had fled to the mountains or crossed the border into France or fled south to Barcelona. The town was quiet for a week or more – no one was sure who would come back or what would happen. The dam was being protected by Franco's soldiers, that was all. Then more of his soldiers began to pile in, and they took over the town hall, and they put up tents on the grounds of the school. Orders were given that shops and bars were to resume their normal hours.

At first, she remembered, people were afraid and stayed indoors. There were rumors that they were all going to be taken away, every house cleared, even the houses that had nothing to do with the war. Under cover of darkness, some people made their way into the mountains or toward the border. Everyone was waiting for something to happen. But nothing happened except that ordinary life came back, or something like it. Once the shops had reopened and there was Mass again on Sundays, the talk was about the dam and how carefully it was being guarded, and about a clearing that the soldiers had made by the edge of the water and the makeshift bar they had built and the fire they lit every night to keep the mosquitoes away. The talk was of the supplies of food they had, and the guitar playing and singing and dancing.

She did not go there at first, but girls she knew did and even some of the older people who wanted to forget about the war.

Later, Rudolfo told her that he had seen her on the street, noticed her as she went shopping with her mother and her sisters, but she did not think that that was true. However, she was sure that she had noticed him the night she first went down to the makeshift bar. It was the way he seemed to be amused by things that drew her attention, the way he smiled. His hair was cut short; he was not as tall as some of the others. He was in uniform, his shirt unbuttoned. As he sat there watching, the soldiers began to play music you could dance to, slow songs. Some of them danced with girls from the town.

There was, she remembered, a swagger about the soldiers, which faded slowly as the night wore on, and there was something uneasy, too, which meant that when the music became sad they all seemed more comfortable, even the ones who were not dancing. When the soldiers were joined by others, who had just come off duty, there were sudden bursts of gaiety – shouting and clapping and drinking. Only Rudolfo sat quietly, observing the scene.

She realized that he had noticed her. Once, he nodded to her. It could have been a casual gesture, except that it was not. She knew that it was not.

After a while, when one of her friends left, she left, too. She did not go there the following night. The next time she went, he was there as before, apart from the others, watching, amused by it all. He did not stir, merely made it clear that he knew she was there; once again, he took no part in the dancing or the showing off around the fire.

He let her know by looking at her that he wanted her and that the rest – the drinking, the dancing, the boyish antics – did not interest him. He was shy, almost retiring, but seemed also entirely sure of himself. She didn't believe that anything would happen between them. She didn't think that he would move toward her or do anything to damage his self-contained observation of the scene around him.

Yet he kept his eye on her, and she returned his glances, careful that none of her friends were looking.

One night, there was a full moon and a clear sky. When the crowd moved to the edge of the water and let the fire die down, neither he nor she moved with them. When he spoke to her, she could not hear him, so he moved closer. She realized that no one had noticed that she had not joined the others by the water. Some of the soldiers there had stripped down and were swimming and splashing. Away from them, close to the dying embers, he touched the back of her hand and then turned it and traced his fingers on the palm.

There was an old ruined building nearby. They walked slowly toward it and when they leaned against the wall she was relieved that all he wanted to do was kiss her and smile at her in between the kisses. In all the years since, she had never forgotten the sweet smell of his breath, his eagerness and good humor.

The next night, he found them a place where they could lie together undisturbed, and that was what they did every night until September came.

Every day that summer she waited for the evening. Her friends knew that she was with Rudolfo, but most of the girls who went to the makeshift bar had found boyfriends among the soldiers. No one ever talked about it. When her mother asked her if she had been to the soldiers' parties, she shrugged and said that she had passed by once or twice, but had walked on with her friends. When her mother asked her a second time, a few nights later, she was careful to come home early for once, so that no one at home would have an idea what she was doing.

She wondered now if she remembered correctly that the weather had changed as soon as the bombardment of the villages on the other side of the river began. Perhaps the man from the electric company would know. The bombardment began, in any case, toward the end of summer. The sound came in the night but often in the day, too, the sound of heavy artillery from up the valley. The villages that had remained with the Loyalists were being attacked.

She remembered her father saying that the soldiers had spent the summer preparing for this assault, that they had been building dugouts and finding the best positions and carrying the heavy guns there. They had left nothing to chance, once they secured the dam. He added that there was no hospital on the other side and no medicine, and the soldiers were letting no one cross the footbridge at Llavorsí or the bridge in Sort. People were trapped, he said, and the injured were dying of their wounds.

It struck her that the parties by the water were where the troops who'd been working all day preparing the guns came to relax. But she did not feel guilty. Instead, she hoped that those who had noticed her presence at the soldiers' bonfires would have their own reasons to keep silent about it. In the years afterward, everyone – even those who had been there every night – pretended that none of it had happened.

It was the change in the weather that changed everything – she was almost sure of that. It was a gray day, with the mist that came over the valley in September, when she realized that she knew only Rudolfo's name and that he came from Badajoz. By that time he was gone, and it struck her that he would, in all likelihood, not be returning. The realization broke the spell that had been cast on her, by the war itself as much as by Rudolfo.

It was not until then that she began to worry that she was pregnant. It was not only that she had missed her period; something in her body had changed. She waited and hoped that she was wrong. She woke in terror some nights, but in the day she tried to behave normally. In the meantime, the war went on up the valley, and jeeps and trucks full of soldiers and supplies drove through the town, and the town was often desolate, the main square empty, even though the bars and most of the shops remained open.

When she was sure that she was pregnant she decided that she would marry Paco Vendrell. For years at the town festivals he had followed her around, offering to buy her drinks, asking her to dance and, when she refused, standing on his own and observing her with a single-mindedness that made her shiver. He was ten years her senior, but had seemed middle-aged even when he was younger. Since he had begun working in the control room of the dam, when he was fourteen or fifteen, he had spoken of little else: the levels of water in the two rivers, or in the lake itself, or the flow of water that could be expected soon, or the difference between this year and last year. Montse's father laughed at him, and for her mother and her sisters the idea that he had been pursuing her since she was sixteen or seventeen was a source of regular jokes. She did her best to avoid him, and if she could not avoid him then she openly rebuffed his efforts to speak to her.

Now she urgently wanted to meet him. For a few days, she watched to see if she could run into him on his way to work. Since she did not see him walking to the dam, she supposed that he was taken there by military jeep now, and brought home in the same way in the evening. No one, she knew, was allowed to approach the road that led to the control tower overlooking the dam. The only time she could be sure that she would encounter Paco, she thought, was at Sunday Mass. She would have to be brave and move fast and not worry about other people watching and commenting. The opportunity to meet him might not come every Sunday.

Fortunately, there was only one Mass on Sunday these days, and the church was more crowded than it had ever been, as the people of the town, even those who had no interest in religion, or who were known to have been with the Loyalists, set out to show the troops whose side they were on now. By the beginning of that winter, it had become clear to all of them who was going to win the war, and it was clear, too, that as soon as the war ended there would be many more accusations and arrests. She understood that there would be little pity for someone in her situation, no matter who the father of the child was.

That Sunday, she went to the church early, walking quietly and demurely in the street with a mantilla on her head and a prayer book in her hand. She was sure that Paco would go to Mass if he wasn't working; he was not the sort of man who stayed away. But she could not remember actually seeing him in the church and did not know if he stood at the back, as many of the men did, or if he walked right up and found a place close to the altar. She would need to find a good vantage point from which she could see everyone, but she could not, she thought, sit at the back of the church, as she had never done so before and might be spotted by neighbors or by her family, who would wonder what she was doing there.

She sat in one of the side pews and was early enough to witness the two priests arriving, the older one, whom she knew, and the younger one, whom she had never met. What she noticed, as they walked up the aisle to go to the vestry, was their bearing, how proud they seemed and severe. They could easily, she imagined, have approached the vestry from outside, but approaching it like this gave them more dignity and more importance.

Soon, they were followed by a group of soldiers in full uniform. For a second, she was startled by the idea that Rudolfo could be among them. She looked at them carefully, however, and did not see him. Even if he did appear, she thought, whatever had happened in the atmosphere between the summer and now would mean that he would not come near her or acknowledge her. She was sure that, even were she to approach him and try to talk, he would avoid her.

She shivered for a moment and then watched warily as the pews began to fill up with people who kept their eyes averted. She wondered when the war would be over and wondered also, as the panic that often came to her in the night returned, what would happen to her if she could not persuade Paco to marry her. It occurred to her that she would be sent away, that her father and mother would not be able to protect her, even if they wanted to.

But how would she marry Paco? How could it be done? She had been so rude to him in the past, so dismissive. How could she make it clear to him that she had changed her mind? What reason would she give? In this uncertain atmosphere, with the chance that many more people were going to be killed or locked up, no one was thinking of romance or marriage, least of all someone like Paco, who was cautious and whose daily work at the dam was likely more and more difficult. But there was no one else she could think of who might marry her.

In the reaches of the night, one other option had come to her, and it appeared to her again now. There was a secluded place above the river, about a kilometre up the valley, where the current was strong and the water deep. Over the years, two or three people had used this place to kill themselves and their bodies had not been found for days. She thought that maybe soon she should go and look at that spot, check if it was guarded by the troops. She closed her eyes at the thought of it and bowed her head.

When Communion was almost over, she saw Paco walking up the aisle. She knew then that he must have been standing at the back. She studied him carefully as he returned. His lips were moving in prayer; his hands were joined. He seemed even odder and more isolated than usual. She almost smiled at the courage, or the self-delusion, it must have taken for him to pursue her the way he had; she wondered what thoughts he must have had before going out on those evenings and how disappointed he must have been to go home alone, knowing that he had no chance with her. It struck her, too, that, since he worked at the dam with the soldiers, he would have known about the parties at the water's edge and might have heard that she was among the girls who had gone there. He might even have heard about her and Rudolfo. It occurred to her as she waited for Mass to end that he might want to have nothing to do with her now. And if he, who had been so enthusiastic, did not want her, then she was sure, absolutely sure, that no one else would want her, either.

She moved quickly as the ceremony came to an end. Paco was not the sort of man who stood at the church gates after Mass with a group of friends. In any case, no one would want to be seen standing around now. When she walked out of the church grounds she saw that he was already a block away. She followed him as quickly as she could, hoping that no one would see her. She had prepared what she would say to him. It was important to make it seem plausible, natural.

When he turned, he gave her a look that was anxious and withdrawn, and then almost hostile, as if to say that he had enough problems without her chasing him down to let him know yet again that she had no interest in him. He turned his back to her before she had a chance to smile. As he walked faster, she grew more determined. If he had wanted her before, she figured, he would still want her now. All she had to do was be careful and hide all signs of panic as she spoke to him.

Eventually, when he looked back again and saw her, he stopped.

"I have to go home to change my clothes," he said, "and then they'll collect me. They are very busy at the dam. Everything has to be noted and written down."

She smiled. "Well, I'll walk along with you so I won't delay you," she said. "We are all worried at home. You know, I have no brothers. And my father says that we cannot go out alone now, not even just to the shops. So I am locked in the house or that's what it seems like."

They continued walking. She feared that if she stopped talking for one second he would tell her something about the dam and everything she had already said would be forgotten.

"If you were free some time, it would be great if you could call at the house and maybe we could go for a walk, if only through the town and then home again. But maybe you are too busy."

"There's a new captain from Madrid and he's a stickler for notes, and they all watch me in case I decide to pull one of the levers when they are not looking. You know, I'm the only one who fully understands the switching system, though the new fellow from Madrid is beginning to get the hang of it."

She wondered whether, if she concentrated hard enough, she might get through to him. But she said nothing as they came to the town center and then it was too late.

"Anyway," he said, "I'd better get going. I can't use this suit in the control room. It's the only good suit I have."

When Paco called two days later, one of her sisters answered the door and did not disguise her amusement or keep her voice down. Montse found her coat and left with him. During the weeks that followed he called every few days. Her sisters and her mother made jokes about him, at first, then expressed puzzlement, and finally grew silent. Not one of them asked her what she was doing walking around the town with Paco Vendrell and having hot chocolate with him in one of the granjas.

He talked to her about the dam, explaining its strategic importance and how old some of the systems were, which meant that only someone experienced could deal with the levers, someone who knew that a few of them would not respond if pulled too fast, and also that if one of them was pulled halfway it would have the same effect as pulling it the whole way.

She already knew that he lived with his mother but found out now that his father had died when he was young. She discovered that he liked routines, liked going to work at the same time every day, and disliked the soldiers' efforts to vary his timetable. Within a week, she, too, was part of his routine. Chatting to her, he seemed comfortable. She realized that he would be content to meet this way for months, maybe even years. He was not someone who would make a quick decision or want a sudden change in his life. And, like everyone, he knew that things would be very different when the war was over. He had a way of addressing the matters that interested him slowly and deliberately. Her efforts to speed things up, to ask him, for example, if he was happy living with his mother, failed completely. He did not register anything that interfered with the current of his own conversation.

When Christmas came, there were more and more rumors. Whole families disappeared, and houses became vacant. Her father said that anyone who had the slightest reason to leave should go now. She continued seeing Paco, although he was more cautious as they walked around the town, hoping not to be noticed by the troops.

One evening as she stood up from the table she saw her mother's eyes resting on her belly. She waited until they were alone in the kitchen.

"How soon?" her mother asked.

"Five months, maybe a bit less."

"Is Paco the father?'

"No."

"Does he know?'

"No."

"Is that why you are seeing him – so that he will marry you?"

"Yes, but he's in no hurry."

"Was it one of the soldiers?"

"Yes."

"And he has disappeared?"

"Yes."

Her mother looked at her.

"Let me deal with Paco," she said.

For the next two weeks Paco did not come around. The weather grew cold and there was snow. Sometimes they could hear rifle fire in the distance, even during the day. Feigning sickness, Montse stayed in bed, joining the others only for meals. She waited for her mother to come into the bedroom and tell her that it could not be done, that Paco would not marry her. She imagined then how she would have to brave the cold and avoid the soldiers, find a quiet time and move as though invisible. She tried to imagine what it would be like to jump into a deep and fast-moving river, wondered how quickly she would sink, how long it would take her to drown. As she lay in bed, another scenario came to her: she would be sent to a convent or an orphanage somewhere and the baby would be taken from her as soon as it was born. She would not be allowed to come home. Maybe that would be preferable.

Eventually, when the house was silent one day, her mother came to tell her that the wedding was arranged. It would happen in a few days in a side chapel and Paco would take full responsibility for the child.

"His mother seemed surprised and almost proud," her mother said. "She thinks the baby is his. Paco said that he has always wanted to marry you, that you are the girl for him, so at least someone is happy. There is a small flat at the top of the building where his mother lives. He is moving furniture in there right now. It would be lovely, Montse, if we didn't have to see too much of him. He has a way of wearing me down with his talk."

When her mother had finished speaking, Montse turned away from her and did not move again until she was sure that her mother had left the room.

As soon as Rosa was born, Paco wanted to hold her. In the days that followed, Montse watched him to see if he was holding the baby merely for her sake. She saw no sign of that, however. When Paco came home from work he wanted to know what the baby had been doing. Even being told that she had been sleeping was enough for him.

As they walked through the town with the baby, Montse was aware that other men were laughing at Paco because of his devotion to the baby. She knew that her family laughed at him, too. But Paco remained impervious to the laughter. When he was at home, he tried to amuse the baby; he soothed her if she cried. And, once Rosa learned to walk, Paco loved taking her out, moving as slowly as she wanted and holding her hand with pride.

Being married to him was strange. He never once asked about the father of the child. He seemed grateful and content with everything. Montse was grateful to him in return, but that did not keep her from feeling relieved when he left for work each day or when he fell asleep beside her in the bed. She was careful to disguise this, though. And slowly, as they had two more daughters and moved to a bigger apartment, she found that being polite to him took on a force of its own. She tolerated him, and then grew fond of him. Slowly, too, as she realized that her parents and her sisters were still laughing at him, she saw less of them. She began to feel a loyalty toward Paco, a loyalty that lasted for all the years of their marriage.

Rosa did not look like Montse or Paco, or her two sisters. Nor, Montse thought, did she resemble Rudolfo. All she had of her natural father was her way of staying apart. She had little interest in the company of other girls and yet everyone liked her. Although Paco was proud of his two other daughters, it was always clear that he loved Rosa best.

While the others settled locally, Ana in Sort and Nuria in La Seu, Rosa went to Barcelona and studied medicine. She married a fellow-doctor and opened a private clinic with him, using money that his family had given them. When Paco was dying, when his heart was giving out, Rosa insisted on looking after him herself. She sat with him in a private room at the clinic day and night. When he opened his eyes, all he looked for was Rosa.

By that time Rosa had three sons of her own, and it was in the sons, especially the eldest, Montse noticed, that Rudolfo appeared again. It was in their eyes, their coloring, but also in the slow way they smiled, in their shyness. Each year, when Rosa and her family holidayed close to Santa Cristina, on the Costa Brava, Montse spent two weeks with them. Once the oldest boy could drive, he would come to collect her. That journey, alone in the car with him, gave her pleasure.

When the man from the electric company came by again, she told him that she did not want to have lunch with him and the general, and that he should not press her as she was not feeling well.

"He will be very disappointed," the man said.

"Yes, I'm sure," she replied, realizing that the edge of bitterness in her voice had given away more than she'd meant to.

"We are all old now," she added in a softer tone, "and we can only do what we can."

"If you change your mind, perhaps you will let me know," the man said. He left her a phone number.

As soon as he had gone she phoned the clinic and left an urgent message for Rosa.

"I wonder if you could come here on the Saturday of next week," she asked, when Rosa called her back. "And if you could come on your own. If you can, I promise I won't ask you for anything for a long time."

"Are you sick?"

"No."

"Is it something else?"

"Don't ask, Rosa. Just come that day. Come for lunch. You needn't stay the night or anything."

She held her breath now and waited.

"I've looked at my diary," Rosa said. "I have a dinner that night."

"Great. So if you leave my house at four or five you'll be there in plenty of time."

"Have you seen a doctor?"

"You're a doctor, Rosa. I'll be seeing you."

"I'll bring my stethoscope." Rosa laughed.

"Just bring yourself."

She came not only with a stethoscope but with a device for measuring blood pressure and a set of needles to take blood samples and a cooler to keep the samples cold until she got back to Barcelona. She made her mother remove her blouse so that she could listen to her heart and her lungs. She drew blood slowly without speaking.

"I'm old," Montse said. "There is no point in checking me."

"You didn't sound well on the phone."

"No one my age ever sounds well on the phone."

"Why did you want me to come today?"

"Because I thought if I gave you an exact day you might be more likely to come than if I said just come any day. I hardly ever see you."

"I wish my husband knew me as well as you do," Rosa said. She seemed to be in good humor.

The table in the dining alcove was already set. Now Montse put a tray of canelones into the oven and brought a bowl of salad and two plates to the table and some bread. She asked Rosa about her husband and her sons.

"They are all wonderful. The only worry we have is that Oriol failed chemistry and has to repeat it."

"Does he still have that nice girlfriend he had in the summer?"

"He does, which is why he failed chemistry."

When they had eaten, she brought Rosa her coffee at the table near the window.

"I found a box of photographs," she said. "Some of them were taken before the war. They must have come from the old house when my mother died. I found them a year ago but I put them away because they made me too sad."

She went into her bedroom, where she had the box waiting on the chair where she normally put her clothes for the next day.

"I wondered," she said when she came back, "if we could pick out the best photos, the clearest, and if one of your boys, when they have time, could make copies for you and your sisters."

She began to put bundles of photographs on the table.

"This was my grandmother," she said, holding one up. "She lived with us until there was a falling out of some sort and then she lived with my aunt. She came from Andorra and my father always thought she had money, but, of course, she had none."

"Who is the baby on her lap?'

"That's me. There was a man who would come once a year with a camera and a booth and people would queue up."

They began to flip through other photographs. Most of them were of Montse and her sisters, taken on summer outings.

"I have some here with no people in them – one of the river when it was flooded, which my father must have taken, and one of the dam being built. I can't remember what year that was."

Rosa moved these aside and began to examine another bundle of photographs of Montse and her sisters and their friends.

"Those were taken well before the war," Montse said. "After the war I don't think people took photographs as much."

Rosa was studying a large-format photograph of a group on an outing with mountains in the background.

"Where is my father in this? Why isn't he in any of the pictures?" she asked.

"Your father always took the photographs," Montse replied.

She reached for another bundle.

"He might be in one of these, but he was the only one who had a camera in the years before the war and he liked taking photographs."

She glanced at Rosa, who was nodding.

"Anyway, if you want to take the whole box and select the best ones – and if the boys had time they could make copies. It all must seem like ancient history to them, but maybe it will mean more when they have their own families."

"I'll be very careful with them," Rosa said, picking up a photograph of herself as a teen-age girl with Paco, smiling, beside her.

"I think I took that one," Montse said.

"I might get it blown up a bit bigger and frame it," Rosa said.

When it was time to go, Montse carried the box of photographs to the lift and Rosa carried the medical equipment. Montse insisted on going down with her to her car.

"If that's too heavy, just tell me," Rosa said.

The car was parked close by. They put the box and the equipment on the back seat, and then Rosa embraced her, before opening the door and getting into the driver's seat.

Montse waved as the car pulled away. She knew that she could easily be seen by anyone approaching. She looked up the street toward the town center to check if there was a car coming. The lunch would be over around now, she thought, and Rudolfo and the man from the electric company would pass by as they drove toward Lleida. She waited a few minutes, but when she saw no car she decided to go back inside and clear away the dishes. Later, she thought, she would walk to the town center and do a bit of shopping.

Soon, she knew, there would be an old man standing at the station in Lleida as the train to Madrid arrived. He would get on the train slowly and then walk along the aisle to find his seat. He would, she imagined, be polite to those around him as he settled in for the journey. Rosa would be on the motorway that led in the other direction, her driving steady and competent as it always was. Montse sighed with quiet satisfaction as she thought of the two of them, moving so easily away from each other; they would both be home before night fell.

TWO BOYS

Lorrie Moore

Lorrie Moore (b.1957) was born in Glens Falls, New York. Her work regularly appears in *The New Yorker* and includes two novels, *Who Will Run the Frog Hospital?* and *A Gate at the Stairs* as well as her stories, the latest volume being *Bark*. She teaches English at the University of Wisconsin in Madison.

For the first time in her life, Mary was seeing two boys at once. It involved extra laundry, an answering machine, and dark solo trips in taxicabs, which, in Cleveland, had to be summoned by phone, but she recommended it in postcards to friends. She bought the ones with photos of the flats, of James Garfield's grave, or an Annunciation from the art museum, one with a peacock-handsome angel holding up fingers and whispering, *One boy, two boys.* On the back she wrote, *You feel so attended to! To think we all thought just one might amuse, let alone fulfill. Unveil thyself! Unblacken those teeth and minds! Get more boys in your life!*

Her nervous collapse was subtle. It took the form of trips to a small neighborhood park, for which she dressed all in white: white blouses, white skirts, white anklets, shoes flat and white as boat sails. She read Bible poetry in the shade on the ground or else a paperback she had found about someone alone on a raft in the ocean, surviving for forty days and nights on nail parings and fish. Mary spoke to no one. She read, and tried not to worry about grass stains, though sometimes she got up and sat on a bench, particularly if there was a clump of something nearby, or a couple making out. She needed to be unsullied, if only for an afternoon. When she returned home, she clutched her books and averted her gaze from the men unloading meat in front of her building. She lived in a small room above a meat company – Alexander Hamilton Pork – and in front, daily, they wheeled in the pale, fatty carcasses, hooked and naked, uncut, unhooved. She tried not to let the refrigerated smell follow her in the door, up the stairs, the vague shame and hamburger death of it, though sometimes it did. Every day she attempted not to step in the blood that ran off the sidewalk and collected in the gutter, dark and alive. At five-thirty she approached her own building in a halting tiptoe and held her breath. The trucks out front pulled away to go home, and the Hamilton Pork butchers, in their red-stained doctors' coats and badges printed from ten-dollar bills, hosed down the side-walk, leaving the block glistening like a canal. The squeegee kids at the corner would smile at Mary and then, low on water, rush to dip into the puddles and smear their squeegees, watery pink, across the windshields of cars stopped for the light. "Hello," they said. "Hello, hello."

"Where have you been?" asked Boy Number One on the phone in the evening. "I've been trying to reach you." He was running for a local congressional seat, and Mary was working for him. She distributed fliers and put up posters on kiosks and trees. The posters consisted of a huge, handsome photograph with the words *Number One* underneath. She usually tried to staple him through the tie, so that it looked like a clip, but when she felt tired, or when he talked too much about his wife, she stapled him right in the eyes, like a corpse. He claimed to be separating. Mary knew what *separating* meant: The head and the body no longer consult; the wife sleeps late, then goes to a shrink, a palm reader, an acupuncturist; the fat rises to the top. Number One was dismantling his life. Slowly, he said. Kindly. He had already fired his secretary, gotten a new campaign manager, gone from stocks to bonds to cash, and sold some lakefront property. He was liquidating. Soon the sleeping wife. "I just worry about the boys," he said. He had two.

"Where have I been?" echoed Mary. She searched deep in her soul. "I've been at the park, reading."

"I miss you," said Number One. "I wish I could come see you this minute." But he was stuck far away in a house with a lid and holes punched in for air; there was grass at the bottom to eat. He also had a small apartment downtown, where the doorman smiled at Mary and nodded her in. But this evening One was at the house with the boys; they were sensitive and taciturn and both in junior high.

"Hmmm," said Mary. She was getting headaches. She wondered what Number Two was doing. Perhaps he could come over and rub her back, scold the pounding and impounding out of her temples, lay on hands, warm and moist. "How is your wife?" asked Mary. She looked at her alarm clock.

"Sleeping," said One.

"Soon you will join her cold digits," said Mary. One fell silent. "You know, what if I were sleeping with somebody else too?" she added. One plus one. "Wouldn't that be better? Wouldn't that be even?" This was her penchant for algebra. She wasn't vengeful. She didn't want to get even. She wanted to be even already.

"I mean, if I were sleeping with somebody else also, wouldn't that make everyone happy?" She thought again of Boy Number Two, whom too often she denied. When she hung up, she would phone him.

"*Happy?*" hooted Number One. "More than happy. We're talking delirious." He was the funny one. After they made love, he'd sigh, open his eyes, and say, "Was that you?" Number Two was not so hilarious. He was tall and depressed and steady as rain. Ask him, "What if we both saw other people?" and he'd stare out the window, towering and morose. He'd say nothing. Or he'd shrug and say, "Fthatz . . ."

"Excuse me?"

"Fthatz what you want." He'd kiss her, then weep into his own long arm. Mary worried about his health. Number One always ate at restaurants where the food – the squid, the liver, the carrots – was all described as "young and tender," like a Tony Bennett song. But Number Two went to coffee shops and ate things that had nitrites and dark, lacy crusts around the edges. Such food could enter you old and sticking like a bad dream. When Two ate, he nipped nothing in the bud. It could cause you to grow weary and sad, coming in at the tail end of things like that.

"You have everything," she said to Number One. "You have too much: money, power, women." It was absurd to talk about these things in a place like Cleveland. But then the world was always small, no matter what world it was, and you just had to go ahead and say things about it. "Your life is too crowded."

"It's a bit bottlenecked, I admit."

"You've got a ticket holders' line so long it's attracting mimes and jugglers." At times this was how they spoke.

"It's the portrait painters I'm worried about," said One. "They're aggressive and untalented." A click came over the line. He had another call waiting.

"It's so unfair," said Mary. "Everybody wants to sit next to you on the bus."

"I've got to get off the phone now," he said, for he was afraid of how the conversation might go. It might go and go and go.

In the park an eleven-year-old girl loped back and forth in front of her. Mary looked up. The girl was skinny, flat-chested, lipsticked. She wore a halter top that left her bare-backed, shoulder blades jutting like wings. She spat once, loud and fierce, and it landed by Mary's feet. "Message from outer space," said the girl, and then she strolled off, out of the park. Mary tried to keep reading, but it was hard after that. She grew distracted and uneasy, and she got up and went home, stepping through the blood water and ignoring the meat men, who, when they had them on, tipped their hair-netted caps. Everything came forward and back again, in a wobbly dance, and when she went upstairs she held on to the railing.

This was why she liked Boy Number Two: He was kind and quiet, like someone she'd known for a long time, like someone she'd sat next to at school. He looked down and told her he loved her, sweated all over her, and left his smell lingering around her room. Number One was not a sweater. He was compact and had no pores at all, the heat building up behind his skin. Nothing of him evaporated. He left no trail or scent, but when you were with him, the heat was there and you had to touch. You got close and lost your mind a little. You let it swim. Out into the middle of the sea on a raft. Nail parings and fish.

When he was over, Number Two liked to drink beer and go to bed early, whimpering into her, feet dangling over the bed. He gave her long back rubs, then collapsed on top of her in a moan. He was full of sounds. Words came few and slow. They were never what he meant, he said. He had a hard time explaining.

"I know," said Mary. She had learned to trust his eyes, the light in them, sapphirine and uxorious, though on occasion something drove through them in a scary flash.

"Kiss me," he would say. And she would close her eyes and kiss.

Sometimes in her mind she concocted a third one, Boy Number Three. He was composed of the best features of each. It was Boy Number Three, she realized, she desired. Alone, Number One was rich and mean. Number Two was sighing, repetitive, tall, going on forever; you just wanted him to sit down. It was inevitable that she splice and add. One plus two. Three was clever and true. He was better than everybody. Alone, Numbers One and Two were missing parts, gouged and menacing, roaming dangerously through the emerald parks of Cleveland, shaking hands with voters, or stooped moodily over a chili dog. Number Three always presented himself in her mind after a drink or two, like an escort, bearing gifts and wearing a nice suit. "Ah, Number Three," she would say, with her eyes closed.

"I love you," Mary said to Number One. They were being concubines together in his apartment bedroom, lit by streetlights, rescued from ordinary living.

"You're very special," he replied.

"You're very special, too," said Mary. "Though I suppose you'd be even more special if you were single."

"That would make me more than special," said Number One. "That would make me rare. We're talking unicorn."

"I love you," she said to Number Two. She was romantic that way. Her heart was big and bursting. Though her brain was drying and subdividing like a cauliflower. She called both boys "honey," and it shocked her a little. How many honeys could you have? Perhaps you could open your arms and have so many honeys you achieved a higher spiritual plane, like a shelf in a health food store, or a pine tree, mystically inert, life barking at the bottom like a dog.

"I love you, too," said Two, the hot lunch of him lifting off his skin in a steam, a slight choke in the voice, collared and sputtering.

The postcards from her friends said, *Mary, what are you doing!?* Or else they said, *Sounds great to me.* One of them said, *You hog,* and then there were a lot of exclamation points.

She painted her room a resonant white. Hope White, it was called, like the heroine of a nurse novel. She began collecting white furniture, small things, for juveniles, only they were for her. She sat in them and at them and felt the edge of a childhood she'd never quite had or couldn't quite remember float back to her, cleansing and restoring. She bathed in Lysol, capfuls under the running tap. She moved her other furniture – the large red, black, and brown pieces – out onto the sidewalk and watched the city haul them away on Mondays, until her room was spare and milky as a bone.

"You've redecorated," said Number One.

"Do you really love me?" said Number Two. He never looked around. He stepped toward her, slowly, wanting to know only this.

In the park, after a Lysol bath, she sat on the paint-flaked slats of a bench and read. *Who shall ascend the hill of the Lord? . . . He who has clean hands . . .* There was much casting of lots for raiment. In the other book there was a shark that kept circling.

The same eleven-year-old girl, lips waxed a greenish peach, came by to spit on her.

"*What?*" said Mary, aghast.

"Nothin'," said the girl. "I'm not going to hurt you," she mocked, and her shoulders moved around as children's do when they play dress-up, a bad imitation of a movie star. She had a cheap shoulder bag with a long strap, and she hoisted it up over her head and arranged it in a diagonal across her chest.

Mary stood and walked away with what might have been indignation in someone else but in her was a horrified scurry. They could see! Everyone could see what she was, what she was doing! She wasn't fooling a soul. What she needed was plans. At a time like this, plans could save a person. They could organize time and space for a while, like little sculptures. At home Mary made soup and ate it, staring at the radiator. She would plan a trip! She would travel to some place far away, some place unlittered and pure.

She bought guidebooks about Canada: Nova Scotia, New Brunswick, Prince Edward Island. She stayed in her room, away from spitters, alternately flipped and perused the pages of her books, her head filling like a suitcase with the names of hotels and local monuments and exchange rates and historical episodes, a fearful excitement building in her to an exhaustion, travel moving up through her like a blood, until she felt she had already been to Canada, already been traveling there for months, and now had to fall back, alone, on her bed and rest.

Mary went to Number One's office to return some of the fliers and to tell him she was going away. It smelled of cigarettes and cigars, a public place, like a train. He closed the door.

"I'm worried about you. You seem distant. And you're always dressed in white. What's going on?"

"I'm saving myself for marriage," she said. "Not yours."

Number One looked at her. He had been about to say "Mine?" but there wasn't enough room for both of them there, like two men on a base. They were arriving at punch lines together these days. They had begun to do imitations of each other, that most violent and satisfying end to love.

"I'm sorry I haven't been in to work," said Mary. "But I've decided I have to go away for a while. I'm going to Canada. You'll be able to return to your other life."

"What other life? The one where I walk the streets at two in the morning dressed as Himmler? That one?" On his desk was a news clipping about a representative from Nebraska who'd been having affairs far away from home. The headline read: RUNNING FOR PUBLIC ORIFICE: WHO SHOULD CAST THE FIRST STONE? The dark at the edge of Mary's vision grew inward, then back out again. She grabbed the arm of a chair and sat down.

"My life is very strange," said Mary.

One looked at her steadily. She looked tired and lost. "You know," he said, "you're not the only woman who has ever been involved with a married – a man with marital entanglements." He usually called their romance a *situation*. Or sometimes, to entertain, *grownuppery*. All the words caused Mary to feel faint.

"Not the only woman?" said Mary. "And here I thought I was blazing new paths." When she was little her mother had said, "Would you jump off a cliff just because everybody else did?"

"Yes," Mary had said.

"*Would* you?" said her mother.

Mary had tried again. "No," she said. There were only two answers. Which could it be?

"Let me take you out to dinner," said Number One.

Mary was staring past him out the window. There were women who leaped through such glass. Just got a running start and did it.

"I have to go to Canada for a while," she murmured.

"Canada." One smiled. "You've always been such an adventuress. Did you get your shots?" This is what happened in love. One of you cried a lot and then both of you grew sarcastic.

She handed him his fliers. He put them in a pile near a rhinoceros paperweight, and he slid his hand down his face like a boy with a squeegee. She stood and kissed his ear, which was a delicate thing, a sea creature with the wind of her kiss trapped inside.

To boy number two she said, "I must take a trip."

He held her around the waist, afraid and tight. "Marry me," he said, "or else."

"Else," she said. She always wanted the thing not proposed. The other thing.

"Maybe in two years," she mumbled, trying to step back. They might buy a car, a house at the edge of the Heights. They would grow overweight and rear sullen and lazy children. Two boys.

And a girl.

Number One would send her postcards with jokes on the back. *You hog.*

She touched Number Two's arm. He was sweet to her, in his way, though his hair split into greasy V's and the strange, occasional panic in him poured worrisomely through the veins of his arms.

"I need a break," said Mary. "I'm going to go to Canada."

He let go of her and went to the window, his knuckles hard little men on the sill.

She went to Ottawa for two weeks. It was British and empty and there were no sidewalk cafés as it was already October and who knew when the canals might freeze. She went to the National Gallery and stood before the Paul Peels and Tom Thompsons, their Mother Goose names, their naked children and fiery leaves. She took a tour of Parliament, which was richly wooden and crimson velvet and just that month scandalized by the personal lives of several of its members. "So to speak" – the guide winked, and the jaws in the group went slack.

Mary went to a restaurant that had once been a mill, and she smiled at the waiters and stared at the stone walls. At night, alone in her hotel room, she imagined the cool bridal bleach of the sheets healing her, holding her like a shroud, working their white temporarily through her skin and into the thinking blood of her. Every morning at seven someone phoned her from the desk downstairs to wake her up.

"What is there to do today?" Mary inquired.

"You want Montreal, miss. This is Ottawa."

French. She hadn't wanted anything French.

"Breakfast until ten in the Union Jack Room, miss."

She sent postcards to Boy Number One and to Boy Number Two. She wrote on them, *I will be home next Tuesday on the two o'clock bus.* She put Number One's in an envelope and mailed it to his post office box. She took another tour of Parliament, then went to a church and tried to pray for a very long time. "O father who is the father," she began. "Who is the father of us all . . ." As a child she had liked to pray and had always improvised. She had closed her eyes tight as stitches and in the midst of all the colors, she was sure she saw God swimming toward her with messages and advice, a large fortune cookie in a beard and a robe, flowing, flowing. Now the chant of it made her dizzy. She opened her eyes. The church was hushed and modern, lit like a library, and full of women on their knees, as if they might never get up.

She slept fitfully on the way home, the bus rumbling beneath her, urging her to dreams and occasionally to wonder, half in and half out of them, whether anyone would be there at the station to greet her. Boy Number Two would probably not be. He was poor and carless and feeling unappreciated. Perhaps One, in a dash from the office, in a characteristically rash gesture, would take a break from campaign considerations and be waiting with flowers. It wasn't entirely a long shot.

Mary struggled off the bus with her bag. She was still groggy from sleep, and this aspect of life, getting on and off things, had always seemed difficult. Someone spoke her name. She looked to one side and heard it again. "Mary." She looked up and up, and there he was: Boy Number Two in a holey sweater and his hair in V's.

"An announcement," called the PA system. "An announcement for all passengers on . . ."

"Hi!" said Mary. The peculiar mix of gratitude and disappointment she always felt with Two settled in her joints like the beginnings of flu. They kissed on the cheek and then on the mouth, at which point he insisted on taking her bag.

They passed through the crowd uneasily, trying to talk but then not trying. The bus station was a piazza of homelessness and danger, everywhere the heartspin of greetings and departures: humid, ambivalent. Someone waved to them: a bare-legged woman with green ooze and flies buzzing close. An old man with something white curled in the curl of his ear approached and asked them for a dollar. "For food!" he assured them. "Not drink! Not drink! For food!"

Two pulled a dollar from his pocket. "There you go, my man," he said. It suddenly seemed to Mary that she would have to choose, that even if you didn't know who in the world to love, it was important to choose. You chose love like a belief, a faith, a place, a box for one's heart to knock against like a spook in the house.

Two had no money for a cab but wanted to walk Mary home, one arm clamped around her back and upper arms. They made their way like this across the city. It used to be that Two would put a big, limp fish hand in the middle of her spine, but Mary would manage to escape, stopping and pointing out something – "Look, Halley's Comet! Look, a star!" – so now he clamped her tightly, pressed against his side so that her shoulders curved front and their hips bumped each other.

Mary longed to wriggle away.

At her door she thanked him. "You don't want me to come upstairs with you?" Two asked. "I haven't seen you in so long." He stepped back, away from her.

"I'm so tired," said Mary. "I'm sorry." The Hamilton Pork men stood around, waiting for another delivery and grinning. Two gave her back her suitcase and said, "See ya," a small mat of Dixie cup and gum stuck to one shoe.

Mary went upstairs to listen to the messages on her machine. There was a message from an old school friend, a wrong number, a strange girl's voice saying,

"Who are you? What is your name?" and the quick, harried voice of Number One. "I've forgotten when you were coming home. Is it today?" Then another wrong number. "Who are you? What is your name?" Then Number One's voice again: "I guess it's not today, either."

She lay down to rest and didn't unpack her bag. When the phone rang, she leaped up, and the leap knocked her purse and several books off the bed.

"It's you," said Boy Number One.

"Yes," said Mary. She felt a small, short blizzard come to her eyes and then go.

"Mary, what's wrong?"

"Nothing," she said, and tried to swallow. When tenderness ended, there was a lull before the hate, and things could spill out into it. There was always so much to keep back, so much scratching behind the face. You tried to shoo things away, a broomed woman with a porch to protect.

"Did you have a good trip?"

"Fine. I was hoping you might be there to meet me."

"I lost your postcard and forgot what –"

"That's OK. My brother picked me up instead. I see what my life is: I tell my brother when I'm going to be home, and I tell you when I'm going to be home. Who's there to greet me? My brother. We're not even that close, as siblings go."

One sighed. "What happened was your brother and I flipped a coin and he lost. I thought he was a very good sport about it, though." The line fell still. "I didn't know you had a brother," said One.

Mary lay back on her bed, cradled the phone close. "How does the campaign look?" she asked.

"Money's still coming in, and the party's pleased with the radio spots. I've grown weary of it all. Maybe you could help me. What does the word *constituent* mean? They keep talking about constituents." She was supposed to laugh.

"Yes, well, Canada was a vision," said Mary. "All modern and clean and prosperous. At least it looked that way. There's something terribly wrong with Cleveland."

"Cleveland doesn't have the right people in Washington. Canada does." Number One was for the redistribution of wealth. He was for cutting defense spending. He was for the U.S. out of Latin America. He'd been to Hollywood benefits. But he'd never once given a coin to a beggar. Number Two did that.

"Charity that crude dehumanizes," said Number One.

"Get yourself a cola, my man," said Number Two.

"I have to come pick up my paycheck," said Mary.

"Sandy should have it," said One. "I may not be able to see you, Mary. That's partly why I'm calling. I'm terribly busy."

"Fund-raisers?" She wrapped the phone cord around one leg, which she had lifted into the air for exercise.

"That and the boys. My wife says they're suffering a bit, acting out the rottenness in our marriage."

"And here I thought you and she were doing that," said Mary. "Now everybody's getting into the act."

"You don't know what it's like to have two boys," he said. "You just don't know."

Mary stretched out on her stomach, alone in bed. A dismantled Number Three, huge, torn raggedly at the seams, terrorized the city. The phone rang endlessly. Mary's machine picked it up. *Hello? Hello?*

"I know you're there. Will you please pick up the phone?"

"I know you're there. Will you please pick up the phone?"

"I know you're there. I know you're there with someone." There was a slight choking sound. Later there were calls where nobody said anything at all.

In the morning he called again, and she answered. "Hello?"

"You slept with someone last night, didn't you?" said Two.

There was a long silence. "I wasn't going to," Mary said finally, "but I kept getting these creepy calls, and I got scared and didn't want to be alone."

"Oh, God," he whispered, a curse or was it love, before the phone crashed, then hummed, the last verse of something long.

In the park a young woman of about twenty was swirling about, dancing to some tape-recorded arias and Gregorian chants. A small crowd had gathered. Mary watched briefly: This was what happened to you when you were from Youngstown and had been dreamy and unpopular in high school. You grew up and did these sorts of dances.

Mary sat down at a bench some distance away. The little girl who had twice spat on her walked by slowly, appraising. Mary looked up. "Don't spit on me," she said. Her life had come to this: pleading not to be spat on. Was it any better than some flay-limbed dance to boom box Monteverdi? It had its moments.

Not of dignity, exactly, but of something.

"I'm not going to spit on you," sneered the girl.

"Good," said Mary.

The girl sat down at the far end of the bench. Mary kept reading her book but could feel the girl's eyes, a stare scraping along the edge of her, until she finally had to turn and say, "*What?*"

"Just looking," said the girl. "Not spitting."

Mary closed her book. "Are you waiting for someone?"

"Yup," said the girl. "I'm waiting for all my boyfriends to come over and give me a kiss." She closed her eyes and smacked her lips in the air.

"Oh," said Mary, and opened her book again. The sun was beating down on the survivor. Blisters and sores. Poultices of algae paste. The water tight as glass and the wind, blue-faced, holding its breath. How did one get here? How did one's eye-patched, rot-toothed life lead one along so cruelly, like a trick, to the middle of the sea?

At home the phone rang, but Mary let the machine pick it up. It was nobody. The machine clicked and went through its business, rewound. Beneath her the hooks and pulleys across the meat store ceiling rattled and bumped. In a dream the phone rang again and she picked it up. It was somebody she knew only vaguely.

A neighbor of Boy Number Two. "I have some bad news," he said in the dream.

In the park the little girl sat closer, like a small animal – a squirrel, a munk, investigating. She pointed and said, "I live that way; is that the way you live?"

"Don't you have to be in school?" asked Mary. She let her book fall to her lap, but she kept a finger in the page and her dark glasses on.

The girl sighed. "School," she said, and she flubbed her lips in a horse snort. "I told you. I'm waiting for my boyfriends."

"But you're always waiting for them," said Mary. "And they never get here."

"They're unreliable." The girl spat, but away from Mary, more in the direction of the music institute. "They're dead."

Mary stood up, closed her book, started walking. "One in the sky, one in the ground," the girl called, running after Mary. "Hey, do you live this way? I thought so." She followed behind Mary in a kind of traipse, block after block. When they got as far as the Hamilton Pork Company, Mary stopped. She clutched her stomach and turned to look at the girl, who had pulled up alongside her, perspiring slightly. It was way too warm for fall. The girl stared at the meat displayed in the windows, the phallic harangue of sausages, marbled, desiccated, strung up as for a carnival.

"Look!" said the girl, pointing at the sausages. "There they are. All our old boyfriends."

Mary took off her dark glasses. "What grade are you in?" she asked. Could there be a grade for what this girl knew in her bulleted heart? What she knew was the sort of thing that grew in you like a tree, unfurling in your brain, pushing out into your fingers against the nails.

"Grade?" mimicked the girl.

Mary put her glasses back on. "Forget it," she said. Pork blood limned their shoes. Mary held her stomach more tightly; something was fluttering there, the fruit of a worry. She fumbled for her keys.

"All right," said the girl, and she turned and loped away, the bones in her back working hard, colors spinning out, exotic as a bird rarely seen unless believed in, wretchedly, like a moonward thought.

BONER MCPHARLIN'S MOLL

Tim Winton

Born in Western Australia, where he lives, **Tim Winton** (b.1960) has written eleven novels (including *Cloudstreet, The Riders, Dirt Music, Breath* and *Eyrie*), four collections of stories, three plays, six children's books as well as works of non-fiction. His work has won the Miles Franklin Award four times, been shortlisted for the Booker Prize twice, as well as the Commonwealth Writers' Prize. "It's the pointless things that give your life meaning," he observed: "friendship, compassion, art, love. All of them pointless. But they're what keeps life from being meaningless."

To say that I went to school with Boner McPharlin is stretching things a bit because he was expelled halfway through my first year at high school. That would make it 1970, I suppose. I doubt that I saw him more than five times in his grotty hybrid uniform but I was awestruck when I did. We'd all heard about him back in primary school. The local bad boy, a legendary figure. And suddenly, there he was, fifteen and feral-looking, with grey eyes and dirty-blond hair past his shoulders. In his Levi's and thongs he had that truckin stride, like a skater's wade, swaying hip to hip with his elbows flung and his chest out. He had fuzz on his chin and an enigmatic smirk. His whole body gave off a current of sexy insouciance. To me, a girl barely thirteen, he was the embodiment of rebellion. I wanted that – yes, right from the first glance I wanted it. I wanted him. I wanted to be his.

I watched him swing by, right along the lower-school verandah with a bunch of boys in his wake – kids who seemed more enthralled by him than attached to him – and I must have been pretty obvious about it because my best friend, Erin, stood beside me with her hands on her hips and gave me a withering look.

No way, she said. Jackie, no way.

Erin and I went back forever. We were at a cruel age when we clung fiercely to girlhood yet yearned to be women, and everything excited and disgusted us in equal measure. Sophistication was out of reach yet we could no longer remember how to be children. So we faked it. Everything we did was imitation and play-acting. We lived in a state of barely suppressed panic.

I was only looking, I said.

Don't even look, said Erin.

But I did look. I was appalled and enchanted.

Boner McPharlin was the solitary rough boy that country towns produce, or perhaps require. The sullen, smouldering kid at the back of the class. The boy too brave or stupid to fear punishment, whose feats become folklore. When he strutted by that day I knew nothing about him, really. Only the legend. He was just a posture, an attitude, a type. He represented everything a girl like me was supposed to avoid. He posed some unspecified moral hazard. And I sensed from Erin that he was a peril to friendship as well, so I said nothing about him. I went on being thirteen – practised shaving my legs with the old man's blade-less razor, threw myself into netball, tore down my Johnny Farnham posters and put David Bowie in his place. I had a best friend – I shared secrets with her – yet they felt inconsequential once I saw Boner. Boner was my new secret and I did not share him.

I don't know what it was that finally got Boner expelled from school. He did set off pipe bombs in the nearby quarry. And there was, of course, the teacher's Volkswagen left on blocks in the staff carpark and the condoms full of pig blood that strafed the quadrangle in the lead-up to Easter, but there were plenty of atrocities he didn't commit, incidents he may have only inspired by example, yet he took the rap for all of it. With hindsight, when you consider what happened later in the seventies when drugs ripped through our town, Boner's hijinks seem rather innocent. But teachers were afraid of him. They despised his swagger, his silence. When he was hauled in he confessed nothing, denied nothing. He wore his smirk like a battlemask. And then one Monday he was gone.

The rest of us heard it all at a great remove. Everybody embellished the stories they were told and the less we saw of Boner the more we talked. Much later, when there was a fire at the school, he was taken in for questioning but never charged. I heard he went to the meatworks where his old man worked in the boning room. That was where the name came from, how it was passed from father to son. On Saturdays Boner lurked in the lee of the town hall or some-times you'd see his mangy lumberjacket wending through cars parked around the boundary at the football.

At fourteen Erin and I began to be dogged by boys, ordinary farmboys whose fringes were plastered across their brows by built-up grease and a licked finger, and townies in Adidas and checked shirts whose hair didn't touch their collars. They were lumpy creatures whose voices squawked and their Brut 33 made your eyes water. We were more alert to their brothers who drove Monaros and Charg-ers. But we weren't even sure we were interested in boys. We were caught in a nasty dance in which we lured them only to send them packing.

The drive-in was the social hub of the town. My parents never went but they let me walk there with Erin and we sat in the rank old deckchairs beside the kiosk to watch *Airport* and *M*A*S*H* and *The Poseidon Adventure*. We wore Levi cords, Dr Scholls and 4711 ice cologne. Neither of us would admit it, but in our chaste luring and repelling of boys, Erin and I were locked in competi-tion. There was a tacit score being kept and because she was so pretty, in an Ali McGraw kind of way, I was doomed to trail in her wake. I kept an eye out for Boner McPharlin and was always thrilled to see him truckin up toward the kiosk with a roily paper on his lip. I kept my enthusiasm to myself, though there were times on the long walk home when I thought aloud about him. I was careful not to sound breathless. I did my best to be wry. I aped the new women teachers we had and adopted the cool, contemptuous tone they reserved for the discussion of males. I was ironic, tried to sound bemused, and while I waxed sociological, Erin lapsed into wary silence.

At about fourteen and a half Erin started letting a few boys through the net. Then they became a steady stream. Our friendship seemed to survive them. I tagged along as though I was required for distance, contrast and the passing of messages. She made it clear she wasn't easy. Nothing below the waist. Friendship rings were acceptable. No Italians. And she did not climb into vehicles.

I must have been fifteen when Boner McPharlin got his driver's licence. Suddenly he was everywhere. He wheeled around town in an HT van with spoked fats and a half-finished sprayjob in metallic blue. That kind of car was trouble. It was a sin-bin, a shaggin-wagon, a slut-hut, and as he did bog-laps of the main drag – from the memorial roundabout to the railway tracks at the harbour's-edge – the rumble of his V-8 was menacing and hypnotic. Sometimes he cruised by the school, his arm down the door, stereo thumping.

Erin and I walked everywhere. Outside of school there was nothing else to do but traipse to the wharf or the beach or down the drab strip of shops where the unchanging window displays and familiar faces made me feel desperate.

I wish something would happen, I often said.

Things are happening all around us, said Erin.

I didn't mean photosynthesis, I muttered.

By the time anything's happened, it's over.

Well, I said. I look forward to having something to remember.

We were in the midst of one of these ritual discussions when Boner pulled up beside us. It was a Saturday morning. We stood outside the Wildflower Café. I had just bought a Led Zeppelin record. In the rack it had been slotted between Lanza and Liberace. Over at Reece's Fleeces people were buying ugg boots and sheepskin jackets. The passenger side window of Boner's van was down.

Jackie, said Erin.

Nothing wrong with saying hello, I said.

Even as I turned toward the mud-spattered car growling and gulping at the kerb, Erin was walking away. I saw the black flag of her hair as she disappeared into Chalky's hardware. Then I stepped over and leaned in. Boner's smirk was visible behind a haze of cigarette smoke. I felt a pulse in the roof of my mouth.

Ride? he said, just audible over the motor.

I shook my head but he wasn't even looking my way. He squinted into the distance like a stunted version of Clint Eastwood. Yet he must have felt something because he was already putting the car into gear and looking into his side mirror when I opened the door and slid in. He seemed completely unsurprised. He peeled out. Heads turned. I clutched the LP to my chest.

Boner and I drove a lap of town in silence. We idled past the pubs on the waterfront, the cannery, the meatworks, the silos. We passed grain ships on the wharf, the whalers on the town jetty and eased up by the convict-built churches on the ridge where the road wound down again toward the main beach.

I tried to seem cool, to make him be the one to break the silence, but he seemed disinclined to speak. The van was everything you'd expect, from the mattress and esky in the back to the empty Bacardi bottle rolling about my feet. Feathers and fish bones hung from the rear-view mirror. Between us on the bench seat was a nest of cassettes, tools, and packets of Drum tobacco. I knew I'd done something reckless by climbing in beside Boner McPharlin. I'd made something happen. What frightened me was that I didn't know what it was.

We didn't stay at the beach – didn't even pull into its in-famous carpark – but wheeled around beneath the Norfolk Island pines and headed back to the main street of town. We slid into a space outside the Wildflower and a dozen faces lifted in the window. The big tricked-up Chevy motor idled away, drumming through the soles of my denim sneakers.

So, I said. How's things at the meatworks?

He shrugged and looked up the street. Erin stood in the door of the café, her hair ensnared by a rainbow of flystrips. Her face was clouded with rage. I wanted to prolong the moment with Boner but could think of nothing to say.

Well, I chirped. Thanks for the ride.

Boner said nothing. He eased in the clutch and scoped his mirror, so I got out and hesitated a moment before shoving the door to. Then he took off with a howl of rubber and I stood there hugging my record in the cold southern wind with a jury of my peers staring out upon me from the café.

In the doorway Erin did not step aside to let me in. She tucked her hair behind her ear and stared into my face.

I can't believe you.

Don't be wet, I said.

Jackie, what did you do?

I took a breath and was about to tell her just how little had happened when a jab of anger held me back. The crossly-folded arms, the solemn look – it wasn't concern but a fit of pique. I'd ignored her warnings. I'd let her walk away without giving chase. And now, worst of all, I'd upstaged her. The realization was like a slap. She was jealous. And this very public interrogation, the telegraphed expressions to everybody inside – it was all a performance. We weren't friends at all.

All I gave her was a sly smile.

Oh my God, she murmured with a barely-concealed thrill.

What? I asked.

You didn't!

I shrugged and smirked. The power of it was so delicious that I didn't yet understand what I'd done. With little more than a mute expression I'd just garnered myself a reputation. I was already Boner McPharlin's moll.

It was a small town. We were all bored out of our minds. I should have known better, should have admitted the unglamorous truth, but I didn't. I discovered how stubborn I could be. The stories at school were wild. I wasn't ashamed – I felt strong. I found a curious pleasure in notoriety. The rumour wasn't true but I owned it. For once it was about me. But it was lonely, too, lonelier for having to pretend to still be friends with Erin. To everybody else her protestations about my purity looked like misguided loyalty, friendship stretched to the point of martyrdom, though from the chill between us I knew otherwise, for the more she said in my defence the worse I looked, and the further my stocks fell the faster hers rose. By the end of that week I wanted the rumours to be true. Because if I was Boner's jailbait then at least I had somebody.

After school I stayed indoors. I went nowhere until the next Saturday when, in a mood of bleak resignation, I went walking alone. I was at the memorial round-about when Boner saw me. He hesitated, then pulled over. I will never know why he did, whether it was boredom or an act of mercy.

He pushed the door open and I got in and through the sweep of the round-about I had the weirdest sense of having been rescued. I didn't care what it took. I would do anything at all. I was his.

Within five minutes we were out of town altogether. We cruised down along the coast past peppermint thickets and spud farms to long white beaches and rocky coves where the water was so turquoise-clear that, cold or not, you had the urge to jump in fully clothed. Wind raked through our hair from the open windows. The tape deck trilled and boomed Jethro Tull. We didn't speak. I ached with happiness.

Boner drove in a kind of slouch with an arm on the doorsill and one hand on the wheel. The knob on the gearstick was an eightball. When his hand rested on it I saw his bitten nails and yellow calluses. He wore a flannel shirt and a battered sheep-skin jacket. His Levi's were dark and stiff-looking. He wore Johnny Reb boots whose heels were ground off at angles.

The longer we drove the stranger his silence seemed to me. I couldn't admit to myself that I was becoming rattled. We drove for thirty miles while I clung to my youthful belief that I could handle anything that came my way. Slumped down like that, he looked small and not particularly athletic. I knew that while he had those boots on I could easily outrun him.

We drove all the rest of that day, a hundred and fifty miles or more, but no beach, no creek nor forest was enough to get him out from behind the wheel. Now and then, at a tiny rail siding or roadhouse, he slid me a fiver so I could buy pies and Coke.

At four he dropped me at the Esso station around the corner from my house. There were no parting speeches, no mutual understandings arrived at, no ar-rangements made. Boner left the motor running. He ran a hand through his hair. The ride was over. I got out; he pulled away. It was only after he'd gone that I wondered how he knew this would be the best place to drop me. I hadn't even told him where I lived. I didn't expect him to be discreet. It didn't fit the image of the wild boy. I was as irritated as I was flattered. It made me feel like a kid who needed looking after.

But that's how it continued. Boner collected me and dropped me at the Esso so regularly that there arose between me and the mechanics a knowing and unfriendly intimacy. They knew whose daughter I was, that I was only fifteen. Like everyone else who saw me riding around with Boner after school and on weekends, their fear and dislike of my father were enough to keep them quiet. Perhaps they felt a certain satisfaction.

My father was the council building inspector. It wasn't a job for a man who needed to be popular. Dour, punctilious and completely without tact, he seemed to have no use for people at all, except in their role as applicants, and then he was, without exception, unforgiving. For him, the building code was a branch of Calvinism perfected by the omission of divine mercy. His life was a quest to reveal flaws, disguised contraventions, greed and human failure. Apart from dinner time and at the end-of-term delivery of school reports, he barely registered my presence. My mother was passive and serene. She liked to pat my hair when I went to bed. I always thought she was a bit simple until I discovered, quite late in the piece, that she was addicted to Valium.

My parents were lonely, they were insular and preoccupied, yet I still find it hard to believe that they knew nothing at all about Boner and me that year. If they weren't simply ignoring what I was up to then they truly didn't notice a thing about me.

I loved everything about Boner, his silence, his incuriosity, the way he evaded body contact, how he smelled of pine resin and tobacco smoke. I liked his sleepy-narrow eyes and his far-off stares. The bruises on his arms and neck intrigued me, they made me think of men and knives and cold carcasses, his mysterious world. Sometimes he'd vanish for days and I'd be left standing abject at the Esso until dark. And then he'd turn up again, arm down the door with nothing to say.

He never told me anything about himself, never asked about me. We drove to football games in other towns, to rodeos and tiny fairs. When there were reports of snow we travelled every road in the ranges to get a glimpse but never saw any. Out on the highway, on the lowland stretch, he opened the throttle and we hit the ton with the windows down and Pink Floyd wailing.

It's not that he said absolutely nothing, but he spoke infrequently and in monosyllables. By and large I was content to do all the talking. I told him the sad story of my parents. I filled him in on the army of bitches I went to school with and the things they said about us. Now and then I tried to engage him in hot conjecture – about whether David Bowie was really a poof or if Marc Bolan (who *had* to be a poof) was taller than he looked – but I never got far.

We drove out to the whaling station where the waters of the bay were lit with oily prisms and the air putrid with the steam of boiling blubber. I puked before I even saw anything. At the guardrail above the flensing deck, I tried to avoid splashing my granny sandals. Boner brought me a long, grimy bar towel to clean myself up with. He was grinning. He pointed out the threshing shadows in the water, the streaking fins, the eruptions on the surface.

Horrible, I said.

He shrugged and drove me back to town.

Although everyone at school assumed that Boner and I were doing the deed every time I climbed into his van, there was neither sex nor romance between us. Erin and the others could not imagine the peculiarity of our arrangement. There was, of course, some longing on my part. I yearned to kiss him, be held by him. After the reputation I'd earned it seemed only fair to have had that much, but Boner did not like to be touched. There was no holding of hands. If I cornered him, wheedling and vamping for a kiss, his head reared back on his neck until his Adam's apple looked fit to bust free.

The closest I ever got to him was when I pierced his ears. I campaigned for a week before he consented. It began with me pleading with him and ended up as a challenge to his manhood. One Sunday I climbed in with ice, Band-Aids, and a selection of needles from my mother's dusty sewing box. We parked out off the lowlands road where I straddled him on the seat and held his head steady. A few cars blew by with their horns trailing off into the distance. The paddocks were still. I pressed ice to Boner's earlobes and noticed that he'd come out in a sweat. He smelled of lanolin and smokes and that piney scent. When he closed his eyes, the lids trembled. I revelled in the luxury of holding him against the seat. I lingered over him with a bogus air of competence. Like a rider on a horse I simply imposed my will. At the moment I drove the needle through his lobe I clamped him between my thighs and pressed my lips to his clammy forehead. He was so tense, so completely shut down in anticipation of contact, that I doubt he felt a thing.

For a few weeks my riding with Boner brought me more glamour than disgrace. The new hippy teachers gave me credit for pushing social boundaries, for my sense of adventure and lack of snobbery. To them my little rebellion was refreshing, spirited, charming. They preferred it to my being the dutiful daughter of the council inspector. I knew what they thought of homes like ours with the red-painted paths and plaster swans. Their new smiles said it all. But when my experiment proved more than momentary their Aquarian indulgence withered. They despised boys like Boner as much as my parents would have, had they known him, and after a while my feisty rebellion seemed little more than slumming. Boner was no winsome Woodstock boy. He was a toughie from the abattoir. My young teachers' sisterly hugs gave way to stilted homilies. Free love was cool but a girl didn't want to spread her favours too thin, did she. I grimaced and smirked until they left me alone.

The gossip at school was brutal. In the talk, the passed notes, the toilet scrawl, I sucked Boner McPharlin, I sucked other boys, I sucked anybody. And more. At the drives Boner hired me out, car to car, Jackie Martin meatworker. Slack Jackie. The slander hurt but I bore it as the price of love. Because I did love him. And anyway, I thought, let them talk, the ignoramuses. Part of me enjoyed the status, the bitter satisfaction of being solitary but notable. I was, in this regard, my father's daughter.

I could bear the vile talk behind my back, but all the icy silence on the surface wore me down. I had enough remoteness at home. And Boner himself barely said a word. I craved some human contact. The only people who would speak to me were the opportunists and the outcasts, boys newly-emboldened to try their luck and hard-faced sluts with peroxided fringes who wanted to know how big Boner's bone was. The boys I sent packing but the rough chicks I was stuck with. They were a dim and desperate lot with which to spend a lunch hour.

At first they were as suspicious of me as they were curious. I was a cardigan-wearing interloper, a slumming dilettante. Their disbelief at Boner's having chosen *me* was assuaged in time by the incontrovertible fact of it, for there I was every afternoon cruising by in the van. I didn't challenge the legend. On the contrary, I nurtured it. By nods and winks at first and later with outright lies. I told them what they wanted to hear, what I read in *Cleo* and *Forum*, the stuff I knew nothing about. It seemed harmless enough. We were just girls, I thought, fakers, kids making ourselves up as we went along. But the things I was lying through my teeth about were the very things these girls were doing. That and much more. And they had the polaroids to prove it.

Only when I saw those photos did I begin to understand how stupid my play-acting had been. One lunchtime five of us crammed into a smoky toilet stall, our earrings jangling with suppressed laughter. The little prints were square, felt gummy in my hands, and it took me several moments to register what I was looking at. God knows what I was expecting, which fantasy world I'd been living in, but I can still feel the horrible fake grin that I hid behind while my stomach rolled and my mind raced. So this was what being Slack Jackie really meant. Not just that kids thought you were doing things like this with Boner McPharlin; they believed you did them with anybody, everybody, two and three at a time, reducing yourself to this, a grimacing, pink blur, a trophy to be passed around in toilets and toolsheds all over town. All the gossip had been safely abstract but the polaroids were galvanizing. With all my nodding and winking I'd let these *creatures* believe that I was low enough to have mementoes like this myself, conquests that would bind us to one another. I'd never felt so young, so isolated, so ill. Those girls had already lived another life, moved in a different economy. They understood that they had something men and boys wanted. For them sex was not so much pleasure or even adventure but currency. And I was just a romantic schoolgirl. Maybe they suspected it all along.

I didn't go to pieces there in the fug of the cubicle but afterwards I subsided into a misery I couldn't disguise. I had always believed I could endure what people thought of me. If it wasn't true, I thought, how could it matter? But I'd gone from letting people think what they would to actually lying about myself. I'd fallen in with people whose view of life was more miserable and brutish than anything I'd ever imagined. It was as though I'd extinguished myself.

I went to class in a daze. The teacher took one look at me and sent me to the sick room.

Are you late with your period? asked the nurse.

I could only stare in horror.

You can imagine how the news travelled. I'm sure the nurse was discreet. The talk probably started the moment I left the class. Jackie went to the sick room. Jackie was sick at school. Jackie was bawling her eyes out. Jackie's got a bun in the oven.

It wasn't that I refused to answer the nurse's question. I was simply trying so hard not to cry that I couldn't speak. And saying nothing was no help at all.

During the final term of that year I went back to being a schoolyard solitary. I spent hours in the library to avoid scrutiny and to stave off panic, and the renewed study brought about a late rally in my marks. I heard the rumours about my 'condition' and did my best to ignore them. The only thing more surprising than my good marks was the new pleasure they gave me. It was all that kept me from despair.

I still felt a bubble of joy rise to my throat when Boner burbled up but it didn't always last out the ride. On weekends, as spring brought on the uncertain promise of the southern summer, I took to wearing a bikini beneath my clothes and I badgered Boner to let me out at the beaches we drove to. I couldn't sit in the car anymore. I wanted to bodysurf, to strike out beyond the breakers and lie back with the sun pressing pink on my eyelids. I wanted him there, too, to hold his hand in the water, for him to feel me splashing against him. But there wasn't a chance of it happening. He let me out but I had to swim alone. The beaches were mostly empty. There was nobody to see my flat belly. The water was cold and forceful and after swimming I lay sleepy-warm on a towel. The best Boner could do was to squat beside me in his Johnny Reb boots with a rolly cupped in his palm.

I began to demand more of Boner. Perhaps it was a renewed confidence from good marks and maybe it was a symptom of a deeper bleakness, a sense of having nothing left to lose. Either way I peppered him with questions about himself, things I hadn't dared ask before. I wanted to know about his family, the details of his job, his honest opinions, where he wanted to be in ten years' time, and his only responses were shrugs and grins and puckerings and far-off looks. When I asked what he thought of me he murmured, You're Jackie. You're me navigator.

I didn't find it charming; I was irritated. Even though it dawned on me that Boner was lonely – lonelier than I'd ever been, lonely enough to hang out with a fifteen-year-old – I felt a gradual loss of sympathy. I could sense myself tiring of him, and I was guilty about it, but his silence began to seem idiotic and the aimless driving bored me. With no one else to speak to, I'd worn myself out prattling on at him. I'd told him so much, yearned so girlishly, and gotten so little in return.

The weather warmed up. The van was hot to ride in. The upholstery began to give off a stink of sweat and meat. I found shotgun shells in the glovebox. Boner wouldn't discuss their presence. I found that a whole day with him left me depleted. I missed being a girl on foot, I wanted the antic talk of other girls, even their silly, fragile confidences. Boner wouldn't speak. He couldn't converse. He couldn't leave the van. He wouldn't even swim.

I tried to find a kind way to tell him that it wasn't fun anymore but I didn't have the courage. One Saturday I simply didn't go to the Esso. On Sunday I helped my startled mother make Christmas puddings. The next week I stayed in and read *Papillon*. I watched 'Aunty Jack'. When I did venture out I avoided places where Boner might see me. It was only a few days before he found me. I heard him ease in beside me on the road home from school. I felt others watching. I leant in to the open window.

Ride, Jack? he murmured.

Nah, I said. Not anymore. But thanks.

He shrugged and dragged on his rolly. For a moment I thought he'd say something but he just chewed his lip. I knew I'd hurt him and it felt like a betrayal, yet I walked away without another word.

Every summer my parents took me to the city for a few weeks. I was always intimidated and selfconscious, certain that the three of us were instantly identifiable as bumpkins, though I loved the cinemas and shops, the liberating unfamiliarity of everybody and everything in my path. That year, after the usual excursions, we walked through the grounds of the university by the river's edge. The genteel buildings were surrounded by palms and lemon-scented gums and here and there, in cloisters or against limestone walls, were wedding parties and photographers and knots of overdressed and screaming children.

I sensed a sermon in the wings, a parable about application to schoolwork, but my father was silent. As we walked the verandahs he seemed to drink in every detail. There was a softness, a sadness to his expression that I'd never seen before. He rubbed his moustache, wiped his brow on the towelling hat he wore on these trips, and sauntered off alone.

What's with Dad? I asked. Did you guys have your wedding pictures taken here, or something?

My mother sat on a step in her boxy frock. Sweat had soaked through her polka dots to give her a strangely riddled look.

No, dear, she said. He wanted to be an architect, you know. Thirty years is a long time to have regrets.

I stood by her a while. Despite the languor of her tone I sensed that we'd come to the edge of something important together. I could feel the ghosts of their marriage hovering within reach, the story behind their terrible quiet almost at hand, and I hesitated, wanting and not wanting to hear more. But she snapped open her bag and pulled out her compact and the moment was gone, a flickering light gone out.

On the long hot drive home that summer I thought about the university and the palpable disappointment of my parents' lives. I wondered if the excursion to the campus had been an effort on their part to plant a few thoughts in my head. Consciously or not they'd shown me a means of escape.

In the new school year I more or less reinvented myself. Until that point, except for my connection with Boner, I had believed that I was average; in addition to being physically unremarkable I assumed I wasn't particularly smart either. The business with Boner was, I decided, an aberration, an episode. For the bulk of my school life I'd embraced the safety of the median. And now, effectively friendless, with the image of the university and its shady cloisters as a goad, I became a scowling bookworm, a girl so serious, so fixed upon a goal, as to be unapproachable. I never did return to the realm of girly confidences. Friends, had I found them, would have been a hindrance. In an academic sense I began to flourish. I saw myself surrounded by dolts. Contempt was addictive. In a few months I left everyone and everything else in my wake.

Of course no matter what I did my louche reputation endured. These things are set in stone. Baby booties and condoms were folded into my textbooks. The story went that Boner had dropped me for not having his child, that he was out to get me somehow, that my summer trip to Perth had involved a clinic. Last year's polaroid tarts were all gone now to Woolworths and the cannery, there was nobody to share the opprobrium with. Yet I felt it less. My new resolve and confidence made me haughty. I was fierce in a way that endeared me to neither students nor staff. I was sarcastic and abrupt, neither eager to please nor easy to best. I was reconciled to being lonely. I saw myself in Rio, Bombay, New York; being met at airports, ordering room service, solving problems on the run. I'd already moved on from these people, this town. I was enjoying myself. I imagined an entire life beyond being Boner McPharlin's moll.

Boner was still around of course. He wasn't as easy to spot because he drove an assortment of vehicles. Apart from the van there was a white Valiant, a flatbed truck and a Land Rover that looked like something out of *Born Free*. Our eyes met, we waved, but nothing more. There was something unresolved between us that I didn't expect to deal with. Word was that the meatworks had sacked him over some missing cartons of beef. There were stories about him and his father duffing cattle out east and butchering them with chainsaws in valley bottoms. There was talk of stolen car parts, electrical goods, two-day drives to the South Australian border, meetings on tuna boats. If these whispers were true – and I knew enough by now to have my doubts – then the police were slow in catching them. There were stories of Boner and other girls, but I never saw any riding with him.

Town seemed uglier the year I turned sixteen. There was something feverish in the air. At first I thought it was just me, my new persona and the fresh perspective I had on things, but even my father came home with talk of break-ins, hold-ups, bashings.

The first overdose didn't really register. I wasn't at the school social – I was no longer the dancing sort – so I didn't see the ambulancemen wheel the dead girl out of the toilets. I didn't believe the talk in the quad. I knew better than to listen to the bullshit that blew along the corridors, all the sudden talk about heroin. But that overdose was only the first of many. Smack became a fact of life in Angelus. The stuff was everywhere and nobody seemed able or inclined to do a thing about it.

It was winter when Boner McPharlin was found out at Thunder Beach with his legs broken and his face like an aubergine. They made me wait two days before I could see him. At the hospital there were plainclothes cops in the corridor and one in uniform outside the door. The scrawny constable let me in without a word. Boner was conscious by then, though out of his tree on morphine. He didn't speak. His eyes were swollen shut. I'm not even sure he knew who I was. With his legs full of bolts and pins he looked like a ruined bit of farm machinery.

I stayed for an hour, and when I left a detective fell into step beside me. He was tall with pale red hair. He offered me a lift. I told him no thanks, I was fine. He called me Jackie. I was still rocked by the sight of Boner. The cop came downstairs with me. He seemed friendly enough, though in the lobby he asked to see my arms. I rolled up my sleeves and he nodded and thanked me. He asked about Boner's enemies. I told him I didn't know of any. He said to leave it with him; it was all in hand. I plunged out into the rain.

I visited Boner every day after school but he wouldn't speak. I was chatty for a while but after a day or so I took my homework with me, a biology text or *The Catcher in the Rye*. For a few days there were cops on the ward or out in the carpark, but then they stopped coming. The nurses were kind. They slipped me cups of tea and hovered at my shoulder for a peek at what I was reading. When the swelling went down and his eyes opened properly, Boner watched me take notes and mark pages and suck my knuckles. Late in the week he began to writhe around and shake. The hardware in his legs rattled horribly.

Open the door, he croaked.

Boner, I said. Are you alright? You want me to call a nurse?

Open the door. Don't ever close the door.

I got up and pulled the door wide. There was a cop in the corridor, a constable I didn't recognize. He spun his cap in his hands. He was grey in the face. He tried to smile.

You okay, Boner? I said over my shoulder.

Gotta have it open.

I went back and sat by the bed. I caught myself reaching for his hand.

Least you can talk, I murmured. That's something.

Not me, he said.

You can talk to *me*, can't you?

He shook his battered head slowly, with care. I sucked at a switch of hair, watched him tremble.

What happened?

Don't remember, he whispered. Gone.

Talk to me, I said in a wheedling little voice. Why do you want the door open?

Can't read, you know. Not properly. Can't swim neither.

I sat there and licked my lips nervously. I was sixteen years old and all at sea. I didn't know how to respond. There were questions I was trying to find words for but before I could ask him anything he began to talk.

My mother, he murmured, my mother was like a picture, kinda, real pretty. Our place was all spuds, only spuds. She had big hands all hard and black from grubbin spuds. I remember. When I was little, when I was sick, when she rubbed me back, in bed, and her hands, you know, all rough and gentle like a cat's tongue, rough and gentle. Fuck. Spuds. Always bent down over spuds, arms in the muck, rain runnin off em, him and her. Sky like an army blanket.

She's . . . gone, your mum?

I come in and he's bent down over her, hands in her, blanket across her throat, eyes round, veins screamin in her neck and she sees me not a word sees me and I'm not sayin a word, just lookin at the sweat shine on his back and his hands in the muck and she's dead now anyway. Doesn't matter, doesn't matter, does it.

Boner gave off an acid stink. Sweat stood out on his forehead. I couldn't make out much of what he was saying.

Sharks know, he said, they know. You see em flash? Twist into whalemeat? Jesus, they saw away. It's in the blood, he had it, twistin all day into hot meat. And never sleep, not really.

Boner—

Sacked me for catchin bronzies off the meatworks jetty. Fuck, I didn't steal nothin, just drove one round on the fork-lift for a laugh, to put the shits up em. Live shark, still kickin! They went spastic, said I'm nuts, said I'm irresponsible, unreliable.

The bedrails jingled as he shook.

But I'm solid, he said. Solid as a brick shithouse. Unreliable be fucked. Why they keep callin me unreliable? I drive and drive. I don't say a word. They know, they know. Don't say a fuckin word. Don't leave me out, don't let me go, I'm solid. I'm solid!

He began to cry then. A nurse came in and said maybe I should go.

Boner never said so much again in one spate – not to me, anyway. I couldn't make head nor tail of it, assumed it was delayed shock or infection or all the painkillers they had him on. When I returned next day he was calmer but he seemed displeased to see me. He watched TV, was unresponsive, surly, and that's how he remained. I had study to keep up with. The TV ruined my concentration, so my visits grew fewer, until some weeks I hardly went at all. Then one day, after quite a gap, I arrived to find that he'd been discharged.

I didn't see him for weeks, months. The school year ground on and I sat my exams with a war-like determination. As spring became summer I kept an eye out for Boner in town. I half expected to hear him rumble up behind me at any moment, but there was no sign of him.

I was walking home from the library one afternoon when a van eased in to the kerb. I looked up and it wasn't him. It was a paddy wagon. A solitary cop. He beckoned me over. I hesitated but what could I do – I was a schoolgirl – I went.

You're young McPharlin's girlfriend, he said.

I recognized him. He was the nervous-looking constable from the hospital, the one who'd started hanging around after the others left. I'd seen him that winter in the local rag. He was a hero for a while, brought an injured climber down off a peak in the ranges. But he looked ill. His eyes were bloodshot, his skin was blotchy. There was a patch of stubble on his neck that he'd missed when shaving, and even from where I stood leaning into the window he smelt bad, a mixture of sweat and something syrupy. When I first saw him I felt safe but now I was afraid of him.

Just his friend, I murmured.

Not from what I've heard.

I pressed my lips together and felt the heat in my face. I didn't like him, didn't trust him.

How's his memory?

I don't know, I said. Not too good, I think.

If he remembers, said the cop. If he wants to remember, will you tell me?

I licked my lips and glanced up the street.

I haven't seen him, I said.

I go there and he just clams up. He doesn't need to be afraid of me, he said. Not me. Tell him to give me the names.

I stepped away from the car.

I only need the other two, Jackie, he called. Just the two from out of town.

I walked away, kept on going. I felt him watching me all the way up the street.

Next day I hitched a ride out along the lowlands road to Boner's place. I hadn't been before and he'd never spoken of it directly though I'd pieced details together over the years as to where it was. I rode over in a pig truck whose driver seemed more interested in my bare legs than the road ahead. Out amongst the swampy coastal paddocks I got him to set me down where a doorless fridge marked a driveway.

I know you, he said, grinding the truck back into gear.

I don't think so, I said climbing down.

I glanced up from the roadside and saw him sprawled across the wheel, chewing the inside of his cheek as he looked at me. The two-lane was empty. There wasn't a farmhouse or human figure in sight. My heart began to jump. I did not walk away. I remembered how vulnerable I felt the day before in town in a street of passing cars and pedestrians while the cop watched my progress all the way uphill. I didn't know what else to do but stand there. He looked in his mirror a moment and I stood there. He pulled away slowly and when he was a mile away I set off down the track.

A peppermint thicket obscured the house from the road. It was a weatherboard place set a long way back in the paddocks, surrounded by sheets of tin and lumber and ruined machinery. I saw a rooster but no dogs. I knew I had the right farm because I recognized the vehicles.

As I approached, an old man came out onto the sagging verandah in a singlet. He stood on the top step and scowled when I greeted him.

I was looking for Boner? I chirped.

Then you found him, he said, looking past me down the drive.

Oh, I stammered. I meant your son?

His name's Gordon.

Um, is he home?

The old man jabbed a thumb sideways and went inside. I looked at the junkyard of vehicles and noticed a muddy path which took me uphill a way past open sheds stacked with spud crates and drums. Back at the edge of the paddock, where fences gave way to peppy scrub and dunes, there was a corrugated iron hut with a rough cement porch.

Boner was startled by my arrival at his open door. He got up from his chair and limped to the threshold. Behind him the single room was squalid and chaotic. There was an oxy set on the strewn floor and tools on the single bed. He seemed anxious about letting me in. I stepped back so he could hobble out onto the porch. In his hands was a long piece of steel with a bronzed spike at one end.

What're you making? I said.

This, he said.

But what is it?

Shark-sticker.

You, you spear sharks?

He shrugged.

So how are you?

Orright.

Haven't seen you for ages, I said.

Boner turned the spear in his hands.

I hitched out, I said.

He was barefoot. It was the first time I'd seen him without his Johnny Rebs. He had hammer toes. Against the frayed hems of his jeans his feet were pasty white. We stood there a long while until he leant the spear against the tin wall.

Wanna go fishin?

I didn't know what to say. I lived in a harbour town all my life but I'd never had the slightest interest in fishing.

Okay, I said. Sure.

We drove out in the Valiant with two rods and a lard bucket full of tackle and bait. Boner had his boots on and a beanie pulled down over his ears. It took me a moment to see why he'd chosen the Valiant. He didn't say so but it was obvious that, for the moment, driving anything with a clutch was beyond him.

Out on Thunder Beach we cast for salmon and even caught a few. We stood a few yards apart with the waves clumping up and back into the deep swirling gutters in a quiet that didn't require talk. I watched and learnt and found to my surprise that I enjoyed the whole business. Nobody came by to disturb us. The white beach shimmered at our backs and the companionable silence between us lasted the whole drive back into town. I didn't tell him about the cop. Nor did I ask him again about who bashed him. I didn't want him to shut down again. I was content just to be there with him. It was as though we'd found new ground, a comfortable way of spending time together.

We saw each other off and on after that, mostly on weekends. These were always fishing trips; the aimless drives were behind us. We lit fires on the beach and fried whiting in a skillet. When his legs were good enough we'd climb around the headland at Massacre Point and float crab baits off the rocks for groper. If he got a big fish on, Boner capered about precariously in his slant-heeled boots, laughing like a troll. He never regained the truckin strut that caught my eye on the school verandah years before. Some days he could barely walk and there were times when he simply never showed up. I knew he was persecuted by headaches. His mood could swing wildly. But there were plenty of good times when I can picture him gimping along the beach with a bucket full of fish seeming almost blissful. No one was ever arrested over the beating. It didn't seem to bother him and he didn't want to talk about it.

I didn't notice what people said about us in those days. I wasn't even aware of the talk. I was absorbed in my own thoughts, caught up in the books I read, the plans I was making.

During the Christmas holiday in the city, I met a boy at the movies who walked me back the long way to the dreary motel my parents favoured, and kissed me there on the steps in the street. He came by the next morning and we took a bus to Scarborough Beach and when I got back that evening, sun-burnt and salt-streaked, my parents were in a total funk.

The boy's name was Charlie. He had shaggy blond surfer hair and puppy eyes and my father disliked him immediately. But I thought he was funny. Neither of us had cared much for *The Great Gatsby*. Charlie had a wicked line in Mia Far-row impersonations. He could get those eyes to widen and bulge and flap until he had me in stitches. In Kings Park I let him hold my breast in his hand and in the dark his smile was luminous.

The first time I saw Boner in the new year he was parked beside the steam cleaner at the Esso. The one-tonner's tray was dripping and he sat low in his seat, the bill of his cap down on his nose. I knew he'd seen me coming but he seemed anxious and reluctant to greet me. A sedan pulled up beside him – just eased in between us – and the way Boner came to attention made me veer away across the tarmac and keep going.

The last year of school just blew by. I became a school prefect, won a History prize, featured as a vicious caricature in the lower school drama production (Mae West in a mortar board, more or less).

Boner taught me to drive on the backroads. We fished occasionally and he showed me the gamefishing chair he'd bolted to the tray of the Land Rover so he could cast for sharks at night. His hands shook sometimes and I wondered what pills they were that he had in those film canisters on the seat. I smoked a little dope with him and then didn't see him for weeks at a time.

At second-term break Charlie arrived with some surfer mates in a Kombi. My mother watched me leave through the nylon lace curtains. As I showed Charlie and his two friends around town I sensed their contempt for the place. I apologized for it, smoked their weed and directed them out along the coast road. We cruised the beaches and got stoned and ended up at Boner's place on the lowlands road. But nobody came out to meet us. In front of the main house stood the bloodstained one-tonner, its tray a sticky mess of spent rifle shells and flyblown hanks of bracken. When Charlie's mates saw the gore-slick chainsaw they wanted out. We bounced back up the drive giggling with paranoia.

In my last term I lived on coffee and Tim-Tams and worked until I felt fat and old and crazy. Charlie didn't write or call. I remembered how short of passion I'd been with him. When he kissed me or held my breast I was more curious than excited. I wanted more but I wouldn't let him. I wasn't scared or ashamed or guilty – I just wasn't interested. There was none of the electricity I'd once felt with Boner squeezed between my thighs as a fifteen-year-old. I felt annoyed, if anything, and Charlie's puzzlement curdled into irritation. I didn't consciously compare him to Boner. Even Boner was someone I could sense in my wake. There was something shambling and hopeless about him now, something mildly embarrassing. I had got myself a driver's licence. I hardly saw him at all.

The final exams arrived. The school gym buzzed with flies. The papers made sense, the questions were answerable. I was prepared. The only exam where I came unstuck was French. I knew I'd done well at the Oral but the paper seemed mischievous, the questions arch and tricksy. It shouldn't have mattered but it made me angry and I tried way too hard to coat my answers with a sarcasm that I didn't have the vocab for. I wrote gobbledy-gook, made a mess of it. I came out reeling, relieved to have it all behind me, and there in the shade was Boner parked illegally at the kerb beneath the trees.

Ride? he murmured.

Thanks, but I'm going home to bed. That was my last exam.

Good?

All except French. I was in *beaucoup* shit today.

Bo-what?

Beaucoup. It's French. Means lots of.

I pressed my forehead against the warm sill of his door.

Made you somethin, he murmured.

I looked up and he passed me a piece of polished steel, a shark that was smooth and heavy in my hand.

Hey, it's lovely.

Friday, he said. I'm havin a bomfire. Massacre Point. Plenty piss. Bo-coo piss. Tell ya mates.

Sure, I said. But what mates did I have?

A teacher came striding down the path.

You better go, I said.

He waited until the teacher was all but upon us before he cranked the Chev into life.

I didn't tell anybody about Boner's party. I felt awkward and disloyal about it but there wasn't anybody I cared to ask. It was so unlike him to organize something like this. He was probably doing it for me and I hated to think of him disappointed.

When I got out to Massacre Point in the old man's precious Datsun, Boner's fire was as big as a house. The dirt turnaround above the beach was jammed with cars and there must have been a hundred people down there, a blur of bodies silhouetted by flames. As I made my way down in my kimono and silly gilt sandals the shadows of classmates spilled from the fire to wobble madly across the trodden sand. I thought of the shitty things these kids had said about us. They were the same people. Fuck the lot of you, I thought. I'm his friend. His only friend. And only his friend.

All of Boner's vehicles were there. At the ready was a pile of fuel – pine pallets, marri logs, tea chests, driftwood, furniture, milepegs and fence posts. Stuck in the sand in the firelight was the school sign itself with the daft motto – SEE FAR, AIM HIGH – emblazoned on it. More like FAR OUT, GET HIGH tonight, I thought.

Beyond the fire was a trailer full of ice and meat. On old doors between drums were beer kegs, bottles, cooking gear and cassettes. There were cut-down forty-fours to barbecue in and a full roasting spit with a beast on it.

Boner's Land Rover was backed down near the water and the tray of the nearby one-tonner was crammed with tubs of blood and offal that boys were ladling into the surf to chum for sharks. Boner had a line out already. I saw a yellow kero drum adrift beyond the breakers and his marlin gear racked at the foot of the game chair on the Landy. Pink Floyd was blasting across the beach. Everybody was pissed and laughing and talking all at once and I was remote from it, just watching while Boner moved from the fire to the water's edge trailing crowds like a guru. When he finally saw me he grinned.

Jesus, he said. You told everyone!

I found a bottle of rum and followed him down to the shore-break to wait for sharks. While we stood there kids burnt kites above us and fireworks fizzed across the sand. The air was full of smoke and of the smells of scorching meat. It was the beach at Ithaca, it was Gatsby's place, Golding's island. My head spun.

About midnight the beef on the spit was ready and we hacked at it, passed it around and ate with our hands. Everyone's eyes shone. Our teeth glistened. Our every word was funny.

Then the big reel on the back of the Landy began to scream. While Boner gimped up onto the tray, a boy from the Catholic school started the engine. Boner's earrings glittered in the fire-light as he took up the rod, clamped on the drag and set the hook with a heave. Line squirted out into the dark. The drum set up a spray and a wake and Boner leaned back and let it run. After a while he banged on the tray and the St Joe's boy reversed down to the water so that Boner could bullock back some line. It went on like that for hours – backing and filling, pumping and winding – until the Land Rover's clutch began to stink and the radiator threatened to boil over. The first driver was relieved by another boy whose girlfriend sprawled across the bonnet to pour beer down his neck through the drop-down windscreen. Now and then he backed up so far that there were waves crashing on the tailgate and I half expected the shark to come surfing out into Boner's lap.

He looked beautiful in the firelight, as glossy and sculpted as the steel carving he'd given me. When the shark bellied up into the shallow wash, Boner limped into the water with his inch-thick spear and drove it through the creature's head and a kind of exhausted sigh went up along the beach.

The fire burnt down. We drank and dozed until sun-up.

Within two days I was gone and it was a long time before I looked back.

During my years at university, I met my parents every Christmas in the dreary motel in the city. We had our strained little festivities, the walks through the campus and down along the foreshore. They told me stories of home but it didn't feel like home anymore. I saw a few old faces from down there but never let them think that I remembered them. I liked the expressions of hurt and confusion that came upon them. I got satisfaction from it. I heard that Erin began teacher's college, but dropped out, married young and had children. One summer afternoon she pestered me on a bus the entire length of Stirling Highway. She was fat. She wanted to catch up, to show me her brood. I got off two stops early just to be rid of her.

When I finished my Honours I drove south just the once to please my parents. The whaling station was defunct. The harbour stank of choking algae. I saw Boner parked in an F-100 outside a pub the tuna men liked. He blinked when he saw me. He was jowly and smelled nasty. He looked a wreck. His teeth were bad and his gut was bloated.

Jackie, he said.

What *are* you doing? I asked, forgetting myself enough to lay hands on his sleeve along the window sill.

Quiet life's the good life, he mumbled, detaching himself from me. Wanna ride? Go fishin?

Gotta meet my oldies in five minutes, I said. Why don't I drive out tomorrow? I'll get you.

No, I'll drive out.

He shrugged.

When I drove out the next day the McPharlin place was even more of a shambles than I remembered. The old man sat on the verandah, frail but still fierce. I waved and went on up to Boner's shack and found him on his cot with a pipe on his chest and the ropey smell of pot in the air. He was asleep. On the walls were sets of shark jaws. The floor was strewn with oily engine parts. I almost stepped away but he sat up, startled. The little pipe hit the floor.

Me, I said.

He looked confused.

Jackie, I said.

He got off the bed in stages, like an old man.

One day I'll kill him, he said. Take me sticker down there and jam it through his fuckin head.

It's Jackie, I said.

I don't care. You think I care?

I went east for postgrad work and then left the country altogether. I did the things I dreamt of, some diplomatic stints, the UN, some teaching, a think-tank. I took a year off and lived in Mexico, tried to write a book but it didn't work out; it was like *trying* to fall in love. I was lonely and restless.

Then my father died and my mother went to pieces. I was almost grateful for the excuse to fly home to escape failure. I came back, sold their house and set my mother up in an apartment in the city. For a while I even lived with her and that's when I discovered that she was an addict. We didn't get close. We'd got a little too far along for that but we had our companionable moments. She died in a clinic of pneumonia the first winter I was back.

For several months I was lost. I didn't want to return to being a glorified bureaucrat. I had no more interest in the academy. I had an affair with a svelte Irishwoman who imported antiquities and ethnographic material for collectors. As with all my entanglements there was more curiosity from my side of it than passion. Her name was Ethna. She must have sensed that my heart wasn't in it; it was over in a matter of weeks but we remained friends and, in time, I became her partner in business.

It was 1991 when I got the call from the police to say that they had Gordon McPharlin in custody. They asked whether I could come down to help them clear up some matters relating to the death of Lawrence McPharlin.

I flew to Angelus expecting Boner to be up on a murder charge, but when I arrived I found that he was not in the lockup but in the district hospital under heavy sedation. The old man had died in his sleep at least ten days previous and an unnamed person had discovered Boner cowering in a spud crate behind the shed. He was suffering from exposure and completely incoherent.

There's no next of kin, said a smooth-looking detective who met me at the hospital. We found you from letters he had. And we know that you went to school with him, that there'd been . . . well, a longstanding relationship.

I knew him, yes, I said as evenly as I could.

He was in quite a state, said the detective. He was naked when he was found. He had a set of shark jaws around his neck and his head and face were badly cut. His shack was full of weapons and ammunition and . . . well, some disturbing pornography. There was also a cache of drugs.

What kind of drugs? I asked.

I'm sorry, I'm not at liberty to say. Ah, there was also some injury to his genitals.

And is he being charged with an offence?

No, said the cop. He's undergone a psychiatric evaluation and he's being committed for his own good. We need to know if there's anyone else, family members we don't know about, who we might contact.

You needed me to fly here to ask me that?

I'm sorry, he murmured. I thought you were his friend.

I am his friend, I said. His oldest friend.

Good, he said. Good. We thought you could accompany him, travel with him up to the city when he goes. You know, a familiar face to smooth the way.

Jesus, I muttered, overcome at the misery and the suddenness of it. I was determined not to cry, or be shrill.

When?

Ah, tomorrow morning.

Fine, I said. Can I see him now?

The cop and a nurse took me in to see Boner. He was in a private room. There were restraints on the bed. He was sleeping. His lungs sounded spongy. His face was a mess of scabs and bruises. I cried.

That afternoon I hired a car and drove out along the lowlands road to the old McPharlin place. The main house gave off a stink I did not want to investigate. All the old cars were still there, plus a few that had come after my time. The HT van was up on blocks, the engine gone. I looked around the sheds and found broken crates, some bloodstains.

Boner's hut looked like a cyclone had been through it. The floor was a tangle of tools and spare parts, of broken plates and thrown food, as though he'd gone on a rampage, emptying drawers and boxes, throwing bottles and yanking tapes from cassette spools. His mattress was hacked open and the shark sticker had been driven into it. They were right, he'd lost his mind. A squarish set of shark jaws lay on the pillow. It took me a moment to register the neat pile of magazines beside it. On impulse I reached down to pick one off the pile but froze when I saw it. This was the porn they'd told me about. The cover featured the body of a woman spread across the bonnet of a big American car, her knees wide. There were little holes burnt in the paper where the woman's anus and vagina had been, as though someone had touched the glossy paper with a precisely aimed cigarette. On the model's shoulders, boxed in with stickytape, was my face, my head. A black and white image of me at sixteen. Unaware of the camera, laughing. I felt a rush of nausea and rage. The fucking creep! The miserable, sick bastard.

I didn't even touch it. I went outside and sucked in some air. I felt robbed, undone. The ground was unstable underfoot. I had to sit down while something collapsed within me.

When I left I hadn't really got myself into good enough shape to drive but I couldn't stay there any longer. I was halfway down the rutted drive when another car eased in from the highway. At least it was twilight. At least I wasn't crying. As the car got close I recognized the cop from earlier that day. There was another detective with him, a taller man. They pulled up beside me.

Everything alright? the cop asked.

Just wonderful, I said, wanting only for him to get out of my way so I could get the hell off the place and find a stiff drink in town.

You need to talk about it?

No, I don't need any talk. I'll be there in the morning. Let's get it over with.

The cop nodded, satisfied. His mate, the tall redhead, didn't even look my way. I wound up my window and they crept past.

Next day I sat beside Boner in the back of an ordinary-looking mini-van with another woman who I could only assume was a nurse. We didn't speak. What I'd seen in Boner's cabin made it difficult for me to sit there at all, let alone make conversation. During the five hours, Boner mostly slept. Sometimes he muttered beneath his breath and once, for about half an hour without pause, he sobbed in a way that seemed almost mechanical. The only thing he said all day was a single sentence. *Eat though young*. Perhaps it was *thy* young or even *their* young. I couldn't make it out. His mouth seemed unable to shape the words. I couldn't bear to listen. I dug the Walkman from my bag and listened to a lecture on Buddhism.

Boner was never released. He didn't recover. Even though I drove past the private hospital almost every day I only ever visited at New Year. I went because I conceded that he was sick. He hadn't been responsible for his actions. I didn't go any more frequently than that because my disgust overrode everything else. When I went I wheeled him out into the garden where he liked to watch the wattlebirds catch moths. He had an almost vicious fascination for the Moreton Bay fig. He said it looked like a screaming neck.

Over the years there were visits when he was hostile, when he refused to acknowledge me, and occasions when I thought he was faking mental illness altogether. He had been lame for some time but after years of shunting himself about the ward in a wheelchair he became so disabled by arthritis that he relied on others to push him. His hands were claw-like, his knees horribly distorted. When I realized how bad it had become, I sent along supplies of chondroitin in the hope that it might give him some small relief. I don't know that it ever helped but he seemed to enjoy the fact that the nasty-tasting powder was made from shark cartilage. It brought on his troll-laugh. He'd launch into a monologue that made no sense at all.

The visits were always difficult. The place itself was quiet and orderly but Boner was a wild, twisted little man; an ancient child, fat and revolting. And of course I was busy. The import business had become my own when I bought Ethna out. I travelled a lot. I sold my house and the weekender at Eagle Bay and bought a Kharmann Ghia and an old pearling lugger. I lived on the boat in the marina and told myself that I could cast off at a moment's notice. I would not be cowed by middle age; I was my own woman. And I valued my equilibrium. I didn't need the turmoil of seeing Boner McPharlin more than once a year.

This year, on New Year's Day, I wheeled Boner out among the roses and he slumped in the chair, slit-eyed and watchful, and before we got to the tree that provoked his usual spiel about his mother's screaming neck, he began to whisper.

Santa's helpers came early for Christmas.

What's that? I said distractedly. I was hungover and going through the motions.

Four of the cunts. Same four, same cunts.

Boner, I said. Don't be gross.

Cunts are scared. Came by all scared. Big red, he's lost his hair. Frightened I'll dog him. Fuckin cunts, every one of em. Come in here like that. Fuckin think they are?

Someone visited? I asked.

Santa's helpers.

Did you know them?

Wouldn't *they* like to know? he said with a wheezy giggle.

I stopped pushing him a moment. The light was blinding. Already his hair hung in sweaty strings on his neck. The sun-light caused him to squint and he licked his cracked lips in a repulsive involuntary cycle. There were scars in his earlobes where he'd torn his earrings out years before. Despite the heat he insisted on a blanket for his legs.

So, did you? I asked. Know them, I mean.

You put me here, he said.

I'm your friend.

Friend be fucked.

Your only friend, Boner.

You see that tree? You see that tree? That tree? That's my mother's screamin neck.

Yes, you've told me.

Screamin neck, not a sound. You can hang me from that tree, I don't care, you and them can hang me, I don't care.

Stop it.

Let em do it, let em see, the pack a cunts. Never know when I might bite, eh. Even when I'm dead. Shark'll still go you when you think he's dead.

Happy New Year, Boner.

Get me out, Jack. Let's piss off.

You are out. See, we're in the courtyard.

Out! *Out*, you stupid bitch.

I'm going now.

You're old, he said mildly. You used to be pretty.

That's enough.

They said it, not me.

I have to go.

See if I fuckin care.

I really have to leave.

Well it's not fuckin right. I never said a word. Never once.

Boner, I can't stay.

Just drivin, that's all I did. Never touched anythin, anybody, and never said a word – Jesus!

I'll turn you around.

Please, Jackie. Let's ride, let's just arc it up and go.

Both of us were crying when I wheeled him into the darkness of the ward. He slumped in the chair. I left him there.

***

A week later he was dead. The hospital told me it was a massive heart attack. I didn't press for details. Looking back I see that I never did, not once.

There were six of us at the cremation – a nurse, four men and me. Nobody spoke but the priest. I didn't hear a word that was said. I was too busy staring at those men. They were older of course, but I knew they were the cops from back home. There was the neat one in the good suit who'd called me about Boner's breakdown. Two others whose faces were familiar. And the tall redhead who'd asked to see my arms when I was sixteen years old. His hair was faded, receding, his eyes still watchful.

I began to weep. I thought of Boner's fire, his twisted bones, his terrible silence. I got a hold of myself but during the committal, as the coffin sank, the sigh I let out was almost a moan. The sound of recognition, the sound of too late.

I walked out. The redheaded detective intercepted me on the steps. The others hung back in the shade of the crematorium.

My condolences, Jackie, he purred. I know you were his only friend.

He didn't have any friends, I said, stepping round him. You should know that, you bastard – you made sure of it.

I'm retired now, he said.

Congratulations, I said as I pushed away.

I drove around the river past my office and showrooms and went on down to the harbour. I cruised along the wharf a way and then along the mole to where the river surged out into the sea. I parked. The summer sun drove down but I was shivery.

The talk on the radio was all about the endless Royal Commission. I snapped it off and laid my cheek against the hot window.

I didn't see it whole yet – it was too early for the paranoia and second-guessing to set in – but I could feel things change shape around me. My life, my history, the sense I had of my self, were no longer solid.

All I knew was this, that I hadn't been Boner's friend at all. Hadn't been for years. A friend paid attention, showed a modicum of curiosity, made a bit of an effort. A friend didn't believe the worst without checking. A friend didn't keep her eyes shut and walk away. Just the outline now, but I was beginning to see.

They'd turned me. They played with me, set me against him to isolate him completely. Boner was their creature. All that driving, the silence, the leeway, it had to be drugs. He was driving their smack. Or something. Whatever it was he was their creature and they broke him.

I sat in the car beneath the lighthouse and thought of how I'd looked on and seen nothing. I was no different to my parents. Yet I always believed I'd come so far, surpassed so much. At fifteen I would have annihilated myself for love, but over the years something had happened, something I hadn't bothered to notice, as though in all that leaving, in the rush to outgrow the small-town girl I was, I'd left more of myself behind than the journey required.

THE WAVEMAKER FALTERS

George Saunders

George Saunders (b.1958) was born in Texas, grew up in Chicago and took a degree in geophysical engineering from Colorado School of Mines before being awarded an MA in creative writing from Syracuse. His work includes *CivilWarLand in Bad Decline*, *Pastoralia* and *Tenth of December*, as well as *The Very Persistent Gappers of Frip*. He has won a number of awards including a MacArthur Fellowship, the 2013 PEN/Malamud Award and the inaugural Folio Prize for Literature in 2014.

Halfway up the mountain it's the Center for Wayward Nuns, full of sisters and other religious personnel who've become doubtful. Once a few of them came down to our facility in stern suits and swam cautiously. The singing from up there never exactly knocks your socks off. It's very conditional singing, probably because of all the doubt. A young nun named Sister Viv came unglued there last fall and we gave her a free season pass to come down and meditate near our simulated Spanish trout stream whenever she wanted. The head nun said Viv was from Idaho and sure enough the stream seemed to have a calming effect.

One day she's sitting cross-legged a few feet away from a Dumpster housed in a granite boulder made of a resilient synthetic material. Ned, Tony, and Gerald as usual are dressed as Basques. In Orientation they learned a limited amount of actual Basque so that they can lapse into it whenever Guests are within earshot. Sister Viv's a regular so they don't even bother. I look over to say something supportive and optimistic to her and then I think oh jeez, not another patron death on my hands. She's going downstream fast and her habit's ballooning up. The fake Basques are standing there in a row with their mouths open.

So I dive in and drag her out. It's not very deep and the bottom's rubber-matted. None of the Basques are bright enough to switch off the Leaping Trout Subroutine however, so twice I get scraped with little fiberglass fins. Finally I get her out on the pine needles and she comes to and spits in my face and says I couldn't possibly know the darkness of her heart. Try me, I say. She crawls away and starts bashing her skull against a tree trunk. The trees are synthetic too. But still.

I pin her arms behind her and drag her to the Main Office, where they chain her weeping to the safe. A week later she runs amok in the nun eating hall and stabs a cafeteria worker to death.

So the upshot of it all is more guilt for me, Mr. Guilt.

***

Once a night Simone puts on the mermaid tail and lip-synchs on a raft in the wave pool while I play spotlights over her and broadcast "Button Up Your Overcoat." Tonight as I'm working the lights I watch Leon, Subquadrant Manager, watch Simone. As he watches her his wet mouth keeps moving. Every time I accidentally light up the Chlorine Shed the Guests start yelling at me. Finally I stop watching Leon watch her and try to concentrate on not getting written up for crappy showmanship.

I can't stand Leon. On the wall of his office he's got a picture of himself Jell-O-wrestling a traveling celebrity Jell-O-wrestler. That's pure Leon. Plus he had her autograph it. First he tried to talk her into dipping her breasts in ink and doing an imprint but she said no way. My point is, even traveling celebrity Jell-O-wrestlers have more class than Leon.

He follows us into Costuming and chats up Simone while helping her pack away her tail. Do I tell him to get lost? No. Do I knock him into a planter to remind him just whose wife Simone is? No. I go out and wait for her by Loco Logjam. I sit on a turnstile. The Italian lights in the trees are nice. The night crew's hard at work applying a wide range of commercial chemicals and cleaning hair balls from the filter. Some exiting guests are brawling in the traffic jam on the access road. Through a federal program we offer discount coupons to the needy, so sometimes our clientele is borderline. Once some bikers trashed the row of boutiques, and once Leon interrupted a gang guy trying to put hydrochloric acid in the Main Feeder.

Finally Simone's ready and we walk over to Employee Underground Parking. Bald Murray logs us out while trying to look down Simone's blouse. On the side of the road a woman's sitting in a shopping cart, wearing a grubby chemise.

For old time's sake I put my hand in Simone's lap.

Promises, promises, she says.

At the roadcut by the self-storage she makes me stop so she can view all the interesting stratification. She's never liked geology before. Leon takes geology at the community college and is always pointing out what's glacial till and what's not, so I suspect there's a connection. We get into a little fight about him and she admires his self-confidence to my face. I ask her is that some kind of a put-down. She's only saying, she says, that in her book a little boldness goes a long way. She asks if I remember the time Leon chased off the frat boy who kept trying to detach her mermaid hairpiece. Where was I? Why didn't I step in? Is she my girl or what?

I remind her that I was busy at the controls.

It gets very awkward and quiet. Me at the controls is a sore subject. Nothing's gone right for us since the day I crushed the boy with the wavemaker. I haven't been able to forget his little white trunks floating out of the inlet port all bloody. Who checks protective-screen mounting screws these days? Not me. Leon does when he wavemakes of course. It's in the protocol. That's how he got to be Sub-quadrant Manager, attention to detail. Leon's been rising steadily since we went through Orientation together, and all told he's saved three Guests and I've crushed the shit out of one.

The little boy I crushed was named Clive. By all accounts he was a sweet kid.

Sometimes at night I sneak over there to do chores in secret and pray for forgiveness at his window. I've changed his dad's oil and painted all their window frames and taken the burrs off their Labrador. If anybody comes out while I'm working I hide in the shrubs. The sister who wears cateye glasses even in this day and age thinks it's Clive's soul doing the mystery errands and lately she's been leaving him notes. Simone says I'm not doing them any big favor by driving their daughter nuts.

But I can't help it. I feel so bad.

We pull up to our unit and I see that once again the Peretti twins have drawn squashed boys all over our windows with soap. Their dad's a bruiser. No way I'm forcing a confrontation.

In the driveway Simone asks did I do my résumé at lunch.

No, I tell her, I had a serious pH difficulty.

Fine, she says, make waves the rest of your life.

The day it happened, an attractive all-girl glee club was lying around on the concrete in Kawabunga Kove in Day-Glo suits, looking for all the world like a bunch of blooms. The president and sergeant at arms were standing with brown ankles in the shallow, favorably comparing my Attraction to real surf. To increase my appeal I had the sea chanteys blaring. I was operating at the prescribed wave-frequency setting but in my lust for the glee club had the magnitude pegged.

Leon came by and told me to turn the music down. So I turned it up. Consequently I never heard Clive screaming or Leon shouting at me to kill the waves. My first clue was looking out the Control Hut porthole and seeing people bolting towards the ladders, choking and with bits of Clive all over them. Guests were weeping while wiping their torsos on the lawn. In the Handicapped Section the chaired guys had their eyes shut tight and their heads turned away as the gore sloshed towards them. The ambulatories were clambering over the ropes, screaming for their physical therapists.

Leon hates to say he told me so but does it all the time anyway. He constantly reminds me of how guilty I am by telling me not to feel guilty and asking about my counseling. My counselor is Mr. Poppet, a gracious and devout man who's always tightening his butt cheeks when he thinks no one's looking. Mr. Poppet makes me sit with my eyes closed and repeat, "A boy is dead because of me," for half an hour for fifty dollars. Then for another fifty dollars he makes me sit with my eyes closed again and repeat, "Still, I'm a person of considerable value," for half an hour. When the session's over I go out into the bright sun like a rodent that lives in the earth, blinking and rubbing my eyes, and Mr. Poppet stands in the doorway, clapping for me and intoning the time of day of our next appointment.

The sessions have done me good. Clive doesn't come into my room at night all hacked up anymore. He comes in pretty much whole. He comes in and sits on my bed and starts talking to me. Since his death he's been hanging around with dead kids from other epochs. One night he showed up swearing in Latin. Another time with a wild story about an ancient African culture that used radio waves to relay tribal myths. He didn't use those exact words of course. Even though he's dead, he's still basically a kid. When he tries to be scary he gets it all wrong. He can't moan for beans. He's scariest when he does real kid things, like picking his nose and wiping it on the side of his sneaker.

He tries to be polite but he's pretty mad about the future I denied him. To-night's subject is what the Mexico City trip with the perky red-haired tramp would have been like. He dwells on the details of their dinner in the catacombs and describes how her freckles would have looked as daylight streamed in through the cigarette-burned magenta curtains. Wistfully he says he sure would like to have tasted the sauce she would have said was too hot to be believed as they crossed the dirt road lined with begging cripples.

"Forgive me," I say in tears.

"No," he says, also in tears.

Near dawn he sighs, tucks in the parts of his body that have been gradually leaking out over the course of the night, pats my neck with his cold little palm, and tells me to have a nice day. Then he fades, producing farts with a wet hand under his armpit.

Simone sleeps through the whole thing, making little puppy sounds and push-ing her rear against my front to remind me even in her sleep of how long it's been. But you try it. You kill a nice little kid via neglect and then enjoy having sex. If you can do it you're demented.

Simone's an innocent victim. Sometimes I think I should give her her space and let her explore various avenues so her personal development won't get sty-mied. But I could never let her go. I've loved her too long. Once in high school I waited three hours in a locker in the girls' locker room to see her in her pant-ies. Every part of me cramped up, but when she finally came in and showered I resolved to marry her. We once dedicated a whole night to pretending I was a household invader who tied her up. In my shorts I stood outside our sliding-glass door shouting, "Meter man!" At dawn or so I made us eggs but was so high on her I ruined our only pan by leaving it on the burner while I kept running back and forth to look at her nude.

What I'm saying is, we go way back.

I hope she'll wait this thing out. If only Clive would resume living and start dating some nice-smelling cheerleader who has no idea who Benny Goodman is. Then I'd regain my strength and win her back. But no. Instead I wake at night and Simone's either looking over at me with hatred or whisking her privates with her index finger while thinking of God-knows-who, although I doubt very much it's me.

At noon next day a muscleman shows up with four beehives on a dolly. This is Leon's stroke of genius for the Kiper wedding. The Kipers are the natural type. They don't want to eat anything that ever lived or buy any product that even vaguely supports notorious third-world regimes. They asked that we run a check on the ultimate source of the tomatoes in our ketchup and the union status of the group that makes our floaties. They've opted to recite their vows in the Waterfall Grove. They've hired a blind trumpeter to canoe by and a couple of illegal aliens to retrieve the rice so no birds will choke.

At ten Leon arrives, proudly bearing a large shrimp-shaped serving vat full of bagels coated with fresh honey. Over the weekend he studied honey extraction techniques at the local library. He's always calling himself a Renaissance man but the way he says it it rhymes with "rent-a-dance fan." He puts down the vat and takes off the lid. Just then the bride's grandmother falls out of her chair and rolls down the bank. She stops faceup at the water's edge and her wig tips back. One of the rice-retrievers wanders up and addresses her as señora. I look around. I'm the nearest Host. According to the manual I'm supposed to initiate CPR or face a stiff payroll deduction. The week I took the class the dummy was on the fritz. Of course.

I straddle her and timidly start chest-pumping. I can feel her bra clasp under the heel of my hand. Nothing happens. I keep waiting for her to throw up on me or come to life. Then Leon vaults over the shrimp-shaped vat. He shoos me away, checks her pulse, and begins the Heimlich Maneuver.

"When your victim is elderly," he says loudly and remonstratively, "it's natural to assume heart attack. Natural, but, in this case, possibly deadly."

After a few more minutes of Heimlich he takes a pen from his pocket and drives it into her throat. Almost immediately she sits up and readjusts her wig, with the pen still sticking out. Leon kisses her forehead and makes her lie back down, then gives the thumbs-up.

The crowd bursts into applause.

I sneak off and sit for about an hour on the floor of the Control Hut. I keep hoping it'll blow up or a nuclear war will start so I'll die. But I don't die. So I go over and pick up my wife.

Leon wants to terminate me but Simone has a serious chat with him about our mortgage and he lets me stay on in Towel Distribution and Collection. Actually it's a relief. Nobody can get hurt. The worst that could happen is maybe a yeast infection. It's a relief until I go to his office one day with the Usage Statistics and hear moans from inside and hide behind a soda machine until Simone comes out looking flushed and happy. I want to jump out and confront her but I don't. Then Leon comes out and I want to jump out and confront him but I don't.

What I do is wait behind the soda machine until they leave, then climb out a window and hitchhike home. I get a ride from a guy who sells and services Zambonis. He tells me to confront her forcefully and watch her fall to pieces. If she doesn't fall to pieces I should beat her.

When I get home I confront her forcefully. She doesn't fall to pieces. Not only does she not deny it, she says it's going to continue no matter what. She says I've been absent too long. She says there's more to Leon than meets the eye.

I think of beating her, and my heart breaks, and I give up on everything.

Clive shows up at ten. As he keeps me awake telling me what his senior prom would have been like, Simone calls Leon's name in her sleep and mutters something about his desk calendar leaving a paper cut on her neck. Clive follows me into the kitchen, wanting to know what a nosegay is. Outside, all the corn in the cornfield is bent over and blowing. The moon comes up over Delectable Videos like a fat man withdrawing himself from a lake. I fall asleep at the counter. The phone rings at three. It's Clive's father, saying he's finally shaken himself from his stupor and is coming over to kill me.

I tell him I'll leave the door open.

Clive's been in the bathroom imagining himself some zits. Even though he's one of the undead I have a lot of affection for him. When he comes out I tell him he'll have to go, and that I'll see him tomorrow. He whines a bit but finally fades away.

His dad pulls up in a Land Cruiser and gets out with a big gun. He comes through the door in an alert posture and sees me sitting on the couch. I can tell he's been drinking.

"I don't hate you," he says. "But I can't have you living on this earth while my son isn't."

"I understand," I say.

Looking sheepish, he steps over and puts the gun to my head. The sound of our home's internal ventilation system is suddenly wondrous. The mole on his cheek possesses grace. Children would have been nice.

I close my eyes and wait. Then I urinate myself. Then I wait some more. I wait and wait. Then I open my eyes. He's gone and the front door's wide open.

Jesus, I think, embarrassing, I wet myself and was ready to die.

Then I go for a brisk walk.

I hike into the hills and sit in a graveyard. The stars are blinking like cat's eyes and burned blood is pouring out of the slaughterhouse chimney. My crotch is cold with the pee and the breeze. The moon goes behind a cloud and six pale forms start down from the foothills. At first I think they're ghosts but they're only starving pronghorn come down to lick salt from the headstones. I sit there trying to write Simone off. No more guys ogling her in public and no more dippy theories on world hunger. Then I think of her and Leon watching the test pattern together nude and sweaty and I moan and double over with dread, and a doe bolts away in alarm.

A storm rolls in over the hills and a brochure describing a portrait offer gets plastered across my chest. Lightning strikes the slaughterhouse flagpole and the antelope scatter like minnows as the rain begins to fall, and finally, having lost what was to be lost, my torn and black heart rebels, saying enough already, enough, this is as low as I go.

A REAL DOLL

A.M. Homes

A.M. Homes (b.1961) was born in Washington DC. She studied with the writer Grace Paley at Sarah Lawrence College. Her novels and stories have been described as controversial, but that has not stopped her work being awarded a Guggenheim Fellowship and, most recently, the Women's Prize for Fiction for *May We Be Forgiven*, in 2013. "I think fiction can help us find everything. You know, I think in fiction you can say things and in a way be truer than you can be in real life and truer than you can be in non-fiction. There's an accuracy to fiction that people don't really talk about – an emotional accuracy."

I'm dating Barbie. Three afternoons a week, while my sister is at dance class, I take Barbie away from Ken. I'm practising for the future.

At first I sat in my sister's room watching Barbie, who lived with Ken, on a doily, on top of the dresser.

I was looking at her but not really looking. I was looking, and all of the sudden realized she was staring at me.

She was sitting next to Ken, his khaki-covered thigh absently rubbing her bare leg. He was rubbing her, but she was staring at me.

"Hi," she said.

"Hello," I said.

"I'm Barbie," she said, and Ken stopped rubbing her leg.

"I know."

"You're Jenny's brother."

I nodded. My head was bobbing up and down like a puppet on a weight.

"I really like your sister. She's sweet," Barbie said. "Such a good little girl. Especially lately, she makes herself so pretty, and she's started doing her nails."

I wondered if Barbie noticed that Miss Wonderful bit her nails and that when she smiled her front teeth were covered with little flecks of purple nail polish. I wondered if she knew Jennifer colored in the chipped chewed spots with purple magic marker, and then sometimes sucked on her fingers so that not only did she have purple flecks of polish on her teeth, but her tongue was the strangest shade of violet.

"So listen," I said. "Would you like to go out for a while? Grab some fresh air, maybe take a spin around the backyard?"

"Sure," she said.

I picked her up by her feet. It sounds unusual but I was too petrified to take her by the waist. I grabbed her by the ankles and carried her off like a Popsicle stick.

As soon as we were out back, sitting on the porch of what I used to call my fort, but which my sister and parents referred to as the playhouse, I started freaking. I was suddenly and incredibly aware that I was out with Barbie. I didn't know what to say.

"So, what kind of a Barbie are you?" I asked.

"Excuse me?"

"Well, from listening to Jennifer I know there's Day to Night Barbie, Magic Moves Barbie, Gift-Giving Barbie, Tropical Barbie, My First Barbie, and more."

"I'm Tropical," she said. I'm Tropical, she said, the same way a person might say I'm Catholic or I'm Jewish. "I came with a one-piece bathing suit, a brush, and a ruffle you can wear so many ways," Barbie squeaked.

She actually squeaked. It turned out that squeaking was Barbie's birth defect. I pretended I didn't hear it.

We were quiet for a minute. A leaf larger than Barbie fell from the maple tree above us and I caught it just before it would have hit her. I half expected her to squeak, "You saved my life. I'm yours, forever." Instead she said, in a perfectly normal voice, "Wow, big leaf."

I looked at her. Barbie's eyes were sparkling blue like the ocean on a good day. I looked and in a moment noticed she had the whole world, the cosmos, drawn in makeup above and below her eyes. An entire galaxy, clouds, stars, a sun, the sea, painted onto her face. Yellow, blue, pink, and a million silver sparkles.

We sat looking at each other, looking and talking and then not talking and looking again. It was a stop-and-start thing with both of us constantly saying the wrong thing, saying anything, and then immediately regretting having said it.

It was obvious Barbie didn't trust me. I asked her if she wanted something to drink.

"Diet Coke," she said. And I wondered why I'd asked.

I went into the house, upstairs into my parents' bathroom, opened the medicine cabinet, and got a couple of Valiums. I immediately swallowed one. I figured if I could be calm and collected, she'd realize I wasn't going to hurt her. I broke another Valium into a million small pieces, dropped some slivers into Barbie's Diet Coke, and swished it around so it'd blend. I figured if we could be calm and collected together, she'd be able to trust me even sooner. I was falling in love in a way that had nothing to do with love.

"So, what's the deal with you and Ken?" I asked later after we'd loosened up, after she'd drunk two Diet Cokes, and I'd made another trip to the medicine cabinet.

She giggled. "Oh, we're just really good friends."

"What's the deal with him really, you can tell me, I mean, is he or isn't he?"

"Ish she or ishn' she," Barbie said, in a slow slurred way, like she was so intoxicated that if they made a Breathalyzer for Valium, she'd melt it.

I regretted having fixed her a third Coke. I mean if she o.d.'ed and died Jennifer would tell my mom and dad for sure.

"Is he a faggot or what?"

Barbie laughed and I almost slapped her. She looked me straight in the eye.

"He lusts after me," she said. "I come home at night and he's standing there, waiting. He doesn't wear underwear, you know. I mean, isn't that strange, Ken doesn't own any underwear. I heard Jennifer tell her friend that they don't even make any for him. Anyway, he's always, there waiting, and I'm like, Ken we're friends, okay, that's it. I mean, have you ever noticed, he has molded plastic hair. His head and his hair are all one piece. I can't go out with a guy like that. Besides, I don't think he'd be up for it if you know what I mean. Ken is not what you'd call well endowed . . . All he's got is a little plastic bump, more of a hump, really, and what the hell are you supposed to do with that?"

She was telling me things I didn't think I should hear and all the same, I was leaning into her, like if I moved closer she'd tell me more. I was taking every word and holding it for a minute, holding groups of words in my head like I didn't understand English. She went on and on, but I wasn't listening.

The sun sank behind the playhouse, Barbie shivered, excused herself, and ran around back to throw up. I asked her if she felt okay. She said she was fine, just a little tired, that maybe she was coming down with the flu or something. I gave her a piece of a piece of gum to chew and took her inside.

On the way back to Jennifer's room I did something Barbie almost didn't forgive me for, I did something which not only shattered the moment, but nearly wrecked the possibility of our having a future together.

In the hallway between the stairs and Jennifer's room, I popped Barbie's head into my mouth, like lion and tamer, God and Godzilla.

I popped her whole head into my mouth, and Barbie's hair separated into single strands like Christmas tinsel and caught in my throat nearly choking me. I could taste layer on layer of makeup, Revlon, Max Factor, and Maybelline. I closed my mouth around Barbie and could feel her breath in mine. I could hear her screams in my throat. Her teeth, white, Pearl Drops, Pepsodent, and the whole Osmond family, bit my tongue and the inside of my cheek like I might accidently bite myself. I closed my mouth around her neck and held her suspended, her feet uselessly kicking the air in front of my face.

Before pulling her out, I pressed my teeth lightly into her neck, leaving marks Barbie described as scars of her assault, but which I imagined as a New Age necklace of love.

"I have never, ever in my life been treated with such utter disregard," she said as soon as I let her out.

She was lying. I knew Jennifer sometimes did things with Barbie. I didn't mention that once I'd seen Barbie hanging from Jennifer's ceiling fan, spinning around in great wide circles, like some imitation Superman.

"I'm sorry if I scared you."

"Scared me!" she squeaked.

She went on squeaking, a cross between the squeal when you let the air out of a balloon and a smoke alarm with weak batteries. While she was squeaking, the phrase *a head in the mouth is worth two in the bush* started running through my head. I knew it had come from somewhere, started as something else, but I couldn't get it right. *A head in the mouth is worth two in the bush*, again and again, like the punch line to some dirty joke.

"Scared me. Scared me. Scared me!" Barbie squeaked louder and louder until finally she had my attention again. "Have you ever been held captive in the dark cavern of someone's body?"

I shook my head. It sounded wonderful.

"Typical," she said. "So incredibly, typically male."

For a moment I was proud.

"Why do you have to do things you know you shouldn't, and worse, you do them with a light in your eye, like you're getting some weird pleasure that only another boy would understand. You're all the same," she said. "You're all Jack Nicholson."

I refused to put her back in Jennifer's room until she forgave me, until she understood that I'd done what I did with only the truest of feeling, no harm intended.

I heard Jennifer's feet clomping up the stairs. I was running out of time.

"You know I'm really interested in you," I said to Barbie.

"Me too," she said, and for a minute I wasn't sure if she meant she was interested in herself or me.

"We should do this again," I said. She nodded.

I leaned down to kiss Barbie. I could have brought her up to my lips, but somehow it felt wrong. I leaned down to kiss her and the first thing I got was her nose in my mouth. I felt like a St. Bernard saying hello.

No matter how graceful I tried to be, I was forever licking her face. It wasn't a question of putting my tongue in her ear or down her throat, it was simply literally trying not to suffocate her. I kissed Barbie with my back to Ken and then turned around and put her on the doily right next to him. I was tempted to drop her down on Ken, to, mash her into him, but I managed to restrain myself.

"That was fun," Barbie said. I heard Jennifer in the hall.

"Later," I said.

Jennifer came into the room and looked at me.

"What?" I said.

"It's my room," she said.

"There was a bee in it. I was killing it for you."

"A bee. I'm allergic to bees. Mom, Mom," she screamed. "There's a bee."

"Mom's not home. I killed it."

"But there might be another one."

"So call me and I'll kill it."

"But if it stings me I might die." I shrugged and walked out. I could feel Barbie watching me leave.

I took a Valium about twenty minutes before I picked her up the next Friday. By the time I went into Jennifer's room, everything was getting easier.

"Hey," I said when I got up to the dresser.

She was there on the doily with Ken, they were back to back, resting against each other, legs stretched out in front of them.

Ken didn't look at me. I didn't care.

"You ready to go?" I asked. Barbie nodded. "I thought you might be thirsty." I handed her the Diet Coke I'd made for her.

I'd figured Barbie could take a little less than an eighth of a Valium without getting totally senile. Basically, I had to give her Valium crumbs since there was no way to cut one that small.

She took the Coke and drank it right in front of Ken. I kept waiting for him to give me one of those I-know-what-you're-up-to-and-I-don't-like-it looks, the kind my father gives me when he walks into my room without knocking and I automatically jump twenty feet in the air.

Ken acted like he didn't even know I was there. I hated him.

"I can't do a lot of walking this afternoon," Barbie said.

I nodded. I figured no big deal since mostly I seemed to be carrying her around anyway.

"My feet are killing me," she said.

I was thinking about Ken.

"Don't you have other shoes?"

My family was very into shoes. No matter what seemed to be wrong my father always suggested it could be cured by wearing a different pair of shoes. He believed that shoes, like tires, should be rotated.

"It's not the shoes," she said. "It's my toes."

"Did you drop something on them?" My Valium wasn't working. I was having trouble making small talk. I needed another one.

"Jennifer's been chewing on them,"

"What?"

"She chews on my toes."

"You let her chew your footies?"

I couldn't make sense out of what she was saying. I was thinking about not being able to talk, needing another or maybe two more Valiums, yellow adult-strength Pez.

"Do you enjoy it?" I asked.

"She literally bites down on them, like I'm flank steak or something," Barbie said. "I wish she'd just bite them off and have it over with. This is taking forever. She's chewing and chewing, more like gnawing at me."

"I'll make her stop. I'll buy her some gum, some tobacco or something, a pencil to chew on."

"Please don't say anything. I wouldn't have told you except . . .," Barbie said.

"But she's hurting you."

"It's between Jennifer and me."

"Where's it going to stop?" I asked.

"At the arch, I hope. There's a bone there, and once she realizes she's bitten the soft part off, she'll stop."

"How will you walk?"

"I have very long feet."

I sat on the edge of my sister's bed, my head in my hands. My sister was biting Barbie's feet off and Barbie didn't seem to care. She didn't hold it against her and in a way I liked her for that. I liked the fact she understood how we all have little secret habits that seem normal enough to us, but which we know better than to mention out loud. I started imagining things I might be able to get away with.

"Get me out of here," Barbie said. I slipped Barbie's shoes off. Sure enough, someone had been gnawing at her. On her left foot the toes were dangling and on the right, half had been completely taken off. There were tooth marks up to her ankles. "Let's not dwell on this," Barbie said.

I picked Barbie up. Ken fell over backwards and Barbie made me straighten him up before we left. "Just because you know he only has a bump doesn't give you permission to treat him badly," Barbie whispered.

I fixed Ken and carried Barbie down the hall to my room. I held Barbie above me, tilted my head back, and lowered her feet into my mouth. I felt like a young sword swallower practising for my debut. I lowered Barbie's feet and legs into my mouth and then began sucking on them. They smelled like Jennifer and dirt and plastic. I sucked on her stubs and she told me it felt nice.

"You're better than a hot soak," Barbie said. I left her resting on my pillow and went downstairs to get us each a drink.

We were lying on my bed, curled into and out of each other. Barbie was on a pillow next to me and I was on my side facing her. She was talking about men, and as she talked I tried to be everything she said. She was saying she didn't like men who were afraid of themselves. I tried to be brave, to look courageous and secure. I held my head a certain way and it seemed to work. She said she didn't like men who were afraid of femininity, and I got confused.

"Guys always have to prove how boy they really are," Barbie said.

I thought of Jennifer trying to be a girl, wearing dresses, doing her nails, putting makeup on, wearing a bra even though she wouldn't need one for about fifty years.

"You make fun of Ken because he lets himself be everything he is. He doesn't hide anything."

"He doesn't have anything to hide," I said. "He has tan molded plastic hair, and a bump for a dick."

"I never should have told you about the bump."

I lay back on the bed. Barbie rolled over, off the pillow, and rested on my chest. Her body stretched from my nipple to my belly button. Her hands pressed against me, tickling me.

"Barbie," I said.

"Umm Humm."

"How do you feel about me?"

She didn't say anything for a minute. "Don't worry about it," she said, and slipped her hand into my shirt through the space between the buttons.

Her fingers were like the ends of toothpicks performing some subtle ancient torture, a dance of boy death across my chest. Barbie crawled all over me like an insect who'd run into one too many cans of Raid.

Underneath my clothes, under my skin, I was going crazy. First off, I'd been kidnapped by my underwear with no way to manually adjust without attracting unnecessary attention.

With Barbie caught in my shirt I slowly rolled over, like in some space shuttle docking maneuver. I rolled onto my stomach, trapping her under me. As slowly and unobtrusively as possible, I ground myself against the bed, at first hoping it would fix things and then again and again, caught by a pleasure pain principle.

"Is this a water bed?" Barbie asked.

My hand was on her breasts, only it wasn't really my hand, but more like my index finger. I touched Barbie and she made a little gasp, a squeak in reverse.

She squeaked backwards, then stopped, and I was stuck there with my hand on her, thinking about how I was forever crossing a line between the haves and the have nots, between good guys and bad, between men and animals, and there was absolutely nothing I could do to stop myself.

Barbie was sitting on my crotch, her legs flipped back behind her in a position that wasn't human.

At a certain point I had to free myself. If my dick was blue, it was only because it had suffocated. I did the honors and Richard popped out like an escape from maximum security.

"I've never seen anything so big," Barbie said. It was the sentence I dreamed of, but given the people Barbie normally hung out with, namely the bump boy himself, it didn't come as a big surprise.

She stood at the base of my dick, her bare feet buried in my pubic hair. I was almost as tall as she was. Okay, not almost as tall, but clearly we could be related. She and Richard even had the same vaguely surprised look on their faces.

She was on me and I couldn't help wanting to get inside her. I turned Barbie over and was on top of her, not caring if I killed her. Her hands pressed so hard into my stomach that it felt like she was performing an appendectomy.

I was on top, trying to get between her legs, almost breaking her in half. But there was nothing there, nothing to fuck except a small thin line that was supposed to be her ass crack.

I rubbed the thin line, the back of her legs and the space between her legs. I turned Barbie's back to me so I could do it without having to look at her face.

Very quickly, I came. I came all over Barbie, all over her and a little bit in her hair. I came on Barbie and it was the most horrifying experience I ever had. It didn't stay on her. It doesn't stick to plastic. I was finished. I was holding a come-covered Barbie in my hand like I didn't know where she came from.

Barbie said, "Don't stop," or maybe I just think she said that because I read it somewhere. I don't know anymore. I couldn't listen to her. I couldn't even look at her. I wiped myself off with a sock, pulled my clothes on, and then took Barbie into the bathroom.

At dinner I noticed Jennifer chewing her cuticles between bites of tuna-noodle casserole. I asked her if she was teething. She coughed and then started choking to death on either a little piece of fingernail, a crushed potato chip from the casserole, or maybe even a little bit of Barbie footie that'd stuck in her teeth. My mother asked her if she was okay.

"I swallowed something sharp," she said between coughs that were clearly influenced by the acting class she'd taken over the summer.

"Do you have a problem?" I asked her.

"Leave your sister alone," my mother said.

"If there are any questions to ask we'll do the asking," my father said.

"Is everything all right?" my mother asked Jennifer. She nodded. "I think you could use some new jeans," my mother said. "You don't seem to have many play clothes anymore."

"Not to change the subject," I said, trying to think of a way to stop Jennifer from eating Barbie alive.

"I don't wear pants," Jennifer said. "Boys wear pants."

"Your grandma wears pants," my father said.

"She's not a girl."

My father chuckled. He actually fucking chuckled. He's the only person I ever met who could actually fucking chuckle.

"Don't tell her that," he said, chuckling.

"It's not funny," I said.

"Grandma's are pull-ons anyway," Jennifer said, "They don't have a fly. You have to have a penis to have a fly."

"Jennifer," my mother said. "That's enough of that."

I decided to buy Barbie a present. I was at that strange point where I would have done anything for her. I took two buses and walked more than a mile to get to Toys R Us.

Barbie row was aisle 14C. I was a wreck. I imagined a million Barbies and having to have them all. I pictured fucking one, discarding it, immediately grabbing a fresh one, doing it, and then throwing it onto a growing pile in the corner of my room. An unending chore. I saw myself becoming a slave to Barbie. I wondered how many Tropical Barbies were made each year. I felt faint.

There were rows and rows of Kens, Barbies, and Skippers. Funtime Barbie, Jewel Secrets Ken, Barbie Rocker with "Hot Rockin' Fun and Real Dancin' Action." I noticed Magic Moves Barbie, and found myself looking at her carefully, flirtatiously, wondering if her legs were spreadable. "Push the switch and she moves," her box said. She winked at me while I was reading.

The only Tropical I saw was a black Tropical Ken. From just looking at him you wouldn't have known he was black. I mean, he wasn't black like anyone would be black. Black Tropical Ken was the color of a raisin, a raisin all spread out and unwrinkled. He had a short afro that looked like a wig had been dropped down and fixed on his head, a protective helmet. I wondered if black Ken was really white Ken sprayed over with a thick coating of ironed raisin plastic.

I spread eight black Kens out in a line across the front of a row. Through the plastic window of his box he told me he was hoping to go to dental school. All eight black Kens talked at once. Luckily, they all said the same thing at the same time. They said he really liked teeth. Black Ken smiled. He had the same white Pearl Drops, Pepsodent, Osmond family teeth that Barbie and white Ken had. I thought the entire Mattel family must take really good care of themselves. I figured they might be the only people left in America who actually brushed after every meal and then again before going to sleep.

I didn't know what to get Barbie. Black Ken said I should go for clothing, maybe a fur coat. I wanted something really special. I imagined a wonderful present that would draw us somehow closer.

There was a tropical pool and patio set, but I decided it might make her homesick. There was a complete winter holiday, with an A-frame house, fireplace, snowmobile, and sled. I imagined her inviting Ken away for a weekend without me. The six o'clock news set was nice, but because of her squeak, Barbie's future as an anchorwoman seemed limited. A workout center, a sofa bed and coffee table, a bubbling spa, a bedroom play set. I settled on the grand piano. It was $13.00. I'd always made it a point to never spend more than ten dollars on anyone. This time I figured, what the hell, you don't buy a grand piano every day.

"Wrap it up, would ya," I said at the checkout desk.

From my bedroom window I could see Jennifer in the backyard, wearing her tutu and leaping all over the place. It was dangerous as hell to sneak in and get Barbie, but I couldn't keep a grand piano in my closet without telling someone.

"You must really like me," Barbie said when she finally had the piano unwrapped.

I nodded. She was wearing a ski suit and skis. It was the end of August and eighty degrees out. Immediately, she sat down and played "Chopsticks."

I looked out at Jennifer. She was running down the length of the deck, jumping onto the railing and then leaping off, posing like one of those red flying horses you see on old Mobil gas signs. I watched her do it once and then the second time, her foot caught on the railing, and she went over the edge the hard way. A minute later she came around the edge of the house, limping, her tutu dented and dirty, pink tights ripped at both knees. I grabbed Barbie from the piano bench and raced her into Jennifer's room.

"I was just getting warmed up," she said. "I can play better than that, really."

I could hear Jennifer crying as she walked up the stairs.

"Jennifer's coming." I said. I put her down on the dresser and realized Ken was missing.

"Where's Ken?" I asked quickly.

"Out with Jennifer," Barbie said.

I met Jennifer at her door. "Are you okay?" I asked. She cried harder. "I saw you fall."

"Why didn't you stop me?" she said.

"From falling?"

She nodded and showed me her knees.

"Once you start to fall no one can stop you." I noticed Ken was tucked into the waistband of her tutu.

"They catch you," Jennifer said.

I started to tell her it was dangerous to go leaping around with a Ken stuck in your waistband, but you don't tell someone who's already crying that they did something bad.

I walked her into the bathroom, and took out the hydrogen peroxide. I was a first aid expert. I was the kind of guy who walked around, waiting for someone to have a heart attack just so I could practice my CPR technique.

"Sit down," I said.

Jennifer sat down on the toilet without putting the lid down. Ken was stabbing her all over the place and instead of pulling him out, she squirmed around trying to get comfortable like she didn't know what else to do. I took him out for her. She watched as though I was performing surgery or something.

"He's mine," she said.

"Take off your tights," I said.

"No," she said.

"They're ruined," I said. "Take them off."

Jennifer took off her ballet slippers and peeled off her tights. She was wearing my old Underoos with superheroes on them, Spiderman and Superman and Batman all poking out from under a dirty dented tutu. I decided not to say anything, but it looked funny as hell to see a flat crotch in boys' underwear. I had the feeling they didn't bother making underwear for Ken because they knew it looked too weird on him.

I poured peroxide onto her bloody knees. Jennifer screamed into my ear. She bent down and examined herself, poking her purple fingers into the torn skin; her tutu bunched up and rubbed against her face, scraping it. I worked on her knees, removing little pebbles and pieces of grass from the area.

She started crying again.

"You're okay," I said. "You're not dying." She didn't care. "Do you want anything?" I asked, trying to be nice.

"Barbie," she said.

It was the first time I'd handled Barbie in public. I picked her up like she was a complete stranger and handed her to Jennifer, who grabbed her by the hair. I started to tell her to ease up, but couldn't. Barbie looked at me and I shrugged. I went downstairs and made Jennifer one of my special Diet Cokes.

"Drink this," I said, handing it to her. She took four giant gulps and immediately I felt guilty about having used a whole Valium.

"Why don't you give a little to your Barbie," I said. "I'm sure she's thirsty too."

Barbie winked at me and I could have killed her, first off for doing it in front of Jennifer, and second because she didn't know what the hell she was winking about.

I went into my room and put the piano away. I figured as long as I kept it in the original box I'd be safe. If anyone found it, I'd say it was a present for Jennifer.

Wednesday Ken and Barbie had their heads switched. I went to get Barbie, and there on top of the dresser were Barbie and Ken, sort of Barbie's head was on Ken's body and Ken's head was on Barbie. At first I thought it was just me.

"Hi," Barbie's head said.

I couldn't respond. She was on Ken's body and I was looking at Ken in a whole new way.

I picked up the Barbie head Ken and immediately Barbie's head rolled off. It rolled across the dresser, across the white doily past Jennifer's collection of miniature ceramic cats, and *boom* it fell to the floor. I saw Barbie's head rolling and about to fall, and then falling, but there was nothing I could do to stop it. I was frozen, paralyzed with Ken's headless body in my left hand.

Barbie's head was on the floor, her hair spread out underneath it like angel wings in the snow, and I expected to see blood, a wide rich pool of blood, or at least a little bit coming out of her ear, her nose, or her mouth. I looked at her head on the floor and saw nothing but Barbie with eyes like the cosmos looking up at me. I thought she was dead.

"Christ, that hurt," she said. "And I already had a headache from these earrings."

There were little red dot/ball earrings jutting out of Barbie's ears.

"They go right through my head, you know. I guess it takes getting used to," Barbie said.

I noticed my mother's pin cushion on the dresser next to the other Barbie/Ken, the Barbie body, Ken head. The pin cushion was filled with hundreds of pins, pins with flat silver ends and pins with red, yellow, and blue dot/ball ends.

"You have pins in your head," I said to the Barbie head on the floor.

"Is that supposed to be a compliment?"

I was starting to hate her. I was being perfectly clear and she didn't understand me.

I looked at Ken. He was in my left hand, my fist wrapped around his waist. I looked at him and realized my thumb was on his bump. My thumb was pressed against Ken's crotch and as soon as I noticed I got an automatic hard-on, the kind you don't know you're getting, it's just there. I started rubbing Ken's bump and watching my thumb like it was a large-screen projection of a porno movie.

"What are you doing?" Barbie's head said. "Get me up. Help me." I was rubbing Ken's bump/hump with my finger inside his bathing suit. I was standing in the middle of my sister's room, with my pants pulled down.

"Aren't you going to help me?" Barbie kept asking. "Aren't you going to help me?"

In the second before I came, I held Ken's head hole in front of me. I held Ken upside down above my dick and came inside of Ken like I never could in Barbie.

I came into Ken's body and as soon as I was done I wanted to do it again. I wanted to fill Ken and put his head back on, like a perfume bottle. I wanted Ken to be the vessel for my secret supply. I came in Ken and then I remembered he wasn't mine. He didn't belong to me. I took him into the bathroom and soaked him in warm water and Ivory liquid. I brushed his insides with Jennifer's tooth-brush and left him alone in a cold-water rinse.

"Aren't you going to help me, aren't you?" Barbie kept asking.

I started thinking she'd been brain damaged by the accident. I picked her head up from the floor.

"What took you so long?" she asked.

"I had to take care of Ken."

"Is he okay?"

"He'll be fine. He's soaking in the bathroom." I held Barbie's head in my hand.

"What are you going to do?"

"What do you mean?" I said.

Did my little incident, my moment with Ken, mean that right then and there some decision about my future life as queerbait had to be made?"

"This afternoon. Where are we going? What are we doing? I miss you when I don't see you," Barbie said.

"You see me every day," I said.

"I don't really see you. I sit on top of the dresser and if you pass by, I see you. Take me to your room."

"I have to bring Ken's body back."

I went into the bathroom, rinsed out Ken, blew him dry with my mother's blow dryer, then played with him again. It was a boy thing, we were boys together. I thought sometime I might play ball with him, I might take him out instead of Barbie.

"Everything takes you so long," Barbie said when I got back into the room.

I put Ken back up on the dresser, picked up Barbie's body, knocked Ken's head off, and smashed Barbie's head back down on her own damn neck.

"I don't want to fight with you," Barbie said as I carried her into my room. "We don't have enough time together to fight. Fuck me," she said.

I didn't feel like it. I was thinking about fucking Ken and Ken being a boy. I was thinking about Barbie and Barbie being a girl. I was thinking about Jennifer, switching Barbie and Ken's heads, chewing Barbie's feet off, hanging Barbie from the ceiling fan, and who knows what else.

"Fuck me," Barbie said again.

I ripped Barbie's clothing off. Between Barbie's legs Jennifer had drawn pubic hair in reverse. She'd drawn it upside down so it looked like a fountain spewing up and out in great wide arcs. I spit directly onto Barbie and with my thumb and first finger rubbed the ink lines, erasing them. Barbie moaned.

"Why do you let her do this to you?"

"Jennifer owns me," Barbie moaned.

Jennifer owns me, she said, so easily and with pleasure. I was totally jealous. Jennifer owned Barbie and it made me crazy. Obviously it was one of those relationships that could only exist between women. Jennifer could own her because it didn't matter that Jennifer owned her. Jennifer didn't want Barbie, she had her.

"You're perfect," I said.

"I'm getting fat," Barbie said.

Barbie was crawling all over me, and I wondered if Jennifer knew she was a nymphomaniac. I wondered if Jennifer knew what a nymphomaniac was.

"You don't belong with little girls," I said.

Barbie ignored me.

There were scratches on Barbie's chest and stomach. She didn't say anything about them and so at first I pretended not to notice. As I was touching her, I could feel they were deep, like slices. The edges were rough; my finger caught on them and I couldn't help but wonder.

"Jennifer?" I said, massaging the cuts with my tongue, as though my tongue, like sandpaper, would erase them. Barbie nodded.

In fact, I thought of using sandpaper, but didn't know how I would explain it to Barbie: *you have to lie still and let me rub it really hard with this stuff that's like terrycloth dipped in cement.* I thought she might even like it if I made it into an S&M kind of thing and handcuffed her first.

I ran my tongue back and forth over the slivers, back and forth over the words "copyright 1966 Mattel Inc., Malaysia" tattooed on her back. Tonguing the tattoo drove Barbie crazy. She said it had something to do with scar tissue being extremely sensitive.

Barbie pushed herself hard against me, I could feel her slices rubbing my skin. I was thinking that Jennifer might kill Barbie. Without meaning to she might just go over the line and I wondered if Barbie would know what was happening or if she'd try to stop her.

We fucked, that's what I called it, fucking. In the beginning Barbie said she hated the word, which made me like it even more. She hated it because it was so strong and hard, and she said we weren't fucking, we were making love. I told her she had to be kidding.

"Fuck me," she said that afternoon and I knew the end was coming soon. "Fuck me," she said. I didn't like the sound of the word.

Friday when I went into Jennifer's room, there was something in the air. The place smelled like a science lab, a fire, a failed experiment.

Barbie was wearing, a strapless yellow evening dress. Her hair was wrapped into a high bun, more like a wedding cake than something Betty Crocker would whip up. There seemed to be layers and layers of angel's hair spinning in a circle above her head. She had yellow pins through her ears and gold fuck-me shoes that matched the belt around her waist. For a second I thought of the belt and imagined tying her up, but more than restraining her arms or legs, I thought of wrapping the belt around her face, tying it across her mouth.

I looked at Barbie and saw something dark and thick like a scar rising up and over the edge of her dress. I grabbed her and pulled the front of the dress down.

"Hey, big boy," Barbie said. "Don't I even get a hello?"

Barbie's breasts had been sawed at with a knife. There were a hundred marks from a blade that might have had five rows of teeth like shark jaws. And as if that wasn't enough, she'd been dissolved by fire, blue and yellow flames had been pressed against her and held there until she melted and eventually became the fire that burned herself. All of it had been somehow stirred with the lead of a pencil, the point of a pen, and left to cool. Molten Barbie flesh had been left to harden, black and pink plastic swirled together, in the crater Jennifer had dug out of her breasts.

I examined her in detail like a scientist, a pathologist, a fucking medical examiner. I studied the burns, the gouged-out area, as if by looking closely I'd find something, an explanation, a way out.

A disgusting taste came up into my mouth, like I'd been sucking on batteries. It came up, then sank back down into my stomach, leaving my mouth puckered with the bitter metallic flavor of sour saliva. I coughed and spit onto my shirt sleeve, then rolled the sleeve over to cover the wet spot.

With my index finger I touched the edge of the burn as lightly as I could. The round rim of her scar broke off under my finger. I almost dropped her.

"It's just a reduction," Barbie said. "Jennifer and I are even now."

Barbie was smiling. She had the same expression on her face as when I first saw her and fell in love. She had the same expression she always had and I couldn't stand it. She was smiling, and she was burned. She was smiling, and she was ruined. I pulled her dress back up, above the scarline. I put her down carefully on the doily on top of the dresser and started to walk away.

"Hey," Barbie said, "aren't we going to play?"

THE TOYMAKER AND HIS WIFE

Joanne Harris

Joanne Harris (b.1964) was born in Barnsley, into an Anglo-French family. She is known to millions as the author of *Chocolat*. Her most recent books include *Blackberry Wine, The Lollipop Shoes, Blueeyed Boy* and *The Gospel of Loki*. She writes in her garden shed. She regularly tweets short fiction #storytime.

There was a man who married for love, but lived to repent at leisure. He was a toymaker by trade, and his passion for precision work was known across the Nine Worlds. It was said that he'd made a mechanical bird that sang as sweetly as a lark, and great battalions of clockwork Hussars with sabres at the ready. His dolls looked as if they might draw breath; his engines blew real steam from their stacks, and were fed with tiny coals by mechanical stokers wielding tiny mechanical shovels. His dolls' houses were marvels in miniature; with tiny gilt mirrors on bedroom walls reflecting tiny four-poster beds and tiny children playing with baby dolls no bigger than a grain of rice. Everything was perfect in the toymaker's world; down to the smallest detail. Well –

Everything but one thing. His wife.

Of course, they'd been in love, once. But now, some years later, the craftsman began to see that his wife was no credit to him. She was no beauty; her judgement was weak; her housekeeping was slovenly. She loved her husband, to be sure, and he loved her too – in his way. But was it enough, he asked himself? Didn't he owe himself more than this?

One day the toymaker noticed that his wife's hair was going grey. It displeased him to see it; and so he made her a new head of hair, spun from skeins of gleaming gold, and stitched it into place on her scalp, as he had done so often when he was making dolls. The wife said nothing, but looked at herself in her dressing-room mirror, and touched the bright, stiff strands of her hair, and remembered a time when he had thought she was perfect in every way.

For a while, the toymaker was pleased. But then he started to notice that his wife often spoke rashly or out of turn, or said things that he found unnecessary, or even downright stupid. And so, as she slept, he cut out her tongue and replaced it with a mechanical one, sleek as a silverfish, crisp as a clock. After that, the toymaker's wife was always perfectly precise in her speech, and never said anything stupid, or dull, or bored him with her chatter.

All was well for a time after that, until the toymaker noticed that his wife often looked at him with reproach, and sometimes wept for no reason. It made him uneasy to look at her, and so he made her a new pair of blown-glass eyes that were bright and approving, and never shed tears, or seemed to express anything but contentment. He was very proud of his handiwork, and for a time, he was content.

But soon he noticed his wife's hands; hands that were often clumsy and slow, and so he made mechanical hands for her, and fixed them into place. His wife's new hands were as white as milk, and as clever as any automaton's, and so he made a pair of feet, and then a pair of perfect breasts, so that little by little, over time, he had replaced every flawed and worn-out part with clockwork and gleaming porcelain.

"At last, she is perfect," he told himself, looking at his beautiful wife. But still, there was something missing. Still, she wasn't quite as he'd hoped. And so the toymaker opened her up to see what part of her inner workings he might have neglected to tune or correct. He found everything in place – except for one thing he had overlooked. One small, insignificant thing, so deeply embedded in the intricacies of clockwork and circuitry that he hadn't noticed it. It was her heart – it was broken.

"I wonder how *that* could have happened?" he said, reaching for his watch-maker's tools, fully intending to make his wife a new heart to replace the broken one.

But then he looked at her, lying so still and beautiful and pale upon the work-bench; quiet and lovely in every way; every part shiny and gleaming.

"Why, you don't need a heart at all, do you, my darling?" he told her.

And so he took the broken heart and threw it onto the rubbish heap. And then he turned back to his wife and kissed her lovely silverfish mouth, looked into her shining blown-glass eyes and said:

"At last. You're perfect."

MARCHING SONGS

Keith Ridgway

Keith Ridgway (b.1965) is the author of *The Long Falling*, which won both the 2001 Prix Femina Etranger and Premier Roman Etranger, *The Parts, Horses, Animals*, and *Hawthorne & Child,* as well as a collection of stories, *Standard Time*.

I am ill. I have been ill for some time. Years now. It has become years.

I believe, though I cannot prove, that my illness is due directly to the perverted Catholicism and megalomania of Mr Tony Blair, former Prime Minister, whom I met once, whose hand I physically shook (at which point he assaulted me), and who, if you should mention my name to him, will tell you that he met me, or that he did not meet me, or that he cannot recall. Because he has all the answers.

My illness is debilitating. It disbars me from work. It prevents any social interaction. It has been, my illness, both misrecognized and dismissed. Misdiagnosed. And dismissed. As malingering; as a problem of my own creation, of my own invention, as if it was my child or my garden or a song I was singing, or something I have idly, on a quiet afternoon say, made up, invented, as a story to tell mental health professionals because I have nothing better to do. It generates anger, pity, bloody-minded stinking compassion, notes between doctors, phone calls and files, avoidance, the disappearance of friends, and all that sort of Englishness. I sit in my chair.

Compassion is a weapon wielded against me. Amongst others.

I'm not blaming you, specifically. I don't blame people, specifically.

However, Islington council, my landlords, my sister (against her entire knowledge), and the NHS are all trying to kill me. Trying to enable circumstances (to arise) in which my death becomes inevitable. They are involved in an unconscious, unarticulated conspiracy to kill me in other words. It's not a plot. It's nothing so straightforward as a plot. No one can be blamed in any individual way. It is an inevitable, bureaucratic conspiracy, so devolved and deniable as to be invisible; so peculiarly set out in rules and procedures and protocols and directives and guidelines as to allow plausible public denial of responsibility on the part of any of the participants at any stage of the process.

Initiated by Mr Blair. Of which I have no proof. A small wart. On my thumb. It sings to me in the mornings in warm weather. My doctor shrugs at it, and no ointment works.

No blame. You understand me. When they write the report, my report, the report into my case, they will find some systemic failures, some culture of this or that, some procedures for tightening, some lessons to be learned. No heads will roll. Dead children. You understand me.

I like where I live. I live on my own.

It's not necessary to be paranoid or to harbour any delusions in order to feel that I have been abandoned by the mental health services. Because I have. They want me to fail, mentally. I have innumerable documents if that sort of thing interests you. Tracing a clear trajectory of discouragement, in which a subtle strategy is discernible. No single thing. Cumulative. Terribly slow, terribly patient. The gentle whisper of the letters and the reports and the assessments. *Die*, they say. You may as well.

My GP, one example, has prescribed to me, for the pain, enough Tramadol to kill me several times over. Go on. Another example, the mental health doctor who first assessed me in Archway had an office on what appeared to be the 12th floor, with a large window, and she sat me within easy reach of the window and also left me alone for several minutes in the room with the window on the 12th floor, which had a view of all of the east or south or west of London from Archway. All that sky, like the city is upside down. So that if you stepped out there you would rise. Several minutes. Perhaps seven or eight. Go on.

I do not have any trouble with my neighbours and I have never had any complications with either the police or the security services, nor have I ever stood for elected office or campaigned for any political party nor have I ever agitated or demonstrated against the authorities in any way, not even on a march – and I never even went on the anti-war march – so there can be no reason for what is happening to me that is public or which may have been expected to arise as a result of my previous actions. I can only assume that the council and my landlords and the NHS have an occult agenda to which they secretly adhere, created for them by the Tony Blair government, to encourage into complete despair any person who does not hold a stake in the national project involving bank accounts for babies, education for profit, and pretending to fight wars – when in fact all that is happening in Afghanistan, and all that happened in Iraq, is that British soldiers are invested in American projects so that the Tony Blair Agenda can feel that it is a stakeholder in the future, which it cannot imagine as being anything other than American, and this is our national embarrassment.

I am not a stakeholder. I hold no stake. I pay my taxes. My taxes buy weapons and arm soldiers. My taxes send the soldiers to Afghanistan and formerly Iraq to be terrified and traumatized, and to inflict terror and trauma upon others, including the killing and maiming of others, and I do not support Our Boys, it is a volunteer army and I believe that every one of those volunteers is misguided and that their innate, childish, boyish attraction to aggression and adventure and camaraderie is being perverted by malign and morally vacant politicians who are not even clever enough to be operating to anyone's advantage, not even their own, who are merely drunk on narrative and who see themselves as part of something bigger, such as the delusion of History, and who are impressive only in the scope and depth and profundity of their stupidity.

He's quite charming, actually, Mr Blair, when you meet him. You can see how he manages to draw people to him. He looks you in the eye. He listens. His smile is warm and he is the right height – neither too tall nor too short. The average height of successful politicians is five feet eleven.

My landlords make noise at a very early hour meaning that I cannot sleep. They also send in the middle of the night an overweight middle-aged or elderly man who tries the steel doors. He rattles them. The landlords, let me explain, have their offices below my flat. I never speak to the head man. He never speaks to me. But I see him, dapper and small, coming and going, and I see how they defer to him and I notice, I have noticed, how he watches me sometimes with half a smile. He has an odd name – Mishazzo. An unlikely name. As if he is a landlord by mistake. His people are very polite, even friendly. But they are, as soon as I am inside my flat, extremely devious in their methods, always doing things that are small enough in themselves but which taken together amount to a campaign of psychological torture, including slamming doors. I think they have fed rats into the cavities. Certainly the cat that used to patrol the yard has disappeared. There are noises in the walls, in the roof, the ceiling. My ceiling is the roof. I hear scratches. Scurries. I hear clicks. I once found a cockroach in my bathroom. I ran downstairs and into the landlord's office but they were not of any use at all to me . . . in me . . . in my horror. Mr Mishazzo was there. His people glanced at him and he smiled. As if he is a landlord because he finds it amusing. Mr Price came by later with a trap. I wanted nothing to do with a trap. I have devices now. Electronic discouragers. Since I have installed them there have been no further creatures inside apart from mosquitoes, bluebottles, wasps, flies, tiny centipedes, moths, a spider.

I have some sort of infection in my forehead.

Let me level with you. Level best and utmost. Let me be as honest as I can be. I know that something has gone wrong. I know that the fault is visible. You can discern it in everything I say to you. In most of what I say to you. In how I say it. I know this. I am cracked like ice. I know this. But listen. Listen to me. This is important. Beneath the fault there is solid ground. Beneath the ice. Under all the cracks. Under all the cracks there is something that is not broken.

I am on the Internet.

You can watch the suicide bombers on there.

I go down to the square a couple of times a week.

Giggling now.

On the Internet, you can watch people dying, all over the place. This is new, isn't it? This is a new thing in the world. On a slow day, when nothing happens, I wait for the news, hoping that there will be something happening there. And sometimes there is. And I like the idea of something happening. I like the idea of it. People don't take anything seriously unless something is happening. My illness makes more sense when something is happening. Against the background of light entertainment and the weather it looks inappropriate. It sticks out. Against the background of body parts and the constant slaughter it looks wise and cautious and who could blame me? I imagine that if there were lots of things happening to me all the time I would like the idea of nothing happening. Sometimes the news is nothing. So much happens and they tell us nothing. I look out of the window.

When I met Tony Blair we talked briefly about motor racing. About Formula One. I don't know why. There had been a Grand Prix that day. It came up somehow. Someone else mentioned it. I said oh. I said I used to watch Formula One as a boy. Not any more? the Prime Minister asked me.

No.

Not any more. Nothing happens now. In Formula One.

Through my window I can't see very much of what I suppose is the world. Some offices. A roof. A sky crossed by planes. I often hear helicopters but I don't see them. There is always something happening. If I press my cheek against the glass and twist my shoulder to the left I can see the elderly or overweight man rattling the steel door. No helicopters. Just the street and the orange lights, wet sometimes. The wet orange street. Shining in the dark and the rattling door.

When nothing is happening we want something to happen, and when something is happening we want it to stop.

There is always something happening on the Internet.

I sit at my kitchen table. I make a cup of tea.

The Zapruder film. Hillsborough. Bloody Sunday. The shooting of Oswald. The audio of Bobby Kennedy's murder. The calls from the towers. The planes going in. The jumpers. The suicide of Pennsylvania State Treasurer Budd Dwyer on live television. He stuck a gun in his mouth and blew the back of his head off. The camera zooms in on his dead face, the blood pouring out of him like the water out of my overfilled kettle. I don't know what to do about it.

The Madrid bombs. Running up those stairs. The Enschede explosion. Laughter then fear then the world just goes dark and sideways.

Tamil suicide bombers flinging parts of their bodies into the crowd like pop stars.

Iraqi IEDs. Hostage murders. Car bombs by the Green Zone.

Hundreds of dead people. Around craters in Baghdad, Tikrit and Ramadi. British armaments. American armaments. You can see the markings and the peeled-back steel.

There are photographs of aftermaths. Blood and stumps and crushed torsos. All the devil's little mandibles. Misery hats. Pockets of tissue. Cups of tea. There are interviews with people in shock. They cannot begin to believe what they have seen until they tell someone else what they have seen. They shout at the camera, they use their hands, they say things over and over. They're actually talking to themselves, and we are watching.

I am talking to myself and you are watching.

In my kitchen I can look at the wall if I want to.

When he shook hands I felt a sort of scratch. A nick. A prick. Something or other. I didn't react. I didn't look at my hand. I was meeting the Prime Minister. But it hurt. Something had. He had. I don't know.

Some device.

***

There are endless car crashes on the Internet. There are head-on collisions, turnovers, side swipes, flying pedestrians. All sorts, really. But it is usually unclear whether there have been fatalities.

I stare at the little wart on my thumb. It's white. Tiny and a perfect circle.

When I go down to the square I take a coffee with me, in my hand. I get it from the coffee shop around the corner. I glance at the machine gun policemen. I walk through the square, as if I have business on the other side. They keep an eye on me. I nod sometimes at a policeman. A policeman sometimes nods back. I haven't spotted the cameras. I expect they will knock on my door sometime. That they will come and have a chat.

I'll examine their cards. Their IDs. I'll look at their faces and their photos. They won't mind me writing down the numbers. I'll do it at the kitchen table, so that they follow me into the flat. Let them have a good look around. They'll stand over me. Looking. Two of them. They'll smell of the street and of cars and of camaraderie in the locker room and the gym and of encounters with trouble.

– You think I don't live well?
– What? No. We're here about Connaught Square.
– About what?
– Connaught Square.
– What the hell is a connocked square?

I'll have them baffled in minutes. I'll speak slightly louder than is necessary. I'll walk them backwards through a prayer. Policemen are standard procedures. There is nothing to them that cannot be confused.

– You took your time getting here.
– What?
– I called you hours ago.
– We're not responding to a call.
– So you know about the windows?
– What about the windows?
– They are haunted.
– Haunted?
– They contain reflections at night other than my own.
– Ghosts?
– What are you going to do about it?
And so on.

I go and sit in the park. There is a view over the City, and to the left, Canary Wharf. The park is full of people looking in the same direction.

Part of managing my illness is to keep. Is to try to keep. Is to try to manage to keep a certain amount of regularity in my operations, my whereabouts. A structure. When the pains allow. When the singing isn't outrageous. I used to work in radio. Everything had a schedule. I try to get up every morning and I do. I get up at eight o'clock and I listen for a little while to the *Today* programme. I never worked on that. I try to have a shower. Sometimes I am in too much pain to shower. Sometimes I just get dressed and think about having a bath later. I never have a bath.

I go to Sparrow's for my breakfast. I have Breakfast #5, except I have black pudding instead of beans, and I have tea and toast. I try to take my time. It costs four pounds. I can't afford to do this every day, so sometimes I stay in bed. The waitress calls the toast bread when she brings it. Not every morning, but most. There is a man there, sometimes, two times in four maybe. A small man in a thoughtless suit, short haired, crooked somehow. I look at him trying to work out what it is. I think maybe he's had a harelip corrected. Maybe it's just a broken nose. Some facial thing from childhood like a ghost. He has scrambled eggs. Every time I see him he has scrambled eggs in front of him. A hill of yellow rubble, as if he's been sick. He has a notebook that he writes in sometimes. Maybe he's a writer or a journalist. I'm trying to work out if he's some sort of writer or journalist. Sometimes he reads a newspaper, a tabloid usually, but he doesn't read the same newspaper every time, which is more evidence that he might be a journalist, I think. He is half ugly half handsome. He looks at his watch. Sometimes he talks on his phone, turning the pages of the newspaper, or writing lazily in his notebook, making humming noises, *yes, go on, yes, OK*. He's the only regular I notice. I don't think he notices me. Who would look at me?

I look at him. Sometimes I think he's crying, which makes me laugh. Sometimes I think that night is day and I look out of the window and everything is wrong until I realize it's night and this is what the night is like.

The man who rattles the steel door and shutters. That's always in the middle of the night. I lift the corner of my curtain and peek at him. He is big. He wears a grey jacket. In the dark it's grey. He just rattles the door, the shutters. He does it and he stands there for a moment staring at the steel. And then he goes away. I don't know what it's about. Perhaps he has a grievance.

When I go outside into the street where I live I am surrounded by people shouting and jostling and buying vegetables. That's OK. Where did they get their lives? Who told them that this was the way to be? How did they learn? They are pushed up against one another with no space for anything. They have become unhealthy and short minded. Things move so quickly that they don't know what to do with anything, other than shout at it or push it or try to buy it.

In the past I drew down from the local people all the things I needed. All the things I needed were things I needed to draw down, to pull down into me, like fruit on a branch. Along my street I met with grocers and barbers and phone-fixing men. I ambled slowly into furniture shops and asked them about the price of hatstands and bunk beds. I paused in butcher's doorways and stared at meat counters, at the cuts of flesh and the granulated blood. I licked my lips in the windows. I walked the street I live on. What is this vegetable? What is this fruit? What is the name you call this? How do I cook it? I took time in cafés where they fed me. I watched other people. I listened in on other people. I read sometimes. I didn't read.

I have lost my place now. I do none of that.

If he is a journalist I might tell him about Blair and the device. A pin. A poisoned pin. Or a miniature syringe. Some sort of nano-technology. His hand was dry. His smile was the one you've seen on the television. The same one. Except we were in a room, and there were no cameras. Odd.

All the deaths in Formula One are on the Internet. Most of them are. Most of them after about 1967. Gilles Villeneuve and Ronnie Peterson and Ayrton Senna. Villeneuve thrown from his car. The medics crouched over his broken body caught against the fence. Peterson pulled burning from a multiple pile up at Monza. They didn't think he was badly hurt. He died hours later when his bone marrow melted into his bloodstream. Senna. Going straight ahead into concrete. They still don't know why. It takes a slow two minutes for the medics at Imola to get to him. On the American commentary Derek Daly worries about the delay. *Where are they?* he asks. Tom Pryce in 1973 – he hits a marshal who is running across the track, the marshal's body spinning in the air like wet bread, his fire extinguisher hitting Pryce's helmet, shattering it, killing Pryce instantly, though his car continues in a straight line. Jochen Rindt, 1970, Monza. It doesn't look that bad. Lorenzo Bandini's Ferrari exploding by the yachts in Monaco. It looks that bad.

Riccardo Paletti on the starting line at Monza in 1982. He slams into the back of Didier Pironi's Ferrari which has stalled in pole position. The other drivers have managed to avoid it. But Paletti doesn't see it. They say that he's dead by the time the marshals and the medics and Pironi get to his car, but still. You can watch the film. You can watch them trying to get Paletti out. You can see the moment when the first flames appear. If you listen to the version with Jackie Stewart's commentary you can hear the panic in his voice when the flames suddenly take hold, bursting over the whole car, sending everyone scurrying, and you can watch then as a collection of flailing useless men try to make the extinguishers work and Ricardo Paletti burns.

Roger Williamson at Zandvoort in 1973. He flips his March on the long corner and he's trapped inside it. A fire starts. His friend David Purley sees what's happened, stops his car, runs across the track and tries to help. He tries to lift the car. He gestures to the marshals to help him. They aren't wearing fire-proof clothing. They hang back. He gestures at other cars. They think it's Purley's car that's overturned. And they can see Purley, so everything must be OK, and they're racing, so they don't stop. Purley can hear Roger Williamson. He can hear him shouting. Then screaming. The extinguisher won't work. There's only one. He tries to get it to work. He tries to lift the car. He can't lift the car. The marshals are standing there looking at him. The smoke is billowing out. The race goes on. He walks away. He runs back. His arms. His shoulders. He can hear Williamson. Then he can't.

You can watch it all. Over and over.

I watch it all, over and over.

Several items arising. The local health and mental health unit of the Borough of Islington have now discontinued my therapy a total of twice on two separate occasions, ruling that I was in both of these times incapable of benefiting, using this deception to cover over like a dog their ineptitude and possible encouragement of my self destruction, ignoring on three separate occasions my stated intention to kill someone, preferably Mr Blair or someone else like that, deciding that these were not serious threats and were instead manifestations of my own particular 'illness', as if the world was separate from the things in it, the events separate from the people, the people separate from the things they do, as if the done things do not come out of thought things, as if there were no traces anywhere, as if we had never noticed dogs and the way they proceed. What a remarkable ambush of shit. What a cloud of frayed cities. What a dust of blood. What a wound. What a pulse of broken teeth. I will fucking kill you. I WILL FUCKING KILL. YOU FUCK.

I am ugly. Ugliness has taken me over. It's OK. The infection in my forehead has spread along the slight left centre of my nose and out into my left cheek. My right cheek. The slight right centre of my nose and my right cheek. I have red cleft marks along my thighs and under my right arm. One eye has failed. It rarely opens now. There is a stench inside my mouth. There are ruins in my corners. I cannot wash and carry on.

There is the problem of money.

When I left my job – left, left, I had a good job but I left – they gave me a certain amount, which I stored in a savings account, an ISA account, where you are allowed to put only a certain amount of money in different ways and you do not have to pay tax on what you earn there. That is my understanding. And the rest of it I put in another account which is an ordinary savings account and it earns interest in there and I suppose that somehow I pay tax on that though perhaps I don't pay taxes any longer. I'm not sure. There's the principle of it though. Then there was the house I had. I sold. I sold the house I had. That's OK. All that money I put mostly in another savings account and another current account and all this money is all nearly gone now I'm sure of it, though my sister looks after my finances for the moment for the most part, and she hasn't said anything, yet, except to get a job. But she says that gently now. These days. I am disfigured.

I will go and stand by the café. And watch them. They come and go. The policemen. By the square. He spent millions on the house. It's in the public record. You can look it up. It's where he lives. With his armed guard and his devices and all his perpetual shame, poor man. Sometimes I feel sorry for him.

Money is a problem. I find that I cannot spend it when I go out. I go out and I go to the shops, for example, and I try to buy food. I walk around the shop, the supermarket, with a basket on my arm, and I put things in it. Milk for example, bread, eggs, some pasta, some mushrooms and carrots, some orange juice, a fillet of fish or a pork chop. I fill the basket. I put in extra things that might be nice like some buns or a cake or a packet of biscuits. Extra things that might be nice. But when I get to the checkout I cannot. I cannot. In the air. My pains all sing their song. I cannot take the money out of my pocket. I cannot take the items one by one from the basket and have them sent under the bleeper. It cannot happen. This is so stupid. This is mad. There is something wrong with it. Something horrible. I don't know what it is. I stand in the queue for a moment, maybe longer, and I try to stay, but I put the basket down and I leave – I go to the door and through it and the security guard looks at me and shakes his head.

Cash. I have a problem with cash.

I think.

In Sparrow's though, for my breakfast, I can do that. Because it is four pounds. £4. It is always £4. So I have that ready. Or, I know the change I will get. A one-pound coin. Or a five-pound note and a one-pound coin. The crooked man in the suit does the same. He knows the price of scrambled eggs. It's the way to do it. It really is.

And I can get a coffee when I go down to the square. I can do that. It is £1.85 in the place I get it. I give them £2. They give me 15p change. I drop that in the glass they leave on the counter for tips.

My bills are paid automatically. I'm on the Internet. And that will do. I have lost weight. My fingers sing to me. My sister comes on Saturdays and she brings what I more or less need.

Once I had an urge for cornflakes, and I stole them from the corner shop. I had no milk. I went back and bought milk. I don't know how I did it. I think I forgot that I was unable to use cash. I think I forgot – so perplexed was I by the theft – that I was mad. I wanted to pay him for the cornflakes too but he didn't know what I was on about, and he shooed me out of it like more than two schoolchildren.

I watch them in the café. By the square. Down by the square. The same place I get the £1.85 coffee. There are several of them. They know I'm there. I'm sure. They have that training. Things attached to their belts. They don't mind me then. They don't mind me so much I don't think. Maybe they don't see me. Maybe it's another division that sees me.

David Purley was born in Bognor Regis of all places. I have never been there.

Soldiers sing as they march. They sing as they march.

In his car as he burned to death Roger Williams sang. David Purley never mentioned it. He thought he was hearing things. He thought, when he remembered it, that he was making it up, that such a thing was ridiculous, that it was impossible, that it was impossible and wrong to remember it, so he never mentioned it. He never said a word. Roger had sung. Sang. Roger sang.

I am going to get better.

He sang a melody that Purley had never heard before. I don't know what it was. Something lovely. Purley sang it himself when he crashed his aerobatic biplane into the sea in 1985. Off Bognor Regis of all places, in sight of home. He remembered the melody that Roger had sung. Sang. And he sang it too. It is a death song, I suppose. Death needs its orders, its boots, its motivations. Death needs its rations.

Poor death.

My sister brings most of the food I need. It lasts the week. I am embarrassed more than anything about my sister. About myself in relation to my sister.

I am tired of talking.

The pains in my stomach are now sometimes unbearable. I listen to them sing. The pains, I mean. They sing. They keep themselves chipper with songs. Because it is hard to be a pain in me. It is hard work. It takes all day to use up a minute of my time. It takes a great effort of all those little pains, working together, to make the song, the chorus, that sounds in my head like a world. These days they have learned their song and they seem happy in their work and they can on a good day lay me low and kill me. They kill me and I die. And I am resurrected.

What did I say to him? To Mr Blair? What statement did I make, what question did I ask to prompt his attack on me? Or was it something in my face or my bearing or in my eyes. Something in my eyes? Was it a story I told, of something in my life? Was it a joke I made? What did I do to Mr Blair? What offence or danger did I present? What was it about me that led to his decision? Perhaps nothing. Perhaps it was an accident of timing. He felt the need to destroy something. Anything. Given his power. It would be a sin, perhaps he thought, not to use it.

Maybe he felt I would be better off.

He thinks a lot, I imagine, about sin. Uselessly.

Death will come to him as a terrible shock, I shouldn't wonder.

Maybe he detected my unhappiness in my work. My unhappiness at home. Maybe he felt that I would be better off with all that misery behind me. Maybe he felt that my life needed shaking up. That I could do with a shock, upending and run through. The pains started the very next day, when I woke. I could not move. I could not move for days. All my limbs, my joints, my knuckles and my hairs, all my ducts and patches. They were all tuning up.

The man in Sparrow's looked at me blankly.

– What?

– Are you a journalist or a writer?

He had a settled face. A man in control of his expressions. I couldn't read anything in there. He'd finished his eggs, his toast. His plate was pushed aside. He had a second mug of tea on the go. Did he do that every morning? I didn't know. He was reading about global warming in the newspaper. There was a picture of a glacier and sidebars with explanations. His phone sat on his notebook. There'd been no calls this morning, and no writing either. His voice was level. I couldn't get the accent. Flat south-east. London, out of Essex or Kent. I don't know. His face wasn't as crooked up close. Odd that. I find it difficult to talk to people.

– I'm neither.

– I thought you might be. A writer. A journalist. With the notebook. You know. He nodded, slowly.

– No.

– OK.

I didn't know where that left me. If he said he wasn't then he wasn't. I couldn't start an argument about it.

– I've seen you in here, you know. With the notebook. Writing. The odd time. I just thought. We're often in at the same time.

He nodded again. Maybe he was tired. He looked tired and sad and red-eyed. He didn't seem to mind, but he wasn't going to talk to me. He wasn't going to ask me to sit down. He wasn't going to ask me to sit down and tell him about Mr Blair and the device so that he could tell my story.

I thought I would tell him my name. I'd say my name, my surname, and I'd hold out my hand for him to shake. And I'd smile, and he'd pause and smile back and take my hand and ask me to sit down. So, *we eat breakfast here*, he'd say. Or. *You must be local, too.* Or something like that. A small talk interregnum. Then down to it. I'd duck into it. I'd use dialogue. I'd speak in dialogue. In lines. *You want to hear a story?* I'd say. He'd shrug. *Politics*, I'd say. *Politicians. Not quite what they seem, sometimes.* I'd pause. *Go on*, he'd say. *You remember Blair? Interested. Of course I remember Blair. What about him?*

And so on.

I didn't know what to say.

– Well. Nice to talk to you.

He nodded again.

– Bye now.

– Bye.

He sipped his tea and looked at me. I walked to the door and out on to the street. I don't know. I don't know what to do with the rest of my life.

Mr Blair is not the owner of his own evil. He is the host if you like – if you want to use the sort of terminology that he has adapted into his own life and heart, the vocabulary of the groping church – he is the possessed corpse of a former human, animated entirely by the spittle-flecked priests of Rome and by miserable justifications, by ointments of the sagging flesh, the night-time coldness of the awful touch. His skin is a manila envelope. It contains an argument, not a heart. But he has made choices and the choices are owned by him, and he owns those choices and he is the chooser of death. He is the chooser of death. He has chosen death and he has chosen to visit it on others when no such choice was necessary. He is the progenitor of the crushed skulls of baby girls. He is the father of the dead bodies of children and the raped mothers and the bludgeoned fathers. He has embraced the murder of his lord, and he has used the people to enact his fantasy and his perversions. He has masturbated over the Euphrates. He has rubbed History against his cold chest like a feeler in the crowd. Like a breather, interferer. Slack muscle of pornography, piece of shit.

I only know what I believe.

I go down sometimes to the square, and I wander with a coffee and I watch and I go around again. Nothing happens. I have to be careful. Even still, I'm sure I'm noticed.

I saw him once. Early in the day as I came from Marble Arch. He was no more than a blur between his house and his car; a man in a suit, moving as if it was raining, crouching out, ducking in. I stopped in my tracks. Words rose in my throat. I had no idea. I didn't know what to do. It was such a beautiful morning.

He glanced in my direction and I saw his face. He did not look at me but I saw his face. He looked terribly familiar. Of course. But no. Not as himself. He wears a state of shock. He carries panic in his eyes. He bristles with tension and fear, as if he knows what he does not want to know – that any moment now, it will be too late.

I went home and slept.

There are too many photographs of David Purley attending to the dying of his friend Roger Williamson. There is too much film. His human body makes too much of itself, changing direction, pausing, giving up, resuming, going back, tensing in fear, resuming, slumping in despair, ragged in despair, resuming, going back, screaming, his voice, you can see his voice in the pictures, screaming, *somebody fucking help me, somebody fucking help*.

There are two sorts of pale skinny Englishmen in my nightmares. One is burned at the edges, frayed by fear, his blistered hands and scorched face taut with the effort of trying to save a life. David Purley. And the other, a coward and a traitor, who set his face against bravery, who embraced the dying man and swallowed his song. Tony Blair.

Tony Blair.

I wake to the rattling and the marching songs.

MIXED BREEDING

Nicola Barker

Nicola Barker (b.1966) was born in Ely, spent some of her childhood in South Africa, was educated at Cambridge and now divides her time between East London and West Sussex. Her books have won a number of awards, and include the collections *Love Your Enemies* and *Heading Inland*, as well as the novels *Wide Open, Behindlings, Clear, Darkmans, Burley Cross Post Box Theft, The Yips* and *In The Approaches*. Originally published in the *Observer*, the story had the subtitle, "A Shaggy Dog Story."

Had Lenny realised that Cassandra's interest in him was based principally upon a sexual fascination with Pike, his German Shepherd/Labrador cross, he would definitely have reconsidered his good opinion of her.

Cass – she preferred to be abbreviated, but was strictly teetotal – had first encountered Lenny as part of a mixed amateur running team (they ran Wednesday nights, mostly around the Epping area) and had been immediately convinced that he was exactly the kind of man who might own a big dog. She was right.

Her parents had both been art teachers. Her father had suffered from an allergy to hair, so they'd kept cats. Cats have fur, not hair, which is a small but significant difference. As Cass grew older, such differences became very much a pre-occupation. But even as a small child, Cass had found felines both sexually unexciting and physically unreciprocal.

Lenny's father was a hospital porter. His mother, Doll, worked off and on in pub catering, Lenny himself was 27 and tender verging on raw following his recent separation from Jill, his superficially angelic, but perpetually philandering, wife. So he was home again, back in his old bedroom where Sam Fox fought nightly duels on adjacent walls with a post-pubescent Glenn Hoddle. Home again, having difficulty in digesting regular meals of fish fingers with chips (never oven-baked) and saveloys with mash. Back home, and right along-side him – trotting, panting, cavorting – was good, loyal, unadulterous old Pike.

Woof! Lenny earned a crust driving his own black cab and was not alone in observing that there are, in general, two kinds of cabbies; those who converse and those who don't. Lenny didn't. It wasn't in his nature to unburden, and anyway, those things buried deep within him – his heart, his kidneys, his pride, his bowels, his backbone – were still much too fragile and tense and jaded for him to even contemplate off-loading.

Lenny was gentle and relatively physically demonstrative, but not in the tiniest bit wordy. And although he could boast of big hands, grey eyes and an almost infallible sense of direction, these characteristics, married with an intrinsic naivety, were rarely sufficient to keep him out of trouble.

Cassandra, on the other hand, was ridiculously chatty. She knew her milkman by his first name (Bud), told people on buses about her terrible appendicitis scars (an "imposter' surgeon had apparently been involved) and didn't hesitate to use the men's toilets when the queue outside the ladies' seemed prohibitively long.

She had short dark hair, big lips, a small nose and a skinny torso which was crowned by two huge pink nipples. These she displayed, unashamedly, like exotic chrysanthemums, as a life model every Thursday night. She found keeping still such a constant struggle that she could often be found sitting hard on her hands, was 23, and fully enrolled in a part-time course to learn the fine art of the masseuse.

One day she hoped to work for the British Olympic team, or in a temporary capacity for a continental soccer club.

Cass always found quiet men a particular challenge. Lenny was surely no exception, but she won him over, finally, by faking cramp in her left thigh towards the end of a seven-mile run. Lenny was already deeply impressed with the stamina Cass displayed by running and talking almost continuously, even uphill. This remarkable accomplishment, she told him, was considerably aided by the wearing of the kind of nasal strip she'd seen demonstrated during the Euro '96 football championship, which served to facilitate the more efficient flow of oxygen directly up the nasal passages and straight down into the lungs. (She had also been known to favour using this particular device during certain types of vigorous sexual activity.) Prostrate in the roomy confines of Lenny's cab, hot and languorous on her way back home, Cass told him how she'd learned – from a punkish American performance artist – to reach orgasm during masturbation without using her fingers, but merely by controlling her breathing in a very particular way. Lenny was perfectly appalled by this revelation and resolved to go out of his way to avoid her at every future opportunity.

But Cass kept turning up. And although it was no instant thing – no fireworks and silver spangles – it took only a gentle nudge here, a canny poke there, the odd bit of honking and parping and timely indication before Lenny was seeing what he thought was the Real Girl underneath all the talk and the trash and the tassles.

If Lenny was a traffic jam, Cass did her damnedest to surreptitiously ease herself in at the front end. But it wasn't all plain sailing. Lenny was still too chafed for full-scale sexual adventure. His jib was still battered, his mast halved. And these particulars aside, there was still his mother to contend with, and she was surely no pushover.

Doll was powerfully built, majestically permed and certainly a proposition. She took against Cass with a vengeance during their very first encounter. Cass's Lycra/cheesecloth combinations were truly a red rag to a cow. Doll lived in nylon and believed – stupidly, vocally – that a compromise between Lenny and his ex-wife, Jill, was still attainable. If only, she'd mumble ruminatively, if only Lenny could learn to accept that trust can always be reacquired following certain kinds of minor sexual indiscretion. Doll was an old fashioned pragmatist and proud of it. Cass, she felt, was horrifyingly arty-farty. On her first home visit, Doll watched with some amazement as Cass fed the devils-on-horseback she'd so painstakingly prepared to lolling, pink-tongued old Pike. And this, even after she'd warned her that virtually all kinds of preserved fruit made him prone to wind. Cass was unapologetic: "I'm a vegetarian, Doll, and something of a body fascist,' she announced, baring a set of teeth as grand, magical and monolithic as the main circle at Stonehenge, "so I'm afraid that you'll just have to take me as you find me.'

Doll found her sorely wanting. She watched suspiciously as Cass stroked Pike from the tip of his nose to the end of his tail and didn't think once of slapping him down when he clambered up all too keenly. She advised Lenny towards carnal reticence. The word "rebound' was rarely far from her commonplace vocabulary.

Lenny smiled. He'd felt under no pressure to be sexual with Cass as yet, and since Cass claimed to be able to reach a climax while watching adverts about car insurance, was aroused by things as everyday as the taste of peppermint and the smell of household disinfectant, she appeared about as sexually demanding as a Pot Noodle.

Doodling in Cass's kitchen one day, Lenny happened to notice a leaflet an the noticeboard for a discussion at the ICA entitled "Where Does Love End and Fur Begin?' And paging through Cass's copy of Madonna's book, *Sex* ("Madonna is the ultimate paradigm of a truly emancipated female'), he noted that one of the pages was especially well-worn. It detailed the Virgin Queen's early experiences in New York's strip joints. There were some pictures involved but it was mainly text, which, Lenny decided, as far as Cass and her proclivities were concerned, made perfect sense.

He fondly believed that Cass, unlike his apparently conventional spouse, Jill, was all talk, no action. She was a chicken waiting to be plucked. But until that time, she seemed perfectly content to simply peck and cluck. What Lenny didn't notice, however, was that on the back side of the well-worn page was another which showed Madonna frolicking in the garden with an exceedingly friendly bitch. And Madonna, the strumpet, was all bare ass and beams.

One Tuesday night, Lenny came home for a quick snack before starting his evening shift and let slip to Doll that he was considering attending a World Music Festival in Reading that weekend. It would be the first night he and Cass would spend together. Cass owned a tent – he dimpled – and she had suggested that they take Pike along with them for the ride.

Pike swished his tail at the mention of his own special syllable and gave an attention-grabbing whine. He was surely the gamest of pawns.

Doll scowled: "But what about his regular Sunday walk in the forest?"

"He'll get plenty of exercise with us."

"He might get lost."

"Lost?!" Cass nearly choked. "Lenny! He's your dog. Tell her that she can either like it or lump it."

Thursday morning, Lenny told Doll that Cass was determined that Pike should attend the festival after all. "This is an important weekend for Cass and me," he said gently, "and it's rather a case of love me, love my mutt."

Doll sucked in her cheeks. She felt a brief spasm of prickly heat beneath her girdle. Then she exploded: "Don't you think Pike has been through enough already over the past few months? He shouldn't be dragged from pillar to post. What he craves is security."

"It's only Reading, Mum," Lenny whimpered, but Doll had already stalked off.

"Oh dear."

Lenny stared at Pike, who stared back and then reached down to sniff his own scrotum.

(Let it be observed that if, at any point, it might have been suggested to Lenny that the conflict between his new woman and his mother was in fact a psycho-sexual one, the suggester would've been the recipient of a grazed jaw. But a secret part of Lenny sensed that this was, in fact, the case, and the private thrill of it made his oedipal juices swish. The silly bugger.) Through the remainder of Thursday and the first mouthful of Friday, Lenny didn't mention the subject of Pike's weekend to either conflicting party. Cass saw no reason to believe that she hadn't got her own way, but decided, just in case, to turn up at Lenny's house a spit before he arrived home from work, so that any disputes between her and Doll could be ironed out in his absence.

Doll had been very busy. She'd taken Pike out that morning for a wade in the more rancid spots of local marshland and had gorged him on smoked haddock for lunch. She answered the door wearing a pale pink housecoat and pop socks. Pike was as high as a rotten potato. Doll – usually houseproud – appeared not to notice.

Cass recoiled. Pike in no way resembled the beautiful firm-nosed, tousle-head-ed, clean-tongued dog of which Anais Nin had written so evocatively in her erotic prose. But these differences, Cass told herself, while significant, were really quite small.

Doll led Cass into the front room.

"I gave Pike a worming tablet just after lunch," she declared, the high colour of battle flaring in her cheeks. "So he might be a little gyppy in the car."

"Oh." "Perhaps he'd be best left after all." "He'll be fine. Maybe we could hose him down before we go?" "No. Tea?" "Thanks."

While Doll busied herself in the kitchen, Cass dumped her suitcase, grabbed Pike's collar and led him, with little resistance, to the front door, through it, and onwards and outwards. "Okay, fella," she told him, once they were settled on the bus, "let's see how you scrub up, shall we?" Lenny arrived home to a scene of sheer bedlam. Doll was rabid.

"Pike's gone!" she bellowed.

"Where?" "She took him! My back was turned for just one moment and then she took him." "Who?" "Cass!" Lenny grinned. "Come off it. Why would Cass take Pike?" Doll threw herself down onto the sofa. "I don't know why, Lenny, but what I do know is that the way she petted Pike and fussed over him every single time they met just wasn't natural."

Lenny was mortified. "Mum," he said quietly, "calm down. You're being silly. She's probably only taken him out for a walk. She left her suitcase behind, see?" He pointed.

"Yes," Doll was triumphant, "and maybe you should take a little look inside."

She sprang up and grabbed Cass's battered old, case, pinged open the lock and pulled it wide. It was empty except for a small, but rather delightful, moth-eaten fur bikini. Lenny was lost for words.

"How's that for depravity?" Doll slammed the case shut with a resolute crack.

Lenny took a deep breath and then spoke: "Have you considered," he cleared his throat, ". . . is it at all possible that you might be feeling just the tiniest bit . . ." he paused, "um . . . well . . . jealous?" Doll blushed the colour of a beef tomato.

"Jealous? What of?"

"Of . . . well . . . of me."

Doll cackled: "Jealous? Of you? Pah!!"

Lenny was visibly withered.

Driving over to Cass's flat, Lenny couldn't help fixating on the way she'd pinned a cuddly puppy calendar above her bed, her collection of studded collars, her great show of excitement when Crufts was televised – especially during the working dogs coverage. He felt sick.

Cass, meanwhile, had arrived home and tried to put Pike in the bath.

He'd proven astonishingly unwieldy. In the space of 20 minutes, he'd sat on her face-towel, eaten a bar of soap, a loofah and several chunks of her best fern. Then he'd shaken himself all over her new living-room curtains.

Things weren't going at all to plan. Pike kept barking at her stereo and her toaster. Three times she'd had to remove her first edition copy of *The Women's Room* from between his champing jaws. He, like Doll, was certainly proving no pushover. Cass inspected her soaking shirt-front and sighed. The whole flat smelled like fish guts and old cardboard. Why weren't things working out? Was it just a lack of organisational skill on her part? Did she possess no real sense of authority? Was it simply this alien environment which had rendered Pike so unattractive, so unmalleable?

"I have the fantastical nipples of a true hussy," she told herself brokenly, then picked up her favourite pair of Hush Puppy suede slippers and threw them violently against the wall.

"Pike. Fetch!" Good as gold, he retrieved them.

Lenny felt like he was driving through treacle. Everything seemed so slow and so sticky. But finally he arrived. He parked the cab, climbed out, stared over at Cass's flat, took a deep breath, walked up to the front door, pushed. It wasn't locked. He steeled himself and then bowled right on in. He froze.

The sight that greeted him made him gasp in horror.

"Pike!" he yelled. "Off the sofa! You know full well you're never allowed to do that at home."

Cass emerged from the kitchen, perfectly cool, holding a bowl of water.

"Hello," she smiled. "I brought him home for a bath. He was absolutely filthy. How was work?" "Work?" Lenny just gaped.

In the cab, after an interval of strained silence, Lenny said quietly: "Cass, you do realise that Pike's been neutered?" "Really?" Cass seemed unperturbed. Lenny studied her lack of reaction side-on. He hated himself for the thoughts he'd been having.

"So you don't think it's cruel or anything?" "What?" Her mind was clearly elsewhere. "Actually, Lenny, maybe we should leave Pike with your mum after all. If it really means that much to her."

Pike sat damply on the back seat, full of beans.

"So you don't think it's cruel? To neuter?" "Cruel?" Cass seemed taken aback. "Hell, no. Cruel? What a silly idea. I mean that's like saying life would be impossible without penetrative sex."

Lenny was suddenly nervous: "You mean for dogs?" "No," Cass looked perfectly calm. "In general."

"But wouldn't life be impossible?" Cass glanced at Lenny's troubled expression. "Good God, Lenny, some of your ideas are so bourgeois."

A gradual change began to take place in Lenny's perception of Cass.

Gradual, slight even, but very significant. Could a person be very sexual, but very prudish, at exactly the same time?

"It wasn't really true about your being aroused by household disinfectant, was it?" Cass wasn't listening. She was debating the small, but significant, difference between reality and fantasy. She was thinking how wolfish Lenny was in profile, how big his hands were, how obliging he could be.

And he had a fantastic sense of direction, which was always an asset in a man.

"Disinfectant?" she parroted finally. "Uh . . . no. Well . . . only pine-flavoured." "And surely you can't actually reach orgasm by simply breathing?" Cass frowned: "I can't if I don't, that's for sure."

Lenny spent the best part of the journey home working out what this meant exactly.

They dropped Pike off. Lenny explained to Cass that it might be easier if she waited in the car.

"Fine." She propped her feet up on the dashboard.

Pike was glad to be home. He blew about like a mad little thistle in a windy gust. Doll was much calmer than she had been previously. Lenny told her that the trip to Reading was still on, but that they'd decided to leave Pike behind after all.

"Fine." She didn't bat an eyelid. "Whatever's easier."

Doll always recognised victory when it bit her on the butt.

Lenny retrieved Cass's suitcase and headed for the door. He felt like he'd really run the gamut. He climbed back into the cab and handed Cass a map. "Just in case," he muttered, and fastened his seatbelt. Cass tossed the map onto the back seat, sat hard on her hands, and spent the rest of the journey trying to scrape Lenny's Thank You For Not Smoking sign off the dashboard with her toes. For once, she seemed to have nothing in particular to talk about. And for once, Lenny felt like he had plenty.

Pike was home again! He was truly home again! Doll was ecstatic. She was so relieved, in fact, that for the first time in what seemed like a very long while she felt able to relax and wind down completely. She took off her housecoat, rolled her pop socks around her ankles and applied a fresh coating of bacon fat to all her main glands.

BEAUTY'S SISTER

James Bradley

James Bradley (b.1967) has twice been named as one of the *Sydney Morning Herald*'s Best Young Australian Novelists and has won the Fellowship of Australian Writers' Literature Award, the Kathleen Mitchell Literary Award and has been shortlisted for the Miles Franklin Literary Award. He is the author of a collection of poetry called *Paper Nautilus* and the novels *Wrack, The Deep Field, The Resurrectionist* and the forthcoming *Clade*. He lives in Sydney with his partner and their daughters.

I was four when I discovered I had a sister. It was winter, the forest outside still and silent, the fire dancing in the hearth.

All morning my mother had been tired, distracted, pushing me away and snapping when I grabbed for her sewing, her frustration with me so palpable that finally I retreated to the other room.

It was darker in there, colder, and so with my doll beneath my arm I clambered up onto the bed. From the next room I could hear the fire, the occasional movement of my mother's chair, but otherwise it was quiet, the only sound that of my father's axe in the distance, the blows ringing through the freezing air.

How long it took I do not know, but eventually I grew drowsy, and slept.

When I woke the house was silent. Rising, I went through to the other room to look for my mother, but the room was empty, the fire low. Thinking she must have gone to fetch wood, I went to the door and looked out, but she was not by the woodpile either.

I had never been afraid of the forest before, but standing there I felt something shift inside me, and so I called out to her, my voice echoing through the silent trees, over and over.

On the ground I could see her footsteps, leading away into the snow. Thinking to follow, I stepped out, but after a few steps the chill of the icy ground under my feet drove me back.

I am not sure how long I stood there, looking out. Long enough for the heat to escape from the house. Long enough, too, for me to realise I could no longer hear my father's axe in the distance. Long enough for me to understand I was alone and to begin to cry.

In my memory the time that followed seems to stretch on forever, though in truth it can't have been more than an hour or two before my father returned home.

Who knows what he thought at first? Aware the fire was dying, I had tried to push a log in, something I was expressly forbidden to do, but all I had succeeded in doing was spilling the pot and spreading ashes across the floor. And so all he saw as he stood silhouetted in the door was the empty hut and the spilled food. Standing there he called my mother's name once, and then again more urgently.

It was only as he came closer that he saw me huddled by the fire. I remember the way he dropped his axe and grabbed for me, the pressure of his hands on my arms as he searched my body for signs of injury.

Perhaps because he was so absorbed with me, he did not hear my mother at the door behind him until she was already in the room. She did not greet us or offer any explanation, just shook off the blanket she wore, hung it by the door, and, taking the knife up from the table, began to carve at the hank of bread that lay upon it.

Placing me on the floor, my father stood to face her.

"Where have you been?"

When she did not answer he moved closer. "Where have you been?" he asked again.

Although he did not raise his voice, something in his deliberate calm frightened me.

My mother looked up. "Out," she said.

"And the child here, alone, unattended?"

She looked at me for a moment, then shrugged and went back to her work. "She was asleep."

"All the worse. Did you not think about what would happen when she woke? About what I might think?"

Turning, she took down the pot by the window. "I'm not responsible for your thoughts."

He did not move. "She could have wandered off and gotten lost, the house could have burned, anything could have happened."

"But it didn't."

There was a long pause, and when my father spoke again his voice was low, trembling.

"You've been there again, haven't you? To see her?"

My mother did not answer. She stood close to the fire now, the pot in one hand.

"Haven't you?" my father said, his voice sharp, and as he did my mother spun.

"And what if I have?" she hissed. "Who are you to stop me?"

My father took a step towards her. He was not a big man, or a cruel one, but in that moment I was afraid of him.

"It shouldn't be me who stops you, it should be the child. You're her mother."

My mother did not flinch, just stood, staring at him. When she spoke again, her voice was hard. "I'm *her* mother as well," she said.

At this my father faltered, and for a long moment the two of them stood, staring at each other. So it fell to me to speak, my voice clear in the silence.

"Whose mother?"

Like any child I only knew the life I was born to. Yet even before that day I think I understood all was not right in our home. It wasn't just my mother's silences or the unspoken tension between her and my father, it was that there seemed to be an absence in our lives, a space that could be neither identified nor acknowledged.

And so, when the sound of the door jolted me from a shallow doze a week or so later, I did not simply roll over and go back to sleep. Instead I took rags and bound my feet, and slipped out after her.

Outside it was cold, the snow luminous beneath the bruised sky. At first I thought she had gone, but then I saw her footprints in the snow, her shape moving in the distance through the trees.

The snow was deep, and she moved quickly, so I had to run, my feet slipping and sliding beneath me. After a mile or so it became difficult, until at last I lost sight of her altogether.

With only her footprints to follow I struggled on, fear rising in me. But then, just as I began to wonder whether I should turn back, I saw the dark shape of the tower through the trees ahead.

I had seen it before, of course: it was visible from the road to town, and from the stream where I sometimes walked with my father. Yet, because I had always been forbidden to leave the familiar area around our hut, this was the first time I had come close enough to see it properly.

It was older than any building I had ever seen, its jagged shape rising high and strange out of the trees, moss and ivy growing in the cracks between the stones. At its base stood a hut, a small plume of smoke coiling upwards from its roof; above it the remnants of a wooden staircase still clung to the side of the tower. Although the ground between the tower and the wall was lined with gardens, the base of the tower itself was surrounded by wild bushes, the thorns on them thick and cruel.

Slipping behind a stone, I knelt down. Ahead of me my mother moved stealthily from tree to tree, her eyes fixed on the tower, until at last she came to a stop behind an elm, and stood, staring upwards.

I am not sure how long she stood there. The forest was quiet beneath the snow, the only sound that of the crows in the distance, and the occasional rustle and thump as a branch released its load of snow. Beyond the wall the tower and the hut were silent as well, and were it not for the smoke that rose from the chimney of the hut, it would have been easy to imagine them empty.

And then, without warning, a voice began to sing, pure and clear. Behind her tree my mother stiffened, her hand tightening on the bark.

Seeing her pain, I wanted to run to her. Yet something held me back, which meant I had time to see the way her face changed when the window at the top of the tower opened, and the girl looked out.

It is the hair most people imagine when they think of her, that impossibly long skein of gold, but it was not her hair I noticed that day. Rather it was her face, its openness and beauty. That and her resemblance to my mother.

I thought for a moment my mother might lift a hand to wave or call out, but instead she just stood, her body straining upwards and out from behind the tree slightly, as if hoping the girl might sense her presence and look her way. But the girl did not: instead she just sat, staring out.

Then all at once I heard a noise, a creaking sound, and a woman's figure emerged from the hut at the tower's base. Overhead the singing stopped, and with a start my mother dropped back out of sight.

Nestled behind my rock I let out a little gasp. I knew who she was; how could I not? On our visits to town I had heard the other children use her name as they might a devil's, calling her down upon their enemies, threatening her ministrations in the night. Some said that in the full moon her house rose up and danced beneath the trees on chicken's legs, others that her eyes were rubies and her teeth cold iron.

My heart beating fast, I lay as still as I could, praying she would not see me. Yet as I lay there I did not see the monster I had heard described. Instead I saw a smallish woman dressed in black, a cloak clutched about her against the cold. As I watched, she tucked a bundle under her arm and, moving with a quick, almost reptilian motion, hurried over to the base of the tower and called up to the girl at its top.

"Rapunzel!"

That was the first time I saw Jinka scuttle up the rope to the tower, but it was not the last, for as winter turned to spring I followed my mother to the tower many times.

Whether my mother noticed I was following her, or whether she knew and did not care, I do not know. There was something occluding about her anger, a sense in which it shut out all else: certainly there was no place in it for me.

The trips to the tower were not the only journeys we made in those months. For, as the weather grew warmer, it became easier for us to travel the three miles to town.

These trips were not always necessary: we had little money, and the forest supplied most of what we needed. Yet still my mother liked the clamour of the marketplace and the company of her friends, and so, as the snow began to melt, she would call me to her two or three times a week and we would walk out onto the road and into town.

At first I avoided the children of the town on these trips. At some point it had become their custom to scream and run away if I looked at them, or to call my name from behind walls. It was nothing, really, just a child's game, but it made it difficult for me to play with them. Then one spring day the baker's daughter Hettie saw me coming and cried out, but as she did her mother heard her, and, grabbing her arm, asked her what she was doing.

"Nothing," Hettie said, straining away. Her mother looked at me, then back at her daughter.

"Have you been tormenting this child, Hettie Prynne?"

Hettie shook her head, but her mother snorted. "Good. Then you won't mind taking her with you to play."

That Hettie was not pleased by this turn of events was clear, but with her mother's eyes on her, she had little choice but to comply.

At first Hettie and her friends did their best to ignore me, but as the morning passed they began to snipe at me again, making private jokes and glancing at me and laughing behind their hands.

Yet it was only when one of them said something I didn't quite hear about the witch that I retaliated, and, smiling coldly, said I had seen her for myself, and not just once but many times.

At my words the girls fell still. Looking around, I could see the way they stared at me.

"Liar," Hettie said, but her speech lacked its usual vehemence. I smiled.

"You think?" I asked.

I do not remember exactly what I told them that day, but what I do remember is the way my words held them. Later I would learn to use this glamour, to weave it close about myself to strike fear into them when it suited me. But that first day it was enough just to see the way they turned to me, to feel that shiver of delight, of power.

I understood it was wrong, of course, even then. Yet as I felt the way my words bound them to me I began to forget the trespass I was committing, to set aside the knowledge that I was violating some trust between my parents and myself. And as I did, I began to add details conjured from my child's mind: a crack of lightning, Jinka's hideousness, Rapunzel's hair.

Whether my parents noticed anything in my manner that day I do not know, but, regardless, it did not take long before my story of the tower spread and came at last to their ears. It was my father who heard it first; he arrived home from the forest one evening and entered the room, his face dark.

"What is it?" my mother asked, but he ignored her, grabbing my arm instead and bending down so his face was close to mine.

"What have you been telling the children in town?" he demanded.

I shook my head. "Nothing."

"Nothing? Are you sure?"

Behind him, my mother stood, watching.

"What is it?" she asked, but my father only shook his head, releasing my arm and stepping away.

"Ask her. Tom says she's been telling the children stories, about the tower, and your visits there."

My mother looked shocked.

"Did you even notice her following you?"

Looking up, I saw my mother's face change, saw the anger I knew so well return. But this time I saw something else in my father's face, not anger, nor despair, but exhaustion.

I heard the story that night, or most of it. Of my mother's first pregnancy, her nausea and wandering. Of her glimpse of the green rapunzel in Jinka's garden and my father's midnight sortie across the wall to fetch it for her. Of his encounter with Jinka as he made his escape.

As he told the story, my father would not meet my eye. "I did not hear her until she was there,' he said, "she was like a devil, close on me. She said she would curse us, curse me."

Behind him my mother sat, her face cold and pale.

"And tell her what you said."

"I told her of my wife at home, of the baby in her womb, of her desire for the leaves."

"And then?"

"She smiled, and said that perhaps she might let me have the rapunzel, and let me have my life, if I agreed to give her something."

"And what was it you agreed to give her?" my mother asked, her voice cold.

For a long moment there was silence.

"The baby," he said at last. "I said I would give her the baby."

Our parents' lives are always mysterious to us, yet in that moment I saw something of who they had been. I already knew some of it, of course, not just the part about the simple woodcutter who travelled to a village fair and fell in love with the local beauty, or the part about the beauty's wealthy father, the town miller, who forbade them to wed, but the final part, about their determination to marry against his wishes, and their flight from his house to the woods. But there was more, I now understood. The shared heedlessness that had drawn the two of them together, and led them to marry against my mother's father's wishes. The delight in indulgence that had led my mother to demand the rapunzel. The callow, careless confidence that had sent my father clambering over a wall into a witch's garden in the middle of the night simply to please his vain and sensuous wife. And what their foolishness cost them.

After that night, I did not follow my mother to the tower again. She still went and so did I, yet somehow it seemed wrong to follow her. And so when I went, I went alone.

At first I only went occasionally, but as I grew older I began to visit the tower almost every day. Exactly why I am not sure: perhaps it was simply habit, perhaps it was from some deeper need; all I know is that I passed many hours in the trees outside the tower, watching and waiting for a glimpse of my sister, or playing quietly amongst the rocks that rose up to its north. With her golden hair and tawny skin, she was as unlike me as could be, but when I was there it was easy to imagine we might be close, to imagine she knew I existed. Sometimes when she sang, I would close my eyes and rock myself, pretend I was with her.

Nor was it just about the tower and Rapunzel. Left to my own devices by my parents, I was learning the ways of the forest: coming to recognise the calls of the birds, to know which plants grew where, and when, to recognise the tracks of the foxes and the other creatures who called it their home. Out there, alone, I began to glimpse the force that moves through us all, to sense the way silence lurks in things, to feel the way the trees connect to the wind and the world. Once I saw wolves feasting on a deer, their long legs and silver fur matted with blood; another time I saw a woman's body half-buried by the autumn leaves.

I did not share these lessons with my parents, not even my father, whom I sometimes followed as he went about his work in the woods. Not, I think, because they would have been frightened, but because they would not have understood: although we still shared a house, and they a bed, when we were together we seldom spoke, my mother sunk in her anger and pain, my father in some deeper, sadder silence.

Perhaps it is strange, then, that I was almost thirteen before I first spoke with Jinka.

I had been in town the day we met. It was hot, the summer air heavy, and, bored with the heat, some of the boys had waded out into the river.

Seated on a rock to one side, I watched them chase each other through the shallows, whooping and laughing as they splashed and fought and fell. The mayor's son, Will, had stripped off his shirt, and as I looked on he wrestled with Tom, the blacksmith's boy, his face alight with the joy of it.

It was Will who won, of course, catching Tom off balance and sending him sprawling.

On the bank a cry went up, and as it did Will turned to face the girls gathered there, opening his arms theatrically and bowing low, as if he were a knight before ladies.

It was a playful move, but a teasing one: from their tittering and simpering it was obvious half of them were in love with him, and no less obvious that he understood that fact. But when the noon bell rang, and the children slipped away, Will did not follow them. Instead he approached me.

"Will you not go home also?" he asked, and I shrugged.

"Perhaps," I said.

"They say you do not have a home, that you live in a lair like a badger or a fox," he said then, and for a moment I thought he meant to wound me, but then he grinned, and despite myself I smiled as well.

"Perhaps I do," I said, and he laughed again.

"You must show me some time," he said.

"Maybe," I said.

The bell rang again. "I have to go," he said, and, throwing his wet shirt across his shoulder, he again gave a bow.

With him gone I felt suddenly empty, restless, and so when I slipped away into the forest I walked towards the tower, hoping to lose myself in the quiet there.

As it often was in the summer months, Rapunzel's window was open when I arrived, and, after climbing the beech I usually sat in, I looked in, but she was nowhere to be seen. Knowing she was not always visible I swung down again and moved along the perimeter of the wall to the next tree and shimmied up.

Again I saw nothing, but this time I was closer to the wall, and so, moving quietly, I clambered out along a limb.

From where I sat I could see down into the space behind the wall, see the rows of plants and trees planted there. And by the tower was Jinka's hut, its door closed despite the heat.

Maybe it was the carelessness of the afternoon, maybe it was curiosity, but as the minutes passed I found myself filled with a desire to enter the garden, to look inside her house. And so, moving quietly, I dropped to the ground and clambered over the wall.

Inside the air was warmer still, heated by the stones of the wall, and thick with the scent of grass and honeysuckle, and the golden peaches on her trees. Taking a peach, I bit into it, feeling the juice run down my chin.

Moving as quietly as I could, I approached the hut. From outside, it looked like a ruin, yet closer up it seemed different somehow: larger, more substantial. Through the window I could see a table and a bed, a fireplace of stone, a pot above it; from the roof and eaves hung charms and talismans: garlands of herbs, a fox's tail, a string of knucklebones.

Outside the door I paused, glancing back across the gardens to the gate. In the distance I could hear a crow calling, but otherwise the air was still. Then, lifting a hand, I placed it on the door, and began to push.

The door swung open, but as it did I felt something behind me. At first I froze, then quickly turned and began to run. But although I was fast, she was faster, and in one sharp movement she grabbed my hair and pulled me close.

"Who's this snooping in my house?" she hissed.

Writhing in her grasp, I did not answer, and so she twisted my hair and pulled me closer.

"Well?" she asked, her face so close to mine now, I could feel the hot fug of her breath, see the filed points of her teeth in her mouth. Afraid now, I fell still.

"What? You thought I hadn't seen you lurking in the trees? That I didn't know you were there?"

I tried to shake my head, the pain of it making me whimper. For a long moment she held me immobile, then with a snort she loosened her grip and released me. Stumbling back, I landed heavily on the path. She stared at me, then she smiled.

"Your mother, too," she said, and laughed.

When I did not reply, she shook her head.

"So what did you think? That you would climb the tower? Visit your sister? You should be glad I don't take you there, lock you up with her."

Pulling myself to my feet, I rubbed my arm where I had fallen on it. "Why? I've done nothing."

She smiled. "No? You've taken nothing that's mine?"

As she spoke, I remembered the peach.

"No," I said.

In a flash she grabbed my face.

"Liar!" she hissed, her nails biting into my skin. "You come into my garden and steal my fruit and you think I am so stupid I will not know?"

I was about to tear free and make for the wall when she paused, and, eyes narrowing, drew me in again. Then, as abruptly as she had grabbed me, she let me go. With a convulsive movement I jumped back, but she made no move to follow me.

"Would you meet her?" she asked.

I hesitated, watching her. Then I nodded.

I wonder now how much of her art was really magic. Much of what she knew was simply women's lore: the knowledge of berries and plants, the making of medicines. Yet there was craft there, too, for she could mix a potion to make a woman throw a baby, or to draw desire from the heart or loins, and in the dark she would mutter spells and charms and curse those who offended her. Beneath it all, though, I suspect she was just cruel, and took pleasure in people's fear of her, in the power that it gave. There was something black inside her, something cold and cunning, and that power pleased it, made it stronger.

Had I been older I might have realised this, and wondered at her readiness to show me her secrets, but that day such thoughts were banished by the idea of what she was offering me. And so I followed her to the tower, watching as she called to Rapunzel to cast down the rope.

She went first, scuttling up the side of the tower like a spider or a rat. From below I watched as she climbed onto the ledge beside the window and unlocked the cage. Then she looked down at me, and nodded.

Before that day Rapunzel had been more an idea of a girl to me than a person of flesh and blood. Indeed, it was not until I let go of the rope on that ledge beside her window and heard her asking Jinka who was outside that it occurred to me she might have her own past, her own thoughts, or that learning there were others in the world beside Jinka and herself might be frightening.

I was nervous, too, of course. Yet as I swung down from the window I could see Rapunzel was far more so, her face pale and body tensed as if for flight.

For a long moment nobody spoke. Then at last Rapunzel took a step back.

"Who's this?" she asked, not letting her eyes stray from me.

By the fireplace, Jinka smiled. "Ask her," she said, the harshness of her voice outside replaced by something cloying and sweet.

Still unwilling to let me out of her sight Rapunzel glanced quickly at Jinka, then back at me again.

"Well?" Jinka said.

Rapunzel hesitated. Up close she was smaller than I had imagined her, slimmer, and, if anything, more beautiful. Then, as if reaching a decision, she gave a small, almost imperceptible nod.

"Who are you?" she asked.

I looked at Jinka. Down below she had made me promise I would not tell Rapunzel anything that would make her suspect we were related.

"Juniper," I said, "my name is Juniper."

Opposite me, Rapunzel nodded.

"Where have you come from?" she asked. "How did you find us?"

Again I looked at Jinka. "I live nearby," I said, "in a house in the forest."

"Mother?" she asked. Jinka smiled, her face cold.

"She means us no harm," she said. "Would I have brought her here if she did?"

Rapunzel hesitated, then shook her head. "No, Mother," she said.

I did not stay long that day: half an hour, little more. Then Jinka bade me leave, and sent me back down the rope.

Outside in the forest I moved lightly through the trees. It was still hot, and although on another day I might have returned home to eat, today I had no desire to, preferring to be in motion, to follow the paths through the shaded spaces of the forest.

It was growing dark by the time I found my way back to my parents' house. Although it was late I knew my father would not be back for another hour yet, for he had been working in a valley to the west. I was surprised, though, to find my mother seated on a log outside our hut, her sewing in her lap. As I approached, she called to me, and I crossed to where she sat.

She did not rise, just looked up, her eyes taking in my dirty feet and ragged dress, the tangles in my hair. In the summer sun my skin had taken on the grey-brown tan and freckles those of my colouring are prone to.

"So late," she said.

I did not answer, and she smiled, extending a hand.

"Come here," she said, "let me see you."

Obediently I knelt before her, allowing her hand to caress my hair, my head.

"You're growing up," she said, and I nodded, feeling her hand come down to cup my chin, turn my face to hers.

"Where do you go? What is it you find out there?"

I shrugged, holding her gaze.

"Nowhere."

"Are you sure? Do you have no friends? I hear you are sometimes in town."

"Sometimes," I said.

For a moment she was silent. "And today?" she asked. "Where were you today?"

I hesitated, my heart beating fast, then shrugged again.

"Nowhere," I lied.

The next morning I slipped out before my mother rose, making my way to the tower through the dawn light. As I came through the gate, Jinka appeared at the door to her hut.

"You come back?" she said, and I nodded.

"Yet I did not say I would let you see her again."

No doubt my face betrayed me, for she smiled coldly. "What? You thought you would just scurry up there, take what is mine?"

When I did not answer, she gave a short laugh. "Stupid child. A witch's gift is never given freely."

I hesitated, but when I spoke I held my voice level. "What is it you would have me do?"

For a moment or two she stared at me, then she smiled. "Not much," she said, "just little things."

That morning the price was two hours spent in Jinka's garden, for which I won another two in the tower. Yet as the weeks passed, and summer faded into autumn, the time I spent with each grew longer and longer. Sometimes Jinka would keep me in the garden, other times she would send me running through the forest in search of bark or fungus, or to catch some wild thing.

Taken on their own, these tasks were not difficult, and, truth be told, I took pleasure in pleasing her. Although her moods still frightened me, she could be kind as well, and somehow the fear of her anger made that kindness all the sweeter. And piece by piece I began to learn something of her craft, watching as she made her spells with strings and bones, berries and bark.

I do not remember most of what we spoke of in those early days. Rapunzel knew so little of the world, and because I feared Jinka's anger I was afraid to tell her anything that might make her wonder about her confinement. And so I answered her questions as I could, filling in blanks with little lies, and telling stories as they came to me.

She did not believe herself a prisoner: Jinka had told her she was the victim of a curse, and if she left the tower she would die, but when I pressed her for the story behind the curse she grew uneasy, and said it was her father's work, that he was a great wizard, and it was only Jinka's love for her that kept him from finding her.

"This wizard, your father," I asked, "have you ever seen him?"

Rapunzel grew uneasy, then nodded.

"Once he came to the gates to look for me, dressed in a woodsman's suit. My mother bade me hide, and drove him off."

Looking up I saw Jinka watching me, her eyes cold, and dead, and in that moment I knew the man she described was not just any woodsman but my father, come to beg once more for Rapunzel's return to him.

"Tell me about your mother," Rapunzel said, and something froze inside of me.

"My mother?" I asked, looking at her.

"Yes," she said, smiling. "What is she like, what does she look like? Why does she let you roam alone in the woods?"

I glanced over at Jinka, who stared back at me. Clearing my throat, I shifted my hands, adjusted my dress.

"There is not much to tell you," I said. "She was a lady once, but now she lives in the forest with my father."

"So they married for love?"

"I suppose."

"And is she beautiful? What does she look like? Like you?"

I shook my head. "No," I said, "not like me."

I wonder now exactly why I gave myself to Jinka. Was it for Rapunzel's sake? For my own? Or was it because I saw in her a way to harm my mother, to make her suffer for her coldness, her lack of love?

Whichever it was, the reckoning was not long in coming. Two months after that first afternoon I returned home one evening to find my mother waiting.

I knew at once, I think. Something in the way she held herself told me without words that she had been at her tree, had seen me in the garden or the tower.

She did not speak as I entered, just lifted her eyes and looked at me. I had thought she would be angry but she was not: instead her face was pale, cold.

"How long?" she asked. "How long have you been going there?"

I shrugged. "A while."

"And the witch, she is your friend?"

Suddenly afraid, I gave a small nod.

"You do her bidding?"

I nodded again.

"Why?"

I shrugged. My mother sat, staring at me, her face pale, as if she had been hollowed out. Yet when she spoke her voice was clear, calm.

"Go," she said. "Leave this house. You are not my child."

I hesitated, but before I could speak she stood, her fists tightening.

"I said go. And don't come back."

When I still did not move, she struck the table.

"Go!" she cried, tears on her cheeks. "I will not have you near me."

Outside it was growing dark, the air already cold, yet as I stumbled through the trees I barely noticed. At first I walked at random, moving quickly, urgently, as if my speed might keep the tears at bay, but in time they caught me, and I broke down and wept.

When at last my tears were done, I rose, pulling my shawl tight against the chill. It was not winter yet, but I knew the forest well enough to understand I would die if I stayed out there alone.

I slept in Jinka's house that night, but after that I took myself away, to an abandoned hut I knew of, off in the trees. It was small, and cold, but with a fire it was enough to keep me through that winter and the next.

Living alone, so far away, my visits to the town grew less frequent. And so it was I did not see Will again until the spring eighteen months after I had left my parents' home, and when I did, it was by chance.

I was on the road, where it bends towards the bridge, when he, on horseback, rounded the corner ahead of me, one of his father's servants behind him in livery. Seeing me there, he grinned delightedly and reined in his mount.

"So, Juniper, you still live!" he said.

"I do," I said.

"I thought of you often last winter, freezing in your badger's set."

"Was it not a fox's lair?" I asked, and he grinned.

"Perhaps it was. Either way, I'm pleased it kept you warm."

"Where are you going?" I asked, and he glanced back at the man behind him.

"To the city," he said, "to see to some matters with my father's man."

I must have looked unimpressed, because he laughed.

"What, you do not think me a man of substance?"

"I think the ladies in the city would do well to watch out for you."

"What makes you think I have eyes for the ladies of the city?"

I looked skeptical and he laughed again.

"Oh Juniper, so young and yet so cruel."

Despite myself I smiled. He leaned back in his saddle.

"Will you wait for me?"

"Why would I wait for you?"

"Juniper, you wound me. Do you think I have eyes for anyone but you?"

I laughed, and he hesitated, watching me. I thought for a moment he was going to speak, but instead he reached for his purse and took out a coin.

"Here," he said, "take this. And do not trust that Tom Varney, he is a man of no morals."

I understood, of course. Even at fifteen I had a power over men that other women did not have. Some think it is beauty we desire, but it is not. It is something else, something less easy to define. We want what is forbidden, yet will have take what is available. And so, while I might not have been the one they wanted to marry, I was the one they would settle for in the meantime.

I suppose I understood what this would make me, yet I was surprised the first time I heard another girl call me a wanton. It was that prune-faced Milly, a girl no man could ever truly want, but still it startled me.

"What did you say?" I asked, turning to her. She did not move, her mouth tight beneath her white bonnet.

"You heard me," she said, but as she spoke I could see she was less certain now.

"I'm not sure I did," I said, smiling easily and moving closer. Beside the pale Milly, my black hair and dirty feet made me look a wild thing. Lifting a hand, I reached for hers, but she jerked it away.

"Witch's slut!" she spat, and for a moment her vehemence and the hatred in her voice startled me. Recovering myself, I pressed closer.

"What?" I asked, and Milly pulled away.

In truth there were not that many men. And none of them mattered until Will came back for the summer. I know men, and I am sure he knew what I was, of the bodies I had known, and yet he took his time coming to me. And when he came, it was almost as if by accident. I was in the woods, by myself, when I came upon him, walking. For a while I followed behind, watching, until at last I grew tired of waiting, and, taking a stone from my pocket, cast it at him.

He turned, his face angry, but seeing me he laughed, and rode closer.

"Little June," he said, "I had wondered how long it would be until I saw you."

"Long enough, with the way you blunder through the woods," I replied, and he laughed again.

"We have not all had your experience in these woods."

"I am sure you move quickly enough in the city."

He shrugged. "Is it true what I hear? That you are already half witch?"

I smiled. "Perhaps."

"Must I fear your arts?"

I pushed my hair back from my face. "I thought you already feared me."

"Perhaps. Or maybe you have already enchanted me." As he spoke, he held a hand out to me. Seeing it I laughed, and, dropping down from my branch, slipped out of his reach.

I have heard people call him a prince when they tell this story, but he was no prince. Yet he was special nonetheless, possessed of that easy beauty and confidence that comes from being unafraid of one's own desires, or the things that are necessary to achieve them. And that summer he was mine, or as much mine as he was ever going to be. In the forest and the ricks we lay together many times, our bodies thrown together, panting and laughing. Neither of us called it love, and so we believed there was an honesty between us, though, looking back, I wonder whether that honesty was merely a clever way of hiding a truth neither of us could admit. Sometimes he would tease me, call me his June and kiss me or touch my lips, and I would feel something between us, some electricity.

Jinka knew, of course; how could she not? Once he came to her gate, and she saw him before I did, and in the time it took me to run to meet him, to steer him away from her, I think she understood everything she needed to. Everything except what mattered.

As the summer wore on, our conversations grew more intimate, each of us telling the other things we had never told anybody else.

Often his stories were about his father, or his family, the future he had mapped out for him, but sometimes he spoke of girls as well, both those his friends had known and ones he had known, until one day he told me of the girl in the city his father wished him to marry, of her kindness and suitability.

When he had finished, I said nothing, just lay looking upwards. Next to me I could feel him listening, waiting for me to respond. When I did not, he placed a hand on my cheek.

"I have offended you."

I gave a little shrug. "Of course not," I said. "Why would I be offended?"

For a long time he did not answer, just lay there, his hand stroking my cheek. And when he did speak again, his voice was different, softer.

"Tell me about her."

"Who?" I asked.

"The witch."

I made a dismissive sound.

"Is it true, what they say? Can she really turn herself into a cat and speak to the dead?"

I laughed, pulling away from him. "Perhaps."

He shifted his weight to look at me.

"And you, June, what secrets do you have?"

For a long time I did not answer. His body was so close to mine I could feel the movement of his blood beneath his skin.

"She has a girl," I said at last, my voice scarcely more than a whisper. "In the tower."

He stared at me, his eyes narrowing in disbelief.

"No."

I did not answer, just grinned.

"You've seen her?"

I shrugged. "I know her."

He laughed, leaning away.

"You're lying."

I shook my head. "She took her, as a baby."

"From whom?"

I hesitated. "My parents."

He looked at me warily.

I nodded. "Come with me and I'll show you".

I sat up, watching him. "Are you afraid?"

He shook his head. "Only of you," he said, although when he smiled there was something behind it I had not seen before.

Why did I tell him? Because I loved him and thought it would impress him? And what did that say about how I saw her? Although we were friends, although I took pleasure in the time we spent together in the tower, talking and laughing, and although it pleased me to see the way she trusted me, there was something else there, too, some sense in which her innocence brought out something cruel in me. It was exciting, knowing she was there, knowing she was at my mercy, and like a child I wanted to share that excitement, to show off my power.

Three days passed before Jinka left for long enough for me to chance taking Will to the tower. Then, on the third day, she slipped away, taking the path I knew led to her traps in the hills, a journey that never took less than three hours.

Will was by the river when I found him and, taking his hand, led him back towards the tower. As we hurried through the forest we barely spoke, but by the gate I looked around at him and was surprised to see him smiling, scared, but excited. Catching my eye he grinned, and I felt a sudden thrill of pleasure at being there with him like that.

Inside the wall, the gardens were quiet, the only sound the buzz of the bees and the heavy hum of the insects, and as I led Will through them towards the tower I watched the way he looked about himself, taking in not just the swelling beauty of the plants and trees, but the charms and talismans hanging from their sticks to scare the birds. To one side a scarecrow stood, a nightmare thing of straw and cloth and crow feathers; by its feet, one of the cats watched us with its fathomless yellow eyes.

By Jinka's hut we stopped, and I slipped in to take the key from its place. Then, emerging into the light again, I motioned him across towards the tower.

I went first, but I did not tell her Will was behind me until he appeared in the window, and I still remember how she took a step away in shock, one hand raised to her mouth.

"Juniper!" she shrieked, but before I could speak Will raised a hand reassuringly.

"Please. I'm not going to hurt you."

Beside me Rapunzel clutched my arm.

"It's all right," I said. "He's a friend."

Although her grip did not slacken, I felt her breathing gradually slow. I saw her eyes fixed on his.

"Who is he?" she asked. He spoke over me, past me.

"My name is Will."

If he was ever mine, I lost him that day. Although she was awkward with him, and shy, it was easy to see the way she bloomed under his gaze, the way his kindness made her smile. Once her fear of him was overcome, she was eager to know all she could, and she plied him breathlessly with questions about the city and the town and the world beyond her tower, her eagerness disarming him, delighting him.

An hour passed, and then another, and then I interrupted them, saying that we had to go. Will looked at me, and for a moment I was aware of how her golden beauty made my thin limbs and ragged hair look.

"Already?"

I nodded, and reluctantly he stood, his eyes taking in the two of us. He grinned carelessly.

"Had you not told me, I would not have known the two of you were sisters," he said.

At his words, something went still inside me. Turning, I saw Rapunzel staring at me in confusion.

"Sisters?" she said. "I don't understand."

Will hesitated. "You didn't know?" he asked.

"No!" Rapunzel said. "You're lying!" As she spoke she looked at me imploringly. I shook my head.

"He's not."

"But I don't understand," she said. "Why didn't you tell me? Why did you lie to me?"

Uncertain what to say, I drew back towards the window. "We need to go," I said. "Jinka will be back soon."

Things were different after that. Although he still came to me, something had changed between us, our bodies no longer congruent, no longer bound. One night we fought, my ill temper curdling into fury at his indifference, and after that I saw him less, and when I did he greeted me as he might any girl.

No doubt my shame and anger showed, for Jinka noticed.

"There is a charm," she said one evening, speaking lightly, as if it were no great thing she was suggesting. "A spell that would make him yours."

I hesitated, feeling the thrill of the possibility, then shook my head.

"No," I said.

"Then we should punish him," Jinka said, the tone of her voice making me turn in time to see the way she smiled. I went cold.

"No," I said again, "not that either." Although I think I wanted to, at least a little bit.

Rapunzel was different as well. For almost a week, the only times I saw her were when Jinka was there, so Rapunzel could not speak. The first time we were alone she stood and backed away from me.

"Why did you lie to me?" she demanded.

I shrugged. "She told me not to tell you."

"So that woman, the one outside: she is my mother?"

"And my mother as well."

It hardened me, to see her wounded like that, to feel the sting of her disapproval. Taking up her needlework, I cast it at her. "Finish your sewing," I said.

There is a potion, the making of which I know, a draught designed to harden the heart, to make one forget that which has been lost. Brewed from belladonna and poppy seed, it is taken sometimes by grieving mothers. Yet its powers are false, for grief withheld is only grief delayed, and by refusing pain we also forget how to love. But I was too young to understand that, too foolish.

And, as it turned out, too blind. For one day, as the summer drew down, I approached the wall to find Will standing by the gate. He was ahead of me, and could not see me, so I slipped behind a tree, and then, after waiting for a moment, followed him.

Inside he moved quickly, certainly, cutting towards the house and stealing in, only to emerge a moment later with the key. Beneath the tower he paused, and, looking up, called for the rope.

As he shimmied up the wall I stole closer, concealing myself by the thorn bushes. From where I knelt I could not see them in the tower above, but even before I heard her cry out, I understood what his visit meant, and how long it had been going on.

That night I did not sleep, just lay awake, listening to the dark. After Will had gone, I had climbed the rope myself, paced about her room, watching her for some sign she thought I suspected, but she just ignored me in the manner that had become her habit since Will's first visit, answering my questions as briefly as possible. Yet in my bed, as I closed my eyes, I could reconstruct the scene in my mind, their nakedness, the closeness of their bodies. I knew them both so well, it was easy to make it real to myself. And as I did, I felt my fury grow.

Jinka was still abed when I arrived the next day; as I entered she hissed.

"It's only me," I said.

"What is it?" she asked, lifting herself to look at me.

"It's Rapunzel," I said.

Even as I spoke I saw the look of fury on her face, the black rage. When I was done, she was silent, then with a shriek she stood, and ran to the tower.

Rapunzel looked confused as we entered, her eyes flicking first to Jinka's face and then to mine. Jinka was wild, terrifying, and as she moved she swayed like a snake.

"What is it, Mother?" Rapunzel asked, backing away.

"You think I am a fool then?" Jinka hissed.

"No, Mother."

"Liar!" Jinka spat, lunging forward with the speed I knew so well. "Faithless child!"

Rapunzel twisted in her grip, but Jinka was too quick, too strong, and before she could get away Jinka had her on the bed, her face clutched in her hand.

"So, you give yourself to him, do you? And lie to me, your loving mother?"

Rapunzel shook her head, fighting against Jinka's grip. "No," she said, but as she spoke her eyes met mine, and I saw understanding appear.

"What did he promise you?" Jinka asked. "And what did you give him?" As she spoke she snaked a hand into Rapunzel's dress, her hand pressing into her, her face thoughtful for a moment, then harder than before. With sudden force, she thrust Rapunzel away from her, sending her sprawling across the bed, then, turning to me, reached into her skirt pocket and drew out a length of cord and cast it at me.

"Tie her," she said.

I worked quickly, binding my sister to the bed. When I was done Jinka produced a pair of scissors, and with rough strokes began to cut Rapunzel's hair away. Then she brushed the hair onto the floor and sat beside Rapunzel, one hand raised to touch her cheek.

"Did you not know your mother loved you?" she asked. Rapunzel jerked her head away, and once more Jinka looked at me.

"Gag her," she said.

It was after midday before Will appeared, slipping through the garden to the hut. As he called her name on the platform beneath, Rapunzel strained at her bindings and tried to cry out, but Jinka just crossed to the window, and cast the rope down.

I did not move as he ascended. And so, when his body appeared in the window, it was me he saw, seated on the bed, Rapunzel shorn and bound behind me. In that moment I understood what I had lost.

"June?" he said, swinging his legs over the sill, but before I could speak Jinka grabbed him from behind and pressed a knife against his neck.

"Come here like a thief, will you?" she hissed, her free hand sliding up until it touched his head.

"What have you done, witch?" he asked, but Jinka only laughed.

"Nothing yet," she said, then with a look at me, she had me fetch the chains she had prepared.

I did not speak as she closed them about his wrists and ankles. I was afraid now.

"You were Juniper's man, weren't you?" she said, standing over him. He looked at me and then away.

"What if I was?"

She smiled a cold, crafty smile.

"She brought you here, didn't she? To show you her sister?"

Will did not answer, just glanced at me again. But it was enough. Jinka looked at me.

"And you: you thought this would be your vengeance?"

I began to shake my head, but Jinka spat at me.

"Save me your lies. I'll deal with you later." Then, turning back to Will, she smiled again.

"So what shall I do with this thief?"

She drew something from her pocket, and I saw she held a black iron needle.

"Such a beautiful boy," she murmured, turning his face towards her. "So easy, so sure." Then with a sudden movement she pushed him from her, and, pulling his head up, pressed the tip of the needle against his eye. Will fell still.

"But a thief all the same. This will teach you," she said. "Let the poison enter you," and as she spoke she took the needle and pressed it deep into his eye.

Will screamed; behind me Rapunzel moaned and strained against the rope that held her. Jinka smiled, murmuring a spell as the needle did its work, then slowly drew it forth. Turning to me she ordered me to help her lift him, and together we dragged him to the window and with a push shoved him out, into the air.

I have heard many versions of what happened next. Some say Jinka slew Will, and cast his body down into the brambles. Others say he went mad from grief, and threw himself out to die. Still others say Jinka pushed him out into the thorns, and, blinded, he wandered off into the woods, to live as a beggar until Rapunzel found him, and her tears healed his sight.

There are other stories, too. About how the woodcutter's daughter fooled the witch, made her say her name, so she was dragged down to hell; about how the girl fooled the witch into drinking poison, or climbing into the oven. About how the dark-haired girl set her sister free, yet was cursed to stay behind.

Perhaps they are all true. This is what stories do, after all: go out into the world, become real. We think we tell them, but more often they tell us, make us theirs. So much so, I sometimes think, that the truth lies less in what actually happened than in the ways we tell ourselves about what happened, the things we need to hold on to.

They are gone now, both of them, passed away with the wind and years, so I could tell you anything, make any story that I wanted to. Yet I will tell you the story as I remember it.

The first thing I remember is the silence, the quiet in the space before he struck the ground below. Then the sound itself, so small, so ordinary. Beside me Rapunzel tensed for a moment, then turned her face away.

Turning back to Jinka, I found her looking at me, her face full of the knowledge of her victory. There was no invitation there to share, just the pleasure of what she had done. And all at once I understood. Not just that she did not love me or care about me but that she had no love in her at all, that all she cared about was power. That all her magic, all her powers were simply ways of bending others to her will. That I had never been anything more than a convenience, a thing for her to play with. And that I hated her.

"Wait here," she said, and, swinging out over the sill, went down towards her hut.

I understood what it was she meant to do, that the herbs she had gone to fetch were ones that would kill the baby in my sister's womb. And so I crossed to where Rapunzel lay, and, moving quickly, unbound the ropes that held her.

At first she sprang away from me and would not look at me. She was weeping, I saw now, silently and furiously.

"Come on," I said. "I need your help."

When Jinka returned we grabbed her. She was fast and strong, but there were two of us, and we had the element of surprise. I held her fast as she kicked and spat and swore, and we wrestled her to the floor.

"What are you doing?" she demanded, fighting and straining.

"Why did you do that? He never hurt you," Rapunzel said, and Jinka shook her head.

"I did it because I love you. Can't you see that?"

Something knotted inside me at her words, but before I could act Rapunzel had lunged forward, and pressed a knife to Jinka's throat.

"I should kill you," she said.

"No," Jinka said, "my child, please, you know I love you. If I erred this time I'm sorry."

"You are not my mother," she said then, "and you never were," and as she spoke she pressed the knife closer, Jinka whimpering at the feel of it, her eyes rolling back in her head.

For a long moment they sat like that, the knife pressed close, Jinka's breath coming sharp and ragged. I think there was a moment when Rapunzel meant to do it, too, but instead all at once she let the knife go.

"Tie her up," she said. "And gag her."

"We should kill her," I said when I was done, "or cut out her tongue and break her fingers."

"Would you do that?" Rapunzel asked, and I looked at Jinka. Part of me wanted to, but instead I took the knife and began to cut Jinka's clothes from her, piece by piece, and with them the charms and talismans she wore against her body. As each one came loose, I placed it on the ground and broke it with my foot, some cold part in me exulting in the way Jinka hissed and bit at the gag.

Rapunzel watched until I had finished. Then she addressed Jinka.

"You will leave this place," she said, "and never return. For if you do, I shall kill you myself."

Turning to her, I said her name, but she lifted a hand to silence me.

I knew then that I had lost her, that whatever came after this was the end for us.

I climbed out, lowering Jinka ahead of me, then, picking her up, marched her out the gate into the trees.

When I removed her gag, she spat and swore, but I lifted the knife and she retreated.

"Where will I go?" she wheedled. "Who will care for me? Please, June, don't.'

But I just threw a blanket after her and turned away.

When I returned, I found Rapunzel kneeling by the bushes at the base of the tower, Will's body cradled in her arms. As I approached I saw him move, and realised he was not dead, and began to run towards them, but as I reached them she shook her head and told me to stay away.

They left that day, Rapunzel helping him back towards the town. Although I did not follow them, I knew they would find their way, and that when they reached the village's outskirts his father's men would find them, bear them back to his father's house, that she would tell them her story, and they would listen in wonder. They would not return for me.

For my part, I busied myself. I made a poultice for his eye before they left, and heard later that, in time, his sight returned, and that they had taken up residence in his father's house as man and wife.

And as the weeks passed and Jinka did not return, I made this place my home, tended the garden. And in time when the village people came to ask for my help I gave it to them, without bullying or fear. And the children began to come as well, and I found stories to tell them, and fruit for them to eat. Sometimes my neighbours came and asked me for the bounty of my garden, and if I could I gave it to them. Yet I was alone, apart; all understood that.

And then a day came when he came through the forest to my house, and with him he had a child, as blonde and beautiful as the sun. She was afraid of me at first, and hung close to her father. About us the day was warm, the trees full of light and air. We did not speak, the two of us, just sat and watched the child. And she turned to me, and smiled, and I held out my hand to her.

NOTHING VISIBLE

Siddhartha Deb

Siddhartha Deb (b.1970) is the author of two novels, *The Point of Return* and *Surface*, and an acclaimed work of non-fiction, *The Beautiful and the Damned*. Born in north-east India, educated in India and Columbia University, he now lives in Manhattan, where he teaches creative writing at The New School.

From the days of the British the collieries in Bihar had pitted cheap human labour and expensive heavy machinery against the earth, so that there was no reason to think the Gajalitand colliery would be unusual or different. I was told that it was much like the twenty other mines operated in the region by the Bharat Coking Coal Limited and that my assignment was routine and uncomplicated; when I arrived there I found that both men and machines had been run dry against that harsh, unforgiving soil.

I took the Coalfield Express from Calcutta to Dhanbad and found a jeep that would let me off at the colliery. The swarms of people at the railway station gave it the air of a refugee camp, and that impression was only confirmed as the jeep entered the countryside. The paddy fields we passed were barren and forsaken, interrupted by dry, rocky stretches of land and deserted slag heaps. Black, unmanned trolleys appeared above us occasionally, jerking along on their wires like old, run-down toys. Gajalitand seemed no better at first sight, with a dog stretching itself under the awning of a little stall near the entrance to the colliery. Across the road, where the land sloped down to a bare stretch of ground littered with fragments of coal before it rose steeply again, there was a small figure bending down, its right hand moving mechanically from the ground to a cloth bag it held in the other hand. From the distance, warped and bent by the heat, it looked like a child, but I couldn't be certain.

The colliery office stood on the hill across from the road, its verandas and the loading station next to it covered with a fine black dust. From there, one could see across the dips and rises to the main pit that fell under the Gajalitand colliery division. Large, strange-looking machines were scattered through the landscape, some of them sinking into the ground under their own weight, the red rust on the machines gradually giving way to the blackened soil that was everywhere. A row of *kamins*, women workers, were silhouetted against the skyline, the baskets on their heads like inverted hats as they carried coal to the platform of the weighing station. A green BCCL truck was backed up under the chute leading down from the weighing station, the rocks and dust unloaded by the *kamins* pouring down in a steady stream, in the background the same stunted figure ceaselessly bending and straightening to the dictates of the bag in its hand. Over all this lay a haze created by smoke from the main pit, billowing out in a thick cloud as it emerged from a rusty funnel, spreading slowly over the *kamins*, the truck and the figure filling the bag, finally effacing the entire scene as if I had imagined everything, including my journey.

I worked in a small room in a corner of the office bungalow, starting early so as to stay ahead of the heat. Pandey and Mukherjee, the manager and assistant manager, came in from Dhanbad around eleven. The engineer, an Anglo-Indian called Coelho, stayed nearby in the company quarters. By the time I made my way to the office, he had already completed one of his numerous descents into the pit and was drinking tea on the veranda, looking sleepless but vibrating with a kind of nervous energy as he sat there with his dusty boots placed upside down against the railing.

The three officials had reacted strangely to my presence among them. Pandey was reserved, even cold; when I introduced myself as the new accountant, he merely nodded and had me shown to my room in the office. A tiny, dark woman, her wrinkled face like a crumpled paper bag, brought me the books in pairs, touching her forehead each time she put them on my desk. Someone had painted a large "Om" with sandalwood paste on the first register, but when I opened it I found that the initial thirty pages had been torn out. It was not an auspicious beginning.

The deputy manager, on the other hand, was an outgoing man. He had arranged for my flat in the colliery quarters to be opened and cleaned, and he came into my office every day to slap me on the back. On a couple of occasions, he even invited me to join him on birdshoots at a lake in Dhanbad, but he was astonishingly vague about his responsibilities or mine. The only man who acknowledged that I had come to the colliery to work was the engineer, and his recognition was a double-edged sword.

Through the open door of my room, I would see Coelho surveying my desk with an intense, piercing gaze. Sometimes he came right in, usually during the long afternoons when I was struggling with the heavy ledgers, their pages mysteriously blank or torn out. He would sit across from my desk watching me as I went through old, bloated folders and tried to figure out from the vague purchase vouchers and invoices what goods or services had been procured and from whom. He wasn't that much older than me, perhaps in his late twenties, and he would have been a welcome presence in Gajalitand if it had not been for his questions.

"Not called the head office yet?" he asked me on an afternoon when Mukherjee and Pandey were absent.

"They told me not to call with complaints," I replied a little tersely. "Perhaps they knew I would achieve nothing."

"What is the grand design?" he asked.

"The only design I see is a big "Om" on one of the registers. Here, take a look."

"But you are in the know surely?" he said. "Certainly, you are quite aware of the plans they have."

"Look, Coelho, I'm here because I applied for forty-two jobs and got one. I would have preferred a bank posting, but in this market you take whatever you get."

"Beggars cannot be choosers, certainly," he said, nodding his head vigorously as if I had offered him some fundamental insight into life. "Yet you are clearly too qualified for this job. We have not seen an accountant here for years. But only now, when there is talk of assessing all the mines, you come down from Calcutta with your coloured pencils."

"Coelho, I don't even have an accounting degree. I'm just a commerce graduate. That's why I'm here, sweating through the evenings by myself, miles from a town where one might find a restaurant or a film show. If I was a proper accountant, I would be with PricewaterhouseCoopers, flying first class to Delhi from Calcutta right now, with Gajalitand a speck on the ground below."

Coelho wasn't satisfied. He sat quietly for a while, pushing his long hair back across his scalp, leaving black streaky trails on his forehead. The office was quiet in the absence of Mukherjee and Pandey, who had left earlier in the afternoon with a fat, mean-looking man they had referred to by the mysterious title of "colliery agent".

"Look Coelho, do you think it's such a bad thing for these mines to be assessed? They can't run on like this, you know." He seemed taken aback, as if I held him responsible for the state of the books I was looking at. "But it's a very good thing," he said. "It should have been done so long ago." Then he looked around him, to the room where Pandey and Mukherjee usually took their naps, lowered his voice, and said, "You would be surprised how profitable the mines are, even if the profits don't show up there." He pointed at my table. "Those books can tell you nothing of how things really are, just as sitting in the office won't help you understand how the colliery operates. The truth hides underground here, invisible unless you look for it. I have seen the truth, and I am uncomfortable with it." He fell silent as one of the women in the office came in with two cups of tea.

I didn't understand the exact nature of Coelho's worries, but there was enough in his disjointed comments to feed my own anxieties. I should have been grateful that I had been left alone by the managers, but Coelho's edginess about the colliery brought to the surface everything I had noticed and then pushed aside. The head office had sent me to create order, to work out a system for the business carried on here, but every attempt I made so far had ended in failure. Numbers and figures tell you a story, even if in a specialised, symbolic language, but in Gajalitand they only revealed a blankness, as if every transaction carried out had resulted in a void. It was not so different from the way things were at the colliery as a whole. As I went about my work, I could hear the whistles marking fresh shifts, the coughing and shuffling of the miners, the clanking of the lift, Coelho's voice ringing out confidently, but at the heart of this apparently ceaseless activity there was only a strange, impassive indolence.

The days were shaped by the rhythm of the heavy blades of a DC fan whipping the air, interrupted repeatedly by power cuts. The air would grow thicker as the fan stumbled to a stop and I would hear Mukherjee cursing and Pandey's voice asking for a wet towel. Cups of sweet, milky tea were brought in at frequent intervals by the women who worked at the office, their bodies so frail and small that it seemed like an eternity by the time they covered the distance from the door to my desk. The women in the office were even smaller than the *kamins* carrying coal; they circulated around the figures of Mukherjee and Pandey like slow, silent dwarfs, serving tea, cleaning the rooms, waiting with mugs of water and towels as the officials finished leisurely lunches brought from their houses in towering tiffin carriers, each carrier consisting of four stainless-steel bowls piled on top of one another.

Coelho and I drank our tea in silence. Then he stood up to leave, wiped his hands on his trousers, and spoke very emphatically. "You will please come down with me one of these days." It sounded almost like an order.

"Go down? What for? It's not my job."

"To see the pits, to get an idea of how things are so you can report to the head office."

"Is it safe?" I asked.

"You are not afraid, surely? Your head office status will protect you from everything."

I ignored the comment.

"How often do you go down, Coelho?"

"You accountants," he said with an uncharacteristic smile. "All you want is a number."

"Don't engineers?"

"An engineer knows that there is a gap between numbers and reality. Between theory and practice. A gap in which the unexpected can occur."

"The unexpected? Like what?"

"You'll see when we go down," he said, not very comfortingly.

2

Another week passed before Coelho reappeared, looking even more manic than usual, though it was difficult to tell if he was nervous or merely overjoyed at the prospect of showing me the truth. "So we will go down now," he said. I had been anxious about going underground when Coelho first mentioned it, but now it seemed like a release, a way of escaping the futility of my work and the absurdity of Mukherjee and Pandey in the next room.

The two men looked up questioningly as I followed Coelho into their office. I was nervous and said I thought it would be useful for me to know a little about the work in the pits. The manager hastily put down his phone and narrowed his eyes, while Mukherjee genially addressed Coelho.

"The accountant down in the pits? Why's that? What are you up to Coelho?"

"A little tour, sir, I thought," Coelho replied.

"Oh yes, I see," Mukherjee said, looking thoughtful. Then he rose from the chair and slapped his forehead in mock admonition. "I should have thought of it. We used to do this before, you know. Whenever we had a new officer joining the colliery. Drinks afterwards, a big dinner, a film show in the open for the miners." He reached for his helmet and stepped out of the office.

A change of shift was going on and the returning workers had spread all over the site around the main pit. Some of them were depositing their equipment to a man who had set up a table in the shade, while others gathered near the water pump, their thin, calloused hands saluting us as we passed. Mukherjee stopped to watch the workers of the new shift. The miners were muscular but small, and Mukherjee towered over them like a benevolent giant, long hair reaching down to his collar, his short-sleeved shirt drawn taut over the expanse of his back.

The men on the new shift began getting into the lift – what Mukherjee and Coelho called the cage – and they seemed more purposeful now, adjusting their helmets and batteries and ropes, torsos bare, legs knotted and wiry below their shorts. A bell rang somewhere as I stepped forward for a closer look, and I noticed a grey sheen on the hands, knees and ankles of the miners. It was the shade of the naked clay one sees on idols or dolls when the paint has worn off, giving the workers an air of unreality and impermanence even as the cage door shut and they began their descent. Mukherjee began walking away from the site, gesturing at us to follow.

"Planned on showing him the main pit, Coelho?"

"Yes, sir."

Behind us the cage dropped into the shaft like a stone down a well.

"Another time, maybe. Today we'll just do Number Two." Mukherjee turned to me. "There'll be less disruption, you see. Number Two's an old pit, nearly worked through."

"I wouldn't know the difference, sir."

"I'm not worried about you. But the workers jump at every chance they get to slack off and I can't hold up production, especially with you around. Number Two's an incline so we can walk down to the seam without interfering with work."

"Why operate it if it's so old and unprofitable, sir?"

"Why?" Mukherjee stopped to look around. "You see all this?" he asked, his tone aggressive. He pointed at the long line of women workers strung out between the main pit and the weighing station, then at a row of Soviet loaders rusting without spare parts, and finally at Number Two, visible in the distance as a black gash in the green scrub. "Dead weight," he said, almost spitting out the words. We approached a shallow canal and prepared to wade through it to Number Two. "In certain societies," Mukherjee said, hitching up his pants, "the weak and the inefficient slow down those who are more capable. They hold you back. Right, Coelho?" Coelho nodded and pointed to the canal. "This is the Katri River," he said in what I had begun thinking of as his confident, engineer voice. "More dangerous than it looks right now. It will become a proper river during the monsoons. Mr Mukherjee remembers when it flooded the pits in '85."

"Ancient history," Mukherjee replied, "like Number Two. Our modern accountant won't be interested in such things."

Two men were waiting at the entrance to the tunnel with helmets, lamps and heavy batteries with shoulder straps. There was a pair of tracks running down the centre of the tunnel, lit by small bulbs along the overhead arch with two rows of posts supporting the roof. It took no more than fifteen minutes to walk down to the seam, although the ground was slippery and wet. The bare-bodied workers at the seam spoke in brief, terse whispers, so that the silence seemed part of the darkness, like a surface of utter absence through which the lights and the sound of the picks and the drills appeared as mere pin-pricks of consciousness. Mukherjee and Coelho offered me many engineering details that I found uninteresting and dull; what I retained was the impression of heavy walls and the curve of the roof, their colour indistinguishable from the darkness that filled all available space, and at some point the sound of my own heart and the clump clump of our feet as we made our way back up the incline.

Two men were working on the tracks, clearing away dirt from the rails. They paused as we came towards them, raising their hands to their helmets, and I felt a little jolt as I looked at the older man. The younger worker had said "Salaam, saab" as we stopped, but the old man stood silently in the half-light, eyes fixed elsewhere. He was shorter than any of the miners I had seen, almost a dwarf, but the broad squat nose, the lines around his eyes like fissures in a rock, and the grey beard that reached to his knees gave him the air of an Old Testament prophet.

"Who's that?" I asked Coelho. "What's his name?"

"Looks like Father Time, doesn't he?" Mukherjee said, chuckling. "Wait, we'll have some fun. What's your age?" he asked the old man, leaning down towards him. The old man's eyes grew wide and he looked away. The younger worker hesitated, as if debating whether to speak out of turn, and then said, "He doesn't know his age, sir. They usually don't." Mukherjee laughed uproariously, the sound of his mirth echoing down the tunnel. "You bet he doesn't know. Draws full pay, doesn't he, for standing around in the tunnel. His name's Ammonia."

"Ammonia?" I asked.

"That's what Mr Pandey calls him. The workers call him Mauniya because he doesn't speak, so Mr Pandey turned that into Ammonia." He leaned towards me and whispered into my ear, "He also changed Coelho into Koila, for coal." Then he slapped me on the back. "Let's not waste time on curiosities like this. Doesn't know his age, probably doesn't know if he's alive. What did I tell you about dead weight a little while ago?" The younger worker shifted uneasily at this exchange but there wasn't the slightest flicker of expression in the old man's face. He stood there rigid, eyes unblinking, pick balanced on his shoulder, and only when we walked on did he move again, bringing his tool down to the rail. Silhouetted in the faint light of the tunnel, he looked not so much like a worker as one of the wooden posts planted along the tunnel, as if he would stand there holding up the roof even when the mining had stopped for good.

3

Certain things changed after my visit to the pit, as if the arrangement of forces around the colliery was shifting gradually in a prelude to some major transformation. The beginning of the rainy season took the edge off the heat, and in the cool fresh gusts of wind that came into the office bungalow, the two managers seemed a little more human. They were friendly, even solicitous, and Mukherjee suggested that all of us should go to his house for dinner at some point.

Perhaps I had crossed a line that made me part of the colliery, although I did not feel that way at all. Nor did Coelho, I think, for his afternoon visits stopped altogether and I took to wandering around on my own. One day I saw him at the tea stall outside the colliery, talking to two men I had not met before. With their wiry build and grey hair they looked like workers, and their manner was deferential as I approached them. "Abdul, Jagdish, this is our new accountant," Coelho said in a slightly preoccupied manner, calling for a cup of tea for me. The men stood up and brushed their pants awkwardly and I was surprised when Coelho said they were union leaders.

"I come here to talk," Coelho said, as if he knew I was surprised by his association with union leaders. "You have definitely noticed there's no social life here. One learns interesting things from them." After a while Abdul began talking, about how long he and Jagdish had worked at the colliery, about the migration of their fore-fathers to the colliery, and of the disputes between the regular workers and the labourers provided by private contractors. "The government's never been very good to us, but now it looks like they mean to make orphans of us." He looked a little embarrassed after he said this, but Coelho encouraged him. "Go on, he will understand. He's not with them."

"The contractors and officers take cuts out of the wages," Abdul continued. "They say sixty workers but hire forty. Then they write down the government wage in the books, but they pay outside workers much less. The difference goes to the contractor and to the officers." Some of the numbers and figures in the ledgers appeared in front of my eyes as he spoke, certain discrepancies I had noticed between the equipment issued to miners and their wages, but their relation to what Abdul was describing was not entirely clear.

"Where do the private contractors get their workers from?" I asked.

"Oh, from everywhere, sir, they round them up in the morning from marketplaces and bus stops, where people wait for the contractors. The ones who get picked consider themselves lucky," Jagdish replied.

"Much migration from other parts of Bihar, especially from the north," Coelho said. "Only seasonal agricultural work, with constant wage disputes, even bonded labour in some cases. The armies of the landlords burn down their huts so they come here to find a better life."

"This is better than the oppression of the landlords?"

Jagdish and Abdul laughed.

"What about the local people?" I asked. "Everybody seems to be from somewhere else." Coelho tugged at my arm, pointing at the figure I always saw on the loading dock.

"You see him gathering coal down there?"

"Yes."

"If you walk around the outskirts of Dhanbad, you will see others like him, both adults and children, selling small bags of coal to people."

"That's how they get it sir, from scavenging around the trucks and the loading stations. The children run behind the trucks, picking up pieces that fall out," Abdul said.

"But what about them?"

"If you look closely, you'll see that they appear different. Very small and dark, and their faces are different, with flat noses. Aboriginal probably," Coelho said.

"Manbhuyias," Jagdish said.

"They are the local people," Coelho said. "They gather small pieces of coal and they sift through the slag heaps for partially burned coal."

"They are the local people and they have to do this? No one gives them jobs?"

"That's the curious thing about our world," Abdul said. "You look down, there's still another man below you no matter how far down you think you are. You'd think the coal belongs to them if they have been here from the beginning but no, it somehow turns out to be the paternal property of Pandey and Mukherjee."

Jagdish, who had been waiting to say something, interrupted. "But they're not like us."

"In what way?"

"We're just workers. But they can talk to the apdevtas," Jagdish said.

"Apdevtas?"

"You have not heard of spirits? The malicious, powerful ones?" Coelho asked.

"The Manbhuyias did work in the mines long ago," Abdul said. "They can communicate with things down there. There would be accidents sometimes, so the coal companies stopped hiring them. They're easy to pick out."

"Some of the very old workers may be Manbhuyias," Jagdish said. "It is said they live longer and that you can't always tell their age. They're not like us."

"Well," Abdul said with a philosophical shrug. "Some say that anyone can see or talk to the spirits if you stay down long enough. That's why miners never really like it in the pits. You don't get used to it. It's not like being a fisherman."

"Perhaps you sensed something, sir?" Jagdish said.

"From my first and only visit?"

"It's well known that the old pit is more full of spirits than the main one. Many of the Manbhuyias worked in the old pit, which became unproductive only when the spirits grew angry with the company. Perhaps the Manbhuyias were unhappy and called on the spirits. Rocks would be thrown around, sometimes even roof collapses. Regular miners and officers would be led astray along tunnels that turned out to be dead ends."

"Stop it," Coelho said. "If there were spirits now, don't you think they would do something?"

The two men fell silent. Coelho began speaking in his usual nervous manner. "Well, the telephone line in the main pit is down and nothing can be done. That's why we are meeting here."

"The monsoons are a bad time to be without the telephone," Jagdish said.

"There is an alarm bell also," Abdul said, "but sometimes it doesn't work."

I thought of telling the head office about the telephone, about the siphoning off of wages, about the account books I had been given. But they knew, just as they had known that there was no point in sending someone as inexperienced as me to Gajalitand.

I left Coelho and his companions with an odd mix of feelings. Coelho called out, "Remember what we said. It may be useful some day." The land stretched all around me, with hardly a human figure in sight save for the boy gathering coal and the three men behind me. The ground below my feet was hard and unforgiving and yet it was better than what lay further beyond, beyond what I could see, where all that existed was the armies of the landlords riding through the night. I looked behind and saw that the three men had gone. The bench was empty, like a little stage prop waiting for the play to begin, while ahead of me, the boy went on, not stopping to look at me, still bending, still picking, filling the bag with all that his world had to offer.

The accident happened on the night we were at Mukherjee's house for dinner, at the end of a wet, chilly day that changed the craters in the colliery grounds into pools of black ink. Coelho had meant to join us later, but no one was surprised when he didn't turn up in what had become a thunderstorm. Mukherjee had been generous with the food and whisky, so that even Pandey finally abandoned his reticence in a flow of religious fervour. He was urging me to read the *Ramayana* when Mukherjee went inside to answer a phone call.

When he returned, he did not address us immediately. It was pouring outside, and the chandelier above us swayed in the gusts of wind, creating shifting patterns of light and shadow in the centre of the room. Mukherjee was a big man, but he looked weak as he clutched at the door-frame for support, his whisky-flushed face slowly waking up to whatever reality had presented itself. He stood there for a while and then walked over towards Pandey. A jeep had drawn up outside the house, its engine running, and they went out to the porch to talk in low voices.

"I am going home, you take care of it," I heard Pandey shout. Mukherjee came in quietly and gestured at me to follow. "Come, come quickly. Something like an accident in the colliery." Pandey squinted at me as I stepped out. "You go straight to your quarters and lock your doors."

"What's happening, sir?"

"There's been an accident in the main pit. This rain, that river." He turned to Mukherjee. "When the police come, send a couple of men to the accountant's quarters."

"Why?" I was beginning to lose my temper. "Why do I need policemen?"

"To protect you, son," he replied.

Mukherjee dropped me off near the office and one of the workers broke away from the group huddled on the veranda, carrying a big black umbrella which he held over my head as we made our way to the officers' quarters. Mukherjee had driven the jeep straight towards the main pit and I kept looking back at him, the man with the umbrella bumping at my heels each time I turned to look. I had imagined smoke and fire, the talk of an accident somehow giving rise to images of a horrific underground explosion, but there wasn't the slightest wisp of steam from the boiler that usually chugged away furiously. All I could see was the rain pouring over the chimneys and pipes of the main pit and changing colour as it hit the ground, as if the rain too was being processed by the Gajalitand machinery into some kind of viscous, potent fuel.

4

I lived by myself in an empty building, with Coelho the only other resident in that drab concrete complex. The building had clearly been constructed to make some people richer rather than because there was a pressing need for officers' housing at Gajalitand, but the management had at last found a use for it. I saw the first column of miners and their families approaching the building around seven, almost noiseless in spite of the children and women stumbling along with their belongings. Soon a man arrived to tell me that the workers were being moved here because there was some chance of their tenements being flooded. Katri River had risen by a couple of feet last night, he said; it was still rising.

As I made my way to the office, the miners' tenements looming to my left, I saw that their shacks were on much higher ground than the quarters they were being shifted to. There were policemen moving things into the shacks, setting up a temporary barracks, even as the miners poured out of them. Behind me, at the gates of the officers' quarters, a smaller group of policemen strung up blue plastic sheets to shelter from the rain.

It was the end of life at the colliery as I had known it, without any further pretence of work on my part. There had never been an active role for me at Gajalitand, but Coelho's death reduced me to a silent observer. Pandey and Mukherjee asked me to sit in on meetings, but information about the accident came largely from other sources. I read the newspapers, watched reporters arguing with the policemen, saw the miners massed near the main pit as six industrial pumps churned out streams of water. I found out that the river had flooded its way into the tunnels on Friday night while the third shift was on and that the men on top had been unable to send the cage down to their trapped colleagues because of a power cut. There was a backup system of operating the cage with steam, but the boiler had failed to produce steam that night. The heavy rain brought the temperature down and the steam condensed, unable to build up enough strength to work the cage even as the alarm rang with the news of Coelho and the sixty four miners trapped below.

These were the facts, cold and irrefutable, but the truth that Coelho had spoken of, where was that? There is much that I don't remember about the weeks after the accident; the different scenes, incidents, little pieces of information are stuck together the way pages in a book sometimes get, so that when you try to pry them apart you often find that the type from one page has become super-imposed upon another.

There was nothing I could do, so I watched. I saw the building come alive as the raggedy children of the miners played on the stair-cases, hiding when they saw me. The pumps continued their Herculean task of flushing out the bowels of the main pit, while the cage went down with unfailing regularity, as if ashamed and conscience-stricken at its inability to deliver at the moment of need. I got used to the thin, shabby reporters from the local Hindi newspapers who parked their two-wheelers near the veranda and said, "Sir, one minute?" before a policeman escorted them to Pandey.

One afternoon a former Bihar chief minister chose to visit Gajalitand with a large retinue of followers. The former chief minister stayed for half an hour, drinking tea with Pandey and Mukherjee and pontificating, while his body-guards stood around on the veranda, also drinking tea and stroking their big moustaches. Of course, when he addressed the miners near the main pit, he gave a fiery speech about the need for justice, punishment and due compensation. The miners clapped half-heartedly and began walking away before he had finished, even though the bodyguards tried to bully them into staying. He had been out of power for a long time.

Pandey and Mukherjee responded to everything with a great measure of calm, simply waiting, knowing that time was their great ally. After the first couple of weeks had passed and not a single body was found, things quietened down. The politicians and the press lost their interest, and only a couple of reporters still hung around the colliery, hoping to discover some new fact that would propel the worn story of the accident to the front page again.

The rain began to let off and the pumps chugged away with greater effect than before, about a dozen of them spread out in the slushy ground. Mining work resumed in Number Two and in some of the tunnels of the main pit. Although the waters of the Katri had subsided, the miners remained in their new quarters, while in their old shacks the policemen set up lines of washing swaying with white vests, khaki shorts and striped underwear.

It was in this state of calm that things began to happen again, a second string of events that started with posters around the tea stall. The police were the first ones to get wind of it and a small group of them rushed to the office to talk to Pandey, rifles clattering behind them. I later went to sneak a look at the posters, even though I was not supposed to go anywhere on my own. Thin sheets of paper with big red slogans on them, the posters had been put up in even groups on the patchwork shutters of the tea stall and on the BCCL signboard at the colliery entrance. "We will act against the exploiters," the Maoist Communist Centre had declared, and with a fine sense of the BCCL hierarchy, they had named their targets in descending order: the absconding colliery agent, Pandey, Mukherjee and me.

The Maoists didn't have much of a presence in the area, but the reaction in the office was immediate. Pandey got on the phone and within hours the union representing BCCL officers had issued statements condemning the cowardly threats. The armed contingent at the gate was doubled, and when Mukherjee and Pandey travelled to and from the office, they were followed by a truckload of policemen.

Then the men operating the pumps, brought from outside the state, refused to work at night. They had been doing round-the-clock shifts so far, continuing under the glare of great big lights as darkness fell. They gave no reasons for their sudden decision and, being outsiders, they couldn't be bullied into submission. The miners had been working in reduced shifts anyway, so the colliery became lifeless after dark. I began to hear stories, of the Maoists preparing an ambush, of the cage operating by itself at night and of the emergency telephone, now functioning again, ringing at the time the ill-fated shift had supposedly been trapped underground. Even the policemen lost their earlier boisterousness and rarely walked around alone, often leaving their post at the gate unmanned.

Finally, one of the reporters who had continued to follow the Gajalitand story got his scoop. It came out on the front page of a Dhanbad newspaper. By the evening, even the television channels in Delhi had picked up the story. The reporter had acquired a letter written by Coelho to the Managing Director of the BCCL. For reasons not entirely clear, Coelho had not sent the letter; the newspaper said he had been waiting for leave to take it personally. There was a photograph of the letter, but because it was in English and had been reproduced badly, the paper had extracted the major points and spelt them out for its readers.

The letter listed everything Coelho had observed in his seven years at the colliery, beginning with the practice of stopping the trucks between Gajalitand and Dhanbad to substitute part of the coal with rocks. It spoke of the lack of safety inspections, of the fact that Pandey and Mukherjee never went down to the pits, and of a steady attrition in the number of regular workers even as the production quota was steadily increased. Coelho also said that his seniors had removed workers from key posts, including the observation post near Katri River which had been set up in 1986.

It was a long letter with many details, and it seemed to seal the fate of the two officers running the colliery. Pandey and Mukherjee, however, were at their most resourceful when under pressure. They showed what they were made of over the next few days, as the reporters came back again, this time having tasted blood. In front of the television cameras and tape recorders, they appeared as hard-working, middle-aged men being persecuted by the press. After dark, they brought in the gunmen to find out how the letter had been leaked to the press. There were four of them, big fellows dressed in loose kurta-pajamas, sophisticated-looking automatic rifles slung casually over their shoulders. As they went about their business in the colliery, interrogating the miners, they brought a further chill to the place.

They were good at their work, so good that they didn't stop to think for a minute that I was present when they stomped up to Mukherjee and Pandey one evening to ask what was going on. Mukherjee had been slightly moody all day and snapped at them. "What d'you mean what's going on? You know why you are here."

"To catch the fellow who passed the letter to the reporter. Not to wrestle with whatever's down in your mines."

"Explain," Pandey said calmly. "Try not to get too excited. It's bad for your blood pressure."

The chief gunman, a thick-necked swarthy man shorter than his companions, wiped his forehead and neck with a handkerchief and sat down facing the two officers. "So we found the reporter yesterday when he was going home, near the mining school. We beat it out of him, who he got the letter from."

"So where's the problem?" Mukherjee said. "You know what to do next."

"No, we don't. The reporter didn't have a name for the person. And I don't think he was lying by the time we finished working on him."

"Of course he wasn't lying," the other men said in a chorus, as if their professional competence had been challenged. The chief held up his left hand and they subsided.

"No, he wasn't lying. He would have told us how he likes to do his wife if we had asked him."

"You know I don't like those kind of references. I am a religious man," Pandey said.

"Beg your pardon, Pandeyji, just habit from hanging around with the low life." The chief gestured at his partners.

"Can you continue?" Mukherjee asked loudly. "If he didn't have a name, you have nothing. Nothing of use at all."

"He gave us a description. And it was as detailed a description as he could make, since we helped him describe."

One of the men in the back cracked his fingers and the others laughed.

"He said he was given the letter by a miner, somewhere near the tea stall. He had never seen the miner before and nothing was said, no money exchanged. It was dusk, and the man appeared out of nowhere and handed him the letter and left. Everything happened very quickly, and he didn't get a good look at the miner except that he was small and had a big beard and that there was something about the way he walked, not like an old man at all."

"Mauniya," Mukherjee mumbled. Then he got up from the chair and began to pace through the room, reminding me of Coelho. The chief gunman watched him keenly, wiping his forehead again.

"Get that attendance clerk here," Pandey said on the phone. "So find Mauniya. What is the problem?"

"We tried," the chief gunman said. "We went to the miners' quarters last night. Turned it inside out. Questioned the miners. The police quarters, we didn't go into. But we told them to look, and they searched. It's their territory. Why should they hide him?"

"They're not hiding him," Mukherjee said. "You won't find him."

"What are you talking about, Mukherjee?" Pandey said sharply. "He's old, ancient, half-dead. Where would he go? They'll find him."

Mukherjee drew his breath. "They won't find him because he's not a miner."

There was a puzzled silence following this remark.

Mukherjee went on, looking at Pandey, speaking in a low voice. "You and I have known for a long time that there was something different happening here, and we didn't care because we were making money. So neither of us asked how Coelho kept things going down there, how he kept the normal rate of extraction with shifts less than full strength."

"Full strength only on paper," Pandey said, but Mukherjee cut him off.

"We have sixty four going below on the night of the accident, sixty four missing on the roster. But did you check with the miners and their families how many of them are actually missing? I did. Forty of them. So where did the others come from?"

"Mukherjee, you know the numbers are only on paper," Pandey said placatingly. "Since when has that been a problem?"

"So if it's only on paper, why do we have sixty four pieces of equipment checked out? Why does the attendance clerk remember Mauniya going down on that shift? Why do we have Mauniya's name on the roster of that shift, along with nearly twenty other strange names that I don't recognise? And why don't those same names not appear on the wage books we have?"

"Mukherjee, you're losing control. We were the ones who arranged for fake names."

"We did, didn't we? But if we arranged for fake workers, we also arranged for them to be paid their wages. That was the point of it. So why would we have fake workers going down and being issued equipment but not given wages? And how do you explain Mauniya? He wasn't a fiction created by us. How is it that we have records of the work he has done, of the shifts he was part of, even an order from Coelho transferring him from the incline to the main pit, but nothing to indicate his wages? What man, fake or real, would work every day in the mines and not get paid?"

There were mutters of "Ram, Ram," from the three gunmen. They were visibly uneasy now and their chief waved at them in a gesture of dismissal. They left the room and waited outside, lighting bidis, and in the inky darkness of the evening the glow of their bidis looked like fireflies inscribing slow, small circles in the air.

The clerk Pandey had sent for was standing near the wall. He had been listening carefully to what Mukherjee was saying and spoke up in a toneless voice. "I remember the bearded one going down before the accident. None of them made it out alive. But now the cage goes up and down by itself at night. Empty. With no one in it. The alarm bell goes off, the telephone rings." He was going to continue but Pandey got up from his seat, walked up to him, and slapped him hard on the face. "You can go now," he said in a quiet voice, and the clerk left, head bowed.

Mukherjee was in some kind of trance. "Who is Mauniya? Who are the others? What have we been playing with out here? I looked at the records we possess, not what was given to the accountant, and I can't find any explanation for Mauniya or those extra workers Coelho used."

There was silence in the room as everyone considered this last bit of information. The chief gunman was the first one to react. He stood up with dignity and addressed Pandey. "This is not what we were sent for," he said. "We're professionals, and we know our limitations. Chasing after shadows in the dark is not our job." With that, he left the room.

"I feel old, very old," Pandey said.

Mukherjee looked at him blankly and then cried out. "And Coelho? What about Coelho?"

Pandey got up and put a hand on Mukherjee's broad back. He leaned towards Mukherjee, but his words were drowned out by the sound of the gunmen's jeep pulling out of the colliery.

The police post at the gate was empty as I walked out of the colliery. The brown stray which slept near the shops began barking as my feet crunched on the gravel, but it calmed down once it saw me and began following me, sniffing at my ankles. Not a soul in that thin, translucent darkness, nothing visible except for the lumps of the colliery buildings and the figure down in the loading yard, already beginning its unforgiving work. Struck by a whim, I walked down the slope towards the boy. Behind me the stray stopped dead, whining. The boy turned when I came close to him but did not utter a single word in response to my meaningless query, meaningless in any time and place, but especially there and then, with the dawn emerging cautiously behind the main pit.

"What is your name? How old are you?"

He looked at me and waited, his right hand in the air. It was an old man's face, rendered expressionless by time, and only when I began to step back did his hand and body move, stooping to the earth once again. I climbed back to the road and began walking towards Dhanbad.

THE DEEP

Anthony Doerr

Anthony Doerr (b.1973) was raised in Novelty, Ohio, majored in history and was awarded an MFA from Bowling Green State University. He has lived and worked elsewhere, notably in Africa and New Zealand where many of his stories in *The Shell Collector* are set. He now lives in Boise, Idaho, with his family. His work has been awarded a Rome Prize, the Ohioana Book Award, a Guggenheim Fellowship and the 2011 Sunday Times EFG Private Bank Short Story Award for the story included here. "When you're falling into a good book," he told an in-flight magazine, "exactly as you might fall into a dream, a little conduit opens, a passageway between a reader's heart and a writer's, a connection that transcends the barriers of continents and generations and even death . . . and here's the magic. You're different. You can never go back to being exactly the same person you were before you disappeared into that book."

Tom is born in 1914 in Detroit, a quarter mile from International Salt. His father is offstage, unaccounted for. His mother operates a six-room, underinsulated boardinghouse populated with locked doors, behind which drowse the grim possessions of itinerant salt workers: coats the colors of mice, tattered mucking boots, aquatints of undressed women, their breasts faded orange. Every six months a miner is laid off, gets drafted, or dies, and is replaced by another, so that very early in his life Tom comes to see how the world continually drains itself of young men, leaving behind only objects – empty tobacco pouches, bladeless jackknives, salt-caked trousers – mute, incapable of memory.

Tom is four when he starts fainting. He'll be rounding a corner, breathing hard, and the lights will go out. Mother will carry him indoors, set him on the armchair, and send someone for the doctor.

Atrial septal defect. Hole in the heart. The doctor says blood sloshes from the left side to the right side. His heart will have to do three times the work. Lifespan of sixteen. Eighteen if he's lucky. Best if he doesn't get excited.

Mother trains her voice into a whisper. *Here you go, there you are, sweet little Tomcat.* She moves Tom's cot into an upstairs closet – no bright lights, no loud noises. Mornings she serves him a glass of buttermilk, then points him to the brooms or steel wool. *Go slow,* she'll murmur. He scrubs the coal stove, sweeps the marble stoop. Every so often he peers up from his work and watches the face of the oldest boarder, Mr. Weems, as he troops downstairs, a fifty-year-old man hooded against the cold, off to descend in an elevator a thousand feet underground. Tom imagines his descent, sporadic and dim lights passing and receding, cables rattling, a half dozen other miners squeezed into the cage beside him, each thinking his own thoughts, men's thoughts, sinking down into that city beneath the city where mules stand waiting and oil lamps burn in the walls and glittering rooms of salt recede into vast arcades beyond the farthest reaches of the light.

Sixteen, thinks Tom. *Eighteen if I'm lucky.*

School is a three-room shed aswarm with the offspring of salt workers, coal workers, ironworkers. Irish kids, Polish kids, Armenian kids. To Mother the school yard seems a thousand acres of sizzling pandemonium. *Don't run, don't fight*, she whispers. *No games.* His first day, she pulls him out of class after an hour. *Shhh*, she says, and wraps her arms around his like ropes.

Tom seesaws in and out of the early grades. Sometimes she keeps him out of school for whole weeks at a time. By the time he's ten, he's in remedial everything. *I'm trying*, he stammers, but letters spin off pages and dash against the windows like snow. *Dunce*, the other boys declare, and to Tom that seems about right.

Tom sweeps, scrubs, scours the stoop with pumice one square inch at a time. *Slow as molasses in January*, says Mr. Weems, but he winks at Tom when he says it.

Every day, all day, the salt finds its way in. It encrusts washbasins, settles on the rims of baseboards. It spills out of the boarders, too: from ears, boots, handkerchiefs. Furrows of glitter gather in the bedsheets: a daily lesson in insidiousness.

Start at the edges, then scrub out the center. Linens on Thursdays. Toilets on Fridays.

He's twelve when Ms. Fredericks asks the children to give reports. Ruby Hornaday goes sixth. Ruby has flames for hair, Christmas for a birthday, and a drunk for a daddy. She's one of two girls to make it to fourth grade.

She reads from notes in controlled terror. *If you think the lake is big you should see the sea. It's three-quarters of Earth. And that's just the surface.* Someone throws a pencil. The creases on Ruby's forehead sharpen. *Land animals live on ground or in trees rats and worms and gulls and such. But sea animals they live everywhere they live in the waves and they live in mid water and they live in canyons six and a half miles down.*

She passes around a red book. Inside are blocks of text and full-color photographic plates that make Tom's heart boom in his ears. A blizzard of toothy minnows. A kingdom of purple corals. Five orange starfish cemented to a rock.

Ruby says, *Detroit used to have palm trees and corals and seashells. Detroit used to be a sea three miles deep.*

Ms. Fredericks asks, *Ruby, where did you get that book?* but by then Tom is hardly breathing. See-through flowers with poison tentacles and fields of clams and pink spheres with a thousand needles on their backs. He tries to ask, *Are these real?* but quicksilver bubbles rise from his mouth and float up to the ceiling. When he goes over, the desk goes over with him.

The doctor says it's best if Tom stays out of school and Mother agrees. *Keep indoors*, the doctor says. *If you get excited, think of something blue.* Mother lets him come downstairs for meals and chores only. Otherwise he's to stay in his closet. *We have to be more careful, Tomcat*, she whispers, and sets her palm on his forehead.

Tom spends long hours on the floor beside his cot, assembling and re-assembling the same jigsaw puzzle: a Swiss village. Five hundred pieces, nine of them missing. Sometimes Mr. Weems reads to Tom from adventure novels. They're blasting a new vein down in the mines and in the lulls between Mr. Weems's words, Tom can feel explosions reverberate up through a thousand feet of rock and shake the fragile pump in his chest.

He misses school. He misses the sky. He misses everything. When Mr. Weems is in the mine and Mother is downstairs, Tom often slips to the end of the hall and lifts aside the curtains and presses his forehead to the glass. Children run the snowy lanes and lights glow in the foundry windows and train cars trundle beneath elevated conduits. First-shift miners emerge from the mouth of the hauling elevator in groups of six and bring out cigarette cases from their overalls and strike matches and spill like little salt-dusted insects out into the night, while the darker figures of the second-shift miners stamp their feet in the cold, waiting outside the cages for their turn in the pit.

In dreams he sees waving sea fans and milling schools of grouper and underwater shafts of light. He sees Ruby Hornaday push open the door of his closet. She's wearing a copper diving helmet; she leans over his cot and puts the window of her helmet an inch from his face.

He wakes with a shock. Heat pools in his groin. He thinks, *Blue, blue, blue.*

One drizzly Saturday, the bell rings. When Tom opens the door, Ruby Hornaday is standing on the stoop in the rain.

Hello. Tom blinks a dozen times. Raindrops set a thousand intersecting circles upon the puddles in the road. Ruby holds up a jar: six black tadpoles squirm in an inch of water.

Seemed like you might be interested in water creatures.

Tom tries to answer, but the whole sky is rushing through the open door into his mouth.

You're not going to faint again, are you?

Mr. Weems stumps into the foyer. *Jesus, boy, she's damp as a church, you got to invite a lady in.*

Ruby stands on the tiles and drips. Mr. Weems grins. Tom mumbles, *My heart.*

Ruby holds out the jar. *Keep 'em if you want. They'll be frogs before long.* Drops shine in her eyelashes. Rain glues her shirt to her clavicles. *Well, that's something*, says Mr. Weems. He nudges Tom in the back. *Isn't it, Tom?*

Tom is opening his mouth. He's saying, *Maybe I could* – when Mother comes down the stairs in her big, black shoes. *Trouble*, hisses Mr. Weems.

Mother dumps the tadpoles in a ditch. Her face says she's composing herself but her eyes say she's going to wipe all this away. Mr. Weems leans over the dominoes and whispers, *Mother's as hard as a cobblestone but we'll crack her, Tom, you wait.*

Tom whispers, *Ruby Hornaday*, into the space above his cot. *Ruby Hornaday. Ruby Hornaday.* A strange and uncontainable joy inflates dangerously in his chest.

Mr. Weems initiates long conversations with Mother in the kitchen. Tom overhears scraps: *Boy needs to move his legs. Boy should get some air.*

Mother's voice is a whip. *He's sick.*

He's alive! What're you saving him for?

Mother consents to let Tom retrieve coal from the depot and tinned goods from the commissary. Tuesdays he'll be allowed to walk to the butcher's in Dearborn. *Careful, Tomcat, don't hurry.*

Tom moves through the colony that first Tuesday with something close to rapture in his veins. Down the long gravel lanes, past pit cottages and surface mountains of blue and white salt, the warehouses like dark cathedrals, the hauling machines like demonic armatures. All around him the monumental industry of Detroit pounds and clangs. The boy tells himself he is a treasure hunter, a hero from one of Mr. Weems's adventure stories, a knight on important errands, a spy behind enemy lines. He keeps his hands in his pockets and his head down and his gait slow, but his soul charges ahead, weightless, jubilant, sparking through the gloom.

In May of that year, 1929, fourteen-year-old Tom is walking along the lane thinking spring happens whether you're paying attention or not; it happens beneath the snow, beyond the walls – spring happens in the dark while you dream – when Ruby Hornaday steps out of the weeds. She has a shriveled rubber hose coiled over her shoulder and a swim mask in one hand and a tire pump in the other. *Need your help.* Tom's pulse soars.

I got to go to the butcher's.

Your choice. Ruby turns to go. But really there is no choice at all.

She leads him west, away from the mine, through mounds of rusting machines. They hop a fence, cross a field gone to seed, and walk a quarter mile through pitch pines to a marsh where cattle egrets stand in the cattails like white flowers.

In my mouth, she says, and starts picking up rocks. *Out my nose. You pump, Tom. Understand?* In the green water two feet down Tom can make out the dim shapes of a few fish gliding through weedy enclaves.

Ruby pitches the far end of the hose into the water. With waxed cord she binds the other end to the pump. Then she fills her pockets with rocks. She wades out, looks back, says, *You pump*, and puts the hose into her mouth. The swim mask goes over her eyes; her face goes into the water.

The marsh closes over Ruby's back, and the hose trends away from the bank. Tom begins to pump. The sky slides along overhead. Loops of garden hose float under the light out there, shifting now and then. Occasional bubbles rise, moving gradually farther out.

One minute, two minutes. Tom pumps. His heart does its fragile work. He should not be here. He should not be here while this skinny, spellbinding girl drowns herself in a marsh. If that's what she's doing. One of Mr. Weems's similes comes to him: *You're trembling like a needle to the pole.*

After four or five minutes underwater, Ruby comes up. A neon mat of algae clings to her hair, and her bare feet are great boots of mud. She pushes through the cattails. Strings of saliva hang off her chin. Her lips are blue. Tom feels dizzy. The sky turns to liquid.

Incredible, pants Ruby. *Fucking incredible.* She holds up her wet, rock-filled trousers with both hands, and looks at Tom through the wavy lens of her swim mask. His blood storms through its lightless tunnels.

He has to trot to make the butcher's and get back home by noon. It is the first time Tom can remember permitting himself to run, and his legs feel like glass. At the end of the lane, a hundred yards from home, he stops and pants with the basket of meat in his arms and spits a pat of blood into the dandelions. Sweat soaks his shirt. Dragonflies dart and hover. Swallows inscribe letters across the sky. The street seems to ripple and fold and straighten itself out again.

Just a hundred yards more. He forces his heart to settle. *Everything*, Tom thinks, *follows a path worn by those who have gone before: egrets, clouds, tadpoles. Everything everything everything.*

The following Tuesday Ruby meets him at the end of the lane. And the Tuesday after that. They hop the fence, cross the field; she leads him places he's never dreamed existed. Places where the structures of the salt works become white mirages on the horizon, places where sunlight washes through groves of maples and makes the ground quiver with leaf-shadow. They peer into a foundry where shirtless men in masks pour molten iron from one vat into another; they climb a tailings pile where a lone sapling grows like a single hand thrust up from the underworld. Tom knows he's risking everything – his freedom, Mother's trust, even his life – but how can he stop? How can he say no? To say no to Ruby Hornaday would be to say no to the world.

Some Tuesdays Ruby brings along her red book with its images of corals and jellies and underwater volcanoes. She tells him that when she grows up she'll go to parties where hostesses row guests offshore and everyone puts on special helmets to go for strolls along the sea bottom. She tells him she'll be a diver who sinks herself a half mile into the sea in a steel ball with one window. In the basement of the ocean, she says, she'll find a separate universe, a place made of lights: schools of fish glowing green, living galaxies wheeling through the black.

In the ocean, says Ruby, *half the rocks are alive. Half the plants are animals.*

They hold hands; they chew Indian gum. She stuffs his mind full of kelp forests and seascapes and dolphins. *When I grow up*, says Ruby. *When I grow up . . .*

Four more times Ruby walks around beneath the surface of a Rouge River marsh while Tom stands on the bank working the pump. Four more times he watches her rise back out like a fever. *Amphibian*. She laughs. *It means two lives.*

Then Tom runs to the butcher's and runs home, and his heart races, and spots spread like inkblots in front of his eyes. Sometimes in the afternoons, when he stands up from his chores, his vision slides away in violet streaks. He sees the glowing white of the salt tunnels, the red of Ruby's book, the orange of her hair – he imagines her all grown up, standing on the bow of a ship, and feels a core of lemon yellow light flaring brighter and brighter within him. It spills from the slats between his ribs, from between his teeth, from the pupils of his eyes. He thinks: *It is so much! So much!*

So now you're fifteen. And the doctor says sixteen?

Eighteen if I'm lucky.

Ruby turns her book over in her hands. *What's it like? To know you won't get all the years you should?*

I don't feel so short-changed when I'm with you, he wants to say, but his voice breaks at *short* and the sentence fractures.

They kiss only that one time. It is clumsy. He shuts his eyes and leans in, but something shifts and Ruby is not where he expects her to be. Their teeth clash. When he opens his eyes, she is looking off to her left, smiling slightly, smelling of mud, and the thousand tiny blond hairs on her upper lip catch the light.

The second-to-last time Tom and Ruby are together, on the last Tuesday of October, 1929, everything is strange. The hose leaks, Ruby is upset, a curtain has fallen somehow between them.

Go back, Ruby says. *It's probably noon already. You'll be late*. But she sounds as if she's speaking to him through a tunnel. Freckles flow and bloom across her face. The light goes out of the marsh.

On the long path through the pitch pines it begins to rain. Tom makes it to the butcher's and back home with the basket and the ground veal, but when he opens the door to Mother's parlor the curtains blow inward. The chairs leave their places and come scraping toward him. The daylight thins to a pair of beams, waving back and forth and Mr. Weems passes in front of his eyes, but Tom hears no footsteps, no voices: only an internal rushing and the wet metronome of his exhalations. Suddenly he's a diver staring through a thick, foggy window into a world of immense pressure. He's walking around on the bottom of the sea. Mother's lips say, *Haven't I given enough? Lord God, haven't I tried?* Then she's gone.

In something deeper than a dream Tom walks the salt roads a thousand feet beneath the house. At first it's all darkness, but after what might be a minute or a day or a year, he sees little flashes of green light out there in distant galleries, hundreds of feet away. Each flash initiates a chain reaction of further flashes beyond it, so that when he turns in a slow circle he can perceive great flowing signals of light in all directions, tunnels of green arcing out into the blackness – each flash glowing for only a moment before fading, but in that moment repeating everything that came before, everything that will come next.

He wakes to a deflated world. The newspapers are full of suicides; the price of gas has tripled. The miners whisper that the salt works are in trouble.

Quart milk bottles sell for a dollar apiece. There's no butter, hardly any meat. Fruit becomes a memory. Most nights Mother serves only cabbage and soda bread. And salt.

No more trips to the butcher; the butcher closes anyway. By November, Mother's boarders are vanishing. Mr. Beeson goes first, then Mr. Fackler. Tom waits for Ruby to come to the door but she doesn't show. Images of her climb the undersides of his eyelids, and he rubs them away. Each morning he clambers out of his closet and carries his traitorous heart down to the kitchen like an egg.

The world is swallowing people like candy, boy, says Mr. Weems. *No one is leaving addresses.*

Mr. Hanson goes next, then Mr. Heathcock. By April the saltworks is operating only two days a week, and Mr. Weems, Mother, and Tom are alone at supper.

Sixteen. Eighteen if he's lucky. Tom moves his few things into one of the empty boarders' rooms on the first floor, and Mother doesn't say a word. He thinks of Ruby Hornaday: her pale blue eyes, her loose flames of hair. *Is she out there in the city, somewhere, right now? Or is she three thousand miles away?* Then he sets his questions aside.

Mother catches a fever in 1932. It eats her from the inside. She still puts on her high-waisted dresses, ties on her apron. She still cooks every meal and presses Mr. Weems's suit every Sunday. But within a month she has become somebody else, an empty demon in Mother's clothes – perfectly upright at the table, eyes smoldering, nothing on her plate.

She has a way of putting her hand on Tom's forehead while he works. Tom will be hauling coal or mending a pipe or sweeping the parlor, the sun cold and white behind the curtains, and Mother will appear from nowhere and put her icy palm over his eyebrows, and he'll close his eyes and feel his heart tear just a little more.

Amphibian. It means two lives.

Mr. Weems is let go. He puts on his suit, packs up his dominoes, and leaves an address downtown.

I thought no one was leaving addresses.

You're true as a map, Tom. True as the magnet to the iron. And tears spill from the old miner's eyes.

One blue morning not long after that, for the first time in Tom's memory, Mother is not at the stove when he enters the kitchen. He finds her upstairs sitting on her bed, fully dressed in her coat and shoes and with her rosary clutched to her chest. The room is spotless, the house wadded with silence.

Payments are due on the fifteenth. Her voice is ash. *The flashing on the roof needs replacing. There's ninety-one dollars in the dresser.*

Mother.

Shhh, Tomcat, she hisses. *Don't get yourself worked up.*

Tom manages two more payments. Then the bank comes for the house. He walks in a daze through blowing sleet to the end of the lane and turns right and staggers through the dry weeds till he finds the old path and walks beneath the creaking pitch pines to Ruby's marsh. Ice has interlocked in the shallows, but the water in the center is as dark as molten pewter.

He stands there a long time. Into the gathering darkness he says, *I'm still here, but where are you?* His blood sloshes to and fro, and snow gathers in his eyelashes, and three ducks come spiraling out of the night and land silently on the water.

The next morning he walks past the padlocked gate of International Salt with fourteen dollars in his pocket. He rides the trackless trolley downtown for a nickel and gets off on Washington Boulevard. Between the buildings the sun comes up the color of steel, and Tom raises his face to it but feels no warmth at all. He passes catatonic drunks squatting on upturned crates, motionless as statues, and storefront after storefront of empty windows. In a diner a goitrous waitress brings him a cup of coffee with little shining disks of fat floating on top.

The streets are filled with faces, dull and wan, lean and hungry; none belong to Ruby. He drinks a second cup of coffee and eats a plate of eggs and toast. A woman emerges from a doorway and flings a pan of wash water out onto the sidewalk, and the water flashes in the light a moment before falling. In an alley a mule lies on its side, asleep or dead. Eventually the waitress says, *You moving in?* and Tom goes out. He walks slowly toward the address he's copied and recopied onto a sheet of Mother's writing paper. Frozen furrows of plowed snow are shored up against the buildings, and the little golden windows high above seem miles away.

It's a boardinghouse. Mr. Weems is at a lopsided table playing dominoes by himself. He looks up, says, *Holy shit sure as gravity*, and spills his tea.

By a miracle Mr. Weems has a grandniece who manages the owl shift in the maternity ward at City General. Maternity is on the fourth floor. In the elevator Tom cannot tell if he is ascending or descending. The niece looks him up and down and checks his eyes and tongue for fever and hires him on the spot. *World goes to hades but babies still get born*, she says, and issues him white coveralls.

Ten hours a night, six nights a week, Tom roves the halls with carts of laundry, taking soiled blankets and diapers down to the cellar, bringing clean blankets and diapers up. He brings up meals, brings down trays. Rainy nights are the busiest. Full moons and holidays are tied for second. God forbid a rainy holiday with a full moon.

Doctors walk the rows of beds injecting expecting mothers with morphine and something called scopolamine that makes them forget. Sometimes there are screams. Sometimes Tom's heart pounds for no reason he can identify. In the delivery rooms there's always new blood on the tiles to replace the old blood Tom has just mopped away.

The halls are bright at every hour, but out the windows the darkness presses very close, and in the leanest hours of those nights Tom gets a sensation like the hospital is deep underwater, the floor rocking gently, the lights of neighboring buildings like glimmering schools of fish, the pressure of the sea all around.

He turns eighteen. Then nineteen. All the listless figures he sees: children humped around the hospital entrance, their eyes vacant with hunger; farmers pouring into the parks; families sleeping without cover – people for whom nothing left on earth could be surprising. There are so many of them, as if somewhere out in the countryside great farms pump out thousands of ruined men every minute, as if the ones shuffling down the sidewalks are but fractions of the multitudes behind them.

And yet is there not goodness, too? Are people not helping one another in these derelict places? Tom splits his wages with Mr. Weems. He brings home discarded newspapers and wrestles his way through the words on the funny pages. He turns twenty, and Mr. Weems bakes a mushy pound cake full of eggshells and sets twenty matchsticks in it, and Tom blows them all out.

He faints at work: once in the elevator, twice in the big, pulsing laundry room in the basement. Mostly he's able to hide it. But one night he faints in the hall outside the waiting room. A nurse named Fran hauls him into a closet. *Can't let them see you like that*, she says, and wipes his face and he washes back into himself.

The closet is more than a closet. The air is warm, steamy; it smells like soap. On one wall is a two-basin sink; heat lamps are bolted to the undersides of the cabinets. Set in the opposite wall are two little doors.

Tom returns to the same chair in the corner of Fran's room whenever he starts to feel dizzy. Three, four, occasionally ten times a night, he watches a nurse carry an utterly newborn baby through the little door on the left and deposit it on the counter in front of Fran.

She plucks off little knit caps and unwraps blankets. Their bodies are scarlet or imperial purple; they have tiny, bright red fingers, no eyebrows, no kneecaps, no expression except a constant, bewildered wince. Her voice is a whisper: *Why here she is, there he goes, OK now, baby, just lift you here.* Their wrists are the circumference of Tom's pinkie.

Fran takes a new washcloth from a stack, dips it in warm water, and wipes every inch of the creature – ears, armpits, eyelids – washing away bits of placenta, dried blood, all the milky fluids that accompanied it into this world. Meanwhile the child stares up at her with blank, memorizing eyes, peering into the newness of all things. Knowing what? Only light and dark, only mother, only fluid.

Fran dries the baby and splays her fingers beneath its head and diapers it and tugs its hat back on. She whispers, *Here you are, see what a good girl you are, down you go*, and with one free hand lays out two new, crisp blankets, and binds the baby – wrap, wrap, turn – and sets her in a rolling bassinet for Tom to wheel into the nursery, where she'll wait with the others beneath the lights like loaves of bread.

In a magazine Tom finds a color photograph of a three-hundred-year-old skeleton of a bowhead whale, stranded on a coastal plain in a place called Finland. He tears it out, studies it in the lamplight. *See*, he murmurs to Mr. Weems, *how the flowers closest to it are brightest? See how the closest leaves are the darkest green?*

Tom is twenty-one and fainting three times a week when, one Wednesday in January, he sees, among the drugged, dazed mothers in their rows of beds, the unmistakable face of Ruby Hornaday. Flaming orange hair, freckles sprayed across her cheeks, hands folded in her lap, and a thin gold wedding ring on her finger. The material of the ward ripples. Tom leans on the handle of his cart to keep from falling.

Blue, he whispers. *Blue, blue, blue.*

He retreats to his chair in the corner of Fran's washing room and tries to suppress his heart. *Any minute*, he thinks, *her baby will come through the door.*

Two hours later, he pushes his cart into the post-delivery room, and Ruby is gone. Tom's shift ends; he rides the elevator down. Outside, rain settles lightly on the city. The streetlights glow yellow. The early morning avenues are empty except for the occasional automobile, passing with a damp sigh. Tom steadies himself with a hand against the bricks and closes his eyes.

A police officer helps him home. All that day Tom lies on his stomach in his rented bed and recopies the letter until little suns burst behind his eyes. *Deer Ruby, I saw you in the hospital and I saw your baby to. His eyes are viry prety. Fran sez later they will probly get blue. Mother is gone and I am lonely as the arctic see.*

That night at the hospital Fran finds the address. Tom includes the photo of the whale skeleton from the magazine and sticks on an extra stamp for luck. He thinks: *See how the flowers closest to it are brightest. See how the closest leaves are the darkest green.*

He sleeps, pays his rent, walks the thirty-one blocks to work. He checks the mail every day. And winter pales and spring strengthens and Tom loses a little bit of hope.

One morning over breakfast, Mr. Weems looks at him and says, *You ain't even here, Tom. You got one foot across the river. You got to pull back to our side.*

But that very day, it comes. *Dear Tom, I liked hearing from you. It hasn't been ten years but it feels like a thousand. I'm married, you probably guessed that. The baby is Arthur. Maybe his eyes will turn blue. They just might.*

A bald president is on the stamp. The paper smells like paper, nothing more. Tom runs a finger beneath every word, sounding them out. Making sure he hasn't missed anything.

I know your married and I dont want anything but happyness for you but maybe I can see you one time? We could meet at the acquareyem. If you dont rite back thats okay I no why.

Two more weeks. *Dear Tom, I don't want anything but happiness for you, too. How about next Tuesday? I'll bring the baby, okay?*

The next Tuesday, the first one in May, Tom leaves the hospital after his shift. His vision flickers at the edges, and he hears Mother's voice: *Be careful, Tomcat. It's not worth the risk.* He walks slowly to the end of the block and catches the first trolley to Belle Isle, where he steps off into a golden dawn.

There are few cars about, all parked, one a Ford with a huge present wrapped in yellow ribbon on the backseat. An old man with a crumpled face rakes the gravel paths. The sunlight hits the dew and sets the lawns aflame.

The face of the aquarium is Gothic and wrapped in vines. Tom finds a bench outside and waits for his pulse to steady. The reticulated glass roofs of the flower conservatory reflect a passing cloud. Eventually a man in overalls opens the gate, and Tom buys two tickets, then thinks about the baby and buys a third. He returns to the bench with the three tickets in his trembling fingers.

By eleven the sky is filled with a platinum haze and the island is busy. Men on bicycles crackle along the paths. A girl flies a yellow kite.

Tom?

Ruby Hornaday materializes before him – shoulders erect, hair newly short, pushing a chrome-and-canvas baby buggy. He stands quickly, and the park bleeds away and then restores itself.

Sorry I'm late, she says.

She's dignified, slim. Two quick strokes for eyebrows, the same narrow nose. No makeup. No jewelry. Those pale blue eyes and that hair.

She cocks her head slightly. *Look at you. All grown up.*

I got tickets, he says.

How's Mr. Weems?

Oh, he's made of salt, he'll live forever.

They start down the path between the rows of benches and the shining trees. Occasionally she takes his arm to steady him, though her touch only disorients him more.

I thought maybe you were far away, he says. *I thought maybe you went to sea.*

Ruby parks the buggy and lifts the baby to her chest – he's wrapped in a blue afghan – and then they're through the turnstile.

The aquarium is dim and damp and lined on both sides with glass-fronted tanks. Ferns hang from the ceiling, and little boys lean across the brass railings and press their noses to the glass. *I think he likes it,* Ruby says. *Don't you, baby?* The boy's eyes are wide open. Fish swim slow ellipses behind the glass.

They see translucent squid with corkscrew tails, sparkling pink octopi like floating lanterns, cowfish in blue and violet and gold. Iridescent green tiles gleam on the domed ceiling and throw wavering patterns of light across the floor.

In a circular pool at the very center of the building, dark shapes race back and forth in coordination. *Jacks,* Ruby murmurs. *Aren't they?*

Tom blinks.

You're pale, she says.

Tom shakes his head.

She helps him back out into the daylight, beneath the sky and the trees. The baby lies in the buggy sucking his fist, examining the clouds with great intensity, and Ruby guides Tom to a bench.

Cars and trucks and a white limousine pass slowly along the white bridge, high over the river. The city glitters in the distance.

Thank you, says Tom.

For what?

For this.

How old are you now, Tom?

Twenty-one. Same as you. A breeze stirs the trees, and the leaves vibrate with light. Everything is radiant.

World goes to hades but babies still get born, whispers Tom.

Ruby peers into the buggy and adjusts something, and for a moment the back of her neck shows between her hair and collar. The sight of those two knobs of vertebrae, sheathed in her pale skin, fills Tom with a longing that cracks the lawns open. For a moment it seems Ruby is being slowly dragged away from him, as if he is a swimmer caught in a rip, and with every stroke the back of her neck recedes farther into the distance. Then she sits back, and the park heals over, and he can feel the bench become solid beneath him once more.

I used to think, Tom says, *that I had to be careful with how much I lived. As if life was a pocketful of coins. You only got so much and you didn't want to spend it all in one place.*

Ruby looks at him. Her eyelashes whisk up and down.

But now I know life is the one thing in the world that never runs out. I might run out of mine, and you might run out of yours but the world will never run out of life. And we're all very lucky to be part of something like that.

She holds his gaze. *Some deserve more luck than they've gotten.*

Tom shakes his head. He closes his eyes. *I've been lucky, too. I've been absolutely lucky.*

The baby begins to fuss, a whine building to a cry. Ruby says, *Hungry.*

A trapdoor opens in the gravel between Tom's feet, black as a keyhole, and he glances down.

You'll be OK?

I'll be OK.

Good-bye, Tom. She touches his forearm once, and then goes, pushing the buggy through the crowds. He watches her disappear in pieces: first her legs, then her hips, then her shoulders, and finally the back of her bright head.

And then Tom sits, hands in his lap, alive for one more day.

THE THING AROUND YOUR NECK

Chimamanda Ngozi Adichie

Chimamanda Ngozi Adichie (b. 1977) is a Nigerian author. She has published three novels, the second of which, *Half of a Yellow Sun*, won the
Orange Prize, as well as an acclaimed collection of short stories, *The
Thing Around Your Neck*. In 2010 she was listed in *The New Yorker*'s
'20 Under 40' Fiction Issue. On writing, she admitted: "I can write with
authority only about what I know well, which means that I end up using
surface details of my own life in my fiction," but also said: "Successful
fiction does not need to be validated by 'real life'; I cringe whenever a
writer is asked how much of a novel is 'real'."

You thought everybody in America had a car and a gun; your uncles and
aunts and cousins thought so too. Right after you won the American visa
lottery, they told you: In a month, you will have a big car. Soon, a big
house. But don't buy a gun like those Americans.

They trooped into the room in Lagos where you lived with your father and
mother and three siblings, leaning against the unpainted walls because there wer-
en't enough chairs to go round, to say goodbye in loud voices and tell you with
lowered voices what they wanted you to send them. In comparison to the big car
and house (and possibly gun), the things they wanted were minor – handbags
and shoes and perfumes and clothes. You said okay, no problem.

Your uncle in America, who had put in the names of all your family members
for the American visa lottery, said you could live with him until you got on your
feet. He picked you up at the airport and bought you a big hot dog with yellow
mustard that nauseated you. Introduction to America, he said with a laugh. He
lived in a small white town in Maine, in a thirty-year-old house by a lake. He
told you that the company he worked for had offered him a few thousand more
than the average salary plus stock options because they were desperately trying
to look diverse. They included a photo of him in every brochure, even those that
had nothing to do with his unit. He laughed and said the job was good, was worth
living in an all-white town even though his wife had to drive an hour to find a
hair salon that did black hair. The trick was to understand America, to know that
America was give-and-take. You gave up a lot but you gained a lot, too.

He showed you how to apply for a cashier job in the gas station on Main Street
and he enrolled you in a community college, where the girls had thick thighs and
wore bright-red nail polish, and self-tanner that made them look orange. They

asked where you learned to speak English and if you had real houses back in Africa and if you'd seen a car before you came to America. They gawped at your hair. Does it stand up or fall down when you take out the braids? They wanted to know. All of it stands up? How? Why? Do you use a comb? You smiled tightly when they asked those questions. Your uncle told you to expect it; a mixture of ignorance and arrogance, he called it. Then he told you how the neighbors said, a few months after he moved into his house, that the squirrels had started to disappear. They had heard that Africans ate all kinds of wild animals.

You laughed with your uncle and you felt at home in his house; his wife called you *nwanne*, sister, and his two school-age children called you Aunty. They spoke Igbo and ate *garri* for lunch and it was like home. Until your uncle came into the cramped basement where you slept with old boxes and cartons and pulled you forcefully to him, squeezing your buttocks, moaning. He wasn't really your uncle; he was actually a brother of your father's sister's husband, not related by blood. After you pushed him away, he sat on your bed – it was his house, after all – and smiled and said you were no longer a child at twenty-two. If you let him, he would do many things for you. Smart women did it all the time. How did you think those women back home in Lagos with well-paying jobs made it? Even women in New York City?

You locked yourself in the bathroom until he went back upstairs, and the next morning, you left, walking the long windy road, smelling the baby fish in the lake. You saw him drive past – he had always dropped you off at Main Street – and he didn't honk. You wondered what he would tell his wife, why you had left. And you remembered what he said, that America was give-and-take.

You ended up in Connecticut, in another little town, because it was the last stop of the Greyhound bus you got on. You walked into the restaurant with the bright, clean awning and said you would work for two dollars less than the other waitresses. The manager, Juan, had inky-black hair and smiled to show a gold tooth. He said he had never had a Nigerian employee but all immigrants worked hard. He knew, he'd been there. He'd pay you a dollar less, but under the table; he didn't like all the taxes they were making him pay.

You could not afford to go to school, because now you paid rent for the tiny room with the stained carpet. Besides, the small Connecticut town didn't have a community college and credits at the state university cost too much. So you went to the public library, you looked up course syllabi on school Web sites and read some of the books. Sometimes you sat on the lumpy mattress of your twin bed and thought about home – your aunts who hawked dried fish and plantains, cajoling customers to buy and then shouting insults when they didn't; your uncles who drank local gin and crammed their families and lives into single rooms; your friends who had come out to say goodbye before you left, to rejoice because you won the American visa lottery, to confess their envy; your parents who often held hands as they walked to church on Sunday mornings, the neighbors from the next room laughing and teasing them; your father who brought back his boss's old newspapers from work and made your brothers read them; your mother whose salary was barely enough to pay your brothers' school fees at the secondary school where teachers gave an A when someone slipped them a brown envelope.

You had never needed to pay for an A, never slipped a brown envelope to a teacher in secondary school. Still, you chose long brown envelopes to send half your month's earnings to your parents at the address of the parastatal where your mother was a cleaner; you always used the dollar notes that Juan gave you because those were crisp, unlike the tips. Every month. You wrapped the money carefully in white paper but you didn't write a letter. There was nothing to write about.

In later weeks, though, you wanted to write because you had stories to tell. You wanted to write about the surprising openness of people in America, how eagerly they told you about their mother fighting cancer, about their sister-in-laws' preemie, the kinds of things that one should hide or should reveal only to the family members who wished them well. You wanted to write about the way people left so much food on their plates and crumpled a few dollar bills down, as though it was an offering, expiation for the wasted food. You wanted to write about the child who started to cry and pull at her blond hair and push the menus off the table and instead of the parents making her shut up, they pleaded with her, a child of perhaps five years old, and, then, they all got up and left. You wanted to write about the rich people who wore shabby clothes and tattered sneakers, who looked like the night watchmen in front of the large compounds in Lagos. You wanted to write that rich Americans were thin and poor Americans were fat and that many did not have a big house and car; you still were not sure about the guns, though, because they might have them inside their pockets.

It wasn't just to your parents you wanted to write, it was also to your friends, and cousins and aunts and uncles. But you could never afford enough perfumes and clothes and handbags and shoes to go around and still pay your rent on what you earned at the waitressing job, so you wrote nobody.

Nobody knew where you were, because you told no one. Sometimes you felt invisible and tried to walk through your room wall into the hallway, and when you bumped into the wall, it left bruises on your arms. Once, Juan asked if you had a man that hit you because he would take care of him and you laughed a mysterious laugh.

At night, something would wrap itself around your, neck, something that very nearly choked you before you fell asleep.

Many people at the restaurant asked when you had come from Jamaica, because they thought that every black person with a foreign accent was Jamaican. Or some who guessed that you were African told you that they loved elephants and wanted to go on a safari.

So when he asked you, in the dimness of the restaurant after you recited the daily specials, what African country you were from, you said Nigeria and expected him to say that he had donated money to fight AIDS in Botswana. But he asked if you were Yoruba or Igbo, because you didn't have a Fulani face. You were surprised – you thought he must be a professor of anthropology at the state university, a little young in his late twenties or so, but who was to say? Igbo, you said. He asked your name and said Akunna was pretty. He did not ask what it meant, fortunately, because you were sick of how people said, "Father's Wealth? You mean, like, your father will actually sell you to a husband?"

He told you he had been to Ghana and Uganda and Tanzania, loved the poetry of Okot p'Bitek and the novels of Amos Tutuola and had read a lot about sub-Saharan African countries, their histories, their complexities. You wanted to feel disdain, to show it as you brought his order, because white people who liked Africa too much and those who liked Africa too little were the same – condescending. But he didn't shake his head in the superior way that Professor Cobbledick back in the Maine community college did during a class discussion on decolonization in Africa. He didn't have that expression of Professor Cobbledick's, that expression of a person who thought himself better than the people he knew about. He came in the next day and sat at the same table and when you asked if the chicken was okay, he asked if you had grown up in Lagos. He came in the third day and began talking before he ordered, about how he had visited Bombay and now wanted to visit Lagos, to see how real people lived, like in the shantytowns, because he never did any of the silly tourist stuff when he was abroad. He talked and talked and you had to tell him it was against restaurant policy. He brushed your hand when you set the glass of water down. The fourth day, when you saw him arrive, you told Juan you didn't want that table anymore. After your shift that night, he was waiting outside, earphones stuck in his ears, asking you to go out with him because your name rhymed with *hakuna matata* and *The Lion King* was the only maudlin movie he'd ever liked. You didn't know what *The Lion King* was. You looked at him in the bright light and noticed that his eyes were the color of extra-virgin olive oil, a greenish gold. Extra-virgin olive oil was the only thing, you loved, truly loved, in America.

He was a senior at the state university. He told you how old he was and you asked why he had not graduated yet. This was America, after all, it was not like back home, where universities closed so often that people added three years to their normal course of study and lecturers went on strike after strike and still were not paid. He said he had taken a couple of years off to discover himself and travel, mostly to Africa and Asia. You asked him where he ended up finding himself and he laughed. You did not laugh. You did not know that people could simply choose not to go to school, that people could dictate to life. You were used to accepting what life gave, writing down what life dictated.

You said no the following four days to going out with him, because you were uncomfortable with the way he looked at your face, that intense, consuming way he looked at your face that made you say goodbye to him but also made you reluctant to walk away. And then, the fifth night, you panicked when he was not standing at the door after your shift. You prayed for the first time in a long time and when he came up behind you and said hey, you said yes, you would go out with him, even before he asked. You were scared he would not ask again.

The next day, he took you to dinner at Chang's and your fortune cookie had two strips of paper. Both of them were blank.

You knew you had become comfortable when you told him that you watched *Jeopardy* on the restaurant TV and that you rooted for the following, in this order: women of color, black men, and white women, before, finally, white men – which meant you never rooted for white men. He laughed and told you he was used to not being rooted for, his mother taught women's studies.

And you knew you had become close when you told him that your father was really not a schoolteacher in Lagos, that he was a junior driver for a construction company. And you told him about that day in Lagos traffic in the rickety Peugeot 504 your father drove; it was raining and your seat was wet because of the rust-eaten hole in the roof. The traffic was heavy, the traffic was always heavy in Lagos, and when it rained it was chaos. The roads became muddy ponds and cars got stuck and some of your cousins went out and made some money pushing the cars out. The rain, the swampiness, you thought, made your father step on the brakes too late that day. You heard the bump before you felt it. The car your father rammed into was wide, foreign, and dark green, with golden headlights like the eyes of a leopard. Your father started to cry and beg even before he got out of the car and laid himself flat on the road, causing much blowing of horns. Sorry, sir, sorry, sir, he chanted. If you sell me and my family, you cannot buy even one tire on your car. Sorry, sir.

The Big Man seated at the back did not come out, but his driver did, examining the damage, looking at your father's sprawled form from the corner of his eye as though the pleading was like pornography, a performance he was ashamed to admit he enjoyed. At last he let your father go. Waved him away. The other cars' horns blew and drivers cursed. When your father came back into the car, you refused to look at him because he was just like the pigs that wallowed in the marshes around the market. Your father looked like *nsi*. Shit.

After you told him this, he pursed his lips and held your hand and said he understood how you felt. You shook your hand free, suddenly annoyed, because he thought the world was, or ought to be, full of people like him. You told him there was nothing to understand, it was just the way it was.

He found the African store in the Hartford yellow pages and drove you there. Because of the way he walked around with familiarity, tilting the bottle of palm wine to see how much sediment it had, the Ghanaian store owner asked him if he was African, like the white Kenyans or South Africans, and he said yes, but he'd been in America for a long time. He looked pleased that the store owner had believed him. You cooked that evening with the things you had bought, and after he ate garri and onugbu soup, he threw up in your sink. You didn't mind, though, because now you would be able to cook onugbu soup with meat.

He didn't eat meat because he thought it was wrong the way they killed animals; he said they released fear toxins into the animals and the fear toxins made people paranoid. Back home, the meat pieces you ate, when there was meat, were the size of half your finger. But you did not tell him that. You did not tell him either that the dawadawa cubes your mother cooked everything with, because curry and thyme were too expensive, had MSG, were MSG. He said MSG caused cancer, it was the reason he liked Chang's; Chang didn't cook with MSG.

Once, at Chang's, he told the waiter he had recently visited Shanghai, that he spoke some Mandarin. The waiter warmed up and told him what soup was best and then asked him, "You have girlfriend in Shanghai now?" And he smiled and said nothing.

You lost your appetite, the region deep in your chest felt clogged. That night, you didn't moan when he was inside you, you bit your lips and pretended that you didn't come because you knew he would worry. Later you told him why you were upset, that even though you went to Chang's so often together, even though you had kissed just before the menus came, the Chinese man had assumed you could not possibly be his girlfriend, and he had smiled and said nothing. Before he apologized, he gazed at you blankly and you knew that he did not understand.

He bought you presents and when you objected about the cost, he said his grand-father in Boston had been wealthy but hastily added that the old man had given a lot away and so the trust fund he had wasn't huge. His presents mystified you. A fist-size glass ball that you shook to watch a tiny shapely doll in pink spin around. A shiny rock whose surface took on the color of whatever touched it. An expensive scarf hand-painted in Mexico. Finally you told him, your voice stretched in irony, that in your life presents were always useful. The rock, for instance, would work if you could grind things with it. He laughed long and hard but you did not laugh. You realized that in his life, he could buy presents that were just presents and nothing else, nothing useful. When he started to buy you shoes and clothes and books, you asked him not to, you didn't want any presents at all. He bought them anyway and you kept them for your cousins and uncles and aunts, for when you would one day be able to visit home, even though you did not know how you could ever afford a ticket and your rent. He said he really wanted to see Nigeria and he could pay for you both to go. You did not want him to pay for you to visit home. You did not want him to go to Nigeria, to add it to the list of countries where he went to gawk at the lives of poor people who could never gawk back at his life. You told him this on a sunny day, when he took you to see Long Island Sound; and the two of you argued, your voices raised as you walked along the calm water. He said you were wrong to call him self-righteous. You said he was wrong to call only the poor Indians in Bombay the real Indians. Did it mean he wasn't a real American, since he was not like the poor fat people you and he had seen in Hartford? He hurried ahead of you, his upper body bare and pale, his flip-flops raising bits of sand, but then he came back and held out his hand for yours. You made up and made love and ran your hands through each other's, hair, his soft and yellow like the swinging tassels of growing corn, yours dark and bouncy like the filling of a pillow. He had got too much sun and his skin turned the color of a ripe watermelon and you kissed his back before you rubbed lotion on it.

The thing that wrapped itself around your neck, that nearly choked you before you fell asleep, started to loosen, to let go.

You knew by people's reactions that you two were abnormal – the way the nasty ones were too nasty and the nice ones too nice. The old white men and women who muttered and glared at him, the black men who shook their heads at you, the black women whose pitying eyes bemoaned your lack of self-esteem, your self-loathing. Or the black women who smiled swift solidarity smiles; the black men who tried too hard to forgive you, saying a too-obvious hi to him; the white men and women who said, "What a good-looking pair" too brightly, too loudly as though to prove their own open-mindedness to themselves.

But his parents were different; they almost made you think it was all normal.

His mother told you that he had never brought a girl to meet them, except for his high school prom date, and he grinned stiffly and held your hand. The tablecloth shielded your clasped hands. He squeezed your hand and you squeezed back and wondered why he was so stiff, why his extra-virgin-olive-oil-colored eyes darkened as he spoke to his parents. His mother was delighted when she asked if you'd read Nawal el Saadawi and you said yes. His father asked how similar Indian food was to Nigerian food and teased you about paying when the check came. You looked at them and felt grateful that they did not examine you like an exotic trophy, an ivory tusk.

Afterwards, he told you about his issues with his parents, how they portioned out love like a birthday cake, how they would give him a bigger slice if only he'd agree to go to law school. You wanted to sympathize. But instead you were angry.

You were angrier when he told you he had refused to go up to Canada with them for a week or two, to their summer cottage in the Quebec countryside. They had even asked him to bring you. He showed you pictures of the cottage and you wondered why it was called a cottage because the buildings that big around your neighborhood back home were banks and churches. You dropped a glass and it shattered on the hardwood of his apartment floor and he asked what was wrong and you said nothing, although you thought a lot was wrong. Later, in the shower you started to cry. You watched the water dilute your tears and you didn't know why you were crying.

You wrote home finally. A short letter to your parents, slipped in between the crisp dollar bills, and you included your address. You got a reply only days later, by courier. Your mother wrote the letter herself; you knew from the spidery penmanship, from the misspelled words.

Your father was dead; he had slumped over the steering wheel of his company car. Five months now, she wrote. They had used some of the money you sent to give him a good funeral. They killed a goat for the guests and buried him in a good coffin. You curled up in bed, pressed your knees to your chest and tried to remember what you had been doing when your father died, what you had been doing for all the months when he was already dead. Perhaps your father died on the day your whole body had been covered in goosebumps, hard as uncooked rice, that you could not explain, Juan teasing you about taking over from the chef so that the heat in the kitchen would warm you up. Perhaps your father died on one of the days you took a drive to Mystic or watched a play in Manchester or had dinner at Chang's.

He held you while you cried, smoothed your hair, and offered to buy your ticket, to go with you to see your family. You said no, you needed to go alone. He asked if you would come back and you reminded him that you had a green card and you would lose it if you did not come back in one year. He said you knew what he meant, would you come back, come back?

You turned away and said nothing, and when he drove you to the airport, you hugged him tight for a long, long moment, and then you let go.

EXTENDED COPYRIGHT

ACKNOWLEDGEMENTS

My thanks are due to: Jason Arthur, Paul Bailey, Roberta Borgna, Antonia Byatt, Georgina Capel, Anthony Cheetham, Sarah Churchwell, Gill Coleridge, Rachel Conway, Sam Copeland, Martijn David, Colin Field, Judith Flanders, David Flusfeder, Georgia Garrett, Robert Gottlieb, Stephen Grosz, Lisa Highton, Victoria Hislop, Amanda Hopkinson, Mathilda Imlah, Melanie Jackson, Clemence Jacquinet, Philip Gwyn Jones, Stuart Kelly, Julie Kemp, Julia Kreitman, Federica Leonardis, Fiona McMorrough, Richard Milbank, Madeleine O'Shea, Cynthia Ozick, Laura Palmer, Max Porter, Clare Reihill, Amanda Ridout, Annabel Robinson, Peter Robinson, Rob Ryan, Rebecca Servadio, Becci Sharpe, Allan H. Simmonds, Alan Simpson, Peter Straus, Bill Swainson, Scarlett Thomas, Salley Vickers, Zoë Waldie, Hannah Westland, James Wood, Romily Withington, and Frank Wynne for their help, and then impositions, outrage, puzzlement, questions, suggestions. Earlier debts of gratitude are due to Peter Brodie, Peter Newman Brooks, Lavinia Cohn-Sherbok, Eamon Duffy, Andrew Dobbin, the late George Matthewson, June Miller, Robert Milner, the late Peter Pilkington, Miri Rubin, the late Mrs. Sprott and the late Jenny Williamson, all of whom – at some stage – encouraged and showed me *how* to read. Blackhall Library in Edinburgh, the library in Burgess Hill, the libraries where I was at school and university and – recently – the libraries in Notting Hill, Hammersmith, and Chiswick, have also been spaces where I've felt hugely at home with the words of others. Perhaps my sons, Freddie and Billy Miller, and my nieces, Tamara and Mariella Coulthard, might enjoy what is here one day: we deepen our knowledge of one another by understanding what we've read together.

There is one name missing from the list above. John Conrad remembered his father saying that, when a friend dies, "each morning one casts a look around to see if all one's friends are there; the older ones go on ahead, the younger ones follow behind and, if all are there, one is content. Then one is missing from his usual place – there is an unfilled space which remains for the rest of your life." As this book neared its completion, the woman who taught me much about love, life and work but, above all, revealed to me how best I could read – and for whom and with whom I worked for half my life – died. She left that "unfilled space" in many lives but, true to form, bequeathed something intangible, yet legible, given she was a passionate, winning advocate for those she represented, as well as dozens of others: a "ghost in the machine" she helped to influence what a myriad of readers over the last fifty years could have read. Amongst other diverse enthusiasms, her devotion to championing the short story and its writer should not be forgotten, which is why this book is dedicated to Deborah Rogers.

THE INDEX

J.G. Ballard

J.G. Ballard (1930–2009) is best known for his semi-autobiographical novel *Empire of the Sun*, filmed to great acclaim. Before his death he was rightly applauded for a late sequence of novels that thrilled in examining the possibility of violence in modern society – *Cocaine Nights, Super-Cannes, Millenium People* and *Kingdom Come*. His stories are sublime, inventive, questing, genre-bending, and he is one of the five writers in this volume when it became hardest to chose the finest as his range is so wide.

Editor's note. From abundant internal evidence it seems clear that the text printed below is the index to the unpublished and perhaps suppressed autobiography of a man who may well have been one of the most remarkable figures of the 20th century. Yet of his existence nothing is publicly known, although his life and work appear to have exerted a profound influence on the events of the past fifty years. Physician and philosopher, man of action and patron of the arts, sometime claimant to the English throne and founder of a new religion, Henry Rhodes Hamilton was evidently the intimate of the greatest men and women of our age. After World War II he founded a new movement of spiritual regeneration, but private scandal and public concern at his growing megalomania, culminating in his proclamation of himself as a new divinity, seem to have led to his downfall. Incarcerated within an unspecified government institution, he presumably spent his last years writing his autobiography, of which this index is the only surviving fragment.

A substantial mystery still remains. Is it conceivable that all traces of his activities could be erased from our records of the period? Is the suppressed autobiography itself a disguised *roman à clef*, in which the fictional hero exposes the secret identities of his historical contemporaries? And what is the true role of the indexer himself, clearly a close friend of the writer, who first suggested that he embark on his autobiography? This ambiguous and shadowy figure has taken the unusual step of indexing himself into his own index. Perhaps the entire compilation is nothing more than a figment of the over-wrought imagination of some deranged lexicographer. Alternatively, the index may be wholly genuine, and the only glimpse we have into a world hidden from us by a gigantic conspiracy, of which Henry Rhodes Hamilton is the greatest victim.

U

United Nations Assembly, seized by Perfect Light Movement, 695–9; HRH addresses, 696; HRH calls for world war against United States and USSR, 698

V

Versailles, Perfect Light Movement attempts to purchase, 621

Vogue (magazine), 356

W

Westminster Abbey, arrest of HRH by Special Branch, 704

Wight, Isle of, incarceration of HRH, 712–69

Windsor, House of, HRH challenges legitimacy of, 588

Y

Yale Club, 234

Younghusband, Lord Chancellor, denies star chamber trial of HRH, 722; denies knowledge of whereabouts of HRH, 724; refuses habeas corpus appeal by Zelda Hamilton, 728; refers to unestablished identity of HRH, 731

Z

Zanuck, Daryl F., 388

Zielinski, Bronislaw, suggests autobiography to HRH, 742; commissioned to prepare index, 748; warns of suppression threats, 752; disappears, 761